The Island of Second Sight

From the Applied Recollections of Vigoleis

The Island of Second Sight

From the Applied Recollections of Vigoleis

ALBERT VIGOLEIS THELEN

Translated from the German by Donald O. White

THE OVERLOOK PRESS
NEW YORK, NY

This edition first published in hardcover in the United States in 2012 by

The Overlook Press, Peter Mayer Publishers, Inc.
141 Wooster Street
New York, NY 10012
www.overlookpress.com
For bulk and special sales, please contact sales@overlookny.com

First published in German 1953 by Drukkerij G. J. Thieme in Nijmegen, Amsterdam
and then by Eugen Diederichs Verlag, Dusseldorf.

This first English language edition published in 2010 by Galileo Publishers, Cambridge,
in association with Isabelle Weiss.

Copyright © 1953 by Albert Vigoleis Thelen
English translation copyright © 2010 by Donald O. White

The translation of this work was supported by a grant from the Goethe-Institut,
which is funded by the German Ministry of Foreign Affairs.

 GOETHE-INSTITUT

Cataloging-in-Publication Data is available from the Library of Congress

Book design and type formatting by Bernard Schleifer
Manufactured in the United States of America
ISBN 978-1-4683-0116-8
10 9 8 7 6 5 4 3 2

umbrarum hic locus est, somni, noctisque soporae
Vergil, Aeneid

for Beatrice

NOTICE TO THE READER

A ll the people in this book are alive or were at one time. Yet they appear here, the author included, in dual cognizance of their personality, and therefore, they can be held responsible neither for their actions nor for any assumptions that might arise in the reader's mind. Just as my ego-deprived characters appear subject to greater or lesser degrees of personal disjuncture, similarly the sequence of events has undergone chronological rearrangements that can even involve the obliteration of all sense of time.

In case of doubt, let truth be told.

PROLOGUE

It would mean commencing this chronicle fictitiously if I were to try now, twenty years after the event, to ascertain which wily fiend plagued me more sorely during that nocturnal ocean voyage: the man-eating common flea inside the sleeping bag I borrowed from a sailor, or the horrendous nightmare that whisked me back to the Nicolas Beets Straat in Amsterdam, where the grave had just closed over a young woman whose cause of death I, her renegade lover's double, had somehow become.

What an intriguing, macabre beginning for a book, one might say. Perhaps, but for the moment this faint flash of lightning off in the distance is all we shall discern. Insofar as I, the author, have any say in the matter, I can safely predict that over the long haul, events here will not turn out to be all that terrifying—except at the unpredictable finish, when bombs start exploding and when hatred, night, and fear—in short, when the arsenal of the Spanish Civil War gets deployed. "Farewell my brothers, aim for my breast!"

Within this breast of mine, as if by a miracle of Santa María del Pilar, my own and my tragelaph Vigoleis' heart keeps on pumping constantly and undauntedly, now as on that summer's day when I arose at dawn from my nautical pallet, rid myself of vermin, a shaggy blanket, and anxious dreams, and shook myself like a poodle emerging from the surf. Our travel companions, who like us had sought refuge in the mephitic cabins from the sudden onset of evening chill, also came alive and were topside on the lookout. Those of Spanish tongue arrived noisily and very much at home on the heaving deck; while I and my ilk stepped forth cautiously with pursed lips, as if groping for a taste of this new world.

Resembling me most closely in this hesitant exploit was Beatrice, who herewith makes her rather unceremonious entrance in my book, and who will not depart from it until the very last page. But she will have to get accustomed to the role I have plotted out for her: as a character in my chronicle. Come to think of it, mustn't I, too? Awkward throughout a life I have never yet got used to, wearing maladjustment like a mark on my brow, a mortal whose wounds can be fingered by anyone and everyone—will I be any more resourceful as the "hero" of a book? It may seem odd that I have borne with me a by no means unremarkable set of events for twenty years without committing them to the literary pickle-jar. Admittedly my origins are anything but distinguished; what is more, my life is strewn with multiple failures. Still, neither these facts nor fear of the printed page has kept me, up to now, from prancing out on the belletristic tightrope. Whereas

Vigoleis occasionally helps me muddle through, Beatrice has constantly had to bear her own cross. That is why I am dedicating my book to her.

Experienced as she was on bigger oceans than the Mediterranean, familiar with foreign languages, schooled for years in contact with various classes and races, her soul divided by Inca blood and thus at once closer to, and at an extreme remove from, the Latin way of life—nonetheless Beatrice seemed just as bewildered as I was when I got up the courage to approach the women's cabins on the ship's gospel side. Beset by fleas and separated by sex—that is how we sailed under Spanish flag and sky toward our Island.

Dreams and mini-fauna had also tormented Beatrice, and while her slumber-time imaginings no doubt differed from mine, the itches she felt were my itches too. Death had likewise entered her sleep, waiting to ambush her mother, whom we had been obliged to leave to her fate in Basel, now blind and the victim of rapid physical and mental deterioration.

Two telegrams, received a few days apart, had brought disorder, not to say chaos, into our life in Amsterdam. The first wire came from Basel, summoning Beatrice to the bedside of her fading mother. The second originated in Palma on the island of Mallorca, and its message was as desperate as it was ultimate: "Am dying. Zwingli"—the name answered to by Beatrice's youngest brother. So now we had to minister to him also. At such a fork in the road, a fond heart finds it difficult to choose the right direction. After consulting with the doctors we decided to leave her mother in the care of her other brother, whose occupation kept him in Switzerland in any case.

With this decision our insular destiny was sealed.

BOOK ONE

Praise be to Heaven and all the Saints
for bestowing upon us finally an Adventure
that shall yield us Profit!
Don Quixote de la Mancha

Puta la madre, puta la hija,
puta la manta que las cobija.
Old Spanish Proverb

Everyone receives his inner sense
of North and South at birth.
Whether an external polarity comes with it
is not terribly important.
Jean Paul

I

Round about us the grey veils of night were lifting as we stepped upon the afterdeck, disheveled and weary from lack of sleep, lightly shivering in the breeze that was now sweeping in from the horizon to reveal the gorgeous spectacle of the approaching steep coastline of Mallorca. On the previous evening a smudging of the heavens had obscured a spectacle lauded in every travel guide: the fabled Monserrat Range sinking into the sea. Now we were being abundantly compensated, and I in particular, for as a rule I take little enjoyment in landscape or the supposed marvels of nature. It is only fitting that the world should display before me now and then, by means of its laterna magica, one of its exemplary picture postcards, for my standpoint is that of a person who can never regard his existence as a little pleasure trip in tweeds and parasol. I am not a parvenu; I have no idea from whence or by what means I might have socially "arrived." But there at the ship's rail, standing next to Beatrice, I was your typical conceited snob who has already witnessed, a thousand times more gorgeous and sublime, the scene that was greeting us. During my lifetime I had in reality seen next to nothing. A few trips in Germany, Czechoslovakia, Holland, and Switzerland—that was the sum of it. And yet that would have remained more than sufficient had I not constantly focused my gaze inward upon my own inner landscape. To be sure, the scenery there offers few memorable vistas to compare with the Loreley Cliff, the tulip fields at Lisse, the Hradchin, or a glacier-eroded escarpment near Lucerne with on-site explanatory lecture by Professor Heim. In view of my own inner glacial escarpment even the most garrulous cicerone would stand there in utter silence, since all there is to see is a slag-heap, one that could never on this earth become the site of an Escorial.

Beatrice's thrill was intense and undivided. No comparisons with the sights she had witnessed on earlier extensive journeys could diminish the joy she felt here at each new emanation of color, at a gull snatching up a bit of bread in screeching mid-plunge, at the gamboling of porpoises, or even at our ship's wake, expanding as it neared the horizon where it became one with an upward drift of light. But just as I am completely unmusical, Beatrice, in keeping with her musical sensibility, is incapable of expressing such experiences with a pen. Otherwise I would ask her right here and now to insert a description of our sunrise, one that would do justice to the excitement she felt at the time, since one reader or another might well be grateful for just such a passage. It would indeed be fitting, even more so when one considers that each passenger must have regarded as unique an event that, given the proper meteorological conditions, takes place each and every morning with a punctuality guaranteed by the captain's chronometer. Be that as it may, the sight transported Beatrice repeatedly into audible rapture—a truly astonishing acknowledgment of Mother Nature's accomplishments by a person who is otherwise so reticent. There are places in the world where The Mother of Us All salves her conscience—a faculty peculiar to Her alone and hardly to be called maternal—by showing off beautiful things that in other places She keeps carefully concealed. A sunrise, for example, at 39°45'16"N and 2°8'28"E could reward me for 365 consecutive solar eclipses in the poor section of Amsterdam's Derde Helmersstraat— assuming that the rising of that celestial body meant anything to me at all. As far as I am concerned the sun can stay below sea level to all eternity, so long as I can scrape up enough money to stoke my coal stove and put some oil in my lamp.

A superabundance of verbiage, I'll grant you, to avoid describing a Mediterranean *fiat lux* that in the meantime has achieved sufficient completeness, midst radiations, irradiations, and transradiations, for it to be said with confidence: "It is Day!" Even the stick-in-beds are now awake and have scrambled up on deck. Topside is now teeming with passengers, shouts go back and forth, and many a mouth goes silently agape, the words of amazement simply defying vocal expression. Such is the most childlike way of reacting to a feature of the world around us, and thus probably the most godlike way as well. We simply lack the courage to react in this manner every time, for an open mouth is considered poor form. Those lacking such courage start describing the scene out loud—without a trace of silent veneration. A host of languages vie with one another, but to my ear Spanish seems to prevail, no doubt because it is still foreign to me. British and American, which I had already learned to distinguish, join the chorus celebrating this Feast of Light, and then German.

The latter was spoken by a quaint young couple next to us, trying with forced casualness to conceal a state of affairs that normally shies from illumination, especially in a setting such as the present one, which had the rapidly ascending solar orb showering light upon us all in majestic abundance. These two, as yet quite ill at ease amidst their obvious bliss, probably hadn't reckoned on the parasites that held sway below-decks. He called her Lissy, and she called him Heiner. Today, provided that they are still among the living, they are doubtless regaling each other with "Elisabeth" and "Heinrich." They were unable to hold my attention any longer than it is taking me to commemorate them here. I'm doing it only for the sake of my cosmopolitan canvas, onto which I shall now quickly daub an oldish British lady who struck up a conversation with Beatrice, and who was ecstatic at hearing her native-born touristic clichés meet with Beatrice's relaxed, polite attention. She was about to "do" the island—yes, alone, and with her floppy cotton stockings and her unshaven chin it's hard to imagine her finding a partner who would ever be willing to add more than conversational "yesses" and "nos" to her life—neither externally (her pension was apparently meager) nor inwardly, where despite her wrinkly smile there was a musty air of petty complacency. Yet never fear: the British are never and nowhere alone, so long as their Empire accompanies them like the proliferating heads on a tapeworm. Since the moment in question I have met many more of these spinsters. They are ageless. Like the English sparrows they are bound to no single place, and they will outlive the era of their arch-enemy, the nylon stocking.

Just as in the compartment of the train that brought us from Port-Bou to Barcelona, here too on shipboard the Spaniards had the big say, though what they were saying escaped my comprehension—and more's the pity, for by nature I am inquisitive. Inordinately shy and a stay-at-home possessed of *Sitzfleisch* in quantities enviable even among brothers, enabling me to become the long-distance translator that I am to this very day, I have made virtue out of necessity: whenever I am forced to enter the company of other people, something positive usually happens to me. Never enough, mind you, to suppress my congenital aversion to contact with the external world, but just enough to catch me up, as in a safety net, in my tumble from solitude. Afterwards I waver like a stand-up doll, until I come to rest in the company of my own sheltered self.

Coils of rope, cardboard boxes, battered steamer trunks, wooden crates and wicker-encased jugs—anything that could serve as a seat had been commandeered like a kind of wagon train by a very numerous Spanish family. This was their house and home, as if they had been preparing for a voyage of weeks rather than ten hours by the clock. The kids were brattish. The womenfolk, varying in age and in any imaginable contest outdoing each other in feminine charm, yakked and griped with tireless verbal energy. One man in particular, to all appearances father and brother, grandfather, brother-in-law, and uncle—in a word the entire clan in one and the same person, dominated the group by reason of physical stature and an authoritative mien that extended to all the four winds.

This was a spectacle more fascinating to me than the wordless matrimonial urges of the young German couple forced out of their fleabag, or the chatty desperation exuded by our English spinster friend—not to mention sun and seascape. As in a provincial theater, I had before me a scene from Spanish domestic life; all I had to do was take my place in standing-room. One thing I noticed right away: all these goings-on were utterly different from anything I had experienced in my parents' home—this joy and anger at the open hearth, louder, freer, more unbuttoned in every respect. If my own father had only been like this man, who with instinctive nonchalance and amazing aim dispensed ringing hand-slaps around the entire circle of his loved ones, without once making the ridiculous impression our Northern bullies always do. Our native variety of father lacks the Quixotic realization that a swipe on the mouth, even one that lands on target, is a swipe into the void.

As he went about dispensing justice in such casual fashion, our Spanish chieftain squirted red wine down his gullet from a very special kind of squeeze bottle, the porrón—about which more in a moment. Suddenly a young male offspring, clearly demonstrating little respect for the older generation and hence hardly destined for a long life, shoved the *pater familias* from behind, in the process diverting the stream of wine in its trajectory. With exemplary aplomb the paternal gorge parried the thrust, catching a portion of the flow as a toad tongues a fly. The remainder sprayed out into the audience, precisely to my standing-room location. Vociferous huzzahs greeted the foreigner's crimson baptism. Having observed the patriarch's astounding agility in the handling of discoloring liquids, it was mysterious to me how his shiny black suit had received all of its thousand disfiguring stains. I was of course as yet unfamiliar with the Spaniards' maxim about not letting oneself be the victim of one's own wardrobe (*no hay que ser víctima de su traje*), though I was later to observe its appropriateness with respect to the jacket, vest, and trousers worn by a limping character to be encountered soon enough in this chronicle of mine.

Just imagine the heights of achievement I might have attained had I been coddled and spoiled by a mother like the one who now confronted the despotic father with the chastised youngster. She too flailed about with whacks to the cheeks, hitting seldom but drawing forth yowls of pain nonetheless. Her swats had different emotional origins—perhaps they came from the heart—and were the practical application of some rather different principles of child-rearing. Parental division of authority is apparently an international phenomenon, and this could make it seem almost humane. In any case, compared to the dynamics of tonality and coloration in this Spanish family, my own had been totally wrong. That is why I have become what you are confronting here in these pages: not a *conquistador*, not a cathedral-steps beggar with the trappings of a Spanish grandee, not an open-air cobbler with more wisdom in the tip of his awl than Vigoleis has inside his skull. This is not intended as a gripe against destiny, much less against Our Beloved Creator, who surely knew what He was about when He failed to set me into His quotidian world as this Spanish brat from the maritime wagon train who, I now notice, is pissing demonstratively against the mast.

The eating that went on in this improvised settler's camp was prodigious. Items I didn't even know the names for emerged from baskets and suitcases. Oil got poured on dark bread, onions and a green vegetable were diced on top. Olives, chickpeas, and small crabs were handed around, a chicken was torn apart and distributed among famished relatives. The rest of the menu was to me anonymous, at least at the time, for then I had scarcely peered beyond my mother's saucepan—whose contents were not all that bad, though emphatically *echt deutsch*, and based patriotically on a certain ubiquitous tuber about which the nutritionist Moleschott, to this day unjustly maligned as a materialist, once wrote that a person fed for two weeks on nothing but the item in question would no longer be physically capable of affording its purchase. That is precisely my opinion, for I dislike intensely this mindless root-plant that has succeeded in undermining all of Western civilization. Perhaps the beetle named after it can now terminate its hegemony once and for all. "Without phosphorus there can be no thought"—I cite Moleschott once more. And without the potato? At the very least it has been able to divert my attention momentarily from an Iberian picnic based on a cuisine far beyond my ken.

People ate differently here, talked differently, scolded differently. I would have to adapt. I realized this within the hour during which I was the wide-eyed observer of this nation's domestic mores, as the *Ciudad de Barcelona* rounded the northwest coast of the island, passed the Cape of Calafiguera, and entered the Bay of Palma. Meanwhile Beatrice lent our British travel companion her ear, an ear well practiced in convenient deafness through experience with dowagers. But she didn't pass up the sight of the island darting ever more rapidly toward us.

With the charming, resigned pride spinsters often show in the presence of young couples, a behavior often tinged with an arrogance born of pity, our English companion departed as I stepped over to Beatrice to invite her to my *al fresco* theater. This would offer her better diversion, for I could read in her stern expression what was happening to her within. The farther we voyaged from her dying mother, the closer we came to her brother's deathbed. Was he still alive? We had requested telegraphic word to Basel, or *poste restante* to Barcelona. But all these many days they had left us completely in the dark concerning his fate.

By "they" I mean the officialdom at the Hotel Príncipe Alfonso in Palma de Mallorca, whose renovator, manager, and Swiss-born panjandrum Zwingli had recently become. The hotel was thus our destination, although it was clear to us that our dying relative could no longer be living there. No doubt he was in a hospital somewhere. No hotel in the world can afford to shelter a morbid case under its roof, not even if it's the boss himself. In such instances the guests, otherwise extremely conscious of their social standing, immediately defy the rules and demand their unwritten rights: the terminal case is transported downstairs and out the delivery entrance like garbage or dirty linen, so as not to sully the people who come and go amid bowings and scrapings at the main door. Shortly before embarking at Barcelona I had wired the hotel to reserve a double room. We would find out more once we arrived.

Our open-air circus reached the end of its program. The tents were lowered, equipment got packed, and everyone pressed to the rail so as not to miss a single episode of the exciting adventure of our harbor entry.

For about an hour the Cathedral of Palma dominated the background, at first merely as a grandiose block of stone, golden-brown and radiant in the sunlight, the structure of its various sections still concealed by the equalizing profusion of solar brilliance. The closer we came, the more clearly we saw each architectural segment. The mathematical orderliness of the building's profile became visible. Its Gothic heavenward thrust—I remember well this first impression—discernable as one approaches the edifice, gradually turns earthward to bind itself to the stone, indeed inside the stone, just as the verse of an Iberian mystic is seldom capable of emancipating itself fully from the word. Confined to the earthly plane, this Spanish spirit is more receptive to heaven than in the less sunny climes of Northern Europe where God is invisible, where mists drift about, and where eye and heart perceive and imagine things that lie beyond the limits of knowledge and love. Imagined as a member of our picnicking Spanish clan, Immanuel Kant would have turned out as a philosophizing tanner's apprentice. Conversely, Saint John of the Cross, under a Teutonic sky, could never have made it past a barefoot existence as a chanting Minorite Brother. Happily for both of these gentlemen, such speculative transplantations can take root only in my world of fantasy—"And there only as withered stalks!" my reader says to himself, as he nurses his abhorrence of wild goose chases.

The crowding on the quay side of our steamer was getting unpleasant. We too had gathered our belongings. The ship slowed down, but now the almost touchable coastline produced the optical illusion that we were gliding closer with increasing speed. The gulls now swarmed in greater numbers. Those at home on the island flew greedily towards the ship, piloting us securely into port. It was six in the morning—seven, according to my own reckoning, putting me ahead of the Spaniards in at least one respect, though only by virtue of my grandmother's First Communion timepiece. The landing maneuver was already proceeding apace, our engines jolted at each shift of the propeller's gears. Shouts, probably professional commands, flew back and forth; chains rattled, winches screamed in their effort; we seemed to be in the midst of burgeoning chaos. Here, as before, it struck me as odd that a habitual procedure, one that requires no close analysis of its component events and is repeated day after day, at the very same hour and with the same motions and shifting of levers—that such a procedure should confront the entire topside and below-decks crew with totally unfamiliar tasks. Our fear of a completely mechanized world will be groundless so long as man can make mistakes at his most regular daily chores. And if he swears while performing them, all is most definitely not lost. A defeated man no longer curses, for who will hear his stevedore's prayers?

Here in the port of Palma there were cusswords aplenty, enough to lacerate the ears of God and the Devil. Too bad I was unable to grasp the literal meaning of all the oaths, but in any event they prevented the *Ciudad de Barcelona* from crashing into the dock. Doubtless I would eventually be able to locate the efficacious vocables in Zwingli's Lexicon of Invective, assuming that he was still alive or, barring that, that his estate could be placed at my disposal. For a number of years this brother-in-law of mine had been working on a multilingual *Compendium maledictionum*, and had already amassed copious material. In fact, my first acquaintance with him came about in connection with this foulmouthed enterprise of his. As a student in Cologne I agreed to collaborate on the German section, and in doing so I made contact, circuitously enough, through his younger brother with their sister. To this very hour I have never once felt the need to grace the latter encounter with a single item from Zwingli's polyglot dictionary.

Now the engines were silent; the deck beneath us turned rigid, almost like *terra firma* itself. The ship was roped to the pier and the landing plank hauled aboard. Police and Civil Guards, in their funny shiny caps with the flattened occiput so conducive to snoozes against vertical surfaces, clambered aboard to collect the passengers' passports. Since we expected no one to meet us at the pier, we had no need of searching the waiting crowd, which meant that the excitement of disembarking was less for us than for others who were using binoculars to locate their loved ones. Our excitement had a different, more sinister urgency. Since leaving Basel we had pictured to ourselves, in long and fruitless conversations, our Mediterranean voyage with all of its ports of call. Once on land in Palma we would hail a cab and drive straight out to the Hotel Príncipe Alfonso, unless we were able to catch the hotel limousine itself. One thing was certain: it was a first-class establishment, located somewhere out of town at the seashore. That was all we knew, for Zwingli's letters in Spanish were limited for the most part to accounts of his exploits with females. The duties and other details of his job, which had taken him unexpectedly from Rome to Mallorca, he mentioned only cryptically. When a person's outward occupation differs from his inner ambitions—and this was the case with Zwingli—it is unimportant how he goes about fulfilling the chores. Eating bread with the sweat of one's brow is only for those who harvest it with their left hands.

But over there on the dock, great Scott, isn't that...! It's got to be, or my name...! I rubbed my eyes. But now wait just a moment! Beatrice can see better.

"Beatrice, over there, at the right! No, farther! Yes, the guy standing next to the one in the white smock, near that handcart and the pile of baskets! Either that's Zwingli or I'm seeing ghosts in broad daylight!"

"Zwingli? You surely are seeing ghosts, Vigo, or somebody's double. Yet I should think that your own ghost back in Amsterdam might suffice for a while. Must my poor, dear brother have one too? Come on, let's watch for our luggage. Wave to a porter! They're called *mozo* here. Let's not lose time! I'm so frightened! I hope we're not too late. This crowd is getting awful! The vulgarity of humankind is nowhere so apparent as in railroad stations and at landing piers!"

While this dialogue was in progress the crowd on the pier had shifted, and no matter how carefully I searched among the heads, there was no longer any sign of Zwingli. Was I truly seeing phantoms? I had no time to linger on such thoughts. Each of us had about six items of luggage of various types and sizes, which I now laboriously pushed forward. Although I shouted the word *mozo* several times over the railing, not a single porter responded. The menials now leaping deftly over the gunwales probably took me for a miserly type. Maybe Beatrice could have better success. She had on her uppity-snooty face, the one she used in protest against the plebeian mob that now had abandoned all etiquette and was straining to get on land as quickly as possible. "If you get shoved, shove right back": neither of us has ever really followed this exhortation, Beatrice on aesthetic grounds, I out of a predominantly fatalistic temperament. As a result we have missed trains and other vital connections in life, and when disembarking we are the very last to cross the plank—which of course lends us a certain dignity after all.

As the pressure increased, as the rabble with its charitable Christian theology of the thrusting elbow pushed me to the tail end and headed for land, I sank deeper and deeper into my own inner world. Suddenly that nightmare once again came to the fore. The thought of Zwingli's phantom transported me instantaneously across oceans and countries back to my little attic flat in the Nicolas Beets Straat in Amsterdam. There I had been the tenant of one Madame Perronet, a French widow who earned her bread as a landlady. For thirteen weeks I maintained lodgings, with permission to entertain guests, directly beneath her sheltering roof. A few days prior to our helter-skelter departure for Basel there occurred the most curious exploit, shocking in its total arbitrariness, and involving my very own double.

It happened on a Saturday afternoon at about four o'clock. I was expecting Beatrice, who planned to stay overnight. Madame Perronet had gone shopping, and none of the other tenants were home. The doorbell rang. Thinking that it might be Beatrice I went to the stair to pull the long rope that opened the front door. Who knows, perhaps she had got off early from her enervating job, which consisted in educating the stubborn children of the Ix family in competition with their barbaric parents.

"Françoise?" I heard from below, but couldn't see anyone. I went down a few steps in order to see who had entered the narrow stairwell. In Holland, stairwells are a product of each individual homeowner demanding his own front entrance—the rear doors being common to all. They are constructed in such a way that from the top of the stairs you can never see who is at the door.

I myself, blinded by the light flooding in from below, couldn't make out who was standing in the doorframe. But I did hear a scream, and then the door slammed shut.

I thought nothing more of it and went back to my typewriter to continue translating the final chapter of a book that I was very busy with at the time, The *Bourgeois Carnival* by Menno ter Braak. I had read excerpts from it in a magazine, was annoyed by its literary technique, and hadn't understood much of it at all. Just the same I went out and bought it, because I was in basic sympathy with its romantic attitude, an effective point of departure for treating, with the one-sided device of a brilliant dialectic, the eternal conflict of mind and soul, life and death, poet and bourgeois. The adventure fascinated me all the more as it pointed in the direction of Nietzsche and, so it seemed to me at the time, Novalis. In order to make the most of this literary encounter I decided to translate the *Carnival* into my own language.

The result was amazing: in eleven days I sight-read, so to speak, into the typewriter a book I thought I didn't even understand. It meant working well into the night, and this led to friction with my landlady, for the gentleman in the next apartment complained about the clattering of my rickety typewriter. So after 10 pm I placed the contraption on my bed, erected soundproof walls of pillows and cushions around it, knelt down in front of it, and pecked away into the wee hours. During these nights of second-hand creativity I noticed that my neighbor, who ran a placement service for German housemaids, was also in the habit of—quite literally—kneeling down to his work, and that he also used his bed for support. But my fellow reproductive artist also preferred not to practice *con sordino*—a carnivalesque touch that greatly amused my erudite author ter Braak when he learned of the nocturnal origins of my translation.

Beatrice arrived at the appointed time and revealed that she had been forced to give notice to the Ix family because they had refused to allow her a few weeks' leave to look after her mother and brother. Anybody can send off telegrams, they told her. This brought about a change in our plans. We decided to leave Holland for good, a country where apparently even the heads of household were not averse to using the rear entrance.

In the middle of the night we were roused from sleep by knocks at our door. My first thought was: the vice squad. Amsterdam has long enjoyed a reputation as an immoral city, although its nighttime constabulary cannot compare in overall charm with its counterpart in Paris. Realizing this, my lovemaking in the gigantic peasant bed Madame Perronet had one day installed in my attic room took on the qualities of a criminal act, like any form of love that treads the paths of the Lord exclusively. At the same instant—our door wasn't locked—the landlady stepped in the room. Her behavior was strange, her dishabille signaled distress; she stood next to our bed with tears flowing down her cheeks. Then she broke down completely. I threw my coat over her shoulders and waited until she took hold of herself under Beatrice's expert ministrations. "*Oh, elle est morte!*" she sobbed repeatedly, "*Morte, la pauvre fille!*" And then she gave us this account:

When I came to her house looking for a rental, she had experienced sheer terror, for I was the spit and image of a ship's officer with the East India Line. He had been engaged to her friend, who lived a few houses down the street. A year ago he had left her, which is to say he never returned and never sent word of any kind. She, Madame, had taken such pity on her friend that on her own she initiated a search for the blackguard, but with no success. She was told that he was still with the same shipping line, but that he was now sailing exclusively in Indian waters. When I had ascended her stairs with my prognathic jaw—"*un peu brutal, mais pas du tout du boxeur féroce*"—she had been able to master her fright only with difficulty. For here he was, the absconded lover, in clever disguise with loden coat and soft-brim hat (my romantic-egghead getup of the period), returning to make her the confidante of his machinations. But as soon as I had come halfway upstairs she realized that it was a case of mistaken identity.

I told her that I remembered the rather unfriendly reception she gave me, but that I ascribed it to my clumsy French. It was, she said, precisely the way I garbled her language that had put me in her favor. My mutterings had displayed such queer distortions and such totally un-Gallic sensibility that she found it charming—"*et elle l'est toujours, Monsieur!*" So she abandoned all suspicion of offering shelter to the double of a mangy *canaille*. One token of the fondness Madame henceforth felt for me was the enormous double bed in place of a single-sleeper.

I knew that since the death of her *pauvre Perronet* Madame cherished only two creatures in this world: her monstrous tomcat Melchisédech and a woman friend, Trüüs, whom oddly enough I never laid eyes on—the jilted fiancée. Our first encounter had taken place on that fateful Saturday afternoon. Madame was late with her shopping, and the girl had come over. As usual, I opened the door from above, and in the semi-darkness of the stairwell Trüüs took me immediately for her lover and thought: back from India and now having a secret love affair with my best friend! Treachery! Back home she wrote a few deranged words of farewell to her parents and then turned on the gas oven. The police and the municipal health authorities were summoned to the scene. They roused Madame from her bed and took her to her friend's house to identify the corpse. Madame testified that the probable cause of Trüüs' suicide was the girl's encounter with me—therefore I had better prepare myself for an interrogation. The following day an officer from Criminal Investigation actually came and looked me over. In profile and frontal view he compared my visage with a number of photographs of the sailor. The session resulted in his complete satisfaction: I had the young lady's suicide on my conscience.

This *Doppelgänger* syndrome, cleared of all the humbug associated with it ever since Samuel Johnson, this thing that had already afflicted me inside my sleeping bag—now it was after me once again at the pier in Palma, triggered by Beatrice's remark about the phantom double, as we approached the landing platform inch by inch. Again I saw myself on the dead girl's album pages, held to my view by a policeman: Vigoleis with the rank of an officer of the Royal Dutch Merchant Marine, with gold epaulets and chevrons and tam-o'-shanter. Even my own mother would have recognized her prodigal son, delighted that he achieved such success—not, to be sure, as a devout parish priest (bearing the bishop's crook beneath his cassock, in keeping with our family tradition), but as a fully respectable, seaworthy subaltern. What mother likes to show around a son who, far from having made anything of himself, chucks the products of his hard work into a coal stove? As a sailor he would travel the seven seas—earthbound, to be sure, and lacking any claim on a pension in Eternity—but not a bad alternative at that. Ah, dear Mother, my breast was too narrow for the clergy, and not tough enough for the merchant marine. A few verses, that's all that has entered it, and a few sparse hairs, that's all to be found upon it. And anyway, Mother would never have approved of a tattoo with the symbols of the cardinal virtues, not to mention a purplish one of a naked woman... My Spanish comrades-in-dreams up on the bridge of the *Ciudad de Barcelona* were doubtless more suave; they also looked more arrogant than us palefaces. They fit exactly the image I had, ever since reading pirate stories in my youth, of the occupation I should have trained for. But because I was neither a Spanish nor a Dutch seaman I had cost a human being her life—that is Vigoleisian logic, which gets less and less convincing as I apply my fantasy to playing tricks on the laws of ratiocination.

"Vigo! *Olá*! Vigoleis! Vigo!"

I had lost sight of Beatrice, and found her again only after hearing my name called. The voice was coming from the pier, and we both looked simultaneously towards the spot where again we heard, "Vigoleis! *Olá*! Vigo! Vigolo!"

Far back in a crowd of people stood our moribund Zwingli, or perhaps someone who thought he was or was pretending to be Zwingli—I must be careful not to breathe life into a spirit that has no such claim. But that fellow over there, incidentally a filthy chap, can't be the Zwingli I remember from Cologne and a polite visit in my parental home, the urbane, sophisticated interpreter for the travel agencies of Kuoni and Cook. And yet, and yet...!

"Beatrice, if that guy over there isn't your brother Zwingli, then I'll..."

Well? What did I intend to do? For the life of me I can't remember. Something quite drastic, though, of that I am certain, for all of a sudden I was absolutely convinced that this man... and then I only had time to lift up Beatrice, who had collapsed on a suitcase. I too was devastated—not by Zwingli's resurrection from the dead, but by the fact that a woman with the most variegated travel experiences imaginable, some of them approaching the uncanny, was sitting there on a piece of luggage like a classic heap of misery. Beatrice was acquainted with a world I knew only in novels. She had served as female companion to the wives of millionaires, women who regarded the marriage bed as a trampoline built for leaps into adulterous pleasures that in turn led to poisonings and inheritance swindles. It baffled me totally that she should now behave like this. Of course, the leave-taking from her mother in the Basel hospital had been awful. Not until the telegram arrived later announcing her passing did she dare to tell me, and then with a depth of sorrow unusual for her, about her last hour at the bedside—and even then she told me nothing new. Meanwhile came our trip, one she was inwardly not at all prepared for, toward yet another separation from a loved one. Her family was disintegrating member by member. Her father died of typhus in the Argentinian pampas. Mother and children returned to Europe, the embalmed corpse lodged in the hold of the selfsame freighter. Later came her life at the side of her beloved Vigoleis, who constantly kept her in a state of febrile anxiety ever since their days in Sacred Cologne, where she once pulled him out of the waves of Father Rhine. In a sudden relapse the irrepressibly cheerful nihilist tried to drown himself, willfully breaking his contract as an easily replaceable stage extra in the Lord's Great World Theater. Strictly speaking, I had committed no such misdemeanor, except in the form of theological rhetoric after the fact. For I stand firmly in the midst of Creation like one of Frederick the Great's corporals, thoroughly hazed until he learns to stand at attention. But with a difference: Vigoleis has learned to endure better than those historical automatons.

"Smelling salts!" my reader will be thinking, "Why doesn't the idiot hold some carbonate of ammonium under his lady's nose?" Kind reader, for the moment I'm willing to overlook that "idiot" business, but smelling salts is truly a mistake. It's not in my pocket calendar under "First Aid in Cases of Personal Misfortune," so I never carry any with me. Furthermore, you must realize that Beatrice would have politely taken the bottle out of my hand and thrown it into the Bay of Palma.

You don't know her well enough yet. She is a modern woman with feather cut and plucked eyebrows, and we ought to show some understanding toward her mild attack of enfeeblement. What is more, with her sense of courtesy, which at times assumes comical proportions and which in reality masks contempt (you'll find this out soon enough), she would beg our pardon for the incident if she sensed that at this moment in her life—which has now turned into a moment in my book—anyone might be trying to stop her from feeling anything like simple fatigue.

"Yes, I'm all right. It'll pass as soon as I can get some hot food in my stomach. Let's go on land, the crowd is gone."

A porter finally picked up our bags. Unsummoned, like one of Cologne's Little Magic Helpers, he lugged everything onto the pier, where that man Zwingli reappeared, shouting commands in resounding Spanish and reinforcing them with authoritative gestures of the outstretched little finger of his right hand. Things happened quickly, and then brother and sister stood facing each other.

It was the Year of Our Lord 1931—owing to the downfall of the monarchy a notable year in Spanish history, and owing to his own downfall into the world of *Don Quixote* an equally memorable year in the history of our friend Vigoleis. Moreover, it was August the First, a day on which a gleam enters the eyes of Swiss citizens the world over, a day on which they take special pride in their status as offspring of their wee homeland. Here were two such offspring, but there was no flag-raising, no blowing of the alpenhorn, nor was even a little hanky lifted to eye—surprising enough when we consider the bizarre reverse entombment that had just taken place.

Vigoleis took a deep breath. He sucked his lungs full of salt-spiced Mallorcan maritime air. For five years he will have the privilege of breathing it, until a *finis operis* will lead him to new adventures in other latitudes and altitudes of body and soul. *Adelante*! Onward!

II

Brother and sister stood face to face, but I didn't have to step aside respectfully and pretend I was busy with our luggage. Nor is my reader required to look up from the page to avoid disturbing an emotional exchange between two persons celebrating a grotesque reunion at the edge of the grave. What kind of angel had pushed aside the stone?

"*Salut*, Bé! *Salut*, Vigo! How wonderful of you to come! When I didn't see you at first in the mob that inundates our island every day, I thought you probably got swallowed up in the Barrio Chino in Barcelona. More people disappear there every year than the police are willing to admit. Did you have a good trip, Bé, in the company of your hermit escort?"

We hadn't seen each other for four years, Zwingli and I. But now we exchanged greetings as if just yesterday we had been in Zwingli's flat in Gravedigger Firnich's house in Cologne-Poll, indexing curses in our lexicon file or philosophizing about Dostoevsky, my young culture-vulture friend's favorite author.

"But Zwingli, what's happened to you? You look just terrible! And what was that telegram all about, the one that said you were dying? How's Mother, have you heard? Any word from Basel?"

"Bice, my dear little sister, *sorrelina*, there you go again, taking me literally," Zwingli replied in a very soothing Italian dialect—Tuscan, as I later found out. Brother and sister, both of them having a gift for languages, always conversed in polyglot fashion without transitions—a fact that impressed me no end, monolingual naïf that I still was at the time. Once in a while, out of patronizing respect for me, the linguist of the book-lined study, Zwingli would deign to speak German. He, of course, had absolutely fluent command of my language, though not without the rolling rrr's and the gargling noises that were, to quote my dear poet-friend Albert Talhoff (who, as a Swiss himself, ought to know), part of his gravelly Alpine heritage.

"You always take me so literally, Beatrice, Bice, Bé. Think of me as a page in scripture, where the meaning is something else again! My dying is of the spiritual kind, or to be more specific, it's psychic in nature. The bitch is totally uneducated. She can't even read or write."

I pricked up my ears. What "bitch"? Aha, wouldn't you know, the cause of his horrifying decline was a woman. Beatrice said nothing. She was pale; I noticed a twitching in the corners of her mouth, which always lie in the shadow of a few whiskers, an unmistakable mark of her race. She had pushed forward her lower lip—this meant that she was registering concern. Zwingli would have to be careful not to overdo.

"Oh, I'm sorry. In bed...," Zwingli went on without pause like someone following the One True Path. "In bed she's superb, a first-class revelation as in the Book of Genesis. But otherwise? That's why I asked you to come. We'll take care of everything, so everybody gets what's coming to him. You'll get a concert grand. Music is what I miss most down here. And Vigo will get a comfy study he can crawl into. See, I've got everything all figured out. My dear sister, let me embrace you!"

Now I was truly frightened. In my opinion Zwingli's brotherly heart, though at times a trifle expansive, was as true as freshly mined gold. Yet at the moment, the outer casing thereof lacked that certain degree of cleanliness that might prompt Beatrice to take it to her own. She abhors dirt; she avoids it wherever and whenever possible. Would she now allow her brother...?

But before any sibling contact could occur we heard a voice: "Don Helvecio!"

Zwingli, appearing to respond to this name, dropped the arms he had raised for the embrace and turned toward a man now approaching him. He was wearing blue denim trousers, a motley waistband, and an even louder ascot tie. The two of them had a brief conference, and of course I couldn't understand a word.

Don Helvecio? Did I hear this right? Was that the name used for my brother-in-law? Suddenly the thought occurred to me that I was once again the victim of some satanic mystification. With a quick glance in my direction, Beatrice, too, let it be known that something was amiss here. Was her sudden reticence an instinctual reaction against this usurper of brotherly attention? Here is an explanation, based on later experience: on this island everybody without exception gave Zwingli the sobriquet "Swiss," a generic term used popularly in Germany for cowherds and in Vatican City for doormen and bodyguards. That is the origin of the appellative "Helvecio," to which was added the "Don," commonly used for persons of higher social standing. The name "Zwingli" can be pronounced only with difficulty by those of the Spanish tongue. Permit me to add here the anticipatory remark that I myself was later referred to, though of course not personally addressed as, the *alemán católico*, the "Catholic German." This was a doubly erroneous title. For if by *católico* people meant "universal," then I fit the description neither spatially nor temporally. As for the other meaning, the capitalized one, "Papist"...that I swear I have never been.

Once again Zwingli lifted the little finger of his right hand as he gave instructions. And now I saw, at the extreme end of the digit in question, the instrument of his power over the elves on this island. It was the nail, a good seven-eighths of an inch long, with the black underside polish indicative of ill-grooming, and bent upward ever so slightly at the end. A piece of scrimshaw of this kind, protected from breakage at night by a silver thimble, guards its owner against all forms of menial work. By the same token it qualifies its possessor for a high standard of idleness, Thus it is a mark of class, and as such not to be scoffed at. Even so, Zwingli's nail was less manicured than I have ever seen on any bum.

It was astonishing to observe the effects of a little horn like this whenever fingers with worn-down nails came in its vicinity. Here at quayside, hands quickly got busy loading our bags in an automobile that immediately drove away with a roar and a cloud of smelly exhaust. Again Zwingli held his nail aloft, commanding a gigantic Hispano-Suiza to drive up. A man in yellow coveralls opened the door. The chauffeur, dressed in white livery and white cap, did not so much as glance at us. Doubtless he noticed that we were the last passengers to disembark, and so we were now his distinguished customers, with time and money to spare. He knew the score. We got in.

"Just look at you!" Beatrice felt forced to say when reunited with Zwingli—Beatrice, who seldom criticizes anyone at all, knowing that most people are hardly worthy of such notice or such well-meant remarks. She must love her brother very much—either that, or he actually looked more fearsome than I have been able to describe. How *did* he look? Well, let's put this brother-in-law of mine under good, close, unprejudiced scrutiny.

When I first caught sight of him near the end of Chapter I, I took recourse to the euphemism "filthy chap" to describe his appearance. And Beatrice, far from greeting him with a kiss or even with a jubilant cry of "I'm glad to see you're alive!"—Beatrice, in a reflex action, had told him he looked wasted. Now, no matter how I might try to begin a closer analysis of his appearance, I feel constrained to state: from head to toe, or in reverse direction from the soles of his feet to the tips of his pitch-black tresses (which hadn't seen a barber's shears for months), Zwingli was all that this embarrassing little word says and connotes: he was filthy, he was a wreck, he had gone utterly and totally to the dogs and all the other lower species, visibly and probably inwardly as well. But for the moment, let us observe only the external Zwingli. Just how seriously the inner Zwingli was affected by degenerative processes—that will become sufficiently clear in the course of my narrative.

A quirk of the blood, measurable not by standards of individual countries, but from continent to continent, had also given Zwingli's physiognomy a distinctiveness that cannot easily be assigned to any specific racial or geographic origin. Viewed from the point of view of ethnography, his was a kind of Latin *passepartout* countenance, one that could stamp him as an Italian in Italy, as a Spaniard in Spain, but by no means as a Federated Swiss in his homeland canton. Possessing a well-nigh phenomenal talent for adapting mentally to the ways of the country he was living in at any given time, he was capable of such amazing feats of mimicry as to make him on Spanish soil into a thoroughly genuine Spaniard—so much so that it became necessary to check his true nationality by looking at his passport. Accordingly, the "bitch" always considered him as a "passage-paid" Swiss, a Swiss on paper only. Like a Spaniard's, his beard had a bluish shimmer when unshaven—and unshaven he had been for several days, leading us to believe that he intended to let his whiskers grow like an aborigine or, as we would say nowadays, like an existentialist, which amounts to the same thing. At fault in this regard was presumably the strumpet, the "bitch." And how do we know? Maybe she wanted something more on her Helvecio to tug on above the sheets as well. Why not? A woman's sense of play is mysterious. A man's is even stranger, especially if he comes under the spell of a hellcat like this one, who isn't satisfied with a single ball of yarn.

I mentioned above that Zwingli held a leading managerial position at a large hotel on the island, the Príncipe Alfonso, an establishment that, following the deposition of the XIIIth monarch bearing that name, now called itself, by dint of a little democratic ruse, the "Principal Alfonso." Inspired by the centuries-old liberal traditions of his homeland, Zwingli himself had come up with this gimmick. A high position in hotel management—it's obvious what that entails: shiny black pumps and black textiles, pinstripe trousers, a swallowtail or buttockless jacket, a shirt with starched front and starched cuffs (minus the little curly doodads worn by ancient schoolteachers who still pull their shirts on over their head). Cravat: a discreet grey modulating into silver, with little black dots, pure silk if possible (purchased at Grieder's Silks in Zurich, of course). Thus caparisoned, and assuming that certain other minimum qualifications have been met, our *hôtelier* stands greeting his guests with a smile, ready to serve the *haut monde* from all over the world. His courteous bows mustn't reach so low as to appear servile; for mere physical tasks, rank-and-file minions exist in abundance. As a symbol of social peerage he wears a carnation in his buttonhole. With true experts in this field, not even the touchy question of tipping can cause the blossom to wilt.

But the "bitch"—my reader will again notice that information gathered later is playing a role in my narrative—this particular individual had transformed the above manager type, certified the world over, into something like a cartoon by Berlin's low-life favorite Heinrich Zille. She added certain touches of Käthe Kollwitz and certain bitter contours of the Galician master Castelão. She had made of Zwingli, one might say, a fellow who refuses to hide his personal opinions beneath a starched linen straitjacket, whose heart, now covered by a torn and wrinkled chemise, no longer beats in anticipation of serving his genteel clients. It was indeed questionable whether his heart pulsed for his own sake. In a word, she had created for him a decidedly unstarched private life. Right now, riding in the Hispano-Suiza, we were about to learn details. Must I really add information about the spots on his suit, his scuffed and ragged shoes, the shirt cuffs that hung limply at his wrists and whose color differed only barely from that of his grease-stained jacket sleeves? I do believe that we have said enough; Beatrice was all the more to be pitied.

Vicinity of the city. Gorgeous seaside location. Spacious park at south side. Five minutes to beach. Tram stop at entrance, etc. That's what we read in the brochure describing the hotel where we soon could wash away, in our "double with bath," the dirt of our voyage and perhaps also the moral contamination we underwent upon disembarking. Our personal fenders were damaged. Worse yet, we didn't have any. This matter would have urgent priority as soon as I found out where we were going and how things would turn out. When I have that comfy study to crawl into—how nice of Zwingli to think of me in that way. He's actually a pretty swell guy—a little seedy, quite seedy in fact. Beatrice doesn't like that. But she really ought to have been just a trace nicer to him, seeing that he wasn't dead and all. That would have been a terrible turn of events indeed. Behind it all is a broad; I can't wait to meet the "bitch." Back in Cologne he had one like that. We students were goggle-eyed. After a while she went to bed with our friend the gravedigger. She was a necrophiliac, Zwingli told us laconically. She craved certain cadaverous attributes he wasn't able to provide. Good riddance! If I were him, I would have got the terminal shivers. Not Zwingli. He packed his bags and headed for Brussels, where another affair started up. After that, he hightailed it to Rome, ostensibly to pursue archaeological interests. But his true interest was in digging up women, or at least it had been. Now he was here on this island, with a woman in quotation marks, and surely we weren't prejudiced? The whole thing looked extremely risky.

Suddenly I was very tired. Beatrice, sitting next to me, was also very tired, and Zwingli, facing us on a fold-out seat, seemed likewise very tired. Here, in back, no one said anything. We couldn't hear the lively conversation going on between chauffeur and *palefrenier* up front. The automobile dated from the days of class warfare; a glass partition separated servants from those being served. There was a speaking slot, but it was stuffed with a purple velvet cushion, making the separation near-total—feudal, one might say. In half an hour, I said to myself, we'll be there and things will get democratic again. A pity, though, for I have certain aristocratic proclivities. I admit that I enjoyed that inside window just a bit, smutty though it was. Was this, Vigoleis, the first rung on the chicken-ladder of your new life?

It was eight o'clock, an hour when the sun has already spread its warm blanket over everything. Old Sol also poked his rays inside our automobile, which ought to have been inching along like the vehicle for the bereaved family in a funeral cortege. Our threefold mood was decidedly funereal: black window curtains and a bit of black crepe, and we would be participating in a first-class interment—except, of course, for the missing corpse. Our corpse was alive, and so the Hispano-Suiza could go full out without showing any disrespect. We were driving at hair-raising speed. We saw next to nothing of all the fascinating Spanish sights whizzing past us right and left. Too bad—I'd like to have made note of this and that for letters to our friends. After three minutes—it can't possibly have been any longer—it suddenly turned dark in our car. On both sides of us, house walls edged in dangerously close to our fenders. I started worrying about scratches and scrapes when we jerked to a halt. Beatrice and I lurched forward. We would have gone head-first through the medieval partition if our chariot hadn't been a deluxe model with ample room inside for passenger safety. At any rate, this method of stopping seemed anything but luxurious. Maybe the hotel lacked an auto ramp to its front entrance. We would soon find out.

"*Nous voilà!*" said Zwingli as he rapped on the partition. He was probably stopping for an errand. Our door flew open.

Beatrice didn't move. Thinking that the siblings should be settling everything between themselves, I resolved to be even more hesitant to initiate action than I normally am. So I, too, remained silent, leaning back in a concave section of upholstery that innumerable well-heeled hotel guests had pre-shaped for my traveling comfort. I love broken-in furniture. It welcomes the sitter with deep-seated hospitality.

Zwingli's magic nail, brandished often as an open-sesame, wouldn't work when it came to our hearts—as he himself realized. So to explain his "*voilà*" he added: "This is where she lives. We have a whole floor up there." After a pause, he went on, "It's just so goddam early! She's still asleep," and he scratched his head in confusion. This released a shower of dandruff. We could have covered an entire Christmas tree with the shiny flakes, and if we added a few candles, we might have had a pleasant family reunion after all. Ah, Beatrice, you poor sister of a brother you love so much!

A bunch of ragged kids squeezed together to form an honor guard as the gentleman and his lady emerged from the limousine to follow their host through the entry. So narrow was the street that the open door of our automobile stuck halfway into this gateway. The perfect way to arrive in rainy weather!

The vestibule, where our baggage was standing in a pile, was cleared of the gang of inquisitive twerps by a few kicks administered in decidedly unceremonious fashion by our host. Our motley porter sat next to the baggage pile rolling a cigarette with his left hand, an art Zwingli had also mastered: no more use of bodily appendages in the carrying on of life than is absolutely necessary. Now, however, neither this kind of dexterity nor his magic nail could lift him out of the funk that seemed to envelop him. He was no longer the sovereign Don Helvecio whose marvelous scepter made the Little Helpers dance down at the harbor. As we followed him up the stairs, he gradually got smaller and less imposing, until finally he disappeared altogether. He had simply taken a powder. To describe such events, the occult sciences speak of the phenomenon of dematerialization. It is reported to happen even less frequently than the appearance of ghosts. With the connivance of the appropriate visible agencies, you can conjure up invisible ones. But to make a man of flesh and blood simply vanish into thin air, a man I have been following up a flight of stairs, that is a very sublime form of sorcery, one that must involve the Devil himself. The Devil? Wasn't it more reasonable to suspect the "bitch," who, equipped with parapsychological powers, may have effected Zwingli's abduction to *Nada* just as she had brought on his metamorphosis from elegant young swain to shabby, smelly harbor rat? And if this Zwingli was in actuality only Zwingli's double, then we were dealing with a case of compound levitation—Something scientists like Driesch or Dessoir ought to look into.

A few steps higher and Beatrice, together with her mediumistic faculties, also vanished. One more step and I saw no more of my own self! Only my heart, pounding wildly from the fright, assured me that I hadn't vaporized or turned into one of Gustav Meyrink's spooks. I didn't have a mirror handy to see if I was already wearing the mask of death—the "Hippocratic aspect," as the physicians so delightfully call it.

This spectral intermezzo lasted but a few seconds. I then heard a noise, an everyday, earthbound sound, like a key being turned in a lock. A door was pushed open, and light entered the stairwell—faint, but sufficient to return us all to the real world. I had overestimated the sleeping woman's spell-weaving powers.

The man with the many-colored cummerbund lugged our baggage once more. When everything was in the apartment, he stood waiting. Zwingli reached into his pants pocket—apparently a very deep one, bottomless even, for his hand got completely lost inside it, made a few twisting motions, and then failed to resurface. My own pocket was not so cavernous, but rather well stocked with pesetas. I gave our Little Helper a handful, and this gesture transposed him out of his fairy-tale existence into his native sphere of plodding corporeality. He took the money, grinned, and disappeared. I stepped into the room. There I was, where "she" lived, aground on the shoals of somebody else's love affair.

Beatrice sat down on a chair and lit a cigarette. Zwingli closed the door. I leaned against the wall. It was just like being back in Cologne-Poll, and yet very, very different.

The street where our limousine let us out was called the Calle de la Soledad. *Soledad* means solitude, loneliness, or emptiness, but it can also signify longing, homesickness, mourning, or grief. It is an important concept in Iberian mysticism. On Vigoleis' Spanish sojourn this street was his first anchorage. It wouldn't remain so for long. The seabed wouldn't hold. His ship of life was soon adrift again, and, unfamiliar with the depths in these strange waters, he soon got beached once again.

III

As the hoop fits the barrel-stave, as the gold band seals a marriage, in just the same way inbreeding relates to an island: in each instance something holds something else together. With animals, humans, and intellectual affairs, inbreeding can bring about superior achievements never approximated by a genetic mix. As examples, we might list the bloodlines of famous horses, the generations of Egyptian pharaohs, the writings of Christian mystics, or, since we are speaking of islands, the population of the Dutch island of Marken, which for decades has been on display in proud local costume to tourists and other visitors. The first time I spent a week among such isolated folk, all of whom are related only to each other, I felt very much like an outsider, which of course I was. During that entire visit I wandered about in shame of my mainland chromosomes. I had nothing whatsoever to offer the natives except my money. Deliberate inbreeding provides proof that chauvinism can go hand in hand with calculated cupidity.

Because Mallorca is an island, we could observe the same phenomenon here, though as time went on I became more interested in its gradations of light than in its people. Its light? Perhaps my reader is taken aback by this remark, for one hardly ever hears about the inbreeding of light. What I mean to suggest is the peculiar phasing of illumination generated here by the varying degrees of shade. On this island there takes place a constant shifting and melding of types of shade: human shadows copulate, so to speak, with the shadows and penumbrae of man-made objects and clouds, to yield the ever-changing mystery of Mallorcan light. Hundreds of artists from the world over, on seeing this kaleidoscope for the first time, have not believed their eyes. Some very few have succeeded in fixing the experience on canvas. Prominent among these happy few is a Japanese painter who lived on the island for many years, and who refused to leave until the Civil War forced him off. His name in translation means "Three Little Clouds." In person he was just as gossamer as his name implies, and his paintings breathed the transparent ether of the island itself. As he once told me, this atmospheric transparency was so unique that not even the luminary marvels of his own homeland could bring forth what I liked to call the inbreeding of light—a phrase that, incidentally, he found amusing.

"Cloudless days: over 170 per year; rainy days: no more than 70; fog: 4 or 5 days." That's what the travel brochures say, and I have altered nothing from personal experience, which like all appearances can be deceptive. There, in raw numbers, is the set of climatological preconditions for the miraculous merger of sky and earth whose charm at any given moment overshadows—if I may be allowed such a jarring reversal of metaphor—attractions that Nature normally takes centuries to bring forth elsewhere.

A trace of this magical illumination was also visible in the vestibule of the house occupied by the individual we were now visiting. I have chosen the word "individual" deliberately, with the pejorative connotations it carries with it. By calling her a "bitch," Zwingli had already degraded—or perhaps upgraded—the character of his female companion to that of a mere "individual," especially if we consider what he said about her bedtime talents. Presumably we would soon find out what kind of bitchery he actually was referring to. Was "bitch" a term of endearment? Or did it designate a common street sister? Did he mean to suggest a woman of slovenly habits? Should we already start turning up our noses?

As I have mentioned, there was a handful of that magical light in her apartment vestibule, and at one and the same time it put me in a mood of both reverence and suspicion. Why were the occupants of this house so parsimonious with the celestial gift of light? Wallpaper, which might be subject to fading, was nowhere to be seen. Instead the walls were whitewashed, a type of finish I associated with root cellars and livestock barns. But my very brief sojourn on this island had already taught me that my personal yardstick was ripe for the kindling pile. I would have to acclimate myself to new standards in the same way as I would have to get used to this odd indoors apportionment of daylight.

Was I bothered by the darkness, Zwingli inquired. Surely I wouldn't want it any darker, he said, and if it got any brighter, we would truly be in for it. Had I never heard of flies? One inch more of sunlight and we could be eaten alive!

Flies! So that was it! The perennial plague of the sunny climes, a foretaste of which we had experienced on shipboard! Flies abhor the very darkness that engenders them in swarms. More than most other species, they are lovers of light, the joy of the sunlit world, the very embodiment of the ecstasy of creatureliness. With their cosmopolitan inclinations and their trillions of progeny, they constitute a fine symbol for a faith in the future that puts to shame those of us humans who are inclined to piety. And yet humans don't like them, particularly when they appear *en masse*. But humans in numbers raised to this power don't appeal to their fellow humans either, to judge from the waves of genocide that we have been witness to. Give us a single human being, and things can work out just fine. Give us a million, and we make the sign of the cross and plot their annihilation. Give us a single buzzing fly on a melancholy summer afternoon, alone with a book of poetry in our private study—who would think of harming it as it flits around a central point not unlike our own spiritual core, the point we can only postulate and never locate with certainty? But let flies appear in multiples, and the swatter will swat and the blood will spurt. Man is to his fellow man a demon. To the fly he is a snapping dog.

By banishing sunlight, the woman of this house had also banished insects. The window shutters with their fixed blinds, called *persianas*, let in only the tiniest sprinkles of daylight. Surely that had something to do also with love. As we all know, love shuns the light. Only red light matches its confused inner urges. It stimulates the biochemical processes required for it to find its way out of platonic abstraction back to passion—though little lamps are in reality rarely necessary. In this context I have always been puzzled by the fact that the lowest color on the solar spectrum was selected as the STOP signal in modern traffic. Otherwise, where red lights emit their alluring gleam, life goes on at its most hectic pace. But this matter is far more complex than simple optical semantics. It is an existential problem, one that Jean Paul Sartre might one day solve for us from the exalted precincts of Paris. Red can, of course, also signify "danger," and thus I should be less eager to claim for the color an exclusively erotic meaning.

My eyes soon adjusted to the soft twilight that filled the room like the glow from the clerestory in a basilica. In this room there was much for the twilight to fill, for it was as good as empty. Because it probably wasn't intended as a room for sitting in, it contained just a very few items of furniture. I have mentioned that it was a "vestibule," though one might even contest this designation. There was a bench whose seat and back were made of loosely woven wicker or straw, a few chairs, a table with sideboard that resembled not so much a bonafide table as a South Sea Island catamaran, and two oversized wooden pedestals supporting artificial palms. That was all. These imitation plants, it must be said, produced more subtropical ambience than the decidedly fake-looking real palms to be seen in the conservatory of Amsterdam's Hotel Krasnopolsky. With phony decorations it always comes down to what purpose they are meant to serve. I know certain people who right now are living out their waxen character so determinedly that no waxworks would ever dare to display the originals on a pedestal. The walls of this room in Palma also had a few paintings, but they were less effective as imitations. Not only did their tropical fruit fail to invite the viewer to take a bite. Even a mind untutored in art history could spot their insipid colors as indicative of cheap commercial reproductions. Suspended from the ceiling was a candelabra that looked like a ham in a butcher shop, especially as it was covered with a cloth sack.

One single fly buzzed around this mummified chandelier. It was evidently a degenerate specimen, for by rights it ought to have shunned the darkness, darted through a crack in the shutters, and joined the legions of its relatives that at this time of day were invading the meat stands over at the city market. Zwingli broke the silence by getting up and stretching. He gave a loud yawn, took off his jacket, and made himself comfortable. After all, he no longer had to treat us to the welcoming ceremonies at some princely hotel. And what about the ceremonies here in the Street of Solitude? To describe these I shall, for a moment, have to tell some history.

In the summer of the year 1601, Archduke Albrecht of Austria, the Spanish viceroy in the Netherlands, took up the siege of the city of Ostende. Isabella, who as daughter of Philip II of Spain had presented the Netherlands to her consort Albrecht as a dowry, vowed never to change her chemise until the city had surrendered to the Spanish army. Albrecht's incentive to bring the siege to a rapid and victorious end was therefore very great, but the princess had underestimated the power of the Ostenders to hold out. The siege ended on the 20th of September, 1604 A.D., with a Spanish victory. Princess Isabella had thus worn her blouse for more than three years, offering proof of her patriotism and moral rectitude. There were solemn fanfares as she publicly dipped her blouse in a washtub. It turned the suds an inky color that today bears her name: a brownish-whitish-yellow tint like café-au-lait, known as "isabella."

Surely no one will doubt the truth of this traditional account, insofar as the precise coloration is concerned. I myself regard the background circumstances also as authentic. Who might ever have profited from inventing such a story? Or perhaps "legend corrects history," as Pascoaes says. I can only agree with him.

Historical authenticity on the one hand, with its dry and rarefied scholarly mission, or on the other hand, legend as leaven for poetic truth: both impulses have combined most effectively here to help describe—but my reader will have guessed what I was getting at—Zwingli's shirt. It was of "isabella" shade from top to bottom, save for blackish areas on collar and underarms. Had Zwingli, too, taken a vow? Had he pledged himself to someone in eternal grubbiness? Was he besieging something or someone, or was he perhaps himself under a state of siege? The subsequent course of events will provide historical answers to all these questions.

Earlier, as we were driving to this domicile where "she" was reported to be so superb in bed, Zwingli had waxed progressively more subdued and faint-hearted. This fact, together with the fruitless reach of his hand into his bottomless pants pocket, had led me to conclude that the uneducated "individual" who was as yet unnamed, or whose identity was being anxiously circum-scribed like the One and Only God of Hebrew Scripture—that this person must be a powerful force indeed. And here inside the apartment I received fur-ther confirmation of this conjecture. Zwingli's shirt, plus the kitsch hanging on the walls—whoever could put up with such menaces must be in possession of superhuman strength.

I might have gone down to defeat at the sight of Princess Isabella's chemise, but I am invulnerable to kitsch. More than that, I love kitsch wherever it is appropriate, which is to say, wherever it fulfills the purpose it is without doubt intended to serve. The important thing, of course, is to understand what that purpose is. The fact that we as yet don't know what its overall objective is, need not deter us from our research. Why, even today, we still have no idea why the common flea, the crabgrass of the fields, or mankind itself stands in the midst of Creation. Were we ever to find out, then at that very hour every-thing would lose its poetic or religious meaning. I regard myself as so immune to kitsch that I would even permit Paulus Potter's *Bull* to hang in my study with no danger to my soul. I have just cited an enormously famous work, one that I consider a classic example of the genre.

The longer Zwingli remained silent, all the louder did those reproductions on the walls speak to me.

"Nothing to eat around here?"

This question, posed by Beatrice although it had been bothering me for quite some time too, put some life back in my brother-in-law. Fruit in a picture frame is lovely to look at, but it remains *nature morte* and in the long run cannot satisfy even the birds that occasionally peck at well-painted grapes. In reply Zwingli put both hands in his pants pockets and pulled them outward in the manner of a circus clown. So I made my second dive for loose pesetas and dribbled a handful on the table.

"Is this what you're looking for? Go ahead, help yourself!" Money rules the world right down to the tiniest corner of our planet, right here to the darkest Street of Solitude. Money can get you anything. Kings and popes have groveled in the dust before it. All that matters is the purchasing power we assign to those thirty pieces of silver. If the scribes and high priests had taken back the blood money, Judas Iscariot would never have strung himself up in a fig tree.

I have seldom observed the power of silver as on that morning when it breathed new life into the ebbing Zwingli. It was clear that with my transfusion of cash, I wasn't mistaken in the blood type. Zwingli took the pesetas and stepped over to the window. As he opened the shutters, light, air, dust, and noise flooded the room. He let out a sharp whistle, shouted a few words down to the street, and threw the money down after. This performance impressed me, even though it was taking place at my expense. That's how the powerful of this world act at great moments in history: they show themselves on balconies and toss gold to the rabble.

"Are the masses standing assembled down there?" I was about to ask, but before we heard any "Huzzahs!" or "Long lives!" the sovereign ruler closed the shutters, and our silent vigil could continue. I'm told that people sit around like this in the waiting rooms of maternity wards. Well then, let's wait for the event that, if our luck continues, is bound to be another miscarriage. "Shall I make some coffee? Where's your kitchen?" Beatrice didn't want to stay idle, but her offer was refused.

"Coffee is on its way. I ordered it from across the way at the club. Our kitchen is over there." Zwingli pointed his thumb at a narrow door in one corner. "But she's going to want to use it right away. I mean, it's still so goddam early!"

Meanwhile it was nine o'clock, quite early indeed in a country where evening begins at midnight and where most people, like the pigs, sleep well into the daylight hours.

Although the two siblings had much to say to each other, they had not yet had a private discussion. Were they inhibited by my presence? Hardly, for over the years I had become just as much a part of their extended family as my reader is doing at this very moment. Even so, I didn't quite fit this melting-pot of a family—though I don't mean to imply that my role was supposed to be that of a simple metal lid. No, for the proper fit I had to be ground to size like an engine valve: a dash of emery powder, a few drops of oil, and the rest is taken care of by rotary motion.

"No mail from Basel?"

Beatrice began talking about their mother.

I stood up and walked across the room. In the background was a third door I hadn't noticed before. It was partially hidden by one of the palm stands, and wasn't easily recognizable as a door because its surface blended in with the whitewashed walls. I thought it would probably lead to that special place one could enter without asking. So I opened it and disappeared without ado into even more intense darkness. Brother and sister, their tongues finally unstuck, had started a conversation. Beatrice was using French, and that meant that matters were serious. Zwingli took refuge in Spanish. That's all I heard, and then I closed the door behind me and stole away as if not wanting to disturb lovers in a tête-à-tête that could make or break their affair. Inwardly surrounded by a murkiness seldom pierced by a ray of light, from childhood on I have been a successful if rather timid groper in the dark. Now this compensatory talent once again came into its own. The wall along which I was fingering my way was rough to the touch, and was probably whitewashed also. I felt a doorframe, then a door that was slightly ajar, inviting me inside. It seemed the natural exit from a narrow corridor that led, or so I believed, to a larger room. The door was of the type with a hinged fold down the center, and when I put my shoulder to the outer panel it stuck a bit, shook, and rattled. As I entered the new premises the gloom became even more impenetrable. Out of habit I felt the wall for a light switch. There was none.

Once as a boy, befuddled by a licentious tumult of his senses, he secretly pursued a housemaid, and while following the scent, was discovered by his mother. Mothers don't approve of such things, and when it comes to housemaids and fleshly impulses, they have ineradicable prejudices. But instead of thrashing him as he had expected, this protectress of filial chastity placed certain obstacles in the path of further premature sexual encounters. This brought on feelings of estrangement that Vigoleis bore with him until long after he had outgrown his steamy knickers.

Vigoleis groped along some more, and there—it felt like warm calfskin, something moist and soft. It was naked flesh, and it rose warmly, nay hotly, to his touch. His breathing stopped. Then the flesh twitched, Vigoleis withdrew his hand, but the flesh remained in his hand as if by magnetism. And then a naked arm threw itself around his neck, and then a word met his ears that he couldn't understand. It sounded as bright as silver, and caused the intruder to shiver. He was overcome. He fled.

Amid stumblings and bumpings I found my way back to the room where Beatrice was talking heart-to-heart with her brother. Zwingli had tears in his eyes. They had shifted into *Schwyzerdütsch*, the language of their childhood.

"Zwingli, what's going on here? Who are you holding captive back there in the little room?"

"Captive? *Quelle drôle d'idée*! That's her kid!"

Down below, the doorknocker rapped twice. We heard footsteps on the stair. There was a knock at the apartment door, and Zwingli opened. A man stepped in, identifiable by his uniform as a waiter. He was of medium height, well-groomed, with a handsome face and pleasant manners. His jacket was a blinding white dotted with gold buttons. He brought coffee, which he poured from a copper espresso pitcher, and warm pastry—the famous *ensaimadas*, an island specialty, a local product which the Mallorcans are almost prouder of than of their greatest son, the poet, mystic, philosopher, and martyr to his own so-called Lullian Art, Ramón Llull. I would soon fall in love with both—the delectable pastry and the *ars magna* of Raimundus.

Antonio—the name of this waiter who was later to become our rescuer—was on intimate terms with Don Helvecio who, after introducing us, clapped him several times rapidly on the shoulder as if summoning up his own courage. Antonio spoke some broken French, so I was able to join the conversation for a while until they all lapsed back into Spanish. I was in the minority.

The wheel on Zwingli's mill was once again in motion, the sluice gates were open and things began to revolve. His nostrils flared, he snorted like a horse, his right hand spread out like a fan. The nail on his pinky was set for further action. Whether it was the coffee or Antonio's superior presence, the depression seemed to have left him—and the rest of us too. The air was suddenly clear again. Even the solitary fly had come in for a landing and was slurping up a spartan breakfast consisting of a tiny grain of sugar. Peace and harmony reigned supreme. Why, when such tranquility is possible on a small scale, cannot the nations of the world achieve it in the large?

There we sat, enjoying the repast, though still rumpled from our nocturnal voyage. But who cared? I no longer thought of taking a bath at the Príncipe, and Beatrice too had probably forgotten that we were supposed to be standing—or with somewhat better luck sitting—at a deathbed. Was she happy to have found her brother, if indeed in a ruined state, then at least not breathing his last? Dirt can be washed away, and one can raise up the inner man to new ideals over which death has no dominion. Would we be leaving by the next ship, or perhaps staying on for just a few days? Let's find out what the two of them are thinking.

"You see, Baby..." Zwingli opted for the English language to explain how his plan had developed. He was great at developing plans, that I knew. He was a veritable genius at envisioning things on a grand scale, but with the details of implementation he was an utter failure. He could hold his own with women in the plural, but with individual women he invariably went on the skids. He began his explanation plainly and soberly, with just a touch of impishness. But soon he donned the verbal cloak of man of the future, so much so that we were no longer anything but an audience for him, an amorphous crowd to be fed a big line and eventually, against our will and instinct, to be talked into agreeing with him totally. "You see...," and we truly saw. That is the amazing thing about people with such oratorical gifts. For a little while, we can actually be won over by their prestidigitation. We follow with our own eyes as the buxom lady is sawn in half in her wooden box.

Back in Cologne I had observed Zwingli in superb form. After a lecture by Professor Brinkmann, we returned to my room to discuss a scholarly problem mentioned by that distinguished art historian. Zwingli knew almost all the art museums in Europe, having shepherded around rich people from the States, and especially from South America, as a tourist guide. His "Tours of the Old World Galleries," which he had organized for groups of seldom more than twelve and with the help of various travel bureaus, were well known and very popular. Over the years they netted him quite a thick wad, which he promptly squandered on women or gave away to struggling artists who acknowledged his kindness with gifts of their own work. His private collection, called "Works of Neglected Genius," was respectable. Where it ever ended up the devil only knows. The knowledge of art history he amassed in this fashion would be the envy of any university doctoral candidate, as was also true of the instructional material he collected for himself. Whenever he stayed for more than a couple of months in a university town, he would sign up for courses in art history and write down reams of commentary and analysis in preparation for the time when he, too, would be a Professor of Art History. That was his life's ambition, and he took as his model the great inventor of the discipline, his own distant relative and ancestor Jacob Burckhardt.

But, still, and yet... Whichever opening qualifier we might choose, the fact remains that Zwingli never got his longed-for professorship. The reason was that he applied for it in the wrong field. For not only was he an extraordinary, fully informed, and much-sought-after cicerone in Old-World Collections. He likewise commanded the most astonishing expertise, down to the nicest details of filigree, in the bedrooms of the same metropolises through which he guided so many wealthy devotees of art and beauty. And the art and beauty he got to observe in such places, whose price of admission was usually quite considerable, was not in all cases free of contamination. Because Zwingli never would praise or show a work of art that he didn't know beforehand, he soon fell victim to certain *intérieurs* that he admired so much on the canvases of the French Impressionists.

Here over coffee and *ensaimadas*, and wearing his shirt of historical hue, standing before two exhausted victims who meant the world to him—here he spread out before us a congeries of projects that would affect our future on the island. To wit: he was planning, with the aid of an American millionaire, to establish an International Institute of Fine Arts, and he wanted us as collaborators. He had already worked out all the details. It was to be an enterprise of such imposing proportions that these days not even Unesco could bring into being. I shall return to this project presently, when I describe the nucleus of the establishment on the Calla Caltrava, where it threatened to degenerate into a *lupanar* and where art verily became impoverished. But as for the immediate future, i.e., what we were to do once we rose from this improvised breakfast table—not one word! It was possible that he had talked over this trivial matter with his sister while my own hands had been otherwise occupied.

"I intend to establish, as an adjunct to the Institute, an academy for the selection and training of nude models. Beautiful bodies are not sufficient for a painter; they must know how to utilize their anatomy, and this they will learn at our academy. I also intend to mount a campaign against the prejudice that nude models meet up with practically everywhere. Down here you can't even get a prostitute to sit for you. Women of all classes will soon regard it as a personal and professional honor to be listed in my files with all their anatomical and aesthetic qualifications and idiosyncrasies!"

"And you, you sly old lecher," I could not resist interjecting, "you'll be the meat inspector for your international model-selection bureau. You have a practiced eye and an excellent grasp of womanhood—just as long as they don't have you by the..."

"Not just a good grasp, my dear Vigoleis! Women are a full half of my life..."

"Sure. The half that lies below the belly-button. And with you, no matter how a mathematician or a geometer might object to the phrase, with you that is the greater half. The other half of you has other preoccupations—art, for example, or at least the visual kind of art. And maybe the Hotel Príncipe Alfonso. Or was that a vehicle from your private motor pool that drove us up the ramp here?"

How rude of me, in light of that classy transportation and the clever style of breakfast, to express doubts about the way he divided up his interests. Zwingli no doubt was about to floor me with a snappy rejoinder. But before he could come out with it, we all heard a noise coming from behind the door that had led me to the enchanting darkroom. This was the prelude to a brand new episode. We didn't have a revolving stage, and we could already hear the preparations going on backstage for the ensuing scene, but this only heightened our suspense. From two sources of knowledge—from Vigoleis himself who experienced the drama as co-actor, and from my superior perspective as narrator—I am aware of what is about to happen. Otherwise I would now be pressing my hands to my heart, just as I did following the shock I felt in the sleeping girl's bedchamber. And already I had to steel myself for a new set of confusions. The door opened, and in came...

During the intervening years I have frequently recounted my Iberian adventures in the presence of friends. People have said that I am a brilliant, indeed a peerless story-teller, the master of a rapidly expiring craft. Strictly speaking, there is no such thing as human achievement, just as there is no true human guilt. Rather, we all act at all times in ways that, mysteriously, have been planned out for us. Thus, without fear of sounding pompous, I surely may be permitted here to display in its best light this particular facet of my talents, one which, by the way, never really compensates for my chronic blockheadedness. I practice this art and heaven-sent skill of mine in an era when its specialists can manage to earn a living at it only on the island of Ibiza. What is more, I am very particular about the circumstances under which I practice my craft. The setting for my performances is by no means always ideal. This is how I imagine the optimum surroundings: a comfortable easy chair, but one that doesn't shift my center of gravity so far back that my ungainly body is unable to rise for climactic moments. A bottle of wine, some candy in a bowl—"No, thank you, I still haven't taken up smoking"—good ventilation, and a small circle of friends. Women? If possible, and if they are pretty, all the better.

I commence with a few introductory remarks, then with rapid strokes I sketch out the setting and add some people. At this point, while still offering a preliminary overview, I can easily get sidetracked. It often happens that an apparently tangential matter can become the main topic, simply because this or that aspect of the subject, some quirk or other that I had barely noticed up till now, suddenly engages my own attention so urgently that it subsequently turns into a complete, unified story. If I sense that my listeners are falling under my narrative spell, then this has a doubly energizing effect. I lose sight of my normal self and begin to embody all the roles that I intend to present in my tale. I turn into a young girl carrying a jar of oil on her head, or an ancient crone surrounded by a cloud of dust and moths that have eaten away the majestic robe she wanted to show off for me. Or I'm a man with an enormous hat, riding with ridiculous boots and spurs astride a puny jackass, a character who was none other than my own self—I mean the man, though in another tale I star as the ass.

All such characters become flesh of my flesh. They are true, real, and believable. My talent for mimicry is equal to any imaginable subject. Even if I start out with a bald head—which in reality I don't yet have—and eschew the makeup-artist's rigamarole, I can conjure the image of a society dame's towering coiffure. I do it with my fingers or something—I'm not really sure how. I can even do landscape. In my writings, this particular element of narration gets treated rather gingerly if at all (my reader will surely have noticed by now which world I am most at home in). But when I tell stories aloud, the physical surroundings around my characters take tangible shape, and it is here, as the effect of my own sorcery, that I begin to take notice of those surroundings myself. Just how do I do it? I don't know. It all simply gushes forth like water from a rock touched by a staff. Good raconteurs have always had an air of magic and mystery about them. And we all know that the origins of poetry are to be found in the ancient creation of myth.

To offer a concrete illustration of what I am trying to say: whenever I tell the story of our arrival on the island—and if the wine is good, if the chocolate is bittersweet (from the firm of Lindt, if I'm lucky), all this served up by a comely hand, and if the legs I see opposite me are of alluring shape—then the moment soon comes when with a single motion of my hand I consign Beatrice, Zwingli, and my friend Vigoleis to mute roles as observers of the ongoing drama. As if watching a cinematic closeup, my listeners now concentrate intently on my every move. I arise from my chair and push it back with my knees. My audience, sensing that I need space, spreads apart to allow me to move to the far side of the room. It is never necessary for me to leave the room entirely to produce the desired effect. I have an uncanny ability to stand against a wall and induce the impression that I am nowhere to be seen. When the moment arrives, all eyes are surprised to see me appear, as if I were stepping forth from behind stage scenery, or emerging from the wall itself, just as our double steps out of a mirror to greet us.

Not long ago I had occasion to perform this scene by candlelight in the private quarters of my friend, the writer Talhoff. As before, I vanished from being into nothingness, and suddenly burst forth from nothingness into the quintessence of the woman I was portraying. As soon as the episode was over, my silent but extremely attentive listener could not restrain himself from crying out, "How does the sonofabitch do it!" Well now, the sonofabitch was already working on a second bottle of Orvieto from the private castle winery of the Marchesi Antinori. No wonder that my transincarnation had come off unusually well. Even without the aid of such an exquisite vintage, I am capable of appearing to everyone's astonishment through that imaginary door. I am ready at any time to match my talent with that of, for example, Christine Brahe at Urnekloster in Rilke's *Notebooks of Malte Laurids Brigge*.

With a single word I indicate that all three of us have heard a noise behind that door, and that Vigoleis has taken his heart in both of his hands. Then I raise my right arm to form an obtuse angle. My lower arm is bent slightly forward, my hand with its raised palm and closed fingers hovers in the balance. Everyone sees a delicate, white hand, the one I am portraying, a hand that by pure coincidence resembles my own in beauty and proportionment—which only heightens the illusion, of course. Then I start walking, or rather striding, with my head raised—a beautiful woman's head, so beautiful in fact that nobody reading these words will ever believe that my unsightly noggin could ever approximate its loveliness. This exquisite head then moves forward to the gentle rhythm of my steps and my extended hand carrying its imaginary vessel. My left hand holds up the hem of my robe, a brightly flowered albornoz. With each step of my right foot I offer my onlookers the glimpse of an immaculate alabaster limb underneath. The delicate pitter-patter you hear is the sound of my little golden slippers, not much larger than those worn by any fairy-tale princess you might think of. By hunching up my left shoulder and taking a deep breath I force my chest forward. No matter what I happen to be wearing—my housecoat, a colorful Portuguese peasant jersey, or a custom-tailored suit—the effect is just the same every time. A single suggestive word, and my audience observes the illusion of something that will, of course, remain decently concealed, but which surges forward beneath the play of cloth folds. One single additional motion, and these breasts would be as palpable as those of Simonetta Vespucci in the painting by the Florentine master Antonio del Pollaiuolo. Yet my reader must not forget that we are in Spain, where women reveal their bodily charms only sparingly. With every second step just a tiny bit of leg—no more than that.

Just one more glimpse of whiteness, and I have reached the far end of our hallway. While making a careful balancing motion so as not to spill the contents of this red-and-gold-painted receptacle, I open a whitewashed door. Suddenly the ravishing vision has disappeared, and with her the chamber pot in her delicate, royal hand.

The person referred to on preceding pages between unkind quotation marks as "bitch" or "uneducated individual," the one we have blasphemously circumscribed (or perhaps circumvented) in analogy to the unnamed deity of the Old Covenant—this person has now made her entrance into Vigoleis' applied recollections in a manner more stately than could possibly be imagined. Again Vigoleis took a deep breath, but this time it was not, as at the close of Chapter I, to fill his lungs with the air that wafted across the island. This time he inhaled a woman's aroma, which beguiled the room he was sitting in. Then with both hands he took his heart, which was up in his throat and choking him, and pressed it back down into his chest.

The child's flesh, which had clung to his hand in the dark—if such a thing can happen with young flesh, then what must the fully mature flesh of the mother be capable of?

If I hadn't been sitting down, it certainly would have been my turn to collapse onto a piece of luggage. Beatrice was staring ahead, and her eyes seemed not to focus on anything at all. But my dear bamboozled Zwingli—where have you gone all of a sudden?

Our good friend, the male concubine, had fled the scene entirely.

IV

The sun appeared to be sweltering in the glare of its own light as, at the apex of midday, we stepped out on our street, which at this moment was living up to its official name. It was deserted, save for a few errant dogs and cats that were performing the service of public sanitation. Growling and hissing, they slunk into entryways and tugged out to the street the contents of garbage cans, cardboard boxes, and crushed paper bags. As we approached, they scattered. When the Calle de la Soledad emptied out on a square surrounded by decrepit buildings, we suddenly noticed, in the expanse of white dust, a crowd of teenage boys and a few ragged kids standing around a lanky young girl. She was dancing, egged on by wild shouts and the wheezy music of a squeezebox, flinging her naked arms upward amid a clattering of castanets. It was a colorful scene. I was just about to join the throng of young onlookers when there was a piercing scream, whereupon these other disturbers of the noontime peace also scattered to the four winds. The square was thus vacated for the passage of our little group *à quatre*.

María del Pilar, as gorgeous in name as in figure, displaying her little Renaissance tummy in precisely the manner savored by Spanish swains (until, swelled up by the Good Lord's annual blessing, it must be replaced by one having the proper proportions), and with the graceful prominence of her pointed breasts, anatomical features that might never spell profit for a corsetiere but could doubtless be abundantly cash-producing for the personage who sported them—

Her Helvecio (a.k.a. Zwingli), so sleekly shaven that his face glistened like a blue shad in a running stream in his Confederated homeland. The man was groomed and, quite contrary to his occupation, clothed only in trousers, glistening white shirt, and white cord sandals, making the overall austere impression of a corpse on a catafalque; a handsome fellow of 25 at the side of a handsome woman who was but one minuscule year his senior—

María del Pilar's sister-in-law, enlisted as her bosom companion, a broad-minded guest in her darkened apartment: Doña Beatriz, trying rather awkwardly to synchronize her broad Northern European gait to the mincing steps of the individual who, here at least, shall pass without the faintest taint of quotation marks—

And finally my humble self, her brother-in-law and would-be heart-throb, her premature obituarist, and the as yet unscathed victim of her connubial prowess: Don Vigo, who no doubt occupies her thoughts just as much as she does his...

Thus this domestic quartet ambled across the square. But then Pilar, too, became aware of the musical entertainers. There was another scream, an echo of the first one but weaker, more like a sob from deep within, like a devout ejaculation uttered in abject despair. And just such an ejaculation it indeed must have been, for it contained the sacred names of Jesus, Mary, and Joseph. All doubt of its reverent nature was removed by the sign of the cross she swiftly made with her right hand over her face, following it up immediately with the larger analogue of the same ritualistic gesture. My own mother used to go through the very same motions when proceeding through the Stations of the Cross—more sedately, to be sure, and with more deliberate gestures of self-benediction, while insisting that her little boy follow and do likewise. But there weren't any Stations of the Cross here. In Barcelona I had noticed that gentlemen tipped their hats when passing a church, and ladies crossed themselves. But here, there wasn't a church in sight. How silly of me to forget that this same symbolic gesture can be used to exorcise the devil or to ground a bolt of lightning! So many oddities and novelties had descended upon me since landing here—I ought to have anticipated such a twist as a public, gratuitous Declaration of Faith in the Triune God, delivered wholly without expectation of reward. And there I was, thinking that I knew all the ins and outs of Roman Catholicism, a cultural institution that, to be truthful, no longer enjoyed my allegiance.

Keep your eyes and ears open, Vigoleis! For now you are living in a hyper-Catholic country, the selfsame land that perfected the Inquisition. Perhaps they will no longer escort you in hair shirt and devil's cap to the gibbet—but be careful just the same! Beatrice, too, must be on her guard here, accosted as she already has been by a terrifying, fanatical glance on that boat on our way over here! Is it obvious from her looks that she is lacking a Catholic baptism? Once again, Vigoleis, take care! You are walking among religious fanatics, oh thou of no faith at all, in an exceedingly religious country. But hold! "Faithless Among the Faithful"—wouldn't that be a dandy title for the diary you really ought to start writing now that you have begun a new life? A new *external* life, let it be stressed, for internally, in your heart and in your soul, let's grant that there's not much that can be done. Pursuant to the promise you made (permit me this gentle reminder!), do send soon a few diary quotes to your dear uncle, the Bishop in Münster who, prior to his summons to episcopal office, himself once traveled through Spain with a hiking staff and a beret that concealed his breviary. How comical were the tales he told of his extensive wanderings in mufti! And yet he can scarcely have ever found himself in such exciting Spanish company as his nephew at this moment, who, smooth-shaven and pressed to the nines, is on his way to buy a bed.

A bed? Aren't you and Beatrice going to reside in the Hotel Príncipe? Or have you decided, rather, to take up quarters in the Street of Solitude? If you are to be the house guests of María del Pilar, then doesn't she have a guest room with sleeping facility? And what about that nail on Zwingli's right pinky? Has it lost its magical efficacy? As is well known, the Little Cologne Helpers are wont to perform their lilliputian domestic favors only at nighttime. But of course there are always exceptions. Besides, they weren't afraid of the light back there at the port of Palma. And Pilar's apartment was just the place for doings in the dark.

Earlier, as soon as the lovers had left the apartment by separate doors, each bearing a different burden in hand and mind, Beatrice had whispered to me, "What a frightful situation this is! Poor Zwingli! It's enough to make you sick. I wouldn't be at all surprised if what we have here isn't a severe case of sexual bondage. When that happens, the victim just gives up taking baths."

"Oh come now, Beatrice, that's nonsense! If everybody who forgets to take a bath is a sexual slave, then I'll be forced to revise my concept of human freedom. Especially my own freedom, because I don't always take baths either."

"This has nothing to do with you. And besides, you have a regenerating skin."

Like that of a Zulu, I thought, but kept the idea to myself so as not to press my luck.

She was right. The situation we found ourselves in could well be described as frightful, particularly with regard to impending developments and threats of disaster. What is more, the situation was critical in more than one sense of the term. To be specific, the household budget was obviously in a terminal state. A third plunge into my trouser pocket, this time yielding a piece of paper currency, had materialized a midday meal, a feast that, it must be conceded, provided delectable proof that Pilar could be "superb" with the cooking spoon. How enormously talented she must be in bed—this I could easily gauge by the fact that Zwingli, an experienced gourmet compared to whose taste my own would then have best been termed porcine, regarded his paramour's culinary skills as negligible. Today, incidentally, my standards of cuisine are rather different. My only continual failing in this regard is in the philology of the printed menu. I remain an easy mark for poetic designations of entrees that, once ordered and served, turn out to be nothing more than variations on the theme of the vulgar potato or some other miserable, proletarian vegetable. This happens even in hostelries that should be ashamed of such shameless sham. It's just one more example of the degradation of elegance in our world.

Here I shall interrupt the course of my memoirs only so long as it will take to report what Beatrice, in *Schwyzerdütsch* conversation with her kid brother, was able to squeeze out of him. I'd better let Beatrice do the reporting, even though it means shifting into indirect discourse. Her account will by no means stray from our main topic.

Now then, we are already familiar with the "frightful situation"; likewise with the prevailing conditions of unwashedness. But above and beyond these givens:

It was not possible, she told me, to achieve full clarity in the matter of Zwingli's job at the hotel, though his professional connection there had not been officially terminated. Since he began cohabiting with the "individual," he would betake himself every once in a while out to the Terreno where the hotel was located, just to see how things were going. Aha, thought Vigoleis upon hearing this. The philosopher Scheler had been right after all, when he responded to the Archbishop of Cologne, who had accused him of unvirtuous conduct, by asking His Eminence if he had ever seen a signpost that had ever gone in the direction it pointed to. There exist certain dictators who can lead entire nations from obscure positions far behind the scenes—why shouldn't Zwingli, the boss in the brownish-yellow blouse, be able to direct the activities of his minions in their lily-white chemises? At the hotel everything was in good hands—that is, in the best of hands apart from his own. Specifically, things were in the hands of his friend Don Darío and a Baltic secretary. His salary was sent to his apartment with a certain degree of regularity, though at the moment a remittance was late in arriving, and thus he was a bit short and somewhat restricted in his movements; how embarrassing it was for him that we chose to arrive on the first of the month.

As for our living quarters, we could of course take up residence in the Príncipe Alfonso; or if not there, then someplace else. He would prefer, however, that we chose a domicile not quite so far out of town. His strongest preference, in fact, was that we should share his own townhouse quarters, for this would be in keeping with the plans he had already outlined. He had indicated as much in the telegrams he had sent, admittedly in somewhat encoded form, but trusting in Beatrice's intelligence to decipher the intended message. As to the person he called the "bitch," the same person whom Beatrice referred to as the "individual"—María del Pilar was a simple girl from a humble background, who was not yet quite what Zwingli intended to make of her, but who was on the way toward becoming the very center of Mallorquine society; only a very few more obstacles remained to be surmounted. She had a certain past—a consequence of her beauty and her liberal attitudes towards living and loving, a state of affairs he was certain we were prepared to ignore. Now it was his intention to obtain access for her to exclusive circles, groups consisting for the most part of the nobility, and surely we could be of assistance in this effort. Music and literature would open doors on this island almost as readily as a master key made of money. He wished to liberate the young lady from the confines of her talent, and educate her up to his own level. This would best succeed if we would consent to move in with him—or rather with her, for she was apparently the one in charge. An increasing familiarity with persons of intellect, good conversation and the like, all this could not help but soften her up for cultural advancement. But we would now have to take an immediate first step toward creating this Pedagogical Province: we must go into town together and buy a bed. We were to note further that the necessary wool mattress, as was the practice here on the island, would have to be custom-made, but that this could no doubt be ready by this very evening...

Vigoleis as the cultural mentor of a beautiful woman, as a prop that was to foster this vine's voluptuous growth—there have been cases when the tendrils have overgrown their artificial support and strangled it completely.

Beatrice thought that we should stay on, for only in that way could she accomplish something for her brother. Did she intend to minister unto him in true biblical fashion, as Martha and Mary had done with their moribund brother Lazarus, *secundum Joannem*? "Lord, by this time he stinketh" was equally applicable to Zwingli, although he seemed to have been dead for longer than four days, and had not been transported by angels to the lap of Abraham. On the contrary, his lap was still very much of this world—more specifically, of this island—most specifically, of this city of palms, Ciudad de las Palmas, a name that refers to the palms of victory planted here by the Roman conquerors of yore.

And it was beneath the city's palms that we now strode forth to purchase a bed, at the hottest hour of the day, a time when anyone who possibly can do so will take shelter in the shade. The well-to-do circles in particular, known on the island by their Catalan nickname *butifarras* (blood sausages), are quite invisible in the noonday sun; they have disappeared behind the imposing portals and closed-draped windows of their palaces, the very abodes that were supposed to be opened up for Pilar by the power of Beatrice's music and my Vigoleisian literature. But wasn't Pilar's beauty alone sufficient to cause this to happen? If I were a king and lord of a castle, with a simple gesture I would have the drawbridge resoundingly lowered just as soon as my tower watchman, with a blast on his horn, announced the approach of such a specimen of pulchritude. And since, according to Schopenhauer's persuasive dictum, intellect is the enemy of beauty, María del Pilar would not even have to be smart in order to subjugate the petty grandees of the extinguished monarchy of Mallorca. If it is true what the chroniclers say about Catherine the Great's thighs (and what earthly reason might they have for telling fibs about such a tangible part of the body?), that she had but to spread them, and whole dynasties would perish—if this is true, then Pilar certainly could at least put her thighs to use forging the little golden key that would defy the craft of the most expert locksmiths. Why employ Beatrice as a cudgel, or Vigoleis as a battering ram? Why Vigoleis, who as yet has no heroic exploits attached to his name, unlike his eponym *Wigalois*, the "Knight of the Wheel" in the courtly epic by Wirnt von Gravenberg? I was not yet aware that Pilar kept a dagger sweetly concealed against one of the extremities in question. Nor did I realize at the time that she had been a registered member of the professional organization that ever since *Don Quixote* has been referred to as the "fair guild," a sodality that maintains headquarters in every city in the world including, of course, Palma—here, as in so many places, in the twilight shadow of the Cathedral. Sin prefers to ply its parasitic trade at the very place against which the Gates of Hell shall not prevail. That is how sin secures for itself an earthly existence unto all eternity.

In a country like Spain, where worldly goods are distributed very unequally, those who cannot afford a siesta comprise a scandalously large majority. In a city like Palma, with well-nigh 100,000 souls, the majority is sufficient in numbers to make the street scene picturesque in the extreme, even during the hour of well-heeled snoozes.

The closer we got to the inner city, the livelier became the traffic, the crowds, the hurly-burly of the masses of scrawny little people who are forever in a rush to get out of the sun—or to get out from under poverty. But sociological conjectures such as this are never very reliable in countries where the sunset turns nighttime into daytime. Little *burros* trotted past with lively gait, everything on them ashake—ears, tail, and the burdens they were made to carry: baskets, burlap sacks, large clay jugs filled with water, mother and child in the perennially touching pageant of a Flight into Egypt, Joseph with his walking-staff taking up the rear. Yet how unsaintly these *patres familias* looked with their motley sashes holding up their pants beneath their overhanging bellies! The biblical ass always and everywhere makes for a charming sight; even outside the realm of literature, Cervantes has granted protection to this animal all over the world against verbal and other kinds of abuse. To me, asses are also a delight in the intellectual-artistic sphere. Their numbers there are probably even greater than in the animal kingdom, where I am told they are doomed to extinction. In art and the life of the mind, they are not bound to a particular climate. Having evolved upwards into beasts of gluttony, they will perish only with thought itself. They are a romantic fauna, and I feel that I have a certain consanguine relationship with them, Is this mystical vanity? Perhaps, perhaps...

It wasn't only the little *burros* that held my attention here in the mid-city. I was registering everything. Each and every step provided me with material for the travel articles I was going to write for a Dutch newspaper. I had already peered into a few courtyards, making mental note of them for special visits later. Then I discovered a merchant who, besides the usual rubbish, was selling devotional wares. His hottest item was a self-illuminating crucifix for one peseta, unmistakably "Made In Germany." If you peeped through a pinhole in a cardboard box, you saw Our Savior surrounded by rays of light. The inventor of this phosphorescent masterpiece, a carpenter's apprentice from Saxony, had become a millionaire in just a few short years. Next to the peddler of sacred images, a commercial scribe had set up his table. A girl was dictating to him— presumably a love letter, and what a shame that I couldn't understand a word.

"Beatrice, come over here and make yourself useful. I am consumed with curiosity as to what that child is getting the old man's pen to write for her. What do you mean, indiscreet? There are a whole lot of other people standing around and listening. It's a public institution here. But what's going on? What's the rush? That bed's not going to run away!"

Zwingli had dashed off on the double, Pilar likewise and, locked arm in arm with her, Beatrice perforce also. Then all three made a sudden turn—eyes right, for'rd *march*! Whereupon the trio disappeared into a murky passageway. I had all I could do to keep up with them. The narrow pavement was cool underfoot. By stretching out my arms, I could touch the houses on both sides. These houses seemed to be leaning toward each other—that's how very tall they were, and that's how very black the strip of daylight was that closed off our view of the sky like a shutter.

I stopped and took a breather in the shade. And then I lapsed into one of those alleyway reveries that befall me whenever I enter such a narrow urban defile. This has happened to me ever since I made the acquaintance, some thirty years ago or more, with the writings of the German arch-lampoonist and "autocogitator" Georg Christoph Lichtenberg. Among his aphorisms concering the human countenance I once found a passage that amuses me even today: "In Hannover I once took up lodgings in a flat whose window opened out on a narrow street that connected two broad thoroughfares. It was pleasing to observe how people's faces changed expression as soon as they entered this lane, where they thought they would be unobserved. One fellow would take a pee, another would adjust his stockings, still another would laugh to himself, and yet another would shake his head. Girls would break into a smile as they reflected on the previous night, and would rearrange their underthings preparatory to further conquests on the adjacent avenue."

It goes without saying that I did not recall this passage quite as literally as I have quoted it here. But I remember clearly drawing a mental comparison between the typical connecting passageway in a typical German town and this Spanish metropolitan chasm that snuffed out one's eyesight completely, blinding one even to the shafts of intense light that held shut each of its entrances.

But of course, I mused, Pilar has to make a habilimental adjustment of the kind that requires women to enter a dark doorway or step behind a lamppost. "Don't look!" cries the purely symbolic lamppost when approached by a woman, who then executes the classic motions of lifting and shifting, perhaps displaying for a split second certain visible attributes that otherwise, were it not for the presence of the chaste lamppost, might cause a minor traffic snarl. I am one of those men who dutifully avert their glances whenever a lamppost forces citydwellers into strict observance of their puny morality. This is an embarrassing vestige of my careful upbringing, the worst imaginable training for the struggle of real life. It was so wrongheaded, and in its wrongheadedness so ineradicable, that it pursued me over and across the Pyrenees as far as—well, as far as Africa, if we grant any credence at all to the theories of those ethnological savants who draw Europe's southern border at the aforementioned mountain range (probably because they know so little about Europe and nothing at all about Africa, which they refer to as "Europe's subconscious").

And thus my childhood superego followed me across the sea all the way to this island, where it was totally out of place. It pursued me right into this confined and confining alleyway, where at this moment María del Pilar—and in spite of the murk and the gloom Vigoleis shut his eyes, just like a newly-ordained curate hearing a young female confess her transgressions against the Sixth Commandment. At precisely the right moment, however, the neophyte priest suddenly loses his resolve, interrupts his pious thumb-twiddling, and peeks through the screen. Vigoleis, too, was unable to resist earthly temptation. He now peered toward the place where a shapely hand was about to raise a skirt and a lissome leg would—but instead he sees both legs, still very much covered, tripping along ahead of him. In fact, to all appearances they have never stopped tripping along. Not a sign, my dear Herr Lichtenberg, of garter adjustment, not a trace of indecent activity of any kind. It remained to speculate whether my dear friend Pilar was having any thoughts of the previous night, or of the coming night. Was she smiling? My only view of her was from behind. And how she did dash onward! All three of them were playing the disappearing act, that was the only word for it. Good heavens, what can possibly be the matter? They shot around another corner and were swallowed up by the next street. Gone in a trice was my quasi-literary reverie, my semi-erotic noonday fantasy and canyon meditation.

After running through the alley and out into the light, I spotted my quick-stepping relatives well ahead of me, so I immediately took up the pursuit. Giving both elbows to fellow pedestrians on the way, I finally got to within a few paces of the trio, only to notice Zwingli taking another right-angled turn, this time disappearing into a store. Pilar, whose regal stride we earlier had occasion to marvel at, sped in after him, with Beatrice, manifesting an air of resolute dignity, not far behind. Willing or not, I followed them in.

The establishment was a furniture emporium, with a selection ranging from potty chairs to bridal beds to caskets—in short, every single item of its kind that might be required by a creature that has descended from the comfort of the treetops to join the civilized world. "So that's it," I thought as I entered. My brother-in-law is actually going to have his measurements taken for a mummy-case! You see, I was still preoccupied subconsciously with the image of Zwingli as a terminal patient. But I soon located the fugitive trio in the sleepware department—of course, that's what we came downtown for. We

were looking for a bed, the biggest bed we could find, one that would at once satisfy one's craving for individual identity, plus the requirements of conjugality. One yard's width for each of us—to me that seemed about the proper democratic dimension for a life of mutual happiness.

We were soon discussing this subject of size with a salesman who, as I could tell by his tape measure and the accompanying gestures, was proposing that each of us sacrifice several inches of our individual liberty. Since I lacked command of the language, my own doctrine of dimensions got nowhere. No one made eloquent pleas for its validity, least of all Beatrice. Back in the Middle Ages, when kings shared bedsteads with their vassals, I might have deemed such parsimony appropriate. Each partner, the furniture mogul was explaining, should be willing to forgo a full twelve inches of space—this would redound to the benefit of nuptial harmony. Pilar contributed expertise in her rapid, euphonious voice. Zwingli flashed his horned pinky and, to conclude the negotiations, I flashed my money. The entire parley had taken up no more than half an hour. But it was too long a time considering what we ended up with. It was not a bed of the sort I was used to, not one of those on which, in my Lower Rhenish homeland, babies get conceived and born, or upon which I myself, Vigoleis, first saw the light of the world. I have in mind my ancestors' gargantuan slumber-chests, which permitted their lovemaking, like everything else in their lives, to be a truly earthbound enterprise. What we purchased here was, instead, the equivalent of an army cot, a frame with wire springs and four metal feet that you screwed up to the desired height. I squatted down to indicate the proper distance from the floor, announcing to all and sundry that this contrivance, which more sophisticated personages might designate a "couch," would be just right for sitting on.

A "couch"? I was strongly reminded of Shakespeare:

> Let not the royal bed of Denmark be
> A couch for luxury and damned incest.

"Incest"? From time immemorial, both civil and ecclesiastical law have sentenced its perpetrators to flogging or to the gallows itself. I could hardly expect anything different, if I should choose to christen this couch with Pilar in the appropriately ceremonious fashion. Would I like to? Did I have any such secret intention? Even before Vigoleis placed the agreed-upon sum in the furniture salesman's palm, he had already incurred—in his imagination, at any rate—the direst retribution in body and soul. *L'acte fût brutal et silencieux*, but at least not on a bare floor as in Zola's *Thérèse Raquin*.

Pilar blushed; she fingered distractedly at her black lace veil, and freed herself from Beatrice's arm. Vigoleis, too, was unable to stop the blood from rising revealingly to the roots of his hair. No one noticed as he slowly released his pent-up breath through his nose. Zwingli, who had reverted to Don Helvecio throughout this entire scene, was already out the door, trying to scare up a Little Helper or a jackass to carry the bedframe. Beatrice was the last to leave the store.

Out on the street she said in a language known only by me—which is to say, in language addressed to me and me only—"I don't like the looks of this." She loves to utter obscure prophecies of this kind, each time in an irritated tone of voice, implying that we shall allow her premonitions to go unheeded at our own peril. Whenever her predictions come true, everyone, of course, suddenly comprehends what she meant in the first place. Prophets are seldom original. If her auguries don't turn out, then she too keeps silent—the inscrutability of all sibyls. The immediate state of affairs "didn't look good to her"—well, small wonder, for I can't imagine what could ever "look good" as long as our lamebrained friend Vigoleis, that arch-practitioner of *Weltschmerz*, has his finger in the pie. Or perhaps rather, in the language of a paltry fatalism, if the pie has devoured his finger.

Come to think of it, our adventures had just begun. Or just begun to begin.

Our sprint through the city of Palma continued, at the hottest hour of the day, and, so it appeared, with ever more burning urgency. Our pace accelerated, and I took pity on our coolie. He had jerked our bedframe to his head, which was protected from the springs and wires only by his jaunty beret. He held the dangerously dipping edges of the cot with outstretched arms, avoiding collisions with pedestrians right and left by means of timely yells. With us in the train, he also took on the role of herald, announcer, and strident dispatch-bearer of our headlong hegira. Oddly enough, nobody seemed to take notice of us. After various detours through alleys and courtyards, at times losing sight of our agile delivery man, we eventually arrived at the next store. Somehow this fellow seemed to intuit our destination, for soon we caught up with him at the door of a fabrics shop, where he stood at attention, presenting arms with our metal bedframe. Apparently he had no interest at all in the courtyards of rich people's abodes. But were they, for that matter, of any interest at all to our family? Without so much as a glance, we hustled our way through this noonday idyll of cats, palm trees, and beggars basking supine on the sidewalks. Those out front gave rapid signals to each other with looks, now and then tossing a quick smile back in my direction, as if to reassure me, then pressing onward in mystifying haste. No slouches they! It was a Saturday, and perhaps that made our shopping tour such a trial of speed.

In this second store we purchased linens and several yards of a kind of ticking, the latter intended as the cover for our woolen mattress. This job, Pilar explained, would be done by a certain upholsterer of her acquaintance, whose shop was located— But *presto!* Our human donkey was already moving out, with our textiles piled on top of the bedframe. So back we went, snaking our way through the commercial district of Palma. Following our leaders into the gloom of alleys, doorways, and twilight patios, now and again we lost hold of any sense of reality. It was all as in a dream. Only our cargo-carrier, who at first had struck me as a fugitive from the realm of spirits, regained his earthly solidity. He had placed the package of fabrics fore and aft on top of the frame, thus giving the whole construction the proper swaying balance. His head pushed up almost to shoulder depth in the center. Once we got this mess

of wires home, I would have to tighten it all up, commensurate with our bed-weight.

From the upholsterer we elicited a vow to deliver two pillows and a filled-in mattress on the same evening.

Passing through the market square on our return trip, Pilar decided that we should get a few victuals for our supper, in particular some meat. As yet there were no butcher shops in sight, but a certain atmospheric aura clued us in that we weren't very far. The booths were shielded from the sun with awnings. The entire area stank like a glue factory. As we approached, the shouts of the proprietors and haggling housewives assaulted our ears. As we stepped into this enclave of the meat vendors, Beatrice gave me a high sign. She was green in the face, just about to vomit. Zwingli had a quick word with his inamorata, whose nose, like my own, was apparently able to withstand a few more degrees of odoriferousness. And thus the couples separated.

Having no less interest in Pilar's flesh than in the flesh offered for sale here in these shops, I gave the girl my arm. The pushing and shoving of the assembled crowds took care of the rest. We squeezed our way from booth to booth, holding each other tightly. Strictly speaking, I ought to have been overcome by tingles of ecstasy, if you realize that I held my right arm in such a position as to allow her left breast to press against the back of my hand, the pressure increasing with the size of the multitudes gathered at the cheaper butcher stalls. I ought, in other words, to have reaped sensual profit from the low-grade viands being hawked at these crowded shops; like the mob surrounding us, I should have been feeling certain inner surges and swellings. Yet oddly enough, my blood pressure remained normal; there was no danger that the channels and spillways of erotic energy might burst. I ought to have been on Cloud Nine; instead, we found ourselves amid billowing clouds of flies. As for the olfactory ambience, I shall refrain from describing it, fearful that I might forfeit readership among those who, habitually and as a matter of principle, suppress all natural fragrances of the human body with the aid of sprays and ointments. And anyway, Vigoleis, you carnivorous old cockroach, beware! The stink of decomposing meat signals without fail the defeat of fleshly pursuits!

We remained arm in arm, a relatively innocuous form of human contact. Finally Pilar spotted the hirsute meatman she had apparently been looking for, and I was glad when she let go of me. Cupid and raw chops are simply not compatible, especially if the noonday sun threatens to scorch the meal.

Despite the advanced hour of day, this shop was still filled with meat products of all kinds. Large pieces of carcass hung from iron hooks, and smaller items lay out on boards. Large or small, nothing in this display gave the appearance of being flesh of its own flesh. The single clue to its identity was the blood-drenched human character standing behind the counter, wielding hatchet, saw, mallet, and long knives. Everything was blanketed by a thick layer of flies; those that weren't busy sitting and sucking were buzzing about, waiting for the change of shift, which was set in motion every time the butcher let his hatchet drop to slice off a new chunk for a customer. Then the protective blanket vaporized, and for the length of a lightning stroke, the customer was able to see a greasy cut of beef, pork, lamb, or fowl. Then the shimmering curtain descended once again. Any particular fly that wasn't on the *qui vive* would have to circle the landing area until signaled by a renewed blow of the hatchet; an emergency landing strip presented itself every now and then in the form of the slaughterer's blood-spattered arm. My fertile mind suddenly conceived the idea of butchers with bovine tails for swatting flies. Why hadn't the Good Lord completed His job when he created Spain?

Pilar blew expertly on a cluster of flies, bringing to light just the cut that she knew would do the trick for our Sunday *fricco*. In addition, she purchased a variety of giblets, tripe, liver, ovaries, hens' feet, cockscombs, turkey wattles, and the like, all of which smelled no sweeter than the more respectable items. I paid a modest sum for the lot, and then it was Pilar's turn to take my arm and press it softly. Did she mean this as a gesture of gratitude, simply for my having provided the few necessary pesetas? Had I been able to speak her language, I would have refused her thanks—Oh please, it's hardly worth mentioning, happy to be of service, and can't we now take leave of this rotten, fly-ridden inferno?

Instead, I contented myself with a tender bit of counter-pressure against a sensitive portion of her body. The girl's eyes, enticingly embellished with pencil and mascara, met mine from below with a glance that traveled up and down my spine, and then down again and up again—strange behavior for a glance, when you come to think of it. So strange, in fact, that I do believe it was the kind of "first sight" at which, as the popular phrase has it, love steps in. Lord, how I began to yearn and burn for this woman! Her sheer presence made me forget the flies and all that they concealed from my gaze, which was busily engaged with other visible objects. The charnel-house stench became a seductive aroma; the package of meat in my left hand I now imagined as a tangible pledge of what my right hand was able to express but feebly. Shoving, getting shoved back, squeezed together and bathed in sweat, we left the meatseller's lane that now took on the aspect of a haven of purest bliss.

If we can believe the Old Testament, which knows all there is to know about such things, sweat is just as integral a component of love as is our daily bread. Be that as it may, huge drops of perspiration now covered my brow. Luckily, Pilar soon spied the siblings sitting in the dusty shade of a sidewalk cafe. Our coolie was with them, drinking weak beer and talking a blue streak. Zwingli was gabbing away at the same time, likewise the waiter, likewise the guests at the neighboring tables, and it was hard to tell which part of the body was more active in conversation, the tongue or the upper extremities. Quite a lively gathering, I thought; one false word and we'll have a donnybrook on our hands. Tables and chairs will start flying out on the street, knives will be brandished, bottles will descend on skulls. Throats that came here to be slaked will be neatly throttled instead.

But nothing of the sort happened. All the noise and gesticulation was simply a public manifestation of Spanishness itself, an outer show masking the peaceable heart that resides within. It was merely a pyrotechnic exhibition, replete with whistling skyrockets and fiery pinwheels, but destined to fizzle out promptly in the midday sun. The little flame glowing in my heart was actually more dangerous. Still waters, as the saying goes, run deep; still fires burn even deeper.

For the homeward trek, which turned out to be another lengthy detour, we grouped ourselves differently. Each male was assigned to his proper female, in keeping with the injunction that thou shalt not covet thy neighbor's. And here I was, coveting like crazy! An exchange of the sort that occurs in certain novels was out of the question, unless Vigoleis was inclined to force the matter. Let him try things out with this babe, just once! He'll soon see how feathers can fly...

Pilar, I mused, as we marched through the streets, had a guilty conscience towards her new female friend. No need, she surely was thinking, to embark right away on adventures with Vigoleis. He won't run away, and tonight he'll be sleeping under my roof. It's just a matter of time until we can say "sheets" instead of "roof." It was as simple as that.

At eight o'clock the mattress would arrive. But before we stretched out on it, we would have a fine feast, including the wine we were buying just now. Zwingli knew all the vintages the world over, and he knew just which one would be best to accompany the contents of the package I held in my left hand, swinging it like a censer at High Mass. The aroma it exuded was, however, different; to me it was a narcotic, and most assuredly not one to give rise to pious thoughts.

Presumably, Zwingli had made use of his Italian to explain to Beatrice the true reason for our zig-zagging haste on this shopping trip. The enigma had the simplest of solutions: Don Helvecio was up to his unwashed neck in debt. Not a single street in Palma didn't harbor some establishment where he had overshot his credit.

And the streets of Palma are narrow. The owners of stores like to sit out in front, and thus it requires a certain amount of strategy and planning if one wishes to avoid one's creditors. "You've got to hand it to me, Beatrice, Bice, Bé. I've done it again! Thanks to my perseverance and knowledge of local affairs, you'll be sleeping tonight on some genuine Mallorquine wool. A fine layer of horsehair will keep you nice and cool, and you'll soon find that you won't want to bed down anywhere else. As for your friend Vigoleis, the congenital pessimist, he can find his peace on any old bunk whatsoever. He's a great guy, but still a little shy. That hasn't changed since the old days in Cologne. We'll soon take care of that. We'll have to get him to do some hard work. First some Spanish, an hour every day. You can teach him the theory, and the practice. The palaver, he'll pick up from palavering. He's not much good at languages; otherwise he never would have started studying linguistics. Or is it the other way around? We Swiss types are born with one mother tongue and a bunch of cousin tongues. But the Germans have to learn everything by the seat of their pants. That's no picnic for a linguistically retarded country. It's only when they get outside their borders that they start coming alive. It's an example of the collective apron-strings phenomenon—pretty sad, really.

"But we'll get Vigo to come around, I'll see to that myself. The main thing is that he has to begin right away to think in Spanish. That's just the kind of purgative he needs, so he can start working on new thoughts. The little phrases he picks up here in the first few days won't be enough to start philosophizing with, so there's no danger of him coming up with some horribly dreary thought-system. On Monday we'll go buy him an inexpensive textbook at a run-down little German bookstore. That'll give Vigoleis a chance to hear some sounds from home, so the transition won't be too sudden. Anton Emmerich hails from Cologne. He's the real, genuine article, born in the shadow of the Cathedral. He's been in Spain for years, but at least once a week he has his landlady cook him up a dish of those awful *echt Kölsch* potato pancakes, and every Sunday he has knockwurst with sweetened rice! Apart from such aberrations, he's a wonderful fellow, and I'm sure that, with time, he'll learn some decent habits down here in foreign lands. He's a good chess player, by the way. We lock horns over the board every once in a while."

It was thus, in direct and uncamouflaged discourse, that Beatrice reported to me her conversation with Zwingli en route through Palma's thoroughfares. Well now, that's just dandy, I thought. We'll be sleeping on wool with a horse-hair filling—without fleas, I presume, without dreams, surely without pajamas and, as far as I am concerned, most definitely without Pilar. Meanwhile I had become so tired that I would have liked to drop then and there on that spanking-new sack and slept a workingman's sleep right in the middle of the bustling city. But our packman-cum-herald wouldn't stand still. Continuing his balancing act, he led us in a mad scurry up streets and down streets, upstairs and downstairs, following precisely the tortuous itinerary dictated by Zwingli's and his concubine's unpaid bills.

Soon we approached, from the other side, the little square we had crossed in the morning coming from the Street of Solitude. We heard music being played in front of a café. Donkeys, tied to rings in the walls, slept standing up. Zwingli drew my attention to this odd phenomenon—if only human beings could evolve far enough to sleep while standing! He explained that he had been practicing this art for some time now; but because our erect human knees were missing a locking mechanism or the clever musculature of the horse, the only way to avoid tipping over was by means of mental concentration. But mental work of any kind was of course non-conducive to sleep. Thus, he was still in the stage of using walls, he explained further, for otherwise...

... Otherwise he'd fall flat on his face, I thought, but any comment I might have made was suddenly preempted. Before us we all saw that girl once more, the very same lanky one of several hours ago. Here she was again, and again she was dancing. A handsome child, with excellent breeding in her whole body. She bent down and rose up again, leapt up in the air and caught herself again in mid-flight. She skipped and showered sparks all about her, stamped her feet and disappeared in a cloud of dust. She couldn't be much older than eleven. At that age, back in my homeland, girls still play with dolls and toy grocery stores. But here, a child like this one drives the boys crazy. And grown men, too, for it is not only the half-pints who have congregated again here on the square, like the flies milling around the potroast swinging on its hook back at the butcher shop. Quite a few adult men were sitting and standing around, unable to take their eyes off of this fiery female phantom in her pinafore.

Pilar, too, noticed the whirling imp, and to my great astonishment, she repeated the pious ministrations of the forenoon: she made a double sign of the cross, invoked the names of saints and Heaven itself, in the process dropping to the ground the straw net containing the accessories for the Feast of Resurrection we were planning to celebrate that evening. It's a lucky thing that I am forever the cavalier in the presence of women, for otherwise our three bottles of Valdepeñas would likewise have bitten the dust and seen their last. Back in the city, I had taken them from her hands—much against her wishes, as it turns out, for she told me that no man carries packages in Spain.

Pilar's petrification here on the square didn't last long. She shot forth like an arrow, and I was just able to make out how the crowd of gaping onlookers closed in on her. I heard shouts, soprano screeches, and men guffawing. The scene ended with a loud report that sounded for all the world like a well-aimed box on the ears.

"Oh, boy!" said Zwingli as he picked up our prandial delicacies. "There's going to be hell to pay. Let's go on ahead. She won't get home until she's caught up again with Julietta."

"Julietta?"

"Right. That's her kid!"

Next to the little chamber where I had my first enchanting encounter with the child Julietta, there was another small room, windowless like its neighbor. This was to be our new quarters. It served as a clothes closet and rummage room. A naked bulb hung on a wire from the ceiling. Once our bed was inside, there would be just enough room to set up some suitcases as a bureau or makeshift night table. I could easily stretch some clothesline and come up with other contrivances, if they would only let me go at it. But Zwingli hesitated to allow this until Pilar returned; he had no idea where to put our clothes and other stuff. Surely we wouldn't mind camping out the first night in the hall?

Beatrice got to work with our luggage, unpacking and transforming the *entrada* into what soon resembled a fleamarket. We had already loaded our bedsprings with gear of all sorts when, at nine, our mattress arrived. So we unloaded the bed and got it ready for the night. Zwingli expressed surprise that we were about to use the sheets right away, so fresh from the store, where they had been touched by who knows how many hands. Shouldn't they be laundered first, and oughtn't we to sleep in the meantime in our clothes? People who never wash have peculiar notions about cleanliness and applied aesthetics. It is not easy to comprehend the principles according to which they live their lives. Just then, Mother and Child made their appearance.

Certain features of body and temperament (my reader will know which ones I mean), certain attributes that in the mother had reached luscious, bountiful maturity, were also discernable in potential, inchoate form in her daughter. Unless my presentiments were sorely mistaken, the future looked truly auspicious for this fledgling that had yet to depart the warmth of the nest. A magnificent offspring, indeed. She stood there now in our midst, shaking her pretty head, stamping her foot, and refusing to greet her new relatives. To think that you, Vigoleis, actually had this bird in your hand this morning and let it fly away! But then again, how typical of you! Anyone else would have sensed immediately, even in the pitch dark, that this little feathered creature in the hand was worth infinitely more than what that miserly proverb says. Take a good look at her now, in the light of day: her hair is black as a raven's, her eyes are like shimmering coals and as deep as the night. Inside them are little stars that glisten when she lifts her dainty eyelids.

I could continue describing the girl in this vein, piling one hackneyed simile upon another until the portrait is complete. The beauty of the human countenance is infinite, unlike the means we use to capture it in words or images. As soon as we attempt to depict something unique for an audience, we inevitably lapse into triteness. This aspiring young soul's outward attributes were quite simply flawless. And that glance of hers! Were it not for my early-morning contact with her, I might have naively assumed that such a way of looking at another person was merely childlike. But in truth I was biased toward other interpretations. I blush easily, and I am not ashamed to admit that at this moment, in Pilar's vestibule, I probably turned red as a beet. It was a risky situation, and not only for me. Pilar realized immediately that her recalcitrant daughter saw in me a target for her incipient instincts, and that she intended to continue her rebellious behavior right here at the maternal hearth, before our very eyes. That would have to be nipped in the bud. And nip it Pilar did, using the technique employed by most mothers in this world: another whack on the face. The girl didn't flinch.

"Julietta," I said in German, forgetting that she couldn't understand my language, "be a good girl and go to bed. Tomorrow is Sunday, and I want you to show me the city." And I held my hand out to her.

Julietta smiled, stepped closer, and gave me her hand. Then she half-bowed, half-curtsied to Beatrice, and disappeared without giving the slightest further attention to her mother or her mother's chum. Pilar entered the kitchen and took up some noisy activity with pots and pans. In spite of the touchy scenes that preceded it, her meal turned out excellent. The wine, too, was good; Zwingli had brought it to just the correct temperature. Temperature, it occurred to me, was the crucial factor in this household. Domestic comfort, not to mention what we Germans refer to as *Gemütlichkeit*, was in short supply here. We were all so busy sorting out the threads of our separate thoughts that none of us was able to tie the ends together to produce meaningful conversation. Even if that had succeeded, being in the linguistic minority, I would have been left out anyway. Zwingli was ever on guard that nothing should get said in a language that Pilar didn't understand. Hence the *lingua franca* of the evening was exclusively Spanish. The reunited Swiss siblings even forgot to raise their glasses towards the Confederated Cantons, where at that same hour skyrockets and patriotic cheers were rising to the heavens. Here in the Street of Solitude, the mood was emphatically earthbound. I don't mean to imply that we took our meal in funereal solemnity, but the crisply broiled viands called for far more cheerful diners than we were. Around midnight, when the street outside started coming awake, we went to bed. Each of us lay where he or she belonged—though as we know, not where each of us might have wished to belong.

Just where might Vigoleis have wanted to spend this first night on the island of his second sight?

In any chronicle that gets written with truthful intent, with the writer's hand, so to speak, constantly pressed to his heart, there inevitably crop up certain incidents that the author, out of shame and an awareness of personal imperfection, would rather conceal from his readers. Familiar as I am with the inward and outward factors involved in the present case, and convinced that hushing up the events of the night in question would vitiate the credibility of all that is to follow, I shall now reveal that our hero slept in the Street of Solitude *sans* pajama, *sans* fleas, and also *sans* dreams. But in addition, *sans* mother and *sans* bewitching daughter, both of whom come under the ancient Spanish proverb which, in order to avoid flinging open the doors of this bawdyhouse all too suddenly, I quoted at the head of Book I under the disguise of the original language: "The mother a whore, the daughter a whore, a whore the blanket that covers them both." In Spanish this adage rhymes exquisitely. But Vigoleis is not yet far enough along to combine sound and sense.

V

We slept well past noon, which shows how Spanish we had become in the space of a single diurnal rotation.

A telegram from Basel had a calming effect on Beatrice, but it also requested immediate word on the conditions we found on our arrival on the island. This was a difficult assignment, not one to be carried out with a few select words of cabled reply. So we wired back that Zwingli's situation gave reason for hope, ending with: "letter will follow." The task of composing this letter fell of course to Beatrice, and I recall that she chewed up half a fountain pen before signing off her report with the familial greeting "*Ciao.*" We all know what she wrote about, though naturally she rounded off countless details and kept to herself her negative assessment of the long-range prognosis. But she also included certain statements of a kind we are as yet ignorant of, and which I myself only discovered when reading over her epistle to the Baselers. For example, I learned that she was resolved to remain on this island at her brother's residence until he was again firmly treading the straight and narrow. Between the lines one perceived a certain tone of maternal solicitude, not surprising when we consider that Beatrice had begun serving her youngest sibling as a mother-surrogate ever since destiny had taken the family into distant regions. She had been unable to carry on this role for very long, she wrote in this letter, and in the intervening years had not been successful at it. On a later occasion, waxing sentimental about what she regarded as her failure at non-professional intrafamilial pedagogy, she once remarked to me that many of Zwingli's transgressions in word and deed had been just as much her own fault. So she kept on doing for Zwingli as much as she could, and as much as Vigoleis would let her do, although the latter, in his proven and increasingly acute guilelessness, continued for the most part to play the role of cautionary advisor. She closed her melancholy positive report with a promise to inform her brother in Basel at regular intervals about our progress. But our progress, the progress we were all to share in, was exclusively of the downward variety.

As we set about to furnish our windowless chamber, Zwingli gave me some enlightening instruction about Iberian domestic customs. I had not known, for instance, that in Spain there was still something called a window tax. In order to minimize this levy on daylight, the less affluent property owners deliberately built their bedrooms without windows, or upon buying a house, walled them up. To me it was clear that such a procedure derived from the Catholic Christian concept of life as a perpetual sin against life. Because the propagation of the human race is bound up in our culture with bedrooms and their attendant malodorousness (exceptional instances *en plein air* are too infrequent to stem the tides of prudishness), it is quite natural to prevent the Eye of Creation from peeking in on the sinful act. Not even Luna, whom we meet so often in poetry as the "eyewitness to love," is permitted to enter the chamber where ecstasy so often becomes a curse, and cursing almost never helps at all.

"What about candles?" I asked. They always get blown out, Zwingli explained, right at the start of things, since no Spaniard was interested in watching himself in love, not even one who has read Schopenhauer. In brothels, on the other hand—but perhaps for that very reason—things went on amid an abundance of candles, multi-faceted mirrors, and copulative positions too numerous and various to count. I remarked that this seemed a fairly sensible method of escaping from windowless lovemaking—though I was quick to add that copulation had, of course, nothing to do with love.

A publisher in Germany was interested in a translation of Menno ter Braak's *Bourgeois Carnival*. I had sent him a sample chapter from Amsterdam, and the writer Franz Düllberg, who did much to introduce German readers to

Dutch literature, had recommended the work warmly to the publisher. The sample I sent pleased the man in Berlin, at least to the extent that he asked me to submit a complete translation, upon which he would base his final decision. My German version was finished, and needed only to be collated once more with the original. I figured that Beatrice and I could get this done in a week's time if we could use the drop-leaf table for a few hours each day. This suggestion, however, met with resistance from our gracious landlady, prompted no doubt by this illiterate woman's instinctual abhorrence of the written or printed word. Be that as it may, Pilar disapproved of my appropriating her table for the purpose of writing. I explained to her that a writer needs a surface to write on, and added that I was a "writer" only insofar as the German passport office was concerned, not in the sense of ever having "written" anything. I hoped that by saying this, I might rise in this ravishing woman's esteem; I would have abjured the entire alphabet, if doing so would place me at her level.

Well then, are you a writer or no writer at all? Let's pay no further heed to what you may have wanted this broad to think about you. Your heart is so abundantly preoccupied with her, that in due course we're bound to hear more about her from your mouth; no fear of missing out on that. But now, pray tell us in plain language whether you are, or are not, a "man of the pen."

Fair enough. Judging by the amount I had already written by that time, I was indeed a full-fledged writer, and a prolific one at that. I had inscribed thousands of pages chock-full with my indecipherable hen-scratchings. Only Beatrice was able to make sense of the mess, and it was only for her eyes that I wrote anyway. Love letters? Well, it began with love letters; that's how I was first lured out of my cave, where, bearlike, I had been sucking my paws in willful hibernation, waiting vainly for daylight to arrive. Strangely enough, I started out using the French language—not because it is the classic medium of love, the language in which, by a fortuitous quirk of fate, the finest love letters of the Western world have been preserved for us: the outpourings of the heart ascribed to Maríana Alcoforado. The numerous attempts at re-translation of her letters into Portuguese are simply unreadable, and in Rilke's German version, an aesthetic veneer has spoiled the radiant power of the "original."

Nor was my reason for writing my love letters in French the fact that I had any particular fluency in the language. That was hardly the case. I had to use a dictionary to express what my heart was feeling, but the required precision was not to be found in the Advanced Langenscheidt Dictionary. Was it that I had made impressive progress as a lover? What I needed was not even available in the massive Sachs-Villette, a work that has otherwise served me superbly for solving linguistic conundrums. One of my most indelible intellectual experiences, comparable in importance to my first acquaintance with Karl May, Schopenhauer, Hamann, and Pascoaes, occurred when one day—or I should say one night—I discovered effortlessly, painlessly, and directly, the language for expressing my amorous sentiments—a language I had overlooked as the result of endless doubts and confusions. This language was my very own German. Suddenly I realized that German was not only good for writing poems. And suddenly I found myself filling reams of paper with my mother tongue—which is not to say that I used the language my mother used; mothers generally look askance at their son's expressions of love for another woman. My average nocturnal emission comprised thirty pages. Once I made it to eighty; twixt dusk and dawn, inspired by the workings of my benighted soul, the words just gushed forth from the Parker Duofold Senior held in my febrile hand, a hand attached to a physically depleted body cowering in the dark, in fear of existence itself. Between God and the Devil, between my heart and hers, from verses of Walther von der Vogelweide to the close analysis of erotic sensations—there was nothing that Vigoleis, like some latter-day Henri Frédéric Amiel, did not commit to paper.

But did all that activity turn me into a "writer"? No, my dear Self, no, and no again, it did not. But then permit me to inquire what other word there might be for such an enterprise. The compilers of *Heyse's Concise Dictionary of the German Language* are quite clear about it: a "writer" is not someone who simply writes, but one who writes "works" and has them published. Had any of my "works" emerged from the press? The only "press" I had been involved with was the press of inner turmoil that had given rise to my writing. Had I been able to gain detachment from all the scribbled pages by having them printed and distributed to a reading public, then perhaps my chronic anxiety might have been curable. A true writer (to continue my thoughts on this subject, despite its having no further bearing on me) who suffers for his work must find a certain measure of surcease by sending it to the marketplace, for otherwise he would hardly go to the trouble of putting his work in saleable form. If God had not suffered during the act of Creation, He would have had no reason to display His product as The World. A "suffering God"—such a notion can shed new light on Creation; it might move you to take pity on the Creator if you were not yourself the most abject victim of the eternal tension between what is and what can never be. By "you," I once again mean my own self, as well as my friend Vigoleis, who is the incarnation of an even more serious anomaly.

My *Epistolarium nocturnum,* and the harvest of my literary frenzy (*furor poeticus*), would have filled volumes if it were ever printed; that is to say, if I had not withheld the inscribed leaves from posterity, and even (I confess it) from their addressee Beatrice, by committing them to the flames. Whatever portion of my "literature" escaped the coal stove was put into service as garden fertilizer. Neither the onion nor the head of cabbage cared much whether the substance that fed their roots was in verse or prose. In whatever style I composed them, my pages ended up providing nourishment for the fruits of the fields. If challenged, I can furnish the names of horticultural witnesses.

Thomas Mann, whom I first met in Locarno in the summer of 1938, complained bitterly about the writing desks provided in hotel rooms. He never found one that suited his needs exactly; the more expensive the accommodations, the less reliable was the furniture for writing on. I found the poet Henny

Marsman to be less fastidious in this regard; he was happy with a slab of wood that didn't wobble. The wealthy Pascoaes, who could afford tables of gold if he wished, is more humble still; he has composed his entire oeuvre sitting at a tiny round table of the type that a magician carries around in his valise— symbolic of a higher art form, perhaps. Other writers have done entirely without artificial support. They gaze into thin air, and become famous by means of works they have literally written on their knees. I am thinking of Camões, Slauerhoff, Peter Altenberg, the Portuguese arch-poet Barbosa du Bocage, as well as certain Old Covenant prophets like Job, who is reported to have penned the chronicle of his trial of suffering while sitting on his dung heap. So we see that the writing surface is unimportant. But in Pilar's house there was no usable surface at all, except for a table that we would have to clear for each and every meal. Where was I going to do my work? I refrain from using the word "writing," now that I have made it sound so suspect in my personal case.

Many other things were missing in the house in question, even certain items that were indispensable for daily living. Having brought a considerable amount of money with us to the island, on the following day we went out and bought all kinds of useful merchandise. By late afternoon, busy hands had delivered them to the apartment. Even a good-sized wooden wardrobe was boosted and thrust up the murky stairway, not without loss of plaster on both walls. Julietta, with whom I had spent all Sunday strolling through the city, came forth with so much eager help and advice that we all forgave her. And it was the evening of the third day. And that's how it went, midst peace and good cheer, for the rest of the week. One item after another was added to the household, and everyone saw what had been accomplished and purchased, and everyone saw that it was good. As in the Creation Account, I have been able to sketch out this initial period in just a few verses before settling down, again taking the Book of Books as my awe-inspiring model, to narrate the events subsequent to this majestic feat of prestidigitation.

Picture Vigoleis as a beginning student in Spanish. He took his first lessons not from Beatrice, and not from Langenscheidt. As Zwingli had advised, he honed his tongue on the little tongue of Julietta, whose early maturity proved itself also in the field of pedagogy. Of course, I don't mean "honed" in the literal sense of one surface rubbing against another, although my schoolmistress tried her best to get her pupil's lips to conform to her own. A professional linguist might contend that Julietta placed particular emphasis on the production of certain plosive phonemes requiring labial closure. But things actually never got that far; our daily exercises never degenerated into the erotic. And besides, I soon got over the steamy confusions of that first day, which is to say that it was no longer impossible for me to concentrate my libidinous longings solely on the mother. My comradeship with Julietta grew stronger once she understood that of the two of us, I was the more childish spirit. Once in a while she played the role of my protectress, and I gladly allowed her to mother me in this fashion. Unfortunately, though, she also soon discovered that she could dazzle me by bringing into play her arsenal of budding femininity. When she found this out, things got stickier for my friend Vigoleis. That's why he was never able to become as one, heart and soul, with Julietta.

I grew up in a family without sisters, together with older brothers who, far from cherishing my company, used to beat me up. My worst torturer was the second oldest, Jupp, who later blossomed forth as an unassuming bachelor poultry farmer with a long tobacco pipe, an enviable annual egg output, and a love for music and all the arts. Incidentally, he is also the breeder of the first non-hybrid German zero-altitude chicken. This fellow was a tyrant, with a dangerous fist that he would raise and then smash down on his hapless victim whenever his bidding was left undone. In this we can, of course, discern the rudiments of his development toward a successful career as poultryman, a boss who dictates to hens just how high they may fly. Flightless chickens for the *Volk ohne Raum*!

A lift of his hand, a look of fury, and a fear-inspiring shout of "Get a move on!" were sufficient to banish any thought of disobedience, and thus little Albert was kept in the vilest slavery. "Get a move on!" was a phrase he had picked up from our father, who often used it for child-rearing purposes and was indeed delighted when things actually moved. Father was an uncommonly peace-loving and amiable man; after a somewhat dissolute, beery stage in his younger days, he had turned rather taciturn, but he was a democrat through and through. He wept when Gustav Stresemann died, and this was the first time I had ever seen that introverted person react in any way to an event in the outside world. I owe a great deal to him, above all the realization that nothing at all in this world is worth hastening one's pace for by as much as single heartbeat. I never once saw him running. What is more, after my ungainly soul ruined a whole series of chances for earning an earthly existence, he financed my university education—likewise a failure. Last but not least, he paid for all the postage that sustained my aforementioned activity as a "writer." Yet all of these parental subsidies had to be earned. Once a week, I was obliged to give the old man a haircut, a radical clipping down to one-tenth of a millimeter. This regular task was my father's discreet method of minimizing my inferiority complex. More than once he complained of how slowly his hair grew. An enemy to all forms of obscurantism, in his enlightened manner he rejected my suggestion to use Salvacran or some other nostrum. As my epistolary literature grew in volume, the good man had no choice but to increase the wages for his court barber. Heaven has rewarded his kindness, his big-heartedness, and his psychologically untutored understanding for his inscrutable tramp of a son, by granting him a painless death in old age.

But to return to my twerpish terrorist brother Jupp: for years I had to share a room with him, and for a time a bed, and thus not even the nighttime afforded protection against kicks and punches. Before the age of mandatory school attendance, I was already aware that man can find no privacy even in the hours of the night. We must retreat ever further into the darkness if we are to escape the wiles of the world. Like the fertile kernel inside the seed prior to the sowing, our secret, safe place can be found only deep within ourselves. Some are successful in this quest for the innermost locus of being; if they are blessed enough to be able to map out this experience for others, as certain artists can, they thereby become immortal. Immortality: to me that is a terrifying idea!

My toys were no safer than I was from the two pint-sized barbarians who were my brothers. They located my most carefully selected caches, and then waited in hiding for as long as it took, until they could revel at the tears that slowly began to flow when I removed my hand from the empty place of concealment. Eventually I decided to react like a chameleon, although this infantile mutation didn't last very long. I started playing with dolls, but shied from the girls who habitually did the same. This behavior elicited nasty teasing and constant reviling from my know-it-all brothers and their equally disgusting neighborhood buddies. But at least there was an end to stolen toys—after all, boys just don't rob little girls.

This is how I learned early on to walk with a pronounced stoop. I sometimes shudder to think what might have become of my gait if my mother had emulated her biblically fertile mother-in-law, who gave the gift of life to nineteen children. I imagine that, having stooped to the level of a dachshund, I would have crawled inside a badger hole, never again to be snagged out, not even by the most bloodthirsty ferret.

At home I was referred to by one and all as "the scaredy-cat," and I have to admit that, with this new name, these anabaptists were right on the mark. And if it occurred to them today to sprinkle me once again with their water of misfortune, I am certain they could still be just as resourceful. It will be apparent that by every significant measure I take after no one in my family. If my reader feels moved to inquire further as to the nature of that family of mine, I'll concede that I would probably be a happier man today if I had indeed "taken after" my family, as one might concede that a stone is happier than a plant. But to answer the query directly, I would be forced to go into further detail about my childhood. That would cause me pain, and I would rather spare my reader a mess of masochistic pottage. I do not wish the application of my recollections to go so far as to include the exhibition of my earliest post-hatching phases. Besides, I am no great fan of childhood memoirs; I much prefer intelligent stories about animals. It isn't important what anyone experienced as a child. What is of importance is how such experiences are interpreted. Since that would entail applying psychology of the depth-sounding variety, for me that would mean nothing but trouble. I confess to being content with a single eviction from Paradise. In terrifying dreams I have often seen Sigmund Freud as a cherub with flaming sword. Poor heart of mine, enshroud thy pain in silence!

Julietta, who has forced me to take this detour into my girl-less childhood, when compared with my own development at her age was already a condemned soul, and not just because the little sexpot had already begun sprouting her quills. My reader will be no more flustered than I was when I report that once, in despair at my bumbling efforts to produce a rolling Spanish *rrr*, she suddenly threw her arms around my neck and gave me a resounding kiss. This brought an immediate end to our experiments with rolling phonemes, and had other things been equal, we ought to have practiced cooing together. Seated on my lap, she plagued me with Spanish verbs, beginning with the classic paradigm of all language instruction: *amo, amas, ama, amamos, amáis, aman.* My rusty Latin readily flew to my aid, and I was overcome with gratitude as I recalled the academic deadbeat who, in the pigsty of a grammar school that I attended under privilege of Kaiser Wilhelm II, beat into our backsides the profoundly sage motto *Non scholae sed vitae discimus.* By the time of my linguistic *tête-à-tête* with Julietta, this cane-wielding taskmaster was already dead, rotting away somewhere like the stuff he was paid to teach us. Had he been still breathing, I would have sent him a picture postcard from Palma, begging his pardon for the impassioned, quasi-atheistic prayer I once uttered in the schoolyard, wishing him a speedy and painful demise. I was joined in this diabolic incantation by the rest of the entire class, with the exception of two execrable teacher's pets. These classmates of ours were also "learning for life," but for a sharply truncated life; they wanted to be priests, and that's exactly what they got.

Julietta was proud of the success her Vigoleis had achieved after only a single week's lessons. He was in command of a handful of polite phrases, was able to exchange a few minimal words with her mother, and had mastered the all-important statement "I love you." Understood purely as part of my language instruction, such an assertion might never have caused complications. But actually it did, because Pilar and I had already held wordless conversations on the same topic. There are glances of a certain type that one can project; one can bring one's shoulder imperceptibly in proximity to hers, and no sooner does limb approach limb when the spark jumps the gap. We shiver, our lungs labor like some old, worn-out bellows, and if language were at all available, it would have to be severely forced. Nature has arranged all this in masterful fashion: when the sexes come near each other, the human animal immediately reverts to primitive behavior.

No, Julietta, there is no need to conjugate that meaningful verb with your mother. What is going on between her and me is taking place in rather special tenses and modalities, in a very tricky form of the pluperfect subjunctive: *Hubiera amado,* "I might have loved"—if I had been lucky. But I hadn't been so lucky, at least not yet. That would require a little more time, the right opportunity, and—"Well, what else, Vigo?" Julietta, my child, you wouldn't understand, even though you already understand more than your mother approves of. The time factor is no great problem; we've got nothing to do here, we're living the life of Riley, *dolce far niente.* It's really a question of opportunity—which, as the proverb says, makes a thief. It can also make an adulterer, though the methods of the two criminal types may differ slightly. Our house is small, we're constantly bumping up against each other. We'll just have to wait; we'll have to put this one on the back burner. Are you familiar with the expression 'the back burner'? Of course not, and I'll be happy to provide a full explanation as soon as my three words of Spanish have turned into three thousand. What I mean is that pretty soon, our little sight-seeing promenades through the city won't involve all four of us adults. Such things are only for the time being. We'll soon be over the stage of being guests who get treated to festive banquets. Soon we'll have our own house key, and all of us can come and go as we please. You know what that means, don't you, you little renegade? Then I'll be ready to start conjugating that first-declension verb with your mother, and nobody will rap my knuckles if I sneak a few irregularities into the very regular paradigm. But that's again too much for you to grasp, *mon poulet*. Just a few more years and you'll be offering a course for advanced students, and that will be so far beyond Vigoleis that he'll go right back to your mother, and that means big trouble. I can see it coming...

"Vigoleis! Don Vigo! Where are you?"

"Julietta, forgive your absent-minded pupil for letting his thoughts wander. Where did we leave off?"

As a clairvoyant observer, Beatrice had long since noticed that I had lost hold of the instructional thread. Zwingli, too, sensed what was going on. In a real school, the inattentive culprit is first given a verbal reprimand, then a note is sent home to his parents, and finally a bad mark is entered on his report card. For life itself there are no marks as such, but that didn't keep Vigoleis from dreaming of an unusually sublime category of marksmanship here in his German-Iberian Arcadia.

Comparing two lengthy texts, for example a translation with the original, is just as time-consuming and tedious as proofreading. Such a chore becomes literally mind-numbing when you are seated at a table that holds pages and pages of your own writing, thousands and thousands of words you would simply like to be rid of, or perhaps never to have set to paper in the first place. This type of post-creative heartburn can become so unpleasant that some writers pass on their manuscripts to a publisher with instructions never to bother them again. Their works are like fledglings that get tossed from the nest to seek the world of art and beauty on their own. No matter if they perish. Next year's mating season is sure to arrive, and after a period of deaf and blind gestation, a new chick is guaranteed to see the light of day. It is different with another species of literary nestling. Besides regular meals at the nipple, this type requires constant loving care; its diapers need changing, its bottom has to be powdered, and you have to offer the supplemental bottle if the little tyke isn't kicking just right. There is trouble all the time, and not only with seven-month preemies that have to spend time in an incubator. Flaubert and Conrad Ferdinand Meyer are prominent examples of writers who have exercised this kind of admirable, expert baby care; both of them pampered their little darlings into solid maturity. The literary infanticides, on the other hand, one of whom was Vigoleis, are members of a category that the scholars have yet to investigate.

As we collated my translation of ter Braak's *Bourgeois Carnival*, I sat at one end of the table and read the text *mezza voce*. The vestibule was dark and cool, impervious to flies and the noise from the street below. The workers in the post office across the way were busy sorting and pigeon-holing without much fuss, which is to say, quietly. María del Pilar was asleep, her "*señorito*" was asleep, and Julietta, who used this term for her house-uncle Zwingli, was also asleep—unless she was lying on her bed watching the crack in the folding door and awaiting the arrival of her new benefactor. For meanwhile, that is just what I had become in her eyes, with my regular good-morning kiss: her fatherly friend, innocent of any ulterior desires. On this particular morning she had not yet received her matinal smooch, for I was mindlessly intoning, like a deacon at solemn high mass, the text of ter Braak's chapter on "The Carnival of the Faithful":

"The love that transcends all reason; the 'light,' the 'word' that 'was with God in the beginning'... and poetry; all of these are revealed to us through hatred, darkness, silence... and bourgeois existence. What meaning attaches to such feeble phrases as 'transcends all reason' or 'was with God in the beginning,' other than that we strive, using the coordinates of space and time, to give expression to concepts that ultimately defy verbal designation?... It is the bourgeois who, by inherent nature, swear by and upon mere words: 'transcend,' 'in the beginning'..."

I recited the Dutch text mechanically, all the while picturing to myself, in another stratum of my consciousness, a less abstract, less dialectical, less doggedly philosophical kind of Carnival. A carnivalino, one without masks, and at the present hour one without costumes, too—or rather, in the costume of Adam, which is no costume at all. I pictured Eve's costume as an even more naked one, although generally speaking the barest woman is one who has yet to let fall her last item of clothing. In order to relish my erotic breakfast-table fantasy to the utmost, I had to imagine her conjugal Adam, him of the luxuriantly hirsute chest and the magical claw, as banished from her enchanting company. At certain moments this mental repast became so delicious that, to continue with my extravagant metaphor, I began to smack my lips. But then the thin partition separating the two regions of my consciousness suddenly dissolved. I stumbled and halted in my chanting of ter Braak's lines, and I heard an objection spoken from the other end of the table, where every linguistic and emotional deviation from the written or unwritten *Urtext* was being duly registered.

As a woman, and on such a morning as this one, one must be firmly convinced of one's own worth, and be in possession of considerable inside information besides, to refrain from throwing every last manuscript page, the book, and the table itself at the dreamy numbskull sitting opposite and shouting, "Go ahead! Move right in with her, why don't you?"

Why didn't Beatrice do that? Was she the masochistic type who seeks to intensify pleasure through suffering? Was she a superior being who was offering herself in sacrifice to Vigoleis, in the grand tragic style: "Tread upon my bleeding heart, pass over my corpse and enter your beauteous lover's bed, that despicable venue of empty infatuation, etc. etc."? To finish this renunciatory outcry of hers, I would have to quote from the novels of Hedwig Courths-Mahler, which I don't have right at hand and wouldn't inflict on Beatrice in any case. Even after twenty years such a comparison would annoy her greatly. If asked to choose between Pilar and Hedwig, she would undoubtedly take sides with the illiterate against the woman who spent a lifetime in concubinage to the alphabet. No, Beatrice is not one to grab at the petty stratagems of bourgeois marital discord. She is, I must repeat, a woman of cosmopolitan background and, most decisive of all, she is familiar with the writings of her Vigoleis. When necessary, she is capable of pulling this fellow back from the edge of the abyss. What means does she employ? Have patience, dear reader! Her curatives differ from those of normal, traditional medicine. We often read the familiar exhortation, "Shake well before using"; with Beatrice, the shaking gets done after the fact, and that is the source of its amazing therapeutic efficacy. Not for nothing is Beatrice the granddaughter of a famous homeopath.

Pilar began to abhor our literary morning devotions. Owing to her increasing irritability, we had switched our collating activities to the later forenoon. I have never comprehended what caused all that anger over a week of boring professional drudgery. Zwingli came forward with an explanation that struck me as patently unconvincing. But then, his knowledge of women was never more than skin-deep, though he had often performed in-depth research on the skin itself. He was, for example, an imaginative expert in the nomenclature of the erogenous zones. He entered long lists of terms in his anatomical atlas, which he intended to put to use, not like Mr. van de Velde in marriage manuals, but for purely aesthetic ends in his future Academy of Nude Modeling—an idea that escaped even Leonardo da Vinci, who overlooked hardly anything amidst the skin and bones of the human erotic machine. With Zwingli's technique, the models were presumably made to assume the appropriate aesthetic attitudes by a carefully mapped-out tickling procedure. And, it is fair to ask, why not?

It was Zwingli's considered opinion that Pilar felt put upon, in fact she felt demeaned in her illiterate womanhood by our constant nerve-racking recitations of literary verbiage in a foreign tongue. What nonsense! But perhaps I am mistaken. To err is human, wrote St. Jerome in one of his letters, a dictum that I, Vigoleis, prefer to revise upwards a degree or so by stating that to err can also be divine, an insight I have attained through unbiased reflection upon what the Creator has made out of me. Anyway, what Zwingli said couldn't possibly be true. Pilar's lack of education in reading and writing actually was a distinct advantage. What is more, it turned out that she got just as annoyed by the tight-lipped, wordless sulk I had been wallowing in for days now. This behavior of mine became all the more obvious, the faster I made progress in

Julietta's oral language method. With Pilar things were now at a standoff. Most people react to the kind of potent abstinence that Vigoleis was practicing by finding it either ridiculous or pitiful. That's not how I construe it. To me, as a poet, it is like the timorousness felt by one rhyming word in search of another.

Still to come was my secret tryst with Pilar, my smuggler's tour to her inner sanctum. I was waiting for the opportune moment, which I foolishly thought of as imminent, once Beatrice and I had finished our comparative textual ordeal. It was as if I were expecting my Carnival ritual to imbue me with the courage to descend into the real world of Ash Wednesday. That was insane, and a palpable example of how one can overestimate the power of literature. And we were still working our way through the "Carnival of the Faithful"— it would be days before we dealt with the "Carnival Morality" in ter Braak's final chapter. Vigoleis was hoping to achieve two goals at once.

"Vigo, what *are* you reading? I can't find anything like that in your translation. There you go again, engaging in bizarre textual behavior!"

"Oh, sorry, Beatrice! I skipped a section, ten whole lines. It's because I have to drone on like this, and it's dark in here. Literature should always be read in artificial light, the same kind it gets written by. But listen to this, ha ha! Here it is, black on white, this is why I got ahead of you. Just listen, and we can go back to where we were in just a minute. Here it is:

"Mysticism is the natural opponent of the Church. The bourgeois community of the faithful can tolerate such an intruder only if the former is willing to forgo its claim to uniqueness in the game of words. For the bourgeois as for the poet, words mean only what is to be found behind them."

Clank, clank! Two firm knocks of the bronze door clapper downstairs always meant Pilar's apartment. Who can it be at this early hour, which according to Don Helvecio's erotic timetable is still the middle of the night? Don't those people down there know that the absentee boss of the Hotel Príncipe can't be roused from his bed by two knocks, especially since he's sharing that bed?

Those people down there seemed to know all this very well. And they were even better informed than that, for they also knew who would open up for them. That's precisely why they decided to knock at this hour.

Just as "those people down there" expected, our door was opened for them—by Beatrice, let it be said, who was just the opener they were hoping for. But it was only one person who had come, a gentleman, a resplendent specimen of Mallorcan male worthiness. He was clothed in a black suit that had shiny spots here and there from long wear. He had on white hemp sandals, identifying him as a member of a lower social class. He spoke fluent Spanish, not the insular dialect that is related to Catalan, and which I, incidentally, despite years spent on the island, was never able to master. This man was polite, in fact he was gracious in the extreme. He had just the proper manners, a not unusual trait among the common people anywhere, and certainly not among Spaniards of his social standing.

This gentleman knew just how to behave in the presence of a woman who appeared before him in her morning negligee. She inquired what he had come for, then listened and watched as he reached into his pockets and took out a clutch of soiled papers. These documents were decidedly greasy. Our messenger must have carried them around with him for quite some time, and surely this was not the first time that he had drawn them out and shown them. He started searching through the papers with his knobby fingers. Oh, please, said Beatrice, just put them on the table and sort them there. So there they lay, next to my manuscript translation of The *Bourgeois Carnival*, which suddenly took on the pale, remote aspect of anemic philosophy.

The man then drew out two sheets from his deck. For a split second I had visions of an itinerant fortune-teller who has a trained canary pull fortune cards out of a drawer. Our own visiting itinerant, whoever he was, clapped one hand down on the two sheets of paper. He didn't mean this gesture in an unfriendly or threatening way. Rather, he remained quite the gentleman and started talking in the most cheerful manner. Soon he would be in a state of pure rapture; you might say that he had foretold his own future with the greatest exactitude. Beatrice and I, intrigued by this strange visitor, recognized the gaudy strokes of Zwingli's signature, the symbol of his extraordinary business acumen, compared to which my own scrawling way of signing documents seemed picayune indeed.

"Debts?"

Not at all, said the dunning agent. That was too harsh a term for the minuscule credit balance he had come to straighten out. And yet, he averred, the time was soon approaching when this matter ought perhaps to be taken care of, for otherwise, mmm...

Mmm... This "otherwise" is an all too familiar expression. In the form of "Get a move on!" Tied to a fist, it had befogged my childhood, and now here it was again, accompanied by a stranger's hand spread out on our table in the interest of an amicable business settlement. Every country in the world harbors these vestiges of the caveman with his club. When we translate their message, it always comes out reading "distress warrant," "bailiff," "debtor's oath," or time in the tower. I understood precious little of what this gentleman was explaining so suavely, but the bills spoke their own clear numerical language. As a matter of fact it was a negligible sum; I seem to recall that a hundred-peseta note would have sufficed to get rid of our intruder.

With his permission, we repaired to a corner for a conference. As it happened, it was the corner next to the corridor door. Beatrice quickly disappeared through the door, and returned just as quickly with the pesetas. She had fished them out of our moneybag.

"You're going to...?"

"Of course I am. He's my brother."

Of course. Some brother! The man took the proffered banknote, held out a few coins in change, and stuffed the papers back in his pocket leaving us the papers with Zwingli's signature, which for him had now become worthless. Here on this far-flung island, we had just rescued the honor of a Swiss national.

Peering carefully at the receipts, and with the aid of my sparse Spanish vocabulary, I discovered that Beatrice had handed over to the man the monetary value of twelve dozen drinking glasses. Drinking glasses?

"Isn't that right? *Copas* means glasses, doesn't it? Or can it mean something else?"

"No, it means glasses. Why?"

"Then the two of them must own some kind of shooting gallery. Twelve times twelve is a hundred and forty-four, right? When we arrived here, there wasn't a single glass in the cupboard. That's what I call the kind of love that knows no bounds. Shall we bound on over to their arcade and try our luck?

The door opened. Zwingli's queen of the night marched through the room. And it was the beginning of a new day.

Never expect any thanks in this world of ours. When Beatrice showed Zwingli the paid receipts, he went through the roof. She presented them to him with a gesture of sisterly confidence, as if to say that such a favor between siblings was the most natural thing in the world, and that she expected no recompense. "But tell me now, twelve dozen drinking glasses! It would be cheaper to buy an electric dishwasher!"

"You mean you actually paid that crook? You are both chumps! You are weak-kneed suckers and greenhorns, the two of you!"

Zwingli's wrath was quite genuine, not the theatrical kind at all. His anger was, however, directed most fiercely at the dunning artist whose nefarious scheme he claimed we had simply fallen into. But this was not the case at all, Beatrice interjected; the man had a perfect right to demand payment. "God damn it all," countered Zwingli, and then he started assaulting the absent functionary with the type of maledictory vocables of which he had made himself a connoisseur. It was as if his *International Lexicon of Invective* lay open before him, supplemented by his domestic *Dictionary of Swiss Dialect Terms*. Just what did that bilking *chaib* think he was up to? He could easily have been left waiting a whole year more, and then either the statute of limitations would pass by or the affair could be settled fifty-fifty out of court. "Just think of it! He comes in here and attacks my sister with business matters that concern men only! And he probably pulled a fast one on you, too. I wouldn't trust a *Glunki* like that as far as..."

But then Zwingli looked over the receipts. When he was through, he not only was satisfied, he was actually beaming. He found a mistake in our favor amounting to 12 pesetas. With pride he announced that we had made a profit for the day.

It's not everyone who can earn 12 pesetas while still in bed. Such things, I said to myself, are possible only in Spain. We really ought to celebrate, I declared in the spirit of my father, who always liked to reach for the bottle and had a marked preference for the more insignificant occasions. I brought forth two shiny silver duros and the remainder in copper coins to cover our little libation. "Manzanilla?" No, said Zwingli, that wouldn't taste right at this early hour.

"Julietta, why don't you zip around the corner and ask the old lady for a bottle of the usual for Don Helvecio. She'll know what you mean. And bring back some eggs and a string of *sobrasada*."

Eggs and sausage, that was the ticket! As the saying goes, where there's a will there's a way. But Zwingli had obviously begun to run out of both, for recently the best will in the world had been unable to provide him with regular sausage. The *sobrasada* Julietta was out fetching was to be paid for with the money that had fallen so unexpectedly into Beatrice's lap.

Those glasses, Zwingli told us, that was a story all to itself. He would be glad to tell it to us sometime, and Vigo would die laughing. You could write a whole book about the vagaries of his life here on the island. But first, he would have to realize his serious plans here, and we ought to drink a toast to that.

Pilar was going to cook up the eggs in Menorcan style, mixing them with the sharply pimentoed red sausages—*à la Général*, as Zwingli called the recipe. When Pilar heard him use this culinary term, she turned livid, and there ensued a rat-a-tat of verbal volleys and counter-volleys sufficient to decimate a whole regiment. I couldn't understand a single word. Beatrice let me know that it was a rather delicate matter, which was why Julietta had been sent out-doors.

Scenes like this one became more and more frequent. Whenever the subject of "the General's eggs" came up between Pilar and her *señorito*, Julietta would be asked to leave. This happened more often than was good for anybody's mental and physical well-being.

Just what was this business about "the General's eggs"—*los huevos del General*?

These memoirs of mine, whose basic outlines I have been planning through-out all the inexorable vicissitudes of my life, were meant to contain a separate chapter on the life and times of our vulture of a hostess, Pilar. My design was to present a unified, coherent portrait of this woman. But I have long since realized that my best intentions in this regard have been for naught. Sometimes the mere lifting of someone's eyelid can interrupt my narration and propel my thoughts in a different direction, just as it happens in real life. Hence, my fre-quent digressions are not the result of tensions between poetry and truth, but arise from a desire to make plausible for my reader the implausibility of truth itself—an ambition that reaches into the realm of theology. "The General's eggs" played such a fateful role in my insular life that I am moved at this very moment, now that Zwingli has ordered them for his table, to serve them up

in their double aspect for the reader's gustatory delectation. Standing here behind Pilar's back as she cracks them into the frying pan, I'll relate a few details
about their previous existence; there's hardly any danger that they will be
spoiled in the process.

Zwingli had named this egg dish after a specific general—a second Benedict,
if you will, although in this case the eponym has yet to enter our gourmet
cookbooks. The General and his unit had their base, or their post (I'm unfamiliar with military usage; perhaps "base" is the more fitting term for the
Spanish army) at the citadel of Mahón on Menorca, the smaller of the
Balearics. And it was in his household that Pilar had the position of kitchen
nymph.

Under supervision of the General's spouse, the girl Pilar developed into a
superb cook, whose skill I have never let up praising to this very day. The Iberian entrees we still concoct, in order to keep the lowly potato from our door,
we owe at least indirectly to the overlord of that little neighboring island. It
was the Commander himself who trained the girl in the other art she was devoted to, and in this effort she likewise proved to be an eager pupil. On one
occasion, however, she was apparently a little careless while washing the dishes
(in Spain, hygienic conditions leave much to be desired). Nine months later
the *Generalissimus* of the Balearic fleet headquarters, first established in the
year 206 B.C. by Hannibal's brother Mago, had a child.

Are we now to picture the assembled uniformed guards presenting arms, as
the General's aide-de-camp appears before him with the official announcement, coming to attention with all the snappiness that Spanish corporals are
capable of? (Not much snappiness at all when compared to the German army,
but nowadays even the Spanish military has been thoroughly Prussianized).
Did the proud new father fire off the few dozen fieldpieces at his bastion, proclaiming to the island and to His Majesty's gunships, anchored in port, that
heaven had sent him, from the womb of his pretty kitchen maid, a child to be
baptized Julietta?

No, dear reader, nothing of the kind. On this occasion the General twirled
his oily mustachios just as on any other day. And just as on any other day, he
made his way to the barracks, the officers' club, or the bordello—the usual
routine for a Spanish general. What did get fired on this particular day was
the kitchen maid. Taking with her all her belongings, her severance pay, and
her baby, she departed the little isle of her misfortune and set sail for the larger
Balearic, where she planned to continue practicing her culinary arts in other
houses.

She had learned her manners at the highest level of the military, and perhaps
this would be of help as she picked up the pieces of her life. I personally have
my doubts on this score, but that's probably because I am prejudiced against
all mercenaries with their flashy gold braids. Our ten-star General naturally
wanted nothing more to do with his child. Generals are persons of privilege,
like priests. When they breed offspring, they do it, as the untranslatable Spanish phrase has it, *a la buena de Dios*, and it's up to the offspring to look after

its own welfare. Generals and priests are in the professional service of death, and why should they concern themselves with every thing that creepeth upon the earth? If there were no such thing as a death cult, no such professions would be thinkable; and but for the Balearic field marshal, there would be no such person as Julietta. But for Julietta, Pilar would have stayed on Menorca; but for Pilar on the island of Mallorca there would have been no Zwingli to cower under her erotic cudgel, etc. etc. There you have the chain of cause and effect that has led right down to this line in my book. In sum: without the General, my second, insular aspect would have remained forever concealed beneath the mask of my first.

It is quite some panorama, when you come to think of it. Here is a high-ranking soldier, beribboned with decorations earned by his saucepan-rattling heroism, sporting the stars of his rank and the stripes on his pants, and con-fident of the respect of his nation. He's stationed somewhere on a romantic island in the Mediterranean. He's bored with his worn-down wife, and so he orders a pert little recruit, in between stretches of K.P. duty, to perform certain types of hygienic drill several times a day. Thirty years later, somewhere in an attic flat in the decidedly unromantic city of Amsterdam, there sits a man by the name of Vigoleis—nary a star, nary a rank on his trousers, only the blotches and rumples of his sedentary lifestyle, and heroic (*sadly* heroic) solely in the pages of his book. He sits and writes himself sick with the ague. If that isn't divine predestination, then I haven't the faintest idea what we mean when we speak of God's miraculous ways. But we haven't yet reached the end of the ways and byways of this island. So let us whittle ourselves another staff and press onward in our text.

It was of course rude of Zwingli to use the term *à la Général* for the egg-and-sausage mixture that Pilar had been asked to prepare after each service maneuver carried out on her strapping body. It was doubly impolitic of him to do so in the presence of Julietta, who was proud of her highly-placed father, a public servant whose career was already giving rise to adulatory legends. How I envy illegitimate children, who can have kings or cardinals as fathers, while the rest of us who are born safely within legal wedlock must forever be content with Smith or Jones. We humble products of bourgeois normalcy are forced to invent our own personal myths, including important elements of our dream-lives, in order to escape the corruption of contemporary society. Pilar was a good mother, this much I can say for her. She was good enough to give her child the General as her father, rather than some bootlicking subaltern. Julietta knew her male progenitor only by means of a magazine photograph, which showed the commander of the land forces standing in full regalia next to his seaborne comrade-in-arms, a Grand Admiral by the name of Miranda (if I remember correctly), who looked like a latter-day Kapudan Pasha with saber and horsetail, ready to take on the combined armadas of the whole world. Legend has it that he performed meritorious service by expanding the harbor fortifications on Menorca. Someone even suggested that as a tribute to this man, the island should be promoted to the geographical status of a continent.

One day I upbraided Zwingli, for although I myself can often wax quite cynical, there were times when I felt he was going too far when conversing about Julietta's relative in the military. After all, I felt sorry for the girl. She was still at an age when she could feel ashamed for being a come-by-chance. But Vigoleis, *mon cher* (this is roughly how her artificial father reasoned with me), Julietta is now approaching the age when she herself will have to start cooking that recipe I have named after her procreator, and she's better off learning about the consequences in advance.

Nevertheless, my scolding succeeded in making the two lovers more careful. The scenes came to an end. What is more, with a single stroke I was able virtually to rehabilitate the reputation of Julietta's father within the family circle. I promoted his press photo to the rank of room ornament, soon acknowledged by all as a secular votive image. This cost me a few pesetas, a sum that, back then at least, was hardly worth the fuss the others made about it. The girl was so delighted that she could scarcely be pried loose from around my neck. At this moment she was again the little child in need of a father she could look up to, even though this father might well be a simpleton.

I cut the General out of the magazine and had him enlarged by a photographer, then tinted and framed. Afterward I gave the original back to Julietta, and it found its way into a cardboard box, where it yellowed in the company of other mysterious trifles of the kind that girls collect when they begin to realize that Paradise is drifting away.

On Julietta's birthday, which as her mother told me coincided exactly with the General's, the icon was unveiled. To dignify the event, I lit a few candles in the rejected daughter's bedchamber. In the dim light, her martial ingrate of a father appeared to gaze down sternly on his child's bed, the logistical focal point of his extramarital campaign. The scene had something of the atmosphere of a burial service, complete with weeping in the congregation. Julietta wept for joy over the symbolic promotion of her *papá*. Pilar wept for reasons we shall leave unexamined here. Beatrice and Zwingli behaved like Protestants at a Catholic mass: they were decorous but uninvolved in the liturgy. And I? My eyes, too, remained dry, but I felt my chest starting to expand and was suddenly seized by the impulse to deliver a short speech, something I hadn't dared to do since I committed an oratorical *faux pas* at my parents' silver wedding anniversary dinner. Here I could make the attempt without causing misunderstandings about my actual intent, unlike on that earlier occasion when, as a growing young man making his first Faustian pilgrimage through Western intellectual history, I had recently arrived at Spengler's morphological theory of the destiny of civilizations. Here in the little bedchamber I was understood well enough, in spite of my stammering and slips of the tongue, precisely because my tiny Spanish vocabulary was unequal to the task. Zwingli came to my aid. Incidentally, this was the first time in my life that I had ever taken part in a military action. The simple ceremony ended amid universal mirth and cork-popping. From that day forward the virginal bedchamber was referred to exclusively as "The General's Room."

This meant that the spicy egg dish had now become anonymous, but it by no means disappeared from our hosts' breakfast table. Pilar was one racy number. She was also apparently insatiable. Nighttime often started over again for the two of them soon after their private roosters had crowed them out of bed; thus the saucepan would get placed over the charcoal fire a second time at about six in the afternoon. Frequently it was I who broke the eggs into the skillet and stirred in the little red sausages to make *a tortilla. Hay que ser hombre,* "You have to stand up like a man," was Zwingli's way of explaining these between-meals snacks that in Spain could—and often did—get ordered in restaurants at any time of night or day. I had learned at least this much: that Zwingli had to stand at attention whenever his chick got horny. On such occasions there could be no loafing, gold-bricking, or deserting—at most perhaps an armistice, following which the trench warfare continued as before. I, Vigoleis, who am also on the skinny side, might devour dozens of the General's pancakes and I still would probably die a hero's death out in no-man's-land, nameless, without eulogy and without posthumous promotion to private.

A few days later another man appeared at our door, again at the time of morning we reserved for our literary chores. Once again papers were shown, bearing Helvecio's signature. This time the amount was appreciably larger, a matter of several hundred pesetas, and this time it was for chairs. This new dunning agent, too, got what he came for, and departed with a grandiose gesture of gratitude.

Zwingli again swore up and down at pushy creditors who could be brought to reason only by making them wait. Spain, he declared, was one gigantic debtor's colony, and who was he to sabotage the customs of his newly-chosen country of residence by sticking to the cheesy scruples of his insignificant little homeland? Then he laughed again like some sea lion telling a dirty joke, and promised to tell us the chair story, too, at some later time.

I was getting itchy about all this, for I was reminded of my paternal grandfather, who dissipated a considerable fortune by buying up things sold at auctions and bankruptcy sales: 500 top hats at one mark each from a factory that went broke! Where else in the world could you get a top hat for one measly mark? A few dozen baby carriages from a furniture store that came under the hammer—5 marks apiece. Where could anybody find a baby carriage with bamboo wheel spokes, safety harness, and diaper receptacle at such a fantastic price? He presumably set aside a dozen or so for his own use, since as I have mentioned, he had nineteen children. Their descendants, including yours truly, are for the most part still among the living; otherwise I would be tempted to make known my conclusions about the old man's rampant collectomania.

Whatever Gramps didn't need, which is to say almost everything, eventually found its way up to our attic. But he wasn't content with just small stuff. A bankrupt velvet-ribbon factory also received his visit and his cash, likewise a broken-down grain-oil mill and a printing press. The latter was actually put back into service later on, and today it is still running under the surname to which I do less and less honor. Even a complete bathroom plumbing outfit joined his other bargain purchases, and this at a time when Gramps' all-gracious and all-worthy Kaiser, his Lord and Majesty, was still getting soaped and scrubbed daily in a washtub by musketeers wielding hog-bristle brushes. The giant bathtub from this bargain set was passed on to my father, and it remains among the most cherished memories of my family home. Reclining in it at 105° Fahrenheit, I had my first intense experiences of German poetry. With a wooden match stuck in the drain plug, and a sock hanging from the hot-water faucet to muffle the drip, I could retreat to another world, my world...

In the fullness of time, God took mercy on our sorely-tried family, and recalled this ingenious profligate to the Great Auction in the Sky, which is, in fact, also a collecting-place for all kinds of junk, none of which costs anything because no one wants to buy it back from the Good Lord.

Was Zwingli, who back in Cologne heard me tell of my grandfather's economic speculations, now going in a similar direction? The subsequent days would confirm my gloomiest premonitions. Our next visit was from a couple, man and wife, acting *à deux* as in any solid marriage. Nothing disturbed their connubial harmony as they presented us with their demand: sure enough, two ice-cream machines, never paid for. This delay was, they said, becoming rather intolerable. Beatrice agreed, and handed the couple the not inconsiderable remittance. Husband and wife expressed their thanks and blessings, then quit the stage to make room for a new debt collector. The next one came all alone, but the bill was all the bigger—and odder. No, it wasn't for baby carriages or ribbon looms, but for small tables with marble tops, two whole dozen in number. And there wasn't a single decent table in the house! Gramps, this would have been something for you, for once you bought up an entire bankrupt tavern and fitted it out with new vats, pumps, and spigots, only to go broke yourself as the result of your own progeny's unquenchable thirst for beer.

Beatrice kept on paying her versatile brother's growing debts. Did she do this to protect the honor of her homeland? If she had, then today a Swiss life-saver's medal would be dangling at her bosom. For she swam farther and farther out on the ocean of her brother's money problems. I registered no objections. To each his own, was my way of looking at it, and let the chips fall where they may. Should I have warned her? Here, too, the Treasury of German Quotations can offer us just what we need: "Can one forbid the silk-worm to spin its thread / as it spins itself ever closer to death?"

We were covering these unforeseeable expenses out of a modest inheritance that had recently fallen to Beatrice. I can't remember just how large her portion of the estate was, but in any case it came to her in the form of Swiss francs. Converted into pesetas it yielded an amount that one might jocularly call a "tidy little sum," using the same linguistic ploy we reach for when we make an "elderly" lady younger than an "old" one—to the delight, no doubt, of many who are much older. Anyway, with this tidy sum we could have kept ourselves going for a few years—not high on the hog, mind you, but perhaps on the common folks' *burro*, in keeping with our bohemian pattern of living. Not like God in France, but maybe like one of his small-time Spanish prophets.

I say "we" paid the bills, for we practiced joint ownership, although my own contributions, coming from the material rewards for my spiritual labors, would have to be regarded in the category of almsgiving. But what, after all, is money when a man's reputation is at stake? Besides, I was expecting a batch of money, yes indeed, and a big batch at that. In words: four thousand Netherlands guilders, payable to me, Vigoleis, from a film company in Berlin. What difference would a few more bills make? That wouldn't suffice to unsaddle us, not by a long shot. Just let Beatrice get her lost sheep back on the right path, and if I can be of help clearing rocks out of the way, I'll gladly do it. It remained to be seen how large an obstacle Pilar would represent. Would I have to help heave aside this boulder too? I had long ago decided to solve this problem on my own. The path to success, I saw clearly, led across the bed of the woman who was forcing Zwingli to overdo everything. There was a possibility that I would be letting my friend Vigoleis do the hard work for me. But in the final analysis it'll be the same, considering that he and I are two in one flesh. And that's exactly what this cutie was out for: two in one flesh.

The manuscript of my *Carnival* translation was finished and ready for the printer. I sent it off to the publisher with a handwritten blessing: "Take ye and read." I also wrote a report to the author on how I gauged the market chances for his unworldly stock issue. He and I had not yet become light and cordial with each other. Dr. Menno ter Braak was an extraordinarily erudite and extraordinarily shy person. He was embarrassed, for example, when, in my garret room in Amsterdam, I introduced him to Beatrice as just what she was. I am becoming more and more convinced that self-contradiction is the very essence of life. We do good deeds with an evil heart, and we do our hating with the best of intentions. The author of this bitter carnival satire on bourgeois small-mindedness was himself anything but a mardi-gras carouser. In history there has been case after case of a free spirit who in everyday life was the victim of the very same inhibitions that he was battling against. Nietzsche, ter Braak's idol and spiritual master, was a taciturn bourgeois once he doffed the chain-mail shirt of the Superman. Count Harry Kessler, who knew Nietzsche personally, once described him to me in just these terms, thus confirming and supplementing the image of the man that anyone can absorb by reading his collected letters. My little portable typewriter was now free for new as-

signments: some travelogues for newspapers, some editorial repair-work for
literary journals, a few opinions on manuscripts for book publishers, a few
pieces of short fiction for the desk drawer containing my other posthumous
works; and finally some letters to my friends, on which I wasted my literary
energies for years on end, amazed as I was time and again to rediscover later
my own statements, sometimes even entire stories of mine, in books and newspapers. To think what I could have pulled in myself with the same material!

For the rest, it was now a matter of adapting to life on this island: the infernal heat, the dusty cesspool that was Palma's inner city, and not least of all
María del Pilar and her libidinous static electricity, which gave me more homework troubles than any other subject in my insular re-education. The voltage
between us was increasing as in a Leyden jar. Pilar was made of pure amber.
His Excellency on Menorca knew very well why it was futile for him to continue rubbing against his marital bedfellow.

And you, my dear Vigoleis, do you now intend to pull sparks from this tinfoil
tart? Watch out that the spark doesn't get drained out of you—it's all a matter
of the proper polarity and insulation. Both of you are charged for bear, and you
have that extra charge that we call book-learning, a force that has never been
of help to anyone in real life. And with a woman? You should know better.

Yes, Vigoleis was fully charged. Just ask Beatrice. But of course you won't
get an answer, so let's look elsewhere to satisfy our curiosity. This will require
a visit to Mr. Anton Emmerich, who at this hour is in his shop down on the
Borne. We already know from Zwingli that he sells books and newspapers,
that he still clings to the potato pancakes of his native city, and swears by
sweetened rice and knockwurst. In addition, he and I are what you might call
close neighbors. For when seen from the perspective of Spain, the mere 40
miles that separate his city of Cologne on the mighty Rhine from my little native burg of Süchteln on the Niers could easily allow us to regard each other
as kissing cousins.

This determination of geographic proximity is, however, as far as we ever
got, for in the larger scheme of things I am nobody's compatriot, and potato-
pancake chauvinism is not my dish by any means. What does "fatherland"
mean, anyway? The events of 1933 in my German "fatherland" demonstrate
clearly how little importance such a concept has for those who trumpet it
about as the promised site of earthly salvation, and how quickly it can get
thrown to the pigs. One of my favorite eccentric philosophers, Wilhelm Traugott Krug, who amusingly enough was appointed to the academic chair at
Königsberg as the successor to Immanuel Kant, speaks of the inherent ambi-
guity of patriotic feeling. There exist, he says, natural, vulgar, and pathological
variants of this impulse, in addition to a higher form which is the only genuinely humane type. Its vulgar manifestation lacks all moral value, and can
occur even among mindless animals. The less educated one is, the less familiar
one is with the qualities of other places in the world: all the stronger is the attraction to the patch of land where one first saw the light of day. In this respect, Greenlanders and Laplanders, Samoyeds and Hottentots must be listed

together with the cowherd on his Swiss Alpine meadow.

This item of wisdom appeared in the second edition of Krug's *Concise Philosophical Dictionary*, printed "in Leipzig at Easter in the year of Our Lord 1833." I wonder what human type Wilhelm Traugott Krug might have mentioned in place of the Swiss cowherd if he had written his book exactly a century later, supported by the "scientific achievements" of the Third Reich.

VI

The house where Zwingli rented a *piso* for his fair damsel was located in a cluster, in Spanish a *manzana*. *Manzana* means "apple," and no one knows any longer why a housing complex of this kind ever received such a name. This arrangement had windows looking out on three streets and the aforementioned small square. Of the three streets, the Avenue of Solitude was the shabbiest. The presentable side of the house faced the Borne. The residents on this side, landlords and tenants alike, could gaze out on spreading palms, rather than into the grubby halls and sorting compartments of the Municipal Post Office. The owner of the cluster was a Count, about whom all kinds of entertaining defamatory stories were in circulation. The rent was collected by an agent who soon arrived to make Beatrice's acquaintance, a visit that was quite flattering for us. He left us with a thick wad of overdue rent in his pocket. I asked him to convey our greetings to the Count. I love degeneracy, and not only in the poems of Quental or Georg Trakl.

Zola would have taken pleasure in the congeries of humanity that entered and exited the Count's "apple" to go about their domestic business—which often enough was monkey business. But the Conde had never sheltered quite so notorious a party under his democratic roof as the confederated Helvecio and his animated partner. This was told to me by Mr. Emmerich, as I sat with him in his bookshop, having sought him out for the reasons outlined above.

This shop is very important for an understanding of further developments in my chronicle, and so I shall proceed to describe it. It occupied the respectable corner of the cluster. To the right of the door, the Calle del Conquistador began its ascent; to the left, one turned into a short street that opened onto the square where Julietta was accustomed to flaunt her nascent charms to the street urchins. Diagonally opposite the shop was the open terrace of a high-class men's club, where the members were always sitting at dominoes, drinking coffee, or just snoozing. The long, very narrow bookshop itself displayed inside, at its extreme left end, a door—and I when I say "displayed," I am not just using fancy language but speaking the truth, for the door pointed to itself with the word PUERTA, which means "door." The former owner had painted it there himself, in red. Behind the door was a spare room, to which had been added, by means of a wall partition, a lavatory. The whole back area had no window, and thus required artificial lighting.

Obviously this was a very simple shop. Mr. Emmerich had installed a small counter, a few chairs, bookshelves against the walls, and stands for newspapers. That was it. His store was still new, and still the only one in the city where the increasing numbers of tourists could buy foreign papers and books for vacation reading. The proprietor was happy with his little enterprise. He was planning to expand by adding a small advertising agency, and perhaps someday he might start up a weekly English-language newsletter for tourists. He was hardly an idle businessman. He would like to have rented the floor just above the shop, but this was still occupied by the former owner of the store space, and the Count couldn't just evict the fellow. He had been served notice long ago, and hadn't paid his rent for quite some time, but... Don Helvecio, Mr. Emmerich continued, was a well-known personality in the Mallorquine business world, and a respected one, although, er...

"Pardon me, Mr. Emmerich, but is the name Helvecio very common in Spain? You just said 'Don Helvecio,' didn't you? Or did I hear you wrongly? I happen to know someone here by that name. He's a Swiss."

"I'll just bet you happen to know him, Mr. Vigoleis! By the way, your own name is a bit out of the ordinary. We don't hear it very often down on the Rhine."

"And less often than that up on the Niers. I was re-baptized with this medieval troubadour's name when I was studying in Münster, the city of the Anabaptists. But that's neither here nor there. So, you know the gentleman we were just speaking of?"

"Of course I do. He's the same one that both of us are thinking about—or rather all three of us, if you'll permit me to say so, because your wife knows him too. You are his brother-in-law."

"How peculiar! How come my brother-in-law is the former owner of your store? Did you take over the business from Don Helvecio? But he's the manager or something of that sort down at the Hotel Príncipe Alfonso. Or at least he was until very recently. But then again, I'm not so sure."

"You're not the only one who isn't so sure. But most people are sure about one thing: that woman he's living with will soon be the death of him with her erotic fireworks. They go popping off up there day and night. Pilar—well, let me tell you: our Cologne hookers can't hold a candle to her, and I'm whispering this to you from experience. And they know, as well as you and I do, that this thing they've got down there ain't no Mary Queen of the May medal."

I had previously bought newspapers in Emmerich's store, but we had never touched on personal matters. Now, however, he just opened up wide:

"As far as your wife is concerned, permit me, speaking as something like the dean of foreigners here on the island, to offer some friendly advice. I don't know what your plans are. Are you going to be staying here very long? Helvecio told me the other day that you are a writer and a professor of literature, and he's going to hire you for his future art academy. As a bookseller, I've never come across your name before, not even in the newspapers. Maybe you use a pseudonym, like so many others. But be that as it may, here on Mallorca

every one of us is a doctor, a *conde*, or a *príncipe*, each according to his taste
and the extent of his failures in life. But no matter who or what you are, if
you're planning on staying much longer in Palma, do have a care for your
wife's reputation. People are already talking, I'll have you know."

I asked Mr. Emmerich to be more explicit. He couldn't, he didn't have the
time right now, a tour ship was in port, the shop would soon be full of customers. Perhaps I could return in the evening around seven, and I could bring
my wife along if she had strong nerves.

"Beatrice, do you have strong nerves?"

"News from Basel? That last letter has me worried. Speak up! You know
I'm prepared for the worst."

"No telegram. And what you're supposed to get prepared for I don't even
know myself. Tonight the man from Cologne at Ye Wee Booke Shoppe wants
to give us a few tips on how to behave on the island if we're planning to stay
for a while. He's written a tour guide to Mallorca. As a long-standing foreigner
he knows his stuff, but I get the impression that he really wants to talk about
personal matters. And what he'll be telling us for your benefit will apparently
require tough nerves. That's why I asked you that strange question."

Beatrice's nerves are like iron. They are constantly in vibration, and emit
tones that are sometimes high-pitched, sometimes muted. But as we crossed
the palm-lined square at midnight, heading for home, the music had ceased
altogether. Mr. Emmerich had treated us to jokes from his beloved home town
of Cologne, which oddly enough he never left as a younger man, and to which
he was just as attached as he was to the indigenous potato pancakes and sweet
rice with wurst. But he had also revealed certain details from the previous life
of the amazingly bed-bound Pilar.

Holy Pantaleon! Holy Kunibert! Holy St. Mary in the Capitol! Santa
Catalina de Tomás! San Antonio de Viana! All ye saints of the God-fearing
communities of Cologne and Palma, whose cathedrals are among the most
famous in the world! Come to the aid of our two heroes, whose bodies and
souls are skidding rapidly toward perdition!

But the spirits we invoked wouldn't listen to us pagans. The one spirit that
did lend an ear was that of my good mother. I felt her wan, troubled, loyal,
and warning glance directed toward me across the ocean, as I strolled beside
Beatrice beneath the palm trees. A mother's eyes can penetrate any darkness.
They can follow a prodigal son up hill and down dale. They can adjust to the
most fearsome foreign climes better than the prodigal himself, who, though
he may keep his eyes open and a firm grip on his staff, is bound to stumble.
On that Mediterranean summer evening my mother's eyes looked straight at
me; I became conscious of them as in second sight. Like the legendary Atlantis,
the island sank beneath the waves. I felt myself floating on a raft, drifting on
the sea of my memory.

Emmerich's narrative, delivered with a Cologne accent and laced with the argot of Cologne's side streets, took me back several years—which was the opposite of what Emmerich intended. I saw my mother standing before me with tears in her eyes. Why are you crying, Mother? Is it because I, your son, am lost, the black sheep of the family, dyed in the wool? I wish now to relate this experience that drove tears to the eyes of my beloved parent and gripped me again on that sultry evening on the island. It will take us from Emmerich's scabrous report back to his beloved city of Cologne. It will become apparent soon enough why this flashback was necessary in order to gauge the ugly, hateful misfortune that ruined this southern sojourn for Vigoleis and Beatrice.

Anno domini... But the exact year doesn't matter. Germany, with blind trust in the *Gott mit uns* slogan embossed on its army's belt buckles, had lost its first world war and was struggling to recuperate. Art, literature, and higher learning were thriving as in a dream-world. Trusting in nothing at all, I had just lost another of my little private wars and was getting ready to begin my first semester at Cologne University, where scholars like Bertram, Scheler, and Nicolai Hartmann would, I imagined, take me by my pale, bookwormish hand. From one day to the next, my parents had decided to accompany me on this maiden voyage to the land of certified higher academics. My good-hearted mother was concerned mostly with my choice of lodging in the big city: no bedbugs, decent bed linen, and the like. She intended to have a serious word with the landlady about my somewhat questionable health (including my physical health), and to offer her some suggestions of a sort that I needn't enumerate here. Everyone who has a mother knows that there is no end of worries when a child enters the wide, wide world.

My old man also tagged along. A markedly unemotional type, for him the trip meant mainly the chance for a tour of the big-city bars, starting with frankfurters and a full liter mug at the Early Bird on Cathedral Square, and ending at Müller's All-Saints Pub with long-necked wine bottles. Cologne never meant anything else to him.

I had clipped some room-for-rent ads from the *Kölner Stadtanzeiger*, and so mother and son set off on the look-see. Together we located the first address in a narrow alley off the Haymarket, in an ancient building with warped stairs and labyrinthine corridors, everything bathed in a twilit gloom that our eyes first had to get used to. Mother said that this was no place for me. We should try elsewhere, surely we could find a more decent house, maybe a bit more expensive, but that was unavoidable. I appeased her by remarking that un-sightly portals often conceal palatial chambers, adding that I thought these surroundings were romantic (I hadn't yet emerged from my infatuation with Romanticism). So I gave a vigorous knock on the first door, hoping to find out which was the landlady's flat.

A half-naked girl with frizzy hair and voluptuous bosom stepped sleepily into the corridor, gave her visitors a look of amazement, and said, "Hi there, little guy! So early? And you've brought your mommy with you? OK, we'll give her a rosary and she can sit on the stairs, my room is a little cramped."

Then she shouted some names down the hallway in her raucous voice, and added some remarks about this kid who was just weaned and wanted to lie at her breast, wasn't that a riot? And how much did they think she could expect from lambikin here? All at once several doors opened, and the hall filled with loose-limbed womenfolk who greeted mother and son in the most cheerfully salacious way imaginable. A torrent of obscenities assailed our ears, as we ran the gauntlet on our dash to the exit.

My mother screamed; there were tears in her eyes. Was she at all aware that there existed such a thing as professional immorality? Probably not; she came from a happy family. I pity the people who frequent such establishments, or who depend on them for their living. But I regard them as much less despicable than professional mass murder, which involves not only mass graves but also ribbons and medals and heaps of money, and which also has to do with love—the pathological form of love that is called "patriotism."

Once we reached the street, we didn't dare to look at each other. It is embarrassing to be taken for a fool with your mother in a brothel; I have never forgotten the incident. I led my mortified parent to a nearby church, leaving her in more comforting surroundings while I continued my search for a room. I found one in a house where I wasn't assaulted by naked women; instead, I was greeted there by a pious old lady who attended Mass every morning, and who took cash from my pocket using rather different methods.

Provincialism will always be provincialism, no matter if it is accompanied by a boxful of highbrow culture. And provincialism will be all the more provincial if this box, before it arrives at its big-city destination, is already falling apart. For I mustn't forget to mention that this journey to my urban alma mater had an ill-starred beginning. Two accidents occurred at my home-town train depot. First, while being loaded in the freight car, the crate containing my books burst its seams. And then, just as I was about to join my parents in their passenger compartment, two gentlemen appeared for a last-minute inspection: our town pastor, and his shadow and evil spirit, a prominent local gossip and threadbare dignitary, a man who survives in my memory solely in a symbolic role: he was the Hagen of the *Nibelungenlied*, but in petty-bourgeois, small-town recrudescence, an elemental German type that has periodically abetted Germany's downfall. These two worthies caught up with me and made a final attempt to dissuade me from my academic apostasy; the salvation of my soul, they insisted, was at stake. They had seen my crate full of books get broken, and perhaps there was still time to reconsider the whole trip... But in an instant the locomotive engineer took pity on me and drove steam into the cylinders. I had escaped the henchmen of the Inquisition. Beatrice would have tossed a bucket of water at these village Torquemadas, as she will do in a later chapter when she sees her Vigoleis in a similarly stressful situation. But I didn't even know her at the time, and thus I had to defend myself alone against the evil eye. In any case, after arriving in Cologne my troubles only began.

That night in Palma, Emmerich's account of Pilar's early career conjured the image of my mother, and I saw her praying for me. Prayer is a form of grace and a source of consolation, but you have to know how to do it. I have mastered it only in rhymed form, in poems, which are of course monologues, expressions of Self distinct from any Thou—which isn't what prayer is supposed to be about. Thus I saw my mother, that good soul, rushing to my aid here on the island; she accompanied us across the square to the woman's abode, where (heaven forfend!) those Cologne chippies would have been made flesh in even more perilous fashion. The words of Scripture fit this Spanish lush like a glove: "For the lips of a strange woman drop as a honeycomb, and her mouth is smoother than oil: but her end is bitter as wormwood, sharp as a two-edged sword. Her feet go down to death."

In place of the word "sword" I would prefer to say "dagger"; and as for her feet—well, we already know that they walk in little golden slippers.

María del Pilar was the daughter of a poor family from the hinterlands of Valencia. As she grew up, her doll-like beauty proved to be more than just a temporary adornment of her childhood. She turned out to be a beautiful girl, conspicuous for her visible charms in a country where, as in all countries, beautiful females are a rarity. While still very young she was raped by her father, and she ran away. A fisherman had pity on her, and took her aboard his boat. Later she worked on Menorca as dishwasher in a tavern. There she was discovered by Don Julio, our General of eggs-and-sausage fame. He found her a job in the officers' mess; then he became jealous of his comrades, and arranged for Cinderella to join his spouse in their own kitchen. Following the adventures related before, she landed on Mallorca, and soon got tired of playing party girl for raunchy sailors in the quayside bars. She was even more disenchanted as an employee in respectable households, where for no extra pay she was continually pursued by turned-on *señoritos*.

A woman as beautiful as Pilar can always use the witches' cauldron of her sexiness to achieve higher pay, though hardly ever without concessions in the form of overt love-making. And without love-making, nothing, it seems, is possible; for otherwise the world would become extinct. Anyway, the Creator didn't fail to include Pilar in His Eternal Plan, for our Valencian beauty soon found herself in the employ of several well-heeled men in succession. A highly-placed prelate of the Church was among those who feasted on this latter-day Shulamite, and it was this *Monseñor*, by the way, who financed Julietta's education at one of the island's convent schools. When his mistress learned that he had disinherited some extra-ecclesiastical children of his own, she threw him out of the red-silk-lined domicile he had set up for her in a Palma townhouse. Shortly thereafter, she was, in turn, set out on the street by the landlord. The nuns wanted to keep Julietta in their school at no charge, but her mother refused: no Peter's Pence for her! Then she found a position in a bordello, where she no longer had to go out looking for paying employers.

Pilar's entry into the Casa Marguerita (I am still following the *chronique scandaleuse* as recited by our friend from Cologne) was an event widely discussed in every Palma club and society. At the time, this was the best cathouse in town; the *patrona* always had first-class ladies for hire, including some from foreign lands. None of the girls was permitted a tenure of more than six years. "A swell establishment," was the opinion of our bookselling informant, who obviously had not passed up the opportunity to check out the mother superior's entrepreneurial success. It was there that Don Helvecio, in his capacity as director, manager, or whatever he was at the Príncipe, made the acquaintance of Pilar while on an inspection tour of the city's sporting houses. In Spain, Mr. Emmerich explained, the assignment of showing male guests through the local love centers was customarily carried out by hotel personnel, from the bellboy to the managing director. One evening Helvecio entered the Casa Marguerita to give some elderly British lords the chance to lavish their wealth in a fashion suitable to their caste. The *patrona* took him aside and whispered, "Something very fine, for very rich clientele, just arrived, and beautiful, bee-yootiful, Don Helvecio! Just one taste, and they'll be back for more! Her name is María del Pilar."

Don Helvecio, mindful of the good name of his hotel, explained to the Englishmen that he had something very fine for them, something exclusively for guests of some means, just arrived, and bee-yootiful! They would, he vowed, not believe their own eyes. "Just one taste, mylords, and you won't want to leave this island for the rest of the season!" But since the gentlemen would need special arrangements in view of their somewhat advanced years, he would first have to make certain preparations personally. In the meantime, would my lords please be so kind as to repair to the reception room, where they might read newspapers or play dominoes. Coffee was also served there, and every now and then a girl would pass through, so they wouldn't have the impression that they were sitting in a railway station restaurant.

Zwingli was in every respect a master organizer. In all my life I have never again run across the likes of him. The girls in the brothels all loved him. Several of them received gifts of money from him, meant to lift them out of their misery and return them to a decent life. He was familiar with their troubles, large and small, but also with their aptitudes in bed. Seldom, he once told me, had he ever sent the wrong man to the wrong woman. Because of his skill in these matters, he stood in high regard in the hotel business. Zwingli's expertise and fetching ways paid off in this activity, as in so many others. He administered tests in person, and then oversaw further arrangements. This new girl from Valencia was "quality product," to judge by the praise heaped on her by the proprietress, who was not accustomed to exaggerate when describing her girls' selling points to the hotel escorts.

Zwingli gave his new female colleague the highest honors possible in his school of sexual studies: his exam went on endlessly. In this particular discipline, as we all know, high marks in the prelims do not automatically qualify for a waiver of the orals. Zwingli's test lasted so long that the lords got impatient; they knocked on the door through which the hotel manager had disappeared. I never learned whether they spent time later with other girls. Probably the hotel limousine returned them in immaculate condition to the Príncipe, together with the flasks of mercuric chloride that you can always see peeking out of Englishmen's pockets when they go cruising.

Late in the afternoon of the following day, Zwingli finally resurfaced at his hotel. "You have to stand up like a man," quipped his bosom buddy, the hotel's co-manager and co-owner (no one really knew exactly who owned or managed how much of the establishment). "*Hay que ser hombre*, Don Helvecio! But this time you come straggling back like a battle casualty, for Pete's sake! Hey, waiters! Get him some eggs, quick! Ham, bananas, champagne! Let's get this man back on his feet! Tomorrow, Conde de Keyserling's coming with his School of Wisdom, and the place will be packed!"

Don Darío knew what a man needs when he has stood up like a man.

During the following night, Zwingli absconded again. When early the next morning the famous philosopher arrived in port to have his even more famous bearlike hand shaken by the hotel manager, Zwingli was nowhere in sight. Don Darío, the short fellow with the limp, did the honors.

It was the same story night after night, and finally Zwingli stayed away from the hotel altogether.

María del Pilar fell in love with Helvecio. She gave herself to him completely, the first time in her life that she had done this with any man. Her much-touted talents were only for show; up to the moment when this fellow from Switzerland entered her life, she had remained untouched. This is how Zwingli himself explained it, and who was I to doubt his word, considering how much Tolstoy and Dostoevsky he had read. You only learn what you truly are when others confirm it for you. Besides, there are more hookers lying in legally sanctified nuptial beds than on the jerry-rigged cots in joy houses—which, incidentally, owe their popular name to a basic misconception.

Zwingli was fascinated; he felt like Tolstoy *redivivus*. He sensed an important new mission in his life, and ventured forth on the task of salvation and renewal. This girl must be lifted out of the morass, the same swamp where he had been spending all this time with her over the past few weeks, happy as a pig. This mud-bath of love would have to be moved elsewhere, for (and this was a somewhat less Christian notion) he wanted this beautiful sinner all to himself. It was a case of Resurrection with interchangeable roles. This too I can understand.

Zwingli rented a second-floor apartment, called a *piso*, and furnished it lavishly. On the walls he hung paintings and drawings by his neglected geniuses. He also dribbled away his money on behalf of his neglected new girlfriend. And thus began their domestic existence together. Julietta added a serious note to the arrangement. The generous nuns had taught her manners, prayers, and craft skills. It was an ideal family, and it lasted quite a while before things started going badly awry. The difficulties began with feelings of jealousy on Pilar's part, and soon Zwingli was smitten by the same madness. This all-powerful impulse quickly brought both of them to the brink of despair; love, hatred, and fear got all mixed together, and before long they started hitting each other. Pilar felt for certain that Helvecio was having his flings down at the Príncipe; she was well aware that those women from Germany, especially, were known world-wide for such tricks, and that they came to Spain for the sole purpose of having romantic adventures. And what was more, she knew full well that her *señorito* worked nights for his hotel, visiting the same kind of houses that he had pulled her out of. The daughter of joy turned into a raging Fury.

Zwingli worked out a new agreement with his hotel. From now on he would appear there only a few hours each day to look around, take care of the correspondence, and manage the world-wide advertising. The remaining time he would spend at the domestic hearth. Daddy would read books on the fine arts, Mommy would knit, or better yet crochet (Pilar was aiming, after all, for finer habits), and at their feet the little bastard-child would play with her toys, the precocious youngster to whom fate had granted a new father—albeit not a new General, for Switzerland does not support a standing army, but an upright member of the Swiss Civilian Foreign Legion.

Conjugal happiness is an art mastered by the very few. Genuinely happy people are as rare as Christians who believe in God. In most cases one goes through the motions, though one can actually achieve a great deal with the use of such camouflage. Pilar was not happy, certainly not "blissfully" happy, because Zwingli was unable to provide for the necessary bliss. She was bored. She couldn't read; if she could, she might have killed the long hours by devouring trashy novels. Trying on cosmetics, using this or that product to stiffen her eyelashes, was after a while just a pain. Could they travel together? Helvecio had a job where the customers did the traveling—he was obliged to stay put. Pilar was an active person, still quite young even by the standards of Spain, where women grow old early. And she had a pretty daughter, for whom she wished the same glorious future that Zwingli was supposed to be providing for his *querida*.

That is why one day, in the increasingly stuffy atmosphere of their home, Pilar tossed out the suggestion, "Helvecio, let's become independent! Let's start a business! A business where I can use my talents, too!"

Dear reader, you are probably thinking exactly what I am thinking. But really and truly, Pilar had in mind only her culinary abilities. The dream of liberty is the primeval ideal of all humankind. Beatrice and I have been considering the same idea over and over again for twenty years, it's just that we can't seem to agree on which of our talents we should exploit. Thus all we've ever seen is a faint, pinkish dawning on the horizon. Down in Spain we sometimes felt that the sun was just about to appear, but then fog always swept in, without fail. As I write these lines we are surrounded by impenetrable haze. Zwingli has been dead a long time, and I, Vigoleis, am not adept at clearing away banks of heavy murk.

Pilar's finesse with pots and pans was fully equal to Zwingli's magic fingernail. I have never tasted such bonito as came from her skillet. Zwingli, in his own mind a neglected genius, was an easy mark for any kind of new business venture. He mulled over Pilar's suggestion, consulted with headwaiters, rooming-house managers, the theories of Pelmanism, and his bosom friend Don Darío, and finally emerged with the idea that an ice-cream parlor, strategically located in the city of Palma, was an undertaking that without the slightest doubt would yield a handsome profit. No need right away for marble fixtures and artificial palms—it was best to start simple: a few potted geraniums, here and there one of those rangy cactuses. "It's a *solid* idea, Don Helvecio," was Don Darío's reaction, and he was the one to know, considering the lucrative part-time enterprise he could be as proud of as a Spaniard (if he weren't one already). In his home town of Felanitx he ran a bullfighting arena where the so-called *novilladas* were staged, the skirmishes involving novice toreros and young steers—the marionette tryouts, as it were, for the big-time national theater. A young man with ambitions to be impaled on the horns of the huge *miuras* in the metropolitan stadiums could achieve early success in Don Darío's sandy pit, especially since the atheistic owner had placed his enterprise under divine auspices. The Mother of God, he claimed, lent her succor to each and every bullfighter; a *novillero*, like any humble beginner in this world, could be certain of her intervention with the Lord. Darío was a devout man, though hardly of the orthodox variety. His atheism was deceptive whenever he started in about his beloved *Virgen*, the Holy Virgin, who in his opinion would also offer her protective benevolence to the new ice-cream bar. It was bound to be a success.

In the Count's housing complex, the couple found a suitable locale on the "respectable" corner opposite the men's club, whose clientele would surely enjoy a dish of ice cream dispensed by Pilar. Most of the club members already knew her from her previous dispensation, and as for the Conde himself—to finish this sentence would be to indulge in mere gossip, which has no place in my chronicle. Antonio, the hotel's majordomo and headwaiter, is responsible for my having started the sentence at all. This is the same Antonio who served us our coffee back in Chapter Three. He was a prince of a man, and he was devoted to Zwingli. Later he took us to his heart. For a few years he had worked as a waiter in Nice, but family exigencies had forced his return to Mallorca. He was a *grandseigneur* in his profession, quite free of the behavioral folderol that makes so many headwaiters objectionable people. Most men in that position, I have found, act like secret agents who are hired to keep a constant eye on you. I'll grant that anyone in a job of this kind has to have a little of the con-man in him. But with Antonio, his native Mallorcan temperament, which he never tried to conceal, served to minimize this aspect of his activity. The superiority of the Southern races over their Northern counterparts, who like to make believe they are some kind of nobility, is most apparent in the servant classes.

On the days preceding the opening of the "Bar Valencia," as Zwingli had christened their new enterprise in honor of his co-proprietor and chief advertising gimmick, there was a flurry of activity. The most active of all was the boss from Switzerland. He had thousands of brochures printed in four languages. He stretched banners over Palma's streets that read BAR VALENCIA. He hired sandwich-men and street barkers. Invitations went out to every exclusive and inclusive club and society on the island. If you know Spain at all, you can imagine what the bills for all this came to. Every hotel, *pensión*, and movie house in town distributed leaflets designed by Zwingli's friend, a German graphic artist in Barcelona known as "Dibujante Knoll," who in turn had them printed by a first-rate Barcelona fine-arts press (Beatrice later paid this bill, too).

Don Helvecio's economic independence was meant to have the stablest foundation possible. Only a natural catastrophe could cause it to fail, one that would simultaneously plunge the entire island into the sea like an atoll. Hadn't the same man, years ago, rapidly resurrected the Príncipe to its present standing as an A-number-one establishment, after it had been plundered by gangsters and avoided by customers lacking sufficient courage? The new owner, who had wrenched the facility from the robbers by means of a naked power grab, hadn't accomplished anything with his new property until Zwingli came along. I have never found out all the details of the transaction, and the wildest stories coursed around the island. The truth is that the filthy-rich owner, one of the most influential lawyers on Mallorca and at the same time the *alcalde* or mayor of Palma, turned over the helm to the completely unknown entrepreneur after a single half-hour conference. That magic nail no doubt played a role in all this—I mean the one sported by Zwingli, for although the crafty solicitor had grown one, too, his just wasn't long enough to solve all the problems of existence. It was Emmerich, by the way, who drew the newly-arrived Swiss citizen's attention to the empty, haunted hotel. Zwingli had come to Mallorca in the season of the almond blossoms "just to take a look around." By Christmas a large spruce tree was brightly lit; German and English carols greeted the Savior, whose birth then got celebrated in sentimental carousing with popping corks, mulled wine, crackling spruce needles, and sparklers that smelled like incense. Power of attorney and a fat checkbook had brought about this yuletide miracle.

This selfsame Zwingli, the man who meanwhile had risen to the dignified rank of a Don Helvecio—wasn't it likely that he could make a go of it with a little experimental dispensary for lovers of ice cream? Particularly with a waitress like this one, who wouldn't emerge from the kitchen all too often, but when she did, would cause commotion among the clientele? With her as a partner, Zwingli could even have risked opening up a kiddies' lemonade stand. Of course Zwingli wasn't planning to have Pilar scooping cones forever. At the beginning, well yes, but later, when things had settled down, he would let her share the management duties. To make this possible, he would have to hire an expert confectioner, a genuine Paris-trained professional from the Valais with international experience. He had already sent off the appropriate advertisements to the Swiss trade journals.

The equipment and accessories were all bought, partly in cash and partly on promise. As Don Helvecio, Zwingli enjoyed almost unlimited credit. One phone call at the hotel, and even an over-cautious dealer would load up his handcart and push it himself to the Conde's "apple," where carpenters and plumbers had been at work for days. If ever the credit confirmation for some reason wasn't satisfactory, Zwingli would appear arm in arm with his business partner, and resistance would immediately melt away, just as the ice cream later did in the super-heated store.

Women should play with fire. That is their element, but never with anything that's frozen—this bit of folk wisdom from Zwingli, whose own account is the main source for what I am narrating here. Emmerich knew only the bare outlines of the saga. The details and refinements were served up by Zwingli, the boss himself. For example, the incident in a well-known mirror factory, Espejo Mallorquin. "You should have seen those *chaibe Siëche* turn into midgets when I showed up with Pilar! They wanted cash before delivery, but my order was in the thousands. Maybe you can sell ice cream at the North Pole without mirrors on the walls and ceiling, but not in Spain. To understand such things you don't have to be Swiss, with congenital experience of scaling glaciers! But just try to explain these subtleties to somebody who has never in his life seen a snowflake melt in his hand! Reflected light creates just the right polar ambience. I had to have mirrors, otherwise the Mallorcans could go on for all time spooning up their *sopas*, for all I cared. In the packing room at the factory, where we met the director in person, there just happened to be some fun-house mirrors standing against the wall. Let me tell you, what with the instant changes we saw from fat to skinny and from tall to squat, we got the credit approval before we even reached the guy's office. Put some products like those in the halls of mirrors at international conferences, there'd never be another war!"

One week later there wasn't one square-inch of wall to be seen in the new ice-cream parlor. It was wall-to-wall crystal.

Grand Opening: Saturday afternoon at five o'clock. Zwingli had hired from the Príncipe a young doorman in blinding blue livery, as well as a bartender from the same familiar source. Pilar's assignment was spooning out the ice cream. She was dressed in fine silk chiffon, an outfit meant to insinuate coolness—quite some feat for this hotsy-totsy, but a fashion designer from Barcelona seems to have done the trick. Zwingli had insisted on this arrangement. He himself was dressed accordingly, his magic nail exquisitely filed and polished, just as shiny as the mirrors, which had no difficulty deciding who was the fairest of them all. He had sent invitations, written in his own hand, to personages of high standing in the community, including the military governor, the civilian governor, the *alcalde*, the consular representatives of the more important countries (the less important ones would come on their own), and prominent foreign residents, of whom there were always hundreds milling about the island. Back then it was de rigeur to have spent time on Mallorca if one wished to make any kind of impression in the grander European salons. Finally, he sent off printed invitations by the thousands to God and the whole world.

In the meantime Zwingli and Pilar had rented the upper storey in the Count's house, an apartment that came with the shop down below but with a view to the shabby side of the "apple." This arrangement, just around the corner and up a flight of stairs, was decidedly advantageous for the new shopowners. Julietta, let us insert here, was also dolled up for the occasion, although she was forbidden to show her face in the new establishment. Nevertheless, this was to be a red-letter day in the life of the General's rejected daughter—but in a different way than her elders had planned.

The festive couple had a late breakfast consisting of a double portion of the General's omelet, and this tells us that Heaven was doling out its grace to them in double measure. They soon left for the bar, where the *botones* had taken care of the most necessary preparations. The coffee-maker was heated up, the ice-cream machines were converting heat into refrigeration. Zwingli was bursting with creative energy, and no doubt also with pride in his accomplishments before breakfast.

Love is unpredictable. It can come flashing down out of a blue sky like a bolt of lightning, infusing everything with its brilliance. I am thinking, of course, of spiritual love, the unutterable, all-penetrating form of love that emanates from the soul and animates everything in its path; it lives in the Other as well as in the Self. Augustine, an authority in the field of both worldly and celestial love, calls it the *vita quaedam, duo aliqua copulans vel copulare appetens...* None of the standard lexicons has much to say about it, since source material is so hard to come by. Poets, on the other hand, busy themselves often with this miraculous phenomenon.

The other kind of love, carnal lust, is easier to fathom. It has virtually no secrets, since everybody in the world can experiment with it, and most people make ample use of the opportunity. If it is spoken of less often, that is because, as I see it, mankind has a bad conscience. We are ashamed of an act which, if it never took place, there would be no "us" to be ashamed of anything. It is not aesthetic, this mechanism that some call pleasure, others call sin, and sobersides don't dare to name at all. One must therefore be careful when treating of matters that concern this wobbly old vehicle. I shall be as discreet as possible, but I've got to keep the wheels moving somehow, for otherwise I could inscribe my *finis operis* right here. One thing leads to another. And whoever is dealing with Zwingli simply cannot avoid mentioning his Pilar. The axles on their sexual vehicle were ungreased, and the result was a little conflagration. Happily there was plenty of ice on hand, so the damage to their bodies could be repaired. What we refer to as the soul was never involved in the calamity.

Zwingli is said to have looked handsome with a pink carnation in his lapel. Pilar was simply beautiful, enchanting, a poem, a midsummer night's dream. Everything about her was gleaming. Her lashes pointed seductively out into the world—bluebottle flies from the marketplace had laid down their lives for this stunning effect. Cosmetic preparations from Rimmel, Quelques Fleurs, and a dozen other Parisian firms provided her elaborate makeup. Sightseers had already arrived on the scene. On the terrace of the men's club, more gentlemen than usual for this time of day, which they normally spent napping inside, were snoozing away. The club personnel had been asked to sound the alarm just prior to the grand opening across the street. The mirrors on walls and ceiling reflected only festive, happy sights; the faces of all assembled reflected nothing but merriness and cheer. No one noticed that the crystal panes had yet to be paid for. Just a single day's receipts would wipe away all debts, and this would happen by virtue of an ingenious man's ingenious fingernail, whose underside today revealed not the slightest inky blemish. Not even the most bilious fussbudget would have had grounds for complaint here.

One more hour, and then we shall join all the other invited guests in making a deep bow. We'll live through a short welcome speech, just a few words, won't even have to listen, we'll all nod yes yes yes, kiss the pretty barmaid's hand, terrific babe, right? you bet, wonder where he found her, you'd like to take her just about anyplace at all, whaddaya mean anyplace, all depends on what you think of how they got together, whaddaya mean, aw, you know, you mean ya don't know where Don Helvecio dug up his Helvetia, no sir, well juicy chicks like that don't grow like cheese in the Swiss Alps, haha, but sex-ee I tell ya, I don't care what stable she's from, and her trainer, not bad how he pulled the Príncipe out of the shit, bet none of us coudda done it. Great country, Switzerland, but if ya ask me their watches run a little bit *too* accurate, *olé* Don Jaime, *olé* Manolo, you here too? and there's our governor over there, yessirree, everybody who's for progress on the island has come over here to get cooled off.

There is a clapping of hands, Antonio and his waiters distribute *café negro*. The snoozers wake up by themselves, rise up in their armchairs, and have to crane their necks. But it's worth the effort: Zwingli and his ice-cream sundae are coming around the corner—

—and disappear into the shop. Then the door designated by the word "DOOR" closes behind them. Final technical inspection, everyone figures, because that was the room that contained all the machinery. The drains have been unplugged, the electric centrifugal pump is humming away to keep the tank under the roof constantly filled. A glass-washing machine, on test loan from the manufacturer (lucky for Beatrice!) needs only to be plugged in, and in the twinkling of an electrical eye it will chase away even the most tenacious bacillus, leaving the glasses germ-free for the next round of customers.

Zwingli must have been rubbing his hands in anticipation. The champagne was at just the right temperature. Pilar, the Venus of the Island risen from the ocean foam, was to let a few corks pop against the mirrored ceiling as a signal that the ceremony has begun. Our theater director thought up this terrific stage effect: first the exploding corks, then, through a crack in the front door, a beautiful hand would appear, followed by a gorgeous arm, then champagne foam would spill on the ground, and finally the Goddess Herself would step forth...

Unscheduled, like so much else in life, there now burst onto the scene, dressed in juvenile ceremonial array, the Goddess' daughter.

Julietta had pleaded with her mother and foster father, amid tears that bespoke her serious devotion to the Fourth Commandment, that her real father —the General, Don Julio—should be allowed to participate in the opening celebration. In truth he would have been in excellent company among the dignitaries who had now arrived in numbers that exceeded all expectations. And if he had brought along his frictionless spouse with her campfollower's bosom, her varicose veins, and her ivory fan, we might have caught sight of that item of the General's house furnishings as well.

But the defender of his Mediterranean redoubt was deemed unworthy to lick ice cream in the new bar named after his resurrected kitchen fairy. Julietta fumed and cried and shouted, she bared her teeth and uttered dire threats (children always have lots of material they can use to blackmail their parents) for weeks on end. But to no avail. The lord and lady of ice cream could not be softened up. Worse yet: as Julietta tried to sneak in through the crack in the afore-mentioned door, at the critical moment just before the champagne foam was to start flowing, her mother shoved her back outside with a hoarsely hissed curse. The poor child was repulsed, disowned before the multitudes, whose eyes had been staring expectantly at the front entrance. No more scenes, Helvecio! Tell us yourself that there's too much at stake!

Children are as unpredictable as the love I was speaking about just a moment ago. And generals are as unpredictable as both together: love and the fruits of love.

Julietta, hurt to the quick and publicly humiliated in her love for her father, ran up the steps of the Calle de la Seo, and just seconds later was inside the Cathedral, lying at the feet of the statue of Our Lady on the Column, the *Virgen del Pilar*. The nuns had taught her how to pray, and she hadn't forgotten. In the ardor of her despair she invoked her father: "Help me, stand by me! I am abandoned!"

Those who, like me, have forgotten how to pray, are all the more fervent in their belief in the efficacy of prayer, since they have no reason to fear the trial of disappointment. Julietta, still in the initial phase of her piety, still believed in the succor offered by the denizens of Heaven. If an entire nation, "in the fear and misery of a war that threatens the very existence of all peoples and all nations," can turn to God with a request to decimate another country, then why can't a little girl place all her trust in the Mother of God, especially when we consider that the latter was the Patroness of her own mother? Julietta never doubted that her frantic prayers would come true, precisely because the Virgin bore her mother's name. When she had finished praying, she immediately stamped her foot, thus putting the Virgin Mary under pressure to act fast. And on her way out of the Cathedral she stopped to put in a brief insurance prayer with San Antonio.

It was Julietta herself who later told me all this. When her tale was done, she said to me, "Vigo, if your mother had done something like that with the Madonna in your parish, then maybe you wouldn't have had such hard times." Oh, Julietta! If you only knew how obstinate our lovely Lower-

Rhenish Madonnas are! You can't force them to do what you want, not even to get you enough money to buy a genuine 13th-century specimen for your living room!

Don Julio was also repulsed, despite his imposing figure with plumed helmet, epaulettes, sash, saber, medals, jackboots, and the rapidly waning glory of his public fame. Yet though he may have been rejected in body, he had very palpably arrived in spirit. His bastard-child had conjured him, though the girl was totally ignorant of occult practices. The Hand of Heaven was without doubt responsible. Thus a dematerialized General came to aid his twice-repudiated daughter, and in doing so foiled his enemies' strategy. Which is what generals are for, after all.

Here at the Bar Valencia, on a Saturday afternoon, one second before a champagne salvo and without the customary *"Tirez le premier, Monsieur!"* Don Julio appeared in a form and with an effect that are probably not even familiar to our most advanced parapsychologists. I am revealing this occurrence here out of a sense of twofold obligation: first, toward Vigoleis' recollections, and secondly, no less earnestly, toward science. Don Julio came, as if conjured by a troll's whistle, or like a cordial to cap off the meal named after him. Just as the Holy Spirit descended upon the assembled disciples, causing them to speak in all languages, so did the General let himself be called forth from his spectral headquarters to visit the couple. And behold, they began to seethe, as if a powerful gale were howling through the back room at the bar, and with all the fibers and tongues of their bodies, they started loving each other.

Zwingli had just enough time to pull the bolt on the door-door—the outer world had vanished, and they knew each other in their flesh. They knew each other, in fact, so intensely that they didn't know themselves any more, perhaps because their bed of love was anything but comfortable—cool enough, to be sure, but not with the coolness of genuine horsehair. Or perhaps because of the darkness in this area, which they were utilizing for the first time for love-making. They bumped against all sorts of paid and unpaid plumbing and machinery. If love-making is to happen in an extravagant location, a padded cell in an asylum would have been preferable.

The Bible tells many stories of how love can be transformed into hatred. Friedrich Nietzsche filled ten thousand or more pages concerning the same problem. Therefore, let us be content here with the brief announcement that Zwingli's love for Pilar, and Pilar's love for her Helvecio, soon reverted to intense mutual animosity. And who wouldn't be seized by a frenzy of anger if, at the moments of highest ecstasy, your skull kept banging against a centrifuge and your foot tipped over a container of ice, causing your limbs and members, throbbing in the heat of lust, to be cooled off with infuriating suddenness, just as Pastor Heumann advises in his *Manual of Personal Hygiene*: Cold compresses! And if hatred has once made its ugly appearance, it strives to do away with its own immediate cause. Spinoza understood this perfectly. The person I hate must be exterminated, he must go, permanently, and there is no other solution: It's either me or him.

There is every indication that our two shop owners behind the door-door had intentions of acting according to this tried-and-true philosophical insight. Each of them wanted to remove the other from existence—a terrible idea right before the festive ceremony, or rather virtually during the ceremony, for the front door had already been opened to allow the champagne christening to take place.

Both of them, the young man no less than the blossoming young woman, wanted to kill each other, and to take with them to their graves all the hopes they had every reason to trust in. How did they plan to carry out this double murder? I happen to know exactly how; I have been able to reconstruct everything, partly on the basis of reports from those who were directly involved, partly by my own conscientious research into the contributing factors. It is not for nothing that I have sat at the feet of the Münster criminologist Profesor Többen and his live subjects at the penitentiary in that august city. But the results of my detective work do not belong here. Even the most scandalous chronicle must have certain limits, within which everyone may freely exercise his own fantasy.

The General had won a victory, incidentally the very first and the very last of his much-beribboned career. He instantly returned on the wings of his emanation to his fortress, and to the murky marital moods of his old lady. Julietta, too, had won a battle, the very first victory of her life. It wouldn't be her last.

The invited guests left the battlefield slowly—the uninvited ones even more slowly. The bartender listened at the door. What he heard was confusing, allowing no firm conclusions as to what was going on inside. Antonio had no better luck when he held his ear to the thin panel, but they both agreed that turbulent events were taking place behind it. But precisely what? If that pump would only stop whining! The two people inside weren't dead, but they wouldn't respond to their two employees' knocking and shouting. Dead people are mute, whereas inside the ice-cream machinery room there was talking going on—and groaning and screaming besides. How odd; such noises do not belong in the copa of a bar. Civilization has provided other venues for such behavior, although often enough people regress to primitive habits and choose just about anywhere to gnash their teeth and wield their tomahawks.

"Ladies and gentlemen," said Antonio, after a whispered conference with the bartender. "Honored guests, there has been a slight mishap. An unforeseen malfunction in our mechanical plant has forced the management to postpone our opening until next Saturday."

Just then Julietta returned to the scene and began to dance. She threw her little arms in the air and snapped her castanets. Music started up, and no one left for home. Antonio served his *café negro* from the kitchen over at the men's club, and more and more people filled the terrace, including individuals who had no membership rights. Pepe, who ran a little *fonda* for donkey drivers and laborers next to the ice-cream bar, waited on the tables in his tavern and raked in the cash from customers who otherwise would never be seen drinking from his glasses. And Julietta danced without a stop. She whirled with flying skirts, approached the men with her hands suggestively at her hips, stamped her feet—a little-girl Argentinita, who today is probably vying with that great star, for I hear that in the meantime Julietta has become famous through appearances at theaters on the Spanish mainland.

Her audience drove her on, *olé, olé!* But she needed no special encouragement to let out all the spunk and snappiness that the General had passed on to her, or the Valencian fire that was her mother's legacy. Her improvised performance reached its climax when a young man pushed his way through the onlookers, took off his jacket and placed it on the ground in front of the dancing imp. He caught her in mid-twist, and like an infatuated dove began dancing in a circle with his dovelet. The audience applauded thunderously, for they had long since forgotten why they had come here. The boy was Pedro, who back then had the ambition to become what he has since indeed turned out to be, a painter known far beyond his native island. We shall meet up with him again often in these pages.

María del Pilar, who wanted to deny this celebration to a child who longed for her father and for art, was treated by Zwingli to ice cream and love in their hermetically sealed love-nest. Amid moans and sighs and repeated invocations of the Virgin Mary, her spirits finally revived, though in a body that by now was black and blue all over, no different from that of her Samaritan partner. In active lovemaking, as in the art of forging steel, the tempering coloration can determine the quality of the product.

At seven o'clock Julietta collapsed in mid-pirouette, and Pedro had to carry her over to the men's club. A doctor quickly put her back on her feet. Attempts to resuscitate the Bar Valencia, on the other hand, were without success; the enterprise never survived the erotic crisis of its whilom founders. It died in labor, not unlike the Asra tribe of Northern Africa, of whom Heine once sang that they die while making love.

Using Swiss francs, Beatrice later had a simple cross placed at this second gravesite with this pious caption: All debts are now forgiven.

VII

Having arrived at this chapter, my reader already knows more than we did at that night-time hour when we took leave of Anton Emmerich with *Tschüss!* and *Ciao!* And I was once again ahead of Beatrice in this lubricious chronicle by a few pages. These were pages that even the dirty-minded fugitive from Cologne considered too risqué to spread out in front of Beatrice. She noticed that her presence was tying his tongue, and so she absented herself for a while. Mr. Emmerich confessed to me straightaway that he was unsure how far her nerves could be stretched. But then he started right in again.

These days Beatrice was letting herself be seen in public with that woman friend, arm in arm. In certain male circles a rumor had arisen that the city's commerce in pleasure had undergone an augmentation; a newcomer of indeterminable yet indubitable pedigree had been observed on several occasions in Pilar's company. No one was quite sure whether the novice was freelancing or, on the other hand, adding yet another exotic fragrance to the bouquet offered by the Casa Marguerita. Perhaps she had decided to reconnoiter the hotels first. People were making conjectures, and he, Emmerich, had learned that certain rich blimps had hired scouts to find out more about this female stranger. It was surmised that she hailed from Switzerland, where the laws of the Confederation permitted only indoor prostitution, but still, one had certain notions concerning Swiss women. And besides, this bird looked expensive...

"Are they talking prices?" Vigoleis could not resist inquiring.

With a snicker, Emmerich mentioned sums that the Mallorquin gentry would be prepared to place on the night table for my unsuspecting consort. Pretty chintzy, to use a favorite expression of those women whose market value was often haggled over shamelessly, as if it were the most natural thing in the world—which, in fact, it was. If Vigoleis had been forced to cough up cold cash for his Chosen One, he would have slapped down considerably more than these islanders, the ones who sat around on their sacks of money and on their club porches. And yet, if truth be told, he could never have matched even what those fatsoes were offering, not even with the discount that he could claim as a private household consumer—never in his life! As for the fact that he was not forced to enter such commerce, this had to do with a certain passage in the Epistle to the Corinthians, where Paul waxes as lyrical as a troubadour. And yet this selfsame Vigoleis, instead of being grateful for having a woman who commanded such a price with strangers—and an even higher fee according to his own reckoning—this same Vigoleis had turned his eyes to that other female, the bitch-in-quotation-marks. In spirit he had already committed adultery—if we can regard as a marriage the bond that tied him to his aforementioned consort.

Adultery, committed already in spirit? Truly in spirit? I wonder whether the Church (I'm mentioning this out of respect for Pilar), having set forth in its canonical regulations concerning marriage the neatest and most meticulous differentiations between spirit and matter, would grant Vigoleis absolution for a spiritual transgression against matrimonial fidelity when, one fine day, he found himself alone in the house with the lusty siren, and then proceeded to do what he didn't end up doing at all. For what did he do by not doing it? That would fascinate me, too, as his sometime double. For as far as I know, when it comes to women, he is as shy as Monsieur Henri-Frédéric Amiel himself.

Judging from what little we already know about Pilar, but also from the abundance of information to be found between our lines, it was probably this woman who had her mind set on action, who couldn't wait until her new victim was maneuvered *in flagrantem*. I can, of course, be mistaken, and where are mistakes more to be expected than in the labyrinths of the heart? What is more, if the paths inside this maze are slippery, a man is bound to end up flat on his kisser.

Everything would indicate that the events involving Vigoleis and Pilar occurred in a manner very similar to the biblical story of Joseph, who, contrary to God's wishes, declined to sleep with his master's wife. I make this allusion solely with regard to the outer circumstances. Vigoleis' inward thoughts are as yet unexplored territory; and anyway, our biblical interpreter of dreams, purchased by Egyptians for twenty silver shekels, has never allowed anyone to look very deeply into his soul, not even his voluble biographer, Thomas Mann. His master's wife is said to have done her utmost to cause the foreigner to yield to her concupiscence. Thus at her words, "Come, lie with me!" we are allowed to peer into the very bottom of her heart. I assume that Pilar made a similar entreaty to Vigoleis, taking him by the scruff of the neck, as it were, and pulling him down on the pallet of her Eternal Spring. Whereupon this fellow with the two souls (alas!) in one breast will have departed in haste, leaving his cloak in her hands. I wouldn't put it past him.

"It wasn't at all..."—at this point Vigoleis begins to speak in person, to prevent any further spinning out of legends at the site of the evil deed. It wasn't at all the way you think it was. I'll grant you that I am a master of the botched opportunity, whether it be with women or with books written by someone else. It's also true that I've made a big mistake in the century to be born in, and in the blueprint of my second sight. But that woman Pilar, who had already had God knows how many gentlemen beneath her little golden slippers—she was not going to escape me. On the afternoon in question all signs were propitious for my ambitions, my animal curiosity, my comparative scientific bent, and my literary thirst for material from the world of genuine human experience—which my imagination has a habit of playing tricks on in any case. All that is clear. What remains foggy is how I found my way into her bedroom. Between the vestibule and the scene of my sinful conquest stood the dark hallway. And that is where we met, for I had awaited just the moment when we would bump into each other's arms. Her mouth was pressed to mine—what's the big deal? The hall was narrow, and then my hand rested on her breast; the cool fabric of her *albornoz* parted; surely the wearer of this garment helped out a little, and as my hand came to rest on her nakedness I began to see stars before my eyes—in the darkness an altogether natural phenomenon, just as the entire sequence of events I am narrating here had nothing whatsoever to do with supernatural forces. Besides, all that was happening was as unoriginal as Nature itself, which, as we all know, must repeat itself over and again in order to remain immortal. I began to sense more and more urgently the wish that the remainder of her clothing might descend as well, and in a trice we were in her room, jostling against her bedstead. The word "magnificent" flashed through my mind, "you are magnificent on your extended *récamier*." Perhaps not the entire world, but certainly Vigoleis will henceforth borrow your name and call the pallet of love a *pilarière*. Just let me get to work. First, all these buttons. It's taking an eternity! You foxy woman, you've sewn them on just millimeters apart! Underneath her *peignoir* she was—well now, what was she? She was the goddess I had been yearning for, right down to her stockings, which were held in place by violet ruffles.

World literature is rich in depictions of two people meeting in the straits of evil opportunity, performing what nature has prescribed for them, as if they were simply flies or squirrels. Poets have exploited the scene, and some of the greatest prose treats of this eternally unique topic. Just leaf through the canon with this in mind, and you will soon hit upon the suggestive line speaking of "broken flowers and grass" and the lava of love, surging over page after page. Albrecht Schaeffer, through all his years of creative activity, had a constantly inventive pen when it came to making two people into one. When I first read his *Helianth*, I waxed breathless in the chapter entitled "Ecstasy": Georg scoots up a ladder and enters Anna's room, whereupon neither the writer nor the couple wastes any time. They go all the way: "He heard her moan softly. He felt pain himself. He was confused. But then arrived the instant of inchoate sobbing. Suddenly he was urged on by some invisible giant fist towards mad spasms of lust," etc.

"The instant of inchoate sobbing"—superb! Experiencing tingles of bliss, I lowered the book. I meditated on this inchoate instant, I let it pass before me; I relished it. The instant became a whole minute, then another and yet another. The couple was already finished, Georg, arising from his depletion and torpor, had long since jumped into his duds and scrammed. But I kept on savoring that instant, I re-read the passage until all of a sudden—the magic burst. What I was reading was a totally banal sentence. I heard a voice urging haste: "Come on, my friend, get on with your inchoate sobbing! On the double!" and I closed the book. If ever you take a word with familiar meaning and repeat it several times out loud, it loses its sense; it says no more, it becomes hollow noise. In just the same way, you can repeat a line of verse or prose to the point of jibber-jabber, and all that remains is pure kitsch. My "inchoate sobbing" had turned into kitsch, just as love itself will, if you film it in slow motion.

What I was sensing there next to my Pilar's *pilarière*, a few moments prior to the crucial one, would, if written down word for word, yield some highly dubious literature. Even in its primordial, pre-verbal state it was problematical enough, but—it was real!

I was still attempting to strip away the last mundane trappings from my goddess, when the Divinity Herself bent down, grasped her right stocking, and drew forth a dagger. I shall be brief, and shall refrain from creating steamy depictions out of this confession of my weakness of the flesh, which was to end in cowardice of body and soul. Otherwise my chronicler might be accused of pornographic intentions, a charge that has not even spared the Song of Solomon. What Pilar held in her hands was a blade of finest Toledo manufacture. She stood there like Charlotte Corday, ready to bless the hot bath before I stepped in. Never would I have imagined a stiletto at such a breathtaking location on the female body! "Breathtaking" is in fact the single appropriate word here, doubly significant in this context. For one thing, the sight of her beauty choked me up; I became almost numb, as if I were standing before the portrait of a solemn, monumental Madonna. And during these inchoate instants of impending suffocation, the tiny remaining gulp of air that might have rescued me also vanished when I saw the glint of steel before my eyes. The knife had caught a beam of light that had crept in through a knothole in the shutter to take part in this biblical tableau. The thought of murder flashed through my mind: a crime of passion! She wants your blood, she's crying for your blood! She wants revenge for having kept her unsatiated for so long! She will make love to you, and then plunge the blade up to the hilt between your ribs. Yet this shimmering Fury could also dispatch you before any thought of climax. Would there be a more beautiful death for a melancholy poetaster?

Before I could answer this question to my own satisfaction, I myself turned biblical. Like the Egyptian Joseph, I fled, but in somewhat variant fashion: rather than leave my cloak in the hands of the chippy, I slipped through her door holding her albornoz, got entangled in the garment, and would almost have collapsed in the hall if a benign spirit had not lifted me up and guided me through the dark passageway, one breathless step ahead of my putative murderess. Great heavens, I have barely escaped the treacherous needle of her unrequited love! You have viewed her nakedness, Vigoleis, and have renounced it. You must die!

Thus far, Vigoleis' own account of these happenings. His appearance here has been just as naked as that of a poet within his own stanzas, which is perhaps the most blatant showcase for human exhibitionism. If questioned whether he still believes that Pilar lured him to her bed in order to get rid of him, he will be in a position to reply that just a few weeks into his Spanish sojourn, he had familiarized himself with the habits of several women. Pilar was simply about to place that avenging blade on her little night table, so as to allow no sharp foreign object to come between herself and her taciturn purveyor of lust. Permit me to add that this episode's hasty denouement diverges in one further respect from the trial of the chaste biblical dreamer: Potiphar threw Joseph in prison, whereas Vigoleis got off scot-free—for the time being. Later, he was to feel the humiliated woman's vengeance sorely enough. A separate chapter will recount how María del Pilar showed Vigoleis the truth of a saying, still controversial among theologians, that has long since found its way from the Bible into sensationalist literature in the grand manner: "Vengeance is mine!"

But now back to the question, *juris utriusque*, that has necessitated an excursus leading us very close to union with a Divinity: did Vigoleis commit adultery in spirit? And this brings us, in strict consequence, to a second question: how, afterwards, did he stand before his Beatrice, who, after all, was not some arbitrary choice of partner who could be casually cheated on with "another woman." To be honest about it, our hero didn't "stand" before her at all, but was lying on the *pilarière* in their own room when Beatrice returned from a walk through the city with Zwingli. She wanted to rent a piano, and had tried out several instruments, but now she came home to some atonal music in ultrasonic registers: what on earth had been going on? Because the apartment alcove was not a tailor's shop, the *albornoz* lying in a heap on the floor spoke the expected volumes, whose pages we shall simply leave uncut. A clever reader can snatch something of their contents by rolling a leaf or two into a tube, and peering through. It is not false modesty that prevents me from employing a page-cutter. It's just that my reader, too, ought to exert himself a bit and apply his imagination. Such cooperative effort can increase the pleasure of reading, as I have myself experienced with others, and engender a certain sense of comradeship that can sustain a spirit of exploratory enterprise all the way to the *finis operis*. Since these pages of mine contain so much talk of coupling and conjugality and cohabitation, perhaps I may be permitted to beg my reader quite unequivocally for a kind of connubial understanding.

In the text I'm speaking of there is one little term that easily stands out because it is printed in bold italics. After twenty years, reproduced verbatim from the source, it now reappears here in these jottings of Vigoleis as a singular indication that, at the time, did not fail to make an impression. That term is: *mal de France*.

Every Spaniard carries this disease, but for centuries now, it hasn't harmed these people at all. They have become immune to the dreaded poison, just as experienced apiarists do with bee-stings. Entire sequences of generations have brought this about by dint of selfless, indefatigable preventive therapy. Their motto has not been "After us, the deluge!" but, more fraternally and humanely, "After us, immunity!" Still, whoever arrives from abroad as yet unstung can get pounced upon by the bacilli, just as flies search out meat in the marketplace stalls. In Cologne I attended a course on the dangers and problems of venereal infection. Right after World War I courses of that kind, along with related medical examinations, were required for students of all disciplines at all German universities. At the time Germany was thought to be the most seriously threatened country in Europe, and as a good European in Nietzsche's sense, I washed my hands religiously. It won't be my fault, I told myself, if the Decline of the West is going to happen on account of *this* disease. I became a syphillophobe, and came to think of myself as already corroded, in fact already eaten up. As gladly as I might often wish to venture beyond the Stygian stream—still, please, not this way! Experts were speaking of the devil, and so I became careful, or if you will, just plain scared. If it was to be imbecility for me, I would prefer to have incurred it as the result of a poetic parthenogenesis.

Is it any wonder, then, that Beatrice's mention of this term electrified me? I flew to the kitchen and began scrubbing my hands like a surgeon before an invasive procedure. Using my feet, I dragged the *albornoz* up to the door of that dangerous carrier of microbes. Let her pick it up and don it again over her seductive leprosy, I shall never again touch the one or the other!

There are certain kinds of window pane through which somebody standing outside a room cannot see in, while those inside can watch everything that goes on outside. Pilar was that sort of thing: a distorting glass, an enticing toxic blossom, hemlock, a center of contagion and a diabolical swamp, a highly evolved plantlet of the family Droseraceae, commonly and eloquently known as Venus' fly-trap—and Vigoleis was the insect whose juices the goddess was going to devour! It was enough to make one speechless. Meals presented a delicate problem. Was it safe to eat off her dishes, with her forks and spoons? Did it make any sense to wipe them off surreptitiously with the tablecloth, as we did in railroad-station restaurants? Perhaps we should place on the table a sterilizing apparatus, just like an electric toaster, and put on face masks and rubber gloves. And then? Then there would be a public fracas. Contagious persons get very sensitive if they notice that other persons have noticed what nobody was supposed to notice. Pilar the Witch realized soon enough that Vigoleis, the fugitive from her bed, always washed his hands whenever she crossed his path. Haha, this little coward is forever washing his hands, in the stupid innocence I was unable to rob him of! Just wait, I've taken care of many another, and I'll get to you in my own sweet time.

"Vengeance is mine," saith the Lord. That is an audacious figure of speech, and it has often given the theologians much to think about. They have come up with an erudite term for the obvious ascription of lowly human feelings to the Divinity; they call it "anthropopathy." But with God we can still negotiate; we can try to change His mind. People ask Him in prayer to keep His eye on their concerns, to send down in the Great Lottery the number we own one-tenth of; to destroy an enemy of ours or to help us pass an exam. If I believed in God, I wouldn't care to sully a feeling of that kind with commercial transactions, but that is of course a private matter. Pilar, who likewise would eventually take vengeance, couldn't be negotiated with, because her emotions were not the subject of learned semantics. They defied any and all systematizing, and could never be lifted out of their natural urgency by means of complex conceptualizations. For this reason she smote Vigoleis, sending him from the frying pan directly into the fire.

The first to pay the price was Zwingli. To be sure, he was the one who had brought to their house these clean relatives of his, with their firm views on hygiene. But beyond that, he was not responsible for my fears, and even less responsible for the term Beatrice had used to send back to her bed of straw the Cinderella we were supposed to be improving and educating. Once Helvecio's bedtime pet, now this animal began sucking the juices from his body. He rapidly lost weight, and neither omelets *à la Général*, wine, nor fancy aphrodisiacs were of any help. He turned into a rattling cadaver of love. If he refused to obey on the *pilarière*, he got stomped on like a bale of peat. Their bedroom was gradually transformed into an erotic clinic. Scattered around lay packets and vials marked with notations about optimal dosages, but none of this helped a bit. More than once, I sat at his bedside offering him pious consolation, and recommending certain home-baked nostrums once employed by a student friend in Cologne who pursued life in all its manifestations. I failed to mention, of course, that the youth in question had been unable to control his progressive deterioration. But Zwingli just laughed at these bits of wisdom from a bookworm's almanac. The "bitch" would never succeed in placing him six feet under. One day, he appeared at table for warmed-over omelet missing his magic nail, and I took that to be an evil omen. I noticed it right away, for that is how visibly this otherwise insignificant horny accretion determined the man's entire bearing. He couldn't have looked more fully disrobed if he had worn a beard and suddenly appeared clean-shaven. He noticed my glance in the direction of his talisman—well, it had broken off in the heat of the fray, just another month and it would be back in all its magical prowess; he'd just have to wait things out *sans* horn. I could not rid myself of the dreadful feeling that he would now go swiftly downhill. And we had not even reached the portals of all the palaces where we were planning to introduce his lover by means of our new-style art. The only progress we had achieved was the piano that a few days from now would resound in the vestibule, to Julietta's delight.

As committed to two-fisted techniques as Pilar was by reason of her profession, when it came to sating her instinct for revenge, she chose other methods. Her second victim was Julietta, who now got slapped around at least once every day, causing her to scream like a sow tied to the carriage wheel while getting ever so slowly stabbed in the throat, a practice still quite common in Iberian climes. Her mother differed from the long-knived butchers only in that she screamed along with her victim, so that an outsider could never tell who was threatening whose life. We knew, of course, and Zwingli knew also, but so little was left in him of Don Helvecio, the Citizen of the Confederation, that he was unable to take up arms against this violation of human rights. His attempts in this direction ceased abruptly after his first fatherly objection, which he meant to sound like a peal of thunder. Heavy objects got thrown to where he was standing; if he hadn't ducked, a motion he fortunately had already been trained in, his handsome male visage would have suffered some damage. Pilar's throwing skills were scarcely up to the legendary Balearic hurling tradition—but then again, she was not a descendant of those famous Balearic Slingers.

Julietta henceforth preferred to go dancing on the street, rather than serve as scapegoat for her mother's erotomania. Yet whenever she got caught doing her precocious turtle-dove turns, the little golden slippers came at her more pitilessly than ever. One such occasion made Zwingli conclude that things had gone just too far, and so he resolved to interfere. If he had acted with swift determination, there would have ensued a three-way bout of fisticuffs. As it happened however, he gave the infuriated woman reason to hurl an unusually massive object at him, the third member of this family triangle, as a signal that he had no right to interfere in her pedagogical methods. She selected a flatiron. Zwingli ducked, thereby keeping his attractive head safe and sound for loftier ambitions. The iron followed a trajectory calculable according to the laws of ballistics, shattered the apartment window, soared across the Street of Solitude, produced a more distant sound of splintering glass, and finally a hard thump. The projectile had zoomed into the Main Post Office, where it came to rest with its sharp point piercing the desk-top of Don Fernando, the Chief Secretary. The following day it was delivered by the district letter carrier at the routine hour, bearing a label that said, "Refused. Return to Sender." Don Fernando, whose acquaintance we shall make shortly, was the author of this little stunt.

The piano seemed to bring salvation. Peace returned to our *bel-étage*. Bach, Beethoven—

Pilar listened with the air of a connoisseur. She soon learned to sit in such a way as to suggest profound comprehension and rapt attention with inner and outer ear. If she could strike such a pose in the palaces and music salons, Don Helvecio was bound to be gratified. She would, he said, be staying right on course for the role his hopes were shaping for her, and which she herself was aiming toward. Just don't applaud, Pilar, even if you think the piece is over. It's those long pauses that reveal whether a listener is familiar with the score, so don't make a fool of yourself! No, Pilar would not applaud too soon, for the simple reason that she never applauded. Her own profession, which deeply unites performing artist and appreciative client, meant that she was accustomed to the noiseless *morendo* that always follows the grand final chord.

Beatrice began to practice. Every day she sat for seven hours at the instrument with a tense, contorted facial expression that was enough to cause fear and trembling. And Pilar feared and trembled. Up to now she had experienced only pianolas, and the bar ladies who would tickle the keys if you tossed them a coin. Here she encountered rather different performance standards, and the whole thing was no less weird and demeaning than watching people compare two texts in foreign languages. And all this under her own roof! No more playing up for little Argentinita's dancing. For a while this state of affairs reunited mother and daughter—a dangerous, because unpredictable, affiliation. The brief one-acters staged in the dormitoire had little calming effect on the irritable woman. On the contrary, the wilder things went on in there—or at least appeared to go on—the nastier the lady snarled in the interim phases; she snapped at anyone who approached her. The atmosphere of jungle and cave became more and more stifling. I caught a sharp whiff of game whenever this lascivious panther strode past me amid the strains of Beatrice's music. When will she raise her paw, extrude those claws, and tear off a strip of Vigoleis' cowardly flesh? One day Julietta said to me, "Vigo, watch out. Mamá doesn't like you any more. And if I were Mamá I wouldn't like you either!"

Oh la la! Daughters who speak their mother's language! Vigoleis, gird on your rapier and stand your ground with weapon in hand!

Now it was impossible to remove Julietta from the streets and the Donkey Square in front of the *fonda*. Spies were set out to warn of Mother's approach; that was exciting, and increased the pleasure of the forbidden dancing. The child had long ago stopped clinging to me with the affection of our military alliance in the General's room, a bond that I had thought was a life-and-death matter between us. But pacts exist to be broken, for otherwise nobody would need to arrange them. Her mother didn't like it when we were often together. She even made certain remarks on this score, which I interpreted as stemming from her lack of education and psychological acumen, until Julietta clued me in: Mamá was jealous.

You see? Our setup was rapidly threatening to go to wrack and ruin. Beatrice now accompanied her reluctant lady friend less and less often on her jaunts through the city. Her musical instrument had now gained the upper hand. Incidentally, the rich geezers' mutterings didn't bother Beatrice in the slightest. In private, this sort of thing amused us both, though I no doubt got more fun out of it than the woman directly concerned. Pilar, however, gave it her own interpretation. If, in addition, she had known that Anton Emmerich had related to us her picturesque life history, there would have been a massacre.

A new ray of hope arrived in the form of a public announcement that three of Spain's most renowned bullfighters were coming to Palma. We decided unanimously to reserve prime seats on the shady side for the five of us. I as a neophyte—Beatrice had already been to *corridas* in southern France—was to be introduced to this national art by witnessing the likes of Lalanda, Ortega, and Barrera. For days we spoke of nothing else. I soon learned the entire untranslatable vocabulary. I knew that the bulls came out of the *ganadieras*; I was told what *cabestros* are, and what a *picador*, a *chulo*, or a *mono* was supposed to do; that there were cowardly and "tired" bulls; and much more. Julietta latched onto me again. She was tireless in explaining and miming for me the various phases of the spectacle. Zwingli, too, began lecturing me, and for a while there he was once again in one of his elements. I had to shout *Olé!* every time Julietta impaled her foster father from the standing position, *al quiebro*. Pilar contented herself with the role of audience—a ravishing audience, by God, in her towering tortoise-shell comb, the precious silk *mantilla* (a gift from the prelate) cascading from it, and her ivory fan, which she wielded with a style inimitable even for a Spanish *señora*.

The ice was broken; on all sides jollity prevailed once more, even in the recesses of Vigoleis' being that Beatrice's ominous pronouncement had up to now kept under sterile quarantine. It won't be all that bad, he thought. But then with the very first approach... Pilar sensed the onset of spring like a June bug in early March. All her nastiness melted away. Her features brightened. For an entire week Julietta was spared humiliating chastisement, and both of their noses, mother's like daughter's, began to sniff around like guinea pigs on a new bed of straw. Even Zwingli began peeking forth out of his bag of woes. The nail on his pinky had grown back sufficiently to require the silver thimble as protection against doubly painful breakage. It had still to achieve its full magical length, but not by much.

On commission from an illustrated magazine, I wrote a sizeable travel article on Mallorca. Zwingli provided me with source material, for up to now my familiarity with the island was pretty much restricted to a single house interior. The editors accepted my article, but requested illustrations to accompany it, preferably line drawings. For this, too, Zwingli was ready at hand: Knoll, better known by his press-artist's name of "tiroteo," would supply the visual material for my reportage. We decided to look him up in Barcelona, a trip of two days' length. The travelers: Zwingli and Vigoleis. At this news Pilar hit the ceiling as if she had been gored. Her tarantella lasted the better part of an hour. She didn't extract her dagger, although the crazed cutie flailed about with her arms, and I imagined more than once that she would reach beneath her skirt and dispatch one or the other of us. Jealousy is a passion that bids no quarter—there are no puns or witticisms in Spanish for such an overwhelming emotion. The battle is fought differently: I'll cut your feet! I'll slice your heels, both of you, and then see if you can traipse off to Barcelona!

Well, nobody sliced our heels. But nobody left on a trip to Barcelona, either. Julietta offered to go along with me, since she had noticed that without an expert guide I could get lost even in a tiny village. This suggestion enraged Pilar even more. I tried to calm her by proposing that the best solution would be for her and me to make the journey and leave the two siblings under Julietta's protection. A terrifying glance shot at me from the implacable woman's eyes. It revealed murderous intent and sexual lust at one and the same time, and it would have skewered me alive, had it not been for the mitigating effect of those long flies' legs on her lashes.

A telegram brought our travel plans to naught. Beatrice's mother had closed her blind eyes forever.

For a week Beatrice kept to her bed with a high fever, nursed by Pilar with rare solicitude. Pilar was good at this type of ministration, something I never would have expected of her. Zwingli remained unmoved. I got the impression that his mother's passing simply hadn't reached him yet, for he was anything but a cold person. Now that peace had broken out, although it was of course an armed peace, he took advantage of the new situation by cherishing his leisure. He began frequenting the Príncipe more often. In a hotel, even when business is brisk, you can always locate a bed somewhere to park your body on. He always returned from these "inspections" strengthened in body and spirit. Julietta made the streets her exclusive home; we hardly saw her any more. I myself stuck to the apartment, though still lacking the private study that Zwingli had promised me when we first arrived.

Eros was banished from the Street of Solitude, and with him the General from the other island. The oil in the frying pan, which had so often mirrored the renowned officer's second visage, turned rancid. Only the fly in the vestibule remained the same. But since one fly resembles any other fly as a fly resembles a fly, perhaps it was a different fly after all. In Spain anything is possible.

Beatrice recovered quickly from the blow. What gave her the most anguish was to have been so distant from her mother during her final weeks, caught up in involuntary adventures that one might call uncomfortable. All of us felt that death had brought release, a thought that caused the woman most directly affected by its occurrence to downplay her own personal concerns. She was further plagued by the idea of having failed to accomplish during the period in question what she had set out to achieve with Zwingli. His own life's path had yet to be smoothed out; to get this done, someone would have to come along with a heavier earth-roller than we ourselves could pull. And to tell the truth, I had become a useless draft horse.

Time, said Beatrice, will take care of everything. First her poor brother's debts would have to be paid off, and then she would see what could be done for his physical and mental well-being. Beatrice as an apostle of salvation—why not? People have made worse mistakes about their own capabilities. It was true that our exchequer was beginning to dwindle badly; soon I would be reaching into my pocket like Zwingli, and coming up with nothing. We would have to lay out considerable sums for gas and electricity, now that workmen had come by one day to shut off both utilities. Several print shops presented their bills and were promptly paid. Vigoleis thought for a second. With that money you could have published your poems in a bibliophile edition, along with a blurb sheet composed by Zwingli, and in no time at all you would be as famous in the literary world as Pilar was in the demi-monde of the island. But fate does not permit such meddling in its affairs, least of all on the part of versifiers who take their greatest delight in watching their works go up in flames. The lyrical effusions of the scribbler in question had nearly all turned to ashes; they were but dust, and unto dust they did return. Some few of them tried to escape this earthly auto-da-fé; they set out for other parts, pleaded with editors and publishers for the right of asylum, got shooed away, and after extended wanderings returned dirty, tattered, and maimed to their progenitor in the Street of Solitude, the scene of agonies and anguish. These stanzas could have had much to say concerning affronts, insults, kicks administered in arrogance, the executioners' sardonic laughter, and so forth—but they remained silent. They were discreet; at most they just shrugged their shoulders as if to say, "We're back! Nobody likes us!" Occasionally the Main Post Office in Palma took pity on these rejected children and allowed them to disappear amidst the frightful welter of confusion that prevailed in that decrepit building. They never resurfaced. With human beings, the legal condition of permanent disappearance used to commence when the missing person would have reached three score and ten years, the statistically assumed point of life's termination. But what is the assumed point of termination for a poem? When must posterity declare Vigoleis' missing verses as non-existent, as "disappeared without a trace"? This is a question that will be answered in near-miraculous fashion in a later chapter. When we arrive at that point, my reader will be advised to recall Pilar's blasphemous plagiarism: "Vengeance is mine!"

One extraordinarily fine day, Pilar and Zwingli had finally attained the moment when they could pass through the city of Palma in all directions without fear of being waylaid by a creditor, getting yanked inside his shop and then confronted with the debit side of their existence. The soft cushion that, according to the German proverb, a clear conscience places beneath our head, ought to have benefitted Zwingli's slumber. But other demons arrived to plague this condemned man's nights.

Our stockpile of pesetas was rapidly melting away, and so we avoided larger capital outlays. Beatrice regarded the healing of her kid brother's economic condition as a matter of highest priority. As I have mentioned before, she hates any kind of dirt, be it in the form of a speck of dust on the piano keyboard cover, or a smudge on the neck of someone close to her. Such grimy deposits were, by the way, regularly removed, and further cleanups occurred daily. Thus the little gold bracelet on Zwingli's left wrist no longer had to serve the purpose of a leather strap around the axle of a bicycle wheel; once again it played an aesthetic role as pure ornament, although it would be incorrect to think of its wearer as a dandy. The bracelet became him, in the same natural way that a nose ring becomes a Papuan or a golden ear chain becomes a Volendam fisherman. Just how Beatrice imagined the installation of an internal sewage treatment system for her brother, she did not reveal to me. She was not inexperienced at this sort of thing, she said, and I ought simply to let her do what she wanted to. I readily obeyed. She headed off toward her goal with the determination of a migrating bird on its way to a remote destination. Any ornithologist can tell you that every year countless thousands of birds end up crashing into lighthouses; nowadays such hazards are illuminated faintly from the outside and surrounded by safety nets. Beatrice had not reckoned with Pilar, our own gleaming pillar. Nor had Vigoleis.

I had sufficient publishers' fees outstanding to keep us alive until the guarantee for an enormous honorarium arrived from the film company in Berlin. But no money found its way to us, neither via the bank nor via the mails. Soon we would be high and dry. Had I been blowing soap bubbles?

There came a dawn like any other: the same sun, the same fly circling around the fleck of sunlight in the vestibule, the same heartache at still being among the living, the same hunger for stupendous literary renown, the same Beatrice practicing her instrument. Yet in one respect this day was different. Beatrice began practicing quite early, explaining that she had to work through a particularly difficult passage. I had long since become used to the idiosyncrasies of practicing pianists, and thanked my lucky stars that Beatrice didn't sing or play the alpenhorn, for in that case I would have taken to the streets with Julietta. So I stayed home, even on this particular morning—a morning that, by Spanish standards, was still in its diapers. I communed with a medieval mystic, worked a bit on my posthumous literary works, conjugated a few irregular verbs with mutating consonants, and wrote a picaresque letter. Time had of course not stood still while Beatrice and I each practiced on different instruments. But I first became aware of this when Pilar, with elevated arm, strode through the room balancing her matinal greeting. Beatrice didn't even notice her; one of her piano fingers was misbehaving.

Later Zwingli came limping in. He too had been practicing, and his legs were misbehaving. Such a workaday family, my reader will be thinking, in which each member crams away separately, riding this or that hobby horse with cries of "giddyap!" and "steady there!" and "whoa!"—trotting off toward some goal or other, with a feedbag that gets emptier all the time. Zwingli's goal on this particular morning, the one that began so inauspiciously, was obvious: eggs, sausage, and wine. And where was that *chaibe* Julietta, who was supposed to go fetch him this stuff? Zwingli had once been what Don Darío liked so much about him, and he had reason to believe he would soon have to be that special something again. Julietta was more eager than usual. She realized what faced her if things went wrong again in there behind closed doors. She'd prefer, she said saucily, a mother who was hitting the bottle. I had given her some money (Zwingli couldn't quite locate any of his own); "she" was in the kitchen, and, well, within the family you just don't bite on individual pesetas. So step on it, girl, this is a rush job. The girl stuck out her tongue and vanished. Everything was happening smoothly.

After another hour Beatrice closed the cover on the keyboard and lit a cigarette—a familiar gesture of hers. She said she was gradually getting her fingers under control. But performance in public, even in front of a tiny private audience, was as yet out of the question. For such things she was still much too rusty; it would be better for her to start taking lessons again. Zwingli told her of a local musical priest, our later friend Mosén Juan María Tomás. The foreign colony on the island, he explained, was enchanted by the good reverend's *a capella* choir.

Julietta was late. Instead of the hoped-for omelets, the two of them ate whatever they could find in the pantry—which wasn't much in the summertime, because they had been forced to sell the icebox. In any case it wasn't what both of them needed most. Pilar's nostrils quivered. With Zwingli, what quivered was the hand that was re-sprouting the magic wand. Beatrice, too, was quivering, but this was a residual tremor from her musical acrobatics. Vigoleis was the only one who, on this forenoon, got the tremors in anticipation of what was about to happen. He suddenly developed the gift for second sight: boy oh boy, if Julietta doesn't hurry back with the necessary provisions, things are going to get very hot in here. Pilar trembled more and more. Zwingli also lost control, and they began a violent verbal exchange that culminated with a saucer of red marmalade, called *membrillo*, getting aimed at Zwingli's skull. Zwingli forgot to duck, and thus the confection ended up sticking to his face. Lucky enough for him, for it might well have been the ceramic side that struck him, in which case some blood would have been shed, and not just jam. For us, this was a signal that Pilar was declaring an end to the meal. We departed discreetly. *Hasta luego! Ciao! Tschüss!*

Spats are the worst thing that can happen inside four walls. It's better to experience a stopped-up drain, a burst water pipe, or a smoky oven! Such things can be repaired. Spats are irreparable. We were just about to board a tram for Ca's Català to enjoy some open-air peace at the shore, when we heard some commotion. A bunch of wild kids were after a girl, Julietta of course, who once again was raising dust on the square. She coursed back and forth with huge dancing leaps, swinging her straw shopping basket over her head. With a daring fling she suddenly tossed it over the heads of her half-pint audience into the dirt. I went up to Julietta with the intention of scolding her. As soon as she saw me, she leaped up and embraced me with such force that both of us almost tumbled into the dust. She called me "Don Vigo," impressing the assembled urchins with her foreign acquaintance. I asked her why she hadn't taken the groceries home. Her impudent answer was, "Whaddya mean?" Those snots over there had filched them from her—and she pointed to her swarm of fans, a horde that was capable of anything. She just didn't dare to go back to Mom without the stuff. The two of them back home, she said, should go ahead without the usual tortilla. "Well of all the...," I thought, and was sent into further shock. I gave her some money, told her to go shopping again for what the gang had stolen from her, not to forget the wine that the kids had swilled, and to get home just as fast as her legs would take her. With a rapacity that was quite out of character, she grabbed the money, brandished it in front of the kids who were watching her every move, and then heaved it among them. They scrambled like cats for the loot, a sight that Julietta seemed to enjoy and that held me breathless. Then the girl began dancing again. The dust clouded upwards to shroud the scene from my sight.

Beatrice had witnessed my defeat from a distance. We gave up the idea of a stroll at the seashore. We went slowly down to the harbor, where we saw the snazzy yacht belonging to a French billionaire specializing in smells—Coty, if my memory serves me right. What a gorgeous ship! Oh, wouldn't it be grand to go aboard and set sail! We saw some people on deck, no doubt millionaires one and all. I was overcome with amazement and adventurous fantasies. Beatrice remained calm and sober. She had already had her experiences on oaken decks such as these. Once, for several months, she had accompanied millionaires from ex-royal families on board a gilded ark like this one, along and across the azure depths of the Adriatic. Never again, not even for twice the wage! She would prefer to drift along, rudderless on a naked raft, with her

Vigoleis! Bolstered by this bright prospect, we returned home. It was a hot day, like all the days here. In the evening the wind subsided, and this meant that the night was going to be unbearable. Since the day we arrived, not a drop of rain had fallen. A remarkable experience for people who, back in Amsterdam, had often been confined to quarters by deluges.

Our expedition took several hours. Time enough, I thought as we ascended the three portal steps, for the domestic storm and its meteorologists to have come to rest. On the stairway we heard piercing shouts. Julietta was yelling. Pilar was yelling. No question about it: mother, the mature plant, was lowering the boom on her daughter, the sprouting seedling. I darted upwards three stairs at a time, flung open the vestibule door, and sprang to the aid of my darling protégée. "Stop! Not one more slap!"

Pilar had already done some bloody work on her child. Julietta lay on the floor, doubled over in pain. Golden slippers can, as we see here, be used in special ways to soften up an adversary. Pilar was fuming. She was out of control. She called upon every last saint of the Church, the immaculately conceived Mother of God, in a word the entire Heavenly Host, to grant their blessing as she inflicted her punishment. Julietta, rather less pious on her part, replied in similarly pragmatic fashion. She took recourse to the proven argot of the gutter, lending her mother the sobriquet *puta*—an enormously significant concept in Spain, one that can facilitate a comprehension of the country in its entirety. In the same breath the child expressed a desire for her own death. "Go ahead and kick me, you horrible mother! Just see what will happen to you if I die!" I was familiar with this kind of suicidal incitement to murder. As a child I had reacted similarly, although the circumstances were never quite so dramatic in our house. There, the eternal mother-offspring hostility centered on a ghastly carrot casserole that I refused to eat, claiming that I would croak if she were to force this mess of pottage down my throat like a goose— and I hoped passionately that I would suffocate on this bowl of glop, just to punish my mother. But she knew just how far one could go when dealing with a squealing captive piglet. Pilar and Julietta were going too far. It tore my heart to see this brat so cruelly mauled. I was a very inexperienced Vigoleis. Amid the ear-splitting clamor of battle, I overheard Beatrice's warning shout, "For God's sake, Vigo, stay out of it!" Like a warrior unaware of his own cowardice, I lunged at the rabid mother.

The Beatrices among my readers, those who are familiar with the world and its noblest product, the human being, know very well what awaited Vigoleis as he set out to drive a wedge between the feelings of mother and child. But for the benefit of the Vigoleises, one or the other of whom may be among my readers, I shall now reveal what happened to our esteemed brother.

Hardly had he touched Pilar's desirable body, and with cries of *"Basta! basta!"* pushed her up against the wall and away from her slavering daughter, when the child, whom an even less experienced referee would have considered down for the count, rose up and jumped me from behind. Whereupon the two of them joined forces and began beating me up: they scratched, kicked,

shoved, and spat, and soon my hands and face were bloody. Pilar grabbed my
shirt and ripped it in shreds down to my belt, and before I knew it Julietta
had torn it completely off my body. I was already bleeding like a galley slave,
when Beatrice came to my succor and intervened in this scene of violent retribution—but in her inscrutable fashion: she shouted a command to defend
the redoubt just a while longer, for relief was on its way. So I held the fort
with rapidly ebbing strength. One of my eyes was already blinded, while my
other eye was seeing double. What it saw was that I would soon be a goner,
unless...

Beatrice ran to the kitchen and filled a large bowl with water, egging on the
faucet with shouts of "Faster!" and "*Allons donc!*" Though a very impulsive
woman, when plotting revenge Beatrice takes her sweet time—a genetic legacy
hailing from the days when the sun god banished her ancestors to an island
on Lake Titicaca. "Get with it! *Allons donc!*"—but the water wouldn't come
any faster. I have mentioned that this was a hot day, and at this hour the
rooftop reservoir was almost empty. Beatrice's Indian imperturbability cost
me a few more lumps and scratches, for compared to the ferocity of the
women's attack, I put up hardly any defense. But then the bowl, with its contents of smothering water, came flying at this brace of bawds.

Mother and child let go of their victim, spat as if on cue in the direction the
decisive missile had come from, caressed each other with words of endearment, and disappeared into the General's room. Pilar's albornoz had once
again been pushed aside, revealing large portions of her bosom. The sight had
no effect on me, a creature of flesh. How strange are the workings of a man's
heart!

Pilar had now been dishonored a second time. Vigoleis, beware!

It was a long time before I was sufficiently mended to go out on the street for
a breath of air. Meanwhile Beatrice hunted for Zwingli, and actually found
him. He was lying on the bed in a state of double defeat: conquered on the
one hand by the emanations of love, on the other by the scourge of hatred.
As he explained in a barely audible whisper to his sister, Pilar had disarmed
him when he ran to the girl's rescue. "Get out of here!" he said. "If she finds
you here, she'll stab you to death! She's out of her mind today, worse than
any day when she's come back from confession. Out, out! *Use!*"

Pilar went to confession often and with pleasure, but afterwards she was
always disagreeable. For the truth is, her confessor was in the habit of tickling
her too.

We brothers-in-law had not been heroes on this afternoon. One of us because he couldn't, the other because he wouldn't, and we shall leave open the
question of whether this second one could have if he had wanted to. I have
never "performed" this particular episode. I have concealed it; it is not in my
repertoire of heroic ballads, and for a simple reason, too. My reader will recall

that in the third chapter I blew my own horn with puffed cheeks, calling myself a raconteur with mimic talents that are a match for any occasion. Very
well then, let's put this storyteller to the test. Make him perform his own self
right here and now, eye to eye and tooth to tooth with the hyenas. Have him
act out a little bloodletting, let him display the stigmata of shame, the witch-
inflicted wounds of whorish calamity. Ask him to show how, with his one
good eye, he keeps a lookout for his Beatrice, who must soon arrive to splash
him out of his misery. But speaking of eyes: maybe he could re-enact the good
one convincingly enough. But not even a shot of the worst brand of garbage-
man's schnapps could ever get him to portray the other one, the protuberating
one, replete with the proper Picassoesque a-perspectivity rendered by a blow
to his cheekbone at the hands of the woman of his sleepless nights. All that
earlier talk of mimic talent was empty boasting, pure ostentation, and purposeful distraction. For this rascal knows full well that his art has definite limits. Incidentally, it ought to puzzle no one that these two ravishing Spaniards
showed such vehemence in bringing down their island guests. It wasn't the
first time that Spain had emerged victorious over Inca blood, which in this
case, in highly helveticized dilution, leaped into the breach or lay gasping on
the *pilarière*. We can just ignore our dreamer from Germany; he can take care
of his own disposition. That is, after all, the tragedy of his nation: it always
hands itself the means to its own defeat.

"Just to muck our way through," I said to Beatrice as we left the battle
scene, where blood and water had streamed forth as at Waterloo, "is unaesthetic. And besides, it's senseless. We must view everything from the lofty perspective of our minds."

"What else? That's why I decided to chuck water, darling. Water is the only
thing. It always works with cats, and it worked with those two meows up
there. One dousing, and it was all over for them!"

I remained silent in order not to clip my guardian angel's wings in mid-
flight. Who knows when I might need her again. To be sure, the water bath
had done its duty with the she-goat and her kid. But it was also clear to me
who had actually done a job on whom, up there in the apartment.

"Come on, let's go to the cathedral and enjoy the ocean view. Tomorrow
Zwingli will have gobbled enough at the trough so that we can make further
plans in peace and quiet. We can't stay in this omelet barracks. Go to bed with
the swine, and you'll stink all the time."

It was touching to behold this unity of ours, in our desire to abandon the
swinish domicile to which we had been lured by a telegram from an expiring
man. My feelings for the bitch, a term that I place here *sans* quotation marks
because not even a full dozen would do justice to the degree of her depravity—my feelings for this morsel of carrion had simply vanished. Mother and
daughter had torn them from my breast together with my shirt. Or perhaps I
should say that they had simply ripped them off my torso, for they had never
been situated root and branch deep within my bosom. It was never more than
a kind of band-aid eroticism: give it a yank, a few hairs will stick to the strip,

and you won't even say "Ouch!" And your skin will soon heal up.

Thus ended Vigoleis' love for the first Spanish woman to cross his path, a dagger inside her garter. He had been found unworthy to die at her hand, this mournful hero.

The space in front of the cathedral was a campsite for the loitering army of beggars crippled and healthy, infirm and imbecilic, the gatekeepers of all of God's houses in southern lands, people who are as picturesque as they are repulsive. No costume expert in the world could ever design a wardrobe of misery such as the one sported by these partners in penury. Spain is crawling with these characters; they constitute a special guild, or more precisely, a professional class of their own. They call down the blessings of heaven upon anyone who makes a donation, but whoever resists their threadbare entreaties with a regretful *Perdone hermano*, "Forgive me, brother," is regaled with curses and revilement. But since heaven and hell are in criss-cross cahoots with these social barnacles, it makes no difference whether one makes a contribution or not—or at least one would think so. In reality most strangers fork over their copper obolus, not out of superstition, but merely to get rid of this plague as speedily as possible.

One member of this reeking league of cadgers had star status in Palma. It was almost as important to experience him as it was to view the cathedral itself, in whose eternal aura of light he collected his alms. He spoke "all languages," which in Spain means German, English, and French, but he also knew Italian. In addition, local legend ascribed to him a command of the classical idioms and Hebrew. It later became apparent that legend had no need to improve on history, for in fact this hunchback could have invoked curses and blessings on his victims in these latter tongues as well. This hunchback: an enormous hump protruded from the tatters of his cloak, camouflaged with rags of various colors. To look at him evoked loathing and disgust. A greenish liquid oozed from his eyes, his hair and beard were lousy, and he stank from every pore in his body and his filthy raiment.

This whimpering king of the mendicants was squatting there as we climbed the steps of the Calle de la Seo to the square of the same name, from which the cathedral ascends in all its majesty. Porfirio—this was the misshapen fellow's name—crawled his way over to us and intoned his little speech in German. I gave him a few coins and received his assurance that heaven would reward me—not up there (his eyes, veiled in green, pointed in the traditional direction), but here upon our earth, "Right now, Sir, today, before the arrival of the evening!"

The sea was as smooth as a mirror. Boats with drooping sails drifted in the void, waiting in vain for a breeze that would take them back into harbor. We found a bench and waited for the air to freshen up. Tomorrow was another day. Everything would work out all right if only we stuck together.

We had been sitting there for an hour gazing morosely out to sea, each occupied with the other's thoughts, when we noticed two persons walking down
the avenue of palms along the quay. They climbed the theatrical staircase that
led to the cathedral—two tall women holding each other close, no doubt a
mother with her daughter. I am not often subject to attacks of sentimentality,
but following those inhumane scenes in the Street of Solitude, where a prehistoric world loudly demanded its rights with tooth and nail, this sight of pacific
familial love touched my heart. Every now and then they stopped; the mother
caressed the tall girl, the tall girl kissed her mother, and then they both looked
out on the seascape and continued their walk up the steps. What an edifying
sight, this exclusive affection of two people for each other, occurring here at
such a romantic place, a spot that no one who has ever stood there is likely to
forget: beneath the gothic arch showing the scene of the Last Supper, the
Puerta del Mirador. Our two incarnate symbols of human concord directed
their steps to this portal in order to enjoy even warmer waves of elation in the
presence of these saintly images with their whitewash of pigeon droppings.
And no wonder, for no one who lives in Palma lets a week go by without
mounting these ramparts to gaze outward to the blue expanse from whence,
centuries earlier, the conqueror approached under sail to deliver the island
from the scimitar of the infidels.

As mother and child came closer, we recognized them as our mother and
our child, the horny nag with her filly. And they recognized us as the infidels,
the Saracens, the pirates, the incorrigibles, the grandparents of the devil—and
who knows what all else. Pilar crossed herself, Julietta spat in our direction—
two gestures corresponding to their respective ages and world experience.
Then they passed on slowly, with the same dignified air as when they arrived.
Soon they will be among the beggars, and before they enter the cathedral to
genuflect before the image of the Holy Maid of the Pillar, they will already
have bribed heaven itself—and with our money, too, because we had been
keeping a common household budget, albeit a rather one-sided one. It remained to be conjectured just how much money they would toss to the mangy
pimps of heaven and hell. Your fate depends on it, Vigoleis! For you must not
forget that heaven hears the pleas of those who sin in its name, and who allow
love to be made in its name, and for the greater glory of the Lord. And do not
forget what you have already been told: that in Spanish bordellos there is a
little shrine in a corner, where the ladies see to it that the eternal lamp never
goes out. In her apartment boudoir Pilar, too, had a little silver vessel with
just such a gentle flame floating in it, illuminating with its golden glow the
many-colored garments of the Queen of Heaven. If the two of them agree to
do business up there on the cathedral square, and if they contribute one single
perro chico (five-centimos) less than you did, then just like Beatrice, who is
superstitious, I will take it as a disastrous omen.

In Pilar's quarters supper was at nine o'clock. We pondered whether we
shouldn't grab a bite somewhere else, and then rush to our room as soon as
we got home. But that could surely be interpreted as desertion, a verdict that,

oddly enough after our virtual defeat in battle, we wanted to avoid. Among humans, all friction is said to arise from misunderstandings—a theory I firmly believe in, because I regard the world itself as a misunderstanding. My biggest misunderstanding was without doubt to have interfered with mother and child at a moment when they were in the process of working out their own little misunderstanding.

When we entered the house entrance and stairwell for the second time on this day, something came whizzing down the dark passageway and landed loudly on the stone floor right in front of us. Another object arrived directly after this one, confirming the laws of free-fall velocity that had given me such torments back in my German schoolroom. Then it rained once again from above; this time something came bounding down the staircase, and then the upstairs door was slammed shut. The lighter elements of this precipitation hovered for a second in the air, then fell slowly downwards like the snowflakes in those magic glass spheres that fascinated me when I was a child. It was leaves—inscribed leaves, literature—that came flying toward us and landed on their originator. For a moment I felt like a tourist feeding the pigeons on the Piazza San Marco in Venice.

Beatrice's and Vigoleis' possessions were being evicted, and the two of them would surely have been tossed out as well if they hadn't exalted themselves above all earthly concerns by tarrying for a half-hour inside the cathedral. What is more, blood would have flowed—not from scratches and lacerations, but from gaping flesh wounds inflicted by that Toledo blade. But as bad as this bouncing of their belongings was, heaven had prevented worse events. I would dearly love to know how much the bitch placed in those gouty palms on the cathedral square. But heaven, at least in Spain, does not permit anyone to peek into its cards. The Civil War gave me the hugest problems in this regard.

A pile of plunder on the Feira de Ladra in Lisbon, on the Waterlooplein in Amsterdam, on the old Jewish market square in Warsaw—just to name a few famous collection points for abandoned household goods—this was the scene of our heaped-up caboodle in the *entrada* of the Count's apartment complex in the Street of Solitude. The owners stood by speechless. But it was only this mute behavior of theirs that made them differ from the dealers at junk sales, whose job it is to fob off the stuff they've bought on even lower types than themselves.

It was nine o'clock, supper time chez Pilar. "Aha," I was just thinking to myself, "there'll be two less place-settings tonight." But wait! What is that sound? It was a low tone, like a gong announcing "Ladies and gentlemen, dinner is served"—and then there was a horrible crash.

"She's destroying my piano, that crazed slut!" Beatrice shouted in French. "Quick, quick, the key to the apartment!"

Beatrice had allowed mother and daughter to commit reciprocal mayhem; she had rescued Vigoleis by applying her Indian stratagem of slow poison; but now that her beloved instrument was having its wiry heart violated, there was no more question of methodical calculation. I grabbed her skirt and held her back. What a superb climactic moment for a small-town, low-budget amateur theater! Minimal props: a few pieces of rickety furniture, some scraps of used paper. But now witness the great scene of our hero Vigoleis—or let's call him Don Vigo for the sake of local color—which the author will now create with bated breath:

> *Thou fool! Thou darest snatch the evil axe*
> *She holds aloft to split thy skull in two,*
> *That maddened maenad? Let her vent her bile*
> *On wood and wire! Desist, if thou hold'st sacred*
> *Thy brother's life and limb!*

But Vigoleis wasn't standing onstage at your local Thespian Club. Instead, calmly and in resigned tones, using the voice of his own small-scale personality, he stated, "Beatrice, just let that slattern up there chop up anything she likes. Nothing can hurt us any more. If you make a false step now, she'll chuck out our dear Zwingli too, and then we will have come to this island for nothing at all. It would be better if he had just up and died, as he promised us in his telegram. But in this accursed country nobody ever seems to want to stick to agreements. Where is that study I was supposed to be occupying? Where is that concert grand for you? That piano was nothing but a miserable honky-tonk upright! As soon as the money comes from Berlin I'll get you your Bechstein, you can depend on that as solidly as you do on your superstition. Let's just take care of our own situation, which now looks pretty grim. We'll have to..."

Once again the second-storey door opened, and once again it rained cats and dogs down on us in the darkened stairwell. Pilar had transformed the piano into kindling ready for the stove, not including a few sturdy metal hinges and bolts—not a bad job of lumberjacking, considering the short time it took her. Only the bronze sounding board and the wire strings had resisted her efforts at demolition. Zwingli later had these carted away. In the aftermath he told us that he thought his final hour had arrived when the wrecking action started. If Beatrice had entered the apartment, he would, he averred, have breathed his last—a conviction that we share with him completely. Pilar had fumed about that wh... of a sister of his and her *boche* of a boyfriend. Not until she began taking out her rage at the musical commode had Zwingli begun to feel momentarily more secure in his own skin.

And so Beatrice had saved her brother's life after all. The power of music.

Upstairs the music had come to an end. Peace again prevailed under the roof of the Conde's "apple." While I certainly would not like to be inside Zwingli's skin, it would be useful to have that nail of his to get us out of this terrible mess. I decided to look up Mr. Emmerich, who had already had many experiences in Spain, and who could probably give us some advice in this perilous situation. With a few brief words I brought him up to date. The scars on my face left him no doubt that I had been waylaid, that the robbers had stripped me, beaten me sore, and left me for dead. Emmerich, a man of imposing words, was also a man of quick action. All our stuff went into the back room of his shop, not the first time that this space had to bear the consequences of Pilar's rabid erotic behavior. Like an energetic ragpicker of my own existence, I schlepped our gear around the respectable street corner, and by eleven the job was done. My fellow-countryman, whose elbow-room was getting tighter all the time, told us about a *pensión* where he himself had lived for a few years. It was owned by an impecunious count from the mainland, who had married the even poorer daughter of a count and countess from the island. It was right nearby, just across the Borne in one of the little streets that lead to the harbor. Should he make a quick call, he asked. Single room, twin beds?

In the Pensión del Conde there was a room for us, a single with twin beds, and we were lying in them by midnight.

On the wall opposite the beds were two wooden panels with burned-in lettering, products from the hobby workshop of our half-Catholic, half-anarchist aristocratic landlord. "The Lord's Ten Commandments" hung where one usually expects to be told to ring once for breakfast, twice for the maid, thrice to make a complaint. The Ten Commandments are no less famous, and so we know exactly what the hobbyist's glowing stylus had inscribed in ninth position: "Thou shalt not covet thy neighbor's wife"!

Vigoleis didn't see the panels until the following morning. Yet even without an Old-Testament warning, during the preceding night he had not coveted his neighbor's wife—indeed, if truth be told, not even his own. He slept, and Beatrice slept, too. Dreamlessly, both of them, for they had each taken a tablet to ward off evil spirits. We should let them have their rest. It had been, as we have noted, a very hot day.

* * *

Three stars, my dear reader, separate us from our sleeping heroic couple, and that is a more respectable form of insulation than three layers of whitewash on an apartment wall. Thus we shall not need to whisper, as we stay together a while to take stock of what's happened, and to make a tentative survey of what is to come.

The first part of my jottings is finished. You have followed our heroes' footsteps through thick and thin, though thickness has admittedly outweighed thinness in this report. You might have expected such a development, however, since the Spanish proverb you saw at the threshold of this work was meant as a clever warning: whoever would prefer not to mingle with such a dissolute brood ought to put the book down and say, "Please, not that kind of thing!" In any case, you are under no coercion to read me, considering that the publishing industry offers you hundreds of authors who outstrip me in every way. And yet you did not take fright at first sight; you joined in on our trip to accompany a relative of the author's on his final journey. Then it turned out that this relative was only seemingly dead. In actuality, he never again became truly chipper. That is to say, in our Fourth Book he will lift himself out of an anabaptism with a grand gesture, and with unabashed audacity. But then we shall already be hearing the first explosions from Morocco, a sign that General Franco has completed his apprenticeship with Mussolini and Hitler, and is handing in his journeyman's test piece. We shall lose sight of Zwingli, and almost of ourselves as well.

This vital toughness of his, his cynical announcement of impending death, when death wasn't close by at all, his appeal to our soft-heartedness and Christian altruism—such behavior has meant bad times for all of us. But for us heroes, things have been a good deal harder to withstand than for you, my reader, who have had the option from the beginning of shutting my book at any passage that strikes you as too extravagant, too shameless, too objectionable, too candid, or too sentimental. As the pacemakers for this story, we have had no such liberty. We were caught in the pincers; we had to stick to the text, which often enough turned out to be an *Urtext* of the most cryptic kind. But now tell us honestly: Haven't we heroes of your book behaved quite courageously? Isn't it true that we have neither kept anything under wraps nor added anything, so help us God? At the moment we are lying comfortably next to each other on our beds in a palace, on mattresses of kelp, the kind that needs no cooling layer of horsehair, and are enjoying a somewhat artificially induced slumber.

Surely you have already noticed: once again they are under a count's roof! Can that be just happenstance? You will recall that Vigoleis once accused himself of aristocratic tendencies, whereas Beatrice is regal by nature and by virtue of her double legacy, as a daughter of the Incas and as a child of the oldest monarchy in the world, whose throne is occupied by a sovereign who rules the world in more than a proverbial sense. Nonetheless, our heroic duo was not led to their new shelter by feudal considerations. They had no time at all to ponder any such subtleties as they departed from the Count's "apple" amid scorn and contempt, unless you imagine that Anton Emmerich, our Little Helper from Cologne, might have nudged their destiny somewhat in this direction. At this point we shall refrain from investigating the matter further. But count's roof or no count's roof, I can assure you of one thing: for quite a while you will see nothing more of the aforementioned brood. In the *palacio* owned by our anarchistic grandee, rabble of that sort are never spoken of— that is, not by human tongues. The fact that a parrot does so, is not without a certain annoyance, but we shall just have to look the other way. This feathered blabbermouth had a faulty upbringing, and now he thinks it is his duty to remind the residents of the rooming house that they are in Spain, in case they may have forgotten, in spite of the heat and the fleas—as is actually the case with Mr. Joachim von Martersteig, Army Cpt. Ret., in Room 13. But we shouldn't reproach this roguish bird—I mean the one from the family of the *psittaci*—for following his nose and telling tales out of school.

In Book Three it'll all start up again. Our heroes will get sent up once more, while you, dear reader, will probably have pulled in your sails. No one will hinder you from casting off this burden. But wouldn't it be better if you returned home right now, seeing that we can't remain travel companions, not even to mention such a thing as friendship? My addressing you as "dear" reader would no longer be appropriate; I would have to ask you to look around for other literary adventures. Your local bookseller can advise you best in this matter.

But—no offense! And farewell! Perhaps we shall meet again. It is such a small world. And what is more, our Vigoleis' name is now linked with that of a Portuguese mystic. As above, your bookstore manager will be happy to provide you with details.

But you others—you readers who are still "dear" to us—we must get on with it. Hundreds more pages lie ahead of us, leading us on countless highways and byways. So now, please, here by the rear stairway, let's enter Book Two.

BOOK TWO

Fortunate is He who receives from Heaven
a Morsel of Bread without having to thank
Anyone for it but Heaven itself.
                    Don Quixote de la Mancha

Come, my sweetest darling fair,
Join me on my pilarière!
                    after Wilhelm Busch

I

When a publisher releases a book, he counts upon a certain number of readers whose interest and purchasing power will allow him to undertake such an adventure of the mind. This implies that it is conceivable to consider readers as the retroactive sponsors of a given work, and that is precisely how I think of them. I don't mean this in the sense of those early-medieval artistic masters who gave their wealthy donors a tiny corner somewhere near the bottom edge of their paintings, showing them gazing devoutly upward at the Community of Saints. No, I'm thinking more of Renaissance artists who placed their benefactors on the same level as the saints and all saintly persons. For this reason, my charitable reader has the right to move about freely in my work. He may even situate himself several levels higher than certain individual characters, a privilege he will surely take pleasure in. It is only natural that I myself remain in control, although as I have said, anyone is free to seek salvation as he wishes. This is especially true here in our rooming house belonging to Count Number Two, a man who tends to attenuate or even abrogate the salvationist claims of his Church on the basis of his anarchistic sympathies.

Beatrice and Vigoleis are asleep, and will remain so until well past noon, but not because they are particularly enamored of Spanish customs. No, they have each taken a double dose of sedative, so that they will remain undisturbed by any outside agency whatever, invited or uninvited. Following their expulsion from the Street of Solitude, they have fully deserved their profound slumber. Let us, then, use this interim to familiarize ourselves just a bit with their new surroundings: their abode, its owners, its paying guests, and its badly paid service personnel.

Once when I was in conversation with the publisher of this book, I mentioned in passing that it would contain a half-anarchistic, semi-Catholic Count. My assertion met with a violent objection on the part of this publisher, the first and most generous benefactor of my jottings. Poking his cigar suddenly in my direction, he cried, "That's impossible! Either someone is an anarchist or he's a Catholic. But both at the same time? You must be dreaming!"

"Mynheer van Oorschot," I replied, "every publisher is at the mercy of the notorious dreams of his authors. And the crazier those fantasies are, the nuttier their ideas seem to be, it's all the better for the resulting book! I assure you that my 'impossible' Count is a pure prodigy of Nature, which every now and then is capable of such marvels. As soon as you reach this spot in my manuscript I trust that you will be convinced."

We have now arrived at this Count, a person even more remarkable than my publisher imagined, as we shall see when we examine his "impossible" trinitarian makeup: a Count by virtue of his father's name; an anarchist in his own right and in the name of the freedom that he loves above all else; and a Catholic in the name of his rather less than pious spirit—although piety and Catholicism are not necessarily complementary concepts, as we can learn from a glance at papal history. If, however, a Spanish grandee turns anarchist, this is a much more instructive kind of metamorphosis than the one involving our little Vigoleis, a.k.a Albert, in those faraway years of his childhood, when he sought to protect his cache of toys from his brothers' tyranny by turning into a girl and playing with dolls. That's why I have been able to move past "little Albert" with just a few words. I shall have to take more time with our *Señor* Conde, although it won't be until we reach the Epilogue that I can do full justice to his true stature and his confusing tripartite nature.

When a Count turns anarchist, he renounces his long aristocratic title. He takes an axe to his family tree. He hammers flat the ring that bears his dynasty's coat of arms. He then calls his palace a "house"—a rather ineffective form of renaming, for under the same roof there is still room for kings and even for God himself.

Our Count thought otherwise, and in so thinking, he constituted a minority of one—which is of course just what he had in mind as an anarchist. The renowned Baedeker, for example, couldn't be bothered about this *hidalgo*'s social transformation. The famous tourist guidebook portrayed his *palacio* for what it was, and referred to its owner as the scion of a *titulado*, who gets a few lines of his own. I, too, have no reason to call this venerable building a house or a cottage, just to suit a certain apostate's whim. In architectural style it could belie neither its glorious past nor the fact that many blue-bloods entered and exited through its doors. They held on to money bags that got lighter and lighter over time, and in the end were powerless to retard the downfall of this particular "house."

"If what you want is loss, then become your own boss," my grandfather used to say. Whereupon he bought his own tavern and hung a sign on the door saying "Make your own coffee!" This pioneer forebear of mine sold boiling water by the measured pint or quart to whole families, who in long processions made pilgrimages to his bar, asking to brew up their do-it-yourself java. But it wasn't actually the hot water that attracted these families. My little home town was situated on the pilgrim road to Kevelaer.

Our Count Number Two was likewise a loser. To be more exact, he was well on his way toward becoming one when I met him. He, too, nailed up a sign at his entrance to lure pilgrims from all over the world into his palace, but not to offer them hot water. He provided passable shelter for a modest price. My reader may expect his sign to have read "House of the People's Friend" or "*Fonda* for Catholic Anarchists," or maybe the other way around, "for Anarchist Catholics." But no, in gold letters on a blue ground his sign bore the reactionary legend Pensión del Conde, "The Count's Boarding House." And behold, it was just as great a success as the hot-water hospice run by a certain Lower-Rhenish speculator in pilgrimages. Beneath the Count's roof there was always a crowd of guests, people who had either seen, or hoped still to see, better days, just as my grandfather's water customers were mostly driven by a promise that beckoned in their direction from the goal of their pilgrimage. The Count had made himself the object of his own disbelief. If anyone had pointed out an anomaly in his commercial house sign, he could well have replied that his abode indeed did not contain a genuine Count—but then again, who could expect to find a specific bird at the cash register of the "Golden Swan Hotel"? Or to be served at Sears Roebuck by a deer?

Don Alonso María Jesús de Villalpando, Marqués de Sietefillas y Conde de Peñalver y Tordesillas—this was part of the dynastically expansive and ramified title of our anarchizing hosteller and friend of the people. Here I shall call him simply Don Alonso, for the sake of brevity, and at the same time in keeping with his own sworn abhorrence of highfalutin' traditions. Don Alonso married into the palace on the Calle de San Felio, and the price he paid for the holy sacrament was Doña Inés, the only daughter and last surviving offspring of a very old family with a probably even longer name. The roots of her family tree were located somewhere deep in ancient Castilian terrain, and the branch that she extended into the world with a certain pious resignation was just as desiccated and unyielding as the soil from which it sprang. One of her chain-mailed forebears had arrived on the island in 1229 with James I of Aragon, the Conqueror, and here the family flourished. But now it was in a state of acute degeneration. Doña Inés remained childless, in sharp contrast to the seven daughters that Don Alonso sported on his flattened-out coat of arms: Marqués de Sietefillas. Extramaritally, however, he exceeded this heraldic challenge. He sired several progeny, by lovers he obtained in order to sweeten a life spent at the side of the increasingly sour, tiny, almost dwarflike, and exceedingly ugly Doña Inés, whose physiognomy Velázquez was able to capture long before her dynasty's final aberration first saw the light of the island near the turn of the century.

Yet as mentioned above, such distasteful matters were never spoken of in the Count's house. Everyone knew that they had happened, and that would have to suffice. If it hadn't been for this marital prize, the Casa del Conde, which the state had yet to declare a historical site, Don Alonso would have left his little housewife in the lurch—where, incidentally, she now finds herself. Who wouldn't do the same to snatch a dowry like this one? I would, at the drop of a hat! In which case I would make just the kind of arrangement with Beatrice as the Count appears to have fashioned with his multiple mistresses. For I have not only aristocratic inclinations, but capitalistic ones as well: Vigoleis as a palace lord! I can just see him reclining in his Hall of Ancestors. Beatrice would finally get her own pipe organ.

Like most Mallorquine villas, in architectural style this free-spirited Count's *palacio* showed a pronounced influence of the Italian Renaissance. And like many others, the edifice was falling apart. In the interior court an arch had split apart, and was kept from collapsing by means of timbers and iron clamps. The open staircase was likewise out of plumb, ditto the gallery that led to the gate of the *piso principal*, the main floor. Everything had to be propped up, until the day when our enterprising anarchist could put together enough of his homemade bombs and infernal machines to blow up the whole island, which is to say the whole world. Over the centuries, the Spaniards have developed a genuine and fascinating mastery in the art and culture of architectural decay, a skill exceeded perhaps only by their Iberian brothers in Portugal. They are no good at restoration, because they are too impulsive, too little devoted to petty matters, and still too rich in the midst of their poverty. Historical conservation requires a sense of having nothing to put in the place of what is in decline. The Spanish are not conscious of their poverty, and therein lies their greatness.

In the courtyard there stood some crippled banana shrubs, recognizable for what they were supposed to represent only by the shape of their leaves. A coat of white dust enveloped these subtropical plants, but every so often they took on a tropical aspect when a wind arrived across the Mediterranean from the Sahara and covered their whiteness with a reddish coat. Above these bushes stood a stately palm tree, just as genuine as the banana plants but, unlike the latter, free of dust. A little monkey, Don Alonso's darling, leaped around the fronds and kept them from getting dusty by busily shaking them. Don Alonso, who was skeptical about mankind and even in despair at times when the production rate of fireworks was at an ebb, sought and found in "Beppo" what Madame Perronet had sought and found in her tomcat Melchisédech and Bismarck in his Imperial hounds. Our Spanish landlord, on his part, had to reach back to a former evolutionary stage of humanity to obtain the consolation he was seeking.

Broad-leafed plants, with above-ground roots of a kind that I never saw elsewhere on the island, were growing here in big-bellied clay vats that had once served as containers for water. These roots were remarkable for the little red blossoms that came forth out of their woody fibers—parasites, as Herr von Martersteig claimed. The courtyard floor was set with sizeable flagstones. In the rainy season, when pools of water collected in between them, to keep our feet dry we had to jump our way across the court to reach the first step of the open staircase. In the background of the patio, where doors led to the stables and storage rooms, was a red-marble dipping well, whose rusted iron framework revealed that it was just as dried up as the house's exchequer.

The *entrada* or entrance hallway was roomy. If upon entrance you looked up at a ceiling richly inlaid with polychrome wood, you were given the impression of grandiosity, of expansiveness, of a style of living that is not constrained to camouflage its four enclosing walls with slaked lime. But we seldom enter a stranger's house with our eyes elevated to heaven; in certain instances we tend to do just the opposite. Stepping into the Count's solarium, our glance went directly to what was no longer aristocratic at all about Doña Inés and her purchased spouse, Alonso. It was not even aristocratic in the sense of those impoverished noble types, who decorate their cramped city apartments with relics of their exalted family heritage. This space was the realm of little people who have renounced a glorious past, but who continue to honor what they have inherited from the bride's father, besides the palace itself. It contained paintings—paintings that were just as unmarketable as I would term them impossible, if we weren't forced to admit that the impossible simply doesn't exist. Don Alonso's father-in-law had daubed these monstrosities onto canvas during a long lifetime as a Sunday and workday hobbyist. Still-life studies with columns, lizards stuck on them, a goat reclining in shadow; pieces of fruit; sunsets that one could interpret as sunrises with no loss of effect; blind alleys showing everything in merciful darkness; portraits of women who, at least as they appeared on canvas, could never count on winning a husband; portraits of men whom one should probably avoid after dark; pictures of children, of whom Beatrice said that if they were hers, she would drown them in a bucket. I supplemented these criminal aesthetics of hers by remarking that there were people who wouldn't shrink from trashing the pictures, too, if they were forced to live in their company—which is exactly what we were about to do. A self-portrait of the artist stood on an easel. That seemed the only way to permit the magic of illumination to play upon his forceful, very Castilian nose. By rough estimate, a good fifty square yards of painted canvas were hanging in this hall—and that, by the very same approximate estimate, was the total vertical surface of the hall itself including the doors, which also had art works on them.

"Ghastly!" Beatrice said when it dawned on her that the paintings were worse than the children she reacted to so vehemently and who, after all, must have given some modicum of pleasure to their parents. "Ghastly! All of them should be burned!"

Beatrice inclines to arrogance. Quite often she is moved to issue unfair, overhasty opinions. I calmed her down a bit by pointing out that in the most famous galleries of Europe, works of no less putrid quality get exhibited all the time. I was thinking primarily of the Mauritshuis in The Hague, and today I can think of several others that I hadn't yet visited back then, when I relied for the most part on Zwingli for my justification of kitsch. If human hair could display an aesthetic reaction, it would often stand on end in art galleries, such as the ones I'm thinking of. But human hair is uneducated; you might say it is crass, or even lacking in respect, for otherwise it wouldn't keep on growing after the demise of its maternal soil.

We must further consider (I am still quoting myself, as I stood in contemplation of the gimcrack art produced by Don Alonso's father-in-law) that world-class collections display their moldy junk mainly for historical purposes, whereas here in the Count's palace, it was shown as a gesture of piety toward the person of its perpetrator, who was still among the living and who resided under this very roof. This state of affairs actually doesn't affect the meaning of the term "inherited," which I have used above. As count and grandee of a historical nation, and as an artist within his own four walls, Don Juan, the father-in-law, had long since ceased to exist. His kingdom was no longer of his own world, and he could be regarded as already interred, if he didn't sit day by day on a stool in the kitchen, peeling potatoes and cleaning vegetables with one blind eye. He himself considered this second, proletarian existence of domestic servitude as an anomaly of his family destiny, all the more so since he could no longer paint, and thus had forfeited his life's golden glory. In a purely physical sense, he was a large man, a veritable colossus with thick, white, close-cut hair. His bushy eyebrows, two bundles of fur with a few bristles sticking out, would have seemed menacing if the eyes beneath them had been similarly piercing. But the left side showed total sightlessness, and all the right one saw was a troublesome blur. It was only after work hours, when the old gentleman rose from his drudgery and took the place of honor in the hall, that he perked up markedly, thus putting certain limits on my prior description of him. The seat of honor was a wicker armchair with wobbly legs; the fact that it was situated next to his self-portrait was a coincidence that gave rise to interesting comparisons. But because in a Spanish household, not to mention in a Spanish boarding house, a day's work ends at around midnight, and because Don Juan had to climb out of the sheets every morning early, he never sat for very long next to this previous edition of himself. Certainly he might have had better reason to veer off toward anarchism than his active, vital, joyful, life-affirming, yet often life-cursing son-in-law, if it weren't for the fact that he, Don Juan, had already entered his second childhood.

I would be doing this artist an injustice if I failed to mention that the remaining rooms were likewise papered with his entertaining colored canvases. The dining room, in particular, contained masterpieces of his appetite-enhancing brushwork. I had the pleasure during our entire stay at the Pensión del Conde, of sitting opposite a fish with an expertly painted, staring, glazed eye that seemed to plead with me, "Please, won't somebody finally eat me up, now that I've been gasping here on dry land ever since my executioner fished me out of his cranial aquarium?" It wasn't lack of air that was causing this fish to gasp, but an ordinary kitchen onion that it held in its maw. To keep the fish within the confines of its frame, the painter had garnished its ventral fin with a sprig of parsley.

If we can speak of a certain lack of genuine art on the part of this family's testator, it was made up for by his heir's practical, applied artistic talents. Don Alonso was skilled in all kinds of crafts. He punched leather, painted on porcelain, burned in wood, made ceramic pots, turned wood on a lathe, etched, carved ivory, and modeled in wax. He was good at marquetry and intaglio, and bound his own books with self-marbled end-papers. In short, there was nothing you could find in a handbook of arts and crafts that this after-hours anarchist didn't practice with proficiency. His workshop on the third floor was equipped with all the necessary tools and machines. I was constantly amazed and, I must admit, envious whenever I watched this master puttering away in his white smock, which displayed, in a kind of batik pattern, traces of all his various enterprises.

Since I was myself an unregistered member of the guild that can make thirteen botched jobs out of a dozen tries, we soon became friends. I was allowed to enter and leave his studio at will, and also to use his tools, once Alonso noticed that I was just as clever at this sort of thing as he was, and that I wasn't about to purloin his precious possessions. This anarchist Count would never have tolerated such a thing.

Only one area was off limits to me, and that was the tiny, windowless cubicle where he devoted himself wholeheartedly to his anarchism. It could be reached only by squirming through garrets, past a pigeon loft, up a set of stairs, and along perilous attic passageways. In the palace it was referred to as the *cámara ardiente*, which in Catholic churches is what they call a chapel with a catafalque for funeral masses. Not unlike the Church, though with much less pious intent, the Count placed his *cámara* in the service of death. This is where the partisans gathered in the evening, men who were convinced that things must not go on as they were, and that something had to be done. Some had read Bakunin, others were versed in Ballanche; all of them were devoted to what they read between the lines in Unamuno and Pío Baroja, and they all dabbled in the manufacture of fireworks and infernal machines with which to undermine bourgeois society and, above all, blow up the churches. The conspirator-in-chief, Don Alonso, demanded that one of these churches be spared: Montesión, where once every year he partook of the Holy Eucharist.

Don Darío, who up to now is familiar to us in word if not in deed, was a member of years-long standing in this league of explosives experts. With some he had a reputation as the group's intellectual spine and unimpeachable brain, for he was a well-read fellow, much traveled, nursing a personal hatred of the Pope, and in possession of the financial wherewithal without which it is futile to foment any conspiracy. But he got thrown out of the nocturnal cooperative as too dangerous a revolutionary. In a later chapter I shall return to this gentleman. But let me explain here why a rich and smart terrorist like him could no longer be tolerated in the Count's powder magazine.

One night the gang, having convened in the fraternal harmony and pacific concord that is essential when dealing with high explosives, was as usual fiddling around with their petards. Don Darío, our crippled hero of the barricades, having maneuvered the secret passageways, suddenly bounced into this chamber of horrors. Upon arrival, he proclaimed loudly that enough was enough; from now on all churches must be leveled, including the Montesión that Comrade Alonso wanted preserved for the salvation of his private soul.

Down with all Your Eminences, one of whom, an eminently grey one, had been living it up for months in Don Darío's hotel with wine and women, but had now vamoosed for the mainland without paying his bill! Don Alonso, it was reported, was at first benumbed by this pronouncement. But then he quickly recovered, and retorted that if Comrade Darío blasted away his church, he would personally light the fuse in the chapel at this co-conspirator's bullfight arena, and send the Holy Mother of God sky-high, so help him God! With a gnashing of teeth Don Darío retracted his threats, only to put forth additional warnings that were worse, because he meant to carry them out right here in the powder room. There was no choice but to gang up on this zealot and transport him out to the street. When we took up residence in the Pensión del Conde, relations among the bomb builders had broken off.

Over the years I saw many bombs from Alonso's atelier go off in Palma. These explosive pronouncements had the best intentions of doing away with the entire clerical clique. But when, for example, they got thrown at streetcars whose passengers were politely asked to disembark beforehand, it still took some powerful anarchists' shoulders to overturn the vehicle. On the other hand, the bombs made short work of window glass. The shattering noise mingled promisingly with the explosion, the bomb-chuckers cheered in the cause of "freedom," cursed the bourgeoisie and the clergy, and then withdrew to a café to discuss their next plot. When Franco exploded the big bomb that turned the whole country into a *cámara ardiente*, Don Alonso and his buddies were forced to realize that what they had been up to amounted to stuffing *butifarras*—about which, more in my Epilogue. For the moment, let us enjoy peace for a while longer. It is so profoundly calming now that the noise of the fireworks has died away.

Doña Inés was love itself, kindness itself, solicitude itself, and she was all these things regardless of the fact that she was also ugliness itself. Having no children, she was as busy as a bee—a cause-and-effect relation that would make no sense in northern Europe. In Spain, mothers with multiple children are condemned to indolence, a result of their tumbling from one trauma to the next as they deal with their offsprings' plight, which is so seldom mitigated by happiness. I never saw Doña Inés with empty hands. She was fierce even with a dust cloth, although she always conducted a losing battle. Her staff knew well enough why they weren't asked to do the dusting. It would have required the entire army of monkeys commanded by the German guest in Room 13 to assist Beppo in keeping the grime from fulfilling its bourgeois function. Doña Inés didn't lay her hands in her lap until the day she died. A few months ago a friend told me of her passing away. She was in her early forties when we committed ourselves to her care. Her hair was already then snow-white, and her face featured a constant smile that wasn't meant to be one. What caused this illusion of merriment was an unfortunate play of wrinkles near her mouth. Perhaps "play" is saying too much, for as an innkeeper she might well have worn a perpetual smile without harboring an iota of good will toward her guests. "Keep smiling"—that's what the Americans call this technique of using a lie to smooth over the rough edges of life. It is certain that I never saw her laughing, but then it was no laughing matter to keep charge of the crowd of bungling domestics who served under her scepter. Come to think of it, she herself served under the cudgel of her gigantic philandering husband, the one who had chopped down his family tree so that he could crawl around all the more conveniently in the depths of the shrubbery.

Among the female personnel, the most remarkable was the cook. She was a short, plump girl with a significant bosom, from the depths of which there rose little clouds of smoke, making her appear as though she were always carrying a steaming bowl of soup. She believed in God with the type of faith that keeps the believer from ever having to blush in the face of the One believed in. We could have thought that she was constantly offering a ritual gift of incense to the Almighty. But this was not the case. As she went about her chores Josefa puffed on a pipe, and she stashed it in her capacious cleavage when working at the stove, while explaining a Spanish recipe to her guests, or while she had to carry in the food herself because the table waiters were off wallowing somewhere else. An expert in matters pertaining to smoke, Captain von Martersteig, later told me that Josefa wore between her breasts an asbestos pouch hand-crafted by our friend the Count. As a reconnaissance pilot in Baron von Richthofen's squadron, Martersteig had enjoyed a bird's-eye view of many events, and thus we can believe that he made reliable observation of the cook's bosom. Unfortunately, his current status was limited to low-level flying of this sort, which is to say... But I am not yet through with our little fireplug of a cook, Josefa.

Everybody in the house loved this little ageless, God-fearing, honest girl with her smoke-producing gentleman's vice. I soon took her into my heart, and more than once she pressed me to her ample cushions. She was a good cook, Josefa was, but always with the same menu—which wasn't her fault. The Count's Boarding House was not, after all, a "Príncipe" with a chef who, if he worked in Germany, would be awarded the title of Privy Councillor or, like some painters in oils, a professorship. At the Count's house the menu had to be inexpensive, in order to keep the price of lodging within reason. The hot water sold by my grandfather was no doubt cheaper still, but I don't wish to make invidious comparisons. At Doña Inés' table no one suffered hunger or thirst. And if the two of us did feel such pangs later, it was not at her board, but out in God's open air.

Everyone loved Josefa, even old English spinsters and even Beatrice, who normally kept in check her feelings for fellow humans. And yet this cook had enemies under the Count's roof against whom she was defenseless. She had two enemies: Beppo the monkey and Lorico, the Inca cockatoo.

Beppo pestered this roly-poly girl. He leaped on her shoulders from behind and groped lasciviously down between her smoke-cured breasts to steal her pipe, a move at which he was sometimes successful. With such an incubus on her back, Josefa could have earned more money in a traveling circus than here in this anarchic island hostelry, where the clients could watch the entertaining spectacle for free. Of course, Josefa hurled choice epithets at Beppo, but the colorful terms she used were not authentic curses, for she did not permit sacred names to pass her lips. Thus she always lost out, and always got pelted by the screeching Beppo with all sorts of objects that weren't nailed down. As if to excuse her defeats, Josefa would say that if only the monkey didn't look like somebody's kid, she would long since have slaughtered him with the big kitchen knife that she whetted every morning on the stone staircase in the courtyard. During this process she was regularly spied upon from up in the palm tree by the crafty Beppo. Too meagerly endowed with human sentiments after all, the sacrosanct temple animal was of course unaware of her sacrificial yearnings. With all due respect for Josefa's man-fearing Christian attitude, it must be said that even without such inhibitions she never would have skinned this monkey alive, simply because he was her master's favorite pet.

Her conflict with the cockatoo was of a different sort, although here, also, human-all-too-human impulses broke through the barriers of animalhood. Lorico had a loose tongue. His former owner, a Portuguese ship captain, had taught him two words that probably meant the whole world to someone who had nothing but water and sky around him for weeks on end: *porra* and *puta*. With these vocables the bird assaulted everyone who approached his perch, each time raising his red and yellow crest feathers as if emitting these words in a state of highest excitement. Not even Count Hermann Keyserling, who on one of his visits to the island inspected the palace of his renegade fellow nobleman, was able to discern whether Lorico was enunciating his words in rage or in jest. Years later he remembered this bird when I mentioned in his presence the phenomenon of animal speech, thinking that I might offer him some novel zoological perspectives for his work on *The Cosmos of Meaning*.

Josefa was hated by this Inca blood, and she hated the bird too, and thus the animosity was mutual. The bird's reasons must remain obscure, but the cook's were an open book. Josefa took offense at one word in the educated bird's vocabulary—a term that is probably the one most frequently used in the whole Spanish language: the little disyllable *puta*. In Spain, nothing at all will work without this word, simply because things will not work without the thing that the word signifies. The more often our distinguished anarchist cheated on his even higher-born spouse with the types thus signified, all the less did Josefa tolerate the use of such colloquialisms in his house, where she went about her work with the touching loyalty of servants who often are more solicitous of their employers' reputation than the employers are themselves. It goes without saying that she also had personal reasons for wishing to gag the bird. Josefa was a chaste person, and her primness was in no way vitiated by the acrid smoke from the noxious shag that at times wafted up out of the crater of her bosom. That nasty word *puta* wounded her sense of shame just as severely as did the monkey's habit of letting his hands rove around in imitation of human lechery.

With the other term that he learned in the Portuguese ship captain's language school, Lorico was rather less conspicuous among Spaniards. A Portuguese Josefa would have wrung his neck on the spot. In Spanish, *porra* can mean walking-cane, truncheon, boasting, obfuscation, thunder, and several more things, but never anything that one wouldn't utter in the presence of the most innocent of young female souls. In Portuguese, on the other hand, *porra* is not presentable. The Portuguese vernacular, by means of an embarrassing process of localization, has confined the word's meaning almost exclusively to its etymological root. Lorico was not a linguist in any academic sense; he used the term in its Lusitanian definition, just as it had been cherished by the old salt who knew his way around all the oceans and all the harbor brothels of the world, and who in all his seafaring days had probably never once heard of semantics or metaphorical discourse. Here on the island, Lorico remained loyal to his original tutor by parroting forth his rudimentary ABC's even after the captain had jumped ship and taken off somewhere with his *puta* without paying the harbor innkeeper's bill. The illiterate Josefa had no inkling of the curious processes that allow a language to use one and the same word to pull the wool over somebody's eyes.

To be honest about it, I wasn't aware of such subtleties at the time, either. But years later I was vividly reminded of our grandee's Inca cockatoo when Pascoaes, whose parents had been close to the Portuguese court, told me the story of how King Don Carlos felt obliged to reject the credentials of an Italian emissary who bore the resounding name of Conte Porra di Porra. From a Portuguese perspective the surname indicated a lineage of the most suspect kind. Might the Italian court, the King inquired with a fine sense of humor, not have sent a less insistent nobleman? A simple "Porra" was perhaps acceptable, but such a painful reduplication, Porra di Porra, was too much of an affront even to the emissary himself.

British ladies, ignorant of the Iberian languages, had great fun listening to this squawking bird, and often inquired as to what it was saying. Again and again I was asked to interpret His Master's Voice, and this was not at all an entertaining assignment. Each time it happened, I was stymied by the inevitable question, "Does he really mean it?"

Beatrice had the same effect on the bird as a red cape on a fighting bull, or the sight of a priest on Don Darío. On the bird's part, it was hatred at first sight, and this drove Beatrice into alliance with the cook. It was probably due to Lorico's alert intraspecific instincts, which sensed in this new guest a degeneration of the Inca bloodline, abetted by an official action of the Immigration Service in Basel. Lorico was outraged at such a corruption of his race. At first Beatrice was oblivious of such connections, but when I explained them to her, she treated this bigoted bird with the same contempt that she was later to present to the Nazis, who would likewise accuse me of "profanation of the blood."

I have yet to mention Pepe, a young errand-boy and jack-of-all-trades, whose extended notions about the meaning of "it all" brought considerable dishonor to a house that he served as adroitly in his blue livery outfit as Beppo did in his scarlet one. Like the monkey, he was a thief. Today it is not easy for me to give an accurate portrait of Pepe. With his agile fingers he already points us in the direction of Portugal and the vintner's palace of the poet Pascoaes, where a similarly caparisoned diminutive lackey was also prone to confusing mine and thine. This Lusitanian Pepe, Victorino by name, with his pranks and his thirteen-year-old bravado, obscures my image of his less cunning Mallorquine counterpart, so I think I will save him for a book on my Portuguese adventures. There were of course differences between them. Pepe got trounced daily by his exalted master, whereas at Pascoaes no one laid a hand on Victorino, since according to the castellan's thesis, proclaimed in all his books, man is not to be regarded as a sinner but as sin itself. Pepe stole on a small scale, Victorino in a big way. The anarchist's clients thought of the modest drain on their funds as a kind of visitor's tax, levied by the management under the table in return for the privilege of witnessing highly dramatic scenes of chastisement that were gleefully applauded by the monkey and the cockatoo.

I never blamed the boy for playing fast and loose with other people's property. What was he to do, living in a community where bombs were manufactured for the violent redistribution of the world's wealth? Unfortunately we were ourselves the cause of Pepe's getting thrown out of the palace personally by Don Alonso. I had left a fairly large sum of money in our room, unlocked, and the little thief's anarchistic tendencies veered rather rapidly toward a dangerous capitalistic karma. He snatched our cash, was caught by a cleaning girl, but wasn't told on until after he had blown all the pesetas. The scene of dismissal was grandiose, and compensated us to an extent for our no less grandiose loss. Pepe scratched and bit and, using Lorico's vocabulary, spilled out to all within earshot the most intimate secrets of his revolutionary employer—this in the presence of Doña Inés, whose morose features remained stony. The cockatoo went wild with joy on his perch; sending his feed pellets flying through the breakfast room, which was the site of these leave-taking festivities. Over and over again the wise-acre bird let go with his two words, which now became truly germane to the situation. No doubt, the parrot felt transported back to his old teacher's below-decks cabin, where goings-on of this kind were the order of the day. Captain von Martersteig, summoned forth by the martial hubbub, shuffled in wearing his huge fur slippers, but he went directly to his room when I told him that Pepe had just been convicted of stealing a considerable amount of money. The old soldier wanted to make sure that the little pilferer hadn't made a visit to his musette bag, where he kept the meager pension sent down to him through special channels by Field Marshal Hindenburg himself. But nothing was missing. The cook prayed. Beppo, waiting in sleazy ambush on the courtyard stairway, tossed dirt in his fellow miscreant's face and then leaped back up, barking and screeching, into the palm fronds. Nevertheless, his simian freedom was not to last much longer. A few days later he was put on a chain, but one that allowed him to continue his business of keeping the tree free of dust.

After all: Beppo, too, was a robber. An English lady was busy painting the romantic interior courtyard when with a lightning leap he went at her hair to swipe a beguiling silver barrette. Instead, her entire head of hair remained in his grasp. The lady became quite exercised, trying with both hands to cover her bald skull, while the shameless thief set to plucking her wig to pieces. For a long time afterward her scalp hung like a hunting trophy from a thin strand of the coconut palm, to the silent amusement of a sickly Dutch plantation owner, Mr. van Beverwijn. He had lived for many long years among the head-hunters of Borneo, probably none of whom was as threatening as his Mevrouw. Mijnheer van Bewerwijn was now reminded of life in the jungle, and for a time he regained his spirits. But then he relapsed and atrophied further like his sclerotic kidney, which was the reason he had left the colonies. I daresay I bestowed some light on his darkened soul during the weeks we spent together at the rooming house. I was the only one with whom Mr. van Beverwijn could hold a conversation in his native tongue. He preferred not to listen to his wife, because she spoke in the tongues of Christian Science. In Book Three we shall again encounter these guests from the East Indies; Mijnheer will be even more withered and lonesome, and Mevrouw will have made further advances in her increasingly un-Christian hyper-Christianity.

II

At about three in the afternoon there was a commotion outside, overpowering the sedative effect of our household apothecary. I woke up, and at first had no idea where I was. But this condition of de-identification lasted only for a moment. My eyelids descended once more, and I dozed on without losing the sound that had lifted them. It got louder; it was a series of reports like the clappers used by penitents during Holy Week. Beatrice awoke too; she went bolt upright and screamed, "*Vite, vite,* Zwingli is being killed! Let's toss some water...!"

Now I was wide awake. I got up and calmed her by placing my hand on her forehead. To this day a laying on of hands is for her the most effective technique for getting rid of nightmares.

"You've been dreaming, *chérie*. There are no Pilars here with daggers and axes. There's a storm over the island, and the shutters are loose in their hinges—*alles kaputt!*"

But outside was bright sunshine, and it blinded me when I opened the shutters. At the very same instant something hit my face, and I was in pain. There was a strident screech, a hairy something swung through the air, and seconds later I saw the glazed rear-end of a mid-sized monkey gleaming down at me through the leaves of a palm tree. The object that had given me this belated matinal greeting, a plaited wicker fan for keeping charcoal fires aglow, fell to the ground. What an ingratiating way of saying hello to new arrivals!

"You stupid beast!" I yelled up to the palm tree. But the reply I received came from down below, from whence I expected to hear nothing from out of the subtropical light-filtering palm branches.

"I beg your pardon?"

Down below stood a gentleman, presumably also a house guest, wearing a white suit that contrasted markedly with his polar footwear, which consisted of animal pelts and, seen from above, looked like two furry plaster casts. He stuck a gilt-framed monocle to his left eye, but then let it drop again on its black ribbon and looked up at me.

"Oh, I'm sorry," I said a little shakily and in German. "I was talking to that fellow up there who just molested me." And I pointed to the monkey, who in the meantime had discovered something on his own person that held his full attention.

"I'm quite sure that you meant that fellow up there, that damned little clown, the guy that all of us hate so much. Well, sir, we'll have to get together and talk about this. Can we wait until later for the introductions? It's unpleasant this way, at such a distance and with the two of us occupying different standpoints. My greetings to your spouse. Just take care, though, let me warn you. Beppo can tell the difference between the sexes, but he has no respect for any such difference. At your obedient service, sir!"

He squeezed the single lens to his eye, let it fall again, and disappeared limping through the house portal.

"For God's sake, *chérie*, did you hear that? This is turning out to be quite something. Once again you are correct with your generalization about my fellow countrymen in foreign lands—the familiar and all-too-familiar ones, and the remote ones, and the remotest ones, too. Either they go crazy from trying to act like foreigners, or they get more and more German by trying to out-German the Germans. The character I just spoke with is as German as he is bonkers—an army officer, or maybe a dueling fraternity student. At least he wasn't able to crack his heels together. He doesn't have any more heels. The army probably marched the heels off of him. He wants me to convey obedient greetings to my spouse. So I obediently suggest that we get dressed, go downstairs, and introduce ourselves obediently. It looks as if we'll be living above our means here, to judge by that monkey and this character with the monocle. But over at Pilar's things just wouldn't have worked out in the long run."

Our room was spacious, and less oppressively decorated than the reception hall—which is to say that it contained only the barest necessities. There was no lack of a sturdy table for writing on; not even Thomas Mann could have found reason for supercilious remarks. It entered my mind that there was even room enough here for a grand piano—and with this thought I had unwittingly brought us back to reality and the events of the previous day. This re-attachment to the world, anchoring us firmly in our insular destiny, forced us into action once again. We had to make decisions. A review of our finances would provide a basis for shaping the future, and now, following such an abundance of misfortune, we had every right to expect better things to come. A trip to the post office, a visit to the bank, a few letters to our creditors...

"Beatrice, that crazed courtesan and guttersnipe may have thrown us out of her house, but she can't toss us completely for a loop. As far as I'm concerned, I'm back to normal. What about you? Have you been able to calm down? You don't seem to trust the air here. You're sniffing around again."

Doña Inés met us in the hall and begged our pardon in the name of her establishment for Beppo's misbehavior. She had received a report on the embarrassing incident from Don Joaquín, a boarder from Germany. She hadn't succeeded in persuading her husband to put Beppo on a chain before it was too late. The little fellow from Java, she told us, was cunning and unpredictable, and she didn't like him either. And might she now introduce us to another honored house guest who spoke our language, Doña Adeleide? The countess pointed to a rocking chair in the shadow of the now-familiar easel. It was cradling the person of an elderly lady, who now applied the brakes, let the chair come to rest, and then said in a very natural yet dignified voice, "I am Frau Gerstenberg, and this is my son Friedrich."

At first we could see nothing of this Friedrich. He had made himself small in a corner of the room that was darker still than the area behind the self-portrait of the distinguished progenitor and house artist, the man who had already outlived himself. Friedrich's chair, too, ceased its rocking, and from it arose this lady's son, a tall, untidily dressed fellow. He was wearing black-rimmed glasses and a matching pitch-black mustache.

"Ginsterberg!" That is how he introduced himself, with the same kind of ridiculously stiff academic bow that I was trying to rid myself of down here on the island.

"To avoid any misunderstandings," the lady now interjected, "permit me to explain that Ginsterberg is the name of my ex-husband. Since our divorce I have legally retaken my maiden name, the one I went under at the *Burgtheater* in Vienna. I was known there as 'La Gerstenberg.'"

As she spoke, her features no doubt turned somber, but we didn't notice, because the aged count's *autoretrato* with its dynastic nose took up all the light here in the hall. Her chair began gently rocking again, as was fitting for her dreams of a distant past.

"Why Madame," Beatrice exclaimed, "are you the famous Gerstenberg, Adele Gerstenberg? If you are, then many is the time I have admired and applauded you!"

The veil of nostalgia that I had imagined descending over Madame Gerstenberg's features was now quite visible on Beatrice's face. What is more, her eyes had taken on a moist gleam that was all too familiar. Thoughts of Vienna always gave her fond memories of her music lessons with Juliusz Wolfsohn, which circumstances had forced her to discontinue. Madame Gerstenberg had caused Beatrice to take a painful look into the past; Pilar and her hatchet-job on the pianoforte were but a trivial interlude.

The ashen artiste rose from her chair, supported by her son. She went up to Beatrice and embraced her warmly.

"My child, do not be angry if I get so emotional. But you are the only person in this anti-artistic country who has recognized me, who remembers me. Oh Golden Vienna, where I was carried aloft! Friedrich, my son, if you don't know it already, here is someone who can tell you who your mother truly was!

I was once 'La Gerstenberg,' and so I could not remain Frau Ginsterberg. And is this your dear husband? Let me welcome you, too!"

I kissed the great actress's hand and led her back to her chair.

"Oh, I am touched by so many thoughts, so much emotion! Herr von Martersteig already told us that you are a writer. That means we make up a little world of our own here together."

"But Mama, Martersteig was exaggerating. You know that the information he gets from Anton Emmerich isn't very reliable."

Aha, I thought. Our *chronique scandaleuse* has penetrated to the rocking chairs of the Count's Hostel! But I took solace in the thought that for Friedrich, it seemed a greater scandal to be a writer than to have been chased out of house and home by a hooker.

"Now son, there you go again. You haven't expressed yourself very well at all. It's not an exaggeration to say that a certain person is a writer. The important thing is what that person writes. And with the best will in the world, I can't say that the Captain knows his limits as a writer. You're acting just like your father, always leaving yourself open to criticism. That worries me. Excuse us, my friends. Here we are once again with our family topic number one. It must seem quite abstruse when we get to arguing about it in front of strangers in a boarding house. Come on, Friedel, let's get hold of ourselves, shouldn't we?"

Mother's and son's chairs cannot have swung back and forth more than a hundred times before we learned in general outline the sorrowful story of these two expatriates. Friedrich's father was a renowned Tübingen cardiac anatomist, who once every month sent them 400 marks, a sum that should easily have kept them going. Yet like the aforementioned Captain, but in a different sphere of activity, this son didn't know his limits. He was consumptive, and had been forced to break off his medical studies before his doctoral exams. They had lived for a year in the dusty Spanish desert of Alicante, where a woman lived from whom young Friedrich simply could not part. Then, for different reasons, they had come to Mallorca, a place that didn't seem to me to be ideal for a TB case either. Swiss sanatoriums, they explained, were too expensive, and "La Gerstenberg" had no desire to remain in Germany. Staying there would surely take a bad turn; they were Jewish. Hindenburg was a military giant with softening of the brain. The insurgent National Socialists, in league with Hindenburg's conservative cohorts, would soon stab the old general in the back, and then all non-Aryans would be slaughtered. Considering that these political speculations were expressed in the summer of 1931, it is amazing how prescient this famous actress was in a field outside of her professional expertise. She had keen insights, and it wasn't for nothing that she kept up with the best of the world's news media. Friedrich was a faithful customer of Anton Emmerich's.

That noontime we didn't meet any other boarding-house guests. Like Beppo, the cockatoo Lorico had introduced himself, and having just arrived from Pilar's lodgings, we heard the sounds of home emerging from his obscene beak. Unfortunately, we had no time to indulge in nostalgia of this kind. With

Pepe's help we lugged our belongings from the bookstore and carefully set up everything in our room. Beatrice is a genius at the spontaneous management of space; she knows how to improvise and juggle things around like no other intellectual woman. She places boxes and suitcases on top of each other according to a precise plan, in such a way that it is always the bottom-most box that contains what we need most urgently. Before entering the *comedor* for supper we had made a home for ourselves from which no one would very easily evict us.

"Captain von Martersteig, if you will permit me, sir. From Magdeburg. Joachim by Christian name—that's why these odd people here call me Don Joaquín."

"Vigoleis, with a soft V, as in 'Hannover.' But I'm from Süchteln on the Lower Rhine, if you will permit me in return."

We made reciprocal bows, very stiff ones—the Captain for reasons that will soon become clear; I myself in a symptomatic regression to childish German manners.

"Vigoleis? And with a soft V as in 'Hannover'? What does that mean? If I have heard you correctly, you have quite a romantic name. Are you related to that knight of Arthur's Round Table, the one with the wheel on his helmet, *le chevalier à la roue, Wigalois*? Medieval Courtly Poetry, 13th century—I own the Benecke edition. Peculiar. Quite remarkable, my good man with your soft V as in 'Hannover.'"

Smart fellow, I thought, this captain with a literary education. I'll have to be on my guard. Give a military man some schooling, and he'll be doubly dangerous. And a Prussian to boot, whereas I am a Prussian only by coercion. Fortunately, the captain was standing before me in civvies, which dampened his pride of caste. Minor nobility, insignificant.

"Related?" I replied to his literary inquiry into my pedigree. "Well, you might say that I am related in spirit to that character in Gravenberg." But I refrained from adding that the wheel borne by my medieval namesake as an ornament on his headgear was something I carried around inside my head, where it sometimes spins so rapidly that I get dizzy. The captain would notice this soon enough if we were to share the anarchistic Count's Round Table for any length of time. "As for the soft V, I'll explain that some other time, Captain. It's a purely Swiss affair. My wife, I should explain, is half Swiss."

"Great Scott!" the Captain burst out. "Then the other half must be a tinge of Indian. When I first saw you, Madame, I immediately thought of the Aztecs—my respects, Madame. Has Madame recovered from the shock of witnessing the greeting her spouse received yesterday from up in the palm tree?"

"Yesterday," I replied in Beatrice's stead, who was reacting to the captain with polite hostility. "Yesterday we got our shocks from some artificial palm trees, and today from a real one. Surely Mr. Emmerich has informed you?"

"Beppo is unpredictable, Madame," the Captain said over my reply. "And he has every right to be. That is his *summum jus*. It's his inalienable right by reason of his belonging to monkeydom, something not even an anarchistic Count can deprive him of. By the way, if that scene yesterday had taken place in a French hotel, I wouldn't hesitate to call it a perfidious manifestation of germanophobia. I do not love my fellow countrymen unconditionally, and at the moment I am in open conflict with the fatherland. But any time at all I'll risk my war-battered spine against the French, the whole crew of them. Not even the gratings of a green cheese..."

His remarks ended with this mysterious allusion, for the dinner gong now invited us to table. The Captain took Beatrice's arm: a handsome couple, two people feuding against their own homelands. It was enough to make Lorico wax indecent again. I followed at a respectful distance—I who, while not yet totally at odds with my fatherland, was in a constant fiery spat with my own personality. Martersteig obediently requested permission to report, *à la prussienne*, that he had taken the liberty of arranging the table seating in such a way that we could form a little group of our own, together with La Gerstenberg and her pampered son, and not excluding Fräulein Höchst from Dresden, who at this time was still doing healthful Mensendieck calisthenics up in her room.

This Fräulein was an academically certified gymnastics teacher, a mannish type with blond hair and aquamarine eyes who spoke no language but German, and this with an inherited Saxon harshness. Otherwise, there was nothing re-markable about her. She kept modestly in the background, and was always happy when she could go outdoors to practice swimming and throwing the javelin. "The Germanic Fury" she was called out on the beach at Ca's Català, where people scrambled whenever she heaved her spear into the ocean and dove in to fetch it like a trained dog. She never took part in mealtime conversation. The patriotic history of German gymnastics was not really a proper subject for our chats, not even in Frau Dr. Mensendieck's diluted modern version.

I would much prefer to have sat at the indigenous side of this *table d'hôte*, where things proceeded much less decorously than in our Nordic corner. But I couldn't have done such a thing to Beatrice. She immediately loses her ap-petite if somebody slurps his soup or pushes a spoon like a coal shovel straight into his mouth—not to mention the artful characters who eat with their knives without cutting their tongues. If industry could ever come out with a "safety knife," such a prejudice would not endure for very long in the books on eti-quette. Which reminds me of a funny story from among the little episodes of our life together. We were at table in Geneva, and the conversation revolved around Hitler and the Third Reich. Miserable victims of Nazism that we were, it was awkward for us there in the midst of a well-heeled though politically neutral gathering, whose members hadn't yet realized that if the German hordes ever came stampeding across their border, the jig would be up for them too. I presented a political-philosophical defense of our position, while Beat-rice remained contemptuously silent. Our host asked her for her opinion. She replied that she was unable to speak at table about Hitler, a man who ate with his knife. At which our host, who had just placed a morsel of food in his mouth with his knife, nearly choked. "*Mais, Madame...*," he said, whereupon the conversation took a sudden turn to the weather and the upcoming grape harvest. It was more than embarrassing.

One master of the skill in question was a boarder from the Spanish mainland, a Spanish Smith or Jones from Burgos, who was vacationing on the island with his wife and two daughters of fetchingly marriageable age. He was not an artist, unlike several who, according to Emmerich, spent time at the Pensión del Conde. But he had connections to the art world as a salesman for Dutch and German paint and brush manufacturers. Everybody who was anybody in Spanish art, Emmerich told us, squeezed paint from this man's tubes and spread it on canvas with this man's brushes. Miró, Zuloaga, Puigdengolas, and Sureda were among his distinguished customers. The Count on the easel, too, used to buy his art supplies from him. His hues had a brilliance that even the Old Masters would have been incapable of mixing. This tradesman of the palette was also an expert at mixing things on his dinner plate. My Spanish was too feeble to allow me to join in the discussion across the table. Friedrich translated a few things for me while Beatrice sat at her place with such disgust on her face that not even La Gerstenberg dared to strike up a conversation with her.

Martersteig explained the menu for us. He was familiar with Spanish cuisine, and was particularly expert when it came to salads—not even the tiniest snail escaped his monocular inspection. He would accept responsibility, he told us, for all the ingredients except the typhus bacilli. His earnest caveats on this score meant that most often he finished the entire bowl of salad all by himself. He owed his kitchen finesse indirectly to General Hindenburg. The Reich President had refused an increase in his spinal pension, and as a result Martersteig had to prepare his own dishes in his headquarters at Deyá. Compared to our Josefa, however, or to a Santiago Kastner, he was a culinary duffer, a master of the greasy spoon.

"Martersteig is a writer, too," Friedrich suddenly said à propos of nothing at all.

"Too?" replied the gentleman under attack, turning around to face the two of us. "This young man no doubt intends his expression 'too' as a compliment addressed to my person. But this young man is apparently unaware that his mischievous little adverb 'too' might also be offensive to you, Mr. Vigoleis. For as we well know, you 'too' are a writer. As for myself, I am not a writer 'too.' I write because I must. I have a task to fulfill. My writing is in an area quite different from yours, but still I would like you and Madame to hear a few pages of my manuscript sometime. I would be grateful for your opinion— I mean, of course, both of your opinions."

"Huzzah! Long live our retired Captain, the generalissimo and head chimpanzee of his own army of monkeys! There they are, standing before us in rank and file, and we haven't even finished our first course!"

It was Friedrich who said this, and it sounded like a victory proclamation.

Frau Gerstenberg tried to pooh-pooh this bit of adolescent raillery. There was, she explained, this constant open animosity between her boy and the Captain, and it wasn't a serious matter. *The Army of the Monkeys* was the title of the novel that Martersteig had been working on for years. He was continually revising his manuscript. His monkey recruits refused again and again to behave in the manner conceived for them by their author, as fully equivalent substitutes for a force of German national conscripts. Her explanation prompted Friedrich to the equivocal remark that this one-time military man was of course writing from personal experience.

Martersteig remained unperturbed by these words, intended partly as pure information, partly as provocation. Silently he shook his spherical head with its snow-white locks deftly arranged to conceal the bald spots. Then he set his monocle, took his fork, and busied himself with boning a red bream, which he then presented to Beatrice.

"Doña Inés is a clever woman," said the Austrian Imperial Actress. "Twice a day she serves fish with dangerous bones. That forces our two fighting cocks to give all their attention to the plates in front of them. Otherwise their constant squabbling would be unbearable. Don't you think so, Fräulein Höchst?"

"Begging your pardon," said the expert fish-boner, thus relieving the young Dresden lady of the necessity of replying. "Just a few more weeks of your patience and I'll be returning to my little mill-wheel castle in Deyá. By then my enemy will have calmed down."

Friedrich, who had finished boning his own bream, started speaking again:

"That enemy of Martersteig's is a writer, too. *Too,* I say. And he too has a 'von' in his name, but not all the time. Right now he's one of the island's most famous residents, although he doesn't look it. His name is Graves, but as the grandson of our noted historian Ranke, he likes to call himself Robert von Ranke Graves. The Captain, who selects his army recruits so carefully, is also very choosy when picking his enemies."

"Ginsterberg is a smart aleck, and he's full of nonsense. By German standards, he's also amazingly superficial and uncultured. Profundity? Not the gratings of a green cheese! They say he used to be a model student, trying to emulate his eminent father. But now he is sick. We'll just have to show some understanding. But now let's change the subject, Mr. Vigoleis. What were you saying a while ago about your soft V as in 'Hannover'?"

"Vigoleis with a soft V? Oh, that was just a little joke. I was trying to come up with something to match your elaborate title, with your Captain, your Retired, your 'von,' and your Magdeburg. And even for this little bit of fun I had to do some borrowing—I could never produce anything of the kind on my own accord. Through my wife I have a certain liaison with the Swiss Confederation—Basel, to be precise. Basel is famous for its humanistic past, but what's left of that famous city now is all paper. Nowadays they more than make up for the loss by celebrating Carnival and, probably in the same spirit, by the games that old families play with their names. The House of Burckhardt—I mean of course the one spelled ck-dt, owes its immortal fame to its greatest son, Jacob. But there's another Swiss family, the k-t Burkharts pure and simple. They've got along without any upper-middle-class alphabetical snobbery, although they have had to take a back seat to the others—'literally literally', you might say. Nobody takes the k-t family for real, and the 'real' ones insist on not being confused with the pseudo-Burckhardts. It's pretty much the same with the Vischers with the soft V, who refuse to be tarred with the same brush as the Fischers from the slums—although it's ironic that a Fischer with his little *guppy-like F* has achieved immortality through Goethe's poem. The Meier family belongs in the same category, with their *ei* in place of the chic *ai* or *ay*.

"My wife had a ck-dt grandmother, and now she has a husband with a soft V. Incidentally, all this orthographic and phonetic pedantry about our pedigree has yet to be declared legal by a justice of the peace, as Mr. Emmerich has doubtless already let you know."

As a matter of fact, everyone in the boarding house was aware that the Knight with the Wheel in his Head and the soft V in his medieval troubadour's pseudonym was living in common-law marriage with his Beatrice, the woman accused by the cockatoo of practicing racial pollution.

The Captain listened intently to my philological, confederative thesis concerning mobs and snobs, all the while gazing fixedly into his glass of Vichy water. Jakob Böhme probably peered in just the same way into his cobbler's lens, locating there all at once the Divinity and Eternal Nature, Good and Evil. Our Captain, rather less wholly transported to the depths of Being, finally lifted his blue peepers and said to us,

"We shall have to go into more detail, Madame, concerning what your spouse has just elucidated. I also have certain connections to Switzerland, though not to your vaunted citadel of humanism. My mother was a von Tscharner. Because if this misalliance, some of the Martersteig aunts broke off relations with my late father, whereas on the other hand, the Tscharners regard our own family as inferior. Are you by any chance familiar with the Bern dynasty of that name?"

Fortunately, Beatrice wasn't. I myself got the name confused with that of an obscure philosopher, von Tschirnhausen, and this earned me a pitying glance from the Captain. But then we were served black coffee, and so this gap in my education was passed over. We sipped our coffee on an open loggia, where we were further able to determine that a certain Viennese dignitary named Martersteig, whose guest lectures I had listened to at the Cologne Institute for Theater History, was unrelated to our new acquaintance, although quite well known to La Gerstenberg.

Friedrich had another dramatic scene with his theatrical mother, and it was interpreted for us by the Captain. Friedrich, he explained, was still tied to the apron strings, but only during the daytime. At night he was in the habit of leaving his own mother aside and harking back to the Primeval Mother, whom he located with Emmerich's help in certain houses frequented by our bookseller. First there would be a game of chess at the "Alhambra," an activity that was in no way deleterious to Friedel's health. But from there he would proceed to an end game with some queen or other, and this was young Ginsterberg's undoing. Then the Captain made a discreet reference to Don Helvecio, alias Zwingli—surely we were following his drift? The Viennese Court Actress was a stunned woman when Friedrich finally picked up his briefcase, and, saying "Good night all," left the scene. Martersteig, too, excused himself to continue writing his Army of the Monkeys. He had just arrived at the passage where the German High Command was conducting maneuvers with the freshly drilled simian recruits—in the Teutoburg Forest, no less. "Kiss your hand" to the ladies, "My good neighbor" to Don Vigoleis, a stiff bow of the kind that was costing General von Hindenburg twenty pesetas a day, and then Baron Manfred von Richthofen's comrade of the clouds shuffled off to do his patriotic duty.

"I don't know which of those two young men is to be pitied more," said La Gerstenberg after a pause. We led her to her favorite place in the shadow of the painted castellan. There, without rocking, she tried to digest what she had heard and what she had eaten. The latter task she could accomplish only with the aid of a medication that Doña Inés had already given her.

"I'm not sure which of them I should feel sorrier for, my Friedrich or Martersteig. They are both on death's door. With his Prussian discipline the Captain will no doubt outlive my son. Friedel is dying of women. Back in Germany it was bad enough, but now Spain is giving him the final thrust. My ex-husband is insisting that he return home, but we don't want him to. In Germany the mob is rising up, and Chancellor Brüning is trying to keep them down by making them wear white shirts instead of brown ones. I'm scared, my dears. I fear for us all."

Our conversation got entangled in politics. I have already mentioned that the old lady had been a success on those other boards that represent the world. Great statesmen and diplomats had paid homage to her. Poets and musicians had frequented her Vienna residence, among them some of the most prominent names of their time: Schnitzler, Hofmannsthal, Richard Strauss, Harry Kessler—anyone could add to the list without fear of committing a mistake. She was familiar with our escapades in the Street of Solitude, but it had not yet come to her attention that the Don Helvecio of the Príncipe was one and the same as our Zwingli. She had lived for several months in his hotel, before the manager abducted his slut. She compared Zwingli's current situation with that of her son, who likewise no longer took regular baths.

At midnight we retired to our room, which was situated next to the Captain's. He was still performing military drill, earsplittingly, on his Orga-Privat typewriter. Friedrich claimed that Martersteig depended on the noise of his machine to drown out the howling of his monkeys—a redoubled clamor of battle, as it were. When the pendulum clock in the corridor struck twelve, his typing ceased. At the final gong, Martersteig picked up the black oilcloth and covered his monkey factory. He was of the opinion that here in Spain the prohibition of nocturnal disturbance of the peace took effect at precisely this hour, and so he now gave his troops the horn signal "Disperse!" and his macaques scrambled out of file. The Captain himself lay his stiff limbs on his bed and dreamt of the attractive boys he could no longer afford on his skimpy war-invalid's pension. His epoch of glory lay far in the past. Only once in a lifetime can one be a corporal in the military academy and the commandant's favorite. Baron Joachim von Martersteig, German Airforce Captain Ret., who had left Baron von Richthofen's fighter squadron at 15,000 feet and fluttered down into enemy lines, was homosexual, just like the long-tailed comrades of his imaginary army. It was a venerable Prussian tradition, but one that, as Don Joaquín, he had to forswear here in Spain. Once again it was the fault of Paul von Hindenburg, German Army General Ret., who as President of the Reich proved to be just as wooden as the gigantic idolatrous statue of him into which we wartime German kids had the privilege of pounding symbolic nails in the war bond effort. Like a beast entering the slaughterhouse, this martial colossus was marked off in zones bearing various prices. Since my father couldn't afford a golden nail, I was assigned an inferior portion of the General's anatomy to drive my threepenny spike into. I was mortified. The biblical Golden Calf was more to my liking.

In Martersteig's universal conscription for his pan-German monkey army, Beppo had as yet been spared. Thus it came to pass that this immoral Javanese simian once again started shaking his ritual clapper, this time at the crack of dawn, which in Spain is the veritable witching hour. He held on by all fours to the window latticework and drummed us out of our sleep. When I opened the shutter, the little devil lurched up to his lair with a hoarse bark, this time spraying down a foul-smelling liquid that I was barely able to dodge away from. Instead, I got hit on the shoulder by a pebble. I decided to close the shutters again.

"Throw some water at him!" Beatrice called from the bed, "They don't like that!" She had taken note of the new offensive tactics practiced by the Count's favorite pet, this plague upon his boarding-house guests, and she now believed that her cure-all against whores and cats would be equally effective in the battle again monkeys. But Beppo belonged to a race of Javanese simians that is not at all hydrophobic, and thus aren't fazed by a few spurts of water. Perhaps we could get some advice from Martersteig, who was so far along in sounding the psyche of his substitute draftees that he was threatening to turn into one of the four-footed mercenaries of his own all-German horde of the future. It wouldn't be the first time that an author identified with his protagonists right down to the bone. When we broached the subject at breakfast, our master tactician told us that there was only one reliable weapon against Beppo's shameless insults and exhibitionistic pranks: poison! As long as that monkey kept up his gymnastic tricks, we would be on the defensive. This was the very reason why he, Martersteig, Airforce Captain Ret., had the intention of sub-

mitting to the Reich heads of state his plan, in the form of a novel, to muster
an army of monkeys. If his idea could be accepted, then there would never
again be a Marne disgrace, never again a Compiègne, never again a deserting
Kaiser. Unfortunately, General Schleicher had not yet given him the opportunity to present his scheme for reform of the military...

But all this, he said, was causing him to digress from our urgent problem.
He advised us that since poison might also harm Beppo's master and benefactor, we should move to one of the windowless rooms on the building's
courtyard side, perhaps switching lodgings with Fräulein Höchst, the bovine
Valkyrie who occupied one of these. Such quarters were, he admitted, unhealthy. But they were conducive to meditation, and thus more beneficial for
mental hygiene. He, too, was living here in a form of retreat from the world;
for him, never again a room with a window, and most definitely not one with
a window on the street, which after dark turns into a staging area for the lowest classes, who arrive on hot nights with mattresses and marital squabbles
coram publico.

Don Alonso was convinced that in just a short time we would get used to
Beppo's style of blowing reveille. Just pay no attention to the little chap, he
said, and he would leave us alone and pick out some other targets. In fact, the
animal did just that: he targeted an irritable old couple, a Spaniard and his
French wife, who lived in constant warfare with each other, and now were
joined by Beppo as a crafty co-belligerent. No one could tell why the monkey
sometimes went to the aid of Madame and at other times gave Monsieur his
support. The gymnast from Dresden couldn't afford the higher rent, and so
we exchanged rooms with this disputatious couple, who in the process of moving were able to keep the peace for a full twenty-four hours. Then their skir-
mishing started anew. As much as I despise marital strife, I'll have to admit
that this pair raised spatting to new levels of sophistication. Beppo now indulged in a period of egregious misbehavior, shaming himself as well as all of
us boarders. The Inca bird, too, had a field day. And so did we, for our new
mystical chamber was about half the price of our previous larger quarters with
the musical shutters.

Half the price: "Beatrice, this will make a difference in our finances. We're
not yet exactly in abject penury, but if we start imagining abject penury in real
terms, for example, as a gutter, then I have no doubt that we'll be lying in it
before long. Our pesetas are shrinking, my manuscripts are getting sent back
to me, and we haven't heard a word from the movie people in Berlin."

No, the lords of the silver screen weren't interested in me. Why was this so?
The originator of this promising venture, a resident of Amsterdam, the novelist, poet, essayist and playwright Victor Emmanuel van Vriesland, wasn't
writing to me either. He had published an important novel that the folks in
Berlin wanted to turn into a film. They had a nose for money and fame, and
both were to be had with Vriesland's book. Vigoleis had translated it, and my
German version was to serve as the basis for a screenplay. The title was *Goodbye to the World in Three Days*, but it turned out to be farewell forever. A

film star had told the writer that it would make a sensational movie. This middleman was actually a very beautiful woman; it was she who drew up the contract. Beauty and the cinema: the most natural match in the world. My manuscript had wandered off to Berlin, where it lay dormant. Where the beautiful woman now lay, I had no idea, but I supposed it was in Amsterdam—a good reason for the creator of the *Urtext* to cloak himself in silence. Recumbent women require loving care—who would ever take umbrage at such a thing? Or take notice of Vigoleis?

The world had forgotten him, just as he might have forgotten the girl Pilar and her eponymous erotic bedstead, if the loose-talking cockatoo didn't remind him of her daily with a word of two syllables. Meanwhile, Beppo had been deprived of his freedom by being put on the chain. He could still shake things, but his pilfering days were over. The English matron had a new wig, and with gentle colors and lines she resumed painting the courtyard fountain, which, at least on canvas, did not dry up. The art-supply salesman and his woman left the scene. Fräulein Höchst gave indications that she had the same thing in mind, but then, because of an injured foot she had to stay on a week longer. Pepe was kicked out amid circumstances that I have already sketched out. Friedrich remained his mother's daily and nightly concern, the increasingly enfeebled pageboy to a flighty queen introduced to him by Mr. Emmerich. Captain von Martersteig was back in Deyá, where his enemy was apparently willing to temper justice with mercy. His room was now occupied by a Catholic priest in civilian garb who was busy negotiating a very complicated probate matter for a mainland religious order. His interest in the female sex was considerable, as was his thirst for wine and free-thinking philosophy. I enjoyed chatting with this erudite man of God. La Gerstenberg became more and more friendly toward Beatrice and me, and in turn, we became more and more fond of her. The half-blind Count went on peeling potatoes, Josefa puffed away at her shag and let the smoke waft merrily from her bosom, evoking our veneration like an ambulatory liturgical thurifer.

And thus things went on, day by day. I read a good deal of Spanish, especially the Old Testament, because that is a book I love and because one can learn to read a foreign language most conveniently with a familiar text. We heard and saw nothing of Zwingli. As if by special agreement, the twin stars Gerstenberg-Ginsterberg never mentioned his name again, and of course our arch-coquette was likewise forgotten completely. Once in a while Julietta crossed our path when we went to the post office or to Emmerich's to buy newspapers and thumb through books by the two writers who represented German literature on the island. Every now and then the bookseller asked me hesitantly when my own name would start drawing customers to his shop. "May I help you?" "Oh yes, do you have the latest by Vigoleis? Simply fantastic! He's all anyone is talking about. What? Are you living on the moon? What else in God's name is a German supposed to read on this island?"

To me it is an exciting idea to be a writer whose works get read, particularly when you hear racy things about yourself when eavesdropping in houses or when, in a bookstore, you observe how your books get snapped up like hot-cakes. Back in Cologne I often visited a tiny shop where Max Scheler liked to browse. The famed philosopher was the main attraction in this establishment, making his appearance sewn and bound on the shelves, and, very much un-bound, standing at the counter with his round metaphysical head lifted from the pages of a book and gazing off with almost animal-like despair, into the void. Otto Dix has captured much of this posture in his frightening portrait of the man, and that is how Scheler lives on in my memory. At his lectures I was so disenchanted with his bald pate, plus the incomprehensibility of his expla-nations, that I soon joined those who helped to thin out the student ranks. By skipping what he said and sticking to what he wrote, I got what I wanted.

At any rate, in this bookshop nobody was asking for Vigoleis' latest, for the simple reason that his latest hadn't yet been authored. It was yet to be born, and in order to be born it would have to gestate a while, and in order to ges-tate, it had to be conceived. The author had come to the island with this pur-pose in mind. There he wandered about in double role beneath the glowing sun, no longer the target of a floozy's anger, no longer Zwingli's object of pitying indifference, no longer Julietta's steamy predator.

No, no one inquired as to Vigoleis' newest book, just as no one ever inquires about the heroic feats of a child unborn. Let us, then, begin a new chapter, one that will give us some glimpses of new light. Frankly, we had expected more at the anarchist Count's boarding house: at the very least a palace re-bellion, with a broken window pane and a hysterical English matron, deciding she would rather live on her own home island with no sun, no oranges to be savored fresh from the tree, and no daily anxiety about the ups and downs of the exchange rate of the peseta.

III

Small causes can often have large effects. Smaller causes can have even bigger effects, and the very biggest effects frequently have no cause at all. Witness, for example, the world. It was created out of nothing, and that has made it the worst calamity the world has ever seen.

Nothing was happening. And because nothing was happening, Vigoleis' and Beatrice's frequent personal financial audits caused us to scowl with increasing concern. Our worry reached a climax the day we were notified of an empty bank account. When such things happen to a business firm, the distinguished gentlemen rub their hands and begin calculating with rapid pen strokes how much the swindle has netted them. A field general spits on his saber, oblivious to how many corpses his day of defeat has cost him. A stoic, assuming that such persons can ever go broke, continues twiddling his thumbs. Because we belonged to none of the above-mentioned types, we would be forced to find another solution to our life-threatening predicament.

Beatrice found it. We decided to keep our room for the time being, just as a roof over our heads, but to renounce all in-house meals except breakfast, which, here too, consisted of café au lait with *ensaimadas*. By means of this drastic cutback, we could go on for a time, but then...? Then the island would sink into the sea.

Out of a false sense of shame, a vestige of our bourgeois mentality, we refrained from informing our fellow boarders about our straitened circumstances. It left us cold to know that people were pointing their fingers at us on account of a doxy's wrath, but we were genuinely ashamed of not being able to pay our bills. We were shameful paupers. If one last, urgent telegram to the movie people met with no success, perhaps we would hang ourselves. Did I just say "perhaps"? Always a Johnny-on-the-spot when it came to quick decisions, it was I who suggested this solution. But Beatrice considered suicide ridiculous and cowardly, and besides, hanging was un-aesthetic; she would leave that to Teamster Henschel in Gerhart Hauptmann's play and similar literary proletarians. If she were ever to do away with herself, she would emulate Sappho, who, still strumming her lute, dove from the Leucadian Cliff into the sea. To this I readily replied that to maintain such artistic standards, we would have to rent a larger wheelbarrow, or better yet a donkey cart, to carry our musical instrument (so thoughtfully disassembled by Pilar) out to one of the promontories to be found everywhere on the island—out at Ca's Català or Porto Pí for example—any travel agency would gladly provide directions. For my part, I would take along my little typewriter, or perhaps my somewhat more portable Parker Duofold pen, which could symbolize my muse with no difficulty at all. And anyway, the ocean probably didn't give one damn what I took along with me to its depths.

By the time Vigoleis had this vigorous discussion with Beatrice, he had long since given up on Schopenhauer. He accused him of betraying his own great creation, a philosophy that in its negativity far outstripped Christianity, by lapsing in his later years into pseudo-mysticism and a stuffy, academic doctrine of individual salvation. At the moment, he was in search of a substitute for this German apostate, and had reason to believe he had found one in a dyed-in-the-wool Spanish mystic. He was resolved literally to delve into this new friend, sound out his meaning, and with every deciphered line to cover up the lie he was himself living, to wit: that he lacked the courage to do damage to his pitiful carcass by his own hand, and was thus under sentence of looking forward to a normal demise somewhere on a bed of straw. What he overlooked, however, was the fact that in the proverbial light of eternity he had much too high a regard for his own taedium vitae—for which, incidentally, he had adopted forms of play-acting that were so amusing to others that they refused to take his despair at all seriously. Such a reaction is doubly painful until one learns to ignore it. Vigoleis ought to have offered proof of his chronic melancholy by putting a noose around his neck, a bullet through his head, or a stiletto into his aorta—to name just a few of the proven household methods. Besides, he possessed dexterity and practical inventiveness far beyond his domestic needs. Placed in the service of self-annihilation, these talents could promptly relieve him of the shock he experienced, morning after morning, at his continued existence among the living, together with his first personality, and in addition to his second.

Pessimists are often the greatest optimists. Year after year, Vigoleis closed his eyes each night with the incontrovertible certainty that this would be the last night of a life he never would have accepted in the first place—if the mysterious procedure for placing orders had allowed him to do so. Thrice already, this devious fellow had tried to end things by his own well-formed, talented hand. But it was at the same time the hand of a seer of ghosts, or of a *Don Quixote*. His moment of departure was yet to come. Perhaps this island would provide an opportunity for a favorable leave-taking. But let us not forget what Vigoleis, once put to the test, is only barely willing to admit to himself, and what he is now trying to shroud in the mists of mysticism: at the sight of Pilar's dagger he ran like a rabbit. That is the time when he should have put into practice his death-wish. That is when he should have bared his body, which conceivably might already have shed most of its coverings in anticipation of a dramatic *Liebestod*. Citing his chronicler's phrase in double inverted commas, he ought to have cried, "Farewell my brothers! Aim for the heart! Stab away, Pilar, release me from this mortal coil!" Instead, he took French leave. Weekend equestrian of suicide that he was, his feet flopped out of the stirrups; at the end of a high trajectory, he landed in the bed of his own makeshift marriage.

It is events like this that should warn us to be on our guard with this fellow. We can't take his *Weltschmerz* seriously until a knife is sticking in his ribs, or until we find him, like the Englishwoman's scalp, hanging from Beppo's palm tree—to the delight of Mr. Beverwijn, whom I have rather lost sight of for the moment, simply because that man's wife is a vicious dragon whose poisonous breath I wish to stay clear of in memory and on paper.

For a week we roamed the city eating out of paper bags. At first we treated ourselves to bread, sausage, cheese, and lots of fruit. Then we cut out the less nourishing, merely filling varieties of forage, and finally we took the grape cure. In our initial enthusiasm, we were actually elated at this latter decision, but soon we had the unpleasant feeling of being vegetarians without subscribing to any philosophy of vegetarianism—an attitude not even worthy of a horse. I know some famous vegetarians who eat their meat on the sly, with no one the wiser. Such little acts of self-pollution contain more vitamins than all your vegetables put together. We felt sicker and sicker, but we didn't die. As for me, I was still far from wishing for the dish I loathed so intensely as a child, and whose alliterative designation makes me shudder even today: "carrot casserole." No, we would be having no such delicacy in the shadow of the Cathedral of Palma, but also no god-awful potatoes and no biblical bread, symbol of earthly penury ever since the first couple was cursed into eating it by the sweat of their brow.

We sat in the shadow of the Mirador with our vitamins. The ocean at our feet was of the incredible blue to be found in the Spanish National Tourist Board's glossy brochures. We spat our grape skins into the hot sand, each shot causing a tiny explosion—little dust clouds arose as if on a miniature battlefield. Our conversations dealt for the most part with prehistoric man, his nature and possessions, and I must confess that on virtually empty stomachs we came closer to ultimate truths than during all our gabfests at the anarchist table in the "intellectuals' corner."

Every once in a while the hunchback beggar gave us his company. Someone had told him of our difficulties, and now he offered us advice on getting by and reaching a ripe old age in Spain with no money. Beatrice usually moved one bench away, but the outcast didn't seem to mind. He was, he said, probably just a trace too bug-ridden for her, but that was simply part and parcel of his earthly sojourn, loved and sanctioned by the Dear Lord. He had stretched out his hand for alms in many countries, but nowhere were people so generous as in Spain. Not even at the portal of St. Peter's in Rome did the blessings flow as copiously. I admired the crooked little man's broad culture, which he couldn't possibly have gathered in piece by piece as with his income from charitable sources. But I was unsuccessful in prying into his past life; he deflected all my inquiries in that direction. Some people thought he was a defrocked priest, or a monk escaped from a mendicant order. Both surmises can lead to further surmises: let's imagine this high-shouldered fellow going into business for himself, placing an ad in the diocesan newspaper: "I hereby notify all devout charitable donors that, upon completion of thorough schooling in the exercise of the vow of poverty, and following faithful execution of the humble beggar's calling under auspices of the Mendicant Order of St. Francis (certified by the Holy See since 1210), I have now placed myself on my own two bare feet. Whoever wishes to demonstrate mercy toward his neighbor may now do so toward me! Eliminate the middleman! Bigger indulgences! On request, mediation with the Devil himself! *Man spricht deutsch*. On *parle français*, etc. Praise be to the Lord Jesus! Porfirio, Beggar of Strictest Observance."

Every time Porfirio returned to the cathedral portal after a brief chat, I had to slap and shake the fleas out of my clothes. We had sworn off insect powder as a superfluous luxury. Beatrice didn't want anything to do with this man whom God had stricken with a hump on his back. But I kept trying to serve as advocate for this Beggar Prince who now, after twenty years, was repaying my intercession by helping me to liven up my narrative at a point when, following the anarchistic count's failure, nothing else was going on.

With a single brush stroke I shall now depict this Minorite's earthly demise. On a certain day he was found dead, lying on a heap of rags in his room. The coroner determined that he had perished of starvation. But during the post mortem, the doctor also made the surprising discovery that the man's hunchback was artificial, a kind of leather rucksack that could be fastened on with a strap. Inside there were banknotes, stock certificates, and promissory notes from many different countries, having a combined value in the millions of pesetas. Papers in his possession revealed that he was a German citizen, whereupon the German Consul instantly confiscated all his belongings, attaching the estate before the Spanish authorities could say a word in their own interest. As usual, the latter bureaucrats were tardy, but they were eventually able to push aside the peremptory German executor. Seeing that no heirs came forward, they raked in millions for themselves.

There was said to be a bundle of manuscript pages in his fake hunchback as well, notes written down by this bogus beggar, whose lame leg was likewise of the removable kind. I was very interested in getting a look at those notes, as was the writer George Bernanos. But nobody got hold of them. The case was the subject of lively discussion in the island's literary circles. Each one of us contributed in no small measure to the legend that now began to be woven around this shabby millionaire in his moth-eaten duds. Was he a priest? A monk? Later another beggar turned up, one with a genuine hunchback, to which he pinned a medical certificate verifying its authenticity. But just as birds will peck at vomit, this guy's colleagues lit into the cripple and banished him from the sacred portal.

I may have contributed a total of five pesetas to the millions in Porfirio's leather sack. As you can see, he has stretched out the thread of my tale to a point where a simple reach into his hump could have sufficed to save us from our grape cure. But then I could write *finis operis* and "happy ending" at the close of this very chapter. The fact is that, on my isle of second sight, one seldom looked in the right drawer. For this reason, Vigoleis cannot yet fade away among the nameless thousands for whom Mallorca serves as a world-renowned source of official stamps on picture postcards, sent to loved ones back home.

IV

In the final chapter of Book One I stated that a certain day began like all other days, but I failed to mention that it would end like no other day before it. I could make the same assertion here at the opening of this chapter, which also will bring a Book to its close. But I shall refrain from doing so to avoid repeating myself. This day, too, began like all others and ended like none before.

As on every morning, we took breakfast in the *pensión*, this time in the company of two artists from the mainland, about whom more in due course. I consider the two of us more important, at a moment when our straits are so dire that our existence could be regarded as an utter failure. Our harmonious closet-marriage was able to withstand the temptations of the outlandish *pilarière*; now it was being put to a financial test, one that I called the "duro test" after the five-peseta coin of that name. The word *duro* means "hard, tough, heavy, difficult"; it can also mean "cruel" or even "heartless." We could already see ourselves as artists' models, assisting in the creation of an eternal monument to our doom: Vigoleis sketched by the jittery brush of the half-blind count, once again putting away his potato peeler for a while in the interest of art, with the intention of crucifying our hero on his easel as a boozer or a Teamster Henschel, as in Hauptmann's famous play. And he would depict Beatrice, larger than life in Sappho's diaphanous robes, painted in oil on a charcoal ground by an even more famous practitioner of genre painting. I have in mind no less a master than Baron Antonio Jean Gros, whose *Sappho*, by a macabre coincidence, resembles Beatrice. The fact that he sought and found his death in the Seine can only recommend him more warmly for our purposes.

On the morning in question, I saw the connection quite clearly. We went to the post office—no money—and then we started our climb to the cathedral, each of us holding a book and a single grape. On the way we ran into our waiter Antonio—"*olá!*" How were we, he asked, and were we still living at the palace anarchist's? Yes, but how much longer, we really couldn't say. Antonio asked some more; his sympathy with our plight was genuine. He felt somewhat responsible, for—and now came a confession—he had intended to send word to Beatrice in Basel that Don Helvecio was not mortally ill but just getting bored with a *querida*. But Antonio's wife had persuaded him not to get mixed up in other people's business. Now he regretted this omission. We explained our situation to him in graphic detail. Oh my, he commented, we must be able to get help somewhere, *caramba*! This just couldn't go on, just let him take care of things! First of all, it was a luxury to be staying on at the *pensión* with that newfangled revolutionary. He knew of a cheaper shelter outside the city, in some ways just the proper place, though in other ways not, but one couldn't afford to be choosy when one's money-bag can't hold its seam. He was friends with the owner, and would even vouch for us on the matter of rent. Then he would ask around in his club whether anyone had a daughter eager to be taught a language—French, English, Italian, maybe even German—"just be patient, my friends, and don't make any hasty moves!" With a handshake we promised this fine gentleman not to do anything that might obstruct, let alone foil, his plans. We should get our things ready. Around seven or eight he would come to the *pensión*. If we were lucky, we could on this very day blow the fanfare for the great removal. Antonio smiled with his thin lips, which he was able to press together in a straight line, causing even the most grandly titled of club members to cower in respect.

On this day we did not finish our climb to the cathedral, nor did we go to the ocean, or visit the bookshop where I was in the habit of flipping through newspapers, and where Beatrice took over for the owner like a born salesgirl. Our everyday routine was thoroughly disrupted. Even the vegetarian touch was spoiled by an invitation from Madame Gerstenberg to a sausage snack in her room. For the thousandth time in her life Beatrice packed luggage; you would have to witness her technique first-hand in order to appreciate it in all its intelligence and meticulousness. Word had got around that the Indian woman and her Teutonic chieftain were moving out, destination unknown.

At eight o'clock everything was ready for departure. Luckily, crates of books from Germany, Holland, and Switzerland hadn't yet arrived. We had sent them to our first island address at a moment when we had reason to think we would be staying on at least a year in Palma, or if it wasn't to be on Mallorca, then on the Spanish mainland. I had no desire to return to Germany. I had left my homeland without shedding a single tear. Whatever German heritage I still carried around with me, except for the language, found its place in a few boxes of books. A few years were to pass before I could take to heart Heine's words, "When I think of Germany in the night, I find I cannot sleep aright." At the moment I was being robbed of sleep by other demons. For me, the present was still mightier than the past.

Antonio arrived with startling punctuality, smiling, smoking, polite, generous. He brought along a quaint and colorful Little Helper, laconic in the language of his broader nationality, but vociferous in the island dialect. Antonio had found us a shelter, out there at that certain friend's place outside the city on the road to Valldemosa. While the *almocrebe* carried our luggage to the inner court-yard where the animals were tethered, we said goodbye to a few people we had got to like. Madame Gerstenberg became emotional; you could see it in her glis-tening eyes. She had prophetic vision not only concerning world politics and her son Friedrich—our departure toward an uncertain future didn't please her at all. "No, dear friends, I have evil premonitions!" Her voice shook. Beatrice had told Madame her exotic mother's life story, including the inevitable ship-wreck on the reefs of the ck—dt clan. She now saw in our exodus from the an-archistic Palace of Peace, behind mules that carried our belongings—not exactly in night and fog, but still suspicious in all its accompanying circumstances—, our doleful actress friend saw in this event a sequel to the Swiss curse once issued by that petty, hyper-religious underworld that doesn't shrink from employing God Himself for the work of the Devil. Friedrich, who knew every detail about our getting bounced out of the God-fearing hooker's house, stated the opinion that after leaving this other place, things were actually looking up for us.

"Children, I'm so sorry for you!" cried Madame Gerstenberg when Antonio gave us the sign to start walking behind the pack animals. "When I see your miserable lot, I can almost forget my own. Vigoleis, what would your mother say if she could see you moving out like this?"

"My mother would not believe her eyes, even if she were standing next to us here on the stairs! My mother's son walking behind jackasses, out into the dreary night! No, she would think it's a phantom vision, a nightmare, a hor-rible joke. Fortunately, a mother's eyes are blind, for otherwise many a mother's eyes would close from grief long before their time."

"Just don't get sentimental!" said Friedrich, who feared that an emotional scene like this could jeopardize his own departure at half past ten. "These two are lucky. They have no idea yet what's ahead for them. In my own case, grop-ing around in the dark was over long ago."

Adele Gerstenberg asked us to come back to her whenever we were hungry. Yes, she had a way of hitting the nail on the head. Of the two of them, though,

Friedrich had the sharper mind for matters of daily living. Accordingly, he suggested to his Mama that we should arrange a particular day of every week when she could provide us with fodder, for otherwise we just wouldn't come. Since she wanted to read us her play anyway, he told us, this would provide a literary excuse for our sausage picnics. "So let's say you should drop by next..."

Madame Gerstenberg a writer too? Here at her very door, as we stood on her threshold, and as a farewell greeting, we were given this astounding revelation. All of a sudden the objectionable little word "too" took on special meaning. Our thespian-dramatist looked at us with disappointment, as if we had caught her doing something naughty. She murmured an apology, not on account of her writing, but because she had kept it a secret. Now this awful Friedrich, she added, he was always so gabby, an *enfant terrible*, it was enough to give his poor mother constant stage fright. And anyway, for the writing of her historical drama about Elizabeth and Essex, she was drawing heavily on her long experience on the stage, and besides, her writing didn't disturb anybody, she did it at night, by candlelight and with a pen...a tragic figure. I was amazed to find such an attitude in this highly intelligent and talented woman. It was most definitely unnecessary for her to imitate some pianist and compose a display piece for her own artistic dexterity. After all, her career was over. I recalled what Brentano had written in his "Story of Honest Caspar and Fair Annie" about writers and their secretiveness: they should admit their calling to all the world. What nonsense: poetry considered as a kind of monstrous goose liver, which of course presupposes a freakish, sick goose! This was emphatically not the case with the dramatist Gerstenberg, "for you see, Madame, art has significance as an illness only if it manifests itself in individual cases. If there were ever an epidemic of it, we would all have to flee. The individual case and quarantine..."

Vigoleis was unable to develop his topic further. Antonio was getting impatient and urged us to get going. Herr von Martersteig, who happened to be in the city, had joined us without saying a word, his crooked spine attempting to maintain the ramrod pose that was just as unconvincing as the pension awarded him by the Reich government that had made him a cripple. Count, countess, and count-in-law were also on hand, and even the cadre of well-bonded servants stood by at attention. We took leave of each and all with dignified, restrained camaraderie. Our farewells were unsullied by any thought of offering tips. Our blue-blooded bomb-thrower offered me his studio for practicing my construction hobby. Doña Inés assured us that her home was ours too. And Josefa, who in the rush had forgotten to hide her pipe in her bosom, reminded us that we were all in the hands of the Triune God. Beppo was on his chain, so we didn't have to fear any surprises from his palm tree. And the cockatoo chattered away in his usual winning way, since one couldn't put a chain on his tongue. Dear Lorico, with his interminable squawking about *porra* and *puta*—how could we have guessed that he was uttering prophecies, and not making snide remarks about our past experiences on the Street of Solitude?

Our exchequer had shrunk to the above-named amount, one quite easy to remember: one silver duro, a coin that can be easily forged by any halfway clever Spanish counterfeiter. The one we owned, minted in such-and-such a year, was genuine enough. If it had been fake, I would be careful not to mention that here, so as not to add poor taste to our poor fortune.

I am trying not to flavor my chronicle with "local color" by tossing in an excess of Spanish vocabulary. The use of such exotic spices would be a cheap way of hispanizing my narrative. A reader who lacks command of the language will get nothing out of such condiments; on the contrary, the recipe could irritate him, just as I am irritated by authors who write dialect. Someone who, on the other hand, is familiar with the country, its inhabitants, and the language they speak, will already know how a given event will have happened in its original setting. I am of course in no position to judge whether I will be successful at recounting Vigoleis' adventures from memory, in a way that will strike my reader as sufficiently Spanish in taste. I trust, though, that the reader will forgive me for using the little word *almocrebe*—for one thing, because the context clearly shows that it designates a donkey-driver, for another and more importantly, because the word derives from the Arabic, where it means "mule-driver." *almokerí*: I delight in this word all the more because I don't know any Arabic. I'm using it now as a talisman to put myself back in the fairy-tale mood I was in as we set out on our journey behind crossbreed quadrupeds. By the way, only two of the four animals carried loads; our worldly possessions, packed in large baskets made of coarsely woven palm fronds, hung from each saddle almost to the ground. The lead jackass bore the more enormous burden, followed at regular intervals by the others, each attached to the one in front by a rope. This procession automatically puts me in mind of the Arabian fantasy world. Ali Baba and the Forty Thieves could serve as an analogy since we, too, were heading toward a robbers' den.

But I'm getting ahead of the nomadic pace of the animals, which is to say, the proper sequence of events. Antonio hadn't said a single word about where we were going. Well, yes, past the city gates to a friend's place—but this hush-hush destination was all we learned for the moment. Rather than ask indiscreet questions, we simply let our fate hang in the palm-frond baskets. We were demoralized, and preferred to wait on whatever surprises the future had in store. We didn't even ask each other where this man was taking us. Questions like that would only reveal a lack of trust in the fellow who had rescued us and was now our guide. So we trudged along submissively at the rear of the caravan, which left San Felio Street to turn into Borne Boulevard, followed the latter straight along, then down San Jaime past moribund palaces, farther past Santa Madalena into Olmos Street, whose elms had long since succumbed to the pestilence. Then we reached a part of town that got more and more unfamiliar to both of us. On our starvation treks we had never gone beyond the bullfight arena and the railroad station square. We left the city limits behind us and followed a road lined with almond trees, tree after tree in full blossom—in this season of the year? And without their narcotic fragrance? We already were familiar with this phenomenon, this fakery of nature that requires you to exercise your imagination a little in the opposite direction— or mobilize Beppo the tree-shaking monkey—in order to return the trees to botanical reality. This road, Antonio told us, led to Sóller, about 20 miles through fields of red earth and past eroded farms, the *fincas*. Martersteig had told us this and that about the little town of that name. Valldemosa, higher up in the hills, we knew from world literature. Our pack animals (I don't know whether they were donkeys or mules; I can't keep the hybrids apart) apparently knew exactly where they were supposed to lug our belongings, for the *almocrebe* had joined us at the rear and was discussing politics with Antonio.

Monarchist anarchy had given way to Republican anarchy. The latter was only a few months old in Spain, and therefore still gave rise to the fondest hopes, whose realization was being championed by the conspirators in the seven-daughtered Count's powder room, a cause that must be fought for by every last person, without exception, that is, by anyone who has an iota of pride in being a Spaniard. Now it would be possible to toss bombs on weekdays too. Think of it: every day of the week a holiday, even for the workers! "If you're planning on staying with us for a while," Antonio told us, "you'll have to start throwing bombs too. Now you know where you can get them." At a Saharan pace, we anarchists, who hadn't ever thrown anything more explosive than water, took up the rear of this romantic hegira. How I would have liked to mount one of the burden-free animals! But I didn't dare to for Beatrice's sake, who suspected that there were more fleas in those gaudy saddle blankets than in the jacket of our backpacking holy man Porfirio. As *Wigalois, chevalier à la roue*, it would be more fitting for me to ride to our new castle than to plod toward it through the dust. A castle? Another castle? I had no idea what was up ahead, but here on the road to Sóller we were, at the moment, on a pilgrimage toward a dreadful stench, possibly a mass grave. It reeked of corpses and carrion. Where were the enchanting fragrances of my Araby?

"The slaughterhouse," said Antonio. "The wind is blowing the wrong way, from the Sierra del Teix. That's unusual. You won't have this pestilence every day."

With five pesetas in your purse, I thought, there's not much hope of fighting a wind from any direction. I glanced anxiously at Beatrice, who was once again getting green around the gills, just as at the meat market. When you set out on a trip, I told her, you just have to expect certain minor inconveniences; back home anyone can seal himself off hermetically—an argument Beatrice refused to buy. "Fine," she said to our guide, "but how much longer until we get past the stink zone?"

"A quarter of an hour," he replied, rolling another cigarette, thin as a goose quill, probably his hundredth of the day. Our *almocrebe* was smoking a clay pipe. The road was still dusty. Not a soul to be seen far and wide. Not only did it smell here of finality and decomposition, the world itself seemed to end at this spot. For a while we hoofed it through the very twilight of doomsday, but then the animals quickened their gait, the ropes between them stretched tight, and each donkey seemed to urge haste and pull the others along. Yet the sudden excitement proved too much: a suitcase slipped out of its girth and crashed to the ground. We stood around in a cloud of dust inspecting the damage. The *almocrebe* swore at the beasts; I thought he did them a grave injustice, for the entire procession had come to a halt, and the animal waited patiently for the suitcase to be cinched back in place. Then with a *heya*! they started out so fast that we couldn't keep up. They've got the scent of their stable, the driver told us. There was nothing holding them now. I wanted to reply that if that were so, we should be all the more grateful to them for stopping while our suitcase was picked up and refastened. But I said nothing, feeling that I wasn't quite up to this particular Arab.

The clatter of hoofs died away, and when the dust cloud cleared we saw nothing more of our quadriga. Ravens were squatting in the olive trees, and some eagles circled overhead, made ravenous by the stench we still had in our nostrils. Up ahead we now saw a large settlement, consisting of various structures built up against or inside of each other, the whole complex dominated by a tower. It wasn't a castle, nor was it a fortress. But it wasn't an ordinary residence either, or any Balearic *finca* of the kind I had already seen. Whatever it was, the first word that entered my mind was "romantic." Add a fiddle, take Beatrice on my arm, sing a little song about God favoring us by sending us out into the wide, wide world to the gates of this human habitation—and I was Eichendorff's *Ne'er-Do-Well* all over again. It was indeed "far, far away," but could this hostelry possibly be meant for us? With five pesetas and a hotel waiter's verbal voucher, it's hardly likely that we could find refuge in such an inviting shelter.

I looked around for a separate cottage, but didn't see any. "Tired?" Antonio asked, then pointed to the tower, bent his head to one side and put his cheek in his hand, mimicking sleep. So it was true! We were at our destination, Antonio was a saint and master magician, and for once God appeared to have taken sides with the poor in spirit. And so I sang His praises with the words, "And were I to perish in this dungeon, I shall return like the phoenix!—Beatrice, we've finally got the long end of the stick for once! And it doesn't smell so bad here."

But that was a bonafide olfactory illusion. Beatrice had just enough time to voice her annoyance at my constantly referring to a God I didn't believe in, and not only metaphorically at that, when a man strode toward us, tall and handsome, like so many men on Mallorca. This one was colorful and picturesque in the extreme, so that my attention was diverted from God to one of his most magnificent creations, one that could earn Him respect even beyond Eternity. Not to mention our respect for Antonio, for the fellow approaching us with brilliant cries of "O, o, o!" barked out like little explosions from the back of his throat—this man was Antonio's friend, the Lord of the Manse, to assign a temporary title to the settlement we had arrived at.

The ceremony of mutual introductions was splendid. Our impression of this procedure's grandiose *courtoisie*, its transmundane sublimity, was heightened by the fact that no names were mentioned—just as at a meeting of kings, where everyone knows exactly how the crown fits. Antonio was no longer a hotel waiter, he was an ambassador at a foreign court. We were not vagabonds with a damaged valise, down to our very last fiver: just behold our cortege! Only titled guests would arrive in such panoply with steeds and knights; the dust on our garments and boots gives testimony to our long journey. Beatrice's sedan chair? A minor accident on the highway—what matter? "Now you are here, welcome to my abode. *Heya*, my good people, get on with it!" The warrior claps his hands, and the broad area where we are standing—half riding arena, half castle approach—is instantly filled with people of all ages and sexes. The crowd of welcomers begins with an infant in the arms of its dwarflike nurse. It includes tittering, awkward teenagers, rises to the more sedate adults, and culminates with the exalted, awe-inspiring, yet also pathetic figure of a white-haired matriarch. She approaches us, accompanied by yapping dogs, with the aid of a brightly polished, high-backed chair that she's using as a crutch. Twice she gives us a toothless "*Bona-nit*," the Mallorcan dialect form of "Good evening." Then the aged woman sits down on her improvised crutch, thus forming the natural center of this biblical tableau. Let us give her, again temporarily, the matriarchal name by which she actually was called: Na' Maguelida, the hundred-year-old. We foreign emissaries bow down before her.

The lord of the tribe was named Arsenio. I might have expected him to bear the title "Don" in keeping with Spanish custom for men of his standing. But he wasn't a count, either; he was just a Mallorcan. Arsenio dominated by his behavior and gestures: a few waves of the hand, and everyone quickly obeyed. Zwingli with his Magic Horn would go pale with envy. In action here at the settlement, he was even more impressive than his torso and limbs might already cause a passive observer to think possible. He looked down on my puny five-foot-ten dimensions from the height of his shoe length. His shoulders were made for putting under heavy pieces of furniture. In a railway switchyard in India he could substitute for a working elephant; in a circus he could assemble singlehanded the iron cages for the menagerie. I could add any number of similar comparisons, but what it all comes down to is this: Arsenio was a giant. And he laughed like a giant. In response to some remark by Antonio he shook with mirth in a way that made us shrink back just a little. But he was at the same time a gentle giant; he meant well for us. He was overcome with pleasure—you could read that in the enormous expanse of his face. Each wrinkle of laughter was a special welcome greeting, "*hahahahaha*, o, o, o, o!" and then he extended his hand toward me, fraternally, jovially. I gave him mine. His monstrous paw closed. We looked each other in the eye, man to man, and when the pressure abated, something bloodless fell downward and swung feebly at my pants seam. But I didn't cry out! Nor did I cry out when, a few years later, my hand entered a similarly vise-like claw, that belonging to the philosopher Hermann Keyserling. You endure such things every time they happen, and every time you are amazed that you've survived without a plaster cast.

I'm forced to admit, though, that I prefer such virile handclasps to the limp extremities some people extend to us, amorphous appendages that feel like some obscene object we aren't prepared to touch.

Beatrice was spared the vise. Our warrior-receptionist bowed down before her, which is to say, he inscribed an arc with his torso, downward and then up again. His right arm made a gesture of homage and hospitality; to make the courtly scene complete, we had to imagine that it held a hat bearing shimmering feathers. What a character for a cowboy movie! In America this guy could make a million, but he's probably not interested in playing a villain. He's content to live here on his estate amid his thriving populace, sans mustang and sans flecks of blood on vest and chaps. I estimated his age at about fifty.

Compared to this Anakite, the lady of the house must be called small. She was rotund, with a pretty face and the soft features one often sees in heavy-set mothers. She wore earrings made of precious gold. She parted her raven-black hair neatly in the middle; it shone like freshly poured asphalt. Like the matriarch she spoke only in the island dialect. Surrounding her were a number of girls—some gorgeous, some ugly—of various ages. All of them were giggling behind raised hands and skirt-hems, just like the adolescents back home. They whispered things to each other about us, whereupon Arsenio thundered at them to desist on the spot. His voice was so persuasive that even some of the dogs fled with their tails between their legs. "Get away now! Enough of this staring! Off to the hall! Go get some wine, sheep cheese, donkey curds, olives, butifarras, grapes, and paté for Madame! Right, Antonio? That's what our guests deserve, arriving here this evening after such a busy day. From Germany and Switzerland, you say? My, my, a goodly portion of the world is assembled here at the tables of our golden island!"

Arsenio, like two of his older sons, spoke in marvelous Castilian, though at times they lapsed into Mallorcan, especially now that our almocrebe had joined us for a drink. The wine was good, an island vintage. What am I saying? It was the house product of our movie villain, who bottled several hundred liters annually. Beatrice took part in the conversation in my stead. The talk was about trivial matters, but the Spaniards got excited nonetheless. Arsenio wanted to know what the "outside world" thought of the end of the monarchy. We couldn't tell him, because we had been too busy coping with our own decline and fall. No offense, and once again they talked about the weather. I was still unable to participate in any diplomatic pseudo-conversations, for my tongue would not obey, no matter how eagerly I might have wanted to contribute my profound thoughts about weather prognoses and the incompetence of every last forecaster, despite all their isobars and isobronts. The most I could add was a single speech-fragment that I tossed into the conversation, one that emerged as I let my thoughts hover around our own private weather forecast. In that realm the wind was still blowing from the direction of Armageddon—it was blowing the wrong way, Arsenio would say, and I would have to agree with him. To this very day, the wind refuses to blow as it should. The ravens are still squatting at the roadside, and the vultures are still circling in the air above.

This house, the proud landlord began in explanation, was known to everyone as the "Torre del Reloj," the Clock Tower, named after an iron rod ce-
mented at an angle into a wall and overgrown with grapevines. A century
before, this rod had been the indicator of a sundial; as a child, the matriarch
had read the passing hours on the tower wall. He, Arsenio, couldn't recall the
rusty metal pointer's horological function. Earlier the settlement was called
"Ca'n Costals," but the true original name, the Giant told us, had dropped
out of memory generations ago. As the place gradually deteriorated, local lore
preserved the quainter designation—oddly enough, for if the sun had continued to tell the hours on the wall, no one would have thought to substitute
"Clock Tower" for "Ca'n Costals." People, he said, often ignore what is right
in front of their eyes. But whether it was "Ca'n Costals" or "Torre del Reloj,"
he assured us that the house, in accordance with the ancient Spanish tradition
of hospitality, was now our house too.

My hobby, the creativity of decay! What a shame that my tongue was still
tied, preventing me from entering a discussion on the topic with an unprejudiced
mind, and adding a word or two about the sinfulness of God and the renewal
of the universe. In any event, at the time I had nowhere near the command of
the subject that I have today, after decades of work with the mystical writings
of Pascoaes. Even now, it's tempting to work out an imaginary conversation
between Vigoleis, the later discoverer, exegete, and translator of the Portuguese
savant, and Arsenio, the cocky part-time philosopher and man of the Spanish
people. To do so would not run counter to usual methods of writing personal
memoirs, as the selfsame Vigoleis would later observe when, as the personal
secretary of a memorialist of world stature, he got a peek into a workshop where
past events were not infrequently simply guessed at. Very instructive indeed;
Vigoleis was continually amazed at what he saw. Details will come to the fore
as soon as Count Harry Kessler gets his own chapter in my chronicle. For now
I would prefer not to stray from the Manse, since Antonio deserves a little more
attention as our savior. He interrupted the Giant politely—he would have to
leave: night duty on the club terrace, where meanwhile even the most habitual
of sleepers had awakened and would have to be kept alive until dawn and beyond with coffee, dominoes, and tales of womanizing.

And so he departed, leaving his two protégés in the care of Arsenio, who
could put hordes of enemies to flight with a single fist. We had no more worries, he declared, and *Bona-nit* ladies, *Bona-nit* gentlemen. As imperceptibly
as his lips pressed into a straight-line smile, he disappeared into the night.

But to what kind of devil's kitchen had he brought us? From what I have recounted up to now, my reader will not have made much sense of the place: The
"Clock Tower," a community of considerable size, neither castle nor fortress
nor even a normal house; a large number of people gathered in biblical solemnity around a matriarch and our solicitous host and benefactor Arsenio; an
almocrebe whose pack animals have their home stables at the Manse. They
serve us wine—by Bacchus, not at all a shabby vintage. And then we are offered
coffee from the espresso containers so tediously familiar to us. Those are the

details so far, plus the remark I let slip above that our caravan was headed for a nest of thieves, not to mention my even earlier statement that the Inca bird with the all-encompassing vocabulary was being prophetic. Where are we?

We rose and followed the lady of the house, who would show us to our room. Surely this would raise by an inch or two the veil of mystery that seemed to be woven around everything here and, for that matter, still seems to be draped over all of us on God's earth. Antonio was unwilling to provide explanations. The responsibility was all his, he said; at the Tower we could rest easy at his expense. He asked only that we return sometime and knock at his basement door—no, no, no thanks necessary. With agile fingers he twirled yet another cigarette, we clapped each other on the shoulder: That's how it was when Antonio vanished into the night.

Now the drawbridge can be hauled up. The campfire crumbles to ashes, and the only light comes from fireflies. And from the moon above. Will the moon remain true to my fable?

Good night. That wasn't just a figure of speech, for the hour was far advanced. Not much longer and the ghosts could make their entrance at our bewitched Manse. But the clock tower was as mute as the matriarch, who had dozed off on her crutch. It was a directorial error of Antonio's not to have twelve peals of an iron bell descend upon us now from on high. Instead, the air was filled with buzzing and fluttering sounds—huge stag beetles with pincer-shaped antlers were flying around above our heads. Fireflies lit up, faded out, then lit up again. Bats as big as pigeons swooped down out of the void, paused in mid-flight, and disappeared with a hoarse screech. All we lacked was the scent of jasmine, almonds, and oranges, to give us a romantic night under a starry Southern sky. But the asphyxiating stench in the air wasn't coming from pretty beds of blossoms. The wind, still from the wrong direction, was blowing its *memento mori* from the abattoir, a penetrating reminder of the evanescence of the flesh, one that might have converted me then and there to a vegetarian life—if only the comestible so poetically named "cauliflower" didn't stink just as horribly.

Walking behind our new hostess, we entered a colonnade and noticed how the moonlight beamed through its vine-covered ribs and arches. Soon we stepped out on an open area surrounded by various buildings. The moon had now fully risen, but still we were unable to tell what kind of structures they were—perhaps stables, sheds, or barns for storing grain. In the background we saw a particularly conspicuous building, one that we hadn't noticed from the road because it was hidden partly by the tower and partly by the main house. Its gables were covered with grapevines that had grown out over the yard to attach themselves to trees and trellises. A wide stone staircase minus a handrail led to a kind of portal, whose architecture reminded me of the horseshoe-shaped gateways of Islam. There in the moonlight our hero and heroine took each other by the hand, as if expecting some nocturnal initiation ordeal. Were new dangers lurking ahead?

Just as the air above us was filled with swarms of winged creatures, the species that creep upon the ground were by no means absent either—thus providing full manifestation of the Lord's fifth day of Creation. Long-tailed rats skittered to and fro, but not with the lightning speed I had observed in countries where people actually want rid of them. Here no one cursed Noah beyond the grave for obeying the Lord's command and taking rats, too, aboard his ark. The beasts weren't exactly well-liked, but they were tolerated; these simple island folk honored the Almighty's sacred decree, though they weren't averse to kicking one of the critters once in a while. But no, the hustle and bustle displayed by these repulsive rodents here on Arsenio's open range must have had intraspecific reasons of an urgency unfathomable to outsiders like us. Perhaps their intention was to reproduce as numerously as possible, requiring that they run around day and night, offering full tits to their insatiable whelps while trying not to eat each other up in the process. I can never forget the old silver-haired witch rat who, in the declining years of her life as a rover and chewer, appeared to have found a peaceful hole somewhere in the hospitable Clock Tower. On that very first night she darted across our path, as if heaven had sent her to us with the divine injunction, "It is well that we are here. Let us make booths!" Later I spied her night after night on the same path near the open latrine, always moving with the same dignity and tail-dragging *gravitas*. At first glance it looked as though she might be part albino, for her coat was flecked with white. But when she came so close that Beatrice screamed and I could easily have counted the scales on her tail, I saw that she had reached an advanced and incurable stage of the dreaded mange. We stood right near her, and one kick would have sent her out of our way and off to the rattish Beyond, but she kept moving at just the same deliberate pace. In fact, our hostess did give her a poke with her foot, but only a gentle one. She shoved the old lady to one side and said that we would soon get accustomed to the comings and goings of the rat population. This old beast wouldn't hurt anybody any more, she told us; even the dogs left her alone.

At Beatrice's request I later sinned against this animal. One clandestine moonlit midnight I did the old lady in—it had to be. Once the deed was done, Beatrice shook my hand in silence. To this very day the poor soul has no idea what I used as a murder weapon. Were I to go into detail here, disgust would again well up in her after all these twenty years. At any rate, I can understand full well how bishops in the Middle Ages saw the necessity of controlling the pests by pronouncing maledictions on rats. Still, such a device for interfering with Creation isn't exactly edifying.

The woman led us up the steps and told us our place was inside. She had arranged one of the corner rooms near the entrance. We would be comfortable there, she averred; a room like this one would surely get more air and light. The main entrance was closed off only chest-high, by a half-door of the kind they often have on old farmsteads to prevent the livestock from strolling in at random. I am very fond of doors like that; to me they symbolize peacefulness and domestic leisure; they seem built to encourage meditation. Here the top half had been removed. It would be replaced in winter time, our landlady explained, probably anticipating an objection from us. That was hardly necessary. Every last feature of this house was material for a whole volume full of objections, as the reader will soon find out.

Ahead of us was darkness, which swallowed up a long corridor that I would later pace off at sixteen of my footfalls, each measuring two feet six inches. In the dim light we could barely make out that there were doors to the right and left, many doors. In fact, the corridor walls seemed to consist of nothing but doorways. Were we standing in a hallway flanked by cells? Monastery cells? As a child I often played in a historical tithing barn used for rolling cigars. I recalled that now, perhaps from a similarity of smell. In any case I immediately associated this place with something religious such as cloisters and storage sheds. By now my eyes had become accustomed to the gloom, and I made out at the far end a large mound. Our luggage, as I determined with a certain measure of relief. We were standing in front of the first right-hand door.

"Where your baggage is, there you shall feel at home," my landlady once declared when I was a student in Cologne. So now we had come home once again. But why hadn't the *almocrebe* taken the trouble to put everything in the room, when helping hands were there for the asking? Oh well, we'd take care of that ourselves in the morning, and we'd do it our own way. But now my typewriter, of all my possessions the one nearest and dearest to me—where is my precious Diamant-Juwel? Ah, that black object up on top! And then I watched as the black object started to move and divide into two, three, four black objects. Was my writing instrument giving birth, and I hadn't even noticed that it was expecting—except of course the progeny of my mind? The pups plopped one by one to the floor and scampered between our legs. Once more Beatrice screamed. Rats again. "Throw water at them," I said, but it was a poor joke. These spreaders of the plague carried on their voracious gnawing even within the sacred confines of a cloister.

The woman—her name was Adeleide, and they called her *Señora* Adeleide because she wasn't of the proper standing for Doña—*Señora* Adeleide opened the door and switched on the light. There in the yellowish gleam of a bulb with the lowest possible candlepower, we saw just how poor we had become and how little our trusty guarantor Antonio was worth, even among friends. "Here's your little room," said Adeleide "How do you like it?" We both replied with a single voice: yes, we liked it, we liked it a whole lot. We were in such a rush to spit out our lie and get rid of the woman, who said "Good night" in Mallorcan and left. We were alone.

Vigoleis, how did you feel as you stood there in Beatrice's way, and as your darling Beatrice stood there in your way, after the door was closed? For we each stood very much in each other's way, contrary to the proverb that says there's room even in the tiniest cottage for two people in love. Didn't our heroes love each other any more? Was it all over, *fini*? Had they grown tired of one another? Had *La Pilarière* undermined their relationship? Was this a whore's revenge, with a time fuse set for the moment when Adeleide leaves the couple alone with two or three creeping creatures? No, kind reader, none of the above. It is rather a purely technical form of repulsion. An architectural disinclination had taken hold of our two friends, or to be more exact: an antipathy based on room design. For where one of them stood, there the other would have to stand also, whereas for both of them to stand on the selfsame spot was a clear impossibility. Therefore Beatrice fell immediately onto the bed; in this little booth every structural detail seemed calculated to force one of the pair to fall on the bed, and the other to fall on top of the first. Once that had happened, the problem of living space was solved in a highly pleasureful manner for both. Because it was night and we needed sleep, we solved the problem exactly in the spirit of the house Antonio had delivered us to. In doing so, we sinned against a certain Judaeo-Christian myth I was quite familiar with, though not in the sense that we sinned against any Tree of Knowledge. I am fond of making love in the shadow of that particular tree, but I resist the idea of being asked to join in the harvest. And I don't like fallen fruit at all.

Beatrice embraced her Vigoleis tightly, and Vigoleis didn't move. He thought he heard her sobbing; he had the impression that her body shuddered every now and then, but these perceptions were perhaps only illusory, caused by the partial dream state he had already drifted into. The wine had been heavy, and now it made him light as a feather. As in classic nights of love, the two lay together and slept the insular sleep of their merged bodies. This occurred beneath the third roof of their continually disrupted Spanish sojourn. Let us grant them peace and privacy, slumber and joyful dreams; it will be morning soon enough. The cocks will crow them awake all too soon, and the asses that led them to this place, one and all under the spell of Arabian fairy-tale magic, will be prompted by the first sign of daylight to trumpet forth their bone-shattering, stuttering yells. Dogs will start barking, human voices will flutter about. Then Beatrice will rise with a start. She will open her arms in fright, freeing her husband from her almost botanical embrace—exactly the opposite reflex to that of the sensitive mimosa plant. Vigoleis, already disposed to looseness in earthly matters, will forfeit his last hold on things—a mere half-turn at first—and then promptly fall out of bed. Then, we presume, he will rub his eyes, but also the back of his head where a bump is beginning to swell...

Let us spare Beatrice the discomfort of having us as witnesses as she drops her beloved Vigo on the very first morning in their new home. Let us, rather, return to the blackness of night—which God the Almighty did not create in order to confound the Day, although human behavior might often lead one to believe otherwise. At this point, and for special reasons, I am more than willing to aid and abet nature's nocturnal schemings. I do so for the benefit of my heroes, for whom this particular night cannot last long enough.

Once again we shall place asterisks at the end of a section of our book—three little stars from among the myriad that have risen over Vigoleis and Beatrice, even though they themselves may not notice them. There are always stars in the heavens that we humans do not notice—perhaps because the world around us hasn't yet turned sufficiently dark. If you look up a chimney on a sunny day, believe it or not, you'll be looking at a tiny portion of the starry firmament. "Twinkle, twinkle, little star, how I wonder what you are...?"

* * *

Three starlets have now been borrowed from the heavenly regions, where no one will miss them as I put them to use as a closure for my Second Book. There they stand, twinkling away, doing their best to fend off the pinions of night, a night that is allowing our heroes some sleep and giving me some time to work out a continuation of our narrative—but now especially to deal with this vexing problem: how can I possibly let our two schlemiels know that they have just jumped out of the frying pan into the fire?

Two customs have now been established quite naturally during the writing of my memoirs: the division of the book into Books, and at the end of each segment of our journey together a detached, philosophical discussion that we hold at the bedside of our guileless heroes—who now are of course asleep. This means that I have now begun a tradition to which I intend to conform from here on in—though I'm prepared to admit that it is questionable to refer to something as a "tradition" that has up to now happened only once. This is not unlike the disturbing but ultimately frivolous puzzle of the creation of a heap. One grain doesn't make a heap; add another grain and we still haven't got one. Even a third grain won't do it quite. When, then, does a heap begin to be a heap, if the addition of a single grain will not suffice to form one? A similar but contrary game gets played by armchair philosophers with the concept—one that is closer to those who derive amusement from such things—of baldness. How many hairs must one be lacking to be considered a *calvus*? For me, such conundrums have long since ceased to be a problem at all—ever since I had first-hand experience of the "heap" of money that two pesetas can represent. That's why I have no hesitation in calling something a "tradition" that has now taken place twice only.

"Insofar as I, the author, have any say in the matter..." —You may recall these words from my Prologue; they are evidence of sheer grandiloquence and authorial hubris, especially considering their markedly declining relevance as we press onward with our story. Therefore, at this juncture, I shall come right out and confess that I have less control over the destiny of my heroes than the lowliest *almocrebe* on this island has over the stubbornest of his jackasses. With any set of memoirs it comes down to a question of the writer's devotion to truth as the basis for the quality of his memory. How easy it would be for me to bend the course of events here and there in a more positive direction! Instead of having myself lie in Beatrice's protective embrace on a shabby, sinful mattress, I could depict Vigoleis reclining in one of Mallorca's palaces, whose gates have been stormed by Beatrice's music and my unchallenged literary talents—in a four-poster, with mosquito netting to shield us from the frantic, bloodthirsty dance of diverse flying insects. Instead of being under a gangster's heel, with a single stroke of my pen I could make myself into the adopted son of a rich and lusty American heiress. I could be luxuriating at Miramar, one of the estates belonging to the Austrian Archduke Ludwig Salvator. Would you ever believe that, dear reader?

Truth demands that the forces of envy will demolish Vigoleis' capitalistic dream in Book Four. Why aren't I carrying out here, on an ostensibly neutral sheet of paper, what I once did to my dear mother—a little act of hypocritical mendacity I am mortified to recall, although I committed it in the interest of preserving her peace of mind? It went this way: I told her that my marriage— which in reality I entered into only in secular fashion under hilarious bureau- cratic circumstances in Barcelona—I pretended to her that this bourgeois farce had received the blessings of the One True Church. Thus far it might have been one of those little white lies that become necessary every so often in our devout daily lives. But no, I traveled farther on the path of iniquity. I wrote down on paper the putative divine message given to us on that happy occa- sion. In the house chapel of a friend, I claimed, a Jesuit priest (no less!) had given us a special exhortation as we set forth on the journey of holy wedlock. In a few pages I gave free rein to my sacerdotal eloquence; I spoke as the Light of the World and the Salt of the Earth, taking as my model Monsignor Don- ders of the Cathedral at Münster, that consummate artist of the Sunday hom- ily. He could have done it much better, of course, but for a layman apprentice—or rather counterfeiter—this was quite an achievement.

So let us stay with the truth, and that means with poverty, hunger, and the Mallorcan underworld. Our heroes arrived on this island and found a roof over their heads. It wasn't a roof of the kind they expected, and yet it covered their existence quite satisfactorily. Heaven soon began to treat them ill. Things had gone badly with the trollop, and they lost the roof over their heads. But soon enough, by dint of a Cologne fellow's presence of mind, they could once again reside under sheltering tiles. Troubles began anew, leading eventually to a day of forced marching, this time behind asses and an *almocrebe*. It should be noted that our two friends could easily have camped out for a while, for ever since they trod the landing plank at Palma's harbor, not one drop of rain has fallen. Nor does it look as if any kind of showers from the heavens are about to enrich their lives. At any rate we should be happy that Antonio, with modest means that can excuse much else, has once again erected a roof over their heads. One doesn't look a gift horse in the mouth, at least not so long as the benefactor is standing nearby. Once the benefactor has left—ours is already at the club cater- ing to the rich old farts—it's probably all right to take a closer look at things.

So let me put this question of propriety my reader: are you willing to be present as I take aside this gift horse at the Giant's Manse and yank open its maw so that everyone, horse-trader or layman, can see plainly what quality of animal we are dealing with? You're not afraid? No moral compunctions? No fear of germs? Excellent! I approve of such companions. Would you even be willing to stay on with us here under our new roof? *Señora* Adeleide will be happy to show you to your room—a single word and she will open it for you! Your revolver? No, you won't be needing that here. Oh, I see, because we were talking a while ago about thieves? It's actually not as bad as that, and anyway, Arsenio has a weapon more deadly than your little pea-shooter. Besides, our heroes are unarmed—we could even call them defenseless in their naiveté. That is what makes them heroes of the praiseworthy Robinsonian kind, those who repeatedly stand their ground in the face of the unknown.

But now you, my dear female reader back home in Germany: I'm not sure I would encourage you to pass your time at a place where the game of shepherd's idyll gets played in earnest. On the other hand, if you do rent a small room, you might be surprised to find friends of yours here. We could produce for you at least one of your dear acquaintances from back home—assuming that you already know Kathrinchen, that charming lady whose husband is an Essen steel magnate with doctor's degree, beer-glass spectacles, and a neurasthenic constitution. Such a reunion is entirely possible here. The world gets smaller and smaller the farther away from home one travels. For example, Beatrice had once met this popular society dame at the home of another Rhenish industrialist. To be sure, on that occasion Frau Doktor was very fashionably dressed, whereas here, though still the same merry and lusty Kathrinchen, she spends a good deal of her time in a convincing state of undress. It goes without saying that Beatrice wouldn't think of revealing this socialite's erotic secrets. And I am obliged to implore my reader to maintain the same discretion that an author of recollections must observe whenever he describes persons who have crossed his path, but who are still happily alive even as he strives to commemorate their deeds for posterity. Count Kessler, when writing his own memoirs, had enormous difficulties with long-lived characters of this kind. In particular, a certain famous princess refused to die, and thus cheated him—cheating, it seems, was her specialty—of some salient passages. He couldn't just put her in his book as "Madame X," Kessler told me, because every knowledgeable reader would immediately realize what species of beast was implied.

Because my characters present themselves in dual cognizance of their identity—for which I wish to express my thanks at this point—my task is rather different, though with some of them it isn't easy to have faith in the ameliorative effects of a memorialist's cleaver. Anyone who has observed the aforementioned Kathrinchen, grunting with pleasure on the butcher-block of her own flesh, will not have received the impression of a split personality.

With the traditional seal of confidentiality now on our lips, permit me to invite my reader to follow me into Book Three—no, not up the wide stone steps, not through that door. Nor are we in league with the limping devil of the poet Don Luiz Velez de Guevara—surely you know the story (Goethe mentions it in a sentence in his autobiography): one night, as a favor to a friend, the devil lifts off all the roofs of the city of Madrid. Even without having signed any diabolical pact, it will still be easy for us, right here and now, to get a bird's-eye view of our heroic duo. For you see, their room at the Manse had no ceiling.

BOOK THREE

I wish purely and simply to be
the animal that, before God and man,
performs the tragicomedy called spirit.
Pascoaes

"Despabiladera" means "candle snuffer" in Spanish.
You'd think it was, at the very least, the word for
Imperial Lieutenant General Field Marshal
Lichtenberg

I

The black-and-blue welt on the back of Vigoleis' head does not play a sig-nificant role in his recollections. Yet because these are recollections of the applied variety, or rather since Vigoleis himself intends them that way, it will be appropriate to include here all manner of experiences and insights, byprod-ucts of his pure, undivided ego, that can be grafted organically or wilfully onto this account of his life. He trusts that these words will suffice to justify a few empirical lines concerning a goose-egg that made him into a bright and clever fellow.

The hummock on my noggin—how did it get there? What I mean is this: from what contact with what object in the space that confined and imprisoned us two mortals, the space that might well be called our death cell? My question is not a frivolous one. It would be if I had simply bumped my head on the floor, a surface made of the traditional local clay tiles. But no, I fell against an object made of metal, one that was located at the head of our bed within reaching distance, like a night table, though it served other purposes—hygienic ones, to be precise. In a room where there was virtually no room at all, this seemed to me to be an impudent luxury—and not just because I came into painful contact with it. Today, of course, I know that this pesky apparatus with its hip-shaped metal basin was just as integral a part of the room as the women who habitually made use of it—astradddle, as prescribed by the Italian term from which its name derives. A *bidetto* is a little horse, a pony so small that when you ride it your feet touch the ground—an extremely apt etymology. On the very first morning of our island sojourn, we (I include my reader, who by now is part of our family, and in whose presence we can discuss the most intimate matters)—we made the acquaintance of Pilar's love-vessel. And now here, at first blush of a new dawning in our existence, we confront a similar object, one that is even less modest, and doubtless rather more expensive, than its counterpart on the Street of Solitude. I gave it a swift kick, sending it clanging against the door. Then I rubbed my bruise and looked around for something cold to place on it. My mother's bread knife came to mind. She used to treat our bumps and bruises by pressing the blade lightly against the affected spot. It eased the pain and helped the blood circulation. We didn't have a knife among our possessions, but why not use the basin itself to cool my skull? As I stood there with my head crowned, steer-horn-like, by this curved feminine utensil, I must have looked like some ancient Egyptian deity. But it worked. The throbbing stopped.

"Just where are we?" Beatrice asked. She had not yet fully awakened to life in our new Paradise. "And why are you wearing that stupid bucket on your head? Cold compresses! Isn't there any water around here? And anyway, what a place! To me it looks like a youth hostel, or some kind of stopover for itinerant craftsmen."

Voilà, there she is again, my Beatrice with her faulty imagination when it comes to the grittier aspects of life. On a purely cerebral level she could have made significant contributions in the field of comparative linguistics. Her extraordinary ability with languages, a twofold inheritance from father and mother, would suggest this kind of career as the most fitting one for her. She can grasp the most remote etymological nuances at a single glance. But we cannot expect her to look at an egg and deduce from it the hen that laid it, or to think back from some chewed-over carrion to the vulture that spat it out, or from Vigoleis to *Don Quixote*.

"Beatrice," I therefore said in the spirit of the Encyclopedists, who crusaded against chimeras and rank superstition, "*la mia Beatrice*, you can chalk it up to my cranial hematoma if I venture to enlighten you while holding this peculiar object to the back of my head. It just seems to me that your choice of words is erroneous, because once again you haven't figured out the connections properly. You speak of 'itinerant craftsmen,' whereas I would suggest itinerant crafts*ladies*. And if you'll permit one further correction, instead of 'itinerant' I would select some term or other that implies a static condition. All this may sound rather pedantic, especially so early in the morning. But don't you agree with me that the solution to this puzzle is more likely to be found among the horizontal *señoritas*—assuming that it is any of our business at all to figure out the social significance of this embarrassing bathing stool? Let's just be happy that we have a roof over our heads."

In reconstructing this conversation with Beatrice I have just employed an obvious figure of speech, one that was not entirely applicable under the conditions prevailing at the time. If our heroes will only look upward, they will find out what we already know: that in that direction, too, not all is as it should be.

Neither of us had yet dared to glance ceilingward. The previous evening, in the murky light, I had the sensation that the space above our heads had a certain infinitude about it. My eyes could not discern any horizontal structural element. Everything here seemed to point upwards, towards the heavens. The entrance to this edifice was markedly unconventional; the corridor led to nameless depths, thus suggesting a cloister-like purpose for the building, a presumption supported by the size of our room with its dimensions of a monastic cell. It seemed only logical, then, that the building's topmost structure should likewise lead one's glance toward the celestial regions.

And it was just so. Our room had no ceiling. The perceiving eye searched long and hard until finally getting lost somewhere up in a jumble of roof beams. The roof itself was outfitted with curved ceramic tiles, in antique Spanish style. And because the roof lining was missing, one could see above the rafters the naked tiles, installed according to the system that the master builders of yore dubbed "nuns and monks": one "nun" underneath, one "monk" on top, and so forth, all for the greater glory of God and to keep mortals from having their pious daily chores rained upon. Many of the tiles were broken, and several had slipped out of their overlapping fit, with the result that narrow beams of daylight penetrated through the open spaces. This lent our cubicle an ambience like that in a cathedral, a play of light refracting into a colored spectrum as it passed through broad areas of cobwebs gently undulating in the drafts of air. On clear moonlit nights the pitched roof resembled a star-studded tent. Little points of light lay scattered out above us, reminiscent of a passage in Immanuel Kant, a statement so cogent as to make one almost forget his reputation as a creative destroyer: "Two things fill my mind with repeated and increasing amazement and awe the more often and intensely I reflect on them: the starry heavens above me and the moral law within me."

But what if it rains? We haven't reached that point yet and probably never will, for the Mallorcan Tourist Office's statistics on annual precipitation would make it totally absurd for any moisture to find its way down through our damaged roof. Moreover, the rainy season wouldn't start until the late fall; until then we surely could make an escape, perhaps even an escape devised in the spirit of Pure Reason—although we can doubtless rely on our friend Vigoleis, the Man of Unreason, who likes to boast of his talent for improvisation. He just won't let rain interfere with the lugubrious workings of his mind, much less with his everyday business.

The walls of our cell were as high as I can reach with my arm extended, which is to say 7 feet 7 inches. The walls themselves were made of boards that partitioned off the whole building into little chambers. The windows were set so high that I couldn't have cleaned them even with the aid of a stepladder. One of these sources of light in the masonry wall, an opening that tapered to smaller size on the outside, was located right above our room. Later, with the aid of an orchard ladder, I transformed this into a storage area for our laundry, not without encountering difficulty with the sharply angled sill. It was a daredevil kind of a job, and it had an effect on my health that ought not to be underestimated.

Our furniture consisted of the barest necessities: a bed wide enough for the shoulders of a strong Mallorcan male, but decidedly lacking his length; a primitive chair of the kind used by the old matron as seat and crutch; the aforementioned bathing stool; and a three-legged metal toilet stand painted in white enamel, whose aperture was no larger than a soup bowl. Beneath it was a pan containing a generous variety of insects, an indication that our cell had remained unoccupied for a long time—or, on the other hand, that the previous occupants were not the bath-taking type. The bait for this swarm of bugs, a repulsive substance of inorganic nature, was stuck to the bottom of the pan. Luckily Beatrice hadn't noticed it.

I climbed on the chair to survey the remainder of the abbey-like quarters we had been assigned to, and counted fifteen gaping tops of cubicles. That meant fifteen compartments, ×2 = 30, and when multiplied according to the dictum that two shall always be of one flesh, the result was a good sixty people, i.e., threescore or about half a gross, that this barracks of love could entertain in one shift. The chamber sharing a partition with our own was furnished in just the same way, and all the others presumably likewise. It was a uniform setup, completely standardized, a clever way to rehabilitate an old unusable barn and turn a profit from it. That is exactly what had taken place here; without any doubt it was a brothel. But why hadn't Arsenio gone ahead and added a few more floors? All at once I saw exciting possibilities that this edifice offered if extended upwards—possibilities for the cheapest and saddest way of fulfilling the command "Go forth and do not multiply." Illumination would be a problem, but for such activity light is not a true necessity; a single bulb, as in our own space, would suffice. Air could be let in through specially installed ducts—but if you ask me, that too wouldn't be a matter of high priority. An entryway built in the style of...

"What do you see up there that's so interesting?" Beatrice said, interrupting my architectural reveries. "Is the box next to ours occupied too? People who come here to live must be very poor."

I couldn't bring myself to tell her what I had seen, and what I now knew incontrovertibly on the basis of all I had observed, including that pan underneath the toilet stand: that we had landed in an establishment of the lowest conceivable price range. Twenty-five pesetas per month is what Antonio paid for this flophouse, which included a towel and probably also the entertainment tax. 25 pesetas for a month of joyless shelter was one huge rip-off.

"I can't see anything at all, *chérie*. So what you say is probably right. We're in a youth hostel, and in summer business is slow. Who would want to go hiking in this heat? In winter it's different, I can imagine that Adeleide always has a full house then. She's probably got just what it takes, a hostel mother with a warm heart and a firm hand."

"Maybe. But that would be the first time I've ever heard of Spaniards who go hiking. The place is probably exclusively for foreigners, and they really don't start coming until winter. What I'd really like to know is, what you think we should do from here on. We have five pesetas left. I won't be able to stand it here very long. It's so awful. I could just strangle that Pilar woman! Go ahead and laugh. I don't see anything funny about this situation of ours. What do I smell? It's probably coming from the toilet!"

There ensued a lengthy tirade in French, one that was not very flattering to me, and in spots even hurtful. To understand all is to forgive all, I thought to myself as I continued my elevated reconnaissance of our quarters. And besides, I thought this thought in French, which reminded me of my grade-school teacher, the one all of us kids were in love with and who spoke these words of wisdom every time my classroom performance left something to be desired. At the time, she wasn't thinking of love but of my stupidity, but now I am constrained to think of Zwingli, who was actually the one who plunged us into this doubly distasteful whorish adventure. Instead of strangling Pilar, it would be more reasonable of Beatrice to consider fratricide. But who can expect logic from a woman early in the morning, still in bed, with no makeup on, no roof over her head, with a well-trampled mattress beneath her, and next to her a man who wouldn't even have been able to come up with installments for the chair he was standing on?

"Our next steps? My love, I can't reveal that to you until after I've been to the post office. I'm going back to the city right away, unwashed and unshaven. My shoes aren't even polished, so you can see what a rush I'm in. You are so very right. Something has got to happen, and something will happen. But don't forget that as a last resort we still have our ropes."

"Our... you're going to...bah! That would be unaesthetic. And then I would just be on my own, trying to get out of this filthy place. Thanks a lot!"

Our ropes—oh my dearest, there you go again getting everything backwards! Once again you fail to comprehend how one thing connects up with everything else, or even that there is such a thing as Providence, which leads us to destinations that Providence itself can envision only at brighter moments. Our ropes! I truly had no intention of stringing them up in the dizzy heights of the roof beams and shoving my neck into the noose. In any case, before I could bring off such a sinister feat, I would break my neck scrambling around in the roofwork. I tried to explain this to Beatrice, but with no success.

I have had suicidal tendencies for quite some time. I have a significant metaphysical interest in the course of my personal planetary orbit, and experience with several botched jobs by way of diabolically conceived attempts to do away with my own person. But this time, any such plausible idea was far from my mind. The ropes were for something else; my idea was to use them as an element of interior architecture, to tie them up not vertically but horizontally, as I then later did. I had a complete picture of how we could convert this box-for-an-hour into a somewhat liveable, perhaps even comfortable habitation. I sensed how, by putting to use all of my failed careers, by combining the intuitions of a paleolithic handyman with the highly involved technical skill available to myself and my century, I could create for Beatrice a home of the kind that otherwise only a Henry van de Velde could offer her. So let us now leave her in her angry mood, pondering her fate with compressed lips (the lower one jutting forward ever so little), with quivering chin, and with one bloodless hand held downward like a fin in a gesture of extreme resentment—but also of extreme misery. Her fate? Having an absent-minded theologian for a father, an exotic cosmopolitan woman for a mother, a Zwingli for a brother, a lady of the streets for a sister-in-law, and me, Vigoleis, the zero-grade writer, for an unmarried husband. Let's hand her over for a good long while to her devastating thoughts, and listen in the meantime to the story of our ropes. It is briefly told.

In Lyon we missed our connection. Perambulating on the railway platform I saw a traveler whose suitcase burst just as his train was pulling into the station. The contents spilled out all over the platform, and in the throng of passengers they got partly trampled, partly kicked under the wheels. The man's catastrophe was complete. He was close to tears, and his train left without him. With a porter's help he collected what was left of his belongings, but since his suitcase was destroyed, all he could do was tie up his things inside his pajamas.

Witnessing this anonymous incident was sufficient for me to take measures to prevent us from ever confronting such a disaster while traveling. Quick as a whistle, I entered the city and bought a few yards of leather strapping, some hemp rope, and some narrow belts with adjustable buckles. All this to the amazement of Beatrice, who trusted in the solid craftsmanship of her Swiss luggage, and thus could say that she had already traveled far and wide without ropes and straps, which is to say, far and wide without anything bursting apart—enough to make her complacent. The fact that back there in Lyon, Heaven had thrust a man with suitcase trouble before Vigoleis' eyes, thus opening them for him; the fact that Providence itself was operative on that occasion—all this did not become clear to us until something of our own burst apart: not our luggage but our entire existence. But I still had the ropes! Here in our naked abbey cell we could now put them to excellent use; Beatrice will soon find out just how clever I was with them. To go right ahead and hang myself with them would, in the light of such possibilities, have been tasteless and, besides, beneath my dignity as an inventor.

"I'm going with you, I'm not staying here. And that smell is back again—sickening! But first let's go get our luggage before the rest gets stolen."

"Stolen?" I pointed upwards, where anyone could enter freely. And then, with five pesetas in our pocket, we set off to greet the thousands more that could have arrived for me that very day at the Banca March. When the need is greatest, God is often very near—I dare not say that at such times He is closest of all, for otherwise He would not have sent us on the pilgrimage to this cloister of lust. Or was He testing us, like Abraham in the Land of Moriah? Whoever in God's world is unprepared for the worst, will find that he can easily get the short end of the stick. And on that late morning the heroes of our story picked the very shortest end of the stick of their destiny. There was no money at the post office; no mail at all had come for us, and at the bank our duro had not spawned any children. In monetary affairs there is no such thing as parthenogenesis, and so we were left with no other choice but to break the duro to purchase some necessities. Necessities? What is a rock-bottom necessity for people in our position? The way we solved this problem will give my reader some insight into the very essence of our psychological condition, now that he has paid witness to this and that event taking place behind the curtain of our unsanctified married life of woe.

In a saloon frequented only by donkey drivers and similarly picturesque barefoot types, we each had an espresso, then another and yet a third, for even though the odor of the slaughterhouse had gone from the atmosphere, it hadn't left our noses, not to mention our stomachs. Three *café negro* can do wonders in such a situation. Then we purchased an alcohol burner, which Beatrice called our "lantern"—the cheapest model, not the kind that explodes. Then we bought some fuel and a long-handled pan for frying, boiling, sautéing, and roasting, since we aimed to limit our culinary needs to a half-pint of milk, a fried egg, a *sobrasada*, and a slice of bread apiece. With our remaining cash we bought a bar of cooking chocolate *à la española*, cigarettes, and some nautical zwieback. That was the extent of our provisioning for the expedition back to our planetarium. Some few items were no doubt lacking, but even without wine and canned sardines, we no longer were drifting in quite such rudderless fashion. After all, I still had my providential ropes, my inventor's brain, and my hopes set on Victor Emmanuel van Vriesland in Amsterdam. Beatrice had what was inimitably hers: music in her head, and the somber premonition that she would never have a concert grand. And yet (she thinks) there will still be music, my dear; you can depend on Vigoleis, who calls himself unmusical. On my part, I think: I'll have to stay ahead of her by one or two paces when we reach that hostel of ours—to remove that trademark from the toilet bowl. First I'll dilute the mess to soften it up.

Without delay we set out homewards, planning to reach the cool shadows of our abbey before the hottest hour of the day. It was then that I first noticed how my eyes kept searching the roadway for useful objects. It was worth my trouble: I found a nail, a piece of wire, another nail, and several more rusty things that seemed promising. Beatrice observed my scavenging without saying a word; she was resigning herself to this new phase in her Vigoleis' life. It was perilously close to taking up the beggar's staff, and if I am to be completely honest, I'll have to admit that it is unclear which of us had brought the other to this pass: was I the culprit, with my chronic dialysis as a hermetic poet and intellectual? Or was it she, with her unconditional sisterly love?

At any rate, as we came within sight of the "Tower," I was just packing away my last find in my book bag when it all started up again with *olé* and *hallo* and how is everybody and we wish you this and isn't that grand and just this way please, Arsenio's huge mouth, prolific as always, once again set and dominated the whole scene. He was the perfect highwayman-in-chief with his colorful silk sash wound around his body at the place where, contrary to all anatomical probability, his belly ended and his thighs, clothed in blue velvet, began. Adelaide, too, made a brief appearance carrying a feeding trough for pigs. That meant that these people kept animals for market, a little farm work on the side for extra income. Here comes the old matron, limping about and yelling at a crowd of kids engaged in fun and mischief. They were playing bullfight with the skull of a real ox, and there was blood on the horns from real lacerations. The old lady was friendly, at once intimidating and amiable. In the course of our stay at this brothel I got to like her very much, although I cannot pretend to have understood her speech on any single occasion. Without doubt, what she had to say every time was profoundly wise. She had grown not only old but ancient in these rural surroundings, close to the heart of nature—or to put it in a more earthbound way, at Nature's bosom. What is more, she had grown bronzed and stooped. Someone like this has seen much that isn't contained in the pandects of my philosophers. This "abbey" of hers enjoyed a special prebend, producing income from mankind's most human activity; this requires plenty of knowledge of the world and its ways. Na' Maguelida certainly had that kind of savvy.

Arsenio invited us to join him at table, but we declined. No, we explained, we had had a copious breakfast in the city, a so-called "fork breakfast," English style—Arsenio was familiar with that, of course? Ham and eggs and all kinds of sharp condiments. No, he said, that didn't quite suit his palate. At this hour he preferred his *sopas*, the Mallorcan national dish, a soup that you fill with so much bread that your spoon stands up straight in it. But he wanted us to know that their kitchen and provision cellar offered nothing but the best, and were at our disposal day and night.

The children crowded around us, more of them than on the previous evening. All of them, without exception, were expected to address Arsenio as "Father," for he alone was their sire. Altogether he had twenty-three under his legal name, and his virility probably accounted for considerably more in the outskirts of his erotic activity. Three sons worked in his business, all of them husky fellows who were perfect for tending to their Dad's affairs. One was in the army, where he was learning to handle powder and lead. But he wasn't in training for the defense of his country; the "Tower" maintained a third enterprise, for which the other two served as a front.

I borrowed a hammer and a pair of pliers, and installed my harvest of rusty objects in our cell. In just one hour every single nail and every last hank of wire was in place and doing its appointed task. Beatrice lay down on the bed and, unaccustomed to meditating or staring into empty space ("empty" is meant here in the non-allegorical sense, although there was more allegory here for her, too, than at any other stage of her life), picked up a book and disappeared from my consciousness. That was fine with me, because I needed privacy for designing our habitat. This was especially necessary since I'm terrible at arithmetic, and our living quarters had to be planned out not with a simple ruler but with a micrometer. Precision work, in a word, requiring tight-fitting joinery. Go at it, Vigoleis! Show us what you can do in a field where nobody thought you were worth anything!

I don't like to be disturbed when I am puttering. I'm ashamed of all the sweating and swearing I do as I fit one thing to another, then take it apart again with more sweating and swearing, and so forth, until finally, based on no particular initial plan, a finished product emerges that is perfect, or in any case better than anything I might have thought through carefully before starting. Such remarks as "What is that supposed to be?" or "You'll never get it done," or "That doesn't look like anything at all"—and the whole thing is over with. I putter in the same way that I write poems. I take the first word that sings to me, often enough some rusty old word or other, and never know at the beginning how it will fit the next one. Somehow I join one thing to another with rhyme and rhythm, and suddenly it's done, there it is. Then it's your business to decide whether it's good or bad. But no matter what, I'm the one who has made it.

When Beatrice awoke from her literary sedation and closed her book because it was finished, my do-it-yourself poem wasn't complete. But at least I had come up with an opening stanza, which normally gives the direction for the further course and pattern of a literary work of art. I used my practiced fingers, which were unhindered by any Zwinglian cuttlebone, Arsenio's crude set of household tools, my scavenger's booty, and the ropes sent by Providence. The combined application of my resources permitted me to elevate these discrete elements into a spiritual dimension, as it were, by imparting to each one a new and higher function, albeit a subservient one. I installed the materials up against the wooden partition in such a way as to yield a practical writing surface—a tiny one, to be sure, but one that was attractive enough in overall aesthetic and pragmatic effect, somewhere between full-fledged Empire and its sober and tasteless German variant, Biedermeier. All that was missing was an inkpot, a goose quill, and a container of sand, and the Right Honorable Vigoleis could have started writing—perhaps an Ode to the Clock Tower, or a Sicilian *canzona* on the thirty cells of love 'neath monk and nun. But at this unlyrical moment in his life he had neither the heart, nor the sensory alertness, nor the soul for rhyming words together. So he confined himself to showing Beatrice their new brothel board, but then he added a solemn pronouncement in Italian: "*Ecco, la mia bella, il bidetto anche per scrivere!*" But Beatrice, too, was in no mood for intellectual feats commensurate with my cultural achievement. She refrained from using the newly created libertine surface to compose a lapidary statement in Latin, *in hoc equidem equuleo...* She didn't even have any florid complimentary words for my skill in cabinetry. She was simply hungry, and she told me so.

Ecco, I'll set our new table for a topping-out ceremony. We brewed up some Spanish national chocolate, which comes mixed with sugar, cinnamon, and other seasonings. Beatrice took the first taste, and thus it was she who, with a grandly vulgar gesture, spat out the stringy mess on the floor. It was a horrid brew. I was forewarned, and so I didn't have to spit. Using a well-known hydraulic technique practiced by infants, I made the substance flow back into the bowl, went outside, and heaved the Spanish national drink into a ditch with a splash. Immediately the chickens came running and clucking, hoping for something to peck. Go ahead and peck, but you'll be better off with a worm. I closed the package and placed it in the single pigeon-hole of our new secretary. Then I boiled some water and we finally enjoyed a hot drink—insipid, but germ-free. Typhus! That was all we needed. Beatrice had terrifying things to say on this subject, and I was familiar with the story she now saw fit to recount once more. Her father had died of the disease in Argentina at a time when she herself had contracted the bubonic plague, the wicked scourge of the Old Testament, the Lord's Avenging Angel, the Black Death. Her mother defeated it by dosing her with homeopathic miracle drops. The local physician, not to mention the populace far and wide, was astounded at this development; he was getting ready to give her the usual lethal injection. Thousands had already succumbed to the epidemic. Not one infected person had survived; they all turned black, began talking gibberish, and that was the end.

No indeed, we were not about to take risks here at the very borderline of perdition, sitting right next to a ditch full of rats. Having barely escaped syphilis as a result of my stringent self-discipline and my rationalized cowardice, we ought not to let ourselves be ambushed by the miasmatic fever in a simple sip of water. As Nietzsche says, "With various little medications you can turn a coward into a hero—but the reverse is also true."

Our grape cure had made us weak, but it had also cleansed our blood so that we were immune from hypochondria—one less affliction. The world around us was hostile; we had to be ready for anything, and that meant we had to think through every next step. By purchasing that chocolate soup we had put our exchequer under unnecessary strain. One more mistake like that, and we would find ourselves at the very rim of the volcano that was already spitting at us. This hackneyed phrase about the yawning abyss is what the rhetoricians call a trope: the transformation of an abstract concept into a graphic image. I am employing such a figure of speech here not just to enrich my prose, but mindful of a very specific hole in the ground that threatened to become an abyss for us, and which to our consternation was actually enticing us. Every agricultural enterprise has a manure pile, and since there were large animals and much human traffic here at the Clock Tower, the installation for excretory waste was correspondingly capacious. Architecturally speaking, it fit in nicely with the monastic ambience, although I would not have placed it quite so close to the open-air staircase. It was longer than it was wide, and its masonry extended about a foot above ground, in keeping with traditional dimensions. What surprised us was that this oblong structure also served as the place of retreat for human beings. Visiting it entailed walking out on a plank laid across the pit, which dipped down precariously under one's own weight and as a result of its frequent use. The place was partially concealed by dangling vines—a gift of Nature that was particularly appreciated by the female population.

During the night the plank was a shadowy rendezvous for the rats. They were reluctant to depart when, in your state of secret need, you walked the plank and sent it dipping up and down with your steps. Month after month I conducted nocturnal observations of rattish behavior, and often regretted my lack of talent for sketching. Yet out of respect for the aesthetic sensibilities we are so often reminded of, I shall refrain from further depiction of the goings-on at the edge of this crater. I shall only add that my regular nocturnal vigils were finally rewarded by the sight of a snarl of living matter, a shadowy black mass of tails and legs and snouts that could be nothing else than the fabled rat-king. Overcome with zoological excitement, I nearly fell into the marl-pit. After this fright, instead of continuing my intense observations and perhaps experiencing the approach of this swarm of creatures towards me on the plank, I confess that I behaved unprofessionally: I leaped up, ran off to Beatrice in our cell, and reported to her that there was something good to be said, after all, about the place that she preferred to avoid for a thousand reasons. "A rat cluster!" I stammered. "Come quick, or it'll be gone! There must be thirty of them, all knotted up together!" Beatrice turned pale and waxen with disgust. A single rat was enough for her. "Not even old man Brehm ever saw such a tight-knit family with his own eyes! Just think what he might have given to hunker down there with me on the plank for an hour or so." Beatrice said something about the bubonic plague that gets passed on by rats, and that there were still cases of it in Spain, especially in Barcelona. I slunk back out to the diving board, but there was no repeat of the miracle. I squatted there with stiff knee joints for quite a while, until someone came and chased me away.

Incidentally, I solved Beatrice's double phobia against pits in a way that once again did credit to my talent for invention. It was a carpenter's stratagem that not even the ingenious architects of the Middle Ages had thought of. After we finally departed this cloister of lust, my contraption was dismantled, and no chronicle, least of all the sketchy present one, will ever again relate the details of my cunning technical-hygienic installation. To this day Beatrice often thinks back to that period of horror and its dark menace, but she is touched to recall with gratitude that Vigoleis never got so cross with her as to chase her out on the plank. No, that he never did. This woman was chased enough to begin with. Love, in combination with inventive skill and a bad conscience, is what led to an appropriately sanitary solution.

Our first day at the cloister ended with us having arranged our moveable goods as sensibly as possible within the immoveable cell space provided. To achieve this I had to nail the chair to wall in such a position that it could be reached when we wished to place it at the desk—entirely in keeping with the philosophy of Either/Or, which under the circumstances must be judged not as a purely intellectual insight, but as an element in the art of living. I hoisted our two large trunks on top of the partition at the places where it formed a T with the neighboring box, thus giving us something like a homey ceiling and made the room feel more like a room. We just had to trust that this invasion of the next-door space—it was a matter of a few inches at most—would not elicit objections. If it did, I would have to screw down those big pieces of luggage, but where would I find screws? Simple: I just removed a few from all over the room. No one ever bawled me out on account of this annexation; there could be no question of a violation of law in the vertical direction, since all I did was take up some free space. Our trunks now towered above us, but we had to tie them in place with the ropes, for otherwise I might have to spend time in jail for manslaughter.

After two hours of moving things around, which meant creating order at one end of the space by causing disorder in the other, we were exhausted. Each of us took a swallow of germ-free water, a ration of biscuit carefully apportioned by Beatrice, and gave each other a germ-free kiss. Then we embraced tightly and fell asleep. The day had been a busy one, and not without its blessings, considering that neither of us considered murdering the other in order to usurp space. We shared it like two people who have not yet arrived at the knowledge of good and evil.

Nothing disturbed our peace. No noise from above descended on our pallet. The encampment was utterly silent. Beatrice was right: the youth of Spain does not go hiking. All the more restless, however, were the rats. Yet their hustlings and jostlings, their scatterings and bumpings were no match for the deafness of our slumber, even though there must have been quite a hubbub when the swarm took possession of our cell. There wasn't much to be had, but enough to keep the indefatigable tooth of a rat quite busy. The sleeping couple did not awaken even when the grisly gnawing horde attacked their stock of provender. Was the mangy old lady-rat among them? I rather doubt it, for she would have to have been tugged up over the walls by the her younger cohorts, as I once observed a suckling mother rat do with her entire brood. The invaders will have been amazed to find suddenly, in this one compartment, more to gnaw on than was to be located anywhere else in the cells. There, they would be happy to come across a banana skin, a piece of chocolate, or a crust of bread. The truly lucky one would hit upon a cardboard packet containing a dose of Vaseline—that oily stuff was yummy, something to bare your teeth and hiss about. Since tubes have come into use, hardly any forager can sniff out this greasy delicacy any more.

The animals paraded in a row along the vertiginous top edge of our partition, their tails hanging down like a single broad band across the upper edge of the wall—could we have watched it move? They sniffed at everything; not a suitcase, not a package, not a book escaped their attention. This cell, and these inhabitants of it, are from now on to be kept under close surveillance. Of particular interest was this small box, shaped like a suitcase. It didn't look easy to gnaw through; one's teeth just slipped across its hard surfaces. But wait—there emanated from inside it such a tempting fragrance that one ought to have a go at the corners. This was the container, at one time used by a Dutch traveling salesman to carry around his samples, where Vigoleis now kept his manuscripts, especially poems, which in spite of his advancing years he still wrote, but which in a spirit of unhealthy modesty he concealed from everybody. Not even Beatrice was allowed access to this little hoard of work in progress. Vigoleis kept alive her interest in his poetic idiosyncrasies by showing her works that had already been stored long enough to mature, or by telling her Herostratic stories about verse manuscripts long since immolated. These were conversations in the realm of the dead, like those famous ones that were popular when Frederick the Great was king.

The morning of the second day found our two anachorites up early. Their bodies were numb from sleep; here and there they had sleep-marks on their skin, and it took a while before they could distinguish which limb was whose. The plunge that then occurred was an intentional one, and it didn't hurt Vigoleis at all. There was no kissing—that would have been a mockery, a virtual desecration of the original cultic motive for such gestures: the transference of energy from one person to another. Not to mention the connotations... But enough, the reason they refrained from kissing was their immediate notice of the havoc visited upon their room during the night. As if with a single breath they both exclaimed, "Now we have nothing to eat!"

Our national chocolate was done for: it was simply inedible, and would be so even if we had put it somewhere less accessible. We wished we could have hurled it at the rats. We were rigid with despair.

Whispering to each other, we pondered what to do. One of us should set off alone for the post office, because we now had to conserve bodily energy. I went and returned with one empty hand, and no trace of the bundle of banknotes we were expecting. In my other hand I held a bunch of grapes I had stolen. I saw them hanging down in front of me as I walked, and so I took them along. Perhaps they were public property, but in any case my conscience was unburdened. The grapes were for Beatrice. For myself, I also brought along some rusty hooks and a tiny horseshoe. These were for my next handicraft project: a rat trap.

Beatrice was lying on the bed, smoking. She wasn't reading. She wasn't doing anything at all. She was on strike.

The rats, she said, had come back. In broad daylight, or at least during the daytime hours in this shadowy cell. She had tossed books at them. Disgusting beasts. She just couldn't stand this much longer. "Did you get the money transfer?"

Here I stand, displaying for her my grapes and my rusty metal, and she is asking me about money?

"Beatrice, you have less imagination than Adam and Eve before the Fall. I pick up a money transfer, and then walk all the way back home carrying this junk?" I placed everything carefully on the *bidetto*. "I would have raced back to you in a Hispano-Suiza, I would have honked the horn, tossed roses to you and abducted you. Maybe tomorrow. But no, tomorrow you want to leave."

"Forgive me. I'm so stupid and tired. Be so good as to pick up all the books I threw at the beasts. They're in the rooms next door."

I clambered through the neighboring cells until I had gathered up our personal library, and then I took the chair down from its nail, stepped up on it, and began a careful repositioning of the trunks. I would rather have read some poems. I imagined myself as Sir *Wigalois*, standing watch over his fair damsel, doing battle with rats instead of dragons.

Today I wish I could retrieve my actual frame of mind at that moment. My book collection contained the first complete edition of poems by Georg Trakl. For the edification of Beatrice from the homeopathic family, *simila similibus curantur*, I could have read her his poem about rats, one that was surely inspired by a "Clock Tower" experience. It's almost all the same: the whistling noise, the empty silence at the windows, the shadows under the eaves, the horrible stink coming from the toilet. Still the "winds that groan in the dark" were not "icy" here; at nighttime they reached temperatures that would have sent us kids in Germany home from school because of the heat. The moon is everywhere white and ghostly, in every poem and in every evening, except when it's a question of making love under a lilac bush. The vision of death that Trakl, with Hölderlinian grandeur and accuracy, conjures up amidst decay, repulsiveness and decomposition, could have given us strength back then when the vermin were plotting our downfall. Beatrice, too, cannot now recall which author she chose do help her do battle with the evil forces in that loathsome house of joy. Perhaps, she says, it was Angel Ganivet's *Idearium Español*. She was smitten by this Andalusian writer and diplomat who, while still young, took his own life in Riga as the result of a love affair. I myself was later much taken by the mystical-religious attitude that led Ganivet to reject Catholicism, while Beatrice's sober, more foresighted mind was captivated by the racial-political reflections that inform that writer's *Idearium*.

We read. But even the most severely addicted reader will drop his book if the flesh is weak. Reading requires a certain minimum of flesh on the bones.

The third day: as far as our practical routine is concerned, it was just like the day before, except that it was Beatrice who made the pilgrimage into town and came back "without nothing." And because she is neither a thief nor a scavenger, her hands were completely empty. There was hot water, each of us picked up our favorite writer, and then we drowsed off into a state resembling sleep, in which clear thoughts played the role of dreams. When we awoke we exchanged our thoughts about these thoughts; Beatrice spoke of "lucid stupefaction," while I preferred to call it "mystical catatonia." It thus appears that starvation was good for something, after all. Then Beatrice suddenly said that she wanted to end her life. I was constantly talking about suicide, she added; she was actually going to do it. I was crushed, for wasn't it Beatrice herself who, just a short time ago, had given me Nietzsche's works as a gift intended to bring a little light into my sullen existence?

Beatrice never gambles. This means that Schiller, in his missionary role as educator of the human race, would deny her a place among humankind, since only that person is human who has a sense of play. And because she shuns any and all gaming tables, she certainly had never gambled with life, much less with any thoughts of ending a life. I mean, of course, her own life, not someone else's, since other people's lives are meaningful only in a collective sense. Which is to say they have no meaning at all, as our wars and the current rapid transition in the Western world from humanism to hominism so amply displays. The fact that Beatrice desired to wring the hooker Pilar's neck is sufficient proof that she has not yet fully abandoned the realm of common humanity or become a sociopath—or should I put all this in the past tense? No, today she remains grounded in the Old Testament, despite the crisis in the Clock Tower and despite all the other crises she has endured through war and escape from war, renewed hunger, and her chronically senile Vigoleis. Her list of potential victims still contains a half dozen names of persons who ought to be eliminated illegally from this world, insofar as this world impinges on her private world. The number remains magically constant, while the names change over time. Some depart from the scene, new ones appear and get on her nerves, and thus there is a quite natural, seasonal continuity to her roster of contemptibles.

I myself do not disapprove of suicide, which Creation itself has demonstrated for us in impressive examples. In fact, I consider the concept of suicide as more sublime than that of a death than can strike us in the form of a flower pot plummeting from the sixth floor and hitting our skull—with God's prior knowledge, to be sure, since He has even included the lone sparrow dropping from the sky in His Master Plan for the Universe. Every human being has the right to do with his own life whatever he pleases; if it pleases him to end it, that is his own business. And yet it is someone else's business whether fellow humans approve of his deed. Most people regard the act as a violation of nature—"What if everybody...?" And there's the rub. It is pure egotism that makes a person who feels superfluous want others to go on living, or to die by their neighbor's hand. "The ethics of any pessimistic religion," Nietzsche says, "consists in excuses not to commit suicide." Even a person who believes in God and attributes solely to the Almighty the right to bring a life to an "unnatural" end before its "natural" one, might be persuaded to see in suicide the Will of God, of a God who in such cases, using a finely calculated and masterly plan, chooses a technique other than a bubonic plague, a Pilarian bacillus, a flower pot, or a Massacre of the Innocents to gather human souls into His presence. In the words of my poet Pascoaes, whose brother was hounded to death as a student in Coimbra by a professor who was his intellectual inferior, "He chose to decrease the distance between himself as a creature and his Creator."

I, too, consider suicide to be a religious variant of the Big Gamble in Paradise. I don't mean the kind that happens when life threatens to choke you, when you leave fingerprints on the cash register, when there's a bank failure, when your wife is sleeping with the chimney sweep (which leaves other kinds of prints), when you just can't stand it any more and reach for the noose. All that has nothing at all to do with suicide, at least not with the dignified, metaphysical type of suicide I have in mind. Those are simply petty bourgeois traffic accidents of a sort that just don't happen in the primeval forest. I'm fully aware that my position on this matter resembles that of a black native who feels superior to the whites, or of one of the "happy few," one who feels more at home in the realm of metaphysics than in the range of experience open to everyone under the moon, who senses the redemptive emptiness that lies beyond this world and desires a foretaste of it, who immerses himself in it and, especially if he has fled from some Pilar, feels the need to stretch out his antennae toward some new form of Eternity, who can hold out for a day and a night, and again for another day and another night, in the awareness that there will once be an end to all this nonsense, with no promise whatsoever of a rebirth or continuation of existence, either in this world or the next. Someone who, by clinging to this metaphysics of *nada*, is just as unoriginal as the antipodes who fall to their knees with utter faith and confidence in the opposite persuasion—those heroes of the battlefield who trumpet forth *fortissimo* their own homeward march, if they haven't died already. And they will have monuments erected to them. None of that is original. But what, after all, does "original" mean? Not even God was "original" when, after the Creation, he delivered up the whole thing to mankind, like some earthly artist in search of bread.

All this is an amplification of the philosophy of the sin of the Creation as developed by my mystical friend Pascoaes, whom at the time I—a novice and myself a flesh-and-blood candidate for suicide in the Clock Tower—had not yet discovered, despite my search through Iberian literature for new ideas, inducements, and stimuli for my notion of nada. But this is an exaggeration, for I actually left it to chance to meet up with the proper adversary. I came close; my Portuguese sage was already on the horizon, and it is one of the rewarding aspects of my Mediterranean guest appearance that I finally did encounter this Lusitanian poet who, without fear, lays siege to the ramparts of his God. The pathway into his presence would take us first to a place that we sorely missed in our Tower. Patience!

I do not disapprove of suicide, because its roots can be located in the big mistake of Creation itself. But was Beatrice thinking of this kind of metaphysically grounded death now, on the our third day of starvation? Did she wish to return to her Maker and then call back to me, "*Ciao*, Vigo! There's hot water everywhere here, and you can have a roof over your head!"—which I have my doubts about with regard to the Great Beyond. Be that as it may, what *did* she want? The word "annihilation" had been uttered. Our values were about to undergo a total revaluation—I was expecting something very final. To be sure, here in the cloister of the horizontal brothers, different standards prevailed. Our cell was proof in and of itself that nothing at all could be depended upon in these surroundings, least of all in the matter of nutrition. How gladly we would have crawled on our stomachs the entire length of the corridor if, at the other end, we had espied a slice of bread, preferably garnished with sobrasada or even a stone-hard *butifarra*. We were now ascetics, wetting our lips with stagnant water. No locusts fell to us from heaven, not to mention manna or wild honey (Velikovsky's *Worlds in Collision* hadn't been written yet). If I were to succumb now, if the strength of my mind were to sink beneath that of my body, then we would have to do ourselves in, hand in hand. And we could arrange that in a romantic way. I had imagination; I enjoyed, albeit within a small circle of acquaintances, a certain reputation as an inventor, and moreover, we were avid readers—Beatrice had in fact read a great deal. Literature could offer us examples of how two people who are tired of living can take leave of this world—Romeo and Juliet come to mind. We know of their fate in the form of Luigi Da Porto's novel, Shakespeare's stagecraft, and Gottfried Keller's dreamy, romantic version.

If I were to yield to my drive for annihilation, I would opt for the Swiss writer's solution, even though Vigoleis and Beatrice were not separated by family hatred, which is always more intense when money is at stake. Something else, though, was separating them from their love, which did not come to an end with Pilar. What I have in mind is the fact that their tragedy, their Spanish auto, was no less worthy of attention, although up to the very moment I write this only a single writer of the most obscure reputation has taken it up as a subject. To be more precise, this writer is right now in the process of laying it all out. Will he conquer the stages of the world? That depends on whether the audiences approve of their method of dying. When the curtain falls, audiences prefer to see the boards heaped with corpses, blood everywhere, swords skewering the heroes' armored breasts, daggers stuck in the enemy's ribs up to the hilt, and the avenger's cry of "How do you like that!"

That is why I said to Beatrice that I had no intention of interfering with her gloomy plans, that I was never a spoilsport except in regard to myself, "and do you know, *chérie*, if I were to approve, if we actually do it, won't that mean that we are admitting defeat? That we are the slaves of our own desires? A marriage built on egotism is corrupt and will come apart. Is that what we want? Over a bit of hot water? In a house like this one, I hesitate to speak *pro domo*, and I could be easily misunderstood. And imagine if I were ever to write my memoirs—how should I handle this chapter of our life? Will I have to suppress it? Will I have to pretend that we never went to the dogs, or should I try to capitalize on this autobiographical detail in the manner of great writers such as St. Augustine? If you're thinking that this is a melancholy idea, then you have to know that such is just the way I am by nature, with or without earthly ambushes by a Pilar or dilapidated youth hostels. It's just that nobody notices. But let me make this clear: I refuse to let my sublime disgust with life be subsumed in your low-grade *taedium vitae*.

"Here's another suggestion, a splendid one, one that comes from a remote corner of my being that hasn't yet been smothered in darkness. Let's not rush things and spoil the handiwork of Divine Providence, which on occasion has a hard enough time of it. Let's be real men and give it an honest chance, one last chance, or maybe two last chances since there are two of us and One of them. That's what you call fair play, *sportif*. Starting today we won't boil our drinking water any more. No more killing of germs, no more prophylactic measures. Let's make a beggarman's contract with fate, the kind that used to be so popular, where you sign up for a process of honest competition. There's a legal word for it, but I've forgotten what it is. All right, the first step will be the intestinal one. The second will be by way of Amsterdam, and for that I'll need a sheet of paper, an envelope, and a postage stamp (which we don't have). On second thought, I'll send the letter without a return address so the addresse will have to pay the postage, which he'll gladly do when he sees *Clima ideal* on the cancellation, considering that it rains all the time in Amsterdam. That's the most reliable way to send a letter, because the post office always wants to get its money. And who do you think I'm going to let the post office press a fine from? One of your victims? Your erudite brother in Basel? My uncle on Cathedral Square in Münster? My dear loved ones in Süchteln on the Niers? Wrong! I'll write to them on some other occasion, and make their eyes leap from their sockets.

Quiet, don't ask. I want to go on being mysterious. This idea has to ripen in me like a potato seed—when it hits daylight it will suddenly turn green. I'll start writing, Beatrice, while you recline exhausted in body and spirit on that cot for wayward youth. It'll be a letter to the single person who holds the little sparrow of our life in his hands, and he simply won't let it fall from the roof. I'm going to write to Vic—or rather, to put it in the arcane and cryptic form of his little country's titular *barème*: to His Excellency the Most Worthy, Highest-Born, Most Erudite Sir Victor Emmanuel van Vriesland, Esquire, Friend of the Fair Sex and Connoisseur of Fine Literature—the first writer of world renown whom Vigoleis ever sinned against before he went over, or is going over, or is about to go over, to self-pollution. For you see, Beatrice, it's all a question of transition, of transcendence, if you prefer to hear such exalted terms from your own transcendent but not at all immanent Vigoleis. I'm going to write to Vic and apply a whole lot of pressure on him, which I'll ask him to reapply to the very pretty lady he's closed the film contract with, and probably some other kind of contract as well. Who besides Vriesland is capable of sculpting on the weaker sex the kind of concave relief that only the ancient Egyptians were the masters of? Over the years the carvings can get clogged up, and you have to use a rasp to clean them out. In his inimitable charming way he will make an impression on this girl and free up the money. It'll be here next week, I swear it! Today is Thursday, by nine o'clock my letter will be on its way to Barcelona. I'm going to take it directly to the harbor so it doesn't sit around in Palma for weeks more on our friend Don Fernando's desk. He's a meticulous worker, and that usually means lots of delays. Next Tuesday it'll be in Amsterdam. By Wednesday Vic will have paid the postage due, and he'll read it on Thursday when he wakes up from the hangover he'll have from his scrounging maneuver. Any objections, *ma chère*?

None. During the course of this optimistic conversation with the pessimistic Beatrice, which found me bubbling over with self-denial, I took the typewriter out of the box that the rats had gnawed at but not succeeded in ripping open. I put it on the *bidetto*, rolled in a sheet of paper, typed out the date "Torre del Reloj, Thursday...," and then came the salutation. Did I write "Dear Mr. van Vriesland," or "Dear Victor E. van Vriesland, " or just "Dear Vic"? I can't recall which degree of human and literary cordiality author and translator had reached at this point in their relationship.

The little machine rattled and banged, the platen with its dried-out rubber roller zipped back and forth, line followed line, and the result was a lengthy epistle. Sometimes misery loves prolixity. Inspiration usually arrives from above; materialistic thinking imagines the creation of the universe, the revelation of the Good, the True, and the Beautiful, the divine enthusiasm of poets, and hitting the jackpot as resulting from an emanation from on high, a kind of bathroom shower with tiny jets whose faucet human beings have no control over, for otherwise there would be no miracle. Here in the Sundial Tower, in this grubby flophouse and eternal trampoline, inspiration reached Vigoleis from below, from the bathroom appliance he was typing at and on. You might say that he was the recipient of subterranean effusions, tellurian impulses that a dowser could detect if he ever found his way into our cell of happiness.

Vigoleis typed away on top of the bidet. It shouldn't surprise anyone that every word he wrote took shape under the aegis of a particular legendary animal, the horse. *Bidetto* means literally "little horse" "little nag," or "pony." One thinks immediately of the winged Pegasus, the symbol of poets the world over, the stallion that created the Hippokrene Spring on Mount Helikon with a stroke of his hoof. Right here and now, our poetizing hero was digging his spurs in the loins of his Dutch colleague, urging him to gallop forth valiantly. And behold! The fabled fountain of Berlin Film Inc. will start to flow!

For a few hours the hallowed halls resounded to the ryhthmic rappings of mechanically activated revelation, without discord of any kind. Beatrice does not snore in her sleep. All the other cells were still empty. My orchestration of our bitter misery thus escaped profanation by the raucous discord that can arise among journeying men when they, too, run out of bread and whip out their switchblades to defend their right to the last available crust. For we must not deceive ourselves about the journeyman clientele under this celestial canopy. Not a few of the establishment's patrons will have dastardly deeds on their record, committed while on their travels under, as the poet says, the benevolent eye of God. It's all a matter of the distance between the Creator and His creature. The only disturbance was the black shadows scurrying along the top of the cell partition. From day to day the rats were getting more insolent.

Tapping a final period into the machine, Vigoleis felt his inspiration suddenly expire. The emanations stalled out completely; from below there now came forth from the mythological bathroom appliance only a faintly putrid stench. And from above, silence descended upon the young man who was daring to enter the lists with fate itself.

On this third day of alimentary fasting—already preceded by a period of moral abstinence—Vigoleis' girl slept the sleep of total exhaustion.

The hygienic pony had done its duty well. For the first time ever, and without bucking, it had tolerated an intellectual burden on its back.

At around 7 pm I went to the harbor. I left a note explaining my departure and its urgent rationale, for otherwise Beatrice might have might have gone into shock thinking that I had taken off to do myself in all alone. March in step, but bite the dust separately—is that Vigoleis' motto?

A vigorous walker with a length of pace like my own should take 35 to 40 minutes to get from the Clock Tower to the mailbox of the Transmediterránea Steamship Company. A more casual loping gait would require about ¾ of an hour. This hike, out and back, took me more than three hours. The letter-carrier took a long rest at the dock, then he started for home with a spring in his step, like a happy convalescent. His thoughts probably oscillated between heaven and earth; today I can easily imagine what at the time I could imagine only vaguely.

Having arrived at the olfactory barricade of the slaughterhouse, I had to break through another kind of obstruction, one that had to be overcome without holding my nose. The highway in the vicinity of the Tower was now guarded by armed men. On closer approach I saw that they had formed a cordon around the Tower premises. Searchlights were scouring the area; beams of light hit me, and just as suddenly let me disappear again. So I wasn't their target. A few mounted men galloped away—was this perhaps a night-time military maneuver? Had they selected Arsenio's handsomely situated fortress as the scene of their strategic exercises? And what does "handsome" mean in this context? But I have no comprehension of martial whims, and maybe it was the local firefighters responding to a false alarm. But then I heard a shout of "Alto!"

"You musn't go any farther, get back, please!" I heard myself addressed in friendly, calm, and clear tones. Mainland Spaniards are capable of this type of command; a German armed guard could never come close to it. When a German guard gives an order, he turns as steely as his rifle. The man giving me an order here was no Mallorquin.

I cobbled together my Spanish vocabulary and explained to the *carabinero* that I unfortunately could not leave the area, that it was imperative for me to enter the premises—yes, the "Torre del Reloj," for that was where I lived with my wife. I used the word "wife" as a diplomatic gesture to designate a private relationship that was none of his business in any case; if this had been a German guard I would have uttered some long bureaucratic phrase.

Instead of arresting me, the gendarme laughed. In fact, he laughed resoundingly, and I would have bet my own head that he was a high-ranking officer, although I couldn't see his stars. He was still giggling when he called over another member of his squad to share the joke with him—"Hey, just think, this guy says he *lives* here with a woman—with his wife!" His colleagued laughed out loud, too: "Oh sure! Who *hasn't* lived in there with a woman?" But then, "Now please leave."

It is not my habit to resist authority. I lack money for doing this, and therefore I lack the courage. What is more, I was very tired, and thus I could be excused many things. But before I acted in obedience to the command to depart, I had a brilliant idea: I named a name. Civil servants of all kinds are impressed by names, simply because they earn their bread by seeking to eliminate namelessness in the line of duty. I told them to apprise Don Arsenio of my presence; what I said was that they should contact him right away and tell him that Don Vigo, the German, the *homme de lettres*, was at the cordon outside, and that Arsenio should identify him.

Thank heavens, they finally understood me. Minutes later I was escorted under armed guard to the courtyard, where a turbulent act of the world stage was being performed. I don't know who was playing what role, nor do I know who wrote the script. But it was clear that the Lord of the Manse was not a mere extra in this drama, to judge from the sweaty and jowl-shaking excitement and bossiness of his behavior ("Just you try...!"). My *almocrebe* was there, too, as well as a few men I had often seen ambling across the Tower courtyard—regular customers, I supposed, for Arsenio ran a café here where you could get things to eat and drink; you just clapped your hands, and the table set itself. And now they were all swearing up and down; nobody understood a word I was saying or what anybody else was saying—which swearing isn't meant to accomplish anyway. When I appeared on the stage, Arsenio swung his hat. I didn't catch the cue from the prompter. And then a captain of the guard came up to me.

This captain—maybe he had one more star, I'm not familiar with this brand of astronomy—greeted me politely, and in his address to me employed the French language. He was neatly combed and uniformed, ironed and polished, and I was unkempt and unshaven, and very, very tired. Oh you brigands, you who wield power, let me pass! What is the password? I want to go to bed. I've just sent a letter to Vic. The letter is already afloat, it's proceeded ahead of you, you can call it predestination of the Lyon kind, everything is fitting together nicely like a worm gear. Why, if the bidet hadn't served me as a burbling fount of artesian inspiration I would still be squatting in front of it with my machine, grasping for fitting words to open the eyes of my colleague—yes, you natty fellows, I happen to be a colleague of Monsieur Victoire de Vriesland, *un homme de lettres, lui aussi.*

What were these official gentlemen doing here anyway, in the calm of night? Everywhere and anywhere in the world, policemen are an embarrassment. The more innocent you are, the quicker you'll get caught, for the true culprit knows how to pull his neck out of the sling. The sling will be pulled tight no matter what, but they never catch the real guy. But now, is it me they want to catch? Or maybe Beatrice? Or one of the ladies of the night, one of the thirty? But now there are only twenty-nine of them; we have, after all, requisitioned a *bidetto* for service in intellectual pursuits—we, your typical representatives of a bidet-less culture. That's it! We are a bidet-less culture! That's what I've been trying to explain to Beatrice. That's the reason why we North People, we who get conceived to the accompaniment of the goose step and get born with trumpet fanfares, that's why we are in such decline! A nation's greatness...

Then the major said he had been told that I was a German, and that I had taken up lodgings with my *Madame* in the Clock Tower. Very well. But was this in fact the case—please understand, just a formality...? Could I provide identification? And, *pardon*, what was I doing at this place, since it didn't seem as though it accepted permanent guests. Or did Señor Arsenio recently... ahem...? There was a long pause, the colonel looked over at the Giant but refrained from slapping his boot-top with his riding whip. He spoke French slowly, correctly, with no grammatical mistakes, although Beatrice probably would have counted up a dozen or more, and then added the ones I was making, and it would have been curtains for both of us. As it was, the officer and I understood each other perfectly. Of course I could prove my legitimacy; my

passport was in our room—should I go get it? And if I may be permitted to
inquire, what was this all about?

That was for the time being none of my business—such, in effect, was the
reply, though it may have been more polite. There was a small complication.
Allons. I climbed the open staircase with the sergeant in my tracks. Not one
rat showed its face. They had all hidden away because the battalion had arrived with dogs in tow, and the gendarmes who weren't standing guard were
patrolling the fields with muskets at the ready. Revolution? But the King had
long since been smoked out. Or was he trying to smuggle himself back in?

A *carabinero* was standing guard at our private chamber. He saluted his superior and gave his report. It sounded much like army headquarters, and my
next thought, so close to the *pilarière*, was: the vice squad, as in Amsterdam
on Nicolaas Beets Straat. Well then, if you want to know, we're not really
married. We're living together in devout congress, and we're at the end of our
rope. Poor Beatrice, a mangy rat hanging from our partition wall would be
better than this. The only redeeming feature of the scene was that the guard
was seated on a chair.

And Beatrice was seated on our cot with her flowery *peignoir*, looking more
exotically beautiful, more Indian than ever. Her right hand—Good Lord, how
angry she must be! "What's going on? Have you been sitting in front of the
door all this time? Are they looking for somebody?"

"What's going on? I was about to ask you the same thing. They're turning
the place upside down."

My sense of security returned. My fatigue was gone. I should have crossed
swords with the general, not chickened out as I did back in Münster when a
fellow student, a member of a dueling fraternity, challenged me, and I answered him in the presence of other habitual duelers, that I was too cowardly
for swordplay, and anyway not the dueling sort. My friends studying in the
theology department were proud of me; they detected in this reply a proof of
my enormous courage. But then I turned cowardly a second time, and didn't
even try to explain to them that I was really and truly a coward.

I handed our passports to the captain outside the door. First the document
from the Weimar Republic and then the little booklet, showing official stamps
from page one through to the end, issued by the Swiss Confederation. Oh, the
lady has done some traveling, said the officer, and I immediately took shame
at the paucity of stamps in my own passport. Everything was in order, many
thanks, but could he just take a peek into our room, though he didn't wish to
disturb Madame, very sorry, he wasn't going to ask any questions, we obviously didn't belong here, "*c'est la vie*," he was just doing his duty. He did it
with a rapid, expert glance inside the cell, then he gave us a majestic salute.
Surely he had the highest rank in his line of service, and without any doubt
he was a man of the world. As such, and dressed in civilian clothes, he returned to the Clock Tower a few days later and made Beatrice a grand-style
immoral proposition. Meanwhile the guard had gone to sleep on his chair. I
let him snooze and closed the door noiselessly.

"House search," said Beatrice as I squeezed my way into her boudoir. "You had just left when I woke up to the sound of a shot. That's when I noticed that I'd fallen asleep and you weren't here. And then you should have seen the spectacle, the uproar—I was crying, shouting, swearing, much worse than that business back then with Béla Kun. I thought..."

"Vigo has gone and shot himself. Cross your heart, who else around here would be interested in shooting off guns?"

"I know you're afraid of guns. I didn't have time to think anything. There was your note, and all of a sudden they started banging on the wall, and I thought all the trunks would come crashing down. Adeleide ran in crying and said nothing was going to happen to us, we should just stay inside, and if I understood her correctly, they were looking for smugglers, and her husband was under suspicion, but he was innocent. That's all she said, because then a *carabinero* took her out and asked me for a chair. That's all I know. But Vigo, I beg you. I can't stay here any longer. We've got to leave. I'd rather die in the gutter!"

That's easier said than done in a country where the gutters are filled with contented bums. I don't even think that there is a single country where you can die in a gutter. That's just a figure of speech.

That night we didn't get any sleep. Instead, we felt a marvelous lightness. We seemed to have sprouted wings, and our ears resounded with shivering, rushing tones. If you need a musical comparison for this, Beatrice would be the one to consult. But that's not really necessary, because these organ-like sonorities came to us not from the upper vaults of our basilica but from our own abdomens. To put it more delicately: the singing arose from the hunger in our blood.

As the meager dawn approached, we dozed off into a semi-slumber that lasted perhaps a second or two, perhaps an hour. But then we heard a noise at the walls of our cell. The rats!

But it wasn't the rats, nor was it an armed battalion. First we saw a little hand reach over the partition, shadowless, like the hand of a dead child. We had no time to cower in fright, though, because the fingers of this hand clearly bent over the top of the wall to get a purchase on it. And then a second hand appeared, grabbing the partition. And finally a little curly head. Only one creature in the Tower had such a head of curls, and that was little Rosario. She peered into our cell.

What she saw appeared not to satisfy her. Far back in her little throat she made a sound like the bleating of a new-born lamb. The others in this soprano choir were apparently standing downstairs in the corridor. The one peeking in on us said, "They're still not doing it!" The little rubberneck slid down from her perch and the mob of kids dispersed giggling.

Oh, my dear children, how I would like to have done you the favor of doing what we weren't doing! For doing it would have meant living not only in a different skin, but in an entirely different flesh, not the martyred flesh we could barely sustain with a few drops of water, dragging ourselves past the stations of the cross muttering "Lord, have mercy on us" and fingering the beads of our agonizing rosary. No one was having mercy on our heroes. But what do you kids know about what's really going on in your father's house? What's really going on, 30 times from door to door—kids, go play somewhere else.

Beatrice glanced squarely at me. "*C'est ça?*"

"What else?"

<h1 style="text-align:center">II</h1>

Except for the usual wailing of the wind and the everyday hubbub on the premises—the barking dogs, the squealing piglets, the braying donkeys, the clucking poultry—all was quiet at the Tower. I stepped outside our door.

Arsenio was strutting around prouder than usual, issuing orders. When he saw me he gave me a conspiratorial wink and called out a few words, as if in rapid summation of the previous night's adventures. Those cops had better go back into training if they think they can catch him—if indeed there was anything to catch here in his personal domain.

At noontime we lay down again, Beatrice on the bed, I on the floor, each of us in the drowsy shadows of our hunger. Then I suddenly heard voices. There was commotion. More and more people had arrived at our cloister, door after door was being opened, the partitions shook. I heard Adeleide's voice. Children were screaming like crazy.

Adeleide was scurrying around in the corridor. At the far end on a small wall pedestal was a statue of the Madonna, the altar in this House of Love, with candles that, when lit, surrounded Our Gracious Lady with a halo of natural light. I peeked through the door. The hostelry matron was arranging flowers and greenery in gilded vases. A palm frond, beautifully woven in on itself, rose up behind Our Lady to the heights, which in this place were, of course, eternity itself. Was it Corpus Christi? I remembered this feast day very well. On the street in front of our house we put up an altar. We kids had to collect rushes and swamp grass to strew on the path of the Most Blessed Sacrament. Corpus Christi: a moveable feast—but this late in the year? The Catholic Church seemed to follow a different sequence of events in Spain; the faith was different here, the relationship of believers to the Almighty was different. But this was mid-September.

"Friday," said Beatrice, "the day the Lord died. You remember it only as the meatless day of the week. In Spain it means a lot more. In some southern countries they still ring the bells of dread the evening before. In Fiesole I was always touched by that custom."

"Bells of dread? Up in Süchteln we had no such thing, and"—I spoke in an aside—"no mantraps with perpetual May altars, either."

On this day we finessed our walk to the post office. The word "suicide" didn't enter our whispered conversations, although we both kept it in mind and sensed it in each other even as we insisted on boiling our daily ration of water. Then we both retired to our separate pallets. We couldn't share the cot any more, since the straps no longer held. Stretched out on my back, protected against the hard floor by cushions made of pieces of clothing, I began dreaming. But of what? I simply can't remember. But we both recall, with the absolute certainty that comes of preserving "vaguely" in one's memory an agony survived in the past, that we felt as if we had temporarily yielded up all of our earthly weight. To be sure, we were unable to fly, but could probably do so soon if we didn't lose our patience and kept on fasting diligently. If Rilke, who loved to reside in palaces and perambulate arm in arm with white princesses, could say that poverty is a great inner glow, then perhaps he was thinking of the starvation that goes along with poverty, which can in fact become an inner source of light. As with the birds of the air, your bones get hollow and turn into fluorescent tubes. As we know, asceticism is partly based on the desire to release man's higher nature by means of self-denial and abstinence. Stripping ourselves in this fashion at the Giant Arsenio's cloister, we never reached the point where we felt so far elevated above the needs of the day as to require his services no longer. Nor was our condition of drowsy bliss so enticing that we ever wished to repeat the experience at a later time by voluntary exercises in fasting.

"More! More!"—but in Spanish, with its long vowel *aaa*: "*Más! Más!*"— that's how the word hammered rhythmically into my semi-slumber. I saw hands reaching toward me, all the cathedral beggars were crowding in on me, an army officer joined in the mob, half of me was myself, the other half Don Vigoleis, the Catholic German. But then I underwent a further cleavage, and I became the adulterous captain of the East Indian freighter. I saw long rows of animals passing by, large jungle ants being led to the slaughterhouse carrying burning candles, it was like a religious procession, and it smelled of flesh and incense. It smelled of women. I heard piercing shouts, a tongue of flame shot up, I was surrounded by monks' cloaks, there was no lack of people wearing *sanbenitos*, a naked female was there (ascetics are famous for their wild dreams) I was being crowded and pushed, in one hand a dagger, in the other a gleaming receptacle. I felt a painful sweetness on my tongue, then I was split from head to toe. My tongue broke apart, I heard the tinkling of a key ring, and again and again: *más* and *más* and *más*... I tried to rise. Then I screamed and woke up.

"You were shouting so loud," said Beatrice as she bent down over me from the bed to wipe the sweat from my face. "What kind of a disgusting dream was that? I woke you up. I should have just tickled you behind the ear so I wouldn't scare you. I've been wide awake for a long time. I know where we are. Can you hear me? I need some cotton to stuff in my ears, otherwise I'll go crazy. This is Inferno itself!"

The space above me seemed to be staggering in faint illumination. Beams of light were drifting off into the infinity of the sky. The bats, whose nocturnal dogfights had kept the fluttering insects at bay, threw ghostly shadows, like monstrous little dragons. And now there began a hullabaloo of bumping and humping, moaning and groaning, cursing and slamming from twenty-nine cells along the corridor. Women screamed as if they were being roasted alive, and the words they stammered forth in their transports of lust only barely exceeded the illiterate minimum of their devout carnality: *Ay Jesús, ay Jesús, Santa María, ay Jesús, María, José*, followed by a seething machine-gun rat-a-tat of lust from 29 different locations at once: "*Más! Más! Más!*"

C'était ça, évidemment!

Our booth shook. They had finally arrived—the much maligned journey-men—but instead of bringing their *Wanderlust* with them, they brought only their lust, and each one a woman. The debauchery screamed to the high heavens as in the days of Sodom and Gomorra, but no Hand of God appeared to smite the sinful multitude. The ridgepole bearing the brunt of these waves of depravity sat firmly on the walls of the Manse. How that Inca bird would have swung around on his trapeze and shouted his *porra* and *puta*! Every once in a while one of the cells ceased to oscillate, only to have another one redouble its rate of vibration. A third cell began to sound like the drawn-out moan of a conch-shell horn. Then came something like a fanfare, then somebody whacked a bass drum, and somewhere underneath all this, you could discern a *vox humana*. Was someone getting beaten up?

The bats were already hanging in the feeble light of the roofbeams when this orchestral performance came to an end. The cacophony of creation gradually gave way to sounds from outdoors, one instrument after another went silent. Here and there one more note, a straggler from the sea of salaciousness, proof that some guy had finished playing a march for his chosen Madonna. Out on the courtyard a jackass was braying loudly.

And yet silence did not reign among the nuns and the monks. Some dreadful snoring had started up, an ear-splitting form of snoring interrupted occasionally by a curse or the sound of a kick.

Beatrice sat on the bed like a corpse—cold, pale, bolt upright, with wads of cotton protruding from both ears. Her whole body was trembling. I rose up from the uncomfortable position I had spent hours in, stretched out my legs, took the chair down from the wall and stepped up on it. I wanted to survey the scene, take in the view across the partitions into the temple to make sure it had survived this primeval night. At the end of a thunderstorm or a flood, people like to set out and view the damage, the news of which, depending on its severity, will get passed from mouth to mouth for generations to come. I am unable to enter into this chronicle what I saw in the neighboring cells; at best I might describe it in a privately-printed pamphlet that in any case would be immediately confiscated by the censors. I was touched—nay, I was deeply moved—by what I espied at the far end of the corridor. The little shrine to Our Lady was smothered in garlands of flowers, waxen votive offerings hung down on strings from the narrow pedestal, dozens of votive candles had burned all the way down into their glass holders, leaving only a single tiny flame, flickering ever so dimly in the upward breeze, as a devotional gesture to the Mother of God. Here in this devout Tower of the Hours, the breezes always went upwards. The wick floated in a little golden puddle of oil in a many-colored glass receptacle, casting prismatic daubs of colored light on the doll-like figure of María of the Pillar, Our Blessed Lady of Love, who had survived the entire past night of libidinous activity. She knew that the candles were not lit to banish the darkness, but to express joy and gratitude for Her humane regard for the lot of humankind, as well as to invoke Her blessing on what many consider to be a sin. She is familiar with any bearing of any cross, with any human destiny, any transgression. You can approach Her with any concern, even with the concerns of the Clock Tower. In Spain, the saints are not just static images of grace; in this country God has not been disqualified and made to follow the whims of theologians; no professor raps His knuckles in objection to philologically questionable passages in his posthumous writings. No one trains Him like a canary. He moves about freely, and is as well off as God in France—the One I know too little about. The fact that His Mother was given such a place of honor in this stable of lust displayed the Spanish national soul more clearly to me than any profound treatise ever could. I had, to be sure, read widely in the writings of Santa Teresa, and that ought to have sufficed to justify the Blessed Virgin's presence in Arsenio's scurrilous cloister.

Around noontime Beatrice said softly but firmly, "Come on, get ready. We're going to the water."

That's what she said: "to the water." Not...to the movies, or to the Café Alhambra, or to the Cathedral. But she also said that I was to get ready—and that meant, no doubt, get ready for the worst. And so I finally started shaving.

The past night was simply too much for her. This much I could understand, but I didn't say anything. Instead, with over-meticulous care I set to removing my stubble. This has nothing to do with class-conscious suicidal customs as practiced by dueling fraternity students, or army officers who dress up for the event in a dark suit and top hat. I was cleaning my face because I hadn't done it in two whole days. I have never been free of vanity as far as my outward appearance is concerned. I'm not the roguish type who always checks himself in the mirror, not by a long shot. But I like my shoes polished, and the creases of my trousers mustn't be allowed to flatten out. If I were a smoker, Beatrice's suggestion would have prompted me to light up a cigarette.

This particular day remains branded in our memory as an unusually hot one, a true dog day, even though the eponymous star no longer prevailed in the sky. Thus my depiction of our passage to the place of self-destruction cannot do without copious drops of sweat and thick clouds of dust. Did we take a final look at our possessions—*adieu*, my little *bidetto*, my faithful little typewriter, my poetic oeuvre; farewell, slipper and collar button, badger-hair brush and brassière, Indian dress and Unkulunkulu (this was Beatrice's umbrella, about which more later), so long to all of you; shall we never see you again? I locked our cell door with the key, something we never did before. But when you intend to stay away forever, you take certain precautions.

The Clock Tower cook, a girl of a certain age named Bet-María, with iron bones and a bosom that extended under both arms, greeted us effusively, pointing upwards where a shimmering haze concealed the azure sky, and intoned words that I shall never forget: "What a glorious day! May the Lord bestow upon us just as much sunlight tomorrow, and may the Purest, the Most Blessed, the Immaculately Conceived Mother of God grant us her gracious intercession"—and she pointed to the citadel of lust from which we were about to depart forever.

Slowly and with dignified pace, like the mourners at our own burial, we entered the city, passed through its streets and headed for the harbor with the intention of leaping into the sea from the farthest end of the pier, where the lighthouse stands surrounded by a raised promenade. First I would help Beatrice, who isn't good at climbing and doesn't much like heights, to clamber over the iron railing, and then I would follow. I, too, am not very good at gymnastics, but a railing like this one wouldn't be any problem. This was, incidentally, a wordless agreement between us, as we figured out in retrospect— one of the many that can illustrate how two people who are devoted to each other in body and soul can, at just the right moment, do just the wrong thing.

As we arrived at the first boat dock, we noticed something that forced us to change our plan. Amid orange peels and sardine cans, bunches of straw, street refuse, and a pool of oil glistening in all the colors of the rainbow, we saw the swollen cadaver of a cat jutting out of the water, and sitting on top of this, a rat eating a hole in its improvised raft. I pointed at this symbol of transience, and was about to start quoting Trakl when Beatrice pulled me away from this view of a form of putrefaction that, to one kind of tooth at least, offered delicate morsels. "...in sweet, stale, rotten flesh / their snouts toil in silence." She was thinking: That's just what would have happened with us—or rather, *pardon*, that's just what is going to happen with us. So we'd better find a rat-free shoreline. "Come on, let's go out to Porto Pí!"

Porto Pí? But of course. That's where a cliff juts out over the sea. We once stood there just like the tourists we decidedly no longer were. The Golden Isle had since become a Devil's Isle, and now it was to become for us the Isle of the Dead. Onward, to Porto Pí.

Did I remember Porto Pí, Beatrice asked. You bet Vigoleis remembered that cliff above the sea! He had stood up there in the days before Pilar turned into a raging bedstead fury. She had stood next to him, the intoxicating one next to the intoxicated, and she touched his arm and pointed to something in the distance, causing Vigoleis to think impulsively of Life and the Ocean and Swimming and all such things that leap to mind when things have come along so far that the two of you can stand and stare together at some distant point. He, of course, did not recognize this spot as suicidal topography, ideal or otherwise. But if Beatrice now wanted to go out there, the overhanging cliff could very well serve as a diving board, though not a very springy one. Still, once in a lifetime one can manage even that. I followed her.

It must have taken us three hours to trudge along the bay to Santa Catalina, the working-class suburb of Palma, then through the village El Terreno with its high-class villas owned by foreigners, then onward and onward on the road to Andraitx and the cliff. At a turn in the path we finally spotted it. Far below us lay the tiny harbor. The sea sparkled with a silvery luster. The cliff rose majestically ahead of us. Just a half-hour more and we would be standing at our diving board ready for the launch.

But "standing" is not the appropriate word after such a strenuous on-the-double march. Once we arrived at the edge of the precipice we would have to rest for a while and take stock of things before taking a dive out of our misery. At the time, there were no such things on Mallorca as catapults for suicidal individuals; the Tourist Office was holding these back until there was official approval of the new gambling casino. This meant that we would have to take recourse to the launching trick used by the bats. Nature knows how to give a helpful shove to the have-nots of this world: we would just let ourselves drop, because afterwards we wouldn't need to scramble back up the promontory.

As soon as we caught sight of our fateful cliff, there also came into our view a certain building, a large palace with a free-standing tower resembling a campanile, covered by what looked like a gigantic parasol. It was the Hotel "Príncipe Alfonso." Is it any wonder that we slowed down our pace? We began scenting like wild game, but what kind of danger were we facing? So we proceeded on our way. We had made a decisive break with Zwingli, so what further concern was he to us? We strode onward. Neither of us had thought about the "Príncipe" when we started out on our journey toward death. But—why should we bother at all about that hotel, and anyway...

It never rains but it pours. For our part, we had already compiled an entire anthology of misfortunes; *porra* and *puta* had descended upon us with a vengeance, we had come face to face with syphilis. So we had no reason to be surprised that the man who was the cause of this final journey of ours was standing in the doorway of his building at the precise moment when we, with our oft-proven somnambulistic timing, chose to pass by—or rather to sneak by, if our linguistic purists are willing to accept the word "sneak" as a description of forward motion with heads held high. For we refused, damn it all to tarnation, to lower our heads on this final trek, and thus we forged ahead step by deliberate step without so much as glancing at that relative with these eyes of ours that were on the verge of becoming sightless for good.

"*Olá*! Hey! You two! Bice, Vigo, what are you doing here? Out hiking in this heat? You're going to get sunstroke!"

Zwingli had more to say. In fact, he gave a whole speech. But having begun with American slang, the remainder of his warning palaver got submerged in Swiss gutterals. We had already crossed the barrier into the realm of real danger, and were deaf to any shouted warnings. Other voices were calling to us, and we were following them.

But then there was a dashing of hasty footsteps behind us, and we felt as if we were being accosted in public. Zwingli caught up with us, grabbed each of us by the arm, split us apart, and it was no help at all that Beatrice kept saying "Stop it, please!" or "Just go away!" or whatever one says under such circumstances—I don't remember her exact words. Nor do I recall the *Urtext* of Zwingli's attempt to drag information out of us. What were we doing out here? Had we or had we not come this way with the intention of seeking him out? I felt acutely embarrassed by this washing of the family laundry on a public thoroughfare—perhaps not so rare a spectacle in Spain, but decidedly *infra dig* for the likes of us Northerners. I hate scenes of any kind; I am much too decadent for robust yelling and gesticulating. Let the two of them go off into the bushes somewhere to deal with their family dirt. But these scrubby pines, one every ten meters or so along the roadway, were public property. Be that as it may, my dear Vigoleis, mustn't you now admit that when your final journey was so unpleasantly interrupted, you were concerned more about yourself than about Zwingli's sister?

Zwingli's behavior makes this question a moot one. He made short work of the two stubborn would-be suicides. He quickly turned both of us around abruptly and whisked us off to his hotel, at first meeting with vigorous resistance, then less and less, until finally there was none at all. He dominated us with his well-fed physical strength and his iron will-power, trained in the school of Pelmanism, and in the end we just caved in. Such is the origin of any and all moral aberration. Viewing the situation in retrospect, I have concluded that anyone contemplating suicide ought first to enjoy a hearty breakfast, if possible with champagne. And one should give consideration to the digestive system, so as to obviate any necessity of emergency measures on this score. Only then might one proceed toward the inevitable. For otherwise—and exactly this happened in our case—some free-roaming brother or other can easily bring your best-laid plans to nought. You will go as limp as a virgin after stammering prayerfully for the third time, "Oh, please don't stop!" She means, of course, her own courage against her adversary, but her adversary thinks she means him, and straightaway the deed is done.

What a cynical attitude! Such, perhaps, is the thought that immediately occurs to a reader who has never set forth from a Clock Tower to a Cliff of Eternity with a beloved woman at his side. If I were a cynic, I would now show Beatrice pushing a wheelbarrow along the Carretera de Andraitx, with myself leaning my shoulder in harness up ahead, the barrow filled with the ruins of the piano previously destroyed by the harpy. In an earlier chapter I made allusion to the Leucadian Cliff from whence the poet Sappho leaped into the sea with her musical instrument. The wheelbarrow/piano combination would not be at all inappropriate, nor would the providential rope I was using to help pull us along. In any case, such trappings of our journey could take effect as products of my abundant creative imagination, which likes to lend biblical ramifications to a given state of affairs. Just the same, I always end up lacking a certain ingredient of talent, for otherwise we would never have foundered on our way to Porto Pí. "Your son," the school teachers told my father repeatedly, "will never pass the class requirements." "Well then, he'll be a cobbler," was the repeated reply from my father, who was a man of few words. Both superiors, teacher and father, gave me their predictions for my future. I never passed the class requirements. Unfortunately, I never became a cobbler either. God had other things in mind for me, even though he could have made out of me a good mender of soles. If now I replace the phrase "class requirements" with the word "cliff," then my father was speaking prophetically. I have never reached goals that others have set for me, and I have been extremely wary of setting out little flags for myself. That cliff was Beatrice's own personal fateful destination, and I went along as an also-ran. Then came the fiasco, and after that no one told us what was to become of us, not even Zwingli, who as Don Helvecio pushed us decorously into the foyer of his "*Príncipe.*"

Our existence was shattered. Our dream of nothingness, our plunge into the waves—all this was now wrecked on an empty stomach! We stood there in shame, and there is no need for me to explain how tired and leached out we looked in the reception area of a hotel where the cheapest attic room cost more for one night than we had on our persons. We were grubby and foul; in spite of my clean-shaven chin I felt utterly filthy. Zwingli could have done a turnabout and said to us, "My gosh, you look just terrible!"

But he, Don Helvecio, who was now once again on top of the heap, said nothing of the sort; it wasn't his way to pay someone back in like coin. He looked elegant in his duds, the tips of his footwear were mirror-shiny, his hair lay flat and curly on his well-groomed head, there were no scatterings of dandruff, his hairbrush had done smooth work. And behold, at the tip of his right little finger the horn once again jutted out into the world, looking even longer now than back at the harbor and on the Street of Solitude. Not a trace of black under the curve of the nail, and all of his nine other nails were spotless, the result of manicures with almond oil, not even a hint of peeling cuticle. Zwingli was now the complete Swiss *hôtelier* much in demand, a man of the cosmopolitan world among his international clientele gathered here now for five o'-clock tea. Yes, five o'clock: that's how late it was on this Saturday afternoon in mid-September. A few weeks more and Vigoleis will celebrate his birthday. But first, let us allow him to celebrate his personal resurrection from the dead.

Zwingli—no, Don Helvecio—lifted his horny finger, and immediately they all entered the scene: tall waiters and squat waiters, a head waiter and a supervisor of waiters and then a supervisor of the supervisor of waiters. They prepared a table in the smaller dining area—"Or Beatrice, would you prefer to dine in the rotunda? That'll be just fine." Another flash of his pinky, and a not quite noiseless rush of personnel—not because they were ignorant of hotel protocol, but because many foreigners enjoy a genuine Spanish spectacle. And with so many Anglo-Saxons on hand to take their afternoon tea, we approved of the shift in venue. Our table would be at the far end of the room, with a fine view of the ocean ("*mare nostrum,*" Zwingli said, and he was thinking of Tacitus; as for us, we were not thinking of Tacitus). "From here the cliffs look especially steep and picturesque. Just take a gander at that one over there. Isn't it grand? Every year it fills our coffers quite nicely."

Yes indeed, with his magic nail Zwingli was pointing to our Leucadian Crag, thrusting up out of the waves, the one that angled out over the water ever so slightly, now gleaming with a russet tint, at its base a fringe of white foam. A shimmering column rose up above the promontory and disappeared in the haze. Our own eyes, too, could perceive only a shimmer, no doubt a symptom of our fatigue. It wasn't until much later that we realized that we were eating our last meal within direct view of our intended place of self-execution.

"Don't you want to spruce up a bit? A bath, maybe?"

We wanted nothing of the sort. We wanted nothing at all. We were void of all wanting. In response to further magical gesticulations of Zwingli's nail, our table was set, gold-braided youths leaped forth, and waiters circled around us balancing viands of various kinds. Should I present a detailed description? Oddly enough I can recall precisely all the delicacies we were served, but they would be just as out of place here as they were back there at the Príncipe. Business was flourishing; hotel guests came and went, many of them greeting the eminent Don Helvecio in their best Baedeker Spanish, while Don Helvecio let it be known with disarming directness that he was busy with VIPs: we were his people, his sister and brother-in-law—no need for vagueness on this point—artists both of them, just come in from a stroll—can you imagine, in this tropical heat? They came up through Génova on their way to Bendinat Castle, and now he was helping them get presentable again. This was a merry fable, meant to entertain the British ladies who with their crooked legs never made it past the trolley stop but—who knows?—on a cool day might risk a similar hejira. Don Helvecio assured them that if they wished to try, he could place the hotel limousine at their disposal.

Was it embarrassment that made him jabber on like this? Not in the least. He even did us the honor of joining us for the meal. And what in Devil's name did I see there on the table before him? It was a plateful of the General's Eggs, and he dug into them with a wine chaser—Julietta's red, in point of fact. It was obvious that he was still, or once again, linked up with a Pilar, yet with a diminished degree of devotion, for otherwise he would never have halted and derailed our funeral cortege in front of his hotel. We ate nothing.

"Dig in! All you can eat! Don't be shy, no need for that here! You're tourists! And you, Bice, no need to hold back. You've sat down to dinner with princes and kings. And I want you to come back here someday and tell Es Mestre, our head chef, all about the Colloredo-Mansfeld Castle where the last Tsar's personal cook wielded the spoon. *Mon cher Vigoló* can't hear about that often enough. But what's eating you two...?"

The torrent of twaddle splashed on. We were silent—what was there to say? We couldn't eat a thing. We asked for tea, waited until its temperature approximated that of our bodies, and then dunked zwieback in it. That wasn't a proper way of dining, but then tourists and artists are quite above accepted table manners.

What was up with us? Would he have to apply thumbscrews to get it out of us? Surely we weren't sore about that stupid business with his Pilar. And where were we living? Emmerich told him that we had moved to the Count's house. He knew the Count well, a fine fellow, a superior anarchist, an artist almost, and with a private gallery of horrors; he intended to go visit us there, just to put a stop to all the gossip. "You know, spread around by dames. But you had already moved out, and Don Alonso didn't know where to. Antonio didn't know anything, either, but people saw you with him often. He's a good guy. By now you've become used to Spanish ways. It happens fast—the main thing is to keep your balance. You have to start thinking in Spanish from the very first day, and then everything takes care of itself."

I told him that we took a room outside of town, in a house called the "Torre del Reloj."

This news almost snapped off our confederated relative's classy fingernail. What, in the "Clock Tower?!" He would never in this world have thought of looking for us out there. Beatrice in *that* place? He took his head in his hands and stared at his sister. As for myself, he was probably thinking that I was right at home in such a location, that I had finally found the cozy study I was hoping for. "It's the most notorious place on the whole island! A flesh factory! Smugglers' den! Flophouse! Headquarters for counterfeiters! Everybody and anybody who shuns the light of day, even if they go about their business at high noon, finds his way under the Giant's roof. Out there you're going to have to be on the *qui vive*. You're going to get in trouble with the police. For years now the police have suspected Arsenio of masterminding the opium traffic in the Balearics. I'm going to tell Don Darío about this. The two of them are old buddies, there's a murder case involved, and the banker Juan March, you know, the billionaire. It's big-time, all of it, with vendettas like on Corsica. And the sex traffic? I've been through it. When the *corridas* are on and the all the troops come down here from the mainland, it's party time out there. The boxes get filled with *picadores* and *chulos*, the whole herd of swordsmen overflows the Clock Tower. We often reserve beds out there for our guests. Ever heard of the Buttlar Gang? Pietism and libertinage combined. But that was nothing compared to the Torre out there with its cabins and the luxury suite for the rich toreros. You should ask Adeleide to show it to you sometime. Cost thousands. Unique on the island!"

Zwingli laughed so hard he began shaking. "'Torre del Reloj'! But wait, isn't there a *corrida* tomorrow?"

So that was the explanation for our Creation Night: the bullfighting troupe had disembarked the day before. Tomorrow the candles would get lit at the Madonna's altar in the bullring. Ave María Purissima.

The hotel guests had left the rotunda. We sat alone together, just a tiny bit strengthened. Oh, to stretch out now and sleep in a real bed!

But we decided to leave, like two dogs after a scolding.

"How's things with your exchequer? Probably not too good. Let's see"—

Zwingli reached into his pocket and jingled some metal. "Here's some change to tide you over, for the tram and such. Later we'll take care of your other debts. What a shame back then, Bice, you with your scruples and all. But you'll be staying on the island for a while yet. We should see each other more often. Let me organize it. I've got plans for you. I'll come out to your Tower sometime soon. Vigo will get to learn a thing or two—I mean for his books. Last year a photographer crawled up onto the roofbeams to get a bird's-eye view the night before the bullfight. He expected to become a millionaire, but the *picadores* spotted him and beat him half to death. I'll be sure to come out, Arsenio has some great wines, and Adeleide is famous for her octopus cooked in ink, *mon cher Vigo!*"

"And ink is what it's all about, *mon cher Zwingli*, especially when things are turning black all around you."

"So long!"

"*Ciao!*"

"*Tschüss!*"

We straggled back to the city without exchanging a word. There seemed to be no longer any connection between us, not even our mutual silence, otherwise so eloquent in itself. We had become enemies; each of us had reached out with a wicked hand, as it were, to prevent the other from doing the deed, and each was now ashamed of the other. Suicide *à deux* requires a perfect *homousia*. In novels, it can easily take place on a single page. For ours we were planning a whole chapter, and as yet nothing had come of it. We would have to start over. When we arrived on the Plaza de la Liberdad, we had just enough time to get to the post office and inquire whether any money or letters had arrived. The clerk in his blue smock didn't know me, and so everything had to happen in neat alphabetical fashion. There was nothing in *poste restante*. I thought to ask whether he had looked really carefully. You can do that in Spain, whereas in Germany I would never have dared. The man in the smock didn't even get angry, and as for feeling insulted—not the gratings of a Martersteigian cheese. He smiled politely. "I see. You think that we can't read because in this office we are the illiterate heirs to the clerical monarchy? All foreigners think that way, and they're all wrong. But please, if you wish to look for yourself—" He pushed a whole bundle of mail across to me and went back to his crossword puzzle, which still had plenty to be filled in.

After some rummaging I found a letter from Stuttgart, from the Deutsche Verlagsanstalt. This had to be the money transfer. "Well now, I see you've fished something out after all?" I showed him my passport. The man said "All very well," and then he started beaming. Just a moment, he said. All the Saints, he went on, must have sent me to him, Would I be so kind as to take the trouble to examine another pile of mail, one that had been sitting there for years? No one knew quite what to do with it, perhaps...? "Perhaps," I said and fingered through the mound of missives, picking out this and that addressed to us, old stuff, long-overdue correspondence. I took it.

The clerk was about to load more and more mail on me, including some packets under heavy seal, stuff that he wished to be rid of. But I refused to be bribed. "Some other time, perhaps. God willing."

"God willing! But please, just one moment!" He pointed to his crossword. "Famous German writer, with double-V?"

"Wigoleis."

"You? Well I'll...!"

"Incognito. So many admirers, you understand."

He didn't really understand. With "Jacob Wassermann" he would have made better progress. He shook my hand warmly.

Beatrice sat beneath the palms of the Café Triangulum and listened to the saga of the wealth that had fallen into Vigoleis' lap overnight. It was a check for a few hundred pesetas, the fruits of his somewhat less than Wassermannian success with the pen, his pygmy efforts at creative writing, the cold-cash proof of his existence as a writer. It had arrived a few weeks late by a quirk of devious fate, the same cabalistic powers that at the very last moment kept us from the final temptation of all, and issued a command to Zwingli to cross our path on the way to the cliff. All of this had taken place without the customary extra insurance premium, starting in the bordello with the Supreme Judicial Court assigned to our case, *à chandelle éteinte*, in a procedure that very closely resembled medieval legal protocol. And when the final candle went out, Beatrice broke down completely. Not a single star appeared in the heavens. In a purely external way, all of this can be explained differently, more simply, without any evocation of a Higher Purpose. The bifurcation of my private personality extends into the realm of bureaucratic documentation. At the time in question, my passport certified only the baptismal half of my existence. In its pages, no trace of Vigoleis was to be found. So it was no fault of the bureaucrats.

Herr Emmerich readily lent us fifty pesetas. I was about to show him the check when he laughed. With him we could charge anything; we looked more honest than most people who came to Mallorca. Why, he would be willing to lend us a hundred. Whoever was willing to go into debt to a free spirit like himself, he said, would never get into financial trouble.

We bought some easily digestible food, a simple soup, the kind quickly brought to heat for hospital patients. A candle, and a box of Oropax for Beatrice, to assure her peace and quiet during a night that we would soon be spending again in the confines of the "Tower," and not in the arms of some undersea octopus. We strode—but no, I mustn't go on talking about "striding"—we hailed a taxi. By coincidence it was the same one in which, in the previous chapter, Vigoleis began boasting to his Beatrice. "Where to?"

"'Torre del Reloj'!" Now we'll see whether the place is as notorious as Zwingli claims it to be.

"'Torre del Reloj'? Good, very good! You have to stand up like a man!" And we arrived in the twinkling of an eye.

Things were hopping at our house of joy. A second-hand dealer had set up a booth for the candy and gift articles adored by girls who would never think of selling themselves for money. Arsenio had thought of everything; anyone who appreciates the human soul will want to take care of the human body as well. We, on our part, were happy to be back home. Unnoticed, we made our way up the open-air stairway into our cell, where we were greeted by a surprising new development. Our sleeping quarters was the scene of a furious paper-cutting fracas. Had we been invaded by vandals? Jagged scraps of paper lay all about the room; the floor, the bed, the trunks—everything in sight was covered with torn fragments of paper. The rats had been at work. My traveling salesman's leather case, the one that I used as a purgatory for my sinful attempts at poetic utterance prior to consigning them to the fires of Hell, had been selected by the rodents as a prime target for their intercessive activity. With their special expertise, but oddly misled by their instincts to assume the actual expiration of the man who was now opening the cell door, they had attacked the posthumous literary works of Vigoleis. "If any man's work shall be burned," says the poet Paul of Tarsus, "he shall suffer loss: but he himself shall be saved; yet so as by fire." This obscure passage, often debated and still not translated into comprehensible language as it will have emerged from the mouth of the Apostle, occurred to me later when I was involved with Pascoaes' *God's Poet*, as pertaining to the condition I found myself in when my work was destroyed, but I myself was saved yet condemned to outlive my own work—the worst thing that can befall a writer. And to think that I was consigned to this destiny not by a jury of my peers, but by the denizens of a bordello.

"Our cheese! Our cheese!" Beatrice shouted, and all at once she was alive again. A light had dawned upon her; the theory of the subconscious triumphed for once over Vigoleis, who has a low opinion of such chimeras. Porto Pí and Port-Bou—what possible connection can exist between the two in the muddy regions of the human soul? With an archetypical cheese? "Cheese?"

"Yes, in Port-Bou! Don't you remember, our Emmentaler?"

Of course. I had forgotten. As far as I was concerned, it had simply dropped out of sight, that wedge of cheese I stashed away at the Spanish border in order to mislead—though not, mind you, deceive—the Spanish customs officials by wrapping it in my poems and placing it underneath my prose, inside the traveling salesman's satchel. But then came Zwingli limping out of his grave; Pilar pursued me with her wormy apple, all the joints of our existence came cracking apart, domestic scenes, eviction—let the reader count up all the events that might have caused us to forget, in the throes of starvation, that we had a sample of the most famous cheese in the world in our private luggage. It was an open-and-shut case of instinctive repression. A race that can commit such a lapse can never endure. "But Beatrice, *chérie*, I can see nothing in any way tragic in this event. There you are, looking as though you were going to tear your hair out. Leave your hair alone. Instead, consider the following: the Old Testament days are over and done with. Those good old times when God could have spoken to me in my sleep, 'Vigoleis, arise, take up thy salesman's valise, rip apart thy poetic oeuvre, bring forth the cheese, eat thereof and offer a morsel thereof to thy helpmate that she might eat thereof, and be of good cheer in this house of iniquity.' God is not with us, Beatrice, in spite of the fact that as a German citizen I can lay a certain claim to the contrary."

"You're making fun of me. You're mind is clouding over."

"Not at all. I have never seen things as clearly as right at this moment. Just you wait, Heaven has certain things in mind for me. The rats took advantage of our godforsaken absence to murder me as a literary personality—that is significant, and cheese is inspirational not only for rats. At this very moment in Germany, people are assembling an entire philosophy based on cheesy ideas. Weissenberg..."

"Oh stop your quarreling, you over there! Life is so grand, and the Spaniards—do they ever know how to be alive! You have to get used to it, though, so quickly from one day to the next. If my husband knew that I am lying here, he'd have another breakdown. As far as he knows, I'm just on a trip. And do you know what? He's right about that..."

We were dumbfounded. This voice, speaking with an unmistakable Lower-Rhenish accent and in drowsy, languid intonation, was coming from the cell next to ours, the one I had peeked into that very morning. It was the voice of the transparent, hyper-erotic subject of my secret, privately-printed essay, now lending expression to the after-spasms in her loins, in the language of my homeland between the rivers Nette and Niers. I have never felt homesick; I am at home anywhere and everywhere, even in a house of joy whose joys I do not share. Such an attitude presumes a vigorous inner life and a large measure of disgust with the outside world; one must avoid perversion and cultivate introversion, but above all, one must not cling to one's own shadow. Yet I'll confess that I was not untouched by the thought that only a single leap over the partition separated me from my dear fatherland, although I could not have brought about this repatriation without a serving of the General's Dish.

Beatrice and I continued our discussion in whispers. Using our camp stove, she cooked a stringy panade with ingredients supplied by her Swiss compatriot Maggi. Looking back, it seems to me a comical turn of events that both of us, having survived such a dire ordeal, got a whiff of our respective homelands while sitting at the very center of a hellish foreign world that had almost been our undoing. In silence we spooned the soup from our bowls. Then I took the candle and approached the shrine of Our Lady of the Pillar, where the eternal flame was still lit. In anticipation of the coming night, many fresh candles had been placed at the little altar—big ones and little ones, white, yellow, and many-colored ones, each according to special need and affordability.

I love candles. I always have several on my writing desk, and keep them lit even in daytime in order to relish the secrets of the flame. As to why on that particular occasion I made an offering of candlelight, I am no longer able to say. Perhaps I did it out of a superstitious belief that bad things could happen to us if we persisted in being the cause of no sound at all emerging from one of the cells, if our abstinence were to transform one of the boxes, the rest of which would soon be resounding like organ pipes up into the rafters, into the source of a mute pedal point—a kind of tuba mirum spargens sonum. By neglecting to join in the concert we would be depriving the music of the special sound that, according to our friend the organist Mosén Juan María Tomás, is the touchstone for all composers. In my home town, on the Feast of Corpus Christi a Jewish family we knew regularly assembled a votive window at their house using items borrowed from pious Catholic neighbors, in order to avoid a conspicuous gap in the row of festively decorated houses. This is exactly what we did in the Clock Tower, and it spoke for a sense of communal spirit in the midst of the diaspora.

With a tender, loving gesture Vigoleis placed his Beatrice on the cot. Then he took up a palm frond, swept up his posthumous papers into a pile, and lay down upon it.

"Oropax" lent Beatrice peace of mind, a peace that the Mediterranean had denied to these two pilgrims who were so thoroughly sick of the island. Peace for one night. But this one night lasted half an eternity.

III

It was Sunday.

We lay there for quite a while with open eyes, gazing up at the vaults of our cathedral, each of us aware that the other was awake. But neither of us moved. It was Sunday.

As a child I suffered from a condition that someone once referred to as Sunday melancholy. Later this affliction extended to the remaining days of the week, and then it was no longer anything special, considering that I had been able to summon a certain amount of energy to counter it. I recall Sunday mornings when the sun shone through the slits in the venetian blind into my room, turning everything into a celebration. Every flower on the wallpaper looked different, even though the pattern replicated them a thousand times. I knew each and every exemplar by heart, and discovered more and more new transformations. On the street outside there was no rattle of trucks passing by: on Sundays commercial traffic was prohibited. Sunday! Gradually my not quite wide-awake brain registered the truth: no school, no humiliation, no teasing, no punishment, no homework, nothing—just Sunday, the most comforting day. But then I burst awake and remembered: You have to go to church! Gone was my summery meadow of a thousand blossoms. All the roses looked alike and crummy and cheap, fifty cents a yard and pasted up at all the wrong angles.

Going to church was a twofold coercion. My parents and my school insisted on it, and the school even took attendance at Mass. Young nitwit that I was, I couldn't make this kind of weekend surveillance jibe with the omniscience attributed to the Good Lord. I also had trouble with the fact that one of our classmates was allowed to absent himself from all church services on the basis of a medical certification. This kid Wilhelm was as healthy as a lumberjack, but his father was the richest taxpayer in town, a millionaire who could afford his own concordat with the church. Our family used the same devout Catholic doctor, but we wouldn't dream of requesting a similar dispensation. My father was not in a salary range that would have permitted him to enter negotiations with God's representatives. When he finally worked his way up to the point where he could have greased the Lord's palm, I had long since sprung free of the whole dishonest mess. It didn't cost me a dime, but it cost me many a sleepless night and threw the course of my education out of balance. For years, Sundays remained poisoned days for me, and for years I nursed a strong mistrust of a Church that I was unable to square with the God who was said to reside within its walls. Then came the day of my First Communion, a climactic moment in the life of any Christian, the most wondrous day in his life.

I gazed up at the vaults of our Mallorcan church, saw the beams of sunlight streaming through the cracks in the roof, the prismatic light of my Sunday melancholy. "Most wondrous day," indeed! I was nine years old and still believed in God, in the same way that I believed in fairy tales. But fairy tales don't impose obligations on a believer. God, however, commanded us to "come forth" into His service with shouldered prayerbook. This most wondrous day: it was preceded then, and presumably still is, by a course of instruction that was supposed to initiate us into the mystery of "transubstantiation," a concept more difficult to comprehend than it is to pronounce. I myself probably didn't comprehend anything at all, but that didn't make any difference. Our pastor gave me the necessary box on the ears, and others got it too. This baleful procedure took place two or three days before the Most Wondrous Day. We were required to stand in rank and file at the altar rail—our food dispensary, as it were— for a "rehearsal." We had to memorize each and every step, each and every segment of the liturgy. The instruction placed particular stress on our behavior when receiving the Blessed Sacrament: bow your head in sincere humility, kneel down gingerly without banging the shins of the kid behind you, fold your hands under the linen cloth at the rail, and then stick out your tongue so as to swallow the Host while avoiding the slightest desecration, such as causing it to drop to the floor. Do not chew it! The Savior will melt on your tongue all by Himself. Our ancient pastor had trained generations before ours, every year the same maneuvers, and he had just as little patience as a humorless drill sergeant. I was guileless, and believed firmly in the miracle that was about to take place. My mother had given me fuller explanations than the pastor did. I would feel a shiver at the moment when I received Our Savior; I would undergo a metamorphosis, I would become a different child—a "better" one, she no doubt said—maybe even an angel.

I was quivering with expectation. All this seemed even more promising than Christmas Eve, which up to then was the Most Wondrous thing I knew. I pitied the poor negro kids in the "Steyl Missionary Messenger" who, instead of receiving the Savior, ate each other up. But if we saved up enough tinfoil and rolled it up in balls and delivered them to the pastor, the kids in Africa could receive Holy Communion too. I collected a lot. I felt truly sorry for the pagan children. Today I feel more truly sorry for Christianized children. In catechism instruction I didn't do very well. God had not granted me enough intelligence to grasp the bounty of knowledge required to receive Him, and on rehearsal day it turned out that I was physically awkward besides. I was a pagan child black as the ace of spades, a kid that the white folks would have to collect truckloads of tinfoil for, before he could approach Our Lord's table.

We approached the altar rail two abreast, as what was called "Communion partners," and knelt down. I folded my hands in the prescribed manner under the cloth, bowed my head, peeked to one side to see when it would be my turn, lifted it again, and extended my tongue. Not very far, it's true, because the pastor might have got the wrong idea—some of the kids stuck out their tongues at him during the communion instruction, just for fun. My own Communion partner was one of the most active in this regard. I was amazed at this kid, my cousin Karl, who was now kneeling next to me and somehow still found the time to pinch me, whereas I was already sweating from anticipation.

The old man walked along the rail checking everyone's posture, everyone's tongue. When he came opposite me he began to fume. What, this rascal doesn't even know how far to stick out his tongue? Farther out! Farther out! And when "farther out" was simply no longer possible—after all, a human being is not a woodpecker—he took his big key and whacked that part of me that was to receive the Savior on Whitsunday morning. My teeth crunched painfully into my lingual artery, and my mouth filled with blood. With the practiced gait that was meant to signify contemplation and inner bliss, I staggered back to the pew, next to me my Communion partner Karl. Karl had observed everything very carefully, and he hissed at me, "Man oh man, why didn't you spit at him? Just let him try that with me. I'll puke out all the blood on his pretty vestments. Just wait, that old bushman's gonna pay for this..." Our pastor's name was Busch.

My cousin Karl died while still young. When he was seven, he claimed to know where babies came from. Nobody believed him, but he didn't care, and it turned out he was right. He never avenged me—how could he have? A kick in the shins? A spritzer of stink juice on the pastor's cassock, the one he said every dog in town should piss on? Was it truly the old man's fault? As one of the Good Lord's legion of accomplices, our pastor was respected in the community, and when he died they put up a nice gravestone for him. He had grown old and grey in the service of God, and was no less brain-dead than a sexton who genuflects before the altar dozens of times every day while thinking of nothing at all. What he succeeded in doing was to single out one of the nameless victims of his pious drill methods during his final season in office, give that boy a well-aimed smack on the tongue with his house key, and with this single blow destroy the mystical edifice of a childlike faith.

Now I was supposed to let the Savior melt on my swollen tongue—not to chew Him! The Host was not a lollipop. And whosoever eateth of this bread hath eternal life. On my way back home from this rehearsal where I had once again displayed my doltish, unheroic behavior, I dropped my cap in the mud, thus furnishing myself an explanation for shedding tears. My nice colored cap! My mother consoled me by letting me know that she had already bought me a new one, a silk sixth-form cap with a stiff wire in it. I told no one about getting whacked on the tongue. It was my secret. I was hoping that Sunday would make everything all right again. I would received Our Savior, and God wouldn't let Himself be diverted from His Divine Purpose by some backwoods priest with stains on his cassock and dirty fingernails.

Whitsunday arrived. I knelt down. My cousin Karl poked me just as I was about to stick out my tongue. Lots of incense, a crowd of people in their Sunday best, the First Communion roasts were already simmering in a hundred casseroles, the organ roared forth, a girl recited some prayers, ushers shepherded the little chosen ones on this, their Wondrous Day. All of a sudden I felt the cool presence of Our Savior on my tongue. Did I tremble? No doubt about it. Was my mouth dry? Of course. And I of course had difficulty swallowing the Lamb of God who taketh away the sins of the world. The sins of this young initiate were now erased, but I sensed no overwhelming illumination. Except for a bland taste of something like cardboard, I felt, to quote Martersteig, not the gratings of a green cheese. I had been deceived. Ex-communicated.

When Heaven fails, Earth can often provide abundant recompense. The giraffe has a long neck in order to pluck leaves from trees. Nature thinks of everything. My Divine Feast was a failure, but my Mom's First Communion meal was of regal proportions. Providence had bestowed upon my father a certain relative, Aunt Hanna, a spinster renowned far beyond our town limits. She was famous as a gossip, one who could take minuscule domestic events and inflate them into epic sagas. Whenever she opened up what she called her "Berlin basket," my ears rose stiff with lust. And she was a great cook. There was never a baptism without her baking something fine, never a wedding without her Sevastopol pudding. Her true specialty: First Communions! This muse of the spinning-wheel had long since got the hang of what God meant by venial sins. She knew what kind of reward was due on these special days, and in my case she provided it in the form of savory dishes, which to this day I can name but no longer afford. Life has gone on, I have had to take many more whacks on the tongue, but there has never again been a tired but happy Hanna Hemmersbach to take her seat at table and accept praise from the assembled guests. And I have never again received rewards for any of my defeats.

The Wondrous Day was also a day for getting presents. My relatives had arrived bearing gifts. My godfather, with his reddish chin-whiskers, his dresscoat, and his self-framed picture of the Sacred Heart (oval, red velvet, the rays in gold leaf), was already drunk by mid-afternoon when I was sent to attend the Service of Thanksgiving. If I had had a choice, I wouldn't have gone. I owed no thanks to a duly ordained Friend of the Children like that old geezer.

It was Sunday. And I didn't have to go to church. The forest is my cathedral, pantheists of all shades are wont to say. We, too, lay beneath a starry dome. Most of the faithful were still asleep. Their snoring chanted harshly throughout the Manse.

Beatrice asked me what I was thinking. I told her the story of the priest who was supposed to prepare my way on the Lord's path, but who instead unloaded rubbish on it that I have never been able to push aside. I have often dreamed of this man, and now, in the Clock Tower, he appeared to me as a monster, half satyr and half shepherd of souls, dressed in a chasuble and chasing a virgin, wielding a huge key with slavering lust. I heard him shouting "Farther out! More!—*Más!*" with a drawn-out Spanish *aaa*. Spain is the land of devout eroticism. Nowadays I tend to doubt whether I would ever have come to an understanding of the great Iberian mystics if I had not undergone my novitiate in the Tower of Tarts.

The main house and all the outbuildings were silent when, after dozing off again briefly, we squinted in the sunlight. Was everybody gone? Was time standing still? Had the tower clock struck its final hour? We got up.

The old crone was all alone, asleep on a chair in the archway. Bullfight day is a holiday for young and old. At this hour in the Palma bull arena, Ortega, Lalanda, and Barrera were confronting the horns of the massive animals bred by the famous Miura. The champions who had exhibited their mettle on Adeleide's mattresses were at this very moment displaying their courage and their *más* at the *corrida*, each according to his assigned role in the complex sport. Each of them could end up biting the dust, despite the candles burning in the little chapel on the Plaza de Toros, where the gladiators kneel before the Mother of God prior to entering the ring to the sound of trumpets and kettledrums. It was these three bullfighting stars that Zwingli was thinking of when he invited us to attend the national spectacle under the expert guidance of his friend Don Darío. Zwingli and his buddy were no doubt sitting right now amid the cheering hordes in the arena bleachers, cheering along with all the rest. Having snagged expensive seats on the shady side, they would be caught up in the frenzy of the bloody moment of truth that arrives in a whirlwind of silk. Hovering above it all, in merciless detachment, there would be the celestial vault and its sun, scorching the less affluent mob in the opposite semicircle of the stadium.

Our own Sunday passed by without incident. Whatever passions were unleashed during the following night in our warehouse of wantonness had no effect on us, and thus are lost to posterity. Our slumber was hermetic. Our keyhole, through which it might have been possible to watch and hear us dreaming, was stuffed with paper. And behold another newborn, chrysalid day, a day for emerging out of hairy, hungry ugliness with sprouting, shimmering wings to enter a new life—lasting a single day. On the third day we felt nimble again, and went to the city. The world had not changed. There was an odor coming from the *matadero* and clouds of dust in the air. We aimed our sharp prow toward the telegram from Mr. Victor Emmanuel van Vriesland. It hadn't arrived. Emmerich got his money back, and then we went to visit Antonio at the gentleman's club "La Veda," which means something like "closed season," and the gentlemen there were decidedly closed-off types.

Antonio advised Beatrice to place an ad for language instruction in the *Ultima Hora*. Sensing that things were urgent, he composed the irresistible text himself. Replies should best be sent *poste restante*; nobody should find out where we had our lodgings. Arsenio and Adeleide were fine people, and the police wouldn't bother us any more; he had told the commander of the *carabineros* the story of our disaster with the minx Pilar. The police would have to check out the Clock Tower every now and then, but no one would pester us again.

Another day, and no dispatch from Amsterdam. Instead, word from Danzas that our large luggage, especially crates of books, was now ready for passing customs in Palma de Mallorca. They found this out in Basel before the fellows at the Palma customs office got word of it. Fee: 1000 pesetas. Books are contraband in a country where literature is assessed by the kilogram—which, when you come to think of it, is not at all such an unartistic idea. I blessed myself: good heavens, will there never be an end to the fees and charges? Did we stay alive only to be plagued by life's miserable appendage, financial worries? But Antonio knew just what to do. He had our luggage shifted temporarily to the duty-free warehouse.

We received more mail; the world hadn't forgotten us. A letter from my father, a delight for the eyes in his meticulous handwriting. How I would love to have penmanship like his—I could use it to earn my bread. What he wrote was just as candid as his calligraphy: It wasn't clear to him what I was doing with my life down here. My reports were ambiguous; between the lines they showed an image of me that he wasn't familiar with. How were things going in Spain? Mother was getting worried. And then a final line bringing the letter to its climax. As with any good writer, the sentence stood there on the page and suddenly opened up vistas across the passage of time, causing the reader to place his hand on his heart. The weather was getting cool, and they had just mailed me a duck, the best of this year's backyard brood, and *Guten Appetit*! I looked at the date on the letter. My shock of pleasure was followed immediately by the discomfort known to any skeptic familiar with the decompositional tendencies of all organic matter.

More mail arrived on this day. But first I must dispose of this duck, and that will mean setting the clock ahead. Two weeks later I received from customs a notice that a package had arrived from Germany, import duty due. To be opened in the presence of a customs official. It was the duck.

There was a certain odor, said the official, polite as the Spaniards always are when things truly begin to stink. Yes, it was the pestilence itself that I now proceeded to open up in the presence of authority. The packaging was first-rate: impregnated paper. I had to unwrap several layers until the backyard bird began to seep. The official nodded, and I replaced the wrappings over what was to have whetted our appetite. The fee was waived. Outside the city gates I heaved the roast into a field. Why didn't I drown it right away in the harbor? My relatives had meant well, but as unclear as their notions about my welfare were, their ideas about the Spanish climate were completely false. Beatrice calculated that the bird would have got us past starvation, but would duck and Emmentaler go well together? Things would have gone much better if we had left Zwingli's bills unpaid. My father was right: never get mixed up in strangers' business. One's own business is strange enough.

The second letter was from a writer, and presented us with another *canard*. Vic had written it, Mijnheer van Vriesland, author of a novel about departure from the world in three days. My father's bird had a greenish tint, but the bird Vic sent me was decidedly blue. The Berlin film company was broke, the glamorous star had completely disappeared, and he was unable to send an advance on the contract since he was himself depending on an advance from his publisher. But my letter! He found it delightful. It was worth more than a whole movie, this story about the trollop Pilar, I should try to market it. In any case, he had made copies of my epistle, and it was now circulating among the literati (the litter-rats?), some of whom had asked him for my address. Thus I shouldn't be surprised if I got asked to produce sequels.

And so my picaresque plea for help had not yielded us any cold cash from the writer van Vriesland, who today, as president of the Dutch and vice-president of the International PEN Club, has achieved the world fame that our abortive movie never gave him. Nevertheless, it was on the basis of my Pilar-iade, composed on a rusty bidet, that I did obtain something of no little importance: my friendship with the poet Marsman, whose verse I knew and carried around with me together with my volume of Trakl.

The third letter we received on this day likewise had to do with ducks, or rather with a duckling: The proprietress of a small hotel in the center of Palma asked Beatrice to come for a visit. She had a young daughter who must be taught to chatter in English.

Our suicide lay behind us, as if it had never taken place. The 4000 Dutch guilders for our departure from the world were sequestered in Berlin by dint of legal injunction, nor were we in a financial position to depart from the island to begin a new life in Toledo, where both of us wanted to go. We would have to wait things out on Mallorca and, worse, in the Clock Tower. So now, Vigoleis, get to work! Develop a new style! Combine the spatial visions of a van de Velde and a Gropius, with the Old Testament insight that life can be tolerable among depraved nomads, provided one has a tent to sleep in. Make a virtue out of necessity! Make a comfy home out of a flophouse!

Vigo took all this to heart. He began to get ideas, and the chips began to fly.

Beatrice got to work, too. That is to say, she got dressed up and went begging to the hotel where the duckling lived. The world was truly upside-down. The duckling's mother, a very prim lady, was named Doña María.

The girl's name was María de las Nièves, Mary of the Snows. And it was she who brought about the miracle that early Christian legend associates with this cognomen: it snowed in mid-summer, or, translated into our insular situation of the moment, money fell into our heroes' laps. Beatrice went to the hotel three times a week to hammer English vocables into this pleasant, but not very talented, daughter of a rich widow. The lessons took place in combination with a *merienda*, a snack—a matter of course, since the teacher lived far out of town, and a hotel kitchen never shuts down. This meant that Beatrice could regularly deliver sample delicacies in a can to her Vigoleis out at the cloister, where the shameless pauper gobbled up the crumbs from the tables of the rich like a flesh-and-blood vegetarian sneaking his Sunday chicken dinner behind closed doors. Once, while engaged in this work of marital mercy, Beatrice got caught with spoon in hand. Her boss confronted her ("What, secrets?"). Did she have a dog? There was enough garbage in the kitchen. All she had to do was notify the sous-chef. As we know Beatrice, she did not reply directly, "Begging your pardon, Madam, my dog's name is Vigoleis." Instead, blushing for mendacious shame right down to her liver, she employed circumlocution: the food was for her husband; we were living outside of town in a rooming house, but "full pension" did not describe the actual state of affairs. The landlady had fallen ill—that's a detail I would have added. Doña María didn't understand completely, but she understood enough to start railing about Mallorquins and their shameless exploitation of foreigners. From now on, at each English lesson Doña Beatriz would be given a picnic basket for her spouse, whom she should ask to come along sometime soon. With thanks for this generosity, Beatrice promised to put me on display.

It is not my intention to accompany this language teacher on her forays to the hotel, much less to guide my reader along into the little room where Mary Snow struggled with a new tongue that she had to learn for her future career as owner of the present hotel, and of a brand new mammoth hotel already under construction. She had a hard time learning, and thus there would be no end of our hiking back and forth again and again, three times a week, from our suburban villa into the city. The Civil War would have already lit its fuses and sent its thugs after us. Any progress we made would reveal the hollowness at its core, and Mary Snow would still be agonizing over the irregular verbs. We actually did make some progress. We buckled down. With blind obsessiveness, we eked our way out of the Stone Age and entered an era that brought us custom-fit shoes and a tailor-cut suit, a thousand books on our shelves, and this and that other item that one wishes for when one is beyond wishing.

During all this time, Vigoleis rigged up our homequarters. Rusty nails, stolen boards, a discarded wheel spoke, our ropes, a hunk of corrugated metal—with millions, anybody can build anything; God created the world out of nothing. Here, everything underwent an organic evolution, following the miraculous purposefulness of Nature—here and there a dead end that Beatrice would point to and ask, "What's that for?" It was like a good book, about which critics might say: not one superfluous word.

Our chair, which was superfluous whenever both of us were in the room, had its firm place up against the wall, where it looked like a hanging epitaph, a Baroque extrusion good for placing objects on. Most often, it was decorated with a tin can containing fresh flowers, and this became a problem when one of us wanted to sit down. I transformed our trunks into chests. Our *bidetto* is already familiar in its new function, but we of course also cooked on it— "brewed" would be the more fitting word, to take cognizance of its dual role. I stretched our ropes across the area where the architect had left a gaping hole, in the manner of clotheslines, but not for drying clothes. Instead, I hung our library on it, plus items we used during the course of the day. All kinds of things bounced above our heads: shoes, stockings, Georg Trakl, brushes, spoons, Nietzsche, Saint Augustine, dustcloths, suspenders, Novalis, detective novels, brassières, Teresa de Avila, St. John of the Cross—our books astride the ropes *à la amazona*. Using special wire clips, I took rejected manuscripts and pages fresh from the typewriter and fastened them to the lines, where, like our victuals, they would be more or less safe from the rats. In old-time printshops, as you can see in early woodcuts, they hung the galleys up on ropes in a similar fashion to dry. If you're willing to blank out such diverse items as sausages, loaves of bread, bags of flour or sugar, a sprig of vanilla, garlic cloves, and bay leaves, you'd think the Clock Tower might be the Venetian printing office of Aldus Manutius.

So now, in place of a missing ceiling, we had an elaborate latticework of lines set out with remarkable skill, one that still allowed us a view of higher things. What writer can boast of a similar working space, where he can receive creative inspiration from above and below at the same time?

Things didn't go very well for us during these first weeks after the collapse of all the hopes we had set on the bottom of the ocean, and on Victor van Vriesland's skills as a womanizer. Whoever puts his faith in hoping ought to consider making a careful selection, and eliminate from the start certain questionable aims. But we didn't complain. We set to hard work—Beatrice with her usual compulsiveness that tastes like "victory," compared to which I feel like a dullard, even when I'm putting my shoulder to the wheel next to her. Like the ants, grain by single grain we built our abode here in the Tower of Iniquity, surrounded by whores and rats, house searches and braying donkeys, candlelight and pious concupiscence, sharing a glass of wine with Arsenio or gabbing with the old crone. Somehow I even found time to play with the kids and sit on the lookout for the rat-king.

One of the kids in the family, Pablo, was slated to learn English so that he could later play a role in his father's business, whose true nature was getting gradually unveiled. Pablo was nineteen, narrow-minded, and wily; his hair was shaved down to his skull, and his breath smelled. He was in the military, but he was bought free to the extent that he could sleep at home rather than in a barracks. Three times a week he hunkered down in the Giant's *fonda* as Beatrice funneled learning into him. For this activity she received 25 pesetas, meaning that we no longer had to pay rent for our cell. The young soldier, who at nighttime went on life-threatening smuggling duty, fell asleep without fail every time English sounds reached his ears. And since it is inadvisable to waken a sleeping soldier, Beatrice, too, regularly fell asleep during these sessions. It is only very great generals who can afford to snooze on the battlefield. The only one who stayed awake was the Giant. He slithered around our little classroom with something on his mind—but what? Every time Beatrice's head fell on the tabletop, she woke up with a start and saw this gang leader motioning to her with a shiny duro—his Adeleide wouldn't notice, and after all, he was the boss here at the Clock Tower. Beatrice could no longer see the forest for the trees, so I finally had to enlighten her as to what this guy really meant by flashing 5 pesetas at her. In my calmest tones I let her know that she had gone down in price since we started living right here at the source. Now that we were housed in a hookshop on the basis of a hotel waiter's ministrations, it was all over with the prices once offered by the gentlemen sitting on the hotel terrace. Beatrice shook her head, and with this gesture she provided the most plausible confirmation of the effectiveness of my interior architecture: she had forgotten that the air surrounding us was unclean. Then it was Arsenio's turn to shake his head. He added a second duro, he went as high as twenty, and then he gave up. We stayed the best of friends. He just couldn't understand why people didn't make use of their most natural gifts.

Why would a woman ever choose to remain fallow?

After a few months, he offered to advance me the amount due at customs for our books. We could bring all of them here, since books were all that we had on our minds. I thanked him with a deep bow, and was given wine. But we refused his tempting offer, for fear of the rats. We knew that there wasn't any cheese in those boxes of books, but we didn't trust for a moment the lemurs in this carnal zoo.

We enjoyed the respect of the permanent Tower whores. They were poor creatures, not all of them beautiful. They were women who got badly mauled by the bullfighters when they wouldn't perform as requested. Their behavior earned them slaps and blows as a bonus for the love-making. They knew that we could hear everything, and they agreed that the whole setup was like a pigsty. I told one *señorita* I had got to know, one who had certain intellectual ambitions, that you can get beaten up in any profession: a rejected manuscript is no caress, either. When I showed this girl our room, she broke out in tears. And then she asked if we had ever seen the Big One.

The Big One in the Tower of Whores was the super-lady, the main attraction, a walking exemplar of eroticism, a living legend of lechery, a second Pilar, a scarlet sister of sainted reputation, Palmira by name, who demanded a cool thousand to stretch out on the mattress of her profession—if we can indeed call a "mattress" the venue where she pursued her business. Her johns, if they weren't the famous *espadas* in person, arrived in limousines. For this queen of the coquettes, Adeleide had outfitted a luxury chamber in the main house. One day Palmira showed it to us, like a proud newlywed showing her relatives around the estate of her nouveau-riche husband. This suite had cost a pretty penny. The four-poster bed stood on a raised platform, the canopy borne by gilded columns. An elegant *mantilla* served as a bedspread. By means of a silken sash, the canopy could be opened, revealing a capacious mirror. Indirect illumination was installed all around, each lamp with its own silken pull. The walls were done in Genovese damask. In one corner stood a shrine with an antique Madonna on the crescent moon, a literally adorable figure. There was a censer hanging on a chain, a lamp for the eternal flame, and an ivory crucifix. A reproduction of Goya's nude *Maia*, not one clipped from some art book, hung on the wall in an exquisite frame. Above the door you saw a shepherd lolling next to his shepherdess, playing her a tune on his shawm. The room smelled of very expensive lasciviousness. An upholstered door led to the bath, which was a masterpiece of the Palma firm of Casa Buades, Plaza Cort 32-35. Baths of such opulence as this one were to be found in only one other location on the island, the *Palacio* of the banker Juan March. Pilar's murrhine receptacle was here made of red marble. It could not be held in the flat of your hand—the single blemish in this exemplary penthouse.

The woman who lent this bed of honor the glory of her body, Palmira, whom some called Doña Palmira, arrived one day at the little room of Vigoleis, whom some called Don Vigo, and asked him straight from her tastefully concealed shoulder, without cooing or lovey-dovey preliminaries, if he would be interested in giving her some company in her boudoir. "I want to sleep with you, stranger man. Why won't you come and visit me? You are certainly aware that people pay handsomely for a night with me, but you are not aware how much I would give for an hour or so with you, my foreign man. My dear little friend, you've come here from so far away. I could give you so much, so much…"—this was the approximate tenor of her invitation—"but of course you wouldn't accept it, for you are as proud as your dear Doña Beatriz. I admire you both for remaining here in this pigsty, for living your own lives that are so much unlike ours, and not giving in to the misery that surrounds you. For you know, my sweet darling, I've heard your story, and I just had to see you up close. So now, come!" The only alluring aspect of her appearance was her eyes, which shimmered behind gilded lashes.

Sweet, darling Vigoleis, her little love-cushion and lustful lollipop, gold medalist in the syphilis sprint and by this time fluent in Spanish, withdrew his desirable body from this dangerous tangle in approximately the following fashion: "*Señorita*, my dear friend, my big little sweetheart from the luxury apartment, pride of the Ivory Tower—you are lying. For if you truly knew of our adventures, you would realize and comprehend that I simply cannot come with you. And since you are bigger than Pilar, I wish that you wouldn't threaten my life. I don't exactly love it, this life of mine, but I am suddenly in need of it again in order to finish a story I'm writing, the story of a poetizing (I said *poetisante*) youth, whose posthumous works were eaten up by rats when they got wind that he was on his way out. But then he survived a leap into the void, and in his leather satchel there was no longer an oeuvre for him to destroy. Now he is making up for lost work. He is writing his fingers to the bone, just look...so let's remain friends. As romantic as it would be to sneak around on the paths of illicit amorousness, it's just as romantic to write about it. My next chapter will be an idyll about Palmira and this far-traveled stranger, and their encounter in the Clock Tower..." But then I noticed that the nymph standing opposite me hadn't understood. She wasn't interested in literature about love. She wanted love itself. She stamped her foot, shook my hand, and departed. No sooner was she gone when I felt the need to wash my hands. But I was ashamed of my twofold cowardice.

Over time we got used to the sounds of nature at the Tower, just as the neighbors of a railroad station become inured to the noise of arriving and departing trains. You subconsciously memorize the schedule and watch the clock on your kitchen wall. As far as we were concerned, this whoretel functioned more like a registry. We got to know several regular customers, and they got to know us: "Odd birds, that foreign couple nesting out there in the 'Torre'—they must be some kind of token respectability." Aristocrats have a way of showing disdain for the mob, even after the mob has long since tossed them out of power.

I think the time has finally arrived to say a word about the actual business conducted at the "Torre del Reloj." Suburban hostelry, produce farm, vineyard, and trading post—all this was, of course, a front. Arsenio stood at the center of an ingeniously contrived ring of opium smugglers, who chose a cleverly orchestrated dealership in contraband American cigarettes as a further element of camouflage. He wasn't completely his own boss, although in the Balearics he was the top guy, crafty and cunning, gifted like no one else with the talents of a field marshal, and equipped with detailed knowledge of the local terrain. The true boss of the syndicate was the noted banker Juan March, nicknamed "Verga," a term that means "rod" or "switch," a cognomen held in honor by the family to commemorate the weapon they used in earlier times to discipline their hogs. March was the richest man in Spain and one of the richest in Europe. "*Enrichi au su de toute l'Espagne par la fraude et la concussion,*" as Bernanos exclaims in his book on the Spanish Civil War, a war that was to a large extent financed by Juan March himself. Today, according to reports from friends in Spain, he is richer than ever before. Someday I would like to write a biography of this American-style gangster, but no doubt a more worthy pen will be found for such a task. In the meantime, a great deal has already been published in newspapers and magazines about this upstart. Yet as far as I know, no one has yet produced the horror story appropriate to the subject. At this point I shall only mention the role played by this political dude during the Wilhelminian World War, which poured the first millions into his piggy bank: grain exports from Argentina to the belligerent countries, paid in advance using neutral bank accounts, protected by neutral insurance companies. The freight consisted exclusively of stones; the ships were sunk by a hired submarine. A brand new game! A brand new kind of luck!

When we arrived on the island, this banker's palace was already standing. But his father still tended the pigs in Santa Margarita, using a method that is just as amazing as the mathematical/philological talents of the famous Elberfeld horses: the swineherd opens a furrow in the field with his verga, and not a single pig dares to cross the line. That's because thousands of years ago the pigs that strayed beyond the line got whacked on the snout, and their descendants still sense this. The younger Señor March, on the other hand, escaped the magic pale and pressed his snout far beyond the limits of the family farm. In fact, he marched over corpses, and that's why he served time in prison when the Catholic monarchy collapsed. But he didn't stay long behind bars. He bribed the prison personnel, from the warden on down to the most menial keeper of the keys, guaranteed a living for all of them in foreign climes, and arranged a clever escape for the whole caravan via La Linea across the border to a ship waiting at Gibraltar. This coup cost the banker several millions. The nascent Spanish Republic was already beginning to topple. Don Darío, who bore a personal grudge against Don Juan as the result of a murder case, suffered a nervous breakdown while the monarchists celebrated lavishly. During this time, Beatrice was giving French lessons to a certain *señorita*. On the day the escape was announced, she received champagne. Her pupil's Papá was Don Juan March's lawyer.

Juan March came up with a brilliant idea for a wedding present for his own daughter: an airship. He commissioned Dr. Eckener to build a zeppelin for her honeymoon trip around the world. Unfortunately, the company in Friedrichshafen was unable to sign a contract, owing to lack of time until the desired date of delivery. In Palma, gossips passed the word that the bridegroom had already crossed the line; even solid German workmanship could not produce a dirigible airship in nine months' time. Don Juan was content with a Super Whale from the aircraft firm of Dornier. For the position of on-board steward he selected a giant Watusi negro, who for weeks was a sensation on the streets of Palma. The smaller wedding gifts were publicly exhibited in a local hall; it was similar to a World's Fair, and people came over from the mainland to take a look. Only Goering and Caligula ever put on such gaudy displays.

There were innumerable stories circulating about the owner of the "Banca March." But then things quieted down for a few years while the man lived in exile, until at the beginning of the Civil War his name started to be mentioned again. After our own escape from the island, when we were living in Basel at the end of 1936, in conversation one day with Dr. Hartmann, the foreign-news editor of the *Baseler Nachrichten*, I ventured the opinion that Franco would never win the war, not even with help from Hitler and Mussolini, because these two potentates had only their own interests in mind and would drop His Excellency the Caudillo just as soon as they had achieved their particular ends. Dr. Hartmann and I were having a meal at an Italian restaurant. He ordered more wine, we drank a lot, and he became more and more pensive. His ruddy face featured a pair of very intelligent eyes behind thick spectacles. These eyes of his sparkled, but otherwise he looked dead. I thought to myself, he's drunk. But no, he was just sad. Like many bachelors, he was a good-hearted fellow, and loose talk just wasn't his way. I continued gushing about the possibilities in Spain, but then he said it was already too late. Franco was going to win. His newspaper had just received a dispatch from Rome that Juan March had arrived at the Vatican to negotiate support for Franco with the Pope. Did that mean that gold would start flowing from the combined sources? "No doubt about it," said Hartmann, taking another doleful swallow. Tipsy though he was, he saw all the connections, and soon things started working out precisely as he had prophesied. A few days later the Concordat was no longer kept secret; it was in all the newspapers. Any church with universal ambitions must be willing to walk over corpses if it wants to avoid having to dig its own grave. That is the bitter truth, but it's also how progress works. It causes weeping only in those who get to feel it. We were weeping too.

At around this time Don Pío Baroja, one of my favorite writers, found refuge in Basel, where he lived in the house, in the shirt, in the trousers, and in the slippers of the oddly totalizing writer Dominik Müller, and ate his heart out with homesickness for Spain. The only element of his clothing that didn't originate in Müller's costume shop was the beret on his head. Don Pío was a very special kind of anarchist, so special that he had enemies in all political camps in his fatherland, all of whom wanted to shoot him, even in the attics of the country's two embassies in Paris. So he fled to Basel's Water Tower area, where Dr. Müller did for this Spanish refugee what we refused to have the *Führer* do for us: he offered him a pair of pants. Pío Baroja accepted. Herr Müller published an interview with this, the greatest Spanish novelist of his time. People who read it and who knew Baroja said to themselves, "There goes another one—Baroja on Franco's side!" It gave us a shock, too, and we sought out this Basque writer. He was, thank heavens, still the same. His Swiss host had played an evil game with the refugee's world fame. I lacked the courage to alert Don Pío to the scam that was going on. He was himself unable to read the words his friend had put in his mouth. Baroja immediately confirmed Dr. Hartmann's dark suspicions, and even without the aid of wine he added, more gloomily still, that he felt forced to surrender. He was old, sick, and exhausted, and without Spain he couldn't go on living. This vagabond genius, this desperado and anarchizing romantic, whose life's work already filled more than eighty volumes, was suffering from the same illness as had befallen his Basque compatriot Unamuno: Spain. Gallows-birds like Juan March, whose biography no one could have written better than Don Pío as part of his series of little-known adventure books, seem able to keep this disease under control. The finest products of the country are the ones who are repeatedly ruined by it—not only in Iberia, although that is where the affliction causes a dramatic level of desperation only possible in the somber shadow of the Man of La Mancha.

Arsenio was not a murderer and not a millionaire, but he was what one might call well off. He could have bought up all the volumes of poetry in the world without becoming one penny poorer. Juan March was the crowned king of the island, Arsenio the uncrowned one. The gang used a submarine, a decommissioned craft of German manufacture, steered by a genuine German captain whom we once met in the Tower, where he always was given a princely welcome. If he happened to arrive without a sailor's bride, Adeleide regularly lent him accommodations in the Big One's commodious four-poster. This fleet lieutenant spoke fluent Spanish, but on one occasion, when something took him by surprise, he betrayed his Teutonic origins by exclaiming, "*Au Backe*!" I immediately replied with, "*Mein Zahn*!" and the introduction was complete. Whenever this dashing pirate turned up at the Tower, a certain excitement pervaded the premises. One week later Arsenio actually told us that we shouldn't be scared if we started hearing guns going off at night. The *carabineros* had gone nuts and couldn't be persuaded that he, Arsenio, didn't have something to do with Juan March's band of smugglers. "Opium?"— "White slavery?" The chieftain slapped his thighs and left me standing alone. In the following night we heard gunshots. There was a hellish to-do, a clattering of hooves, women screaming (but not in the boxes), dogs barking, and flares shooting up in the sky. Vigoleis and Beatrice were unharmed. Antonio's connections with the police were reliable, and, in any case, we had such a reputation as bohemians that we could have walked the depths of Hell unscathed, like angels on a guided tour. Arsenio and his two older sons were taken into custody, and that evening the English lesson in the *fonda* was canceled. But the three rogues wandered home the very next day—lack of evidence. So Arsenio blew his loud horn: wine, octopus, *pavo real*, *turrón*, with the lady and gentleman from Box I as guests of honor. For once, Beatrice didn't need to enter the little hotel with tin can in hand; this time her dog was given the juiciest morsels right from the spit. But we drew up short of drinking to companionship and brotherhood. We stuck with the formal titles Señor Arsenio, Señora Adeleide, Doña Beatriz, and Don Vigoleis. A toast to you and to us!

Years later when visiting friends we were told a highly romantic story. Half an hour outside of the city there was a mysterious site called "The Clock Tower"—not exactly a *finca*—a set of old buildings with a stumpy tower. This place was the subject of the weirdest rumors. The owner was said to be an accomplice of Juan March, a flashy cowboy type who ran a brothel as a front, sold wine, had a *fonda* on the premises, and also rented out mules—an altogether shady operation. Well, for a period of time a German-Swiss couple lived there and maintained contacts in foreign countries. They spoke many languages. Drug dealers. International criminals. Search warrants. But they suddenly disappeared without a trace. Juan March probably put them to work somewhere else—either that, or they took their loot and decided to go live someplace else under fictitious names. Think of all the riffraff that washes up on the shores of this island!

Hearing this tale we were overcome with fear and trembling. To be sure, we had heard of Juan March and his moles; why, you could almost find them in any Baedeker. But we knew no details. Surely the Germans were behind the whole thing, this time with a U-boat and its swaggering captain—what a scoop for one of the Berlin magazines! We should try to get the captain's name, because names are what sell magazines, even if they're the wrong names. No, "von Borck" was definitely not this guy's name—and I almost let the cat out of the bag. It wasn't "Kraschutzki," either, as some denizens of the German colony thought it might be. Kraschutzki was the navy captain who claimed to have started the sailors' mutiny in Kiel. He was living peacefully in Cala Ratjada weaving straw or breeding chickens, but in any case not shooting off torpedos full of opium.

Later, when we settled down to something approximating middle-class existence and began socializing in the "upper circles," I identified ourselves as the notorious couple from the "Torre del Reloj," the roomers in Adeleide's house of bawds. There was consternation among our distinguished hosts. Daughters pricked up their ears and wanted to hear details. Proof! Doña Beatriz out there among the whores? Impossible! Our reputation was at stake. But our hosts were dyed-in-the-wool monarchists—like Juan March, who also led a double life. Everyone on the island had his second aspect. We were not shown the door.

How often have I kidded Beatrice about this Anakite giant and his duro! Why, she never figured out what the guy wanted to buy with his 5 pesetas! But then she has replied, "Haha, *mon pauvre petit*, and you with that fertile imagination of yours! What was it that Arsenio was hoping to get out of you? I'm the one who had to explain it to *you*." It's true. While I had taken a peek over the partitions of depravity, I had never looked farther. For weeks the gangster paced around me, interrogated me, put me to the test to see if I was eligible for a job as a middleman in the drug business. We learned this from one of his sons, shortly before the outbreak of the Civil War. His Papá had certain plans for me (like my own father). I looked promising. I could do a whole lot. But he soon noticed that I was too stupid for this kind of shady commerce, yet not stupid enough to be sent out as a stooge. It was the same old tragic story: too stupid and not stupid enough. An entire life can be a shambles as a result of this predicament. *Can* be?

IV

If I decide at the last moment to make up titles for my chapters, this one might be called "Vigoleis in a Dress Suit." Because the event to be described took place before the advent of Hitler's regime of Strength Through Joy, it will be free of ludicrous elements in and of itself, but in particular, it will lack the singular clownishness of the German peaked military cap. The Germans are so methodical in their ways that they always invent a uniform to symbolize their own degradation. In any case, mine wasn't blue but black.

In an earlier chapter I mentioned in passing the silver wedding anniversary of my parents, and how in front of all the guests, who were expecting something special, I stammered so badly that no one understood a word I said. On such notable occasions even the blackest of black sheep get to turn white; for about an hour the people are proud of you. But of course it went all wrong, and there I stood in the expensive dress suit that my father had asked a tailor to custom-fit to my hopeless frame. I can still see myself standing there in my snazzy threads. But this isn't about me. It's about that suit, which I stashed in moth balls in my luggage. Would I ever put it on again?

"Put on your black one," said Beatrice. Vigoleis buttoned himself in, and off he went at the side of his Beatrice in her Viennese finery to Doña María's hotel, where we were invited for dinner by a certain Don Felipe, the manager of the establishment. A "certain" Don F. He had something going with the proprietress, Mary Snow's mother, but otherwise he was insignificant. Short, with yellowish skin, smug, very well dressed, on his business trips this man was often a guest at the hotel where he later kept the books. No doubt he took notice of the widow, and she of him. They probably worked out an estimate and did some checking, and soon enough Don Felipe stood at the counter wearing even nicer duds.

The meal was excellent. The chubby lady liked me at first sight. I noticed this right away, whereas Don Felipe surveyed my person several times to figure out whether I might be of use to him—but I didn't realize this until much later. Our hosts were of course curious about Beatrice's lap-dog, but despite Doña María's cordial hospitality, this was not just a repast in honor of the spouse of Mary Snow's private language teacher. I sensed that it had some other purpose, but I was wrong about what that purpose might be. Both of our hosts seemed to want something from me, and since they seemed to be in agreement with each other, it had to be something quite innocent. They watched every bite I took. They perked up at every word that left my mouth—was I being interrogated? After the second course they knew quite a bit about my past life, in fact more than I did myself, and they seemed satisfied. Seeing that my wife had command of ten or more languages, how many did I know? Was I a wine connoisseur? Could I interpret a dinner menu, drive a car, keep accounts? And how did I get along with people? I didn't score very well on any of these points, but the two of them seemed pleased by the way I skirted embarrassment—the widow more so than her cicisbeo. For me, the main thing was the meal we were eating, whose separate components I would not recognize on a menu for what they really were. Finally to have a decent meal, with food that wasn't prepared on a bidet! I had to control myself to avoid regressing into my Clock Tower table manners. Beatrice had no such difficulty, because even when seated at a bidet, she doesn't abandon propriety. My suit, both of our hosts said, was a fine fit. I explained that I had led my parents to the silver altar wearing it, a remark that touched our listeners' hearts. Even the merriest of widows will turn silent for the length of a breath when the god of marriage places a wreath at the bedpost of a 25-year-long union. The wine was delectable.

The invitations multiplied. The feasts became more and more informal, and before we noticed it, they had become a tradition: once every week an abundance of food and drink. Don Felipe remained reserved, observant, and polite, until one day he felt that the moment had arrived to unpack what was on his mind. And here is how the sly imp went about it...

He was the manager of this small inn for traveling businessmen and other middle-class clientele. We were further aware that Doña María was building a hotel in El Terreno that would meet their steadily increasing needs, a few hundred beds, private beach, private funicular, and its name was to be "Majorica." It would be ready in a few weeks—that means in about a year, I thought to myself— and then would come the time for greeting the first guests. One whole floor was already reserved—so perhaps "a few weeks" was right? Fine, but now he was ready to hire employees in the higher ranks, and we had come to his attention. Beatrice as manager and hostess. In her free time she would have use of the grand piano. He would insist that she function not as an ordinary receptionist, but as an elegant lady, and that meant no black dresses with dainty white collars framing a widow's countenance. Don Vigo would be employed at the reception desk. In the morning he would betake himself to the harbor to welcome the foreign guests, but for the rest of the forenoon he would be free of further duties and could devote himself to his literary labors. He should be present in the dining room during mealtimes—I suddenly imagined myself as a glad-handing maitre d'; as a child I always wanted to be something like that. But that wasn't what he had in mind. I was just supposed to be on hand if anyone needed an interpreter, since the headwaiter knew only English and French and that was all. On occasion I would have to perform certain minor chores—but of course, I nodded—such as holding a bowl, assisting a guest with a chair, explaining an item on the menu— that sort of thing, surely I knew. Don Vigo knew. They would need to obtain a hotel library (he actually said "obtain") in the most important languages, and I would have a free hand: newspapers, magazines, a collection of records for the phonograph. I pointed to Beatrice, and said that she was the expert in that department. And then at night the hotel guests would want to visit the typically Spanish attractions. Especially the guests from England would not want to miss any of these, and Don Vigo would act as a cicerone—did he understand? Don Vigo made a gesture that satisfied Don Felipe, although he failed to say that it was on the basis of his ability to understand that he felt obliged to understand everything he was told here. No one would expect, of course, that I would be a perfect hotel man right away; I should just be myself and go ahead and tell lies, if what was at stake was the truth. Don Felipe was ready to admit that he would be competing with the "Príncipe"; over there they had this amazing man, a genuine Swiss, Don Helvecio, who had put the hotel back on its feet, and now it was thriving—ah, the Swiss (he turned to

Doña Beatriz) knew how to run a guest house. He didn't suppose that we knew this fellow-countryman of hers, did we? No, Beatrice didn't know him. We had been there once, but hadn't noticed anything Swiss. Don Felipe: that's right. Don Helvecio looks just like a true Spaniard. So now, would we accept his offer in principle?

Our heads were swimming. This would mean a real room, real food, a real bed, bath, running water, hot and cold. Don Felipe explained quite clearly: our room would be on the top floor, our bath would be a stand-up shower, and at the beginning our salary would be more like pocket money. Do you accept?

By now I had myself completely under control. It was important now to avoid a misstep; we must remain cool in the face of this cool calculator who was putting us to the test. One false move, a premature leap from the plank, and the miracle would disappear like Arsenio's rat cluster. Furrow your brow, visibly tighten your concentration on an invisible goal: in half a year, nine months or so as hotel receptionists, we would have enough money for two *burros*, and could wander through all of Spain writing travelogues from the donkey perspective. I had it all worked out. How much do you suppose a beast like that costs?

Perhaps, said Don Vigo, we might be willing to reach an agreement. In three of four days we would let him know. We would have to think things over, make some arrangements in literary affairs, send a few telegrams. Above all, a certain film company in Berlin would have to be informed that a commissioned script would not arrive as soon as expected, but—Don Felipe could surely understand that if I were to make such a change of profession, I would be doing so with the hope of collecting material for new novels. Studying the people who frequent a hotel is always a lucrative enterprise for writers—but on second thought I shouldn't have said this, considering Vicki Baum, Ernst Zahn, and such people with dual professions. Afterwards, out on the street, Beatrice said that Don Felipe hadn't noticed. Doing Palma's night life with pilarizing British gentlemen—there's a novel in itself.

Our homeward trip was like walking on air. We would be finished with our Tower Period and its tin cans, its bidet, whores, gangs of rats, weekly police raids, and monthly *corridas* on 29 mattresses. We would switch residences to a part of town where the broads—in this case the ladies—were taught to waltz without recourse to a little shrine and candles. —"Did you notice, Beatrice, how important it seemed to Felipe that I'm a Catholic? He didn't care that I don't practice any more. He doesn't either. He said that's part of being a Spaniard. They're a Catholic country." My baptismal certificate and my dress suit, two pieces of equipment from my homeland, were now clearing my path to a glorious future. I would casually pocket all the generous tips. I would consent to sleeping with a pickled old lady if she promised to make me her sole heir, as happened around the same time with a young Swiss elevator operator in the Grand Hotel... With such thoughts in mind, we passed through the moonlit peristyle of our cloister, whose first right-hand cell we would soon no longer be desecrating with our sublime asceticism.

On this particular evening, Mary Snow was the only one who had no cause for turning mental somersaults. She would have to continue cramming English verbs and learning etiquette. Up to now she was lacking all the attributes of a *grande dame*; the child was still in sticky diapers.

If all else fails, become an innkeeper; in between, do some literature. And if that, too, comes to naught, you can put your hair shirt back on.

The three days we requested as a pretense to mull things over seemed never to end, but I filled them with purposeful activity. I practiced being Major Domo at my hotel. I made polite bows in all directions, gracefully accepted bows from others, and made the appropriate remarks in the languages I would be expected to use the most frequently. Beatrice, who was doing our laundry on a stone at the water trough, was my most cherished customer, a guest of many years' standing who wouldn't flee the scene if I made some mistake. On the contrary, this guest was so much a part of the household that she could offer corrections of my behavior and my grammar. While there was much to be corrected in the latter respect, my deportment as a receptionist left nothing to be desired. The Tower kids stood around and had the greatest time watching us. They thought I was playing theater with Doña Beatriz when, with professional expertise, I conducted her through the gauntlet of house rats, roof rats, and nomad rats, up the outside staircase, down the darkened corridor, and into our pen, as if she were the spouse of a celebrated writer and I were guiding her with the proper decorum to the room reserved for her famous husband. "But of course, Madam, we shall be happy to shorten the table legs! I shall take the measurements right away, and we shall be glad to allow room for the gentleman's knees—I understand perfectly, intellectuals have certain quirks... Noise? No reason for concern, Madam, everything here is soundproof, double doors, cork floors, partitions with horsehair lining, and up above, if you would be so kind as to see for yourself, there is a clear view to eternity itself—a little extra perquisite for creative guests. This innovation is unique to our establishment. Word is getting around, and once writers have experienced our roofless ambience, they refuse to seek out accommodations at any hostelry but ours."

"And that can down there? It's disgusting!"

"Oh, the one for vermin on the floor? It will be removed. Our manageress ought to have been more observant, but of course, she can't be everywhere at once..."

Doña María and Don Felipe were happy when we gave them our decision. There was much to discuss. The proprietors considered it most important to plan an elaborate opening-day ceremony. It should be an event worthy to be entered in the house annals. We were asked our opinion, we made suggestions, I came forth with some daring ideas that delighted Don Felipe's ears. An invitation should go out to the German philosopher Conde de Keyserling, and we could ask him to deliver an inaugural address. Would he come? And how he would come! But it would require a great deal of wine.

Don Felipe made notes, he calculated, crossed out some things and added others, and was not without ideas of his own. But he asked me in passing if I had ever organized such a celebration before. I couldn't reveal to him that it was Zwingli's ice-cream bar premiere that was serving as my model. I hid behind the fact that any writer must at any given moment make things up out of whole cloth, even an opening-day celebration, if one of the characters in his novel suddenly decides to start up a hotel—which of course the next-best floozy could sabotage in the twinkling of an eye.

Invitations were sent out. Advertisements in all the newspapers announced the day and hour of the inauguration ceremony, Saturday at 5:00 pm. On the list of invitees we noticed the name of Don Helvecio. Just wait till that guy sees me in my monkey suit from my parents' silver wedding, and his sister playing with a big key ring and a grand piano! Too bad that we were still on the warpath with him—but were we? We had been driven apart by special circumstances. As soon as Pilar gave Zwingli his walking papers so she could return to the streets, everything would be as it was back in Cologne-Poll with Gravedigger Firnich.

I composed an inaugural speech for Don Felipe, one that in my opinion downplayed intellectual aspirations in favor of the man's cosmopolitan ambitions as an entrepreneur, yet without eschewing artistic aspects altogether. My idea was that an innkeeper can become anything he wants to, and so to the pair of *burros* Beatrice and I were fantasizing about, I added a third beast of burden, a sturdy mule. Don Felipe liked the speech, but felt constrained to excise or correct certain details and add certain others. The result was a *Vigoleis castratus* for the hotel's middlebrow, but lucrative, clientele. I was more fortunate with my text for an advertising brochure. Employing a romantic palette, I presented an image of the Golden Isle so authentic that not even a museum curator could distinguish original from reproduction. Don Felipe, in particular, didn't notice how I had violated certain details of geography. There was no need to cite my Swiss brother-in-law, the professional *hôtelier*, in learned footnotes; it was all my own work, inspired by the hygienic Pegasus in our Tower cell, and by my ardent desire to lure the richest people in the world into the "Hotel Majorica." If I perchance lavished excessive praise on this or that feature of the island, I could always moderate this later as *chef de réception* and impresario. After all, few people are capable of reading an advertising prospectus correctly, and fewer still know how to compare a text with reality. Hotel advertising is essentially the same as party politics; it's not the platform that matters, but the slogans. From day to passing day, I, Vigoleis, felt more and more in control of the promising situation. Finally I had produced some writing that would go out into the world without my having to go without food to come up with the postage, and without the risk of having my text returned to the sender like a rejected manuscript. This text would end up in other people's wastepaper baskets.

One by one, the days leading up to the hotel opening fell from the calendar. We had not yet seen the new building, but a day before the celebration Don Felipe took us along to El Terreno to show us the palatial edifice; on this occasion he would give us our rooming assignment. We agreed to wait until after the ceremonies before moving in.

I can leave out the details of our tour through the enormous building. It still smelled of workmen, but in the prevailing heat it wasn't necessary to provide for temporary rent-free tenants to help dry the masonry. Here and there workmen were busy sawing holes in the sandstone walls for windows—easily done to correct minor mistakes made by the architect. The rest was all finished, and we could stage the grand opening with a clear conscience. Whoever thinks that any opening ceremony is a fraud, has no proper sense of dynamics. Bunting, a bevy of costumed girls, top hats, a little verse intoned by an innocent child, a fluttering parade of dignitaries, and the laying of the keystone, the launching of the new ship, can take its impressive course. There will be speeches and toasts and choral singing, and afterwards the hammering and riveting and plastering will continue. Back in 1928 I had the opportunity, as a humble research scholar, to march behind Mayor Konrad Adenauer and other notables and attend the opening of the "Pressa" Exhibition in Cologne (30 million deficit). The event was still vividly present in my memory. I can testify that twenty-four hours before the sluice gates were opened, our hotel on Mallorca was farther along than the Cologne affair had been, even if you consider that Doña María's shekels were by no means squandered as freely as those of then Rhenish Cathedral City's fatcats.

We had little time to look around our room, which was commodious and bright. Beatrice wanted to press a few keys at the concert grand, but Don Felipe was nowhere in sight. It wasn't until we were on our way back home that the light finally dawned. Beatrice suddenly stood still, as if struck by a beam from above that couldn't be caught hold of while continuing in forward motion. In a frightened tone she asked me, "Did you get a good look at our room?"

"I just glanced in. A pretty nice room, not some garret like the one at Pilar's, not to mention our dismal pigsty in the Tower. We've come a long way."

"A long way? Did you notice any wardrobe?"

I conjured up my image of the room, measured it inch by inch, let my memory touch it up and down, and finally I had it all together: it did not contain a wardrobe, but something like a metal chest with little curtains in front. Surely the wardrobe was of the built-in type—just press a button and the clothes racks would come bouncing out. Drawers would pop out by themselves, and every time you opened or closed them you'd see the dust from little dead moths—in the Tower it was the bats who kept those little butterflies away from the love boxes...

"Don't kid around! You'll see, those people won't give us a ward-robe!"

"Those people," indeed. It wasn't nice of Beatrice to talk this way. She was being very pessimistic. Why on earth should "those people" withhold a wardrobe from us, when they were investing millions in this enterprise? Millionaires, it is true, march over corpses—but over wardrobes...? This was my argument on behalf of grand-style capitalism.

"It's precisely because they've put millions into the building that they are cheapskates when it comes to adding a box for clothes. You can't teach me anything about millionaires!"

That was far from my intention. On the contrary, my intention was to plumb the depths of their psyche, or better yet, the depths of their cash register. A clothes chest as an instrument of power in the hands of a millionaire—Beatrice could recount certain experiences of her own in this regard. Inside the home of one of these types, she once was poisoned and, comically enough, a clothes closet played a major role in the adventure. That is where a strange man hid himself when not in the company of the lady of the house, the mistress who had hired Beatrice. So now, under the circumstances, I said that it was best to make inquiries, under the assumption that Beatrice was unwilling to play the role of hotel hostess without a wardrobe in our room, and I told her that I had given up the idea of being an erudite hotel flunky in a monkey suit. "When you come to think of it, *chérie*, we don't need anything of the kind."

"That's what you're saying now, but as soon as we get there and start negotiating with them, you'll chicken out, leaving me in the soup all by myself. You'll start feeling sorry for those poor folks, or else you'll get all mystical, and I don't know which is worse."

Sorry? Well, anyone who feels sorry for himself can feel it for others, too. But "mysticism"? That hurt, and all I was able to say was, "Come on! We're going to that hotel to have it all out with Don Felipe. If you prefer, you can wait outside. Don't you worry, I am not going to go transcendental on account of a wooden box. You know what they can do with...?"

But before I could specify a destination for the wardrobe, we had already reached the Calle San Nicolás and stood at the door. Just a few seconds later, we were in the little man's little office. During those few seconds I gave myself an inward yank. My spinal column was stiff, but not inelastic. I was prepared to enter single combat against a million pesetas.

Beatrice's suspicions were confirmed in full. There was no wardrobe in the room, neither in the form of a piece of furniture nor in the form of a wall closet. Would we eventually get one? No, not in the foreseeable future. In the meantime, surely we could use the metal chest. Wood was expensive on the island...

Beatrice shot flames at me with her Indian eyes, and this spurred me on immensely. I most decidedly did not chicken out; the two of us, certain of victory, started tugging hard—but at the wrong end of the rope. My mysticism remained earthbound in an Iberian way, whereas Don Felipe's heart remained as stony as that of the king in the famous ballad.

Then the little guy started getting edgy. Was he perhaps interpreting our behavior as an attempt at extortion? He got mean. The tiny golden pencil that up to now had tapped out the Morse code of his impatience on the desktop suddenly disappeared inside his fist, and his fist hammered down on the blotter. *Caramba*!—this was the Devil himself who now was reading me the text. Then he arose, but since he was unable to stretch up to his full height, he looked rather comical as he approached me with his shoulders hunched forward and his head drawn down. What kind of a game was this? What was this insolence of ours supposed to mean, a veiled threat? On the eve of opening day? "Do you want money from me? Are you both crooks (*gentuza*)?"

All indications were that Vigoleis was about to get his face punched in. Beatrice took the necessary emergency measures. She was familiar with Don Felipe's irascible temperament; in addition, he represented his patroness' millions, and so he was doubly dangerous. But there was no violence. The Spaniard discharged his fury by thundering, "*Me cago en Dios!*" In the presence of a woman this utterance was in fact worse than the act itself. He was wishing me dead.

Thus Vigoleis passed his first important test in the struggle for a human being's right to a dust-free wardrobe, an object to which we can, without exaggeration, ascribe a symbolic value. He didn't get a punch in the nose, nor did he get the wardrobe. Using his hors-d'oeuvre Spanish, and eschewing blasphemous actions like the one with which he had just been regaled, he let it be known to this Philip fellow that, under the prevailing circumstances, he must decline to place himself at the service of the hotel, and furthermore, even if Don Felipe were to reconsider, acknowledge his error, and come forth with the item of furniture in question, even then, there could be no question of cooperation in the enterprise. The conversation had opened up a gap; now there was an abyss between us, an unbridgeable one. What was more, Vigoleis knew he had the complete agreement of his Beatrice.

Doña María, alerted by the noisy argument and informed in a few words as to its nature, immediately offered to have her own wardrobe transferred to our room. But her suggestion came too late; I had peered too far down into the cesspool of a capitalist soul, and it made my flesh creep. If ever I were to fulfill my life's dream, would I act in similar fashion, haggling over a few pieces of wood? Doña María had no recourse but her own nerves, which now conveniently collapsed. Her cicisbeo caught her as she fell, and hotel personnel rushed in from their listening post behind the door. Smelling salts, emetics, expert hands helped loosen the stays over her bosom. We departed. In this place there was nothing left for us to do.

Upstairs in her little room, Mary Snow snapped shut her English textbooks. She liked Beatrice as Doña Beatriz, but not as *profesora*. But was the *profesora* now satisfied with her Don Vigoleis? The way he gave it to "those people"? Not yielding an inch in their categorical demand?

We were on our way back home, out in an open field but surrounded by the stench of the slaughterhouse, a reminder that all is transitory, animal life as well as wooden clothes chests. Suddenly Beatrice acted up like a little puppy. She embraced and kissed Vigoleis, her armorless knight. He had really stuck it to those people!

What else did you expect? What do you suppose those people thought about where we were coming from? Foreign trash—or doesn't the word gentuza mean the common mob? They have only themselves to blame for this fiasco. There will be no opening-day tomorrow. "The damage will be in the thousands, and what does a wardrobe like that cost?" Although they were still the disgraced lodgers at a whorehouse, Vigoleis and Beatrice were finally on top of things again.

Mary Snow was a cute child, but not a dancing dervish like Julietta, who in a similar situation would have dashed off to the cathedral to force the Virgin into approving of her nifty new dress. Nièves had as yet no such compensatory concerns.

The hotel was not consecrated. As a result of unforeseen technical difficulties, the inaugural ceremonies were postponed indefinitely. Vigoleis needs only to brandish his lance, and already his enemies' weapons split apart.

We had to pay for this paupers' pride of ours, but never for one second did we regret our stupid little prank. We are idealists. If amid the perfidious vicissitudes of fate suddenly a wooden cabinet is transformed into a divinity, we shall worship it to the point of utter renunciation. The first result of our fearless stand was three days of total fasting.

Herr Emmerich congratulated us. He had heard rumors that we had landed splendid jobs. The charm of any rumor consists in the fact that everything about it can be either true or false; there is always "something" in it that corresponds to reality. When I reported to him that we had told those people to go stuff their jobs, he wondered whether we had received the money from Berlin and were about to go waltzing through Spain on donkeyback. The titillating news of Vigoleis' latest quixotic caper spread like wildfire. There was a shaking of heads, viz.: the heads of Gerstenberg and Ginsterberg, Antonio, the noble anarchists, Captain von Martersteig, and the gangboss Arsenio, who renewed his prowling around with silver duro in hand. We were considered heroes.

I have never owned a wardrobe. That's because, since the mystical moment in question, I have always refused to forfeit any portion of myself for the sake of four boards, be they for holding clothing or for housing my eternally unclothed person.

At this point I must not conceal the fact that a few months later Doña María begged us to excuse the boorish behavior of her business manager Don Felipe, and that she asked whether Doña Beatriz would be willing to resume lessons in her home. In the meantime Mary Snow had gone through two other English teachers, and she wanted Beatrice back.

Beatrice agreed. My dress suit was put back in mothballs, and we continued our daily grind at the Clock Tower.

One day was like any other, and what reason was there to expect that tomorrow would be any different? Every day was a day in a cramped cloister, with cramped food in a cramped room on a cramped bed, constantly gazing up at eternal goals, at the musty rafters and the beams of starlight that seeped through the spaces between nuns and monks above the motley wreck of earthly love.

We had strapped ourselves early onto our cot, and were harkening to the waves of lust that reached our ears from the neighboring cells, the ebb and flow of human passion, the now familiar play of the nearby surf.

Untrained though I was in things musical, my ear perceived what sounded to me like a wave of atonal sonority coming from two, or at most three, pigsties down the hall from us. She must be lying there now in her shimmering white Rubensesque plumpness, the mannish Kathrinchen, giving her groaning self to some dark-skinned bull—how fortunate for her that her lawyer husband's nerves were still in a shambles! As long as that's the case, she can get off on her own and live it up royally. There's no lethargic Freddy around to tell her, "Not tonight, honey," because tomorrow there's this all-important conference, and after tomorrow's conference, he's so used up that it's still no use. You've found just the place here at the Clock Tower. There are no conferences here except those that take place at night *à deux* in narrow cubicles, and the conference partners are of the prize-stallion kind. They may arrive with the faintly acidulous smell of a cow-barn, but you are long since sick and tired of your Friedrich Wilhelm's fragrance of baby soap. To be sure, you must take precautions that your conference partners don't present you with a certain kind of gift; the Essen coal-and-steel community would notice right away that your kid came not from your own local master-miner, but from a Spanish sapper.

Just as I was mentally sneaking over into the white-hot next-door cell and was about to suggest that the blond child of the Lower Rhine ask the Tower madam for some stain remover, there was a knocking at our wall. Adeleide had a message for Beatrice: there were two gentlemen waiting in the tavern who wanted to speak with her on an urgent matter. "At this time of night?" Were they out of their minds? No, one of them was a soldier, a buddy of her son's. The other one, in civilian clothes, she didn't know.

What do they want with me, asked Beatrice as she donned her *albornoz*. When I replied that it was obvious what they wanted, she said that, first of all, I should be ashamed of myself, and, secondly, they wouldn't arrive as a pair, and, thirdly, one of them was a comrade of her English pupil.

Arriving in a brothel as a pair—back in Cologne I had done just that on my mother's arm. And as far as shame was concerned, here in this accursed red-light joint, there wasn't a single corner free for the satisfaction of such moral exigencies. But Beatrice didn't listen to my compunctions. She walked the length of the corridor down to the eternal altar to the month of May, and located the secret door that led directly into the *fonda*. At night it was impossible to get her to go out alone to the rat nests.

From the cell where the Valkyrie was being anointed by some Iberian sailor or *almocrebe*, there again arose the familiar voice: "You over there, are you arguing again? Do you ever do anything else? You don't have to come to the Tower for that. You can do that back home!"

Before I could launch a reply over the partition, I was interrupted by a muffled scream of pleasure. In Spain, the *jus primae noctis* is a plural concept. In this case, a certain kind of erotic stopper was preventing our Menapic Katha-

rina from giving full effervescent cry to her ecstasy. I am already calling her
"our" Katharina, long before we have made her vertical, fully dressed
acquaintance at the side of her burned-out spouse. Needless to say, we shall
refrain from revealing to the latter person what we know all too well about
the former. We will wink at each other now and then, and here in the Clock
Tower winking will convey a message something like this: what we see there
curving up under a hand-knit blouse from Casa Bonet for 100 pesetas is something that we have already viewed in its pristine, divine, paradisiacal, untouched state, gleaming with dewy freshness. That is, we could say we have
viewed it in this state if we make the effort to erase from our thoughts an
insatiable Spanish pig and his grubby hands—which we truly must do if we
wish the word "untouched" to have any but second-hand connotations.

In the following chapter I hope that we will progress far enough to get to
see Kathrinchen without climbing up on a chair. When the time comes, she
will no longer be a juicy piece of wild game, but rather a tame gentlelady. But
now, Beatrice was staying away a long time.

I had the *pilarière* all to myself.

Lying on my back, I gazed through our latticework ceiling into the heavens
above the barn. In the next cell a sailor, one who apparently hadn't put into
port for quite some time, was exerting himself strenuously. The partition shuddered, and the ropes and everything hanging on them were making obedient
bows. My manuscripts rustled softly, and my shoes dangled up and down on
their laces. The longer the swab next door blabbered on in a language unknown to me, seeking compensation (perhaps even more) with his saved-up
pesetas for many a lonely night on the high seas, the more macabre seemed to
me the ebbing and swelling of the Baroque rigging above me. Moonlight
seeped down through the perforated cupola and combined with the glow of
the corridor shrine to form a melancholy twilight, glistening dimly in the os-
cillating ropework.

It is at such moments that I have made poems, the best and most beautiful
ones of my lifetime, which reveal the locale of their origins only insofar as I
step forth in them more naked than the divine Rhenish child three boxes away
from me. These stanzas of mine mark significant beginnings, they allow certain chords to resound that might almost have given meaning to my life. But
these products, too, I committed to the flames with a firm hand when it
seemed to me that their time had come.

While Vigoleis, released from all earthly bonds and with strange flesh heaving all around him, thus experienced his moment of transcendence, downstairs
in the *taberna* the Fates were spinning new threads. That is to say, the yarn
was already spun at the beginning of time, and all that was necessary was to
mount warp and woof on the frame so that the shuttle could start on its zigzag
journey.

The two men who had arrived at this hour, which was for us still the dead of night, were Pedro, a painter, and his brother-in-law and friend Fernando.

Pedro wore the uniform of the Spanish army. He was a common soldier, not one on bribed leave, serving his time in the army with a peevish and scoffing attitude. He was an intelligent young fellow whom the curse of civilization had not yet turned into a fool. Like all men of his rank, his head was shaven bald, for the military debasement of the soul is quickly given its outer mark of Cain. If you're being trained to shoot at your fellow human beings, what right have you to walk around with a full head of hair exposed to the omnipresent lice? "Poor guys," said Beatrice, who had never seen a prisoner in a German barracks brig. Arsenio passed around smuggled cigarettes and poured them a vintage from his cellar, otherwise served only to the gentlemen who arrived in Rolls Royces and U-boats. Don Fernando, Beatrice told me, actually looked nice. And it was no wonder, compared to the two other good-for-nothing ragamuffins.

Here is the story: back at the barracks, Beatrice's somnolent pupil had sounded forth the praises of this private teacher who was coaching him in English, something he was decidedly less good at than he was with telling tales out of school. Everybody knew, of course, that the Clock Tower was a cheap doss house, and Don Fernando's comrades-in-arms began wondering about this exotic coozy who was earning extra pesetas by selling another one of her natural talents. And from England, of all places. Or was she? No doubt a prostitute who was dishing out a story to Pablo that he wasn't supposed to pass on, even after several months—but one mustn't look for guilt inside a shaved head. A uniformed companion of his, Pedro, also bald but bright, had been looking for a teacher, one who was good but cheap—two qualities seldom combined by Mother Nature, who isn't exactly generous in handing out her oddments. Out here at the Tower, Mother Nature relaxed her standards somewhat, so much was clear. But was Pablo's teacher good? She surely must be cheap, and that's what Pedro needed because he was very poor. He was nothing more than the son of an even poorer father from a highly aristocratic family, an impoverished island dynasty with historically significant lineage. Some of the ancestors are hanging in the Prado with pleated millstone collars, their hands on their swords or at their breast. Pedro's brother Jacobo was rumored to have become a successful painter, married to a rich American woman. They had a house in Génova, C'an Boticari, that was frequented by the art-loving foreign colony that spoke only English, which is why Pedro wanted to learn the language. Pablo had been raving about his teacher, but surely he never said where or how he was sleeping with her, since his lessons always took place at a marble table in the Tower *taberna*, pitifully illuminated by a lamp thickly coated with fly droppings. Don Fernando, Beatrice reported, spoke fluent English and was a much-traveled man; I must know him: he was the thin, greying fellow at the post office whom we often overheard offering consolation to English ladies concerning lost correspondence. His title there was Secretary, next in the post office hierarchy after Director, a position that

was unfilled. His wife Pazzis was a sculptor, one of Pedro's apparently numerous sisters, and there were even more brothers. A flourishing family...

In two hours a lot can get said. Beatrice gave me a report down to the last
detail. I listened to her like a child at the feet of a crone telling fairy tales while
rain patters against the window panes. The men in the cells were doing another kind of pattering, but this didn't make the scene any less magical and
lulling. Every once in a while Kathrinchen added a Rhenish squeal of pleasure
to the Spanish drumbeat. And Beatrice talked and talked...

Don Fernando and Pazzis, who was lust for life incarnate, became our
friends. I recall Pazzis as a highly talented artist on the morbid side, with a
face covered by freckles. Whenever I was in her presence I felt a lump in my
throat. Often it was only a dumpling that prevented me from speaking, but
Beatrice said that I was in love. I knew what it meant to be in love, when your
throat and your mouth tighten up simultaneously. No, it was something else.
Later, Pazzis took her own life. And then I realized that I had sensed her presence as a counterpart to myself.

Don Fernando had a high-pitched voice; his manners were quite un-Spanish
in studied imitation of foreigners he had observed, and he had salt-and-pepper
hair that must have given Beatrice pause for a second or so. Moreover, he had
a sarcastic way with his sketching pencil, which he wielded at any and all society gatherings on the island. As a marvelous complement to his eccentric
personality he owned a little Fiat in which everything was loose that was supposed to be tight, and everything that was supposed to move was stuck tight,
so that the car had to be pushed. The more Don Fernando kicked and swore
at this vehicle, the more immoveable it became. On the other hand, as a postal
official he demonstrated a gift for cosmopolitan inventiveness. He distributed
gratuities to the conductors on the Génova tram line, so every day at quitting
time he hitched his Fiat to the last car. Out at the terminus he was greeted by
his mongrel Perna, so named after the leg that it lifted on everything in sight,
including its master's own leg. Upon arrival he asked kids to push his Fiat up
to his house, the residence of artists. Don Fernando liked to have himself
chauffeured around like a satrap. The next morning the kids turned the car
around and set it at the top of the street, and Fernando descended noiselessly
through clouds of dust to his place of work. In El Terreno he had to put another gang of kids in harness to get him across a level stretch. There, too, Fernando exercised his regal prerogatives. He employed this commuting
technique for years until Pazzis finally was able to show him down to the last
penny that the bribes, gratuities, and motor vehicle repair costs—the only constant and reliable aspects of owning this vehicle—were costing him more than
he would spend if he took a taxi every day. If five passengers got together for
a taxi ride to Génova, each one would be paying the equivalent of a single
fare on the tram. So Fernando gave up his car, but then fell into a fit of melancholy. People said that he even began neglecting his postal duties—that is, if
a Spanish civil servant can ever be said to "neglect" his duty. At the time when
Don Fernando came to look over the educated prostitute at the Clock Tower,

he still was in possession of his Fiat, which meant that he was at the height of his potency. He was of course convinced that the teacher didn't know a word of English, but he was genuinely curious as to how she went about practicing her other profession, her Tower trade, and he wanted to find out for himself. This he confessed to us later, but he need not have.

Don Fernando was such a sophisticated postman and civil servant that he survived the shock of learning that Pablo's *profesora* was the sister-in-law of the doxy who lived in the apartment across the street from his office. Once this mutual acquaintance was established, the conversation took an easygoing, cosmopolitan course, partly in English, then in French, and again in Spanish. Don Fernando was familiar with the biography of Zwingli's mistress. He knew Zwingli, too, but only as Don Helvecio, though he would never have guessed that the man behind the name was actually Swiss. "But listen," said Beatrice, "this Tower here is even worse than we imagined. People get killed here!"

"People killed? What else is new? But of course, you've never climbed up on the chair and seen bodies lying flat in rows. That's pretty old stuff that your two friends are dishing out."

"No, Vigo, you don't understand. I mean real murders! These guys aren't at liberty to express themselves clearly. Arsenio kept pacing around the table. He didn't trust these visitors. And the Chinaman who helps out in the kitchen isn't just some shipboard coolie. Adeleide told me that he's an important contact in the opium trade, and the international police are looking for him!"

"Well, they'll have a hard time finding him. The 'Torre' is the best alibi for respectable people. For example, who would ever guess that we live here? As for that stuff about real murders—wouldn't that be a great plot for a trashy novel? The title, usually the hardest part of any book, would be the easiest thing to come up with: '*The Clock Tower Cadaver Murders.*' How's that?"

"Cadaver Murders?"

"Of course! I mean the corpses that get pre-slaughtered by the pious girls in their boxes with the aid of the Sixth Commandment. Then along comes a sadistic smuggler with a mask and completes the job. As for getting rid of the bodies, a piece of plotting that most writers of thrillers lose sleep over, I'll leave that to the rats. Brehm reports about a case in which a gang of these rodents devoured alive three of young Hagenbeck's circus elephants. When they all work at it together, they can take care of a stiff in the course of a single night. All that's left over is a bunch of bones, and if necessary I'll grind them up in Adeleide's flour mill, in a chapter where the author steps forward to manipulate the plot so as to avoid the premature revelation of the culprit and to prevent the novel from ending too soon. Our horny friend Kate over there..."

"Shh! What if she's listening?"

"She's all finished, I made sure of that. Now she's lying there like a pile of rotten wood on a sultry summer evening. So what do you think? Wouldn't a great murder thriller like this one bring us some money?"

"I'm all for the theory, but the problem is how to put it into practice. What I mean is, that the rats would gobble up this manuscript, too, before the first murder takes place. But you know better than I do what purposes you have in mind for your writings."

"Beatrice, *chérie*, I swear to you a sacred oath that this time..."

"No swearing! We have sworn to each other never to swear anything to each other. Have you had any sleep?"

"Did some reading."

"Nietzsche?"

"More profound than that! The Book of Nature. It's quite amazing when all the cells are cooperating in the work of Creation. Everything fits so nicely together, it's enough to make a believer out of you. In any case, it's given me a whole lot of inspiration. Two poems! A lullaby filled with sweetness, and a dirge filled with jarring hiatuses. They were all finished in my head. All I had to do was to reach for a pencil. But as you know, I never do that. The seismometer announced new temblors, even your Unkulunkulu started shaking, which it usually doesn't do unless the boxes are filled up. Such things get dangerous if you're on a bridge, and that's why you should never go across in march step. And here? Wow! Blondie over there started yelling for her mother, so you can imagine what her mood is like. Now she's quiet, but there are always aftershocks. Tell me more about those two guys downstairs."

"Tomorrow. The painter strikes me as pretty far gone. By the way, he looks just like the ex-King of Spain. The very same face."

"And the other guy, Don Fernando?"

"What about him?"

Hmm..., I thought. Instead of "What about him," Beatrice could have gone on to say, "Oh, that one. Well, he's elegant, a little crazy, in a raw-silk suit, steel-blue eyes, Basque blood, and hands like a vampire."

Reclining now on our chaste pallet, we abandoned all further considerations to the care of the night. The moon had departed, the candles in the cells and on the pedestal of Our Lady had all gone out, and since the seismograph was inscribing its perceptions into thin air, there is nothing more to report concerning lingering tremors. If I were determined to record a single word, a single blissful moan uttered by my Kathrinchen, I would have to reach back for earlier statements or ejaculations of hers; what I would write may be true, but it wouldn't be historical. She herself is historical. She has left traces in the Essen Registry of Vital Statistics, and she left impressions on her mattress in the Clock Tower that I shall never forget. Surely it does not behoove me to impugn her credibility in my jottings simply in order to lend contours to her figure by having her utter in a barely audible wheeze, "Man oh man, I'm all done in! Now I've had enough for three whole days!" (In chaste parentheses: the next day she was at it again.)

We don't even know if the rats got what they were after, during that night when Don Pedro José María de Lourdes Juan Celerino Roman Miguel Bruno Ramón León Ignacio Luis Sureda de Montaner Bimet de Maturana y Vega

Verdugo de Rousset y Lopez da Sousa y Villalonga de Alba Real del Tajo made his shaven-headed entrance into the Recollections of Vigoleis.

When Beatrice conceded her poverty award to Pedro, she was familiar with only three centimeters of his name, for otherwise she would have subtracted a few pesetas. For the longer the name of a Spanish grandee—some of them take up the entire page of a book, and I have rendered Pedro's only in its minimal, albeit historically most significant, form—the poorer its bearer turns out to be. They seldom suffer from a dearth of ancestors. Pedro, with a lordly gesture, reduced everything to "Sureda" on his visiting card.

The English lessons took place at the home of Pedro's parents. And it was there that Beatrice got to know the numerous clan members. "It's a crazy place," she said. "It would be impossible to make them all up." Once again I was forced to restrain my novelistic curiosity. It was weeks before I was introduced to Pedro and his tribe, of which he represented a quixotic offshoot. With regard to the other members of the family, I am tempted to write that he was "the most quixotic," but this superlative form of the adjective is not very elegant linguistically, and besides, it would imply value judgments that I prefer to avoid. In what ways, for example, was Pedro battier than his father? I shall stick with the simple term "quixotic," which will allow me plenty of room for doing justice to this new character in his superlative deviancy as an artist and as a human being.

We frequently took advantage of La Gerstenberg's invitation to join her for a snack in her room at the Pensión del Conde. This was, of course, the kind of "snack" offered by persons of means, and it far outpointed our usual main meal of the day in terms of nourishment.

We had to return her invitation, and thus there arrived the great day when Beatrice held her *jour* in the Clock Tower. Adele Gerstenberg was touched— "But children, no need for that! And for heaven's sake, don't go to great construction for an old lady like me." She asked what our living quarters were like. She was curious about this ever since her Friedel told her that the estate out there was a highly romantic place, and Vigoleis himself had already planted hints in this direction. One day she almost hiked out there by herself to make a surprise visit, but her kind son was able to quash that idea. "But Friedel, why not?"

Her son kept the answer to himself. But now we had issued the invitation, and all that remained was for the scales to fall from her eyes.

We chose a day for our little dinner party when the mattress transactions would be at a minimum. There were in fact certain days when no one at all made use of the cells, allowing us exclusive enjoyment of the celestial premises together with the rats and the bats.

We arranged everything in the most attractive fashion. We unscrewed the chair from the wall, and our natural disorder was transformed into unnatural order. Beatrice was in charge of the change of sets. She had her own notions and experiences concerning a *jour fixe*. I had none. There was no such thing in my parents' home; there, every single day was a fixed day, and that was that. In the first months of her marriage, my mother tried to arrange some such thing with the aid of her well-to-do farmer relatives, who planned to arrive at our house in their coaches drawn by heavy draft horses, dressed in stiff silks and furs and velvet. Among them was a filthy-rich hermaphroditic cousin, Aunt Molly, whose marriage turned into a tragedy—a novel in itself. But at the birthing hour, my father stuffed this tradition's head back where it came from. If this nonsense came about, he would sue for divorce. This was a remarkable form of mutiny for a small-town couple who, on their wedding day, took a donkey ride up Dragon's Crag on the Rhine. My father simply didn't like any kind of "fancy stuff," and thus he deprived me of *jour* experiences, leaving me to depend on my own imagination and on passages I read in books. I wondered how Madame de Staël or Bettina Brentano might arrange a reception if they lived like us in Robber Arsenio's castle of whoredom. But Beatrice wasn't to be deterred; she developed her own style of entertaining company. Her standard was not to be found in the palaces of the princes and captains of industry where she had been present for tricky conversation, delectable pastries, and poisoned tea.

Our sty looked less piggish once her aesthetic hand rearranged the stuff on our clotheslines in a more pleasing order, just as, when company is expected, you might place knickknacks on a highboy next to a silver swan with peacock feathers. The bidet was concealed with an Indian shawl, although it was my intention to reveal the whole truth to my fellow author La Gerstenberg, ever since we had our conversation about how, for a writer who plies his craft by hand and outside-in for hours at a time, writer's cramp is best overcome without the aid of psychoanalysis.

We picked up our guest at her *pensión* and walked with her casually to our *jour fixe*. I carried her folding chair, which she made use of repeatedly during the journey. She didn't like the heat; on a hot day she felt as if she had been strapped in a harness that impeded her freedom of movement. This was an oppressively hot day. The highway was veiled in clouds of dust, and the slaughterhouse was making propaganda for a vegetarian lifestyle. Adele, even more prone than Beatrice to feelings of disgust, started shivering. I told her that this was a stroke of bad luck; it didn't smell like this all the time—the wind was blowing in from a certain range of hills and bringing certain things along with it. Surely she knew the poem "Harbingers of Spring" by her friend Hugo von Hofmannsthal, where the wind wafts through bare boulevards carrying strange things in its course. There was a similar stanza in Mörike: familiar fragrances glide ominously through the land, just as we were experiencing here. "Great poetry, *chère Madame*, can encompass the entire globe. No matter which poet pumps the bellows, his breath can grasp the heart of any receptive creature."

The two ladies would have preferred to grasp their noses, but such a gesture is bad form in better society. Before our tragedian friend's cheeks could take on a greenish tint, we were already at the entrance to the Manse. I didn't have to announce, "Here we are!" Instead, La Gerstenberg cried out, "Oh you *dear* people! No, Vigoleis wasn't exaggerating. This *is* a romantic place. I'm going to have to sit down."

I placed her folding chair beneath her, and now she sat there like a field marshal surveying the battlefield, commotion all around her, aides-de-camp scurry to and fro, there is a clatter of hooves, a blaring of bugles, adjutants surround the general's chair, ready to pass on the latest action report—"Yes, over there to the east there's that thousand-year-old carob-bean tree. On moonlit nights you can see the dust rise up from the explosions. Our accurate catapults toss cocaine shells onto the field, and trained dogs fetch the booty. I've been able to reconstruct the whole strategy. We now can predict with certainty the night when the ship captain will shoot a torpedo filled with drugs onto the coast, and dozens of women will clamber over crags and crevasses to—how's that? Those black birds? Those are ravens. There are still a few colonies of them that nest on the island; they'll be extinct unless another war comes soon. Do they belong to the Manse? No, our robber boss hasn't yet been so successful that the birds of the air obey him in biblical fashion. He'll go a lot farther with his henchmen and Juan March's gold. The ravens always feed at the burial pit over at the *matadero*. I've even observed some vultures there. Can you see any, Beatrice? They're said to be dangerous; besides goat kids and lambs, they can carry infants off to their aeries. Arsenio shoots them down whenever he can. They hinder his work. I think they spook his dogs and prevent them from pointing properly—something like that. I'm no hunter. And see that ivy-covered projection up there on the tower? Originally, it was probably a spout for dropping hot pitch; now a lookout sits up there and counts the catapult missiles as they arrive."

La Gerstenberg was thrilled. "But Vigoleis, why don't you write a book about the 'Torre'? You must write one. You must! Just the way you're telling me about it now!"

I exchanged glances with Beatrice, which spoke mutely of *the cadaver murders* that took place in the Tower. "But, *chère Madame*, up to now you have received only an impression of the external business. What goes on inside the Manse is also worthy of being depicted, although it is less original in concept."

"It's wonderful how each and every stone here cries out for literary portrayal! How happy a writer must be that fate has inserted him in such a place! Now I understand a great deal, Vigo, and I'm almost tempted to say that the two of you should be grateful for your destiny. Shall we go in? I am so relieved for your sake!"

Inside the walls of our robbers' ranch there was the usual hubbub, the kind you would find in any household with lots of kids and domestic help on any baking-hot late afternoon. The old matron was leaning on her crutch, roasting fish on a spit over a grapewood fire. Using a calabash, she dripped wine onto the roast—no easy matter since the fish, wrapped in strips of bacon, tended to fall apart. She greeted us and, employing sign language and words mumbled into her long whiskers, let us know that we were all invited to partake of the meal. Arsenio strode across the courtyard accompanied by his barking herd of smugglers' hounds. He was wearing his blue vest with its red sash, resembling down to the very lacings of his raffia *espadrillos* the image of the Lord of the Island that I had sketched out for our tragedian friend. All he needed to do was clap his hands and call out "Hey, let's have some wine and anything else you'd like!" A girl came running, and for a split-second Adeleide poked her head through the fly screen at the door. With a wave of my hand I said "No, thanks," and explained that today Doña Beatriz was having her *jour*, and that this lady was a great friend of ours from the land of the waltzes that Mr. Arsenio loved so much. Immediately the Giant began jumping around in the rhythm of the Blue Danube. He started whistling the tune that drove Beatrice crazy night after night as it resounded from the red enamel bell of the cylinder gramophone. "This is so cute!" said La Gerstenberg, who usually couldn't endure noise of any kind. "Beatrice, Vigoleis, how could I possibly have felt sorry you for even one night? When I remember how you got evicted with no money at all, and there you were, marching behind a team of loaded donkeys..."

"That's because Madame Adele Gerstenberg has forgotten that here in Spain, when the play is over you don't see horse-drawn cabs driving up to the theater exit."

Beatrice made herself scarce, trotting off to take care of this or that with no servants to help out—ladies comprehend such a move without exchanging words. In any case, it was better to get on with no help at all than with some Spanish maid with a tragic history—

—and now, following a brief pause, it was Beatrice who clapped her hands in a dignified, almost soundless way, although the sound had to travel around the corner of the house that separated us from her *jour*. There she stood, the *grande dame*, up on the open staircase poised for the grand reception. Poised? Beatrice? They were both poised, the staircase and the lady who now descended two steps to greet her guest—"Once again, a warm welcome to you *chez* Vigos."

I offered the tragedian my arm, and felt no less equal to the task than Beatrice with her wide-ranging experience. It was the first time in my life that I had ever "received," much less at my own place of residence. I no doubt relished the delight that takes hold of a stork when it locates its own special wagon wheel and never gives it up. *Weltschmerz*, where is thy sting? It was a powerful moment indeed: not a distortion of the actual past, not a pipe-dream of the future, but a singularly pleasant experience of the present, arm in arm with a star of the stage.

The Giant tried to disperse the crowd of gaping kids, but happily they disobeyed and remained under the spell of our grand occasion. They were determined to witness our spectacle. To be sure, they did not strew flowers and marsh grasses on our path. But they did even more, these snot-nosed half-pints, some of whom were dressed in chemises that didn't even reach to their navels. This was apparent only to someone who looked at them carefully, for the cloth had assumed the color of camouflage. La Gerstenberg thought that they were all naked. This is what they did for us: they screened off the manure pile and scattered the rats that, day after day and even at high noon, held their own *jour* on the plank amidst garbage and offal. Infected by the pestilence, they had gradually lost their fear of humans. Tame rats are death itself!

"What magical, natural grace Spanish children can have," said our guest. "Where we come from, all that has to be trained and rehearsed, and it is always so stiff and straight-laced. Down here, everything is already fit for the stage."

"If you'll permit me to say so, that's just why you never get to see it on the stage. In Madrid you will have noticed what Martersteig has told me—no, not the Captain but the Privy Councillor—the stages in Spain are god-awful. Nothing but cheap melodrama, or if you will, just play-acting."

We had reached the top of the stairs and let our guest pass in front of us, although I ought to have preceded her into the dimly lit nave. It would have been all too banal for me to say with Schiller, "Through this narrow pathway he must arrive." We knew that the actress wasn't fond of theatrical quotations. In any case I couldn't think of any more edifying apothegm from the classic stage tradition, least of all the motto from Dante that would have been most fitting for this place, the one that admonishes anyone entering to abandon all hope, so inexorable in its Italian vocalization: *Lasciate ogni speranza, voi ch'entrate...* But this would be valid only at the portal to Cell No 1; in the others, hope began swelling immediately upon crossing the threshold. It's wonderful to have a wise poet's line of verse, a divine proclamation, or a well-turned curse for every occasion in life—it makes things easier. Entire professions thrive on catchy phrases uttered by the masters and prophets. Here we had to do without one of Büchmann's "Winged Words," but we got along nicely.

Adele Gerstenberg, after being distracted for a moment by the glimmering brightness at the end of the hallway where I had lit a candle at the little shrine, took a look at our room. She gazed up at the suspended netting, and before her eyes could focus through the gridwork at the dome of our private cathedral, she did something that I can describe only with a hackneyed phrase: she turned into a pillar of salt. The blood congealed in her veins, and, as if halted by a supernatural force, she stood there rooted to the spot. Tremors will have been visible in the plaster mask that was her face. Since we were standing behind her, we could not see this change in her features, but it is familiar enough as an image of sudden fright. Nevertheless, her condition of total stupefaction did not last long. In fact, it was a lucky thing that we were standing behind her, for when the spark of life returned to the actress, it was barely sufficient to pass from petrification to yet another commonplace state: the very picture of misery, one that we were just able to prevent from collapsing in a heap. This was first-rate theater in the finest Viennese tradition, but there was no applause. I held the lightweight woman under her armpits while Beatrice lifted our chair over our heads and placed it in the corridor—thus removing the single chair from our salon. where our *jour* had gone to pieces before it even got started.

So this was our triumph, our grand premiere with the celebrated artist from the Vienna Burgtheater. She sat there and wept tears that not even a Nobel-prizewinning dramatist could ever squeeze out of her. We let her have a good cry, stepping back from her with the discreet, empty gesture of mourning used by heads of state when they place a wreath at the tomb of the Unknown Soldier. But no, I'm being unfair to ourselves; we by no means had such cynical thoughts as we witnessed the genuine pain felt by our horrified friend.

In the meantime the water had started boiling in our genuine Dutch-made whistling teapot. The steam escaped first with a hiss, and then came a piping noise that got louder and louder as it resounded through the whole barn. Adele, sensitive to noise, suddenly cringed, and it took a few seconds before she cleared the entrance to our cell. I flew into our sty and immediately shut off our "end of the day shift" signal.

In the next cell, too, things were coming alive. Our teapot could have resurrected the blessed dead, and now two of our neighbors had been wakened from their erotic burrowings. Yet before we were treated to another Spanish theater scene—Sudermann with an Iberian cast—we took our guest out to the courtyard where she perched herself on a wine barrel. She refrained from reciting the line from Rilke's poem on Confirmation Day—though she might well have cited it while remaining in character: "The feast is over. There is noise in the house / And the afternoon passes more sadly..." The three little dots are by Rilke, too. Our feast was over, but not quite yet.

Adele Gerstenberg grasped our hands and remained sitting, mute, overcome, and as if aged by several years. Adeleide inquired whether something had happened to our guest—a heat stroke? Arsenio, busy unharnessing his nag, suggested a cold drink. "Bring her right away to the cellar where it's cool," he said. Beatrice calmed him down: "She just wasn't feeling well. She'll be fine." Without a word, the Giant hitched his gelding back between the wagon shafts. Taking a palm frond, Adeleide dusted off the seats. And then Arsenio stood waiting like an official coachman. Thus our guest from Vienna got her horse-drawn cab after all, and Beatrice's "day" ended in less than total disaster. One of the Manse's hired hands drove us back to the city. The tragedian didn't want to go directly home—what about a visit to the Alhambra? We accompanied her. A little later, Friedrich joined us at their usual table.

He arrived in a good mood and with lots of gesticulation. Right away he inquired whether it was nice out there in Grinzing, but he was visibly taken aback by his mother's dusty appearance. "Begging your pardon, Maman, but you were determined to go out and visit the Tower."

"It's not what you're thinking, my son. That's not what bowled me over out there. I am familiar with vice in all its manifestations. But that these people have to live like that, and that they haven't done away with each other—that's what truly got to me."

After a short time we were joined by the fellow from Cologne, and later still by Captain von Martersteig, who was back in town with his air of suffering and his complaints about new outrages committed by his enemy Robert von Ranke Graves. And then came one of Friedel's friends, one whom we hadn't met before: a professional Czech or Polish optician. *Tout Mallorque*, Adele told us, gazed at the world through his spectacles. She gradually regained her composure, and she became almost merry when her son, no longer than a minute later, started bickering with the retired aviator.

Before we took leave of each other, we agreed on a date for a return visit to the actress. A *jour* is, after all, a *jour*. As far as I was concerned, this was a stylish way of arranging things. She promised to read us a few scenes from her play, and yes, she would expect Martersteig to attend if he happened to be in Palma. That is one more reason, he replied, to stay in the city. And when, she asked, would Vigoleis give her the pleasure of reading from his own works?

"After you, Herr von Martersteig! First the regular troops, then the home guard. After the capitulation of your Monkey Army, my Cadaver Murders in the Clock Tower!"

V

Don Fernando summoned me to the post office secretariat so that he could give me a few tips about how to make sure we could receive, without undue delay, more than half of the items that arrived in our name. That was a decent proposal, and I agreed to it—by return mail, so to speak. Don Fernando knew his way around all the various postal departments; he knew all the tricks practiced by his employees and all the holes in the floor of the crumbling post office building. The proverb O chão não tem buracos—the floor has no holes in it—which the Portuguese like to cite when they can't find something that has fallen to the floor—was not applicable to the main post office barracks in Palma de Mallorca. There the floor had real holes in it, though perhaps it wasn't the floor that we would have to search to locate them. As General Secretary, Don Fernando exercised oversight over these leaks within his official quarters.

I was led to his office down a rickety staircase. He greeted me with effusive congratulations for having arrived without breaking my neck, and was obviously impressed by my daredevil balancing skills. Then we descended farther through dark hallways, stumbling over canvas bags and stepping into mounds of paper—the packing room, said Don Fernando, where lots of mail got left unsorted. It just couldn't be helped. That was the first hole in the floor. The second hole, a more dangerous one, was one of the colleagues, a professional postal clerk in a blue smock, the most feared postage-stamp thief in all Mallorca, as ineradicable as quack grass or mildew. In the normal course of things, a postal employee will concentrate equally on sender and addressee; this blue-smocked fellow had eyes only for return addresses. Stamps that were missing from his collection, or that he needed for swapping, he loosened from the envelopes using his own method, and they disappeared. If the loosening technique didn't work properly, he would take a pair of sewing scissors and simply cut away the stamps. Letters or packages that got seriously damaged, he threw away. Over time, he established for himself a proprietary privilege that the post office administration was unable to deny him. After all, he represented a lesser evil amid the egregious large-scale inefficiency of the Spanish postal service, a state of affairs that corresponded exactly with the country's illiteracy rate, as Don Fernando was able to show me on the basis of statistical studies.

I was introduced to the stamp thief. This is not the place to set forth a description of the ideal type of the philatelist. I shall mention only this man's beard, which actually wasn't a beard at all and wasn't meant to be one: it was ten-day stubble. It served him perfectly; he kept it that way so as to take the postage stamps from their soaking and hang them on his facial bush, where they dried off and eventually fell away. More than once I observed him with stamps in his beard that got stuck in the whiskers. Like all robbers, he was a friendly guy, but woe to me if... He knew me and was interested in my dealings with the Netherlands, but he immediately complained that I wasn't getting much mail from there any more; couldn't I do something to improve the situation? Holland had just issued a new series, and he was missing a few items. In the presence of Don Fernando we made a gentleman's agreement. I promised with a handshake to show him all the postal items addressed to me, and to let him keep the stamps. I rented a postal box, an *apartado*, which made it easier to keep our deal. Not that I would ever be tempted to break it: I am a collector of nothing at all, not even experiences, and thus not even money. But I can imagine that a serious collector must live constantly on the edge of crime. What seems so attractive about this activity is the prospect of cheating—either cheating the other guy or getting cheated oneself. There is always this tension: is that pot genuine? Did Van Gogh paint that bridge himself? Is this bone fragment truly from Saint Kunibert's tibia? Is this iron nail really from Christ's cross? I have enough to contend with regarding my own authenticity. Incidentally, my Mallorquin drybeard friend ended up paying dearly. Shortly after the Civil War broke out he was eliminated, as the current phrase would have it, by another stamp collector from whom he had been stealing for years. One of the most praiseworthy aspects of all civil wars is that they develop their own drumhead justice to handle such internal matters, thus relieving the juntas of much superfluous work.

In numerical terms I can report that on the basis of my agreement with the postal clerk, seldom more than 36% of our mail got lost in the shuffle.

It was Menno ter Braak who drew my attention to the writer Slauerhoff. I came upon Albert Helman by myself, whose stories impressed me greatly. His pseudonym concealed a Surinamese writer about whom it was rumored that at age seventeen he was still climbing trees in the jungle—no doubt an exaggeration, but he couldn't yet be badly spoiled by our civilization. I wanted to reach him concerning the German copyright to his jungle novel *The Quiet Plantation*, and one day in the university library I took a seat next to a young man who was obviously translating something in a book. It was *The Quiet Plantation*. At the time, I was struggling with Menno ter Braak, the West Indian's recalcitrant, trouble-making antipode, and his *Bourgeois Carnival*. My new library acquaintance and I got talking. He was a brand-new German Ph.D., and he was in fact translating Helman's book into German. Probably, he said, we would be at loggerheads about my own intellectual barbarian ter Braak. This Dr. NN was a reticent, well-read philologist, the recipient of a Catholic stipend that allowed him to purchase books and sufficient amounts of food—an ideal situation for a literary person, whereas I was living on garbage like a stray dog. But this I must now explain. I worked a lot, but got almost no pay. Moreover, I am a voracious carnivore, one whom the vicissitudes of life have often coerced into becoming an abject omnivore. I refuse to let this get me down, but I am filled with remorse by my awareness that Nature can turn certain creatures into bad dogs. To be sure, the Miracle of Creation exhibits worse cases of corruption than a meat-craving Vigoleis with his seven meatless days each week. I found out that a butcher in my neighborhood sold scraps for dogs at ten cents an ounce. I became a daily customer of his. It's for my Doberman, I told him, a smart, sweet, huggable animal if there ever was one, trained to the nines, a good watchdog, virtually quivering with pedigree. The butcher and his regular customers couldn't wait to see this canine miracle. It was not readily noticeable that I myself was the dog in question, for I performed my metamorphosis inside my rented room, where I prepared these somewhat questionable delicacies using rare Indian spices that cost much more than I could afford. The other little doggie had none. But in his state of non-existence, he was actually better off than his master.

Every day at the butcher shop I reported the newest training triumph of my pet pinscher, and I reached the point of having him begin to talk—at the time there was only one other talking dog in Amsterdam—when a stupid grocery clerk entered the discussion and killed my dog Mickey dead right in the middle of the shop. This guy was eating all the scraps himself, she shouted, the *stakkerd*!

She had the laughing crowd of customers on her side. *Stakkerd* means imp, bum, loafer, tramp, and moocher. But before I could investigate mentally the word's etymology backwards from the Old Norse and then up through the centuries to Vigoleis, on through the incarnate essence of all of the term's nu-

ances and into the very blush of my cheeks, I found myself standing out on
the street with my ounce of flesh, betrayed by a maiden—just as, months later,
Beatrice was caught holding a spoon by Doña María. Her dog was also named
Vigoleis, which is further proof of his unique brand of double identity. I pulled
the brim of my floppy hat far down over my brow, hunched up the collar of
my loden coat, and snuck away like a culprit. That was the end of my peppered adventures with the frying pan. In total humiliation I reached for the
potato, and came to despise it even more ardently. I avoided the scene of my
abasement, although by rights I ought to have avoided my own self. I kept a
discreet distance from the butcher shop. I behaved like Zwingli, or rather—
keeping things as close as possible to the first person—I conducted myself as
the Vigoleis of my own self will have to behave in the following chapter. Everything has already existed, says Uriel da Costa.

The Ph.D. wanted to obtain a fellowship for me from the same Catholic organization that was financing his existence, but I would have to declare ad-
herence to the Creed. As tempting as his offer was, I preferred to remain
faithful to my pinscher: for every Sunday Mass, days and days of living it up.

I also maintained my fidelity to Dutch literature, whose rich corpus of verse
makes up for its almost total dearth of "great" prose. I discovered Henny
Marsman, bought his books of verse and poems by other writers—you can
buy little books by scrimping on food, one of the fine advantages of poetry.
This entire harvest was now hanging on the ropes in our cloister cell, although
at the time I had no idea that our adventures in the Clock Tower would one
day be the very thing that started my friendship with Marsman, the great carnivore who loved solitude, but only if there was a butcher shop nearby. In my
biography of Marsman I intend to relate how, in a restaurant located in the
shadow of the Goetheanum in Dornach, and featuring a life-size photographic
likeness of Rudolf Steiner with his theosophic gaze, the entire clientele of an-
throposophers turned to stone as Marsman, speaking through Beatrice as interpreter, asked the waitress to bring him a bloody rib roast. *Pace* Uriel da
Costa, such a thing had never existed before. We had to leave the premises,
and in Arlesheim "At the Sign of the Ox" we finally were served what we
were dying for. No one there raised an eyebrow, no one raised a scolding finger, no one pointed to a likeness of Steiner, and no one declared with the voice
of an avenging bouncer/angel, "Rudolf Steiner says..."

With all due respect to anthroposophy, its Founder never listened with sufficient intensity to emerge from the Seven Regions of his spiritual realm to
pass into the Eighth Region: our "Clock Tower," where I can survive on little
nourishment, just as I did on Nicolas Beets Straat in Amsterdam, and where
I make literature and then destroy whatever the Tooth of God has not already
destroyed. Slauerhoff's novel *The Forbidden Empire* made such a strong
impression on me that I inquired about the copyright, and began translating
it during the hours that Beatrice spent in the city giving language lessons. Of
course I never succeeded in finding a publisher for this novel on the life of
Camões, although I spent a pretty penny on postage for this manuscript. In

addition, there were my intermittent poetic blood-lettings, my satirical stanzas, my dark-hued ballads: all of these got hung on the ropes, where they could dry out like slabs of Swiss smoked ham. The rats sniffed at them, but not because of the poetry they contained—I can't boast of any such success. Scraps of food and edible provisions also hung alongside them on our lines, which I stretched loosely enough to prevent the beasts from dancing along them. I placed insurmountable obstacles, made from tin cans, at strategic points where the ropes crossed each other. This infuriated the pestilential horde, but they devised a way to get around it. They chose a subterfuge that must have involved insight and ratiocination: standing on top of the partitions, they gnawed the ropes. One night whole portions of the contraption collapsed. We two slumbering human beings were victims of the disaster, and everything in the cell went higgledy-piggledy. It was like a replay of the scene at Pilar's on the night of our eviction. Not a single rope that held only literature had been touched! Since I still considered myself more intelligent than the most brazen smarty-ass among the rats at Arsenio's whorehouse, I suddenly had a brilliant idea. Putting index finger to temple, I thought, "Wire!" On my tramp-like wanderings I never found pieces of wire long enough to create a network entirely of metal. So I made do with lengths of wire as end-pieces for attaching the ropes, and slipped the necks of bottles over them. Now show me a rat that will dare to step out on this tightrope! Beaming with pride I displayed my new brainstorm to Beatrice. A gnaw-proof hanging library! But I was jolted back to sober reality when my woman remarked laconically that, while she never wished to interfere with my technical experiments, she had never quite understood why I hadn't thought of using wire in the first place. My hopes that one day during my lifetime an English lord would offer to purchase one of my teeth to fashion a ring from it—a story they tell about Isaac Newton—were immediately dashed. Worse yet, it would be like pulling every last one of my own teeth to become master of this murky, misty realm of the shades. I had no profit from Beatrice's retroactively obvious solutions.

Our heroic couple was not lacking in diligence and ambition. Beatrice gave language lessons inside and outside of the notorious Manse, while Vigoleis led his less lucrative, sedentary literary life in our thinking room. Occasionally, the kids peeked through the partition to observe his production of world literature, and the big kids often arrived with their even bigger playmates to engage in their bumping, groaning business next door. This was just as much a part of the daily routine as the braying of the donkeys or a courtyard conversation with Arsenio. Every once in a while the Maiden from the Lower Rhine sounded forth with her silvery peals of joy. One day, when I perceived these blissful yelps issuing forth from the neighboring box and felt a waning of the literary inspiration descending upon me through the webwork above—our *bidetto* wasn't yielding anything more than hollow, tinny trotting sounds anyway—I decided to step up on our chair and take a peek into the next-door cubicle. What met my eyes was a vision of the purest splendor; reaching my glance from the bedstead in all its glowing, shimmering clarity, the sight penetrated all the gloomy regions of my heart. Yet moments of mystical vision are like all moments: they don't last. This one was over in a trice: all at once a shoe came whizzing at me, and I had to crawl back into my private underworld. The *almocrebe* who was her companion of the moment had aimed poorly. His missile struck the barn wall, loosening a centuries-old film of dust, caromed off, and did considerable damage inside my sty, though not the kind of damage that this off-duty teamster had in mind: he had aimed at my head. My airy archive was set in motion. Ropes snapped, and it was hours before I could re-arrange everything in its proper order. During this repair job, I of course had to keep my skull below partition level, for otherwise it would have been sudden death. Next door, Katie had a giggling fit, thus deriving a bonus of pleasure from the situation. What was I thinking of, violating the unwritten regulations of a whorehouse? The Spaniards are the most chaste people I know. A professional Spanish prostitute—perhaps I have said this already, but in any case I'll mention it soon again—feels mortally insulted if a painter asks her to pose as his model.

Our respective jobs didn't bring us much money, but whenever we scraped up the real and fake duros that came our starving way, they were sufficient to meet our current expenses of sending out manuscripts into the world and heating our stew over our little camp stove. Meat? Not even on Sundays, the day when even the poorest of the poor can find traces of fat in their soup. We could smell meat, but only as its fragrance wafted toward our cell from the abattoir, from the neighboring cells, or from the old crone's barbecue spit. We were invited once a week to visit our friend, the Royal and Imperial Court Actress, to partake of a meal and reminiscences of Old Vienna. This was always a feast day for us; there was wine, good talk, Inca squawks, monkey business, and lots of handshaking and shoulder-clapping with friends and strangers. And one day—lo and behold! It wasn't Schiller's famous Cranes of Ibykus. It was Katie, the coal tycoon's spouse from Essen! The rocking chairs wouldn't stop rocking. There were shouts and laughter. "Yes, indeed, my friends! Beatrice, Vigoleis, finally I've got you together with a few of Vigo's compatriots. I've already told them about you. Please, Friedel, you do the introductions."

All of a sudden the big, wide world became a mere nutshell, a tiny thimble. This beautiful and imposing lady, her Rubensesque bosom covered by an expensive embroidered Mallorquin blouse, came up short when she stood facing Beatrice. And Beatrice, too, mentally shielded her eyes. Now where had the two of them met before? In Berlin, of course! No, beg your pardon, it was in Düsseldorf at the Becker Steel stockholders' meeting. "Friedrich Wilhelm, isn't this amazing? We meet again here on Mallorca!" Her spouse, the Herr Doktor, the steel magnate, was not sharing the thrill of this re-encounter, and so the lady felt it necessary to apologize for her slight breach of etiquette, based as it was on a total memory blackout. Her husband's eyesight, she explained, had deteriorated since that time—when was it? Of course, 1928, when the serial murderer Kürten was loose in Graf Adolf Park—the mention of this notorious fellow with the blood-stained jacket helped to patch over an embarrassing moment. "He's over-worked," the lady added, and La Gerstenberg, once again rocking in her chair, whispered to Vigo as he bent down to listen, "Nervous breakdown"—a diagnosis that I discreetly passed on to Beatrice. Whereupon all of us assumed a mien of great seriousness, as is appropriate in the presence of a fellow human being gone to rack and ruin. Only the Inca cockatoo refused to respect this minute of silence; he squawked forth his unchaste battle cry, and in so doing was, of course, very close to the truth at hand. Mr. Heavy Metal took off his thick spectacles and wiped them ceremoniously on his jacket lining, although when he put them back on, he couldn't see any better. He had aristocratic hands, probably as a result of his ailments. He was also markedly taciturn, and to cap his misery, he seemed to have picked up a flea somewhere, for every once in a while he secretly scratched himself under his belt, the place to where the little animals love to migrate; they feel sheltered in the warm space between clothing and skin.

We took our seats around the self-portrait of the illustrious Sureda father-in-law. The robust Rhine maiden sat opposite me, and her silken blouse caused me to become just as tongue-tied as the gentleman from Essen. My inner world, too, had now increasingly shrunk—not to a nutshell, but to right-hand Cell No. 2 in the Clock Tower, and I was straining to accustom myself to the sight of the fully dressed woman. So that's what you look like, you steamy nympho, when you've had your fill and then stride forth out of the sin bin to return to the myopic glances of your mucked-up Freddy Boy and give him some line about "going shopping," while your *almocrebe* once more licks his chops at the thought of the beauty spot so magically located on your left breast. Has your honorable husband ever noticed it? I'll bet it's not listed in your passport under "identifying marks."

"Vigoleis, you're so quiet today. Is anything wrong? Poems? Creative block?" inquired Madame Gerstenberg, for whom my silence was particularly odd, since I was the one who usually was expected to take center stage with my story-telling.

"No, neither the one nor the other, and most certainly not the third thing, either. I'm still enough of a mime to be able to conceal such afflictions from other people. Otherwise I could never step out in public."

"Was there another flood out there where you live?" asked Friedrich. I replied that maritime conditions at the Torre del Reloj were still favorable—sometimes low tide, sometimes...

"The Clock Tower!" shouted the magnate's wife, and turned as white as her now-clothed body. Her features collapsed and her eyes turned hollow, but she quickly regained control and continued in a joking vein, "Oh, 'Torre del Reloj'! Back home we call it a church steeple, and that's probably what it is. But now, speaking of clocks, a glance at my watch (a costly object set with diamonds, which she never wore in bed—her johns would have a taste for such items, too) tells me that we're going to have to leave. My husband is ex-pecting a call from Germany. Darling?"

"Well," said the tragedian as heavy industry made its hasty departure. "What would Herr Doktor do without the ministrations of his little lady?"

"And what would Frau Doktor do without Spanish subsidies in the Clock Tower," added—not Vigoleis, who could have verified this brown-on-white, but Friedrich Ginsterberg, La Gerstenberg's sassy, savvy son.

"Now Friedel! Do you have to spill the beans all the time? Besides, speaking in asides isn't the fashion any more, except perhaps in cheap melodrama."

"It's just possible, Mama, that this is a cheap melodrama," replied her son, who knew the score. With that he had the last word. Bowing in all directions, he went his own way, a way that was to lead him without delay or hesitation to many similar towers, and before very long to the Alicante cemetery.

The telephone message from the homeland, the one the Frau Doktor remembered so suddenly on the basis of my prompting, appeared to have thrown her ailing spouse completely for a loop. The industrial couple sent a note to La Gerstenberg, saying that an urgent family matter required that they return for a time to Germany, and then they boarded the next steamer for Malaga. The mild climate and the famous medicinal wines will have put Friedrich Wilhelm back on his feet, and Katie no doubt also found in Malaga what she was in need of.

I wonder whether they are still living—he with countless professional entries and titles in "Who's Who?" and she, nameless and identifiable only by a beauty mark on her left breast? We shall meet up with her again, once again denuded, but not in her own nakedness.

The tycoon couple ought to have stayed on to hear Adele Gerstenberg read from her play, but as the insatiably curious Friedel had found out, they were already floating somewhere on the Mediterranean. Thus the audience was confined to the persons originally selected: Baron von Martersteig, Beatrice, Vigoleis, Mr. Emmerich, the optician, and Friedel, his mommy's son.

The author read aloud for two whole hours, with a brief intermission for seltzer water between Acts Two and Three. We had been told that she intended to read only a few scenes; no one was prepared to hear the entire drama. The historical model is a familiar one: the chaste Queen Elizabeth, a miracle of moral righteousness in her own time, managed a "Clock Tower" outside the city gates, where *almocrebe*s and bullfighters likewise derived their entertainment. To be sure, this cost Essex his head. I can't recall whether La Gerstenberg lent this hackneyed material a specifically Spanish flavor; I am myself too poorly schooled in history to tell, and even less curious about necrophilia. In any case, the effect of her reading was overwhelming. But to say this, is not to apply a value judgment to the literary qualities of her play. A talented elocutionist can transform the kitschiest doggerel into veritable pearls of poetry, and send immortal literature into the trash bin.

There was no applause as the tragedian's head sank to the tabletop. Friedel remained seated, and so we assumed that her gesture was part of the *mise en scène*. But this wasn't playacting at all. I was deeply moved by this display of emotion. Why had this artist taken leave of her stage career? When Adele finally lifted her head with a smile, wiped her brow, and with another gesture swept away everything in the room that seemed alien to her feelings, her appearance was once again almost true to reality: grey, wasted, old. The first to speak up was Friedrich. He asked us to leave his mother by herself. We crept away on tiptoe. Downstairs in the hallway we sat together for a while until Spanish guests arrived. We then decided it was time to go. But before we left for home at the "Torre," we heard the actress's cane tap-tapping on the floor tiles above. She called me. I followed her into her room.

"Please don't leave without saying something about my play! Was it so bad, Vigoleis?"

I cannot recall verbatim what I replied to her, but in a general sense this is what I said: she, Adele Gerstenberg, had also departed without a word after witnessing our misery in the Clock Tower. Tower or stage drama—it was all the same tragedy...

I kissed her brow and left.

A week later it was my turn to read from the original works of Vigoleis. But what was I to read? In front of such a privileged audience it could only be un-published material, and since my oeuvre contained an abundance of this sort of writing, my selection ought not to have been difficult. Poems? All I had to do was reach up to our clothesline. But poems are a tricky matter. When recit-ing them, I feel as if I'm wearing long pantaloons for crawling into a hole in the ground, while the ground refuses to reveal even the tiniest fissure for me to sink into. Prose? That's innocuous enough—perhaps a chapter from *The Cadaver Murders*, or—"Beatrice, do you think that it's proper to appear before La Gerstenberg with corpses? Ones that don't have any historical patina to make them seem housebroken?" At the time, I was very hard at work on the manuscript for this tome. The crimes were already multiple; "Vig-otrice" comprised an inseparable pair of detectives; and the super-whore, the doxy of doxies, had the name María del Pilar. But was this appropriate for the Count's *pensión*? I decided to write something custom-made for this event. I wrote the history of my and my brother Jupp's murder at the hands of a priest. Here's how the saga goes:

The "respectable" elementary school in my home town, the scene of my first elemental failure in education, existed under the aegis of Kaiser Wilhelm II—not in itself a fact of earth-shaking proportions, since he lent his august name to some much shoddier enterprises. For the ceremonies for the opening of the school, when I had to recite a patriotic poem, he sent his regrets, pre-ferring to be represented by an oak tree (*Quercus pedunculata*) that was planted in front of the entrance, in the presence of the highest local authorities.

The tree didn't take well to the soil and perished a few years later during the Wilhelminian War, a time when perishing was the order of the day. Since a dead Wilhelminian oak is not an adornment for a Wilhelminian school, and since it might have been taken as an evil omen, the tree was secretly replaced by a hardier local species. This was of course a superfluous act, for soon afterward, the entire Hohenzollern family tree was chopped down for good.

None of the above was in the story I read; it is only now that I'm bringing it back to mind. The story itself concerns the principal of the educational institution in question, the Reverend Dr. Kremers, who caused much trouble for the Holy Father in Rome and for my episcopal uncle in Münster. A notorious man, one who had to submit to ecclesiastical disciplining, he entered history as a behind-the-scenes accomplice and string-puller of the Rhenish Separatist movement, which collapsed in 1923 after proclaiming an independent Rhenish Republic in Aachen. I loved and respected this teacher of mine. He was an excellent pedagogue, not a brute like the other elementary drill sergeants on a staff that consisted wholly of scholarly failures. It was he who opened my eyes to philosophical questioning, to literature (insofar as this didn't come to me through the Rhenish songwriter Hanns Willy Mertens, who was also a member of the Wilhelminian faculty), and to a cosmopolitan attitude that to this day I call my own. He had become a priest against his will, had a less than exalted opinion of his profession, and made no secret of this. For this reason, and on the basis of his increasingly audacious political activism, he was the best hated man in a town that prided itself as a citadel of Catholicism, but which at bottom was just as worm-eaten as the Arctic Imperial Oak. As soon as the first shouts of "*Heil Hitler*" resounded, the town capitulated, and the mendacious edifice of faith failed to collapse in a heap of ruins. A Catholic town expects a priest to become a hypocrite. If he is sleeping with his housekeeper, he should at least do the citizenry the favor of calling her his sister or his niece. My beloved teacher was not of this ilk; he put his trust in the Pope, who was arrogant enough to prefer scandal to lying.

My parental home was one of the few in town that remained open to the school principal. He took frequent advantage of our hospitality, and we welcomed him warmly each time. He also appreciated our wine cellar and the box of 500 cigars into which any male guest was free to grab. I have the fondest recollections of these evenings with Father Kremers.

My brothers and I liked to go out collecting plants and flowers with our principal. We took bicycle trips to nearby Holland, paid visits to the Missionary Headquarters in Steyl (Father Kremers was a member of the Society of the Divine Word), and explored the borderland area between Venlo and Roermond. Once in the month of May—I had already left the school—Father Kremers suggested a bike tour to Roermond, saying that he wanted to show us something very nice there. The group was to include my brother Jupp and a classmate of his named Erich. Departure time: 3:00 am. We arrived at the principal's door right on time, but Erich was nowhere in sight. I was sent off to yank this lazybones out of bed. I swiftly pedaled to the outskirts of town where he lived and gave a whistle under his bedroom window. Erich's father, a short, know-it-all factory manager, stuck his head out the window and cursed me and the clergyman; his son wasn't coming. That school principal wasn't proper company for a decent student, and I should go to the devil. Erich was what you might call a sissy, but his father, who was a tyrant, wasn't aware of this.

So we were a threesome for the bike trip, with Father Kremers dressed in civilian clothes. Born in the neighboring town of Dülken, home of Goethe's Academy of Fools, he had scouted every last corner of the Schwalm valley. He knew by heart all the flora and fauna of the region including, to my particular amazement, plants and animals that were not listed in Brehm's *Guides to Nature.* During this day's exploration we agreed on a plan to write a cyclist's handbook of local zoology, with the title "What's Missing in Brehm." By dusk we were near home, our baskets full of specimens. On a wooded hillside just outside of our "Town Amid the Forest," we were met by the principal of the Protestant school, a friend of our own Catholic principal. This man handed his fellow clergyman a black biretta and a black loden coat, explaining that it would be best not to appear in town in mufti. Then he gave him the news that his father, old Severin Kremers, had been discovered dead in his bed. He advised him to change clothes in his school, which was located just outside the town limits. Rumors were going around. We boys were asked to stand aside, but we overheard enough to give us the feeling that we were becoming protagonists in a cops-and-robbers story—that Reverend Kremers, who didn't get along very well with his father, had killed the old man and tried to escape at an early hour in civilian garb. He had, the rumor said, abducted two of his favorite students, and the group had been sighted leaving town. A third student named Erich was forbidden by his father to take part in the suspicious bicycle tour, and thus escaped certain death. The two other boys—the rumor continued—were already dead. The loathsome priest had strangled them and buried them in the forest near a large anthill.

A fine kettle of fish. Inquiries at my house produced the information that the two boys had gone to Holland—across the border!—with the priest. This was sensational news in a town that, apart from the occasional suicide, was unfamiliar with violent death. My aunt Hanna Hemmersbach, introduced in a previous chapter as the cook at my First Communion festivities, immediately went into action. Eye for eye and tooth for tooth! For her it was an open-and-shut case: this dreadful man of the cloth, already well known for pederastic proclivities, had lured the boys across the border into the Holland heath with the intent of purging his parricidal guilt with the blood of us two innocents. Crowds gathered at every street corner. The police were placed on alarm status. Sabers rattled, and like destiny itself, they were borne along the cobblestone streets with serious, desperate mien. Our sacrificial blood cried up to Heaven. My selfsame Aunt Hanna convinced my mother that I had been murdered. My other aunts, Aunt Mina and Aunt Lena, joined the ritual of mourning, stalwarts of automatic sympathy both of them, ambulatory dispensers of caffeinated consolation who, no sooner had they arrived in our house, reached for the coffee grinder to brew up a cup of extra-strong java for my pitiable mother, Johanna Scheifes. Lord knows, she could use it!

Born in the Scheifes cottage in St. Hubert, having spent long winter evenings as a child in the spinning room together with maids and farmhands, my mother heard frightful tales of one of her uncles, her father's brother, who had been slaughtered in the dark of night by a crazed man. We kids were also familiar with the story, and for me it had an especially intense meaning. One day I discovered in my grandmother's chest of drawers this great-uncle's death certificate, printed in black and silver on hand-made paper and framed under glass. I hung it on my bedroom wall beneath the awful plaster statue of my guardian angel that I was still too cowardly to take down. I smuggled into my story the text of this document, so beautifully penned by my great-grandfather's hand that otherwise was used to grasping only a plow, and so moving in its intimate statement. Did I say smuggled? It was only later that I realized to my amazement that this kind of creative appropriation, so common in our profession, is nothing more than a casual crossing of borders. Literature by nature lifts all barriers, not even to mention these current applied recollections of mine, in which the author is not constantly sure of the ground he is standing on. I shall therefore insert the appropriate requiem right here:

JESUS, Maria, JOSEPH! HUBERTUS! GOD!
Look down with Your grace upon this boy

HEINRICH HERMANN SCHEIFES
departed while still so young.
Our Lord Jesus Christ deemed it proper
to deliver him to the hands of the unjust
and to have him endure the agonies of death.

The deceased, born in St. Hubert on March 4, 1823, had not reached the age of 21, when, at 11 o'clock on the night of October 8, 1843, on his way from the village of St. Hubert to the Scheifes homestead, he was attacked and stabbed in his side. His agony grew worse and worse; death rose up inside him. He received the final sacraments, gazed up to his Redeemer in heaven with contrition, and on the third day after that fateful night, at around 12 noon, passed away amid his family's prayers and the ministrations of a priest bearing the Cross of Jesus. The Good Lord will never scorn his youth, his innocence, his kindness, or his childlike love.

At this young man's grave, his parents, overcome with grief but trusting in the abundance of divine grace, stood with their surviving four children and prayed to God that He might, in His infinite mercy, forgive the man who had fatally wounded their dear son. Thereupon they commended their beloved deceased to the prayer of the faithful:

MAY HE REST IN PEACE.

(Incidentally, God forgave the murderer. But the earthly judges strung him up on the same tree under which he committed his heinous crime.)

But now, in the third generation, once again blood was shed most cruelly and cried out for vengeance. Johanna's children—all three of them! For rumor counted my other brother Ludwig among the victims of the bike trip to the heaths of Holland. My mother Johanna, piously accepting the inscrutable will of the Almighty, broke down completely. My father, clamorously summoned from his office desk, is reported to have said, "The principal may occasionally swipe a bottle of wine or sleep through Mass, but he wouldn't do a thing to his father or my children." For him the case was closed, and he calmly returned to his job, while all the relatives cursed him as mean and heartless, thus piling tragedy upon tragedy in my mother's house. My mother began imagining, with help from the aunts, a mound of earth at the scene of the crime, topped by a crucifix inscribed with a plea to all who pass by to say an Our Father for the souls of the innocent youngsters murdered on this spot by the hand of an ignominious priest...

It was a bitter pill for the devout citizens of the town when they learned that the principal had brought these youngsters home safe and sound, except for a punctured tire on one of the bikes, that no such dire funerary monument would be necessary, and that Old Man Severin could be proven to have died of natural causes. Many of the clergyman's political enemies never forgave him for refusing to be a blackguard. His father's funeral was attended by just a few friends; it was like burying a dog. Following these incidents, my admiration increased for this hated priest. A year later he was suspended from office.

It took me a day and a night to write down these reminiscences in our Tower cell. I chose the form of a framed narrative: a university student reports the events of that tragic day to his episcopal uncle and friend, events that made a lasting impression on the young man who had already lost his faith at the hands of another priest. This Prince of the Church, uncommonly open-minded and urbane for a Catholic clergyman, interjects questions to clarify certain details, while the student, in his eagerness to get the facts told, never notices that the Bishop already knows more about the case than he can imagine. At the end, the Bishop asks one of his curates to fetch the Kremers file from the archive. Only then does the student realize that years ago, in his capacity as ecclesiastical authority, his uncle had dealt with the case of the disciplined priest.

I recited my story—hot off the *bidetto*, as it were—and received applause. I was both pleased and crushed by the book dealer's comment: the wily cockroach, he said, probably copied it out from somewhere, because a writer whose name is completely unknown, that is, one who isn't a writer at all, and yet can produce such a thing within twenty-four hours—such a writer is darned suspicious unless he is willing to lift his pseudonym, in which case we should all drink a toast to him. Such was the gist of the judgment handed down by the man from Cologne. Madame Gerstenberg, too, had her doubts. "Honest now, just who are you?" What sort of man is this, that even winds and sea obey him? It was the kind of question posed perennially by those of little faith. But only by those of little faith? Vigoleis sat in his author's chair, blushing crimson with embarrassment. He pondered, ruminated, pondered again and re-ruminated all that he had ruminated before, and finally, as he set out to depart with Beatrice for the Tower, he made a decision then and there to take his manuscript that very night and toss it to the rats, for now it wasn't worth the proverbial tinker's dam. So Vigoleis copied it all out? Peeked over somebody else's shoulder, just like a kid in my school with a worm-eaten oak tree as a symbol of Imperial education? Will he never, ever graduate from school, not even here in Spain, the land of Quixote? Over and over again, whenever he received one of his rare decent grades, his teachers suspected him of copying other kids' work; that was their constant attitude toward him. Those sadists never realized that this pupil of theirs was too cowardly to peek at the work of kids sitting in front of him, behind him, or next to him in class. Copying is a talent we learn not for schoolwork, but for life itself.

During the ensuing night Vigoleis staged an auto-da-fé with the fruits of his addled brain. He considered it too risky to tear up the pages and throw them to the rats in the pit for post-mastication. This story of his had to disappear completely from the world. Not one fragment of it must survive for the winds to scatter. Copied! That was the final blow!

Even so, this literary soirée had important ramifications. My reader is probably thinking: of course, a fight on the *pilarière* with Beatrice, who thinks that the process of self-mutilation has simply gone too far. Wrong. To step out on the path of Providence, we must now sidle up to Captain von Martersteig. I assure you that this will be much more rewarding than if you were to remain a mute witness to Beatrice's despair. So let us return to the actress' apartment, where Vigoleis is still seated in the reciter's chair which, as a result of the bookseller's suspicions, has turned into a court dock.

The Captain, asked for his verdict as a fellow wielder of the pen, inquired politely if he might take a look at the typescript. He checked it over very carefully, flipping through the pages as all eyes focused on his lips—which were pressed together and refused to open. After a while, Joachim let his monocle drop into his hand and returned the manuscript to me. I was fully prepared to hear him pronounce my grade, "C minus. Sit down!"—the type of evaluation that all teachers use when they can't keep up with their pupils. Our friend the fighter pilot started discoursing on problems of style and the neglect of narrative frames in modern literature. He even cited the famous but trite saw of Buffon, according to which *le style c'est l'homme même*, and as for my own style, it was—

"Like a trampoline! Go ahead and say it, *Herr Hauptmann*! Or perhaps you prefer a somewhat more profound simile, such as 'It is dreadful to cross the moor / so gloomy in the mists of heather.' Or maybe something botanical, if that will be of help: the common shave-grass..."

"*Equisitacae*, cryptogamous class of the subspecies of vascular cryptogamous plants," interjected Friedrich, who had just passed his medical exams.

My style, the Captain said, was immature, or perhaps overripe. It was spiky and thorny, it was undignified and—but he didn't mean to criticize, he was not a literary scholar, but only a retiree interested in *belles lettres*. But no doubt about it, the manuscript was neatly typed in triple-space, making the text clear and easy to read, with plenty of room for corrections. His own typescripts, he told us, were an unholy mess; he had a hard time finding things in them, and he had been searching for a long time for someone who could type out clean copy, triple-spaced. He could scrape up the funds for the extra paper, unless his enemy forced him to absent himself from Deyá for long periods of time. Then he reset his monocle at his vacant eye and awaited my reply to his question, formulated so hesitantly as to be unworthy of a professional dive bomber: "Don Vigoleis, would you be willing to become my personal typist?"

When your own efforts go astray, look for success in the work of others. Vigoleis would have no reservations about entering the Captain's service if he could be told what the gentleman was willing to pay per page.

The retired flyboy said that he had no idea what the going rate on the island was. Perhaps Mr. Emmerich...

Emmerich decided to play King Solomon of Cologne. Two such masterful writers as these, he said turning to our hostess, are surely not going to start picking nits over each other's work. He could supply paper at a discount. Hurray! And so long, everybody!

No agreement was reached; the case remained undecided. The Captain's assessment of my style was not far off the mark, but it would have been more accurate to describe it as "cactus style": it formed branches and offshoots at random, like a cactus with its urge to sprout buds just where you would never expect them. But this occurred to me only later, on the way back home. One more reason to destroy my manuscript.

Robert von Ranke Graves had metamorphosed into an anaconda, hissing at his enemy Martersteig on the public thoroughfare in Deyá. The latter, not yet immune to the British-German venom that was unavoidable on Spanish soil, decided to seek shelter a few weeks longer at the anarchical rooming-house in Palma, and this prompted La Gerstenberg to ask him to be the next to read from his work in progress. After that, she said, he could return to his mountain retreat, and if she ever encountered Graves in the "Alhambra," she was determined to give him a piece of her mind. This met with a protest from the Captain, who insisted that in true-blue Prussian fashion he was quite able to defend himself. As for reading from his "Monkey Army" manuscript, however, he would be more than happy to be of service.

A week later the Captain mustered his legions of apes in the actress' apartment. He recited badly. Again and again he lost the thread; it was obvious that his text was badly in need of decent retyping, this time triple-spaced. Nevertheless, what he had to say was well worth listening to. Damn it all! I had not expected the likes of this from the crash-landed fop Martersteig. Page after caustic page, Prussian militarism was castigated here in all its inhumanity, its absurdity, its stupefying emptiness. This was coming from a fellow who knew what he was talking about, and it reached a climax that took my breath away: the monkey battalions parade through the Brandenburg Gate; the German people, unaware that its soldiers in the Kaiser's uniform are in fact of the simian species, march along in exact rhythm, with shouldered umbrellas. Brehm and his books on the animals of the world were no longer of any use for this work. Protocols of the Teneriffe Chimpanzee Station of the Prussian Academy of Science were creatively exploited here; even a layman could tell that Martersteig's monkeys behaved as monkeys should. A new Clausewitz was born. The renowned German land of poets, philosophers, and field marshals had brought him forth at a time when the emergency gripping the nation, despite the application of a thousand suction cups, had not been able to suck a single heroic thought out of the country's citizenry.

"Well—?" The Captain aimed his monocle right at me. What did I think of his style? Was his stylistic amateurism, he asked, getting in the way of his message? Before I could reply, "Hmm...Your style? Very nice, but that's not the point...," La Gerstenberg said, "Very nice, if you ask me." But, she added, she didn't know much about literature, and nothing at all about military matters.

Herr von Martersteig picked up his manuscript and placed it in a ring binder, closing it with an angry snap. Only then did he send out a somber gaze at his audience. Focusing his monocle on the actress, and speaking in the now familiar barrack-room tonality of his Clausewitzian chimps, he said something like this: "My dear Madam, I am most grateful for your evaluation, which is without question more favorable than I might have heard from the mouth of Vigoleis. 'Very nice,' you said. Why not? This is, after all, an opinion—a verdict, and an annihilating one at that. 'Very nice'—well, well. Then you will now permit me to take my leave..." But before leaving, he asked Vigoleis if he would kindly come to his room for the briefest of discussions of certain technical matters such as a retyping of his "very nice" novel. With that, the mortified Prussian soldier departed from us—not before we noticed his leaving, for he was too lame for that, but a good deal more rapidly than was his wont. A minute later I heard a toilet flushing—aha. Or was he sending his manuscript the way of so many manuscripts? I myself, upon hearing such a verdict from the tragedian, would have ripped up my text in a thousand pieces right in front of her eyes.

La Gerstenberg wondered out loud whether what we had just heard was more than just a pastime for an officer of the air force who had force-landed. "Vigoleis, now you say something!"

"Dear Madame Gerstenberg," I began, in an attempt to defend my literary colleague, "Martersteig's style is, as you say, 'nice.' You took the word right out of my mouth, but coming from my mouth, it would have meant something different. I would have added, 'Very nice, indeed, when observed with the eyes of a writer whom you have outpointed, Captain, with your own style. Many people know how to write, but very few have anything to say. You cannot write, but damn it all, you have everything in the world to say.' Your book is superb. Whoever reads it will be rid of any notions about making war. Our neo-Clausewitz will have one thing in common with the New Testament: it will never find its way into a soldier's musette bag. Yet I fear that hardly a week afer it is published, our friend Martersteig will be the victim of an as-assassination. Those guys will search him out in his lodgings in Deyá and string him up in the nearest olive tree. He'll lose his spinal pension, but his royalties for the book will outdo what he could ever squeeze out of Hindenburg."

How much should I charge him per page? What was the going wage on the island for such secretarial drudgery?

Meanwhile, it was too late in the day for financial negotiations with the author. Strengthened in body and spirit, we made our way homeward—yes, homeward to the Clock Tower, where we now actually felt at home, cosmopoli-tans that we were. When you come to think of it, if you subtract the naked joy from a house of joy, what you're left with isn't necessarily naked misery.

As we hiked out from the city, Beatrice asked me what I really thought of the Captain's "so-called writing." She thought that his style was frightful, and the rest insignificant. Bitter thoughts of a failed soldier, one who curses the troops but is offended if you don't address him with his military rank. I agreed with her on this point, and remarked that the Captain hadn't yet tossed his medal *Pour le Mérite* on the dung heap. "Nobody will read that stuff," Beat-rice went on. "It's just so meaningless." And then she added, this time in French, that she had been wrong about my taste.

If you're holding hands as you stride toward a Clock Tower, if you know that just an hour later you'll have night all around you, if the aroma of the slaughterhouse is coursing over the fields, and rats are scuttling across your path, if the mute stars are skewered on the dull firmament of nothingness like the fearful many-faceted eye of the Creator—then you don't tell lies.

And so I said, "Beatrice, *chérie*, if I can persuade that aviator to fork over fifty centimos for each page of monkey fiction, then I won't care the gratings of his own green cheese what kind of style this stupid Prussian writes. With his style, he isn't paying much honor to the officer class he once belonged to. The real Clausewitz, Moltke, Gneisenau—those were first-rate classical styl-ists, models for anyone who wants to learn how to write good German. It's just that the things they wrote down on paper don't interest anybody any more. They don't interest me; they don't interest anybody anywhere. What Martersteig has to say will still be meaningful tomorrow. And if you'll permit me to turn prophetic, it will be meaningful as long as there's a place called Germany with German soldiers that are all monkeys, from the privates right up through the sergeants and the field marshals. Tomorrow I'm going to start negotiating with him about typing his novel. The author will provide paper and ribbons. I'll provide the machine and the triple-spacing from my own resources, and..."—lifting my gaze to the stars, although Beatrice didn't notice—"if my name ain't Vigoleis, for the first time ever, world-class litera-ture will get written on my Diamant. I hope that Vic van Vriesland will forgive me, and ter Braak and Slauerhoff, too, and all the lesser writers who have constantly been helping me to run away from myself. I'd even do it for 30 centimos, even for a single real, but the Captain doesn't need to know this."

Beatrice didn't need to know that I would do this job for a *perra gorda*, that is, 10 measly centimos. For a 500-page manuscript, you can figure it out yourself: that would amount to two months' rent in cash. We would be rid of that worry until year's end, even considering that Pablo was no longer falling asleep under Beatrice's pedagogy. It was already close to the end of October.

And so in our nocturnal conversation on the way home, I ended up lying after all, although I meant it only to conceal my real thoughts. But there was no concealing them from the many-faceted, starry eye above us. Now it was that eye's turn to make a move on the chessboard of our destiny. We were playing black, and we lost.

Negotiating with the writer was a long process. My hopeful suggestion of 50 centimos met with decisive rejection. No, he couldn't pay me *that* much. 250 pesetas? Did I realize that a sum that large meant a whole month of hostility from Graves? And, if he might be permitted to inquire, was I crazy? So I started haggling and underbid myself by 10. No! Not the gratings! Another 10. This would still force him to take up a beggar's staff; not a pretty state of affairs, since, as an officer, he was used to leaning on his ceremonial saber. Besides, it was his enemy who was constantly forcing him to live beyond his means. In the long run, he simply could not afford commuting back and forth to the Count's redoubt; he rejected the idea of responding, and, in any case, this accursed Tommy was in the stronger position. So in his guts he was pondering final departure from the island to move to Ibiza or Alicante. Should he decide to make the move, and although it was painful even to consider it, he would sell all his belongings, and he had a commode, a "chest" as we might prefer to call it, a masterpiece of cabinetry that he would gladly offer as compensation for my typing. "Madame, dear Madame Beatrice, what a blessing it is that you came along today! You see, your Vigoleis—I like him. He's a fine man, but he's not a very practical man. Please, no objections, let's call a spade a spade. With his metaphysical twists and turns he's placing obstacles on the path to his own well-being. If you ask me, and I beg your pardon, you will both end up in a barrel."

"We're already there, *Herr Hauptmann*! But now that you have sounded this alarm, permit me to inquire: how far does a Vigoleis have to drop before he's eligible for a hero's pension?"

Herr von Martersteig gave me a pitying glance through his monocle, and then continued speaking in his elegant way to Beatrice,

"... and that is why we must be very careful, for Don Vigo might well choose to type out my manuscript for no wage at all, and of that I would not approve!" The Captain made a dismissive gesture that included his fur-slippered feet, which were still a part of his militarily unfit body, though only barely recognizable as such.

He would hate to part with this chest of drawers, a Martersteig heirloom that he had arranged to be sent down from Magdeburg for reasons of nostalgic ambience. He was, he said, a man who clung to the proper environment; he was still unable to get used to Spain. This chest was a piece of the homeland. Vigoleis may go ahead and smile—lucky is the man who can carry his homeland around with him in a little suitcase. He was in need of very special kinds of homey surroundings. Was I able to empathize with that, he asked?

I was indeed. I knew that there are some writers who can write only when they hear a tomcat purring on their laps, one that every now and then will lift its tail to wipe the drops of creative sweat from their brows. Other writers are in need of a woman instead of a cat, a woman who under certain circumstances can relieve them of creative agony along with the sweat. Josef Roth got along with strong liquor; Hemingway takes a complicated bath-cum-massage when he is working. For his struggles with the demons of creativity, Teixeira de Pascoaes requires a few dozen pencil-thin sticks made of precious wood and with little gold feathers at their ends, which he places like oversized toothpicks in a special quiver. Dante had his Beatrice, and Vigoleis no less. François Villon kept his divine lamp lit by means of highway robbery. Was the Clausewitz of the 20th century likewise using this hunk of antique German furniture, yanking forth from it the energy to animate his four-legged army recruits in a campaign to purge the German nation of its mission to redeem the world?

While describing his armoire, the Captain was overcome with emotion, and we couldn't help but be moved in turn by every one of his feelings and little delights: exquisite marquetry, hardware of forged metal, an antique lock with a secret mechanism, according to Martersteig's informants the work of the Nürnberg master-carpenter Hans Ehemann; a warped drawer, one slightly damaged hinge. Vigoleis could take care of that with one blow of a hammer in the anarchist's workshop. What unrecognized genius would ever refuse to type out the ± 500 pages of his Monkey Army for the price of this masterpiece of a *cassone*? After just a few weeks, he explained, the item would pass from the Martersteig estate to that of Vigoleis; and, come to think of it, the raised-intarsia family monogram with its "V" as predicate of nobility could henceforth be construed symbolically as a quaint form of parody of the new owner's initial "V" (pronounced as "F," to be sure). The Captain closed his melancholy encomium by stating that he was unfortunately unable to produce the heirloom right here before us, but that I should not have the slightest reservations concerning the agreement. Would we care to visit him in Deyá to become convinced of the chest's value? But now Madame must not look so worried—we would of course be his guests, and as for transportation, he could make the following specific recommendation: by rail as far as Sóller, then over the mountain—"Just a short hike, Vigoleis, I make it easily, even in my lame condition"—down into the next valley, past his enemy's house, and—

Before he could transform this business trip into a pleasure jaunt, I interrupted him, and surely not without a show of deep emotion on my part:

"Herr Hauptmann, I am at the moment unable to envision the consequences of your practical romantic offer. Thank you very much for the invitation. Even sight unseen, I would have accepted the Martersteig chest as payment, but perhaps I can set you at ease by telling you that we never buy a pig in a poke. So I say, off to Deyá!"

Beatrice replied—not spontaneously, not at all jokingly, but with emotion, as always when the talk came around to travel plans, and missing the correct pitch by a half-tone, and thus making her question sound midway between a request for calm and a reproach: "And the money for the train fare?"

As always, it was a matter of money! No sooner has the soul started ascending like a lark into the twittering blue, when it reaches the end of its song and plunges back to the fields of common potatoes. If the Dear Lord had created only one fewer species of animal and, as compensation, permitted humankind to produce its own hard cash without resorting to counterfeit, things would go much better from day to day here on earth. But no, He had to go and make insects and vermin in untold millions that defy all attempts at categorization: the bedbug, the common flea, the man-eating flea, beetles with gigantic pincers that no scientists know what to do with—much less the beetles themselves, not to mention millipedes that could easily reach their destination with 30 fewer feet. And now Vigoleis doesn't know how we can scrape up train fare. Human history has yet to come up with answers to certain questions, for the simple reason that humans are too shy to ask them. The ostrich is the only animal in Creation that has not mistaken its true reason for existing. It provides human beings with a useful symbol. As for this train fare, here in the presence of an officer of the air force we stand ashamed at lacking an organ that would get us two third-class tickets Palma-Sóller. Every spider is capable of spinning a thread on which it can descend at will, whereas an aviator crash-lands with fatal consequences for his sanity. A caterpillar rolls itself up when it gets tired of its own ugliness, and then soars away with enhanced value as a butterfly, whereas I—but I mustn't go on with such thoughts; they will cause a darkening of my mood, and besides, this is not the place to pick a bone with the Creator. As a layman in such disputes, I know I would soon lose the argument, and what is more, we would lose sight of the commode on which whole generations of Martersteigs had their diapers changed, in which their crown jewels were stored along with any number of *billets doux* stemming from domestic dalliances, and finally the Monkey Army. Now, however, this piece of furniture has taken on prime significance for our heroes, probably even greater significance than that hotel-room wardrobe a few chapters ago.

Beatrice did some mental addition. Like a good *Hausfrau* she conjured up in her mind's eye our provisions hanging on the ropes in our cell, and then pronounced the result: In three weeks we could save up enough for the fare. Her tone of voice revealed to me that she had actually squirreled away more than that, and sure enough, she was including a glass of lemonade for each of us at the railroad station restaurant.

Beatrice had no intention of slapping a donkey's behind at the Manse to make him extrude pieces of gold. For purely aesthetic reasons, she would never stoop to such a thing. She was thinking exclusively in terms of frugality. For each and every cubic centimeter of that commode, we would have to go without certain items of nourishment, pull our belts one hole tighter—to the very last hole of all. Then, and only then, would we get to see the ancestral chest face to face. For the moment, we could have the pleasure of living in hopeful expectation. We had, of course, already divided up the bearskin before Bruin was slain: Beatrice would get all the drawers for her underclothes—this I generously allowed her, while claiming for myself only the secret drawer. "You are aware, *chérie*, how urgently I am in need of a tabernacle for my poems. It's so painful for me to see my most sacred feelings hanging there on the clothesline like a shirt. And anyway, with underthings one usually expects a certain amount of decorum—just think of brassières and other suspensory articles that any lady, who is truly a lady, hangs up only in a darkened chamber. I suppose I could write my reflective verses with some kind of invisible ink, but that Martersteigian heirloom seems just the right thing for my purposes. First-hand inspection will reveal whether it will be necessary to bore a few air holes in the drawer to prevent moisture and mold from accumulating during storage. We can ask Adeleide whether she'll let us stand the piece out in the corridor. But what it all boils down to is this: this bartering deal is going to force us to look for some other living quarters. If we could only open up our folding cot somewhere else, we could consider this chest of drawers as an example of divine intervention."

Emmerich had already got wind of our proposed junket to Deyá for chest-inspection. Deyá, he told us, was a damp, highly romantic burg, three stars in Baedeker and special praise for the cemetery. We mustn't forget to look up a famous Japanese painter named "Three Little Clouds" who was a friend of Martersteig's. Sóller: marvelous, glorious! The superlatives in the tourist guidebooks, Emmerich told us, couldn't begin to describe the valley and its tiny harbor, an exquisite study in white, blue, and olive-green. And anyway, we had now lived on the island long enough to start exploring its inland attractions. We should be quick to load the armoire on the return bus; at the last minute our pilot could be overcome with regret about parting with it, obsessed as he was with keeping personal junk, such as his *Pour le Mérite*, his Iron Cross First Class, and similar crash-landing decorations. Every time he came to the bookshop, he blabbered on about Germany, the German forest, the German spirit, and German furniture. This from a Cologne native who couldn't survive without potato pancakes.

Just two weeks later Beatrice had saved up the money for our trip. Marter-steig planned to keep us in Deyá for four days; thus, we could avoid expenses for food for an entire week by fasting totally one day before and one day after the journey. He explained to us that he lived very simply, but that we wouldn't starve in his little mill tower. Well, we weren't starving in our own Tower refuge, either, but in fact—no offense to the military man intended—we were looking forward to putting on a little flesh during our stay in Deyá.

We took an early train. Our leader, stiff in the joints as usual, was abnormally quiet. He dusted Beatrice's seat with insect repellent, thereby exposing himself and me to attacks of vermin. Then he dozed off grumpily, cradled and shaken by the 3rd class coupé. By unhappy coincidence we found ourselves sitting directly above an axle. The Captain's air cushion provided only a little comfort, and when it burst a few minutes later—it was not made for the tropics and had dried out—his mood turned sour. The thought of going home seemed to depress him. Who knows what tricks and shenanigans his enemy would have thought up in the meantime? We left Martersteig to his morose cogitations, his aching back, his increasingly ominous premonitions, and an army of fleas that went on the attack in our compartment. Beatrice was the only one who didn't get bitten.

The trip was worth the money that we had scraped together by going hungry. We rode through several tunnels, an experience that can make any landscape, no matter how intrinsically dreary, become a series of pleasant vistas. This landscape, in its fabled luxuriance, could boast of being the most beautiful and fertile region on the whole island. Olive orchards followed upon groves of almonds, palms jutted out from orange plantations, and yet the effect was not of the tropical sort in this southern clime. Everywhere you looked you could see merry black wallowing Mallorquin pigs, exemplars of a world-famous culture of gastronomic swine-breeding, based on a diet of apricots. More than the palm trees, the Aleppo firs, the araucarias, the carobs, and the tangerines, these animals gave me a sense of being very remote from my homeland and its pale prize-winning German hogs.

Sóller is a lovely town—if you are willing to accord any meaning to the word "lovely" under the hot Spanish sun—situated at the bottom of a colorful valley. A visitor wouldn't mind settling there in one of the white-walled cottages amid cats, orange groves, and in the little front yard mothers suckling their young with their gleaming golden breasts. The morning we arrived we didn't get to see much of this orange-producing town, whose product can be found in gift baskets of fruit anywhere in the world. The Captain was in a rush to get home, and that meant that we had to step on it, too. He wouldn't even let us saunter through the streets, take a peek at the Franciscan monastery, visit the market square, seek out a wayside shrine—none of all this. We had to speed home—I almost wrote "home to the Motherland"—and so we trudged along donkey paths across rocky ground, past boulders and over mounds of talus, up into the range of hills that led from Sóller to Deyá.

I am incapable of describing landscape, for the simple reason that landscape doesn't speak to me—or to put this more modestly, it doesn't say very much to me. For this reason I could now make good use of the pen of the Archduke Ludwig Salvator of Austria, who lived on this island for decades. He is the author of the definitive work on the Balearic Islands; he knew how to capture the archipelago in word and image. Copy his text? Oh, if only I could locate one or two pages of his to plagiarize so that my reader might receive at least a remote impression of how magnificent our hike was, far above the pulsating flanks of the ocean, parallel to a shoreline incised with fiords and inlets that beckoned to the blue swells of seawater. Anton Emmerich would of course immediately say, "Copied out!" And Lord knows I wouldn't deny it, although I would never even dream of stealing from Emmerich's own "Guide to Mallorca." If you wish to deck yourself with borrowed plumes, you won't wait around until a moulting sparrow sends you one of its tail feathers. With all due respect to that Colognian's business acumen, his "Guide" was a mess. So a few dabs of color from my own personal palette should do a better job.

The Captain's feet were shod in a pair of sealskin moccasins, prescribed for his journey to Spain by an orthopedist in Germany. In the Count's rooming house he always wore slippers made of cat or rabbit fur, which were no doubt beneficial for his gouty extremities, but were anything but moth-proof. Up here on the donkey path he shuffled along, every once in a while emitting a groan that signaled a pause to rest on a knobby pine branch. This we did gladly, for we heroes were also tuckered out from hiking, especially me with my congenital aversion to long foot marches. It wasn't our footgear or our feet themselves that limited our endurance up here in the hills. As a Swiss citizen Beatrice is quite used to taking miles and miles at a stretch, and with her Indian heritage she could have snuck her way all along the trail. Moreover, the balancing mechanism inside our ears remained undisturbed, unlike the aviator, whom we had to lash to a rope whenever we had to eke our way past a precipice. "It's a case of acrophobia, Madam, and it becomes acute on donkey trails like this one. Terrible. But neither of you has ever crash-landed from 9000 feet. Down there..."

Martersteig almost audibly clapped his hand to his eyes, for "down there" was a yawning gap of about a hundred meters. To crash land down there without eligibility for a government pension? The worst way for a famous fighter pilot to get shot down, I thought, was if he did the shooting himself. But by then, we had successfully roped the airforce retiree past another steep cliff. Loose rocks tumbled down the incline into the abyss below. Our ailing, stiff-backed leader, who at any moment could plunge to the depths, thanked us with a glassy stare. "Your fatherland's gratitude is certain"—isn't that what the poets of his homeland were so fond of singing?

The sun, too, offered no mercy. It glared down upon us with ferocious strength in spite of the lateness of the season. Apart from a couple of brief drizzles that passed over the island, it hadn't rained at all. The Captain, like all sufferers from gout a walking weather prognosticator, said that we could expect real rain very soon; he could feel it in his sealskin footwear. And then we would get to see what it was like when an entire island is inundated; we would learn what rainstorms can do in Spain.

After many hours of forced marching, slipping, sliding, and stumbling, we finally reached the village of Deyá, located on a mountainside in the midst of an orange grove, just as picturesque as Baedeker said it was. Martersteig came back to life. Stealthily, like a hunted game animal, he took Beatrice's arm and whispered, "It's down there, no, a little farther on, more to the right—no, farther still. Do you see that spruce tree standing alone? That's it, right there. And who do you suppose lives there?"

Beatrice made no reply. Peering along a raised index finger with its bitten nail, she could focus her glance only on the landscape as a whole, not on some single house or free-standing spruce tree within it. I raised my own well-kempt index finger and said quickly, "Your enemy, Herr von Martersteig, our literary colleague Sir Robert von Ranke Graves."

"Let's move on, just a half hour more, and then we'll take a rest beneath my spruce tree."

This remark was controlled, to-the-point, and strategically significant. That's how I imagine a ground observer communicating with his pilot: one kill. Next enemy, please.

His calculations worked out to the minute. After the announced interval, we were sitting, bathed in sweat, on the wall that surrounded the old house where the Captain had set up his command post. This is where he conjured up his imaginary army of Barbary apes, where he entertained his imaginary ephebes, his imaginary enemies, and his imaginary hatred of Germany, capable all the while of mustering as weapons for the great battle only his damaged spine, his knotty gout, and his worries about his pension. But we mustn't forget that his arsenal also included his wooden ancestral shrine, which had gone before us like the Star of Bethlehem during our entire miserable cross-country trek, and which each of us imagined as sharing in equal parts: Beatrice for her underclothes, Vigoleis for his sacred cache of poetry. He imagined the key to the secret compartment as made of pure gold—the Nürnberg master surely would not have been content with anything less.

"Welcome, my dear guests," said the Captain, as he opened the tower door with a creaky key.

The *entrada* was cool—more than that, it was ice cold. Whitewashed like all of the rooms in the house, it was completely bare except for a small jewel box set in a wall niche. A large spider with its notorious hairy legs (its bite can be fatal to man or horse, the encyclopedia says) was crawling back into its lair between wall and ceiling beams. Our host flipped a wall switch. No electricity.

The heart of a pessimist really starts pumping when everything goes wrong, especially in the presence of witnesses. "Madam, Don Vigo, you can see for yourself. Try the switch. No light! Do you need any more naked proof of my enemy's wickedness? Robert von Ranke Graves wishes us to sit here in darkness! His spies will have reported our arrival to him. He wants to humiliate me in front of you, but—I have some candles!" This sounded triumphant. O death, where is thy sting, O grave, where is thy victory now? Robert von Ranke, where is thy poetic imagination? Joachim has some candle stubs! In a soldier's musette bag such things can be more important than a field marshal's mace.

While we recovered from the agonies of our journey—our host opened up chaises longues in the shade of *his* spruce, or was it a palm tree?—Martersteig busied himself in his kitchen. On the way to his house he had purchased three good-sized sardines, and now he was roasting them on the grill. The smell penetrated everything around us, including ourselves—right down to the marrow. Nothing stinks worse than sardines as they slowly roast to a crisp; it is a fiery purgatory for all the slime of the primeval world. Science is still trying to figure out why the sardine, next to the earthworm the cleanest animal in existence, stinks so much, whereas a pig that has wallowed in mud all its life has such a sweet fragrance on the spit. "He should put his kitchen on the roof," said Beatrice, and then she was silent. She had turned green, and I wasn't feeling any better. But the snack did us good, and then we fell into a deep sleep. Afterwards, we went into the village. It was late in the afternoon when the shadows were getting long.

To cite Baedeker further, since I'm unable to do any better, Deyá is simply a fantastic place, unique, highly attractive and truly rewarding. I can't quote any more, because I have just found out to my amazement that my 1929 Baedeker covers the village with exactly three-quarters of a line! Be that as it may, later guidebooks put the artistic activity in Deyá in the same category as Worpswede and Ascona. I don't know Worpswede, but Ascona offers more naked flesh, more bedroom scandals, and less artistic activity than Deyá had at the time, when some world-famous painters were still living there. It also sheltered a few writers of note, a few philosophers, the odd vegetarian, a Rumanian soothsayer, and an Italian coloratura soprano whose ornamentations had long since broken off, so that she now exercised her God-given talent only on bright moonlit nights while sitting alone on a stone near her house; a dozen sculptors, a portrait photographer much in demand, a Russian. Graves lived at one end of the village, Martersteig at the other end. In between were the domiciles of international artists, some living there with their fame, others with their failures, their envy, their hatred, and their gossip. And then, of course, there were the indigenous citizens of Deyá, who for a long time now hadn't been able to figure out just what they were still doing there on their mountainside strewn with orange trees. Many of them readily posed for painters—*qué remedio*? What else is there to do?

But now, did a famous writer like Graves truly feel the need to torture an un-famous writer like Martersteig? Lay traps for him? Drive him out of house and village?

Robert Graves was already famous by this time. His *Goodbye to All That* had a reputation as one the best British war books. It had appeared in German with the title *Strich drunter* ("That's it, period!"). Like Joachim von Martersteig, Graves was an officer in the Wilhelminian War and served in France, the country that Martersteig still hated more than any other. But one day each of them said, "That's it, period!"

Their soldiering days were over, their colorful uniforms in tatters, and depression overcame both the victor and the vanquished. *Omne animal post coitum triste, praeter gallum qui cantat*, says Aristotle: after the sexual act every animal is sad, except for the rooster, which crows. Or perhaps it sings, like our two writers from hostile camps. They devoted themselves to literature, Graves in a fashion that you can read about in any history of literature, Martersteig in a manner that the world has yet to discover. His image as a fighter pilot was already yellowing in the pages of the illustrated magazines. To display the new Martersteig to the world, the Clausewitzian Martersteig, it would be necessary for the canny Vigoleis to type clear copy from his "Monkey Army" manuscript. Each of these literary competitors could boast of a German particle of nobility in his name, and both had selected Deyá as the scene of their pacifistic post-partum labor. And now comes the almost incomprehensible state of affairs: despite the similarity of their background, neither of them would have anything to do with the other. They avoided each other. Graves gave the crippled Prussian veteran the complete silent treatment, as if he didn't even exist. On one occasion the Englishman apparently tried to walk right through the man from Germany, just as you read about in the Bible and in ghost stories. Yet since the Captain, in spite of his spiritualized old-Prussian sense of duty, was not made of pure spirit, it came to bumpings and shovings on the public street of the village, and it's irrelevant which of them won the skirmish. Anyone who knows Graves or has given a cursory look at his picture in Penguin Books, can confirm what I know first-hand: the poet-officer beat up the officer-poet mercilessly. He knocked him out. He roasted him like a young herring and then, once again, as in the title of his book: "*Goodbye to All That*!"

Martersteig gave us a melancholy report of this affront, this provocation, this insult that he fell victim to. But judging from what I heard, it seemed to me that the Martersteigs had fallen victim to a great deal more than this. "He's making things up," said Beatrice, who came to dislike him more and more. I, too, had my doubts about the public scrimmage. Certain events may have taken place solely within our friend's concussed cranium; later conversations with Graves confirmed these doubts, although the British all-around man never came forth with the whole truth. For Martersteig, Graves was apparently what horny dream images were for the pious hermits in the Desert of Chalcis. If a naked woman appeared in a dream to a stylite when he dozed off after his meal of locusts, we can have no religio-historical doubt at all that 99% of the saints tumbled off their pillars in a fit of repressed sexuality. Saint Jerome experienced things like that, and reported them convincingly. And he never even climbed up a pillar. Herr von Martersteig, predestined to crash-land, fell to earth with every step he took.

As for the blackout: at that time the village Deyá had a small unit for producing electrical current, a primitive affair that was in private hands. There was a little generator in a little shed, attached to a tiny two-stroke motor. Day and night it rattled away, and day and night there were breakdowns. But since the current was stored in batteries, there was no interruption of service. I can't recall whether Graves had a financial interest in the power company, or whether he was just friends with the guy in charge. In any case, whenever Graves got angry at Martersteig, then out of sympathy with the Englishman the Spaniard cut off the German's electric lights. And the darker things got in the Captain's house, the angrier he became. It was the same technique as in the bull ring: before the fight the bull is harassed in the darkened *toril*. And it was like old family feuds, in which no one remembers who started it all and what the original reason for the dispute was; everybody just spits at everybody else. Martersteig was in command of whole regiments of gossiping monkeys, and they impugned the honor of Mr. Graves as often as they could—stories about women, mostly. And Graves countered by cutting off the electricity. But the Germans are not only the inventors of gunpowder and the printing press, but also of a light source made of wax. Martersteig had candles.

That evening, in the light of just one of these German inventions, we sat in the hexagonal study of the creator of the new German army. This room deserves a careful description. The walls of this turret-like space were whitewashed; the beamed ceiling was low, the stone floor covered with the customary palm-leaf mat. In the middle stood a large round table made of darkly stained wood, split on the diagonal. Into the split the owner had stuffed some envelopes and a wire fly swatter. Three high-backed chairs were placed around the table, and on the table's surface there was a metal holder containing the single wax candle. In one of the walls there was a small hole, and the plaster was peeling around it. Somebody, the Captain explained, as if making an excuse, had tried to drive a nail into the wall, but without success. The walls themselves showed neither bloodstains nor squashed mosquitoes. How did he do it? He killed the mosquitoes on the fly. But of course, the Richthofen Squadron! The Vigoleis Squadron kills mosquitoes using a soft clothes brush instead of his slipper, and that, too, leaves no traces of murder. A naked light bulb hung from the ceiling on an electric wire.

This spartan cell is where the general of the monkeys developed his strategy. This is where the Macaque Army was engendered, where Clausewitz hatched out his plans for cutting and slashing and emasculating the enemy. And this is where we now sat stiffly on chairs after a second starvation ration, listening to a man's life story that bordered on the uncanny. It was enough to give us the shivers. The Captain drummed on for hour after hour, sitting somewhat bent forward to alleviate the pain. He stood up just once, to take a new candle from a drawer; he lit it and set it on top of the still burning stump. My legs had long since gone to sleep, and I was unable to move. But I wouldn't have dared to in any case.

Martersteig's father was a tyrant, an iron Prussian pedagogue who would have admired a teacher at my own imperial educational barracks, who, to teach us a lesson in endurance, marched us into a growth of nettles and commanded us, "Up! Down! Up! Down!" And woe to whoever started whining and pulling his sleeves over his hands like mittens. That kid was given some whacks and ordered to stay after school—down among the nettles. In the Martersteig family, too, there could be no thought of complaining. Germany needed heroes, and heroes grew up only under the parental rod. Daddy had many titles and many obligations. He was a Privy Councillor, possessed a high rank in the military, and wore a slew of decorations that jingled tunes about service to the People and the Fatherland; he may have even been a general. His civilian profession was the law. He held two doctorates and was a State's Attorney, Superior State's Attorney, perhaps a District Commmissioner? This, too, I have forgotten. Let us just assume that this father was something very big, very imposing, very fear-inspiring, for his business concerned nothing less than so-called Final Authority. Whoever didn't pass muster with Old Man Martersteig could just string himself up on the doorpost, or somebody else could string him up. In either case his life was over. Everyone in his house knew that the decisions he made were of the life-or-death variety.

A late marriage to a Swiss woman beneath his social rank gave rise to tensions in the family tree and in the family's fortune, but happily for the future, the marriage seemed to remain childless. Scandal causes deafness. Or perhaps the Privy Attorney was so busy with his court cases that he forgot to sleep with his bride from the Alpine meadows. The latter is my own theory, but the son of this father expressed it differently: his progenitor didn't know the word "love"; such a thing didn't exist for him, neither in spirit nor in the flesh. Nevertheless, late in the marriage, and in a moment of weakness, this stern husband spilled the seed that became Joachim.

Joachim attended a humanistic high school and had what the Dutch call a *studiekop*, that is, a head for book learning. Translated into the ridiculous, it means that he was purely and simply a brain.

When his father ended 25 years of service to the Empire, he was showered with honors, new decorations, an ornate chair in his office and banquet in the Martersteig villa with servants and printed menu, with braided uniforms, cutaways, naked shoulders, Martersteig diamonds, a Swiss Alpine necklace, a Hungarian fiddler, some dull-witted convent canonesses, and monocles. Someone taps on a glass; all rise and gaze into the silvery eyes of the celebratee. "A toast to many more years!" The band plays a fanfare, outside the rockets soar into the sky, 25 of them, and then the worthy judge raises his glass to his lips and expresses his thanks to one and all. He takes one sip. He staggers. A servant catches him up. There is a hubbub in the room, someone shouts, the ladies grasp at their diamonds. But no assassin or thief has entered the premises. The celebratee had only taken poison, and the curtain came down.

His posthumous papers contained a few words to his family: after twenty-five years, a German judge who has done his duty before God and the Fatherland has but two options: either resign from office or take poison. He preferred the latter choice as the more decent, courageous, Prussian solution, so help him God.

God helped him very effectively. The dosage was exactly proper for the Judge's constitution, and so he immediately collapsed as if struck by a bolt of lightning. The proper Prussian military method would have been to use a bullet, but the old gentleman was also an aesthete; he didn't like the idea of blood on his white vest, and perhaps he thought that the explosion of a pistol would be drawing too much attention to himself. I don't know whether at that time suicide was regarded as a crime in Germany; in any case a civil servant was constrained to follow definite regulations concerning the cause of death: he had to kill himself in keeping with his status in society, for otherwise his widow would forfeit his pension. At the very moment when his father toppled over and there was panic in the hall, a deaf-and-blind Countess von Martersteig and the goldfish in the festively illuminated aquarium were the only ones to maintain their composure. Someone cried out, "Poor Joachim! Now he can't go to the university!" In fact, Joachim's mother received no pension at all.

Certain aunts of his pooled their resources, and he was sent to a Royal-Imperial military academy—a "brain crusher," as the Captain described it, using a term that was flattering for such an institution since it assumed that there was such a thing as a brain. What he probably meant, was that when the cadets were grown up and entered "real life," they had no brain left in them. I can no longer recall whether it was the academy in Berlin-Lichterfelde. While describing life at this place, Herr von Martersteig started shivering, insofar as his bones permitted such motion. If anyone wishes further detail concerning such educational penitentiaries, he should consult Count Dr. Dr. Werner von der Schulenburg, who likewise spent several years in one without getting squeezed flat by the brutal guards. But these are amazing exceptions. Christianity, which developed so gloriously and so naturally out of the starvation edema of humankind, has degenerated at the hands of its own unnatural, self-satisfied, conceited scholarly theology. In similar fashion, Germany has gone to the dogs as the result, speaking with Nietzsche, of its unnatural methods of education. Instead of learning the Greek and Latin classics, philosophy, and psychology, which his talents directed him to do, Martersteig studied generalship.

Then came a war, and the young cadet rose in the ranks—never becoming a true officer, for he made it only to a captaincy, whereas in a war everybody else is named at least a sub-general. No, Herr von Martersteig was attached to the fighter squadron of his colleague Manfred von Richthofen. As an observer he got to see a lot—enemy territory mostly, a bird's eye view of hell. Not many people had such a chance. That is why, afterwards, he was able to peer into Josefa the cook's bosom and identify her little asbestos bag as a fireproof receptacle for pipe ashes—without, incidentally, being in any way aroused by what he was looking at; he loved only boys. Then he was brought down out of the skies. One shot sufficed to verify his status as a hero—it is like the shooting gallery at the county fair, where for a dime you can aim at a clay pipe and, bang! the whole array of stuff starts dancing and prancing, things start leaping and twisting and doing somersaults, it's a high time all over, your audience is amazed. You leave the scene feeling like a hero with your head held high, and you enter a booth and treat yourself to a pickled herring and a mug of beer. It would be a macabre joke of history if the Tommy Robert Graves (minus the "von Ranke"; *à bas les boches* was still the byword) was the one who shot down this particular enemy, for Martersteig crashlanded behind enemy lines near a unit of French forces where Graves was posted at the time. And he actually landed, that is, he didn't penetrate the French soil like an artillery shell. He had this lark-like hovering descent to thank for coming out of it with his life, his dislocated spine, his fantasies, his Hindenburg pension, his love-hate of his homeland, his "Farewell my dear homeland," and the inspiration for his army of monkeys.

The full moon had risen. It was long past midnight, and the stump of the last candle had long since died out in a pool of wax. Our story-teller rose achingly to his feet and paced back and forth noiselessly in his slippers, talking all the time. He did this for a while, then took his seat again. His story was apparently at an end; there seemed nothing more to tell. His pause for thought was, so we thought, the end of his song.

Before we went to bed, Joachim, overcome by his own personal account, one that he often recited silently in his mind but seldom with audible voice— Joachim told us, begging our pardon, that he had decided not to leave the island after all. He would stay in his *atalaya* in spite of his arch-enemy, the humidity in the valley, the spiders and scorpions, and—he now felt that he could not part with the piece of family furniture; someone had found his father's final poison inside it. Would we be angry at him? Now that we had seen the commode for ourselves, surely we could understand his misgivings about letting go of it.

"Seen for ourselves?" asked Beatrice. "But we haven't seen your chest yet, Herr von Martersteig. We haven't been in all your rooms." It certainly wasn't in our bedroom.

"Oh Madame, you are too kind. 'How nice'—isn't that what you said when you saw the niche in the entryway, just as we came in? The secret compartment is where my father kept my destiny, the powder he used to bring his brilliant career to an end and to force me into mine. No, I cannot part with that piece as long as my work remains unfinished."

We left the house early the next morning. A few meters above Martersteig's little castle, the road made a dangerous curve where drivers sometimes lost control and ended up in the Captain's front yard. This, too, he seemed prepared to live with for the foreseeable future. Our host stood at the top of the curve like a traffic cop and waved down a truck that was on its way to Palma via Valldemosa.

Our leave-taking was polite. In a single night we had come so close that each party now felt the need to say goodbye as quickly as possible. As we entered the dangerous curve in the road, we saw the castellan's monocle drop to his anemic hand, and then we could see only dust, chickens, jars of oil. We closed our eyes.

The Captain stayed behind. Now he was 1000 meters back, 1001, 1002, it went quickly. The distance grew between us and the chest with its secret drawer that was to contain my meditative poems. The commode had such small dimensions that not even the art of perspective could make it appear any smaller. As far as my own valuables were concerned, a single poem, folded like the little packet containing a dose of poison, might fit inside the secret cubbyhole. Beatrice might have found room in it for a silk kerchief, a single gossamer item of underwear, her good-luck sturgeon scales, a few trinkets. One of the Captain's polar-bear slippers was larger than the inlaid drawer with the lock forged by the Nürnberg master Hans Ehemann.

The day before, during our walk through the town of Deyá, we paid a visit to the Japanese painter Three Little Clouds. I chatted with him about the qualities of light on the island (not those in Deyá), admired his delicate, elfin French girlfriend as much as his diaphanous drawings, and poked around a bit in his studio, very much under the impression of his and his artist companion's similar coiffure: they both wore their hair in bangs, as if they were made for each other. Three Clouds wanted to sketch Beatrice's portrait, and Aimée asked if she could paint my likeness on ivory on the following day. But then came the night with its cup of poison, and so we departed in an ancient Ford, bouncing and shaking amid poultry, rabbits, black piglets and tomatoes. The only work of art we took with us was our lilliput dream commode, *en pensée*.

We didn't see the Captain for years afterward. That is to say, if we met on the street or at the anarchist's rooming house, we looked right through each other. When the wound caused by the monkey business with the armoire finally healed, and we could have made friends again—although we never really became enemies, our neo-Clausewitz experienced a new shock. Robert Graves had learned of our visit for chest inspection, and thus he found out something that was not to be found in Baedeker: that a man named Vigoleis did typing work for pay. So instead of *The Monkey Army* by Joachim von Martersteig, I made a clear typescript, from squiggly handwriting, of *I, Claudius*—a work of the enemy.

Thus we gradually lost sight of our crash-landed friend. But as soon as Germany awoke to the first state-sponsored scansion of the refrain "Germany awake, Judah perish!" and things became very serious for Judah, our Joachim reappeared, and we shook hands in the face of a more powerful enemy, one that was flexing its sinews to leap at us here in our island redoubt. All three of us now castigated the Reich, lamenting how this frightful disgrace was sweeping over everything we held dear—for otherwise, why didn't the spectacle just leave us cold like some massacre among the Botokudes? We felt we must completely swear off this dishonored fatherland, not only with our hearts, but in our deeds. Beatrice and I kept to this oath, right down to the last Brown Shirt menace. After just a few weeks the Captain was tripped up by a mug of German beer and two German sausages. But the details of this baronial Martersteigian monkey-business will have to wait for a later chapter. Let us close the current one with Vigoleis and Beatrice, who are now lying next to each other on their mattress at the Clock Tower. Their eyes are directed upward to the webbing containing their bodily and spiritual bric-a-brac. But their minds are still mired at rock-bottom, near the keel of their ship of life, where the bilgewater collects. Only rats can live there; never, or almost never, a human being.

VI

It never rains but it pours.

On the night when the Captain conjured up his father's chalice of poison; when an item of ancestral Martersteig furniture shrank from a respectable hardwood commode to the miniature dimensions of a jewel box, the kind that gets placed on top of a respectable commode; when we slept in a genuine bed for the first time in ages, but without ever getting to sleep—on that night, all the stars rose in the heavens and the moon did its utmost to save the lord of the *atalaya* the price of a candle.

On the following night we exercised our settlers' rights at the whorehouse, and in the adjoining booths certain fellows feathered their own nests with exemplary gusto.

Around noontime the sky became overcast. The old crone predicted rain, and you didn't need a century's worth of meteorological experience to agree with her. But as evening arrived, the wind from the Teix blew apart the clusters of clouds, and since we had no crops of any kind to harvest anyway, we ignored whatever the heavens had in mind, went to bed, and slept.

One second later—one hour later?—we were awakened by a cannon shot. Great Scott, has Arsenio now decided to roll out Big Bertha? Isn't he satisfied with his U-boat? The report echoed loud and long. A storm hovered over the city. Bolts of lightning illuminated the cathedral vaults, our walls started shaking under some higher power, and all of the stuff above our heads began to oscillate. Now whistling, now with a hollow roar, the storm sped through our books and writings—how we wished we owned a wooden chest for preserving them smooth and clean! As puny and miserable as a human being may feel when the elements decide to break into an uproar, one of those oaken commodes that my grandmother had back at the Scheifes homestead could have given us significant moral support during this riot of inorganic and organic nature. From all of the occupied cells we heard not the great kettledrum of lust, no raunchy Kate groaning for more, no *almocrebe* clicking his tongue. Instead, there were entreaties to the Mother of God, begging her to lend succor against lightning and conflagration. Yet the name most often invoked was that of Saint Barbara, that glorious lady who is listed among the Fourteen Intercessors ever since she performed a miracle ages ago to save the life of a certain Hendrikus Stock in the town of Gorkum in Holland. This is something the local hookers were of course not aware of, but I was informed in no uncertain terms that their Saint Barbara could do more to ward off lightning and fire than the Mother of God Herself.

During the current emergency, and amid deafening salvos of thunder, I was glad to have a cookie from Cell No. 2 tell me just how the Celestial Fire Department worked: who manned the buckets, who stroked the pump, and who wielded the hose. The pious whore knew all about these matters; she didn't hurl a shoe at me when in all the confusion I happened to gaze down on her across the partition. I had to rearrange our ropes, for otherwise the tempest would have scattered all of our carefully stowed possessions all over the cubicle. In a state of semi-undress, the girl was kneeling in prayer at her *pilarière*, her eyes raised to Heaven and thus to me, although I was in no position to perform miracles. Her bull lay asleep on the mattress. Only a direct lightning hit, or a renewed invitation to the dance, could have lifted him out of his snooze. She asked whether my girlfriend wasn't afraid, too, that the world was coming to an end; she wasn't screaming or praying, and we hadn't lit a holy candle. No, I explained, my girlfriend had long since conquered fear. She wasn't much for praying, and anyway, God didn't care much for mockery.

No sooner said, when a bolt of lightning hit the barn. I tumbled back off the chair on top of Beatrice, a loud peal of thunder rocked the Manse, the rafters shook, and piercing screams went up all around us: the Torre is on fire! The place smelled of sulfur and the cheap laundry bleach "Legia," the scourge of all foreigners who cannot afford new clothes every six months. Underneath me Beatrice was trembling from head to toe, and I myself was trembling under the mess of our belongings that this celestial knockout punch had sent down on me with our network of ropes. For a split-second that seemed like an eternity, all was quiet. And then the clouds split apart. Rain splashed on the roof. Nuns and monks started dancing.

If this were a novel and I its author, I would now introduce the *filles de joie* one by one and have them tear each other's hair out over the question of who was responsible for seizing that lightning bolt and, in the very last fraction of a micro-second, flinging it outside the barn at the carob tree—was it Saint Barbara or Our Lady of the Pillar? *O Santo da porta não faz milagres*, says a Portuguese proverb: the household patron saint doesn't perform miracles. In this barracks of sin there was no shrine to Saint Barbara, and thus it was she who had prevented the disaster. The Tower was not consumed by flames, although the carob tree was now two carob trees.

Nevertheless, this meant an end to love-making. This, too, makes my jottings different from a novel, where the writer would show his little couple sauntering across some field or, in a higher-class plot, have them mounted on horseback, both of them filled with glowing ardor and quivering emotion. Then with a swift change of mood the author would make a storm appear. At the first big raindrops he would have the two of them head for the nearest haystack. The heavens would open and pour down oceans of water, a second Great Flood. But our two heroes would remain neither soaked nor satiated; they would make love endlessly, as if there were no such thing as hay since Adam and Eve... Unfortunately, I can't depict such a scene for my own little couples, because there are too many of them, and I wouldn't know where to put them. Outside it's pouring cats and dogs, and inside the barn too. Even if the nuns and monks had allowed all the stars and planets to enter the Manse, they would have been powerless against the waters. The water level was rising in the cells. *Sauve qui peut*! *Après nous le déluge*!

The electric wires shorted out. I lit candles—not holy candles, but working candles: man the pumps!

Deploying our raincoats and Beatrice's miraculous Unkulunkulu, I was able to divert the torrents; at least we were now protected from the worst inundations. All around us was chaos. My poems, my great prose, my published renderings of other people's writings, our sugar, our sprig of vanilla—all this had now turned into a soggy, dripping, watery mess. The sole survivor of this catastrophe was a little spray of domestic parsley that Beatrice hung on the ropes to ward off vermin; it devoured the moisture, turned greener than green, and emitted a delightful fragrance as in the month of March.

I spent the rest of the night squatting like a hen on my typewriter, trying to protect it from the liquid elements. Beatrice cowered under her exotic umbrella, fast asleep. The outcome of this cloudburst in our palace of God-fearing lechery was bound to be either renewed suicide or a double case of pneumonia.

As dawn arrived at our hovel, I made a firm decision: we must leave this place. Out of this pigsty! Away, as fast as possible!

My reader will be thinking: who is he to be making decisions? He's quick to find words, but just where does he think they can go, Vigoleis and his girl, seeing that he doesn't even have money enough to take a trolley to the terminus of his own life, not to mention the train fare to Deyá to negotiate for a commode? Another reader will recall his mother always telling him that moving three times is just as expensive as having your house burn to the ground. Yet another reader, a classically educated one, will start murmuring, "Oh," or rather "*Evoe! Plus salis quam sumptus habebat.*" Be that as it may, my dear reader, we would simply have to leave this water mill.

"Beatrice, *chérie*, Bice, Bé," I said, as it began raining underneath the Kaffir god, "my dear, unlike the feathered fauna, we lack a preen gland with which to oil our beaks and then smear each and every feather until we are as waterproof as a burkha. I've been thinking. While you were asleep I went deeply into my soul, and have returned with certain insights. During our very first night here, when the tempests of human lust raged all around us, we decided to go jump in the sea holding hands. But the ocean depths rejected us. Now that the waters are threatening us from above, don't you agree that our neighbors' libidinous yawpings are more endurable?? Or should we go kill ourselves again? The mysterious Heraclitus once said, *panta rhei*, everything is in flux, you can't step twice into the same river. I invite you to join me in pondering this matter. Do you think that the Captain still has a tiny bit of his old man's anniversary poison left over? Somebody ought to take that secret compartment and bang out all of its contents. Or wasn't it perhaps an act of Divine Providence that we were cheated out of the chest? Under the present circumstances, a chameleon would start evolving gills. But unfortunately we're not that kind of lizard. Nevertheless, I sense a miracle in the offing!"

Beatrice wasn't interested in developing gills, or in putting a noose around her neck, or in poison. And unlike the flounder, she rejected the idea of a moveable eye in order to face misery from only one side of her head. In a word, she didn't want to take her own life again, and this meant that I had to preserve mine to remain with her. This was Point Number One of our watery breakfast chat. Point Number Two emerged, and ended, in a single word. "Antonio!" we cried out as if with one voice. How could we have forgotten that good man for so long?

Antonio said that now that the rainy period has arrived, earlier than usual (honestly), we could no longer remain at the Torre. The barn would get cold and drafty, Arsenio wouldn't have the roof repaired—"Tell us about it," I thought to myself—and so it was time that we looked elsewhere for lodgings. So our camping days were over! Antonio advised us to rent a small unfurnished apartment. We could scour up some furniture somewhere, time would tell. In a country where time has no meaning, this was a somewhat risky proposition—but the water was rising. Don Vigo would have to go looking, upstreet and downstreet; vacant *pisos* were always indicated by a piece of white paper in the window or tied to the balcony. Then he would enter and start asking about how many rooms, whether there was running water—but we already knew about such things. It was no doubt the same in other countries. I assured Antonio that it was no different than in Holland—and started thinking about Madame Perronet, a long staircase, a ship captain in loden coat and floppy hat, a girl's corpse...

The *Encyclopedic Dictionary* of Wilhelm Traugott Krug offers information about more things than a normal human being needs to know, in order, consonant with a very broadly conceived *polypragmosyne* (check it out in Krug), to reach the end of his days. Yet this superb reference work contains no advice whatsoever concerning how one should conduct a search for a *piso*—either systematically or by violating all rules of civility. This is probably the case because both methods are subject to happenstance—not an appealing matter for Krug, who was a genuine philosopher. Nonetheless, following Beatrice's suggestion I scoured the entire city of Palma, carrying a map and a street index, checking off each street, alley, bridge, square, and so-called island as I investigated it. There was no dearth of white paper in windows and on balconies. The city was undergoing a building boom. The island was flourishing. It was bustling with activity that was already beginning to concentrate in the capital, and it was expected that the island's population would double in the next 30 years. Here as elsewhere, human reproduction was largely an arbitrary matter, but this technique can also fill the world systematically with new progenitors. Besides, the Spaniard loves to change his whitewashed walls frequently. Moving his household will give him, it is true, the same whitewashed walls as before, but in different dimensions and with new neighbors and new excitements. He loves the street, not cozy togetherness at home and hearth. He loves his club and the bordello. The women can be depended on to frequent the church.

My Spanish had improved to the point where I could haggle without difficulty. I climbed upstairs and downstairs from morning to night. Many apartments in many sections of the city stood empty; I stuck my nose into all of them and cringed at the prices, but without anyone noticing my horror. No, I said, this was too large—just the wife, no kids and only two maids, one of whom slept at home. How charming, I said, a poem, a little gingerbread house, but unfortunately too small—seven kids, the eighth on its way, three maids, a cook, and we were expecting the in-laws from Paris soon. My family situation became more and more complicated. During this search I got to know my Vigoleis truly well for the first time. My profession changed with the changing circumstances. And it occurred that by mistake I looked at the same apartment twice, telling the landlady a different story each time—"What? Last week I had three kids and now I have seven? Well, yes, four from my first marriage that I had asked to join us"—and I was gone. Once I was confronted by the house-owner himself and subjected to a cross-examination. He asked me one question after another, each one more compromising than the last, and finally I sensed that he actually knew us—which was true. He demanded the gospel truth, he was in the know, I was the pimp for some *puta* out there, what I wanted was to drag his house down in the dirt, he knew all of us including Don Helvecio of the Príncipe— but perhaps we could make a deal: 1250 pesetas a month, 3 months in advance, *hay que ser hombre!* If something is very expensive, the Spaniard says it will cost him *el ojo de la cara*—the eye in his head. For me at the time, the cheapest apartment was so pricey that I would have had to toss down both of my eyes.

Weeks later I finally located an apartment in the Old City. I encountered only cats and nuns. The apartment was just right for us, and not too expensive—I would have lost one eye and closed the other. The owner was a pleasant fellow, a book printer, and his workshop was in the same house. I figured that we might collaborate, since he always had proofreading to get done. I rented the flat with a handshake and sprinted out into the darkening street. The cats scurried away and the nuns blessed themselves. A thief? An adulterer? Before they could recover, I was back at the Clock Tower fetching our passports for the rental contract. When the printer saw our documents, he hesitated. Was the Madame my wife or my "relationship"? Since she was neither the one nor the other, and since I couldn't conjure up the appropriate term in any language, I responded to the severe glance of the man's pince-nez by saying that Doña Beatriz was my wife. "Legal?" "No." "So?" "Yes."

A man, he said, could have as many lovers or mistresses as he wanted. But a woman must be married. I could move in any time at all with my *querida*, but with a doubtful wife—he must have consideration for his own spouse, the neighbors, and his Catholic printing house.

So once again I missed the boat. It was too late to explain to this moralist that my wife was my *querida*, my doxy, my hooker, my concubine and my Pilar, tell him that we were coming straight from the Clock Tower slut hut, and ask him where I might continue my search. Too late; I was shown the door. The owner wanted things above-board.

Once again I ran myself and my heels ragged for weeks without finding anything acceptable. But then one morning Lady Luck smiled at me. I am not superstitious, but if at the crack of dawn a rat with a white tail runs over your body, it can only mean good luck. I found a *piso* that seemed just perfect for our morganatic bond. The landlady was friendly with me. I was friendly with her. The apartment was newly whitewashed, making it look like friendliness itself, so I said I would rent it then and there, but—I would quickly return with my wife to show it to her. As soon as the landlady saw Beatrice, she made the sign of the cross and slammed the door in our faces. A neighbor who had been watching came forward with the explanation: that lady in there was a *beata*, a bigoted witch who was always telling lies. To the landlady, my companion's short hair was the Devil in person. The Church forbade mannish haircuts. Pious women had often blessed themselves when they saw in Beatrice an emissary from Hell. Everyone has his or her own ideas about the celestial and the infernal Beyond and its denizens. As for myself, I cannot claim to be able to distinguish an angel from a devil. That's why I never slam doors in people's faces. That is my undoing.

In the earliest movies, where it was always raining and the actors went through their mute and jerky paces as if in constant fear of themselves, the passage of non-filmworthy time was indicated by a placard saying, "Years later..." Heart-rending music underscored this rapid flow of time. One saw clouds drifting past, the snow melted off the garden gate, the trees came into blossom, a newborn lamb skipped into the world. And then, suddenly, the rejected lover made his reappearance. In the meantime he had bumped off his rival and made a bundle in the States, while his girl had gone off with somebody else. The dance could continue.

Our existence on the island, likewise eternally rained in, eventually reached a point where I could say, "Weeks later..." Three or more dots can indicate the occurrence of nothing much at all. Beatrice gave language lessons, and we made up with the hotel owner Doña María; the Captain's armoire joined Don Antonio's hotel-room wardrobe on the junk pile of furniture we got cheated out of—the Fates that rocked our cradles just didn't include these items in their list of goods we would obtain on earth, and to this day we have got along without them. Over and over again I took my *Sitzfleisch* for long walks through the city, with casual stride but acutely observant like a policeman on his beat, constantly on the lookout for anything resembling a white piece of paper. Palma was abuzz with moving vans. I knocked on many doors. I learned a good deal about municipal architecture, and like the gas man, I poked my nose in countless households. And found nothing. Oh, Unku-lunkulu, Thou god of the shiny-skinned Kaffirs, Thou shelterest my Beatrice from the rain, but when wilt Thou perform a miracle for me? I beseech Thee, lead me on the right path, one, two, three flights upstairs...!

During the hours when I squatted in our cell, I wrote reams of airy stuff, finding my subject-matter mostly somewhere beyond the clouds. But can a true poet ever let a cloud bank cheat him of his creativity? Too precious for putting on paper, too lousy to get published—"So he'll be a cobbler," my father used to say, and if I had taken his advice, I wouldn't be sitting in a brothel. I would long since have sewn up enough shekels for an armoire and a wardrobe with built-in mirror. One publisher to whom I sent a set of stories wrote me a cordial, encouraging letter: not quite what he needed, but he would bear me in mind as I kept him informed concerning my "growth" as a writer. I did no such thing, of course, but I kept on applying fertilizer to my little plant. Lord knows my life provided me with plenty of manure.

Three times a week Beatrice went to the Suredas' house, where she got to know the whole clan. Papá, she said, seemed to be even crazier than Pedro. It was now time that I, too, made their acquaintance. Yet as far as craziness was concerned, I had best put my own house in order, which I proceeded to do.

With a clear conscience I could pass through all of the streets of Palma with one exception, a place I just mustn't dare to go. Every person has a dark spot in his past, and I was no different. My dark spot had the name Villalonga, and the street where the man lived, the one I had to avoid, was the Calle del General Barceló, just a few steps past the anarchist's palace. Dr. Villalonga was one of those specialists for anatomical cavities who, if he's treating you, can cause the cessation of hearing and sight. I owed him money. The dust on the island had stopped up my ears; I was deaf. Don Alonso recommended the doctor just around the corner. The treatment was exemplary. Back in Cologne not even the Professor of Otolaryngology had squished out my ears as elegantly as this fellow. His fee was a mere 10 pesetas. I intended to pay up without delay, but was asked to come for a follow-up in two weeks' time. Dr. Villalonga had studied medicine in Germany; he was fond of digging up memories, and told me the names of his old professors. I still remember one unusual clinical case he mentioned: a soldier had been shot straight through the head, and the professor had patched him up successfully; whatever was said to that man afterwards went in one ear and out the other.

By the time my two weeks were up, Beatrice and I were on our grape diet, and I was unable to pay my bill. Like Zwingli, I now avoided the street where I had no business being anyway. Then came the period when I wandered the streets looking for white sheets of paper. I didn't dare to enter General Barceló, for fear that I might meet up with the doctor. For me and my strategy, the city map of Palma was reduced in size by one street.

There are writers who use many words to say little, others who say much with few words, and still others, rare ones, who can say everything with a single word. Let the reader decide to which category Vigoleis belongs, for I am unable to decide for myself. One thing about me is clear, however: I shall never inscribe this single word. I prefer to circumscribe it, paraphrase it. That's why I have constantly altered my mode of expression when describing the brothel, since what I have tried to express was, once we got accustomed to the variety of tones emitted inside its shaky walls, so mind-numbingly monotonous.

I have employed a host of synonyms to designate our accommodations at the lecherous bandits' redoubt. In private, Beatrice and I referred to it for a while as the goat pen, after a billy-goat one day leaped up the open staircase, and on his second jump landed right in our cell, causing such havoc that even I, old apocalyptic pessimist that I am, started weeping copiously. Perhaps "hellhole" is the proper term, but it never occurred to me—or perhaps I have simply avoided naming our misery in such radically precise fashion. Yet now that our lodgings were no longer waterproof, now that the rats patrolled the partitions more brazenly from day to day, now that the moisture drove gout into our entire bodies, now that the storms raged and Beatrice arrived at such a slough of despond that she spent an hour every day in tears beneath her Unkulunkulu, threatening to manifest a malignant form of hispanophobia, whereas by rights she ought to have burst forth with the symptoms of acute Vigolophobia—amid all of this, I suddenly called to mind my little friend from the Street of Solitude: Julietta, I thought in a mood of inward jubilation, child of a general who brought you such joy when you were a little child—why shouldn't Vigoleis, too, place his final bet on red trouser stripes and stars on his *guerrera*? What's sauce for the goose is sauce for the gander.

Without mentioning my audacious plan to Beatrice, I betook myself with the courage of her despair to the street I had so long been avoiding, one that was so short, narrow, and shady that it doesn't offer many possibilities for increasing my reader's suspense—what's in store for Vigoleis this time? Will brigands descend upon him and beat him to death, poke into his empty pockets and leave him to be taken to his grave on donkey-back? Will a mule kick backwards and shatter his kneecap? Will women of loose virtue seduce him to a *pilarière* and filch his last peseta? Or will the Fates put Dr. Villalonga in their employ and have him scream at him, "Finally, my little friend! Now I've got you! Out with those two duros, or else I'll strap you to my chair and yank your forgetful brain right through your natural orifices, just the way they do it with mummies!"

Nothing of such a highly dramatic sort happened. A few nuns passed by me with lowered glances. Black-clad priests are said to bring bad luck, but nuns...? Hardly had I taken fifty paces into this danger zone when my courage found its reward. A yellowed sheet of paper was fluttering on a balcony. I was startled, but took hold of myself and entered the first-floor hallway. It smelled of fish and very small people, but not of whoresflesh. One minute later I had the key to the apartment and unlocked the *piso*. Two studios faced the sunless street. There was a long corridor with two sizeable rooms adjoining, and then a large room with a French door that opened on a spacious yard. What met my eye was an expanse of palm, cedar, orange, lemon, banana, and almond, whatever flora one might hope to find in a semi-tropical environment, an oasis in the urban canyon. There was a narrow passageway leading to small pantry space, and even a well with a bucket for hauling up the water. The kitchen featured a built-in cast-iron stove and two charcoal grills, plus running water. Finally there was another room with windows looking out on the yard, like all the windows in this part of the house. Seventy pesetas a month was the price for these sumptuous lodgings; the owner himself lived in the same building, the garden of delights was his property also, and his wife, who had followed me during my survey of the premises, pointed out the patio where at the moment a few girls were having a quarrel—these were the privileged daughters of the landlord who would be accepting our rental payments.

I neither walked nor ran back to the Clock Tower—I flew. Seven rooms at 10 pesetas apiece, one room larger than the next, each room with its own ceiling, polished floors, running water, a well, an Eden of palms, and in the leafy shade, classic golden oranges, everything that had incited Goethe's yearning for the South and lent him immortality: "Thither, thither will I go with thee, my beloved!" The sight of all this lent me wings.

"Beatrice, 7 rooms, 10 pesetas apiece, a ceiling and a roof, my darling! On the most taboo street in all Palma, the General Barceló, where Dr. Villalonga rinses out people's ears—you know, in one ear, out the other—just a few doors down, nuns and monks live there, the street was black with them, and I am no longer a cowardly toad. Now if I were a pelican, I would make the legend come true: I would tear open my breast and feed my brood with my own blood!"

Beatrice stared at me. She is not afraid of spiders, whom she counts among her allies, but she cowers in the presence of madmen. Had I gone crazy? Had something happened to me? Disappointing mail?

Quick, put on dry clothes. We were going to leave our aquarium, and I would show her a terrarium. And besides, I was more sober than usual, but also more elated.

When just a few hours later I again unlocked the *piso* to show it to Beatrice, the rooms had become noticeably smaller. The studios were nowhere to be seen, the two rooms adjoining the long corridor turned out to be tiny, windowless boudoirs like the "General's Room" on the Street of Solitude, and the other rooms could be measured with just a few paces. As for the ceilings, they had in fact remained in place, but were now considerably lower—you could forget about doing a pole vault inside the *piso*, though you might try a somersault. Still, in the yard nothing had changed; the display of blossoms had not withered, the well had not gone dry. On the contrary, Beatrice discovered there some greenhouse rarities and other botanical wonders whose names I had never heard of. Nevertheless—

"70 pesetas, *chérie*. We've got to have the pesetas. It's a matter of life or death."

I rarely invoke the names of the Saints, but Beatrice's sobering reply brought from me this joyful outburst: "Holy Saint Barlaam, have mercy on my poor, wretched soul!" Beatrice had kept some savings!!! Three exclamation marks, one per each 10 pesetas.

"But Unkulunkula, how on earth did you do it? Did you have that much when we were about to plunge into the ocean? I wouldn't put it past you!"

The expenses that arose from our suicide would have to be covered by the sale of our combined belongings, for it was not until the night of the tempest at the Tower that Beatrice decided to scrape little coins together. Having no head for figures smaller than those with six zeroes, I of course hadn't the slightest idea that at certain times we could have afforded one more drop of oil in our saucepan, or one more postage stamp for my intellectual commerce with the outside world.

While Beatrice exercised squatter's rights in the empty apartment, I sought out the landlord, whose name could easily have caused the superstitious Beatrice to change her mind about renting the place at the last minute. His name was Aguado, which means "filled with water." As I have said, it never rains but it pours.

One after the other, maids led me from the entryway down several corridors and through several hallways to a family room, where I was presented to a short gentleman. He was in the presence of his pretty daughters, who by now had quieted down. His wife was also there, together with a number of other women, all of them relatives—twelve souls all told, and I made bows to every last one of them.

Don Jaime asked a few polite questions. His French was as fluent as water; he was an educated man, and expressed particular interest in that part of my person that did the writing. His grandfather, he explained, was a writer, and one of his daughters wrote poems—probably the one who was now blushing as I glanced with interest around the circle of females. He was a great lover of literature. Then he asked to see our passports. He made no embarrassing inquiries, perhaps out of consideration for the daughters standing next to him, or perhaps because his penchant for literature elevated him above bourgeois prejudice. The official stamps of our respective consulates were sufficient for him. We were welcome as tenants. And then came the great moment, the most momentous moment of this thrill-packed story: Don Jaime asked one of his beautiful relatives to calculate how much I should pay in advance, until the beginning of the next month, when we could start regular payments. It seemed just fine to him: he would draft a rental contract starting next January 1st. Did we intend to move in before Christmas?

Christmas. We were three days away from the Birth of Our Redeemer, 9 days away from the end of the month... Out of Beatrice's stocking I pulled forth 22 pesetas and 50 centimos and was presented with a receipt signed with a Spanish flourish. A maid again accompanied me through hallways, corridors, and piles of rubbish to the majestic portal. My mood was so bouyant that I could have kissed her. One kiss for each peseta saved? That would have meant 57.5 kisses.

I gave Beatrice several of them, twice over. It was only the matter of the remaining pesetas that made her lose her composure. She was quite aware that Christmas was just around the corner. That, she said, was something she wanted to keep quiet about, so as not to make me go into a fit of melancholy. She knew that this could easily happen with Germans when they are off in foreign lands. "And how is it with Swiss citizens who have Inca blood," I asked, but there was no reply. Landlords often make mistakes in arithmetic. But this time, the addition was correct to the last centimo: twenty-two fifty.

VII

Now that we had become bonafide residents on a street in town, we felt that we must carry ourselves with heads held high, in keeping with the street's heroic name: Calle del General Barceló. For this reason I took 10 pesetas out of Beatrice's knitted strongbox and ambled ten doors down to the office of Dr. Villalonga, who greeted me wearing his Cyclopsian head mirror.

"*Olá!*" he said. "My German friend! I've been expecting you for a long time, but..."

I blushed and stammered some mendacious story about illness, an urgent trip to Barcelona. The doctor took no notice of my excuses. He handed me a picture postcard and asked me if I was familiar with Düsseldorf, and if I knew a certain intersection of the Graf-Adolf-Strasse and a certain house there. The house was illustrated on the postcard, one of a thousand street-corner houses in Düsseldorf. Without any doubt I had seen this one dozens of times, and I told him so. It was a stately house indeed, and so I quickly invented a story that included, of course, the Bank of Barmen and a street urchin somersaulting on the Königsallee. With a gesture of relief, Dr. Villalonga thanked me. Then he asked me to translate for him the German message on the card. He knew the language but wanted to be sure, since it was a matter of nuances. The card was from a woman. My *ipsis verbis* professional translation of the text seemed satisfactory. The upshot was that something was afoot, or at least had been afoot at one time, between the sender and the addressee. The doctor put the postcard back in his pocket. Then I reached into my own pocket and begged his pardon for the delay. My duros landed on his glass tabletop with the sound of genuine cash. "Ten pesetas?"

Dr. Villalonga could not recall that I owed him any money, and money that he couldn't recall was not money that he could accept. Be that as it may, the information I had given him was worth more than the two duros that I should put right back in my pocket. Then he quickly pushed a funnel into my ears—all clear. I was well acclimated, but whenever I needed a rinsing out, I was to come visit him! Yes, I said, that was now a simple matter. We were now neighbors, just across the street. In keeping with Spanish custom, I offered to welcome him in my house. He offered to welcome me in his, and each of us stayed where we belonged.   ·

On the very same day postcards and letters got sent out into the world with our new, firm, unalterable address: Calle del General Barceló 23, for anyone who wanted to visit us. Our post-office box number remained the same: *Apartado* 112. The postage for all these missives reduced our savings to zero.

Both Julietta and Vigoleis can tell tales about generals who offer aid in emergencies. Julietta told such tales on the public streets. Vigoleis, less impulsive than she, prefers to confine his tales to the pages of his personal jottings.

What a swashbuckler he must have been, this Sixteenth Intercessor with the rank of a general!

After leaving the post office, we went to the Veda Club to inform Antonio of our impending relocation. He was standing on the terrace, waving his napkin. "Good news!" I called up to him, and asked him whether he had a minute. In Spain one always has a minute. Everything gets postponed to the following day, including whatever got postponed the day before. *Mañana*, "tomorrow,"

is the first Spanish joke learned by every foreigner. Zwingli's successes in this country were in part the result of this *mañana*; he was always wishing that he had done yesterday what he was doing today, and so he was constantly ahead of the natives by one day. Women were his undoing, because in bed they were conscious only of today. Thus this Man of Yesterday experienced failure after failure, until he had no Tomorrow at all.

Antonio listened to our story. He showed no understanding for Dr. Villa-longa's satanic 10 pesetas, my reason for refusing to enter Barceló during my search. The apartment had stood empty for months. Antonio wasn't thinking about Providential intercession; he was thinking about furniture.

Beatrice has a memory that never loses sight of even the most immediate matters. Our couch, the one with the woolen mattress and its cool horsehair lining, our *pilarière*! Pilar would have to hand over our furniture, which had escaped my memory entirely. Beatrice was simply not prepared to forfeit our bed, our bookcase, our laundry, 7 clothes hangers, 1 sugar bowl, 1 darning egg, 9 safety pins, 1 comb, 1 pair of shoes, 1 writing pad—all these items were inscribed in gold in the network of her brain. She would forfeit nothing to "that woman"—her use of this term, which can otherwise be suggestive of dignity, turned it into the epitome of disdain and degradation. The person so designated became a specimen of vermin, a maggot, the dregs of humanity. Fine, this bird would have to hand everything back to us. But how? Burglary? Antonio's gang could take care of that with a one-time operation.

But Beatrice wasn't for violent action. She asked Antonio to send one of his pageboys from the Veda to her brother's house and have Zwingli reclaim our belongings. She had spent thousands for Zwingli, and even now, if a late-coming creditor were to make an appearance demanding repayment, she would readily take care of it. But as for that "woman"—she insisted on getting back everything down to the last safety pin.

Antonio shook his head. Everything had changed in the meantime. Don Helvecio no longer lived in the *piso* around the corner. He and his wife and child were among the missing. No one had seen them for weeks. An inquiry at the post office yielded the information that for quite a long time no missiles had landed there and no screams of fury had been heard from across the street. The concierge was queried, and he called the police. A small crowd of gendarmes gathered at the apartment door and gave the secret knocking signal: no answer. They were presumably all dead. Groups of curious onlookers formed on the Street of Solutide. All of them dead! A cry of "bloody deed!" spread like wildfire in the Count's "apple." Barricades. The apartment door was kicked open and the homicide squad entered the Pilarian love nest, taking professional care not to disturb evidence. But there were no corpses to stumble over, no puddles of blood to step in, no dangling bodies to bump into, and Julietta was not discovered in the laundry basket with a gag in her mouth. No trace of a final communication, no greeting to dear ones on the island, or in Basel and environs. No last will and testament containing Vigoleis' name as heir to a collection of works in the history of art, the manuscript of the Lexicon of Invective, or the coveted Swiss army knife. Instead, the floor was filthy; wherever the murder specialists stepped there was a mess. They lifted finger-prints from all the doorknobs, but where were the matching fingers?

The tenants had flown the coop; as in a case of loss of hair, all that was left were bare spots. The *hermandad* was confronted with a mystery. Zwingli told us later how he had arranged the whole thing, but I shall refrain at this point from inserting details of that nocturnal escapade. We ourselves must concentrate on a relocation that will have to take place in broad daylight—one that turned out to be a little triumphal procession.

Antonio contacted the Príncipe, where the Swiss panjandrum was likewise regarded as disappeared and already struck from the list of missing persons. The message Antonio got was to the effect that Don Helvecio was welcome to stew in his own juice wherever he was. In a normal situation, of course, things happen in quite the reverse fashion: the person departing the scene leaves word for those who remain behind. But when it comes to womanizing, the Spaniards display an amazing degree of solidarity. They do their whoring hand in hand, and never rub the other guy the wrong way.

The next day, Antonio found out where the *pilarière* was located. A little later a messenger came to us with the news that Doña Beatriz'mattress was already on its way to our new apartment, balancing on the skull of a street loiterer. The *señora* had, however, not been willing to part with bed linen, pillows, the darning egg, the comb, etc. Antonio, the psychological anthropologist, advised the one woman to refrain from provoking the other. In good time we would have everything back. *Mañana.*

I then went to the customs warehouse, where I obtained the release of three of our crates of books, under the proviso that the rest of our belongings would remain there as surety.

The thieving couple at the Tower was saddened to learn that we were going to leave our cell the very next day. This calls for a celebration, said Arsenio, and asked us to attend a party to which Antonio would also be invited.

We had leg of lamb *à la mode bisaïuele*, plus two dozen other dishes, including donkey cheese for Beatrice. There were toasts to our prosperity on the Street of the General, as well as to the well-being of the Tower and all it stood for. After midnight we were joined by the sea captain, who had a drink with us and then quickly disappeared. Whenever this underwater smuggler was at the Manse you could be certain that some important job or other was being pulled. But this time his haste was due to the babe who was waiting for him on the bed of luxury. He was getting signals to dive.

No sooner had he left when Arsenio came forth with a question that had been on the tip of his tongue for a long while. I was finally to come clean, no more secrets, no further need to hide anything from each other. I knew very well what he was up to, and why the *carabineros* always kept an eye on him. But, by all the Saints, he hadn't any idea what my game was. What Antonio had told him about Pilar—whom he knew, by the way—could well be true, but he thought that this story was a feeble kind of make-believe. "So now, out

with it, Don Vigo! Who are you, and what kind of a double life are you leading at my place, in the city, on the island?"

I told him the truth. But that isn't what he wanted to hear. Anybody, he
said, can make up nice stories. He was hurt; it was a matter of confidence for
confidence. "Go on now, don't leave me hanging. Or do you want me to tell
you who you are and what you are up to here on my family estate?"

"By all means, go ahead and tell me."

The Giant sipped his piping-hot coffee and enlightened me concerning my
Balearic mission.

Unlike his boss, he was not illiterate, although he had not read a book in
his entire life. But he knew that there were such things as books, and such
things as people who wrote them. His security department had investigated
my case, and here was the result: I was a writer, I had never denied it, and one
look inside our cell was enough to confirm the nature of my profession—by
reading the clothes hanging on the line, as it were. There were well-known
cases of people who wrote books and who took jobs as waiters or cabin-boys,
as grape-pickers, or in the Foreign Legion, or anywhere at all, and then acted
as buddies just so they could collect material for their work. It was no doubt
my intention to write a Spanish novel of manners, and that's why I decided to
move in at his place of business. A Spanish writer would do the same thing in
Germany, but with this difference: he would leave his wife back home. He
laughed, we laughed too, and then he continued: now I was finished collecting
material, tomorrow I would load all our stuff on a wagon, his wagon—"No,
no, that's fine with me, it's a question of honor"—and then I would start writing my novel in our new lodgings. "But please, caballero, not one line about
me as long as I am still alive!"

We toasted Vigoleis' novel, the *Clock Tower Cadaver Murders*, a few soggy,
rain-smeared chapters of which hung on the line as we spoke. Before I sent
them off to the publishers, I would have to squeeze them through the wringer.
Prost!

By naming Arsenio's name in these pages twenty years later, I am not breaking my promise to him, for the robber chieftain was eliminated in the first few
days of the Civil War. His death must have been dreadful; I have heard several
versions of how it happened. He was not even given time to escape in his U-
boat. Which is to say, his ship-captain friend decided to return to snorkeling
for Germany.

We allowed ourselves a few hours sleep, and then we began dismantling our
hovel. I untied the ropes and carefully pulled each nail out of the wall, placing
all of them, straight or crooked, in my pocket. I also took along the boards and
fence pickets that I had found on the grounds of the Manse. I regarded them as
my own property on the basis of the right of salvage, whereas previously they
only fell under beachcomber's rights, unqualified by any whore's notions of pri-

vate ownership. I was touched with melancholy as I took apart our universal bidet. Where would my inspiration come from in the future? While packing our books, I started leafing through familiar works that were always the source of new discoveries. But Beatrice, who can spend whole days packing books, urged me to make it a rush job—no time for that now, on Barceló there would be so much to set up. "And besides, tonight is Christmas Eve!"

Christmas Eve—and the trees are in blossom.

A hired hand loaded the wagon. We took leave of one and all, large and small. The crone wiped a tear as she turned a fish on the spit in the acrid smoke; she was the only one who probably never had a single thought as to what we might be doing there at the Manse. For her we were just there, friendly foreigners who never got in the way, never betrayed her boss to the police, never tried to blackmail him. Like the rats and the hookers, indeed like herself, we were simply part of the household, with no apparent purpose except to turn the spit. Why does any given tree stand in the landscape here rather than over there? One just accepts it like Nature herself; one doesn't puzzle over it. Whoever tries to will go insane, and most people would rather not. Only when the tree is cut down do we notice that it is missing, and often not even then. The cloven carob tree—to which, incidentally, my Notice to the Reader at the beginning of this book does not refer—was soon dug up by Arsenio, and no one seemed to mind. The bandit had designed another kind of tree for the guys who manned his catapults.

Adeleide returned a few pesetas to us as overpaid rental—a little gift that made us beam with pleasure. The boss hitched his shaggy draft horse to the wagon. We took our seats in the quaint coach, and *Tschüss* and *Ciao*, Palace of the Whores! People waved and shouted, dogs barked, maids came by and bared their teeth in merriment, children turned somersaults. The century-old matron picked up her chair and limped out to the highway to see us off. A brood of black piglets scurried off across the field with people chasing after them. Dust, and more dust, behind which the "Clock Tower" then disappeared.

Now cross your heart, Beatrice: you were ready to blow up the whole Tower any day when the rain came down on our cot through the canvas and your Unkulunkulu, when the moisture gave us bone cramps, when mold started growing between the typewriter keys, and when your Parisian hat started growing a beard where the fashion designer never would have put one. And when the big bat got caught in our hanging library, to your great shock, and contrary to all the textbooks of zoology that say that a bat is incapable of making such a mistake, you were ready to jump out of your own skin—but you stayed in it. Admit it: it was nice there after all, and we led a peaceful domestic life there beneath the nuns and the monks.

How quickly all the misery can disappear, how easily an ordeal can peel away when you have a goal in sight and a work horse in harness in front of you. Arsenio clicked his tongue louder than a whip. The hooves sped on; sparks flew.

Our arrival on the General's street caused no little commotion. Word had got around that a foreign couple was moving into the empty apartment. If the street hadn't been so narrow, the neighbors would have lined up on both sides to greet us. So they stood in a cluster of curiosity on the convent patio across the street and observed each piece of the action with such attention that we felt quite flattered. This time we drove up to an apartment without a *palefrenier* in tow, but Arsenio made an even bigger impression. Turkeys were gobbling away on all the balconies, as if to celebrate our arrival.

But hold on, *cher* Vigoleis, we are not interested in how, step by step and hoist by hoist, your belongings got lifted off your prairie wagon and taken inside your new *piso*. Or how an old granny came up to you and told you that you would find a bed in the entryway that was meant for the new tenants since she didn't know what to do with it otherwise. Some other time you can tell us how the old lady's husband introduced himself as fellow tenant and professional custodian; he claimed to be well over ninety but still on the job as gatekeeper over at the convent. Who would have thought this of the wizened old gent? At twelve, as the little bell sounded at the convent, the street suddenly emptied. Not one soul was interested any longer in the German writer who was arriving with a cart full of stuff and a brain full of ideas, waiting for the time when he could sit down at his typewriter and set to work creating his *pilariario íntimo*. But now, you clever scoundrel, perhaps you could at least tell us what you said in reply to Arsenio's question, "What about your furniture?" "Our furniture, Señor Arsenio, is at the customs warehouse. I hope that we can fit it all in, because the rooms are smaller than they looked when I first inspected them. It's Swiss furniture, by the way, a small fortune in freight, insurance, packing, and customs! If we had got to know you sooner, we could have brought it all on land the back way. Your ship captain could have torpedoed our furniture piece by piece onto the beach into specially constructed padded docks."

For days and weeks prior to the birth of the Redeemer, households are oddly busy preparing elaborate celebrations of this feast of the poorest of the poor. We had to compress all this work into just a few hours, for that's all the time we had between arrival in our new digs and the moment when the little bell under the Christmas tree would signal the sharing of presents. A pair of pants, a shirt, and some underthings were deployed as dustcloths and scrubbing rags. I skated across the black-and-white square floor tiles and gave them such a glossy sheen that the Christ Child Himself, if He had dropped down from Heaven again, could have seen his mirror image in them. But since He had his own experiences in a stable with oxen and donkeys and a crib of straw, He studiously avoids the hovels of the destitute and prefers houses that have Persian carpets on the floor. Beatrice cleaned the kitchen, which was redolent of the previous tenants' cooking habits. We didn't have any incense, but used orange peels for the same purpose. I roasted them over a manuscript that was ripe for immolation. Then I arranged things in our bedroom. A couple of hoists and snatches, and the job was done. Two more heaves in the roomy sala with its view of the idyllic yard outside, and our miracle of the boxes and suitcases was complete. In order to vanquish emptiness you need a special sense of space; it helps to be familiar with the secrets of Gothic structures. I put the rest of our stuff in one of the windowless alcoves. Then I made myself scarce. Beatrice, too, had errands to do.

I knew a spot near the harbor where there was a stand of cactus, the common *opuntia*, a giant variant growing on a dangerously steep incline. Twice I came roaring to the bottom with landslides, but on my third attempt I got a firm foothold and, not without loss of blood, came away with a large central trunk with two offshoots that looked like ears. I filled a bucket with soil and returned home, grubby but happy. Our Christmas cactus stood one meter tall. I melted down two candles left over from our rage at the Madonna for sending rain to the Tower, twisted a few wicks, and shaped some pencil-thin tapers that I stuck on the cactus needles. If in all your misery you are still clever and buddy-buddy with the Muses, you will take Rilke's *New Poems, Part Two*, thin-paper edition, out of a box, tear out the already foxed blank flyleaf, and write on it your own poem "For Beatrice," a work that bears (or rather *bore* since it no longer exists) the same relationship to Christmas Eve as a Spanish fig-cactus does to the German Christmas spruce. Just don't start wallowing in potato-pancake nostalgia! Just don't remind yourself that somewhere on the Lower Rhine a home-grown goose is getting roasted to burnished yellow-brown crispness, yet not too soon for the ceremony of gift-giving.

Employing my South European palette, I composed a thoughtful letter entitled "Christmas in Spain," with the intention of diverting my parents' and my brothers' attention from the domestic goose. Instead of singing *Stille Nacht, heilige Nacht* with half-crocked solemnity, I meant them to break out in a fit of envy: how they would yearn to be down here with me, ambulating under the palms, standing at the blue seashore, letting the sun beat down on their skin, while up there—damn it all, somebody go check!—it's about five below zero, and what'll it be like when the privy freezes up? They don't have to know that down here in the Southland, their Prodigal Son's pipes froze at well over 100° above, that the two of us were skating on a different kind of thin ice, or that before we could exchange Christmas presents, we had to hang a shirt over our window so that the young ladies in our back yard couldn't peek inside to watch our private celebration. Or that when our candles have gone out, we'll be sitting in the dark since we have no money for a light bulb— but would they actually believe all of this? It's possible to boast romantically of even the direst poverty. Successful writers are fond of depicting their youth spent in misery: lousy grades in school, quitting school at thirteen, paper boy, scrounging for food, time in prison (the latter is particularly popular nowadays; no writer can be taken seriously who hasn't spent time in the pen). I can just hear someone urging me to add this question to my seasonal letter: "And do you, too, have roast turkey in your casserole?" This "someone" will know that for Spaniards the Christmas goose is invariably a *pavo*. And which vintage had we chosen? A Malvasian from Bañalbufar?

Suddenly there are footsteps in the corridor—*porra!*—it's Beatrice. "Stop, don't come in! I'm busy! What are you thinking—that this place is like some poor people's house where the Christ Child is lying on his tummy with the whooping cough? Just hand me one of your slips. I have to cover up something. Fine, now you can come in..."

Then it was my turn to be invisible; the gift Beatrice was bearing for the Feast of Lights also looked imposing. I went into one of the front rooms and peeked through the blinds to the street outside, where *padres* were coursing back and forth in their picturesque cassocks. On Christmas Eve these gentlemen have more on their minds than just some pagan tree symbol.

Beatrice arranged a dining space on top of our book crate. In conjugal harmony we sat on the edge of our bed and consumed our Christmas Eve repast. Like laborers at a construction site, we ate off paper. This comparison with professional carpenters is not at all far-fetched, for the two of us were, after all, construction workers: we were building our home and our future on the island.

When it got dark, I lit the candles, not without some difficulty keeping them upright. Then we exchanged presents.

I had fastened my stanza to a spine on our brightly lit cactus. Thus illuminated, the single sheet of bible paper looked elegant indeed; but did it also have a solemn inner glow? I could only hope so.

My present lay underneath Beatrice's slip: a book, one that has passed through how many hands? The paper was yellowed and dog-eared, but from every last page there came forth an intense light: *Las Moradas, The Interior Castle, of Santa Teresa.*

When our candles burned down to the last stump, we went to the cathedral to attend the "Missa del gallo." According to ancient custom, so we were told, at the Christmas Mass a Moorish boy would intone Moorish chants. It was an experience. The brightly lit cathedral, the little black boy warbling his sing-song from up in the pulpit, the ladies with elegant *mantillas* on top of towering combs, and right in front of us a man stretched out on the pew, snoring away the Holy Night. I had to think of Felix Timmermans and a louse-ridden tramp from my childhood, the one we called King of the Bees because of the insects that inhabited him. He spent his nights inside a small forest shrine, and in my childish ignorance I considered that the profanation of a sacred site. The local police smoked out this bum, but not for reasons of sacrilege. The snoozer in front of us took up the space of five seats during his silent, holy night, and nobody bothered him. Everyone celebrates the advent of the Redeemer in his own fashion, and this fashion apparently struck everyone as not the worst way to celebrate. For who knows? Perhaps this tired fellow, already beyond his last crust of bread, was in his dreams a shepherd keeping watch over his flock by night. And, lo, the angel of the Lord came upon him, and the glory of the Lord shone round about him, and he was sore afraid. And in his slumber he heard the sound of wings, and an angel descended and said unto him—but you can read the sequel in the Gospels, unless you know it already by heart. This particular angel will have spoken to our local deadbeat in Spanish, or even more likely in the Mallorquin dialect. All of a sudden the whiskered snoring came to a halt; the star stood still above the stable, and our dozer caught sight of Mary, Joseph, and the Child lying in the crib, and he emerged unblushing through the strait gate to Heaven. And the other shepherds returned to their flocks, fanning the flames and glorifying and praising God for all the things that they had heard and seen, as it was told unto them. Then our man turned over on his other side and resumed his snoring for the length of three whole Masses.

The streets and alleyways were alive with people. In Spain Christmas Eve, the Night of the Rooster, is not a time for quiet contemplation or for decorous quaffing of spirits at home in the family circle. Not after the Christ Child has been placed back in His manger with fresh diapers.

Taking a long detour, we too returned to our domestic hearthside. We now knew just where we belonged, and that we were all by ourselves as soon as we closed our door. No rats, no riotous shouts from 2 x 29 throats, and not only a ceiling but also a blanket over our heads. No donkey to wake us with the gentle wafting of its biblical exhalations, rather than with bone-shattering screeches.

Vigoleis had saved one more candle. He stuck it on the topmost spine of their *opuntia natalis* and lit it. He hoped that its little flame would send some light out into the empty night. He dotes on this tragic mood of hopelessness. Once in a while he likes to turn over his egg timer and watch the grains of sand trickle down for no reason at all, just as the days of his life trickle away, grain by grain, for nothing and for no reason at all. Just as the stars twinkle in the firmament, eternally and without any meaning.

On this night, too, the heavens were dotted with little lights. Since it was a remarkable night in his lifetime, he looked up and lost himself in the sight of eternity, a spectacle that never fails to convince him to the point of physical pain that there cannot be a benevolent Father up there. One star might contain God, but millions and millions of them...? On a Night of the Redeemer like this one, you've got to be wearing a golden tiara as a protective helmet if you don't want to feel like reaching for the bottle...

Vigoleis closed the window. The night's breath was cool. He turned around to his Beatrice, but she was gone. She was lying on the bed, and he was just about to check under her pillow to see if she had placed his stanza there when he remembered that the accursed Pilar hadn't forked over their pillows. Doctors will tell you that it's healthy to sleep without a pillow, and these are the same doctors who say that the vegetarian regimen is better for you than meateating. On this particular night, what would Vigoleis have sacrificed for a crisp roasted goose, the fragrance of which reached his nose in rather unChristian fashion several pages ago? Saint Teresa's *Interior Castle*, perhaps? Perhaps. Or his last shirt.

He covered Beatrice with the cloak of Bethlehemite charity and lay down next to her fully dressed. And there was peace on earth at this spot, where two persons of good will were one: on the Street of General Barceló, in house No. 23, second floor, in the room at the end of the corridor, where I had to close the window to keep out the chilly air from the palm-adorned night.

Let's hope that we don't catch cold!

A special star, dear reader, shone over the night with which I am bringing this Book to its close. So let's have a little asterisk stand here as a typographic symbol for its ending. It is the same star that legend tells us led the Magi from the East to the stable of the Redeemer; it's also the star that pricked the conscience of a young man from the Swiss cantons, urged him to rise up from his *pilarière*, put on his pants, and head for the Street of the General. His footsteps did not echo through the house, for he was shod with *alpargatas*. He knew that two people were abed in a *piso* at this location, and thus that they had found a place to lay their heads, but that's all they had found. The young man regretted this very much, for he considered himself responsible for the fate of this couple. He didn't plant a candle-lit Christmas tree in front of their apartment door—that will be taken care of in a later chapter by an American millionairess, or rather by her servant. This Swiss fellow, not a millionaire, but just a few zeroes away from it as long as he lived, slid an envelope under their door. Inside were a few hundred pesetas and a note with the words,

> *Merry Christmas! You'll hear from me*
> *as soon as the bitch lets me go! Zwingli.*

Our heroes discovered this belated Christmas present the next morning as they padded through the empty house. It was a long time before they heard from Santa Claus again. When he finally surfaced, it was already high time for our heroes to intervene: Caesarian section! They performed this operation with great care after disinfecting the area completely, and although Vigoleis was confronted by Pilar's drawn dagger, he did not run for it. He did not flinch. All of this will be put on paper in good time. At this moment we are taking a breather. There's no reason to rush things, for our couple spent nearly five years under the same roof.

You, perdurable reader, may continue to follow their footsteps, or you may choose to go your own way on the path of other characters by other writers, just as you like. If you knock, it shall be opened unto you. On the other hand, you might find the door already unlocked. The key is of the old-fashioned kind. It's huge and unwieldy, not a work of art like the ones produced by the Nürnberg master Hans Ehemann. This key is one that you'd rather not take with you when you go to the store run by the pretty Angelita or to Don Matías the baker, who is in reality not a baker at all but a great philosophizer. You're probably thinking: aren't there burglars on your island? No, the Barceló is one of those streets where, at its far end, people live who would sooner hack off their own fingers than stick them in other people's pockets. Later, around about the end of 1933, things will get different; spies will make their appearance everywhere, political flunkies doing their job at the behest of a man they worship as their glorious Leader, checking things out in the so-called German Colony in the Balearics, a community to which our Vigoleis also belongs on the basis of his German birth. To them he looks suspicious. So they'll break down his door with a crowbar and sniff around inside: what's this guy writing about, anyway? Stuff against our *Führer*? A *Führer* is not some god you can believe in or not as you choose. So behave yourself, little man, or we'll take care of you! —"A Yale lock," said Beatrice, "and always hook the chain."

But that came sometime later. I'll give you due warning when the *Führer*'s local henchman rises to power, so that you'll know that he's after you, too. And a few years after that, when the Caudillo starts shooting and once again you start getting hot feet, you'll want to be right there along with the rest of us. You won't be able to breathe free again until we are all on board a British destroyer that will take us away from an island that has become Hell on earth.

Steamy adventures, loose women, candles for María del Pilar: is this the end of it? Yes and no—I'm not making any promises.

Let us not profane Christmas Eve with jarring previews of later chapters. We must allow the angels to sing their eternal hymn of glory to God in the highest and peace on earth to men of a kind of good will that, unfortunately, nobody believes in any more.

BOOK FOUR

Ecce homo—ecce demens
after Unamuno

Homo homini homo
after Vigoleis

I

If the world contained nothing but famous people, it would long since have dribbled away like dishwater and left nothing behind but slops in the cloacas of the Last Judgment. God the Inscrutable has seen to it that His creation has not attained the supreme heights, and that the supermen have not sprouted forth in such abundance as to grind lowly humans down completely as they goose-step onwards into eternity. History tells us that humanity is stronger than its yea-saying and nay-saying geniuses, its saints and heroes. Both types are freak occurrences that either threaten us or beguile us. It seems as if the nameless drift of society can at times suddenly bring forth a profusion of great individuals whose names are destined for immortality. When this occurs, rational people take fright, wring their hands, and ask, "Will this never end?" For the most part, such fears are baseless. How many truly great Popes have there been? None of them has been able to topple the Church from its rocky heights. Not even an Adolf Hitler has succeeded in driving Germany into a cesspool from which it can never arise again. True greatness is to be found in true anonymity, in the mode of existence of the vermin of this world. The Spanish all-around genius Gregorio Marañón has written some very readable ideas on this problem in his book on that Great Nameless One, the Man on the Street, Henri-Frédéric Amiel.

I am writing these thoughts on greatness and fame in the city of Amsterdam, in a house situated on a street named after a famous writer: Jan Frederik Helmers. I'll have to confess that I have never read a single line of Helmers, and in my circle of literary friends I have yet to meet anyone who knows who Helmers was, much less has read him. And yet this bard is so famous that the Amsterdam city fathers have named not one but three streets after him. This is more than a writer has a right to expect after his death, especially one who then goes completely out of everybody's sight. My friend Pascoaes, the mystic and vintner whose works and wines I continue to advertise shamelessly, was overcome with dread when he learned that potentates in his home town of Amarante wanted to name a street after him. "Don't they want to read me any more? If my work is not of a kind that is cherished by posterity on its own merits, then let it perish. I do not wish to be buried alive as a street."

The fame enjoyed by the Dutch writer Helmers on the city map of Amsterdam far exceeds that of the Spanish General Barceló in the eyes of the Mallorquins, for only a single street bears his name. It is a thoroughfare that would hardly deserve the designation "street" if it didn't widen out slightly at its upper end. At the point where it merges into Calle San Felio, it is inhabited only by the better sort of people, such as the wealthy Dr. Villalonga in his old palace and, kitty-corner across the street, by Mosén (Monsignor) Juan María Tomás, a heaven-inspired musician and one of the finest characters we got to know on the island. At its bottom end, the street becomes narrow and snakes off into sheer poverty, presenting nothing at all worth commenting on. Little people live there, the kind who see to it that the island doesn't become extinct. Two cloisters are located there, showing the street their gloomy facades and their consecrated portals, the one opposite our house for male inmates, and the other, farther up the street and with better exposure to sunlight, for the female variety. I am unable to verify whether the two pious establishments are connected by an underground passageway. This is, however, the case with most Spanish or Portuguese cloisters.

I once entered such a subterranean tunnel in the former convent of the Sisters of Santa Clara, the "Casa da Cérca em Cima" in Amarante, now the residence of my motherly friend Doña María da Gloria Teixeira de Vasconcellos Carvalhal, the sister of the writer Pascoaes. Standing there in the tunnel, I envisioned the pious parade passing back and forth, and it is no wonder that I came under the spell of the delightful lunar eroticism that I have otherwise experienced only in early Iberian mysticism. For the history of love-letter writing, it is fortunate that the Convent of Conceição in Beja, where Sor Maríanna Alcoforada served the Dear Lord, lacked such a corridor to the realm of the monks, for otherwise this Portuguese nun's letters would never have been written—if indeed she wrote them herself, which I doubt.

Presumably General Barceló was born on the street named after him. Or perhaps he died here, because I can't imagine why the city didn't pick a better spot to perpetuate his fame. He lived from 1717 to 1797, the great son of an island that has produced many great children. He cleansed the Mediterranean of the plague of piracy which, with billowing sails, infested the high seas at the time. Antonio Barceló succeded in sniffing even the most dastardly corsairs out of their coastal lairs, forcing them out on the main and blasting them to the salty depths. He was no less victorious on dry land. You can still hear today a popular quatrain composed during the hero's lifetime: "If the King of Spain had four like Barceló, Gibraltar would belong to Spain and not to the English, *No!*"

Don Francisco Franco, himself a general of the most superlative type, once a much-feared freebooter in Morocco and a man who now has the most elegant *avenidas* in the whole country renamed after him, has yet to grab Gibraltar from the British. Thus he actually pales in comparison with his historical comrade-in-arms, General Barceló. No one knows how many General Francos Spain might need in order once again to sing "Not to the English, *No!*" And if anybody did know, he would be shot anyway. Be that as it may, this is not of much importance for my story, whose course is just as void of great individuals as human history itself, within which it is a mere leaf drifting in the wind.

In a dismal stable on our street there lived a shoe repairman, who kept himself alive with his awl and the sale of charcoal and olive-wood, the island's fuel of preference. We soon started calling him "Siete Reales," seven reales (one real = 25 centimos), because he always miscalculated prices to his own disadvantage—quite a feat when dealing with Vigoleis, who never got past the basic times-table. Siete Reales was illiterate, but he spoke a spotless mainland Spanish, and that is why I enjoyed chatting with him. I even profited from his philosophical insights, and this led to friendship—though we never went so far as to clap each other on the shoulder, for this would have raised too much charcoal dust. With the baker Matías—who wasn't a baker at all, but a schoolteacher, and hence Don Matías—who ran his shop a few houses down the street in the shabbier direction, I regarded this indigenous gesture of eternal friendship as less unpleasant, although not entirely innocuous. At any rate, with him the dust clouds were not of the sooty type. I shall return to this flour-bedecked fellow, with whom I enjoyed a similarly philosophical commercial relationship, as soon as the Nazis emerge from their historical hinterlands and send one of their Mata Haris on a special Balearic mission to turn men's heads before they get their necks wrung.

On a nearby street, the Apuntadores, there stood a little shop owned by two elderly ladies, one of whom had two beautiful daughters—one of whom, in turn, waited on customers in the store. This was Angelita, whose eyes were larger than the most alluring night-time sky. Every time I stepped up to the counter, she fluttered those teasing eyelashes with their fly-leg adornments, and I immediately forgot what I was supposed to bring home. I heard a buzzing noise around me, as if the flies were still alive whose legs made this little she-devil so dangerous to someone like me—who grew up on the banks of the Niers and whose Mama once took him through bordellos looking for a suitable apartment. Under such glances, everything collapsed. By the way, Beatrice was of the opinion that Angelita's lashes were natural—she didn't have to hurt a single fly to turn into a she-demon. As for myself, I prefer her, even just the memory of her, with fly-leg eyelashes. And she didn't have to go far at all to lay in a supply of such a cosmetic: right next door was a butcher shop presided over by a sour old hag, where we sometimes went to buy a cut of lamb. This butcher-lady was crabby, and barked at anyone who came to disturb the peace and quiet of her swarms of flies. One day she was found dead behind the counter, and now it was her turn to be covered with flies. This was in mid-summer. Such an edifying end for the proprietress of a butcher shop: to get buried by flies in her own store. The shop lacked a meat cooler; if it had one, she could have slumbered off flyless into the Great Beyond.

I believe I have paid my proper and sufficient respects to our Street General, so that he need not feel outpointed by Julietta's father. But the real reason why

I spent so much time on the various streets of the town is that in our house there isn't much to see. It is an empty house—that is to say, an empty apartment. The money that Santa Claus pushed under the door would have been enough to equip the rooms with the necessary furnishings. But we considered it more advisable to buy back our books from the customs office before they got eaten by rats. For 300 pesetas we were able to repossess our world of print. The remainder of our belongings wandered off into the same furniture warehouse where we went with the whore to buy our sofa bed. We purchased a rickety table and two old-granny style chairs, and this left us with a few measly coins for a postage stamp and a loaf of bread.

Such was our modest debut: a table and two chairs in the kitchen. Krupp's beginnings were more meager than that, and even Diogenes found shelter in a barrel. We were lacking many things, but in our condition of enforced asceticism we never went so far as to take pleasure in our lack of pleasures. On the contrary: we were jubilant whenever we undid the knot in our money stocking and poured out enough change, *calderilla*, to afford a cooking pot, or perhaps a knife. On such occasions we would look deeply into each other's eyes, down to where you can espy a mysterious glimmer, and would say, "What do you think? We've got by for so long without a cooking pot. How would it be if we just waited a few more weeks? And do we really need a knife? Or a spittoon (an item that in Spain is almost more urgently necessary than cooking utensils)? What do you say we go out and buy a book?" A book! That's it! And then we would fall into each other's arms, which we kept clean despite our destitution, and would feel that we had hit the jackpot.

The better I got to know our new language, the clearer it became to me that there were untold treasures to be unearthed here. I discovered writers whose very names were unknown up in the North. Spain? That meant Cervantes and the classical dramatists, and that was all. I was thrilled by the prospect of reading Saint Teresa, the Confessions of Juan de la Cruz, and Fray Luiz de León in the original. I didn't dare to even think of reading *Don Quixote*, however; that seemed to me to be an assignment for a more mature spirit than my own, just as it is only now, at the threshold of my own half-century of life, that I am able to read Goethe with profit, if not yet in the classy Artemis Edition. I should probably wait until I am a hundred—but then again, I don't think Goethe is worth that. We literally ate our way into Spanish literature, simply by eating less. Each of us had a special field. Beatrice delved into history, while I, with my aversion to all forms of tradition conserved in books, plunged into the immutable imaginative world of rhymed and unrhymed poetry. I can be fascinated by historical writing if the historian has a one-sided view of things—if, that is, he writes with one eye to the ground, much as a chicken must look down in order to see the sky above—if, that is, the historian can elevate history into legend, thus redeeming it from so-called professional scientific accuracy, which in any case never can exceed astronomical approximations. Thousands of works have been written about Napoleon, and the literature on this rewarding subject keeps growing. But what do we know about him? Who was Napoleon? Every biography has to create him anew from the germ cell of a human existence, perhaps his own. According to the latest calculations, the world in which we bring up such questions can expect to last another 20 billion years. Or maybe it's only 15 billion. And there's the fly in the ointment: Napoleon was a savior, but it's also possible that he was a criminal, or perhaps it's the other way around. Whoever enters "history" has ceased to be himself.

Chatting for hours in this fashion helped to slake our hunger for "real" food, the pangs of which were often painful. I was the advocate for poetry and legend, the champion of a form of truth that resides in the clouds. Beatrice clung with a physical and mental sobriety to historical reality; with her sharper intellect and with the help of her frightening, emasculating erudition, she defended what I, in my impotence, insisted (and still insist) on calling the Historical Lie. Will Vigoleis one day be her victim? It was hard to stand up against her—or rather to sit down against her, for I was sitting and Beatrice was sitting, too. During such disputations we both squatted in a mood of harmonious hostility on boxes of books, later on our rustic chairs, which after a time sported a coat of paint. Later still—indeed much, much later—we sat in real living-room chairs made of straw. Two years (the chronology is not very precise) had to pass before we could afford such lacy sitting-baskets. But no sooner were they broken in, when they collapsed, and we reverted to our primeval style of living as box-squatters. Our edifying literary discussions did not suffer from the change, but our ability to expand our library certainly did.

Our living room, pantry, kitchen, and bedroom were situated one adjoining the other, and as I have explained, the windows and the large French door of the sala looked out upon the yard. Nobody could peer into our kitchen or bedroom, and there we had wooden shutters for blocking out a blinding sun or curious onlookers. Things were worse, though, in our living room, which was at the same level as an outside patio. We couldn't reach the patio from our floor, since it was separated from us by a light-shaft that was like a castle moat. And besides, the patio was not included in the rent. In addition, we were separated from the world of the proprietary class by an iron fence. Our view was usually blocked by laundry hanging on a line. In the South one does the laundry every day, with cold water and on a stone. So there was a constant fluttering in the breeze, large bedsheets and the little things that lie closest to the body. I was soon able to assess the cup sizes of Mother and her daughters, and also of the maids, besides which I learned the schedule of their lunar phases and eclipses. It was embarrassing when we invited company and saw these pages from the domestic calendar hanging on the line outside. At first, Beatrice was upset at this spectacle. I didn't mind it so much. I didn't exactly think it was beautiful, but was my clothesline-full of poems back at the bordello any more stylish?

What was truly disturbing was the source of this open-air exhibition, the daughters of the house who emerged onto the patio several times a day. Without fail, they sent their curious glances into our room, and were always amazed to see nothing but boxes of books and our Christmas cactus, which, by the way, was starting to sprout. What—hadn't "they" moved in yet? Have "they" just thrown down their stuff here while they live somewhere else? For- eigners act strangely on Mallorca—everybody knew that, and everybody dis- approved. One day one of the *señoritas* screwed up her courage, spied me out, and asked me straightaway, "Are you here yet?" I was standing at the fence, gazing at the exotic display. In the bourgeois way that I have with little matters that are of no concern to Vigoleis, I began to fib, thereby committing the sour sin of cowardice: I fed her the same story that I had already handed out to Arsenio, about our furniture that was waiting to be processed at the customs office. To be on the safe side, I transplanted the whole saga of forms, declara- tions, value estimates, oath-takings, and deposits to the city of Barcelona, for it was possible that this little lady's Papá knew the Customs Director very well. One false word, and all our stuff would be out on the General's Street before sundown. When chance and coincidence have repeatedly tripped you up in your lifetime and caused your prospects to shrivel away, you get over- cautious—and end up in the soup worse than ever. "Barcelona?" our neigh- bor's daughter asked. "Papá knows the director of the Main Customs Office. You should talk with Papá, all he'd have to do is say the word, and all your stuff would get sent over on the next ship. It must be terrible to live without any furniture! I mean, you can't even..."

Which saint should I have implored for aid against this kind of proffered assistance? I wasn't aware of a single one that specialized in such complex matters. And Beatrice, who invoked Saint Anthony for any and all problems, wasn't within earshot. So I kept on lying. I thanked the girl for her kind offer, and told her that our most recent communication from Customs gave promise of the release of our belongings in short order. It was only our Bechstein piano that would be kept under bond, since we owed 3000 pesetas in duty.

"3000 pesetas?"

"3000, as I say. And at the moment we haven't got that much."

After this conversation took place, we bought some drapes as a protection against the prying glances of the considerate daughters. I hate drapes. They remind me constantly of how cramped this world of ours is, and that I am too poor to keep it at a distance. I would give anything to have a private study on the top floor of a skyscraper. And please: no drapes at the windows—get away from me with your gypsy-wagon puffery! My life is one uninterrupted battle against the potato and bolts of chiffon, both of them symbols of an Icarus who can't even fly high enough for the wax on his wings to melt.

In the Count's *pensión*, Madame Gerstenberg hosted a farewell dinner. She could no longer endure life on the island. She was suffering from insular anx- iety, an affliction that had escalated into insular rage, a dreadful illness that later would befall Beatrice, too. There are only two types of cure: leave the island, precipitously if need be, or bang your head against a wall. Our dowager tragedian chose the deck planks of the Ciudad de Alicante, and departed with her son to Alicante, from whence they had once arrived. It had simply become unbearable to her to be separated from the world by an ocean. She felt as if she had been locked in a pillory. I tried to reassure her with the sophistical remark that one can never be quite sure at what point a continent begins, geographically speaking, to get demoted to an island; science just hadn't progressed far enough to set standards on this subject. And then I unloaded on her my monetary theory: an island was actually no more unbearable than any arbitrary point on so-called *terra firma*. All that was necessary was sufficient wealth to afford a motorboat or an airplane, like the banker Don Juan March. Why, that man could enjoy a more serene existence on some coral reef than Adele Gerstenberg could experience in Alicante.

Instead of replying, Madame Gerstenberg just gave me a look with her yellowish face, causing me to fall mute and feel like a simpleton. Captain von Martersteig, the only true Icarus in our local flying circus, had not come to the festivities, although he was still in town. Doubled up with gout and heroism, he sat alone in a bedbug-infested apartment, and to make matters worse, agonized over an open letter of ultimatum to President Hindenburg: either the calcified old Field Marshal must raise his pension as a war invalid, or—but no one ever found out what dire consequences lay in store for the Reich President if he should refrain from appending his martial signature to an edict of augmentation. The reason is that Adolf Hitler made short work of this particular little paper tiger. He bought our old air warrior's loyalty for the price of a glass of beer, two Frankfurt sausages, and a dollop of mustard.

I exchanged a few letters with Madame Gerstenberg, but then the intervals increased to the point where both of us stopped writing to each other. Friedrich died of tuberculosis, and half a year later his mother followed him to the Realm of the Shades. *Terra firma*, it turns out, was even more confining than the island. Both of them lie buried in the Alicante Cemetery. The Captain, on his part, will inter himself for a few more years in his ghostly palace in Deyá. There he will live on as if in a cremated state, nursing his pique in a dank and barren cell. Not even his arch-enemy von Ranke Graves will be able to scare him away. His pension will once again be reduced by a few marks— and that says everything. But now let's leave him alone to gather mold; soon enough the *Führer* will appear on the scene and yell out to the whole world, "Germany, awake!" This clarion call will in fact awaken our Captain, and he will reappear in these pages with his monocle, his fur-lined Turkish slippers, his *Pour le Mérite*, his bottles of poison, and his winged words about the gratings of a green cheese.

Anton Emmerich will now gradually disappear from our view. He has big plans, and hankers to get out into the world. He is not suffering from insulitis, but he simply has had enough of this grubby island Paradise. He offers us his shop for a song—Zwingli's debts to him came to a much larger sum. But since we couldn't even cough up a song, since in fact we were poorer than the people in the folk ditty, "Please give us a penny—Sorry, haven't any!"... In brief, this crafty potato-pancake German patriot departed from the island after selling his business to a new arrival from the homeland. This gentleman came from the banking business, had a few shekels, and was remarkably short in stature. Behind the counter he looked as if he were standing in a trap door. And a trap door was to be his insular destiny.

Now that we've swept away our friend from Cologne, I have room for more characters.

If my extrapolations are correct, I have already used up more than half of this book to depict the consequences of our shipwreck—which, strictly speaking, was not a shipwreck at all, since we lost our footing as soon as we stepped on the island. Our existence became grounded only after we moved into No. 23 on the Street of the Hero Against Piracy, which then led to a fierce struggle for our daily bread. This struggle lasted years, and ended with complete victory: we finally bought a bathtub. This was possible only on the basis of several uneaten meals and several unpurchased books. For me, the bathtub meant much more than a vessel for cleansing the body. Seated within its walls, I experience the Archimedian Principle in its spiritual manifestation. Beatrice, as jaundiced as our friend the dowager tragedian, has cursed the island more than a thousand times, and more than a thousand times I have implored her: "Do not curse the island, curse *me*, your Vigoleis; curse Vigoleis, who is not just an avatar of myself, but rather my self's court jester, even if I'm not wearing a fool's collar and a cockscomb. Take him as the symbol of an attitude that is sufficient unto itself, and therefore sufficient for self-induced implosion. Sure enough, I probably continued, the Spaniards have a lot to learn. They aren't housebroken. If you don't have a spittoon handy, they spit on the floor, and they mess up your apartment with cigarette ashes. A house and a public street are all the same to them. But is it all *that* bad? I clean up after them every time. Like the circus clown who runs behind the elephants with dust pan and broom, I follow our Spanish house guests around all the time. And frankly, I get a fright every time the doorbell rings and you open up to welcome not some dear friend of either sex, but a company of spitters, ash-droppers and butt-tossers. Why, to look at you at such moments, you'd think that these guests of ours were about to lift their legs and have a go at our deluxe Bible-paper edition of The Great Philosophers."

"Oh, this accursed island of Balearic polluters!" you once said, my dear Beatrice. And I could only repeat: "Oh, this polluting scoundrel of a Vigoleis! Why doesn't he finally write a poem that will buy us a doormat, a spittoon, and an ashtray? Just you wait, *ma chérie*, you'll see how life can get transformed when a guest of ours gets up out of his chair, walks over to the corner, and with an audible splash and visible gratification spits his load into a gracefully tapered vessel. Sometimes he might aim wrong and return to his seat with a shrug of his shoulders. In such cases I will get out the broom, and we should be grateful if about 30% of all shots hit the bullseye. Day and night, my dear, I wrack my brain to figure out how to invent something truly great that will earn us 1000 pesetas—in writing: One Thousand! Just imagine if I ever succeed in working out the formula for my fluorescent printer's ink. Henceforth, mankind would be able to read in the dark. It would mean an end to bedtime squabbles when one of the partners wants to read and the other wants to go to sleep. But nobody is willing to recognize my genius, not even you—and that is a bitter pill to swallow."

Let the reader be aware that I have just recorded thought-patterns and snatches of conversation that move far ahead of actual events. For up to the present moment, no Spaniard has ever had an opportunity to spit on the *ladrillos* on our apartment floor that we polished so assiduously with our shirts and pants. Besides, *entre nous* (although I could announce this in public, since Beatrice has known all about it for a quarter of a century): what I wouldn't give to have been born with such intrinsic greatness as to permit me to spit on anybody else's apartment floor, to eat with my knife even when nobody is looking, and to walk into my house without scraping the mud from my soles! Why hasn't Vigoleis achieved anything in life? Because he doesn't spit, that's why. Because he behaves himself. Because he insists on wearing buckled slippers even in his miserable garret at 3E Helmersstraat, Amsterdam. I am singing the praises of public spitting, and I am fortunate enough to have found a publisher for these jottings who is a full-throated master of this art. It's hard to say what the result will be. After all, it's a little late. And a little early for an unknown writer to come forth all of a sudden with a heap of jottings.

Well, here's Nietzsche on this subject: anyone has a right to produce an autobiography after his fortieth year, because even the least among us can have had close-up experience of something that is of rewarding interest to a thinker. During the period in question, I experienced my Vigoleis in extreme close-up. And if you, dear reader, are the thinking type, then we are on just the right path and I can continue my wandering. Therefore, let us consider it a compliment if I allow Pedro Sureda the privilege of being the first Spanish *hidalgo* to spit in our *piso*. This is, as Beatrice has just remarked as she spies over my shoulder at my manuscript, not historically accurate, because Pedro himself came from an un-Spanish household. I think it would be a shame if Pedro were not a born spitter, and so I'll make him into one right here. History, let me repeat, is not a waxworks museum where every birthmark gets pasted on where it belongs. Herodotus is guilty of much worse historical transgressions. And just think of all the things the authors of the Old Testament make Yahweh do, not to mention Christian Morgenstern with his Palmström! What, my friend Sureda was never a spitter? Why shouldn't the world that matters to us be a fictional one? Doesn't your friend Nietzsche say so?

If you have ever seen portraits of Alphonse XIII, the last King of Spain, then
I needn't go into specifics about Pedro's appearance. He was the (forgive me!)
spitting image of the great Bourbon. His mien was more intelligent, and he
lacked the effeminate arching of the brow. His glance was livelier than that of
his King, and his nose was pinched slightly to one side. But otherwise he was
the very likeness, the mildly distorted mirror image, of the monarch. This often
led to misidentifications that Pedro handled with regal aplomb, and the re-
semblance led also to gossip. For how can somebody have a king's face, when
he ain't no king? It would be nice for the island of my second sight if Pedro
stood in the same relationship to the King of Spain as Julietta did to the General from Fort Mahón. From a sociological perspective, this would expand
considerably the circle of my intimate relationships, and today I could only
regret the fact that I never embraced the coalman Siete Reales simply for lack
of a romantic opportunity—Vigoleis enjoying converse with charcoal merchants and royal offspring in the lofty regions of the island. It just wasn't to
be. Not with the man in black, because of the dust, and not with Pedro—no
disrespect for the King intended—because as we know, kings aiming to freshen
up their bloodline are wont to use the servants' stairway, whereas Pedro's
mother was in her own right the progeny of ducal nobility. "But that's no argument!" say the genealogists, people who are habituated to grafting branches
onto family trees at will. True enough, but this particular Spanish princess is
still among us, living out her waning years on her island.

On his mother's side, Pedro hails from ancient Iberian nobility. His family
flourished on the banks of the Tajo under Carlos V, and later under Philip II,
the one with the name that is so abhorrent to the Dutch. Even if we discount
such questionable royal connections, Pedro's lineage on the paternal side
points back to the Spanish mainland. The ancestors of the Suredas arrived on
the island with James the Conqueror in the year 1229, the year that is sacred
to all Mallorquins. After a long siege, on the 31st of December of that same
year, the Christian king delivered Palma from the hands of the Moorish dogs.
Pedro's ur-grandfather was on hand for this. Clothed in a coat of mail he raged
furiously among the heathen hordes, for he had a specific grudge against the
moros: to this day the family bears the name "Verdugo," which means executioner, hangman, or beheader—to memorialize the bloody deed that kept
the clan in fealty to the Spanish Crown.

I'll relate the story in a variant that comes closest to satisfying my penchant
for gothic sagas. In Don Paco Quintana's version, fewer heads roll, but otherwise every detail is exactly the same. It's the thirteenth century. The castle
of the Suredas is undergoing siege, and we hear the battle cry, "Death to the
Castilians!" Battering rams wham up against doors, gates split apart, black
devils clamber up the ramparts, a massacre commences. The lord of the castle
falls under the swipe of a scimitar. The noble lady and her children, the sole
survivors of the blood bath, are brought before the Sheik. The latter pronounces his decision: "Death to the Castilian infidels!" —But with this
proviso: if the mother will behead her children with her own hands, one *hijo*

varón will have his life spared. The lady agrees, but it is not she who decides which of the children is to survive the infanticide. She places her children around her in a circle, lets herself be blindfolded, picks up a sword, and whirls around several times, swinging the weapon like the hand on a clock. When she stops twirling, the blade points to a *varón*, a boy, the one selected to continue the noble line. She kills all the rest, and then herself.

I have often recounted this ancestral saga, and have yet to meet a mother who says that under similar circumstances she would act the same. To kill for love—is that so difficult? Or does a mother's love not extend beyond the grave? Death is a good thing only when the masses say it is.

Pedro from the House of Verdugo is tall, a born dancer. He has beautiful hands that move in enchanting ways. He has a pleasant singing voice, and prefers the old songs of his island. His lungs are messed up, his stomach likewise, and his heart is enlarged. He is an accomplished actor—not on the stage, where he would no doubt be a failure, but in real life, where this art earns more, especially in Spain, where the theaters are bad because they pretend to be good. At the time when we made Pedro's acquaintance, he had not yet made a final decision about his career, and no one was pressuring him about this. He had certain ambitions as a writer, but even stronger inclinations to become an artist with pencil and brush. But first he had to do his military service. I have never been a soldier, but I know that an army recruit is worth less than a head of cattle. Beastliness has stuck to mankind ever since we emerged from the primeval slime, and that's why nearly all of us go right along whenever we get the call to don a snappy uniform. Anyone who refuses is put up against the wall. As soon as someone puts on a uniform, he ceases to be what he is. Pedro from the House of Verdugo—let this be said to his credit—tried to preserve his human dignity even as a soldier, and at the time in question this was still more or less feasible. He accomplished this when it came time to get dressed. Arriving at the quartermaster's store, he fished out a jacket with the arms too long and the collar too wide, a pair of trousers whose hindpart reached to the back of his knees, a belt that he had to wind twice around his waist before he could find the proper hole. His headgear would have been too large even for his heraldic progenitor.

Beatrice met him when he was garbed in this fashion, and she claimed that he was daffy. I got to know him in the same *Landsknecht* outfit, and as soon as I grasped his hand, I knew: this is a man after my own heart. As a citizen of Switzerland, Beatrice had no idea what it meant to be a soldier. The handful of guys who, to the annoyance of their neighbors, pop off musket shots every Sunday in their cantons while smoking their stogies or between hands of cards, and who in a war emergency can plant a land mine or do some border patrol while remaining free citizens of the Swiss Federation—these types have no say in the matter, although they would like to think they do. Whenever they get tired of the charade, they toss their gear at the feet of the Division Commander, and are never put in front of a firing squad. Pedro himself could have a say in the matter, whereas in Germany—and I believe Captain von Martersteig's every word—such behavior would land a soldier in front of a military tribunal for sabotage of patriotic duty. "What a disgusting sight, these monkeys in the Spanish Army!" Pedro was not the only one who kept his dignity by flouting regulations. Martersteig: "For each missing button, solitary! For pants that slip down, the brig! How can they ever expect to advance in formation toward the enemy when they have to hold their pants up? And what can be done with an army where the generals put up umbrellas as soon as it starts to drizzle?" Napoleon, I replied, did this, too, and still he won battles. At Waterloo he just didn't have a *parapluie* close to hand, and things went badly for him. I have seen many Spanish generals, but I've never seen one with an open umbrella. If I had, I would have embraced him. I felt vindicated when I once ran across an illustrated article in a Portuguese newspaper: a review of the national troops in pouring rain. The entire General Staff was sitting on kitchen chairs under open umbrellas. And these officers didn't even have their batmen hold their umbrellas for them; no, the latter were back home taking care of the kids. My heart is touched at the sight of so much humanity in an inhumane profession. The Negus of Abyssinia carries his umbrella with imperial majesty. But maybe that thing is considered part of the royal insignia.

Just a brief moment more concerning the defense of the badly shrunken Spanish Empire: Pedro's grandfather, Don Jaime Montaner y Vega Verdugo etc, was an admiral who earned his stripes in the otherwise rather ignominious Cochin China campaign. When still in the bloom of his youth, he was in the thick of things when the Spaniards tried to wrest Ceuta from the Riff pirates. From then on, he added one piping after another to his uniform; one gilded star tinkled next the other, so that the sea-warrior's aged breast was overflowing at the gunwales when I finally met him in person in his palace. I was awestruck by this Balearic Nelson; his jacket fairly glistened with molded hardware. And such a confession is no doubt surprising coming from me, since I am much more often prone to ridiculing any and all manifestations of secular and ecclesiastical masquerade. Shall I give you an example that speaks volumes? Here it is:

I was to make a formal visit to my episcopal uncle in Münster, whom I had never met. I only knew his aged servant, a fellow named Jean, just like his employer. The two of them were bosom friends, since the elder Jean had once served as a coachman for the bishop's father. For this reason, the servant felt completely free to drag the high priest down from the pulpit if, upon checking his pocket watch, he determined that the boy's sermon was lasting too long, and that he would have to reheat the coffee in the sacristy. This impressed me: my uncle paled in significance when compared with his loyal menial. It is true that Uncle Jean's prestige rose mightily in our family after he was named to the office of diocesan shepherd. Up to then, the issues of the "Steyl Missionary Messenger" and the "City of God" had displayed to one and all my parental household's piety and modest literary taste. But now such things became of secondary importance. The Titular Bishop of Cestrus overwhelmed the popular Catholic press with his staff and his miter.

I was a non-believer in the sense of Berdiaev's "non-tragic theology," which rejects all forms of supplication. It was thus my intention to appear before my uncle as an "enlightened" citizen, as a person in my own right, as a young relative of his from the provinces, presenting myself to him as a fellow human being, as someone who recognized his own servant as a person to whom he was in the habit of bowing down. I knew that you were supposed to kiss a bishop's ring—Mother really didn't need to insist that I followed this custom. Yet I also knew that I didn't care the gratings of a (to me, as yet unfamiliar) green cheese about such medieval malarkey—although I kept this knowledge from Mother. Thus fortified, I entered No. 30 Cathedral Square in Münster with my head full of Nietzsche and Schopenhauer and similar weaponry, expecting to press the flesh with my relative: "Hello, Uncle. Here I am, Johanna's son from Süchteln. How are you? Greetings from Dad and Mom. If you'd like to come visit us, you can say Mass in the hospital across the street, if Jean will let you. After Mass the nuns will give you some coffee in the rector's office..." But at the door of No. 30 the lady told me, "His Excellency is not in. Come back tomorrow around eleven, that'll be fine. And who should I say has come calling?"

Punctually at the appointed hour I betook myself to the small palace. A large crowd had gathered at the entrance—but surely not because of me? Or was Uncle Jean, following instructions from my Mother, going to perform a public conversion, with a procession and a Te Deum to follow? Unfazed, I strode through the waiting crowd and the portal into the palace garden. As I entered the vestibule I was intercepted by a young curate, who said that no matter who I was, I had arrived at the wrong time. His Excellency was about to say his first Mass in the Cathedral—would I be so kind as to... And then I heard voices and footsteps and the swishing of vestments. His Excellency the Auxiliary Bishop was descending the broad staircase in full panoply, surrounded by hands busy with adjusting this and that detail in his raiment and ornaments. The garments of Church dignitaries are just as seductive as those of a *femme du monde*. The unexpected sight of this pageantry caused me, in spite of the safety pins being attached to him as he strode forth in all his dignity, to lose my composure to the extent that I no longer saw in front of me my Uncle Jean but a Prince of the Church. On a sudden impulse, I stepped up to him. No sooner had he reached the bottom step when I cast myself down on my knees before him, grasped his hand and attempted to kiss his fisherman's ring. The Bishop remained my Uncle. My gesture hadn't surprised him in the least. He covered the ring with his other hand, drew me out from the circle of his vassals, and said, "That's what Johanna told you to do. But with me you don't have to. We'll do it all differently. Come around tonight at seven. You see that I'm in a hurry. Look, they're still trying to get me dressed on the stairway." "*Propinquus meus*," he said to a foreign-looking monk. It sounded like an apology. And then my theatrical relative disappeared.

I've never forgotten that gesture with the ring. Needless to say, by making it, the bishop had won the heart and the trust of an infidel, although he had not won a disciple.

Uniforms and vestments are as dangerous as the war paint on primitive tribesmen. One must be very strong to resist them. Have I been any more successful at this than the missionary who, at the sight of a gang of painted Africans, was overcome with doubt concerning his sacred assignment? Like this man, I soon regained my confidence. Neither of us got eaten up, but we both had succumbed in our own fashion. Full-dress uniform is part of everyday business, even pious business. The Protestant Church is losing its hold on the faithful. I can't help thinking that if the big-time non-Catholic professors and spokesmen of God's Word were to put on a little warpaint, if they would don some colorful garb, swing a censer now and then, and talk in a foreign language, their cause would soon reap its proper benefits. They wouldn't have to carry things so far as to fear being mistaken for dolled-up matrons, as once happened to the Patriarch of Lisbon on the island of Madeira. But a little more color wouldn't do any harm. What I mean is that it wouldn't harm their church, because for a long time none of this has had anything to do with God. God is under church arrest, and to the Protestant theologians He has no greater significance than what Nietzsche said books meant to most people: mere literature. And that is as it should be. In the Catholic Church, on the other hand, the same primeval myth is still as alive as the one that prompted the first African to put a ring in his nose. In our own day and age, as we witness the beginnings of an "a-perspective" era, such things can still produce daily miracles. But my friend Don Juan Gebser, the inventor of the era I am speaking about, knows much more about these things than Vigoleis.

So now I have introduced Pedro Sureda to my reader, establishing connections that stretch across the centuries. Heads had to roll, veils had to get lifted, a king's name had to be conjured up to facilitate the description of a face, an admiral had to be resurrected from the dead and asked to jangle his decorations, and a heretic had to grovel in the dust before an elaborately caparisoned Servant of God. If I had depicted these things strictly according to nature, we would now be further on—that is to say, I would have used fewer words. But I deliberately dispense with such methods, for I lack command of the writing art. It is difficult to paint the portrait of a person in words in such a way that, if an artist were to illustrate the work, the original character would remain genuine. I once amused myself by comparing the illustrations in the earliest editions of *Don Quixote*, created before the visual appearance of the Knight of the Mournful Countenance as we know it had developed. Even today, it costs me some effort to imagine the features of my *Don Quixote* while only reading the text. The later goateed depictions of Cervantes' protagonist repeatedly get in my way. It's the same thing with Christ. It's well-nigh impossible to extricate the genuine article from behind the fossilized Beautiful Man with the Jesus Beard.

As you can see, Vigoleis has no lack of connections on the island. Battle commanders on land and sea have handed him their letters of credential; he is recognized and registered in the best whorehouses in the city; a Catholic bishop's official letter has recommended this young man's scholarly ambitions to a bosom friend of Pedro's Papá, the Archepiscopal Bishop of Mallorca, and the latter has applied his official seal and signed it in his fine, somewhat trembling hand: *Joseph, Archiepiscopus, Episcopus Maioricensis.* And by an odd coincidence, it turns out that the exhibitionistic young ladies on our patio are related to Pedro.

"You know these *señoritas?*"

"On this island everybody knows everybody, although sometimes it's best to pretend that you don't. What's more, we are all related. But between me and the Aguados there's a double remove."

And yet it remains a lamentable fact that Vigoleis has been unable to transform all these high-sounding, anointed, palace- and bordello-born connections into cold cash. Not from connections that point to Heaven, not from connections that point to Hell. Even the connections that point nowhere at all haven't yielded up a single peseta. If you want to find ore, you have to dig shafts in the earth. Vigoleis' shafts are leading nowhere, just as always.

"Don't you have any furniture at all?" asked Pedro, who as a pupil of Beatrice's had arrived for his maiden lesson, and finally to get a look at the man who couldn't afford the chair that his nature dictated he should be squatting on.

Beatrice had told him about our fateful odyssey. If two people sit opposite each other three times a week for an hour at a time, teaching and getting taught, then certain things will emerge in conversation that can allow an alert learner to reconstruct and ponder pretty nearly the whole saga: the whorish comedy with Pilar, the feral Julietta, the ingenious Zwingli, the "Clock Tower," the army of monkeys and the poison chest, the twofold refusal of a wardrobe. And the pupil, with his artist's eyes, will of course gaze at Vigoleis and, if he has a promising visage, will take up his pencil and sketch the schlemiel with a few deft strokes.

Our first conversations took place in a mishmash of Spanish, English, and French. The formal and familiar forms of address were glossed over, or got so mixed up that we chose to use the more intimate pronoun henceforth. The British are so lucky. From cradle to grave they use "you," and the hapless translators into "du" languages are forced to intuit the moment when things get cozier between the interlocutors.

I don't know which is worse: not to have a shadow, or not to have a face. Nobody can steal my shadow. I cast it ahead of me as I move along, I cast it behind me, and most often it swallows me up. It is always there. But my face? On a certain occasion the ownership of it was challenged. By Pedro, of course, who walked around with the face of his deposed King. The artist in him gave rise to the confusion.

Unlike Madame Perronet and her lady friend in Amsterdam, Pedro didn't dress me up in a Dutch naval officer's uniform and picture me as I set my deceitful course through the Straits of Macassar. Instead, the artist Pedro, the son of a king, detected noble blood in my veins, despite the fact that my nose is not at all aristocratic. So he focused on my chin—poor Vigoleis, will there never be an end to this? Who besides Beatrice had ever reached out for my chin? And he said,

"Your nose is not of the worthy type *(castizo)*. But your chin, and your marvelously curved lips! Welcome to our island, you Bamberg Knight of ancient German lineage!"

I was a marked man. Pedro held the stirrup for me, I leapt into the saddle and sat there, a hero rattling my saber, gazing off to distant horizons. Vigoleis Imperator. Vigoleis Magnus Dux. Vigoleis Dominus et Rex. But Vigoleis still didn't own a chair, not to mention a loyal vassal who could assist him in toppling Pilar from the pillar of her innocence and snatching a wardrobe and bedclothes from her apartment.

"So you don't have any furniture? Not even a couple of chairs? Hold it there, Vigo, just a second, don't move, your head is just right..."

Pedro went on sketching. Presumably he had now espied a facet of my Bamberg countenance that revealed a *soupçon* of Hohenstaufen arrogance, rather than some bastardized distortion that would ruin this whole artistic enterprise.

"We don't have many chairs in our house, either. One chair for the three of us. That's why we're all so much on the move. But in Valldemosa, in our *feudo*, Papá has hundreds of chairs. Valldemosa is a village up in the mountains, and that's where our castle is, the one we had to vacate—debts, lousy management, women. Papá, you have to know, is hornier than a billygoat in springtime when the leaves start sprouting. I can't wait to introduce you."

"A hundred chairs? Just like that?"

"Yes. Papá saved them when the Sureda fortune crashed. There isn't one of them that hasn't been sat on by some famous personage or other. There are tags on all of them, with names and dates. Miguel de Unamuno, Rubén Dario, Alphonse XIII *El Rey*, Chopin, Luis Salvador, the Duke of Austria, George Sand. Ever read any of her books?"

"Not one line. I only know that Nietzsche called her a horrible scribbling cow, and that she wrote a book on Mallorca that everybody here seems to be reading. In the German bookshop she represents world literature."

Pedro went on sketching. We chatted on, but then I had to shut my mouth because the contour of my Bambergian upper lip, shaped after Cupid's bow, was giving the artist some difficulty as it kept moving up and down. Beatrice went back to reading her detective novel, unperturbed by our conversation and my Habsburg bloodline, which years later in Portugal was to blossom forth in unexpected glory.

Pedro tore the sheet from his drawing pad and stuck it on our cactus plant. In *Poetry and Truth* Goethe relates that owing to a midwife's blunder he was considered stillborn, and that it was only as a result of strenuous efforts that he actually saw the light of the world. What got reborn here on Pedro's sheet of paper—as dubious as a *Doppelgänger*, a hybrid of Goya's ghost and some medieval German masterpiece—was simply not viable.

The constellation was not propitious. Beatrice turned away in disgust and left the delivery room. Woe to him who portrays her Vigoleis as uglier still than Mother Nature saw fit to create him! The artist, offended, asks me for my opinion. I have often sat for artists. It is always a difficult moment when they ask this question, or when they glance back and forth between the canvas and the model. I gave Pedro my honest opinion, right to his Bourbon face. If, I said, I wrote as badly as he sketched, I would throw myself down in front of a trolley car. Pedro turned sour. He was proud of his Bamberg Knight, and as an excuse he said that he was only just a beginner. His brother Jacobo was making much better progress, and his mother, the amateur princess...

No less sour, I replied that I, too, was just a beginner, and was beginning to fear that there would never be an end to beginning. And then we gave each other a hug. Would I care to exchange my pen for his pencil? Tomorrow he would bring me a pad full of jottings, aphorisms mostly. Would I be willing to read them through and tell him if he should switch from drawing to writing? But those damned army barracks! An hour ago he was scheduled to stand watch in some filthy guardhouse. He was late for duty, and didn't have a cigarette to bribe the officer in charge to look the other way. "What would insubordination like that cost you up there in Prussia? A whole pack of cigarettes, I'll bet you!"

I gave Pedro a bribing cigarette from Beatrice's stash. "It would cost me my head, my friend. And it would cost my family everlasting shame unto the seventh generation."

"A great people, the Germans! Papá admires them, especially if they're Catholic. He's against Luther, and he knows German, too. He learned it in the john."

"In the...? How do you...?"

My philological curiosity was awakened. I was familiar with several methods of language learning, and a few chapters later I will invent a new one myself. But I had never heard of the one that Pedro just mentioned. Beatrice, a certified foreign-language teacher, had surely never heard of it, either. Unfortunately, Pedro could not be persuaded to stay on. That would have cost Beatrice two cigarettes. He had no money, he said. And we didn't have any, either. And so he left to loaf through his guard duty. We parted as friends for life.

Only after the door closed behind him did it occur to me that he had not once spit on our floor. As I have already indicated, this is precisely the way I wanted to present him here—with his superior Spanish manners. In this sense, he left nothing behind. But his sketch of me still hung on our cactus plant, and that was just as bad. I took down the sheet and placed it in a folder. But maybe I should have left it in place and invoked Goethe: "Oh, Beatrice, if you were a German instead of this Swiss hodgepodge of ck, ck-dt, and Indian squaw, I would quote the Sage of Weimar, who once told his friend Eckermann that the Germans didn't know how to respond to strange occurrences, and thus they often missed out on higher things in life without even noticing. Goethe went on, and I quote verbatim: 'Any fact in our lives is not of value because it is true, but because it is significant.' Pedro's sketch and my ugliness, which can never be disguised as some Bamberg Knight, are facts, but they have no significance whatsoever."

I spoke these sublime words to the wind, for Beatrice entered the room, scrutinized the floor, disappeared again and came back with the pair of pants we used as a cleaning rag. Frowning tightly, she began wiping the floor.

"Now you see how these people can mess up your whole house. There's no end to cleaning up after them."

Whenever female intellectuals go on a cleaning rampage, it's a signal to take off. And if they don't, then you just have to go to the dogs in your own filth.

But then she, too, noticed that Pedro hadn't spit on our floor, and her mood changed.

"He must have had a good upbringing. As crazy as they are, those Suredas are first-class people."

"It's all a matter, my dear, of his royal blood. Kings spit on their subjects, but never on the floor!"

II

B eatrice, Pedro has an idea how we could earn some money."
    "You've had certain ideas, too. But all right. I'm curious. Tell me what he has in mind."

"Prostitution!"

"Oh, thanks a lot! I rather thought it might be that. You're impossible, the two of you. Just like smutty-minded little boys. So you want to send me out on the street?"

"Right! Out on the street, but together with me. The two of us, get it? We're going to pull the big trick. We're going to be *Führers*."

Back then the word *Führer* was already somewhat in bad odor, but only mildly so—like the place on a pork chop near the bone, where the smell begins. *Führer*: the term evoked ridiculous images such as a silly toothbrush moustache and a faggish lock of hair, a madman's eyes, and all of this stuck in a uniform to bring out the comedy and raise it to tragic German heights. This man was an easy mark for the international humor magazines, though considering that thousands of murders had already been committed in his name, he ought to have been looked into by criminal psychologists such as the famous Dr. Orthmann, director of the insane asylum in my home town of Süchteln. But in so-called heroic times, blood must flow in torrents before anyone realizes that it is blood. Germany itself had to become an insane asylum, in order that the prophecy might be fulfilled: that guy was going to end up in a padded cell.

And thus Beatrice and I became Tour Guides, meaning that we were now "*Führers*" minus the quotation marks.

Pedro introduced us to the manager of a travel agency, a German-Spanish enterprise called Baquera Kusche y Martins. The boss was a German with strong left-wing ideas and much bitterness in his heart. Apart from this, he seemed to be a kindly sort. His birthplace was Hamburg or some other north German town where they sssspeak with sssstrong ssssibilants, and he enjoyed teasing me about my sing-song Rhenish cadences. We got along very well, and we signed a work contract. His company organized group excursions with Woermann Travel, and led tours in Palma and to other points on the island. Each "*Führer*" was given a number to be displayed in a conspicuous place, and a company armband, and each evening, after the tourist hordes had jostled and questioned him half to death, a wage of 25 pesetas. To us that was a lot of money.

Some people enter this life as Guides and Leaders, able to lift the world right out of its hinges. But it also is possible to learn to be a Leader of the masses. A Leader, a *Führer* who learns on the job, goes through life with an aura of amateurishness, as with any occupation that one prepares for by sheer drudgery. He goes through the motions, satisfies his customers and earns his wage, and that's about it. How different it is with the blessed ones who are born to lead others. Everything they do comes naturally, and if their chosen profession brings them into direct contact with people—if, for example, they are murderers, or officials who serve the public from behind post-office counters— then their work is simply a form of play. When human lives are part of the job, they play with those too, just as if they were engaged in some shrewd card game or other.

Accepted for service as Leaders, we took the oath of fealty with a handshake. We had certain definite qualifications for this line of work: our ability with languages (especially Beatrice's ability) and our educational backgrounds. Our boss even complimented us for being "cultured individuals." Our outward appearance: satisfactory. He gave us a tour schedule which we were to study carefully. In case we hadn't already done so, we were to familiarize ourselves with the points of interest on the island—though as the manager said, we surely had lived here long enough for that. He could also provide us with descriptive literature. There was a "ssssstrict" rule to be followed. A Tour Leader must never leave unanswered a question from one of those he was leading! "*Der Führer* knows everything! Just remember that, and you will be excellent Leaders!"

I already knew that a *Führer* not only was supposed to know everything, but that he actually knew it. To come up with proof of that insight, I didn't have to reach very far back into my Vigoleisian past. Let's go just four short years back to 1928. We're in Cologne on Germany's Great River Rhine (but, unfortunately for some, not Germany's Great Western Border), in a former army barracks. There I find Vigoleis as a scholarly tour guide in the Hall of Cultural History at Cologne's renowned and fiscally ruinous "Pressa," the enormous exhibition devoted to the public media. For months he had worked on the staff assembled by the academic historians Karl d'Ester, Günther Wohlers, and Albert Bruckner, and had helped them put together their portion of the exhibit. Vigoleis knew exactly what lay or stood in every single glass case, and consequently he knew that everything in them lay or stood wrong. "Let's not lose time with trivial details," said a relaxed Professor Günther Wohlers, the greatest and most amiable beer-guzzler ever to grace a German university faculty. "After the opening," he declared, a full liter mug standing within easy reach on his seminar desk, "we'll change everything around. The politicians won't notice a thing. Not a single one of those bigwigs will notice anything while they're getting pushed through the halls on opening day."

Even after opening day, things stayed just as they were; Professor d'Ester was muzzled by his garrulous colleague. Thus our exhibit displayed the false cheek-by-jowl with the genuine, as is fitting for scholarship in general and for the discipline of history in particular. Then I made the discovery that a guide, i.e., a *Führer*, is an authority and has immense power. I invented explanations out of whole cloth, and soon I was the most sought-after tour guide—and the most knowledgeable. When famous visitors came, or especially learned or picky experts, the call went out for Vigoleis. Now there was a fellow who knew so much about all branches of literary and press history that he never was at a loss for an answer. That made him the ideal candidate for doctoral oral exams, and that was the very reason he never took them. Superannuated Cologne pols, Mayor Konrad Adenauer himself, and scholars from the world over, all shook his hand at the end of the tour. Dreyer of Dreyer Films wanted to hire him on the spot as a writer and narrator for his educational movies. Bodo Ebhardt wanted him as a scholarly assistant for his ritzy tours of castles and his phenomenal library at Castle Marksburg. The cruise-ship mogul Krone thought he could do wonders for his world-wide advertising. A laundry-soap company wanted to engage him as a factory tour guide for visiting housewives. An ordinary Cologne housewife asked me to visit her evenings after her husband had left for the night shift...

All this expertise began to give me the shivers, and eventually I quit. But not before the crown of scholarship had been placed on my head by the Berlin Institute for the History of the Press. The director of this illustrious enterprise came to Cologne one day with his students and joined in on my tour—incognito. At the end he presented me his business card. I knew his name, of course, from the scholarly journals. He asked me to take his place for a session of his Berlin seminar with a talk on a particularly knotty problem I had alluded to in the Broadsheet Room—a place where my imagination had an inordinate tendency to run riot. I stammered a few words in reply and was about to explain that not everything in the glass cases was entirely correct, when it occurred to me that this fellow hadn't noticed anything wrong at all. So I said nothing, and that evening I consulted with Dr. Wohlers, whose star pupil at Münster University I was at the time. Wohlers said, "Go to it, show them just what a *Führer* can really do. When this farce is all over with, you can get your degree with me with a thesis on 'Historical Hoaxes.'" I passed my Leader's exam at the exalted seminar in Berlin, and later received handwritten certification—from Prof. Dovifat or Prof. Heide, I no longer remember which.

"See?" said Günther Wohlers when I showed him my letter from the Berlin Institute. "That's how things are in this racket—just like a traveling circus. You just can't let up with the whip, that's all. You can always put things over on the biggies. It's the little two-bit know-it-alls we have to watch out for."

It was just such a half-pint smarty-pants, a high-school teacher from the Rhineland backwoods, who was almost my undoing. He arrived with pince-nez, salami sandwich, knapsack, puttees, and his eleventh-grade class. He tripped me up in the Napoleon Room. A Napoleon expert on the side, he was specializing in the Wartburg Festival and the book-burnings that had taken place there. A dangerous amateur historian.

In our exhibit on "Napoleon and the Rise of German National Pride," we had done more violence to historical authenticity than had already been committed in reality. During my spiel the teacher kept frowning and rubbing his sandwich paper against a glass case that was bursting with historical fakery. Then he started objecting: "Enough of this violation of German liberty!" The eleventh-graders, up to then more interested in a class of girls nearby than in my soporific lecture, suddenly were all ears. The teacher took the floor, pushing me against a wall that likewise bristled with distortions of history. The kids all grinned. The reputation of the exhibit was at stake, and along with that of the entire scholarly field of press history. More than that, my *de jure* employer, Mayor Adenauer of Cologne, would stand or fall with the fortunes of his brainchild, the "Pressa" exhibition. This mutiny, incited by a mere corporal in the ranks of public education, had to be nipped in the bud.

In front of his class I asked this puny know-it-all to take over the tour in my place. It was obvious, I said, that he knew much more about this stuff than Professor d'Ester, the doyen of our fledgling discipline. "Please, sir, go ahead and explain this document to your young gentlemen. It is the most important piece in the entire exhibit, but historically, also the most difficult to interpret." I led him to a case containing a single and very significant-looking document. It was significant, too, not because it was in the Italian language, but because it belonged in a completely different room. The caption was also totally wrong, though beautifully calligraphed on a gold card in Ehmcke Gothic, inscribed by one of Ehmcke's glamorous pupils. His artists had painstakingly lettered these gold cards by the thousands. Our archive contained stacks of them, but nobody knew where they all belonged. Not one of the professors could unravel the mess. Karl d'Ester, arriving one morning with egg on his face from a hurried breakfast, wrung his hands. Economists with doctor's degrees came by and weren't any help either. Finally Wohlers came to the rescue: "Put out cards in all the cases. If some are left over, get rid of them. Wrong cards can get changed around later." König, the archive messenger, brought in a bottle of beer, and all was hunky-dory.

But now it was the high-school teacher's turn to get egg on his face. To be brief about it: no matter how close he stuck his pince-nez to the glass, he couldn't make head or tail out of what he saw, and no doubt he couldn't read Italian anyway. He was just about to apologize in front of his whole class when another bevy of schoolgirls, led by a decorous nun, noisily entered this hall of dubious science. The eleventh-graders switched battlefields. One single zealot, a pimply kid with spectacles, stayed with us, making careful notes for his history essay. In the next room, another guide had started his lecture. Back in those days nobody felt obliged to shout "*Achtung!* The *Führer* is about to speak!"

Having once again demonstrated my prowess as a Leader in the field of applied science, how could I possibly fail here on the island? Beatrice studied hard. She devoured books, copied out excerpts, memorized dates. Then, like a good student, she scouted the city, visiting all the main attractions. As for me, I read nothing and visited nothing, for I have no memory at all and don't believe in marble tombs. The day before any tour, I could orient myself just a bit so the customers wouldn't end up at all the wrong places.

A few days later we received our marching orders. A Woermann ship was arriving. About twenty guides were signed on. At seven in the morning the rented cars stood in long rows at the pier. The tour director distributed lists, armbands, and written instructions. Each of us was assigned to a group of 20-25 people and told which car to use. Among the guides were some professional interpreters who had hold of the basic 1000 words in each language, and a few could actually speak them. For years they had been dragging foreigners, people whom as native islanders they despised, across the insular landscape—and holding out their palms at the end of each excursion.

Like all slogans, the one propagated by the Spanish Tourist Board, "*Mallorca clima ideal*," is a fraud—or shall we say, is based on a faulty conception of nature's meteorological vagaries. In any case, thousands of tourists have spent their time on the island in a driving rain. Let us concede, however, that on the day of our maiden tour, a hot sun and hot dust descended on all and sundry. The steamer dropped anchor in the bay, the harbor police climbed aboard, and longboats, sloops, and dinghies headed out to take on the passengers. Then the first batches came on land and fanned out. Each excursion participant had been assigned to a particular automobile. All they had to do was find the right number, or call it out as they came on land.

The Germans are great organizers, though they have never trusted their own organizations. A mad dash commenced. People bared their teeth, yelled, bumped up against each other. Each one wanted to be the first, wanted the best car and the best seat in the car. Fathers pushed mothers aside; daughters forgot their deportment-class manners; sons with facial scars, imagining that they were back in the Heidelberg dueling lists, flailed about trying to snag the snazziest car for their elders—why else travel First Class? In a shipwreck, scenes like this one are kept under control with a pistol. We weren't allowed to carry any, and so we had all we could do to deal with these high-paying German gentry. "Your number, please? Oh, I'm sorry. Yours is the next car, there, see the number on it?"—"What, that old jalopy? We're not getting into that thing, no sirree! That Schulz family over there, they got that big Mercedes. Are they any better than us? Do you know what kind of people the Schulzes are? Where can I register a complaint?"—"With your Guide, or with the company president in Hamburg. It'll go faster with the Guide."—"All right, then where's the Guide, otherwise they'll drive away right under our noses. We're First Class, in case you didn't know. Where's our *Führer*?"

"At your service, sir, and I'm happy to inform you that the car we have selected for you is an unusual one, with a very special feature."—"Liesl, come over here, the Guide here says that our car has some kind of special feature. Let's hear about it. The hell with the Schulzes." Liesl comes over, also two daughters and a son. I explain: "This old jalopy was formerly a luxury limousine, as you can see for yourself. It once belonged to no less a personage than the banker Juan March—you know, sure, that's the one. The special feature is the motor, 200 horsepower. The old rascal had it custom-installed for his drug-trafficking. Just between you and me, it's seen its share of cadavers. Later on I'll show you some bullet holes. A historic automobile, believe you me–if that sort of thing interests you." The family hesitates, but finally is cultured enough to enter the historic gangster vehicle.—"The one occupied by the family you have jokingly referred to as 'Schulz' may look better, but the motor's all shot. I know that car from a hundred tours and more. Breaks down every fifty miles."

Our driver gets in, I sit next to him. In the back seat Daddy and Mom are all smiles. Son and daughters on the fold-out seats are all smiles. After all, they've done it once again! They've picked a true Leader!

For a while now they can relax. Before we drive off, they'll write a quick postcard to Aunt Amalia back in Germany: "Dear Auntie, guess where we are! We're sitting in the *Führer's* limousine, haha!"

Now I have to leave the car again, down the way there's another insurrection, they're almost into fisticuffs. It's Beatrice's group! Beatrice is standing in the middle of a rude throng. In her excitement she's talking French, and that works miracles. These are all people of culture, after all. They've studied foreign languages, so they become as gentle as lambs and summon forth their meager fragments of French. "Oh please, Madame, keep on speaking French, we all know it and it's easier for you as a Spaniard, though I must say your German isn't bad at all—a little bit of an accent, but it sounds delightful. In Valencia we had another guide who spoke French, maybe you know him, real swarthy type, you know, and he was wearing..."

I am able to catch Beatrice just long enough to belch out a string of pithy Dutch expletives. These sons of bitches, let's drown the lot of 'em, shoot 'em all, string 'em up in the baobab trees! But Beatrice, so very touchy about spittle and footprints on our polished apartment floor, acts here as if transformed. She is even able to calm me down, by pointing out that this crazed multitude is traveling First Class. Really decent passengers, Third Class, would be arriving soon enough, and they'd be easier to deal with. Then she was gone, chasing after a woman about to dispense blows with her purse in retaliation against a Spanish driver. No sooner had this luxury-class fury taken her seat next to him, she gasped, than he tried to pinch her in a certain place—*jawohl*, and she was not going to tolerate such behavior! Other ladies were furious because no one had tried to pinch them—why go to all this trouble and travel through Spain as an unattached female? Both factions were right, in my opinion. All of the ladies should have been spirited off to the Clock Tower and thrown to the bulls. But on their chartered tour they all eventually got what they paid for. Those Spanish drivers are fairly bursting with virility. And the way they drive is tantamount to seduction itself: one hand on the wheel, the other on the female client. Lots of squeals and shrieks, especially in the curves, where hip contact naturally gets closer. Oh, I wish them all a safe journey! Still, in all my years as a *Führer* I never once heard of an accident arising from customer service of the kind under discussion. Well, perhaps a scratched fender here, a torn undergarment there...

A tourist disembarkation at the harbor in Palma takes the better part of an hour. Finally the masses have dispersed to the waiting automobiles. The tour director gives the high sign, and the first cars start out: Group 1, Guide 1, then five minutes later Group 2, Guide 2, and so forth, until the snake is winding its way across port city and island.

First stop: La Lonja, the ancient trade center, an eloquent witness to the former wealth of the city. "As you can see, ladies and gentlemen, this is a large Gothic sandstone building with small minarets, 1st half of the 15th century, built by Guillermo Sagrera, richly ornamented with sculpture, four octagonal corner towers, connected by an ornate parapet with turrets. Inside—just follow me, please, but be careful, chips of stone have been known to drop down—here inside, the vast interior is divided by two ranges of three spiral columns. Especially notable is the collection of paintings from the 15th, 16th, and 17th centuries. A spiral staircase—up there, you can see it from here— leads to the roof and from there to one of the corner towers, whence a fine view of the city, the harbor, and the bay is obtained. But we won't be going up, much too dangerous. Not too long ago an elderly lady, handicapped, fell from the parapet down to the street. Too late to save her, unfortunately."

Dead bodies always make a big hit. The remainder of the above text can be found in *Baedeker's Spain*, 1929 edition, pp. 124-25. Some guides, Beatrice without a doubt, passed on this information *ipsis verbis*. But I didn't, for the simple reason that this sort of stuff bores me to tears. As a *Führer* my chief aim was to enter that building a few paces ahead of my charges, and with my panoramic *Führer's* vision determine in an instant what things were all about. Then I collected my group and explained everything according to the dictates of my fancy. After a few introductory remarks, this fancy of mine transported me without ado back to the golden age of Mediterranean piracy. Inside this palace, I then elaborated, the pirates used to divide up their spoils. Abducted women were raped on the spot; the unattractive ones were sold as slaves. Up there in the corners were four small rooms for making gunpowder. And then I would introduce my favorite general: "He took care of the whole mess! Barceló cleaned up the entire *mare nostrum*! Those paintings over there were done in commemoration of that savage era. Take a look at them, but you won't see much. Covered with age-old patina. All right, let's move on!"

The next guide is already coming near, and so I have to shield my own people from questionable elucidations. So far, so good. They liked my story. And that's enough for me. The little gang of tourists got what they paid for. But wait—a little old lady with her nose in her Baedeker comes up and tells me that the book has it all different—isn't this the "Lonja"? Another lady, this one even older (I had winked at her during my brief lecture) asks abruptly which of the two ought to know better, our *Führer*, a local resident after all, or that foreigner Baedeker? Hadn't I been in this profession for quite some time? "Not only that, Madam. I have also been commissioned by a publishing house to edit a new guide to Mallorca containing hitherto unpublished material, most of which I have myself unearthed. And I intend to publish my findings despite a certain sensitiveness on the part of the island natives in historical matters."

"Daddy, did you hear that? Our guide is going to publish a brand new book all about historical sensitivity on Mallorca! He's our *Führer*, so let's buy it! OK, Dad?"

"We certainly shall, Agnes. These people are pioneers of German culture abroad, and they are contributing to our nation's prestige in foreign climes. After our tour we'll ask him to join us in a toast to the fatherland. I'm sure he'd like that. But now pay attention, Agnes. This is not just a pleasure trip. We're here as part of your education. Travel is more educational than home and school combined."

"Excuse me!" Somebody comes up to me, interrupting my victims' discussion about culture and education. "That painting over there in the right-hand corner. Isn't that late Van Dyck?"

"That one? No, it's early Hodler. But I'm grateful to you for asking such an intelligent question. Up to now no one has been able to establish just how that work of art ever got here to Mallorca. The Cantonal Museum in Bern is still investigating. Professor Iselin—surely you've heard of him—has come down here himself. He and I are working on it together."

"Many thanks, very interesting. I think I've read about that somewhere."

"Don't mention it."

Without stepping on the Swiss art expert's toes, I was unable to add a single thing more to this story about where the painting belonged. A very distinguished-looking gentleman from the group stepped forward and—I could see it in his eyes—was about to ask me a very tricky question. Before he came anywhere near, I was already sitting in the car, and we coursed through streets and alleys toward the Cathedral.

I did know a thing or two about this building. I remembered a few architectural details from our mournful starvation walks in its vicinity. But—who was slumbering within the many sarcophagi; how wide, how long, how high; how many columns, when it was built, why it was built, with whose money, with whose sweat, who designed it, when the deterioration had set in, when it would be restored, how many people could fit inside it—Please, ladies and gentlemen, for God's sake (that's probably why it's standing here) don't ask, because I simply don't know and I'd have to concoct stories to come up with answers. I'd rather you pray to your *Führer*. Churches are meant to be prayed in, not studied. Most people forget that.

We have half an hour for the Cathedral. I ask my group first of all to let the colossal space take its effect, which they all do; they crane their necks like chickens being eyed by a hawk. "Simply colossal!" "You're so right!" Then comes the first question: why are the columns that support the central nave angled slightly inward? Damn it all, I never noticed that. They really are bent inward. My brain comes up with the Leaning Tower of Pisa—can I use that here somehow? Call it a "partial inclination"? But first I throw in the jazz that never fails to do its stuff: "That's an excellent question, one that shows unusual powers of observation. Are you perhaps an art historian, and a very original one at that?" The young man nods assent. I'll have to be careful. Even on well-trodden paths there can be traps. Dad and Mom take one step forward and eye their son proudly for asking such a smart question. This evening the whole ship will know it: that young fellow will go far—he knows how to get at problems, and how to embarrass a tour guide. But wait just a minute. I make reference to one of the Pre-Socratics, who once said that the right question is half of its own answer. Still, I go on, in art history this maxim didn't always hold, and most surely not in this particular cathedral. At this, the student's parents' eyes glaze over. The student himself says, "I beg your pardon?" and I can tell that with my remark I have threatened his pride as well as my own. But I continue: we could take two basic ideas as our point of departure: a religious idea and an architectural idea. To me it would seem more appropriate to combine the two, for as we know, the great cathedrals of the world were conceived as amalgams of religious-rhythmic contemplation and secular-technical visual acumen. For this very reason, our own centuries have no longer produced cathedrals. People in my group nod their heads. And they nod even more energetically once I start using motions of the hands to illustrate my assertions. Especially effective in this setting is what might be termed the "pumpkin outline," employed as an indication of the cathedral's limitless dimensions. It never fails.

But this student just wouldn't let go. He pestered me no end with his insistent prodding, and when several more tourists rejoined my group and started listening intently, I had no choice but to start talking in earnest. I abandoned all rationality, donned the mantle of smugness, and found the solution in a flash: mystical inclination. The columns inclined that way as an expression of a mystical tendency. This kind of statement must, of course, be delivered with loudly echoing chest tones. Then it does have its effect. "*Inclinatio mystica*, sir! Surely you are familiar with the concept. We have before us here the sole example of medieval mysticism translated directly into architectural space."

The young academician motions to the intent crowd that he is, in fact, familiar with the tendency in question. Ten minutes more of reverberating rhetoric, and I have explained how the medieval technicians were able to raise the columns without causing the collapse of the whole edifice. One of the tourists, probably an architect, pointed out that the damned columns were not only inclined inward, but that they were positioned asymmetrically to the central line of the nave. Vigoleis, once again into the breach! Hod carriers! Vigoleis mobilized thousands of hod carriers to fill the entire nave with sand, thus preventing the columns from falling. To me it seemed like a perfectly cogent explanation. But now there were audible skeptics. Even some of the uncultured faces started grinning. One gentleman pulled out a pocket slide rule and said, "Now wait, my good man, how much sand? I'll have that figured out in a second." My knees turned to rubber. Slide rules aren't reliable beyond the decimal point, and even in front of it they leave much room for the imagination. But I was about to be exposed, and all I was doing was making up stories for 25 pesetas. Never let a question go unanswered! *Der Führer* knows everything!

"Well now, my good friend, it figures after all. Congratulations! When the Suez Canal was built..."

All ears were on the Suez expert. I took a deep breath. I was liberated. The crooked columns collapsed, the Cathedral of Palma sank into nothingness, and nobody noticed at all. For meanwhile, an argument had started among the gentlemen over whether Ferdinand "von" Lesseps, the architect of my savior the Canal, wasn't himself a German, and whether an envious world wasn't trying to rob Germany of his accomplishments, too. It was, somebody piped up, the same as with Johannes Gensfleisch, known to posterity as Gutenberg. Those goddam Dutchmen were always claiming that their man Coster...

God was with me, and against my German clients. Who's to say that He doesn't abide in the houses named after Him?

We continued our tour. I pointed to the rose window and explained that German stained-glass artists had had their hand in the brilliant result—a remark that didn't fail to win approval. After that I again lapsed into fiction. Things got especially hairy when we came to the marble sarcophagi, whose separate contents I mixed up hopelessly. Not one carcass stayed in its proper holy place, and none got correctly ascribed to the person it had been in real life. No one noticed, for somebody in the group mentioned that German carcasses were much better anyway. Comments like this diverted attention.

Things proceeded in this fashion, beyond our allotted time. I made springs gush forth where there were no springs, I pulled stars down from the sky, entombed living persons, all for 25 pesetas. But happily, people who travel First Class are so very cultured that they'll swallow anything.

Up comes a gentleman, introduces himself, we shake hands, he offers me his cigar case, genuine German Brasil, or would I prefer a throat lozenge? He compliments me on my absolutely superb explanations. *Donnerwetter*, he says, that's the best thing he's had on the whole trip. Surely I was aware of the ignorance that you meet up with nowadays in the field of tour guidance! Unbelievable! Then he takes me by the arm and gets confidential. I think to myself, now he wants to know the way to the nearest house of bawds—I'll be happy to send him to the Clock Tower with my compliments. "But do you realize, Herr *Führer*, what kind of people you have as clients? I mean, have you noticed just who is here among us?"

I confessed that I hadn't noticed. I wasn't about to tell him that I regarded the whole lot of them as idiots—I wouldn't mention that until tonight at the pier, when we would be saying *adios*. All we were told was that this shipment contained nothing but academicians and high-class types, but that you could spot that right away by the way they disembarked. After all, the disciples at Emmaus also had an idea who was standing among them. The gentleman puts his mouth to my ear and hisses forth his secret: "Von Puttwitz!"

"Von...?"

"Exactly! The general! I'm afraid he's in another group, but I'll get him over here. I want him to meet you. You know, he's the one with the..."

"Oh, that one? With the two...?"

"Two? What do you mean, there were three!"

"Oh, of course, if you look at it that way."

"Nowadays that's how you have to look at it. Otherwise the German nation is lost. We have very hard times ahead of us. But Puttwitz..."

I knew less about any General von Puttwitz than I did about the builder of Palma Cathedral or the corpses that repose in its vaults. I had noticed a middle-aged man with dueling scars and a Vandyke, accompanied by two women. That one could very well be a general, and that is why I was about to ask whether it wasn't the one with the two ladies that this guy was talking about. But in General von Puttwitz' life the number three was apparently the magic digit. Maybe he had been divorced three times. Or jailed—for political reasons, of course. Or maybe he had made three attempts on the *Führer's* life, or on Poincaré's. At any rate, this conversational misunderstanding brought the two of us only closer together.

"By heavens," I said, "Ill have to report this to my friend Martersteig this very night!"

"Martersteig?"

"No less! Baron, or General von Martersteig. He holds claim to both titles."

"You don't say! Wait a minute: Battle of the Marne..."

"Sorry, von Richthofen Fighter Squadron."

"Oh, of course! That's where he was. Great flyer. He's living here? Recuperation?"

A small group of tourists had come close by, so I put a finger to my mouth and whispered into the gentleman's ear, "Secret mission!"

"Aha! I understand. And you?" He winked at me. I winked back, and pointed meaningfully at my official Guide number. Our confidential bond was established—not, to be sure, at a table of regulars in some rustic German inn, but in patriotic surroundings at one of the frontier outposts in an anti-German world. My fellow conspirator bowed slightly; he would report to the General and bring him over to my group with a few other colleagues. "And then we'll drink to our *Führer*!"

I bowed. "Oh sir, you are too kind!"

But this was yet another misunderstanding. For the *Führer* he was talking about was not Vigoleis, but that other *Führer*, the non-quixotic one. It was Adolf Hitler.

My skull fumed, my stomach churned, my mouth filled with a bilious liquid. And this was only the beginning of the tour.

I drummed my people together, gave each one of them a kindly word, and received thanks and peppermint candies in return. Not one of them gave me 25 pesetas. If any had, I would have sped homeward right then and there.

Mom, Daddy, Trude, Lore, and Fritz had taken their seats in the car. They smiled at me; now I was one of the family and was offered chocolate and cigars. "Thanks, but I don't smoke."

I could take it easy for a few minutes. The papal maxim "Rather a scandal than a lie" is convincing, but only if you're a pope. I couldn't afford a scandal; I had to lie for my 25 pesetas, and this day had to end sometime. "I am better than my blather," we read in a story by Bjørnstjerne Bjørnson, in a context about cowardice. But Vigoleis is definitely a coward.

The continuation of our trip, taking us through the city and up into the mountains to Valldemosa, proceeds very slowly. Each column of cars has to wait until the dust settles from the column ahead.

Before leaving the city we visited the San Francisco Monastery, where the mystic Raimundus Lullius is said to be buried and probably even is. To this man's spirit I devoted a few words that were genuine in every sense, but which did not fall on such fertile ground as had my fantasizings at the Trade Center and the Cathedral. General von Puttwitz—or was it von Puttkammer?—arrived and rescued me from the fetters of truth. We shook hands like old friends; there was no need for lengthy introductions. Each of us conversed with the other using subtle hints and allusions, and it worked to perfection. Germans are always more at home in miasmic fog than they are on the sunny byways of the diaspora. That's why their attempts to conquer *Lebensraum* have been such washouts.

We left the city. How long would I be able to doze on the way to Valldemosa? An hour? Not one second! Turning around toward the back seat, my neck craned at a painful angle, I had to submit to a barrage of questions. My own personal data were now more interesting to the tourists than the Mallorcan landscape with palms, oranges, olives. A troop of black piglets gamboled across the red soil, but only Trude showed any interest; the others harkened to the words coming from my bone-dry mouth. Before the car started climbing the foothills, my passengers knew that their *Führer* was born in Spain, but that he had grown up in the care of a blind aunt in Germany, in a little town on the Lower Rhine known for the erstwhile good works of a Christian saint and for its annual yield of carrots. My father, Consul in Malaga, had been killed in the famous train wreck. My mother, now remarried, lived in Burgos.

"Destiny," said the man in the back seat. Mom fully agreed with him, because Fritz had a friend whose father was a consul in Turkey and had also died there.

"Destiny," I said, and turned around to grab a snooze. But once again I had to open up my personal file. This time it was about one of the other Guides, a lady who looked like a gypsy. Did I know her? I did indeed. She was the daughter of an attaché at the Peruvian Embassy in Madrid, had been living for years on the island with her Swiss mother, and was bored stiff. She was acting as a tour guide just to pass the time. Her brother, an airy chap in every way, was the famous balloonist who just recently had risen in a paper-clad *montgolfière* and set a record for Alpine hovering. Did news of that reach Germany? Daddy vaguely remembered reading about it in the Neue Zürcher Zeitung. I was glad to hear that he had.

Our chauffeur was superb. He took the curves with typically Spanish death-defying velocity, but also with typically Spanish driving skill. If I owned a car, I would let it be driven only by a Spaniard or a Portuguese. The chances of breaking our necks with this expert at the wheel were small indeed, which meant that I would have to bear with the other passengers for the remainder of the trip.

We were approaching one of the farmsteads called *fincas*, and right away the questions started. What kind of a country estate was that? This by no means simple question came from Trude, the one who had spied the black piglets. But her mother promptly reprimanded her: did she expect our *Führer* to know every detail about everything? Then, turning to me, Mom explained that Trudi was on her first trip away from Germany. In my opinion, Trudi's question wasn't in the least annoying, and I came near to begging their pardon for knowing all about this particular *finca*. Then I started in. I spun my tale slowly, so as to make it last until we reached Valldemosa. Two hostile brothers, romance in dark forests, a dastardly deed under a mulberry tree, a Corsican-style vendetta—"Really? That sort of stuff still going on in the Balearics?"— "Only on Mallorca. Did you see that big cedar tree? It was planted when the families were reconciled. The writer Mario Verdaguer has written a novel about it, that's how I know."

Valldemosa! Everybody out!

The high spots in Valldemosa are the Carthusian Monastery and the cells where Chopin and George Sand lived in the famous winter of 1838-39. I would be giving myself a guided tour of the place.

Pedro had told us a few things about the property his family had to auction off, and so I was acquainted with the town and the monastery without ever having set foot there before. The rousing story of the Verdugian matriarch now came in very handy—my listeners shuddered. How can a mother possibly...? The castle turret where Pedro had done his painting provided me with an occasion to tell about a friend of mine who had climbed onto the King of Spain's family tree, and how as a child he had played football in the monastery garden with Moorish skulls, until Don Juan put an end to this un-Christian behavior, appropriating the skulls for his meticulously labeled, bizarre collection: Ibn Mohammed Bar.

I let my charges stretch their legs, take a few inane pictures, and eat oranges.

Then I hauled them into the *Cartuja* in the prescribed sequence: church, sacristy, colonnade, and cells. There wasn't much to explain in the church. Some saint or other stands on a pedestal holding one eye in her hand—anybody could interpret that one blindfolded. Architecture: I estimate early 18th century, an ugly commission of the local bishop's treasury, one that no doubt pleases God more than it does modern man with his vast sophistication in matters of art history. I will have to admit, however, that some buildings are beautiful just because they are standing in Spain, just as some rubbish takes on value when it doesn't deny its age.

My group squeezed into the sacristy. I had fallen behind by entering a technical discussion about raising tomatoes on Mallorca, finding to my surprise that I knew anything at all on the subject. "Oh yes, of course, the *sacristia*, let's go give it a look." I was the last to enter. That was a mistake, for now I could only pray that I wouldn't get any premature inquiries.

I saw glass cases containing vestments, chalices, monstrances and the like, old missals, things I was familiar with from my one-mass tenure as an altar boy. *Oh how far away, how far away...* and I commenced: "Over here, please, ladies and gentlemen..." But apparently no one was interested in what their *Führer* wanted to show them. They had discovered something on their own— the echt German spirit in the outside world, showing its indomitable, pioneering vitality even on a vacation trip—Herr *Führer*, could you please tell us what this is?"

The sacristy lay in semi-darkness. I couldn't quite make out what it was they were asking me to identify. And I didn't dare to part the crowd and walk over to that pointing finger, aimed at some object behind glass. The frame was thick and black. The object, about one span wide, was also black. Everything was black, black as the ace of spades. What can that possibly be?

I had no idea of all things it *might* be. But what it *had* to be—that I knew in an instant. The idea came to my mind as swiftly as lightning, by way of one of those baffling thought reflexes that keep psychiatrists from starving. Something pitch black, I thought—and suddenly I had it. I could begin my speech.

Well now, I explained—with the infallible instinct that has made our German nation the foremost nation in the world, my devoted followers had picked out at first glance the one item in the collection that made it worth our while to spend any time at all in the sacristy. All the other objects in the cases and on the walls were of no account, the usual *sacralia*, but that item over there— and then things went black before my eyes, jet black, my mind blackened out the sum of 25 pesetas. But then came the second bolt of lightning: The Black Death! God's Avenging Angel! Angels of the Lord wreaking Heaven's vengeance on earth! Let them perish by the plague, these sinners, unmourned and unburied, and let their bodies litter the fields as dung and a feast for the birds of the air!

In just a few seconds it all took shape as in a dream, across centuries and continents, a crazy jumble of thoughts and images: the Justinianine Plague of the 6th century; passages from the Old Testament; scores of woodcuts from the broadsheet exhibit at the "Pressa" in Cologne; the devastating Black Death of the 14th century, thinning the ranks of Europe's population almost as efficiently as a mechanized war. I waxed as eloquent as an Old Testament prophet; they hung on my words, no one paid any more attention to the black object that had spread the Great Dying all across the island. Here in the Valley of Muza, the sheik who had given his name to this place, Vall-de-Muza, here in this valley the Grim Reaper had raged more fiercely than anywhere else in these parts. People died like flies, the area stank like the pestilence, healthy persons simply collapsed dead in a heap, and their boils burst open, emitting fumes of new death. Blasphemers turned instantly into pious worshipers, god-fearing monks cursed the Lord, devout believers echoed Job on his dung-heap.

This went on for years, I explained further. If it had lasted one or two more years, Mallorca, the Golden Isle, would have been like an extinct volcano. But behold, in the classic hour of direst need, a priest ("old and gray," naturally) received a miraculous inspiration: a penitential procession! Amid lamentations and sacred hymns, amid prayer and self-flagellation, let all the able-bodied pass though the mountains at night and implore Heaven for surcease, and the Mother of God for Her succor: Lord, have mercy on Thy suffering children from the Valley of Muza!

The image I sketched out of the nocturnal cavalcades was gruesomely appealing: plague victims straggling in long lines through the very landscape that the tourists could see around them. Imagine that it is nighttime: dark clouds scud overhead, moonlight hovers over the scrubby pines, the chalky ridges, the desolate palms. There is a smell of death.

Slowly, I backed up toward the exit, hoping to draw my rapt audience away from that accursed black object before I let go with my punch line. For once that was out, all eyes would of course turn again to the object just explained. "Lo and behold, ladies and gentlemen, the processions hadn't taken place but a few nights when the Avenging Angel lifted his hand from the tormented Valldemosans. Fewer and fewer of them died, and then suddenly there were no more deaths at all. Their wounds healed, their scabs fell off, only their terrible scars remained as testimony to the disaster. The last bodies were buried, and they threw their plague-infested garments into the fire. The Black Death had been conquered! But not before he demanded one last sacrifice: the old, gray priest. He died like the wizened old mother in Goethe's famous poem.

"Centuries later, as a memorial to the devout processions, one of the monks in the Charterhouse carved in miniature a torch just like the ones fueled with pitch and carried at the head of the procession on those nights, adding their eerie glow to the mournful tones of the *Miserere*, and visible far and wide in the mountains. The Archbishop of Toledo blessed the replica before it was framed and exposed to the reverent attention of the faithful. Once a year this so-called *taeda pestis* is shown in the open air. And every 13th year this eloquent relic is carried in solemn procession over the very same route as that followed by the Valldemosans so very long ago. May the Good Lord preserve us from hunger and pestilence, Amen!"

Round about me it had become perfectly silent. You could have heard the proverbial pin drop, but only if somebody dropped one. And besides, outside in church and colonnade we could hear the tumult of the tourist mob, munching figs and oranges and drinking beer from bottles and wine from calabashes. Several were already drunk. They were thus doubly out of character, for a Spaniard never gets soused on fermented spirits. He has other means of intoxication.

No sooner had I capped my pious fable with the final "Amen," than I heard another guide noisily approaching the sacristy. It was a Spaniard, and he was doing his level best with his German and his Germans. He trumpeted forth: "Lady anda gentaman, nowa I showa la *sacristia* witha genuina naila froma True Crossa ofa Christa ina beautifula frame-a!"

I broke out in a cold sweat. A nail from the Cross of Golgotha! Oh Lord, Who wert crucified for us, why hast Thou forsaken Thy Vigoleis? The most obvious answer—why hadn't he thought of it? Long ago Schopenhauer put his finger on a peculiar defect of the Germans: that they can't see what lies at their very feet and go looking for it in the clouds. And the same Schopenhauer also realized that any charlatan could lead Germans by the nose if he just kept on mouthing nonsense at them. Was there something of both in Vigoleis: a charlatan and a man of the clouds? Is Vigoleis' personality bisected in this authentically German way, as with the incomparable Nietzsche, Heine, and Börne, and on down to the dullest German teutonophobes? Be that as it may, I had done a masterful job of spouting nonsense!

I was able to evade the Spanish *Führer* and lead my group out into the fresh air. No one noticed anything amiss.

Outside I sat down on the parapet. The Avenging Angel came within an ace of snatching me up and flinging me into the abyss. I was already starting to hear my bones rattle when Beatrice came over to me with a smile. I never would have thought that prostitution would give her such pleasure. But she had "charming people" in her group, she told me. Why, there was even a publisher among them, and she had mentioned my... "But Vigo, what's happened, you look awful!"

"Beatrice, I've just escaped the Black Death!"

The Peruvian ambassador's daughter stared at me, then she quickly sprang to the rescue. "You come with me, over here in the shade! I think you're getting sunstroke!"

"Ah, *chérie*, the emergency is over. I've already had a stroke. Just let me sit down. Tonight I'll explain everything."

"A woman?"

"Much worse! You'll hear all about it tonight—that is, if I'm able to talk any more." Before Beatrice could push a wedge of orange into my mendacious mouth, we were surrounded by a circle of gentlemen: General von Puttkammerwitz and his Staff.

"Aha, now we've got him, our disappearing artist! A little flirting, eh? *Jaja*, great landscape, as I'm beginning to notice, odd similarity to certain chalk deposits in the Dolomites, could this be the same strat...? *Ach*, I beg your pardon, didn't mean to disturb..."

"Not at all, *Herr General*. Permit me to introduce you."

The daughter of the Peruvian diplomat in Madrid had no objection, and behaved in keeping with her background. Herr von-zu-und-auf-Putt-und-Kammerwitz cracked his heels together. Not only he, but the entire Staff clicked to attention and each member barked out his name in turn. I remember only one: Lieutenant von der Hölle. Beatrice made her "snooty" face, and the General Staff seemed to appreciate that, though they were somewhat less charmed by the fact that she preferred to speak French. It was a first-rate scene, and they all racked their martial brains to recall "who we have sitting over there (they meant in Lima) at the embassy." But before they could agree on a qualified diplomat, an elderly lady appeared, walked up to Beatrice with a glowing smile, and in purest Swiss German began an earnest conversation with the Peruvian woman, beginning with "Do luege Sie emol" and continuing out of earshot of the General Staff.

In fact, Beatrice left the scene with this Frau Sopzin, or Sarasin, or Phischer (ph as in "photo"), or whatever. The gentlemen in the company of Herr von Witzprittkammer put on amazed faces—now then, wasn't that Swiss German we just heard? I enlightened them: "Her mother's Swiss." —Ach so! And then they wanted to learn more about my "secret mission." Although I had given my word of honor, this much I could tell them: never again a Marne outrage, never again a Compiègne. I was about to add "Never again a Kaiser on the lam," but caught myself just in time to avoid such a gaffe. For all I knew, these guys might be members of a monarchist cadre serving under the man from Braunau.

"Gentlemen, it has been an honor! *Führer* duties, you know how it is. But by all means don't miss the little town of Deyá, on the left up on a hill—I'll tell your driver. That's where he lives, our Herr von Martersteig, in a tower called *Atalaya*. Within the foreseeable future Germany's fate could well be affected in no small measure from that little place, where a great man still exercises quiet heroism. His enemy lives there, too. Surely you all have heard of him: Graves, Robert von Ranke Graves?"

Someone slowly puffed air through his lips, and then said, "Good-bye To All That?"

"The very same."

"That miserable swine?"

I heard no more, for again I made myself scarce, leaving the General Staff to itself in the shadow of the Charterhouse, which in its day had dealt with other powerful personages. Pedro's Papá surely would have liked to speak a word or two in that gathering, and to show around certain objects bearing labels.

In Sóller new challenges awaited the *Führer*. The farther this tour took him, all the more tenuous did his hold on German culture become. We were to have our noontime meal in this town, which we knew from previous visits. The tourists were distributed according to precise lists among the restaurants and *fondas* of the little railway junction. The train station, of recent vintage, had a very good restaurant named "Ferrocarril," where up to a hundred guests could be fed at a given time. The tables were already set, an elating sight for starved, dusty, sweaty tourists. The guides had to direct the guests to their tables: You over here, you over there. Truly a game of patience. I had to accompany ten people to a small *fonda*, which I myself couldn't locate without the help of a street urchin. It was an ancient house with a dining terrace not much lower than the roof that covered it. Grapevines were everywhere, their fruit hanging in huge bundles right down to the tables. There was a glow and a fragrance over everything; it smelled of wine and olive oil. Dust and flies filled the air and covered the entire scene. It couldn't have been more Spanish. But my guests turned up their noses. Protest! Were they worth any less than the people eating in fine style over at the "Ferrocarril?" And did their *Führer* realize how much they had paid for this trip? A thousand marks per, *jawoll*! And did he expect them to be fed like common laborers in some greasy spoon? Where were the complaint forms?

Actually, only one man had spoken up—in such situations it is always one man who does the talking, the lead stallion who sets the more or less melodious tone. Later all the others chime in together in uproarious babble. It was no different here. Leicas got put back in their cases, jackets got thrown over shoulders *à l'espagnol*, and even less well-to-do travelers knew pretty exactly what their tourist-class tickets were *supposed* to be paying for. The Guide was requested to lead the group to the train station so they could have a decent meal. He was to see to the necessary arrangements—they were hungry! What a scandal, to eat in such a filthy dive!

Here in the land of saints, I again found myself in need of someone to protect me from this mob of philistines. No saint appeared. So I thought I would give my home town's patroness, St. Irmgardis, a try. Legend has it that she miraculously pulverized the castle of some robber knights who were pursuing her with dishonorable intentions. "Blessed Irmgardis, come to the aid of thy servant Vigoleis!" I calmed down, my fever abated, and I clearly saw ahead of me the path that I should follow. It was the path of money. I was going to have to do some arithmetic for my rebellious clients.

"Excuse me, sir, but did I hear you correctly? 1000 marks?"

"Well, what did you think? *Jawoll*, a shiny G-note! You can go cheaper on the Monte Rosa, or didn't you know?"

Oh, I do know. But now tell me, do you know Bielefeld? Ever heard of it?"

"The city? I know it on a map. Why?"

"How many of you know Bielefeld?"

Not one of them knew the city. I'd never been there either, but that was beside the point. Then I asked what city the rabble-rouser came from. Central Germany, so now I could figure out roughly what it would cost him to go First Class by train to Bielefeld: 20 marks. Now the electric railway from Palma to Sóller, I explained, was a product of German ingenuity, designed and built by Siemens & Schuckert. The train station: German enterprise, German architecture. The station restaurant: German art and, coincidentally, built by the same architect who did the railroad station restaurant in Bielefeld, only there things were a little larger in scale. The food at the "Ferrocarril" was good, you might even say excellent, but 1000 marks was much too much to pay for it. The same was true in Bielefeld, and there the beer was no doubt much better, Dortmund Union brand. When in Spain one ought to do as the Spaniards do—drink wine instead of beer, and instead of parking oneself in a German railway station diner, one should take one's place on the terrace of a *fonda*. And this particular *fonda* was world-famous to boot.

They pricked up their ears. Famous places can be photographed. A wave of questions came at me.

"Well, you see, in this house, and on this balcony, Cervantes wrote his *Don Quixote*, in 95 nights by the light of an oil wick. During the day he slept, as many writers do. This is sacred ground. Surely I need say no more."

No one noticed that the ground beneath my *alpargatas* was getting very warm. A few seconds passed. Nobody raised any objections to my travesty of literary history. On the contrary, they were already busy taking snapshots of the holy shrine, doffing their jackets again, examining every stone and every wooden beam with the intentness of connoisseurs. I gave a sign to the proprietor, who had been watching the proceedings with interest, to bring out our meals. I explained the various dishes, recommended them all without reservation, and they thanked me. The women went wild-eyed: what a marvelous *Führer*!

When a German sits down at a historic place, he takes a deep breath, rolls up his sleeves (if he hasn't done so already), yanks forth his automatic pencil and writes a picture postcard. That is the way it has been ever since the world has known Germans and picture postcards, two creations that supplement each other. In the *fonda* where Cervantes wrote his *Don Quixote* my German clients behaved no differently. The owner brought over his box of pictures, people licked their graphites, and soon the homeland would be all ears:

"Dear folks, we owe these special greetings to our *Führer*. We're writing this at a historic place, which is something our *Führer* got us into. It's where Don Bosco wrote his famous *Infant of Spain*, all at night. Our *Führer* told us all about it, and we'll tell you more when we get home. Oranges are more expensive here, and the beer back home is a lot better. Love,..."

"But Richard, look at the mistake you made! The guide didn't say Don Bosco. It's Boskop, or something like that. You know, that famous name!" What did she mean, Richard protested; he was sure it was Bosco. Then turning to me he explained that his wife was thinking of those apples in her garden, Noble Boskops. But wait, wasn't Bosco the guy who sailed around the world? In school they read his travel books.

Navigare necesse est. A little education can't hurt either.

I wanted to hunt out the tavern assigned to the General Staff, join in with the gentlemen and do my bit to ensure a glorious future for the Reich. So I took leave of my own group, placing them in the safekeeping of Cervantes' ghost as they ate, wrote postcards, and prided themselves on the greatness of the historic moment.

At the entrance to another *fonda* the proprietor stood wringing his hands, protecting himself against two tourists who were apparently about to attack him. As a *Führer* I intervened in the fray. Ah, said one of the Germans, finally a guide shows up! And did I realize what a scandalous mess this place was? "Just come with us!"

This *fonda* wasn't as emphatically romantic as the Cervantes Inn I had just left, but it too was typically Spanish, even typically Mallorcan. Three dozen tourists fixed me with fire in their eyes. Had there been a holdup? Rape?

"Herr *Führer*, are you a German?"

"Spanish, but I grew up in Germany."

"Then you are familiar enough with our language to know the word 'swill.' This stuff here is swill. It belongs in a pigsty."

The spokesman for the mob pointed to his plate, which contained a broiled fish biting its tail in desperation; in the language of *haute cuisine* it was "curled." I knew the dish; it was rather bland, though tasty enough if you added lots of lemon juice, and it had a high protein content, very nutritious. In a small town like this one, when thousands of tourists have to be fed on short notice, the cooks often reach for this fish, one that can be netted easily and in large quantities. The inn owner couldn't make himself understood. The waiters threw hostile glances at the foreigners, who like a gang of convicts had now gone on a hunger strike. Back home they thought nothing of a meal of pickled herring and sauerkraut. I would have to act. Blessed Saint Peter, come to the aid of thy servant Vigoleis! I tapped on a glass and asked for their attention.

The Germans, I said, were a great nation, a gifted nation, a clever nation. The whole world, though it may not want to admit it, owed much to the Germans. The tourists' faces brightened a bit. True enough, I wasn't able to transform the curled fish into pig's knuckles and sauerkraut, or even into pickled herring. Eschewing such miracles, I decided to go the route of heroism—always a sensation for my fellow Germans. The ancient Germanic tribes, I proclaimed, were extremely fond of fish. The Rhine-Valley tribe of the Bructeri had gone so far as to elevate the salmon to the status of a divinity (murmurings of "Hear, hear!" from my audience). During the World Conflict, I continued, German U-boats under the outstanding leadership of their heroic captains had dominated the world's oceans, not only destroying enemy tonnage, but also causing the man-eating shark to flee for its life. Not one of the world's oceans was safe from the German undersea navy—except for the peaceful, golden, sun-drenched Mediterranean. The sharks got wind of this and swarmed into the *mare nostrum* through the Straits of Gibraltar. Accordingly, the science of marine biology listed this sea for the period from 1914 to 1918 as a new habitat for the notorious man-eater.

Ladies and gentlemen, what you see before you on your respective plates is the killer shark, but at an age when he is as yet quite harmless. In these parts he is considered a rare delicacy. In Paris, *Chez Nogarette*, a meal like this would cost a fortune. And incidentally, you are lucky that you didn't arrive here one month later. This is the peak of shark season for the Balearics. The neighboring island of Ibiza lives almost exclusively on the infant man-eater. Note particularly the somewhat gamey taste. With a sip of Felanitx white you can lend this dish a piquant note that not even the Parisians can emulate. Shall I order a few bottles of Felanitx?

Within seconds all plates were clean. Not a man-eating shark in this world could have gobbled its meal as fast as these sauerkraut connoisseurs finished theirs. People called to the waiters for more shark, more Felanitx, and postcards. They wrote, "Dear Aunt Gertrude, we are in a fabulous Spanish restaurant in Sóller. You'll never guess what we just had for dinner: curled shark with a very gamey taste. As we ate it we thought of you, and we hope you are well. Our guide told us all about this special treat. Later we're going swimming in the Bay of Sóller. I hope there aren't any sharks there. Our guide told us about an uncle of his who got eaten up by one."

The owner of the inn embraced me in sight of the voracious throng and pressed two shiny duros into my palm. Then he pulled me into the kitchen. I had to explain to his help how I had converted the barbarians. A miracle at high noon! "*Hombre*," he cried (and that means "man" to the highest power), "we almost lost the whole show! Nobody's got sick? You probably know that shark is really a rare item. The fins are a gourmet's delight." This was an indication of how close I had once again come to the abyss. St. Peter, the miraculous fisherman, had held me just above water with his angling rod. But meanwhile I had myself become nauseous. I departed from the Curled Shark Inn and went in search of a place where I could lie down flat for an hour. My appetite was gone.

Out on the town the Master Race held sway. They were tipsy, some of them blotto. I hid my face. They were behaving just like back home; after all, this was only Spain. No one could begrudge them their patriotic songs, I suppose. But there under a blistering sun and palm trees, their "Blonde Rhineland Maiden" sounded even odder than "*Deutschland über alles*." Oh, my dear fellow Germans, if only you would stay at home! For this you're shelling out a thousand marks?

I had no luck finding a place to snooze. "Herr *Führer*!" It started up all over again. "Over here! They're trying to gyp us. They want three pesetas for this thing! Back home we could buy it for half a mark!"

You stupid nitwits, I thought. The very fact that it's "Made in Germany"—that's precisely why it costs three pesetas here! The talent for haggling is a matter of human self-respect. I don't have that talent, and never did have it. I can't haggle with God, or the devil, or with a vegetable hawker at the Saturday market. I always pay the advertised price in full, and as I walk away God, the devil, and the vegetable hawker chuckle to themselves. Nevertheless I was able to arbitrate this particular marketplace dispute—in favor of the Spanish salesman and in disfavor of the German invaders. I ascribed to the desired commercial article such a unique value that the tourists were eventually willing to pay nothing but the stated price. The sidewalk merchant flourished.

Soon thereafter my gifts as mediator and fount of information came in demand in a much more sensitive area. A tourist called me over, rapped his Baedeker and asked, "All right, you expert, tell me a thing or two that's not in Baedeker!"

"Be happy to! I have a *Führer's* license and I'm enrolled in a special course on unexpected tourist inquiries."

"Fine. Then kindly inform me where I can find a decent..."

The gentleman's language suddenly became cryptical. But I knew very well what he was in search of. Back at the Cathedral I had already had occasion to give a couple of clients some discreet hints as to where they might locate certain *casas* that catered to their wishes. After a plate of curled shark, this guy had begun to feel certain urges. He was out for something quite gamey and man-eating, something that could fight him with fin and fang. But I had no addresses in Sóller.

"Where I can find a decent place to take a leak?" the urgent fellow concluded his inquiry.

In the course of the centuries the little word "decent" has undergone significant semantic chànges, and we can observe further change in our own time. Therefore, it was still not clear to me what the man meant by "decent" with reference to his particular desire. Did he construe the word in a patriotic sense? Probably. I told him that the appropriate facilities at the railroad station had been built by German experts in sanitary installation. No danger of infection, in case he was wary about such things. "But look, just ten paces ahead, that palm tree—just be careful, the Spaniards are a little touchy about their trees. Don't forget, we're not back home in Germany."

The man lifted a finger to his pith helmet and disappeared behind the palm. I turned around, and there was a lady in front of me. "Oh, pardon me, Herr *Führer*, but I feel the need..."

For the love of God, I was all confused. Surely I couldn't direct her to the same palm tree! What was this, a kindergarten? Fortunately, all she had in mind was the need to offer me her thanks for my wonderful explanations of all the sights. I was, she said, so very convincing (thank God!), and the whole experience was so educational. Yes, she did travel often, but to find someone who was so well-informed in so many fields of knowledge, and who knew how to stress the most important aspects of every place we visited—she shook my hand tightly and long. There followed an inquiry as to my nationality. Was I German? Just an hour ago I had claimed Spanish citizenship; now I renounced it in favor of the country of my actual birth. We were fellow Germans. How very nice—and she shook my hand anew. I bowed and thanked her for the pleasure of being her fellow countryman, and asked how I might be at her service. Well then, seeing as I was German, did I perhaps know Herr Müller in Barcelona?

Now it should be understood that every single German has, in his lifetime, known a Herr Müller, even if only a solitary individual of that name. I know one such person very well, seven others more or less well, and two dozen more who may have touched the periphery of my existence. As far as I was concerned the Herr Müller in Barcelona could well belong to the latter category, and I promptly said as much to the lady tourist. Mutual acquaintances are surely one of the finest things we can share in this life. The Herr Müller she had in mind was this tall, dark- haired—no, you're quite right, he's blond and wears his hair combed smooth, no, right, that marvelous wavy hair of his, the Spaniards are always so amazed, and those blue eyes, no doubt about it, it was our mutual friend Müller. What a small world! This lady's needs were easier to satisfy than I had originally feared.

A tall, skinny fellow, stripped down to his trousers, came running across the square, his monocle hanging on a black string and bouncing up and down on his chest like a scapular. He was looking for something or somebody. His *Führer*, perhaps? "Oh there you are! Where have you been keeping yourself? Come join us for a few, Herr *Führer*!"

He belonged to von Kammerputt's clique. The Officers' Club, some of them shirtless and with beet-red faces, but as class-conscious as ever, had set up headquarters over beer at the Bielefeld Station Canteen. The beer was terrible, they said, pure horse-piss. Didn't this backward country know how to make a decent brew? In accordance with my secret mission I reassured the gentlemen by again passing on some confidential intelligence. This miserable state of affairs wouldn't last long, I told them. Negotiations were in progress with a major German brewery to begin exporting a special heat-proof lager product. The contacts went through the Consulate General in Barcelona, where my personal friend, Consul General Dr. Köcher, had taken a special interest in the matter. Because of the water situation, they had given up the idea of moving an entire brewery to Spain.

Nods of approval. Yes, yes, the Foreign Office was on its toes. They almost always had the right man in the right place—almost! Mugs were raised to our revered fatherland, our up-and-coming *Führer*, the new Germany. I much preferred my desperate palm-tree man and the lady with her Herr Müller. I made a mental note to ask Martersteig what breed of sectarians and degenerate aristocrats these were who would travel to Spain to take beery oaths on that resentful proletarian Hitler.

I went out behind a cactus hedge and threw up. Now I had earned 12.50 pesetas. In half an hour my fellow citizens were to be at Sóller Harbor for a ten-minute stay, then we would drive back through Sóller and on up to the summit pass, the Coll de Sóller, 1848 feet above sea level. But now the tour director is drumming his guides together and announcing a change in schedule: a two-hour stopover here, and that means water sports in Sóller Harbor. Arriving at the porto we guides shouted it out: "time for a swim!"

For a swim? Nobody has brought bathing gear, and so there is a general stampede to the single rickety rental booth. Within a few short minutes they have demolished it. Middle-aged men, hefty women, kids, all chase and claw each other over a bathing suit. Men undress on the march and stumble over their own pants; women brandish their ample bosoms; a Spanish bather pulls out somebody's whimpering kid from where he got stuck under a tent. People knot handkerchiefs together to gird their loins. Modesty compels each one to turn the other way, but no matter what direction they turn their backsides, there is always someone else in front who also turns away. A few shamefaced individuals bend low and sneak into the cooling briny *sans* figleaf. A handful of professional nudists stride upright into the Mediterranean. The Spaniards are shocked. They are a prudish people and will not tolerate nudity. They protest to the tour director, but he is powerless to halt this natural catastrophe. Nor are we Guides able to put an end to the sinful spectacle.

A couple of tourists have now started a fight over a pair of bathing trunks. Two elderly ladies go off hunting their automobile; they wish to leave this very minute. But their driver can't understand what they are saying, for one thing because he doesn't speak German, for another because he's fast asleep. Only von Kammerwitzputt's General Staff, men who are, after all, inured to ambushes, melées, and naked violence, continue drinking beer and mixing the ingredients for their creation of the new German Reich. Lieutenant von der Hölle is on a one-man reconnaissance mission with binoculars. He has a fabulous broad in his crosshairs—marvelous superstructure. Back on board ship there might be a chance for some close combat.

The owner of the shore restaurant reports the theft of napkins and table-cloths—purloined no doubt in the interest of chastity. The tour director makes note of every detail; the company will make full restitution.

The two hours are up. Time to leave. No one pays a bit of attention. They're too busy splashing around and getting sunburns. The car horns let out cacophonous blares, but to no effect. A Guide yells out oceanward: whoever is not in the car in five minutes will be left behind, and will have to arrange return transportation *at the traveler's own expense*. That does the trick. People torpedo onto the shore, pull their togs over their wet bodies, leap into the nearest car, and off they go.

Every single car has now left for Sóller except mine. The restaurant owner had let me take a nap in his kitchen. Our driver rushes in to tell me that one of the *señoritas* is missing and the parents are frantic. I dash out to find them on the beach, and they start beseeching me, "Where is our daughter?" I ask for Daddy's binoculars, and start scanning the mirror-smooth ocean. Not one young lady to be seen. "Can she swim?" I ask. "Like a fish," says Mom, but she didn't have her bathing suit, and without one... No daughter of theirs would ever, not in a million years! The way people had behaved here, she adds, was absolutely atrocious! I wasn't to imagine that these savages represented Germany.

But I'm not imagining anything at all, just looking. Our driver is getting impatient. I give him one of my duros from the Shark Cafe. He goes back to sleep. Then a blood-curdling scream from Mom's throat. She has found a pile of clothes—the shame of it! Trudi went swimming naked! And at that moment the prodigal daughter reappears from her fugitive swim and steps out on the sand. Mom, with her broad back, tries to shield from curious glances this Birth of Venus from the Mediterranean Foam. Luckily, Lieutenant von der Hölle has departed with the General Staff and at this moment is nearing the mountain summit. As a *Führer* I have not only obligations but also certain privileges, and so I make sure to observe the dressing procedure—from a discreet distance. What I see convinces me that unless Mom keeps her spunky daughter on close tether, some fellow might make a very fortunate catch. I certainly don't wish it for the execrable Lieutenant.

Daddy, who meanwhile has tipped the driver for waiting, tells me I won't regret having neglected my duties to the other tourists for his daughter's sake. I am unable to think of an appropriate *Führer*-like reply, so I stand smartly at the side of the car, open the rear door, make a formal bow, and as I motion Trudi to enter, she gives me a mischievous smile. Now I can understand her interest in black piglets. Mom spoils the situation by insisting that this is Trudi's first and last trip abroad. Daddy vigorously agrees. Brother and sister, soured by the whole scene, say nothing. The mood in the car is awful.

I leave the family to their own affairs. Thanks be to Trudi and her threadless enterprise, for now I can snooze in peace until we reach "Alfabia," where we are going to look at subtropical gardens. Oh, I muse to myself, if only Trudi had shed her clothes as soon as we left Palma Harbor! In my thoughts she writes a long, long letter to her girlfriend back home, a letter in which "awesome" is every other word. And I am flattered that she mentions me: just imagine, he knows everything! And he didn't leave me behind! But is everything he tells us true? Daddy says it has to be, cuz otherwise he couldn't keep his job for one week. People would notice if he was making things up, and some of the tourists are real experts. What's amazing is that he's been doing this for seven years! I'd go nuts...!

You would *go* nuts? Trudi, between you and me, your *Führer* already *is* nuts, but go ahead and tell your girlfriend everything else about your trip as you see it. It's true, and if you need more material for a gushy paragraph about the landscape, just keep your eyes open. The drive up to the summit is extraordinary, and not only in Baedeker. From the top you can see the plains and the ocean far down below. Tourists often get tears in their eyes, the view is supposed to be so splendid. *Supposed* to be? Exactly, for I'll be seeing it myself for the first time today. It is my maiden voyage, too.

We stop at the summit. But the ladies and gentlemen prefer to stay put in the car. "Let's keep going." And so we careen down to the depths around countless hairpin turns.

Dozens of cars are still standing in front of the country estate "Alfabia," and this tells us that we have made up our lost time. But the distraught family won't get out here, either. Punishment for Trudi! What will become of her? She'll end up in a brothel! Perhaps so, but then only in the "Torre del Reloj," on the majestic mattress.

So we zip past the Moorish gate to the gardens. I've taken off my number and *Führer* emblem. I'm on strike, and from now on traveling incognito.

Our leave-taking at the pier was strictly pro forma. Mom avoided me altogether; brother and sister said hasty goodbyes; Daddy kept his word and pressed a 25-peseta note in my hand. That's how much he was willing to pay for his daughter's exposure. He did this, incidentally, with practiced sleight of hand; the driver, who had an eye out for his own gratuity, didn't even see it.

Trudi was the only one who gave me a warm farewell, and in doing so elicited a poisonous glance from Mom. I was about to wend my way homeward when the girl cried out, "Oh no, my bathing suit!" "But you didn't have any!" "Yes I did, I always do. But I didn't want to use it, so I hid it in the car." "Then I would advise you to hide it even better right away, otherwise Mom is going to skin you alive!"

Vigoleis was dismissed. He went home, pulled the shades in the bedroom, and threw himself down on the *pilarière*, sunburned, lacerated in body and spirit, tormented, filled with disgust at the behavior of the human herd. Heine, Nietzsche, and Schopenhauer had each told bitter and biting truths about the Germans. How might they have let go with all barrels if they had ever played tour guide to Germans for an entire day around the island of Mallorca? Did I say *played*? And yet my first experience as a *Führer* was in fact child's play compared to the tours with the packs who arrived later on Strength Through Joy ships and infested the island.

Beatrice returned exhausted but not demoralized, much less in desperation. I'll admit, she said, that these Germans were riffraff one and all. Crowds of them are repulsive, they have no idea how to behave in a foreign country, and that scene in Porto de Sóller! No other nationality in the world would behave that way.

"Not even the Swiss? Or will they only start behaving that way when the franc takes a nosedive?"

For a while longer we tore into our respective so-called fatherlands. That pulled me out of the slough of humiliation. Then out of a blue sky I asked, "Tips?" and proudly smoothed out before her my 25-peseta bill. Beatrice fished around in her purse and came up with 2 reales, which equals 50 centimos. A lady had pressed the coins in her hand, while the others had preferred not to tip.

"A German lady, of course."

"I'm afraid not, she was Swiss. But," she added as a mitigating point, "from Basel."

"ck....dt or photo-Phischer?"

"More or less, and filthy rich."

"But in Valldemosa you said that your group was so charming!"

"The charming people are neither Germans nor Swiss. The charming ones are always whatever you aren't, Austrians for example. Didn't you know that?"

Over the years we led tours of this kind regularly, also for other agencies, and made good money at it. But I never got rid of the disgust. Starting with the third one I had to throw up even before I hit the streets, and this happened every time. Basically, this technique of preventive purgation worked out better; it was an expression of my cowardice, for anyone else who reacted as I did might have wanted to spit in the tourists' faces or quit on the spot. Gradually I got to know the places we visited inside and out. I not only knew the names of the paintings, but also which ones were genuine and which were forgeries, just like a professional art historian. I knew who was buried in which tomb, whether he died of old age or had been poisoned or skewered with a blade. I knew why a certain church stood here and not on some other spot.

I learned all these data with the aid of tradition and scholarship. But still I kept on fabulizing for my clients, and my reputation grew. On one occasion, angered by the behavior of the philistine mob, I gave forth the unadorned truth—and they grumbled at me. The masses have an unerring instinct for the tawdriness of real history. As in Cologne at the "Pressa," here too I was asked to take over for VIP visitors. Among others, I guided (and misguided) abdicated kings, archbishops, chairmen of the board, generals, prominent whores, millionaires, and world-famous artists. I didn't get rich doing it; I don't even possess a single autograph. After that first tour nobody dared to offer me a tip, and that disturbed me. Guides who clung to the stupid truth pulled in huge harvests of tips—a psychological injustice if there ever was one.

The 100-peseta note I once received from a business magnate was not meant as a tip, but as hush money. It was none other than the owner of the passenger line for which I was inventing all the pertinent history not to be found in Baedeker. He was traveling with his own wife, his own daughter, and his own ship. I was assigned to him as a personal guide—that's just how important a man he was. He would be taking the same tour as everybody else, but our agency boss insisted that he was under no circumstances to be allowed near the common tourists. He hated that sort of thing. He wanted to be undisturbed, but I would have to explain things as usual.

The Chief Executive Officer himself took me aside and told me emphatically, but amiably, to keep the camera-carrying hordes away from him and to spare him the long lectures; I wouldn't regret it. Astute businessman that he was, he named the amount right there and then: that evening at the pier his secretary would hand me 100 pesetas for my trouble. Or rather, he could take care of that himself, right here and now. No sooner said than done. His wife and daughter went along with the scheme, only here and there they asked a timid question or two, which I then answered—truthfully, but also very briefly and in a conspiratorial whisper. The most exquisite automobile in running condition on the island was chartered for this tour designed to foster the Chief's meditative experience. Somewhere at the shore we stopped for a picnic. I ate up heartily, the ladies decidedly less so, and the Chief didn't touch a bite. He sat off to one side on a rock and contemplated the blue horizon. Possibly he was in love, or maybe his flotilla was foundering.

In Sóller we did have a run-in with the madding crowd, but there were no serious consequences. The driver stepped on the gas, and we disappeared in a cloud of dust. We arrived on the dot at the Palma pier where the ship's longboat was waiting. The Chief's secretary came up to us with a mournful look to render a brief report on the day's receipts, and a few items didn't add up right. Pointing to me, the Chief said that his guide was to receive 100 pesetas. All day long I had been on my best behavior, but now at the final minute I made the stupid mistake of explaining that Mr. Chief Executive Officer himself had already taken care of this small matter, but now had obviously forgotten. What a fool I was! If only I had kept mum there, too—seeing as where I had been hired to play a mute! "Talk is silver, silence is golden" indeed.

Walking homeward Vigoleis swore to himself that he would keep his mouth shut forevermore, for by doing so he might soon advance to Chairman of the Board himself. But this went the way of all good intentions. To this very hour he has advanced to nothing of importance, because he's always opening his big trap at just the wrong time.

III

Pedro arrived in civvies; the time for wearing his humiliating carnival costume was over.

We celebrated the Feast of the Miraculous Disrobing with *sobrasada*, wine, and bread, and we gave a toast to freedom. The food resembled the General's Eggs, but it didn't serve the same function. Pedro picked up his pad and began sketching: Vigoleis as Tourist Guide. A second sheet: Vigoleis as Padre with Cassock and Biretta. A third: Vigoleis as Spanish Army Recruit, Engaging in Mutiny. The fourth sketch showed him as a knight with hand to breast, ruff collar, and saber, freely after El Greco. This fellow was a talented artist, but he never succeeded in depicting Vigoleis as Vigoleis, despite hundreds of drafts and sketches for a grand portrait. Later, when he took lessons from the German refugee Segal and asked me to pose for him, a shadow of my second aspect gradually merged into my primary visage. But before the work could be completed, Segal packed up his utensils and left the island, and I fled soon after him.

It wasn't only Pedro Sureda who had returned to humanity. We, too, had reached a tolerably humane level of existence, thanks especially to Beatrice's persistence in hammering several languages into some very resistant brains.

She made a name for herself in Palma. Our house became a crowded place. In her field, she was just as much in demand as I was in my capacity as a cicerone. Prosperity lay just around the corner. In our kitchen there was a real saucepan on a hook, and each of us had our own pillow. We no longer had to roll up our clothes. We even had bedclothes, including a woolen blanket, an attractive second-hand peasant model that cost us more to de-flea and de-Pilarize than a new one would have. But easy come, easy go; our common oddball vice, books, was the reason why we still had no doormat. At the foot of the bed lay my old black loden greatcoat, as spooky to look at as some trophy from the hunting grounds in a world of ghosts. On our bookshelf one Rivadeneira classic stood next to another. We also spent quite a lot on clothes; in the South, more than in most other places in the world, clothes make the man.

I began translating Spanish literature, first only for myself as an exercise in getting to know the texts, but then in order to create an audience for Iberian literary art in Germany—I should say more modestly, a larger audience. I translated works by Padre Feijó, Baltasar Gracián's *Criticón*, novels by Pío Baroja, a few books by Mario and one, a gem of a book on the art of pipe-smoking, by Joaquín Verdaguer, the relative and literary *confrère* of the great national poet Jacinto Verdaguer. And some other things that I can't recall. Pedro helped me tirelessly with linguistic difficulties; Beatrice, the walking dictionary, provided the solution in doubtful cases. I started up a busy correspondence with publishers. Our private exchequer shrank in direct proportion to the German publishers' regrets that at the moment they daren't get too close to Spanish material.

Was this a reflection on the quality of my translations? Later on, Professor Karl Vossler had lavish praise for my ability to render the spirit of Iberia.

I remained faithful to Dutch literature. At the beginning of an earlier chapter I mentioned the name Slauerhoff; it was ter Braak who brought him to my attention. But no sooner did I write down his name than I got sidetracked to my own literary dog food. That's how it always goes in the life of Vigoleis, and thus that's how it goes, necessarily, in these pages. But now I can report I completed a German version of Slauerhoff's unique novel on the life of Camões, *The Forbidden Realm*. I expended a great deal of time and care attempting to emulate this writer's famous chaotic style, and I was proud of my chaotic German version. The first publisher to hold my manuscript in his hands dropped it on the floor and lifted those selfsame hands to the heavens. Back to the sender. Other publishers rejected it on the grounds that nationalistic circles could take offense at the novel's title; the "Third Realm" was about to come out of the forge. The Great German Carnival was about to happen, and that is why a dozen publishing houses also gave political reasons for refusing Menno ter Braak's *Bourgeois Carnival*. People were being careful. Even Verdaguer's little book on the tobacco pipe, which finally came out in Germany around this time but not in my translation, caused one publisher to go into a world-historical fit. Even as a non-smoker I knew that you can burn your fingers on a pipe. But for political reasons? Simple: Hitler didn't smoke.

Vriesland's *Departure from the World in Three Days* was taking an eternity to write. It was sent to me down on the island in separate waves. In the first line of the book a Jew makes an appearance—and on the horizon the Forbidden Reich was about to dawn forth.

"If you keep putting your own stuff into the fire," said Pedro, "why don't you try translating cheap novels? For that kind of stuff we have our own Pedro Mata."

Pedro meant well, but I felt that I meant even better, so I persisted in translating for the highbrows: Eugenio d'Ors, Angel Ganivet, Miguel de Unamuno—all for naught. I didn't even dare to produce an uncensored rendering of writings by my Santa Teresa de Ávila.

Don Quixote had his windmills, and now Vigoleis had his publishers. A non-Iberian evolution.

Beatrice's consumption of literature is so huge that not even a rich man would find it easy to keep her book bin filled. She has a literary tapeworm, and occasionally I envy her for it. This is the reason why we scouted around for a lending library. Pedro recommended the "Casa del Libro" on the Borne. There I entered my name in the membership list; their catalogue seemed to justify such an adventure. The fee was manageable; we would just have to send off two fewer manuscripts per month. The library manager was a short, fat man with a mild speech defect. He had an inimitable bleating laugh that drove milky-white bubbles of saliva into the swarthy corners of his mouth. His name was Mulet. From the second day of our acquaintance I felt constrained to pay special attention to this man. In the forenoon he was smooth-shaven, but by five o'clock he had a stubbly beard. At ten in the morning I asked him for a certain book, and he said I could pick it up at five. At five, he couldn't remember a single thing. One forenoon he accidentally twisted his hand so that it turned black and blue; by afternoon the injury was invisible. Once I saw him sitting in a café on the Borne; I waved and went on my way. When I arrived at his shop, there he was. For a long time I remained the butt of jokes, some of them quite clever, perpetrated by the identical twin brothers Mulet, much to the amusement of the *tertulia* that met at the "Casa del Libro" around the writer Verdaguer, the tobacco-pipe Verdaguer.

A *tertulia* is a circle of people that can open up and then close again quite casually, a lodge for empty chitchat, a forum for plying one of Spain's favorite social vices: verbal idleness. Its particular attractiveness as an institution derives from its higher aimlessness, its unique method of killing the already dead hours. No one can resist it who has even the slightest taste for the void. For me the void is its own purpose; I am a stick-in-the-mud and shy, and therefore the *tertulia* went straight to my heart. In Spain some *tertulias* run in 24-hour cycles, at full strength. But to belong to one of these you must have a fat purse, a big mouth, and a willingness to put your shoes on a new polisher's box every few hours. All *tertulias* have their own bootblack, a fellow who usually is the center of the group's attention. His opinions about all kinds of daily and nightly matters are as respected as those of any successful writer. Famous Spanish statesmen have attended a *tertulia* before launching a coup d'état, checking things out with the *limpiabotas* before staging their revolt. In Spain, the man of the people is not to be confused with the "man on the street" in other countries. My barber José was a philosopher whose spoken Spanish was just as pure as Unamuno's or Pedro Sureda's. Only he didn't write down his thoughts; for him, he told me, what grows on top of people's heads was more lucrative than what was inside.

At Mulet's *tertulia* I regularly met a young man who drew my attention by the careful way he filled his pipe. He would start "really" smoking it only when it came time for him to leave. Cleaning, blowing through the stem, tapping the tobacco in the bowl, extruding the tobacco from a sack made from the scrotum of a fighting bull, rubbing, partially filling, completely filling, pushing down—he went through all these motions as if they were a liturgical ritual, with long pauses for joining the conversation with his invariably witty sarcasm and dreaded mockery. This was Don Joaquín Verdaguer, the only writer I know who actually follows the path he recommends in his books. He had already written his treatise on *El Arte de Fumar en Pipa*, and now he was living a life devoted entirely to this archetypal art. It didn't bother him at all if he burned holes in his pants. Once his pipe was in his mouth, he never lost his composure in front of the students he had to teach in German, English, French, and social economics, or when faced by the super-challenging writings he translated by Nietzsche, Zweig, Dickens, Papini, Mann, Kipling, Istrati, and other fellow-smokers. When he learned that I was a non-smoker, he reacted with a *broma*, a witticism. He could accept the fact that I was a writer, but the idea that I could translate without smoking a pipe—as a German I would of course use a long one—this presented him with problems that he was unable to solve even with his own pipe. "How do you do that and not go crazy?"—As a Spaniard it hadn't occurred to him that you could take on such a challenge in the aforementioned condition. My double-sewn leather *Sitzfleisch* took care of the rest.

His brother Don Mario was at that time working on his translation of *The Magic Mountain*. Thomas Mann had told him in a wonderful letter that he was unwilling to explain breakneck passages to his translators. So I took over this job, while Don Joaquín helped me in turn when my cart got stuck, and even Pedro didn't dare to pull me out of the mud. It is with pleasure and sorrow that I recall those years, when the course of world literature got decided in a little lending library, urged on by the bleating mirth of Mulet, the man with the magic beard. As the sole representative of the Nordic branch of literature, I didn't have an easy time with these indigenous *tertulians*, whose ranks included notably the two Villalonga brothers, Don Miguel, Army Captain ret., and Don Lorenzo, physician and psychiatrist. Both of them were well-known writers, especially Don Miguel, who is certain to enter Spanish

literary history as the "Mallorquin Proust." This man was, if not the ambulatory, then the sedentary quintessence of melancholy, a satirist who could
hold his own against the likes of Lichtenberg. A few chapters later, Count
Harry Kessler will take flight from his presence. And Verdaguer's pipe went
out whenever Don Miguel started airing his bleak mood, in the back room
where the elite of the *tertulia* gathered, a group to which I wasn't admitted
until after a year. That's when I finally had sufficient command of the language
to take up a cudgel for my own brand of *Weltschmerz*. Incidentally, I tried to
stir up interest in Villalonga's charmingly scandalous *Miss Giacomini*, but
with no success.

Some also-rans: Don Felipe, a botanist and astrologer; Busquets, a rich wine
merchant who as a typical Spanish autodidact compiled in his *bodega* an Ara-
bic-Spanish dictionary that was prized by specialists. Whenever he hit upon a
word he didn't know, he sailed to Morocco, got the answer from sheiks he
was friends with, and returned with a bag full of the most amazing stories. I
must resist the temptation to relate them here. This "Arab" took on special
importance for me, because in his library he had the poems of Pascoaes.

The manager of this literary cabaret seldom showed up. His interests tended
more toward high-level politics than to the liberal arts, although we gave
plenty of attention to political affairs in our conversations. A genuine *tertulia*
doesn't shrink from any topic; the more vigorously you shoot the breeze, the
more convinced you are that you hold the destiny of the world in your hands.
When contrary to all rational expectations the Third Reich emerged from its
baptism of fire and blood, I was elevated to the position of expert on domestic
German affairs; I became purely and simply an authority. It was only when I
started prophesying that my prestige diminished, in contrast to the true
prophets like the one who was the cause of defeats such as my own. Thus I
was forced to realize that I was unaccepted even outside my own country. My
clairvoyant eye lifted the veil from things too horrible to contemplate: new
Battles of the Marne, a new Compiègne, the *Führer* flees the scene leaving
Germany as a heap of rubble—unless Baron von Martersteig can make a
timely appearance on the scene with his Army of Monkeys. I permitted myself
this minor proviso; the prophets of the Old Covenant also kept their back
doors open. Captain Villalonga, who had served for several years in Africa
and had first-hand knowledge of monkeys while his German colleague was
merely consulting Brehm, presented the case this way: I must dismiss from my
mind any of my friend's notions about recruiting monkeys. Germany had produced a Goethe, a Bach, a Nietzsche, and so forth, and the country wasn't
about to go to pieces because of some army private. Don Lorenzo, the scientist
of the human soul, supplemented this assertion by saying that as is well
known, insanity begins inside the head; a nation is no different. The bottom-
up insurgency that was happening in my *patria* would never affect the brain;
it was nothing but mud, and it would forever remain weighted down by itself.
Erudite as these brothers were, there followed a hail of learned quotations.
But Vigoleis stuck by his guns. Since when can soldiers and psychologists claim

to know anything about the human soul? Both of them move along in trenches that are forever colllapsing, so there is never an end to the shoveling.

One day I was out for a stroll with Pedro on the Borne. This was at the hour when the Mallorquin either takes his promenade, or rents a metal chair from the Tourist Office and makes the pedestrians run the gauntlet. We had no money for a chair, and so we bumped our way through the crowds. Suddenly there was a commotion. The promenade came to a halt, and all eyes went upward. A bird of prey of the falcon family came plunging out of the blue sky, aiming for a domestic pigeon. The pigeon made a few twists and turns in the air, and then fell among the crowd as good as dead. The attacking bird broke its plunge just above our heads and soared away into the air. The pigeon lay on the Borne with outstretched wings. This aerial combat took place so rapidly that the Spaniards had no opportunity to cheer it on with "*Olé!*" Now everyone was gazing at the lame and frightened bird. Then a new hubbub arose on the boulevard. An elderly gentleman in a white linen suit and with an armful of books was running as fast as his long legs could carry him straight across the Borne; the throng parted to let him through. He narrowly missed crushing the pigeon with his foot. Some people laughed, others cursed. A boy picked up the pigeon and carried it safely away from further attempts at assassination.

"Great heavens, Pedro, just take a look at that sprinter all dressed in white! I wonder who's chasing him?"

"Nobody's chasing him. That's Papá. He's racing over to the 'Circulo' to read French newspapers. He's just finished reading the English ones in some other club, and afterwards he'll race off to grab the German papers. It's high time that you were introduced to Papá. You'll take a novelistic interest in the man. No one could ever invent such a character."

It was Don Juan Sureda Bimet of the House of Verdugo, the wacky aristocrat who in his youth had been one of the wealthiest landowners on the island. He became so important for my own intellectual development that he deserves his own chapter in my recollections. I shall make no attempt to give shape to this balmy *hidalgo* beyond his own anecdotal self, nor do I intend to out-gossip Diogenes Laërtius, the ancient inventor of the historical *bisbigliamento*.

IV

Was it a coincidence that I made the acquaintance of Don Juan Sureda at the time when the intelligentsia of the Western world was gearing up to celebrate the 100th anniversary of Goethe's death?

The book dealer Emmerich had a bottle of bubbly in readiness for offering toasts with his customers to the greatest sales triumph of German literature since the beginning of the "Library of Golden Classics," whose interests he represented in the Balearics. In Mulet's *tertulia* I was asked to say a few profound words, and chose as my topic "Goethe and Germans in Foreign Lands." Mulet was thrilled, and asked me to write down my speech so that I could deliver it as a bonafide *conferencia* before an invited audience. Nothing came of this, because in this case Mulet was his twin brother, and the other Mulet, to whom I handed my essay a few days later, corrected by Pedro and neatly typed out, didn't or couldn't know anything about this arrangement since he probably wasn't the right Mulet anyway. The Goethe celebrations reached their climax on the evening of March 22nd, the unforgettable date when we were invited for a stand-up visit with Pedro's parents.

Beatrice was a frequent visitor in this apartment, so she was familiar with the customs one had to observe in order to avoid being odd man out. She knew, for example, that there was only a single chair in the reception room, one that had never been sat in by any famous personages, for the simple reason that it had only three legs. In this townhouse it stood against a wall, not in the company of its one-hundred kinsmen in the Sureda arsenal in Valldemosa. Pedro's mother, the princess, Doña Pilar by name, was of course a consummate hostess. But she was not only a representative of the highest aristocracy, she was also an artist, and as such she possessed a different sense of social hierarchy, and at times forgot to observe the niceties. It was up to her, for example, to indicate to her guest with a smile that he should take his seat very carefully, placing the weight of his so very welcome body as far as possible toward the back of the chair, so as to prevent it from tipping forward, since oddly enough there was a leg missing and no one knew where it was. Usually the guest would say, "Oh, that's quite all right, I'll manage just fine, thanks." But things wouldn't go just fine at all. It takes practice to sit down politely on a three-legged chair. But the family was used to such mishaps; they always stood in front of the guest with open hands, ready to catch him as he fell or at least to warn him by means of this gesture to lean back against the wall. This usually succeeded in keeping him put. Beatrice knew how to take her seat, but getting back up was always a problem. Still, her years-long experience with the Mensendieck technique of gymnastics came through at the critical moment: just a quick lunge forward, and you're already standing.

Pedro had also instructed her in the second rule of decorum among the Suredas: when asked if you would like some tea, you must say, "Oh no, thank you!" There were no useable teacups in the house, since famous people had drunk from them and now piles of them were preserved in moldy straw out at the Valldemosa arsenal. Papá could never bring himself to free them up for domestic use, and ever since they were forced to vacate the Valldemosa palace for lack of funds, famous people no longer came to visit them in their townhouse.

Don Juan and Doña Pilar welcome their son's language teacher's husband. The latter glances intently at the parental couple. He is standing. Beatrice takes a seat on the chair as Vigoleis presses it firmly against the wall, smiling all the while as if he were having his picture taken. Down deep I am not in a light-hearted mood. I know Beatrice. She has no technical savvy, and in the heat of her conversation with the princess, in French, she will forget that there are certain laws of statics that must be observed. And sure enough, the moment arrives when she starts getting up to approach our hosts. With remarkable presence of mind I place one foot on the chair brace. It cracks, but equilibrium is maintained. No one pays any attention to the little accident—a bagatelle for these aristocrats who have already had an entire palace come crumbling down on them. People like me, who come from the bourgeois milieu, can be disturbed by the merest ripple of trouble.

Pedro's mother is a small woman who dresses very casually. She was respected as a portrait painter; the King posed for her at a time when portraits of kings were only copies made from postcards. It was rather confusing that her name was Pilar. For me this name had become a symbol of merchandized carnal lust, whereas this woman could not deny her dignified lineage even when dressed, as she was now, in an artist's smock smeared with blobs of paint. Unlike the slut of the Street of Solitude, she obviously rejected the idea of standing on a pillar.

Behind her stood Don Juan.

In his hand he held a trumpet and, prepared as I was for all eventualities, I imagined that he might treat us to a military march or a romantic song from *Des Knaben Wunderhorn*. If he were to do so, how could I keep from laughing? When I feel that I can't behave, it usually helps if I press the nail of my middle finger under my thumbnail. But here? As a precautionary measure I stiffened the part of my body that ought to have been relaxed, and asked the aristocrat, "Oh, you play a wind instrument? Please play us something!" The *grande* placed the mouthpiece to his ear and the bell to my mouth, and said, "How's that?" He was not a musician, but simply deaf.

Now the conversation became loud. Don Juan swung his trumpet like an elephant's trunk; now he held it to this person's mouth, now to someone else's, in order to take part in the repartee. His comments revealed, however, that he wasn't very quick on the uptake. Pedro explained to him that I was the Catholic German he had told him about. Papá didn't catch this, so Pedro shouted, "*El alemán católico!*" The horn conveyed this information effectively; the old gentleman nodded with satisfaction and then explained to his wife that the first phase of the visit was complete, and the guests could now follow him into his study. This was a small room piled high with books, most of them old folios. And behold, it contained some real chairs and a canapé. We sat down with no danger of breaking a leg.

Pedro tooted into the trumpet that this Catholic German knew everything—all he had to do was ask him questions. Then he took Beatrice's arm and led her out of the study. It would be better if Papá had his German all to himself.

Don Juan shifted a pile of books, drew forth a stool, and sat down facing me, ready to receive information. With my weak lung I have often had doctors sitting in front of me like this with their auscultating apparatus in hand, asking me to take a deep breath. Don Juan placed his mammoth stethoscope near my breast, but first set about wheezing and sputtering himself. Then he said, "Goethe is dead."

The trumpet bell was now at my lips. Don Juan closed his eyes and held his head with one side turned upwards, so that part of his face was before me as in a concave mirror. It was yellow and wrinkled. A sprig of hair jutted from one nostril, and it moved up and down in rhythm with his breathing. When this fellow is dead, it won't be necessary to hold a feather under his nose to check whether he's still alive. Long, stiff hairs also protruded from his ear and covered the bony mouthpiece of his hearing apparatus. I remained silent, and the old deaf gent thought his trumpet might be plugged up. He banged it a few times with his hand, stuck the mouthpiece more firmly into his fur, and repeated the century-old communiqué that Goethe had died.

I was quick enough to reply, in English, with the almost century-old expletive "Dead as a doornail!" The *hidalgo* nodded. I had hit the nail on the head. After a pause for reflection there came the first question, one that caused me no little amount of confusion: "Now that Goethe has been dead for a hundred years, what influence do you think that this has had on his style in his later years?"

I made no reply. Don Juan continued: "As a German you will have pondered this problem. *Ich bin ganz Ohr.*"

The German he had taught himself in the john and with a program of reading at the club was not all that bad. To be *ganz Ohr*—this was no mean feat for a Spaniard. On the other hand, if a deaf man says that he is "all ears," he means of course his trumpet. To prompt a reply, Don Juan poked my chest with it a few times, then placed it again at my mouth and closed his eyes. "Well?"

At the very same hour when I sat facing this aristocrat's reverse loudspeaker, getting taken to the cleaners more pitilessly than any student at an oral exam, all over the world distinguished speakers were standing next to pitchers of water holding forth in honor of Goethe—all the Bertrams, the Heuslers, the Ortega y Gassets, the Gundolfs (if he lived long enough to take part in this celebration), the Gides, the Schweitzers. To be sure, a hundred years after the Olympian's death, Goethe scholarship was still in its Wertherian phase, and none of the professors would have been able to blast forth any great wisdom into the Great Sureda's trombone. So it's no wonder that the likes of me had to take recourse in empty blather. I did so for a whole half-hour. Don Juan shook his brass instrument frequently, he repeatedly poked the earpiece into his hairy orifice in order not to miss a single word of my anniversary oration. He nodded in assent, as if to indicate that my jerry-built disquisition was taking the words right out of his own mouth. Deaf people are mistrustful, but if they are convinced that their amplification apparatus is working properly, they can become as gentle as the blind. I passed my orals with distinction. How amazed Don Juan would have been if I had already made the greatest contribution of the current century to Goethe scholarship, my discovery of Goethe's conversations with Mrs. Eckermann, my surprise gift to the professorial guild on the occasion of the poet's 200th birthday!

When, at the end of my improvisatory rope, I brought my declamation to a close, I was hoarse. Don Juan set down his trumpet and thanked me. I looked over at the door with the intention of escaping, but the grandee held my arm, pulled a small poetry anthology from his pocket, and asked me to blow forth a few poems as the final gesture of our celebration. He checked off the poems he wanted to hear, and now he heard them: *durch das Labyrinth der Brust – wandelt in der Nacht*. Oh, thou eternal hour! When silence returned, Don Juan glanced at me and said with emotion, "Goethe is alive. You have brought him back to life! A great spirit!"

Who, Goethe or Vigoleis?

In the Book of Joshua it is reported that seven priests blew seven trumpets of rams' horns, and the walls of Jericho fell down flat. That is amazing. But it is no less remarkable that my blowing into a deaf man's horn reawakened the dead Goethe, and on the very same day when the scholars were pummeling him with all due solemnity.

Don Juan was an erudite grandee, and travel had further educated him. I don't know if Ernst Haeckel ever sat on one of his chairs, slept in one of his beds, or ate from one of his plates, but a copy of that writer's *Miracles of Life* with a dedication from the author, written in large script across the whole fly-leaf, was in the *hidalgo's* library. Yet more important than the library was Don Juan's collection of tickets from all the trains, trolleys, toll bridges, ships, theaters, museums, and the like that he started amassing at a certain point in his life. They filled dozens of boxes and gradually displaced some essential items of furniture.

A brief word in this connection: during the last decade of the previous century, Don Juan made a trip to Germany. At the time, a criminal case was in all the newspapers. A certain man was accused of murder, convicted, and sentenced to death. He maintained his innocence, although he couldn't prove it. He claimed that on the day in question he wasn't in the city where the crime was committed, but in the distant town of X. Shortly before his execution, his defense lawyer, conducting another search through the man's house, found one of his defendant's old suits. In one of the pockets he came upon a ticket for a horse-drawn tram. He ascertained that it had been issued on the fateful day in the town of X. The man was acquitted.

Don Juan, who followed this case with increasing dread, began imagining himself the potential victim of a miscarriage of justice. The Dreyfus Affair was also in the news at around this time. The public was getting nervous. It was felt that it was important to have an alibi at all times. Don Juan returned from this journey with a suitcase full of material that would save him from the gallows. He insisted that his relatives never take a single step that they couldn't document years hence.

His mania for collecting extended also to newspapers, and in this regard he doubtless exceeded my mentor Karl d'Ester, the professor of journalism whose students even had to protect their sandwich wrappings from his prying fingers. Don Juan had once read of a case in which an entire year's worth of a particular weekly suddenly became critical evidence and was worth thousands. Ever since then, he kept all periodicals and subscribed to a host of obscure serials.

His archive was stored in crates, suitcases, baskets, and cardboard boxes, in drawers, cabinets, under beds, and in corners of rooms where there was always space to spare. After a time it started competing for *Lebensraum* in the Suredas' apartment, since Don Juan decided to bring to Palma the portions of his collection that had been stored in the wet nurse's quarters in Valldemosa. He was planning to compile a general catalogue of his holdings, and asked my advice concerning the best system of classification. I recommended a pocket-sized microcard file; in two or three years the job would be finished, and then I could only hope that Don Juan would be accused of murder. That would be the most fitting way to put the catalogue to its proper use.

Like the *fiumare*—those rivers that carry water only in the rainy period but then swell up to become dangerous torrents—Don Juan's life saw the regular recurrence of hectic activity that destroyed much in its path but left behind, in the river bed of his mind, a fertile layer of mud. I am now about to relate the story of how the *hidalgo* learned German, an account that is as fundamentally important for these pages as it is indiscreet. Perhaps my reader will catch my drift if I say that I wish him to become privy to this story; once we can get past the "privy" part, it will be clear to my reader why it is that my ears pricked up when, for the first time, I heard the name of the Portuguese mystic Teixeira de Pascoaes, the man who has played a central role in my life ever since.

Hemorrhoids are, apart from the discomfort they cause, an indecorous affliction. The euphemistic designation "golden veins" does nothing to remove the stigma. Don Juan suffered from this ailment to an extent that forced him at times to sit for hours on end in an unmentionable location in his house. Under such constraint the pious monk Caesarius of Heisterbach would have pondered the question of eternity. But Don Juan, citizen of a country of autodidacts, pondered his own education. During these hours of outer and inner coercion he drove himself to learn two languages: Greek and German. Since his ailment was chronic, he reached his goal. Still, everyone knows that it isn't possible to learn a language silently; one must declaim everything to get used to the new sounds. That's just what Don Juan did, and because he was hard of hearing, he did it very loudly, considering that he couldn't shout the lessons into his own trumpet bell.

If you will now picture the site where this self-teaching went on, and picture further a housemaid from the countryside, you can imagine that after a few days this maid will start getting the willies. He locks himself in and yells out gibberish—you, too, would pack your things and leave your new job before real insanity broke out. None of these hired *criadas*, Pedro told me, lasted more than a week, and so Doña Pilar was forced to abandon her easel again and again to do common housework. Her art suffered as a consequence, but

Don Juan suffered even more, for over the years the rectal clusters multiplied. From a solely linguistic standpoint, the golden knots that disfigured Don Juan's second visage were quite beneficial. Over time, the entire household became exclusively oriented toward the grandee's philological vein.

When we got to know him, Don Juan was already an advanced student. In German he was quite fluent. His affliction worsened, and his family feared that Papá might start teaching himself Chinese. His doctors weren't much help. As with cases of the flu, they advised waiting until the illness cured itself.

Whenever Don Juan finished a relieving session on his linguistic perch, he left the throne room with his textbooks stuck under his arm, holding his drooping trousers with one hand, while with the other hand keeping his underwear from touching the sensitive spot, and shuffled across the hallway into his bedroom. The bedroom was small, and he had long legs, so he had to keep the door open with his legs projecting out into the hall like a roadblock The family was by now accustomed to this new phase of his malady, and they hurdled over these paternal stilts as a matter of domestic routine. "Learn to suffer without complaint," was the doomed German Kaiser's motto, and our family doctor had it posted on his office wall for the edification of his patients. Don Juan suffered while learning.

Once Pedro installed an eternal lamp in the hall, no one stumbled any more. A wealthy aunt donated the oil, but not out of Christian charity. No, this was a preventive measure to avoid hospital bills that might otherwise ensue. But the eternal flame was unable to prevent a worse calamity.

A British lady commissioned Pedro to paint her portrait. Friends of hers had recommended the "famous Suredas," and by mistake she approached the nameless Pedro rather than his brother Don Jacobo. Pedro was thrilled: Heaven had sent this errant non-beauty to him and his easel! Art history can point to several instances where such mistakes have given rise to immortal masterpieces. The rich lady from England was willing to pay the price that Don Jacobo would have asked—a few thousand pesetas. All of us shared in Pedro's excitement: thousands of pesetas! The sittings were to take place in his parents' flat, mornings at eleven in the little room where I had held forth on Goethe. Pedro outfitted the study as a studio, and at that hour of the day the light would be just right for the job.

But this was the same hour when Don Juan conducted his one-man sit-down seminars. There was a way, they figured, to steer clear of disaster. Pedro's mother and a number of siblings agreed to keep Papá in check and, if necessary, squelch his loud verb conjugations. I myself offered to stand guard, or to divert Don Juan from his sanguine preoccupation by conversing with him on his favorite topic, Original Sin. But Pedro, trusting in the resourcefulness of his own family, said that my services would not be required.

On the evening of the first day of posing, Pedro visited us, and I could tell right away that something untoward had happened. Those thousands of pesetas had slipped through his fingers. As a proud Spaniard, the kind you read about in books including this one, he didn't cry. But you could infer from his quivering lips that down deep in his gut he was plotting dastardly revenge. If only he had left this English dame to his brother and shared the loot with him afterward!

"How come?"

"Papá!"

"*Good gracious*!" cried Beatrice with the emphasis of a dyed-in-the-wool Brit who has just had the death of her favorite cat predicted by a soothsayer. As in a movie, she immediately sensed what had gone wrong, while I was still groping in the dark.

The dowager arrived at the appointed time. The princess welcomed her and took her to the studio where Pedro had hastily covered one wall with a bed-sheet. This had the effect of dividing up the room and gave the illusion of space. One of Doña Pilar's masterpieces, perhaps the best painting in the entire *piso*, was duly admired by the lady from England: a portrait in blue of an old friend of the family, Don Miguel de Unamuno. Then Doña Pilar left the room, and Pedro gave posing instructions to his very first paying victim. Using the few snatches of English that Beatrice had taught him, he started a conversation, but soon he went silent. He sketched out some contours, and perhaps even started applying some color—I don't recall any details of his technique.

Then: intermission for the model. Why of course, she could simply relax. Should he fetch her purse for her? Oh, she must have left it in the *entrada*—if she wished to get it herself, it was just across the hallway. The lady ambulated out of the studio. She was an elderly personage wearing the familiar English stockings. The ensuing scream was ear-splitting. There was a noise as if someone were stumbling over something, and then an urgent summons to "*Dear God*!" Pedro heard a shout of the English vocable *umbrella*, and then the front door slammed shut.

Pedro, standing at his easel, turned into a pillar of salt. "Papá!" He didn't even need to go out into the hall to be certain of what had happened. The grandee lay prone and bare-bottomed on his bed, his legs stretched out across the hall carpet, loudly conjugating verbs. Can there be a more dreadful, a more fear-inspiring sight for a lady who came to have her portrait painted? And apart from the sight, this incomprehensible yelling coming from the oblivious old man's mouth—German, or perhaps Greek, Homer, Goethe, Hölderlin...? The domestic guards had let down their guard, leaving Papá alone to follow the nameless urgings of his philological passion.

It speaks for Pedro's virtues as a human being, and as the son of his father, that he refrained from whacking the old man over the head with his palette. Who, in a similar situation, would not have spit a wad, or at least tossed a shoe tree at the naked old gent lying there?

We were shaken.

"There's nothing for it," said Pedro, bringing his account to a close. "Vigoleis... What would you have done?"

"I would have locked Papá inside and left the scene."

"Locked him in? You idiot, it's obvious that you come from a country where not only philosophical systems, but also doors can be 'locked.' Did you ever run across a door in our *piso* that can be properly locked? The bathroom door, for example, can be locked only from the inside, and even for that you have to know just how to do it, or else you'll never get out again. If it were any different, that thing never would have happened to Mamá's nun."

I listened up. The princess has a nun? One to whom embarrassing things have happened? I have always been interested in nuns. Once, a nun was deeply in love with me and wanted to sleep with me. Another nun once stole a blackbird I had carefully tamed—she killed it, fried it, and ate it. Since then I have looked upon these black-veiled ladies as the archetypal manifestation of corporal and mental aggression. At my insistence Pedro told us a remarkable story, and in the telling he forgot his own frustrating escapade with the English lady. When he left after midnight he was his old self again.

After escaping the fateful apartment, we later learned, this British portrait dame leaped into a taxi and asked to be driven to His Majesty's Consul. There she filed a charge stating that under pretense of having her portrait painted she had been lured to a dark house on a dark street. There she was greeted by a short woman and led into an artist's studio that, as she later realized, was not an artist's studio at all.

This short woman then showed her some blue man she claimed to have painted herself. And then the real painter came in, claiming to be the famous Jacobo Sureda. He stood behind an easel pretending to paint her portrait. Then this awful thing happened—we wondered just how she depicted it to the Consul.

That same evening the British lady left the island, in flight from the tortured buttocks of a Spanish grandee. Incidentally, the grandee himself never learned the mischief he had caused with his philological blood. Deaf or partially deaf persons always have the last word—the only word they can be sure of. In the story of the nun, this word once again belongs to Don Juan Sureda, although it was Pedro's sculptress sister Pazzis who rescued the cloistered lady in question.

Having strewn about so many hints, I can no longer hold back from giving an account of this tragedy. Besides, I am of the opinion that by relating such quixotic adventures, I can offer my reader a clearer image of Don Juan Sureda, a man who gave my own existence such a significant new direction, than if I were to linger over a description of the double bags under his eyes, or over the fact that owing to my Habsburgian donkey's chin I was often taken for the son of Papá Sureda himself, whereas his true son Pedro had to go on playing make-believe in the kindergarten of the Thirteenth Alphonse, the King of Spain, *El Rey*.

The princess never kept a nun in her house in the same way a prince of the Church keeps a house chaplain. Doña Pilar was ill, and preferred to be under the care of a nun rather than any of the numerous members of her family.

Nurses visit many households, rich or poor, and they can adapt quickly to local conditions. They don't ask many questions. In the Sureda home, Sister Amalberga was put on her mettle more severely than in most other houses. Soon she figured out which doors could be opened, and which it was best to leave closed. The problem was finding out how. She located the bathroom all by herself, but no one instructed her in the tricky matter of the inside lock.

The mishap occurred during her first night in the apartment.

Pedro shared a bedroom with his older brother Juanito, a student of jurisprudence. His academic specialty was Canon Law, but his chief field of interest was a form of pious idleness.

It was perhaps around midnight when Pedro was awakened by a noise. He listened, and it sounded as though someone were knocking. Was it a nocturnal bird pecking against a shutter? All he could hear was his brother snoring. Pedro turned over and tried to get back to sleep, but now he heard this rapping noise more clearly. He listened again, and this time there was no mistake: someone was knocking! But who? He immediately thought it must be the nun, locked in the bathroom and unable to get out. Damn it all, nobody told her how to do it! What now? While he was no left-winger, Pedro was no particular friend of the Church either, and thus as far as he was concerned, Sister Amalberga was a subject of strictly clerical interest. So he shook his brother awake and said approximately as follows: "Juanito, stop that un-Christian snoring! There's a cloistered woman in our house who right now is in cloistered distress. Listen!" The knocking was still audible; it was louder but still restrained. Juanito agreed at once with his heretical brother's assessment of the situation: no doubt about it, Sor Amalberga was locked in the throne room!

The brothers sat upright in bed and listened to the knocking, which could now be heard at regular intervals. After a while, Pedro said that it was Juanito's job, as a Catholic, to liberate the nun. Juanito was not so firmly convinced of such a doctrinal obligation; he defended his position by alluding to both prevalent modes of jurisprudence, although Canon Law would have sufficed to justify his preference for malingering. Then Pedro had a brainstorm that once again showed him to be a faithful son, this time on his mother's side. In the current situation, he said, it was probably not the nun who needed help, but their mother who needed help from the nun. But then it would be Mamá who was knocking, said the clever student of the law, and the scales of justice sank for a moment in his favor. Silence. The brothers tried to figure out whether the knocking was coming from their mother's room. The ghost decided not to do them any such favor. There was more knocking, this time louder than before, and it was coming from the bathroom.

Pedro: "Maybe Mamá is too weak to give a signal. What'll it be like if something happens to her while the nun just stepped out to the john?"

Juanito: "God forbid! But I don't believe in such diabolical coincidences. But how about this: why doesn't Pazzis just let her out?"

Pedro: "Pazzis is at the Carnival Ball. Tomorrow is Ash Wednesday."

Juanito: "Tomorrow? It's already past midnight, and the big fasting has begun. The time for repentance has commenced. So come, dear brother, let us both arise and together release the nun from her penitential plight, so that in the fullness of time we may be forgiven our sins."

"Amen, you Jesuit," Pedro might have said if he didn't actually say it. In any case, the lazy brothers got up and marched in their pajamas to the bathroom. Juanito addressed the sister: "Sor Amalberga, listen carefully. We want to help you. Put your right finger at the left under the latch, down where it's broken off, but not all the way in the slot. With your left finger give the spring on the clamp a little push upwards, but don't press too hard. It'll be easier if you use a match. At the same time, press against the door with your foot, let go of the latch, and the lock will click open. We should have shown you this before, but you can do it."

The nun had no match, no technical dexterity, and no memory for verbal instructions. So she couldn't do it. Moreover, she was ashamed to ask the *señoritos* for more precise directions. So instead of making any reply, she prayed.

The brothers consulted with each other, faced now with this cloistered stubbornness. Pedro offered to climb through the bathroom transom, which was missing its pane of glass anyway. Or rather, he offered to climb up, hang down through the transom, and with half of his body show the imprisoned lady how to work the latch. But the nun rejected this idea. "*Señorito*, in Heaven's name do not come at me through that little window! I prefer to wait here and pray until morning dawns and I can obtain help from someone else. God does not abandon those who are close to Him in prayer." But Juanito, for his part, could not agree with this plan, for he said, "Sister, please consider that Mamá could be in need of your help. If you will just step up on the toilet and stretch your arms through the transom, we'll be able to pull you out. Bind up your skirts, and we'll have a table ready for you to land on."

Sor Amalberga regarded this suggestion as even more impertinent. She would rather die than be pulled out of a bathroom by two young gentlemen. I can see her blessing herself at the very idea of such a maneuver. So the brothers had to consult again while the nun, resigned to her fate, prayed on.

Suddenly Pazzis burst into the house, in the merriest of moods after dancing through the night, covered with spangles and with confetti in her hair—the same artist who with her gouges carved marvelously sensual Madonnas out of olive wood, and who turned my head with her beauty and an intensity of *Weltschmerz* that was eventually her fatal undoing.

Pazzis was never at a loss for advice for anyone or anything except for herself, and that is what made us so similar. After just one glance she diagnosed the situation, laughed at her incompetent brothers, and spoke a consoling word to the nun through the peephole. Then she said, "That big log in the fireplace in the *sala!*" "Ram it in!" she added when her brothers still couldn't grasp what kind of strategy she had in mind. "Let's break down the door!"

This log had its own special history. It was indeed inside the fireplace, but woe to whoever would think of burning it up! A note attached to it announced that it was the last remaining piece of the tree under which their grandmother had given herself to their grandfather—if only in the form of her verbal consent to marriage.

Sor Amalberga received new instructions, this time of the sort that would be neither difficult nor sinful to obey. She was to stand up on the toilet bowl and press her body firmly against the back wall, with her back to the door so that she wouldn't get hurt when the door burst in. The nun did as she was told, relieved to hear a helpful female voice. All right, now she was on top of the bowl and facing the other way. She kept on praying. The brothers grabbed the log and swung it back and forth, at first to get the heft of it. Then Pazzis counted one—two—three, and on three there was a loud bang. Not only the tricky lock but the entire door split apart, and they barely missed sending the pious lady off into the Great Beyond. Her natural padding withstood the onslaught, and she didn't even scream.

At this point I must confess to delaying a dramatic stylistic coup in my account. Following the bashing of the bathroom door, instead of lingering with the pious lady I should have gone on this way: there was a frightful crash, and as the door was smashed apart, another door opened, the one to Don Juan's room. Dressed in a shirt that reached to his feet and pale with fear, the grandee dashed out into the hallway swinging his trumpet and calling out with a croaking voice, "Revolution! Revolution! Every man for himself!"

Before his children could inform him that no new tyranny had broken out, but only that a small palace revolt had been successfully quelled by his daughter's intervention, the old gentleman was already on the stairs. And he ran through the night-time streets of the city announcing the bloodbath: "Revolution! Revolution!"

Pedro kicked in what remained of the bathroom door, and the nun was free. With pale dignity she stepped down from the toilet bowl, offered the siblings a grateful "Praised be Jesus Christ!" and returned to duty at the beside of the ailing princess.

The foregoing account is a description, fashioned from a variety of perspectives, of the place that was to facilitate the Occidental mission of the mystical writings of Teixeira de Pascoaes, whom I was about to discover.

V

Have I mentioned that the mysterious Count, the proprietor of the "apple" in Book One, was Pedro's uncle? Yes indeed, he was a *tío* on his mother's side, from the house of Alba Real del Tajo. I can't remember why he was going through life simply as "Conde" and not wearing a prince's crown on his head, although Pedro once explained this to us. In Spain there is a great deal of commerce in noble titles; it's possible to exchange them within families, and you can raise or lower your rank as your sense of snobbery dictates. From the standpoint of hereditary biology, this is a healthy form of simony, one that is also widely practiced in Portugal, but it hasn't put a stop to the overall decline of the nobility. This whole subject has now re-entered my mind with the same casual spontaneity as my inclusion of Pedro's uncle in my island adventures. Let me add that the bronze knocker on Zwingli's front door was a copy of one of those snooty Carthaginian divinities that you can see so many examples of in the museum on Ibiza. Was it perhaps Tannit, the guardian of heavenly love, who was summoned to drive out the tenants from their *pilarière?*

The knocker at the entrance to House No. 23 had no such art-historical value; the builder found somewhere an iron hand that corresponded to the tenants' social class. The noise it made was, however, the same. Because we occupied the *bel-étage,* a single knock sufficed.

Just one bang!—and it was for us. Seconds later the bell at our apartment door was given a twist. Who could that possibly be on a Sunday afternoon? Pedro used a special signal. I opened up.

"Santa Barbara!" I cried like a devout Spanish lady in a thunderstorm. It felt as if lightning had struck me. Pilar was standing at our doorstep.

María del Pilar, the woman who was Vigoleis' libidinous undoing; the raging scourge of Zwingli's bed; our collective misfortune. My brother-in-law's degenerate concubine looked at me with eyes reddened from weeping, and said, "Come quickly, before it's too late!" She handed me a note. In my brother-in-law's no longer elegant handwriting I read the words, "Am dying. Zwingli."'

Oh sure, my dear fellow, we know what your dying is like! You have every good intention, but intending is as far as it ever goes. You can't fool me this time. I handed this premature obituary back to Pilar and said something like this: give him our best wishes for a blessed death; perhaps some other time. But the woman grew very angry and gave me a piercing look. She stamped her foot, which was shod in a shiny little golden slipper, and yelled, "Where is Beatrice? Your brother is dying! Follow me!"

This was not an act; I went in and told Beatrice. She put on a mantilla, and we followed the bearer of tragic news.

The novelistic tradition contains many examples of relatives hastening through night and wind, over hill and dale to the deathbed of a dear one, and usually they arrive just in time to look soulfully into the eyes of the dying one, grasp his quivering hand, or hear from his lips, "I did it, I buried the body, God be merciful to my sinful soul..." On such a journey the relatives have plenty of time to conjure up whole other novels: the dying man's life passes in review before their mind's eye. "Oh Lord, if Thou wilt but spare his life, we shall make peace with him. All shall be forgiven and forgotten!"

We were not allowed time for such emotionalizing, for Pilar raced like a weasel with us in tow, down Barceló and then left into the Calle San Felio, second house on the right, next to our pharmacy—we were already at our destination. So this is where the loving couple lived, where in fact they had been living ever since they secretly left the Count's apple, just a hundred paces from our own house, and yet we had never crossed paths! Let no one ever say that we were lacking a benevolent guardian angel when we moved to the General's Street.

Zwingli was lying on the *pilarière* with his head hidden in the folds of the pillow. I would have bet my own head that this time he was really dead. His beard was Christ-like, his cheeks more sunken than in real life, causing his cheekbones to appear more Indian than ever before. His white hands lay on the blanket. Oddly, all of his nails had grown out, exceeded in length only by the one on his pinky, which now was bent slightly upward, as if commanding one final measure of respect before getting placed under the earth along with the others. All the magic was gone.

I have never witnessed a human being getting born or dying, and thus as a poet I couldn't have much to add to what Rilke already said in the words of his Malte Laurids Brigge "One must also have seen dying..." Now I was at least in the presence of death itself.

The room was darkened, and yet I could still make out our wooden wardrobe from the Street of Solitude. Aha! The death of my beloved maternal grandmother, who suddenly passed away at an old age on Christmas Eve during our notorious "turnip winter," as presents were being exchanged under the tree, gave rise to an ugly dispute over her estate. The altercation actually started at her wake. I was still too young to grasp the value of her earthly belongings, but too old not to be deeply shaken by the rude estate-grabbing indulged in by a devout, doctrinaire uncle, one whom I often saw crawling in the dust before our family Bishop, kissing the ring of this blood-related eminence of ours. Yet Uncle Jean, that wonderful man and expert in human nature, never pushed him away with his other hand.

Now, however, I myself began feeling a certain mercenary urge in the presence of my relative's corpse. The slut hadn't given us back our wardrobe, or our table, or our bed linen, which she could now use to wrap the cadaver. But just you wait! The Finger of God can reach farther than your whored-out Helvecio's magic nail!

Beatrice's eyes, too, lit upon the wardrobe. But since they slowly filled with tears, she had only a blurred notion of the legal ramifications. Poor Zwingli, she not only thought it but said it, too—in French, which for me had the effect of increasing the misery she was feeling. We stood at the foot of the bed—as we forgive those who trespass against us, and lead us not into temptation...

The widow Pilar was weeping out loud, at times crying out in pain, "*Ay Jesús, ay Jesús!*" Then she threw herself down on the corpse, shook it, embraced it, squeezed it so hard that if her lover were not already dead, he would be completely out of breath. "Beatrice," I whispered, "let's leave her alone in her sorrow." But Pilar was thinking the very same thing. She rose up and left us alone with our sorrow and with our relative. "If he had only called us sooner!" Beatrice groaned.

Then the dead man opened his eyes, exhaled long and hard through his waxen mask, and, for once forgetting his international prestige, said in Swiss German,

"Is she gone? It was getting to be too much for me with that fucking woman!"

Won't this man ever die? Does he just want to go on dying forever? Now that's going simply too far! I felt like hitting him over the skull with the shoe tree that Pedro failed to hurl at his spoilsport of a father. Then we would have an end to these constant false death alarms.

Beatrice, in attendance for the second time at her darling brother's resurrection, went deathly pale. Even her lips were now white. She didn't move, she didn't cheer. She said nothing. There was no water handy to toss at this jackanapes, as if he were a cat or a whore. But as might be expected of her, Beatrice was in control of this kitschy situation.

Pilar came back. Zwingli immediately closed his eyes, but rather than play dead he started breathing audibly. These were the "sporadic sounds" of the deathbed which, according to Rilke, a poet must harken to for the sake of a good line of verse. This part of the scene, at least, worked out to my benefit.

Doubtless already accustomed to such spontaneous resurrections of her bedfellow, the woman didn't collapse in a heap. "Water," the dying man now wheezed. Pilar shot from the room.

"I don't want her here. I've got to talk with you two. Send her off to a drug store far away."

Beatrice wrote down a prescription, and sent Pilar to the Calle San Miguel to buy some homeopathic drops. Vigo would go get a doctor while she stayed on at the bedside.

A Spanish woman's tears can dry up faster than they can flow. Pilar set off on her mission. Besides buying the medicine, she would no doubt return with ingredients for the General's Eggs.

In addition to his considerable, very masculine amatory woes, Zwingli had contracted another serious ailment; in fact, he was in desperate shape, not far from giving up the ghost. "Down there," he said, "everything's on the fritz." He would have to say goodbye to the island, and the best thing for him would be to give up on Spain completely and return to Switzerland to undergo a full cure. But he could do this only if he chose to escape. We were supposed to help him with this plan, and it would have to be done with the greatest of care. One false move, and all three of us would get a shiv in the ribs. Zwingli turned his miserable head to one side and pointed to the night table. There lay the Toledo blade, ready for wielding.

"But there's something even worse than the dagger and almost worse than my health. There's a card stuck in the mirror over there. Read it and you'll see why I have to get the hell out of here."

The card was alarming. It came from a small village in the hinterlands of Valencia, where Pilar's parents and siblings lived. The note said that they had sold their property and were about to board ship for Mallorca, where they intended to spend their retirement at their daughter's house! Pilar had at one time informed her family that she was married to a famous hotel manager and had a large *piso*—and her relatives were expected any day now. All of us cringed at this news. Forgotten were all the spats and conflicts, now it would have to be clan against clan. The two Swiss citizens renewed a historical oath: *Ça? Jamais! Niëmols!*

My sense of family cohesion is poorly developed, and my patriotic consciousness is best described as atrophied. But to stand together like this at the hour of need—even I thought this was admirable. So as the third member of the cabal I swore an oath to lend a hand and deliver Zwingli from the whore and her hinterlands.

"Once I'm on shipboard," Zwingli said, "Knoll will help me get out of Barcelona. Then you can pick up your stuff here, and especially, Vigo, my library, my collections. All of it is in my office, part of it still packed in boxes. Nothing must remain here. The combined value is in the thousands. That bitch...!"

But then the bitch herself returned, and Zwingli went back to dying. The pharmacy was of course closed, but Beatrice, who saw through the bitch right away, offered to prepare some Künzli tea—this would work as a purgative and have a calming effect at the same time. In fact it was a miraculous brew, one that outdid the expectations of even old Pastor Künzli, the herb expert who invented it. It was agreed in guttural Alpine German that on the following day Zwingli would sneak over to our house for further discussion of our plans.

Then we departed, leaving the moribund Swiss citizen in the clutches of the vampire. Yet now the spirit of the Rütli patriots hovered over the chamber of death.

Back home we trickled out our pesetas; we would have just enough for a sail to Barcelona. Spain, said Beatrice, was Zwingli's undoing. Now it was up to us to rescue him at any price. But then he must never return to Spain.

Zwingli arrived stealthily at the appointed hour. Not with the springy gait of a conspirator, to be sure, but with the haggard limp of an emaciated Lothario who is already toying with the idea of entering a monastery. He was accompanied by a street urchin carrying a large but light suitcase. As usual Zwingli reached into his pocket, but all the bravado of that gesture was now a thing of the past. I bedded down our friend on our mattress since he couldn't keep standing up. Bedridden for weeks, he had wanted to send for us, but the bitch would have nothing of it. When he learned that her relatives were going to move in, he staged the dying scene. A Spanish proverb has it that the greatest obstacle in life is the family. One can manage with *putas* all right, but not with their hangers-on...

Julietta was gone. Following an almost fatal beating, she had left the island. Some "uncle" had offered to take in the saucy and promising young kitten. He was having her trained as a ballerina in Barcelona.

As physically wretched as he was, Zwingli still commanded active mental powers. And since there was now no Pilar around to interrupt him, he started emoting about his plans for an academy. The initial concept was all worked out, and soon a lengthy memorandum would be sent to an American financier. In addition, he had in mind setting up a shoe factory and a horse-racing stable.

We had the hardest time focusing his attention on the one immediate, central idea: his escape. He had forgotten all about it.

Because there were no ships leaving for mainland on Sunday, we settled on the following Saturday as our day of our departure; that way, Zwingli would be one day ahead of a possible pursuit by Pilar. He arranged the following: she would go to the movies with a girlfriend of hers, and after the show she would wait for him on the Plaza Santa Eulalia. The doctor would give him some injections to make him more or less fit for the trip. Pilar, a movie fanatic, wouldn't have the slightest suspicion. As far as she was concerned, everything would be fine as soon as her Helvecio once again stood up like a man. She even went back on the street to raise money with her heaven-sent talent for the General's Eggs.

Zwingli thought it was too dangerous to enter his real name on the passenger list; he feared that Pilar would inquire right away at the shipping line. For this kind of camouflage he didn't need to search very far. His father, schooled in Christian patristics, had let him be baptized with a plethora of first names including, among a few concessions to bourgeois normalcy, such echoes of Renaissance Humanism and the Reformation Era as Erasmus, Melanchthon, and Oekolampadius. The latter, a Basel reformer and one of the most feared religious gangsters of his fanatical time, carried the bourgeois surname "Hausschein," and it was under the name of an obscure "Señor Hausschein" that Zwingli intended to make the trip to the mainland. It was his hope, of course, that such an erudite disguise would put Pilar and her confederates off the track. But on the day of our departure Zwingli sent me a note asking me to go right ahead and buy his ticket. I did so using my own name, Vigoleis— which amounted to a double deception, although at the last moment the game took on a certain legitimate aspect when I draped my loden coat over the escapee's shoulders and propped my floppy hat on his brow.

It was a favorable moment for an escape. Fog lay over the seascape, concealing the harbor and the low-lying section of the city where we lived. Beatrice said goodbye to her worrisome brother, who was now barely distinguishable from myself, either in clothing or in mood. Then, *ciao*! and "Don't forget to write!"

We walked separately. Ahead of me in the mist walked my loden coat under my symbolic floppy hat. But the Vigoleis who was propelling this getup along seemed to be either congenitally lame or plagued by the same affliction that caused Don Juan Sureda to speak in so many different tongues. If Beatrice had not found just the right word at just the right time back on the Street of Solitude when I was lusting after my brother-in-law's wife, I myself would now be plodding along like a crippled capon behind my own double.

I said goodbye to Zwingli before we reached the dock; I didn't dare follow him to the brightly lit gangplank. Zwingli gave me some good advice: don't be a stick-in-the-mud, take good care of Bé, and get his archive away from the bitch, even if it meant calling the police...

"Should I go find a bullet-proof vest?"

"One night with her and you'll have everything!"

"A knife in the ribs, or syphilis?"

I received no reply to this superfluous question. My double had disappeared.

As I turned the corner into Barceló, a foghorn started wailing. The *Ciudad de Palma* had weighed anchor and was steaming toward Barcelona.

Now Zwingli could shake off Vigoleis and climb back into his old, tortured skin. I see him standing in front of me like a horse being brought to stable. He never learned how to sleep standing up, but he was certainly an expert in the horizontal position. We wondered whether he could truly get mended in Switzerland. His intention was to have himself de-pilarized in the clinic run by a well-known homeopathic specialist and friend of the family, old Dr. Scheidegger. His entire family was committed to homeopathy; one of the grandpas had achieved a certain notoriety in the field. His "Home Guide to Homeopathy" was a bedrock of the siblings' private library, and they consulted it for any and all ailments. Beatrice owed her life to homeopathic drops. Surely this potent liquid, dribbled into a glass by an expert hand, could do the trick against the Pilarian toxin. Since the treatment is based on the principle of similarity, he would have to remain for a while yet under that woman's scourge— but such a method could make the withdrawal cure all the more humane.

After arriving home, I barricaded the door. We realized that Pilar would immediately suspect us of being accomplices to the escape, and that she was capable of asking pimps to help her force an entry. I knew that she still maintained cordial contacts with the Mallorquin underworld.

That night, our lives weren't worth a fig.

A few days before, a bloody drama had occurred on our street. A man discovered his wife in bed with another guy. This is called adultery, and for people who haven't thought much about the ways of the world, adultery is a rotten spot in Eve's apple. Our neighbor murdered the violator of his putative personal honor, dispatched his wife with a second blow of the axe, and with a third, the sister-in-law who lived with them. Blood flowed in torrents down the staircase, a crowd raced to the scene, a few butchers' dogs had to be chased away, and kids were kept from viewing the carnage. As a relative of the murdered sisters, "Siete Reales" knew the details, and thus I got a full report from an unimpeachable source. Above and beyond the metaphysical blindness of the perpetrator, I took a special interest in this case as a study in ethnology. The police locked up the murderer, who hadn't even tried to escape since, as the shoemaker explained to me, every Spanish married man has the right to kill his wife and her other bedfellow if he catches them *in flagrante*. A few days later the judge set the man free, and all his neighbors accompanied him in a triumphal parade to his house, which some helpful ladies had washed clean of any trace of the deed. Not long after that, this defender of his personal honor took another lover to his bed, someone else's wife, a woman he had been "visiting" for quite a while previously—a likeable young lady, by the way, who whitewashed walls for us in our apartment. Nobody could white-wash like this adultress, who charged only two reales per hour.

Blood—and this is all that I have meant to convey by telling the story of this petty bourgeois tragedy—had already flowed copiously on the Street of the General. Was our own blood now to be shed in all innocence? Was our blood to attract the frightful curs of Palma, the progeny of the hordes of canines that ravaged the city at the turn of the century? These hounds were housed in a kennel owned by Don Juan Sureda, who kept them as guard dogs for himself and his increasingly numerous relatives. At that time he still was living on Calle Zavellá, in the town palace named after his clan. Every evening the hungry pack was let loose, and instead of protecting life and limb of the nobility, they swarmed out across the city, raided private houses, and had a particular weakness for butcher shops that were kept open to take advantage of the cool night-time breezes. On these nightly self-service expeditions, the bloodhounds provided themselves with the food that their kennel master no longer could offer them, since by this time Don Juan was already among the aristocrats who could afford to make bets at his club like the following: "Do you want to bet that I can make an omelet that will cost X thousand pesetas?" Take a frying pan, an egg, a drop or two of olive oil, stir constantly over a low flame fueled with hundred-peseta bills. —Whenever the barking band of beasts descended on the city, there was general panic. For years afterward, the population had memories of the widespread outcry, "God help us, the Suredas are on the loose!" On one occasion we ourselves were the cause for the general alarm getting spread almost daily on our street.

I had agreed to type out some manuscripts and do some partial German translations for an English travel writer. Her husband was a war invalid, suffering from a strange form of the gout that could be cured, or at least made bearable, only by constant moisture, and for this reason the couple always sought living quarters in a humid environment. This didn't help much. So the determined wife bought a tiny sailing sloop, stuck her gouty spouse in the little cabin, set sail, and in this way evolved into a popular author of travelogues. *Hydrophilus* was not seaworthy, the owners even less so, and this meant that on their voyages they had to stay close to the coastlines. But this, too, was dangerous, since the chubby lady didn't know how to sail, and the crippled warrior was no help in any case. So the intrepid voyagers bought two Great Danes and trained them to leap to the other side of the boat to keep the balance every time she tacked.

They had already explored all the French and German rivers, testing them for humidity, and now they arrived in the Mediterranean to check out its literary and hygroscopic possibilities. They made the passage over to Mallorca roped to a freighter, then they got towed around the whole island and finally threw anchor and moored their floating sanatorium at the Paseo Sagrera dock in Palma harbor. The lady's stories were pure kitsch, miserable pulpy stuff, but since she always staged her plots on the ocean, they were grabbed up by the maritime-obsessed English public. In Emmerich's shop her books went like hotcakes. No wonder this writer, whose name I have forgotten, was able to pay me well.

The lady always arrived in the company of her Great Danes—that is to say, her dogs dragged her to our house and then proceeded to riot in front of our door, scratching the varnish and tearing apart the doormat we had purchased after so much physical and mental sacrifice. What is more, lacking any house to live in, they were not housebroken. Even before running amok on the landing in front of our apartment, they created havoc on the street outside. Like heralds of the court they swept a path for their mistress. Our peaceable neighbors, who loved to sit on low-slung chairs near their doorsteps and knit, mend fishing nets, or—their favorite activity—do nothing at all, gathered up their children and belongings at the first sound of barking and rushed into their houses. Chairs were scattered on the street; degenerate dogs that didn't realize quickly enough what was in store for them, got bitten to death. Cats hissed and scrambled up the naked walls. Nuns blessed themselves and instinctively pressed their flat bosoms against the wall. And then the writer herself came on the scene, a pith helmet propped on her weathered coiffure and tied under her chin with a veil, carrying the large palm-frond basket that contained her manuscripts. She readily paid for minor property damage that neighbors complained to me about—such things, she said, were material for a good story. But once when a child got bowled over by the Danes and had to be taken to the hospital with internal injuries, this was a bit much for the lady from England. We made an agreement that henceforth I would fetch her manuscripts from on board their sloop and later return them there. From then on—and this is why I am telling this story—there were no more shouts of "God help us, the Suredas are on the loose!" on our quiet street. As in days of yore, the neighbors sat calmly on their chairs mending and knitting, cobbling, sewing mattresses, tying fishing nets and nursing their babies.

Later the British lady geared up their sloop and set sail again with husband and canine herd. For a while longer her travelogues appeared in the magazines, but then her byline disappeared and their little boat was never sighted again. Presumably the Great Danes committed a nautical error during a difficult maneuver, consigning themselves and their masters to a glorious mariner's death at sea.

Blood, then—I am reaching back a few pages—blood that attracts dogs: would it start flowing again from House No. 23, this time from Vigoleis' and Beatrice's veins? Will Heaven not grant surcease? I preferred not to trust to a Higher Power, but far and wide there was no sign of a whore coming to flash her blade. I could have spared myself the effort, but I quickly changed my mind when we entered the bookshop around noontime. "One minute sooner," the proprietor told us, "and a crazed fury would have skewered you both!" Pilar had come by and made a search of the premises, thinking that Zwingli must be hiding somewhere in the ice-cream bar copa that they both knew so well.

The man who reported this to us was no longer Emmerich from Cologne but his successor, a short, ash-blond, very friendly fellow from Swabia who learned only too late that he was not made for Spain. It cost him his nerves, his health, and his own and his wife's savings. He was still quivering over his whole body, and I, two heads taller but no less fearful of raging whores, now likewise felt the touch of cold steel at my back. This time someone was bound to end up lying flat on the battlefield, rubbed out either by Pilar herself or one of her kind. Zwingli once told us that Pilar had stabbed more than one individual. Mortally? My gooseflesh told me: mortally. The new owner of the bookshop hadn't yet learned a word of Spanish, so all he knew was that on this particular hunt, we were the prey. He was, of course, familiar with the details of our whorish adventures, right down to the matter of the rapidly abandoned deathbed. It didn't cheer him up at all when Vigoleis was asked, "You're still here? I could swear that I saw you just last night on board the steamer, wearing a loden coat and a floppy hat, when I was taking some last-minute mail down to the ship."

But then I told him our story. He and I were in great excitement, whereas Beatrice started calmly leafing through books on the shelves. Antonio came over from across the street, where Pilar had also made a visit, and warned us, "Watch out! That woman is unpredictable. At any minute the dagger can pounce from her stocking!"

That evening I once again barred our door and installed a clever alarm contraption that would wake us up immediately if anybody started fiddling with the lock. But the contraption didn't spring into action until next morning when the milkman arrived. No sign of María del Pilar.

No hay mal que por bien no venga, goes a Spanish proverb: "misfortune can have its good points, too". Beatrice wasn't feeling well—nothing serious, but she decided to stay in bed.

Her bed rest saved our lives, or at least one of our lives.

The whore arrived at noontime. I immediately fainted, and was still shaking as she shouted to be let in. With the clear conscience enjoyed by all atheists, I rapidly set my affairs in order with the Powers Above. Just let her approach, dagger in hand! I could have wished a nobler form of widowhood for Beatrice, but such things lie beyond the control of man.

"Do you want us to go back with you? Is your Helvecio dying again?"

She had arrived, she declaimed, to settle matters, but now with both of us. No more fooling around. Where was Beatrice? These words spewed forth from her pretty little mouth, from beneath her quivering little nose. She had forgotten to powder it, which she suddenly realized when I focused my eyes sharply on it. Women don't like that.

My cosmetic ambush gave me an advantage.

If she came to settle matters, I said, then she would have to betake herself into the back room to Beatrice's bed. Beatrice was sick.

Fearing the worst, Beatrice had been listening at the door and now dove back under the covers as we entered the bedroom. I let the vengeful woman go ahead of me. Our apartment was like a cave animal's burrow, with the nest at the end of a set of tunnels: you couldn't go astray. But this wasn't just a casual hunting expedition.

My own back was secure from the dagger's thrust—but what about Beatrice's breast?

The woman stopped at the bedside and hurled her customary hate-filled glance at Beatrice—or was it a lethal glance? Hardly lethal, since she possessed other means for killing. Before we knew it, Pilar reached under her skirt and pulled out this dagger that by now is probably so familiar that it has lost its effect—stylistically, I mean. As a weapon it was still dangerous.

Beatrice remained motionless, lying in wait. Perhaps she had secreted some weapon of her own under the bedspread, ready to brandish it at the proper moment. Or perhaps she knew from reading detective stories that it's difficult to stab somebody through bedclothes and pillows. Nonetheless, I grabbed a kitchen chair to smash the whore's skull with. This chair, however, was badly carpentered; as I lifted it, a splinter went straight under the nail on my middle finger. I yelled "Ouch!" and dropped the whole chair. At the very same instant Pilar shouted at us that Helvecio was gone and she had come here to...

"... to murder us, too," Beatrice interjected coldly, as she rose up incautiously on the bed. "We know the whole story. The police have been here. They're looking for you. Who else but you can have killed my brother, *sale femme*!"

Who would have expected this of Beatrice? Instead of water, this time she was hurling an accusation! Pilar turned rigid; the dagger fell from her hand. She called out the names of her loyal Saints, then groaned "*Ay Jesús*!" and threw herself down on the bed. She started weeping so violently that it almost broke both of our hearts. The murderous crisis was over; the arrow had flown back to hit the archer.

We let the poor wretch wail herself out. I offered to brew us some coffee. Beatrice asked for a cigarette.

I gave Pilar a briefing: we knew that Helvecio was missing. According to rumors, he had been done in by a jealous concubine. The police were notified. When Beatrice heard the news, she lost consciousness. Bad heart attack. There she lies.

Pilar threw herself down on the floor and beseeched me with choking voice not to believe that she ever laid a hand on Helvecio. Helvecio, the only man she ever loved! The scene was frightful in its phony melodrama. The woman literally coiled up on our floor. I thought it best to go into the kitchen and heat up the stove. Beatrice got up, and I noticed that she pulled a dust pan from under the covers—she probably meant to use it either as a shield against the dagger or to smash the fury's nose in. Now she calmly replaced it on its hook, but not before sweeping up demonstratively a few bits of dust. María del Pilar took no notice of this; she was busy with her own misery. Jesus, Mary, and Joseph came to her aid, and she was soon over the worst.

Had the police been there, she asked? Yes, but not on her account; they came in connection with the murder a few doors down the street. But where was Helvecio? She had just visited the steamship office and asked to see the passenger list. He wasn't on it, not even under the name Zwingli. What could she do? Would we help her relocate her man? All these questions were interrupted by sudden bursts of tears, moans, imprecations, vague gesticulations. She powdered her nose, applied rouge, made hesitant suggestions. I advised her to flee before the authorities started a serious search for the missing Swiss citizen. Go in hiding? But where? In Barcelona, of course, where no one would find her, but where she might find her Helvecio. She liked this idea. She would dissolve her household immediately, sell everything, throw it away for cash to the highest bidder. Would we...? Why not? We would like to get our few pieces of furniture back—our wardrobe, especially our table, and our bed linen—you remember, don't you, little Pilar, back then—? Renewed sobbing, Ays, invocations of the divine intercessors. What was I thinking, now, at this moment of her great sorrow, her desperate situation, her unbearable solitude—to have the nerve to bring up long-forgotten stories! Pah! She was right. It was cruel of me to come at her with the apple of discord. Things would go better if I paid mind to the old saw about building golden bridges behind the fleeing enemy. This harlot has fire in her eyes, Vigo. You won't be safe from her until the Mediterranean Sea lies between you.

"Fine, Pilar. We'll buy a few of our... er, pardon, a few things from you. If you have, let's say, a wardrobe and a serviceable table, one that I could do my writing on, and some bed linen—how would that be?"

We agreed on a price between friends, plus a small amount in consideration of her emergency situation, inclusive of moving costs.

Our leave-taking was memorable. The two women embraced and kissed each other on the cheeks, their eyes partly tear-filled, partly glazed over. It wouldn't have surprised me if one of them fell over dead with a knitting needle in the aorta. Vigoleis stood by and wondered whether "that woman" was going to throw herself around his neck, too. But the horny *pontifex* had no need to build such a golden bridge as this one; he gave her one final handclasp and a glance that takes us back to Book One and the Street of Solitude, when the insatiable doxy tried to lure the stranger to her poisonous bed.

Before my eyes could focus again properly, she was out the door.

"Oh ye olde whorish glory, whither hast thou gone?" I whistled. Then the doorbell rang. I opened up. *Porra!* Pilar!

María del Pilar was smiling. My resistance crumbled. Now or never—but not here! On your *pilarière*, Pilar, just around the corner, I'm coming... Then she asked me for her knife. She had forgotten it in all the excitement.

Beatrice fetched it from the rubbish can.

Cleaned out of house and home, Pilar left the island. Our furniture deal went through before she departed; the Swabian book man lent us the money.

Zwingli's archive had disappeared. We never found out who the bitch might have sold it to.

We received a postcard from Zwingli in Switzerland. This time he was not on his deathbed but on clean sheets in Scheidegger's homeopathic clinic in Basel. Old Grandpa's drops and his millionaire godmother's francs would, he wrote, soon have him back fit as a fiddle.

Now we had the island all to ourselves.

VI

Render unto the Kaiser the things which are the Kaiser's, and unto God the things that are God's. No believing soul would ever have difficulty rendering unto God what belongs to Him. But to render unto the Kaiser the taxes he demands: who hasn't spent sleepless nights over this problem? To this day my head spins whenever I fill out a tax form. I have had to do this in many different countries and languages, and each time I have been confronted with the same riddle: why all this gibberish that a normal human being cannot understand without crib notes? Nowadays the latest literary fad is "hermetic" poetry. Isn't all poetry "hermetic"? But for me, plumbing the depths of a poem is child's play compared to puzzling out a tax form. I filled out my first Spanish form to the best of my knowledge and with the worst conscience imaginable.

The tax agency chose to ignore my poverty status and demanded that I pay hundreds of pesetas, or else... The letter ended with a threat signed by some bureaucrat. I was stunned. This was just like Germany.

We hadn't regained our composure when Pedro came by and asked us if we had been visited by some new misfortune. Pilar was gone, Helvecio was gone, and we had the whole game to ourselves. But then he spied the tax man's letter. Aha, he said, that's a bit of a problem. We would have to figure out some way. Foreigners on the island could expect harsh treatment. There were too many suspicious cases among them; so many of them came here under questionable pretenses.

Pedro took out his pad and began sketching Vigoleis as a victim of abrogated civil liberties. Then he drew Beatrice with shorn locks, incarcerated in a Tower. Finally he told me to meet him at the Palma City Hall—he knew a few important people there.

The most important person's office was a reflection of his rank: large and empty. Or almost empty, for it contained a diplomat's desk and along the walls, in keeping with Mallorquin custom, a few dozen handsome, uncomfortable, upright chairs that had leather seats and leather backs with embossed coats-of-arms that pressed into the flesh of anyone sitting on them. The walls featured impressive paintings that fascinated me as a tour guide, but happily I was not obliged to offer any explanations of them. If I had, I would have listed them among the greatest Spanish masters. The gentleman seated on the heraldic throne behind the desk had the appearance of an old El Greco. And it seemed to me that he knew this, or rather that he knew he looked like the real thing.

On the surface of his desk were to be seen a gold cigarette case, a little silver bell, a book with gilded margins and bright-colored bookmarks, and the important person's right hand, pale and tired from signing so many documents.

Pedro had not briefed me concerning what he, I, and the important person were to talk about. I had to rely on my instincts as a tour guide, but I soon realized that the owner of the pale right hand was likewise a born *Führer*.

Don Francisco was enormously pleased to make the acquaintance, finally, of Don Vigo. He had of course heard a great deal about him—wait, what had been the occasion? Had he read him? No, in all honesty not one line; even educated Spaniards had no knowledge of German, Spain was oriented more toward France. A zoologist, of course! Don Vigoleis was a scientist of animal life. Don Francisco nodded appreciatively at Pedro's explanations; he seemed captivated by the whole story. I was no less intrigued by these revelations about my own career, and Pedro was doing quite a fine job of making it all up. I have always had a weakness for animals; as a kid I kept quite a few of the smaller varieties. I trained jackdaws and starlings, I bred budgerigars and meal-worms, kept canaries, moles, frogs, salamanders and pet fishes, rabbits, hamsters, squirrels—a stinking, squeaking, copulating, expensive, noisy and silent menagerie. I could well have turned out to be some kind of expert in zoology–why not? And now that's just what I was. My hobby, Pedro explained, was the flea. "Go ahead, Vigo, tell Don Francisco something about your latest scientific findings in this field that concerns us all!"

Don Francisco made a welcoming gesture and offered us cigarettes. "Fleas?" He was very interested, if only from a scientific standpoint. These tiny animals were what had brought me to Spain? Remarkable, very remarkable.

The flea, I began, was an anabiotic incarnation—I ought to have said "as we all know," in order to lend credence to my thesis, but my Spanish wasn't yet good enough for that. But I got by with some famous names: Haeckel, Darwin, Bölsche, Aristotle. I spoke of occasionalism and prestabilism, Mendelism and pseudo-ovulation, fabricating the evolutionary story as far as the kangaroo, the focal point of my research: the flea as a degenerative mutation of the *marsupialia*. My investigations would lend support to the theory of degeneration, according to which the entire world of fauna originated through the progressive deterioration of the most highly evolved creature, *Homo sapiens*. For purely economic reasons I was conducting my research with the flea, a more accessible animal than the kangaroo. It had become apparent that the Iberian flea, and its subspecies the Spanish, Balearic, and specifically the Mallorquin flea, *Pulex irritans maioricensis*, were best suited as guinea pigs. My research station was located on Barceló Street, and my research assistant was the daughter of a Swiss scientist who had made his name in a different, albeit no less flagellating, field of inquiry. I was preparing a lengthy study on my topic, under sponsorship of the Union Internationale des Recherches Zoologiques in Geneva, at whose most recent congress I had delivered a paper on the pouched flea. The press had printed detailed reports of my discoveries. Don Francisco recalled seeing my name in the papers.

I need not emphasize that during this disquisition I felt as if ants were crawling over my entire body. From my very first day on Spanish soil I was plagued by fleas. Not a single page of these jottings of mine, at least in their Iberian aspects, was lived through without flea bites, although Beatrice somehow was spared this pestilence. The bubonic plague made her immune to many things, but also allergic to a host of other threats. Keating Powder was actually beyond our means; we went through a whole can of the stuff in a single day. And Zwingli's godmother hadn't yet financed the invention of DDT.

Don Francisco listened politely and, feigning real interest, asked me a few questions. He expressed his hopes that my research could proceed undisturbed, if not un-bitten. The island, he explained, offered not only the necessary fleas, but also the appropriate degree of tranquility. This was the moment when Pedro chimed in and pointed out that certain untowardnesses had already occurred. Don Vigo was involved in an unpleasant matter concerning taxes, one that made doubtful his permission to remain in Palma. He was being asked to remit horrendous sums to Internal Revenue; weren't scientific stipends regarded as tax-free? "Vigoleis, do you happen to have the documents with you?"

He had them indeed. Don Francisco's expression turned mournful. After a moment's thought he ventured the idea that the flea professor had no doubt, out of absent-mindedness and modesty, neglected to introduce himself to the island's Governor. It was important, he said, to know how to deal with official agencies as well as with fleas. He might be able to do something about the present case. He rang his silver bell, a functionary entered, and the two of them whispered something to each other in Mallorquin dialect. My documents then disappeared with the functionary. Our conversation continued. *Clima ideal*, bullfights—my flea circus was at an end. The functionary returned with a file folder. Don Francisco glanced through it to see if it was the right one. Then he dismissed the functionary, stood up, and said approximately as follows: "Don Vigoleis, you may rest assured that we Spaniards are proud to have such an eminent pulelogist in our midst. Our country has a glorious history; it has enjoyed world-wide prestige under a monarch on whose empire the sun never set. Today we are perhaps not at the height of our power in the political sense. But in matters intellectual and scientific we outclass the rest of the world. La Cierva, Marañón, Unamuno—you surely know the names. As far as your personal research is concerned, you shall not be further harassed by the tax authorities as long as you are our guest."

With these words Don Francisco tore up the file and threw it in the wastebasket that—I forgot to mention this—was also in his office. We were dismissed. You could tell from Don Francisco's behavior that he didn't want to waste any more of his time with us. And for our part, we were eager to leave this citadel of bureaucracy. Down in the hallway, Pedro danced the bolero and sang a picaresque ditty. I maintained my professorial decorum until we arrived at the Plaza Cort, when I, too, finally let loose. Beatrice, far from embracing us in our triumph, said that she didn't believe a word of our flea story. Be that as it may, in all our later years on the island no one ever again sent us a tax form, much less a process server.

I was deeply impressed by the sophisticated manner in which a Spanish civil servant had fallen for some hare-brained nonsense. This was Spain in its quixotic unpredictability, one of those mild attacks best described as half insanity and half clownishness, although there is really nothing ludicrous about them. *Don Quixote*'s foolish mistakes can appear ridiculous only to someone who thinks he knows the limits of being serious. I loved that Spain, and still love it for its mystics, its ecstatic poets, its morbidly erotic priests, for its Pedros, and for Pedro's philologically tortured father, for its God-fearing whores of the streets, and for the cheap hotels that light a candle to the same Virgin to whom the torero dedicates his life before he walks out to face the bull's horns. I love the stubborn pride it displays in the face of the ridiculous, and the absurdity with which it confronts the obtuseness of the world. I love it for its "*mañana, mañana*," for the simple reason that every Tomorrow will without fail turn into a Today. How would a German tax administrator have reacted to getting an erudite flea planted in his ear at Pedro's instigation? He, too, would have tapped his little silver bell. But instead of some office minion, two guys would have appeared, strapping fellows both of them, pointing to Vigoleis and saying, "This the one?" And they would have taken him away in a paddy wagon. And amid shouts of *Heil dem Führer!*" he might have been released as "cured" sometime in the year 1933.

Shouts of "Hail to the *Führer*" had been resounding in my fatherland for years, but the new Savior was not yet officially recognized. Up to now, the only one who had resurrected and commercially patented the historic Roman Greeting was Mussolini, who had acolytes in Spain and on the island of Mallorca. They were few in number, only a tiny coterie gathered around the fasces. And oddly enough, unlike in Germany, it wasn't representatives of the underworld who sided with the insurrectionist leader. The first followers were from the aristocracy who were betting on the future. I say "oddly enough," but why, exactly? The nobility's purses were empty, too.

Beatrice's fame as a language teacher was rising, like my own star as a flea scientist. So for a while we both shone brightly in the firmament. She drummed respectable languages into Mallorquin brains manifesting varying degrees of density. Meanwhile, she also began teaching at a lycée, since she had excellent recommendations, plus an even more valuable Swiss diploma. This school admitted only daughters of the richest, most prestigious families. Founded by Germans, it was still called Colegio Alemán, although its ownership and direction had long since passed over into Spanish hands, those of an intelligent and pedagogically talented woman, Doña María, who had many names, many children, and many grandchildren. One of whom, a wild *mestiza* of enchanting beauty, presented her with vexing problems. Doña María was urbane, much-traveled, and married to an ailing husband who, nevertheless, was a wine connoisseur, fond of offering copious quaffs to guests at his table. Doña María had discovered this new teacher, Beatrice, and hired her on the spot. She dismissed in silence rumors that her new *profesora* had once been of the ilk of the Pilars.

Pedro had opened up for Beatrice the palaces of the impoverished nobility. Each one was occupied by uncles, aunts, and cousins whose consanguinity was even more tenuous than the ancient, traditional labels named after parts of the body. From the head to the tip of the middle finger, there was at one time such a thing as a "fingernail cousin." Beatrice gave lessons in all of these domiciles, showing the *señoras* how to decline and conjugate. Some got left by the wayside, others took their place, and Pedro told all of them that Doña Beatriz had a husband who was worth looking into: a little crazy, a little shy, very learned, and not very handsome—which a man doesn't really have to be. There was a statue of him in a German cathedral. This aroused the young ladies' curiosity. They urged their parents to send Don Vigo an invitation. It happened, and he accepted. He found the girls charming, and not at all so abysmally stupid as Beatrice had described them. He engaged in polite conversation, blushed readily for no discernable lubricious reason—an annoying legacy of Original Sin—and at times caused the young ladies to blush. Those were very pleasant moments in the *palacios* listed in every Baedeker, homes that we now could enter for reasons rather different from what Zwingli originally had in mind for us and his concubine.

One of these citadels of pedagogy was the *palacio* of the Count de la Torre, situated on Portella, the "Casa Formiguera," which was connected by an archway above the street with the Casa Marqués de la Torre. During my first visit, walking through abandoned rooms we spied priceless treasures dating from a time when the island was owned by a half-dozen of these grandees. We also met a genuine matriarch, whose age I estimated at a few hundred years. She seemed so very authentic in these authentic surroundings that I could have converted then and there to a classicistic theory of history, until the Count told me that this was his own mother. Had she been artificially fossilized? Her son was scarcely older than I was. He had many children, very many, perhaps in deference to the name of his dynasty, Formiguera, which means "ant hill." The girls were learning French and English. One of the older daughters, perhaps the oldest, was married to a captain who, although a soldier, was not the worst specimen of his kind. His private cook was particularly good. Soon we were clapping each other's shoulders in friendship. I told him how I had restored honor to a Spanish general, while not concealing that I didn't think much of the military. Whereupon this officer invited us to his fortress, and ordered the casement cannons to be winched up to their threatening positions above the ramparts. These were his pride and joy. Just a few more stars, and he could have been Julietta's father. Later his cook/aide-de-camp sprang into action. In peacetime, the trench surrounding the fort served for the most part as a rabbit trap. We ate *râble de lièvre au Madère*. My compliments, Captain!

The Counts de la Torre had a friend who likewise belonged to the military caste, and about whom they liked to tell stories. As a strapping young officer he had participated in the Moroccan Campaign, after which he was immediately appointed commander of the military academy in Zaragossa. As ambitious as the famous Corsican, he strove for higher and higher ranks, and his model was Il Duce.

Like so much else, I knew the Italian dictator only from the newspapers. What he was aiming for was unclear to me, but how he was going about it couldn't have been more obvious. Since everything was happening in uniform, his movement was distasteful for me from the start. Beatrice didn't like Il Duce either, although her antipathy was based on personal experience. She had lived for a long time in Italy and witnessed Fascist acts of terrorism at close range. Her years in Florence were particularly clear in her memory, when she and her paleographic brother belonged to the intimate circle of the historian Guglielmo Ferrero and Dina Ferrero, the daughter of Lombroso. Ferrero was on the Duce's blacklist, and thus exposed to harassment that also extended to members of his family and their friends. Beatrice couldn't take a step without being followed by one of the sbirri. She was taken into custody several times and interrogated, then released as a Swiss citizen and threatened with deportation. But before she could be accused of subversive activities and driven out of the country or dumped into the Arno, she had accepted a position as companion to the wife of a German millionaire who, it must be recorded, poured arsenic in her breakfast coffee—which was surely just as bad as getting pushed around by the Fascists. That is why she responded to the Spanish count who was pounding Il Duce's drum, "No Duce for me, thanks!"

One day the Formigueras sent us an invitation to a party in honor of their friend, the aspiring Duce Don Francisco Franco y Bahámonde, who was vacationing with his wife in their house on the island. They explained that it would be necessary to hold a conference to practice the protocol for the event. We were both expected to attend, especially Don Vigo as representative of a nation that was responding so positively to the Italian Duce.

Don Francisco Franco, General of the Infantry, had been sent in 1931 from Azaña to the Balearics as Military Governor, but he soon returned to Morocco. In the Formiguera household he was referred to as the *Cabdillo* or *Caudillo*, which means "chieftain"or "gang leader": Il Duce.

The word "practice" gives me a bad taste, no matter whether it is applied to the times table, a machine gun, or the Communion altar rail. It conjures up visions of Vigoleis' predecessor, and how an aged priest wielding the Key of Saint Peter whacked his tongue for not sticking it out far enough, with the result that he never again joined in the singing of Aquinas' wonderful hymn of praise, *Pange lingua gloriosum*... And now I was expected to show up to practice lifting my right arm and shouting *"Ave Caesar!"* to a general. But let's go anyway. It won't hurt to take a look at this nonsense.

Young people were gathered in the halls of the residence. There was dancing and flirting, people made grandiose declamations into the void, and then the guests practiced saluting a make-believe general. All it took was one go-through, for after all, inside every human being there sits a monkey.

It's strange, but even in jest I couldn't be persuaded to step up to the straw man, lift my arm, and say *"Viva Franco! Arriba España!"* Sometime later—not in this book—I'll relate how I did this very thing years later at a Spanish border station, dressed up as a general. We let it be known that we would not be attending the party. We didn't want to be spoilsports, especially since it now seemed to us that for all these people, playing at Fascism was a bloody serious affair.

"Just as you wish," said the grandee from the House of Formiguera, who earned his bread as a subaltern in a bank. "But later you will regret having failed to make the acquaintance of a future man of prominence. Hitler or Franco—we'll see which of them hits the top first!"

The general appeared, and the party was a huge success. For days afterward, the daughters kept telling Beatrice how much we had missed by being so strangely reluctant to attend. What the *señoritas* had in mind was not so much the political aspects of our refusal to come to the reception. They were thinking mostly about the glamour, the show of wealth, the erotic game-playing with *mantillas* and clattering fans. Despite their fascistoid parade of the capes *(suerte de capa)*, how could these girls or anyone at all know that four years later this glory-seeking general would bear the superlative title of El Generalissimo?

Vigoleis, the champion of missed opportunities, with books as with second-hand women, with his choice of a century to live in, and with the narrative of his second sight—the later world-famous Caudillo is not in bad company with this tissue of failures. But Vigoleis has never shed a single tear over this particular fiasco.

Who has never heard a washerwoman boast that she works only in the finest houses? Seamstresses, midwives, and hired butchers all have their pride of place. Beatrice makes no special claims for her professional standing, in fact she would rather get paid one duro less for working in a faded palace, than be given wads of money by some belching *nouveau riche*. Common folk, who were intelligent and eager to learn, left their cottages to come to our apartment on Barceló, bearing with them even less than a duro, but gifted with the bright alertness and appealing decency that you can still find in the lower segments of society. All of them, with or without money and with or without brains, dirtied up Beatrice's living quarters, but that had nothing to do with education. It had to do with the doormat that still was nowhere to be found at the entrance to our apartment. Books were more important.

The houses that I frequented were not rich, and certainly not elegant. I was often drawn to the charcoal bin and cobbler's shop occupied by "Siete Reales" for a bit of conversation, centering on the inner world experienced by this sooty man, who enunciated his sentences word for careful word, and who could well be regarded as your "man on the street" for the simple reason that he had no door to separate him from it.

And then there was the bakery! The *panadería* was an even greater attraction for me, but before this could happen, the baker's wife had to die in childbirth and leave her five famous little worms and her little pink infant motherless in a cruel world. This is an old story, and I wouldn't be able to give it a new twist even if I tried. Life goes on via the back stairway of death. God wished it so, and Jaume the baker yielded to the will of the Creator, in Whom he believed less and less. But he had no time to give serious thought to his fate. For whereas God reigns unapproachable in eternity, and whereas to Him one day is like an hour or an eon, these kids kept screaming their heads off, the dough had to be kneaded, the apprentice had to be slapped around, and loaf after loaf had to be put in the oven. And there were always these customers! Women from the neighborhood took care of the kiddies; if one of them had just given birth herself, she would put the strange infant to her breast. Poor people aren't finicky about such things. Where one baby is slaking its thirst, there's room for a second. See for yourself: a contented lower-class mother will open her dress, proudly lift a heavy sphere out of its covering, and with practiced hand squirt a stream of milk against the wall. That's persuasive. As prudish as Spanish women can be, as soon as they become mothers they lose all traces of modesty. Breasts are an ornament that they display like a farmer showing off a particularly luscious turnip. In Spain, mothers often nurse their kids for three or four years. This can result in amusing scenes, as when a thirsty tyke takes things in its own hands, pulls forth the spigot, and starts sucking away amid curses and screams like those of the Inca cockatoo. It's an undying privilege of babies to press their demand for the nipple. It took me a long time to get used to this everyday manifestation of maternal happiness. With these Madonnas, the miracle of the female breast, which invites conception and then sustains what was conceived, lost its mystery and became nothing more than an udder.

In this fashion, Jaume's youngest little worm was nurtured along with other infants. He lacked for nothing; he screamed along with his siblings and joined in their chorus of giggles. He was bent on enjoying life as long as it lasted. In these countries it is always doubtful how long that will be. There are deaths in many families where a dozen children is the norm; God giveth and taketh away, in His inscrutable fashion. Whatever remains will eventually engender another dozen. But for Jaume the real problem was the customers who came to his shop. They were more important to him than his God-given family nest. Matías took care of them for him.

Matías was the brother of the baker's deceased spouse. His left leg was shorter than his right one. He had entered the world with this deformity, and so he became a teacher. As a teacher he had claim to the title "Don." I made Don Matías' acquaintance at his sister's funeral. He was dressed all in black. If I had got to know him a year sooner, he would likewise have been dressed in black, and a year earlier than that: also in black, although the shine on his suit would have been less scuffed. His appearance of perpetual mourning stayed the same.

Pedro once explained to us that the average Spaniard never emerges from *luto*, and thus never really doffs his black suit unless he deliberately scoffs at the idea of mourning and an age-old tradition that dictates just how many years, months, and days must pass between "heavy" and "light" mourning, calibrated according to the degree of relationship with the deceased. Sometimes a person who has walked around for 20 or 30 years buried in black will tell himself that the time is up. Just 23 more days, and finally he'll be able to put on a bright new suit. He goes to the tailor, gets measured up, chooses the fabric, and senses that this time it's going to work, unless he himself dies and ends up all in white in a box. And then an obituary notice arrives in the mail— *caramba*, a long forgotten uncle seven times removed, related to the cousin-in-law of a long since deceased great aunt—this will cost him three weeks! The tailor undoes the stitches and sends the fabric back to the dye works.

With his pedagogically trained eyes, Don Matías noticed right away that I was a foreigner and the only "intellectual" among those attending the funeral. He was limping along beside me; I shook his hand, and he learned that I was Vigoleis, Don Vigo, a practitioner of the writing trade from the nation that cradled poets and thinkers. For him this meant consolation on the day when he was burying not only his sister, but also to his hopes of wearing a white suit again anytime soon.

From among my poets he was familiar with Goethe and, from among my thinkers, with Krausse. "What was that name again?" "Carlos Cristiano Frederico Krausse."

Aha, Krause. I had never read a line of his writings, and had never "had" him at the university, unless I was absent the day he was mentioned. Krausse? When I get back home I'll have to look him up right away, no doubt he's in Sternbeck. But because it is a cardinal principle of philosophy to tell the truth, or at least to aim in that direction, before the corpse was placed in the earth I confessed to her mourning brother that I was basically unfamiliar with this fellow "Krausse." Don Matías immediately stood still in this crowd of gabbing, smoking, joking funeral guests and, supported by his cane, looked at me as if yet another of his hopes had been dashed to the ground. "What? You don't know him? Is it possible that a German doesn't know his own Krausse?" I maintained my philosophical composure and replied with the bitter truth, "Sorry, no!"

Don Matías approached his school authorities and was granted a period of so-called hardship leave, which would permit him to help keep his brother-

in-law's shop going until a permanent replacement could be found for the
deceased woman. It was good for me to know this, for it meant that I would
be seeing Don Matías every day and would have to be on my guard. To soften
the blow to my intellectual pride, I could have blathered something about
"Krausianism" to a German professor of philosophy. But I had to be careful
in the presence of a Spanish *aficionado*, an amateur who devoted himself with
passion to philosophy. Just think: a *Krausista*, a Neo-Krausian! It was stupid
of me to spill the beans, telling this fellow right away that I was a writer and
that I didn't know Krausse. I am normally so wary about associating myself
with a profession that, in my hands, amounts to nothing. My indiscretion
resulted in our eating bread from another bakery for three days—three days
of boning up on Krause. Beatrice never saw me studying so hard! But now I
could calmly approach Don Matías and orate to my heart's content about
Krause's primeval being, his primeval inwardness, and his pantheism, without
fear of a failing grade. And in the process I could buy a loaf of bread from him.

"But Don Vigo, you told me that you didn't know Krausse."

"You Spaniards say 'Krausse,' whereas we Germans say 'Krause.' It's a
pardonable mistake, considering that we were in the middle of a funeral
procession."

Don Matías had already considered the possibility of mistaken identity; for
him it was axiomatic that any German would know his Krausse—no other
thought was possible. From my reference books I learned that Krausian philosophy had achieved a particularly strong following in Spain. At Madrid University there was even a professorial chair of Krausism, which was the
springboard for an indigenous political-ideological movement. Its adherents
were called *Krausistas*, they counted in the thousands, and Don Matías was
one of them.

Nonetheless, our second encounter did not take place under the aegis of
German philosophy. Had I tortured myself in vain for three whole days with
that Masonic pantheist? Don Matías took only superficial notice of my
re-Krausification, and immediately began declaiming an ecstatic lecture on
Spain's greatest lyric poet of the previous century, José de Espronceda, who
considered himself the Spanish Byron: a seducer of women, hero of the barricades, political conspirator, and pioneer of *Weltschmerz*. "A model to be
emulated, Don Vigo!"

Sitting on a sack of flour behind the shop counter, Don Matías delivered an
emotional recitation of this poet's controversial stanza about a cemetery that
he claims to envision, one filled with corpses: *de muertos bien relleno, man-
ando sangre y cieno, que impida el respirar*. There are stronger passages in
Espronceda, and the scholars aren't sure whether the one I have quoted is
original or spurious. But coming from Jaume's flour sack, it became moving
poetry. It was incisive, no matter how many corpses it contained. One mark
of great poetry is that it holds nothing back. Only Jaume himself and the ladies
and girls in the shop thought that his Dance of Death was out of place, especially in a house in mourning. The Week's Mind Mass had not yet been cele-

brated. Some of the women blessed themselves, saying "But Don Matías!"
From below, too, came the admonitory cry of "Matías!" From below—that
doesn't mean from the Nether World, but from the oven room situated adjacent to the spacious retail shop, but lower by about a man's height and separated from the shop by a metal grill. This was the realm of Jaume the widower,
who from morning to midnight and often beyond, in the broiling heat amidst
his vats and pans, earned his bread by baking it himself while watching his
brother-in-law and that foreign *intelectual* sitting up above on his flour sacks,
gabbing away about matters that transcended by far the subject of one's daily
bread. He didn't like this one bit, but he kept his peace; his house was still in
mourning. His brother-in-law, on hardship leave to keep the shop going, was
taking great pains to solve the world's mysteries along with one of their most
insignificant customers: half a loaf of bread a day. The creator of biscuits and
rolls had figured out that this was what the two of us were in fact up to,
though he was oblivious to the wonderful, if only temporary, solutions we arrived at. Needless to say, as solvers of the world's problems we made the flour
in the sacks musty. We were all for sacrificing the Good in favor of the Better.

During these first days—more precisely, prior to the Week's Mind Mass—
Don Matías sat on his sack in his close-fitting black suit, serving the customers
with the politeness proper to a teacher on leave from the classroom. Later he
neglected to brush himself off—what for, anyway? Flecked in white, he delivered his orations or listened to my disquisitions, selling baked goods in between. Then the heat in the shop got to him. First he shed his collar and black
tie, with the result that he lost none of his imposing, magisterial mien. As a
symbol of eternal mourning, he kept two black buttons on his white piqué
shirt, which he seldom had to change because at his new job it remained snow-
white. Things went this way for a while, until one day I came upon him without his jacket on, and in place of his shirt he had on a wide-mesh wrestler's
jersey. He wore a scapular around his neck, but the one sported by this Krausist did not contain a picture of the Mother of God. Inside the little golden
capsule was a photograph of his fiancée, the fabled Doña Encarnación—Carnita, "Little Flesh"—about whom more later.

Like any Spaniard who can read and write, and who thus stands above the
masses and is devoted to things of the mind, Don Matías also wrote poetry
and short prose works. He collected these products of his ecstatic moments
together with certain sarcastic analyses and pantheistic effusions in an oilcloth
folder. By the time I got to know him, he had filled several dozen paper pads
with his writings. He told me that they were stored in his library in the *pueblo*,
the village where he worked as a teacher, and where he figured he would
resume working once Jaume had found someone to replace not his wife, but
him, Matías.

He told me that he would go out and get these folders, since he wanted to
get my opinion. The drawer under the shop counter was also soon filled with
home-baked literature, and on a shelf behind our flour sacks some metal cans
got replaced by a small personal library. Thus whenever our conversation cen-

tered on a writer whose work Don Matías "had somewhere upstairs," he didn't have to limp up to his room; he just reached up behind him, and in a cloud of flour dust we both bent over the passage in question.

In this way, a small-time bakery in a poor section of Palma became an intellectual focal point of the highest significance.

I was able to draw Don Matías' attention to a few aspects of the original Krause that he had overlooked. The bakery business suffered, but that was unavoidable. Hadn't Catherine II once mocked the incurable world-improver Diderot, by saying that his grand ideas would yield fine books but a lousy economy? What hopes did we have, two unpublished writers, of exerting a meliorative influence on this woman-less bakeshop? One thing was in our favor—or rather in favor of intellectuals who chose to converse amidst sacks of flour: Pío Baroja, the great novelist, was in his younger years not only a physician but also a baker. In spite of his ck-dt pedigree, Jacob Burckhardt had engaged in some of his world-historical reflections while seated on a sack of flour in a house in the suburb of Sankt Alban where he rented a room. I was, by the way, delighted to introduce that cultural historian to Don Matías, explain Beatrice's relationship to his clan, and point out this remarkable detail of his biography.

The relationship between the two brothers-in-law deteriorated as a result of the teacher's ineptness as a shopkeeper. The clientele threatened to take their business elsewhere. Beatrice, too, took umbrage at the intellectual substitute baker. It piqued her that my shopping for half a loaf of bread kept me from doing other important things, and also that on the way home I so often made a detour to the Municipal Library to fill gaps in my education. For me nothing was more embarrassing than to step into Don Matías' presence like a schoolboy who hasn't done his homework. At Mulet's *tertulia* I was never grilled so thoroughly as when sitting on Jaume's flour sack.

But now it was Beatrice who put new life in the bakery business, and she did it by becoming an inventor—which is supposed to be my own forte. Here's how it came about: it was taking me too long to come home with our half a loaf, and Beatrice decided to go fetch it herself. She entered the bakery at a moment when Don Matías was reading aloud from one of his works. Besides myself the audience consisted of a bunch of women and kids from our neighborhood, who had come not for literature, but for bread. Instead of yanking me by the collar and dragging me home with the bread, as many a plebeian wife would have done, Beatrice reached out by herself for a half-loaf, her lower lip pushed forward menacingly. From my stories and my hunger for learning, she already knew of the local schoolmaster and his Iberian mission, and she didn't want to interrupt his recitation. In this respect she was acting like the other women, who listened open-mouthed to the brother-in-law's declaiming, while down below Jaume kneaded dough, weighed it hastily, and threw it with a loud and angry report onto the mixing table. Beatrice, not the least interested in the oeuvre of my *praeceptor Iberiae*, grabbed our bread from the shelf, paid at the counter, and disappeared. This was the signal for the other customers to follow her example, and it left no one but me to hearken to the rhapsodical verses of the Krausist in the wrestling shirt. There ensued a siege of the shelves. People took what they came for, one girl turned on a machine and pared off the thin slices she wanted for today's *sopas*, and one by one they paid their money and left the shop. It was the world premiere of the self-service store, a triumph of remarkable female audacity—inspired, to be sure, by my own—that is, a born fabricator's—absorption in abstract spirit. Today such stores can be found the world over. The Americans and the Swiss Migros boss Duttweiler are competing for ascendancy. The patent belongs to Beatrice.

Because this shop was patronized only by little people, there was practically no cheating and no checking up on the customers. Don Matías was grateful that everything around him went so smoothly, for this meant that he could devote himself all the more passionately to his philosophical and belletristic endeavors, and pursue his studies to his heart's content. Sitting as a shop regular on my personal flour sack, I remained loyal to him. Then came the day when he began writing at the counter. Not ordinary literature, not *l'art pour l'art*, but love letters! He was not just a theoretical love poet, he was actually in love.

His girlfriend filled his entire being. He called her his own, although according to Spanish custom he would first have to conquer her. This task served as an impetus for his thirty years, his nimble pen, and his winged spirit. The girl's name was Encarnación.

Can there be a more beautiful name for a beloved woman—Love made flesh and blood? Three times a week, Don Matías carefully shook the flour dust from his shirt, from the chest hair beneath it, and from his trousers, threw his black jacket, a so-called *americana*, over his shoulders, stuck his guitar under his arm, and waved *Adios* down to his brother-in-law in the oven room—he was off to the *pueblo*. There, where he taught school, is where she lived, and one day she was meant to fulfill the biblical injunction, implied by her name, that she and Don Matías should live as one flesh. But Jaume would bake many sacks of flour, and I would purchase many half-loaves of bread, before the amorous schoolteacher would let me peer into his heart. On one occasion, filled with ardor but free of any tinge of jealousy, he showed me the contents of his scapular medallion. People who are receptive to poetry, mysticism, and philosophical ruminations are often quite shy and reticent when it comes to interacting with their fellow men. But once the veils are lifted and the dams breached, there is no holding back the floods of emotion. What I am reporting here is the result of a long-term friendship and secret literary/philosophical conspiracy, kept alive by means of our daily bread. It could serve as a refutation of my own theory concerning bread as the most graphic symbol of poverty. Let us bear witness:

Encarnación was the daughter of a general—incidentally, the fourth man of this rank to make an appearance in these recollections. Heaven had bestowed upon her many charming features, but left one of her eyes out of alignment.

Her mother died shortly after giving birth, and the baby was given over to the care of an Indian *ama* who carried her only on her left side. Her father, who thought of Carnita as the apple of his eye, likewise was in the habit of holding her only by his left arm. But while the nurse acted only from thoughtlessness or force of habit, for the general this was a matter of sheer necessity. His right arm was missing. So the infant would wander from the left arm of its nurse to the left arm of its father, until it finally reached the age when it no longer wanted to be carried. By this time, however, Carnita was seriously cross-eyed, and the general was told that there was nothing to be done about it, although the condition might correct itself as the years went by. In a civilized country, any number of techniques would have been applied to bring her eyes into line—special glasses, for instance, or Christian Science, or homeopathic henbane in the proper dosage. But little Encarnación was an exotic flower not only as a general's daughter; she had entered the world inside an authentic buffalo-skin wigwam high up in the Honduran Cordilleras. This took place around the time when her father lost his arm; it was the price he paid for heroism. But he had not yet attained the rank of general.

Don Matías didn't know whose praises he should sing more ardently, those of his true-love-become-flesh or those of his future father-in-law, Don Patuco, who was responsible for the miraculous Incarnation.

Don Patuco, the Honduran general, was tasting the bitter *sopas* of exile on the island of Mallorca. As a young soldier he made his name protecting the construction of the Inter-Oceanic Railroad against attacks by brigands, losing his right arm in a skirmish. He battled gangrene in stinking field hospitals, and finally won. Once the stump healed, he began his rapid rise through the ranks. His country's supreme command sent him from one endangered borderland to the next; wherever the *manco* made his appearance, the one-armed warrior, the enemy retreated. He played a role in every insurrection and *pronunciamiento*, and it wasn't long before his name came to stand for a free, united Honduras, under God and beholden to no other power. In the 1920s a carefully planned coup d'état failed as the result of the bribery of one of the conspirators. Don Patuco and a small band of followers were forced to leave the homeland soil that contained his arm and his wife. Deported by the neighboring countries, and after indescribably difficult wanderings, this stateless group of warriors eventually landed on Mallorca, in the same village where Don Matías was struggling to wrest the younger generation from the Spanish vice of illiteracy. I never learned the general's real name, since he was living incognito. Don Matías would reveal only that the father of his future bride was a direct descendant of the Zambo general Guardiola, a famous personage in Honduran history.

Since time immemorial priests, generals, and whores have been the great sources of energy and progress in the Southern lands; their history can never be written without giving close attention to this Trinity. Don Matías and I did just that during our sessions on the flour sacks. We determined, for example, that two of the categories were subsumed and united under the third, whereas enmity could prevail between the servants of a militant Church and those of the state. This play of forces makes the South more attractive for me than the sun, but not more attractive than its wines.

Don Matías shared my antipathy to the clergy, although he was not as enraged as I was to see representatives of this caste pursuing women with flowing cassocks and fanatical leers, then seeking out the next best church, casting themselves down before a crucifix, and flagellating themselves. Matías had his own experiences with Men of God, and I had mine. "Be on your guard against generals with two arms and priests with forked tongues!" he said to me one day when waves of political excitement entered the bake shop and raised much dust—though not the peaceable white dust from which bread is made.

I knew several priests with forked tongue, but I couldn't quite figure out what Don Matías meant by two-armed generals. He explained this eloquently, using as an example Don Patuco, who had passed on the maxim to him:

A general must display his courage in front of his troops; he must leap into the breach, race across the savannahs, and aim straight for the enemy's heart. "None of your remote observation posts for field marshals, Don Vigoleis, none of your map-room strategy! Don Patuco won all his victories with his sword in his fist. It was only natural that certain limbs might remain behind on the battlefield. When the militiaman Don Patuco chased after the brigands to rescue the pouch containing funds of the Inter-Oceanic Railway, a bandit sliced off his right arm. The robbers were close to being victorious, but after the field surgeon bound off Don Patuco's arm stump, our hero declared that he wanted to fight on, and someone handed him a sword. But then an amazing thing happened: Patuco refused to re-enter the battle without his own sword. So they looked around and found his blade still in the fist of his severed arm. In their haste they were unable to loosen the rigid fingers from the handle. Patuco, mindful of bloody old myths of the Mosquito Coast *mestizos*, took the other sword and with a single blow separated his former hand from his former arm, grasped his dead right hand with his fearless left one and, sensing now a double unity with himself and the spirits of his forebears, he cried out, 'Follow me!' Before sundown the railroad funds were again in the hands of the Trans-Oceanic Company. Patuco was promoted to sergeant."

"What a glorious hero's life! What grand material for a mythological-religious epic! Isn't there any Honduran bard who can render this in rhyme and meter for posterity? The whole epic tradition pales in comparison, the Germanic and Greek heroic sagas and even the astral myth of Gilgamesh. You are the one, Don Matías. You must compose this song of the double-fisted sword. You owe it to the father of your Little Flesh!"

Don Matías gave me a pleasant smile. And then he picked up his cane and, as if it were a scimitar, slammed it down first on my flour sack, then on his own, raising such a cloud of dust that we disappeared for a few minutes from the censorious glances of the baker down in the underworld. When we finally surfaced from our mythological mist, white-in-white like the shades of another world but plagued by a very earthly attack of sneezing, he said to me in a con-spiratorial tone, "Don Vigoleis, my Teutonic friend, before the flour in the sacks we are sitting on has been baked into bread, I shall introduce you to the poet of the Honduran national epic. All things take time. Poems that are meant to outlive the generations do not simply grow like the blossoms of a single summer!"

I wrapped up my bread, paid at the counter, and rushed home. At first Beat-rice just shook her head, then she shook me. I had never before returned from the bakeshop so completely covered in white. "Did the bakerman finally chuck you out? If I were he I wouldn't have just kept gaping s-o-o long at the two of you!"

Just shake me as much as you want, I thought to myself. You'll be as-tounded as soon as I start telling you my Wild West story. "Don Patuco..." But my tale of derring-do made almost no impression on Beatrice; she would have preferred any dime-store detective novel. She already knew South America. As a child she herself had raced bareback across the savannahs and herded cattle with cowboys. Without doubt, she said, my "General" Patuco was known in his home country as a much-feared and much-sought-after cattle rustler, one of the big-time sort who ravaged entire ranches. And we were supposed to think that he was the savior of his country? All right, why not? Any dictator we could name was also a cattle rustler, and the South American variety had plenty of models to take after, most of them beasts of the pure-bred sort.

"But what about the Honduran national poet, the one who is writing the saga of Patuco? Aren't you touched by that idea?"

That she would have to see with her own eyes, said the Swiss theologian's daughter, all at once renouncing her own Indian heritage and her wild chases across the savannahs. That's what makes her so complicated: her unexpected transitions, her wavering between Basel and the Inca lakes.

Was it two sacks of flour that got baked into bread, or was it more than two? Far be it from me to take literally Don Matías' prediction, one that he uttered in a rush of enthusiasm for the Honduran national cause. But I actually got to meet the poet.

For me, meeting a poet is always a moving event. Poets embody all that transcends mere reality—as long as one doesn't get too familiar with them. In my lifetime I have met several of them, great and not so great, published and unpublished. None of them has ever resembled the Honduran poet I met on my flour sack when on this particular day I entered the shop for my daily bread.

He was a pale, thirtyish fellow, dressed in black, with hollow cheeks that seemed cadaverous, but in his case were no doubt the mark of his Muse. His cheekbones projected sharply, his mouth was puffy, and a delicate mustachio followed the contour of his upper lip. It wasn't his melancholy expression that made me realize who this new customer really was; rather, it was the signifi-cant look with which Don Matías greeted me on this occasion. What ensued was a rendezvous of the unpublished poets. Beatrice had sent me here for a half a loaf of bread and a pound of flour. But just how important are bread and flour when the inchoate murmurings of a national saga are sitting on a sack in front of you?

Don Matías rose up ceremoniously, took his cane, and limped from behind the counter to effect the introduction: "Don Gracias a Dios, *poeta*—Don Vigoleis, *poeta*." We bowed to each other—I, for my part, with a deep bend of my torso, Don Gracias a Dios less deeply since, doubtless taxed by his patriotic visions, he chose to remain seated on his white throne. Today I am amused to recall this encounter, but at the time I was deeply affected by it. Here we were, all three of us prodigiously gifted poets, all three of us showing great promise, if not the greatest talent. Three poets, three destinies. When would the world sing our praises? Or rather, when would we start singing to the world?

Unlike Vigoleis at various times, Don Gracias a Dios was not one to curry favor with book publishers or newspaper editors. He had a loftier mission; his recognition as a poet would not emerge from the waste-paper baskets of third parties. An entire nation was looking to him, and thus he could keep his mind focused inside himself—which he now did on his flour-sack perch.

"Books have their own destiny," says a well-known maxim of a certain Terentianus Maurus. But aren't the destinies of those books' authors also worthy of a classical quotation? With Don Gracias a Dios this was surely the case, in spite of the fact that his work wasn't published. For this reason I shall now tell his story, which Don Matías revealed to me on the occasion in question. With a wave of his hand he asked me to free up some space for him on a flour sack, and as the self-serving customers came and went I learned what the Norns are capable of spinning if they have some halfway decent thread on their spindle.

The poet Gracias a Dios was the child of a mother who with annual regularity gave birth to a stillborn baby. This had occurred six times, and her seventh was imminent when a miracle happened: she came to term and bore the child, and it lived. "Thanks be to God!" she rejoiced, "my prayers have been answered!" Hence the boy's name: Gracias a Dios.

It soon became apparent that little God-be-Thanked was unlike other little children. As the first to emerge safe and sound from his mother's womb, he was born for higher things; as a poet he was meant to join the ranks of the eternally rejected. He combined in himself the energy of all six of the babies who preceded him but never took a single breath, and the result was that he harbored a longing for all that is infinite and inexpressible. This became manifest when he entered puberty—pale, driving because he was himself driven, brooding with hot breath in the superheated air of his unhealthy homeland. Don Matías pointed to the counter drawer where he kept a notebook containing God-be-Thanked's earliest responses to divine inspiration. Eventually, he said, they would be preserved in his country's Pantheon. I remarked that they had a more tragic effect sitting inside a baker's drawer, and both men agreed. With a dejected gesture of his pale hand Don Gracias a Dios wiped some flour dust from his mustache.

Then came Patuco's insurrection and defeat. God-be-Thanked's father perished at the barricades, perforated by bullets of the government forces. Mindful of the miracle of the "living birth," the general urged the boy to unite his destiny with that of the men who had now become stateless. Henceforth he was to be their guiding spirit, their migratory talisman. Filled with renewed inspiration, he agreed. Has a poet ever failed to comprehend special voices that speak to him from no matter where? Gracias a Dios said farewell to his bride, his lodging, the soil of his homeland, all that was near and dear to him. Sooner dead than slave! And with the others he went into exile, into a transcendent new realm where the destiny of his nation could—and would!—prevail in his verses. For was it not, Don Matías continued, a poet's mission to seize meteors that plunge through the universe and restore them to the sacred cosmic order? They would return victorious, the band of men declared to a company of weeping women and girls as they secretly embarked at a coastland hideout. They would be back, it was only a matter of time. They would reappear suddenly, and the trumpets would blare for their arrival! They're at the Mosquito Coast! Don Patuco, Manco, Maneta, the General, our Savior!

Matías portrayed the scene in the most colorful language, surely not without unconscious allusions to the Napoleonic legend of the March to Paris after the hero's resurrection from the Hundred Days of banishment. God-be-Thanked had reached this phase of the national saga in his notebook. To compose the final stanza he would have·to await the fanfare of freedom.

Down below, Jaume toiled by the sweat of his cheese-colored brow, struggling more with his repressed anger than with the viscous mass he was supposed to knead to provide food for the masses up above. He was lacking the proper insight, for surely it is the masses that poets sing and tell stories for, the masses that heroes die for, and the masses that call forth new heroes and new poets. All Jaume could see was the kneading board under him and the time-wasting blabbermouths above him. He sweated all the more, and Don Matías continued:

After the band arrived on Mallorca the poet lived in the *pueblo* where Don Patuco bided his time and kept his blade sharp, while his daughter Encarnación created a flag for the *prununciamento*. (This was the design: from out of an undulant Sea of Freedom a fist juts forth, holding another fist in its iron grasp; the second fist holds a battleaxe, and the scene is crowned by a rainbow in the Honduran national colors.) Then Don Gracias a Dios was ordered to Palma, where he could more readily scan the international press for news of Honduras and gauge public opinion concerning his fatherland. As minimal as this information was—the world hardly took notice of his puny country, no matter how explosive things were, God-be-Thanked's poems gave reason to believe that the Great Day would soon arrive. The poet's fingers were literally itching to write his final stanza. "As a fellow poet," Don Matías added, "Vigoleis should know about such things."

And how I knew about such things! But I didn't notice that Don Gracias a Dios had itchy fingers, unless his nail-biting—in which many poets engage—was to be taken as a harbinger of future glory.

With his pallid complexion and his consumptive ardor, Don Gracias a Dios struck me as the affecting epitome of the patriotic young firebrand pining away for his humiliated homeland, awaiting the hour when his nation would rise up as one man, and on the wings of his own song would carry him home as the once-banished troubadour of his people. From my own experience I am unfamiliar with such homesick love for the fatherland, even though for several years I have eaten the so-called bread of exile, which for me has never tasted more bitter than wherever in the world the bread of poverty tastes sour. It's possible to live it up even in exile. I know several such persons who back home never had it so good as in their stark new surroundings.

But I am interrupting Don Matías's account. I meant only to point out that in conversation with the bard of Honduran national shame and rebirth and his Spanish friend, the suitor of the cross-eyed embroiderer in the *pueblo*, I once again had occasion to point to the Western literary heritage. I could name any number of historical models. I could tell these men about German greatness and German love of Freedom, about the German night and German grave-digging, about emergence into the light of a New Day, about ethnic and patriotic poetry, about lyres and swords, about Körner, Schill, Arndt, and the latest German uniformed seer Ludendorff. That got their attention! It roused the youth on the flour sack from his lyrical reveries. His eyes took on a fiery cast, and he was about to rise from the sitting position. But apparently his legs had gone to sleep—like my own—and he dropped down again against the metal grill. For a while he was hidden by flour dust—one no longer saw him, but heard his voice intoning an original stanza out into the bakeshop, upwards and downwards. Just a single stanza—he had to conserve his energy. When he again became visible, his singing had already died away.

Don Matías, moved by the puzzling outburst brought on by my German *Sturm und Drang*, now came into action in his steamy wrestler's jersey. With one swoop he pulled open the counter drawer, fished around in it, but couldn't find what he was looking for: his own contribution to this memorable moment. Probably he had left it in his classroom desk out at the *pueblo*.

I leaped into the breach—which I was able to do since I happened to have with me the Insel edition of the collected works of Hölderlin. I had already told Don Matías about my thin-paper philosophy, and he declared that he also wished to possess a volume like this one on *papel biblia*. "Death for the Fatherland," I began, "by Hölderlin." This majestic, cynical stanza has probably never had such a rapt audience as these two men, Gracias a Dios and Matías, sitting there on Jaume's moldy flour sacks. Speaking for the German Parnassus, I urged youths to descend in waves from on top of their hills to engage with the murderous enemy rising up from the valley below. I infused them with the soul of their own youth and enjoined them, like a band of magicians, to do battle in their just cause. And their patriotic songs—Gracias a

Dios knew this just as keenly as Hölderlin, who was close to insanity—weakened the knees of the dishonorable foe, and finally victory was ours: "Live on, O fatherland, / and do not count the dead! For you, / beloved country, not one too many has fallen." Not one – i.e., none!

I recited these verses first in German. Not very well, not like Wüllner the professional elocutionist, although like him my hair was white. Then I translated word for word. I received sincere applause. Even Jaume down below was clapping, but not for me; he was slapping mounds of dough into a trough. I made my biggest impression on the two poets with the line about not counting the dead. How far would we get if people started counting them? Don Gracias a Dios explained that beginning with his very first *pronunciamiento*, Don Patuco had made it a sacred principle never to count those left behind; only in this manner would the battle for freedom be won. I agreed, although Hölderlin hardly needed my support. A soldier fallen on the field of battle is of course only a legend. He becomes real only on the pages of written history. If it were any different, how many youths would be willing to descend from the hills in waves? We should leave counting to the chroniclers who juggle and manipulate numbers according to the particular philosophy of history they serve. How many soldiers fell on the fields at Chalons, at Waterloo, at Stalingrad? Only a worrywart carves notches in his rifle-butt. *Me gusta ver un cementerio de muertos bien relleno*, Don Matías was now declaiming in the words of his pseudo-*Espronceda*, and it was just as convincing as my Hölderlin.

The hoarse bakeshop doorbell jingled incessantly. The little people, the cannon fodder of our patriotic songs, came in for the bread they had been toiling for ever since that unholy story about a woman and a snake, one of which stepped on the other's head while the other snapped at the first one's heel—it has never been cleared up which was which. Their domestic labor was at least as strenuous as that of Jaume, who was now baking their bread while muttering curses.

Don Matías later explained to me that the Honduran youth's sallow complexion was not only the result of patriotic fervor and homesickness. Gracias a Dios had an inamorata in the city of Palma, a girl he sang to while standing under her window, like the thousands of other mortals who night after night lift their gaze to their beloved until the girls, chased away from the window, move over to the next house so the serenade can continue. Gracias a Dios was used to this game; surely it helped him cope with his sorrow, and it kept the embers of poetry alive in him. All the situation needed was a puff of air, and the torch would again burn brightly—for Honduras!

Well then, said Don Matías, now that we had talked over so many things and, as it were, given heaven and earth a good preliminary plowing to reveal what the noble bonds of humanity and friendship could achieve, he saw no reason to conceal from me the final truth, insofar as I, a *poeta*, had not intuited it already. Don Gracias a Dios also had a genuine, home-town girlfriend named Asunción (Ascension or Assumption), whom he intended to marry when he returned to Honduras with flying colors. He thought of her every single day—and this was weakening him.

"*Hay que ser hombre*, Don Matías," I said. "You should stand up like a man, even in exile!"

Like bosom comrades we clapped the flour dust from each other's shoulders. I strode homewards carrying my bread, while Matías remained seated on his sack behind the counter, still in trouble with his brother-in-law Jaume, who thought that things were getting more and more out of hand.

For a few pages now I must leave Don Matías out of sight, but not the cause of Honduran independence, as I introduce my reader to another exiled combatant from the one-armed general's platoon. His name, borrowed from the geography of their home country like those of all their fellow conspirators, will in my hazy memory always be associated with Reinhold Conrad Muschler's novel *Bianca Maria*. This new fellow was the cobbler Ulua.

Ulua not only had two names—that was normal for an insurrectionist—but two professions. Besides being a shoemaker he was a petardist, or perhaps I should say a *petardero*, since in Spain the word *petardista* is reserved for a crook or extortionist who secretly lights fuses and blows up whole houses with his home-made bombs, the petards. Ulua was no extortionist, though one might say that he was extorting himself, which is true of any good revolutionary or blind adherent of a militant political movement. There can be no victory without idealism. But we shall go no further into that.

Ulua had fought at the side of Patuco; he had undermined many a stretch of railway and filled many a hollow bone with explosives. This was in fact his specialty: bombs made from bones. As soon as he was appointed chief fireworks expert of the Honduran national movement, Don Patuco's fame rose as the most feared cattle rustler in Central America, a development that brought discredit to his *pronunciamientos* for quite a long time. Ulua needed cattle bones. He sneered at the paper bags that others, Don Alonso and his gang among them, were always glueing together. For him that was child's play, whereas "we in the Cordilleras, we in the savannahs..."

Ulua lived in Palma in one of the dilapidated houses lining the square near the dilapidated post office and bordering the more elevated portion of the city—the square where Julietta used to dance. It took courage to risk your life clambering up four floors on rotting stairways. His wife was the daughter of Mallorquin immigrants, and it was she who advised our freedom fighter to take residence on the Golden Isle to await the Great Day. Their marriage was blessed with a son named Sacramento. While still young he began to abjure the God to whom his pious mother had dedicated him at his baptism. His name, meaning "Holy of Holies," no longer quite fit his nature, and so he latched on to "Pablo" as an innocuous substitute since no one associated it any longer with the Prince of Apostles. He had just turned twenty, but like all of these kids with mustaches, he looked older.

Gracias a Dios took a room in Ulua's house, thus closing the circle.

My first meeting with Ulua's son took place of course on Jaume's flour sacks. Pablo himself initiated our second encounter by rapping the iron fist at our front door. "Welcome, Don Pablo! Beatrice, here comes a combatant from Don Patuco's legion. Up to now he's only been a punctuation mark in the epic poem of our mutual friend Gracias a Dios, but soon, who knows...?"

"*Enorme!*" cried Don Pablo, "*enorme*, Don Vigoleis, a punctuation mark! And perhaps only a question mark! And that's why I have come. Doña Beatriz, I would like to learn English, for quite frankly I don't think much of this mania of our old guard for upsetting the world with hollow bones. Every month a revolution, and then once every year Holy Communion at Easter time—*enorme, enorme*, but that's not getting us anywhere. I want to go to England, and then to the States."

This was Don Pablo the skeptic, the young man who doubted the revolutionary efficacy of hollow bones. From then on we called him Don Enorme, because this was his every second word, and that is what he was in every respect. He worked as a clerk in a shoe factory. In his free time, which in Spain means during working hours, he occupied himself with literature and philosophy. He had learned German by reading, and for this it wasn't necessary for the god of language to enter his Golden Vein. He was of course a Krausist, he knew his Nietzsche inside out, and Stirner too, whose maxims he had taken to heart: "For me nothing is more important than myself." He dismissed Ortega y Gasset, the darling of the philosophical set, with a few barbarisms, only to sing the praises of Count Keyserling's Latin American confessions—"*enorme, enorme!*" Now that we had staked out the landscape a bit, he asked how much Don Vigo would charge for philosophical instruction twice a week. But please: I was to understand that what interested him most in German philosophy was whatever seemed most obscure to the teacher himself; the two of us could make an attempt to find our way together on the basis of our very different intellectual backgrounds and attitudes.

Things became more enormous than ever when I suggested that we collaborate on an anthology of German octopus philosophy. We would work together on the Spanish translation, then translate from Spanish into English, from English into Italian, and through further antagonistic languages eventually back into the original German. The resulting work, a dilution and distortion containing many new gems of wisdom, I would then recommend to a publisher as a collection of aphorisms by a long-lost Sanskrit philosopher of personal redemption.

We did not end up undertaking this philosophical chrestomathy, long a favorite project of mine. Rather than tempt the gods, we stayed with the tried and true. Until the outbreak of the Civil War Pablo remained my indefatigable disciple, and a dangerous one with an enormous brain that absorbed and assimilated everything with frictionless rapidity. On only one other occasion have I ever dealt with such a quick-witted, exotic thinking machine with interchangeable gears and dust-free lubrication vents: the aforementioned Surinam writer Albert Helman. I stand in amazement at these prodigious cerebrators, and not without trepidation at witnessing forces at work in them that the Western world has long since lost sight of.

Now one might suspect that Ulua and Don Patuco would be proud of such a champion of their national uprising. But no. Don Gracias a Dios, pining away in pre-matrimonial love for the fatherland; Encarnación, sewing away at the national banner; and a certain Don Sulaco, a drug dealer with connections to the Clock Tower who provided the group with the necessary financing—all these received more attention from the crippled warrior than the philosophy student who could never wield a sword, much less hurl a petard stuffed by his father's swarthy thumb, without blowing himself to smithereens in the process. His conflicts with the Old Guard were approaching a crisis, and the shoe factory paid a minimal wage.—"Doña Beatriz, a year from now I must know English perfectly!"

Ulua was getting less and less pleasure from his Sacramento. The latter, not a stick-in-the-mud like his philosophical preceptor, who is more afraid of unexploded bombs than when they actually go off, was growing tired of the "old guys" constant nagging him about creating a revolution. He said that the next bomb to go off in Palma would get tossed by his own hand, in front of pre-arranged witnesses. Would I care to be on hand?

One day he came for a lesson and instead of taking a philosopher out of his briefcase he pulled out a bicycle-racing cap with blue and white stripes. Tomorrow he would be on the Plaza Cort at 12 noon wearing this cap as a signal to his cohorts, and would throw a powerfully loaded bone into the Ayuntamiento. "The Spanish revolutionaries can take care of the rest, I'll have nothing more to do with it. Everything has been carefully set up. Later you'll have to let Don Patuco know through a third party that Ulua's son will stop at nothing." He gave a thunderous laugh, and then we lost ourselves in a discussion of *Cogito, ergo sum* and its bearing on anarchism.

Sacramento, Ulua's son, threw his bomb at the stroke of noon. It did no more damage than the local petards from the workshop of the anarchist Count. The insurrection was put down with a few rubber truncheons. Sacramento escaped. He threw away his racer's cap together with the explosive bone—an ingenious double stratagem by the philosophically trained terrorist. We harmless passers-by, surprised by this revolt on the streets, noticed a pickpocket lifting up the cap and heading off in the distance. But a policeman with lightning-fast reflexes immediately put bomb and cap together in his mind; since a bomb obeys laws that hardly concern a Spanish policeman, he chased after the thief, whose legs, unfortunately for him, were shorter. He was dragged over to the constabulary. It wasn't until much later that the actual cause of the disturbance was ferreted out.

Don Patuco was said to be amazed, indeed moved in his patriotic heart by this baptism of fire of Ulua's offspring, who had been given up for lost. I myself was surprised by the un-Spanish punctuality with which the bone got tossed. Later that evening Pablo told us the revolution had failed precisely because of this punctuality, because the main actors were still sitting in a café when the internal marrow blew apart the bone—and nothing else.

"Anarchy and punctuality! Don Enorme, *voilà*, there's the topic for our next lesson!"

"*Enorme*, Don Vigoleis, *enorme*!"

Ulua as cobbler: in the opinion of Don Matías, the spiritual advocate of all Honduran affairs, his work was of the finest custom craftsmanship. "Elegant fit," the increasingly feeble bard added. "Not as bad as one might expect," said the shoemaker's own son, who preferred his employer's mass-produced footwear to his progenitor's hand-sewn products.

My own homegrown shoes were long since worn down to the inner soles. In summer and winter I now wore nothing but *alpargatas*, the footgear of the little people, 50 centimos the pair. Yet there came the day when we had saved up enough to afford a pair of shoes for myself—ordinary shoes, nothing special. But just a few months more, said Beatrice, and we could place a custom order—with Ulua the cobbler! So we waited. This was as natural as the black powder in the shoemaker's hollow bones.

Our links with the Honduran cause were meanwhile so close that even without an awareness of certain prospects I would not have offered a commission to any other craftsman. What was the nature of these prospects?

Don Matías left for the *pueblo* not only to serenade his beloved, teasing notes from his guitar that were meant to soften the girl's heart and direct her healthy gaze at his eyes full of yearning. During each visit he also met with Don Patuco to report on world events, insofar as they affected Honduras. Enfeebled though he was, albeit not in the heroic manner, over time he came back into the general's good graces, and now exercised the office of messenger and advisor. After the revolution, he was slated to enter the Ministry of Culture as specialist for combating illiteracy. All this was contained in the as yet unwritten new Honduran Constitution. At the very next opportunity Don Matías intended to bring "my case" to the General: I was to be appointed attaché for Western European intellectual affairs, to the extent that they had bearing on Honduran matters. My philosophical attitudes, my antipathy to Church and State and their forked-tongue, two-armed emissaries, my inventive talents, my *Sitzfleisch*; Doña Beatriz' half-Inca heritage, her half-Swiss allegiance—the latter important with regard to the gold reserves behind the Honduran *lempira*—all of these qualities increased my chances as a member of the revolutionary government. It is no wonder that I started picturing myself in Tegucigalpa, sitting in meditation behind an empty diplomat's desk made of solid rosewood, 3200 feet above sea level and immeasurably far above my own self.

This was not the first time in my life that I came in line for a government job. "My good man," my teacher and friend Dr. Wilhelm Kremers said to me on more than one occasion, back in the days when he was recruiting up and down the Lower Rhine for his Separatist coup d'état, "My good man, I can use someone like you when we proclaim our Rhenish Republic. I'll need you for our Ministry of Culture!" At the time, I was either a weaver or a mechanic, but wasn't interested in upward mobility. On the contrary, I was hoping to enrich my biography in the opposite direction. Nevertheless, this prospect of official employment hung by a single hair—a fateful state of affairs, since the hair in question was one of those that grew back on the previously tonsured pate of the lapsed priest Kremers, and it didn't have much tensile strength. The Separatist *Putsch* in October was an immediate failure. Dorten and Smeets, Kremers and Pepi Matthes had built up their ideas for a Rhenish Free State in league with boozehounds and beer-bellies, phony beards, swindlers, pimps, and degenerate army veterans. It's common knowledge that priests and soldiers create havoc when they engage in politics. But perhaps it's different in a Wild West country; Don Patuco would have to test this out. In the case of the Separatist Kremers and in the current case of the one-armed general, it is biographically significant that everything be planned far in advance, and that the leaders have a talent for picking their co-conspirators. Once in power they must be able immediately to appoint major and minor functionaries, or else their coup will be a flop with the direst of consequences. On the day of the Röhm *Putsch* in Germany, Count Kessler, who was quite shaken by the event, asked me this: if Hitler were ever actually toppled, what then? The German emigrants were ineffective; they were a phantom element, and there was no one to depend on inside Germany. Don Patuco would not be a phantom, I said. Don Patuco? Who was Don Patuco? So I told him a few things about the fate of my Honduran friends, about the *tertulias* and Jaume's flour sacks. For the author of *Notes on Mexico*, none of this was out of the ordinary. "Since the publication of my *Notes* there's been a price on my head in Mexico. But speaking in general, I think all of us should emigrate to South America."

So I would order my new shoes from the cobbler Ulua, with or without the promise of a government ministry.

This was the beginning of exciting times. The Swabian bookshop owner, once he was duly clued in about the goings-on, willingly provided us with foreign magazines. Don Pablo brought us illustrated catalogues from his shoe factory. Pedro, beholden to his art and to nothing else, came forth with some designs for my new footwear. Vigoleis compared, considered, rejected, selected. Beatrice was listened to. And eventually we arrived at the solution which tended from the very beginning in the direction of the point-toed shoe.

I know of no other country outside of Spain that gives as much attention to shoes. They must fit exactly right, they must be polished to a mirror shine, three or four times a day if the shoe tips get dusty, or if one hasn't anything else to do. For every Spaniard there are 100 generals, for 50 Spaniards there is a *cura*, for every 10 a *limpiabotas*, and for each and every last Spaniard—general, priest, or bootblack—there is one María del Pilar.

I could have climbed the stairs to Ulua's workshop to issue my official commission. But no, I preferred to savor the whole idea; I postponed the day when, with my elegant new footwear, I would saunter among the beautifully shod citizens of the island. I let a month pass by in cognizance of the fact that the journey is more fulfilling than reaching the destination, that the hope for redemption is more blessed than redemption itself, as the Old and New Testaments both assert. But then the time came after all. Philosophically schooled readers are familiar with the phenomenon of intellectual hyper-pregnancy (superfoetation), which I chose not to forego just for the sake of a pair of new shoes.

Ulua was a shoemaker of a definitely original cast. There was nothing at all mystical about his craft, and he didn't possess a crystal ball. His tripod was squeaky-clean, a sign that his manner of sewing leather was conscientious. He had a remarkable thumb, unmistakably a thumb for mixing and tamping gunpowder, one that could fit into even the largest hollow cattle bone. As I entered, Pablo's mother, a native Mallorquine, quickly stuffed a clump of horsehair back into an upholstered stool and asked me to take a seat. Our conversation immediately took flight—to be precise, we landed at 3200 feet in the center of the capital of the embattled and besieged Central American homeland that was waiting for its liberator. Then we hovered back over the headlands where the ghost of Karl Marx lay in wait for us. Just as Don Matías had stopped in his limping tracks in the funeral procession when he learned that I had never read a line of Krause, now Ulua stared at me when he learned that he was sitting opposite a man who had not only never read Marx but wasn't about to do so, either. My candid confession resulted in a lengthy summary by Ulua of his "Carlos'" aims and goals in the world. His dissertation, plus a mug of *pulque* and a few slices of *turrón*, made me forget why I came there in the first place.

A second visit to this versatile craftsman's workshop was devoted to the clarification of fascism. Several monasteries would get blown up, the Jesuits once again banished from the country, Juan March hanged, and his millions funneled over to the Honduran Freedom Movement. Ulua was prepared to accept responsibility for all of this. Not wishing to remain idle or to seem cowardly, I volunteered to rip the ribbons from every general's uniform and the red stripes from their pants, just as I had witnessed in 1918 as a schoolboy in Germany. But with these suggestions I had come to the wrong man; after all, Don Patuco, the future breadwinner for all of us, was also a general. But the anarchist's disappointment rapidly subsided when I told him that it was only the two-armed generals I had in mind, and more specifically the Prussian-German exemplars of that caste. I named name after name, and was back in my interlocutor's good graces when I remarked that very soon an army of monkeys would be ready to march in Germany. On this occasion I also learned that Honduras had swiftly declared war on my Kaiser just as he was getting ready to pack his bags. Then Ulua took my foot measurements. He praised my noble nether extremities—not a single bunion. They had never felt the pressure of army boots.

It wasn't until my third visit that we settled on the material. I sat on the stool and listened to long explanations of the various types of leather. I checked them over, and was told at the very beginning of our workshop conference that Europe had no such thing as good cattle. This was puzzling. Mussolini had already forced millions into his black-shirt legions, and Hitler was about to brand the entire herd of the German people with his hissing swastika. But of course, Master Ulua meant the skins. Good skins were to be had only on the savannahs! If Ulua were a Mongol he would place all his bets on the Upper Tartar water buffalo. In the end I decided on Czech uppers, German inner linings, and soles curried in genuine Spanish tanning bark. This was, Ulua said, the most expensive combination, but I would never regret having chosen it.

I could expect my custom shoes to be ready in about a month, provided that no unforeseen political developments forced the shoemaker to stuff bones or to—but who could dare to take this thought to its conclusion? Certain things were going on; there was once again unrest at the Mosquito Coast; people were rebelling against the Yankees who had established themselves in the region. A certain double-armed general and certified doctor named Don Tiburcio would have to be eliminated. I learned from Don Matías that Carnita was staying up late nights bent over her embroidery frame, sewing the complicated coat of arms on the flag, and that Gracias a Dios was deeply immersed in his heroic life as a *pilarierista*, yet not without intoning a daily tribute to his far-off political fiancée. I can still see him before me on his sack of flour, this anemic human vessel into which the final, as yet unrealized stanza of the Honduran Horst Wessel Song will soon be poured. Ripeness is all, said Ulua in the melancholy tones of an exile who will soon rush forth into freedom, but who hasn't seen things go so very badly for him away from home. In my selfish way I replied with the hope that the course of world history would allow Master Ulua to put my shoes on his last before the big bone went off. "And then, my good friend, I can use my new soles to make my entrance at the Cultural Ministry of the Honduran Republic."

I don't like bread. To me it is as insipid as the potato, and because it lacks nutritional content you have to fill your belly with large amounts of it to stave off rumblings that can happen at just the wrong time. Nevertheless, we filled our bellies with bread; during the weeks preceding delivery of my new shoes we didn't have the necessary pesetas for more nourishing fare. The Czech upper leather was beyond our means, and we had to save up for it by stuffing ourselves and going without real food. Jaume made a profit on us.

I quizzed Don Matías intensely on the status of our business. When did he think things would start up? Over and again I steered our flour-sack discussions toward Tegucigalpa; together we worried about the chances of success with the bone-tossing that was supposed to bring about a change in both our lives.

Sometime during this nerve-wracking period of bread-eating, Don Pablo casually interrupted our philosophical musings to mention that my shoes were ready. The Master would be honored if he could bring them to me himself... Oh my noble foot, thine hour is at hand!

Ulua appeared in his Sunday best, a large package under his arm—his masterpiece, wrapped in the *Diario de Honduras*. We greeted each other with the cordiality of old fellow-assassins. I had obtained cigarettes and coffee, a Costa Rican blend since the only decent kind, the Honduran variety, was sold nowhere on this island of ours behind the moon.

No longer a child, I suppressed my curiosity. First, while still wearing our alpargatas we bestrode with giant steps the paths of politics, clarified certain major aspects of the *pronunciamiento*, filled our state treasury with other people's money, imposed German language and literature as required subjects at all Honduran educational institutions, settled minor border disputes with Nicaragua, and discussed this and that concerning Don Patuco. Then the Master unpacked my shoes. A page was being turned in our history, and you could hear it.

When Beatrice returned from one of her distinguished houses, Ulua had already left with his reward and my assurance that the shoes were *enorme*, and that he shouldn't apologize for billing me extra for adding reinforcements for my perfectly normal feet—a pittance. We parted as friends with a handshake, a clap on the shoulder, and a huzzah for the Revolution.

The cobbler had poor eyesight, and that was lucky for me, for he didn't notice how close I was to tears when I caught sight of the monstrosity that emerged from the *Diario de Honduras*. Were these the pointed shoes we had spent weeks saving up for with bloated bellies? These were indeed pointy-toed shoes, but there are many kinds of points; it all comes down to your personal idea of what a "point" looks like. Ulua had not emulated Pedro's artistic notions, but rather Nature itself. He had taken as his model the bill of the pelican, whose massive lower jaw is a network of folds of skin. That is what my "pointed" shoes looked like. Instead of an elegant narrowing towards the tips, these "points" gradually broadened out like the open maw of a hippopotamus jutting out from a putrid puddle in a zoo. Yet since the hippopotamus is not indigenous to Honduras, even this allusion to Nature was distorted. What is more, during the months of planning and design the cobbler's documents containing sketches and measurements had somehow got mixed up with other *papel*, with the result that, to be on the safe side, the Master had added a size or two when he put leather to last. Later, when his son asked me in passing how I liked his old man's handiwork, I replied, "*Enorme.*" "*Enorme*? How so?" He was surprised, for while his father was good at making revolutions he didn't know how to make shoes. I was his very first customer for custom work, and I was a German! Ulua was bursting with pride, and Gracias a Dios was going to put this event in the annals. When in exile, don't just twiddle your thumbs—this, too, was a Honduran trait.

"Don't cry, darling," said Beatrice, "We'll get over this calamity, too. I saw a pair of shoes at the *Sindicato*, and I'll give them to you for Christmas. Until then you'll just have to keep wearing your *alpargatas*."

I embraced the woman, not because she promised me a new pair of shoes, but because she refrained from adding the usual consolation that walking on *alpargatas* was healthy. I am aware that everything poor is healthy. Kaiser Wilhelm's turnips were also healthy.

The first time I put on my Uluas was the day we left the island. Their size was such that I could place in each one an insole made of forbidden literature.

In these unrhymed recollections of mine there are two names that can be said to rhyme after all: Ulua and the writer Muschler.

A friend of mine from my Hunnish home town, a fellow named Matthias who has lived for many years in Mexico where, as Don Matías, he had met his share of Patucos, Pilars, Sacramentos, and Uluas—how I envy him for this!—this friend once recommended to me Muschler's novel *Bianca Maria* as a literary delicacy. I made a note of this "White Mary" for a later time when I would be in need of mental diversion. This moment arrived during our exile in the CantonTicino, in Auressio. I had translated Pascoaes' *Hieronymus* into German and Dutch, an accursedly difficult exercise in "applied" mysticism. I was exhausted. Christmas was just around the corner. I felt that I couldn't stand to look at a single other book. But such a spiritual fasting never lasts long with me. Whatever I started to read, it would have to be simple and refreshing. Then I remembered *Bianca Maria;* the hour had arrived for me to indulge myself with a pleasure I had been postponing for years. My friend Peter Jud, a book dealer in Locarno, Libreria Internazionale "Under the Arcades," had it in stock. I ordered it. Beatrice remarked that I probably knew what I was doing and what I was picking out as a means to spoil the Christmas season, be it Muschler or marzipan. Besides, she said, Muschler was now a Nazi bigwig. "Just think of Ulua!'"

"Ulua?"

"*Nous verrons!*"

In the meantime, my Uluas had been expertly reworked by the cobbler Schira in Loco into hiking boots that could withstand glaciers and granite. I now wore them every day. What did Beatrice mean by her warning? These clodhoppers were still giving me excellent service.

Christmas Eve in the Casa Peverada, beneath a crumbling ceiling covered with prancing cherubs, in front of a crackling fireplace and within decaying walls that you could see through to welcome all the Good News descending from heav'n above and the snow-topped Salmone—on this Holy Night the big present waiting for me was Muschler's novel. I hadn't yet got indigestion from the sweets sent with the book by the bookshop owner Barbara, a kind mentor to all the starving writers who lived down in this part of Europe. I threw my legs over the arm of the rickety easy chair, got good and comfy, and started making the long-sought, long-delayed acquaintance of White Mary. Beatrice also had a Christmas writer, and each of us a seven-armed candelabra.

One page tells you nothing about a book. Twelve pages don't tell you much about a book. But Matthias—were you pulling my leg back then, exactly ten years ago? Books do not ripen like wine and women. Whatever is contained within their pages can undergo transformation only within us readers. In themselves, books are dead. I was holding a corpse on my arm.

I was overcome with sorrow, in combination with hot flashes and a desire to drown myself. Beatrice peeked over at me from behind her own writer, to see how my encounter with Bianca was getting along. But before this woman with gold in her heart could look up the aforementioned symptoms in a medical book and pour out some drops of *Aethusa cynapium* into a glass, I tossed the hunk of trash into the fireplace. We didn't have any Karl May at hand, but we had some grappa and a sheaf of galley proofs.

"Don't cry, darling," Beatrice said, "you'll get over this calamity, too."

White Mary was ablaze in the fireplace, our candles were burning down in the Christmas Eve drafts seeping through cracked walls into the sala where Marsman had done some writing.

If someone wants to get far in literature, says Don Quixote, it will cost him time, sleepless nights, hunger, and nakedness; it will cost him a swirling head and stomach cramps and other things connected with the above-mentioned symptoms.

Perhaps I can be permitted, as Sancho Panza, to supplement the Knight's insights by averring that a writer who produces works in the manner described can have similar effects on his reader—*ecco*: Bianca Maria.

VII

Mémé, her grandchildren called her. She loved this childlike name which stood in such marked contrast to her austere, passionate, uncompromising nature."

With these words, Count Harry Kessler begins the first volume of his memoirs. I am copying them down now for the thirteenth time. The first twelve times, I did it from the author's manuscript, emended many times over. Now I am using the printed text, which incidentally is nearly identical to the one I remember from the days when I took a step upward and became the exiled writer's secretary. Both he and I often stumbled over that opening adjective-appositive proper noun, but Kessler could not bring himself to write simply, "Her grandchildren called her Mémé." When he sent off the typescript of his memoirs, he had a weak moment: he reinstated the somewhat inelegant version of his opening sentence. Mémé retained her place of honor as an ornamental initial, a detail the rather humdrum Fischer edition of *Times and Faces* fails to highlight. When Kessler showed me his author's copy, he was pale with rage and literally trembling over his whole body at the unauthorized textual alterations the publisher had made out of fear of the Nazis. He said to me, "They couldn't even leave my first sentence alone! How could I have ever let pass such a monstrosity?" He was disconsolate, until a letter from his dear friend Annette Kolb revived his spirits. This writer praised Kessler as the superb stylist he in fact was, pointing expressly—I haven't forgotten it in all these years—to page 13 of the book. Right here, she wrote, we are confronting a great master of German prose style.

Aha, my reader is thinking, finally a character of world renown in the Recollections of Vigoleis, after all these dubious types like Zwingli, Arsenio, Ulua, or whatever their real or manufactured names are! But please be patient; Harry Kessler is going to get a chapter to himself, maybe even two. As yet the Nazis haven't chased him out of Germany; the madhouse hasn't yet flung open the doors of the solitary cells. The Count's head is, for the moment, only on somebody's blacklist somewhere. In our next chapter we shall hear the crazed shouts calling for Germany to awaken and for Jewry to croak. Patience, please! I needed the reference to *Times and Faces* in order to introduce into my narrative another Mémé, our own Mémé—a personage who, I'll grant you, wasn't quite as beautiful as the Count's mother, and whose name, to be honest, was a little different. But all we need to do is change two letters, and to avoid objections from syntactical nitpickers, I won't put her name at the beginning. In all other details I can easily borrow from Kessler. And that brings us to the true beginning of this chapter.

Her grandchildren called her Mamú. She loved this childlike name that stood in such marked contrast to her austere, passionate, uncompromising nature. Austere? Did Mamú have an austere nature? Right away our description is beginning to get shaky. And when Kessler goes on to say of Mémé's childlike name, "She seemed to cherish it as a cloak and a shield against a hostile, cold world," our reservations begin to multiply. For to the very end of her life, our Mamú used a different method to defend herself against the world's enmity. With the aid of Christian Science she erected about herself a fortress replete with embrasures, moats, and spouts for pouring down boiling pitch. Her ramparts were patrolled by a squadron of aged and aging ladies who were devoted to the same science, who sang its hymns badly out of tune, and who took care that no un-Christian influences ever threatened their recent converts' trust in Scientism or, what would be worse, ever prayed their way into her fortune of millions. Yes, Mamú was a millionaire. As such, she had an easier time than most in making progress within Christian Science. Faith is difficult with no money at all. The Vatican would long since be a heap of rubble if the rock on which Peter's church stands didn't have veins of gold that can even withstand the *aqua fortis* of hypocrisy. But let us remain for the present with our high-carat faith in Mamú. Soon enough we shall see that sham and pretense can also exist outside of the various established churches.

"Until her final hour," Kessler continues in his description of Mémé, "she was and remained beautiful and regal." If we just delete the words "beautiful and," his words again fit Mamú. She *was* regal, but with a light tinge of Viennese coloration, which is what made her so irresistible.

What Kessler goes on to say in praise of his mother is irrelevant; from here on I shall have to be content with my own recollections.

In Mamú's retinue there was a Parisian cosmetician, who herself embodied the worst kind of advertisement for her profession. She was beautiful, and had no need whatever of salves and lotions; *sans* rouge she had rose-colored cheeks. She never used lipstick, yet she sported the kissable cherry lips illustrated in the marketing brochures she passed around. Her eyebrows were thin lines that required no plucking, and not one single false lash disfigured her eyelids. The girl's bosom—a poem, whose accents took full effect without the aid of foam rubber. She possessed, of course, noble fetlocks and marvelous hands; her hair was of iridescent chestnut hue. She had turquoise eyes that deep down harbored obscure secrets. Who would be the lucky treasure hunter to explore their depths? Her voice—to continue in this fanciful vein—was like the murmuring of a conch shell. Of course many men had put this shell to their ears, but the one she actually permitted to do so was a Spaniard, and then he did it all wrong. The girl was not a Spanish beauty; she came from the opposite end of Europe, from Finland. She laughed at us when we complained about the millions of mosquitoes on the island. Back in her native Nordic lake district, she was used to them by the whining and biting billions that darkened the sun. This exemplar of pulchritude, this hovering goddess with so much experience of mosquitoes, this natural beauty who challenged Nature itself, and whom a Spanish suitor desired with such desperate passion that he turned more and more ashen as time went on—this young woman's name was Selkä Kyliki. In Mamú's house she was called "Auma."

Before we could call her by that name, the Finnish girl came to our house to learn English. She already spoke Spanish and French fluently, was able to get by in German, and knew the many dialects of her homeland.

She often talked about her friend Mamú, and as such things will happen, she told Mamú a lot about the two of us. Mamú wanted to get to know us, she said, and this matched our own desire to pay a visit to the elderly lady. But then we would have to hurry, Auma said, and Mamú almost didn't dare to invite us. But if we were in fact the "nice people" Auma told her we were, then she wanted to meet us before she died, and we would have to promise to stand at her bier when it was all over. Such was, in outline, the nature of her wish, which was for us of course tantamount to a command.

Mamú had kidney trouble. The doctors, reputable specialists of whom there were a few on the island, had given her up. A German professor of medicine had concurred with their death sentence, and thus we could be certain that Mamú's days were numbered. As is well known, one doesn't play games with kidneys. The physicians decided that this *caso* could live another two, at most

three weeks at the maximum, though they feared for their professional standing by saying so. One month, and then Goodbye Mamú! This was a harsh
calculation. Anyone who has ever taken a vacation knows how quickly those
few days are over.

That is how things stood with this very ill woman. We called her "Mamú"
in our own conversations well before we were actually summoned to her bedside to submit to her special test: were we in fact "nice people"? Were we nice
enough to be on hand when the time came, and then to accompany her to her
grave? A woman of this type, a 72-year-old dying woman who requests the
company of a Vigoleis and a Beatrice for her final weeks—people she knows
only from hearsay, but whom she asks for, out of thousands of possibilities,
just because they are reported to be "nice"—a woman who desires the presence of strangers at a time when most people would want a priest, the immediate family, or the family lawyer? A human being of this kind must, I told
myself, be in possession of practical wisdom and quixotic gifts to a degree
that not even a busted kidney could impair. Let those doctors say what they
want about your chances, Mamú, but in the meantime keep on consulting
Higher Authorities! When would you like us to visit?

The practitioners of medical science, myopic as ever, had zeroed in on renal
cancer. But they overlooked another science, Christian Science, which also
had its claims and demands. This latter science of course cannot raise the dead,
but it is capable of postponing death within certain limits. It is vital to know
something about this special set of beliefs. Ignorance of it can lead to blindness—not the blindness of fate, but of those who write out prescriptions in
defiance of fate.

It was the third time that we were summoned to a deathbed on this island.
Is it at all surprising, then, that we were less than deeply touched as we bowed
to the old lady laid out before us under a palm tree in her garden? Was it
heartless of us not to be overwhelmed by the event, but instead just curious
about what it might lead to? "Laid out before us"—that is of course an allusion to death, which is precisely the topic at hand. In reality, the ailing woman
was resting on a chaise longue, an American patent model with dozens of ad-
justments. One shift of the mechanism and presto!—just the proper angle for
breathing one's last.

It had been several days since Auma had practiced her cosmetic art on
Mamú's face, and as a consequence we could plainly see the effects of physical
decline. I estimated her chances at less than a week. Beatrice, a pessimist in
matters of the short run, gave her two weeks. If we could have had any idea
of the stony accretions inhabiting her kidneys at the time, we might have expected her to succumb during our very first visit.

Several women ministered to Mamú during her final days: an elderly, experienced German nanny, a Mallorcan housemaid, and of course Auma, Mamú's
Finnish light of the sun and "beautiful little darling." In addition, there was
one of Mamú's daughters, an imposing boxy woman with a bust of the type
one often sees behind the ticket counter at a circus. She had been summoned

by wire from Paris, and had now taken charge like someone used to having her tune danced to. Another daughter, married and living in Budapest, was expected any day, as was Mamú's only son, who lived in the United States. Mamú wanted her children, her children's children, friends, and nice people near her as she joined the choir invisible in the classic manner we read about in novels: with laying-on of hands and final blessings. After it's all over, let the descendants squabble over the inheritance. That is an ugly prospect, so it's better to die beautifully, if at all possible. Mamú wanted very much to die in this fashion, and yet in all probability she would never perish as gloriously as her husband had. We soon were told about his unique manner of joining the majority, but I wish to save that for later. Right now I am about to take Mamú's heart by storm. Quite literally I am going to spit my way to the heart of a dying woman.

This is how it was done: just as Mamú was not an ordinary mortal, neither was she an ordinary "terminal." The way she received us was stylish, the style being that of the upper crust, the only class that could do justice to a situation of this kind. Mamú's daughter, the busty one whose front end supported some genuine diamonds, had ordered the kitchen help to wheel out some very fancy hors d'oeuvres on a sideboard. There were mixed drinks, too, of a variety to please every taste. Madame la fille was sure that everyone would just adore the tomato-juice cocktail she had prepared herself and was now offering to all assembled. I had no choice but to accept, *naturellement*. No sooner had I taken a swig of this concoction—too big a swig, I confess—when with an even more natural reflex action, I discharged the entire mouthful onto the greensward.

This was an awkward moment. I had misbehaved. Everyone's eyes were on me—something I like even less than tomatoes. "Rotgut!" was my contribution to a conversation being conducted in French. I turned as red as a tomato. The dying Mamú heard me. And with queenly *politesse* she said to me in German, "Just what are you doing? Expectorating on my lawn? What's the matter? Don't you like that tomato brew either? Or did it just go down the wrong way?"

"No, not that," I stammered, my face redder than ever. *Madame la fille's* eyes stabbed me to the quick. I wasn't the first *boche*, she said, whose barbaric palate never got beyond *choucroute*. Now this was a dastardly affront. What would Baron von Martersteig do in a situation like this? Would he draw his sword? Bow politely and leave the scene? I myself haven't much of a sense of etiquette, and what little I have isn't much help with tomato-juice cocktails. So all I could do was blush and remain silent.

Mamú, now turning to Auma, continued, "So that's how he behaves on his first visit? Auma darling, he's priceless! I thank you from the bottom of my heart for bringing such a splendid fellow to my house to brighten up my last days!" Then she spread her moribund arms and called out, "Don Vigolo, come and give me a hug! I, too, think those cocktails taste like spew!" Bedazzled and maladroit, I bent down to the expiring dowager and received a kiss on the mouth that tasted of the apothecary shop. Her arms clung to me. The Ninth Symphony! "Embraced by millions"!

"You priceless fellow—*goldiges Mannerl!*" Mamú, the American millionaire, preferred to speak Viennese German. For years she had held court in Vienna at the side of her famous spouse, who sported a Hungarian noble title in addition to Mamú's checkbook. He was the scion of a lineage that included princes as well as counts. Mamú's own bloodline was princely enough. Her forebears had used the intimate *du* with the Austrian Emperor Franz Joseph.

Mamú's daughter, insulted twice over, had gone back to the house. A nurse pushed the patented chaise longue farther down the yard. Auma whispered to us that we should go along with Mamú; the injection would hold for another half hour, and then she would suddenly fall asleep. Mamú doubtless wanted to put Beatrice to the test now—Vigo having passed his with flying colors.

During the minutes that followed, Beatrice was likewise deemed worthy to stand at our new friend's grave. To gain Mamú's blessing it was unnecessary for her to break any rules of etiquette—which Beatrice never would have done anyway. She and Mamú had mutual acquaintances in Vienna. Just imagine, Beatrice's piano teacher Juliusz Wolfssohn—how often hadn't that man played at Mamú's little villa on Schwarzenberg Square! Beatrice also got a kiss, a buss on the cheek. But just barely, for just as the ailing woman was bestowing it, she suddenly faded away. If Auma hadn't alerted us to the medical injection, we would have thought that she had passed away in our arms. Just before she drifted into slumber, she asked us in a final whisper, and in English, "Do you believe in healing by spirit?"

Mamú's automobile took us home. Her chauffeur, a Mallorcan, had the very same Christian name as the gallant Mallorcan cavalier who was Auma's suitor. This led to some comical, and at times unpleasant, misunderstandings. As my reader will have guessed, Mamú didn't die. And because Auma's suitor, a genuine lawyer, was a daily guest at Mamú's house, there was no choice but to give the chauffeur another name. Neither the driver nor his mistress had any notion about the magic of names, and so they settled for just plain "Miguel." They might just as well have chosen "José" or "Francisco," but José was the cook and Francisco was the gardener.

During the English lessons that followed our visit, Auma had much to tell. We gave her our impressions, and she put in its proper context the question Mamú had asked us—whether we believed in healing by spirit. Mamú, Auma told us, was going to be healed by spirit. By what kind of spirit, I wanted to know. Foolish question!

A Dutch lady, Auma explained, an adherent of Christian Science, had accepted the mission of playing tricks on the medical profession, specifically on that certain German professor. A faith-healer, a German woman, was already contracted for and paid in advance. Now it was only a matter of trust. Mamú, the "terminal" patient, must also have firm belief in a miracle, for otherwise the Great Spirit could be of no avail. We were dealing, after all, with cancer, and this meant that extreme measures were in order. Was it expensive? Yes, but money was no object. A human life was at stake. Of course. And besides, Mamú was a millionaire.

I was suspicious. A Dutch lady? Was it the Dutch lady from the anarchists' *pensión*, Mevrouw van Beverwijn? The very same. Did I know her? Hmm... well, yes. And I told Auma that the medium's husband was suffering from sclerotic kidneys. Couldn't he be faith-healed too? These Dutch plantation owners surely had enough money for that? Auma said—and she was no doubt right—that the husband probably didn't believe in the power of prayer. In the absence of true faith, the Dutch lady had told Auma, no amount of prayer, direct or indirect, could be of any help. Old man van Beverwijn was not a believer—that we could all understand. To be married to a woman like that one, and then to believe in anything at all any more—that was too much for science to grapple with, even the Christian variety. That man's life consisted of nothing but knuckling under to his wife. If he ever dared to resist, he got hissed at. The poor fellow. His marriage was so hopeless that his kidneys were atrophying in response.

Thus our good friend, the ever-alert Mevrouw van Beverwijn, had Mamú's kidneys as her chief concern. While her own husband's analogous organs degenerated beyond recall, she devoted her magical talents to those of the American heiress. And lo and behold, Mamú got better! We can't say that she got *all* better—she was too old for that, and she had lived too extravagantly for a total and permanent cure. But her health returned to the extent that she was again able to eat and drink whatever she wanted, or almost. She could again enjoy the company of us younger folk, and she avoided older people more and more. I can attest to this transformation, just as I can confirm a "miracle" of Our Lady of Fatima, one that I witnessed later in Lisbon. Certainly the testimony of a non-believer is worth a great deal in cases that involve miracles.

It is beyond doubt that Mamú got better. Were the doctors wrong with their diagnosis? Were the people who lived with Mamú mistaken all along? Mamú herself told it this way: she had faith, and therefore nothing stood in the way of her being healed by the spirit. There was no earthly way of explaining it. Come to think of it, it's also not possible to explain a poem: one has faith in it, unless it is simply too awful a poem. But what did Mamú, the atheist, have faith in? In the World Spirit? In Don Matías' pantheism? In the ogress Mevrouw van Beverwijn? No, her faith was in a potent tale told by this Dutch busybody, a hair-raising verhaal of the sort one used to find in old household devotional handbooks, but which actually took place on the plantation owned by the van Beverwijns in the Dutch East Indies. Mamú once told us the story, but I also heard it from the mouth of Mevrouw van Bewerwijn herself. The two versions differed in certain details. Mamú's version was benign, and not designed to convince anyone. Mevrouw's variant, on the other hand, coming from a fanatical and evil-minded priestess of the cult, had the ring of Eternal Verity about it: woe to those who will not believe!

On the day before our visit, Mevrouw had arranged a conversation with Mamú, who told her that she was going to die within days. In fluent English, Mevrouw preached Christian Science to Mamú, concealing all the while her own husband's kidney problem and tossing in, as an example of the healing power of the spirit, a story about a dog.

These Dutch planters had a dog that always went along when they visited neighboring farms. During one of these visits, contrary to their own custom, they tied the dog to the back of their car. On leaving for home they forgot to take the dog back with them into the car. At the time, she wasn't at all sure how such ghastly negligence was possible, but later she understood it as a form of Divine Intervention. The poor beast was dragged behind their vehicle for many miles, which is to say that the dog suffered horribly in tongue and lung for the entire length of the involuntary sleigh ride. Once arrived at their plantation, the couple discovered the whimpering animal behind their car, half dead, covered with blood, a total mess. His fur had been scoured away over large parts of his body. But the worst damage was to his paws. They had disappeared. Only bloody stumps were left. Native servants nursed the animal, but no one thought he would survive. And yet he didn't die. He recovered, but as a pathetic cripple.

A nearby planter, who practiced Christian Science and proselytized for the creed, offered his services as a faith-healer for their dog. There were skeptical smiles. The paws had gone, they would not grow back— after all, a dog is not a salamander. But why not let this man of religion do what he wants, they thought. There's nothing to lose. With his prayers, the healer re-created the dog's paws and claws. According to Mamú, the healing process lasted but an instant; Mevrouw van Beverwijn herself, on the other hand, said that the Spirit took a month to regenerate the tissues. The photographs that Mevrouw presented as proof of the miracle didn't show how long it took for the cells to develop into skin and fur and claws. Mijnheer van Beverwijn couldn't remember at all how long it had taken, although he did remark—albeit not in so many words—that their dog had better luck than his own kidneys. As usual he deferred to his wife. Like a dog.

At the time of the Byzantine Iconoclasm, the Caliph of Damascus ordered that the Church Father Chrysorras have one of his hands cut off for alleged high treason. The worthy Father asked for the return of his severed hand (oh, Don Patuco, it has all happened before!). He then pleaded with the Virgin Mary to aid him in his struggle against the iconoclasts, and to let his hand grow back again as the only means of proving his innocence. The hand grew back. Or so the legend has it. With the Lord nothing is impossible. And a dog, Mevrouw van Beverwijn said, is neither closer to nor farther from His omnipotence than a human creature, be he a sinner or a paragon of piety and virtue.

The dog got well. I have seen photographs of the four paws. Mamú got well, because she believed in the restored four canine paws. How to explain this, the devil only knows.

In those days, when Mevrouw van Beverwijn had joined with God or the gods in the struggle for Mamú's kidneys, a wave of faith in miracles swept over Mallorca. A mother's son—I'm telling this in biblical style, which is how it came to pass—had died, and he was taken out to the cemetery to be buried. In southern countries, because of the heat, dead persons are often buried on the very day of demise, or at least they are brought to a mortuary. This youth was therefore taken to the morgue on the graveyard premises and had to wait while the earth was opened. His mother was an extremely poor woman who had lived on her son's earnings. Now she was penniless. Should she go begging at the cathedral? She prayed to the Lord, Our Lady of the Seven Sorrows, and the Heavenly Hosts, that her son might be returned unto her. And Heaven heard her plea. When the men came and lifted up the casket to place it in the earth, the miracle had already taken place. From inside the coffin the pall-bearers heard a knocking sound. And they were sore afraid, though they were rough men used to handling dead bodies as if they were inanimate objects—which of course they are. One cannot expect a gravedigger to have respect for the dead. The men were, I say, sore afraid; they dropped the box and fled. As it hit the ground, the box burst open and the dead youth fell out. His mother, who had gone to her son's burial with trust in the Lord's great power, was not surprised when she heard the knocking, for it was as if she were just wait-ing for the moment when the casket would open. She picked up the boy in her arms and carried him back to the ossuary. There she laid him down with maternal care on a wooden scaffold. The youth raised his arm, as if to strike or caress his mother. She, whose faith in the Lord had moved Him to make manifest His omnipotence, prayed in a loud voice, sang hymns of praise, and thanked the Almighty. The future would take care of the rest. The main thing was that her kid was alive.

News of the miracle spread throughout the city like wildfire. Great throngs of people streamed out to the cemetery, some discussing the marvelous event among themselves, others singing hymns of praise. A number of ecstatics beat their breasts and openly confessed their sins. An unsolved case of robbery that had taken place years before found its solution here: the thief chastised himself in public. At length the authorities saw the need to intervene. Physicians were alerted, in particular the one who had made out the death certificate, and whose career was therefore in jeopardy. No one wants to be buried alive, but doctors ought not to be blamed for every little mishap. The doctor in question pronounced the boy dead a second time. "But how dead is he?" the Palmesans inquired. Surely not as dead as Dickens' old man Marley, who was as dead as a doornail. "As dead as a coffin nail!" said the doctor. He stood by his diag-nosis, and as far as he was concerned, the case was closed.

But not as far as the boy was concerned. Every once in a while he raised his arm—one could never quite determine whether this signified a blessing or a threat. At other times he even sat up. His mother never left his side. Because she was poor, she was unable to persuade the authorities to have the boy taken to her home. The death certificate had been issued, so the boy was supposed to be dead. Just who did this young fellow think he was? Who was he protesting against? Why, he wasn't even eating anything.

The professor of medicine from Germany, the one who made such a grievous error with Mamú's kidneys, learned of the case and examined the young man. This time he made no mistake. The boy was alive, he declared, but he would soon die unless taken immediately to a hospital, or if necessary to his own, the doctor's, residence. Clinically dead? No, very much alive, but totally gone to the dogs. He offered to treat the patient for no fee. Once again the authorities intervened. This German professor did not have a license to practice medicine in Spain. He had a reputation as a quack, but they let him continue examining the boy anyway. Colleagues had arrived from the mainland. They percussed and stethoscoped the patient all over. Their victim remained motionless throughout, except for an occasional arm-raising and now and then a twitch that went through his whole body. The diagnostic literature on "twitching" could have been amplified significantly there at the cemetery in Palma, for the dead youth kept on living and twitching for a full six weeks more. Then a sudden, universal twitch shook his entire body. He was now so very dead that Professor Hufeland himself, Germany's famed specialist in clinical death, would have attested to this agonizing *exitus* in writing and without the faintest scruples.

The pilgrimages to the cemetery were taking on dubious forms. At the gate, religious hawkers were selling chewing gum, holy pictures, *turrón*, roasted chestnuts, white mice, lemonade, holy water, and rosaries. My grandfather would certainly have nailed up his coffee sign. The excitement in the city grew. Holy Mother Church remained silent, awaiting further developments. As much as She welcomes any and all true miracles, She is strict about such things and refuses to be misled by a simple case of clinical death. With this in mind, I discussed the case with one of our neighborhood *patres*, and I quickly let go with the assertion that when it came to clinically dead people, the Church—how could it be otherwise?—was cruel and lacked imagination.

Proof? Years ago I had heard a bell tolling, but I no longer remembered precisely where it hung. The good Father kept prying, and so I gave him the story of a canonization that failed. In the heat of our theological disputation, and urged on by subconscious feelings of regional chauvinism, I decided to have things center on a certain Electoral Bishop of Cologne. This servant of the Lord had accomplished more than the required number of miracles for canonization. His name was firmly anchored in the minds of the faithful. The *advocatus diaboli* had raised no objections. A papal bull recounted the life and deeds of the candidate for sainthood. Everything was shipshape—no doubt even more so than I reported in my story.

Only one act remained, and that was to exhume the bishop's mortal remains in preparation for his "translation" into a special vault. But when the stone tomb was chiseled open, the priests and prelates were seized with horror: the candidate was lying on his stomach! That is, the skeleton showed unmistakably that the corpse had been set in its final resting-place in prone position. Was that a proper way to bury a Christian? Clerical minds started working feverishly: what had actually happened? Holy Mother Church came up with a clever way to wriggle out of the embarrassing predicament these prone bones had put Her in. The bishop, She declared, had been mistakenly buried alive. Waking from his rigid state, he had been stricken with fright and started blaspheming. He ought, of course, to have yielded to the will of the Almighty and awaited the hour when it would please the Lord to lead His servant out of apparent death into the arms of genuine death. Yet instead, the bishop tossed and turned in his tomb until, lying on his belly—an outrage to all sainthood, a slap in God's Eternal Countenance—he breathed his unworthy last. It would be unthinkable to canonize such a sinner! God forbid! And so they plugged the almost-saint back into his stone box.

Now wasn't that a case of hard-heartedness and failure of imagination? How did I think things had really happened, my priestly interlocutor wanted to know. This way: when the man awoke from his rigor mortis and was about to rub his eyes—"Where am I?"—his hands hit the coffin lid. Buried alive! Having survived this moment of mortal terror, the saint thanked his Creator for granting him this final trial, one which he, in his steadfast faith, was to endure before he should meet his Heavenly Father face to face. Bedded softly on luxurious ecclesiastical textiles, with head raised, as comfortable as one can be inside a granite container, he lay there and started thinking. Not frantically, for he knew what was proper for a future saint. It was his desire to die humbly, as he had lived. With one final effort, he twisted around to the lowly belly-down position, one that is indeed dishonorable for a bishop, and gave up the ghost. The Lord took him unto Himself. Holy Mother Church anathematized him.

The priest listened to my legendary version of the legend, shaking his head all the while. Then he said gently that I had things quite wrong—not about the Church, but about the saint in question. That man was, he said, the author of *The Imitation of Christ.*—"What? My fellow Lower Rhinelander Hämerken?" —"Hämerken?"—"Yes, Thomas à Kempis?"—"The very same!"

I was astounded. My fatherland had manufactured a stab-in-the-back legend about its war heroes, and now I stood at the cradle of a belly-down legend about a Christian saint! Not just any saint, but my mystic friend whose *Imitatio* hung in the handiest position on the line back at our Tower of Meditation...

The Palma cemetery administration, yielding to pressure from the populace, permitted the mother to set up home next to the youth's body. There she sat, waking and praying. God, who had given her son back to her, would surely be willing to pester some official into declaring the death certificate null and void. That is what the mother, not a very intelligent woman, was hoping for. The Lord had done what He could, the rest was up to human beings. But humans, especially if they are officials, seldom cross the narrow borders of their own stupidity. A certificate is a certificate. Doesn't God know that? Well then, we now have before us the age-old question of Job, which my mentor Pascoaes answers so beautifully.

No one wanted to bury anyone any more. Many people didn't dare to lie down to sleep, for fear of waking up in a coffin. Some of Beatrice's pupils called off their lessons, refusing to learn anything more until the miraculous youth was either truly dead or truly alive. In the midst of this mania there arose anguished notions of self-chastisement, fear of the Lord, the devil's touch. Mamú's household also had come profoundly under the influence of the chiliastic movement spurred on by the boy caught between death and life. Mevrouw van Beverwijn came along with her legend of God's mercy to canines, and threw it into the heady brew of pious hopes. Not all threats of death bring death itself! Behold the youth at the Palma graveyard! Her story of her dog and his four paws fell on well-tilled soil. Mamú announced that she was willing to have her kidneys prayed for.

Afterward she confessed to us that without the twitching youth she never would have fallen for the Christian Science rigmarole. The boy had dropped out of his box just in time. *No hay mal que por bien no venga*—this saying was getting truer and truer on our island.

Mamú thus became a devotee of Christian Science—not what one would call an impassioned believer, but a very active and hard-working member. For the Mallorcan chapter of Scientism her house became what the cottage of Lydia the dye-seller at Thyatira had been for the early Christian movement of the Apostle to the Gentiles: a church.

Our second visit to El Terreno took place at a time when Mamú, in the opinion of all her doctors, ought to have been dead or at least in an ambiguous condition somewhere between extremes, perhaps lying next to the youth at the Palma cemetery. But she was alive and chipper. Her features, formerly distorted by the imminence of death, now had a kind of sallow plumpness that was to stay with her to the very end. Her abdominal cramps had ceased, she had no more hemorrhages, her entire arsenal of medicines went into the garbage can, and her live-in nurses had been dismissed—with a generous bonus, of course. Such was the scene when we revisited Mamú. We celebrated privately her resurrection. Her cocktail-mixing daughter had left, and telegrams had been sent to her other children: "Alarm over. Mamú prayed to health. Death nowhere near. Live Mamú welcomes visitors." They never showed up.

Mevrouw van Beverwijn told her that spiritual healing was not connected with diet. Intercession with divine forces had nothing to do with recipes, so long as no one ever laced meals with poison. This was an important matter for Mamú, for she very much liked to eat good food. At one time she had enjoyed the same close relationship with Madame Sacher in Vienna as her late princely spouse had enjoyed with Franz Joseph, the Austrian Kaiser. Despite the fact that I have never been at all close to such prominent individuals—which I did not hesitate to confess to her— I, too, am dreadfully fond of excellent cuisine, and thus our ancient heiress was all the warmer in her feelings toward me. In the course of time Mamú discovered further amiable qualities in her friend Vigolo. For example, that he had had some intriguing experiences during his brief life span, and that he was capable of recounting them with spicy affability. That there had been adventures, for example, regarding a genuine Spanish *puta*. That in my student days, arm in arm with my mother, I had visited the mothers of the City of Cologne. Or again, that the "Torre del Reloj," a Mallorcan cathouse, had sheltered us for months beneath its extremely porous roof. Mamú beamed. I was the "nice man" who would have been welcome at her interment. But she liked me better at her table and in relaxed conversation.

José, the Catalan cook, Monica, the part-time cook from Santa Catalina, and Celerine, the assistant cook, all performed their assigned duties as in the days prior to Mamú's horrendous disease. Only Anna, the nanny from the Black Forest, crabby like all servants kept on beyond retirement age, wasn't pleased with the new dispensation. She thought it was just fine that her mistress was still alive—that was the proper thing for a mistress to do. But that Mamú had found religion—this turn of events she liked less, and even less than that, the constant fuss about "The Science" and the hymn-singing ladies. Nowadays, she said, the house was chock full of Bibles, and the Lord's word was getting bandied about here in all kinds of foreign languages, whereas she, Frau Anna, approved of it solely in Martin Luther's version. But what she liked least of all was the presence of that man Vigoleis, who kept telling stories that in her opinion had precious little to do with Christianity. But on this point this simple, extraordinarily diligent old lady was quite mistaken. Francisco, the gardener who had already discussed with his mistress the details of landscaping her grave, tended the grounds, Mamú's "park," with the same adeptness as before. There is little to report about her other maids, a seamstress, and a young messenger, except that they were collectively louder than one might expect in a wealthy household. But Mamú was living in Spain. Miguel, the chauffeur, had his own opinion of the crones who lately had become his chief passengers.

This was the start of a marvelous epoch. We spent every weekend with Mamú. Sometimes Miguel picked us up, but usually we walked the narrow boardwalk along the bay with its rippling waves of not quite pure sea water, a route that now has been transformed into the Paseo Marítimo. We had the key to a gate in her "park" wall.

At the beginning of every week Mamú came to Barceló Street to discuss with me the menu for Sunday. With time I got more and more fastidious and adventuresome in gastronomic matters. My revulsion against bread and potatoes grew stronger, and this meant that we had to shop for ingredients from many different countries. The *calmados* in Palma didn't sell such delicacies. Mamú had shopped at gourmet retailers all over Europe. She owned a huge library of cookbooks in a variety of languages. Now and then, after the spirit had brought her back to health, she regarded these extravagances as sinful. I soon recognized the danger that threatened this new domain of mine, and quickly talked her out of such silly notions. I had never eaten bear's paws, and was curious to get a taste of them, or at least to find out whether it was only snobs who sang their praises.

It was reasoning of this sort that led me to recommend to Mamú a kind of compromise: she should buy a set of Bibles in the languages represented in her gastronomic library. Mamú thought that was a fascinating suggestion, though hardly a Christian one. Right away she sent word to her book dealer in Vienna to take care of everything. Her Portuguese Bible served me well when I later studied the works of Pascoaes. This, too, was a manifestation of destiny, as Mamú wouldn't deny. The youth with the twitching arm, the dog's paws, the Portuguese Bible—everything on this island had a dual essence, a twofold incarnation. Still, one had to be careful with such things. Islands themselves have their own ways about them.

Mamú's bookcases contained not only cookbooks, and Frau Anna didn't only trip over volumes of Holy Scripture. Mamú owned a first-rate collection of contemporary literature in many languages. She knew most of the writers personally. Take any book from her shelf: there was an autograph inscription. Or Mamú would say, "What's that you have there? Oh, Blei!" And immediately she would tell a story about Franz Blei, one in which she herself was a star performer. "Fülöp-Miller?"—Mamú hadn't exactly unraveled this writer's bibliographic snags as he was working on his book on the Jesuits, but she had used her connections to help him out, connections that extended to some very obscure ecclesiastical archives. She had known the unpronounceable Stanislaus Przybyszewski, a writer I much admired, and she once had entertained him as a dinner guest. And of course our friend Madame Gerstenberg, but also the great Frenchmen Gide, Valéry, Romain Rolland, the great Englishmen, the great Americans. Gabriele D'Annunzio, Papini, and Pirandello, who had just been awarded the Nobel Prize—they all were alive in Mamú's amazing memory and in her even more amazing library. In addition, a certain number of deceased authors, she claimed, had entered her abode. That didn't bother me, though it did Beatrice, whose memory is as solid as it is merciless.

All of these exalted personages had at one time been Mamú's personal guests, either in her *palazzino* in Vienna, at the estate of her late husband somewhere in the Hungarian hinterlands, perhaps on one of her father's farms in New York State, or in her Paris apartment on the Quai d'Orsay, designed by Henry van de Velde. It is not uncommon for an American heiress to marry a Hungarian prince. Yet with the downfall of the Austro-Hungarian monarchy, this particular prince forfeited all his property. He was able to polish the tarnish off his title with dollar bills, and Mamú used hard cash to buy back his castle. In those years, the feudal Europe of yore was literally haunted by tradition-starved American heiresses of Mamú's kind. It was even plausible that her Hungarian Count or Prince—her deceased spouse sometimes surfaced with the one lineage, sometimes with the other—had not been a wastrel, but an extremely gifted architect whose talents had bestowed upon the citizens of

America the Metropolitan Opera, the Waldorf-Astoria Hotel, and a few dozen skyscrapers of somewhat lesser distinction.

When Mamú, in our presence, ascribed the Metropolitan Opera to her late husband, the man who had died such a beautiful death, Beatrice, who is a devotee of world history, started figuring out dates. Did she perhaps think that Mamú was faking? A millionaire heiress, I was convinced, had no need of such charades. Only poor people tell lies. For 25 pesetas you could buy a lie from any tourist guide.

Mamú was a millionaire. How many times over? For someone like me, someone who is forced to stick with the second-grade multiplication table of daily existence, it is immaterial how many million times a million his friend owns. A single million can suffice to hone away the rough edges that so often plague a friendship. Be that as it may, Mamú was a thousand times a millionaire.

Her father, a typical American, invented a baking powder. Twofold genius that he was, he gave his invention a majestic name: Royal Baking Powder. It was a success the world over, putting Dr. Oetker's continental products to shame. In no time the inventor's business flourished, and he became a billionaire. Mamú was an only child, and a veritable deluge of wealth cascaded upon her. She went to the very best schools, and spent her vacations on long cruises on her father's yacht. In her own words she grew up in a timeless world, just like a millionaire's daughter in a novel. As we all know, life begins to get interesting only when it touches on poetry.

Her father, she told us, died during the First World War, when she was already living with her children in Vienna. Meanwhile she had married the Hungarian aristocrat and put him back on his feet. A building contract detained her Prince in Barcelona. Returning to New York in wartime was impossible, although neutral diplomats offered their services. For the entire duration of the war her husband was listed as missing. In fact, he had gone to Mallorca to wait out the end of the world conflagration at the estate of his friend, the Archduke Ludwig Salvator of Austria. But the Archduke had already left the island in a submarine. Either he was now residing at his royal-cum-imperial summer home, or he was dead.

1918: Armistice. Mamú flies (in the sense of hastens) back to America, searches for her husband and finds him, searches for her multi-million inheritance and doesn't find it. "Vigoleis, do believe me, that was quite a blow!"

"I can't think of a blow that *hasn't* hit you!"

"Oh, you're just being nice. But listen..."

Anything having to do with the Baking Powder millions, Mamú told and discussed only in English.

Irregularities had occurred within the company. It all went into the very high numbers, and what those numbers meant was that she, the sole heir, had been bilked of her Baking Powder shares. There was talk of dastardly deeds; perhaps her father hadn't died a natural death. A certain cousin of hers was thought to be behind it all, a fellow she had no hesitation in calling a gangster.

Many years ago he had courted her and her millions. For doing battle with the company thieves, she had recourse to smaller sums that were invested elsewhere, a drop in the bucket when compared to the bakery hoard, but a cool million nevertheless.

Her lawyers encouraged her to sue. Her son, at the time just beginning to grow whiskers, said, "Shoot 'em, Mamú!" One of her daughters urged settlement out of court. The other daughter, who had wedded her own millionaire, shrugged and told her to do whatever she wanted. Wisely enough, the Prince was not asked for his advice. Since she had the money for it, Mamú sued. She pressed her case with elegance, vigor, patience, and all the other necessary qualities for that sort of thing. What she lacked was a good lawyer, and of course she had totally mistaken notions about the type of justice that gets practiced and perverted in courts of law. True enough, she had read Kleist's *Michael Kohlhaas*; I spotted a copy on her bookshelf. But that was only literature, she said, and anyway, all Kohlhaas fought for was a few horses, whereas in her case it was a matter of millions of dollars. That was grotesque logic, but I accepted it. The company that was her antagonist in this affair was working against her with a frightful weapon, one whose natural and insidious deadliness Mamú never recognized as clearly as we did. Had the Royal Baking company bought her lawyer and the judges? It was as simple as that.

Her children grew up, married, had children of their own, got divorced. While the suit was still in progress, her husband died in the aforementioned "beautiful" manner (in Mamú's Viennese it was "*ein scheener Tod*"). Stones started forming in her kidneys; cancer made its appearance and ate at her innards. If it hadn't been for Mevrouw van Beverwijn's powers of persuasion, Mamú would have died with her million-dollar suit unsettled, and the Royal company would have gleefully won the case *de jure factoque*. The Dutch lady thought Mamú could go on for another twenty years, and thus it made sense to start working again in earnest with the legal documents. Mamú put herself to it with renewed energy and with the counsel of the Spanish prosecuting attorney who was courting Auma. This fellow knew a lot about law, but he had never seriously studied gangster methods—and anyway, his mind was more on the young woman from Finland. Still, he helped to fill reams of paper with figures—figures about interest and compound interest, dividends and margins, profit-sharing, and other fancy concepts that are beyond my understanding. Mamú had studied up on these things, and so the prosecutor was able to broaden his professional horizons at the same time that he could keep an eye on Auma. She was still maintaining her distance, however, and we wondered why. The two of them were in such a state about each other that it was painful for us bystanders to observe. As with Mamú's court proceedings, love had come to a standstill. They talked and talked and got nowhere. Mamú's monthly income was substantial, though by a multimillionaire's standards it amounted to peanuts. The legal fracas was taking its toll. Other American millionaires on Mallorca behaved very differently. They arrived with sumptuous yachts, traveling private casinos, and stark-naked women, whereas Mamú had to get by with a rented automobile and well-dressed domestic servants.

It wasn't only the court battle with the Royal Baking Gang that was eating away at Mamú's bank accounts. She was having a great deal of trouble with a brother of her late husband, an odd bird indeed, old, over eighty, he too a prince, and living in princely dissolution. He resided in Budapest, and each year was required to pay enormous sums in child support as a result of his habit of siring progeny all over the place—not only in Hungary, though that was his main hunting preserve. Mamú had sworn to her husband that she would pay debts, *coûte que coûte*, for his profligate brother Ferencz. And she kept her promise, despite the constant flurry of new paternity claims piling up on her lawyer's desk in Vienna. "If only the old lecher would just go impotent!"—how often Mamú expressed this wish with a sigh when mail arrived from Vienna. I told her she should cut him off totally, but Mamú was not one for the scalpel. This meant that her financial condition was in flux and unpredictable. She had already rented out her palacete in Vienna and used the income to pay the smaller child-support claims.

We ourselves would soon feel the effects of this ancient brother-in-law's second adolescence. But first we must let Mamú's husband die his "beautiful" death.

Mamú and her prince had gone to a little town in the hills near Vienna—I don't remember its name. They were on a walk, and stopped at a stone balustrade to gaze at the landscape below them. They noticed a little church with a cemetery next to it down in a valley, and in the cemetery a couple of men who, from this distance, looked like little ants working at the ground. From their motions, it was apparent that they were digging a grave. Mamú's husband, who had built skyscrapers and opera houses, who as a dynast had the privilege of being interred in his forefathers' mausoleum, who furthermore could afford the most expensive style of cremation in the States—this man now went weak, got tears in his eyes and said, "Ethel, down there, see that churchyard? That's the kind of world-forsaken place where I would like to be buried. Will you promise me that, darling?"

Mamú, deeply touched, made the promise, and they continued their walk. They had gone just a few paces when her husband suddenly felt ill. He grabbed at his chest, had trouble breathing. They spotted a bench. She led him to it. He slowly sat down, fell over, and was dead.

Mamú bought the grave plot, which on the following day was to have received the remains of a well-to-do local citizen. She also paid a huge sum for maintenance of the gravesite for decades to come—I think it was for 50 years. She signed the proper papers, and later she stored them in a portable metal safe.

What I have just recounted would have occupied many pages in a written version of Mamú's story. For Mamú had a wonderful gift for storytelling, comparable only to one other person I have ever known, though not of quite the same caliber in matters of romantic impact: the mother of the writer Pascoaes, Doña Carlota, about whom there will be much to report in a later book. Mamú also wrote down a good deal. She told us that stacks of her diaries were in safe keeping in New York. But ever since that business with her kidneys, she tired easily, a behavior Mevrouw van Beverwijn hadn't been able to pray out of her. And so one day Mamú asked me to enter her service as her chronicler. She would recite for me the novel of her life; I could freely rework everything, add excerpts from her own notations, and generally shape it as I saw fit. For this collaboration we would have to be together all the time.

The idea arose, as do all great ideas, out of the void. It came to Mamú one day as she was carving a roast capercaillie. It was a daring idea, fully worthy of this grand woman. Beatrice, who thinks "the void" is a concept for cowards, later said that the idea certainly came more from Mamú's heart than from the roast bird; the woman was obviously in love with me. In any case, from whichever source, heart or roast grouse, the idea had arrived.

Near Valldemosa lies the large estate known as Miramar. Ludwig Salvator, Mamú's late husband's friend and Archduke of Austria, had purchased it along with other landholdings, then renovated and enlarged it. The legal circumstances were obscure. The Archduke had sown his wild oats on the island, there were paternity suits, and now no one knew exactly who owned the property that was once the archducal demesne. One of the country houses at Miramar, a small summer residence praised in Baedeker, was for rent or sale. Mamú decided she just had to have it; there the three of us would live. The roast game bird stuck in my mouth, something that doesn't happen to me often.

Auma's prosecutor started negotiations with attorneys for the Archduke's heirs, and we went out to examine the castle by the sea. The premises were ideal for our trio. I was familiar with the various portions of the estate from my days as a tourist guide, when I had explained the sights in my own fashion.

Beatrice would get her concert grand if she promised to play for Mamú every day. If everything went well across the ocean with the baking powder concern, she would install an organ, Beatrice's second-fondest wish.

"And my dear Vigolo, what would you like?"

"A donkey, Mamú."

Did Vigoleis intend to become *Don Quixote* and Sancho Panza at one and the same time, here on his mirror isle of Barataria? Yes. *Don Quixote* because of the millions that now, with the aid of some majestic baking powder, beckoned like a mirage. And Sancho Panza on account of the wooden peg to which he would have to bind the Knight, for the latter was such a fool that he was constantly and literally fit to be tied. And furthermore, neither of these two fools had much over the other one.

Mamú expected me to say that I wanted an automobile. She obviously didn't know me well enough to realize that I wouldn't bother mentioning something I took for granted.

It wasn't until the final months preceding the outbreak of the Civil War that Mamú's marvelous plan developed to the point where we could prepare for the actual move to Miramar. Her finances permitted such a momentous change of abode. We were to commence with the writing of her life story before the grape harvest. I was determined to give it the title *The Royal Baking Gang*. But we ought to wait a bit on that, the multi-millionaire heiress said. For a title she would prefer something "beautiful."

Her daughter in Paris was against our plan, likewise the daughter in Budapest, likewise her son, likewise the bristly German nanny. Without exception they regarded poor Vigoleis, in whom Mamú was plainly infatuated, as a fortune hunter. Mevrouw van Beverwijn, who hated me because I refused to swallow her story of the Miracle of the Four Paws, went after Mamú with all the tricks of her pseudo-science. Mamú stood fast. Arguments from envy couldn't touch her. The fact that all of us on our island were soon to become failures was a matter of separate destiny, one that bore the unique and unmistakable features of a two-armed general.

Thus, in place of Mamú's memoirs I am setting before the reader the applied recollections of her friend Vigoleis. Here we have been unable to tell the story of this enchanting fourflusher with the amplitude she so fully deserves, for better or worse. But there is surely enough in these pages to show how greatly I loved her. Never have I enjoyed so much being led down the garden path by a person who was my friend. Not one bad dream has ever darkened my memories of her.

On the other hand, as I look back in careful judgment of those experiences, there is one figure who returns to memory as fundamentally wicked and mendacious. It is the person who constantly prayed for her human and animal fellows, Mevrouw van Beverwijn.

VIII

1933

In a southern country you can get along best if you succeed in switching off completely your sense of time, and as completely as possible your ideas about space.

Sometimes it is already tomorrow, when you would swear that it is still yesterday or the day before or, on happy occasions of absolute temporal confusion, no day at all. You can always cancel out Today; that is a mere philosophical abstraction. Iberian Man—and that is the character we are talking about here—is at all times standing on his earth made of clouds.

During our seven years of politico-poetico-mystical exile in Portugal, at Pascoaes Castle in São João de Gatão—our Mediterranean island and all of Spain were already behind us, Switzerland too, France too, plus the anxious hours of our second escape through Spain. One day I said to Beatrice, looking up from my manuscript, "When is Easter? I'd like to send Mother a Resurrection message up there in her *deutsches Reich*, which is getting bigger and losing more blood every day."

If sent by telegraph, my time-conscious Beatrice replied, tongues of fire might arrive just in time. We were three days away from Pentecost.

Even with this hyper-Iberian compression of time, there was a certain amount of loss due to friction, for we eventually figured out that the Outpouring of the Holy Spirit would be taking place the very next day.

That's how late it was, and we hadn't noticed anything. While we were snoozing away on our island amidst the raucous daydreaming of the Mamús, Patucos, and Uluas, the vagabond Suredas and Pedro (constantly making progress as a painter), surrounded by *porras* and *putas* and Pilars, corpses that weren't dead and living persons who refused to die—Germany had awakened. And because an awakened Germany meant a Jewry that must croak—there's no heroism without sacrifice—the nation of poets and thinkers, which is also Hagen's nation, was joining up with the *Führer*.

How large was the number of people who were slated to die with their limbs sticking out rigidly from their bodies? Millions, probably. Two of them could already be stricken from the list. The *Führer* needn't worry about them any longer. Adele Gerstenberg and her son were resting from their own death in the cemetery over in Alicante. Millions minus two—does that make any difference? If one million people kick the bucket, are two people of any consequence? If everybody goes along with the plan, the nation can get things done with no trouble at all. Everybody has to help out, everybody! No one can shirk from the business of murdering, for whoever does will get whacked himself. That's what Hitler and history have in mind. And here is Vigoleis, still insisting that he doesn't believe in history. Just don't count the dead: that's what Don Patuco and Hölderlin teach us.

After years of national humiliation, ethnic snubbing, and darkness across the entire country, the German dawn was finally approaching—the Dawn of the Gods, an uprising of house and home and kit and caboodle. Now there could once again be collective rejoicing, a closing of the ranks for an orgy of fun-making. The more people who got murdered, the more heartwarming it all was. And because Joy gives rise to Strength, the process was given a name: Strength Through Joy. With the strength that proceeded from joy, the populace embarked on Strength Through Joy ships—for wasn't our country also a *Volk ohne Raum*?

The newly awakened nation also found its way to Mallorca, the end of the world, the hinterland, the underworld—but still world. Here was a scene to be gaped at. You could have joy at the sight of the lowly, such a stark contrast to one's own cultural heights. Everything is better back home! But things will improve here, too. What a mess! They don't even have beer! "Oh *Führer*, sir, where in the name of the *Führer* can one get a halfway decent...?" But before

I, as the local Herr *Führer*, can pass on these fellow-countrymen's complaint to the *Führer*, I have to make sure of just where we stand.

This I learn from Herr von Martersteig—an informed source, for as I have mentioned, it had finally happened, and we hadn't noticed it. We didn't subscribe to any newspaper. My home-town gazette arrived irregularly, and at the German bookshop we read only the literary stuff. At Mulet's *tertulia* international affairs were discussed with intensity, but only in their timeless aspects. Mamú's easy chairs gave us glimpses of royal baking powder on the rise, Jaume's flour sacks were a site for deciding the fate of Honduras, and on the Suredas' three-legged chair we discussed the fate of the Sureda family. Everyone was concerned solely with his own little world. Thus I had no idea that overnight I had become the citizen of a master race, and that my *Führer* in quotation marks was the image of the Lord Himself.

It was an ordinary day, and an ordinary crowd of people was strolling to and fro on the Plaza Cort at the late-afternoon hour when the paper boys hawk the *Ultima Hora* with their lusty, high-pitched, singsong paeans to *Uultim-mooooooooo-ra!*—the genuine swan-song of the "final hour" of world history. Whoever has heard this will never forget it—*uultim-mooooooooo-ra!* But now, whoever was that man limping out of the Colmado Parisién, where only Mamú and other millionaires and perhaps Robert von Ranke Graves did their shopping? It was Baron Joachim von Martersteig, more sallow of complexion than ever, more furrowed of feature, more crippled of gait. We hadn't seen each other for an eternity. Were things going badly for him here on the Golden Isle, where it is always Blue Monday? With his old, familiar gesture of amazement he placed his monocle to his eye and let it drop again, but this time he had to reach out farther to retrieve it.

"Don Joaquín" "Don Vigoleis!"

Like all of the foreigners, we enjoyed playing Spanish. Before we could shake hands, the Captain tried to hide from me what he had just bought in the store. Instead of the gratings of a green cheese, he had bought an entire sapsago. So apparently he wasn't worse off financially. Presumably Hindenburg had finally yielded to his pestering about the pension for his war injury.

"Have you heard the news?"

I was startled, because I hadn't heard. But instinctively I assumed it had to do with his enemy Robert Graves. For Beatrice and me, it would be a blow if anything had happened to him. Probably got in a fight and smashed his writing hand! Oh ye Muses, preserve Robert Graves until he has finished *I, Claudius*!

"Hitler has taken over. Germany has ceased to be what it was. Heads are already rolling!"

With God and with history, nothing is impossible. Nevertheless, I was stunned.

"Thunder and lightning, *Herr Hauptmann!* What a grand opportunity for you! The uprising of the Browns changes the entire strategic situation overnight."

Martersteig gave me a twinkle with his healthy eye. Then he cocked his other eye and started sparkling at me with that one, too. He asked stiffly if my intention was to insult him.

Not on your life, I replied. I was merely thinking of his monkey army and his years-long difficulties with recruitment. Now he wouldn't have to pound his impressment drum in the jungle. His conscription commissars would no longer have to use bananas to lure the recruits down from the trees, for now, "from the Adige to the Belt, from the Meuse to the Memel," he could count on mobilizing an abundance of material for his long-tailed regiments. Whereupon the Captain completely lost his composure, hissed an unkind word, hunched himself upright in military fashion, and said with contempt, "I forbid you to insult my monkeys by means of a comparison that you probably mean to be witty! It's Germany itself that is at stake! The mob is crushing everything that has been built up over generations. A mere corporal...!"

We stood there for a long time debating the coup d'état that claimed to be none, but which for that same reason was all the more dangerous. We parted in disagreement. Both of us rejected the new political style; both of us refused to accept the new myth that, in the absence of Jews, made us into "Jew-influenced Aryans." Martersteig rejected such a notion by reason of his Prussian military attitudes, myself on the basis of my Quixotic, all-too-human nature. Which is to say, my cowardice. Something in me shied away from wringing the neck of a Jew, from forcing him into a condition of nonexistence, as my fatherland's new political program was demanding of every loyal citizen. And although he had been trained to kill, the Captain wasn't fond of this idea, either. But his refusal was only his way of avoiding getting his hands dirty. Once again, this time with certain questions on his mind, he approached his General and Field Marshal Hindenburg. Was Hindenburg suddenly no longer just a slob?

Beatrice connected this piece of news with Martersteig's enemy, precisely because I had heard it from the Captain's mouth. Had something happened to Graves? Had he left the island? What a blow that would be to my typewriter! After all, what was of any importance to Martersteig besides his apes and his enemy?

This enemy had approached me. In the German shop, he had been told that I would definitely be available to type a manuscript. In our doorway stood a tall man with rugged features, squinting eyes, and a dark tan. A lock of hair hung across his face. He was wearing a colorful checked shirt, an even more colorful shawl, and an odd straw hat. Was I the person he was looking for? he asked. I confessed that I was indeed that person. The man spoke English. My first thought was: Arsenio, drug dealing, U-boat captain, they're pulling a job and need a stooge, and they've found me. But even before this pirate uttered some phony name, I knew exactly in whose presence I had the honor of standing: Robert von Ranke Graves, the enemy, the lord of 115 volts and 7 watts. One flick of his bison-like brows, and all of Deyá is plunged in darkness! Has he come here to hook me into his shady business?

There are many different ways to introduce yourself to your fellow human beings. None has ever impressed me as much as the technique used by my friend's enemy. He said, "Graves," and then he said in German, "*Strich drunter*!" This was a spoken visiting card—and what a card it was! How picayune by comparison is Burckhardt with ck-dt, or Meier with an E, or Vigoleis with his soft V! "Graves, *Goodbye to All That*"! Such an introduction precludes any mistaken identity. One knows immediately whom one is dealing with. Voltaire, too, preferred clarity in personal introductions. This great enemy of the Church and baiter of the Jesuits had his own private house-Jesuit named Adam. When introducing him to his guests he would say, "*C'ést le Père Adam, mais il n'est pas le premier homme du monde.*" It's a simple matter for people who are known for their books. "T. Mann, *Royal Highness*! Heinrich Mann, *Loyal Subject*! Klaus Mann, *Mephisto*! Or Vigoleis, *Vigoleis* —but for that, this book would have to be already published.

Was Graves collecting witnesses against the Captain? A trial? Why doesn't the man just dispatch him with a stab in the neck? It was a clever move of Graves's, one that I recognized as such too late, to begin his visit on a literary mission with a literary allusion. He had not come as a bully. He had written a new book, whose title would probably be *I, Claudius, Emperor and God*. Would I have the time and the willingness to type out his manuscript? This sounded peaceful enough, and it was a paying job.

Robert Graves' handwriting was rather difficult to decipher. He asked me to read aloud a few lines. I was only moderately successful; I would have failed any school exam. But the enemy was not as petty as Martersteig made him out to be. I could, he said, take my time to get used to his script, and anything I couldn't figure out I should leave blank. I wasn't to add anything of my own, for that would cost him time when it came to reading proof. Did I have a decent typewriter? "Brand new!" Could he please take a look at it so he could check out the font size? It was, I said, still at the factory, a Spanish *teclado*. I was having the German umlauts and the Dutch "ij" installed. Wasn't that a quick-witted lie on my part? I hadn't the courage to show this dashing writer my rickety Diamant-Juwel.

We quickly reached an agreement concerning my wage. I named a rather large amount, and Graves found it acceptable. He would let me buy the paper myself, and he asked if he should hand over some money for that purpose. The writer reached into a pocket and came forth with a sheaf of bills. My eyes darted from their sockets. Did this writer-colleague of mine spend his free time as a highway robber? Was he dealing in drugs? Was *Goodbye to All That* the source for this heap of dough? For such a wad I would gladly say "goodbye" to all of my own past life. He was as trustful as they come. One further sign of a great man: he left his manuscript package with me, a stranger! It was the sole extant copy.

On his way out he asked me whether I knew Deyá, where he lived. A pleasant artist colony like Worpswede—I should come out for a visit. Well, yes, I told him, I had been out to that swallows' nest for visits with Three Little Clouds and the German Captain von... What—? Did I know that fellow, too? But who didn't know him? Graves added in Spanish as a farewell greeting, "*No pinta mucho!*"—Martersteig wasn't worth very much. Neither of us ever mentioned his name again.

From a lie to the truth is but a single step. Beatrice was teaching a certain Señor Alvarez, Don Alejandro, owner of the "Casa Barlock," where he sold typewriters and office equipment. There I purchased, on the installment plan, the machine I lied about preemptively, and was given 100 pesetas for my worn-out Diamant—a merchandising challenge if there ever was one. Don Alejandro was up to the task. He knew a young man who wrote poems but was otherwise quite normal and had some money, and who could make good use of my old rattletrap. So my writing apparatus simply changed hands, and everything remained as it had been. I often wonder if that Spanish son of the poetic Muse got more out of the machine than I did.

I opted for a Continental, the latest model with all the fixings except the ones I had dreamed up myself but couldn't find in any catalogue. It took some time to alter the letters. Don Alejandro had to order new combinations from the factory. As we waited, he let me use a machine on loan, and I started familiarizing myself with Graves' handwriting and, engrossed by his manuscript, by his English. What I found was not an army of monkeys marching toward a commode from Martersteig's ancestral attic, but He Himself, Tiberius Claudius Drusus Nero Germanicus, marching towards a Continental typewriter. That is why I cringed when the Captain told us the news, and Beatrice felt the same way: nothing must happen to Graves. For if anything did, it would be curtains for our new machine.

"It's odd, Beatrice, but I was thinking the very same thing: the enemy and the installment payments. If Graves were to die, it would be a catastrophe for us. But it's a lot worse than that. The National Socialists are now at the helm, and now they'll start doing what La Gerstenberg was so afraid of: they're going to kill all the Jews. Hitler has been proclaimed as the God of the Germans, and as you know, thou shalt have no other gods before him. The first heads have already been lopped off. The first un-German cadavers are floating in the Rhine, 'Germany's river but nevermore Germany's border.' Patriotism is once again official public policy. You're supposed to take your hat off when you hear the national anthem. This is weird. It's like in the jungle. You can't tell when the dance is going to start up, and you'll have to put a ring in your nose so as not to be conspicuous. And Martersteig was a little strange. He's no longer so anti-militaristic, although he rejects any comparison between his monkeys and the hordes of brown-shirt apes. He thinks that great times are ahead. You'll see—he'll get his pension raised! I saw him coming out of the Colmado Parisién, where a slice of Edam costs 50 centimos."

This marked the onset of political discussions on the Street of the General.

Whereas previously we had talked only about generals, we now chatted about a certain corporal, for whose sake the *Ultima Hora* came out a whole hour late on the day when he announced his plans to upend the whole world. Verdaguer, an energetic co-worker at this newspaper called *The Final Hour*, told me that such a thing had never happened since the paper's very first hour.

We talked a great deal, and eventually even Beatrice began to lose her faith in historical progress. I was the optimist, she the pessimist. I insisted that a hundred or a thousand people might go crazy when commanded to, but not an entire nation of 70 million. And after all, the Church was still there. The Church would surely have a thing or two to say about this development. It was the beginning of great times for the Church—"Saint Boniface..."

"... This time Saint Boniface will go along with the barbarians. At the moment I consider it more important to figure out what we're going to do about our typewriter."

"What has that got to do with the Third Reich?"

"It's very simple. Every German mark that we spend on installments will be converted into Nazi poison that can get thrown back at us sooner or later."

The next day I explained our situation to Don Alejandro. This Barlock type-writer man thought I was nuts. What was I trying to do, be more popish than the Pope? A puny private boycott of this kind would not alter world history by a single iota. Nevertheless, even though it meant taking on a somewhat higher debt, we shifted our order to an American Royal.

With this move we declared war on the Third Reich, breaking off trade relations with the newly awakened Germany just twenty-four hours after it commenced its thousand-year-long history.

The newspapers informed us that the world at large was still unsure about how to respond to Germany's brownshirt *pronunciamiento*. Governments were taking matters under advisement, diplomats were hastening back to their capitals for secret briefings, spies were getting bonuses, and the code machines were tapping furiously day and night. The world hemmed and hawed, preferring to wait things out.

To this very day we are under no illusions concerning our swift and correct decision, which was easy enough for us to make. We didn't believe in God, nor were we nominal Christians, and this meant that we felt responsible only to our own conscience. We had no need to keep up appearances or protect a private fortune.

Our conscience said no, the world said yes, and so more heads would roll. Diplomatic relations were not broken off, and it was the same with trade relations. In this regard we stood quite alone there on our isle of second sight. The Vatican signed a Concordat with the brownshirts. Christ and Antichrist ambled off arm-in-arm on the safe middle road.

As a child I worked up for myself a totally false conception of God, and that is why this life of mine on God's green earth has veered off in the oddest directions. My devout mother, concerned for the eternal salvation of her four children, detected signs of this oddity early on, and in her old age still finds repeated confirmation of her forebodings. I never became a true-blue Nazi, nor did I ever turn into what I like to refer to in summary fashion as a general manager, that is, somebody respectable and adaptable in human society. All I do is vegetate at the side of the road. Any passing goat can eat me up, any passing cartwheel can crush me. In a word, one that my own family is prone to use, I am a good-for-nothing. No marksman's badge, of no matter what regiment, decorates my chest.

When the burnt-out pastor of our home-town parish gave me that bang on the tongue with his St. Peter's key, my little edifice of inchoate, mystical faith came crashing down. No matter how hard I shoveled, I couldn't get rid of all the rubble, and in the ruins I recognized God. God had ceased to be a mysterious being, unapproachable, nameless, unthreatening, sacred and demonic. My innate longing for the darkness from which we all proceed led me to the path of poetry.

The world around me, the tiny world of a tiny town, kept on talking about God, but this wasn't the same God that I failed to stretch out my tongue far enough to receive. The war presented me with further problems that the curate who gave religious instruction at our school wasn't able to solve. Wasn't it blasphemy if "our" soldiers had the name of the Almighty on their belt buckles and, "God With Us," slit open the bellies of the Frenchies who weren't wearing such divine armor? It wasn't until years later that I realized that the Prussian King Friedrich Wilhelm's motto "God with us," cheaply reproduced by the millions in its metal belt-buckle version, was remarkable in religious history for being the only blasphemy ever to receive the imprimatur of all the churches. And wasn't it blasphemy to celebrate victories by bellowing forth the name of God? I had a lot of stupid questions like these, and the curate ended up by punishing me. He sent a written notice to my parents, and the religious school principal, the same man who was expecting to be named president of the "Rhenish Republic," had some devout advice for me: "My son, just don't confuse our teachers with pointless questions. If you keep this up, you'll never amount to anything, and that would be a real shame. Once you have outgrown school, you'll realize that there are certain questions that a person should ask only of himself. And you have to find the answers by yourself. Anybody else would have to lie about them. You got that, you little snot-nose?"

I lied and said, "Yes!"

In the tenth grade I switched to another "Christian" seat of learning. At this one the religion teacher had the title "Professor," and he was feared for the questions he asked during the tests at Easter. He never gave answers. He was just as unable as his curate colleague to tell me why God had singled out German bellies for wearing His slogan, and he drew a blank at other queries about things that gave me concern. Upon hearing my third hesitant inquiry, he made sure that I kept seated in class forever. From then on, he gave me the go-by. Erich, who sat next to me, likewise got the go-by. So there we forever sat, two hopeless but by no means mendacious cases.

The Kaiser gave up the war. Instead of counting the corpses, he counted his money and left the fatherland. In those days, George Grosz drew the crucified Christ wearing a gas mask. A storm of protest broke loose. The Belgian artist Albert Servaes delivered his Fourteen Stations of the Cross to their destination, the Carmelite church in Luythagen. Public indignation at this Expressionist depiction of the mystery of faith was so vehement that the Pope himself was asked to condemn the work. That was in 1919.

In 1933 Christ was nailed to the swastika amid the thundering jubilation of millions and the tacit approval of billions. People were not as narrow-minded as after the Imperial War. They all went along with this newest Expressionist work of art—all but a few of them, the obtuse art-lovers you can always find, the hecklers and fault-finders. Such people just don't count. Vigoleis and Beatrice didn't count, either. They got the go-by.

If on the day Hitler seized power all the people in Germany who called themselves Christians had acted in the spirit of Christianity, then this man made in the Lord's image would have wandered off into a sanatorium to be cared for at state expense until the end of his days. The *Führer* would be a case study for university professors, a laboratory specimen for students to learn from. But there were no more Christians in Germany. God was dead, Christ was dead, only the *Führer* was still alive. When people woke up from their frenzy and their rigid fast, it was too late. Heart failure.

The history of National Socialism can never be written as long as Christian hypocrisy persists. Such an invasion of pagan barbarism would not have been possible without the de-Christianization of Western Europe. But we are still far from realizing that ours is no longer a Christian world. Theology is still getting taught, and the name of God is still invoked for a morsel of bread. Bones are filled with gunpowder, and swords are forged in juicy streams of blood.

The year 1933 was also a milestone for us on our island. What business of ours was that mess, Don Matías asked, so far away from the scene? He was wrong. Hitler was no Don Patuco. Even though he could lift only one of his arms, that one arm of his reached much farther than the Honduran warrior's. Soon he had the island in his grasp. Fellow countrymen who every day made the sign of the swastika in the name of the divine *Führer*, Amen, wanted to kill Vigoleis and his suspiciously un-Aryan-looking Beatrice because we were refusing to tithe to the new God. Apart from the fact that it was filthy, we didn't believe one word of this swindle. We would sooner have believed the Beverwijn dog story. Mevrouw van Beverwijn herself immediately believed in the new Savior. She became angry once when I made fun of the *Führer* before an audience of female Christian Scientists. Many of these enthusiastic ladies, who were already piqued because Mamú didn't eject me from her house, be-came ominously starry-eyed whenever there was talk of the Redeemer of the

Germans. It wasn't possible just to keep silent about the man, as one did with Don Patuco. The Honduran wasn't one for counting corpses, either, but otherwise he seemed to me to be doing everything wrong, while Hitler was doing everything right. The German *Führer* had figured it all out right away: God is dead, not a single soul believes in Him any more, but they all keep on acting as if they did, so this is my big chance.

But what did Mamú think of all this *Führer* business? On this matter, too, she was marvelous. In spite of her millions, in spite of the important market for the baking powder that was still *her* baking powder, she rejected the Savior of Germany. She felt pity for the ladies of her bible-study circle, explaining that you can't change the ways of old spinsters. They had missed their chances all through their long lives, and now, as things were heating up, they were beginning to feel warm and cuddly. There was, Mamú added, a purely sexual explanation for this phenomenon. She was quite familiar with such symptoms of repression. She had known Freud very well, and often cited his opinions. Weren't the ladies getting enough satisfaction from their Biblical Jesus? Wasn't he beautiful, too? Mamú put her finger to her lips and said, "You bet your life!"

The nanny, who wanted nothing to do with Bible Science, but who came from the Black Forest, worshiped the *Führer* as a leader after her own heart, a heart grown senile in foreign climes. All at once she wanted nothing more than to return to Germany. And suddenly she perceived it as an ethnic disgrace that she had let herself be persuaded years ago by her mistress to become an American citizen. She constantly badgered Mamú to forbid us from entering the house, for she regarded it as the height of depravity to believe neither in God nor in the *Führer*. Mamú raised her wage and things stayed calm for a while.

The state's attorney, pleading his amatory case so poorly that he was still unable to hold Auma's conch shell to his ear in a way that would have been good for both of them, likewise declared for the *Führer*. Auma was against him. This increased the tension to the point where they began to hate each other at the same time that each one's unpolitical flesh desired the other's more than ever. The pair was approaching the boiling point. Mamú would have liked to toss them both into bed together—the way things like this got done in Vienna. But in Spain? Not on your life. I have no idea how the Finns handle such a situation.

At the *tertulia*, as I have mentioned, I was considered the spokesman for German destiny. They thought of me as something like a prophet, albeit a bad one. All I did was take at face value the daily pronouncements of the *Führer* and his propagandists, which pointed to war as the goal of all national uprisings. This was the reverse of insurrections of the Patuco variety, which begin with a ruckus that stirs up nationalistic emotions, which in turn don't last very long because they soon unleash just another ruckus.

Following extended flour-sack discussions, Matías and Gracias a Dios turned anti-Hitler and more and more pro-Patuco. Patuco: for them he meant

Honduran Liberty, Equality, Independence, the chance finally to marry those brides yearning for them so chastely all this long time, an end to their impotence one way or the other, peace at the point of a sword wielded by a doubly armored fist.

Pedro Sureda remained unmoved. German saber-rattling made just as little impression on him as had his soldier's colorful uniform. It simply wasn't his affair. Papá, on the other hand, was delighted. He thanked his lucky stars during his daily blood-letting that now he could read the *Völkischer Beobachter* in the original. He also approved of the Catholic Church's pact with the heathens. Our discussions got louder and louder. Finally I had to bellow like a Nazi to make myself understood through his stubborn horn.

The German shop adopted a wait-and-see attitude. A businessman must not show his political colors. The little Swabian maintained a busy silence. Two new arrivals, business partners of some kind, huge fellows, Germans from head to toe, sensed the profit to be earned by declaring in favor of the swastika. But they, too, kept their own counsel. There was jubilation in the palaces of the counts, the princes, and the vice-princes. Soon their own Don Francisco Franco would also be a *Führer*! And he was a general to boot, not some measly corporal. When that happened, woe to the sub-human Germans!

As a child, I often put carnivorous beetles in a box. In a very short time they ate each other up. I repeated this cruel experiment many times, because I just couldn't imagine that all of them would die. One of them, I thought, must stay alive: the strong guy, the hero, the Chosen One. If I had continued on with my research, I would have discovered the secret of Nature. But I just wasn't sadistic enough. The problem went unsolved. It was too dangerous to ask the curate or the professor of religion about it; they would have eaten me up. And so, after leaving school and in the years of my maturity, the answer was revealed to me by the current, future, and faded *Führers* of all countries.

Germans were leaving the Third Reich in droves, seeking refuge in the neighboring countries. Once resettled, they pondered their fate and the closely related question of money. Whoever could do so, moved on. Spain? Why not? You don't need coal there in winter time (they thought). And Mallorca? The island still enjoyed a reputation for its ideal climate and its even more ideal cheap living. Hospitality was somewhere in between, insofar as the islanders offered any hospitality at all. Refugees from Germany who found their way to Palma also soon made the further short journey to the Librería Alemana, and there they told their stories, countrymen to fellow countrymen. If they spoke with the easy-going Swabian proprietor of this bookshop, they were told to ask for directions to Barceló, just a few streets farther on. There, at No. 23, lived another German who could offer advice. No, not another emigré. This fellow was an old island hand, with very special island experiences.

The first victim of Hitler who was directed to my door was a Jew.

His case was resolved quite simply, and with a logic that could have led to the purest insights if it ever emerged from the obscurity it deserved.

The gentleman was about sixty years old, highly educated, as I soon found out, and dressed in black, so that he looked to me like a Catholic clergyman—which he in fact turned out to be. He had forsaken his rabbi and entered the One True Church of Christ. He took his first vows when he was nearing fifty. He had been a lawyer before he fell into the hands of "the false messenger of God." The Nazis wanted to lynch him because, as a Jew, he was hearing Aryan confessions. I told him that my uncle, a bishop, once was likewise almost lynched because he gave Extreme Unction to a construction worker who had fallen from a scaffold. Someone had summoned him to attend to a dying man. In such cases a priest doesn't ask, "Are you a Catholic?" The worker was a Jew, and the pious mob grew restive. My uncle came within an inch of being stoned. There was no lack of stones at the building site.

My story was no consolation for this emigrant priest. He refused to go back to the jungle. I began swearing at the Catholic Church for tolerating Hitler instead of excommunicating every Catholic who lifted his right arm. In his own particular case, the exemption bordered on the criminal. The convert didn't share my opinion. On the contrary, after arriving so quietly and submissively at my door, he suddenly broke out in a Jesuitical tirade that was not nice to behold. He defended Rome's position. The Church must survive, even if that meant marching over corpses—his own, for example: *Ad maiorem Dei gloriam...*

"Reverend Sir," I said, "why didn't you stay in the Reich? By now, you would be in the appropriate cadaverous condition. And why have you come to me? Did the little Swabian bookseller suggest that I could whisk you off painlessly into the Great Beyond? Or would you prefer that a silken rope be placed around your neck? Go visit the savages in Africa and get yourself converted once again, this time by your Protestant competition. The only thing left is poison. Right around the corner is a *farmacía*. For insomnia they'll give you veronal without a prescription. We don't have a bed for you here. But if you want to stay, we share meals and chairs in ancient Christian style."

If the Salvation Army had maintained a station on Mallorca, I would have sent this errant fellow to visit them. He wanted nothing more to do with his *confratres*. I spoke with one of the *padres* from the monastery across the street, and he offered to help out. But the Jew helped himself. In an obscure apartment house he took his own life. The matter was hushed up. Neither the secular nor the ecclesiastical authorities wanted anything to do with this *marrano*.

In fact, many emigrés now began throwing their lives away, which made them unpopular in foreign lands. First you welcomed them, and then they messed up your household and caused all kinds of trouble. They seemed unwilling to give any consideration to the locals.

Along with the first refugees, the first spies arrived on the island, followed by the murderers sent to rub out dangerous opponents of the National Uprising. Life again became exciting for Vigoleis and Beatrice. To swim against the tide, you need strong arms. We could have got as rich as Croesus—there was no lack of opportunity. Just lift your arm, Vigoleis, just pretend, and then cash in. Nobody is interested in what you really believe.

The first time I was asked to be an altar boy for Mass in the hospital chapel—I was ten—I admitted to the priest, who was also my friend and the principal of my school, that I hadn't yet learned the Latin responses by heart. An orphan boy had skipped his turn, and I was supposed to take his place. The priest then said—both of us already had our vestments on—"My son, just mumble any old thing. That's how I do it."

The prayers don't matter at all. If all the priests who stand at the altar believed in God, the Church would long since have gone up in smoke. The bell was rung, and I mumbled something inside my scrawny neck. Just pretend... I was well trained. To this very day, I am grateful to this priest for his candid advice at God's altar. So then why didn't I mumble *"Heil Hitler"* on Mallorca?

A new German Consul arrived. His predecessor was a pencil-pusher, a dyed-in-the-wool chargé d'affaires and bureaucrat, a conscientious public servant who always kept his stamp pads moist and wouldn't hurt a fly. In the colony he was known as "Potato Bud," because even in the golden sunlight he failed to get a tan, and always looked as if he had just been pulled out of long-term hibernation. This gentleman gave up his post, or it was given up for him, and then he washed his hands in innocence and went back to selling oranges wholesale. His successor, likewise, did not emerge from the bright sunlight, although he was brown—first to look at, and then by political conviction. Just a slight change of color, and he had it made. We got to know each other well. He stood far to the left, and started out as a minor employee in a travel office, good at languages and aiming high. He landed the job as director of the Agencia in Palma that I did my lying for as a *"Führer."* He approved, since that was a good way to be a *Führer*. For quite a while he worshiped the hammer and sickle, but then he discovered another path to salvation. I sought my own redemption first in poetry, then in roasts at Mamú's house. Later it appeared in the form of the donkey at the seaside castle of the Archduke, and again and again it was the bullfight. Many times we saved up money for the tickets by going hungry. Beatrice, clad in a *mantilla*, was transformed on such occasions into a genuine daughter of the Incas. As soon as the bovine colossus entered the white-hot ring, she lost all traces of her Basel origins and their ck-dt's.

One day the Consul summoned me to appear before him in his official capacity. Now completely brown, and very important as he sat there under a picture of the *Führer* and singing the *Führer's* praises, he gave me an official pronouncement: it was his duty to monitor me in the interest of the Party, and would I kindly sign this—some document or other declaring loyalty to the *Führer*, unconditionally. Without hesitation I left his office. Now the Consul knew what kind of person he was dealing with. "Don't leave out a single answer," he once said to me. I had answered every last question of his. But I wasn't shot on the spot, for the Consul knew what I knew—and since, to be clear about it, he was himself on the spot, he chose to be careful. All the more careful now, since during our first conversation I didn't hide from him the fact that I came from the same region of the homeland as Joseph Goebbels, that Goebbels and I once sat together—not in school but in the closer quarters of a university literature seminar—and that, as he no doubt realized, both Goebbels and I were failed poets and philosophers. I intimated that Goebbels and I were bosom buddies. From bosom embraces to denunciation is but a single step—Hagen's people! You don't have to be very bright to discover that in a regime of terror nobody trusts anybody else. That is why the Nazis didn't shoot us dozens of times. Spies never earned a penny on me or on Beatrice. We made no bones about calling the bastards bastards. And so the spies thought, "They must be spies!"

Otherwise the new Consul was a fine fellow. The *Führer* handed him a billy club for "monitoring" the Germans on the island—I'll say it in Nietzsche's words—with a blast of trumpets and with the connivance of the sheep, the jackass, the goose and everything else that was incurably stupid and loud-mouthed and ripe for the booby hatch of the Great Modern Idea.

Meanwhile, Martin Heidegger had added a new dimension of "submission to the fate" of his "being on hand" of existence by genuflecting before the *Führer*. And Thomas Mann, who had left Germany for good, sat in his villa on the shore of Lac Léman, taking good care of both of his aspects, as ter Braak put it: that of the artist and that of the bourgeois. There was quite a stir over the fact that he let his newest books appear in the S. Fischer publishing house in Berlin. With Heidegger we at least knew what the man was about. But with Thomas Mann? Few people understood, and nor did I.

Dr. ter Braak had given up his university chair to accept an appointment in The Hague as Henri Borel's successor as arts-and-literature editor for the prestigious newspaper *Het Vaderland*. He became one of the sharpest and cleverest opponents of the National Socialist doctrine of rancor, and over time earned a name for himself as a cultural philosopher. His books could no longer appear in Germany, nor could he himself—he would have been put to the sword. Busy with my Patucos and Uluas, I had forgotten that some of my translations from Dutch and Spanish, plus certain other literary jetsam, were languishing in German publishers' desk drawers. As soon as the *Führer* blew reveille, the troops mobilized for the Big Clean-Up. Publishers rushed to "coordinate" themselves, and Vigoleis was either returned to the sender or, in the form of manuscript, immolated in the mini-Auschwitz of the editor's office.

The first volume of Thomas Mann's *Egyptian Tales* was published by S. Fischer in Berlin. The book found its way to the *Vaderland* to be reviewed, and ter Braak sent it over to his local Amsterdam specialist for German literature, Dr. F. M. Huebner. The latter refused to review a book by a writer whose works were still appearing in Germany, but who was complaining about the *Führer* in foreign lands. Huebner was afraid he would be shot if he took on this prickly assignment. The Nazis gave no quarter. No one wants to get shot.

Ter Braak found a way to get what he wanted. He remembered his German translator on Mallorca, and sent him a telegram: would you be willing to send us reviews of books by German emigrants? I telegraphed back in the affirmative. I soon received a long letter explaining all the technical details of my cooperation. Ter Braak suggested that I choose a pseudonym to avoid getting shot. I agreed. Thus I opened up a little market stand at *Het Vaderland* under the innocuous name "Leopold Fabrizius." I wrote down exactly what I thought about every book and author that was sent to me. I didn't think very much of several of these, and I said so. Writers don't care a fig for what reviewers have to say, but publishers like to hear praise in superlatives; it makes good copy for blurbs. With certain other authors, I thought to myself, what a shame it was that the German emigration has nothing better to offer, and that some writers were being published simply because they were anti. Again and again I had to deal squarely with the problem of love for the fatherland, the homeland. How ridiculous such a feeling was, and how dangerous! Where does "the fatherland" begin? When is it synonymous with "home"? And when is it synonymous with—us?

Deported and emigrated writers were now everywhere, sharing the fate of a Heinrich Heine, a Ludwig Börne, and a Gracias a Dios. They wrote, and they kept on writing.

Again and again, the books I reviewed presented me with the opportunity for digressions about general human affairs. But what I wrote got interpreted politically. If I wrote that Hitler was guilty of crimes against humanity, the tritest expression of truth imaginable, I was wrong, and the editor scratched it out. Ter Braak then quickly sent me his apologies. He himself would have let it pass, but his *Vaderland* could not countenance any dishonoring of the head of state of a friendly nation. The Pope, too, was apparently among the infallibles, for when I was sent a novel that provoked me into making certain statements about a Concordat that drove millions of unsuspecting Catholics into the arms of the *Führer*, this too was excised. I'll admit that I expressed my opinion not in clever paraphrase, but in clear language: the Holy Father was handling his Divine Lord's monstrance as if it were a *sputino*, and acting with authentic Roman *grandezza*. It was censored out. I was told that I ought to have circumlocuted on this subject, in the style of Loyola—surely I could emulate that kind of prose. This may not have been the way for me to write, but it was definitely the way to act. Today I would no longer make such mistakes. I have learned a few things in the meantime, though not all that much.

Until May 1940, signing on as "Leopold Fabrizius," I kept open my stand on the Dutch *Vaderland* market square, sending in chronicles from Spanish, Swiss, French, and Portuguese "soil." My comments were always edited—apparently the mesh on my muzzle was always too wide. I forgot one thing: the Third Reich was a huge market for Dutch vegetables. Mr. van Beverwijn, the colonist, having got rich on sub-humans, was of the opinion that if Holland made the *Führer* angry—then what was to be done with all the cauliflower? The editors had no need to censor my final book review—that was taken care of by the friendly Dutch nation itself. And since the nation in question is known for its meticulousness, no one in Holland was surprised that their whole country got censored. Vigoleis-Fabrizius, who never considered himself intelligent, thought to himself: were the Dutchmen really so stupid? No, they were no more stupid than the French or the British. It's just that their market for vegetables was bigger than they were.

Before Menno ter Braak could be snagged by the Nazis, he took his own life, on the day in May of 1940 when the greatest consumer of Royal Dutch vegetables completely turned the tables on his neighboring country.

The Consul kept picking at me. Our relationship was reciprocal: I was a Leader for his tours, and yet he wanted to lead me. He was dealing with a stubborn guy, one of those who resist their own chances at happiness. He sent observers to my house, and they reported to him that I had no secrets. Everything was displayed out in the open, the poverty as well as the political opinions. So then the Consul decided to issue warnings. He waxed paternal and, while maintaining diplomatic severity, he remained almost friendly. He also outlined certain plans for me. It was a shame, he said, that I was getting nowhere with all my latent talent. My strengths ought to be put to use for the national movement in Germany. After all, the Reich was not shabby in its preferences. Now wouldn't that be grand, I said. The shabbiest of them all, refusing to be called shabby! My Spanish had become quite fluent, schooled as I was at *tertulias*, on flour sacks, and in daily converse with the Sureda family. One more reason, the Consul remarked, to place my tongue at the service of the *Führer*.

Instead, my tongue as well as my pen kept active against the *Führer*, with the result that our notions of what constituted hunger had to be expanded. In Germany, the Consul said, people would be put in jail for what I was up to, maybe even shot, and here on the island—he was warning me. He himself refrained from taking certain measures, but fellow party members, spies, and murderers were spread over all of Spain to rein in undesirable elements. And people were getting killed.

In our case, it began with a boycott. We suddenly noticed that our income was diminishing. The elegant people in the palaces started backing off. Had their daughters already learned enough? No, Pedro told us, but all over Palma we were rumored to be Communists. In stores we refused to buy German products, and for that we would have to pay. Communism always had to pay; the world was far from being able to afford such a luxury. Doors were getting closed at our approach. We were getting avoided like Don Juan Sureda's pack of dogs at sundown. Vigoleis, the Catholic German, and Doña Beatriz, that snobbish product of incest between Basel and Lake Titicaca, were finally unmasked: Communists! How cleverly these types worm their way into big capitalist houses and princely palaces! How well they know how to balance on three-legged chairs, with the intent of undermining society! Was society not yet hollow enough for them? And just consider the final blow they are aiming at—Christian Science, of all things! Can such goings-on be allowed to continue? That's what everybody was wondering, and with good reason.

Mamú was approached with the Christian admonition to bar us from crossing her threshold. The spokesperson was Madame van Beverwijn, and behold, she now had on her side her old seneschal, the miserable renal case who was impervious to any kind of prayer, and of course all the biddies. No "heretics" must ever enter a house where the Mother Church of Christian Science installed a Bible and a squeaky little organ! Every day they are committing sins against the *Führer* and capitalism—out with them!

Mamú, who liked to take charge, and who herself represented capital, even though the Royal Baking Gang was challenging her for it—Mamú was not intimidated. She wasn't afraid of us, and she wasn't afraid of the biddies, unless in their anger they decided to pray the stones back into her kidneys. In this regard Mamú was not so firmly convinced of the Christian motives of her clucking flock. She remained loyal to us even when we pleaded with her: "Let us depart in peace! Your house has become a place of worship, and we do not wish to make it into a scene of discord. Besides, your internal secretions are in danger. Those ladies are capable of anything."

"Upon my life, you stay!"

A German lady, wearing the swastika at her bosom and claiming to be the wife of the Swedish consul, was the first to leave the bible-study group on our account. Then some others strayed off; half a dozen of them. Then a dozen decided to go pray somewhere else. They were replaced by new recruits, including some who had fled Germany and had terrible things to report about the *Führer*: he didn't like Christian Science, and was persecuting them just like the Catholic Church, the PEN Club, the lodges, and the Rotarians! This came as a shock to Church Matron van Beverwijn. God was putting her to a severe test. While the pious old hags sang hymns in Mamú's salon and quarreled over the question whether the *Führer* was sent by God or perhaps by the Devil, the old gentleman with the ragged white beard and a Royal Dutch signet in his buttonhole sat beneath a palm tree in the park, day-dreaming of the headhunters back on Borneo. He praised the *Führer*, but he was honest and, oddly, smart enough to admit that this was all in the interest of vegetables and the Royal Dutch Bank.

Destiny is an octopus. It has many arms, and they are equipped for grasping. There was no need for the *Führer* to lift his own arm in order to shake the foundations of the Mother Church.

First there arrived an anonymous letter: Mamú's private church was stirring up unrest among the inhabitants of El Terreno. She must close her temple and desist from her blasphemous activities. Catholic Spain could not tolerate heathens. Signed: a Catholic Spaniard who reveres the Fatherland and the Church.

This threatening letter was tendered shortly before the divine service. Mamú, who was already seated in her matriarchal chair in the midst of her devout adepts, asked me to translate the text into English, the language used by the congregation. I did this slowly and with diabolical glee, and surely not without mistakes. The Scientific quails immediately started fluttering about like a row of hens—"Heathens? Us?!" A decrepit English spinster swooned and had to be carried to the kitchen, where the cook sprayed water on her. Most of the ladies simply wept at the bitterness of it all. "Us, heathens?" Yes, I said, *paganos* means heathens, no doubt about it. That's the "gentiles" of the Bible, the ones who were a thorn in Saint Paul's side.

Mevrouw van Beverwijn leaped up from her chair. As white as the biblical wall, she pointed directly at me and said: there he is, the low-down slanderer, the writer of that anonymous letter, Mamú's friend! She tore the letter from my hand—a grand gesture in this place of worship. I was trembling over my whole body, but before the pious hyenas that were still conscious could pounce on me and skin me alive, in my usual cowardly way I had already fled the scene—one more bit of evidence that I was the source of the evil calumnies.

Mamú groaned, and she, too, had to be ministered to. Auma and Beatrice assumed this duty. Everyone thought that Mamú was about to die, and she wouldn't have a beautiful death after all, giving up the ghost here, amidst swooning old ladies. Was this a sign from God? Wasn't it obvious that we were Communists? Out with them! Nevertheless, our Sunday roast tasted quite good.

No sooner had the flock reassembled on the following Sunday for devotional services, when a new calamity befell the bigoted band. Calpurnia, one of the housemaids, came running to the palm tree where we were chatting with old man Beverwijn. The local pastor had arrived and wished to speak with the mistress of the house. He couldn't be turned away. As soon as the maid made this announcement, the cassock-clad gentleman himself made his appearance. I introduced myself as a friend of the household and inquired as to the purpose of his visit. He had come to warn Mamú, and to request that she remove the church advertisement from her front door. Our pagan activities were causing ill-feeling all over the Terreno. The Spaniards, he said, had rather different ideas concerning the House of God. "I do, too," I replied, and asked the man of the cloth to follow me into the house. Like a wolf entering a herd of sheep, this certified man of God stepped among the heathens precisely at the moment when they began intoning a hymn of praise. One lady from Geneva, who possessed more Swiss francs than musical talent but whose son was a famous constitutional lawyer, was seated at the harmonium pumping away. Devoutly out of tune, the air entered the pipes amid jarring staccatos, for every now and then the lady gave herself a shot of morphine through her dress into one of her pumping legs—she had not yet been prayed free of her addiction—whereupon God's praises resounded anew in all registers. The saints sang away with a conviction exceeding that of the Bremen Town Musicians. Then it was quiet again: they caught sight of the man in black, plus the black-hearted Vigoleis.

The pastor delivered his message in French, tactfully and sympathetically. He was, he explained, a tolerant man, while other clergymen were less so, and the Church authorities least tolerant of all. The tablet at the front door would have to be removed, and the meetings would have to cease. He was aware of the heathen nature of Scientism, and he was willing to commend them all to the Lord's mercy. Praise be to Jesus Christ, he added. With my response, "To all eternity, Amen," the noontime phantasmagoria was at an end.

Nobody fell over dead, no one had to be resuscitated with a spray of water. And yet this was a fierce blow! God had once again sent a sign that worked out in Vigoleis' favor. Mevrouw van Beverwijn extended her hand to me and begged my pardon. She was willing to take back her accusations, and she was going to pray for me. She said this in Dutch, whereas English was the customary language for discussing God and His Science. I was happy to reply in the same tongue. "Mevrouw," I said, "please don't bother. My mother has been praying for me all her life, and it's never any use. I suggest that you pray for yourself instead. Ask your Creator to let you live long enough to see your friend Hitler start up his war, inundate your Dutch fatherland, and slaughter everyone who refuses to collaborate with the mighty Behemoth. When this happens, think of that poor fool Vigoleis on Mallorca, and think of this moment in Mamú's house. And if you still have enough strength and enough money in your bank account to go on believing in God, then say your prayers for the Kingdom of the Netherlands!"

"How marvelous," said Mamú as we treated ourselves to her Sunday meal. Once again José had outdone himself—which is to say, for the first time he prepared for us the legendary, ancient Mallorquin dish called *erissó*, using a secret recipe long thought to have disappeared. It was a sautéd sea-urchin of such delicacy that it seemed almost like a stroke of Divine Providence to be savoring it on the day of my Christian rehabilitation. "How marvelous were those things you said in my Mother Church!" But that business about Mevrouw's bank account—that was going a bit too far. Still, otherwise...

"Mamú, it's pretty obvious that Vigoleis is a priest manqué. If you can locate the proper church for him, he'll turn out to be an excellent confessor and proselytizer."

To accompany the *erissó* José offered a Portuguese vintage that grows in the sands near Collares. He always came out to serve special dishes himself. Mamú liked that.

IX

Beatrice kept slaving away in one of the palaces that stayed loyal to us, trying to teach a *señorita* whose kitty-cat memory couldn't retain a single item of vocabulary. The work didn't enlarge our income by much, since the girl's noble parents were so impoverished that they had no fear of the specter of Communism, and since their palace had already reverted to bank ownership. I kept seated at my machine and wrote for eternity. Then the man arrived.

Why deny your own name when standing in the doorway of your own apartment, if you aren't a crook? Yes, I was Vigoleis. And the man said triumphantly, "Finally!"

He was poorly dressed; short and skinny. He was draped in loose-fitting Mallorquin homespun. His cheeks were hollow, and he was unshaven. His hair was white, the skin of his hands sagged over the bones. He handed me a note, asking if I recognized and acknowledged the signature. I didn't recognize it; it was dark here in our *entrada*, and as for "acknowledge"—this began to sound like Zwingli. A tardy creditor? I felt that I had to humor him. "Sir," I said, "I'm glad you have come. I can inform you that Don Helvecio hasn't lived on the island for quite some time now. You see, he was dying, and he had himself transported to Switzerland so he could be treated by Professor Scheidegger, the detoxification expert. He's going to get well, and in his case that isn't just some medical figure of speech: you see, homeopathy..."

At this the man said, in a tone of indignation that I would never have expected from such a cockroach, "What are you talking about? Homeopathy? Don Helvecio?" That was none of his business, he had nothing to do with such stuff. Doña Beatriz had signed this piece of paper—was he at the correct address or wasn't he?

Beatrice, going into debt in my immaculate name? My heart stopped. This was serious. The daily rag in my home town used to publish humiliating notices sent in by respectable citizens, warning readers that they were not responsible for any transactions effected by their wives. How I empathized with the disgraced husbands, especially if I knew them personally! And now I was in the same kind of situation. Beatrice! I led the gentleman into our apartment.

First of all, he spat a wad on our floor. If I hadn't been so familiar with Spanish custom, I would have been doubly enraged by such contemptuous behavior. I'll wipe it up, I said to myself, before Beatrice arrives. Just don't let her arrive before I get to it, because no doubt she'll make a big scene. "Please," I said, "do have a seat. What can I do for you?"

The man not only had bad manners, he also was cruel and calculating. His explanation was so overwhelming that I had to lean against the wall to keep from falling over. In brief, he was demanding 3000 pesetas for a demolished piano. O whore Pilar! Your urge for revenge extends all across the ocean!

"Pay up!" the man said, "or else you'll face a court-sponsored auction of your belongings!"

I told him that I couldn't pay, which meant that everything would go under the hammer. Now in control of the situation, I said "Do what you have to!" How could I have been so petty as to suspect Beatrice?

The man stood up and said, "*Momento*"—a term readily understood by anyone. But what then happened was again incomprehensible. He went to the door and entered the corridor. Gone! I thought. I relaxed and wiped the floor. Now Beatrice could come back any time. But instead of Beatrice, it was the man himself who came back, with a bunch of other men in his train, strapping fellows, every inch of every one of them a Robert von Ranke Graves. I thought my final hour had arrived. But no matter how often and with what metaphysical yearning I might have longed for this moment, this wasn't at all what I expected.

The man said that he had given the matter further consideration. Court case? Enforced auction? Lawyers? All this was nonsense. We could earn the money for the piano ourselves. I immediately thought of Mamú's agonizing baking-powder affair: no, let's avoid a legal suit at all costs! The man nodded and made a sign to the others. They were well trained; muscle-bound though they were, they quickly assessed the situation in our apartment. Amid a banging of doors they carried what little we owned out of our *piso*. He was willing to leave us our bed, but wanted all our books. They weren't really worth anything, he said, but—at a wave of his hand the thugs headed for our makeshift bookcase. I rushed over to stop them. "Don't take those! I'll hand over our bed and my black dress suit!"

"As you wish. As it is, your junk will cover only one-sixth of what's due. I'll come back when you have settled in again." He bent down and tossed our doormat to his gang. We had owned it for three whole days.

Easy come, easy go. The expenses for lawyers and legal perquisites would have amounted to much more. That bloody whore!

"Is that bloody slut back on the island?" I asked when the man was already on the stairs.

"What do you mean, slut? There ain't no slut. The law's the law!"

"If the law's the law, how did you find out my address if Pilar didn't give it to you?"

"Make a note of this, Don Vigoleis. In Spain the worst evils are politics and the family! *Adios!*"

"The Nazis!" I thought. This was the *Führer*'s first attack on our private property! But he didn't get our books!

The damage, though hard to estimate and in any case not covered by insurance, was extensive enough to make one wring one's hands. I wrung mine all right, but not for long; this was a time for action. Beatrice must not get to see the filth all around our apartment. Like a licensed maintenance man I swept and wiped. The place was sparkling when Beatrice arrived, battered and mauled by her drudgery in the upper-crust palace, a line of work that she pursued with such energy that even her students took fright.

Catching sight of our empty apartment, did she think that I was going to surprise her with a relocation to a more respectable part of town, as in the golden days of our move from the Clock Tower? She spoke French, and that means that she felt dark premonitions. We walked across the apartment over to the room that had been our dormitory.—"Well?"

I let out a deep sigh and explained to my *chérie* that it would have been best if we had jumped into the sea from our Leucadian Cliff. That way, the long arm of the *Führer* never could have reached us.

"The *Führer*?" Beatrice had tears in her eyes, and more tears were dripping down her cheeks; one of them fell on our spic-and-span *ladrillo*, and she wiped it up.

"The Nazis, my dear. The *Führer*'s cossacks sent a piano man over here with a demand for 3000 pesetas for your wrecked piano. I took care of the matter and prevented a legal suit that would have cost us a whole lot of money and trouble. This *encargado* said that after we got settled back in he would come back, then four more times, and then the whole thing would be paid off. But by that time Hitler will have had us shot. What happened today is just a warning. You watch, this is only the beginning."

"That's just about what I was thinking."

This was a stroke of luck in the midst of disaster. For whenever Beatrice "just about" anticipated some calamity, we were already on our way to preventing it from happening. What, she asked, was I suggesting that we do?

"All I need to do is say the word, *chérie*, and the Consul will offer me a job in the party's foreign service: Madrid, Barcelona. He has said so several times, and there's no doubt about it. 1000 pesetas a month, minimum. We could leave this place. The piano man wouldn't get a cent."

"*Jamais*!" Beatrice said.

"*Nunca jamás*!" I replied, using the more emphatic Spanish expression of denial.

That night we slept on a pile of clothes. We could have asked Mamú for help, but Mamú was having trouble enough of her own. The split within the Mother Church was getting more serious. She had received upsetting news from her lawyer in New York. Her daughter in Budapest reported that her lecherous brother-in-law had booked some more children on Mamú's family charity account. Her attorney in Vienna announced that the mortgage payments on her little palace would no longer cover the increasing expenses. Mamú was desperate. This time I told her that she should insist that the dirty old man in Hungary wear a permanent chastity apron, or she would cut off his funds. Mamú didn't know what a chastity apron was. I gave her a historical explanation, adducing the Etruscans. She thought that the image, when applied to her brother-in-law, was quaint, and she perked up a bit. She hadn't come to Barceló Street for several weeks—why discuss menus when there's no money to pay for the ingredients? Pigeons from Brindisi, morays from Tartessos, cranes from Milo—all this was past history. Without compromising his art, José was having to make do with the local fare. It was all right with us that Mamú didn't visit us any more; we just couldn't ask her to sit on a wooden box.

Pedro was speechless at our naïveté—more specifically, at mine. That piano man would have been satisfied with a single chair, provided that I had promised him all the rest with the great eloquence I was surely in command of. What a failure! And I had been in the country for such a long time! Pedro shook me. "We're going to go see that man. It's not too late yet. I know the company. Lladó pianos are famous. It's an old company, right nearby on Rambla, right-hand side."

Inside the spacious hall at street level there were many instruments in various stages of playability. A very old lady was sitting in a wing-back chair in the middle of this world of music. She was paralyzed, and wore a straw-colored wig that made no pretensions to authenticity. Right away, like the monkey Beppo, I felt an urge to swipe it from her head. She was the piano company's inheritor, and the piano man was only her factotum. He built, sold, and auctioned off the instruments. Evidently, the company was not having the best of times. The lame old lady was very friendly. With the healthy half of her body she pointed out a few instruments that were already varnished. She thought we had come to buy or rent a piano. She pounded the floor with her cane, at which sign my piano man came shuffling over, the same *encargado* with whom I had concluded our friendly financial settlement. Pedro, the born haggler, took the man aside. He pointed over to me. The man scratched himself in several places, nodded his head wordlessly, and then came over and shook my hand. I was, he said begging my pardon, a big idiot. Why hadn't I protested? Turning then to Pedro, he reported that I had said, "Do what you have to," and so he brought in the movers. The lame lady nodded. She was very attentive, knew exactly what was going on, and agreed to everything. Several times she raised her good hand to an itchy spot in her wig—an odd, touching regression to the times when she still sported a full head of hair.

Unfortunately, the man had already sold the ruins of our piano for junk, making less profit on it than he had expected. He was disconsolate about this sad affair that involved, as usual, a whore and high-level politics, but what was he to do? Here, too, Pedro knew just what was to be done. Lladó & Co., Pianos Lladó, Palma de Mallorca, Baleares, gold and silver medals, etc., must place a Lladó at the disposal of the plaintiff Don Vigoleis on behalf of Doña Beatriz, pianist, pupil of Juliusz Wolfsohn. No rent would be charged during the first months—this would count as restitution for the hasty removal of private property. Doña Beatriz had come to select an instrument. The man agreed, and was greatly relieved. Full of bluster and self-assurance when he first arrived at our apartment, now he was suddenly pliant and deferential. His only aim, he said, was to serve art. The old lady nodded and scratched herself once again at the place where, a half-century before, she felt an itch. The smashed piano was now likewise a thing of the past.

Stepping out onto the Paseo de la Rambla, I ventured the opinion that the piano man was crazy. "No," said Pedro, "but he's well on his way to getting there. All of us here on the island face that prospect. Whenever people get that far, there's not much that can be done about it. The best time is the transitional phase. Papá has got worse over the last few years. You haven't noticed because you didn't know him in his great period."

As a matter of fact, the piano man later became a clinical case of insanity, as Joaquín Verdaguer told me when I asked. "*Se volvió loco. La fábrica ya no existe*"—gone mad, the company doesn't exist any more. Period.

A few weeks later some men came by and, using a huge belt, heaved a Lladó into our apartment. The emptiness there was extraordinarily beneficial for the acoustics. Day by day, Beatrice's playing kept the name of Lladó alive and well. But first, another man arrived.

This other man was a gentleman who did not spit and did not scratch himself anywhere. He was tall, well-fed, robust, nattily dressed in an expensive tropical suit, and carried a briefcase that was too large for a traveling salesman and too small for a captain of industry. What did he want of me? Was he an insurance man? Unlikely. Such companies employ agents who dress differently depending on the clientele they serve. This visitor didn't seem to be observing any rules of social mimicry. Was he a writer hoping I would type a manuscript? That would be a blessing. The piano man hadn't taken away my typewriter— I told him that it wasn't my property, that I was paying off installments on it. Businesses are willing to respect such arrangements. No, this new gentleman was not a writer in my exalted sense of the term. He came from the Reich; the Consul had sent him to me with greetings and a cordial inquiry as to how things were going. As he spoke these words I led him into our bare living quarters, and he looked around with quizzical glances. I hastened to ask him to ignore the sparseness of our surroundings, adding that we were expecting painters to arrive tomorrow to do the whole flat. Tomorrow? Well, within the next few days; here in Spain one must learn to be patient.

The gentleman from the Reich: "Our Consul has not misinformed me. Your situation is lousy, and you have a certain quick-wittedness about you. Painters or paper hangers tomorrow? Clever of you. That's why I'm here."

I: "Begging your pardon, but a person is either quick-witted or he isn't. By saying I have a 'certain' quick-wittedness you're offering me the chance for a retort. Do have a seat." I gestured toward a wooden box. The gentleman sat down.

The gentleman: "Excellent. You're my man. Permit me to explain what I have in mind and to show you some documents. May I spread them out here on the floor?"

I: "By all means. Do what you can under the circumstances."

The gentleman from the Reich was a member of the Party, Old Guard, Honorary Dagger, Blood League, Street-Fighting Ribbon. He also held a doctorate that, while earned under the former regime, still came in handy. He held a high position, if not the very highest, in the Executive Commission of the Hamburg branch of the National Socialist Party Foreign Service. He presented his credentials, taking his long pencil and pointing to documents as he set them down on the stone floor tiles. I began to take a liking to this fellow; he had a sense of humor. He had arrived from the embassy in Madrid where, if memory serves me correctly, a certain Count Welsceck represented the interests of the swastika.

"Well?"

"You'll see in just a moment. I'll take things up one step at a time."

This he did with aplomb, displaying papers that gradually covered almost our whole living-room floor. They were looking for someone with attested verbal and written fluency, in particular someone with command of Spanish, preferably with a university education, well-mannered, confident, good conversationalist, imaginative, neat appearance, married—preferably to a Spanish woman, under no circumstances to a German. That's the kind of person they were looking for.

"Wonderful, wonderful," I said. "It's an enviable man who could meet all of your qualifications. What do you have in mind for such a person?"

This person, the gentleman explained, would be put in charge of a German newspaper in Madrid. In addition, he would be sent on lecture tours throughout Spain, speaking at the German enclaves and also to audiences of Spaniards. The Consul in Palma, who like all consuls was asked to provide information, had submitted my name along with certain personal data that had been supplemented by research at the office in Hamburg. The agent took some more documents from his briefcase and passed them to me. "Here, have a look."

I read the material slowly and with deliberate care. Apart from minor details, everything was accurate as concerned my several failed attempts at fashioning a career, although a few facts were jumbled up. It was true that I had taken theology courses in Münster, but theology was not my main field. "Good work," I said as I placed the incriminating documents on the floor next to the other papers, "except for one thing: the Consul has neglected to inform you that I am an outspoken opponent of your *Führer*. I am unwilling to go along, and he knows that."

The gentleman reached once again into his briefcase and pulled out some papers that he kept in his hand. "I'm afraid you are mistaken. As a matter of fact the Consul did report this to us, and besides, we are in possession of a political assessment of your person, provided by the authorities in your home town. They are keeping an eye on you there, too, in connection with your correspondence. Your father has already been issued a warning."

"I'm aware of that. But that is his own business."

"That depends. We offer no quarter." He had decided to come over from the mainland, he explained further, to speak with me in person, since of all the candidates recommended to him I seemed the most qualified. My uncle was a bishop. I was imaginative, no question about it. This he knew from confiscated personal letters as well as from satirical poems—here a quick glance at new documents—in the collection entitled "Party Comrade Newt." These poems were evidence of genuine talent, although it was talent that had been expended in a void. At the word "void" he again looked around him in our empty apartment. This fellow also had talent, but perhaps he didn't have an uncle who was a bishop.

The mention of the name "Newt" made me a bit worried. I had circulated a series of rhymed satires, among them "Party Comrade Newt" with swastika, honorary dagger, and "bloody claims / to achieve the *Führer*'s aims," who behaves like a wild man and, in the final stanza, "joins up with the vultures / to honor Western culture." Damn it all, they must have found this out! And I will be really in the soup if these guys know that I am the writer of a parody of the Horst Wessel Song.

I was poor, the Reich Commissioner continued, as the result of matters beyond my control. My wife, or the lady I was living with, was, to be sure, not Spanish, but she held Swiss citizenship, came from a well-known dynasty of scholars, and was of partly Indian ancestry...

"And if the Incas, Herr Doktor, were not of Aryan stock? That would be the end of the whole matter!"

"It is not as you might think. You would of course have to marry, not on our account, but because of the Spaniards, their society, and the Church. The Inca question will be decided by the appropriate government commission. You needn't have any concern on that score. Who is and is not an Aryan—that is determined by the *Führer*."

We agreed upon the following: I would take the position in Madrid with a starting salary of 1000 pesetas per month, free rent with furnishings of my own choosing, an advance of so-and-so-many times 1000 pesetas, all expenses to be borne by the Reich. Once a year I would be expected to travel to Hamburg to deliver a personal report, rail first-class, all expenses paid, two months vacation per year, free travel on all lines of the German National Railway, and on non-German lines 60% discount in the form of travel vouchers. Moving expenses? They would be reimbursed, of course. We both smiled. We quickly understood where both of us stood.

"Do you have any further questions? Anything else you would like to add?"

I stood up and said very calmly, "I have only one further question. Just what gives you the nerve to come here and throw me this line of hogwash? Please leave our house at once!"

Vigoleis was courageous. How did this come about? Had he been drinking *cascarilla*? Was Don Patuco exerting heroic remote control on him? This was the same Vigoleis who took it on the lam when he saw Pilar's dagger, who ate a sumptuous final meal instead of jumping in the ocean, who handed over all his property to a half-demented auctioneer, who suffers hunger and goes on a grape diet, who doesn't own a bed, who hasn't finished typing out *Claudius, Emperor and God*, and how can he go on typing without a table to type on? And now comes the Third Reich in the shape of a man with titles, decorations, legal prerogatives, and money—heaps of money—and says to him, Vigoleis, we don't care what you think of our *Führer*. It's what you can make others think of him—that's what we're willing to pay you for, because we have a billion times billions. If he just would say the word, Vigoleis could name Beatrice as his secretary, his own private secretary, the kind that people have who have something to hide, and the 500 pesetas per month could easily be arranged. And this is the same Vigolo who now stands up, calmly makes a pile of the papers on the floor with his foot, and says, "Get the hell out of here!" Has he gone mad? Was he already a victim of the insular malady?

The man from the Reich remained seated, lit a cigarette, and leaned comfortably against the wall. "You have courage, too. That's important. I shall give the *Führer* a personal report on our conversation. He is..."

Screaming now, I told this guy that if he didn't leave at once I would throw him out. And then the happy phrase suddenly occurred to me like a cue from out of my subconscious, where it had lain dormant for years. "Get a move on!"

During this historical, courageous moment in my life, my vision suddenly blurred. I saw before me the image of three clenched fists: the double fist of the Honduran general, and the no less frighteningly cramped fist of my brother Jupp—*Oh childhood, oh disappearing world of charm*! The Nazi recruiter must have also seen this last magical fist getting clenched, for before I could shout my thundering threat for the third time, this time in a powerful baritone, as if I myself were the master and he the muzhik, the slave, the ox under the yoke, the man had already tossed all the documents into his briefcase and snatched up his hat. At first trying the wrong door, since our place was uniformly empty, he finally hurried away muttering dismal threats. I shall refrain from recording those threats here, for we shall later have the opportunity to recount how they were put into practice.

The Reich Commissioner left his cigarette case—it was made of pure gold—on our book crate. Without claiming a reward, I returned it the next day to the consulate. But the gentleman had not forgotten to take his precipitous leave with a ringing "*Heil Hitler*!"

Beatrice came home earlier than usual, so I didn't have time to polish the floor. With her strange notions of floors and how to walk on them, she immediately reached for the waxing mop. I gave her the latest news, explaining that once again I had just tossed out the window a com-pletely furnished apartment, 1000 pesetas a month, and a genuine Reich Commissioner.

Beatrice sniffed, catching the aroma of the expensive cigarette.

"Bullet-proof vests—that's the first thing we have to go out and buy. Right now that's more important than a bed."

I begged to differ. Bullet-proof vests? Nonsense. On this island the Nazis are using poison.

My prediction that in the long run events here would not at all turn out to be terrifying appears to be incorrect, for long before the Civil War broke out, we arrived in very dire straits. Have I consciously misled my reader in order to keep up his interest? And what's with that boastful business in my Prologue about "my having a say in the matter"?

That's not working very well. For one thing, I have overestimated my powers of memory, and for another, I have underestimated the Nazis. Yet in order to detoxify the atmosphere I shall now introduce a harmless youth who also smokes expensive cheroots from a golden quiver. He will get a chapter all his own, and even his own chair to sit on.

X

The youth's name is Hutchinson, George Brewis Hutchinson. "George" is common enough, there's nothing special about it. But "Brewis" was a Christian name I had never heard of. I learned that it meant "brew," as in soup— a kind of bouillon from meat extract. And this was the name he went by.

He's an American, he's consumptive, he is in possession of a college degree from Princeton University, as well as of a head of fiery-red hair that would be the envy of any woman who sought salvation in cosmetic rinses. But perhaps it is best if I put all of this in the past tense, for he died long ago. His tuberculosis was not of the benign sort, and he was given to profligate habits beyond those of the intellectual kind. It even seems likely that it was his organic degeneration that drove him into an adventurous life with women, with a knowledge of eternal, transcendent matters, and, for that matter, with the likes of Vigoleis. Yet we shall not allow suppositions concerning his later destiny to prompt our memorializing of the man by name. The split within his personality was at the time so marked that it could have given rise to all kinds of misdeeds. Besides, in these recollections every person makes his appearance with the features that he himself presented to me.

No, I have nothing scandalous to report about this young man, no incidents that would prompt the future student at a German university to cross swords with me or, since he was a Catholic, to engage me in fisticuffs. Quite the contrary: I owe to him the idea for one of my inventions. My inventions! They would deserve an entire chapter of my recollections, but here I shall mention them only in passing. Vigoleisian inventions have not taken human progress a single step further, but only because they have never been put to practical use as I conceived them. In cases where they have benefited civilization anyway, such as gunpowder, they were invented by someone else. Nevertheless, I have repeatedly experienced the elation of creative moments, and that is what is most important to me.

While I'm at it, I should add that right at the beginning of Hitler's war I got a whiff of the whole tragedy of Vigoleis' career as a failed inventor. The two of us, every day becoming more and more stateless as victims of the brown behemoth, anxiously followed the reports of the increasing threat posed by German U-boats. In those days we were living with tacit political reservations, but with personal security, in Portugal at the viticultural and poetic Pascoaes Castle, a name that has already made fleeting appearances in these pages. The master's aged mother—she was approaching one hundred—liked to gather numerous important people at her hospitable table—to the consternation of her son, who constantly tried to avoid such invasions, many of which occurred with the purpose of seeing him up close, the great mystic, and listening to his prophetic pronouncements.

At one of these magnificently improvised meals, arranged by the fascinatingly ugly, perky, and almost dwarf-sized Doña Carlota, the widow of the last peer of the last King of Portugal, I had the opportunity to expound, to an audience of several dozen attentive listeners, my theory of underwater breathing mechanisms in diving vessels. My ideas arose during the act of speaking, from sheer ad-hoc inspiration. It was a display of technology tinged with mysticism, abetted by my consumption of exquisite food and drink—or did I not owe my eloquence, rather, to Justina, the head cook, who may have been in league with the Devil and his Black Art of culinary wiles? My solution to the problem was as follows: build anti-submarines with a long hose attached to a buoy floating on the surface. The hose would serve as an extended air passage for renewing the oxygen supply, obviating the need for the vessel to surface. I vividly recall that I got this idea from seeing Doña Carlota's garden hose, several hundred meters long, lying totally useless in her yard summer and winter with a thousand punctures and leaks, stretching from her *fonte dos golfinhos* to her beds of roses and groves of fig trees, an element of Nature like a root or a vine. My lecture, which I illustrated with clever waving of my table napkin, made sense to many of my listeners. A navy lieutenant in particular, who was famous for having suppressed an uprising on the island of Madeira within firing range of his pocket destroyer, nodded in assent. Dependent as I am on an echo for igniting the spark of my inspiration, I got more and more excited. After just one or two more gulps of wine my invention was complete. It was up to the admiralty to put the thing into practice.

Accordingly, I expressed the desire to rush immediately to Lisbon, about 500 kilometers from the scene of my hydrostatic "Eureka!" using the *senhora's* automobile—with her kind permission, of course. I would go to the capital and visit the British Embassy, where I would offer His Majesty's Navy my invention, still warm from the incubator and as belated thanks for my evacuation from the Island of Second Sight. That trip would mean the triumph of my idea. But this request of mine had a sobering effect on the assembled dinner guests. As raptly attentive as they had been during my presentation, now they began to think I was crazy. They whispered to each other that I was a jokester, a comical fellow who had gone through all kinds of madcap experiences on the island and who was obviously capable of creating such antics right here and now. At this moment the little dinner waiter Victorino was serving the guests backwards with his right hand, because with his left hand he was trying to cover a hole in his trousers, although his white glove was just as conspicuous as the shirt flap it was meant to conceal. The guests urged him to refill my glass. No one was willing to court embarrassment among the higher authorities on my account. All of a sudden the Pascoaes Castle, normally the scene of all kinds of excess, became a bastion of prudence. This turn of events quickly sobered me up, too. And as always when I have plunged from the heights of creativity, I considered both myself and my brainchild completely bonkers. I mumbled something about the *ratonera speculum* of the poet Pio Baroja (a mousetrap invented by the poet, designed to make the animal fall on its mirror image), and reached for consolation to the source of my inspiration, the dinner oporto, the wine from the sands of Collares that we already knew from Mamú's table, and the heady, fruity *Vinho Verde* from Pascoaes' own castle vineyard, a label already familiar to us from feasts at Mamú's. Pascoaes, an Icarus-type himself, reassured me by referring to that misunderstood mythical genius, and by holding forth on the dubiousness and futility of all technological activity, a subject that looms large in his works. Be that as it may, he writes these works not by candlelight or in the glassy twilight of the tear-shaped lamps he praises so often, but beneath a naked 100-watt Philips bulb.

Everyone knows that the "snorkel" was invented and deployed a few years later by the German Navy. There can be no question of a theft of intellectual property—or was my idea somehow leaked from the dining hall of the Casa de Pascoaes to the *Führer's* main headquarters? Besides, the British naval attaché would hardly have considered me a "man of the moment." *Enfin*, you are a clever inventor, Vigoleis, but what has all this got to do with the youth who was supposed to be the subject of this chapter? Well, not much, I'll admit. This youth was the point of departure for another kind of snorkeling expedition, one that can once again reveal the melancholy misapprehension of intellectual endeavor. And the fellow who came away from it in sobered condition couldn't even seek solace in a wine glass.

I think it was a morning in November. At any rate I am certain that the first year of the Third Reich was not yet behind us, and I was standing on the jetty that stretched far out into the Bay of Palma, watching intently the difficult docking maneuver of the Ciuda de Palma, which ferried passengers to and from the mainland. I was expecting a guest I had been corresponding with on literary matters, but whom I had never met in person. The person in question was the writer Albert Helman, whom I have mentioned before. His pseudonym was by this time as transparent as the secrets it was meant to conceal. Disgusted with the culture of Holland—he was a native of Surinam—he was living in voluntary exile, perhaps the bitterest form of banishment, on a hilltop near Barcelona, out in the uplands of San Cugar del Vallés. A few days earlier I had received a postcard in his minuscule hand, announcing his arrival. He would be sailing with the *Ciudad de Palma*, and I would recognize him by means of an albatross. I found this odd—not because of the animal qua animal, but because of this particular animal. We can never visualize Saint Jerome without his lion from the Desert of Chalcis. The writer of the Apocalypse is often depicted with an eagle hovering above his head. Bjørnstjerne Bjørnson has entered literary history with his cockatoos and his araras, which were most definitely not his inspiring muses, as one envious rival once claimed. Minnesingers look out at us from the illuminated manuscripts carrying sparrow-hawks on their outstretched fingers—so why not Helman with an animal, too? But an albatross? He would be carrying the bird under his arm, if I had understood his postcard correctly. I knew the West Indian stories by this exotic fellow, *Het euvel gods*, and above all his masterpiece, the dramatic short novel *Mijn aap schreit*. Thinking analogically, I expected that if the writer were indeed accompanied by an animal, it would be with his pitiful monkey on one shoulder. Yet ever in search of variety—this was his lot in life—he had no doubt traded in his humanoid pet for the bird that traverses the world's oceans. The very idea of domesticating such an animal was enough to command deep respect. Be that as it may, monkey or albatross, it would be well-nigh impossible to mistake him as he stepped out on the gangplank.

Meantime the docking process finished. Many people streamed forth on land, especially foreigners, for Mallorca was getting more and more popular. The international travel agencies were touting the Balearics as a rendezvous for their customers. Only a few proud Spaniards could be sighted among the passengers, and most of these were carrying turkeys under their arms, culinary delicacies that they snapped up more cheaply on the mainland than on the island. I have already mentioned that the *pavo* is the Spanish equivalent of the Northern European holiday goose. Tied by foot to an apartment balcony, the incessantly gobbling turkey cocks are force-fed in the open air. You need only to have spent the season of Advent in the old section of a Spanish city, gobbled at from every level of houses whose balconies feature cacophonous turkey debates from early morning to sundown, to prefer the Feast of the Resurrection of the Lord and its festive bullfights to the miracle of the Savior's Birth. For long before the wattled bird has been shoved into the baker's oven, you have become so heartily angry at the beasts that you lose all the joy of the meal.

In any case, if Helman had chosen a turkey instead of an albatross as a poetic travel companion, I would have had a very hard time picking him out in the crowd. Assisted by my buddy Pepe, a harbor rat from Barceló Street, I kept a strict lookout for the fowler from the West Indian jungle, but we espied not a single poetic personage with an albatross under his arm. But wait! Maybe he had the bird attached to a string like a kid's balloon, so it could circle around in the air above everybody on the dock! If we followed the string down to the man's finger, it would be a simple matter to single out our exotic traveler from amongst the surging masses at dockside. Pepe must have been thinking the same thing, for we both looked upwards to the shimmering white sky, where the only circling fauna were the squawking seagulls, none of them connected by a string to anyone's finger. I was about to turn on my heel and leave the scene when Pepe tugged my sleeve and pointed to a distinguished-looking gentleman, and I mean a truly elegant fellow. Like all street loiterers, Pepe had a weakness for distinguished-looking persons. Was this the guest I was expecting? The young gentleman strode down the gangplank, but minus any pet animal. We kept him in sight.

He was wearing a light-grey felt hat, the hairy kind preferred by the British, on a full head of fiery-red hair, shiny black shoes with white spats and, apparently in studied color combination, a leather greatcoat with a fox-pelt collar the same color as his hair. This coat would be the envy of any East-Elbian landowner, even down here at 40° latitude, if it were not for the fact that wolf-skin had meantime become the swashbuckling fashion in such circles. In his left hand our man was carrying a suitcase. And what did I see? It was unquestionably a Saratoga bag, all the more certainly since a colorful serape, looped casually through the handle, was hanging down almost to the ground. I must confess with shame that up to that moment I had known such items of baggage only from novels and from a crazy journey once undertaken by Don Juan Sureda. Today I myself own a Saratoga travel bag, and while it may be an exaggerated sense of possessiveness on my part, and although it is long since cracked in several places, I would not give it away for anything. This unique object came to me from the Brazilian estate of Count Werner von der Schulenburg, who at the time was still among the living. He was a member of the Protestant branch of the family, and upon another occasion I shall tell the story of how I inherited his possessions *ante mortem*.

Pepe and I were the only ones who were slaking our boundless curiosity by observing this unmistakably dandyish personality. Both of us were loiterers with higher aims in life. Pepito's ambitions were confined, enviably, to doing nothing at all, whereas I, a wretched practitioner of German thoroughness, was still aiming to achieve nothingness by means of action. Our friendship can be explained on the basis of this concept of *nada*, and our camaraderie lasted until Pepe's death when the Civil War demanded its hecatombs.

The finery worn by this foreigner, who wasn't Helman, was just as poorly adapted to the climate as the pith helmet sported by the German who descended the gangplank right behind him. But in contrast to such headgear, he at least didn't seem ridiculous. This fellow in the greatcoat had style; he exuded the special charm you can encounter in the works of the Portuguese novelist Eça de Queiroz. In his free hand he carried an open wallet out of which, with magical motions of his fingers, he was compensating for whatever he lacked in familiarity with *1000 Words of Spanish*. He evidently lacked a great deal, to judge from the number of coins he dropped into the palms of the fellows who always stand in wait at landing piers. He was distributing pesetas in a way that I have always imagined stock dividends getting distributed. To this very day I regret that my personal destiny has been that of a floundering loiterer among mankind rather than a prosperous stockholder or pension swindler.

There I stood, agape. There Pepe stood, agape. Another Spaniard came down the gangplank, holding his *pavo* so tightly under his arm that the wart-covered bird was pale with near-asphyxiation. Then came a spindly English lady, carefully tapping her way down the plank with her umbrella. Next, a few porters, a pile of baggage, and suddenly the *Ciudad de Palma* was empty. No sign of Albert Helman. On the way back home I couldn't help thinking of that young fellow in the fox-trimmed overcoat who had set foot on our island bearing a quite amazing suitcase.

A few days later I received another note in Helman's handwriting. This time it was a letter with a musical emblem printed at the top that made me think of boy-scouting, a mode of existence that is completely lacking in Helman, either genonymously or pseudonymously. Indeed, in spite of his extensive travels and his cosmopolitan ways he is anything but a guitar-strumming hiker in this world. The letter bore the cancellation: Valldemosa. The writer expressed his regrets at not having met me at the pier, and since the only address he had for me was that of my post-office box, he was unable to look me up. Now he would be expecting me at such-and-such a time at the Café Alhambra. I would recognize him by the means he had previously indicated, except that this time the albatross would be lying open on the marble table at which I would easily find him, although I might mistake him for a Spaniard.

The albatross on the table?! Open?! Had he slaughtered the bird? His jungle instincts had obviously won out, finally smothering his sense of Western high culture. But before I collapsed from fright at the thought, before I could envision a writer tearing the heart out of his Muse in the cruel Mayan cult of his race, the scales suddenly fell from my eyes: Helman's albatross was a book. It had to be a book! And with the jubilation of a triumphant explorer I cried out to Beatrice, "Beatrice, Helman's albatross is a book! The writer is traveling with a book!"

"Of course it's a book. An Albatross Edition. What did you think it was?"

Of course it's a book. A writer travels with a book, not with a *puta* or with an animal under his arm. I was the incorrigible ignoramus, a guy eternally slow on the uptake and with frightful gaps in his education that were embarrassing even amid an ambience of palm trees. This was the year 1933, I was already thirty years of age, and I still hadn't realized that books got printed in editions other than the old Tauchnitz series. As yet I knew nothing of the growing menagerie of animals in the publishing world: the Penguins, Zebras, Albatrosses, Salamanders, Kangaroos, Bantam hens, and Owls. What is more, if I may be permitted this damning admission, I was fully conscious of my ignorance. Such willful stupidity is bound to backfire sooner or later. It can get you into unpleasant situations, and is easily misunderstood. There is always somebody ready to raise a finger and single you out as woefully uninformed. For Vigoleis the only remaining pious consolation lies in occasionally being ahead of the others on the basis of his second, prophetic sight, not the sight that peers through the eye-slits of a mask. For instance, at this very moment I have a feeling that somewhere in the world a publisher, bankrupt from trying to sell volumes by precocious young poets, is preparing a series called "Mole Editions," with which he will blindly attempt to tunnel through the steadily increasing mounds of masterpieces of world literature, in the process throwing up mounds of his own that will indicate exactly where the digging is good, with the result that literary merchants from all continents will follow him with their shovels at the ready. Poor Vigoleis! You can have such vague dreams, but your mediocre education has blinded you to what any educated man should know.

Having now mentioned this gap in my education, I sense that the moment has once again arrived for my reader—whom I continue to address, although he ought not to concern me personally at all, in a style that was common and pleasing in a past century—to confront me with the vexing question of just what an unfortunate gap in my education and my relations with the writer Helman—whom I met at the appointed hour at the Café Alhambra, seated with the mien of an intellectual and with Spanish nonchalance at a marble table, a modern-day Ancient Mariner casting his roving eye past his Albatross toward any stunning female who might enter the premises—it's again time for my reader to inquire just what these topics might have to do with the young man and his Saratoga bag. Come to think of it, what does anything in this life of ours have to do with anything else? What has the snorkel got to do with Helman? Or Helman with the young man? Or again, the young man with Vigoleis? If all of this were not connected somehow to the idea of education, I could easily separate concept from content. But I prefer to approach the heart of the matter using the same method that I apply in all my attempts at gaining knowledge as well as in the process of forgetting what I know. We must all have patience. As so often, the detour will prove to be the quickest way. Our present detour can lead us directly back to our domestic quarters on the General's Street. My reader has nothing to fear. No more gobbling turkeys will cut the thread of my narrative, although there are plenty of them tied to the balconies around us, fattening up for the Holy Night of their sacrificial death.

This was a time when we had not yet obtained new furniture. Our apartment was as virginal as on the day we first moved in. Wooden crates were the best we could do to simulate bourgeois respectability. Only the Lladó with its beauteous sounds hove up like a bowsprit above the swells of the void. The little Swabian and the two tall North Germans, who collectively called themselves "Hasenbank, Schmidt & Kleinschmidt, German Booksellers" with limited liability and unlimited trustworthiness, provided us with scrap paper for a few centimos per kilo, most of it unsaleable newspapers from the Third Reich. Scrunched up in a pile of clothes, this made for a quite comfortable bed, one that we could easily fluff up with just a few kicks, although the arrangement had no further advantages at all. My reader can no doubt imagine what it means to go on living after you have lost practically everything. Today, when the world around us is a heap of rubble and people are living in caves, this may not seem like such a dreadful set of circumstances. But at the time we had no psychological recourse to "normalcy," such as is felt by someone whose house has been bombed to the ground. Thus we lived on in the metaphysical space that is situated somewhere above the worldly struggle for existence, the place that Nietzsche, that bourgeois anti-bourgeois, calls the only proper setting for obtaining an education. In this sense, Vigoleis can be said to be a truly educated man. But rather than being a consistent disciple of the great iconoclast Nietzsche, he was a fellow equipped with a talent for clever mimicry, and as such a faithful pupil of the philosopher Max Scheler.

But let us pass over these hybrid intellects. They could once again retard our current chapter, and perhaps I can give them their due in a later section. It is high time that I introduced Mister Hutchinson. As an island customer with an open wallet, he deserves certain privileges. Besides, by letting him finally take the stage I shall be fulfilling my duty of politeness towards my reader. The American, on his part, fulfilled his own polite duty by announcing his name "Hutchinson," as if responding to a stage cue. I myself—dramatist, actor, and prompter all in one person—had no need for a special cue. I bowed slightly and said, "Vigoleis." Both of us were very pleased to meet each other.

"Very pleased"? Why am I trying to conceal my true feelings by the use of a phrase that gets tossed off thoughtlessly every day on streets and thresholds all over the world? "Pleased"? Yes, I was pleased, but it's better not to inquire how utterly overwhelmed I was. To be truthful about it, I was so shocked that I fell against the wall. I just couldn't believe my eyes. Standing before me there in the dim light of our apartment *entrada* was that same young man from the ship, my substitute Helman *sans* albatross, and now *sans* Saratoga bag but still dressed in the fur coat that thousands of moths were just waiting to gobble up. The seconds that followed were like a confused dream. This stranger was appearing before me as part Helman, part Saratoga youth, and it is certain that he gave me a winning smile, for that was his customary way. I just stood there with mouth agape. Heaven, in its infinite wisdom, can arrange everything so that even inside a pauper's cottage, when an event takes place that exceeds in shock value all that is imaginable, it will still provide a door that can be opened. And thus our visitor stepped into one of the seven empty apartment rooms adjoining our *entrada*.

As on the day we moved in, we had distributed boxes and suitcases around the rooms where "we're expecting the paperhangers tomorrow." A Spanish family, for whom the *piso* was originally built, would have achieved the same effect with children. But since we had no children to offer, we at least gave each of the rooms a nice name. Names can imply value judgments. Any mystic knows this, while philosophy hasn't quite sensed it. I knew a man in Amarante by the name of Homem Cristo, "man-Christ" or "Christ-man." He owned a tavern, and he himself was his best customer. Things were always busy there. Whores and pimps held their rendezvous within its walls, and it was moving to hear people call out the name of the proprietor. There is a millionaire who lives in Lisbon and whose bank bears his name: Banco Espírito Santo e Commercial. The man's name is Espírito Santo, Holy Spirit, and in free translation the name of the bank is Holy Spirit and Commerce Bank, a title that does full justice to the spirit of such establishments: Bank of the Holy Spirit of Commerce. I like very much to maintain contact with higher powers in this way. By giving our rooms suggestive names I rid them of their yawning emptiness. I turned suitcases and book crates into godparents. One room was christened after the luggage company Mädler, another was called "Bible Paper" after our multi-volume edition of German philosophy. We had a "Sala de Africa," named for a the popular soft drink, and a "Cabin Room" that we nicknamed "ck-dt" because it contained one of our overseas trunks labeled "ck-dt." For our bedroom, which for reasons mentioned above we heretofore had simply called our *dormitorio*, we invented the name "The Newsroom."

Feigning self-control, I led the stranger into the space that we simply called The Room, since it contained the only piece of furniture that could have made it into a true *bel-étage*: an authentic Mallorquin chair, the product of a local craftsman, painted red and blue on a simulated gold ground, on loan from one of our palaces, but later the legal property of Vigoleis. I beckoned the young man to have a seat, and asked him what had brought him to us.

Well, he said, he was coming directly from the German Bookshop on the Borne. My name had been mentioned there as a teacher of German. He was intending to stay on the island for a half-year or longer because of his lungs, which could benefit from the Mediterranean climate. Then he would move on to Heidelberg to continue his study of philosophy. He had a degree from Princeton and a certain familiarity with the works of Kant, but was having difficulty reading him in the original. And so the gentlemen at the Librería— if I might have the time and interest—philosophy being my field...

Yes, I had the time, I was interested, and philosophy was, *cum grano salis*, indeed my field. We agreed on a wage and a schedule. He would come three times a week for an hour each. We could start the very next day—preferably in the evening because of the heat. Hutchinson thanked me for this consideration, which he interpreted as being offered because of his lung condition, which was in such contrast with his fur coat. In Spain, even if you don't have TB you prefer to conduct all your business in the natural shade; it's only a bullfight that is in need of direct sunlight above the zenith. Our newcomer of course didn't realize this. What he took for a gesture of solicitude and concern for his damaged pulmonary passages was merely an appeal to local custom and my own personal comfort.

Now German is a language I think I know a little about, although for years now our private language has been Portuguese, and Portuguese is the language I think and curse in. German is and will remain my mother tongue. Besides, I have had a very active intellectual relationship with it. I can read Goethe without scholarly annotations, Stefan George without getting a stiff neck, and Kant without recourse to a medical or liturgical *miserere*. On the other hand, I am no good at offering anybody linguistic instruction. To do that, you have to have a completely different attitude toward language, and under no circumstances the meditative approach that is my own. Still, what this eager student of philosophy wanted was so-called "conversation," which was fine with me since it is just what, from the very beginning, so many people have found me good at. For the most part I just blabber away as if my conversational partner were either myself or Don Matías or, to name a very special case, my mystical friend Pascoaes. Chats with him reach for the stars... but now I was being offered cold cash for this virtue of mine. And why not? I was, after all, a *Führer*. Moreover, this conversation business struck me as having a less than rigorous aspect. It was not bound up with any pedagogical method, much less with any school furniture. Free association inside a free space—that was something I could venture upon using the only chair we owned. "Then we'll see each other again tomorrow, right? Fine, at six. Goodbye."

Following this visit Beatrice and I had a conversation that was strategic in nature. Its focus was our sole existing chair. At the dialectical periphery stood a second chair that we would have to purchase, and somewhere else, in realms beyond the breathable atmosphere, there hovered a table—would it ever descend to us? It dissolved in mist when I explained that my pedagogical talent was so untrustworthy that I deemed it advisable to wait before making any more purchases—perhaps a month. If my pupil was then still willing to risk his lung and my tongue on the island, we could go ahead.

And how, pray tell, did I intend to teach a pupil with only one chair? Just how did I imagine doing such a thing?

At such moments of hesitancy and cowardice I am in the habit of playing certain pious trump cards, although they seldom faze this prodigal daughter of a theologian, while to me, the heretical nephew of a bishop, they come automatically: "We are in the hands of God, chérie. What harm can mere mortals do to us?"

We shall soon see what mere mortals can do to us if we neglect to take preventive action. Let us now re-enter the room where the pupil is waiting for his teacher, so that our plot can continue.

During our first lessons we engaged in little skirmishes of politeness. The youth, from a good family and thus possessed of fine manners, refused to take a seat while his teacher stood. But the latter coerced him, with a smiling word or a philosophical maxim, into utilizing the single sitting surface in the apartment, which was crafted at the precise anatomical height that has been standard in all of human history. He sat, but in a pose as if ready to leap up again at any moment. I noticed this.

One day—we had meanwhile sounded each other out discreetly, and certain personal matters had entered both sides of our conversations—the young fellow hazarded the cardinal question: what was the deeper meaning of this confusing arrangement of our apartment? He apologized profusely for asking. He was quite embarrassed, and added, "It causes me increasing discomfort to be seated, that I must be seated, while my tutor remains standing."

. So there it was. It had to happen sooner or later. Now it was up to me to remain, or rather to become, master of the situation. Beatrice had predicted this moment—naturally, for she is also a teacher—and had pleaded with me to invent some excuse in order to avoid a surprise attack. But instead, I trusted my lucky stars and my instincts as a *Führer*, and made no preparations. Now, however, I would have to set sail and head out into the unknown.

By inquiring as to the "deeper meaning" of the interior architecture of our classroom, a query obviously predicated on the assumption that profundity is an *a priori* characteristic of all things German, Hutchinson handed me a cue that set me off on the slippery slope of mystification. This was a fortunate choice of terms. It served me as a pilot. I followed my inspiration of the moment, which now bore connotations of watery depths. It was the same train of thought that had granted me a vision of the snorkel, the self-inflating brassiere for flat-chested ladies, or the self-erasing rubber collar for men with a compulsion for cleanliness.

"My dear friend,"—this is approximately how I began my confabulation— "you may wish to ascribe it to my inborn sense of modesty that I have hitherto not revealed a certain aspect of my personality. "I am"—and here I bowed to him—"the inventor of the Single-Chair Method, a technique that does not yet bear my name for the simple reason that it has yet to be publicized. No one knows about it. I myself regard it as too premature, too poorly systematized, too loosely conceptualized, and too scantily tested using significantly large samples of unpredictable student reaction to inform the scholarly world of pedagogy of its advantages. For the moment I am limiting myself to small-scale statistical and pedagogical-psychological experiments. You are experiencing the last of these; soon I shall proceed beyond these low-level investigations. Now you, sir, as an open-minded representative of the scholarly world overseas, are particularly welcome as a participant in my experimentation, unencumbered as you are by shoddy and obsolete European models of pedagogy. It was Heaven itself, and not the bookseller on the Borne, that has sent you to me and my naked miniature lecture hall. The book dealer has served merely as the blindly obedient agent of a Providence that is intent upon encouraging the higher development of pedagogical methods inspired by Pestalozzi."

The youth listened intently. His green eyes took on the glow that appears in the eyes of children when they approach the shooting gallery at the fair. His interest was all the greater since his synthesizing American mind was taking in my Single-Chair Method as if it were the strains of lovely music. He remained all eyes and ears.

Now what were the basic principles of this technique? "Listen. Every object, or rather every thing in the world that surrounds us is a world in itself. Speaking solely of the field of linguistics, each new language that a person learns comprises a world in, and of course also of, itself. Today we speak quite generally of a language's 'world view'—in your country, too, I would suppose?"

"Indeed we do, although we have another term..."

"'Behavior,' right? Very good. These two worlds, or to phrase it in Aristotelian fashion, these two categories..." My pupil gave his nodding assent to this lofty gobbledygook—Princeton had not outfitted him with the means to unmask me as an incompetent charlatan. "If allowed to meet, these two categories come into conflict with one another, which unfailingly occurs whenever a pupil confronts a new thing, which is to say, a new world."

Hutchinson had a crystal-clear understanding of all of this. I continued:

"From my many years of experience as a linguist"—still today I am amazed at the cheek with which I uttered such a bare-faced lie to my pupil and to myself, but it just had to be—"I have come to realize that what can best improve the receptivity of a pupil is a progressive sublimation of his environment. In Germany, as a student of Max Scheler, I first arrived at comprehension—insofar as anything was comprehensible in seminars with this philosopher—that the object sphere must be torn forcefully from our circumconscious—not our subconscious, mind you—if we are to arrive at pure perception. In other words, my friend: the less environment there is in a classroom, the smaller will be the coefficient of distraction in the learning process, whereas at the same time we must also acknowledge that the pupils themselves constitute an environment, the so-called meta-environment, which in turn is subject to its own laws. Up to now scholars have avoided this complex state of affairs like a hot potato. And yet we must strive toward a Jaspersian absolutization of anonymity if we are to prevent the universal pedagogical possibilities slumbering within my method from being tossed out of the bath water along with the baby."

I fed my pupil this and similar pseudoscientific balderdash with grandiloquence, at certain points stammering and at a loss for the clearest phraseology, as if groping for words to express the ultimately inexpressible. It all made sense to the young man. He was now quite excited; he took quick, deep puffs on his cigarette and nervously flicked the ashes into the cuffs of his neatly tailored trousers. The climax of his feverish enthusiasm—I estimated it at about 102°F—came when he leaped up from the single chair that had lent its name to my system. Caught up in the momentum of my own mischief, about to perceive a kernel of truth amid all my nonsensical blather, and starting to give credence on my own part to the parthenogenic origin of my ecological fantasies, I reared back to deliver the crowning declaration. I summoned the wise Peripatetics from the arcades of the Hellenic Lyceum to our miserable emigrant lodgings on Barceló Street. These mild-mannered strollers from Aristotle's school of philosophy had excellent reasons, or so I claimed as I myself paced to and fro in front of my pupil, for holding their colloquies—in such sharp contrast to the "lectures" given at today's universities—while ambling through the public galleries rather than sitting in enclosed spaces where one's eyes would tend to focus—nay, would tend to remain fixed—on certain objects, causing the mind finally to cloud over and shut down if it had not already been occluded by the environment itself. All of this has implications, I added, for an entirely new approach to Classical Antiquity.

Hutchinson smoked more and more hectically, like a circus monkey that has snapped up a burning butt.

Over the decades, I explained, over the anguished decades of my struggle towards knowledge and the ultimate perfection of my inchoate ideas, through years of misunderstanding and even hostility, I had decided to remove gradually all superfluous objects from the space in which I offered instruction, with the same methodical care as a zoologist might exercise as he organizes his experimental station, thereby reducing the hazards of "environmental squeeze," one classic victim of which, I added incidentally, was my own humble person. I had made a beginning by stripping my lodgings of pictures on the walls and bric-a-brac on the shelf behind the sofa. "Surely you now understand, Mister Hutchinson, why it is that in the monks' cells—you recall yesterday's discussion of the origins of the cult of the cloistered life—or in the so-called 'lodges' of the desert anachorites during the early phases of the monastic movement, the eyes that search for God must focus solely on naked walls? These sainted, or as good as sainted, men learned how to come into the presence of God, and only of God. The noted Saint Simeon Stylite was the one who, sitting and praying on his famous pillar, rid himself most radically of the environmental encumbrances that we are talking about."

Unfamiliar with early Christian literature, the young man told me that he would like to learn more about the fascinating ascetic personages of the Wild East. I promised to fill him in at a later date, but quickly inserted an account of the historical anti-Vigoleis, the pious Roman deacon Arsenius, renowned for his erudition and appointed by Emperor Theodosius as tutor for his son Arcadius. Theodosius was in such awe of this priest, who was reputed to be of saintly character, that the prince was allowed to receive instruction from him only while standing upright. Arcadius, already the recipient of the title Augustus, regarded this decree as a humiliation and sought to eliminate the palace pedagogue. Arsenius escaped princely vengeance by fleeing into the desert. In this story the roles were reversed, I explained, adding that Mister Hutchinson had nothing to fear. I had no intention of doing away with him. "But please, remain seated. Now where were we?"

"All the pictures," he said in English.

"Oh yes, all the pictures had to go..." So then my walls were completely bare. The next things to be jettisoned were the drapes, the pipe holders, the bridal wreaths, my diplomas, the cuckoo clocks; and then the chests of drawers, the stands for the flower pots—everything flew out the window. My young friend could surely understand that this process did not occur without instances of controversy. But in order to maintain the integrity of the German spirit I assured him that my enraged erstwhile landlady on Klinkhammer Street in Münster, who sued me for "environmental vandalism and property damage," was a shameful exception to the rule.

Here in this room and at this very time, I now explained, I had again taken extreme measures, acting, as it were, as a Simeon/Vigoleis in this century of ours that shows so little inclination to asceticism. Continuing with legendary comparisons I said that at the birth of my radical pedagogical method I had performed a Caesarian section. "In this space, dear Hutchinson, you will be confronting only yourself, your chair, and your teacher. I ask you to convince yourself that your chair and your teacher are the sole remaining necessary props for this system of teaching. It is my hope that in the course of time even these two annoying objects can be sublimated, so that we can eventually attain a Paradisiacal setting for modern linguistic pedagogy—Adam prior to the creation of woman, given over exclusively to monologue."

The historic era we are living in, I explained in concluding this private tutorial, was no longer tolerant of the ambulatory method of teaching and learning. This was particularly true of thickly populated areas where tramways and subways effectively deprived peripatetic candidates of the necessary ascetic environment.

The American, accustomed to traffic accidents in his home country, agreed that this was a perilous state of affairs.

And finally: taking notes on your knee, a technique enforced by my method —the youth became quite skilled at this, like a born aphorist—was by no means to be regarded as such an inconvenience as it might at first appear. It was, after all, the pupil's own knee that would serve as the writing surface. With this sophistical capstone I closed the final overarching vault of my Single-Chair Method.

The American, who is now doubtless well past 39, slapped his thigh with glee and gave me a round of unphilosophical applause. Then he jumped up and began a long harangue, forgetting that our peripatetic *lingua franca* was supposed to be German. He would immediately have to send a report on my method to a professional journal in the States. He would broadcast my name in the American scholarly community, and I myself would have to cross the ocean and introduce my method at American colleges.

"Just a moment, my friend! Your perceptiveness reflects your overall receptivity to the general precepts of our Western culture. But we must not inhibit the growth of our pedagogical seedlings by premature publication. We are not insured against the hailstones of stupidity. My method still has certain points of weakness: its cranial fontanelle hasn't yet closed. What is more, I myself intend to write a monograph on the Single-Chair Method. It will be published by a university press in Münster with a foreword by Rudolf Pannwitz, who has already declared himself in favor of my system. Afterwards, my friend, you will be at complete liberty to report to the world concerning your meetings with me and my chair."

Our hour-long tutorial had stretched into two or three hours, and we were both at full speed. The young man donned his fur coat with panache and returned to the Hotel Príncipe, and then he came back regularly for more lessons, each time likewise with panache. He learned with extreme rapidity. Our conversations dealt with increasingly wide-ranging and complex subjects; no topic was too intimidating for us—which is of course what doing philosophy is all about. Yet as if we had made a tacit agreement, the pedagogical system that gave rise to these successful colloquies never again came up for discussion. We were like lovers who keep their secret to themselves, like conspirators, like mystagogues who do not need so much as a twinkling of the eye to keep the magic alive.

To lend some kind of purpose to our free-wheeling digressions, we decided that we should select a text, on the principle that the student could best reach his goal by a process of reading and interpretation. I suggested Schopenhauer's "Aphorisms on Wisdom," for one thing aiming to show the American that there were German philosophers who wrote in a style that was readily accessible, if not fully comprehensible, to anyone. In addition, Schopenhauer's subjects touched on ultimate truths, which meant that we would not be setting limits to our peripatetic urges. I recommended the pocket-sized Reclam pocket volume, in case Hutchinson was not prepared to purchase all of Schopenhauer in the Grand Duke Wilhelm Ernst Edition.

With this practical suggestion, my attempt at educating the future student of Jaspers and Heidegger came to an end. George Brewis Hutchinson never again found his way to the Street of the General. Our single chair occupied its space in a more orphaned condition than ever before. Likewise orphaned was Vigoleis' wallet, and this was a cause of concern to both of us. What had happened? Had my promising pupil burst a vein in his lung? Had he engaged in less intellectual pursuits and received a fatal stab wound at the hands of a *femme fatale*? In common erotic matters the fellow was not choosy, but he was still insufficiently familiar with the customs of a country where a beautiful lady's stocking could conceal a dagger. Had his father's bank cut off his allowance overnight? We pondered these questions intensely, but my pupil remained among the missing.

This is what had taken place: from our apartment to the bookstore was but a stone's throw, hardly a three-minute walk across the Apuntadores and past Doña Angelita's little shop where Hutchinson liked to stop, buy a little something, and admire the pretty clerk. Still glowing from our intellectual ruminations, still walking on air from our tutorial, the youth entered the bookstore and ordered Schopenhauer in the thin-paper Insel Edition, bound in leather. This was, incidentally, the largest order ever placed at that establishment. The owners beamed, and inquired whether their customer was satisfied with his teacher.

The American, too, was beaming. Satisfied? Why, he was at a loss for words to express his gratitude for having referred him to such a unique pedagogue. There was surely no more fitting referral on the whole island, or in the whole world! This Single-Chair Method was the wave of the future. Hamilton, Jacotots, Berlitz, Toussaint-Langenscheidt, Gaspey-Otto-Sauer—clumsy amateurs, all of them! The modest abode on General Barceló would in future times carry a plaque that said, VIGOLEIS TAUGHT HERE.

Apparently it took a while before the three booksellers suspected a fly in the ointment. Then they must have burst out in gales of laughter, which the American completely failed to understand until they explained everything down to the last detail. This inventor of a pioneering new method of language instruction was a highly imaginative writer of verses, a failure at everything he undertook, not to say a clever con man. As for his teaching method, it was named with his typical wittiness after the single piece of furniture that Don Vigo owned, because he was living in very dire straits. Things would get even worse for him if he didn't soon declare loyalty to the *Führer*. Happily, though, there were still ways and means to remind a German living in foreign climes of his patriotic duty. We're all familiar with this now-broken record, one that is getting glued back together again as Vigoleis writes down these words.

According to reports, the American broke down in tears. First of all, because his dream had been shattered, and also because he no doubt felt sorry for me.

He had indeed taken a strong liking to me. His character was soft and as yet unspoiled by his encounter with Europe, and thus my joke affected him all the more bitterly. In the midst of his tearful anger and impotence, he showed them his father's checkbook, explaining that he was a millionaire. Just a single word from me, and he could have furnished my entire apartment, easily ten times the value of the single-chair classroom. But now this! "What a shame!" He could never look me in the face again, I had betrayed his confidence, I had exploited his thirst for knowledge and, worse still, his ignorance. He felt just generally ashamed, of himself and of me. His world was collapsing...

Let us put it more calmly: the only thing that was collapsing was our borrowed chair.

Thus far the report from one of the three German bookstore gentlemen.

I do not know what later became of this duped hero of my recollections. In any case he left the island immediately in disgust. Did he remember his teacher on the General's Street, holding forth as he paced back and forth in front of him? Did he later sit at the feet of Jaspers and Heidegger, those two luminaries of decidedly non-improvised existentialism, and listen raptly as they held forth on "the being-at-hand and being-on-hand of our state of being thrown into the world"? Without any doubt, my private seminar was more digestible. On the other hand, our chair broke down under my disciple, just as if it were the three-legged one from the House of Sureda.

"Few people write," says Schopenhauer in his treatise on writing and good style, "in the way an architect builds, by sketching out a preliminary plan and thinking through every detail. Most writers go about their work as if playing dominoes. In this game, one piece fits another partly by intention, partly by chance. And that is how their sentences and their context follow one upon another. They hardly ever know what the finished product will look like, or what it will all mean. Many of them honestly don't know, and they write the way coral polyps construct their colonies, by adding sentence to sentence and clause to clause, according to some inscrutable divine design..."

The coral polyp that constructed our insular destiny, setting storey upon blooming storey in such a way that we often wondered what it all meant— this metaphorical animal finally located a table to add to our chair. That is to say, it caused me to locate one, and I paid for it with money that I amassed by my mendacious career as a *Führer*, working now more crassly and angrily than ever as a result of the triumph of that other *Führer*. It was a remarkable table, and not only because of its origins. It served as a writing surface for the poet Marsman, who later became my great literary friend, and also for other notables of Dutch literature, all of whom wrote immortal words on it. It was used by the imperial-democratic Count Harry Kessler for part of his memoirs, and by the transhistorical Count Hermann Keyserling for a postcard sent to his wife, who was being held hostage by Goebbels inside his own "School of

Wisdom."

And Vigoleis?

He, too, added sentence to sentence and clause to clause on this tabletop, and he rhymed "love" with "stars above" and "newt" with "shoot" and many other things besides. None of this granted him immortality, but it made him a fitting target for the Nazis' bullets.

XI

The young American remained among the missing; our single chair remained an orphan. Worry held sway in our apartment, along with sadness and a mood of *Quo vadis?* Then Pedro arrived, danced his *paso doble* for us, snapped his tongue and his fingers, and said, "Come with me to Valldemosa! Why stay here without any furniture and without a bed? We still own a cottage in the village that used to belong to a nanny. It'll be swell out there. And it's about time that you made the acquaintance of Don José, the former private physician of His Royal-Imperial Majesty, Archduke Ludwig Salvator of Austria."

He didn't have to say this twice. We locked the apartment and went out to Valldemosa, where Chopin and George Sand spent their famous tragic winter of love in the Sureda family cloister, and where now a small colony of emigrants were causing no less irritation than the hard-pressed lovers had done a whole century previous. George Sand strolled around the village wearing trousers, and hiked across the moonlit mountains in no more than a shirt. Now, Pedro told us, a German nobleman was trying to emulate her by claiming that he was the son-in-law of Franz von Papen. He didn't wear trousers, and the shorts that were meant to cover his aristocratic nakedness were tailored in such a way that the legs ended exactly where they began; out came His Excellency's long, hairy gams, always powdered to prevent premature tanning. Tanning drove him crazy, because it reminded him of his "brown" father-in-law, whom he would rather disown except for his stable of racing horses. Otherwise, this powered nobleman was a friendly fellow who bred poultry, collected stamps, and taught German to our friend Paquito, the son of the ducal private physician. Teaching German is what almost all the emigrants did. They converted their mother tongue into a tongue that would earn them their bread, for most of them had been unable to smuggle anything else out of the Third Reich.

The nanny's cottage, now the property of Don Juan Sureda, was on the Calle de la Amargura, Number 11. *Amargura* means "bitterness, sourness," but also "worry and trouble, woe, weariness, and lovesickness." It connotes all that is in the highest degree painful, anxious, and objectionable; with some authors it means disease, distress, and dismay, displeasure, discontent, and disaster. That little word contains so much, and much of what it contains is what the Suredas had to go through: Papá, Mamá, the deceased, the living, and the surviving children. This gives them the right to have a little street named after their fate, especially when you consider that in Palma a whole palace still bears their family name.

An old, dented, sickly-blue bus stood with a head of steam on the Plaza Olivar when we began our journey with our minuscule baggage. Because of the steam, we couldn't depart. The engine was overheated, bursting the radiator. They would have to do some drilling, boring, hammering, and soldering, the bus-line manager told us. He used this opportunity to change a tire, too; that would obviate the need to perform this operation on the way to Valldemosa. The tire, he said, was bound to blow out otherwise, without any doubt. "Any doubt about it?" he asked a passenger whose expression doubtless conveyed certain doubts. This fellow shrugged his shoulders, walked three paces to the nearest tavern, clapped his hands, and was served his coffee. The Spaniard likes to have his café close at hand, and his bus stop close to a café.

Beatrice was annoyed. She was still unaccustomed to Spanish schedules, although she ought to have been thankful that nobody observed them. How many pesetas did she earn over the years by teaching pupils who were always punctual with their payments, but hardly ever showed up on time for their lessons so that their teacher could follow her own pursuits? Day after day she came up with dire epithets to hurl at her tardy students. I myself, who had only a few pupils, cursed every one of them who, contrary to custom, arrived on time. Whoever stayed away from my classroom gave impetus to my private life.

There on the Plaza Olivar I would like to have offered Beatrice some consolation for her "vapors," as was customary a hundred years earlier in my fatherland. But I didn't have with me the Complete Works of Ludwig Börne. They were inside a crate in our *pisa* on Barceló Street. The priceless "Monograph on the German Postal Snail," Börne's contribution to the natural history of mollusks and *Testaceae*, could easily have blown away the clouds of her impatience.

An hour later, Pedro showed up carrying an easel and other painting gear. "One hour late," he said glancing at the bus, which meanwhile mechanics had completely taken apart, "and obviously a couple of hours too early. That's fine. Yuñer and Puigdengolas will still make it. They're coming along, and they always figure on a three-hour delay."

Yuñer and Puigdengolas—weren't these the two painters who were introduced to us at the Count's rooming house? Exactly. They had returned, one of them from Barcelona, the other from Paris, to capture the light of the island on their palettes in Valldemosa. The stone-deaf Yuñer was occasionally successful with subjects that eluded Puigdengolas, owing to the fact that the latter's preoccupation with film had given him a rather different attitude toward sunlight. We were in excellent company.

Around noon the bus manager sent street urchins out to alert the scattered passengers. Just an hour more, and the bus would be repaired to the point where they could hazard a departure. But in the meantime his customers had gone so far afield, or had become involved in such gripping conversations, that we thought we would be traveling alone. Pedro, versed as he was in the ways of the local bus companies, pointed to a group of passengers who had been standing on the Plaza with kit and caboodle, waiting for the departure of a bus that was scheduled to leave one hour after our own, but which had not yet returned from Sóller. These people would now take advantage of the marvelous opportunity of leaving on schedule with our vehicle. This kind of schedule-shifting took place all day long. It was only in the evening hours that passengers were left stranded, forced to spend the night on the street and wait until the following day's mixed-up schedule. By one o'clock the two painters had not yet arrived. Pedro gestured to the bus manager: as far as we were concerned, they could start out. The engine snarled at idle; the mechanics smiled and accepted plaudits from all sides. They were experts, after all! The jacks were carefully lowered, and everybody waited tensely for the moment when the weight of the vehicle would hit the newly replaced tire. It didn't burst. We could get on board.

It was a glorious trip, and all the more glorious since I didn't have to play "*Führer.*" We putt-putted past all the celebrated sights, and I wasn't required to explain a thing. Everything stood there like Creation itself, *l'art pour l'art*, including the clouds of dust. The mood among the passengers was excellent, especially since most of them, contrary to their expectation, sensed that they would be arriving early at the destination. Indeed they would have, if the mechanics hadn't changed the wrong tire. At the Son Puig Estate, up in the heights, the correct tire let us know with a loud report that it was, after all, the wrong one. The manager, who was at the steering wheel, took a deep breath. The bus hit a tree and was stuck fast. We were out of danger. There was yelling and wailing, and everybody got out to inspect the damage. The driver said that he had a strange feeling all along; that *tonto* of a mechanic picked the wrong wheel, and he just knew that something would happen. But he said that we had him to thank that we weren't all lying in a ditch with smashed bones. The engine was steaming again, but now it had time to cool off. Everybody tried his best to get comfortable. Pedro entertained the passengers by telling gruesome stories about trips to Valldemosa in the good old days, when it took braces of mules a whole day to reach the mountain heights. Back then there had been loud bangs, too, but they came from highwaymen with their muskets. A peasant in picturesque native get-up, who made this trip often and knew that mistakes were made all the time, took down his basket from the roof of the bus and started a picnic to which he invited everyone to partake of his *tinto* from Binsalem and smoked chicken. Pedro and I set to eating. Beatrice lost herself in contemplation of the landscape. Landscape is something, I said, that wouldn't run away, whereas I had never before tasted smoked chicken. The *porrón* made the rounds, with each diner letting his portion stream down his gullet. This was a wine to make note of: a Binsalem.

The remainder of the journey went off without incident.

On the way, I made friends with the Mallorquins who were sitting next to me, behind me, and in front of me, as well as with those who had shared the chicken, and with Amilcar, the bus manager to whom we owed our lives because, angry as he was, he had driven our vehicle with special care. I made friends with everybody, and these were friendships made to last a lifetime. Cordiality of this kind, which is common in Spain, never disappoints. There is never another meeting, and thus there is no temptation to lend your *amigo* money or, in case of a literary *aficionado*, books. Beatrice was the only one among us who refused to dirty her hands with smoked chicken or hearty handshakes. Accordingly, she was treated with special respect. Ordinary folk can tell right away if a person has mistakenly entered a Ford jalopy instead of his own Rolls Royce.

The Street of Bitterness didn't look as bitter as I had expected; it probably spoke only for a low-grade form of *amargura*. On the contrary, it seemed friendly, clean-swept, and populated with more cats than Beatrice wanted to see. A few natives, squatting in front of their doors, gave us mistrustful looks. These were progeny of the Valldemosans who made Chopin's and Sand's stay in the Valley of the Muza so miserable that the lovers decided to pack their valises soon after arrival. Incidentally, those two were the first tourists in the history of the island. The natives didn't profit much from them, whereas in our own day the cash registers were already overflowing from the mobs of foreigners, especially the machine at the entry to the cloister where the famous couple devoted themselves to art, love-making, and sin. You can visit their cells. This is how they are compensating for what they did wrong. Posthumous fame is always more lucrative than fame itself.

Pedro showed us to our room right away, on the second floor. It was a dank space, stuffed with boxes, suitcases, and assorted junk. In the middle there stood a small mountain that reached almost to the ceiling, a veritable pyramid of a bed. That is to say, there was no point at the top, so I should rather call it a desert mesa made of mattresses. I shall explain everything, but not in my capacity as a *Führer*. No, I shall do so in accordance with the truth, which can sometimes be pleasant and is never boring when it has to do with the illustrious House of the Suredas.

Pedro's father Don Juan had become a beggar overnight, ripe for a lucrative squatting-place in front of the cathedral. This fact, in and of itself, is nothing original. Most of the island aristocrats suffered the same fate, and all of them bore it with the unbowed dignity of a Spanish grandee, one of whose traditions is never to impede the progress of degeneration. Don Juan Sureda became a pauper in exemplary fashion, displaying more imagination than one might expect from a denizen of Iberia.

Don Juan was the landlord of the former cloister. His father had held the same position, and the tradition went back through many generations of fathers to the moment when it turns murky and becomes a playing field for historians. Back then, what is today the *Cartuja* was still a royal palace, headquarters of the Kings of Mallorca, founded around the year 1320 by Sancho I, who suffered from asthma. The next to occupy the fresh-air castle was Don Martín I of Aragón, likewise Mallorcan King, which he ceded in 1399 to the Carthusian monks as a charterhouse. The regulations of Saint Bruno "Hard Fist" stipulated that each monk was to prepare his own meals in his cell, and so the monumental palace kitchen was remodeled into a chapel. Where previously people baked and fried, they now prayed and fasted. In 1835 the monks were driven out. Pedro's grandfather returned the ruins of the Chapel of the Hair-Shirted Brothers to its secular purpose. But in place of a kitchen—there wasn't much left to eat in the house anyway—he had a ballroom erected on the premises. Anyone can dance anytime, and pray anywhere.

The cells were rented out, and among the tenants were Chopin and George Sand. In the House of Sureda, they say that it was some mercenary French woman who first came up with the idea of displaying, for an entrance fee, the cells where the consumptive composer linked the name and the person of his girlfriend, the enterprising "literary cow" (Nietzsche), to his own greater immortality. Tradition does not reveal exactly which cells they lived in, but that is unimportant. History, with its pronounced instinct for local accuracy, will always find a solution to such problems, as it did with the exact location of the Garden of Eden. All you need to do is announce to the foreigners in a firm voice, "And here, ladies and gentlemen, you see the cells in which Chopin and George Sand..." The tourist will start sniffing, and sensitive as he is to fine fragrances, he will capture the fleeting scent of *fleurs d'amour* permeating the walls that formerly kept the pious brothers healthy by exuding the smell of garlic. "We," Pedro told us, "were always proud to show the historic cells without asking a centimo. But Jacobo"—Pedro's brother, whom I hope to bring on stage before a *finis operis* closes the door of my recollections in my own face—"Jacobo once charged a duro to take a look at the place, thereby dishonoring the name of Sureda once and for all. Papá would have shown him the door, if he hadn't already been standing outside. And because Jacobo was already out in the world and got around a lot, he knew that back in Valldemosa things could work out in an emergency, even without charging a duro. And there has surely been no shortage of emergencies."

This was the time when Papá started laying plans for all kinds of emergencies. When Don Juan went bankrupt and his banker alerted him with the customary local tardiness, his reaction was not to feel knocked down by a feather—or rather, he did feel that way, but only by his surprise that things had kept going for so long. Even the banker couldn't explain how the calamity had happened. In such cases, nobody really knows whom to blame. I myself was convinced that the family must have arrived at beggary in the most honest and proper way. Pedro informed me that Papá's lively imagination played a role in the process, since it wasn't only gambling and women that had undermined his fortune. Don Juan let himself be robbed in style. He kept silent in style when told that his own majordomo had cooked the house's books and built himself a country estate with the proceeds—"Oh, what's the difference?"

I admire this kind of attitude, one that leaves the big hole unmended and lets the little hole grow bigger, and you gradually get poor without sacrificing your self-esteem.

Later, at Pascoaes' palace in Portugal, I learned what it means to live in style in an expensive abode. The person in charge was the aforementioned prehistoric mistress of the house, whose true age was undocumented, and which I can best convey by describing her diamond ring. It was an heirloom, and she had worn it day and night since childhood. The stones were worn down to the metal setting. This was her perpetual calendar, with the pages torn away one by one. The sight of this ring on this hand had the same overpowering effect as the sight of the armchair in which the poet Pascoaes sat and wrote, and in which he still sits and writes. The arms were completely ragged, the polished wood peeked forth from behind the desiccated horsehair chair-back, making it appear like the tonsure on a mystic's head.

One day I was a witness as a distraught daughter and a distraught son announced to their mother that 100 contos were missing from their safe. 1 conto de reis = 1000 escudos. "A hundred contos?" asked the old dame. "Children, are you sure you counted correctly?" The children had done so, with the help of the family's completely honest financial manager. The money was gone. Doña Carlota burst out laughing and said, "Well now, make a note of this: if Doña Mariola (a wealthy friend who lived on a nearby wine-producing estate) got such news she would faint dead away. And with good reason, because then she would be broke! I can afford a loss such as this one. Ask Americo to bring the car. I'm going over to tell Doña Mariola in person, and I'll ask her what it would be like if such a thing happened to her." Before leaving she snuck into my study to ask me what I would do if I discovered that someone had robbed me of 100 contos. After duly congratulating her on her sudden loss, I said, "Dear, revered *Senhora* Doña Carlota, on the island of Mallorca I lost my house and all my possessions. What are 100 contos to me? And my friend Don Juan Sureda Bimer of the House of Verdugo, as a Vasconcellos an ancestral relative of your own family, lost very, very much more than a few measly contos, namely an entire palace, and still he didn't fall over in a faint. True nobility comes into its own when the foundation starts to crumble."

"You lost everything on Mallorca? Everything?"

"Everything, *minha Senhora*!"

"Then it's too bad that you didn't steal the 100 contos!" And with that, she left to avoid being outdone by her own reputation. In the evening I gave her a long, drawn-out account of the subject at hand.

Don Juan's splenetic temperament and Doña Pilar's passion for art, a trait that her husband shared with her, not as a practicing painter but as a connoisseur, hastened their financial demise. Matters were not helped by their tradition of holding large parties, though this was nothing out of the ordinary: a palace is just the place for large receptions. Things begin to get doubtful, however, if, an hour before your guests are expected, you tell your majordomo that the two of you are going out to catch some fresh air for a few minutes and will return in good time, and that the Princess will give him further orders. Everyone knows how strenuous the preparations are for such a feast, particularly if you are dependent on a passel of servants who, though carefully trained, are yet Spanish servants with idiosyncratic notions concerning party-giving and the following of orders. Doña Pilar had to take care of all the preparations herself. Everything was all ready except for the sheep cheese from Mahón—it didn't taste as piquant as usual, and perhaps the chef was forced to substitute a Mallorquin variety. Oh well, one cannot be everywhere all the time, especially if you are a painter. The servants were aware of this, too, so then our Princess went out the door on her somewhat bent-over grandee's arm.

A clip-clopping of horses' hoofs. Equestrians? A berlin comes speeding up, there are shouts of *olé!* and *olá!*—"We know you, neighbors from Son Maroig, Miramar, Son Tatx, Es Mirabo! Where are you off to with your steaming steeds?" "To Palma, to the ship!" "The ship? To Barcelona?" "Yes, and then on to London, art exhibition, Tate Gallery, Turner!" "Turner? *Caramba!*"— "Won't you join us? We're in a hurry!"

Papá and Mamá are one heart and one soul, and both of these organs throb only for art. They get in, the carriage rushes on downhill. In Palma the members of the Art Club board the ship, in Barcelona the Suredas purchase necessities for the remainder of the junket, and in London they get undressed, then re-dressed in the proper outfits.

Back home the majordomo greets the first guests—and also the last ones, as the perfect guardian of door, home, and entire premises that he is. His livery buttons shine. His mutton chops are at the ready for all eventualities. Just a short while, then just a short while longer—the Princess and Don Juan should be back any moment now. Yet no matter how politely this loyal servant repeats his announcement of "just a short while," the hour finally arrives when even the greatest time-killer is forced to notice that the clock is no longer striking. Besides, empty stomachs are making their presence felt.

As the moon rose at midnight and climbed above the Teix to enclose with its ghostly light the Valley of the Muza and the Royal Suredan charterhouse, the majordomo finally declared that the "short while" had expired, and that the host and hostess were now surely on their way home. But they didn't come home. Had something happened to them? Had they fallen into a gorge? Why didn't the servants go outside with lanterns and search for the princely couple in the darkest declivities? Oh, those two! They are both romantic souls, nothing is wrong. They've probably decided on the spot to saddle up a pair of donkeys, clamber up the Puig Mayor, and enjoy the world-famous sunrise. Or maybe they've gone off to play *l'hombre* at their neighbor's palace, or… or… there were so many possibilities, and why should anybody worry? Finally, general departure: the horse carriages are summoned, those who arrived by donkey throw their legs over the *albarde*, and now they all leave fond greetings to Doña Pilar and Don Juan. Bona nit!

The majordomo locked the doors, dismissed the servants for the night, and lay down on his pillow. The next day, he continued to follow his orders: the Princess would give him further instructions when the couple came home. He waited.

A few days later a brief message arrived from Papá and Mamá to the children from Barcelona: they were on their way to London. "Turner!" "Turner?" The majordomo, too, had no idea what this meant. But he had his orders: wait for more orders. Which he did. Then the children heard nothing more. No one heard a single word from the parents who had absconded from the palace. Were they really in England? And who or what was "Turner"? The curate in Valldemosa, an educated man, figured out meanwhile that a *Turner* is someone who does gymnastics. It was a German word, coined in Germany. So now Don Juan and his princess were doing gymnastics in London—and why not? This wasn't the craziest thing they had ever done.

Each servant, male and female, was assigned to one of the children. There were more than a dozen to be taken care of before winter arrived. The parents were simply gone. The majordomo obeyed his orders, refusing to act contrary to the wishes of his master and mistress. The servants dispersed and sought employment elsewhere, in order to share their bread with the abandoned children. For their part the children got older, went wild, and turned into a marauding band that came to be feared in the whole valley, not unlike the horde of Sureda dogs that had menaced nighttime Palma. Pedro said that this was the greatest time of his life, this interregnum with no Papá and no Mamá, no hearth and no home.

This paradisiacal situation lasted two years. Then their parents came back home, artistically edified and enriched. Besides Turner, who was in fact a painter and not the gymnast that his name would suggest, they had seen a great deal of art: the Elgin Marbles, Sir Joshua Reynolds's portraits of children, the portraits of aristocrats by Thomas Gainsborough. Time passed quickly. They picked up their children from the servants living nearby. How they had grown! And almost all of them, Jacobo, Pedro, Pazzis, were doing art! It had to be in the blood. Several children had died, and this cast a temporary pall over the happy reunion.

The majordomo delivered his report: nothing had happened. "You faithful servant!" cried Don Juan. "You heart of gold," the Princess added with emotion. "Unlock the door!" The mutton-chopped steward did as he was bidden and cleared the table, on which certain things had changed over the course of two years. The silver was tarnished, the damask tablecloth was yellowed, and the flowers wilted as at an abandoned gravesite. Underneath the covers, the *faux* sheep cheese from Mahón sat in mummified condition. There were dead flies, desiccated spiders, bees, wasps, cobwebs, the smell of decay. In a word: a pitiful *memento mori*.

Some weeks later, Don Juan's personal spoils from their artistic voyage arrived in Valldemosa. Heavy crates were carried into the cloister. The Elgin Marbles? No, it was a cargo of exhibition catalogues, theater programs, tickets, menus, newspapers, and brochures. Two years' worth of alibis for Don Juan. Had there been a murder? Was somebody plotting against him? He needed only to reach into one of his crates from England, and his head was free from the noose. Neither Don Juan nor the Princess was ever accused of a crime committed during their two-year absence. And no one came forward to accuse them of a crime against their own family.

That's how people get poor. And yet the final collapse arrived unexpectedly.

The banker dispatched an urgent messenger to the Palace of the Kings of Mallorca in Valldemosa, where Don Juan was reading his Quevedo, where the Princess painted her pictures, and where Pedro and his brothers played soccer with the skulls of dead Moorish sheiks, Fatimas, and eunuchs that they had dug up in the crypts, to their father's horror. The banker's emissary was a classic Messenger of Doom, the kind one reads about in novels or, better yet, gets to see on the tragic stage. His arrival had an effect like a sudden smack at a beehive. People began rushing about, back and forth. They bumped against each other. They shouted. They issued orders. It was like the old times of the Moorish hegemony, when the family first took on the cognomen Verdugo. Had the infidel once again arrived at the gates? Could one again hear shouts from the ramparts: "Death to the Castilians! Death to the Suredas!"?

The event signified peril for the House of Sureda, but this time Mohammed had not sent his Moorish scimitars to besiege the charterhouse. Instead, he sent one of his minor prophets, the *botones* from one of the Palma gentlemen's clubs, to deliver the sad news. The cloister would be foreclosed the very next day, the entire property auctioned off. Don Juan! Save all the irreplaceable works of art that you can!

Don Juan's banker had got wind of the enforced auction, and decided to warn his friend.

Don Juan Sureda Bimer of the House of Verdugo sounded his horn and called down from the battlements of his castle, "The enemy is approaching! Save the valuables of the Palace of the Catholic Kings of Aragón and Mallorca! To the boxes!"

Large and small, major- and minor-domo, *botones*, hired hands, maids, hangers-on—each was given an assignment. Don Juan personally wrote out tags to be placed on beds, chairs, plates, and platters which famous personages had slept in, sat on, or eaten from. Then everything was carried over to one of the nursemaids' houses at 11 Street of Bitterness. The naming of this street was a triumph of local political premonition, for now a nameless destiny was being fulfilled within its confines. Every single item that was of value in Don Juan's eyes got lugged over to the nursemaid's abode and deposited there, piled up in wild haste. The treasures were heaped on top of each other; the floors sagged under their weight; chairs and baskets jutted forth from the windows. There were boxes containing porcelain, hundreds of salon chairs, armchairs, and stools, plus mattresses piled one upon the other like so many layers of fossilized strata. And then Don Juan's anxiously hoarded collection of alibis: boxes, more boxes, chests, packages—the sweat poured all night long.

Anyone observing these nocturnal goings-on would have to conclude that a palace was being plundered by a mob. Down with feudal domination! To the gallows with the princes, counts, and barons! Death to the Suredas! Afterwards it was determined that plundering had in fact taken place, although the items stolen were among those that the master of the palace had designated as unimportant: the treasures of the Kings of Aragón and Mallorca. To him, the most valuable property was the chairs that had been sat upon by celebrities, the cups from which they had sipped their coffee, the mattresses they had lain upon either alone or in company of others.

When the *embargador* arrived the next day, he found the site empty and deserted. Apart from a lone chair, he could identify nothing fit to be auctioned. He had to settle for the immoveable parts of the estate, the buildings and grounds. And when he sat down on the single remaining chair—now a prop in a tragedy different from the one Vigoleis was living through—with the intention of writing down his official report, he ended up flat on the ground. The chair had only three legs. With this gesture, the civil servant brought to completion all that the now-defunct charterhouse had to offer.

Don Juan escaped to the hills, his children resumed their marauding, and the Princess continued painting. The three-legged chair did not wander off with a special tag to the arsenal on Bitterness Street. Instead, Don Juan remained true to his custom and had it taken to Palma, where relatives of his had meanwhile rented an apartment. Life went on. Now the family was "tenement nobility," and the three-legged chair represented their best effort at displaying high style. Was there a shedding of tears? Spanish grandees don't cry over minor matters.

"Wait, Beatriz. I'll go get a ladder next door. They're always willing to lend us one when we have company. Then you can get that topmost mattress ready. It's the one that was slept on by Don Ramón del Valle-Inclán. I know you're not much of a fan of that writer, but it'll be hard to haul anything else up there to sleep on that would be more to your liking. Let's just see..."

This mountain of a bed, consisting in layer upon layer of mattresses, bore tags that exhibited the following strata of famous slumberers: Don Gabriel Alomar—Don Felix Rubén Darío—Don Miguel de Unamuno — S. A. R. Luis Salvador—Don Federico Chopin—Jovellanos—Mother Ey—Don José Miralles—Archbishop Obispo—Don Antonio Gelabert —Azorín—Don Ramón del Valle-Inclán. I would have liked to lie on top of my fellow-countrywoman Mother Ey, about whom Pedro told us some fascinating tales, whereas Beatrice announced a preference for Chopin. But rearrangement of the mattresses was as good as impossible without emptying out the whole room. So we decided to accept the stratification as it came about hastily during the wild night of enforced removal. And anyway, this mountain of mattresses had attained its size according to certain laws of destiny. For example, the one labeled "Alfonso XIII *EL REY*" did not end up in our largely democratic heap of pallets.

One aristocratic trait in Mamú's personality that I admired greatly was this: she couldn't sleep in strange beds. She therefore took her own bed with her on her travels—or rather, she owned several such personal beds. She always sent one of these ahead together with her load of large baggage. Other people, on the other hand, are proud to be able to tell their grandchildren that they have slept in beds in which kings, popes, celebrated whores, saints, or dictators have sweated out their lust and their fear, their piety, hypocrisy, death agony, or contempt for the Divinity. Beatrice also doesn't like strange beds, whereas I myself hover too insecurely between the earth and the sky to have much concern about the surface I sleep upon. On this evening in the Sureda panopticon, before climbing on top of the Valle-Inclán mattress, Beatrice took a sleeping powder, not for fear of any infra-poetic vapors emitted by that romantic libertine, but out of sheer terror that she might hit her head against the ceiling if our own body heat should cause the ghostly pile beneath us to come alive, much as fleas can be animated by the scent of human blood. I took no such precautionary measure, with the result that I received a bump on my forehead when the souls underneath us got restless, making me have vivid dreams about what each of them was going through as they slept on Sureda mattresses. Mr. Silberstern, who will make his appearance in a later chapter, would have hit the ceiling with his belly—that is how narrow the space was between Valle-Inclán and the beams of our ceiling.

Next to our sleeping quarters was a room full of chairs. Although the eviction from the castle had taken place two or three years previously, it was impossible to imagine how anybody could have piled up these hundreds of chairs in such a way as to avoid getting buried beneath a cascade of tumbling poltronas. The room was chock full. Not all of the chairs in this collection were catalogued. But every last one of them had, at one time or another, served as a place of repose for some notable personage—and who, in Spain, is not notable? Don Juan at first intended to put labels on the unidentified items, but then he decided against it for two reasons: he did not want anyone to accuse him of historical falsification, and he simply could not face the idea of returning to the Valley of the Muza. And besides, a sufficient number of chairs were already tagged with famous names in the interest of posterity.

In the presence of these thousands of chair legs, it once again became apparent how false and mean the suspicions of Mamú's Christian ladies had been that Vigoleis was a Communist. For now he would have to be overcome with distress at the thought of his one single, borrowed chair. Here the chairs were struggling beneath their own weight, as well as under a heavier mythological burden. I felt not the slightest twinge of envy; I remained as cool as a historian registering facts, so long as they were certifiable as such. This, too, was a Waterloo, and that was all it was. It was difficult to reconstruct what had happened at the site.

Another room was reserved for the crates and baskets containing historical porcelain and flatware, as well as for the bedclothes, blankets, pillows, and bedspreads, all of them in bundles bearing labels. Most of this collection had already been consumed by moths or gnawed by mice and rats. I rummaged out several boxes filled with gold and silver livery buttons. When their shine suddenly faded and their heraldic symbolism disappeared, Don Juan removed these buttons with his own hands, but permitted his servants to keep their uniforms.

Dinner jackets, hats, ladies' suits, children's clothing—a theater wardrobe
of astonishing variety lay in a pile beneath the staircase, covered with burlap.
And in a special box, carefully packed in straw, the noble family's chamber
pots. Among these there was one worth mentioning, not for the personage
who utilized it—a tag revealed the name attached to this most private of utensils—but for what was visible inside it. But let me quickly prevent any misunderstandings. In a later chapter a similar misunderstanding will prove
absolutely crucial, but in the present instance I wish to draw attention solely
to the decoration and inscription inside this ethnologically significant household item, to which we must give our attention anon.

Paintings by El Greco and Murillo; Italians, Dutch masters; incunabula,
manuscripts, the entire palace library—Don Juan was unable to rescue a single
item. One shudders at the thought of sardines being grilled and *paella* simmering on cottage hearths all over the Valley, over flames fueled by irreplaceable treasures of the nation's past. And yet we ourselves, we who call ourselves
representatives of the great Western cultural and intellectual tradition, we who
boast of our command of the alphabet, who read books and perhaps even
write them—were we any different from those Valldemosans who didn't care
a fig about frying their fish on a fire produced by a first edition of Quevedo?

We had, as it were, no money. And without money even the most sublimely
educated person will revert to the hairiest barbarism, unless he prefers to
adopt the glassy-eyed look of an ascetic and simply starve. Our pesetas were
just enough for an *olla potrida*, the popular stew, but not enough for us to
buy fuel for an open hearth.

"We'll consume a historic chair!" Pedro always came up with the right expression. I tugged a chair from the bottom of the pile. It was hard going, but
I did it so well that a whole bunch of chairs came plunging down from the
top. We had to barricade the door to avoid being buried in an avalanche of
furniture.

Since we were lacking a hatchet, Pedro was about to kick the chair apart
when I stepped forward to prevent such an irreverent act. I put the chair on
the firestone of the capacious hearth, which was separated from the rest of
the kitchen by a low partition. I set it afire, using material purloined from
Don Juan's archive of alibis: theater programs from his "Paris" file. Then we
began wagering over which direction the burning chair would start to lean.
This was exciting business, and we repeated the ritual before every meal. I recall
one elaborate chair whose name-tag had been gnawed away. Although it
burned with blinding flames, it leaned neither to the right nor to the left, nor
did it bend forward or crash down backward, nor did it crumble in on itself.
It simply carbonized without losing its shape, leaving only a black skeleton.
At the beginning of the process we joked about this special saint getting
burned at the stake. But then we turned silent, because things were becoming
uncanny. Beatrice, normally so very rational, claimed to espy the outlines of
a human figure in the little blue flames shooting out of crevices in the chair.
The smell of resin and incense was so strong as to take our breath away.

We concluded that higher forces must be at work here, occult powers that Don Juan held in command by keeping them in chains. It was likely that this poltrona had once borne the weight of the Mallorquin mystic Raimundus Lullius, the originator of the Great Art. Pedro did not dispute this assumption, for the sage Raimundus had in fact frequented the palace and conjured up spirits for the ancestral grandees. Unfortunately, our house did not contain a bell-jar large enough to cover the carbonized skeleton. Otherwise we would have conserved it for posterity. Smaller glass covers called *redomas* were plentiful in the *entrada*, containing under their mildewed domes such things as sprigs of myrtle and bridal wreaths, little collections of shells and coral, miniature Stations of the Cross replete with colorful penitent folk, and even more numerous insects, all of them on their way to this Calvary and unable to escape. Death, a common theme in this kind of popular art, had come to these household pests unexpectedly, and now they lay there as if the pious artist had intended all along to include them in his kitschy tragic tableau. Pedro said that the palace servants were very fond of these scenes, and that was why, when Don Juan enjoined everybody to rescue the most important contents of the palace, they had removed them to safety. And anyway, why should a painting by Velázquez have greater value than an insectarium, at a moment when a palace is collapsing? Incidentally—this occurs to me as I write these words—the fall of the House of Sureda coincided with the dethronement of the Bourbon Dynasty. All this feudal magnificence then dried up under a redoma, augmented by the vermin that always find their way to the scene of decay.

We prepared our meals in long-handled pans. Using a copper kettle that hung on a hook over the hearth, we boiled water against typhus and the plague.

We lived this way for three weeks, yanking many a chair out from under the spectral buttocks of some celebrity or other, but we never again got to see one of them in the little blue flames.

On the first evening, when Beatrice was about to wash our dishes, Pedro told her not to bother. We were not on General Barceló Street, he said, but on the Street of Bitterness. He went to the WC, which was separated from the kitchen only by a curtain, opened a little window and tossed the entire set of dishes into the cloaca located far below the house, which was built on a cliff. "We've got plenty of dishes. There are more than ten crates full of them in the attic. Papá thought of everything. Let's not pretend that we're poor. Take an example from Vigoleis."

I had tossed a fresh chair onto the embers to warm up a bowl of water for shaving. I wanted to confront the private physician of Ludwig Salvator with a clean-shaven face. Should I bend over and poke through the ashes? I had spent enough of my lifetime in the bent-over position. Now I intended to enjoy life to the full. I had discovered a silver bowl from which, according to the inscription, no less a spirit than Don Gaspar Melchor de Jovellanos had drunk the bitter gall of exile. This statesman, politician, and writer, Mallorca's greatest exile next to Kessler, had spent part of his incarceration in our cloister. I used the bowl for my shaving water.

"Let's go!" said Pedro. "Don José is waiting. He knows that I'll be bringing you along."

I picked up a knobby rosewood cane with an ivory handle and a whole bunch of tags hanging from it like multicolored ribbons on a guitar. "We're off!"

"What are you doing with that horrible stick? You're always making fun of people who use canes, and now you're going out with one yourself?"

"Beatrice, what you see is no longer a cane. Like everything else here it has long since lost its original function. It is my fly swatter, and it will come in very handy. Here, I've found something for you, too."

I handed her a yellowed pair of unmentionables that, if the labels hadn't got switched around at the "Pressa" in Cologne, had once enclosed the aristocratic corpulence of Spain's greatest woman writer, Doña Emilias de Pardo Bazán. "You can use this as a fan when the hot wind blows in from the Teix. Shall we go?"

Don José, private medical consultant to His Royal Highness Archduke Ludwig Salvator of Austria, was also in fact a doctor. He was also an impassioned collector, though he never let his avocation get the best of him. He collected postage stamps, examples of human behavior, and human embryos in the phase of development when they are no longer fetuses. He preferred the embryos of twins and triplets, although he confined himself to these specialties on the basis of availability rather than scientific speculation. Multiple births are rare, and rarer still is the opportunity to put one up in a jar. Don José never got beyond triplet specimens. He was familiar with the Hameln Septuplets, so famous and notorious in the Middle Ages and featured on a fearful broadsheet that we exhibited at the Cologne "Pressa." But he himself could never dream of obtaining such an impressive rarity to put on his shelf. Nowadays this forward-looking physician would have his little moon-calves encased in plastic. At the time, he was limited to the use of pickle jars from his kitchen, which he sealed with the skin of pigs or fishes. Like the Rhine Maidens, these wee people floated in their bath of alcohol, and it was possible to put the specimens to a test of the principle known as the Carthusian Diver. Anyone wandering into this copa had to be in a good mood, with nerves strengthened to avoid spoiling the appetite. The copa is a pantry adjoining the kitchen, which also serves as the area for preparing meals. Standing next to home-made pickles and delicate aspics, the embryos led their melancholy existence beyond the reaches of space and time, weightless, free of sin, and blissful in their cradling, paradisiac, briny bath. People came and went around them all the time. No sooner had one made the acquaintance of an onion, a *truite* or a *langouste en aspic*, when Doña Clara appeared to fetch its neighbor and place on the pantry counter some new, no less succulently prepared dish, which likewise eventually went the way of all earthly things. All that was left over was us.

On certain occasions these Rhine Maidens—the very personification of humility and watery contentment—became a nuisance. There was, for example, a woman from England, one of the thousand old and decrepit ladies who came across the Mediterranean to Mallorca every winter with the regularity of migrating birds. This one had been coming to Valldemosa for many years for recuperation in Don José's abode. Doña Clara, the physician's niece and caretaker, had converted the property into a *pensión*, a kind of private sanatorium named "*Hospedage del Artista*," which she presided over. Not everyone was permitted to enter a name in the guest book; you had to be an artist, or an invalid, or mentally ill. Once these conditions were fulfilled, you could enjoy a heavenly stay with Don José and Doña Clara. This British hybrid lady too, partly splenetic and partly diabetic, referred to the amazing couple's *hospedage* as her second home. But she had never been inside the copa. As a proper lady she refrained from such forms of domestic intimacy. Then one day she had a moment of weakness and entered the pantry to sneak a bite to eat—Don José was keeping her on a strict diet—and what did she see? Her gaze suddenly perceived a preliminary phase of human existence, slowly revolving twofold upon itself in a shimmering greenish medium inside a glass jar, as in a dream. Was this salmon in vinegar and oil? Curried lobster in jelly?

The lady screams and faints away. Tumbling to the floor she knocks over a pot of marinated olives, and then she herself metamorphoses into a ghostly Rhine Maiden. The house personnel rush to her aid. Don José, who cannot bear the sight of a corpse, is staggering. Paquito and Manolo, Doña Clara's very grown-up sons, give their attention to the doctor. Clarita, as her friends call Doña Clara, bends over the lady who is presumed dead.

Bobby, a German friend of the family, a poor emigré artist with Valldemosan experience who, to the delight of the establishment, was a walking expert in first aid—Bobby soon revived the lady on the floor. She immediately called for a taxi to Palma, and on the very same evening she boarded ship for the mainland. Mandrakes with bulbous heads do not belong inside pickle jars, much less in the copa of a convalescent home.

"That's how it goes," said Don José, "when patients don't follow my instructions. Now she'll never come back, and I could have made her healthy."

No patient had ever died under the hands of this physician. How many doctors can say that of themselves? Does this suggest that Don José was a miracle worker, or rather a fake and a quacksalver perhaps in league with Mamú's Christian Science ladies? Or was his success due to the fact that he had no patients except for His Highness, who had long since laid himself down to die at Brandeis Castle? Don José had more patients than was beneficial for his hobbies, and in a larger area of the island than his mule could reach: in the Valley, across the mountains, in Sóller, in Deyá, even in Palma. His name was in excellent repute everywhere. And yet he hated the sight of blood, and looking at a dead body was the living end for him. A person, he said, should die alone; dying was a completely personal matter. Like the animals, no one should make a fuss about it. He was a great friend to mankind, and all the more so in order to speak and act as he did.

Whenever he was summoned to the bedside of a patient whose hours were numbered, whose fate was already in the hands of Almighty God and who had begun the death struggle, our doctor always fainted. On such occasions the peasants or fishermen had a hard time lifting this portly gentleman, and in the process forgot about their own dying relative. It is well known how dependent poor folk are on the local doctor, pastor, and schoolteacher, especially in countries where these are the only people who can read and write, and sometimes not even that. They would feel relieved if Don José came to with the aid of age-old nostrums and magic amulets and, strengthened with a gulp from the porrón, could finally be heaved up onto his mule. "Hurrah, saved again!" How awful it would be if the doctor had croaked under our noses! Croaking, in the meantime, had been taken care of in selfless fashion by the patient, thereby fulfilling the will of the Almighty, who disdains the ministrations of even the most expert of medicine men. This, by the way, was also Don Juan's opinion as a strict Catholic, and it was a view shared by our own private physician in Palma, the equally congenial Dr. Solivellas, who never concealed from his patients that he was first and foremost a Catholic, and then a doctor.

Don José collected stamps the normal way, with the aid of a scalpel that feared the sight of blood. And he collected specimens of human nature with the aid of a wax nose. He practiced applied psychology, but without succumbing to the ridiculous ambition of competing with his bottom-feeding colleagues in a search for the primordial origins of human consciousness. He was at a far cry from such presumptuousness. He did not plumb the depths; he avoided the abysses where physician and patient become indistinguishable, and out of which they emerge with transposed heads, requiring both of them to undertake an even more dangerous descent into the inferno. Don José put all such experiments behind him. He had studied it all in Barcelona, where he was respected for his scholarly publications and deemed worthy of an academic career. The great histologist Santiago Ramón y Cajal had just taken notice of him when the calamity occurred. Don José fell in love; he looked deeply into the eyes of his *novia*, and even more deeply into her soul, but failed to observe that at the surface his girlfriend was attached to another guy. This discovery broke his heart and shattered his trust in the science of the human soul. Henri-Frédéric Amiel went through similar crushing experiences, but his natural cynicism provided him with a diving suit resistant to the pressures of the depths. Don José was no cynic. He remained outwardly calm, made no further mistakes, left the mainland, became a country doctor in Valldemosa—and took care of the rest with his wax nose.

We are seated at table, delighting in the exquisite tiny morsels Doña Clara is serving up at a meal with at least 24 courses. Her cooking is famous on the whole island. The diners are chattering and arguing, there is excellent wine and carefully prepared dietary dishes for the clinical guests. Suddenly Don

José arises and leaves this *table d'hôte* that he insists upon for the main meals in his establishment. We all assume that he has gone out to saddle his mule and ride off to visit a patient somewhere beyond the hills. But he returns after only a few minutes, and resumes his seat at table. But look—what has happened? Don José's features have changed. Is he the victim of a spontaneous hypertrophy of the bodily extremities? Doctors speak of "acromegaly" when certain parts of the body suddenly become enlarged as a result of a disease of the pituitary gland. This is a mysterious organic process, as yet little understood by the medical profession. Don José's nose is swollen, reddened by a network of capillaries, and now three or even four times as long as before. Don José performs his transformation into a carnivalesque pathological specimen, but not by means of a clever tweaking of his hypophysis—that would mean plunging into the inscrutable depths. No, for this purpose José installs a prosthesis, in common parlance a wax nose, and one might say that there is no more superficial solution to the problem. Don José is interested in the reactions of ordinary people who visit his house, most of whom are his patients, to this miraculous change in his appearance. He then draws his conclusions, which can be called infallible. He is particularly pleased by reactions of acute fright. He told us of one instance—thereby violating medical secrecy out of sheer professional egotism, a trait that he normally lacked—when the sight of a new nose emerging from behind his handkerchief suddenly caused a lady of high noble standing suddenly to pass a tapeworm. Which is to say, the nose had an anthelmintic effect, whereas traditional applications of anesthetics had been unable to dislodge the parasite from its aristocratic hostess. On another occasion, Don José forgot to remove his waxen proboscis when, while sipping his *café negro*, he was suddenly summoned to attend to a patient. The patient took such a fright at his appearance that it was no longer necessary to apply the leeches he had brought with him. The blood clot broke up by itself, and the patient recovered then and there.

During the years when Don José worked as a physician and inspector of public hygiene in Valldemosa, the mortality rate declined by half. In addition, like any good country doctor, Don José knew a thing or two about agriculture and animal husbandry.

Since he disliked death, he was always reluctant to fill out death certificates. So it was lucky for him that as a result of the declining death rate, this mournful obligation was also curtailed by half. But then came the Civil War. People died in the thousands—of heart attack, it was said, right here in Valldemosa, and Don José was forced to certify this epidemic cause of death for the authorities and for the historical record. This is a customary procedure in all civilized countries, no matter how bestially the populace might start massacring one another. Whatever is dead must be confirmed as dead in black and white by an expert, and once it is confirmed it stays confirmed. The young epileptic in Palma had six weeks of experience of this phenomenon. And incidentally, Don José claimed that he could have revived the fellow from his pseudo-exitus by means of his wax-nose shock therapy—and I believe he could have.

And so Don José wrote out death certificates in mass-production. There was no end to it, for the war was not just a one-time *pronunciamiento*. It attached itself to the population like a parasite, and murder was a natural component of its metabolism. Until one day when this physician refused to fill out any more such certificates, and started swearing as only he knew how to swear. On top of everything else, he said, he was a Catholic Christian. The others were Catholic Christians, too, and because they were in the majority they murdered Don José for refusing to be their brother. If only this wonderful man had heeded the maxim of Don Patuco, many of whose exploits I recounted to him: "Don't count the corpses, my friend! What's the use? Nature doesn't count your individual life!"

Delivering babies was likewise not a forte of this physician. He held the sane opinion that Nature was much better at this procedure if left to itself. One could perhaps assist with a few chores, such as heating some water and keeping towels and a sponge ready, and soon the new citizen of the world would emerge on its own and start crowing plaintively. My grandmother would have been an ideal midwife for Don José, for she liked this job and did it all by and for herself, with increasing skill from newborn to newborn. After her final self-delivery, as she showed the little heap of human misery to her amazed husband, she said, "Wöllem, count 'em up. Is this number twenty?" My grandfather reached for the bottle and drank himself, uncounted, under the table of his own tavern.

Thus it is quite understandable that one day Don José said to his German emigré assistant, "Bobby, I'm going to train you as a midwife. In six month's time you'll be initiated in the secrets of human birth, so you can accompany me when I go out on deliveries. I'll wait outside until you're finished. Or better yet, I'll send you out all by yourself right from the start. That way we'll need one less mule."

Bobby, who was born in Essen, grew up in the shadow of the Ruhr factory chimneys. At the age of twenty he was already the youngest, most talented, and most promising teacher at the Folkwang School. His specialties were photography and calligraphy. For purely aesthetic reasons he wrote everything in small-case letters, with no concern for the philological problems that this usage might give rise to. His penmanship caused the Nazis to suspect him from the start, for their own custom was to write everything as big as possible, if necessary with blood. Bobby stuck by his habit of writing in minuscules and with home-made ink. This got him branded as a cultural Bolshevist. "Concentration camp! Shoot him!"

Bobby fled to Paris, after having enlisted the aid of a high party functionary in converting his savings into foreign currency and transferring them in monthly installments to France. For this, the functionary was shot. But Bobby had money and, as such things go, he eventually landed on Mallorca. There he fell into the hands of a kleptomaniacal German woman, who in turn was in cahoots with a kleptomaniacal Spaniard, who in turn was involved in odd jobs for the German consulate. His story became a rat-cluster of forged signatures, confiscated letters, and extortion, until the Spanish police finally stepped in and liberated Bobby from the hands of the crooks. The Consul wanted to have him deported at the expense of the Third Reich, which would have snuffed out the whole case along with Bobby. Then Manolo appeared on the scene. Manolo, Doña Clara's son, a painter and a man of artistic sensibility, said, "Bobby, you dare not go back home to the Reich. Come to Valldemosa. You're much too precious for Nazi bullets." The old jalopy of a bus provided transport. Bobby became the darling of Don Juan's household, and he continued writing everything small, subject only to his own self-criticism.

This German fellow was skilled not only with pen and pencil, but also with hammer and saw, awl and paintbrush, glue pot and asparagus knife, grafting tool and soup spoon, enema syringe and larding-needle. Don José noticed all of this. Bobby was inventive, too—just the right combination of talents for any respectable doctor. Why shouldn't he also learn to handle delivery forceps, too? "He will be my assistant. No one else is going to take over my practice."

At that time, former judges of the Reich Court were eking out a living on the island by selling sauerkraut and chickpeas. Famous U-boat captains were smuggling opium and cocaine. University professors were tilling gardens and making apricot jelly. Clergymen were reaching for vials of poison. Famous physicians wearing false beards were sneaking through the night to patients whom they could not treat in broad daylight for lack of a Spanish medical license. A German whore, on the other hand, could walk with pride the streets of the Borne, as if she were on the Friedrichstrasse in Berlin. And Bobby of the Folkwang School now refused to accept an honorable job! He eventually did put on a white physician's smock, but instead of holding visiting hours or going off to treat patients, he painted the entire *Hospedage del Artista* in *Folkwang* hues, and created for Doña Clara a brooding Madonna *al fresco* on the wall above the staircase. But he went no further. He had no desire to assist a woman in her hours of labor—I won't speculate about women in their hours of relaxation. Don José was desperate. His intuitions about human nature had failed him. His wax-nose method had no effect on this beleaguered German emigré. Bobby remained true to his artistic calling. He never again took up serious painting, but his hobby was serious typography. Today his name is well-known. He is presenting his business card with the type design of these jottings of mine, as evidence that nobody shot either him or his author.

When we first entered the doctor's house, we met with turmoil that was unusual even by Spanish standards. Don José was passing through all the phases of annoyance and displeasure, from simple vexation to unbridled anger and wild, passionate fury. Don José the Wise? The friend of mankind? Had he been bitten by a tarantula? Pedro was certain that this raging individual was in fact the physician. His coat-tails were fluttering and his mustachios were aquiver, but he was still a handsome man having a handsome fit. Had someone stolen a three-penny Mauritius from his collection? Had someone damaged his pickled multuplets? He ran into the house, then back out again. He waved his arms around and shooed away people who were trying to calm him down, they too cursing and waving their arms. We were given a display of the strict family hierarchy of helpfulness: first Doña Clara, then Manolo, then Paquito. They shouted a mixture of Spanish and Mallorquin; I couldn't understand a word, so I was at a loss to figure out what kind of catastrophe had befallen the *hospedage* at the very moment when we were to be introduced as new guests. This was embarrassing. In situations like this, one doesn't know how to behave, and thus one doesn't behave at all—which is exactly what we did. It usually turns out later that this form of sympathy with distress has created bonds that not even apparent death can break asunder.

Beatrice listened carefully to the tumult happening around us, and began some cerebral analysis, dissecting the fragments of language that to my ears were simple noise and inarticulate grunting. She then tied them back together to shape an initial hesitant hypothesis: something awful must have happened in the doctor's office. A pail of bandages...

"Stop, *chérie*! Don't say one word more! I know everything! That pail! Don José has discovered in his pail a human body. Some frightful mother has smuggled the fruit of her womb into this most innocuous of places, and now Doña Clara is refusing to hand over one of her pickle jars."

"Yuck!"

"What do you mean, 'yuck'? Don José is an embryophilogist, so what else would he want to pickle—herring, maybe?"

But this was something different. There was no need for the courts to step in. No mother had committed a crime against a burgeoning human life. Beatrice could now hear certain things more clearly: the doctor's office assistant must have forgotten to empty the hermetically sealed rubbish pail. Don José, Inspector of *sanidad*, was understandably incensed by this dereliction—but why was he so wildly out of control? In Spain? Messengers were sent into town to fetch the assistant. Don José was still fuming. He took no notice of us whatever.

A short, fat, roundish, thoroughly pudgy woman, Doña Clara, greeted us cordially. We were welcome as friends of Pedro's, but this unfortunate incident... "Pedro, take my place for just a minute, I..."

There was renewed commotion in front of the house—which is to say, the commotion was coming from the direction of the village and getting closer. Now they were chasing some poor dog! The dog-chaser was a pale young fellow with long legs and pitch-black hair: Paquito, Clarita's youngest son, who had been fleetingly introduced to us during the earlier attempts to calm down the physician. Everybody was shouting: "You coward! You bad dog! You miserable beast!" So now, in addition to everything else, their dog had run away. It never rains but it pours.

From one moment to the next, Don José stopped his raging and was once again the dignified private physician of His Royal Majesty. He stood still, smoothed his laboratory smock, pulled out a red handkerchief, and blew his nose with a loud report. A small crowd gathered reverently around him, and at his feet lay the whining bitch. The office assistant seemed completely forgotten; a greater crime was here awaiting its punishment. Spinning on her own axis in the dust of the road, the dog wagged her tail and cowered as people berated her with epithets. The anathemas were uttered in Mallorquin dialect, so I didn't understand a word. But the dog seemed to know exactly what was meant, even though, as I later found out, she wasn't a native Mallorcan. She came from Ibiza, the little island of the Balearic Group, and she was a purebred Izibenca, from a race of some of the most beautiful dogs I have ever seen. She was a bit like a short-haired greyhound, ocher-colored with white spots. One characteristic of the breed is that it is confined to Ibiza and can procreate only in that environment. Even the short move to Mallorca can shorten its life. The ancient Carthaginians knew this dog, praised it, and ate it.

"You miserable cur!" Don Juan probably was shouting. "Just what do you think you're doing, running away like that? So that's the thanks we get...!" There followed a list of the reasons why the dog should feel grateful to its master. And then the doctor's mood softened. That was the end of his moral diatribe. "*Adelante!*" he shouted, "Onward!" The Ibizenco registered her master's change of tone, wagged her long, sickle-shaped tail in joyful obedience, and jumped up at the doctor's denim trousers. But Don José shouted, "Get away! Do your duty!" and pointed sternly in the direction of the house. Pistola obeyed, thankful for this resumption of trust. With a single bound she leaped over the window sill into the doctor's office.

Pedro motioned us closer to the window—it would be worth our while to watch the proceedings. The dog stood in front of the pail, placed one paw on the lever at the bottom, and pressed it. The lid lifted slowly, and Pistola began emptying it. Beatrice screamed with disgust. Now sick as a dog, my wife had to submit to pharmaceutical treatment by Don José.

This performance, which to me seemed like a perfect display of animal training, was in fact an example of Ibizencan dilettantism. Attracted by the contents of the hygienic container, the dog had taught herself the trick of opening it. She didn't even belong at this house; she didn't have any home, but just strayed around the village. For years now she had been performing this minor service in Don Jose's office with amazing punctuality. The only times of irregular rubbish removal, said Pedro, occurred when the dog was in heat. Incidentally, the doctor had no other clinical assistant, and this was one further reason why he wished to take on this German Folkwang School fellow as an apprentice. What the dog did for him, Bobby could do in his sleep.

Don José never considered me worthy of donning the clinical smock, even though on a number of occasions I offered him proof of my skill as a handyman and a quick learner of matters technical. Besides, as a university student I had dabbled a bit in medical subjects and even taken first steps toward starting a collection of embryos. I wouldn't have rejected such a career. It would have given my life a new direction. But then Pascoaes would have remained undiscovered and this book unwritten—which of the two would be worse?

We stayed in Valldemosa for three weeks. I finally became acquainted with the Charterhouse that I had so often shown off to other people. Pedro explained everything to us, including the nail from Christ's cross, which was Don Juan's property and only by chance had not been taken to the nursemaid's home by his pious servants. Some ancestor of the Suredas had gone off to the Holy Land on a mission of piracy and brought home the nail as a relic. Since I regard Pedro as a better *Führer* than myself, I had no reason to doubt the authenticity of this sacred piece of hardware. Nevertheless, on my own tours I stuck to my legend of the plague torch, which never failed to grab the tourists—and that's what my employers wanted. There are thousands of Nails from the Holy Cross, but my *taeda pesti*s was unique.

We also got to know a postman who was no less crafty and resourceful than the bitch Pistola. He was of course illiterate, but he had the capacious memory of such lucky souls, a phenomenon that historians often underestimate because it doesn't fit in with their theories. The postmaster, who knew how to read and write, sorted the mail and read off the addresses in the sequence of the delivery route. The letter-carrier memorized the names and delivered each item without ever making a mistake, which certainly can't be said of your run-of-the-mill literate postman.

We took hikes down to the Valldemosa *cala* and caught fishes and turtles. Our nets didn't trap any man-eating sharks, not even the little sharks that my touring compatriots tucked away with such relish when I told them that they were not the common fish you could buy cheaper and better in Germany. We camped out, collected driftwood, and cooked our meals over it. Because of the mosquitoes, we kept the fire burning day and night. Pedro told us pirate stories and filled in the history of his family, supplementing his chronicle with romantic, classical, and heroic medieval details, and arrived at the tale of a certain uncle, a *tío* twice removed, who met his death in the belly of a sea monster. In the waters of Cabrera and Conejera, the island homeland of Hannibal, a shark swallowed this fellow whole, skin, hair, and bones, with all of the debts, shady dealings, disappointments, and hopes that clung to him as a Sureda from the House of Verdugo.

Pedro was ten years old when they took him to the little island populated by goats, where the funeral was held for a gentleman of whom it can at least be said that he knew how to hide from the prying eyes of the world—which, by the way, seems to be a talent that this dynasty passed on by inheritance. At the back of the procession was the wobbling casket, which had been caulked with pitch, just like a sea-going vessel. Now it stood on a cliffside in the midst of the bleached bones of the 8000 French soldiers who were abandoned here on Cabrera after the Battle of Bailén. One cannot imagine a more appropriate final resting place for a phantom corpse. The devout family was of the opinion that the fish would eventually deliver up their uncle, since his body contained a soul, and since he was, after all, not some insensate being that one simply devours in order to stay alive. Once he was spewed up on shore, a family member would have to arrive at the spot immediately to place the cadaver, which would no doubt be in sorry condition, into the coffin with the customary Christian ceremony.

Despite their intense patriotic piety the Suredas did not believe that Almighty God would go so far as to keep their uncle miraculously alive in the sea monster's belly. Perhaps they were also aware that their uncle's pattern of living was such that he was undeserving of being spit out whole, and that they would have to be content with his return in any shape whatsoever. I don't recall how long the island vigil lasted. In any case, the uncle never showed up. But every so often people caught sight of a shark's fin, a dolphin's nose, or the tail of some unfamiliar sea animal. Whenever this happened, the lookouts would catch their breath and think: if only this were our uncle! Then the sea would close up again, the waves would resume their rhythm of breathing with the air that coursed above them. The loyal family made the sign of the cross, ended their long wake in the name of the Lord who giveth and taketh away according to His will, and rowed back to Mallorca.

An aged fisherman, who was familiar with the ways of man-eating sharks, explained to the Suredas that all of their watching and waiting was useless. One simply could not expect that the fish that had swallowed the gentleman would ever vomit the gentleman out again. If some mysterious case of nausea were ever to cause the shark to do so, then it was certain that one of its less finicky cousins would immediately rush to the scene to devour the gentleman for a second time, and in so doing would turn over on its back, making the attack all the more grisly to behold.

If this uncle had been a prophet, the fish would in all likelihood have spit him back up onto the beach, permitting him to fulfill God's mission on *terra firma*—just as had happened with Jonah, who, after his release from probationary imprisonment, went on to spread God's words of anger against Nineveh more eagerly than ever before. But this Sureda fellow was only a Spanish grandee, a debtor to boot, and on top of it all a man in the habit of writing down his weak-willed, desperate thoughts in letters that later fell into Pedro's hands. From these, Pedro concluded that his uncle had every good reason to turn himself into a missing person. There was little doubt that he had decided to take up his hiking stick and beat it far away from his island homeland, at the very same time that his relatives put on mourning and had Masses read for him, and as little Pedrito sat on the desolate cliffside weeping because the big fish wouldn't give him back his uncle.

"Did you cry a lot over your lost uncle? And didn't you think a lot about the biblical story of Jonah, who was also swallowed by a big fish?"—I could just see the pageant of yesteryear, painted in bright Mediterranean colors: a weeping boy sitting next to a coffin on a rocky, weather-beaten cliff that juts up from the surf, like Salas y Gomez in Chamisso's poem, the sea gnawing eternally at the shoreland.

Pedro hadn't thought of Jonah, but he was reminded of the three youths in the burning fiery furnace, Daniel in the lion's den, and Lazarus in the state of decomposition. And he hadn't really cried, since he didn't even know that uncle of his. All he did was keep a lookout over the ocean. Perhaps this relative that the family was telling such tales about might come walking on the waves, a *puta* on his arm. For even then, Pedro sensed that some woman must be part of the story—a rather advanced apprehension of human nature for a ten-year-old.

When I was as old as Pedro was then, I wasn't sitting on a cliff next to an empty coffin, waiting for some up-chucked uncle. I was sitting obediently on a much too narrow bench at school, listening to our religion teacher, who was trying to sow the seeds of biblical truth into our souls. Since this priest lacked real experience of God, his instructional method was patterned on the reform-school model. His approach to the Book of Jonah was to portray it as the saga of a minor prophet's mission, disobedience, and punishment. He claimed that the great fish was a whale, and that in addition to the insolent prophet, it also swallowed a table and a stool for him to use inside its roomy guts. This was a time when one of our classmates' fathers was in prison for having neglectfully caused a fellow-worker to fall into a ditch, an accident that had a lethal result. We kids were terribly stirred up by this incident, and when the story of the minor prophet's imprisonment came up in religion class, we imagined Jonah as being like Otto's father and vice-versa, with the sole difference that Jonah could not get to see visitors through iron bars. Later, when I started dabbling in theological matters myself, I learned to my amazement that it probably wasn't a whale at all but an authentic man-eating shark, or according to some expert zoologists the feared Jonah Shark itself, *Carcharias verus* L., which rendered full credit to its scientific name by gulping down that very prophet. Back then, I believed every word of what the priest told us, even though I knew from reading books that a whale's esophagus has only enough room for a middle-sized herring to pass through. The miracle—and this aspect of the story is what the Church deemed important—seemed all the more miraculous.

Our priest wouldn't have been able to hoodwink Pedro with such a tale. At ten years of age he was so mature that he was already visiting bordellos in order to familiarize himself with that national institution. We boys up in Germany, holding our teacher's hand, visited a traveling menagerie. We got to see a flying dog that didn't fly, and a rattlesnake that didn't rattle, all for the 10 Pfennig that Mommy had given us. For 10 centimos, which he stole, Pedro too went with his whole class, but *sans* teacher, to a menagerie of lust, and made his first grab into the bosom of Mother Nature, who had not yet decided between animal and human characteristics. In order not to lose out on more lucrative business, it was usually the proprietress herself who undertook the erotic initiation. She sat on a chair, loosened her garments, asked each of the inquisitive rascals first to drop his coin in her hand. Then she made certain gestures and said, "*Basta, otro!*" and in this fashion serviced entire grades of school kids in just a few short minutes. As soon as you pass beyond the borders of your home town, things become radically different: here is Jonah at latitude 52° N, sitting obediently on his stool in the belly of a whale, waiting for a bell that will signal his release. And at 40°, in the Mediterranean, here is a boy sitting on a tiny island waiting for a fish to spew up a real Jonah who happens to be the boy's real uncle, though twice removed. And to think that fate had already permitted this selfsame boy to touch a woman's breast, an object that some of us kids in the German school may have imagined to exist, but which our religion teacher denied under threat of extra homework. Not even Eve in Paradise had a breast. Her kids were fed from a bottle containing Soxhlet-brand formula—that's what I, too, believed. The Bible as a collection of tales from *A Thousand-and-One Nights*—it's a ticklish subject, even today.

Quite apart from the purely geographic separation between Pedro and me during puberty, I could never have had a real Jonah for an uncle. Pedro is the scion of a dynasty that helped to write world history, whereas Vigoleis comes from a family whose name is at best good enough for a modest role in a village chronicle. His was a dynasty that enjoyed a certain earthly stability, owing to the fecundity of his father's mother, who planted a total of nineteen seedlings in the local soil. On his mother's side, two bishops arranged for the necessary linkage to Heaven Above. These achievements can, to be sure, serve as cozy intrafamilial mementos, to be placed and admired in photo albums and on mantelpieces. But will they have any value as history without adding some fictional spice to make them seem important? Hardly. In one other respect, too, they seem to lack real significance: as documentary underpinning of these jottings of mine. Just imagine for a moment the nature of my situation as the authorized biographer of Vigoleis. I have let my brother Ludwig periodically check through the manuscript of this book. When he reached the part where I first mention our grandmother's 19 children, he wrote in the margin, "*Wrong! Only 9! Typo in the death notice! according to Uncle Joseph.*"—each lapidary remark outfitted with an exclamation point as evidence of this reader's glee at catching the author in a typographical mistake. It is only Uncle Joseph as the source of this corrective information who escaped Ludwig's sardonic jibes, for he regards Uncle Joseph as beyond criticism—which he no doubt is, since this particular uncle of ours is a printer, and he is the one who probably used his father's press to print the death notice.

Well now, I thought, this is going too far, this is irresponsible pedantry. With a single stroke of the pen, ten children are eliminated from the list—this comes suspiciously close to a modern Massacre of the Innocents. Has King Herod returned to wield the Lord's scourge once again? Ten too many children! And to think that Granny was hoping to make it to the round number of twenty, in order that she could get to see her Wöllem sporting on his overcoat lapel a decoration from the Kaiser for productivity! Granted that if it ever came to a vote, nine children would still be in the minority. But such an act of decimation is still much too harsh. I wrote to my brother, the decimator: what a fine family this is, where you can't even depend on what's said in the death notices! I refuse to liquidate a single one of the 19 children; I shall defy the printer's devil and insist upon the existence of all of them. Have you, my Idumaean brother, considered that among the ten you have slaughtered we might have to count our own father? What, then, about us? Nineteen children—isn't that more exciting than quintuplets? And just think: almost all of the great geniuses of history came from families with numerous children, usually more than 15. It's all the more remarkable that no genius has yet come forth from our own family. Let's assume for a moment that those ten don't exist, and never did exist. As a long-time fan of circuses and county fairs, you must be fully aware of the attractiveness, for the minds of the common folks as for the great philosophers, of "what doesn't exist." Any carnival manager can vouch for this fact any night after the show is over, as he sits in his trailer sipping potato schnapps by the light of his kerosene lamp, counting the day's box-office take.

There were no further editorial objections. My brother kept his own counsel. Perhaps he was ashamed for being of little faith. Besides, he is not enough of a historian to insist on mobilizing a single dead typographical error against nineteen living persons.

In spite of our numerous uncles—oddly, none of the girls ever reached the age sufficient to make them our aunts—not one of them had the right stuff to be swallowed by a fish, and not only because the little creek that for centuries has coursed through our historically somnolent home town has no pretensions to reach an ocean. Our single mentionable uncle is my godfather, who like all of his brothers was beholden to the bottle and was otherwise a bookbinder, but a man who hardly ever glanced at the contents of what he was binding. Which means that he was highly reliable in his profession, just as an illiterate typesetter can be depended upon to keep strictly to what is in a manuscript. This merry fellow represented me at my baptism and, in the process, lent me his Christian name. Albert—it means "of brilliant lineage." Unfortunately, I have never detected any of this brilliance in him or in myself. The brilliance must have got diluted or vaporized by the baptismal waters. In any case, once Christ's work of redeeming my soul was accomplished with my uncle Albert's assistance and oath-taking, once all of my sins and my eternal punishment for them were washed away and I could partake of grace, illumination, and consecration in the Holy Spirit, thus becoming a child of God worthy of reward in Heaven—spiritual gifts that we no doubt deserve as we are placed into the vale of tears that is this life of ours, but for which I expressed my gratitude by bawling and wetting the ceremonial object I was lying on, a brocade baptismal cushion from my mother's Scheifes cottage. In brief, as soon as I became a full-fledged Christian soul, the members of my baptismal party felt that they, too, had a right to partake of certain blessings. They betook themselves without delay to the nearest pub in the vicinity of the church, which was the one run by my grandfather. They placed the baptized infant on the counter and started drinking. After this interlude they visited one watering-hole after another. My godfather got more and more crocked, while the baptismal infant's face became redder and redder, but there was no letup to their alcoholic anabaptist ritual. My father, my other uncles, other so-called uncles and family friends had no objections, and they drank, too. Soon they drank themselves out beyond the town limits into the outskirts, in each of the taprooms placing the "bearer of brilliant lineage" on the bar, where he screamed for his mother's breast, until at one of these establishments they finally just left him there. They completely overlooked the original sin that was the trigger for the Christian mystery that had just been accomplished with my person, and, wiping the beer foam from their Kaiser Wilhelm mustaches, reverted to pagan liturgy, victims of the concupiscence that Christian baptism fails to eliminate. They drank without me. And without me they all returned home. Where was their new little Christian child?

Somebody sounded the alarm. They retraced their steps through the various bars, miscalculating now and then, but at none of the stations of their reverse journey declining the bottles that had to be drunk from once again. After hours of intense searching, a local constable succeeded in spying out the bar counter where this little heap of Christianity lay in his soggy, stinking swaddling clothes, abandoned by God and his godfather. I was returned to my mother for the price of a bottle of aged-in-the-cask brandy—but was I still the same person? Hadn't my baptismal procession crossed another equally un-Christian baptismal cavalcade on its journey from bar to bar? Was I some stranger's infant, one that, following the sacred ceremony, likewise got carried to the beer spigots? This question has worried me all my life long, and it is one of the reasons why I seek protection behind my Vigoleis—not to mention all the mythological implications!

"So swiftly," we are told in the first chapter of Pascoaes' book on Napoleon, "did the birth proceed, that for lack of a cradle the newborn had to be wrapped in a tapestry woven with many-colored scenes of warfare. This account has the ring of both legend and truth. Truth is, after all, no different than legend. It is intriguing to speculate about the influence that these embroidered scenes, perhaps depicting events in the Iliad, might have exerted on our hero's destiny. In contrast to many living things, dead things can have a vitalizing effect. The child's very first glances took these images into the misty regions of his soul, where character and personhood were still slumbering, waiting for the first ray of light that would awaken them. This is the hour that gives shape to the Self, when form after form slowly accretes around a central point, giving rise gradually to a more or less definite whole."

When I translated this page years ago at the writer's house, I was reminded of how my own baptismal tapestry, with its smell of overnight schnapps and beer, tobacco and other incense, that penetrated to the misty regions of my developing personality. It was a dubious ray of light, but nonetheless a ray. Even someone who is averse to mythological trends of thought will readily interpret my aversion to beer and inferior forms of brandy as what it in fact is: an intellectual acknowledgment of the lessons derived from my experience of a profligate anabaptism. Of course this has no bearing on the identity of my personality with my Self. It serves only to confirm that, in keeping with the laws of entropy, I was handed over to destiny while lying on a counter in a bar.

Among the books in my personal library there is one that I cherish very much, the illustrated Handbook of Geography by Professor Daniel, who was part theologian and part geographer. The fact that in Book One I was able to compare Pilar's kitchen table to a catamaran is a detail that I owe to my god-father, who, no doubt guided by his innate sense of *panta rhei*, bound this book in such a way that his binder's needle failed to penetrate fascicle 42. When he delivered the finished product and I happily began leafing it through, the native Carolina, Palau, and Sandwich Islanders immediately fell out. After that, every time I consulted the Book of Daniel I had to replace these sinister characters between the pages, with the result that their threatening visages re-mained indelibly imprinted on my mind.

I gave Pedro accounts of this and similar details of my family dynasty, which was never menaced by the maws of a sea monster or by the drawn scimitar of an angry Moor. I told him about the petty citizens of a petty town, people who printed and bound books or, like my father, owned books but never read them: people who lived, made love, drank, and then drank some more, right out of the bottle or from expensive glasses; people who then died, every one of them with the conviction that this was the Will of the Almighty, every one of them a person whom nobody outside the town limits cared two hoots about.

When we left the tiny hidden cove of Valldemosa and clambered back over loose gravel and breakneck goat paths to the fresh-air resort of the Kings of Aragón and Mallorca, we were lugging with us a huge, heavy object: a sea turtle, the largest specimen that had ever been caught at this coastline. It was of extreme old age and, as we learned from a fisherman who was not much younger, not indigenous to Mallorquin waters. It had probably migrated from the great ocean depths near Menorca which were still home to such giants. The one we caught had presumably fled the distressing site of the famous 1756 battle between French pirates and the English fleet under the tragic John Byng, and paddled across the ocean to spend its waning days in the Valldemosa inlet. We now presented this tortuga as a gift to Doña Clara. With the aid of her cook Toninas, she made some delicate dishes from it, including a so-called turtle soup with little turtle sausages and turtle eggs in Madeira *au four*—a meal for gourmets whose taste hasn't been ruined by the likes of Maggi. Doña Clara's *tortue au naturel* will reap praise long after she has passed away, but with turtle it helps to be a connoisseur. To others I recommend the imitation item you'll get out of a can. The one from the Valldemosa *cala* tasted like mammoth from the Arctic permafrost.

We were still seated at our antediluvian meal when a telegram arrived for Beatrice. Was somebody dying again? Or was someone already dead? No, it was just a hasty sign of life, and it came from Paris. The text: "Coast clear? Zwingli."

De-Pilarized by potent ministrations of Professor Scheidegger's homeopathic science, my brother-in-law was once again heading for the southern latitudes.

Beatrice now decided that living in this house of art was no longer for us; the place to confront real danger was one's own house and home. So we left Valldemosa and its heights of historical mattresses and sank back down on the nameless heap of our own poverty. Pedro wanted to give us chairs to take along, a bed, some crockery, a box full of alibis. That's how a friend behaves when he is at the same time a Spanish grandee. But Beatrice and I, still two very un-Spanish little people, declined his offer as an offense to the Sureda dynasty. Immune to such bourgeois temptations, we were satisfied just to shake hands and clap a grateful drumbeat on shoulders all around. I took one last look at the sleepy pickled euphoria of my embryos: "*Adios*, my friends. Don't worry, we'll be back!"

Six hours later, we were sitting in boxes in our bible-paper room and chatting about how wonderful it all had been, about the immense fortune the Suredas had squandered, how everybody up there in the hills seemed crazy, crazier than here in the capital, and—"Now Beatrice, you'll have to admit that genuine turtle soup is pretty terrible. Your Swiss friend Mr. Maggi found this out, and was smart enough to put his mock turtles on the market." Then our conversation turned to the other citizen of the Swiss Confederation, the one who was inquiring whether the coast was clear.

"What he means by a 'clear coast' is obviously Pilar, but he's not asking whether Pilar herself has been de-Pilarized. What are you going to do? The telegram came with paid-up reply."

"I'm going to send a telegram."

"Fine, but what are you going to say? I'll keep out of it. You must act according to your conscience. That's what we always do, and that's why we can rest so comfortably on our pile of newspapers. Think it over while I kick our bed around a bit. Tonight we'll again be sleeping on our own empty life history."

"But after all, he's my brother!"

"That sounds like an accusation. That's not how we want to play the game, and I've never been a spoilsport when it comes to other people."

Beatrice wired Zwingli that the coast was clear—which it in fact was, as far as the tootsie was concerned.

Doña Clara had given us a basketful of food and a bucketful of turtle soup with huge gobs of turtle meat in it. This kept us in *haute cuisine* for two weeks. Two weeks of *haute cuisine* are the equivalent of the price of a table and, if you know how to haggle, two chairs. Let's keep this in mind. We'll endure the odor of a prehistoric mammoth by holding our noses—"Just a couple of weeks, Beatrice, and we'll have finished consuming the entire beast..."

XII

During the starvation years of the Wilhelminian World War, when my father lost two-thirds of his body weight, when my grandmother sat down to die before losing all of her body weight, when the high nutritive value of the common turnip was discovered by the same caste of scientists who later declared the common Hitler Turnip as a vitamin-rich fodder for the people, I had already become so skeptical that I no longer believed in the miracle of the loaves, although I still thought that the God we called our own really ought to do something for His chosen people. Or did He perhaps intend, by distributing a few million breakfast rolls, to spare the experts at the Kaiser Wilhelm Science Institute from everlasting shame? This question concerns only bodily hunger, which has never made me into a true grouch. I have long since counted the miracle of the loaves among Creation's lesser magic tricks. I didn't even long for it to happen when we went starving for days in the Clock Tower. No, what I have in mind is "the sacred power of genuine, true hunger" that Wilhelm Raabe has his "Hunger Pastor" write about, and that makes me yearn again and again for a multiplication of bread loaves: if only a Savior could appear on the scene and increase my library, decimated by war and persecution, by a factor of a thousand! All the while, then as now, here on the street of the poet Helmers, as formerly on the street of General Barceló, in order to buy books I have had to stint on food. No miracles happen in the house of Vigoleis.

In a word, from the tiny amount we saved by consuming the leftovers of saurian soup, we deducted a certain allotment for books. Language is feeble when it comes to expressing minuscule numbers; the diminutive of "an amount" is "a tiny amount," and that's the end of it. The Portuguese are better off in this respect. They can reduce a "tiny amount" ad infinitum, a skill that paradoxically can have a very grandiose effect. The formation of diminutives sheds a great deal of light on a language—a phenomenon that has been largely overlooked by the philologists. A Lusitanian citizen cannot buy a loaf of bread for 1000 reis, nor can he buy a book for 20,000. Our own tiny amount was situated so far below the borderline of diminution that we would have to buy a table and a chair not just second-hand but fourth- or maybe even tenth-hand.

Pedro knew of a rummage dealer on the Rambla, located below ground, a kind of catacomb of junk that, among other things, offered for sale vegetables and live poultry, rabbits, wine, crockery, and brushes.

Every country has its own morality as regards taxation, an attitude that gives rise to tax laws that invite secret and open fraud. Just as government ministries commit fiscal mayhem by means of bills pushed through the legislature, the individual citizen sets traps for the internal revenue office. Every more or less civilized country is familiar with this type of guerilla warfare. In Spain, store owners had to pay a store owner's tax, no matter what, how much, or how little they sold. For this reason, all store owners sold everything: the butcher sold vegetables and *alpargatas*; the greengrocer sold firewood, underwear, holy pictures, and bread; the coal dealer repaired shoes; the cobbler made bombs in his spare time; in the brothels, besides girls you could consult the latest newspapers. In Palma we bought the best nougat in a bookshop, where you could also lease a donkey. Besides tending to churches, the clergy was known for maintaining bordellos, bullfight arenas, and railroads. Thus it was no surprise to me when, arriving at this junk dealer's premises, I saw fresh fruit, small animals, and brooms for sale. A quail was wildly whirling around in a small cage. Quail stands in high regard in Palma. Some say that it brings good luck; others tame the bird as a lure for catching other quails. Their meat is also prized. Mamú's cook roasted them on a spit, and this was my favorite way of cooking them.

"*Duck-duck-duck, duck-duck-duck,*" said the bird in oddly onomatopoetic fashion, as I ducked down to enter the basement store. Even so, I hit my head against a crocodile that was fastened above the door. I took this as a good omen, and clapped my hands.

An old lady weaving straw in the doorway told me that if I was looking for Doña Carmen, I would find her down in the gallery. I should go right in, she said, but warned me that the monster over the door, though quite dead, could still be dangerous.

So even before descending to the depths, I knew the identity of the person who would sell me my junk. When dealing with a bureaucracy, it's best to know beforehand the name of some clerk to look for. Yet on this occasion I placed greater trust in the song of the quail than in the revelation of the name Carmen.

I clapped my hands, and was already inside the store. It was suddenly darker in front of me, and it took me a while to adjust my eyes to the twilight. It was only after my third palmada that I heard a female voice in the background asking who I was and what I had come for. "Vigoleis," I announced. "I've come to see Carmen." I was told to wait patiently for just a moment.

The sum at my disposal was 12.50 pesetas; I wanted to buy a table and two chairs. I wasn't prepared to haggle—I'm too proud and too stupid for such things, just as the old German proverb says: pride and stupidity were cast in the same mold. The objects I could make out in the darkness all looked more expensive than 12.50. A mahogany armoire, for example, was a cabinetmaker's masterpiece, and must have belonged to a Sureda. It couldn't have crossed the threshold for less than 1000 pesetas.

Doña Carmen had a large selection of all kinds of goods. There were cheap reproductions hanging on the wall next to genuine oil paintings that were, in turn, obvious forgeries. Potted palms rose up in royal splendor toward the ceiling, one of them set at an angle because it was obviously meant for higher surroundings. Old porcelain, clasps and brooches from the Bronze Age, green glass beakers, revolving coat racks, doorway transoms with cute painted Rococo scenes, stuffed armadillos—still plentiful on the island—votive altar pieces, gaming tables covered in green felt, walrus teeth with scrimshaw carvings, mirrors, the first typewriter ever manufactured, more mirrors, clocks, suits of armor, buckets, easy chairs, chests and *pilarières*, candelabras, porcelain cherubs, bird cages, eyeglasses, gems, a stork's nest, an electric generator, and a prayer book. Absolutely everything under the sun was here, including its opposite, its supplement, its pendant, the reverse of itself. Certain items were available only in partial form; it was as if each part, once separated from its former whole, was yearning for a new completeness. What is the opposite of a sewing machine? I don't know, but Doña Carmen would not only know, she'd actually have it in stock—perhaps not a vista, but she would drag it out from under an upside-down tin bathtub or a top-hat box. And she had a thousand other useful items—rats, for example. Three of them, if I counted correctly in the dark.

And besides, she had herself, the Queen of her own realm.

The fact that her name was Carmen is not particularly significant. Most Spanish women go by the name of Carmen, unless they were lifted out of the baptismal font as Dolores, María de los Dolores ("Mary of the Sorrows"), or Pilar—Our Lady of the Pillar. These are extremely popular names, though not as common as one finds in books about Spain whose authors, engaging in excusable exaggeration, attempt to be more precisely Spanish than the Spaniards themselves.

Doña Carmen was a voluptuous woman whose appearance could still knock a man's socks off. I say "still," because she was majestically approaching sixty. Zounds! Just imagine yourself thirty years earlier descending into this catacomb to meet her, to the accompaniment of that quail's song: Oh my Carmen, my Carmencita, Carmencitiña, Carmencitilla, Carmencitititilla! I would have diminutized you down to everlasting sin on that Louis Seize canapé beneath that balding stuffed sloth! But this giant doll of a woman just stood there with her pompous dangling bosom and did nothing to conceal her age. As far as I could tell in the dim light of her shop, she hadn't even made up her classic Carmen countenance. She didn't need to, for she was a personality who spent her life amid the changeless conditions of life. On her brow, however, she wore the familiar curl, the upside-down question mark that is still used in Spanish typography and that facilitates the comprehension of complex sentences. When you see it at the beginning of a statement you know that the whole thing will be called into question. Was this the case with Doña Carmen, too? She wore a black silk *albornoz* with roses pinned on it, an adornment so attractive you felt like stealing it, or at least buying it outright—a practice that is by no means unusual in businesses like hers. The customer comes first—and in this case thirty years too late! But still early enough for a table and a couple of chairs. At this time of day, maybe even a bit too early.

I stepped forward out of the sunlit doorway and headed through the piles of assorted stuff to approach the shopkeeper. I made a bow, told her that I was pleased to make her acquaintance, and that her bazaar had been warmly recommended to me.

In reply to her query, "by whom," accompanied by a gesture of invitation, I could have reported truthfully: by my friend Don Pedro Sureda, el de los Verdugos y Alba Real del Tajo, thereby making an aristocratic impression right from the start, though perhaps not an impression of wealth. My pauper's instinct urged me to say quickly, "by Don José," and I probably meant the most recent of the Don Josés to course through my thoughts, the private physician of Ludwig Salvator of Austria.

"Don José?" Another hand gesture, this time not indicating welcome, but pleasant surprise.

Every Spanish man is named José, unless he is a Pedro or a Pablo. Hence every Spanish woman knows at least one José. Doña Carmen knew one, too. We would soon find out whether we were talking about the same one.

"Don José? You don't say, sir..."

Instead of replying, "Yes indeed, the very same, Don José Giménez de Oliveros," as if stung by the tax man's flea I chose a name at random and said: Don José Montodo y Lopez Grau, or Don José Nicolao Campaña Campins, or Don José Portella de Marmolejo. I made up some beautiful-sounding name for this beautiful woman—any name at all. Perhaps it was that of my friend the art historian at Salamanca University, the one that Professor Brinckmann had recommended me to: Don José Aranda y Bustamante—which would have sounded convincing enough.

Whoever this Don José was, Doña Carmen knew him. Her eyes took on a shimmer of emotion, and in the conversation that followed it turned out that my Don José knew Doña Carmen very well indeed, and Doña Carmen—Oh good Lord, she said, how time does pass by! What woman who is not a true character will make a point of the transitoriness of time? It was, she went on, as if it were only yesterday that Don José entered her late father's store... ah, those were the days... and the excavations he was interested in seeing, and that he visited with shovel in hand! He dug around Ibiza and Formentera searching for remains of Punic culture (Who did the digging, Don José or her father?)—"oh, and now he has sent you to me." So my Don José was an archeologist. "How wonderful that he still remembers me!"

"Who, my dear Doña Carmen," I said with no need to prevaricate, "would not remember you? Don José sang your praises—you should have heard him!" Doña Carmen closed her eyes, made a half turn of her head, and paused for a long moment in the melancholic pose of self-mystification.

I was a Mallorquinist, I told her, with a wide-ranging field of professional interest, though not a specialist, and most definitely not the kind of specialist who picks up a pot, and while gazing at the pot focuses on a shard, and while gazing at the shard focuses on a tiny scratch that simply must be there if... I was writing a book, I explained, and Don José had suggested looking up his friend Doña Carmen. At her shop I was sure to find material for my research, and of course I would also find Doña Carmen herself.

Doña Carmen reopened her eyes. Unfortunately, at the moment she didn't have anything Punic or Carthaginian in stock. Don José must have been exaggerating. She had already sold all that—the foreigners were especially interested in antiques of that kind. But faience, majolica, things made on Mallorca—she waved a hand around her shop—such items she had in abundance. Vases and plates with Moorish motifs, granite vessels with leafy ornaments, fragments of mosaics—I looked to where she was pointing, but couldn't locate what I had come here for and what my 12.50 pesetas could pay for. But I hadn't even begun with my own type of excavation. All I had done so far was to make a few digs with the spade and push aside a bit of dirt. The hard work still lay ahead.

The things Doña Carmen was showing me weren't useful for my research. I of course found words of praise for each single item, examined everything with the expert eye of a connoisseur, ventured certain doubts concerning authenticity, and offered certain suggestions concerning provenance. In this fashion we edged our way through her inventory, engaged all the while in animated scientific shop talk. Now I felt obliged to praise a washtub, now a rare Catalan votive picture depicting The Virgin Mary Offering Her Singlet. I clambered over cushions and rolled-up carpets, let out a connoisseur's whistle at the sight of a little votive altar replete with burning wick floating in rancid oil in a silver-plated lamp—a priceless item—: "Spoils from the Burgundian Wars?" I stumbled over a child's coffin that was propped up on a bidet stool. It fell to the floor with a bang. I kept on digging, and we kept on talking.

We eventually reached Doña Carmen's living quarters. A Spanish screen served as an implied rather than an actual separation between her bedroom and the less intimate area full of bric-a-brac. Inside, she explained, I wouldn't find anything more that was pertinent to my field of research—just ordinary, everyday objects such as a bed, a table, a few chairs...

"We mustn't look down on everyday objects! A table, a chair, a bed—these comprise the foundations of human social interaction. If we were to remove them from our lives it would mean an end to all moral behavior. We would sink back to the level of the Neanderthals." Besides, I went on, just look what can happen. At home we had this maid, a real peasant type, a mindless workhorse, a born-in-the-flesh milkmaid, and illiterate—which wasn't the worst of it. Her muscles, Doña Carmen! You should see what those muscles of hers are capable of! They can destroy anything in the house that isn't fastened down. Dinner plates? We're down to using exclusively enamel. Doña Carmen opined that I didn't have to tell her the rest; it was the old song about an age-old grievance. We agreed that we were dealing with a cosmic outrage of culture, or a cultural outrage of cosmic proportions. But we would never make any headway, I said, by giving this nuisance a name. My wife was getting blue in the face with her daily complaints of Na' Maguelida this, Na' Maguelida that, and by now our apartment furniture was in danger. The maid was dusting them to pieces. Wanton destruction of a magnitude no less severe, at times more so, than my loss of self-control, and now—I hefted a bronze wash basin in the shape of a griffin—"Doubtless Islamic influence, Ibizencan?" I asked casually, seeking to conceal my irritation. For at this moment I had finally spotted what my scavenging eyes were looking for, the very reason for this excursion: a small but very sturdy table! The Germans are fond of the saying "kill two birds with one stone," and sometimes they even act on it. Now, intent upon applying this idea contrary to Spanish custom, I pointed into the private quarters of Doña Carmen's *bric-à-braquière*. The table wasn't large; the top measured at most two feet by three, but it had a drawer and strong legs that were roughly carved to resemble Gothic pillars. I could already see myself writing on it, eating from it, using it as a workbench, receiving guests and offering them meals at it, and killing a thousand flies on it with a single swat. And so I said to Doña Carmen: that rugged table over there is just what we need for our maid. Would she permit me...?

I moved ahead in the direction of the table, but the lady immediately blocked my path, partly with her bosom and partly with an outstretched foot: stop where you are! "Oh, I beg your pardon," we both said to each other, Doña Carmen adding that the miserable table was not what I was looking for. She had a round one made of macacaoba with a ritual tripod base, just the thing...

"Doña Carmen, I'll take that rustic one or none at all!" I summoned up my courage and took another step forward. Doña Carmen's bosom retreated, taking all of Doña Carmen with it. She spread out all her fingers as if defending herself against an angry mob, and repeated, "Please, no farther!" Undaunted and intent on examining the table, I took an even more daring step in the direction of the antiquarian lady. She's behaving quite oddly, I thought, as Doña Carmen emitted a tiny scream in inverse proportion to her corpulence, just as she might have done 40 years previous as Carmencita, fending off another kind of attack. Now, however, it was only mice that could elicit such a strange reaction—or was she convinced, once I had identified myself as a German, that I was about to violate her? Did she read books? Was she familiar with the works of Haarmann, Grossmann, Kürten? Hitler's bloody ethnic mysticism? Medieval vendettas and the national uprising? That table had a spacious drawer, room enough for manuscripts, tools, bread...

My third forward step, and this time she screamed out loud. Doña Carmen threw her hands forward and covered her face while calling upon her Savior, "*Ay, Jesús*, have mercy on my soul!"

Women are unpredictable in their chronic climacteric nature. It often happens on trains that the emergency brake gets pulled and a lady tells the conductor that some man was about to rape her. A great to-do ensues, involving written reports and schedule delays, and later the aggressive gentleman is either missing his billfold or he has to pay up some other way, since his alibi is the lady herself even though he had no interest at all in doing her any favors. What would happen if Doña Carmen were now to pull the emergency brake—

a specimen of which she no doubt had in her junk collection—and run out on the Rambla yelling bloody murder? It would be curtains for Vigoleis. The situation was critical. Doña Carmen reached for an area of her bosom that was the true or implied location of her heart, and begged the importunate Mallorquinist one last time, "Señor!" I, too, had taken hold of myself, but instead of reaching for my heart, I took the final step that separated me from the coveted table, and grabbed the knob of the drawer. "Ha! A compartment!"

Doña Carmen screamed so loud that it echoed throughout her cavern as though she were the Witch of Endor. She collapsed on some antique or other, and it broke under her weight. I had pulled out the drawer. It was a deep drawer, not one of those skimpy things that are impossible to close after you put in one tablecloth and two napkins.

Inside the drawer was a chamber pot. I felt a *frisson* of joy as I examined the darkened inside of this vessel: I had finally found one of the celebrated pots that have an eye painted on the bottom, a motif called "The Eye of God," and beneath it the stenciled legend, "*Yo te veo*," or "*Yo te veo bribón*"—I see you, you rascal, I see you! For a long time I had been looking for just such a mystical receptacle, and now Lady Luck was kind to me! Yet at the same moment when I felt sure that I was seeing the divine symbol, my nose told me that I was on the wrong track. I quickly shoved the drawer back into the table and suddenly felt pity for the Eye of God, which is forced to let itself be sullied in order to fathom the mysteries of its own Creation.

Professor Stuhlfauth interprets the "Eye of God" as symbolizing God the Father, insofar as it occurs in the typical form of a human eye inside a triangle. Although the origins of this emblem are unclear, you can find it on altars, pulpit screens, shields, and gravestones, on the title pages of books, and in Spain even in chamber pots. The Hispanic variant presumably has something to do with sorcery, a bizarre manner of warding off the evil eye, since the *iettatore* or the *iettatrice* remains seated above the eye until the latter is darkened over and no longer capable of seeing clearly. A renowned Spanish ethnologist, Professor Ismael del Pan, once had the kindness to inform me that he regarded the "Eye of Providence" located inside this domestic utensil as an element of exorcism traceable to Judaic and Moroccan religious roots. The progressive hygienization of private bedrooms has caused these vessels to lose their practical value while preserving their magical qualities. Even today a bridegroom will present one, wrapped in cellophane and trimmed with pink ribbons, as an engagement gift to his bride...

When I first entered her shop, Doña Carmen had been exercising her rights, as a dealer in antiques, to the private use of her wares. She was enthroned on one of them when I first clapped my hands to announce my presence. At my second clap she had extended her owner's rights to the table drawer, quickly pushing the chamber pot inside it so that, when I clapped my hands for the third time, she was able to come forward with a smile and accept Don Vigo's greetings from Don José Saavedra de Casas Novas. Whereupon destiny, which can be called blind by whomever it pleases, took its course, step by forward step, with a most evil eye directed toward the Eye of the One and Only, which to my misfortune turned out not to be God's Eye after all.

In the throes of disappointment I had slammed the drawer shut with such force that a little accident occurred inside the table. Doña Carmen momentarily overcame the dilemma of her dual role, and casually pushed aside the offending piece of furniture with her foot. The damage was done. Even a woman must at times stand up like a man, and from then on everything played itself out just as Schopenhauer describes it, albeit in a rather less noxious context, in his doctrine of the Affirmation and Negation of the Will to Life. The Will to Life asserted itself emphatically here in the junk shop. Doña Carmen was again in complete control of herself and her collection of reliques. She stood there with inscrutable, elemental mien; she was the most authentic item in her own bazaar.

Next to the table, which not even three Maguelidas would be able to demolish, stood two rustic kitchen chairs made of knotty pine still oozing resin: a pair of items exactly to my liking. Mumbling words of praise for this and that object on display, I approached the catacomb exit, reached into my pocket, offered two duros for the table and the chairs, hoping that she would agree on the price. I said that I would just step outside and fetch an *almocrebe*.

When I returned with a donkey, Doña Carmen had already placed the furniture outside her door on the Rambla. While my servant hitched the items to his animal, I placed the pieces of silver on top of a crate containing hopping rabbits and, maintaining a gallant distance, kissed her right hand, which had of course been so closely involved in her dethronement. Smiling, she asked me to convey her greetings to our mutual friend Don José Toboso y de Tembleque from Toledo—for surely that was the person who had recommended her to me.

I am a talkative fellow, and that means that I am no worse than the next guy at keeping secrets.

Beatrice's eyes lit up when the *almocrebe* unloaded our complete set of kitchen furniture and accepted his 50-centimos wage plus a princely tip of two pesetas. Such joy when she noticed the drawer! Her first reaction was, "So deep!" Just to think of all the things one could put inside it—bread, cheese, greens for our soup, her entire sewing kit—"Vigo!" Her dream had come true. She kissed me.

But my lips were burning with more than her kiss. From inside the drawer, the "Eye of God" was insisting that I give notice of its presence. I gave a full dramatic account of Doña Carmen, myself, the quail, the child's coffin. I clapped my hands, made bows, reiterated my remarks as a connoisseur, peered into the twilit back area of the shop, restaged my somnambulistic steps toward the table, described the table, the drawer, opened the drawer—and Beatrice fainted. This was the second time on the island that she lost consciousness.

Using bicarbonate of soda, boiling water, scented candles at nighttime and the rays of the sun during the day, ammonia, *Legia* detergent, vinegar vapors—I scrubbed the drawer over and over again for an entire week. If I had remained silent about Doña Carmen's Affirmation of Life, I would have been spared a whole lot of irritation, drudgery, and one duro, the price of a novel in the Espasa Calpe edition.

Talkativeness is a symptom of deep-seated pessimism. Without it there would be no pessimistic literature.

Strangely enough, it was Beatrice who insisted on owning a "look-see" chamber pot. I had also entertained the thought, but didn't dare to broach the ethnological subject for fear of arousing olfactory responses that could be dangerous for a woman so highly susceptible to allergies. "There, do you smell something? I smell something again. Has a cat sneaked in?" Then her nose hit the table drawer that meanwhile contained not bread and cheese, but products of my intellectual activity.

"Vigo, darling, do you know what I would just love to have, and which I think we can now afford...?"

"Wait, let me guess. You'll see that I am capable of reading your mind. Van Dine, *The Scarabs Murder Case!*"

"Wrong! Higher! And in a different genre."

Quick-witted as a born *Führer*, and making a sudden leap upwards from the underworld, I said, "Either Burckhardt's *Cultural History of Greece* in an uncut edition, or a pair of shoes to go with your Indian dress, made by Ulua and nobody else."

Beatrice shook her head. "You can get all of those things for me later. Now I would love to have one of those receptacles, you know, the kind with a motto printed inside and a Cyclops eye...?"

I embraced this woman whom I had so often accused of deficient imagination. "You sweet one! You want an eye? To look at, eye to eye...?"

"Not quite that kind, darling. What I'd like is an umbrella stand to put in the *entrada*. With a ring on top."

"So the eye will always stay moist. Right, I understand."

People who have an inferior conception of divinity might consider it heretical or repugnant to adorn a chamber pot with the Eye of God. One must not forget that Spaniards often take the name of the Almighty in vain, since they maintain what amounts to a personal identification with Him. Who wouldn't be knocked flat upon a first hearing of the Spanish curse *Me cago en Dios*, a phrase that is best rendered by three little dots? I have heard priests shout it in heated discussion, and I am convinced that cardinals also use it. No one thinks anything of it. And after all, who thinks anything of God's name? Just behold the state of God's world!

"Beatrice, I shall not rest until the Eye of God looks constantly upon our *entrada*. And woe to whoever drenches it in tears with other means than an umbrella!"

After careful calculations we set aside five pesetas for our celestial *objet d'art*. We could save this up by the end of the month, but until then we would have to get by without the evil eye. As it was, things had gone badly enough for us without it for quite a long time.

Now wherever my steps took me, I was obsessed with The Eye. Or rather, since I am for the most part a sedentary fellow and spent most of my time typing my own or other people's literature, The Eye constantly peered over my shoulder at my text—a form of intrusion that is very much to my disliking.

Alcoholics and serial killers are familiar with the sudden impulse to chug-a-lug a stiff one, the irresistible urge to squeeze somebody's throat before they explode. Whereupon they calmly get up from where they are sitting and go hunting for a victim. Off they go to a bar or to the city park.

That is how I felt about The Eye. It was absolutely necessary that I betake myself to wherever I might find it, which is to say, where I might locate the receptacle that contained its steady glance. There were five pesetas in our drawer—not meant for a pot but for our daily bread. The Eye of God beckoned me to take the money—for the Eye of God. What if I could get one for one peseta? What if, for once in my life, I were to stoop to commercial haggling, knowing that Beatrice had fallen in love with a Cyclopean eye?

I knew well the City of Palma's junk, trash, and plunder market, located on the Plaza del Olivar; I had already fished out a number of items from its abundant offerings. But Pedro told me that the chamber-pot dealer had his stand on the square called "Ses Enremades." There I would be sure to find the Eye I was looking for. But, Pedro said, I should be careful. "En Xaragante" was a crook who chopped up pig cadavers to make sausage out of them. This news didn't bother me so long as, in addition to any number of blind chamber pots, the crook in question had a seeing-eye crock he would be willing to sell me.

The sun was searing down on a tattered canopy, beneath which En Xaragante sat guarding his collection of crockery. He was very fat and poorly dressed, not at all typical for a Spaniard. The holes in his shirt revealed skin encrusted with grime or thick body hair. The man's sombrero provided shade in places where the sun leaked through the awning. Seated on a crate with his heavy body all folded up, he was taking a nap, if this term is adequate to describe a condition accompanied by loud snoring.

Next to the sleeping man who looked like an African tribal chieftain dressed in European garb, stood a large round cage that was missing so many bars that a chicken could easily walk out of it. But the black bird sitting inside and getting roasted by the sun couldn't escape. Profoundly reconciled to its fate, it didn't even try. From its ebony beak to its drooping tail it was a good two feet long, and as an experienced breeder of birds I estimated its wingspan at two yards or more. It was a raven, *Corvus corax*, one that had seen its better days, like everything else that was offered for sale at this location. Unlike its owner, the bird was not asleep. It was unhappy. It seemed to be pestered by vermin, thirst, and a yearning for carrion, but with the wisdom that is natural to all ravens it was keeping its composure. Perhaps it was also aware that its battered wings would never again lift it into the heavens. All around this sleepy focal point lay the vessels I had come for. Fragile as they all were, En Xaragante had spread them out on a piece of canvas. The receptacles for nighttime use stood out conspicuously among the collection, like owls in broad daylight.

Destiny—once again I feel obliged to employ this pretentious term—has often pulled the chair out from under me, forcing me to look for something else to sit on. I have often had to switch residences, and thus have lived in various places in the world. Wherever I have been lucky, unlike my Vigoleis, I have found the familiar little table next to my bedside, and inside it the handy receptacle for emergencies. People who disapprove of such domestic utensils can pay for their aesthetic indignation with kidney stones. Others are grateful whenever, under protection of darkness, they can consult the convenient vessel. That's how civilization has arranged things, and what concern is that of ours? I am familiar with the Dutch *mevrouw*'s robust *kamerpot*, the solid ceramic vase of the German Hausfrau, and our Swiss landlady's rustic earthenware urn, omnipresent in every one of the cantons. I am familiar with the predilections in other nations; I have held in my hand the exquisite vasosinho belonging to a delicate Portuguese *menina*—and I must continually agree with Vigoleis, who tends to reduce his chamber pot to its practical utility. For him, a chamber pot is a useful object so long as it conceals what it is used for.

I had never seen an umbrella stand containing the Eye of God. Would En Xaragante have one for me? More than a hundred vessels of various inviting kinds surrounded the trader and his raven. Would an eye in one of those containers open up and say to me, "Vigoleis, I see you"?

The raven lifted its glance from the contemplation of its own disheveled fate and was now watching me with its brown-on-white eye—taking, as it were, a bird's-eye view of the proceedings—as I gingerly storked my way through its master's crockery.

Corvus corax wasn't the only one monitoring my cautious rummaging. Dozens of flea-market shoppers lined the edges of the crockery stand and observed my every step. I had become a focal point of public attention, and was struck with acute agoraphobia and nettle rash. Whenever this happens, I immediately undergo an inward collapse. My innards blush, while my outer complexion stays pale. And the *Führer* in me starts gabbing away.

All of a sudden I saw The Eye. I quickly bent down, lifted the grail out of the jumble of inferior receptacles, and my two-eyed glance met that of the Mystical Eye. I was in Seventh Heaven.

There was loud applause. The snoozing tradesman woke up, and the raven crowed. Only the painted-enamel Eye remained silent, but the caption beneath it spoke volumes: "You scoundrel, I see you!"

If I was to avoid being attacked by the environment, I would have to start haggling. In my mind's eye I saw Beatrice seated before me. But no, sorry, not seated upon The Eye, but slaving away in some palace or other offering language instruction to elaborately cosmetized *señoritas*. I had sworn eternal love to her, and here and now I could prove that I would march over chamber pots for her. Over ceramic and clay pots, over pots made of enamel and pots made of stone—among these piles I even spied a finely polished granite Celto-Iberian urinal—I slowly advanced toward En Xaragante, held my chosen pot under his nose, and asked, "How much?"

"One duro."

"Just because of the Eye? It has a crack in it."

"The Eye is two, Lady Hamilton three pesetas, that makes five, Sir."

Lady Hamilton? What does, or did, Fanny Hamilton have to do with this piece of crockery? I began to have indiscreet thoughts. Don Juan Sureda would have put a tag on the handle that told this story.

En Xaragante said that he no longer knew exactly how it went, but an Englishman had told him that this pot was doubtless from Lord Hamilton's collection. And so it was only natural that his wife...

Peals of laughter emanated from our audience of curious, pressing onlookers. To my consternation I spied an acquaintance among them, a robust fellow wearing a colorful kerchief and a shopping hat: my employer Robert Graves, who didn't let on that he knew me—for which I was grateful. As an art collector, historian, and Englishman he had a threefold interest in this transaction. Not a collector myself, I was unmoved by the patina attached to this chamber pot, a feature that testified to Lady Hamilton's versatility. I desired the pot simply as a medium for The Eye. I would gladly pay two pesetas for it, but not some extra charge for historical considerations.

In the negotiations that followed, I was the loser; my skills as a *Führer* left me in the lurch. The audience was thoroughly amused at the expense of this foreigner who was trying to haggle with the greasy tradesman while brandishing a chamber pot. Urchins who knew the pot's secret were teasing me: *Yo te veo, bribón,* "I see you, you rogue!" The raven squawked and flapped its wings, rattling the cage.

"God lives in every pot," is how Santa Teresa de Ávila famously put it, and this assertion of hers quickly came to mind as I realized my ridiculous situation. But this mystical insight was of no help. I started wishing for the proverbial hole in the ground where I could disappear together with the accursed eye-pot. But the earth did not open up to receive me. The fat salesman was getting impatient, telling me to make up my mind—he didn't like wasting time with customers, and especially not with the likes of me. This I could understand. There's not a junk dealer in the world who feels he must get rid of his stuff—that is the secret of their success. As a sign that neither I nor anybody else was of further concern to him, En Xaragante once again closed his piggish eyes. I ought to have set God's Eye back down on the ground then and there and walked away. But I was under a spell. I stammered, "And your raven? Marvelous animal! I've never seen such a large one. Where I come from, they aren't any bigger than a fat crow."

The *potier de chambre* reopened one of his eyes and peered at me. My praise for his shaggy critter touched a place in his heart as yet unsullied by commerce in such disreputable merchandise. He stretched a hairy arm to the cage and raised it up to be admired. The raven opened its beak, thinking that it was about to get a *sobrasada* from En Xaragante's carrion kitchen.

"Is he for sale, too? How much for a devil like that?"

"He can talk. One duro per language, *basta*."

"How many languages does he talk?"

"Three, and that makes 15 pesetas. A treasure for your whole life long. This guy will live to a ripe old age. Your grandchildren will still be enjoying him."

The onlookers shouted "*Olé, olé!*" and came in closer. The spectacle was getting to be more and more fun, but no one came across the barrier formed by the mute crockery lying on the canvas.

The raven's decrepit master, who now opened his second eye, put the cage back down and egged me on. "Well?" "Stand your ground, *señorito!*" shouted the audience. The sweat was pouring from my brow. My brain was boiling. I grabbed the handle of the round cage and held out the animal in front of me, as if to gauge its value. There I stood, in one hand the disreputable pot with its Eye of God gazing at me; in the other, the cage with its mite-infested inhabitant giving me wary looks.

"I'll take the pot," I said to Fatso. I placed the vessel on the ground, took the duro from my pocket, and tossed it to the scoundrel. But now the crowd went wild, much as they would at a *novillada*. My mistake was having the duro in my right-hand pocket and neglecting to set down the cage. "A magnificent animal," I said as if offering an excuse for not buying the bird as well. "Three languages—that's a lot! I know a cockatoo that can speak Spanish and Portuguese."

One of the street urchins piped up: "And you speak Spanish like a raven!"

At this, even the junk dealer had to bare his rotten teeth and laugh. Was Robert Graves still standing there? Don't look, Vigo! To top everything, I had now failed a philological test, too, and that spelled my utter downfall. Holding the arch-raven in my left hand, I stepped over the pots to the edge of the junkshop arena. The fat man was yelling something after me that I couldn't understand. I was completely dazed. The audience was clapping. It was an edifying exit.

I noticed too late that I had botched the whole affair. I was followed by a mob of cheering kids; *Corvus corax* squawked for all he was worth, and this brought even more kids into the jubilant chorus. They accompanied me with their yelling all the way to the General's Street, offering practical suggestions all the while as to the proper way of training the beast, how to feed it one live rat and assorted carrion every day, and how I could expect to find lice on it that would gradually eat away all its feathers. I had already noticed this phenomenon, but assessed it as merely a case of natural molting. The kids estimated the squawker's age at 30 years. For the moment I wasn't worried about such things. I was finally home. But what now?

My arms were stiff, my joints ached, my billfold was empty. I placed the cage on Doña Carmen's table and started talking to the bird. He answered in his indigenous raucous lingo, refusing to respond in anything resembling a human tongue. I was experienced with members of the *Corvus* genus, so I knew that he would first have to get used to his new environment and his new master. Besides, he seemed to be feeling what I myself was feeling: hungry. As they say on the farm: first the livestock, then the hands. Within minutes, this guy devoured everything we had on the kitchen shelf. It wasn't much, but it would have yielded a modest meal for the two of us people. And still the bird wasn't full. Certain omnivores consume a multiple of their own weight in a single day. We could simply never keep up! The Eye of God would have been cheaper to maintain. And like all omnivores, this bird stank to high heaven, and he was impudent to boot. When I held out a fly he hacked at my hand with his powerful beak. "A fly?" he probably was thinking. "Who needs a fly? I want carrion, pounds and pounds of carrion, or better yet, *sobrasada* made from pigs' cadavers!" En Xaragante had all such stuff. If I had only let him keep the bird. And what will Beatrice say?

I threw a cloth over the cage, sat down on a crate, and began meditating. Oh Eye of God, why hast Thou cast false glances at me?

Beatrice drew in her breath through her nose and said, "What smells so strange here? Has Pedro brought in another model who never takes a bath? I won't be able to stand this much longer."

Pedro had outfitted one of our rooms as his studio, with his easel and a sheepskin for his models to sit on. One of his nude models was named Joan. Joan hailed from Ireland, and she had a decidedly illegal smell about her. A degenerate aristocrat who was in love with her also had evil body odor, and he asked Pedro to paint his portrait, too. —"But this time, Beatrice, it's not Pedro's models. It's the typical gamey aroma of all carnivores. And just imagine, this bird can talk in three languages!" I added that he ate every day as much as three people could eat. But Beatrice was no longer listening to me.

I uncovered my present: not a gift from Heaven, but a diabolical feathered monster. And I spoke approximately as follows: "Beatrice, *chérie*, it was my intention to offer you a surprise with the Eye of God, but no such luck. While negotiating with the salesman I lost my concentration. The guy must have had more than 500 pots for sale, and now we have a genuine raven, *Corvus corax* L., but the price was the same. I didn't let the tradesman gyp me. On the contrary, he was asking three duros for this prize specimen! I got him for just one duro, and he's a bargain!"

"That was our last duro!"

"Darling, I know. But this was a unique opportunity. It will never come around again."

Beatrice made no more inquiries. She didn't even ask if I had gone mad. One glance at our table revealed that the bird had already consumed our supper. She had some leftover lice repellent, and she emptied it over the raven and covered over the cage. In a harmonious marriage, one should never quarrel over a pet raven. Besides, I quickly offered to visit Don Matías to buy a loaf of bread on credit.

Don Matías listened to my bizarre story. He suggested that I put the raven out on our balcony and dust it with wood ashes to ward off vermin. Then he gave me my loaf of bread and a handful of mice that Jaume had whacked with his dustpan. One of them was still wriggling, and Don Matías said that this one would be a special delicacy for our raven of misfortune.

He meant well. Our gallows bird didn't touch the proffered mice. He squawked for carrion and gruel. Since he could no longer fly, we couldn't get rid of him by releasing him to the winds. Pedro said, "Give him away! A raven still makes a marvelous gift." —"Mamú!" I cried out. "How could we have forgotten Mamú?"

It would soon be Mamú's birthday. I had already composed a poem for her, and now I learned it by heart. It was a very atmospheric piece, with the moon sailing like a barkentine through a sky filled with little white clouds... The raven would be a more original idea. It was, after all, the first time in my life that I would be reciting a self-created poem to a millionairess. Besides, Mamú was already spoiled by such poetizing friends as Rilke, Hofmannsthal, Werfel, and others. So I didn't hesitate for a moment to exchange my lyrical product for the raven, which I had already substituted for the Eye of God. Beatrice gave her approval, but expressed her regret that Mamú hadn't come into the world just a few days earlier.

Mamú was inundated with presents. Telegrams arrived from all over the world. The Christian Science ladies sang a chorale with organ accompaniment. Auma looked her luscious best, and the state prosecutor seemed ready, as always, to gobble her up. The chef prepared something in secret, while the nanny remained sour and dull even on this special *jour*. Then Vigoleis and Beatrice arrived with the bird. The cage was polished clean, the crooked bars were bent straight, and a pink ribbon decorated the handle on top. Fastened to the ribbon was a tag bearing the name we had hurriedly decided to give the ravenous beast: Rabindranath.

Rabindranath literally hacked the eyes out of all the other birthday gifts. Mamú wept with emotion; the tears flowed down her rather wobbly cheeks like drops of candle wax. The ladies sniffed the odor of game and garbage, and closed their Bibles with a snap. Mamú's pekingese had a nervous breakdown.

"Vigo, my Vigolo, you marvelous fellow! A raven from A Thousand and One Nights! Tell me how you caught him!"

I gave her an account of En Xaragante and his Cyclopic chamber pot. The scientific ladies took further umbrage at this story, since they were convinced that magical chamber pots were my own invention. I gave the saga a somewhat mendacious twist, allowing myself to leave the battleground as a hero. This angered the praying biddies; they would have preferred to kill me off. Such incorrigible hypocrisy made me furious, and so I decided to go on the attack and get rid of this science once and for all. I took the birdcage and set it down right in the midst of the pagans. This raven, I explained, had unfortunately lost his three languages. Would anyone volunteer to pray at least his mother tongue back into him? In the eyes of the Lord, a bird is, after all, worth at least as much as a dog.

That hit the mark. There was a sudden rustling, as if of wings. The pious old crones departed the scene forthwith, while Rabindranath continued his inarticulate squawking. Mamú was even more grateful. The feast could begin.

Rabindranath was given a *volière* in the yard, and a meal such as he would never have been able to scavenge together in a natural setting: raw meat, Vienna pancake with filling, Quaker Oats, and eggs *à discrétion*. His feathers lost their shabbiness and turned smooth and glistening, his beak took on a polished gleam, and the whole bird, including his soul, reverted to intense, ravenish black. With Mamú's pekingese it was a case of hostility at first sight, and nothing could be done about it. Mamú's turtles left him cold. He never could be trained to let someone hold him on his hand. On the contrary, he became more and more ornery and pecked at any hand that was offering him something to eat. An authentic gallows bird, he was fixated on human blood.

Shortly before we left the island—Mamú had already fled—I released Rabindranath. Now, finally, he could follow his man-eating instincts, for in the meantime our island had become what Bernanos chose as the title for his book on Mallorca: *The Large Cemeteries under the Moon.*

Les grands cimitières sous la lune: with its funereal message that is a good title for a book in which, from the first to the last page, a mortuary mood of human slaughter prevails. Nevertheless, the title presents a slight shift in imagery. A cemetery is a place where the dead are laid to their final rest. It is a place set aside for personal liberty, where in earlier times even criminals were safe from pursuit, where one could rest in peace. On Mallorca, however, the holy war claimed so many victims that they couldn't get buried even by adding nighttime shifts of gravediggers. They remained where they had been slaughtered, or where trucks dumped them by the thousands, day after day, as carrion for the birds.

It was likewise left to the birds to carry out the practical work of human decency, which the Church lists as the Seventh Work of Mercy that it recommends to the faithful: Bury the Dead. By letting my Rabindranath return to the skies, I partook ever so marginally in this act of divine mercy, one that had to be ignored by those who piled up corpses in the name of the Lord. Later, when evil emanations began to threaten public health, the cadavers were strewn with lime. The feathered gravediggers no doubt resented this action by the Chief of Public Hygiene, for this meant that they, too, would soon go the way of all flesh.

XIII

I am writing this 13th chapter on the 13th of the month, which also happens to be a Friday. In it I intend to report the sad story of how Vigoleis, the friend to all children, planned to accept a child in place of a child, and how his plans came to naught. But I'm going to play a trick on the superstition concerning the number thirteen. Immanuel Velikovsky, in his earth-shattering book *Worlds in Collision*, has this to say about Egyptian mythology: "The 13th day of any month is a bad day. On this day you should do nothing. It is the day when Horus entered battle with Seth."

On this 13th day of the month I shall therefore tell how Rabindranath, our ruinous raven, entered battle with T'uang, Mamú's golden-tressed darling doggie, and how this event brought undiluted joy to our hero.

"How did it go?" asked Beatrice when I returned from the Immigration Office. "Our papers are all OK, right?"

"Yours are just fine. As a Swiss citizen you're welcome all over the world. My papers are something else again, and it doesn't look too good. They want to deport me as a troublesome foreigner, but I wasn't able to get any details. What's certain is that the Nazis are behind this, the German consulate, the local Reich Leader who was fired, and officials back home. They're all working together hand in glove. Anybody who is against the *Führer* will be eliminated like some second-rate sheep. The herd is what counts."

My residence permit wouldn't be renewed. They had received a denunciation telling them that I was an *elemento dissolvente*—a corrosive, destructive element. "Element" meant, of course, not a basic component of the physical universe, but simply a "guy." My catalyzing powers were apparently dangerous. I must admit that it was a master-stroke of the Nazis on Mallorca, at a time when everything in Spain was in a state of dissolution, to single out Vigoleis as a source of threatening ferment.

The official advised me to leave the island voluntarily, for otherwise I would get into hot water. They didn't like keeping files on foreigners who didn't get along with their consulates. That meant trouble, and trouble meant work, and work was unpleasant. This was The Golden Isle, and that was the end of the matter.

At this pronouncement I ought to have slipped two duros beneath the official's desk blotter. The German Consul would have come back at him with three duros, but I would have gained some time, probably a full half-year. But I left the office without offering such favors. So now things were lousy for me, and that meant also for our German-Swiss concubinate.

Don Matías, duly informed of our threatened situation, immediately offered to mobilize the Honduran Freedom Movement on our behalf. Don Patuco, he said, had at hand a talented imp who specialized in such cases. He would be given an assignment to make our immigration file disappear, in the same way as happened with our tax documents. I approved of the plan. Matías took down some notes in his poetic portfolio, and while doing so, came upon his latest lyrical creation, which he proceeded to read to us. I praised his effort with the mute glance of a fellow poet who is not unwilling to acknowledge another person's creative achievement, this time implying my amazement that such a masterpiece must remain hidden in the counter drawer at a bakery. Don Gracias a Dios said he would ask his fiancée to pray for the continuation of our marital concord on Mallorca. Don Pablo Sacramento promised me a powder-filled bone from his father Ulua's arsenal. Pedro just shrugged his shoulders. Mamú, on the other hand, was seized with fright when I told her that the Nazis had set a fuse to our modest insular idyll.

We were seated beneath a palm tree that, despite the drought-like conditions, still did its work of warding off the hot sun by pretending to create a park. Auma was present, as was her fiancé. Even Mamú, an expert in matters of the heart, could no longer tell which of the two of them was living in the shadow of the other. Soon neither of them would cast any shadow at all, for their Finnish-Mallorcan erotic fever was visibly consuming them both.

Mamú suddenly clapped her hands, which were white, soft, and covered with brownish age spots. She began to totter, and her chaise longue was shaking. Her gerbil-like cheeks, lending emphasis to her gesticulations, wobbled as she cried out, "T'uang!" The creature bearing this name had the same flaming red hair as my pupil Hutchinson, the same crisis-prone nerves as the coal-and-steel tycoon from Essen, a pedigree never gnawed at by any hint of anarchy, and the four paws that were the pride of the Bewerwijns' tropical hound prior to his sledding party and the Scientific Christian miracle. He was a pekingese, and as such he had a peculiar, droll manner of walking that aroused my sympathy no less than his facial expression, which was a constant meld of almost tearful sorrow and unreasonable, condescending arrogance. Maybe T'uang had worms. He definitely suffered from migraines.

Mamú lifted her beloved canine onto her lap, and held a long colloquy with him in Viennese dialect. The upshot of this dialogue was that the dog was supposed to explain to me that he was no more ludicrous a creature than a poodle or a Basedow pinscher, that he was his mistress' darling, and that he had cost her $5000.

That was it. His price was $5000, certificate of pedigree included. He hailed from an aristocratic kennel owned by the Esterhazy dynasty, the most famous dog-breeding facility—I'll take Mamú's word for it—in all of old Europe. His family tree had its origins in some foggy prehistoric forest, where not even the most savvy canine genealogist could find his way through the gloom. Family trees don't mean much to me; I'm not in the habit of peering into their leafy crowns, and that's why I felt such glee when the Nazis, with their racial laws, led the entire science of genealogy down the path to complete absurdity. But T'uang was proud of his eugenic tree. If he were a human being instead of just a degenerate dog, he would have hung a replica of that tree on his living-room wall, just as a butcher does with his guild certificate, or a Spanish doctor with his academic diploma. And why not? No matter whether it's a pinscher or a human being, a Harz Mountain canary or a German Noble White pig, it's always good to know why one chirps, oinks, or drools in a certain way and no differently, and why one is superior to all the other chirpers, oinkers, and droolers. I am always deeply moved by the sight of a colored-in family bush. I bow in reverence before such a naive display of faith in marital constancy—a virtue that, at least with a dog, can be sustained by means of a leash. Humans love freedom, as a result of inborn urges that certain people seek to rid them of, sometimes with complete success. But for the most part, humans

are responsible for certain gaps in the foliage of their ancestral cult. There are
the notorious areas where the genealogical traces disappear, where even the
most assiduous of professional researchers come up with blanks, and defer to
their patrons' sense of patience, discretion, and propriety. At such moments
the only solution is a grafting operation. A well-known botanical genealogist,
who was capable of pursuing the pedigree of any plant in the world back to
its roots in the Tree of Jesse, once told me that his art consisted in the clever
invention of an ancestor for those spots in the family tree where, when you
push the branches aside for a better look, you discover certain horny offshoots
that could endanger the entire structure of the family registry. I offered this
scholar the consoling observation that while human beings are definitely
rooted in their ancestors, not every ancestor confined his climbing to his own
family tree.

When I started poking fun at this petty-bourgeois genealogical nonsense,
Mamú assured me that T'uang's pedigree was absolutely authentic. It was
not something cobbled together by some clever professional researcher, and
that was why she rejected the idea of coupling T'uang with the pekingese
pooch owned by the Commissioner of the Immigration Police. This man had
been pestering her for a whole year with his genealogical ambition: he
wanted offspring with T'uang's bloodline! Mamú humored him all the
while, and eventually refused to allow his canine bastard to enter her house.
I knew all this. The Police Commissioner visited Mamú often. He was a
flamboyant fellow who, apart from his own love life, was wholly absorbed
by the amorous affairs of his four-legged pets. He was bound and determined
to soften up Mamú for a copulation deal. Whenever he came for a visit, his
chauffeur waited outside with the rejected bride. Don Fulano did Mamú certain favors with regard to her non-Spanish domestics. And now, with a regularity dictated by the estrus cycle of his pekingese bitch, he was courting
Mamú. As a policeman, he knew fully well that the quarry was bound to
fall into his trap eventually.

Mamú indignantly refused his first proposition, pressing T'uang protectively
to her bosom as if to say, "My poor little doggie, they want to make you
mate!" Her entire household shared her repugnance at such an idea, including
the members of the pagan coterie, whose profound concern for the heavenly
purity of T'uang's behavior arose from the fact that it was a miraculous dog
that had permitted them to erect their Ark of the Covenant in Mamú's house.

Then the two of us arrived with our own rather different life-and-death
emergency, and Mamú, filled with dire premonitions, clapped her hands.
T'uang came waddling toward her, was taken up into her lap, and learned of
the calamity about to befall his aristocratic lineage. This occurred with a great
deal of cuddling and Viennese sentimentality, but also with Viennese *sang
froid*. In the presence of witnesses, and in unequivocal language, the doggie
was informed that he would have to commit a sin against his pedigree. Upon
being told the identity of the dubious young lady who for the longest time had
been awaiting his advances, T'uang looked into Mamú's eyes with the languid

expression of his noble race, and gave his nose a twist exceeding the one which he had inherited. Fortunately Mamú overlooked the despair that spoke through her darling's eyes. She turned to the state's attorney and asked him to get in touch immediately with the Police Commissioner.

The fortress had been conquered. The mob that was raging in the Land of Poets and Thinkers was demanding its victims here on the island, too. And we, all of us, approved of the betrayal of T'uang's loins.

The Man of Power arrived at Mamu's house, desperate but thrilled. His *cadilla*, he explained, was not receptive; it would be a while yet, and could he then reach Mamú by phone? It was agreed that, if possible, he would call one day in advance, since Madame would have to make certain preparations. The latter consisted exclusively in my plan to ask Bobby, the Folkwang School artist, to be on hand to make a photographic record of the proceedings.

Pollution Day fell on a Sunday. At an early hour we left with Bobby for El Terreno. We made ourselves comfortable beneath the park palm tree and waited for the Mother Church to finish its service. Mamú dismissed the ladies; under no circumstances were they to hang around for secular chit-chat, as they normally did. Auma, too, was asked to leave. Mamú suggested that she and her state's attorney visit the park at Belver Castle, a refuge that was, in any case, too sparse of foliage to permit any double wedding.

We had an excellent meal; Mamú's exchequer was once again solvent. T'uang was served beef bouillon with sliced-ham crèpes, and as always he was permitted to lick the blood from the edge of the carving board. The conversation at table centered on remote subjects. Not a single one of the diners dared to make the kind of off-color comment that is so common at wedding feasts. Beatrice and I were filled with reserved expectancy, just as if we ourselves were the ones who would soon be introduced to the greatest of Nature's mysteries. Our insular fate was to stand or fall with T'uang's stamina and acceptance of contamination.

The Commissioner was announced, and Mamú asked that he be shown in. Never in history has a happier father carried a more reluctant bridal daughter in his arms. As this Power Man bent down to kiss Mamú's hand, all we could see was a patch of glistening canine fur with darker streaks. But this sight sufficed to make us comprehend Mamú's qualms about the imminent wedding ceremony. Even a non-cynologist would be forced to conclude that Túang's bride had worm-holes in her family tree. Her parents had not been consistently kept on a leash. T'uang himself, despite his royal lineage in the Empire of Central Europe, would be unable to guide this blood in more suitable directions. Only Dr. Baruch from America, another friend of Mamú's, could have provided the proper advice, as one might expect from a professional diplomat. I came to admire this gentleman when he was the U.S. Ambassador in Portugal, and we were in a position to observe his behavior quite closely.

During Hitler's War, Portugal was germanophile, and opposed to America. Dr. Baruch had a difficult task, although the worst was already over. He was a Jew, but that doesn't bother the Portuguese. They are too dignified for such an attitude, and besides, they have never forgotten that, since the expulsion of the Children of Israel, their intellectual achievements have declined.

Dr. Baruch was already an elderly gentleman when in February 1945 he presented his credentials at the *Necessidades*, with a large white flower in his buttonhole. The Portuguese were less than impressed by his chrysanthemum. The title "Dr." is not worth much in a country where anyone who has attended a university can expect to be addressed as *Senhor Doutor*. If Dr. Baruch had been of noble lineage, a Baron, Count, Prince, or some other kind of top-to-bottom decadent blue-blood, he would sooner have found favor with the descendants of the fabled Portuguese tribal chieftain Luso. Yet this American was cleverer than all the citizens of Portugal. He knew just what caliber of artillery he should deploy on the banks of the River Tejo. I saw him a few times. He reminded me very much of Count Keyserling, with whom he shared his given name. But Dr. Herman Baruch wished to remind people of a much more significant personage, and he singled out no less a figure than Jesus Christ. With the aid of a whispering campaign, he began circulating the legend of his descendancy: the origins of his fleshly nature were to be found, he claimed, in Jesus of Nazareth, by way of Mary, and further, along theologically very confusing genealogical paths through the House of David, and further still in the scrolls of pedigree to Heli and Matthat, Levi and Nathan, and finally to Baruch, son of Neria, the magnanimous companion, fellow sufferer, and biographer of the prophet Jeremiah.

This biblified story made the rounds in the aristocratic salons and tearooms, the *Casas de Châ*, and became clearer in the telling. Jesus came more and more into focus, while Baruch got increasingly blurred. By the time my Portuguese friend Belita ticked off the list of Adam's progeny down to Dr. Herman Baruch, behold: the diplomat had lifted his other leg up out of the morass of the Old Testament and now stood securely with both feet on the firm ground of the New. His ancient ancestor was a brother of Christ! As a devout lady from Belita's circle of friends told me, anyone who attended a garden party at the American Embassy and shook Baruch's hand was actually reaching across two thousand years and shaking the hand of Jesus Christ. When I gave the lady an incredulous look, she snapped at me and asked if I doubted what she had just told me. I replied that I was convinced that with God nothing was impossible, but—and suddenly a number of people started looking at me. As a friend and translator of the national genius Pascoaes, I enjoyed certain privileges, and thus I could utter things for which other persons, even princes and kings, would get tossed off the premises. —But did we in fact know that Jesus and his brother ever shook hands? Maybe they weren't even on speaking terms. Hostile brothers: it's a popular motif in the Bible...

At this point in our discussion of Baruch's christological myth, Belita's mother, the austere Doña María Augusta, felt it her duty to intervene with all the imposing strength of her personality, which was all the more awe-inspiring on the basis of her income from the Quinta do Vesúvio, where Portugal's finest port vineyards are located. She felt insulted by the barbarity of this American fable, which touched on matters of faith and morals. Another elderly aristocratic lady went even further, declaring that she had heard from an unimpeachable source that the Ambassador could trace his lineage directly back to Christ Himself. Old Dr. Baruch himself could not have worked things out with such precision. He could be satisfied with the genealogical seed that he had already sown.

It would be just as foolhardy to cast doubt upon the historicity of Dr. Baruch as it would be to call into question the nature of the historical Christ. Christ's fate as a historical person, along with its much-discussed Palestinian local flavor, is certain. And that is a shame, or perhaps even disastrous for humanity. For if Christianity had based its mission on nothing at all, it would only be a dream, a figment of the imagination or of poetry, and it could never have degenerated to the degree that we are witnessing today with fear and trembling. In the book he wrote about his own experience of Christ, "The Christ of Travassos," my friend Pascoaes makes a statement that is a significant step toward the mystical de-historicization of the figure of the Savior. He says that Christ entered the world with the first tear that was ever shed, at a place that was later to bear the name Bethlehem. The Christians of the Crusades, the ecclesiastical battles over politics, and the Holy Tunic of Trier are unwilling to accept such an insight. They need the open wound that they can place their fingers into. That is human nature. But every religion that traces its origins to a human founder has failed precisely as a result of human nature.

Mentir comme un généalogiste, a French proverb proclaims. Baruch's cleverly planted family tree was a first-rate diplomatic achievement, one that contributed more to the Portuguese citizenry's understanding of the American people than all the cultural missionaries sent to the country. Until his arrival, whoever judged the USA on the basis of its "crippled" president, the "gangster" Roosevelt, now had to concede with surprise and shame that there were people living in the States who had a lineage that was pleasing to God, people with mammoth family trees that were just as firmly rooted as any in the Old World, trees that no conceivable windstorm could topple. Reaching up into the heavens, such trees, fertilized by countless human corpses, were totems around which one could dance the Dance of Death, a favorite form of sacrifice for any and every god.

"Love is blind," says an old adage that has so often proven true that it has entered the universal consciousness and is cited in all the compendiums of famous quotations. Accordingly, the Commissioner of Immigration Police for All the Balearics was blind in his love for the little bitch he was still cradling in his arms. What a miserable cur this was that he adored so much! What kind of ancestors might Dr. Baruch have dreamed up for this flea-bag? Next to such a mutt, Mamú's Imperial lap-dog looked decidedly regal as he approached his little mistress on his invisible walking-props.

The Commissioner set the bride down on the lawn next to T'uang, who provided himself a parasol by raising his tail above his back—a most majestic gesture. It wasn't until I saw T'uang next to the policeman's nameless pug that I understood why, for millennia, the Chinese emperors imposed the death penalty on anyone who exported this race of dogs. It seemed certain that anybody smuggling the Police Commissioner's deviant canine variant into the Central European Reich would likewise fall under the executioner's axe.

As I have explained, Mamú's yard was a park, albeit a very small one. Rabindranath, with the ludicrous dignified gait that is natural to his species, was able to cross it lengthwise in just a few minutes, and could get across the breadth of it in no time at all, with the help of a few hops and a flapping of wings. In the photos that Bobby took for Mamú's family album, this tiny plot of earth takes on the dimensions of the palm grove at Elche; a flower of the order *scorsonera*, photographed from the top of a ladder, gives the impression of a segment of the Garden of Eden. The photographic plate is, after all, much more of a liar than the so highly suspect printed word. Don Juan Sureda knew very well why he didn't include a single photograph in his archive of alibis. What judge would ever base his decision on a photo as evidence? Not even spiritualists would dare such a thing.

As soon as T'uang figured out why an in-bred mongrel was getting placed in front of his snooty nose, he scurried away to find a hiding place in Mamú's primeval park of beautiful illusions. Neither Joseph at the house of Potiphar, nor Vigoleis on the Street of Solitude, had acted any less instinctively, although their proffered mates were of a rather different species. No matter how much he might enjoy sniffing or even mounting a canine female, Mamú's Pekingese was responding to his own millennia-long bloodline. Now, confronted by a strange bitch and threatened with a *Maríage de convenance*, he balked and simply took a powder.

Mamú was ecstatic. "Children, those five thousand dollars were worth it! Here you have proof of the blue blood from the kennel of my friend Nikolaus!" But Mamú's children were anything but ecstatic when they saw T'uang creeping off into the bushes.

When the rejected bride, whose progenitors seldom felt a leash around their necks, attempted to dart after the cute little lap-doggie, the Police Commissioner grabbed her by the fur and held her back. He knew what was right and proper behavior for a bridal ceremony. This was a sign for Bobby and me to intervene. We did what hunters do in similar situations: we beat the bushes. But the little Imperial guy was nowhere in sight; we would never catch the escapee without ruining the manicured shrubbery. Bobby, the refugee from the Folkwang Art School, put on his Cultural Bolshevist face, made a few silent calculations, and then started poking a long bamboo pole into the bushes. His microscopic left eye, doubtless the secret of his success as a typographer, but at the time a detriment to his hunting skills, took on a look of desperation. That little Chinese twerp was evading the attempts of a kid from the city of Essen to jerk him forth from the greenery! Then he skidded into a hole in the ground left by Mamú's pet rabbits. What now? That's when I had my Great Idea.

The raven has had a terrible reputation ever since the days of the god Odin. With his jet-black coloration he is the incarnation of evil itself; he is said to be capable of hacking out the eyes of his own progeny. If he ever becomes extinct—which Brehm says is quite likely—all of civilization will have lost its most graphic symbol of the battlefield. On the other hand, the raven has also been clever enough to gain renown as a beneficent creature. Mythologists can point to ravenous escapades that are little short of ingenious. Apollo employed ravens as divine messengers. Lusitanian charcoal-burners sing the praises of ravens that fly ahead of lost hikers, guiding them to the nearest human habitation. And then there is the bird's amazing memory. The raven is a maniacal scavenger, one that can locate hiding places years after the fact. And besides, this particular raven had taken a strong disliking to Mamú's Asiatic doggie. I cried out, "Rabindranath! I'll release the raven!"

Such an instinctive solution of the problem would have been beyond the ken of Bobby's Folkwang School, even in its Cultural-Bolshevist heyday. I deduced this from the expression on Bobby's face, whose good eye was now also beginning to cloud over. Envy is a common vice among artists.

My plan was a dangerous one, but I saw no way around it. A single peck of the raven's bill would suffice to exclude T'uang forever from Imperial Succession. Mamú broke forth in loud lamentations. The Commissioner turned even paler when he learned that "Rabindranath" was not a famous Indian writer but a bird of prey. He picked up his bitch, and once again cradled her in his arms. Mamú made a grandiose display of compliance and willingness to trust the two trustworthy Germans who would accept all the responsibility. The wedding must not be called off just because the bride has fled the coop.

When I opened his cage, Rabindranath hopped off his perch and strode with pompous gait directly to a place where, every day, he stashed a half-pound of raw meat, only to discover each time with his characteristic aristocratic nonchalance that parasites had completely consumed his hidden snack, meaning that the meat never reached the desired degree of decomposition. Then he retrieved T'uang's little silver bell from another place, took immediate fright at the sounds it made, and hid it in a crevice in the palm tree. These were two oft-repeated capers of his, and he always performed them with a sour mien and much angry squawking. Everyone in Mamú's household was familiar with the routine except T'uang, who was kept inside whenever Rabindranath was let out of his cage. (When the raven became capable of flight, I outfitted him with wing clamps). Only then did he approach the rabbit hole, which presented interesting possibilities of its own. And behold: with hoarse barks, the little canine shot forth from the cave and streaked past the bewildered bird like a bolt of lightning. Only after returning to his perch did Rabindranath regain his composure, while in the meantime Bobby was able to grab the runaway pooch by the pelt. Once smoked out of his lair in this fashion, he was carried over to Mamú, who now had to decide on the further sequence of events.

I said, "Mamú, the only solution is brute force. Consensual union is out of the question. We have made a pact without consulting the Emperor of China himself. And who knows? Perhaps the doggie is so frightened now that it has affected his loins, leading to... shall we say... immobility. There are certain phenomena..."

Mamú herself had experienced all the phenomena that life had to offer, and all of life's phenomena had visited her. Every Sunday her ladies arrived with new miraculous happenings. There was no need for lengthy deliberation. With firm resolve, she snatched up her pooch: "To the dining room, come on!" We followed her like a company of truculent pimps, determined to rescue a potential deportee while at the same time aiming a blow at the *Führer*.

The Police Commissioner set down his morganatic chippy on the dining-room carpet. T'uang, likewise placed on the rug, where he was expected to effect the peaceful consummation of his wedding with the comely T'atsu, immediately darted under an armoire. Was he in terror at the sight of so much Pekingese ugliness? Was he appalled at his own mirror image? I suddenly considered myself already deported from the island. We could hear him growling under the furniture. This was a provocation!

At this moment I felt like a true German, like a dyed-in-the-wool, no-holds-barred Teuton, refusing to be intimidated by anyone or anything under the sun. And I knew I could depend on Bobby—he, too, a true-blue, resolute German. More resolute, in fact, than I, for he was already on all fours under the commode, dragging forth the reluctant bridegroom. It was now our intention to intrude upon Destiny Itself.

"You mean you're going to...?"

"Yes, Mamú. It has to be. Otherwise I'll be deported. The *Führer*, too, gives no quarter. *C'est la guerre!*"

In that case, Mamú replied, the Spaniard would have to leave; there was no need for him to watch the proceedings. But she herself wanted to be present. "But not on my carpet, Vigo! Put the bridal couple up on the table, and bring my chair over. Bobby, go ask Calpurnia for a damask tablecloth."

This was not the first bridal union that Mamú had set the stage for. "*Dô het er gemachet alsô rîche von bluomen eine bettestat,*" in the words of Walther von der Vogelweide, and I sang them for Mamú. "It's an unjust world, Mamú. T'uang will know his T'atsu upon a cloth of the finest weave. I know some people who make do with a pile of newspapers."

I indicated to the Police Commissioner that his presence during the wedding ceremony was not desired. I gave him my word of honor that I would report the outcome in exact detail. Since the gentleman was unaware that I was identical with a certain subject under threat of deportation, he accepted my offer. In this manner I retained my second aspect in order to salvage my first.

T'uang was still unwilling to cooperate, even on the luxurious oriental carpet. Bobby grabbed the bride by the neck, using the skilled hand motion admired by everyone who has seen his calligraphy. I stood at the opposite end of the table. Mamú was seated in her place of honor, her lorgnette focused on the bridal couple, looking no different than if she were attending a premiere at the Metropolitan Opera House built by her princely spouse.

The two animals made strange noises that none of us could interpret. Using her Viennese inner-city dialect, Mamú egged on her little darling. But it was no use. I was resolved to break my word of honor if nothing happened between the matrimonial couple. This was all so ridiculous! We felt like bailiffs at some court proceeding, using miniature models to demonstrate how a train wreck had occurred. Bobby stood his ground—which, after all, was his main job in this situation. But I was suddenly overcome with rage, and made a quick grab. "Oh, my poor little puppy!" Mamú cried, dropping her opera glass to the floor. "I saw a jiggle! Vigo, you can stay on Mallorca!"

Mamú was a highly educated person, but any street urchin could have set her straight. I, too, knew a thing or two about such procedures. After all, I had raised rabbits, and never in a random way, but always according to the book, a certain volume of the *Guild Masters' Library*. This, the most dog-eared volume in my teen-age collection, contained an unforgettable, lapidary sentence: "If the male then makes a leap, one can be sure of success." But Belgian Giants are not Pekingese Dwarfs. Besides, Asiatics are inscrutable, and it was I myself who had caused the leap.

Twice more I let T'uang experience his one second of bliss. Each time, Bobby caught the jolt with knitted brow. I knew that as an artist he was intolerant of mere scribbling, and what was going on here, although we were writing in minuscules, wasn't a demonstration of elegant calligraphy. So let's just get it done and strew some sand over it! It is a terrible thing to break one's word as a German, just because of some tripe-eating animal.

The nanny had already prepared a bath for T'uang. The wedding table was cleared, and then disinfected.

"All right," Mamú said to the Commissioner, who had spent tortuous minutes beneath the palm tree. She raised four fingers of her right hand. "Caramba!" was the overjoyed official's reply. "Fine job!" I said, and congratulated him. He then told Madame that he was grateful, adding that if ever he could do her a return favor...

Mamú was of the opinion that I ought to tell the man straight out exactly what he must do for me. Upon her life she would never be willing to submit her doggie to such swinishness a second time. But wasn't it *scheen* after all? I took Don Fulano aside and explained to him the precarious situation that a friend of Mamú's was in. "No problem at all, my friend. Here, give the gentleman my card, ask him to present it to our clerk, and the problem will be solved once and for all. Four times! *Caramba!* I would have been satisfied with just once!"

The Immigration Police never bothered us again. We were now tax-exempt honorary citizens of Palma de Mallorca. I wish to add that Don Patuco's spy reported to his general that the incriminating registration card was missing from the file. By means of an authentically Llullian feat of prestidigitation, we had been effectively dematerialized in the sense of legal accessibility. When the Civil War broke out, this would save General Franco two bullets.

Now we had no aspect at all any more. And we had beaten the *Führer* at his own game of racial humbug.

The state's attorney later reported to us that the Commissioner's dog had given birth to a litter bearing the unmistakable earmarks of T'uang's Imperial lineage. The proud breeder had let it be known all over the island and beyond that his T'atsu had produced offspring of T'uang.

Would Mevrouw van Beverwijn now...? Was this evidence for the validity of her Christian Science? If so, I would have to do a lot of apologizing.

XIV

I have a friend in Spain who is sad whenever he thinks of the hour of his death. Not that he is afraid of dying. A brave fellow and a swashbuckler, on research trips he has come to grips with Red Indians and predatory animals, and on one occasion, strapped to a martyr's stake, he thought his final hour had arrived. He has two children whom he loves more than himself, although he remains the self-admiring type. He loves them more than his treasures and his real estate, which together amount to a sizeable fortune. When he dies, his children will be as poor as churchmice, for out of the thicket of anonymity there will emerge the more than thirty illegitimate children that this man, still leading a life of Old Testament fecundity, admits to having engendered in his home country alone, and they will all claim their share of his estate. He has taken no measures to prevent this from happening. The earlier count of thirty has in the meantime risen to fifty and more. His devout wife, who he believes is still ignorant of his profligate paternity, prays every day, beseeching God to take all these bastards unto Himself, begging Him to visit a plague upon them and annihilate them as products of her husband's lascivious habits.

When Vigoleis closes his eyes forever, no one will contest ownership of his repeatedly decimated personal library, so often replenished by means of starvation campaigns. It is the single item of value that he will bequeath to the world. With its dispersal, all of his forms of existence will come to their final end. Anyone who claims to descend from him will be a liar, and such a lie will not even be useful in the search for truth, as was the case with Dr. Herman Baruch.

I have remained childless, by reason of having transcended on a metaphysical plane the cunicular Christian pattern of sublimation. But I love kids just the same. And in order to have one without committing a sin against my own convictions, I chose the route of adoption.

Adoption, the scholars assert, is an imitation of nature, and hence a problematical matter if one is willing to admit, as any primitive human and any Naturalist writer can confirm, that nature is very difficult to imitate. That is why the Ancients decreed that no *castrati* could adopt children—a wise move if you bear in mind how an adolescent son's voice will change in comparison with his father's. Such considerations were irrelevant in Vigoleis' case, although he was blacklisted by the Nazis on the basis of having committed racial contamination with Beatrice. One day he found a warning in his post-office box: the Reich Gelding Commission was keeping an eye on him. His Janus-faced character—a poetic aspect together with an innocent, boyish nature—would remain intact, and he could go on writing. What was alarming was the official stipulation that no poor citizen was permitted to claim a rich citizen as an adopted child. This legal detail set the stage for a thoroughgoing perversion of the natural course of events.

Fantasies about synthetic paternity clotted my mind as Mamú's lawyer investigated the matter of whether, how, when, and where I could be adopted by Mamú. If the case ever arrived at a favorable result, I would be an American citizen, and thus could marry Beatrice with no need for her to exchange her innocuous Swiss passport for one printed on criminal brown paper.

My wild, free-wheeling marriage, which continued to gnaw at my mother's heart, was in the eyes of the Children of the Mother Church in Boston more than just an annoyance. They regarded it as one more piece of evidence for our debauched nature and satanic wickedness, curable only in the fires of Hell. As soon as this bluestocking coterie heard about the adoption plan, as a result of Mamú's and my own blabbermouth habits, their sense of outrage knew no bounds whatever. To them, this amounted to a bare-faced attack on the Royal Baking Powder millions, engineered by a couple of beggars who slept on torn-up newspapers. They would have liked to tar and feather me, or better yet, put me in a cage together with Rabindranath. Nevertheless, Mamú remained firm.

What would these guardians of morality have said if they knew that Mamú's prospective son was himself aiming to adopt someone?

As the island's most expert tourist *Führer*, I was of course aware that Mallorca was in the business of exporting children, in addition to its more famous products such as the delicious bacon derived from the Mallorquin sweet hog *(Sus dulciculus maioricensis V.)*, prized since the days of the Roman consul Caecilius Metellus (nicknamed Balearicus), a delicacy that has placed the cuisine of the Adlon Hotel in Berlin far above the average for German hostelries—as Count Keyserling well knew.

This particular feature of Balearic commerce is overlooked by all of the available travel guides—but then again, the shortcomings of our Baedekers are all too familiar. The only person who could have written a truly comprehensive guide to the Island of Mallorca was my dear friend and journalism teacher Günther Wohlers, a scholar specializing in Joseph Görres and an expert on women and spiritual beverages. He died as a result of his own versatility, at about the time when a Baedeker discovered him. After his death, in my estimation it was only Don Vigoleis who could stand in as a worthy successor in matters of Mallorquin detail, albeit one who was at several removes from the original when it came to all-around vagabond tourism. In fact, Don Vigoleis had already taken up Wohlers' scepter in the form of hundreds of letters to his friends, letters that were often copied out and sent to friends of these friends, with the result that he could lay claim to being the most widely read picaresque epistolographer of the entire Mediterranean world.

Don Flugencio's Children's Aid Agency—Established 1876, Gold and Silver Medals, References Upon Request—was not among the attractions one must visit if one wished to have "done" the island.

Pedro told us about a certain fellow on the island, drawing sketches of him in a variety of professional poses, who plied the trade of *corredor de niños*: Supplier of Children. In Mulet's *tertulia* there had also been talk of some such business, but I hadn't been able to form a very clear picture of its operations. In my mind's eye, I saw a large knife with blood on its blade, the blood of a child. And weeping mothers surrounded by innocent kids at play, kids who were destined to fall victim to the well-honed blade. Was my thought process too German, too sadistic? But if so, then the *tertulia* attendants were equally guilty, because they always "ventilated" such matters in such a way that the wheat got thrown out with the chaff, leaving no useful grain behind. In the South, the sky is chock-full of stars and saints. Similarly, on Southern *terra firma* there is an overabundance of words, even from the mouths of people who are constrained to reticence by pipe-smoking—as in the case of Don Joaquín Verdaguer—or by gout and other ailments of a former military career—as with Don Miguel de Villalonga.

By no means did these men shy away from discussion of the ultimate and eternal problems of life, of which the case of Don Fulgencio was a prime example. Besides, it was only a small step from this mysterious entrepreneur to the mystic Nun of Ávila, a step no greater than that between any case of mundane adoption to the subject of becoming a Child of God. Yet despite my profound admiration for the Spanish habit of lifting any subject at all to the level of philosophical discourse, I soon noticed that, in this respect, none of my fellow *tertulia* participants was quite the equal of our beloved Santa Teresa. This woman, the patron saint of all Spain and the *enfant terrible* of the Catholic Church, must have received the gift of philosophical intensity as a baby in her cradle. Quite simply, she was one amazing lady. Her writings, between the lines, have revealed to me a great deal concerning the Eternal Feminine, in an unchaste style tailor-made for the Vatican Index. With amazing frankness, she stirred the pot in God's and her own convent's kitchen and was inevitably misunderstood, especially by pious types who never looked at her original texts. Whenever I read her, I am reminded of the words of Hamann, the "Magus of the North," who said that his mediocre mind could never imagine a creative genius as lacking genitals. My own imagination is insufficient to grasp Iberian mysticism as the pure voice of divinity.

One particular day, this fruitful subject of conversation—which, by the way, I never tried to explain to Beatrice—took a turn from abstract literary discourse and impinged directly on the life of Don Vigo, which is why I am able to report on the matter first-hand. I received a letter, the contents of which, in summary translation, were as follows:

The undersigned was in a position to make me a very favorable offer concerning the legal adoption of a child. Through his professional informants he had learned that I liked children, but also that I was a metaphysically and politically persecuted individual, disenfranchised, humiliated, and deprived if the blessings of progeny—a situation that the Church regarded as sinful and the State as unhealthy, but one that was commercially favorable to himself. He would be delighted to provide me a pathway to reconciliation. By following the precepts of common sense and accepting foreign blood, I could rectify the failures of my own blood. This pathway led to his Brokerage for Children, to which was attached an Agency for the Arrangement of Catholic Marriage. For certain personages to whom Nature had been less than kind, a natural child of one's own could easily become a moral burden, not to mention the financial consequences, whereas an adopted child was an encumbrance only for those who refused to give credence to the saying that where there is food for two, there is enough for three, (or enough for four when there are three, or for five when there are four, etc., i.e., when there are two there is enough for five—I don't believe in this multiplication of the loaves, since the two of us often had meals that were insufficient for one cat).

Furthermore, Spanish law guaranteed that an abandoned child, one who could well have been engendered by noble parents, would receive the patent of nobility, which is to say, that of a *hidalgo* (i.e., *hijo de algo*, "somebody's son"). Fulgencio's Children's Brokerage dealt exclusively in abandoned infants, the so-called *expósitos*. The undersigned was now constrained, he wrote, by advancing age and the lack of personal offspring to dissolve his business. He had unfortunately failed to provide himself with children of his own, or to secure a *hidalgo* for the continuation of his firm. Rather than consider his own welfare, he had devoted all his efforts to the well-being of others. This statement was followed by a passage from the Epistle to the Romans—which gave me pause, since at the time in question I had just discovered Pascoaes' *Saint Paul* and was immersed in Pauline lore. Apparently this broker was a connoisseur of the Bible. Upon request, the orphans he obtained fresh from the convent would be accompanied by trained nannies. A limited number of items remained in stock, and he was recommending that I make my selection soon, within the means at my disposal. The times, he continued in this hand-written missive, were indeed confusing; the State frequently discouraged the production of natural children, and besides, he was aware that I had been threatened with forced sterilization. Thus I would be well advised to act before forfeiting my right to personal adop-

tion. If I was voluntarily refraining from adding to the human population
in a world where human life was no longer the Lord's reflection and
image— well, that was strictly my own affair. Each and every one of us was
master in his own house.

This letter, a calligraphic masterpiece, ended with the abbreviations still customary in Spain: *s.s.q.e.s.m.*, signifying that the writer was the devoted servant
of the addressee, and offering a hand in friendship. This particular hand was
being presented by:

Fulgencio de la Fuente y Carbonell de Lladó,
Corredor de Niños

For the sake of caution, before entering into this pact I showed the letter to
Beatrice.

"Read this, and if you then persist in thinking that the Spaniards' sole aim
in life is to kill time, I will never cease complaining about the holes in your
national cheese."

Beatrice just ignored this childish threat of mine; she was in no mood at all
for instant capitulation. She took the letter and read it. I prepared my defenses,
fully expecting to demolish the arguments that in just a few seconds would
descend upon me and the broker's epistle. And I say "in just a few seconds"
advisedly, for although the broker's solicitation was couched in long-winded
prose, I knew that Beatrice would devour Fulgencio's manuscript in an instant.
Her eyes are not only well-practiced in reading. In addition they have a
remarkable talent for digesting a reasonably narrow-set text and, with a single
glance, transforming the visual image into meaningful language. She reads
lines of text in just the same way as they drop out of a linotype machine. A
diagram of the movements of her pupils would thus not be zigzag, but rather
a steadily descending straight line. Such acuity of perception brings about an
amazing rate of reading speed, but what is more, her brain keeps pace with
her optical prowess. Like a mowing machine, her eyes simply slash the words
down, line by line. As for myself, I read very slowly, and I prefer books in
which what I am looking for is contained between the lines, books that burst
out beyond the printed page and force me to stare into empty space. Thus
it should be no surprise that Beatrice and I have never adopted the custom
of married couples who share literary tastes and read to each other while
lying together on their *pilarière*. In such situations, each of us has his or her
own book.

If we add to Beatrice's optical agility her elephant-like memory, we can understand how she can ingest, digest, and store up for later use enormous quantities of printed material. During this process, her psychic retina remains
unaffected. All of this reading has by no means made her more stupid—oh,
begging your pardon, I mean that it hasn't made her stupid. And that, too, is
a phenomenon that makes me pause and reflect. I hope that this state of affairs
can continue into the indefinite future, in order that the equilibrium of our
marriage, based as it is on contrast, can remain undisturbed.

As far as stupidity is concerned, I consider the type of ignorance one obtains from excessive education a great deal worse than the congenital manifestation. The latter is basically harmless, as long as it does not join that of some fellow human or other to incite a chain reaction, in which case the result can be the establishment of dangerous political regimes. I have had occasion to observe from close proximity how the minds of overeducated individuals can get squashed flat by omnivorous reading, but I failed to recognize the true danger posed by this process. What I have in mind is the German academic type who can be bamboozled by any Kaiser, any sleazy prophet, any charlatan who comes along spouting forth some gimcrack philosophy or other. For these professors, knowledge can become the blind spot of their profession, just as the concept of "God" can, even more tragically, escape the understanding of the enlightened theologians of higher journalism.

Once long ago—oh, so very long ago!—after arriving in Cologne with my busted box of books and, together with my Mom, passing the bordello test that all academic greenhorns from the provinces have to go through (the only test, by the way, that I ever passed), I threw myself into the arms of the professors with the thought, "Here I am! Now create me anew in your image!" I was no longer a little boy, but actually not yet old enough for this kind of re-creation. My true nature had already taken shape, but unfortunately the wrong way around. I looked up to my intellectual guides as if they were superhuman. I was astonished at the amount of their knowledge, which they not only set down in books but could also, at least in some cases, deliver impressively at the lectern. Even more impressive were the private libraries in their erudite households, collections that, following their decease, were submitted in toto to the local antiquarian bookshop of K. E. Koehler & Co. How great was my pleasure at poring over catalogues of old books! A scholar who never once in his career experienced an embarrassing moment must have felt the pinch after his death, when the contents of his book collection were revealed for all to see. But what amazed me most of all was the procession of Ph.D.s emerging one by one from the seminar rooms, wearing borrowed suits and with *summa cum laude* diplomas in hand. The sight of this academic conveyor belt in operation bore serious implications concerning the highest aims of life.

I signed up for course after course, educating myself with a genuine *furor teutonicus*, and continually extended the goal-markers on my intellectual horizon—given that there was no upward limit to my seeking. It was when listening to the professors of divinity that I first realized that certain things were not quite right about the German system of higher education so prized by Goethe and his humanistic contemporaries. I was crushed to ascertain that the teachers of theology had no sense whatever of religion. Instead, they were the mathematical purveyors of dogmatic theorems into which they inserted statements about God. They derived the cubic root of God, and raised God to the desired power—which is to say, they held on a leash the entity they referred to as their Creator. Those who allowed this entity the most slack were the ones who attracted the most students, but it was easy to see that the leash had a finite length. Sooner or later the leash would go taut, and the game would end with a jolt. Johannes Hessen was one such theological gamesman, whose lectures were exciting to listen to. In the halls of academe it was an open secret that he constantly stood with one foot in the papal dungeon. He warned us against Rilke's dangerous pantheism—Rilke, whom I considered more religious than the entire Bible.

In other academic departments, it took me longer to figure out that German scholarship was a malleable science, one that always gave way to stronger pressure. Thus I was not at all surprised to witness the universities falling victim to political *Gleichschaltung* in 1933. In fact, most of the learned gentlemen were willing to forego their customary privilege of waiting the "academic quarter-hour"—no one wanted to be left behind. Having studied their way into "frigidity and impotence," these erudite fellows kowtowed to patriotic fervor, and kept on teaching with half the normal professional achievement (nationalism always means doing things in halves) and in constant fealty to the ineffable omniscience of the *Führer*. The rest of the world greeted with astonishment this newest patent, Made in Germany. Rather than threaten imitators with lawsuits, the Reich actually encouraged them; whoever was unwilling to imitate was a loser. Great writers shrank to midget size and joined the ranks of the Reich Chamber of Literature. I had been among their admirers, but now they had gone stupid and fell for a country-fair barker, just as the tourists on Mallorca fell for a certain other *Führer's* swindle. Both *Führers* had this in common: they detested the rabble and reacted to them by vomiting—each in his own fashion.

The higher the degree, the weirder they be: Schopenhauer, Lichtenberg, Nietzsche. Who wouldn't have certain qualms when it comes to scholars who wind themselves up inside a cocoon or hide inside a shell, lacking the kind of spiky tooth that every fowl embryo comes equipped with, to peck its way out of its prenatal housing? Kierkegaard, too, meditated on this subject and wrote about it. Take, for example, Professor Wernicke, who made a name for himself as a scientist investigating the higher cognitive processes of human beings. A specific area of the brain has been named after him, and this will remain in mankind's memory longer than any city park that bears his name. This man, so very familiar with the brains of his fellow countrymen, is reported to have said that twenty-two percent of German university professors were feeble-minded. In issuing this report, Wernicke clearly echoed statements made by Nietzsche in *Beyond Good and Evil*. Whoever feels personally offended by this ought rightfully to put his head in his hands. If he is unlucky, he will find himself touching the Wernicke region of the brain. Damage to this area of the cerebrum has as a consequence the inability to understand simple language... I intend to pursue this matter further, because rumors of this kind do not arise merely by accident. Indeed, there are rumors that have more truth to them than the events that gave rise to them. One example: how human beings actually became human.

Count Harry Kessler, the Kaiser's adjutant during the Wilhelminian World War, shared with us similar horror stories about the cerebral zones of members of the General Staff. When the papers reported the death of Joseph Pilsudski, he told us how in 1918 the Kaiser had given him orders to free the Polish conspirator from the Magdeburg citadel, a mission he accomplished by disguising himself as a prison guard. Continuing on the subject of stupidity as a way of life, I asked him whether this phenomenon, stupefaction as the result of over-education, was visible among the leading officers of the German Army. Kessler flashed a glance at me with his hollow-set eyes, but he was too polite and too set in his traditional ways to reply, "Hold on there, my friend, don't ask such stupid questions!" Instead, he simply explained that the officers in question manifested a form of stupidity that stemmed from sheer military obstinacy. As a mitigating factor, he cited the fact that even these gentlemen sometimes regarded events at the battlefront as stupid, but then they would take up their rifles and go off duck-hunting. The enemy would suddenly break through the defense lines, and the Kaiser would quickly cashier these generals, the ones who meanwhile had chosen to take potshots at a different kind of enemy. "And which one was the stupidest of them all?" we wanted to know. Kessler explained that there had been a good deal of rivalry for this distinction, but that we should now just be patient. If the Nazis kept their hands off of our island he, Kessler, would let me type out the names to my heart's content. But he added that he planned to take up this topic only in the fourth and final volume of his memoirs.

Count Kessler never got past the first chapters of Volume Three. Thus I have had to compile my own list.

It wasn't until I started living in foreign countries that I became aware of how disreputable these German scholars were who, gorged by the extent of their own knowledge, maintained contact with the world around them exclusively through the prism of their narrow specialties. What they thought and said had precious little to do with genuine human affairs. That is why Hitler had an easy time stringing them one by one, these bogus pearls of German scholarship, onto his Nazi necklace. I was once witness to the first personal encounter of two famous German professors who over the previous twenty years had exchanged professional ideas in letters and scholarly journals. I mentioned to the professor from Munich that his colleague from Berlin would be attending the conference. "Oh, fine, " he said, "it's good that he'll be on hand. That means we can ask him directly. It's not possible to clear these things up by writing letters." When they finally met, there was no evidence of real pleasure. They shook hands with each other—an anemic gesture resembling nothing so much as two slabs of veal getting placed one on top of the other. Not one personal word. I stood by watching in horror. This, I thought, is how a victorious general and his conquered counterpart might behave at an armistice negotiation. There's no denying that scholars of this type play a role as catalysts in the advancement of "pure science." They serve as activating parasites, like the millions of larvae that aid the digestive process in the stomachs of elephants. As long as scholarship continues to go on, this brand of specialized scholar will always be on hand, though it will never occur to them that their true role is that of a purgative. Hitler despised these learned puppets within his movement just as deeply as the Christian churches he continually toyed with.

Beatrice had long since stopped sketching with her imaginary pencil. She put aside the broker's letter and said laconically, "Pedro! And you're falling for it, too?"

"Pedro? What's Pedro got to do with Don Fulgencio? Can't there be anything at all unusual any more without Pedro being involved in it? Just because he's a Sureda?"

This was the attack I was fearing, but it was coming from an unexpected direction: from above. I had to devise a cautious defense of my friend, and try to fend off the worst. If this new model of his started smelling, that would irritate Beatrice, and she would toss out the both of them together with sheepskin and easel. But then what about Pedro's art? Pedro liked Beatrice, but Beatrice liked Pedro less and less, the closer she looked and sniffed at his artistic trappings, and the odder the people were that he brought to our house. These characters were in fact quite impossible if you insisted on judging them by non-Spanish standards—as Beatrice did. That's why she wasn't getting any fun out of the jokes Pedro was playing with his victims.

Here is an example which, while again diverting our attention momentarily from Don Fulgencio, will eventually make his case all the more comprehensible. Pedro knew a pharmacist whose mind worked in ways that were not altogether compatible with the production of pills. This man boasted of being able to tell at a distance of twenty yards whether a woman was, as they say, immaculate. The fellow later became the victim of his own talent, but that is yet another story with a fatal ending. Pedro told this seer about this German friend of his who wrote poems, and who showed other signs of not being quite mentally sound. For example, whenever this friend was introduced to someone, he broke out into gales of laughter. He would get veritable laughing fits. But then, polite fellow that he basically was, he would try to suppress his mirth, and this made the situation all the more embarrassing. Would the pharmacist care to make this gentleman's acquaintance, Pedro asked? Indeed he would, was the pill-pusher's reply, whereupon Pedro told me the selfsame thing about the apothecary's strange habits and asked me the same question: would I be interested in meeting him? The meeting took place in our apartment, unfortunately at the very moment when Beatrice, in despair over the linguistic ineducability of the Mallorquin populace, entered the house. She joined us just as we were standing in the doorway laughing uproariously at each other. Pedro, working his sketch-pad with abandon, winked at both of us in turn: "What did I tell you!" Each of us reacted to the event in the precisely appropriate fashion—most appropriately Beatrice, who turned livid.

It was episodes like this one that, in the course of time, made us constantly wary of Pedro as a house guest. That explains why Pedro had to be suspected of setting us up for this prank with the broker's letter—I myself, good German that I was, had fallen for this nonsense just as all the Germans had fallen for Adolf Hitler. This was a direct hit! Then began our domestic political feud. Beatrice called my gullibility very German and very Catholic. Just one more step and I would land in the bosom of both *Führer* and Pope, the two medicine-men of organized mass deception. Well now, I said, how very Swiss-Reformed of you to think that way. Just one more step and... But then I was silent, because, for one thing, I couldn't really imagine where one next step might take a woman like her, and for another, because I thought we shouldn't be arguing at all about the Nazis—those people would soon enough find a way to drive a wedge between us. Each of us should go off into a corner and be ashamed of ourselves. But now, what about the kind offer being made to us by the aging broker, the worker of miracles?

Pedro, Beatrice continued calmly, had known for a long time about my interest in this fabulous child-dealer, or child-strangler, a fascination that Mulet's *tertulia* had kept at high pitch, probably with the intention of pulling one over on me. It was easy to think that Verdaguer might do something like that. Later he would write a mysterious short story about Don Vigoleis, the guy who believed in everything except God. But the *tertulia* crowd was made up only of literary types; Pedro wouldn't hesitate to go farther. Not only did he invent people, he actually brought them to our house. I should be on my guard. Pedro wrote the letter. Tonight he would show up at our place all a-twitter. As always he would start sketching, and he would listen carefully to our chatter to find out if we had taken the bait. "Just let him come," said Beatrice. "I'll go off to bed."

"My dear Inca maiden, Pedro will arrive tonight just as surely as he did yesterday and will again tomorrow. He's a persistent guy. He aims to wear you down, but he's using the wrong technique. Don't worry. I have no intention of revealing the secret ways of winning over a transalpine squaw. And besides, with all due respect for his thoroughly un-Spanish inventiveness, he would never be able to concoct such a letter."

Beatrice reached for a book, which promised better entertainment than a discussion of the case of the child-merchant. Summoning up my courage I continued, "Let's talk about reality. This letter is extremely clever and subtle. The deceptively blue coloration is bluer than the German Romantic poets' blue flower, the one whose fragrance we perceive at the source of all forms of deeper knowledge. It is pregnant with cadaver murders as at our Clock Tower. It is a double-edged entity conceived in the dreams and waking hours of the poets. Everything else in the world pales in significance whenever reality begins to bring forth stories—not history, but stories— plotless stories, random stories, just-so stories, stories that don't care who gets to read them. *L'art pour l'art*, but with cosmic import. Reality can accomplish anything. It selects topics that our poets do not dare to contemplate. It writes about me, for example, *la mia bella*. Or about the Don Fungencio Lladó of this letter here. It has the greatest store of experience, of the kind that Novalis or Rilke expected any true writer to have. And it never tells lies, even though its texts may cause us to have certain doubts, just as you yourself are having right now. But then again, you are a theologian's daughter. You could never resist taking peeks behind the scenes of your Daddy's study as he composed his Sunday sermons or his university lectures, earning bread for his family in the employ of Heaven itself, just like any other Daddy earning his family's keep. Such a family background is enough to give a precocious child a life-long complex.

"Now you are no longer a believer in divine revelation. And that's understandable, given a father who pronounces the Word of God on Sundays, and in mid-week lays down household cash on the table for Mother—what an impossible situation! The Catholic Church has arranged these things much more intelligently and meaningfully—with more eternal significance, I am tempted to say. Or do you perhaps think that the Church invented its rule of celibacy and defended it down through the centuries against all kinds of attacks, simply because the Church's own virginity required a virgin priesthood, or perhaps because it feared financial burdens on the hierarchy, a debt that would of course grow to gigantic proportions if the clergy, from the village curate to the Pontifex Maximus himself, had to contend with wife and children? Ignatius of Loyola might have devised a militant solution to this problem. No institution in the world outdoes the Catholic Church in combining opulence with beggary. You are well aware that I am still searching for any Servant of the Lord who might actually still believe in this Lord. I am a huge fan of miracles. Romanticism is in my blood."

Such types as believing priests must actually exist, I went on, but it was difficult to fish them out of the mass of clergy because of their talent for camouflage. They were recognizable only by the radical colors that some of them wore, the ones who like Savonarola got swiftly burned at the stake. I added that she herself, Beatrice, the daughter of a pastor and patristic scholar, constituted a welcome confirmation of my theory that the children of Men of God can easily fall victim to the devil, atheism, and hypocrisy. How could it be otherwise? It was simply unthinkable for a man to produce children, go through the daily drudgery of heading a busy household and family, go for walks with a pregnant wife, and then climb into the pulpit every Sunday and break the sacred bread. To me this seemed like a form of blasphemy. Nevertheless, I explained, it was not my intention to cast aspersions on her esteemed father—at least no more aspersions than I was casting in her own direction.

I had read most of his books, and I had never forgotten what she once told me about this poignant incident in her father's den, where the devout scholar was in the habit of writing at a stand-up desk. Sometimes when her mother wanted to be rid of her for a few minutes, she would let her enter her father's study. On one such occasion, while Daddy was busy composing his *History of Revival Movements*, she began systematically removing the page slips from all the books she could reach on the shelves. Clueless in matters parental, yet always kind to children, her erudite father could think of only one way to handle this little intruder short of kicking her out of the room: he lifted the girl up to his stand-up desk, set her down on his manuscript, and went to another table to continue his work *ad maiorem Dei gloriam*. Fearful of falling down from her perch, the little tyke sat there as quiet as a mouse. We can ascribe to simple human nature what then ensued: Beatrice went about anointing the covenant that her father had entered into with his Creator. Later, Professor Adolf von Harnack, who often checked over his favorite student's manuscripts before they were sent to the printer, noticed the strange aroma emitted by this particular sheaf of pages. Harnack, more acclimated to the refined fragrances of the German Kaiser's household, probably interpreted the odor as the ordinary mustiness of a Swiss pastor's dwelling.

I concluded my endorsement of this remarkable letter from the broker by saying that I myself had grown up in a totally unscholarly household devoid of books. Never, ever had I enjoyed the privilege of doing my business while sitting on a sacerdotal throne. At such a tender age I never committed transgressions against what was held sacred.

"And now you are making up for it, *mon cher*!"

"There is a time and a place for everything, *ma chère*. Sooner or later each of us will have his tongue rapped with a key, and then it will be obvious whether or not he will remain in divine tutelage. I left the State of Grace forcibly but willingly, whereas your departure had other reasons. Now we're in this mess together, and we seem to be getting along okay—not brilliantly, but okay. That's what happens when people are coerced into attending service on the day when the Lord took a breather. But that's a whole different story. Can you imagine a God who designs and creates entire universes and then on the seventh day, like any upright citizen, takes the day off? Do your Papa's posthumous manuscripts contain anything on this subject?"

"Vigo, you're hallucinating! What's all that got to do with this letter? It's from Pedro or one of his henchmen. And in order to avoid admitting that once again you're the fall guy, you start lambasting the two Christian religions, whose melancholy products we both are, and setting them one against the other. And in the process you get things all confused."

"I am by no means getting things confused. It will very soon be apparent to you how all these things are connected. I've told you a lot about my uncle the bishop, who was in truth a great man whose mind was in no way affected by having to wear his precious miter cap. In his house in Münster, Am Domplatz 30, I got to see certain things that went on behind the scenes in the residence of a Higher Deputy of Jesus Christ. Let's assume that all of these relatives of ours, each of them having his exclusive place amid the heavenly hosts contending for eternal salvation, were honorable men who put their intellectual and humane talents to work in the service of a cause that, to put it mildly, has very little that is intellectual or humane about it when politics demands its due. Just think: my Pope is already negotiating with Hitler, which means that belief in God and worldly expediency are in the balance. My Uncle Jean was well aware of the dilemma he would face as he was elevated to the rank of Bishop. In fact, he refused twice to accept the shepherd's crook. When I asked him—he was by then a Bishop—whether he believed in God, he gave me a look that would have revealed all my misery to me—if indeed I felt miserable. He said, 'I pray a great deal, my son.'

"Your Papa must have experienced similar crises of conscience, but soon enough he decided to get away from the sterile and musty air of Basel intellectual circles. Surely he felt uncomfortable there, for otherwise why would he have gone off to the pampas to spread the Word of God to the gauchos and the Indians of the savannahs? I'm impressed by the thought of the scion of an age-old scholarly dynasty abandoning his stand-up desk to lift himself up onto a mustang and start baptizing Araucans and Tehuelches. That cost him his life, but at least he escaped the fate of getting swallowed up by Nestlé Theology."

"By what?"

"By Nestlé Theology, an important branch of Swiss seminary pedagogy. It's concentrated, it's germ-free, and if you keep a lid on it, it will stay useable for years. Every country brings forth its own special type of industry, with its own brand name and with no imitations permitted. This is a gripping story for which I have already found a title: God's Gravediggers. I chatted a lot with Uncle Jean about these matters—always behind closed doors, so his butler wouldn't hear what we were saying. One false word, and we would have a scandal on our hands. My uncle was a tolerant fellow, and he let me bring up any subject I wanted to. Only once did he get mad at me, and that was after I heard lectures by Barth and Mausbach. I recommended that he commission the writing of a modern theodicy, a justification of God not because of the evil and suffering in the world but because of the existence of theologians, who for me were convincing proof that God couldn't exist, for otherwise He would have long since, using Old Testament techniques such as brimstone or plagues of locusts, got rid once and for all of these detractors."

"That poor bishop! Did he come back at you by saying that God is immune to attacks by Men of God, especially when you consider that He Himself saw them coming, or even made them what they are? The gates of theology shall not prevail against God. I'll bet your uncle blessed himself three times whenever you came to visit."

"You're mistaken there, too. He and I got along just fine. He never even tried to convert me, since he himself bore a heavy burden of respectability. That miter alone must have weighed ten pounds. One time he put it on my head, and it gave me a dashing look. Just imagine: Vigoleis as an *episcopus*, *in partibus infidelium*, with a princely wine cellar, with chamberlains, a personal confessor, confirmation ceremonies—or wait, let's leave out the confirmation ceremonies, they can do any bishop in, they're too much for even the strongest stomachs—and with a 13th century Lower Rhenish Madonna in a niche in the library..."

"But leave me out of this!"

"You would regret it, because you would get to play an organ even finer than the one played by Mosén Tomás of the Capilla Classica."

"*Mon chéri, tu es maboul. Je n'ai pas le talent d'être la maitresse d'un évèque.*"

I would like to have replied that she had never experienced a temptation of this sort, even though she had lived long enough in places where Princes of the Church were conspicuous if they didn't sleep in a double bed. But I kept silent. How could I defend myself against this siege in the French language? My French was, is now, and will forever remain barbaric, and not only as regards my accent. The failure of German-French entente is a matter that concerns the philologists more than it does the politicians. But it's always the wrong people who try to bring about ententes—just look at the mess I got myself into by attempting to bring my child-broker down to earth from out of the clouds of mystification. I had ended up by crushing him!

"Beatrice," I interjected, "I won't ask you again whether this offer interests you, considering that you have your doubts about the very existence of this man's business. I will simply go to the address we have, behind the Archepiscopal Palace, and seek out the proof in person. Perhaps I can discuss with the broker some matters that can give a new direction to our lives. On the way back I'll visit Angelita; you can stay home and practice."

"Go ahead! You won't find the broker. I'll do the shopping myself, because as soon as Angelita gazes at you with those angelic eyes of hers, you'll lose your equilibrium, and who knows what you'll bring home with you. It's just that tonight I'd like once again to have a genuine meal. There are two pesetas left."

"Don't worry, there is only one Rabindranath, and if those aunts aren't in the store, for our two pesetas Angelita will sell me more than we can gulp down in two whole weeks. That girl is truly an angel, and not only in name."

"And you are truly a utopian, and not only on paper. Those aunts are always in the store."

"If so, we would long since have starved to death. I'm on my way, and don't forget: my ways, too, are sometimes miraculous."

I had emerged from our theological disputation not exactly victorious. And to be truthful, I was myself beginning to doubt the existence of Fulgencio. Doubt can be the first step toward knowledge, but there was no point in worrying; the Calle Morey would provide the precise information we were looking for. On my way there I again studied the broker's missive, which I now regarded as a kind of test for a lower-level course in psychology. Certain turns of phrase in it were formulated in a scurrilously elusive, overwrought style reminiscent of Unamuno—was this Pedro's doing? Pedro was a master stylist, as I knew from reading his remarkable diaries.

At this point I wish to append a further detail from the broker's letter, one that I discovered only while perusing the text more closely: our entrepreneur was offering me a monthly clothing allowance of 10 pesetas, to be paid out of a special fund for hijos de algo in cases where the adoptive father lacked the means to clothe his adoptive kid. In order to feed the kid, we could depend on a pious Vincentian foundation. But in both cases we would have to provide proof of my penury. Far from regarding this clause in the agreement as a personal affront, I thought it was quite appropriate. I may often be the victim of my own misery, but never its true cause—a state of affairs that Beatrice could corroborate if she were ever in the mood to do so. As a heavy consumer of crime novels she is aware that each and every word "will be used as evidence against her." And as a human being among human beings, I am aware that where there is no food, there can be no kid—although the reverse is usually the case.

Perusing and meditating, I wended my way to the Calle Morey, past the Cathedral with its coloration of burnt earth, the earth of Mallorca. I quickly located the broker's house, a mummified palace from the Moreto epoch, modified in later times and resulting, through a patina of decay, in a combined style that was not without a certain unified effect. In Spain, this crumbling and erosion of masonry under the influence of sooty time begins at the moment when the architect hands over the key to the owner, just as a living organism taking its first breath starts breathing its very last. In Portugal, such fatally creative decay—creativity, as always, considered as a form of decline—begins with the laying of the cornerstone—a fact that could lead us to even more telling analogies in the human sphere. As I grow older, again and again I see more and more clearly that the preservation of human creations is an exercise in intellectual impoverishment, a tragic admission of impotence and impossibility, a futile attempt at rescue. To avoid sinking, all we need is a slab of wood. No sign of the grand gesture arising from personal initiative: people saw things apart, they glue things together, they take a thousand shards and stick them together to remake a Madonna, and we heap praise on the clever fellows who show so much patience. As for myself, I love to watch things collapse. In the noise, the showers of ashes, and the clouds of swirling dust I can suddenly discern a gesture, witness the emergence of a word and a deed that captivate me. In such events I detect a tone that, in my enraptured state, can lead me toward the ineffable more readily than the sight of anything that is firmly grounded, supported on all sides, anchored, held fast with mortar and pitch. In the realm of language, poems by Trakl can have this effect on me. In the absence of words, gestures, or sounds, I can still sense the fantastic metamorphoses that take place amidst all the rubble.

Lost in thought, I found myself standing inside the palace courtyard. Fiery-eyed cats slunk around in the hot sun, like the demonic veiled *beatas* and the erotic priests in their Faustian cassocks—a dozen from among the thousands that make up the veritable feline zoo that is the City of Palma. Cats, *padres*, and nuns give the streets of Palma their characteristic stamp.

I had to climb three flights of stairs to reach the *porche*, a narrow arcade that led to a dull mahogany door with a bronze knocker in the shape of the nest of a bird of prey. To the left of the entry I spied a sign set in the sandstone masonry—behold, the salesman's name replete with all the honorifics of his lineage. So Pedro hadn't duped me after all! And as for Beatrice's instinct for truly criminal machinations—why, she was deceived by too much literature! I would simply never be able to put her on a trail that began with any measure of improbability. It was humiliating to discover that my Inca maiden was proof of my contentions—not in black and white, to be sure, but in close approximation of that graphotechnical figure of speech. And just look, the sign contains more information: *Corredor de niños*, and beneath this, *Gran surtido en ambos sexos*. Of course, with a single glance Beatrice would have deciphered these words while I was still preoccupied with the cats—I, *Vigoleis triumphator*, who shall now read the text and translate: "Large Assortment of Both Sexes." We know from the letter that he is already sold out, with the exception of the single item that has led me upstairs to this official sign. Underneath the sign was an enamel plaque, apparently added as an afterthought and depicting the Divine Friend of Children—nothing unusual, by the way, since nearly all Spanish households have a contract with Heaven, the least expensive Watch and Ward Society. Under the picture was the obligatory ejaculation to the immaculately conceived Mother of God: *Ave María purísima sin pecado concebida*. But where I expected to read further, "...pray for us," there stood, penned out in an approximation of calligraphic hand, the words, "Please knock." This was a discreet hint that apart from paying tribute to the Almighty, the urgent concerns of everyday commerce were to be observed here as well. And so I knocked.

A maid appeared, an island native in the familiar costume of the servant class: a kerchief of white tulle tied under the chin, called *reboçillo*, a long pigtail, and a little cap. Thus far, nothing out of the ordinary. Every halfway respectable family had a bunch of these servant maidens. The only thing unusual about this girl was her bosom, which was in constant motion and which moved me, too. I therefore made a bow that was too deep by a few vertebrae, still caught up in that transitional phase between the ludicrous German bowing of my student days and the natural casualness of Mediterranean greeting customs. I had not yet advanced to the universal shoulder-drumming, dust-producing embrace, which in any case would have been out of place with this girl. I simply presented her with my card, which contained a single word of identification: Vigoleis.

This domestic servant—and yes, that is what I wish to call her instead of "maid," a term that all too quickly reminds me of the girl made famous in a poem by Christian Morgenstern, the "maid" who secretly had to nurse a baby "with a head made of cheese," a mental association that could prove deleterious to my admittedly dubious intentions upon entering this house. Besides, I had no particular need for this associative borrowing from Herr Morgenstern, the creator of the *Gallows Songs*. Using his own inner rhyming dictionary, Vigoleis was perfectly capable of filling psychoanalytical gaps of this sort. And as far as this particular girl was concerned, he was determined to set a personal example, no matter if she was a "chaste, self-styled kitchen maid, /

neither clean nor bright, / brazenly deceiving her employers / in plain sight"
and was not nourishing a cheesy brat at her bosom. If I were writing as a
Romantic, having come into the world a century earlier, it would be almost
automatic for me to spice up these jottings with rhymes in the manner of
Eichendorff's *Ne'er-Do-Well*, who every few pages breaks out in song. Such
exuberance has been out of fashion, indeed it has been considered shameful,
ever since people no longer hike their way through the wide, wide world but
instead take elevators and are constantly fleeing from potentates. Poems have
in fact become literary contraband. Our publishers are anxiously on guard
against verse getting smuggled into prose, which is what they make their
money from. In the realm of rhyme, as in so many other ways, the Romantics
were closer to reaching the Blue Flower than we starless descendants in our
century of literary sham.

The domestic servant read the single word on my card. Why, she could
actually read! She looked at me, then again at my card, smiled, and asked me
something that confused me even more than her bosomy appeal: Was I a
Vigoleis? Indeed I was, and decidedly so, I said after a moment's pause during
which I pondered myself as if suddenly casting a bolt of light on my own person. But then I realized that her question meant something rather different. A
"Vigoleis"—she interpreted the word as a title, a designation of profession,
an indication of social rank on the order of "Voyvod," "Padishah," or
"Mahonda," someone before whom one must sink to one's knees if one
weren't such a pretty girl with flirty eyes and a long pigtail that stuck out
stiffly in back and that had at its very end an even stiffer piece of string that
signified her boss' dignified rank. "You wish...?"

I handed her the letter, explaining that this was why I had come. She asked
me to follow her. We entered a room that contained, besides a cuspidor, a single mouse. The latter skittered away, leaving me alone with the ceramic pot,
while the domestic servant disappeared behind another door. She soon re-entered and, still smiling, beckoned me into an adjoining space, the waiting
room. The servant girl retired. I made another deep bow.

Now I was free to examine the testimonials and letters of gratitude that
were displayed on the walls. The sequence of documents had been arranged
with the skill of a museum curator who knows just how to force a visitor to
wander along the exhibit, taking everything in and educating himself in the
process—art for art's sake. The arrangement forced me in addition to pursue
a train of thought concerning the psychology of the waiting room—a subject
that cries out for scholarly investigation. Generally speaking, the installations
range from that of a pre-torture chamber to a Shrine to the Blessed Mother of
Merciful Succor, and on to the boudoir of a wealthy bordello madam. Don
Fulgencio apparently aimed for a synthesis of all such types. I didn't mind
waiting.

The texts of these testimonials were instructive. Two of them, in particular,
caught my attention. The first was written in the hand of His Royal Highness
the King—a clear refutation of Robespierre's claim that kings were illiterate.

The letter was a request to Don Fulgencio that he provide a child free of hemophilia. The man who wrote this was already living in exile, perhaps now liberated from any worry about the mysterious corpuscles whose lack of coagulatory capability may have had no influence at all on the fall of the monarchy, as was bruited about among utopian monarchists during the early years of the Republic. The second document informed the reader that an order of nuns in Alicanta was willing to entrust all the orphans in its care to the good offices of Don Fulgencio.

As in an art gallery, I made the rounds of this exhibit, but without a printed catalogue and unhindered by a pressing crowd of visitors incapable of adapting to the tempo dictated by the works of art—or, to put it more accurately, the tempo that the art works would require if today the picture-postcard aspect of art had not become predominant. To appease this trend, all curators have installed postcard stands at the gallery exits. Don Fulgencio had a different idea. Scarcely had I studied the final line of text when she again appeared, my bosom friend from *1001 Nights*, to guide me through a dark corridor and into a spacious room. An elderly gentleman stepped toward me.

This was the master of the house. There was no need for the domestic servant to whisper it to me: this was the legendary Don Fulgencio.

And what a Fulgencio he was! Such masculine effulgence! I estimated the age of this phenomenon, this flesh-and-blood personage out of the mythological mists, at about 80 years, although I must admit that I am seldom correct with guesses of this sort. If my own exact age down to the minute were not so fully documented by oral tradition and, even more reliably, by the official stamps so prevalent in our time, I would never come near to surmising it, whereas the age of my Vigoleis, whom I myself baptized, is beyond any calculation. When it comes to women, this matter can become acutely embarrassing. Not, of course, with women like Mamú, who at any age can contradict their own birth certificates, women who at 50 have no need for facial alteration or whose mouths at 80 still display their eternal youthful smile. No, the women I have in mind are those tragic, ghostly ones who, with valises full of cosmetic nostrums, approach the borderline where birthdays are no longer celebrated and where the tortoise veers between the purely vegetative and the purely animalic state. Once arrived at the 50-year checkpoint, they apply makeup in order to pass for thirty-something, with the result that they look like ladies in their seventies on Ash Wednesday.

Much too little attention has been paid to this subject. It has given rise to murder and manslaughter; marriages have broken apart long before their time; the masculine world has been forced to stand witness as an entire generation has been passed over, just as certain kids skip a whole year in school. Ladies who, fretting over their crow's feet, rush out to buy salves and ointments, will never reach their goal. Indian fakirs go about this with herbs manipulated beneath magical textiles; they, too, achieve amazing sudden shifts in age. I dare say that the renowned forger Van Meegeren, if he had ever set his sights on the cosmetic mystification of women's faces in a beauty salon in Paris or

Amsterdam, could have become a very rich man. It would have occurred to him to adorn the abandoned mistress of some Monte Carlo billionaire with a masterful Mona Lisa smile, so that whatever remained of her gilded undercoating would be revealed only within the confines of a *chambre séparée*. Instead, by deploying his divinely inspired artistic fakery, this man succeeded in confounding the academic expertise of art connoisseurs the world over, in the process nailing them—and himself—to the cross. And there they now hang, as tokens of ignorance and fanatical ambition. Meanwhile, stock in the fine arts keeps rising in value, in reverse proportion to the decline of artistic discrimination. For the genuine comprehension of art, it is necessary to approach it from inside, with the heart, and not with the aid of litmus paper and X-rays. Specialists in the epidermis of art who stumbled over *The Apostles at Emmaus* are the very same ones who now have discovered primitive man's *l'art pour l'art* in the caves of Altamira, Valltorta, Covalanes, and elsewhere. They have yet to arrive at the caves of Mallorca, although there, too, the Van Meegerens of the Ice Age did their work... But enough on this subject for now. At the moment I am eye-to-eye with Don Fulgencio, and my digressions could make him disappear in a fog.

Don Fulgencio was busy blowing his nose, but otherwise seemed to want to address me straightaway. I felt no need to snap out of my meditative mood for his sake, and yet I had no desire to fritter away the time. Besides, certain noises at the door indicated that the servant girl had taken up a post just outside, eager to learn what kind of business this strange mahatma intended to discuss with her boss. But before I allow these two dignitaries to enter conversation with each other, I wish to offer a description of the gentleman about whose existence Beatrice had serious doubts.

The man's overall bearing was stiff, although when walking he manifested a certain insecurity about setting down his left leg. I don't mean that he dragged this leg behind him, only that the left didn't seem to function as well as the right. A cane would have been of some help, but he would have rejected such a support on the basis of an old man's vanity. Field Marshal Hindenburg was a shining, internationally acknowledged example of this kind of proud senility, an attitude that cost Germany dearly. Don Fulgencio's hands were attractive but unkempt. I studied them carefully, purely on account of their shape. Very few people have beautiful hands, and there are even fewer artists who can paint a human hand. Don Fulgencio was annoyed by my constant gazing, which he misinterpreted. He quickly set about removing the grime from under his nails, employing other nails on each of his hands that served this specific purpose. This he accomplished skillfully, as if he had spent a lifetime in practice. Incidentally, this was not the first time that I, with my mania for observing hands, became the mute agent for an auto-manicure. If only people would realize that, far from wishing to cause embarrassment, my interest in dirty nails stems from a very personal envy of such persons. They embody an attitude toward life, a measure of pride and self-confidence that I have never achieved. They keep dirt for themselves, where it's meant to be kept.

.

Don Fulgencio offered me a chair, and again sat down behind his desk, which was covered with a large plate of glass. Underneath the glass were letters, picture postcards, newspaper clippings, a lock of hair, handwritten poems—a veritable herbarium of yellowing testimonials to his sentimentality. The walls of his office contained calendars with pull-off pages, showing a plethora of past and future appointments. Clearly there was a reason behind such a display in this decaying palace where nothing, not even my own self, seemed left to chance. Opposite me, above the old man's head, was a richly carved Black Forest clock; as I watched, the cuckoo flew out of the little window and started squawking. It squawked four times, with a beating of wings.

Immediately Don Fulgencio drew from a pocket in his embroidered vest a snap-top watch, and checked the time. "Accurate to the second, sir," he said, and these were the first words he spoke. "Here, see for yourself."

He extended the golden timepiece in my direction, and I quickly affirmed his declaration. He was absolutely right, and because he was right, I suspected right away that something must be wrong. Black Forest cuckoo clocks are notorious for their inaccuracy. In my family household each member had his or her own cuckoo clock—hasty purchases made during the inflation, which entered its most murderous phase just as we were spending our vacation in Triberg. Each cuckoo had its own sense of time, which every day sent my meticulous father into a rage, while I thought it was romantic and natural. No two thermometers or hygrometers ever show the same degrees. At Fulgencio's house, however, apparently a stray bird had flown in to show the Spaniards just what German punctuality is all about. In Spain, as is well known, it is only the bull fights that begin on the dot. Amazed at this attack against the Iberian sense of time, I asked the gentleman to explain the origins of his aberrant clock.

"This masterpiece," Don Fulgencio said as he replaced the watch in his vest pocket—making it necessary to pull in his belly just a bit—"This work of art is a gift from a happily married couple in Titisee. You know, in the Black Forest. Thirty-seven years ago I gave them a child with smooth black hair and a fiery temperament, who adapted well to the Teutonic bushlands. I should add that this was my sole export arrangement with Germany. The transalpine races seem to prefer Nordic suppliers. There was a good reason why I simply gave away this young orphan, but that is neither here nor there. When the girl was four years of age, her parents sent me this clock. Ever since then it has never once stopped—to me, an excellent sign that she is getting along just fine. If it ever stopped running, it would mean that her life's thread would have unraveled."

"But what if you forget to pull up the weights? If I understand you correctly, you have a human life in your hands."

"If someone might ever neglect to wind up the clock, it would imply a cause-and-effect relationship with the destiny of that child. In that case, forgetfulness would be tantamount to destiny."

I would like to have continued chatting with this Spaniard about accidence and providence, hoping to make some gains in personal awareness—all the more so, as neither of us was a professional philosopher with the typical penchant for disputations that are as interesting as they are futile. Such colloquies resemble a game played with several balls, many of which remain suspended in thin air. It is a matter of daily practice to see how many balls one can juggle at any given time. Born philosophers are rare. Most of them grow on trees, and that is why almost all of them need the greenhouse ambience of universities, "Schools of Wisdom," or scholarly articles in print.

But I remained silent. Don Fulgencio gave me time to digest what he had just said. The emptiness of his glance beneath his furry brows told me that he was mentally up there in Titisee. Was this pure superstition on my part? In my younger years I was quite snooty toward superstitious persons. Back in those days, on the basis of my bible-paper philosophers I believed that certain effects result from certain causes. I regarded superstition as a pathological excrescence, as a kind of myoma that attached itself to true knowledge. Nowadays I am cured of such dreadful notions. Besides my reading in the Occidental mystics, above all Teresa de Ávila, my recovery owes much to my years-long sojourn in Catholic Iberia, where an apostolic-nihilistic inclination towards superstition is often mitigated by a very moving form of humaneness. It must be apparent from much of what I am recounting here, concerning my own or Vigoleis' life experiences, that it is no accident that I have become the translator of a mystic, Pascoaes. For this I was predestined. This gift was placed with me in my cradle.

Here in Fulgencio's office it was as quiet as a monastery. The clock ticked softly with its little balance wheel. The cuckoo was perched expectantly behind its little window, and behind the office door crouched my host's domestic servant. Don Fulgencio was still far away in the Black Forest. I waited until he could finally return to me from the thickets of Northern Europe. As one born to wait, I would make an ideal prisoner with a life sentence in solitary, an ideal obedient monk, or a constantly praying hermit. But in order to enter prison I would have to commit a crime against a fellow man. To enjoy cloistered solitude I would have to commit a crime against myself.

All of a sudden Don Fulgencio was back with me, and so we proceeded to the business at hand—a business the nature of which was still unclear to me. The proof of the pudding is in the eating. My special mission had achieved fulfillment when I reached the top of those three flights of stairs. Beatrice's incredulity was refuted by my sighting of the company's sign at the door, and Pedro had been washed clean of any suspicion. I could have got up and left. I should have. I was in serious danger of having a child foisted on me by sheer garrulousness. Rabindranath is still a fresh memory for all of us. But I stayed on, and like the cuckoo, I became a cog in the snail-like motions of the cosmos.

For Don Fulgencio, however, I was at this moment simply a potential client waiting for an attractive offer. To signal my inner relaxation, I sat with one leg crossed over the other, but in reality I remained the gullible simpleton, miles away from being the Padishah imagined by the servant girl who was still eavesdropping at the door and was now about to learn what was what.

Don Fulgencio must have been a resourceful businessman, to judge by the furious efficiency with which he now set out to make our deal. A racing oarsman at a *feria* couldn't have done it much better—which makes me think I should retract my analogy with Field Marshal Hindenburg. The boss succeeded in explaining what seemed to me an attractive offer. I found myself concocting arguments that I could later use against Beatrice, in case I once again returned home with an anthropomorphic raven. Incidentally, the abandoned child now under discussion was of the male sex—somewhat disappointing for me, since I would have preferred a little girl to play with. Pre-natal determination of sex is still an obscure area of science. But in the present instance, post-natal sexual identity was a bitter *fait accompli* that I had to accept.

I allowed myself to be persuaded that the child should be set aside for me for a few days. In a short time I was to inform the broker whether we would take the boy. I forgot to ask the tradesman to show me the object of our negotiations, so overwhelmed was I by being outmaneuvered. How often I leave a store with a purchase I had no intention of making! I rose. Don Fulgencio stepped forth from behind his herbarium, and I heard the servant girl flit away from her listening post. Cats sped across the courtyard, and then I was standing out on the street blinking my eyes, as the day had lost none of its dazzling brilliance. I folded my beret to give it a visor, and made my way home.

I chose a long detour as the shortest way, given that I had to ponder my strategy for any and all further negotiations arising from the promise I made to the broker. I did this more for my own sake than for Beatrice's, who would be shocked. First a raven, now a kid.

On the way I met a German war invalid, a fellow whose heroism (Iron Cross, Second Class) had now drifted over into the "Never-Again-War!" movement. He suffered from hay fever, or *catharrus aestivus*, as he himself preferred to name his affliction, but except for that he was living happily and contentedly with his Spanish wife, who ran a millinery store. Anyone who wanted to be seen on the streets of Palma bought her hats from this woman. The injured German veteran, whose father was a schoolteacher and a creator of (rhyming) word games, made his own purchases in Paris, and that was a huge mistake. His fear of aggravating his hay fever was so great that he avoided all contact with flowers, even artificial flowers, the idea being to preclude any thought whatsoever of blossoming meadows. His wife had to switch to selling brassières, stockings, and the like, since no one wished any longer to wear her neurotic hats. Beatrice was her last victim.

I completed the remainder of my homeward journey in my usual state of absent-mindedness, which turns me into a dangerous pedestrian. I probably wasn't even thinking of the state of fatherhood that the gods of the island were plotting for me.

I found Beatrice sitting on a box, absorbed not in some murder case, but in Padre Feijó, whom I had started translating in order to acclimate myself to the misty atmosphere that surrounds his world of thought. I was copying the technique used by underwater workers, who first enter a compressed-air chamber to exercise their breathing before descending in a diving bell. This is the only way I know of to adapt to a foreign mentality. I would like to have produced for a German readership this Benedictine monk's great essay on the mischief committed by nationalist zealotry. Of course this would get nowhere in the Third Reich, but perhaps there was a market for it in a periodical run by emigrés? I corresponded on this subject with Klaus Mann, who, I assumed, would welcome with open arms for his journal *Die Sammlung* such a contribution on nationalistic superstition. But he, too, had no room for a three-hundred-year-old voice of the spirit against the anti-spiritual.

"Well now, has Vigoleis made a successful business deal? And how did Pedro wiggle his way out of it?"

"I'm not at all sure that what I have just accomplished can be called business. As far as Pedro is concerned, you can rest assured. I didn't see Pedro, but instead went straightaway to Don Fulgencio. As you know, he lives on Morey, in a *palacete* that's swarming with cats and domestic servants. That's the street you've always shunned because of its questionable elements. That's where he lives, and nailed to his door is the Sacred Heart and a palm branch. What did Angelita sell you?"

"Some goat cheese from Menorca, some soaked garbanzos, and a can of squid in their ink."

"I just... But guess who I met."

"Bobby, fleeing from Don José's gynecological machinations? So then he'll be here tomorrow. I'll keep the chickpeas and my portion of the squid for him, as long as he spares me his abstract art."

"Our young friend from the Folkwang School can certainly get by for a week in Valldemosa without applying the forceps. No, I met Mr. Hay Fever!"

"Oh my God, you just can't escape bad luck! Did he bore you to tears?"

"He complained bitterly about the failures of medical science. They can't find anything to cure him of his malady—not even the Germans, and for him that's the worst part of it. But since Hitler, he hasn't been swearing so loudly that there'll never again be a war using weapons filled with flower pollen. But at the moment the important thing, it seems to me, is that I made an agreement with Don Fulgencio. You can see in me the Angel of the Annunciation, you may speak your Ecco ancilla, and our plundered apartment will be our Bethlehem. I'm going to zip back to the adoption agency. But don't we still have a drop of Felanitx around?"

Beatrice handed me the bottle in silence. I placed it to my lips as she, standing at the hearth, stirred the calamari a few times in their ink. I was prepared for anything, for heavy artillery and for some French sniping to underscore the seriousness of the argument. *Allons-y!*

"Well then, it seems that this time I've come out OK. To be honest, I was preparing for the worst, especially after you sent me Mr. Silberstern with his disgusting money and girl problems, a trampish pharmacist, Kitschoffer the exhibitionist (this was an unfortunate Spanish schoolboy whose Swiss forebears were named Kirchhofer), the unwashed Miss Joan, *en chaleur perpétuelle*, and instead of my longed-for grail with the Eye of God, a mangy raven. Now it's just a kid? You're running out of ideas. Are you sick? What are we going to do with the brat? I hope it's already housebroken and won't mess up my newspaper. We can find some milk, but I refuse to wash diapers."

This was, in the form of a politely delivered speech, a rebuff—a blow with the flat of the blade, to be sure, but a blow in any case. I parried with a gulp of Felanitx. For ulcers of the spirit, alcohol is still the most beneficial balm, and the brand I'm talking about had 16% of it.

If what I am recounting here were pure narrative fiction, something made up, I would now let you hear a knock at our door and the special doorbell signal used by Pedro, who has a key when he comes down the corridor to our apartment. Or I'd have Mr. Silberstern (may Beatrice forgive me) demand immediate entry with four rapid knocks, to tell me of some new sexual quandary and ask me to help him out, or at least listen to the details. Beatrice would dash away, absolving me of all further explanations concerning the orphan. But unfortunately, these jottings are beholden to reality. Here I am endeavoring to depict everything that happened in those days, down to the last pictorial detail and the most insignificant area of shade, against the background of our furniture-free everyday existence. Beatrice is not some wispy phantasm. And provided that the phenomenon of existence can tolerate being set in the comparative, Don Fulgencio is even less so—although Beatrice would have liked nothing better than to wave him off into the realm of fable and Pedro's masquerading intrigues. Least of all, myself—although I must confess that I have lived through moments when I felt like some monster's sweaty dream. But who would ever want to have a fool like me in a dream? That, too, is something I must take care of on my own; I must be my own nightmare and torturer. There's no one to blame except Creation itself. "Shame, shame—that is the history of mankind!" Thus spake Zarathustra.

Beatrice's unexpected agreement moved me deeply, but at the same time it forced me to make a difficult decision. I said, "Fine, then this evening I'll go right to the agent and set the day when we can make formal acceptance of our *hidalgo*. In three days I'll have put together a crib. Angelita will give me a few empty boxes, and will she ever make eyes!"

Beatrice is not attached to kids. That is why for years she was a teacher who was deified by her charges. She knew how to treat them. She made her decisions with the secure firmness that over the long run can lead to friendship and love, a process that impresses me in certain stories in the Old Testament. At times, the Lord seemed to be speaking through her. Was that now the case, too?

From out of the kitchen of the fisherman's family living below us came the fishy essence of roasting sardines. The girls in our back yard were in a loud, screeching spat over some triviality. In the upper storey Pepa, seamstress to the upper crust, was leaning out the window discussing matters of high fashion with one of her customers across the yard—it was a familiar scene of rich and poor in their customary exchange of ideas. Nothing has changed. Tomorrow it will all be the same, and the day after, too. Only then will the world in our *bel-étage* cease to obey the Copernican laws of orbit and gravity. The lord of our universe will be our adopted kid. Will it succeed in curing me of my *Weltschmerz*? My hare-brained penchant for self-destruction? To wish one's own perdition, says Kierkegaard, is too sublime for the likes of humans.

It was late when Pedro arrived. The bottle was empty, the mollusks had been consumed together with their murky juice, the yard girls were long since lost in sweaty slumber, each one yearning for the embrace of her *novio*, even though she would have been content with a quickie with some guy from the "Tower" gang.

Pedro sensed that something was afoot, but as usual he pulled out his sketching pad and started penciling our images. He casually inquired about Beatrice's stubborn pupils, about my newest inventions, about Mamú, Rabindranath, and Bobby. I showed him the broker's letter, telling him that Beatrice suspected him of being its author. Our artist, crazy in love, *gallant*, and as always in the pose of a bolero, expressed his heartfelt congratulations and, with just a few lines, made a sketch of this new son of ours who would soon enter our impoverished little world. The image was that of a little fat monstrosity of a child—which immediately soured Beatrice's notions of him once again, although she was on the point of forgiving him for having suspected him of perfidy.

The sight of Pedro's sketch made me suddenly aware that I had neglected to inquire about the age of our prospective new family member. After a long debate, we agreed on 13 months. I planned the dimensions of the cradle accordingly.

Do I have to describe the days that followed? How they were filled with hectic preparations? Once again, Beatrice had more layaway cash on hand than I suspected. Pedro's excitement was contagious; again and again he arrived at our apartment carrying useful items. First he brought a baptismal cushion bearing the Alba coat of arms, 300 years old. Another time, he unpacked a pair of underpants whose label revealed that they had been left behind in the charterhouse by Fortunato, a saintly monk, when the tonsured squad was expelled. More significant still was a bottle containing a half-inch of wine left undrunk, as Don Juan's inscription informed us, by Rubén Darío, Antonio Gelabert, and Paco Quintana during a stay at the castle, *anno* 1913. This vintage had had twenty years to improve in the bottle—what cellar in the world could have offered a nobler baptismal quaff?

Paco Quintana is familiar to many, and Rubén Darío is known the world over. But who was this other member of the triumvir, Antonio Gelabert?

As a barber, Don Antonio had several generations of Suredas under his razor, but it was as an artist that he enjoyed the privilege of sharing a bottle with the above-named notables. Moreover, it was as an artist that he was close to the Suredas. Don Juan Sureda was his bosom friend. He began in ceramics, and as a painter he ended in obscurity like Van Gogh. Today his oils are demanding unheard-of prices. He lived in Valldemosa with a maid and a circle of reliable customers. Tired of wielding the scissors, he bought a little house in Deyá and lived there, an artist among other artists, devoted solely to his housemaid, whom he married; to painting, with which he lived on in even more serious libertinage; and to his own ugliness, which inspired him and which might even have captivated a Goya. Weary of all this, he took a rope and hanged himself in the stairwell. The rope was braided from his maid's hair. Thus Don Antonio had returned to his original occupation.

We were also touched by the solicitude of our neighbor Doña María de los Angeles, an old gout-twisted lady who lived in abject poverty since the alcoholic death of her husband in jail, where he squandered the remainder of their savings with some of the guards, and since the death at sea by drowning of her three sons, fishermen and drug smugglers in Arsenio's gang. Someday I shall perhaps tell the life story of this once wealthy, once beautiful woman. She offered to take care of our child—a gesture of friendship in gratitude for the food we had long been sharing with her.

For the adoption itself—or, more elegantly, for our "optation"—we agreed upon a Saturday at one hour before noon. The ceremony would be over with by the time Count Kessler arrived for our usual dictation session on his memoirs. He would be given a sip from the bottle, whereupon we could return it to Don Juan, its label adorned with yet another famous name.

In the previous night there occurred a cloudburst such as Palma had not experienced in decades. Our General's Street was thick with mud from the torrents that swept down from the higher districts all the way to the Plaza Atarazanas. After Beatrice swept the floors, I polished the tiles with a contraption invented by myself for just this purpose. Then Beatrice covered them with a runner made of old newspapers. This would no doubt give rise to comical scenes with the Count, who would of course not comprehend such an improvised technique as the lesson in thoughtful hospitality that it might be for any Spanish guests. Nevertheless, he felt embarrassed to dirty up our apartment, knowing as he did that we had no money for domestic help. In this regard we shared the same degree of penury. Time and again I tried to dissuade him from taking off his shoes at our *entrada*. It was only later that we hit upon the idea of using felt slippers, the kind handed out to tourists at island castles, in place of doormats.

On the day destined by the stars to bring us disaster, Pedro appeared bright and early with a steaming tray of *ensaimadas*. He helped us put newspapers on the floor, and then pinned a sign to our corridor door with the mysterious letters NHN, which I had often seen at other people's entryways and which I had always misinterpreted. The letters do not stand for *Nil homo nequit*, "nothing that is humanly impossible," but for *no hay nadie*, "Nobody home." It was our desire to remain undisturbed for the solemn acceptance of our

Vigoleisovitch.

If today, twenty years after that crazy forenoon, I ask myself whether I was excited, I can aver without exaggeration that the hammer-blows of my heart did not cause me to collapse in a heap. Yet I must admit that on that morning I did not approach our door over pages of the Deutsche Allgemeine with the same habitual, casual stride I used whenever the milkman brought us our milk, which was always at the same point of turning sour. Beatrice was nervous—in fact, too nervous to start an argument with Pedro; she was in the pre-stage of fury that could turn her into a mute pillar. Pedro was simply Pedro, full of silliness even at this highly dubious moment.

A loud knock at our door echoed up the stairway. And just as we might count the seconds between a flash of lightning and the thunderclap, each of us counted the tapping steps as they approached our landing. Now—now! Pedro lifted his hands as if starting a dance, spreading all his fingers. And then the doorbell rang, thrice.

"*Ave María purísima!*" said Pedro. I responded like an altar boy, "*Sin pecado concebida!*" and I went to the door.

If I were a novelist, at this juncture I would plant some doubt as to whether it was truly Don Fulgencio with our child who was asking for entry despite the letters NHN, thus granting Beatrice her little triumph: Aha, it's all a swindle! It's only the night watchman who's come to pick up his weekly pay! Yet historical veracity demands that I open our door for the broker to enter. It's odd, though, that he appears to be rather taller than I remember him from his *palacete*. Perhaps this is because the dimensions of our living quarters are giving rise to optical illusions. Everything looks big to little people.

Don Fulgencio filled up our door frame completely. I even feared that he might hit his head against the upper molding. Would he allow me to precede him into our apartment? Then I espied a second figure—probably the chauffeur, while down below the carriage waited with our kid and the servant girl. This second visitor, smaller than his putative boss and rather less imposing in dress and manner, looked well into his sixties, although probably he was only fifty. He clicked his tongue, suggesting that I was correct in identifying him as the coachman. He made a bow—something a Spanish *cochero* never does, but—all right, let's enter the room where Beatrice and Pedro await the visit with poorly feigned nonchalance. If I say "poorly feigned," it is because no one ever approaches an encounter with another person without fearing a violation of one's own selfhood. There were no mutual introductions. No one asked about the child. If Don Fulgencio had lit up a party cigar or if Beatrice had started yodeling—she never yodels—all of us would have welcomed this as a perfectly natural prelude to the festivities. Instead, Pedro began humming softly his favorite *copla*: "*Ay si, ay no, ses at lo tes em dinen, que'l m'ham de teiar...*" The coachman belched resoundingly and spat with *grandezza* behind our piano. I didn't dare to look at Beatrice.

We chatted about the weather, last night's thunderstorm, the newly rinsed palm trees in the beautiful girls' yard. Then someone piped up about political matters and that fellow Hitler who seemed to be sitting more squarely in his saddle and was now further than ever from getting tossed out, contrary to what Don García Díaz, the Berlin correspondent for the paper *El Sol*, kept prophesying to his readers every Sunday. Don Fulgencio's opinions were more remarkable than I had recalled them from our exclusively personal conversation at his herbarium. They were decidedly not my opinions, but at least he seemed open to discussion. The nameless fellow whom I still took for the coachman—though now, standing in full illumination, he looked more like an accountant or a bailiff—didn't open his mouth except to burp or spit, further proof that he represented some anonymous authority, perhaps a notary who had come along to make official the transfer of the child. His faulty upbringing was of course his own business.

My immediate train of thought led me from coachman to dray horse to civil servant to red tape. Even in Spain, where people were not yet degraded to cannon fodder and the civil servants were still bribeable, you could still meet up with an aberrant representative of the official sphere who would insist on rubber stamps, illegible signatures, and above all on the proper document—what the Germans call a Schein. The meaning of this German word, which originally signified brightness, glory, and brilliance, mutated in the late Middle Ages into a designation for "written proof" or "documentation." Spoken threateningly by a civil servant, it is among the most fearful words I know. "Do you have a Schein?" I have only the most dreadful memories of my school years and my teachers, with the exception of our principal, Father Kremers. I would prefer to end my days in a ditch rather than relive those years in the classroom and get harassed by slave-driving teachers. Even so, I am never tortured by nightmare memories of school. In their stead, what often awakens me in a cold sweat is being pursued by civil servants. I fear asphyxiation, and I cry out. Over the course of the years Beatrice has become used to these nocturnal attacks, whereas I myself am repeatedly the victim of such ambushes. You simply cannot become inured to bad dreams, no matter how often they occur. Those who explore the depths of the human soul might conclude that instead of "sharing my bed with my mother," I had shared it with a civil servant. "Try to shuck off the burdens of the world, and you will have to bear them. Let someone else succumb." The goblins won't leave me in peace. That's why St. Augustine's City of God stands on feet of clay. This precursor of modern psychology refused to employ civil servants in his civitas, not even in subaltern positions. The civil servant is the very salt of the state, its very own salt-lick. My own personal Oedipus once confronted me in the following manner (I hope Don Fulgencio will forgive this digression back to Cologne, where this Oedipus of mine held sway behind a counter in the Municipal Post Office).

I was a freshman at the university, and I was overwhelmed by new experiences. I wanted to purchase some stamps, but the counter window was lowered. I knocked ever so discreetly on the glass. It was 2:00 pm, the time when the public was permitted to do business. Behind the dull glass I saw a dark, roundish shape that could only be that of the clerk's head, apparently awaiting the victims of his afternoon shift, his moistened pen already in hand. Suddenly the window opened with a bang. This servant of the Reich poked forth his skull, which was adorned with the same bellicose brush haircut as the portrait of Hindenburg on the stamps he had to sell, and he snarled at me, "What are you, illiterate? We are closed until two!" The window snapped shut with another bang, much like a guillotine. It failed to decapitate this particular post-office terrorist only because, with reflexes closely resembling those of an aged pensioner in a split-second I succeeded in retracting my head into my collar. In my fright I took a step backward, causing me to step on the foot of the customer behind me. This fellow, in turn, gave me a quick shove forwards, making me lurch into the counter. These post-office counters were built in such a way that the clerks lacked a completely clear line of fire. The principle of free-roaming, introduced decades previous in zoological gardens by Hagenbeck and Lutz Heck—the zoo visitor can stand eye-to-eye with the wildest of animals and not get eaten—had not yet found its adherents among the architects of public-service accommodations and their counters.

Be that as it may, my would-be Hindenburg had now delivered a shot with his Prussian muzzle-loader, and now sat smoking behind his window, which still rattled from the preceding fracas. Suddenly the official clock, set just a few seconds behind my grandmother's First Holy Communion watch, tolled twice. The counter window leaped upwards, and the selfsame Reich bloodhound who had barked at me asked in the politest of tones, "May I help you?" In between the rifle shot from in front and the shove from behind I had forgotten what I wanted. I stammered something, heard the fellow behind me grumbling, and fled the scene. It took months for me to muster the courage to approach another post-office counter. A fellow student consoled me. He had just flunked his all-important state exam with the philosopher Scheler, who on his part had offered solace to his student with the phenomenological dictum that in order to understand him, Scheler, one must be literate. Was the post-office clerk aware that I, too, was a student of Scheler? And did he possibly think that I understood him?

Without a doubt, this Oedipus at Cologne contributed toward my decision to escape into foreign lands before the counter windows closed on the Weimar Republic, long before Adolf Hitler, the Master Civil Servant of the Reich, stepped into office behind his frosty pane of glass, holding a watch that was a good deal slower than my own—slower by centuries.

Satellites are often just as important as the planets toward which they always show the same face. Sancho Panza is an immortal example of this phenomenon. In this regard, let us examine more closely our coachman/civil servant before he signs on the dotted line and disappears into the anonymity of his ledger books—which can also serve as a hiding place.

With such a patently earthbound character, let us begin at the bottom of his feet and proceed slowly upward along his rumpled trousers, across his woolen sash and up to his open shirt collar, from whence there protrudes an impressive goiter, above which, finally, we behold an unimpressive head. Let us begin, that is, at his soles and not at the crown of his scalp, considering that a pedestal is often worth more than the entire statue. Memorable quotations and a bas-relief frieze are meant to distract an observer from the depicted figure, who in bronze is more amazed at his own heroism than he ever was in real life. This coachman wore the hemp sandals of the little people, albeit with Catalan laces. This brand is somewhat more expensive, but for a man of his standing...?

"Take this, " Pedro said. He tore a page from his sketch pad and gave it to me. He had drawn our mysterious visitor on the scale of 1:10, paying more attention to his head than to its underpinning. Only after glancing at the portrait did I begin to notice certain contortions in the corners of the man's mouth—facial gestures surrounded by stubble and reinforced by wrinkles in the neck. One look at the real-life model convinced me that the artist had seen things clearly, and that I—where had I seen such a visage before, so different from a genuinely human countenance? Why yes indeed, at the prison in Münster, where in a lecture room behind bars Professor Többen was exhibiting his "cases" to us students.

The broker was conversing with his companion notary in Mallorquinian. The latter, getting impatient, stamped his foot hard enough to raise some dust, made a grotesque smile, and swore through his nose, an action that gave rise to a bubble that, no bigger than an egg, quickly burst into spray. I nearly collapsed. Were we going to have a unique, profoundly significant act certified by a notary-public who lived at the borderlines of imbecility? This could result in black-on-white disaster for all concerned! I glanced around the assembled company, looking for allies. Beatrice pulled a wooden box over to the Lladó, tipped it up, and opened the top of the piano. Was she going to start practicing? Now? Very well, I would do it all myself. Making a quick decision, I asked the broker to show me, finally, the child. But if the imbecile was not a coachman after all, there would be no coach down below, no servant girl, no *hijo de algo*...

"Don Fulgencio," I said, "let us proceed directly..." But I got no further. With a piercing screech the goitrous fellow leaped to embrace me. Did he take me for a king, the kind of shaman whose "royal touch" some old stories tell us can make a goiter disappear?

This was a primal scream. All of us have used it at one time or another. Without it, the race of mankind would never have degenerated into human beings, but would still be squatting in trees or paddling along in the glassy primeval ooze. Mankind would be at an end, because billions of years ago it would never have got started. There would have been no need for a Jesus Christ to come and redeem us, for pessimists to rake us though the coals, or for non-poetic existentialists to bother themselves with our latter-day enlightenment. The notary cried out, "Papá!"

Strictly speaking, dear reader, what transpired following this brutish shouting in our bible-paper living quarters, the place that was supposed to have been the scene of my most gratifying optation, belongs not in these applied recollections at all, but in a handbook of psychiatry. Here I shall append only the remarkable external events and explain how all of us became the victims of a feat of legerdemain, the consummation of which was abetted by Beatrice's deep-rooted skepticism and lack of imagination, unmitigated in this case by any sight of reality, as well as by my own, perhaps misguided, ambition and my inborn playfulness, arising from natural melancholy. Not to mention my poetizing idealism, which comes dangerously close to being simiesque and can easily be stimulated by sheer curiosity.

Don Fulgencio de la Fuente y Carbonell de Lladó was a common, ordinary employment agent. Housemaids, waiters, *botones*, kitchen help, wet nurses and the like were the raw material of his business, commodities that no doubt were not always easy to deal with. At the beginning of his career he developed his talents on the mainland, with headquarters in Barcelona. Later he settled on Mallorca, where he had grown up. He came from Son Ferragut, a village in the interior of the island. Once by accident he received an indirect commission, on behalf of a childless English couple who regularly spent the winter months in the Balearics, to locate an orphan, a *hijo de algo* of questionable origins, an *expósito* of the kind that still today are taken to convents to rescue them from even more fearful destinies. The foster parents' gratitude knew no bounds, as the girl turned into the glory of their barren marriage and kept alive their bonds with the beloved Mediterranean, even when they lived on their estate in England or when traveling. Over the course of the years Don Fulgencio, despite his commercial shrewdness a man with a warm heart, arranged several further adoptions. Inclined to hyperbole, harmlessly whimsical like most of his fellow-countrymen, but probably also with the intention of lending his trade the aura of sanctity, he placed his business under the sponsorship of the Divine Friend to Children. Yielding in his later years to a progressive penchant for mendacity—*pseudologia phantastica* in still scarcely studied manifestation—he forged for himself several resounding testimonials from personages of high standing. We have already seen and commented upon his royal missive, which managed to express with heavy-handed irony an antimonarchist's unrelenting anger after the collapse of the throne. Presumably it was only Vigoleis who took this bogus document at face value, just as he does his own self, day in and day out.

It was known all around town and across the whole island that Don Fulgencio allowed himself certain irregularities, that he liked to step forth in borrowed plumes, that his ambitions exceeded what a business agency such as his could ever achieve, in spite of gold and silver medals. Yet the authorities never felt the need to go after this merchant in human lives. They turned a blind eye to him, winked at each other, and were no doubt happy that, so far, they had themselves been spared this variant of Mallorcan nuttiness.

Our employment agent's life was further complicated by the simple existence of a feebleminded younger brother, who was in his personal care following the early demise of both their parents. Fulgencio's move back to
Mallorca can probably also be explained by his new legal status as his
brother's keeper. This brother remained a child, one of the poor in spirit
who were—and presumably still are—destined to enter the Kingdom of
Heaven. He was Don Fulgencio's albatross. I know of no other calamity as
dreadful as being burdened with responsibility for someone who is mentally
retarded. My whole being rebels against such an insane twist on the part of
Mother Nature, who even under normal circumstances is insane enough.
No one knows when Don Fulgencio first hatched the idea of selling off his
brother, who in the meantime had reached full-grown adulthood. It is unclear whether the broker came up with this notion at a moment of profound
depression and urged on by his superstitious visions, or whether he had abet-
tors, evil acquaintances bent on making him a laughing stock. I have never
been able to establish the truth of the matter. Was Pedro, after all, part of
such a plot, in so far as he suggested me as the proper father for the man's
goitrous brother? Puzzle upon puzzle!

On the eve of our departure from the island, at our last gathering at a café
on the Borne—at the next table sat a genuine general with his Pilar—we were
reviewing event by fascinating event, in joy and in sorrow, the story of our
sojourn on Mallorca, the times of near-starvation as well as our days of plen-
itude at Mamú's. I inquired, "Pedro, What about that business with the *hijo
de algo*? Were you involved in that?" He did not reply, for at that moment
the general pricked up his ears like a guard dog. Had the writers and philosophers of Mulet's *tertulia*, loyal to us right up to the end, done anything to
push this little scheme along? Verdaguer? Don Jaime Escat, the Villalonga
brothers, or in particular the specialist in depth psychology who could have
had a professional interest in the case? It is useless to try to find all this out
at this late date. For in my memory the events of our island period, which
one or another of my readers may find amusing, have taken on an aura and
coloration of sorrow and melancholy that will forever remain constant from
top to bottom, no matter how rationally I might try to link together all the
strands of so-called cause and effect. I now believe less than ever in the psychology of the moraine and the mythologizing attempts to unravel human
pre-history, both of which methods operate hand in hand in the frightful
lower depths of existence. Perhaps Vigoleis can be forgiven if he has the conceited affrontery to say that he is too fervently devoted to poetry for such
tactics. As I continue to observe him while writing, I discover that Vigoleis,
as prone to shame and embarrassment as any fool, has up to this very moment never veered off—or, let us say, degenerated—into abject despair. His
merry *Weltschmerz* has made of him a plaything of destiny. If, like a football,
he sometimes flies out of bounds, it cannot be said that he ever gave himself
that extra kick. Though continually shoved around, he has never felt that he
himself was doing the shoving. Those who wander at the periphery of exis-

tence, where no one believes that the instinct for self-propagation can bring about the fulfillment of what is unfulfillable, no matter how sacred that goal might be or how much inner commitment it might entail: such persons simply cannot accept the burden of fostering a child. This non-child's name, by the way, was Olimpio.

XV

As the child-of-nobody hurled himself with a shriek to the bosom of his cuckoo of a father, his lips were bathed in foam. Beatrice withdrew in disgust. Her Lladó remained silent.

We took the broker and his white elephant, now reduced in price, to the Plaza Atarazanas and loaded the two brothers onto a cart; Pedro insisted on doing the driving. As a businessman, Don Fulgencio was dead; he was a dead man. Olimpio was delivered to an institution, Fulgenico to his palace.

I went back home. I was incapable of clear thoughts. I felt as if my mind were in a vise. All I could do was make a sudden decision: Matías! Go buy some bread from Don Matías! I sank down on the flour sack like... an empty sack of flour.

"The Nazis?" the baccalaureus asked. "Have you locked horns with the Consul?" I told him I would explain things tomorrow. I bought a loaf of bread, and went back home where Conde de Kessler would be waiting for me. But what would Beatrice say?

She greeted me with a look of such dark, smoldering despair as I hadn't seen in her eyes since the ordeal with the whore Pilar. The sight of foam at the mouth of the goitrous cretin had stifled every last trace of maternal feeling before it could express itself. Besides, our corridor was now filthy, and our bible-paper apartment had saliva on the floor. But even so—all had ended peacefully. I gave her a questioning glance, and she replied with the oracular assertion, "So that's what we get!"

She had squeezed up the newspapers in our bedroom to make a place to sit down. And there she now sat, like a mother bird in the nest. "Never again will I let that guy in our house!" she continued. "You'll just see what happens!"

"Do you mean Kessler? Our schedule for today is pretty full. He and I have a whole lot of solecisms to weed out. Kessler will be punctual as usual, and after this deluge he'll have mud on his shoes."

I could tell by her glancing at the ceiling that Beatrice meant neither Count Kessler nor Fulgencio's boorish brother. Whenever she has fits of superstition, she is unbearable. On such occasions, I feel like grabbing her and dunking her in a cool bath of reasonableness. But—with what strength, and with what justification? So then I, too, lifted my eyes to the ceiling, only to notice that he was really gone. Empedocles! I, too, took fright, but was suddenly thrust back to reality by the ringing of our doorbell.

Whenever I take up a new address, I conduct a test to see if it really works. I issue what I call my Spider Edict.

At the post office I send myself two postcards, each with the notation "Return to Sender." As the "sender" I put down my own name, one with my old address and one with the new. The second card gets sent a few days after the first. The mailman does the rest of the work. He observes that Vigoleis doesn't live at the address indicated, and puts the card back in his bag—"return to sender." On his next delivery round he goes to that address, with the same result. Thus card No. 1 becomes a dead letter. Card No. 2 has no stamp on it, requiring the postal service to make repeated attempts at delivery in order to cash in the postage due. In this manner, delivery eventually takes place, and after I arrive it works like a charm. I owe this clever method to Don Fernando, the General Secretary of the Palma Post Office. It has worked in several countries, even in the Canton Ticino.

My "Spider Edict," so named after the opening words of the text *Sollicitudo omnium aranearum*, has other aims as well. I have always been poor. Poverty breeds emergencies. Emergency is the mother of invention. When I move into a new apartment, I make sure that it isn't swept too carefully, and immediately I pronounce the Spider Edict. I return all rights to spiders, just as Napoleon's clerical adversary did with the Jesuits in 1814. The spiders must henceforth spin their webs and, on my behalf, catch flies and mosquitoes. I keep them—in southern climes, of course—just as the ancient Egyptians kept the sacred ichneumon as a mouse catcher. In particularly bothersome locations such as above our bed, at my desk, or in our reading space, where the incidence of biting and stinging is unusually high, I have them spin their webs. To this end I open the window, allowing free access to all the flies of the neighborhood. In places where I wish the spiders to settle, I spread honey on the wall or on little sticks that I deploy for just this purpose. The flies immediately form black swarms that serve as bait. Then I release the spiders, which I have captured and assorted according to type and size. One out of ten will begin attaching its web just where I want it. Sometimes it takes weeks for the spiders to take up ambush positions at all the important points.

The first spider I trained in this fashion to keep watch over Beatrice's reading site was baptized by her, a Bible expert, with the name Mephiboseth. When one day the spider disappeared without a trace, Beatrice said that this meant bad luck—and it did! From then on we christened our chief spider Empedocles, because it kept disappearing into thin air. Some women cannot bear to hire a maid, and Beatrice could not stand having spiders in our employ. That is why I later gave her a mosquito net as a present. It was less romantic, but more reliable. Still, if a mosquito ever finds its way inside the net, there's hell to pay.

Empedocles was at once poet and philosopher, a kind of wandering redeemer, physician, and multiplier of loaves. He read and ate with his hands,
and if we can give credence to legend, one day he suddenly disappeared. Some
say that he jumped into the crater of Mount Etna in order to enhance his reputation as a divine being—since gods also like to eliminate their tracks behind
them. But the mountain seems to have played a trick on this super-guru—he
flourished around 500 B.C.— for the story goes on to claim that the crater
spewed out the miracle man's slippers, just to show him who was who. And
that is why we picked out this ancient Greek guy's name for our head spider.

Once when things were again going badly for Count Kessler—he had
received a snide letter from Goebbels, threatening him in ways that could be
fatal for our work on the memoirs— I told him about my Spider Edict. It
cheered him up for a while. And because he was superstitious in a manner
deriving from Classical Antiquity, he believed the story about the disappearance of Empedocles.

Vigoleis, the enlightened pessimist, gave his own special spider the name
Spinoza.

XVI

In place of the absconded Empedocles, another ominous "star" soon made
its appearance over our heads. It was a gruesome animal—not one that captured insects, but nevertheless one that spent its entire life in cahoots with vermin. Its professional specialties were wine and women. It came from
Würzburg. Its name was Adelfried Silberstern, and it was the legitimate
brother of Privy Councillor Silberstern, whose first name was Brunfried.

"Vigo, do me a favor and ask the milkman to give us a whole liter today, and
not just half."

"He won't know what's come over us."

"*Ciao!*"

"*Ciao!*"

I had started a novel, a caricature of the Third Reich in my home town of
Süchteln an der Niers. My working title was "*Hun-less Tombs of the Huns.*"
On the basis of a draft chapter and through the good offices of Menno ter
Braak, the Amsterdam publisher Querido had accepted it. I worked and
worked on it during the hours when I wasn't working and working for Count
Kessler, and when I wasn't composing letters to high mucky-mucks of the insane German Reich. I wrote and wrote like a man possessed, and worse yet, as
a man who thought that he could swim against the tide. A human being is not
a salmon; if he swims along with the crowd, he'll always be going downstream.

The doorbell! What did Beatrice tell me? Oh yes, no milk today. I'll just finish writing this sentence... And then, the doorbell again. That guy is in a hurry—I guess he's worried that his milk will go sour before he's had a chance to deliver it. Just type out one more sentence... but then our impatient visitor rang for a third time. I leaped to the door and called out my message into the dark stairwell: "Two liters today, milkman! Just a minute, I'll go get our can!"

The milkman was hard of hearing and invisible. Was he already on the flight above us? But then a voice spoke to me in a south German accent, "Permit me to introduce myself. I am Silberstern from Würzburg, Adelfried Silberstern, wine and spirits, brother of Privy Commercial Councillor Brunfried Silberstern from Würzburg. We're both from Würzburg."

My mind was still back in my home town, where on Sundays the pastor would announce the banns of marriage: "With the intention of Holy Matrimony, Peter Joseph... and Anna Maria..., both of Süchteln. Should anyone have reasons why this marriage should not occur, he is by conscience bound to come forth..." My novel had to do with a marriage taking place in the Third Reich, one that had reasons for not occurring, reasons that carried the death penalty. It's no wonder that my thoughts continued in this direction as the milkman spoke. But surely my engaged couple wasn't from Würzburg...

It was only when our milkman stepped toward me—something he had never done before, preferring to keep a milk bucket's distance between us—that I realized that I wasn't in my home town with the heros' tombs, but on the Street of the General, House No. 23, an address that the man from Würzburg had picked up at the German Bookshop. Gradually he emerged out of the twilight of our corridor, with a torrent of words and displaying a fat belly, making me take a quick step backwards.

I turned on the light. The visitor gave his full name once again, and once again explained his connections with the Privy Councillor. They were Silberstern Bros. from Würzburg, Wine & Spirits. Instead of a business card, he handed me a brochure and said, "Here, this is us! You can read it through, but I've come for a very different reason. Are you listening?"

His accent was distinctly Franconian, just as my own was distinctly Lower Rhenish. His secret "brother" came out as "pruzzer," and his brochure was an advertisement for that fellow's "pruzzerly" enterprise, the production of wine and brandy under a franchise from Würzburg University.

Herr Silberstern stood one-and-a-half heads shorter than me. He had a keg-shaped paunch, in front of which, once he had deposited his briefcase on the floor, he kept his hands discreetly folded. He forgot to remove his expensive hat. Then he started twiddling his thumbs, forward and backward. He addressed me as "Herr Doktor," just as every barber in every university town does with every customer. Several times he lifted his hat to brush back his sort-cropped but somewhat disheveled hair, talking all the while as if he intended to wear me down with palaver. Whereupon he ceased twirling his thumbs, since he needed the latter digits to fit under his armpits as, with expanded chest, he began moving his fingers in wave-like motions. We were still standing opposite each other in our *entrada*. While I must have missed certain details of his story, this much was clear: Adelfried had fled his homeland just as soon as Hitler has seized power. The SS had found his 2-yard-wide bed empty, the one in which he was in the habit of sleeping with Aryan women who preferred to ignore the racial laws. He had left a fortune behind in the Reich. Countless women were lamenting his fate. All five of his brothers bore exceedingly Aryan given names ending in -fried, -wolf, and -helm, and they had a sister named -linde. In spite of all such precautions, all of their lives were at stake, although his entire family still trusted in the *Führer's* generosity. He would not have left the country so precipitously, he explained, if it had not been for the fact that he was a whole-sale practitioner of racial defilement. I also learned that there was a certain Nina. "What a babe, my dear friend!" She was from Cologne, and she repre-sented the erotic apex of his entire life, the triumph of his metallic bedstead. Her father was dead, having twice fallen beneath an oncoming train. The first accident cost him a leg, the second his life. Her mother was still alive as the widow of a railroad-crossing attendant, still lifting and lowering the barrier and eking out a living with a few geese, a goat, and her daughter Nina. "What a woman, Herr Doktor! And she's Catholic, and she's taller than you are!"

It wasn't at all clear why Mr. Silberstern had come to see me. Instead of tossing him out of our house, I led him to my study. To this very day, as I sit here writing my account of this encounter with the lecher Silberstern, Beatrice won't forgive me this huge mistake.

On many occasions I had already given practical advice and/or monetary help to Jews who fled to Mallorca, sometimes even offering them our last duro. They arrived in a state of confusion or intimidation, sometimes pressing their case obstinately—each one according to his or her personality, level of education, or financial wherewithal. One very prominent legal official from Berlin, arriving on the island with his hugely imposing wife and with a daugh-ter right out of the Song of Solomon, gave me a detailed description of his sit-uation. He had foreign bank accounts and personal connections in many lands—just the kind of life I was hoping eventually to lead myself. His plan was to stay on the island for a restful few months, and he asked me about the local German consul: what was that man's attitude toward Jews? I quickly gave this Berlin judge the true scoop. This particular consul wasn't of the kind who ate Jews for breakfast. His diplomatic rank had gone to his head, but otherwise he remained in fear of the Party and its snoopers. If he could help Jews in their attempts to emigrate, he would readily do so. But they mustn't start railing against his *Führer*, as I myself had done openly. "Well yes," the judge said, "no doubt your tirade went much too far. After all, we are speaking about Germany. This *Führer* is a historical accident."

The two of us went at each other tooth and nail, and parted as enemies. From the top of our stairs, I shouted down to this Berlin judge that he should use his money to get on to Brazil; all of his people were bound for extinction one after the other, and those with cash would be hounded out like pigs for the slaughter. A few days later I met the judge's wife in the German Shop. She

begged my pardon for her husband's unseemly response to my frank explanations. The fact was, she said, that her husband was terribly nostalgic for
Germany. He couldn't live without Germany; most of all he wanted to go back
to Germany, to Berlin. A month later I received a letter from her with a fictitious return address: the judge was in a concentration camp.

Be that as it may, the misery of the German Jews had never before brought
us in personal contact with the likes of this charlatan brother of the Privy
Councillor from Würzburg. He enshrouded me with a tangled web of chatter,
mainly concerning the finest specimens of naked German women, among
whom none could compare with his favorite Nina, who was educated and as
dark-skinned as a Jewess, but completely Aryan and Catholic. She was a
dancer, and a model at Cologne's most fashionable Hohe Strasse department
store. And because she looked so Jewish, she was fired from the store and
even threatened with stoning. "Can you imagine that, Herr Doktor? In
Cologne, where every year people celebrate Carnival?"

"Carnival? In 1928 I was an eyewitness in Cologne when Katz Rosenthal
(or was it Rosenstein?) had his hot-dog stand demolished because a customer
found a mouse in his meal, a mouse that a certain journalism student at the
university, a friend of mine, had secreted into the menu. As a result, my friend
Dr. Ley spent half a year in jail. But if I have understood you correctly, Mr.
Silbersteg, you're visiting me because of a certain Nina from Cologne?"

"Stern, please! Silberstern."

"Fine, Silberstern. But I'm sorry. I lived in Cologne for quite a few years,
but—Nina? But now wait a minute—you're quite right, I must know her. A
tall swarthy type, looks like a Jewess, quite a babe? And wasn't her father a
high mucky-muck in the Reich Railway?"

"Please, Herr Doktor, it's not because of Nina that I've come to see you.
The reason why I've come has to do with a very urgent matter. It has to do
with my pooks. And her mother told her: Nina, this Mr. Silberstern, he's such
a fine gentleman, he's so educated, he's from the best of families..."

"Ah, I see. You have come here at the suggestion of your prospective
mother-in-law, a woman whom I also don't know personally. But tell me now,
isn't she likewise a rather full-bodied, imposing personage? But of course, her
husband was a gravedigger in Cologne-Poll by the name of Firnich! Am I
right? You're speaking of Mrs. Firnich!"

"You're not listening to me. I'll tell you once more: I've come on account of
my pooks, and we drove in my own car down through all of Germany. Thousands of kilometers with Nina always at the wheel, and we spent our nights
only in the finest hotels. But just think, Herr Doktor, she never let me really
have her, that's how proper she was, not the kind that puts out for just anybody, and then Nina said when we were in..."

"I understand, Mr. Silberstern. You've come to see me because somebody
somewhere doesn't let somebody have her, and so now I'm supposed to..."

"You're making a joke out of it, but I'm deadly serious about my pooks.
You've got to help me! You're a writer, and you're an Aryan!"

He was seeking me out on account of his books. Apparently it was an urgent matter. But my manuscript was also urgent. I had reached the passage where the manager of the municipal de-braining department has placed an awl up against the Lord Mayor's occiput and is already banging away with a mallet, causing the Lord Mayor's grey matter to spill out into the official Municipal Bucket. A little kid asks his mother, "Mom, what's that awful man doing with his hammer? He's going to bash in the Mayor's head!" "No, no," his Mom answers, "he's just letting the mayor's brains drain out of his head." Where-upon the kid asks the childlike question, "And what about you, Mom? Do you have brains, too? And is he going to bash you too?" Before Mom can reply that the *Führer* does all her thinking for her, the Lord Mayor has already been politically coordinated, and a sprig of mistletoe is placed inside his wound. He leaves the scene amid the thunderous applause of the masses. Feel-ing the urgent call of nature, he goes behind a tree, where he thinks no one can see him. He lifts his hand to the back of his head, and... it's gone! Where his cerebrum had been, there is now a Hitlerian void. *Ach, mein Führer!*

"But I beg you! You're not paying attention to me. Repeat what I just said!"

I cringed as if caught in some naughty act, and almost stammered, "Oh, sorry, Mr. Stern. Actually I was listening very intently. I'm crushed by what you've been through. Nina has stolen your books, and you want me to find you a Spanish lawyer. That I can do. I'll write a few words to a state prosecu-tor I know, and everything will turn out just fine."

The words poured out of me like an avalanche, but behind me I sensed new danger approaching: Beatrice. If she were to come now and catch sight of the newest star in my little cosmology, a comet sporting a ghostly Nina in its tail, and if he were then to say, "Good day, Madam, I am Mr. Silberstern from wherever, and with this and that, and for whatever...," and if at the same moment his Amazon friend were to show up—there would be hell to pay!

"Mr. Silberstern, your case is urgent, but mine is, too."

"Then come with me right away. We must set an example."

As I put on my *alpargatas*, Silberstern took off his hat and, at a record pace, told me the life history of this head-covering, where he got it, how he haggled down the retail price, all the places where he had forgotten it, how often somebody took it by mistake, how it once got stolen but was recovered with the help of his brother Muthelm Silberstern, attorney in Frankfurt, mar-ried, three children, divorced, Juris Doctor—"and also, get this, a Doctor of Philosophy!"

I let him lead the way. As we walked, I was told in passing what he wanted my help for. His main topic was the love lives of the famous conductor Furtwängler and the famous surgeon Sauerbruch, both of whom had entrusted to him the management of their wine cellars.

Four crates of Silberstern's books, I learned, were sitting in the customs warehouse, branded as prohibited literature and hence confiscated. Through all of his torrent of words concerning women who did and women who wouldn't, I probably picked up the term "prohibited," thus got sidetracked from my manuscript. For I am not so cowardly as to give full attention to everything any crack-brain has to say to me.

But how did a lecherous, completely sex-crazed wine merchant like this Adelfried ever get hold of politically suspect literature? But of course, it must be those brothers of his! He's working for them. Together they intend to unseat the *Führer* and establish Jewish world domination, with the Island of Mallorca as its capital. But the customs administrator is sharp enough to nip this plan in the bud. I told my companion that we would soon take care of the whole matter. I was, after all, Professor d'Ester's assistant, I was Professor Wohlers' left- and right-hand man, so I knew my way around such things. What's more, I was a consultant to the Honduran Freedom Movement under Don Patuco. Silberstern already knew about this connection; my reputation had preceded me. The German Bookshop, he explained, had passed on certain personal data, but was I aware, he asked, that Furtwängler did not sleep with the soprano Marietta Kefer-Froitzheim? "I'm telling you he did not sleep with her, and this was the greatest shock to the German musical world since the war, because that Ninth of his in Würzburg...!"

"Please, Mr. Silberstern, wait here outside the warehouse. I'll go in first and talk with the officials, and they won't be interested in Furtwängler's Ninth. Madam Froitzheim is another matter entirely. I know her personally, and in the Gürzenich cafeteria we often had knockwurst and beer together."

At the customs warehouse I knew just who to go to. It was the friendly fellow who had arranged customs for our stuff with Antonio. He dealt with the most serious cases by waving his hand and going back to sleep. But he wasn't there. I asked for the Customs Director. What did I want from him, I was asked; the Director wasn't to be disturbed except in highly unusual matters. I told the fellow that my client had just such a highly unusual situation. "There he is, standing over there, the stocky little gentleman with the fancy hat." The customs officer, taking one look at Silberstern, laughed. "That guy? What a pain in the ass! What a pig!" I motioned to my "client" to be patient a while, and walked to one side with the officer. "What's up?" I asked.

I was given the following explanation. Some books had arrived from Germany, from some place called "Furzeburg," addressed to a "Mister Silbersterren" at the *Pensión* "La Sagrada Familia" in Palma. The customs inspection had revealed an entire collection of dirty literature— pornography. The warehouse walls turned red at the discovery. "It was such a pile of smut, Señor!" But interestingly enough, nobody here realized that there could be such an enormous number of dirty books. The Germans, he said, were very meticulous people. But filth is filth, and we foreigners would just have to learn to abide by the rules of his Catholic country. Then the customs officer snickered, and I snickered back. We both knew all about Catholic manners.

Hiring an interpreter at 10 pesetas an hour, Mr. Silberstern had already started negotiations at the warehouse. The interpreter, a Spaniard in the employ of Cook Travel, got nowhere, since he, too, was mesmerized by the filthy books instead of palavering them out of the possession of customs, pocketing his fee with a redoubled grin. He sent the German pornocrat to the Tourist Office, where the boss was a German who had been in the Spanish tourism business for more than thirty years. He wanted nothing to do with the affair, and sent the emigrant to the German Bookshop, which in turn sent him to me, right up to the edge of my Tombs of the Huns.

"There's nothing we can do," said the officer. "The Director has confiscated the entire shipment, which is now under lock and key. In what capacity have you come here?" I had no idea, so I went outside and asked the brother of Attorney Muthelm Silberstern from Frankfurt, Dr. jur. and Ph.D., to tell me quickly what my duties were to be in this morality play. "Haven't you understood? You are my legal consultant."

I relayed this information to the puzzled customs officer: I was the *jurisconsultus* of the gentleman from the city whose name, when pronounced the Spanish way, sounded faintly shabby. My credentials, I explained, consisted in the fact that I was standing here discussing the case. This he seemed to comprehend, and so he went off to notify the Director. He asked my client to enter the building and take a seat. Under my legal guardianship, Mr. Silberstern's case was becoming official.

The crates containing suspect literature, he then told me, represented only a portion of his personal library—basically just the more frequently consulted volumes. The remainder of his collection was being shipped together with his brass bedstead and his automatic wardrobe. The confiscated material was a small collection of (here Silberstern raised a chubby index finger) scientific erotica, assembled for scholarly purposes.

The Customs Director asked us into his office. I introduced myself as *procurator* and *prolocutor*, pointed to my client, and reached for my breast pocket. But the Director didn't want to see my papers. I said, "Please tell me what's going on here. My client is experiencing harm by being barred from consulting his scientific literature. In the name of free scholarly inquiry, I wish to protest!"

The Director laughed. Did I want to know what was going on here? "*Momento!*"

He pulled forth a huge tome, slammed it on his desk, opened it to a dog-eared page, and then slapped the volume with the flat of his hand. "*That's* what's going on here, sir!"

Pink like lard or marzipan, the buttocks of a beauty queen peeked forth from her discreetly lowered lace panties. Bent over forwards, she turned her head to the spectator, revealing at one and the same time both of her very similar visages. It was only the smile on her second visage that looked any better than the other one.

My client's eyes swelled out of their sockets, gazing in watery glee at the illustration. I remained in control of the situation. I wasn't standing in some steamy apartment corridor with María del Pilar. I was legal consultant for scholarly research on the subject of sleaze. So I replied with confident dignity to the Director's impatient query, intoned as he again slapped the picture, as to what I thought that was supposed to be.

"Director, Sir, what we have here is the hindquarters, shorn of their usual covering, of what I take to be a French virgin—plus a view of her countenance."

"Aha! Here in Spain we call this stuff filth, horrible filth. The worst kind of filth that anyone can imagine." Once again his hand slammed down on the *corpus delicti*. My client asked me to translate what the Director had said about the picture. So I translated, and that brought Mr. Silberstern to life. His eyes bulged out even farther, but now it was from sheer indignation. "The worst kind of filth, you say? Well now, let me show you what's in *this* volume!" With a flip of his practiced hand and without the aid of a dog-ear, he laid bare a page where things were really going strong. This time it involved a couple, a she and a he. Once again my client's expert eyes took on a moist gleam. It was such a long time since he had lost sight of his beloved bare-asses.

The Director clapped his hands a third time, now as a sign for his assistant to go fetch the "whole pile of crap." Soon the top of his desk was completely filled. The smutty evidence spilled over onto the chairs in his office. Wherever we looked, we saw naked babes, savage pimps, and horny chambermaids in the most flagrant poses, all of them openly engaged in love-making of the most unbridled sort. The owner of this scholarly collection pointed out some particularly significant specimens, naming secret sources, prices, and the availability of discounts for serial subscriptions. Then he asked me to inquire of the Director if he might be interested in subscribing.

Meanwhile several other customs employees had entered the office. Volumes and sliced-out pages from the collection were making their way from hand to hand amid chuckles, brief discussions, and appraisals, just as at the pre-sale confabs at an auction. They all agreed that this was filth, and they were appalled that it was made in Germany. I noticed that certain officers were stashing some smaller specimens in the pockets of their smocks. The Director then made up his mind: "*Quemar!*" I translated: "Burn it all!" My client blanched —but not on account of the threatened auto-da-fé. Dripping in sweat, he rummaged among his treasures, pulled forth a few books that had already passed through the officials' hands, and began furiously thumbing through the pages. "Right here, Herr Doktor! Look here! That's exactly where the very best of it was, and these gentleman have used their pen knives to cut them out. You must register a protest!" So I enunciated a formal protest: willful larceny of an entire corpus of intellectual property. The Director laughed and said, "Maybe some judge will fall for that one. We make autonomous decisions." He went on to explain that he himself had cut out the most blasphemous examples, spending whole nights working through the collection. Remaining calm and matter-of-fact, relying on my experience as an assistant to German university scholars, I inquired of the Director just what, in light of a unified concept of erotic scholarly research (difficult to put into Spanish, but I managed), he meant by the word "blasphemous." By employing this term, I added, he was giving the entire case a theological turn. Was he aware of the possible consequences?

He had a ready answer. He reached into the breast pocket of his elegant jacket and produced a few pages that even a Professor Karl Kerényi would have a hard time interpreting in mythological terms. At the sight of this fraud, a quivering Mr. Silberstern stammered, "One thousand marks each! Tell him that we protest in the name of literature! I'll sue him for damages!"

The Customs Director simply snickered. "A thousand marks? In Paris you can get stuff like this much cheaper, *en nature*. We know all about it, we were over there once in our younger days. Nowadays, with a wife and kids..." He replaced the porno sheets inside his jacket pocket, and declared the meeting finished. His verdict was laconic: the entire lot was to be burned. I threatened to inform the Consul. Consuls and Customs Directors need each other. We were granted a delay of 24 hours.

Don Joaquín Verdaguer was not only a professor, a writer, and an expert in tobacco pipes; he was also the Ecuadorian Consul. It was he, of course, and not the German Consul, that I had in mind. I explained the case to him, requesting his aid in the name of erotic science.

At this, Don Joaquín turned morose. He showed me his official Consulate rubber stamps, now twisted and desiccated from disuse, including the dried-out stamp pads, the yellowed Consulate letterhead, and the empty Consulate cashbox. For years, he said, he had been the local representative of the glorious Republic of Ecuador, just waiting for someone to come along and request his protection. But now I had arrived, and I wasn't even an Ecuadorian! I was to go visit his German colleague, who would treat it as the simple matter it was: a delay in the name of the German Reich, investigation by the proper legal authorities, and consultations with experts at the Biblioteca Nacional. That way, we could gain time. The German Consul would pursue the case with vigor and if necessary send a telegram, at my client's expense, to the German Foreign Office. But—was this such a serious affair? The Spanish nation was accustomed to all kinds of questionable goings-on. The Barrio Chino in Barcelona was like no other place in the world, including Paris and Marseille. —"And blasphemous? The very worst kind of stuff? What can that possibly be, the 'worst kind of stuff'?"

I reached into the inside pocket of my decidedly un-elegant jacket and pulled out a page. "This is what the blasphemy in Mr. Silberstern's collection looks like." It was the most titillating specimen in all of Western art: the Mona Lisa's enigmatic smile, seen from behind.

Don Joaquín sucked on his pipe, and retracted all he had just said about vice in Barcelona. "Pilfered?"

"No, not exactly, my friend. Using a stratagem of my new profession, I took possession of it as a form of official credentials. Now I can present myself anywhere as my Jewish client's *procurator* and *prolocutor*."

"Did you say Jewish?"

"I did indeed. And that's precisely the fly in the ointment. Silberstern is non-Aryan, and the reason for his escape was profanation of the blood. So he can't expect his own Consul to offer him protection."

The Ecuadorian Consul explained that if a Jew still had a valid passport, he Consul was obliged to assist him.

With my credentials in my jacket pocket, I went to visit "our" Consul. I explained that if he did not handle this matter with dispatch, his official prestige was on the line; that I had discussed the case with my friend Verdaguer, the Consul of Ecuador, and that by tomorrow morning each and every accredited consular official in Palma would be aware that the German Consul didn't know how to run his business.

The Consul replied that he knew his business inside-out. A Jew was a Jew, but Justice was Justice. He was, he said, the representative of a nation based on laws. "So let's get at it!"

The warehouse Director stuck by his guns. To him, filth was filth. He took forth certain volumes, slapped page after page of unveiled hindquarters and forequarters, mixed-company frolics, and erotic trapeze exploits. But the most incriminating specimens had disappeared, for by now the duana officers of Palma were swimming in a sea of porn. Still, what the representative of the Third Reich got to see was enough to place him in a moral dilemma. "It's horrendous!" he said. "For heaven's sake, just take a look at that!" It was material for scientific research, I retorted, and the one thing was not mutually exclusive of the other, quite the contrary. Wasn't he familiar with the classic dictum that we are all born twixt urine and feces? This, I elucidated further, was the tragedy of humankind, the source of all human error, the vital subject of artistic endeavor, and nowadays the reason why the waiting rooms at psychiatrists' offices were filled to bursting. It was indeed difficult to overcome this natural heritage. In a small voice, the Consul said, "You know me well enough to realize that I'm not a scholar but a businessman. But if this stuff here is supposed to be scientific material, then I'll be a monkey's uncle. Back home in Germany this is what we call sheer crap."

I responded that what he and I regarded as crap back in Germany might not be one and the same thing. I asked him to telegraph the German Embassy in Madrid, at my client's expense, and request a delay against the private verdict of the Palma Director of Customs. I myself would send a registered letter to Miguel de Unamuno, informing him that now Spain, too, was starting to burn books just as in the Third Reich. Unamuno replied with a sarcastic postcard, saying that in Spain a much bigger fire was about to break out. There were arsonists at work all over the place, he wrote, and may God save his beloved homeland.

The Director of Customs expressed his regrets to the Consul of the Third Reich; his Bull of Immolation was already formulated and signed. He showed us the document and then put it back in his pocket, covering with it the naked backside of some whorelet—a symbolic gesture if there ever was one. Case closed: on to the pyre for an auto-da-fé. At my insistence, the German Consul suggested that the crates be sent back to the return address in Germany. "Impossible!" said the Director. This filth would never leave the warehouse. I leaped into the breach with a request in my client's name that the scientific material, the entire four boxes full to bursting, be sent to the National Library in Madrid as a donation from Señor Adelfredo Silberstern from Furzeburg.

That was the straw that broke the camel's back. It was stupid of me to make such a suggestion. The larceny of the skin pix would come to light, and the Director and his staff would be reprimanded for purloining piggish printed matter. The Custom's Director's scolding was anything but music to the ears of the *Führer's* representative: how could he, whom the Director had thus far considered to be a person of sterling qualities, stoop so low as to defend such trash?

The Consul left the scene. He had suffered a defeat.

I stayed on. I at least wanted to save the pigskin and calfskin bindings, as well as certain innocuous title pages. But I was shown the door. I left the scene. I had suffered a twofold defeat.

My client wrung his hands when I reported the ineffectuality of my efforts on his behalf. I mentally estimated my legal fee at 100 pesetas, but Mr. Silberstern saw no reason to pay me. He never so much as asked what he might owe me for my consultative services.

The *auto-de-castidad* took place in the Customs Office courtyard. Valuable first editions, a number of out-of-print volumes and pornographic rarities, but also such harmless books as Fuchs' *History of Morals* and illustrated editions of Boccaccio—every last tome was put to the flames, including a monograph on the Oberammergau Passion Play, illustrated Bibles, plus a textbook of gynecology. My client observed the immolation of his hobby through a knothole in the fence. He figured his loss at 25,000 marks.

My friend Mulet from the *tertulia*, who had a close acquaintance at the Customs warehouse, observed the execution of the books as a representative of the intellectual segment of Mallorquin society. He took a handful of the ashes home with him in a little cloth bag. One charred page still showed a fragment of naked flesh, but not even the horniest Spanish lecher could have established with certainty where, within the framework of the entire human anatomy, this particular view of unadorned epidermis had originally exerted its stimulating effect. But he consoled me with the revelation that not a single full- or half-page illustration had been lost. He himself had observed how, previous to the burnt offering, everything of value had been carefully removed from the volumes, so that the Customs Director was now without doubt the owner of the best collection of visual erotica in all of the Balearics. He was, after all, an old connoisseur... "And not only on paper!" came a shout from the back room, where the *tertulia* was in session.

The most faithful customer at the German Bookshop had the alert, beady eyes of a dog in heat, and he had a long, black beard. His hairy garment was held together by a rough piece of rope. He was as poor as the mendicant order to which he had dedicated his life.

This monk was a subscriber to certain Parisian journals which displayed a eat deal of unclothed flesh. He arrived at the shop several times a week to inquire whether his orders had arrived. If they were on hand, hidden behind the counter, he snuck briefly into the backroom, the one we already know about as the venue for erotic adventures in natura. He always paid his bill promptly. Acting from pure Christian brotherly charity, little Mr. Hasenbank allowed him a discount for needy clergymen. But when the heavy-set and very wealthy co-owner of the shop offered this destitute man of the cloth a shiny duro and a particular street address, Pater Pachomio declined in the Name of the Lord. A bordello was a den of iniquity, he explained, and he wouldn't think of entering one. But as for a cloistered brother taking occasional peeks into illustrated magazines, the Good Lord would not think it amiss. Besides, he regularly confessed to a *confrater*, a colleague who suffered from the same urges and who, incidentally, shared the price of their Parisian magazine subscription.

I presented Mona Lisa's second visage to this mendicant fellow, who was living under an eternal vow of chastity. He blessed me right in the middle of the shop, before the eyes of all three of the German booksellers. Of all the thousands of people who have tried to decipher La Gioconda's smile, it is solely Pater Pachomio who will have figured it out in the privacy of his cell.

XVII

H *eil Hitler!"*
"Good morning."
The German Consul had summoned me to ask a few questions.
"You wish?"
"Do you have certain enemies back in your home town?" The Consul had put on his official face, one that always failed to impress me. He shuffled papers in the officious manner, and this too left me cold. The time was past when I felt the urge to flee the presence of a bureaucratic jackass. "Yes," I replied, "I'm surrounded by enemies."
"Can you name the persons who wish to do you harm, and their reasons? It's important."
"You bet I can, Herr Konsul. But it will take time for me to list all of them. You can start taking notes: my enemies are the gravedigger and all his minions, each and every hick and bugger and whoremaster, all women typists, all clergymen of whatever shade of belief or disbelief, all greengrocers and all salesgirls, cobblers, tailors, sextons and pharmacists, the madam at an exclusive brothel and her staff, the mayor, the director of rubbish collection ..."
"Don't joke around with me. What are you getting at? Answer my questions! I am asking you in my official capacity."
"But that's it exactly! Let's see, where was I? Ah yes, the garbage men, the town accountant, the dairymen and the alpine herdsmen, all tax assessors, tax collectors, and tax embezzlers, all children with the exception of..."

The Consul objected angrily to my ridicule of the Reich. I was guilty, he now said, of slandering the *Führer* on German soil, since his office was sovereign territory. I knew this already. Then I was informed that my father had been detained by Party operatives for the purpose of quizzing him about his degenerate son. If I persisted in sending my relatives slanderous letters about the *Führer*, the Party would find it necessary to take retaliatory measures against the life and limb of my family. I was to consider myself forewarned.

"Herr Konsul, are you telling me that as a result of my complaints, which I do not deny having made, my people will be put in harm's way?"

Apparently this was exactly the case. The Third Reich was a merciless place, and my name was on the list of persons harmful to the state. The authorities in my home town had already recommended my elimination. "Do you understand?"

This Consul, prior to his swift decline an unassuming, polite, well-bred and friendly German on foreign soil, had by now turned into a true big-shot of the unfriendliest kind, every inch the uptight subaltern of the Nazi movement. As he rose from his chair, his scalp almost touched the frame of the *Führer*'s portrait behind his desk. I remained standing and said, "Herr Konsul, my family has flourished for centuries on the banks of the Niers. Our name Thelen can be traced back to earliest prehistoric times. In Middle High German our name was 'Diuten,' and among the Anglo-Saxons we were known as 'Gédithan,' 'Thedoan,' and 'Thiudan,' and some tribes called us by the name of 'Thiudisk.' In Old Norse we find an early branch of the family by the name of 'Thiuda,' which means 'people,' Old Irish 'Tuat,'meaning 'he who is at home on this land, who thrives on the land, who raises his family on the land, who owns the land.' It also meant the same as 'heathen.' So at the beginning we were heathens, too, German heathens to boot, the kind that Nietzsche relates to the idea of *täuschen*: deceptive types, dissimulators, charlatans. What it comes down to is this, if you will permit me: 'Thelen' is a synonym for 'German.' To this day, as you know, the Italians still call us 'tedeschi,' which is to say, 'Thelens.' And here's something you may not know: we have connections far over into Portugal, where the bloodthirsty Doña Leonor Telles murdered her way into the queenship".

"This brief plunge into the murky swamps of ancient history is simply meant to show you that I have a very long pedigree. Although I must admit that, with the exception of the questionable Gothic King Theudis, the tribe of the Thelens has not brought forth the kind of heroes that bards and minstrels keep singing about after all these centuries. But along comes Adolf Hitler, who is giving us benighted latecomers our great moment. My relatives love the *Führer*. They've written to me about this. They will be delighted if they can give their lives for him and his cause. They've written that, too. My mother includes the new Savior in her prayers. If there is anything I can do to see to it that my loved ones back home may fulfill their patriotic wish to become fertilizer for the soil of the fatherland—then, Herr Konsul, I am not so perverse as to deny this to them! I am the black sheep of the family, and now, as I refuse with all my might to put on the color brown, for them I have become blacker still. The people in my home town are ashamed of me. You may report to the local authorities up there that I'm in agreement with their plan. Right away I shall send my father a letter with the same message. Would you like a copy for your files? So then—*Guten Morgen!*"

"*Heil Hitler!*"

As I exited, the Consul called after me, "The day after tomorrow the *Monte Rosa* is arriving with 2000 tourists. So I'll need you again. You're my best *Führer!*"

"Thank you for the superlative compliment. I'll be out there at the pier, right on time. And once again: *Guten Morgen!*"

"*Guten Morgen!*"

A few chapters back I startled Beatrice with Captain von Martersteig's query as to whether she had heard the latest news. She hadn't, and so I told her that Hitler's Third Reich had just begun its thousand-year history, and that heads were rolling, just as the *Führer* had promised the German people. Beatrice, whose fascination with history extends even to the kind that gets written against the grain, asked me this rather startling question in return: "Well now, I'm curious as to how your folks are taking all this. Are they going along with it?"

Like all history buffs, Beatrice is impatient with fragmentary situations.

I have a rule of thumb, one that will often enough rescue me from one miserable situation only to plunge me into the next one. That is why to this day I have never made it as a general, a company executive, a cardinal, or a university professor, but only enjoy my status as a jester at my own private court and as the chronicler of the applied recollections of Vigoleis. This life-sustaining maxim of mine is as follows: in case of doubt, let truth be told. And it was in light of this motto that I proceeded to unveil for Beatrice the situation at hand. My family was going along with it—my father with a certain amount of hesitation, my "Get a move on!" brothers with all the excitement their nationalistic short-sightedness could muster. But Mother? Hers was a simpler case. She refused to lift her right arm, and would sooner bite off her tongue than shout "*Heil Hitler!*" For behind her stood centuries of devout Catholic tradition, the unshakeable doctrinaire beliefs of the Scheifes clan. What's more, she was a member of the Mothers' Society, and she wasn't about to dirty her hands by murdering Jews. She was practicing passive resistance, she wrote me, adding that if all the mothers in all the Catholic Mothers' Societies in Germany did the same, Hitler would soon be history. Beatrice shook her head and said I was still the same incorrigible utopian.

It took five days for mail from the Lower Rhine to reach Palma de Mallorca. So five days later I found a letter in our post office box, and a little later Beat-

rice found me squatting on a crate in our apartment, with an empty stare and
with my prominent lower jaw rattling audibly. Among the Neanderthals the
woman of the family would have snuck into the bushes, fearing a vicious club-
bing. But Beatrice was all solicitude. "Darling, what's wrong? Food poisoning
from the octopus?" (Only one in 30,000 octopuses is poisonous). "Quick,
where's our medicine book?" Then she noticed the letter. "From your folks?"

"Yes, and now they're all in it together, even Mother. They're 'politically
coordinated' one and all. A disgusting letter. The Beast of the Apocalypse has
won out."

In brief, my folks had decided to march along with Hitler. They hung out
the flag. They were singing the songs of the Brown Revolution. To put it even
more briefly, they had completely lost their senses. And yet this was just what
I expected. The worst of it was surely my mother's contribution to this missive.
This devout woman hadn't echoed the chauvinistic rhetoric of the others. She
was unaccustomed to extended writing, and anyway she was surrounded by
wiseacre menfolk who knew how to express themselves readily, with conviction, and in passable prose. She penned just a few lines, explaining in simple
words that she, too, was now committed to the *Führer*. Writing to her so very
distant son, she gave voice to her joy at Germany's return to prominence in
the world, and to her dismay that this son of hers wasn't there to experience
all of this with them back home.

Beatrice pulled out our medicine book. But in all of nature, Dr. Hahnemann
and his homeopathic school hadn't discovered an antidote for nationalistic
toxins. I started explaining that no such discovery would ever be possible. But
she was already busy doctoring me. "Mother, too!" I lamented, my jaw still
aquiver. She felt my pulse, counted the seconds, and lifted my eyelids. I rolled
my eyes. She took a pile of clothes and bedded me gently up against our whitewashed wall.

"You're having convulsions. Internal ones, too?" "Yes." "Strong ones?" I
was shivering mightily. "It could be tonic spasms, or maybe colonic ones. Does
it feel as if the back of your nose is pressing into your head?"

In case of doubt, let truth be told. "No, just the opposite," I said. My nose
feels as if it's leaving my head, along with my brain. Am I turning into a German chauvinist, too?" "Do you feel something warm rising up from your
abdomen, causing shortness of breath?" "We haven't eaten a thing all day, so
there's nothing down there that could rise up. But my breathing is kaputt."
"Aha, you see? Then you must have a tickling in your neck, as if there's a
thread hanging from your throat down into your gullet." "Several threads,
Beatrice, thick as ropes. My father writes us that Uncle Josef has also started
hanging out the flag, but not at half-mast. A Catholic Center Party man, a
pillar of the Church, the most respected guy in the city—but down he goes!"
—"How about pains?" "I can now say with Unamuno: *me duele Alemania.*
Germany gives me a pain. It's funny that I'm feeling this way. I'm seeing double." "That always happens. I'm going to give you some *cuprum aceticum.*
Hahnemann always used *cuprum metallicum* in cases like this, and Grandfa-

ther, who liked to argue with Hahnemann about such things, would have prescribed *cuprum ustum D4*." "My grandfather would prescribe a generous shot of schnapps. The *Führer* would prescribe for me a bullet in the head."

Beatrice fetched forth her Grandpa's homeopathic traveling kit. This satchel had already proven its efficacy at the sickbeds of a King of England, the Sultan of Morocco, the Tsar of Russia, a President of the United States, and other world potentates. It was the treatment of choice for cold patches on the soles of the feet, a condition that commonly worsened between 11:00 and 12:00 o'clock at night, as well as for cases of flatulence aggravated by anger—and it is men of power who often go black-and-blue with rage. It was prescribed for the ingestion of eggs during the autumn months, or for the imbibing of stale beer, as well as for halitosis, an ailment the patient never notices himself. In short, this famous man's homeopathy was a remedy for the German national disease, a condition that Hahnemann never identified.

Beatrice lifted a vial from her little valise and poured a few drops into a tumbler. It was high time, too, for now I felt the incubus of hunger rising up inside me—an event that never fails to disquiet me, desperate fellow that I decidedly am. "No alcohol, no coffee," Beatrice warned. "Otherwise this dose won't work. Keep lying down. I'll go get you some bread."

After she left I took our bottle of Felanitx and swigged down the golden drops left in it, letting the *blanco* roll around where the threads were hanging down in my throat. I heard it hit the bottom of my stomach. When Beatrice returned I was again feeling top-fit. "You see?" she said. "With homeopathy it's all a question of the correct diagnosis. My family tells me that Grandpa was better at such things than any of his teachers."

I embraced her, and assured her that both of our grandfathers knew their way around with medicinal drops. Then I composed a letter to my dear Mother of the Catholic Mothers' Society, a letter that has become renowned within the family. And I received a no less remarkable letter in response. The prodigal son was carrying on correspondence with his prodigal mother.

I argued that "*Heil Hitler*" would mean the death of millions of Jews. All the rest, all the so-called political aims of the Nazis, didn't concern me in the least, as I had no comprehension of them. I had never read the editorials in newspapers anyway, and had never gone to the voting booth because, seeing that I was never able to get straight about my own self, I doubted that I could play any constructive role on behalf of an entire nation. Catholic Center? Social Democrats? Communists? Nationalist groupings of all stripes? I had got to know good guys and bad guys in all of these sects. But: "Let Judah perish"? No, no! A thousand times No!

After the fall of the Spanish monarchy, the mob started harassing priests and nuns in public. Miguel de Unamuno, the arch-enemy of the monarchy and the clergy, hung a big crucifix around his neck—and woe to whoever dared to point a finger at him! *Abajo el Cristo*? "Let Christ perish"? Nevermore, said Unamuno. But as for priests who financed bull-fight arenas, brothels, and railroads in Christ's name—down with them! In my letter to Mother

I mentioned this exemplary form of tolerance. How can somebody's mother shout "*Heil Hitler*"? My filial communication ended with the announcement that as a result of the German Revolution, no one should expect me to return home within the foreseeable future. I suggested that they wait until Hitler had prepared, unleashed, and lost his war. If I hadn't been made to perish by then, I would come back home. But of course I would telegraph ahead.

The *Führer* kept his word, but Vigoleis did, too. Mother received the telegram. She had waited eighteen years for it. Bombed out of her home and starving, she fell into my arms—the return of the prodigal son to a prodigal hearth.

The reply to this letter caused Beatrice to reach once again for our self-help medical book. Although our copy was the 11th revised and expanded edition, she hunted in vain for the drops that would cure my symptoms. She looked up under "anguish," "anxiety," "distractedness," "fluids, loss of," "hair, greying of leg," "hair, sudden rising of head," "homesickness," "shaving, avoidance of," "mouth, sudden closing of with danger of biting the tongue"—and she found nothing. My syndrome was beyond the purview of the great guttologist. He prescribed *mercurius* to counter the ill-effects of eating beef, but what to do for the ill-effects of bull-headedness? Or for infamy? My bile was aroused mainly by Mother's pastor, who had heaved the mothers of the Catholic Mothers' Society onto the patriotic track. Mother wrote me that she was a simple woman, ignorant of politics. She was only following her pastor's recommendations from the pulpit. The Church did not condemn the *Führer*. She, Mother, was praying for him—and for me and Beatrice, since we were in need of divine grace. Our counterfeit marriage was sinful...

The murdering continued in the Reich. Christ and the Antichrist: *ecce homo*, Pascoaes says. Beatrice decided to try out *antimonium crudum*, as my tongue now had a coat of white fur.

"When I think of Germany in the night, / I find I cannot sleep aright." The verse is by Heine, and after 1933 they were his most-often-quoted lines.

My grandfather proved his Christian worth by providing hot water for Kevelaer pilgrims, showing that he was a man of action. But he also became a man of words when he bought an old printing press at an auction, started a newspaper and, with the aid of a deaf, dumb, and blind woman of prodigious muscular strength who could yank the press lever, produced every separate issue. This little operation was the forerunner of our town's regular paper, a Catholic sheet that, together with "The City of God" and "The Steyl Missionary Newsletter," represented periodical world literature in our household. My father sent it to me regularly in Mallorca, which is how I learned of the "political coordination" of my home town, a community that sports in its coat of arms the image of a chapel dedicated to a virgin whose holiness is confirmed in the *Acta sanctorum* of the Bollandists. The little place of worship is located on the wooded slopes outside of town, where you can also find a famous mental asylum. The Director's kids were schoolmates of mine, as were the kids of one of the teachers at the institution, and that's how I eventually got to enter a place where the human mind goes off in strange directions, just as it has so frequently done with geniuses whose acquaintance I have made face-to-face: Napoleon, Nietzsche, Buddha, Christ. I spent time with inmates at the asylum, as I did with the crippled wreck of a man who did the hoeing in my parents' garden. Each one of these people had his own Mémorial and his own St. Helena. Once in a while a patient escaped and ran through the town chased by orderlies, causing the populace to disperse like the citizens of Palma at the approach of the Sureda's stampeding dogs. On one occasion a patient ran amok, brandishing a fence-post as his make-believe Malaysian dagger. The panic was indescribable. The only people in town who kept their wits about them were two policemen, who calmly drew near to the places where rumors told them the madman was lurking.

Wherever this doubly insane fellow had passed, so the local stories had it, he left corpses in his wake. Eventually members of the asylum staff were able to subdue the escapee, and the town could breathe free again. Many people considered it a miracle that nobody had run afoul of the sick man's dagger. It's so easy to stab somebody to death.

When Hitler ran amok with his patriotic rage in 1933, the asylum opened all its cells and released the inmates into our town. From the Mayor on down to the lowliest Town Clerk, from the Pastor on down to the smallest altar boy, everybody was caught up in the crazed St. Vitus dance. A few normal types unaffected by the epidemic were taken into custody. I read about this in my hometown paper. Every day a new miracle, every day some new recruit for the Party. Everywhere you looked, people were shucking off the old inner man and putting on the new outer man. To me, as I harkened here on Mallorca to the echo of my country's self-debasement, the greatest miracle of all seemed to be that our town's patron saint, the noble Irmgardis, Countess von Zütphen, Mistress of the Townships of Rees, Emmerich, Straelen, and Süchteln, was no longer performing miracles. According to legend, she lived in pious seclusion inside a hollow tree in a nearby forest among the deer and the owls, the otters and the squirrels. Once she was pursued by lascivious knights, and a single word from her mouth sufficed to make these libidinous barons' castles suddenly go up in flames. Ten centuries later, as the walls of the towns under her blessed patronage echoed shouts of "Heil!" the saintly virgin's word remained unspoken. Just one single word, I thought, and my home town would be reduced to a pile of ashes, Germany would reconsider, and a minor saint would have rescued the entire nation! But our little saint remained silent. She had no power over the Knights of the Crooked Cross.

My homeland was now "coordinated." Overnight, the Movement got moving, and the populace of my home town was scrambling all around. Everybody is familiar with the experiment: take a water glass and a handful of hay, place the mixture out in the sun until muck starts to form, and then put a drop of it under a microscope. You will witness a back-and-forth teeming of the organisms called "infusorians." When an entire country begins to putrefy, it likewise gives rise to infusorians, the swarming animalcules of the Movement. But these are visible to the naked eye. When they scramble toward you, and you refuse to lift your arm, they reach out and strike you dead.

My home town was beginning to fill me with dread. Whenever I thought of Germany in the night, I found that I couldn't sleep aright.

But now, instead of writing a book about Spain, a country I was beginning to love and to understand, I was writing one about Germany, a country I never loved and was having a harder and harder time understanding.

"*Die kleine Stadt*: 'The Little Town' —Wouldn't that be a good title for your book?"

"It would be excellent, if Heinrich Mann hadn't beaten me to it. I'm just going to call it '*Hun-less Tombs of the Huns*.'"

My outline: Hitler sends out an order that all civil marriages were to take place with patriotic trappings. The magistrate performing the ceremony must appear in his finest livery, the city hall must be suitably decorated, and the bridal couple must step forth in accordance with ancient Germanic custom, amid moon-gazing, the sacrifice of small animals, unrestrained consumption of mead, worship of the goddess Nerthus, de-braining of tribal elders by one-eyed demonic cadavers, followed by priestesses performing auguries over the mass of collected brains. Following a torchlight parade around World Ash Tree Yggdrasil, once upon a time known as Saint Irmgardis' Linden, the wedding night was to be spent beneath the holy tree. Heidhrun, the *Führer's* sacred goat, and Saerhimnir, the *Führer's* sacred pig, would eat out of the wedded couple's hands. The presiding magistrate would ride the stallion Svadilfari, the Mayor would be astride the eight-legged Sleipnir. Then the march of the mistletoe legions would resound. Prisoners of war would be displayed, and Nidhögger, the Dragon of Envy, would blast his fire against Judah. There would be a commotion in the heavens: wing-flapping Valkyries would start singing the "Horst-Wessobrunn" song. The Fenris Wolf would be on the prowl for tasty morsels, but anyone who was "coordinated" would go scot-free. In order to seal the neo-pagan wedded union, a Christian was to be slaughtered at the runic stone next to the forest spring known as the Siep, and his bones scattered to all the four corners of the globe to ward off evil spirits. Finally, a wreath would be placed at the Tomb of the Unknown Brain.

The local Gauleiter then discovers to his consternation that there is not a single Christian left in the community. The blood-wedding, for which thousands of participants were expected from near and far, is threatened with cancellation. The Jews, who might have been a fitting substitute, have already all been killed. At this moment, so very critical for the prestige of the vainglorious Reich, the bridegroom raises his arm, commands silence, points to his bride and then to himself. He makes the Sign of the Cross. He and his girl have remained Christians in secret; they have not abandoned the faith of their forefathers. There is general amazement. A rattling of shields. Ravens start crowing. And then the cry is again raised at the World Tree: "Slaughter them!" The mayor lifts the giant hammer Mjölnir, and slays the groom, Hinnes the weaver, and the bride, Minchen the flax spinner, whose combined weekly wage is 142 marks. When the Mayor, unaccustomed to committing murder, spies the two corpses lying beneath the sacred ash tree, he is seized with terror. He lifts a hand to the back of his head and notices for the first time that his brain is gone. If he could still think, he would be thinking along these lines: "What the hell, the *Führer* will do my thinking for me!" But this couple here—they can't have any children! Still, the Reich Master of Funeral Ceremonies knows just what to do. Using a hemp rope, he leads Audhumla, the Primeval Cow, to the scene and lets her lick a salty block of ice, out of which steps forth Buri, the first-born brainless *Homo hitlerius*.

Secondary incidents were contained within my plot, plus certain statements made by leading citizens of the town, quoted verbatim from the newspapers. The names of all the active characters are real, since it would not be possible for me to invent them so convincingly in all their self-revealing infamy. This novel of mine was finished except for the final chapter. But the ending, for the novel as well as for its heroes, came unexpectedly.

"And why are you calling it '*Hun-less Tombs of the Huns?*'"

"It's meant as a purely poetic analogy to Buri. Do you remember that hilly stretch of woods north of the town, the one called 'Süchteln Heights'? There are quite a few Hunnish tombs and so-called 'Huns' Beds' up there, the sepulchral chambers of my Stone Age ancestors. But they don't contain skeletons or urns with the remains of immolated bodies. No, these giant 'beds' were the ingenious invention of a town citizen with piles of money and imagination— two things that seldom occur in unison. Only it's too bad that this finance manager never consulted a professional menhirologist, for if he had, then even the most erudite Sunday hiker would have been filled with awe at the sight of his bogus gravesites. The very same philanthropist had a sunken church named after him; all you can see is its weathervane, poking out of the surface of the lake. When I was a kid I thought a lot about those empty graves, and about that church symbolized by a barnyard cock. Such were the origins of my mystical speculations concerning the creative potential of non-being."

"If I've understood you correctly, that local saint was also a fake, conjured up by your enterprising philanthropist."

"I'm afraid not."

"Why 'afraid'?"

"You can look her up in hagiographies. She actually lived, and kept herself alive in the forest with snails and herbs. Like all saints she could talk with animals, but not with human beings. She kept those robber barons away from her skirt, and did a whole lot of other things besides. Someday I'll write her biography, in mystical-mariological style, to shield her from her own sanctity. For if she had never lived, she still would have been able to perform miracles."

"Your people will strike you dead if you take away their saint and the annual church fair devoted to her."

"Go visit the Consul, and he'll tell you that I've been condemned to death even without a biography of the Countess of Aspeln. It's in the documents. If a person is unwilling to shed his shell like a crab, they'll break it open for him. We're lucky that we're staying on this peaceful island."

"Peaceful? What a joke! As soon as we get some money, we should buy a deadbolt lock for our *entrada*. I can't forget what that Andalusian gypsy prophesied for us. It's really frightening. And the nightmares you've been having recently! If only Mamú had already adopted you, and we could hide away in Miramar as American citizens! It's all taking so long!"

In addition to our medicine book, Beatrice also owned a dream book, the text of which was almost more exciting than homeopathic diagnoses and prescriptions. She guarded it like the apple of her eye until the time arrived when, having entered her mesalliance with Vigoleis, both our sets of eyes were so overburdened that we couldn't think of reading any books at all. Our very lives were in danger, so both books got put away.

The dream book was a personal gift from Grand Prince Alexander of Russia, who in his Paris exile wrote mystical treatises on the merging of dead souls with the Lord. He dedicated one of these works to Beatrice's mother.

The gift was an Italian dream book from the 17th century. Its amazing treatment of symbols was along the lines of biblical exegesis: long, hard objects were not yet considered as the phallus, and soft, round, hollow ones weren't yet the female genitalia. In other words, this was a book for the sensible interpretation of dreams—insofar as one could sensibly recall their contents. If things turned out differently anyway, it wasn't the fault of this Venetian oneiromantic. Rather, it was owing to one's own faulty dream life. We always came up with correct interpretations, but our dreams were all wrong. As soon as I started having the right dreams, our Italian book was a failure. Beatrice had all she could do to towel up the sweat from my body. In one of my nightmares, Sigmund Freud appeared as an angel with a flaming sword, threatening to drive me out of Paradise. Poor Freud! He was now harmless in comparison with the demons who were pursuing me in real life. The Teutonic savages in my hometown, licked forth by Audhumla from the ice block of the National Revolution, were driving this erudite Jewish pig out of house and home, and robbing me of my peaceful slumber:

I'm seated in our *piso* on the General's Street, but at the same time my feet are stretched out under Mother's kitchen table back home. On the table there's a dish of sauerbraten and a bottle of *Felanitx blanco*, and around the table is my family, trying to figure out the prodigal son. I'm explaining that Beatrice, as a result of her Indian genes, is considered by Aryans as an outlaw and a criminal. My brothers rise up from their chairs and start shouting, "Get a move on!" They raise their right arms, and I cringe to avoid the blow. But instead, they just start shouting "*Heil Hitler*," and then they try to force me to do the same. I hear myself crying out, "Never!" in Spanish, and then I see myself fleeing the scene. Cowardice is an inherited trait in my clan, and that's why it's taking so long for it to die out. I'm racing across the entrance to our house. The family sits down to their sauerbraten meal and lets me escape.

Across the street from our house stands the "Blothus," formerly the mayor's office and now the Nazi headquarters, and next to it is the Catholic Hospital, where I was a failure as an acolyte. I'm trying to start breathing free, but I sense the hot pursuit of new enemies at my back: three ur-Teutons, hairy guys wearing hairy pelts and with their red locks bunched together at the back of their heads. I recognize them immediately, just as one always recognizes enemies in dreams. It's our town mayor, the Catholic pastor, and the pharmacist. Each of them is threatening me with his special weapon: the hammer of Thor; the keys of St. Peter—the very same ones that had attacked my tongue so convincingly that it could no longer intone the *Pange lingua gloriosum*; and the bronze apothecary's pestle. I run to the intersection and catch a trolley driven by a weaver friend of mine. I leap aboard, and my pursuers are able to jump onto the rear car. At the next stop, they step to the front car and start observing my behavior. I raise my arm—not to make the Nazi greeting, but to grab hold of the leather strap. The triumvirate goes into a huddle: is he going to salute, or is he just hanging on there? If he's only hanging on, we'll kill him in the name of the *Führer*. "Kill him," says the mayor. "Kill him," says the pill pusher. They enter the car to execute the sentence. Their murder weapons slice through the air, and there is a huge crashing sound. The trolley hits a tree and breaks apart. I wake up, and instead of finding my killers bent over my corpse, I see Beatrice mopping me with a towel. I am saved.

Instead of writing a book about Spain, a country I was loving more as I got to know it better, I wrote one about Germany's self-induced downfall, a process that I experienced through the degradation of my little home town and its citizens, people who outdid themselves in self-humiliation. With enormous expenditures of energy, they trod the bellows of the national organ, pulling all the stops to boom forth the funeral march for their own abasement. And just as today they are taking up arms for the fatherland, tomorrow they'll be at it again for God Almighty—that is, if they think that in doing so there's something to be gained for their beer halls, for their old-age pensions, or for the long night that will inevitably follow. Pious bellows-treaders that they are, they will go on pumping air for Heaven's sake, panting like big-bellied stallions until the organ pipes burst. Such small-town zealotry could make one smile if it did not continually lead humanity into rivers of blood and tears. Love of God and love of Fatherland—unless you go along with these, may you end up in the gruesome grave amid carnage and spoliation. Thus spake the Lord.

As I was busy on the island of Mallorca writing my *Tombs of the Huns*, German ingenuity was thinking up the fiery ovens at Auschwitz.

When I think of Germany in the night, I find I cannot sleep aright.

XVIII

At times when the source of my lyric creativity threatened to dry up, when it brought forth only meager droplets and when all of the pails I lowered into it didn't come up with a single line of verse, when I consoled myself by thinking of other poets who also went through long periods of drought, such as Rilke and Marsman—during all such fallow times, Vigoleis the Inventor came into his own.

I have invented so many gadgets that my memory is unable to find room for all of them. "Write that down," Beatrice would say. "You're terrible, you never make any notes. You throw away complete poems. Other people use index cards. They write down everything, and they keep what they've written. You put everything down the toilet, or you go around telling everybody about your inventions, and then when you read in the paper or in the patent notices that somebody else has used your idea. Then you get melancholy and start griping about human depravity. Just dictate your ideas to me. I'll know right away what's what."

Mamú, too, was intensely interested in my talent for invention, and like Beatrice she deplored my unwillingness to broadcast my ideas. It had already become a Sunday custom to give her a progress report, after the Amazons of the gilt-edged Bible had squawked forth their last hymn. As a savvy U.S.A. business woman she thought over each of my inventions carefully, approving, rejecting, or offering suggestions as she saw fit. In my creative habits I had advanced to the point where I wrote down everything and pinned it up on the walls of our bible-paper room—great minds will always find a way—replete with drawings made with an artist's pencil borrowed from Pedro. Inflatable pyjamas, containing equally-spaced holes for the evaporation of sweat and which could also be used to prevent drowning in deep water, gave rise to general accolades. This idea was born inside the head of an idiot who didn't even have a bed of his own. At Mamú's expense, a prototype was put under contract at a Palma rubber factory. I entered prolonged negotiations with a technical specialist there, who called me the "rubber man of the future." But the factory burned down, producing such clouds of acrid smoke as to plunge the city into darkness for several hours. It looked as if the end of the world had arrived, as at the eruption of Krakatoa. But it was only the end of my pneumatic pajamas.

So I made another invention: the self-sharpening pencil for students of the Bible who get ideas while reading and want to write them down. I showed Mamú a small sketch of what I had in mind. At first she couldn't quite make things out, but then she quickly figured out what I was getting at. She stepped over to her desk, saying, "This is probably the kind of thing you're thinking of. They're extremely practical!" And she placed my finished and manufactured invention into my open palm. Christian Science had beaten me to it, though of course only in a technical sense. Whenever she passed out Bibles, she added automatic pencils along with them. The brilliance of my idea was confirmed. But who had stolen it from me? "Sue them!" said Mamú. Fine, but who was "them"? Was it the Christians, or was it their Science?

When once again we had starved long enough to save some money to buy a few yards of cloth to make a sheet for our newspaper pallet, I couldn't wait for Beatrice to finish sewing the long hems around it. So I picked up needle and thread myself, and started in sewing a hem on the opposite side. Between us lay an expanse of white silence. I thought to myself, "There has to be a better way. One of us, or both of us, are bound to give ourselves a painful jab with the needle. What we need is a mechanical contrivance, a sewing machine! Not some unwieldy object that's no better than a Singer or a Madersperger. No, something like a wheel no bigger than a human hand, which we could push along the edges of the cloth like a perforating device for paper, but which would leave simple stitches." I pursued this idea for several days; even the berserk wild men of my home town had to take a back seat for a while. I put together a big, primitive prototype. At first glance it looked like a cross between a lawn mower and a pneumatic drill. But it worked like a charm. As I write down these jottings, my Vigoleis Kwik-Stitch Wheel®j (j = junked) is lying amidst all the other detritus of our island sojourn: our dreambook and our medicine book; some books of poetry; some short, some longer, and some very long volumes of prose; about 3000 other books; an autograph (perhaps the sole extant one) of Clavijo (Goethe's *Clavigo*); a copy of Count Kessler's memoirs; an unpublished manuscript of the Grand Duke Alexander of Russia; and every last piece of Vigoleis' unpublished writings.

Then one day back then, as I stood beneath the just-completed model of my special new umbrella, naked as a newborn babe and feeling the naked euphoria of the successful inventor, in walked Count Harry Kessler.

Beatrice already owned an umbrella, an object she clung to like her books. It was a gift from her mother, a valuable piece of property whose history would take even me too far off the track. In brief, this umbrella's handle was a clump of honey-brown, lightly flamed amber containing a fossilized insect, a millipede, but one that had lost a few hundred legs—a feature that made it even more remarkable from a zoological standpoint. It's possible that some child of the Eocene who wasn't familiar with the maxim "Never pull an insect's legs, or you'll end up in the dregs," had yanked out the missing appendages. My first meeting with Beatrice, in pouring rain in Cologne, took place under this roof. But soon I became jealous of her umbrella, since I got the impression that she loved it more than she loved me. She gave it constant attention, adoring it with a kind of silent and unseen worship, just as the Kaffirs revere their highest divinity, the Creator of the Kaffir universe, the god

Unkulunkulu. At the time, I was searching for a decent religion, one that wasn't mired in externals, sanctimonious cliquishness, and money-grubbing, petty-bourgeois hypocrisy like the one I grew up in. So I was reading a lot about belief systems and superstitions among the primitives, and hit upon Unkulunkulu, a god who isn't served by any visible cult. The Zulu who worships this god is never tempted to feign anything to guard his reputation. This made an impression on me, and so I christened Beatrice's umbrella "Unkulunkulu."

Unkulunkulu was made of silk, with opalescent green and gold on the surface and blood-red inside. But now I must digress for a moment on the subject of this play of colors.

One of Pascoaes' brothers, João Pereira Teixeira de Vasconcellos, spent twenty years in darkest Africa hunting elephants, purely for the sake of adventure. I often sat at his hearth, listening to his hunting stories. When asked about my umbrella god Unkulunkulu, he told me that in the forests of the district of Inhambane he had met up with Vatzua tribes who call their god Inculuculo, using the name of the bird "culuculo" or "inculuculo," an animal sporting brilliantly colored plumage. Its feathers were green on the outside, and its head was blue, but when this bird spread its wings and took flight over the sweltering savannah, when seen from below it seemed to glow with the color of blood. I never found any reference to this natural connection between bird and divinity in the books on religious history that I consulted. I was deeply touched by the fact that when Beatrice's umbrella was opened it glowed as red as blood. I had instinctively given it the correct baptismal name.

But her umbrella's days were numbered.

I screwed off the amber handle with its entomological contents and hung it around Beatrice's neck with a string. This gesture pacified her somewhat for the destruction of her beloved Unkulunkulu. She didn't wish to concede immediately that the invention I was working on was of the epoch-making variety. Her domestic instincts were even less thrilled when I told her that I would have to use our only piece of cloth, the sheet for our conjugal newspaper pallet, for my technical research. She objected to this move—in French, no less. But I remained firm. I explained that bed linens were unnecessary household items, citing the ones that María del Pilar had purloined from us. With our fabrics in her possession the whore had regained her independence in Barcelona and now, with the use of our sheets, things were going much better for her than for us on our jerry-built bedstead. Beatrice shook with disgust, but now I had the cloth I needed for my expanded Unkulunkulu.

I cut the sheet apart, and sewed on a curtain that extended from the edge of the umbrella to the floor. By manipulating a network of strings and by pressing a spring, the curtain could be made to descend, allowing the user to stand under it with full protection from the elements down to his ankles. Three pushes on a mechanism set into the umbrella's shaft sufficed to raise the curtain to its original position. The thinner the fabric, the smaller was the roll of cloth that formed on the closed Unkulunkulu. My prototype was ungainly; the umbrella's skinny rods barely supported the weight of the curtain. But it worked, and it would work even better if the curtain were made of the finest silk and with little sewn-in transparent windows—plastics didn't exist at the time—and a small reading lamp clamped to the shaft for nocturnal readers promenading through a rainstorm. "Book production will rise, Beatrice, and the book prices will fall. Maybe someday readers will be demanding to read Vigoleis under an Unkulunkulu, in the softly falling rain."

I am no fan of nudism, although I can't say that I prefer the sight of fully-clothed human beings. When the weather gets too hot, I strip off. As an emergency measure, not on philosophical principle.

It was a doubly hot day when I put the finishing touches on my Unkulunkulu prototype. I was red-hot from the insular sun, and white-hot with the success of my invention. And there I stood in my barest humanity beneath my African deity. The curtain was lowered—one push on the spring, and with an audible click I was closed off from the rest of the world. In my confining twilight I savored my triumph: Beatrice's sacrifice had not been in vain. Then I heard voices in the corridor. Were they speaking French? Was it Beatrice talking to herself? That's not her way; I have never caught her doing such a thing, not even uttering a curse, the briefest type of monologue. She had got over the loss of her umbrella, but she apparently missed the only bedsheet we ever owned in our gypsy marriage. Was she now sending forth streams of French invective at my creative achievement? But that's not her way, either. With her dignified Indian genes, she knows when to keep her mouth shut. But now she just burst forth.

"*Chéri*, it's Count Kessler!" There was noise in the hallway. Sweating under my Unkulunkulu, I heard it, and also the squeaking of our glassed-in double door, and I said to myself, "That damned door! I really ought to plane off the edge. But Unkulunkulu comes first. *Porra* and *puta*! It worked a minute ago, and now it's stuck!"

The heat underneath the glistening wings of the bird Inculuculo was becoming African in intensity. What was Beatrice saying? Kessler? And: Count? "Open, Unkulunkulu!" But the god wouldn't move. "Get a move on! But is somebody else here?" I yanked the curtain strings and said, more for myself than for Beatrice, "Hmm..., Kessler and Count—that's something you can only find on Mallorca. A 'Kessler' is either a professional tinker, a 'kettle man,' or he's a Protestant reformer. If it's the latter, then he's a religious gangster, and we'd better be on our guard. And a 'Count'? That's the least that anybody can be on this island, and nobody will doubt you. But what about me, *chérie*? Look out, I am Unkulunkulu, and it's only the Kaffirs who believe in me! Watch, just one bang on my drum here, and you'll see! Damn it all, the spring is stuck, the curtain won't go up! I swear on your millipede-in-amber that it was working just a minute ago. If you had arrived one second sooner, *porra*! It would have gone without a hitch!"

Profound silence. Was Beatrice still in the room? Was I hallucinating? Was I, without my knowing it, a Vatzua, under the spell of the bird Culuculo that personified the forest divinity? We didn't have any pots and pans for some tinker to work on; we did our cooking in tin cans, and... Damn you, Unkulunkulu, if you refuse to go up now...

I couldn't budge the spring. "Beatrice, be patient for just a minute, and it will work like a top hat—assuming that I owned one... And now..."

I pulled up the curtain from below. "Beatrice, uh..." And I was thunderstruck. Next to Beatrice stood a gentleman—tall, slim, somewhat bent over, with blond hair mixed with grey, faint blue veins in his sagging cheeks, and holding a cardboard folder and a panama hat— but wait, what I've just written is pure fiction. All I could see was the outlines of a human figure, one that was standing petrified and staring at the naked white deity who suddenly appeared below the curtain, and who just as suddenly went back out of sight behind the rapidly descending cloth. I wrapped the stupid Unkulunkulu around me like a toga and staggered away, like some rainmaker taken unawares by a cloudburst. Was that laughter that I heard behind me? I threw Unkulunkulu on our bed, and there he lay, one piece of junk on top of another, an object now denuded of its grandeur and practicality, having once again become a god of the jungle whose worship nobody can witness. As for myself, the blaspheming skeptic, I quickly got dressed. My skull was about to burst. Kessler? This can't be Nietzsche's friend from Weimar! That's ridiculous! The founder of the distinguished Cranach Press in Weimar? Nonsense! Germany's last patron of the arts? And wasn't there a book by him on Walther Rathenau? Concealing the naked savage beneath my Mallorquin denim suit, I emerged into our bible-paper room and stood across from a fellow in—a simple middle-class Mallorquin denim suit. Was this the democratic camouflage of a man who was once close to the powers-that-be in the German Reich?

"This is Count Kessler from Weimar," said Beatrice. "He would like to have something translated into Spanish."

"I beg a thousand pardons," our visitor said, "for bursting in on you like this, Herr Thälmann! Your wife has explained everything. Do you think it might be possible? I'm rather in a hurry."

Thälmann? What's this all about? Just who am I, anyway? For years I've been Vigoleis, Don Vigo. As "Thelen" I appear only in the thermal bath of my dreams, and just a minute ago I was some degenerate oaf with the pale skin of occidental technology, metamorphosed beneath our Unkulunku into the supreme divinity of the Kaffirs. And now I've been transmogrified or bewitched into Ernst Thälmann, the leader of the German Communist Party, Hitler's number-one enemy? I bowed, and gave the gentleman my real name. But of course, he said, that was of course my name, a thousand pardons, that's the name here on this piece of paper, how embarrassing.

Beatrice, misinterpreting my own embarrassment, went on by way of explanation: "You know, the *Josephslegende* ballet with Hofmannsthal and Richard Strauss, and..."

"Oh, yes," I interrupted her bibliographical prompting. "And the *Notes on Mexico* that you've had for years on your list of books to buy." Turning to Kessler, I said, "Second edition sold out, right? You see, your reputation has preceded you into this scrubbiest of domiciles. But at the moment all we're reading is Iberian mystics and detective novels."

"This tells me that you have a remarkable gift for adaptation, and I'm envious. Especially in this day and age, when all of us are being forced to adapt."

Not one word about Unkulunkulu, the kettle-maker's profession, the gangster/church reformer, or nudism! The person standing here in our presence wearing cheap homespun represented the *grand monde*; he was a *grandseigneur* who harbored within his person the cultures of three fatherlands, nurturing them to sophisticated perfection in a manner that is rare in German climes. His garb was, to be sure, somewhat soiled and worn—it was obvious that he had been unable to bring his valet along with him into exile—but it was distinctive nonetheless. True Mallorquins used their picturesque sashes as trouser belts. But like a bullfighter, Count Kessler had pulled up a pair of cotton underpants that reached above his belly button, and folded them into a roll. At first I thought this might be a nautical life preserver—not a bad invention for a diplomat fleeing his country. The Count's hands were particularly attractive, the kind of hands that even good writers often refer to as "spiritual." It was inevitable that they should look this way, for who if not the fastidious intellectual Count Kessler could ever have such beautiful hands? At any rate, Count Hermann Keyserling's hands were very different, which is why Goebbels had such huge respect for them.

This first encounter with Count Harry Kessler was so bizarre that while committing my Vigoleisian jottings to paper, more than once I've asked Beatrice whether my dream life hasn't been playing odd tricks with reality, causing me to produce here what sensitive readers would call "sheer fiction." Not a bit of it. She's sorry, but when she introduced me to Kessler I was actually standing under Unkulunkulu. But she then adds that the contents of the amber handle was a common, ordinary insect. My "millipede" was make-believe.

"Maybe so, but it's one I don't want to give up. I need it for that Child of the Eocene, and I need the child in order to prove that prehistoric man was governed by bestial instincts, and that therefore the ovens of Auschwitz, concentration camps, and atom bombs aren't to be understood, as they sometimes are, as monstrous products of our Christian civilization."

Count Kessler presented his request. As we were perhaps aware, he had fled from Germany, going first to his sister in Paris, a place where he had been a regular visitor, working in well-known circles as an advocate for international understanding. Then he decided on Mallorca as the place to settle in exile; Catalan friends, or perhaps it was Keyserling, had made this recommendation. Later we made the acquaintance of Kessler's sister, a plain woman whom I at first took for the Count's messenger or domestic help. My intercourse with Spaniards, and in particular my friendship with the noble Sureda family, had once and for all made me ignore any and all barriers between classes of people.

I regarded any shoe-shine boy as a king, and any king as a beggar. In school I had never grasped the simple rule whereby two quantities can equal a third quantity, even when equal to themselves. This I didn't begin to understand until I was confronted by Spanish quantities. All beings born upon this earth, I thought, are situated on the same level of humanity, a level that, as I learned in the meantime, is not so very lofty after all. That is how I avoided committing a *faux pas* with Kessler's sister, the Marquise de Brion, who idolized her brother and who, with all the sacrifices that she made for him, cannot be ignored in any consideration of Kessler's life's work. Now he was a guest on this island, one emigré among so many. He explained that he was living in a house in Bonanova, just outside Palma on the road leading to Génova.

I told the Count that I was not an emigré in the strictly political sense of the word, since I had left the fatherland well before the official de-braining of the country. But I explained further that you would never find me inside the *Führer's* deep-sea diving bell. Kessler looked over at Beatrice and murmured something like "*naturellement.*" I said to myself, hmm... This experienced diplomat may be thinking that Beatrice is Jewish, and that this might be the reason why we didn't want the rest of the Jews to perish. So we had to clarify matters, which we quickly did by citing a few facts concerning Beatrice's Swiss 'ck-ck-dt' family history, as well as the fossil Inca prince who played Indian tricks with Beatrice's bloodline. Whereupon we learned to our surprise that Kessler considered it possible that back in Berlin he had once met Beatrice's father, the patristic scholar who, to the consternation of the Basel ck-dt's, had been a pupil of Professor Harnack. "Adolf von Harnack and Kaiser Wilhelm—*naturellement,*" said Count Kessler. I remained silent because I wasn't sure what was so "natural" about this pairing of names. Later, Beatrice cleared things up for me: "*Gott mit uns!*"

The old diplomat and utopian man of international peace expressed admiration for my equations: *Heil Hitler!* = May Judah Perish, May Judah Perish = Crime, *ergo* whoever says "*Heil Hitler!*" is a criminal. He said that if all Germans could see things so clearly, Hitler would long since be in an asylum. "Exactly," I replied, "but now it's us who are in the asylum." What I meant by this was the island of Mallorca, but I kept an embarrassed silence under the gaze of this guest of ours, who hardly five minutes before had found me standing in embarrassing circumstances under the Unkulunkulu.

The Nazis had charged Count Kessler with tax evasion. Since they were no longer in a position to hang him, they at least wanted to grab his fortune using legal means. He was accused of selling a painting from his collection—was it a Renoir? I can no longer remember—for a million, and reporting the sale for a much smaller sum. His German lawyer had asked him to make out a sworn statement in the presence of a Spanish notary, but this wasn't possible given the linguistic deficiencies on both sides. Kessler spoke just a few words of Spanish, and the notary understood nothing but Spanish, not even Latin. The Count had obtained my address from Zwingli; Keyserling had recommended the Hotel Príncipe to him. I bowed and said that he had come to just the right man, but would he kindly call me Thelen and not Thälmann. And I explained that Beatrice was Zwingli's a.k.a. Don Helvecio's sister.

Count Kessler looked a bit startled, but he took the documents out of his folder for us to translate on the spot into Spanish. It was the first time I had ever observed a diplomat at work. In this case, the work was admittedly in his own personal interest, but with a man like Kessler there will not have been much difference between a formal state conference in tie and tails and an attempt to prevent extortion while wearing a Mallorquin canvas suit.

He asked how much he owed us. I mentioned a price reserved for needy emigrés, but he would hear nothing of that. All of us were poor, he said, and he went on to say that I was no doubt poorer than he was, since he was still receiving a monthly check. I replied that he was probably right, but that as soon as my Unkulunkulu went on the market, I would be a rich man, and then it would be an honor for me to take him in under my umbrella. At this the Count laughed out loud. His final thoughts must have concerned the strange detours one is forced to take when in exile.

Scarcely had our door closed behind Kessler when I said to Beatrice, "See? Unkulunkulu performed his black magic. Just when I wanted to raise up the curtain, he tangled up the strings. But now the Count will be thinking that he's come out of the frying pan into the fire. Was he standing in our doorway? I was so excited that I overheard the bell ringing. And now the whole contraption is lying off in that corner over there!"

Beatrice had met this gentleman on the Apuntadores, just as she was emerging from Angelita's store. In broken Spanish he told her he was looking for General Barceló Street, and Beatrice, replying in French, said that she was headed that way, just a few steps. What number was he looking for? 23? "*Mais, comme c'est drôle,*" said Beatrice, adding that they could walk there together. Arriving at the house, they discovered that they both were headed for the second floor, but Beatrice told him that he wouldn't find up there the man named Thälmann he was looking for, but rather me. One glance at his notes gave him the assurance that I was exactly the person he had been told to consult. In his confusion he began to speak with a mild stutter. Then came the weird scene with the umbrella. Beatrice had almost fainted with embarrassment: there I stood, buck naked underneath that stupid contraption. The gentleman had seen it all, and he would surely have run away if he could have. He just stood there like some primitive idol—an image that amused me no end: a god and an idol together in our miserable hovel, staring bug-eyed at each other. I asked Beatrice if she had recognized him right away. Yes, she said, but meeting him on the street was a mere coincidence. On her way home she had learned at the German Shop that Count Harry Kessler had been living on the island for quite a while. So the man she met could only be him.

Beatrice, who has made a hobby of politics, had read Kessler's biography of Rathenau. And since, for her, music was an even more impassioned hobby, she was also familiar with the Strauss-Kessler ballet Die Josephslegende. All I knew about the man was his reputation for versatility. I hadn't read a word of his writings, and now I would probably never see him again, never again touch the hand that closed Nietzsche's eyelids. But hold on!—I didn't know this at the time. Kessler told us about it much later.

On this historic day I did no more work on my Unkulunkulu invention. The grandest product of my creative ambitions now lay in a corner of our *sala immaculata*, tangled up and shorn of all its glory. Had Vigoleis too, its last worshiping Kaffir, lost his faith? Not quite. It was my firm intention to start fiddling with it again the very next day. But the very next day, Count Harry Kessler returned with a thousand apologies and asked me if I would be willing to be his amanuensis.

Whenever Beatrice left the house on errands, she never took with her our large-sized apartment key. We arranged a bell-ringing signal, and I would open our door in whatever get-up I happened to be wearing—which very frequently was my Adamic costume. When the temperature reached 100 degrees that was invariably the case.

I heard the agreed-upon signal, ran to the door, opened it, and had to acknowledge two things at once: that I was as naked as a jaybird, and that I was not a born nudist. The old Berlin rooftop-nudologist Richard Ungewitter, the author of several treatises on the unclothed human body, would have stood right there at our entrance in all his bearded dignity and with the folds of skin that enveloped his torso like a toga, and received Count Kessler like any person in full formal attire. But I, with my Adamic inhibitions, took a powder and hid behind the door.

"A thousand pardons!" said Count Kessler, "Once again I've arrived at the wrong time. But please don't be embarrassed, it doesn't bother me a bit."

"But it bothers me!" I took my raincoat from the hook and wrapped it around my nakedness. Unkulunkulu would have been a better camouflage. I was more than ashamed. But now our visitor, seeing me for a second time in all my earthbound divinity, immediately helped me overcome this moment of mortification. He pointed out the window to our sweltering back yard, where one of the pretty girls' pet armadillos was lazily ambling along. I heard him say that he was enchanted with the way we lived here. From the outside one would never believe that in this house, on this street, there was a rear view of Paradise itself. "If it's Paradise," I cried out, "then my state of undress is excusable."

The Third Reich, Count Kessler began, would last a very long time. Distinguished emigrés, among them Georg Bernhard, Leopold Schwarzschild, and whoever else, were underestimating Hitler and, even more so, the German people. Things would go on like this for years. Then would come a war, and finally a horrible end to it all. He explained that he was a pessimist, but amid his pessimism he had become an optimist, for he had started writing his memoirs. That is to say, he had begun sketching them out a good deal earlier, but here on the island he intended to work on them full-time, no matter what was happening in his beloved Germany. With his life's forward path now barred to him, he would start living backwards. And he hardly dared to inquire whether I would type out his manuscripts for him. Typing was, he knew, something frightful, a form of penal servitude. But—

I reassured him. Once again, I said, he had come to just the right man. I was now hardened by experience, since a few other writers had kept me at the machine for months. It had even been a pleasurable, exciting task to type out manuscripts for Robert Graves, although Laura Riding's were generally boring. With Laura, you always knew what was coming next.

I began by copying out the first volume of Kessler's memoirs. I suggested to him the same fee arrangement that I had made with Graves. He agreed, although the Englishman probably had an easier time coming up with money, since Harry Kessler—yes, Count Harry Kessler, this fascinating literary stylist, this master of the German language—had fastidious taste when it came to paper and to his personal scribe. He used small-format linen stock with a bluish tint, which he no doubt ordered through his sister in Paris, for no such luxury item was available in Palma, not even in the elegant Casa Mir. For his manuscripts he used German script, but preferred roman cursive for his correspondence. This was symbolic of the impressive artistic and intellectual division within his personality. In his letters he was a thoroughgoing cosmopolitan by reason of his lineage, his exquisite international education, his gift for learning and his wide-ranging travels, his career as a diplomat, his way of dealing with people who lend the world their special stamp, questionable as that may be, and through his relationship with the world of Antiquity (he read Latin and Greek authors in the original, better than others are able to read in their own tongue). He was a man who stood above other men and above any and all fatherlands.

He actually had three fatherlands, together with their languages. But it was only German that he acknowledged as his "mother tongue," based on decisive experiences in Hamburg that forevermore made him feel that he was essentially a German. Goethe's concept of *Humanität* and the spirit of Romanticism guided him as he underwent a by no means painless rebirth. As a writer he became a citizen of the tragic country of his choice, more and more so as his destiny led him onwards. This soon brought him in conflict with his ideas about German liberty. "How has it come about," he asks in his memoirs, "that in Germany, the homeland of Schiller, Kant, and Fichte, such degradation of character can have occurred?" As I typed out his words I hazarded an answer to this question: because we Germans are also Hagen's nation, a people that likes to sing for a fee about "honor," a "disloyal nation" as Ernst Bertram once called us, a purblind collective that for the *Führer's* sake was taking the side of the Angel of Darkness. Kessler once wrote that in order to measure the greatness of Walther Rathenau, one must always add that man's personality to whatever he said and did in his lifetime. Or on the other hand, one must subtract that personality from his achievements. This is equally true of

Rathenau's biographer, who lived and accomplished more with his imponderable artistic sensibility than with a calculating mind.

Over time we grew closer, one to another. I gradually got to see his true face beneath the mask of *politesse*.

I was now typing like some ink-crazed coolie—if you will permit me this odd simile, since it was only the author who was making the ink flow. Kessler's script wasn't always easy to decipher, but Beatrice helped me out. I delivered the typed results with the proper gestures of humility, and a few days later, with the proper gestures of humility, they came back to me together with fresh pages of manuscript. Each time this happened, I was asked to grant the author a thousand pardons—which I willingly did, although it was no circus to retype pages and pages incorporating emendations, additions, and deletions in gothic script. In this fashion there arose a multitude of different versions of Kessler's memoirs, variants that text-critical scholars like to designate with letters of the roman alphabet. That is how the scholars do it; for me it meant difficulties of the purely mnemonic sort. There were versions of certain sections that reached the letter M. And to change or add anything, even a single word, meant retyping the entire page with several carbons. But it was only in this manner that the author could gain clear oversight over what would eventually become the "final edition."

Epochs and faces, nations and fatherlands started spinning madly inside my brain. It was like a parade of jumping frogs, but one with many leaps backward and very few that went on ahead. How I longed for a return to my Unkulunkulu or to my stupid Huns, both of which I had abandoned. Are we a "disloyal nation"? It all depends. Count Kessler was punctual with his fee payments. The further the variants reached in the alphabet, the more I earned as a typist. Kessler will have been thinking: this guy is half crazy, so he's the ideal copyist. I began to comprehend the scribal playfulness of the medieval monks to whom the German language owes its cockamamie orthography. But unfortunately I was not permitted to indulge in such aesthetic games. On the contrary, I was obliged to consult meticulously the Duden Dictionary, because Count Kessler wrote Imperial Austrian German, and soon enough I was confused as to whether the word *Thron* is written with an h or without, whether Kamel had two e's or just one, or whether *Gränze* was the correct spelling of the word for "border." During this process, "Thelen" most often got spelled as "Thälmann," but I soon made my peace with this third dimension of my Vigoleis, with no hurt feelings.

Everything, or almost everything, was now democratized in accordance with the regulations of the Association of German Book Printers, Inc. I had a free hand. The final judge was our mutual friend Dr. Theodor Matthias, whose competence Count Kessler doubted from time to time but, like a good German, accepted as our authority, thus relieving him of one worry. We had a harder time with Gustav Wustmann, whom I knew only by name, since I never had much scholarly interest in that man's book *German Language Blunders*. Language is custom, and as such it can never avoid blunders. On the contrary, it has made great strides in the direction of blunders, even so far as to engender de-humanized human beings.

Once I had become used to Kessler's little manias and literary tricks, one day I took it upon myself to point out to him, as discreetly as I could, a few stylistic glitches—offering apologies if I had misread his handwriting. But these were genuine howlers, he said, and asked me to be so kind as to look them up in Wustmann right away. I didn't own a Wustmann. "What!? And you claim to be a writer and a Germanist!?" I was a failure at both professions, it seemed, probably because I had my own ideas about languages, blunders, and similar synonyms. "But that's terrible! We must get you Wustmann's *Language Blunders* right away," said the Count. I was told to go visit the little Swabian at the German Shop and order the book at Kessler's expense. He was unwilling to lend me his own copy, which lay ready at hand on his desk. But how come...

I ordered the book, but the course of history had seen to it that the older *Blunders* were out of print. It took months for a new edition to be released, one adapted to the universal blunder of the Third Reich by a certain Herr Schulze, and containing an obligatory motto ascribed to Hermann Goering saying that it was a particularly noble task to foster pure language that was understandable for the masses. Obviously the linguistic purifiers had said "yes" to the Hitler regime. When I showed Count Kessler this genuflection of the German language to the German *Führer*, he took fright and with a visible attack of embarrassment said that it would be an insult to present me with this book. A thousand pardons. I countered by saying that in spite of my dubious university training as a Germanist, I was at least aware that the people who take delight in pointing out linguistic mistakes are the ones who commit the very worst ones. Then I asked him if I could write down something to this effect in his book. He firmly rejected this idea, saying that it would be tantamount to speaking of the devil. This was a smart move on his part, since the exiled Count's memoirs were due to be published in Berlin by the renowned Samuel Fischer.

I have a faulty memory. Printed matter doesn't stay with me very long. After a single month I can re-read a poem or a novel that impressed me, and it's as if I were seeing it for the first time. This forgetfulness of mine is no doubt an obstacle to critical penetration into a given work. But my preferred reading matter is the mystics, and it's no accident that I am the translator of Pascoaes, the thinker who has brought the long line of Iberian mystics to its culmination. Still and all, despite the crevices and non-functional synapses in my brain, over time I knew the memoirs of Count Harry Kessler by heart. After a half-dozen retypings I had it down just like Goethe's "Erl-King," though with this difference: I learned Goethe's classic spooky ballad in the final version approved by the author, whereas the Count's recollections of peoples and fatherlands, having solidified in my brain to a kind of geode, were still very much in a state of flux. Although I can type pretty fast, I do it with two fingers only, and my eyes are always focused more on the keyboard than on the text. In this case, the result was that Kessler's newest version kept slipping back to an old one.

Ignoring his corrections, I re-inserted his erasures, sometimes leaving out whole words and phrases. Kessler called this a form of creative collaboration, for which he was grateful. The earlier version, he often said, was the better one. I was praised for my putative sense of good style and my Wustmannian acuity.

Hearing this, I blushed crimson at my shameful, sieve-like memory, doubtless also in acknowledgment of the fact that it never functioned like a guard dog for my own writing activity. I refused to accept the borrowed plumes the Count was offering me, and begged him to pardon my wayward ways at the machine. Pardoning me, I said, should be doubly easy for him, seeing that he himself had warned me about the slavish work involved and that he had been a student of the psychologist Wilhelm Wundt, under whom he had earned his doctorate. From that time onward, Kessler often called me, in jest, his personal Wustmann. Our discussions of stylistic matters will remain in my mind as the most rewarding and instructive I have ever had. Thälmann was effectively repressed, and receded into the background. Professor Wilhelm Wundt would have had a ball with his electrical affect-sensing apparatus!

The first volume of Kessler's memoirs came out in print, and with the proverbial courage of desperation I set to work typing out Volume Two, with the aid of my internal and external Wustmann. This new volume contained his accounts of the origins of the American aristocracy, including MacAllister's famous "400." He reported on his own lonely nights in Canadian cabins, where Kessler's father owned a bear-hunting preserve as big as all of Bavaria, and on the naked girls in the upper-storey windows of bordellos in San Francisco—a lascivious custom that set the tone for other cities with the exception of Amsterdam, where vice gets displayed on the ground floor, although climate and Calvinist tradition prohibit a degree of undress worthy of the name. I of course applied my stylistic talents to the various versions of the manuscript. The Count later presented me with two copies of *Times and Faces*, one bound and the other in a cardboard cover, neither of them containing an inscription. He told me that he had pondered for a long while whether I would be willing to accept the "final edition" of his book, since I was no doubt thoroughly sick of it, and in light of the fact that three more volumes were yet to follow.

With the church reformer Johannes Kessler of St. Gall in mind, Beatrice baked some St. Gall *Biber* to celebrate the publication of the Part I of the Count's memoirs. Beatrice now habitually spoiled Kessler with pastries and French conversation. Kessler, who suffered from homesickness, waxed sentimental and inscribed two dedications, one in gothic script, the other in roman. The gothic one was for his private Wustmann, his technical assistant in the production of the book. The other inscription was for Beatrice, who, tenacious as she is on all such occasions, insisted that he write one expressly in her name. But behold, the great diplomat and chronicler of peoples and fatherlands made a slip of the pen: Thälmann made a sudden reappearance, flowing from the Count's pen with the radical-leftist's proper name. When he noticed what he had done, Kessler was mortified. I burst out laughing. Beatrice, now caught unawares with her superstitions, turned pale and murmured something about evil omens. But because no events in this world can have so many bad outcomes as Beatrice is wont to predict for them, I was unfazed. Nonetheless, Count Kessler was upset, and took his leave soon after our little celebration, a feast that our Portuguese friends with their penchant for self-deprecation would call a *copo d'agua*—which is what it almost amounted to. Hardly had he left when Beatrice grabbed the book and disappeared into the kitchen. Years later, when we got to talking about this remarkable name-switching, I told her that instead of burning the entire book she at least ought to have salvaged the page containing the dedication. But apparently evil magic must be destroyed down to the last trace. Worse still, our other copy of *Times and Faces* got lost with other important and irreplaceable items during our escape from the island, whereas I took with us in our paltry bundle of possessions, of all things, the politically coordinated Wustmann. Well, as they say: books have their fate, although they have an easier time of it than the people who write them.

You can read in Kessler's memoirs that his family came from the region of Lake Constance, near St. Gall. The first mention of a "Kessiler" occurs in a document from the year 1282. This man had an estate in Stodon, between Feldle and Vonwil. An ancestor of our Count named Heinrich Kessler got involved in one of the many conflicts of the period and was killed in a 1372 battle, as a miles in the army of the Imperial Cities—not a terribly distinguished occurrence. It wasn't until the fourteenth century that the family, situated in and near St. Gall, began to flourish. His forefather Johannes Kessler was born in 1502, a religious reformer who did battle against the dreaded aristocratic abbot of the St. Gall Benedictine Monastery. The chronicles of the city of St. Gall shower praise on this gentleman's broad education, his refined taste, his simple, gentle, noble, and amiable character, and his exemplary life. Kessler quotes this passage verbatim. This ancestor of his wrote a set of memoirs with the title *Sabbata*, in which (I'm following Kessler) he recounts how, on his journey as a young student to the university in Würzburg, he met Martin Luther at the Black Bear Inn in Jena, when Luther was staying incognito in the nearby Wartburg under the alias "Sir George". Gustav Freytag retells this story in his novel *Scenes from Old Germany*.

For my novel about the Hun-less Tombs of the Huns, I had myself done a certain amount of research into my ur-Teutonic forebears on the banks of the Niers. It wasn't easy to find the pertinent material, since I was able to consult only private libraries. Somewhere—I think it was in Don Juan's highly erudite bookcases—I found a copy of Freytag's *Scenes* in German, and it proved very useful indeed. By sheer coincidence, I read in it the account of the St. Gall reformer Johannes Kessler, and this happened in the days when that man's great-great-grandson was wending his way to General Barceló Street. I had never heard of this harmless religious radical who played no role in the bloody 16th century battles of the theologians. To call him a "religious gangster," as I did under the sweltering Unkulunkulu, was worse than slander. The pious fellow, who scrambled his way up from lowliest beginnings as a saddler's apprentice to a career as a distinguished clergyman, didn't deserve such an affront.

Kessler was a regular guest of ours for over a year, but he never once referred, not even obliquely, to the circumstances surrounding our first encounter. I once asked him if he thought I was completely batty when he saw me standing there under a bedsheet, naked, cursing all the tinkers of this world and singing the praises of Unkulunkulu, a god that only Kaffirs could believe in.

Well then, he said, if I wished to bring that matter up again, he would have to admit that he couldn't believe his eyes, and that he would prefer to have taken his leave immediately. But that would have been impolite toward Beatrice, and besides, he couldn't make any sense out of my rhyming harangue about the church reformer Kessler. Not one in a thousand persons was aware that the religious purifier from St. Gall was an ancestor of his. As I might well understand, this coincidence had given him pause.

"So I can thank Unkulunkulu for the fact that I am playing a peripheral role in the creation of your memoirs?"

Count Kessler, too intensely concentrated on his own world, a world that was causing him more and more anguish as he surveyed his past, simply pointed to Beatrice and began talking French with her—thus avoiding a reply to my mystical gibberish.

Yes, I said, Beatrice was a wonderful woman. She may not appreciate my enlightened Unkulunkulism, lacking as she did any sense of technocratic mysticism. But she tolerated it, and that was saying a great deal. Whereupon I enlightened the Count by explaining that just a few days before his arrival, in pursuit of even battier historical documentation, I had chanced upon the old reformer Johann Kessler in Freytag's *Scenes*.

Sometimes if certain pages had many corrections on them, Kessler wanted them retyped right away. On such occasions I retreated to our kitchen with my typewriter, letting him continue his writing at Doña Carmen's clunky table. I informed him, of course, that the drawer had formerly done service as a tabernacle for our "God's Eye" grail. This bit of news amused him greatly; his eyes squinted with mirth. He liked to get cheered up every so often by a picaresque story—if it wasn't too long, because he was always in a hurry. He was now living solely for his work on the memoirs, and he was huddling in for this task as if for an endless winter. He was scarcely alert to current political happenings, especially those in the Nazi Reich. Which is to say, he deliberately kept out of touch as best he could. But sometimes his best was not good enough, and this caused him a considerable amount of trouble. We owned only one table, which we placed in our bible-paper room when he came, leaving me to work in the kitchen on a board that the little Swabian had given me for a completely different purpose. When Kessler became aware of this state of affairs, he preferred to go to the Café Alhambra or one of the clubs on the Borne, where he joined the other elderly gentlemen. But instead of just lounging in an easy chair, playing dominoes while half asleep, or having his shoes shined ten times in succession, he continued working on his memoirs. He would suddenly notice that on page 206, nine lines from the bottom, the word should be "hurried" instead of "ran." And then a *botones* from one of the recently organized squads of messengers would run—or was it "scamper"?—to the General's Street, where his scribe dutifully entered the emendation in the proper manuscript variant, while forcing his memory to keep silent.

In those days Ernst Thälmann was already in a concentration camp under a death sentence, but strangely enough still among the living. The left-wing Spanish newspapers discussed his case extensively, and the anarcho-syndicalists printed broadsheets and staged parades with flags and banners saying, DOWN WITH HITLER! IN THE NAME OF HUMAN RIGHTS WE DEMAND THE RELEASE OF THÄLMANN! This also took place on a particular Saturday. Kessler had been at our apartment. Beatrice was barely able to persuade him not to take his shoes off for fear of soiling our floor, which was carpeted with old sheets of the *Deutsche Allgemeine Zeitung*. He was worried about spoiling things for us little people, who no doubt wanted to keep things clean for Sunday. After dictating a few letters and finishing a portion of his manuscript, he left for the Alhambra. Half an hour later a *botones* appeared at our door in great haste, presenting a letter in a bluish, lightly perfumed envelope—but I may be mistaken about the perfume—that began, "My dear Thälmann..." It went on to say that he hoped that the boy would arrive before I started typing, "because on page... it should read..." There was no rush with typing his letters. He wrote further that he would not be returning to Barceló Street as agreed upon, but was going back home to Bonanova.

Thälmann hadn't been around our house for quite a while. My first visage had completely repressed him, and Kessler had no idea at all about my second visage, or rather, he had only got a glimpse of it when it was overshadowed by Unkulunkulu. But now, all of a sudden, the notorious "red sub-human" Thälmann reappeared, and I was frightened. For as comfortably as I was wont to play my role as Vigoleis, what was I to do with the "arch-egalitarian" inside me? I would try my best to limit the spread of this Kesslerian rash to the less sensitive parts of my body.

Kessler's Spanish housemaid came by at an unusually late hour, bearing a second letter. It was urgent, she said; the *Señor* Conde had returned home in great excitement, and she would wait for our reply. I broke open the envelope and, now addressed as "Dear friend," I learned that the undersigned knew very well that I was not named "Thälmann" and that I wasn't Thälmann himself, but that the undersigned could not remember my true name. All this, he went on, was extraordinarily embarrassing for him—begging a thousand pardons—and one day he would explain everything. His *servante* would wait to receive my kind reply.

By this time of day I knew that a protest demonstration had taken place in Palma. There had been some violence, and the rally had ended in the usual fashion with arrests. A handful of gunpowder-filled bones, Don Pablo Enorme told us, prepared for the occasion by Ulua, failed to go off because the bone-tossers were too involved in political discussions at some café or other.

I own, or I should say I once owned, several letters from Kessler in which I am called Thälmann, as well as several others in which he retracts my anarchistic anabaptism, substituting my true name, the one from which I had long since de-baptized myself, for the crossword puzzle that my person often presented to him. He never did offer the explanation promised in his night-time express letter. It wasn't until many years later that I learned the truth, this time from another Count whose acquaintance we made during our Swiss exile, in the town of Auressio that I have already mentioned in these jottings. It was Count Werner von der Schulenburg, who lived a few hundred meters above us and the rest of the world in his wonderful writer's domicile named La Monda (later the hermitage of the Dutch poet Marsman). He was reduced to a refugee's diet, *sans* German shepherd and *sans* direct outside contacts, but in the company of his wife Maríanne from Düsseldorf who, while she was much too classy to do the proverbial city-street cartwheels, was likewise the object of my admiration. During the Röhm Purge of 1933 the Count was scheduled to be made a head shorter. But, old conspirator and *condottiere* that he was, a type that not even crafty Nazi huntsmen could drive out of the thicket of his political intrigues, he now sat up there on the hill in his overalls and was writing comedies for the stage. As good Germans we at first avoided each other, each suspecting the other as a spy carrying a concealed dagger and in league with the dreaded Consul in Lugano, Captain Rausch.

But then one Easter Sunday—the Risen Lord was making the rounds of the houses with a blessing for each and every one—we both realized how ridiculous this situation was. There were but seventy hearths in the village. Everybody knew everybody else, and everybody knew whether anybody else had ever murdered someone (in the Onsernone Valley the traditional vendetta was still a local custom). Each evening Schulenburg and I stood together down at the roadway waiting for Mella, the postman, sexton, gravedigger, miner, and discreet purveyor of gossip in one and the same well-groomed person, to distribute the mail. Then, keeping a mistrustful distance, we would climb the stone steps that were carved out of the ledge and kept slippery by the local cattle, up to the village.

Things just can't go on like this, I thought to myself. I sent the Squire of La Monda my just-published German translation of Pascoaes' St. Paul. The delivery was put in the hands of Emma, the aristocratic couple's maid, a calm and reliable child with the blank gaze of a grazing cow and a heart of gold that belied the character of her father, the most feared tyrant in the valley. An hour later His Royal-Imperial Excellency appeared in his heavy loden cape and hunting cap, every inch of him an indication that my T'uang theory was dubious, and that the Almanach de Gotha does contain a few pearls after all. To put it briefly, not even Martersteig's snippety old maids, who grumbled so fiercely against the Tscharners, would have anything to criticize about our visitor, except perhaps his sparse growth of hair and his wife Maríanne.

Maríanne was an actress, and she was Catholic. She embodied the proverbial radiant glow in the lowly cottage. But how had she entered Count von der Schulenburg's life? Quite simply: this Count, flexible as he was in all situations, had lowered himself to let her in. He now introduced himself with all his titles—academic, heraldic, genealogical, and literary: Schiller Prize, Goethe Medal, most frequently produced playwright, Senator of the Halcyon Academy. The best I could do to match these honorifics was to present myself just simply as Vigoleis with a soft V as in "Hannover" but lacking the renown of that city, a name that Beatrice's ck-dt relatives in Basel were reluctant to accept since it intruded on their prerogatives. In any case, Count von der Schulenburg instantly ignored me and turned his attention to Beatrice. He insisted on having met her before—but where? Two such well-traveled individuals might have crossed paths in many places in the world. "In South America, by any chance?" our blue-blood guest suggested. Yes, said Beatrice, that's where she spent part of her childhood—but then she retreated into her Inca fortress. The Count went on guessing where the two of them could possibly have met, while I remained for him just so much air. It was established that they actually did know each other, but that the how, the where, and the when would only emerge with time. But wait, I thought: in cases of doubt, let truth be told, and so I had to take action. I went to our bookcase, took out our Jacob Burckhardt, and opened a volume containing a youthful photograph of Basel's most famous sainted scholar. I showed the picture to His Royal-Imperial Excellency, about whom I knew that he had written a biography of the younger Jacob Burckhardt. "This is where you had your first mysterious encounter with Donna Beatrice from the House of ck-dt!" It is a fact that the young Burckhardt looks just like Beatrice.

A citizen of Basel would have countered my exclamation with "*Däwäg*!" Count Werner von der Schulenburg... but to continue would take us too far afield. By the time he left us after three hours, we realized not only that he had drunk the last of our wine, eaten the last of our salami, and destroyed all our hopes for a quick downfall of the Nazis, but also that our list of encounters with remarkable personalities had grown by two. There developed a see-saw traffic between the meager hut of the struggling writer and the lofty residence of the great one. In fact, many things developed. I told the Schulenburgs about my Spanish adventures, I unplugged the Count's bathtub drain in La Monda, told tales of the priest in the neighboring village—which led me to add some whoremongering stories from Mallorca. "It's amazing how you do that!" said the Count—and for displaying my talents I was rewarded with Valpolicella and roast goat or, most delectable of all, Onsernone fox. Since one cannot go on forever about *porra*s and *puta*s even when the subject is Spain, I told him that I had been Harry Kessler's scribe and what one might call his last secretary, adding some highlights from Kessler's workshop of world history. In the process I also regaled Schulenburg with the story of my third visage, the one that I had worn on the island, albeit only briefly: Thälmann.

Count von der Schulenburg's gaze darkened, while retaining its aspect of firmness; it was a convincing and almost fear-inspiring glance of the kind that only an ages-old aristocratic family could bring forth. "What?!" he cried. "Do you mean to say that you did all of these things, and yet now that you're almost starving you've never put them to your advantage, you've never written a book or even a brochure about the final years of the self-styled Count Harry Kessler from the house of...? You fool, you dimwit, you dunderhead, you!"

"Er—how's that again? Did you say self-styled? And from the house of...?"

"From the Principality of Reuss! It's an old story: illegitimate son. Not very complicated, either. Other people have had a harder time getting their noble titles." I'm quoting exactly what Schulenburg told me, only he presented the story in wittier fashion and with greater precision, without mixing up the Reuss dynasty's elder and cadet branches. I recalled having heard similar gossip on Mallorca concerning my employer's sinister bastard blood, rumors that were outdone only by others having to do with his beloved sister, who was said to be the natural daughter of Kaiser Wilhelm I. Kessler would never have written such a grass-roots correction of Gotha into his memoirs. But permit me to ask my curious reader: doesn't a nightingale have the right to sing a song that the sparrows are already chirping from all the rooftops? Captain von Martersteig, for example, was just such a blatherskite. I believed his very word, all the more willingly, considering that I was myself switched as a baby and then taken for someone I wasn't at all. Confusions of this kind can happen even in the loftiest regions of society, starting with the Imperial *pilarière* and extending to princely and ducal bedrooms or the estate stables. I myself, a person possessing no family tree but only a horoscope whose aberrations apply equally to someone else, have never taken such matters very seriously. Cadet Branch or Elder Branch—parthenogenesis happens with crabs and little worms, as well as in stories told by wet nurses.

But what Count von der Schulenburg, a man who sat firmly in the saddle of any and all genealogical discussions, went on to say about that other mystification, my friend Count Kessler's fixation on Thälmann, knocked me for a loop, for his explanation entered the realm of psychoanalysis. Harry Graf Kessler, he said, had once stood on the barricades in Weimar in 1919, wearing a red shirt. And Schulenburg asked me to guess who had stood next to him defending the fatherland. I thought for a while; I was always lousy in history, and so I wasn't able to get beyond Rosa Luxemburg. But Beatrice chimed in right away: "Thälmann!" It was him. The rest of the story played itself out according to the laws of subconscious repression. On Mallorca, the phonic similarity of the names Thälmann and Thelen had caused the red-shirted agitator to resurface—surely I understood, said Schulenburg. Hadn't I studied psychology?

Indeed this was a persuasive explanation, even for someone who doesn't believe in such eruptions of marsh gas from the depths of the human soul.

Kessler's close friend, the Belgian architect Henry van de Velde, who played such a significant role during his Weimar years and whom I met during the writing of this book in connection with the disappearance of Kessler's posthumous papers, was a modern Pantagruel,. ninety years of age, dressed in a cleverly designed zippered suit he had invented as a final transcendence of *Jugendstil*, he almost persuaded me to join him on the carousel at the church fair in Zug. Professor van de Velde, too, found the Thälmann story captivating, but he doubted that Harry had ever stood on a barricade anywhere. He couldn't recall any such thing, and it was he who ought to know about such things. As for myself, I don't consider it odd that a Red Count would lend a hand at a street blockade. A red shirt would have fit him just as nicely as those Mallorquin canvas duds. Professor van de Velde was gathering material for his own account of his friend's final years, and when I told him that Kessler wrote parts of his memoirs in the Alhambra or any of the thousand other cafés in Palma, the old Kessler connoisseur said that it had never been Harry's custom to hang around and write in cafés. If I hadn't been working on a delicious rack of lamb at the moment, I would have replied that no matter how firmly rooted in his own personality a man might be, he could still be easily shaken into oddball behavior by two types of situations: marriage and exile.

Count Harry Kessler was a bachelor, but he didn't escape the experience of exile.

But now Harry Kessler was said to be a gorgeous late blossom on the venerable Reuss family tree, blooming forth above peoples and fatherlands? And why not? Nothing is impossible in this world, and anthropology and genealogy have no doubt had to solve some even more vexing riddles involving love children. As long as human reproduction doesn't take place in numbered copulation sacs as with the silkworm *Bombyx mori*, official family trees should be banished into the realm of superstition. Still, I would be the last to deny that a Mr. Jones Jr. is in most cases the bona fide offspring of a Mr. Jones Sr.

Harry Kessler was one of the most polite persons I have ever met. But was his politeness a consequence of his elite education? Was he a man of the world because he was a child of the aristocratic court? When he was about to take his shoes off so as not to dirty up our apartment—was he fulfilling Beatrice's secret wishes because he knew that we couldn't afford a housemaid? Or can this be explained, rather, as a manifestation of genetic impulses that formed his character? The science of eugenics is still in its cradle; in 1933 no less a personage than Eugen Fischer proved this to be the case. No one can have much confidence in its findings, perhaps none at all. Things have become a little clearer with the research of Szondi, the Hungarian scholar working in the field of human destiny, and his theory of unconscious drives that lurk within a family. Be that as it may, it makes me wonder when I read a certain passage in the memoirs of the church reformer Johannes Kessler, a passage that his dubious descendant Harry quotes in fragmentary fashion. It's where the young theology student Johannes K. tells of entering the Black Bear Inn in Jena with his travel companion. Sitting there comfortably and eating a hearty meal next to them was none other than Martin Luther. The innkeeper, a jovial fellow, encouraged the young scholars—"Come right in, gentlemen!" But Johannes Kessler, a child of humble origins who had just recently abandoned an apprenticeship in saddlery for the study of theology, felt embarrassed because he was wearing muddy shoes. Whereupon he performed the same act for his new religious idol that, four centuries later, Harry, the child of ennobled parents, would repeat on General Barceló Street: he started taking off his footwear. "For our shoes were (Johannes K. continues), if the reader will permit me to say so, so shamefully covered with mud and dirt that we could not simply enter the establishment. Thus we crept behind a door and sat down on a little bench..."

Harry hadn't crept over to a bench, for the simple reason that Vigoleis, the proprietor at the General Barceló Inn in Palma de Mallorca, didn't own a bench for his *entrada*.

XIX

Reticence is a conspicuous and frequently humbling trait of Vigoleis—humbling for his own person, of course. A shy person is convinced by instinct and experience that humans are often all-too-human to other humans, and this insight has the effect of restricting his behavior in the presence of others. Having had his fingers and his tongue slapped as a little kid by godforsaken schoolmasters and by even more hopelessly godforsaken priests, just for having raised a few impertinent questions about basic matters, having been sent into the corner, into the darkness, where he learned to answer these questions by himself and achieve his own salvation in the process, he finds that he has the pusillanimity of his educators to thank for the smidgen of floating earth he now occupies in comfort and safe-keeping, though he remains constantly worried that his little island could someday simply melt away beneath the soles of his feet. This explains his penchant for metaphysics. "Oh," Nietzsche says, "if only someone could narrate the history of that exquisite feeling called loneliness!" Right here, dear reader, an attempt is being made in just that direction: a lonely Vigoleis among his friends on Mallorca, where he practiced reticence in the company of those friends, but not with his enemies. But after all, the Nazis were not humans. They placed themselves above humanity, thereby becoming bestial. That's what we had to watch out for.

Don Matías was my friend. We were one heart and one soul, and together we shared in divine concord the flour sacks at Jaume's bakery, thus transforming them into much more than the background and basic ingredient for the daily bread and Sunday *ensaimada* of our ongoing Spanish *tertulia*. We shook hands warmly and clapped the flour dust from each other's shoulders until no dust was left. But we never kissed each other—that kind of activity we left to the ardent members of the famous 18th-century Göttingen Poets' League back in Germany, whose antics were the subject of many of the stories I told Matías. We Brothers of the Flour Sacks loved freedom more than we loved each other. This was a satisfying type of bond, one that could hold its own against any other, and one whose third member was still Don Gracias a Dios, "Mr. Thank God," who in increasingly fervent ballads, and with increasingly copious shedding of tears, kept on lauding the goal of freedom for his Honduran pampas.

All of this took place one bread-shopping day after another, over the course of many such visits to the bakery. Then one day I noticed how Don Matías, after glancing straight at me, suddenly looked right through my eyes and off into the void behind me. This was a kind of ominous ocular legerdemain I had experienced a few times before, in particular in the presence of poets who were entering a state of inspirational bliss. Don Matías was also a poet, one who at times dealt with the ineffable, but I had never seen him go into a trance. He was, after all, an Iberian, and as such predestined not only to have moments of mystical afflatus, but to write about them too, as if they were the most natural thing in the world—just like Santa Teresa. Was his brother-in-law involved in an affair? And if so, was the lady going to enter his orphaned conjugal bed and, by the same token, fill the vacancy behind the bakery counter? Would Don Matías have to start teaching class again?

Mr. Thank God, too, was looking at me with the eyes of a cow, and this frightened me. His attitude completed the aura of misery that now filled the shop, with Matías sitting there on his sack, while at the same time he seemed somewhere off in the distance. My two friends kept staring straight ahead. With a gesture of petty-bourgeois neatness I brushed off my seat, then noticed too late that it was a sack of flour, so now I stood transfigured in a cloud of white dust. The three of us had departed the confines of earthly existence.

What had got into these guys? I could have asked them, but my accursed reticence prevented me from penetrating the mysterious silence. If we were truly friends and in league with each other, sooner or later they would have to start talking. So I sat down on my hundredweight of flour.

Was it some new worry? Had an emergency arisen in Honduras? Should I start offering them friendly consolation, seeing as where Germany was also undergoing an emergency? Was the savannah beckoning to them, at a time when these heroes were unable to girt sabers or display a banner of the peasant's revolt? Were they perhaps so downhearted because they lacked money for the ocean voyage? Was it Ulua? Had his gunpowder gone moldy? Was it Don Patuco? Had some over-zealous Christian faith-healer charmed his missing arm back onto his body, bringing a sudden end to his stumpy military prowess? And what about Pablo, Don Sacramento, alias El Enorme? Was he now behind bars as a ringleader of the Thälmann demonstration in downtown Palma?

The two fellows still sat there as if bewitched. Not a word. Not a single movement. Should I grab my bread and go home, leaving them to their fate? I stayed on, and began telling them the story of my advancement to the position of writing assistant to the German emigré Conde de Kessler. In the telling, I of course elevated my job title to that of Private Secretary. The old gentleman was writing his memoirs, I explained, and needed help mining the ores of language, and sometimes panning for golden words, and always in the context of world history. That's how I narrated my story—not entirely in accordance with the truth, since as Private Secretary I was sworn not to tell tales out of the scriptorium.

"Thank God" was the first one to pull his glance back from infinity and focus on the image of the Conde that I had conjured up, here among the flour sacks. Thank God that at least one of them was willing to see beyond the stars of his own destiny. In my narrative I soon recounted how Beatrice had baked especially for the Conde the Basel and St. Gall specialties *Biber* and *Leckerli*, pastries that I had sometimes asked Jaume to put in his oven for us. The mention of this brought Don Matías, too, back into the real world. He said, immediately *ad rem*, that the next time I brought around some of those *Totenbeinli* he would have to take a taste of them, seeing as some world-famous personage had liked them. But he added that he had never heard of this world-famous personage "Kessler." "How about you?" he asked, turning to Thank God, who had never heard of the fellow, either.

The patriots' memory obviously needed some prodding. It was impossible, I said, that they had never heard of the Conde de Kessler. That man's name was practically synonymous with Western culture; he had written a famous book about Mexico, and he had closed Nietzsche's eyelids not long after the philosopher opened them up to see him. All they had to do, I insisted, was poke around in their memory, and they would surely find this or that nugget, this or that event that now, set down on paper, was embedded in Kessler's recollections. And behold, it wasn't long before my two Hondurans began to see the light. Like a prestidigitator pulling a worm from some dupe's nose, I helped them along, and soon enough the renowned man's momentous achievements lay there in our midst. First of all, there was the Agadir Affair of 1911 or thereabouts, the first bolt of lightning on the political horizon, the first skirmish of the Wilhelminian War, the German panther's leap to Morocco, tension with England concerning the naval fleet, panic in the stock exchange, panic in the Louvre, where someone had stolen La Gioconda—a feat that certain newspaper pundits interpreted as an evil omen; unrest in Lisbon, unrest in Mahón, the largest naval port in the Mediterranean, where our General began feeling ever greater hunger for his favorite omelet dish. That was the moment when Count Harry Kessler first stepped upon the stage of world history!

Don Matías and Don Gracias a Dios now recalled these events with great clarity. The literary world, to which they both belonged, could never forget the famous letter of gratitude that Bernard Shaw had sent to the German count for having preserved the peace. They weren't aware that the letter was printed by Emery Walker—but I didn't know that, either. Kessler the patron of the arts, Kessler the discoverer of Aristide Maillol—lights were now flickering on among the flour sacks, and all eyes hung on my every word. Kessler was a thief? The fact that he liberated Pilsudski from the Magdeburg Fortress—that didn't make him into a thief, did it...?

Maillol had the "somewhat un-artistic" habit of chipping away at his statues after they were cast, which failed to improve them. Kessler once commissioned him to create a sculpture —as far as I can remember it was The Boxer—and he bribed the foundry manager. Before the artist could begin his late-term chipping, Kessler and his accomplices had the pouring form secreted out of the factory inside somebody's coat. In the Count's presence the statue was broken out of the form and taken to his apartment. When Maillol was told of the thievery, he was enormously upset. Kessler was immediately summoned. He put the Master at ease, took him home with him, and showed him a work of art that was exactly to his liking.

My Honduran revolutionaries were thrilled. Maillol, they cried, none other than Aristide Maillol must create Don Patuco's Statue of Freedom for the Plaza de la Liberdad in Tegucigalpa! On the day it gets unveiled, all of us, led by Kessler, would break open the form. "A cire perdue!" Don Matías interjected, and I said, "I'm amazed at all the things you know!" I of course offered my services as an emissary to the French sculptor through Kessler as intermediary. And once again, this time with his wrestling sweatshirt even tighter around his belly, Don Matías swore with a handshake that he would see to it that I was appointed Honduran Special Attaché for Occidental Freedom Movements and Monument Production. That very evening he would visit the general and give his report. Then came Kessler at the League of Nations, Kessler as the pioneer of bible-paper printing, the Grand-Duke Wilhelm-Ernst Editions—surely they had heard of these things? They had indeed. So now we discussed the prospect of Honduras' classics on bible paper, published exclusively by the Cranach Press—but hold on, for patriotic reasons there would have to be another name for it. I suggested Ediciones Maneta, "One-Armed Classics" in honor of Don Patuco.

Kessler's life and deeds filled the bakery. Down below, Jaume kneaded his bread loaves and shook his head—was he doubting our sanity or just shaking the sweat from his brow? The customers were serving themselves. There was a coming and going, until I started telling how Kessler (the Hondurans knew it already), dressed in a jailer's uniform with hitched-up collar (I used an empty flour sack to illustrate my story) and carrying a key-ring and a lantern, had freed Pilsudski in Magdeburg. A car bearing the Reich Imperial insignia was waiting outside, and together they sped off. Then the Polish general snuck like a ferret behind the Polish front. It was an action similar to the somewhat later one involving another Count, Schulenburg, who acted as intermediary for the same progressive Kaiser in allowing Lenin to sneak out of Switzerland and return to Russia.

During my thespian presentation of scenes from Kessler's World Theater, the bakery customers forgot that they had come to buy loaves of bread. The Hondurans conceded that there still might be important lessons to be learned from an otherwise contemptible European Continent for their own goals of national liberty. My personal prestige rose to gigantic proportions; all that was missing now was the accursed *pronunciamiento* in Tegucigalpa, and all of us—Ulua and Thank God; Sacramento; Conde de Kessler with his Private Secretary; Beatrice with her busted Unkulunkulu; Don Patuco and his chaste, immaculately conceived daughter as the prospective bride of Don Matías; Pedro Sureda with his nature-conservancy plans; his father, the collector Don Juan; Mr. Silverstar from Furzeburg; Ludwig Salvator's personal physician with his assistant Bobby—all of us would be setting out for Honduras on board a sleek caravelle. And Mamú? Well, Mamú would blow the financial winds into our sails with her Royal Baking Powder blessing, which surely was overdue to prove its culinary efficacy...

The Christian Science ladies would be left behind in their state of blind gullibility, until one day their beloved ersatz savior Hitler would have them all hanged as sub-Christians.

Flying off in advance of our barkentine would be Rabindranath as the Eagle of Liberty; Empedocles and Spinoza would be waiting inside their matchboxes for the swarms of insects on the Mosquito Coast.

No sooner had I ended my theatrical presentation when my two friends once again sagged down on their flour sacks and resumed their vacant staring. Were they seeing ghosts? I took my loaf of bread, paid up my real, and departed.

"Seeing ghosts?" said Beatrice. "You're just as crazy as those guys. It's got to be women!"

"Some Pilar, do you think?"

"Can't get any better."

It was in fact a Pilar who was behind all this, but a Pilar who was in the diplomatic service—that is to say, one who could act as a double agent of fermentation.

The world can collapse on account of women, some philosophers have maintained. But unfortunately, women can lift the world back up again.

At noon I met up again with the Honduran guerilla brothers on the Plaza Atarazanas. They had exchanged their flour sacks for chairs at a sidewalk café, and were sitting in the blazing sun—two melancholy patriots gearing up for a life in the tropics. Arsenal Square was depopulated; Pan's hour had already passed, but not a single *burro* was to be seen far and wide, not even a human being. And what were these guys drinking? Something was foaming up inside their glasses: milk of magnesia! That's good for the stomach. It can cause healthy elimination and help keep you in good cheer. On this urban square and at this hour of the day, the only discernable movements were the gastric ones inside Don Matías and Don Gracias a Dios.

"*Olá*, friend! *Olá*, friend!"

"*Olá*, my friends!"

I sat down with my friends, clapped my hands, ordered something that never came, and yet I was happy. The tables reminded me of Zwingli's ice-cream parlor and the whore Pilar. To start a conversation I said that round marble tables always led me to baleful thoughts. My two friends seemed to be reacting similarly, for they both cringed and, each in his own way, started moaning, "Eva! Eva!"

Two hours later I tried to offer Beatrice a triumphant explanation as to how I had maneuvered the proud Tegucigalpians into passive, blank-eyed silence. "And our bread?" asked Beatrice. "Where's our bread?" I had forgotten it. To be on the safe side, she decided to go fetch it herself, and I suggested that she take a short detour across the Plaza Atarazanas to see Eva's two victims cowering there, just like Rabindranath on the lawn in front of Mamú's chair, his head bent to one side, his beak bleached by the noontime heat, one eye looking up to the sky, the other down to the ground—the epitome of torpor. But Beatrice just wasn't interested. She was tired of stories about whores—*putas* over and over again, as if nothing else existed in Spain. I told her that this was just it: whores were the salt of the earth, and without them Spain would taste terribly bland. But I also excused her from listening to the story of this thousand-and-first Eva, for I knew I would find a more grateful listener in Pedro.

This was only half true, since Pedro had already made the acquaintance of Eva. But he hadn't collapsed, although this was the fate that appeared to be looming for the two Honduran rebels. A Sureda can conquer even the portals of a bordello. They are a very ancient family, with a resourceful woman to be espied at the blurry dawn of their history, with a quiver-bearing ferret in their coat of arms, and with the contentious family motto "Who will retrieve it?"

Eva was entertainment that occupied an entire evening. No wonder, said Pedro, considering that she displayed her abundant nudity at such a small *fonda*. And besides, it was always the same sets of eyes that were glued to her voluptuousness: Don Matías, Don Gracias a Dios, Don Sacramento, Ulua—in a word, all of Honduras.

"So you know the story?"

Pedro knew only Eva and her worshipers, among whom my bakery friends were the most devoted—that is, they had been, for Eva was now gone. Higher authorities had ordered her to get dressed and leave the island.

Too bad, but that's all I was able to get from my friend Sureda. He knew his half of the story better than I did mine. So I went to Mamú, who had the talent and an educated ear for risqué tales that revealed people as something slightly less than socially presentable. Especially now, for since her escapades with the biddies of Christian Science she cherished a calm immersion in a world that, with its off-color hues, reminded her of Vienna.

Mamú chuckled with delight at my story. I hadn't disappointed her. As a reward she promised me roast pigeon *à la Binisalem* for the coming Sunday, and for two weeks hence I requested roast suckling pig *à la broche*.

"And in return...?"

"You'll get the highly piquant tragedy of Adelfried Silberstern's latest sexual calamity."

Eva was entertainment that occupied an entire evening.

"Yes indeed, Mamú. 'Occupied' in the double sense of filling both the stage and the audience, and all the more effectively, since the two areas weren't separated by any kind of rood screen. Eva was much too gregarious a person to allow any such barriers to interfere. She needed to maintain touch with her artistic surroundings. But you mustn't imagine this scene as being similar to La Patti at your departed prince's Metropolitan Opera, or to La Gerstenberg as Maria Stuart at the Burgtheater. No, it was much smaller, Mamú, cozier, more intimate. She displayed herself at a certain Café Cantante on San Miguel Street. Completely undressed except for a bile-green powder puff pasted in front, some rouge on her backside, and around her neck a scapular that was stuck to her skin with tape, so that it stayed anchored to her bosom during her wildest dances. Spanish men love scapulars, and Eva was familiar with this form of etiquette. She sang and recited her own poems in French—not just doggerel, but profound lyric verse. I'm going to get some copies. They say that Eva was a second Vittoria Colonna, and behind the stage there was a back room, something with a curtain where she had her *pilarière*. She lay there resting during the intermissions in the company of her visions, or maybe with some aesthete who was interested in her visions and her poetry."

"During the performance? How exciting!"

"Oh no, Mamú. She never let anybody get close to her. Pedro told me so himself. It was all in the service of art for art's sake."

"*O, mon pauvre Vigolo!*"

"I'll put my hand in the fire for Eva, Mamú. If she had ever let anybody come near her, it would have meant the end of her career. She was always diplomatic. In this exposed position in the German diaspora she was working for the *Führer*."

I then told Mamú the whole story in every last detail. Rabindranath listened in, as did Mamú's pekingese. The two animals had long since concluded a truce, largely in consideration of their mistress' paradisaical park, which with the chattering of many budgerigars and pink parrots had taken on the aspect of a jungle. The official bird-tender was of course Vigoleis. But Mamú was piqued at Eva for failing to do the honors in her own Paradise, since basically Mamú was too immersed in her gilded Bible to imagine that there could be such a thing as an *Eva immaculata*, an unblemished woman on an unblemished bed of love *für Führer und Vaterland*. But then, Mamú was an American and a millionaire, born to bottomless riches, lacking tradition, spoiled by Vienna, and lifted up by her Hungarian dynast to a social rank that she deserved to attain in any case, without the aid of this special liaison.

A blind guitar player and a deaf tenor provided the musical background for Eva's performances. The singer never heard a note of what the guitar was playing, even though he bent down close to the instrument. This acoustically necessary form of acrobatics forced him to sing downwards toward the floor, instead of out into the audience or directly to the racy, shimmering chastity of the Special Female Envoy of the *Führer*. The guitar player, on the other hand, couldn't see what was going on around him, clothed or unclothed. He plucked away at his violent, melancholy *canto hondo*, his blank eyeballs focused on a blind spot which, if he had been able to see, was Eva's sickly-green powder puff. The audience, made up mostly of members of Don Patuco's circle, stayed on into the wee hours, and they, too, kept staring at this ominous green spot.

As a nude model Eva was, according to Pedro, *cojonudo*—we should probably use the more acceptable term "simply fabulous." But then again, things were not quite that simple. Pedro had a whole bevy of Evas, whose faces he rendered only in vague outline. Come to think of it, for any artist specializing in nudes, the model's face is irrelevant. Still, I could have used some more detailed information, since Eva is to be counted among my squandered opportunities.

A Jewish gentleman of German nationality had recently arrived on Mallorca from the Cape Colony to recuperate from a serious illness, and he intended to continue on to America on business. He was a diamond merchant. The German Shop sent him to me for political advice. He was very rich. Every word of his personal explanation was false, and he wasn't even in need of telling me anything. It was immediately clear to me that he had fled from the Cape Town Nazis, who were after his non-Aryan blood, but also after his diamonds. I advised him, free of charge, to leave the island as soon as possible, because just a few weeks ago a murder had taken place in Palma, a poisoning that was immediately hushed up. It took place in a lithograph studio, a place that contained enough bottles decorated with skull and crossbones to dispatch whole crowds of human beings into the Great Beyond. The police were conveniently silent ("Who needs overtime?") about this matter, which was connected with the sinister machinations of the Nazis on the island. The Jewish gentleman told me, not without a measure of boasting, that he had a sufficient supply of English pounds on his person to buy out the entire island and send the Nazis packing. This was, of course, one more reason for him to skedaddle. I had no idea, I told him, how much his life was worth, but it would be a shame if the thugs were to get hold of all that sterling in the bargain. "Take the very next ship! It'll be sailing in just a few hours!" It was only natural that I started cursing the Germans who were letting Hitler get away with all kinds of mischief, and letting the whole world know how proud they were of it. The gentleman objected to my insinuations against his fatherland—I was to understand that he still regarded himself as a German. Before 1933 he was never aware that he was a Jew. In his heart—that is, underneath the thick wad in his *porte-monnaie*—he was first and foremost a German. What was the German Consul like, he asked. Not the type who ate Jews for breakfast, I told him; he had nothing to fear on that account. Whereupon this German petty chauvinist with a heart of diamond returned to his hotel.

A few days later he was just where the Nazis wanted him. "Suicide," the police declared. But they weren't really convinced of this, and began snooping around, since not only the foreigner's life, but also his money was missing. It wasn't long before they detected in this affair the heady fragrance of Eva's sweat. They decided to conduct a fully-clothed investigation of this naked item of Teutonic public relations, and they soon discovered that a woman can conceal an abundance of charms within her own wardrobe. Having duly inspected and disinfected her green puff, the bailiffs said, "All right, get dressed, we're taking you downtown!" Dressed or not, she was surrounded. The officers of the famous Spanish Civil Guard never cracked a smile, not even when they took her on board ship. Two more officers appeared at the quay in Barcelona. Again there were no smiles, and this is how it went through the various stages of the journey. Up in France, Eva again got the chance to display her puff on behalf of the *Führer*. The Spaniards were delighted to be rid of a spy and poisoner.

"Eva" was her *nom d'artiste*, her Second Aspect. Her green powder puff was an ineffectual disguise for her primary occupation, which consisted in ecstatic moaning and groaning underneath the *almocrebe*s and *picadores* at the "Clock Tower." "My goodness, these guys are good!" she used to say. "If my husband ever found me here...!"

In keeping with her policy of patriotic lubricity, her husband never got to see her practicing the horizontal profession at the Clock Tower or at the tasco cantante. Her husband stayed on in Essen. Over time, his nervous breakdowns gave way to a total recovery of sheer nerve, which he placed in the service of the fatherland. His personal motto: Guns, not butter.

Oh, my beloved Kathrinchen! How I would love to have shared just once the secret confines of your *pilarière*, just once touched your green spot!

"You mean her *brown* spot, don't you?" Mamú said. "But you never would have done it."

Mamú was right. This Frau Doktor worked shamelessly for the *Führer*.

The very first time Don Matías attended one of Eva's nude dances, his heart was sold. Likewise Don Thank God, for whom the green puff became a blind spot in his character, which tended toward enthusiasm to the point of patriotic enfeeblement. Fate, once again in the shape of an Eve in full heat, had seized hold of these two fellows, so much so that they put their own fiancées out of heart and mind. For them, the world revolved around the first female *homo sapiens*. Don Matías was her chosen partner. His lame leg gave him certain advantages behind the curtain. "Thank God" would stoop down in front of this curtain and start suffering. In his mind's eye, he saw his friend Don Matías just as I myself see him, with bloodshot eyes and with his bum leg drawn up part-way onto the *pilarière* where she is lying. His brows are aflame, his hands are steamy and moist, the better to leaf through Eva's poetry manuscripts, the very texts that Don Matías was intending to translate and publish.

Would Vigoleis have reclined differently next to this verdant meadow? Would his temples have pulsed less feverishly? Would his hands have been less moist as he turned the pages of her scrapbook? His eyes, too, would have leapt from their sockets, and he too would not have noticed that he was being spied upon. Like Don Matías, he would have unpacked in every detail his dealings with the traitor Don Vigo from the General's Street, the guy who just happened to be Count Harry Kessler's secretary. Nobody who sees red when he sees green would have been aware that this lady in the shimmering white skin was entering all this information in a separate scrapbook. Like Don Matías, I would have been thinking: my God, during intermission she writes poetry! She's a naked, unblemished instrument of Eternity!

When I again met up with the two thwarted suitors on the Plaza Atarazanas, they were purging their sorrow with milk of magnesia. On the previous evening, Eva had been deported to Barcelona. When Don Matías limped behind the Spanish screen, her *pilarière* was empty. The blind bard was strumming his lyre, the deaf tenor was singing his gargled flamenco. There was no audience at all, for nothing was left on the stage to focus on. Thus the musicians had plenty of time to rehearse; surely it would now be possible to harmonize the lyrics with the strumming of the guitar.

Don Matías gradually recuperated in the bakery from the damage to his heart perpetrated by the *Führer*'s blonde beast. Once again he returned to philosophy, insofar as it was obtainable on paper, to Honduran political topics, and to his Honduran fiancée. This woman, who did not possess any visible green powder puffs, was still busy embroidering the banner for the *pronunciamiento*. I eventually learned that Eva had quizzed her adoring acquaintance about my humble person. With a gesture of desperation he beat his brow, and said he had been a traitor. I salved his conscience by asserting that Kessler was fully able to take care of himself, and that as far as my own welfare was concerned, surely he was aware that I had no intention of keeping the sensational secret with which Eva surrounded herself. He must not forget, I told him, that I regarded Hitler as a gangster from the very first day of his regime, and that I had always acted accordingly. Furthermore, he mustn't forget that as a student I had given a whole lot of attention to criminal psychology, next to theology the field that was my world and my underworld. It was only natural for the Nazis to think that someone who curses the *Führer* so openly must have some organization behind him. Who is he spying for? Goering? Goebbels? Hess? Any of the above, each of whom would love to see the others hanging on the gallows?

Intellectual feats of this kind, rather amazing for Vigoleis, actually saved our lives. On separate occasions I was able to play one criminal against another, in Spain, in Switzerland, and especially later in Portugal. That's why the stupid Huns in my home town haven't been able to bury me in one of their Stone Age sepulchers.

Don Matías was grateful. He shook my hand, and we looked each other squarely in the eye. His own eyes were aflame with memories of the Honduran savannahs, yet at times obscured by the insect swarms that the winds brought to the Mosquito Coast. But what was Don Matías seeing as he peered into my eyes, and through them into the bottom of my soul? Following one of our conversations about Germany's decline, he told me that inside my pupils he could see the gigantic menhirs of the distant Nordic past—tombs of the Huns. I stopped him short: "Please, Don Matías, if you value our friendship—no Huns! No Huns, because the time when the cemeteries will be full to bursting with cadavers, as in your *espronceda*, is already on the march. I can already hear the tramping of the rosy feet of the twilight of the idols."

One week after Eva's deportation from our island paradise, someone broke into our apartment.

XX

If the captain of the *Ciudad de Palma* wasn't still swinging in his hammock *pilarière* below the bridge with his lover, a personage who without fail had an astatic effect on the compass needle (as was carefully explained to me by my battiest pupils, William and Charles Batty, compass adjusters for the British Fleet during the Wilhelminian War), then the ship would be tying up at seven o'clock at the Palma wharf. By eight o'clock, our apartment bell would let us know who had come across the Mediterranean, and for what purpose.

On the stroke of eight the bell rang. Was it our milkman? A telegram from Herr Silberstern asking to be rescued from an erotic cul-de-sac? Nina trying to escape from Silberstern's sexual advances? Count Kessler fleeing from my double Thälmann? An emigré? The Dutch writer Marsman, who was expected any day now?

It was Zwingli, our absconded Melanchthon ("black-earth man") and Oekolampadius ("house illuminator," also baptized as "Martinus"), alias Don Helvecio.

Yet it wasn't he who was standing at our door—not yet, anyway. It was only his shadow, which he had sent ahead in the shape of a muscular guy, who now asked me if I was Don Vigo. When I said yes, he pointed to the dark stairwell and said that all the stuff belonged in our apartment, plus everything that was down below. Before I could ask him who sent the stuff, I was pushed aside. "Sent?" Our Don Helvecio of the Príncipe was back again, he said, and ordered me to lend a hand. "There, that box. It's got books in it. He's starting up a university."

No sooner had I uttered the word "Jeez!" when Beatrice came and said, "Jeez! It's not Zwingli, is it?"

"Who else? Heaven is once again being merciful, sending our prodigal brother back into our arms. Open up the box."

"But I don't understand this at all. Why has Zwingli come back to Spain, and why us?"

"Probably to make sure that the coast is clear, as you told him in your telegram."

"Well, he's my brother, after all."

"And that makes him my brother-in-law—maybe not officially, but in a definite moral sense. He takes lots of stuff with him when he travels—it's probably an Inca family trait. You know, whole caravans of buffalo. Your forebears weren't cheapskates. I'll bet you that he's also got some woman camp follower along with him, a suitcase full of homeopathic antidotes, and a valise full of Künzli tea for bathing in. His new amante is probably downstairs right now, putting on some rouge, and if we're in for a really bad break, she's putting some on her behind."

But Zwingli had arrived unaccompanied. His pockets jangled with cash, and his get-up was pure haute couture, custom-fit by Barcelona's leading haberdasher. His pinky nail was clean and polished to an impressive shine. It was Don Helvecio in person. For the trip from Barcelona he had reserved a first-class cabin for himself, but on the way over, out of sheer love of neighbor, he had shared it with a female French painter.

"*Olá*, Beatrice, Bice, Bé! *Olá, mon* Vigo, Vigoleis, Vigolo!"

So here he was, now with an even more probing nose, with shinier black hair, with the familiar fiery look in his eyes, and once again with a sack full of moola. In his current condition he could easily convert his guttologist grandfather's staunchest opponents to the homeopathic faith. Professor Scheidegger had given back to our island a detoxified Zwingli. Such de-pilarization is surely one of the most impressive feats of this medical discipline—on a par, as far as I can judge, with Beatrice's rescue from the bubonic plague.

Brother and sister, both of them living witnesses to the efficacy of a much-maligned science, now embraced each other and shared a microbe-free kiss. The Old Testament and its legendary scourges were a thing of the past. I was deeply moved by the scene—I, who grew up in a little house where we had the mumps or chicken pox and could never afford the services of a university professor. We had to make do with the ministrations of a pious local medical flunky, a fellow who in some cases actually achieved success, but whose allopathic itemized bills did their best to wipe out our recovered sense of well-being. Incidentally, this sawbones was the first extortionist whose connivances

I was able to study from early childhood on. As I got older, he liked to converse with me in Latin—to the horror of my father, who, lacking formal education, realized right away that this technique of healing by means of academic discourse would cost him a pretty penny. And indeed it did.

Zwingli inquired about my literary activity and Beatrice's music—how were things going? "Badly? And you don't have a telephone yet? Well, it's good that I'm back. All that will change now. But tell me, Bé, have you got anything to eat?"

The two of them had switched roles. Beatrice had asked her brother the very same question on that morning of our arrival on the Island of the Great *Puta*.

Besides a wad of money, Zwingli brought with him a whole set of new plans. Naive as I am, and easily hoodwinked by the mysterious ways people attain the ownership of hard cash, I asked him to open his wallet. It was chock full of Swiss francs!

"What's happened? Did you submit your godmother to another blood-letting?"

Zwingli's godmother had the reputation of being Basel's highest taxpayer, a desirable acquaintance in a city of more than 400 multimillionaires, no matter what they looked like underneath their gilded apparel. I never knew her, but I was told that she was not only rich but attractive, though not without a proclivity for shady dealings of the sort that can never be proved when multimillionaires are concerned. This aunt of his had financed his de-pilarization, thus offering her services to science and bringing off another of the philanthropic achievements for which she was well known. We need only mention the pesticide DDT. But now, Zwingli said, it was all over with, and he screwed up his *conquistador* nose in fretful wrinkles. There wasn't one *Fränkli* more to be had from that source, not even one *Räppli! Fini!* When a millionaire snaps her purse shut, there's no way in the world to get her to open it again except—money.

I always admired Zwingli. He was a genius. But he never really understood millionaires. I'm not so sure that my own understanding of them is the correct one, and I'm willing to wait until I can test it out on myself. But I had one advantage over Zwingli: I didn't know a single millionaire. Count Kessler had at one time been one, and Mamú would, we were hoping, be one once again. So we can ignore these two personages. Hence I had an untrammeled perspective on such individuals who, if I understood correctly a lecture I heard in Cologne by the economic historian Professor von Wiese und Kaiserswaldau, were to be regarded as having the mental capacities of boyish pranksters. Later I would have the opportunity to show Zwingli that my economic theory, scraped up during my exposure to three different academic departments, was right on the mark.

Zwingli had earned all his dough in Cologne, Amsterdam, Brussels, and Paris, all of it *en passant*. The bulk of it came from an American art collector. Zwingli had given this man a few tips and taken him from one art dealer to another, and in Brussels was able at the last minute to dissuade him from taking a phony Cranach back across the Atlantic. When this Yankee boarded ship at Le Havre, he simply left his little Opel standing at the wharf. "Take it!" he shouted down to his Swiss interpreter, who acted without hesitation and later sold the vehicle in Barcelona using the same underhanded tactics as when he smuggled it across the border. I, who lack the courage—or am simply too proud—to sneak a pack of cigarettes across any border—I admired Zwingli.

He unpacked his gifts. Books, more books, and sheet music, still more books, and still more sheet music. Knowing my predilection for the *enfants terribles* of Church history, he presented me with an exquisite anthology of the Spanish mystics: Santa Teresa in an old, unannotated edition, causing me to give forth a full-throated *"Porra!"* Beatrice's only comment was, *"Buschibuëb!"* And that was saying a lot.

Zwingli inspected our apartment and decided he wanted the two rooms looking out on the street. *"Bei Chrut und Uchrut,"* he swore, this place was just what he needed.

"For what? Are you going to stay on the island?"

"On the island, in Palma, and here with you. It's not the snazziest address, this pirate's street of yours, but *enfin*, it'll do just fine as the germinal cell of the General Secretariat of my International Academy of Art History. Later we'll move somewhere else."

"Not a bordello? Professor Scheidegger has fixed you up so well for new mattress escapades that your General Secretariat will turn out to be the waiting room for what's more like you: a School of Lust."

No, said Zwingli. He would never touch a woman again. But he had something special for stick-in-the-mud Vigo. He showed me a briefcase, causing me to emit gurgles of pleasure. "Guanaco leather? Genuine? My guess is it cost 5000 pesetas."

"300 francs. Llama, Zurich, Bahnhofstrasse. Since you're a connoisseur, you can keep it. But it's not the briefcase—it's the contents that are important."

This was the Zwingli of olden times talking, when he regarded women as sexless entities, apparatuses to be manipulated, objects to be placed on the shelf according to their beauty and practicality. He was charming, clever, generous. If necessary he'd give you the shirt off his back. But if the shirt turned Isabella-brown, it was all over with him.

This briefcase contained packets of herbal tea, blends for every age and sex, all bearing the Künzli trademark, and in addition the bearded pastor Künzli's magnum opus Chrut und Uchrut. Zwingli was now frequenting all possible paths of rejuvenation. He no longer smoked. I'm always amazed when someone says, "No thanks, I don't smoke." He still had his expensive Chinese cigarette case, and as he passed it to us I was forced to say, "No thanks, unfortunately I'm still a non-smoker." (But because my metabolism doesn't get rid of the nicotine in our food, every once in a while I get an injection of nicotine. That explains the word "unfortunately"). Beatrice was allowed to keep the cigarette case.

Now reconciled in the most heartwarming fashion, brother and sister together drank some brew from their mountainous homeland. I stayed with wine, but at the risk of offending Zwingli I offered a toast to the famous philanthropic Swiss herbophile Künzli. Not that I meant any offense to that pious fellow, either. On the contrary, I have a high regard for the man as a man.. it's just that I don't like his tea. If all the theologians had given their attention to the flowers and the grasses instead of God, Christianity would never have gone to the dogs. To be a specialist in herbs, one must harbor an abundance of love for nature and its Creator; one must possess an uncomplicated mind, a willingness to serve one's fellow man, a generosity of spirit, and humility. Humility above all, which can merge into genuine modesty. Perhaps one in a million clergymen goes off into the forest to collect herbs; the others prefer to stay in church. To this very day, I prefer wine to herbal tea, although I am willing to concede that when administered correctly, herbal tea can make just about anything disappear, beginning with gallstones and extending to evil thoughts. The mystic Albert Talhoff has very good reasons for lacing his tobacco with a pinch of Künzli tea. But he keeps his posological secrets to himself.

An hour later some workmen arrived. Plaster fell down from our walls. Our apartment echoed to the sounds of labor and hearty curses. Zwingli's nail gave the commands. Everything was new, everything was nicely matched with everything else. Though he lacked a woman, Zwingli had culture. The desk, the bookcases, the filing cabinet, the divan that with a simple mechanism could be transformed into a *pilarière*—every item was from the Vienna Workshop and paid for in cash.

Yet another hour later more workmen arrived. More plaster fell from our walls, but this time they brought with them office machines for typing, calculating, copying. Plus one of those little, gaudily decorated strongboxes in Emmanuel style. Just the thing for my posthumous manuscripts! And everything paid for in cash.

Had Zwingli bought the bogus Cranach himself and then shoved it on to some museum for a cool million? Before our expert could offer some comment along these lines, the doorbell rang again. It wasn't more workmen, just a man. All alone, short, limping, and dirty: Don Darío.

Yes, good reader, it was one and the same Don Darío from the Príncipe, Don Helvecio's personal spokesman, the crippled goad to his virility, the originator of the winged words about a man having to stand up like a man to avoid falling down; the anarchist who had been tossed out of the Conde's gunpowder chamber, the sworn enemy of the Pope and all of God's black-robed subalterns; the owner of a bullfighting arena in Felanitx; the political schemer, the man who swore bloody revenge on the banker Juan March. It was the man, in a word, who was everything but a martyr to his wardrobe. Just to imagine that I almost missed out on this character! This book of mine has grown in size; chapter has followed upon finished chapter. But Don Darío has been seemingly reluctant to submit his person to my chronicling research. Just a while ago I promised my reader to stage a special parade in which he would appear in the festive get-up of his filthiest suit, a set of duds to which I might attach a fleck of Juan March's blood as a decoration *Pour le mérite*, the highest order issued by the Mallorcan vendetta.

Well, here he finally is, a latecomer, just in time. His murderous intentions haven't mollified his awkward limp, but you can easily read them in his glistening eyes, as always just visible behind his permanently fogged-up pince-nez. He is given a cup of coffee, and straightaway he spills it. He smokes a clumsily rolled cigarette, and lets the dropping embers burn holes in his pants, his underpants, and his skin. He refers to this behavior proudly as his own form of Inquisition, a quest for liberty, backed up by a sizeable bank account—though decidedly not one at Juan March's bank.

Beatrice would never touch Don Darío with a ten-foot pole. Happily, she didn't even have to try, for Don Helvecio had his rooms in a part of the house that was several flea-jumps away from ours. Don Darío had fleas, too. And because there is nothing in the world more infectious than these animals, Beatrice was already imagining that her beloved Zwingli was scratching himself again. "No doubt it's typhus," she said. "Just you wait."

The two gentlemen slunk around like conspirators inside the lavishly furnished General Secretariat, making obscure remarks to each other. At my inquiry as to what they were planning, and what my function might be in their International University, I received a reply that sounded like a rebuke: "First we're going to get legally incorporated. Then things will start up." It was Zwingli who made this announcement. Don Darío seconded his partner's plan, and added, almost like a command, that they would start out by testing the utility of certain inventions—"Let's see your list!"

My hour had arrived!

I brought them the list of all my inventions, which by now had grown to considerable length. From my doodad for factory outlet shops to my revolutionary thingamabob for book production, it contained a broad display of possibilities for a company with limited liability and unlimited resourcefulness.

Wielding a silver automatic pencil, Don Darío checked over everything. Far-sighted businessman that he was, he crossed out anything he "felt rather sure" had already been invented—which is how he expressed himself, probably to avoid offending me. He didn't know me, my notions concerning creativity, or my lyrical tendency toward excessive modesty. In short, he didn't know Vigoleis. Nevertheless, quite a few items remained on the list; apparently my inventive vein hadn't dried up like Zwingli's godmother's largesse. I recommended that the Sociedad Anónima test out my idea for an adhesive writing tool, a gizmo that today is known the world over as a "ball-point pen" and can be had for one Mark. A soda bottle with its neck broken off just below the stopper gave me the idea of having a spherical stopper rotate inside the point of the pen, an economical way of supplying ink. To Beatrice's amazement, I succeeded in scribbling something on our whitewashed apartment wall using the bottle. But Don Darío and Don Helvecio were skeptical. My ink-delivering sphere, they opined, would be practical only as a micro-mechanism, and such tiny balls were impossible to manufacture. So—cross it out; it's only a toy; we are a serious enterprise. I insisted on the practicality of my invention. What were the advantages of an adhesive pen? I explained to the terrorist that it could be used to write under water, based as it was on the principle of adhesion. All that was necessary was waterproof ink and waterproof paper—essential materials for anarchists who suddenly are forced to submerge. Pearl fishers, coral divers, or sponge gatherers could calmly take notes under water; victims of shipwrecks could preserve their diaries. There were hundreds of possible applications above and beyond traditional handwriting, which was in itself a strong recommendation for my invention.

"Cross it out. Typical German *pobretería*!" Likewise my self-watering flower pot, my compressed-air bicycle wheel spoke, my Unkulunkulu, my Kwik-Stitch Wheel, my fluorescent typewriter platen for composers of late-night love letters, my zippered envelope—these all got crossed out. My city map with electrical direction indicator? Don Darío swung his pince-nez and asked me to explain this contraption. The unlimited entrepreneurs suddenly came alive. Zwingli went out on the balcony and whistled to a passing beggar boy: "Wine, coffee, on the double!" Coins bounced on the street below. Using a hotplate, he brewed himself some ascetic tea. I delivered my report, drew some sketches, and demonstrated my technical brilliance down to the last detail, before I let the wine plunge me into the ecstatic notion of possessing millions as a result of what these two coldly calculating businessmen would accomplish with my invention.

Some months later, the first automatic city map in the world was hanging on the wall at the Café Alhambra. And the world didn't even observe a moment of silence, as happens at the grave of even the most unknown soldier. The Spaniards up on the terrace kept on drinking their *café negro*, kept on playing billiards, and kept on gabbing about their whores. The famous writers kept on writing their undying works: Marsman, Kessler, Keyserling, Helman, Graves, Miomandre, Don Gracias a Dios, Martersteig, Franz Blei, Verdaguer, Bernanos... But why list them all, when there were countless more of them? Down below, the nameless inventor stood in constant awe of the streets, squares, department stores, and touristic sights of all sorts that he illuminated with the press of a button. The commercial circles of Palma had given generous support to this installation. Any business that wished to appear progressive rented a little square on the electric board, and was given its own little lamp within the maze of the city plan. The legal rights to the invention had already been sold to Barcelona, Madrid, and Buenos Aires. Why varnish the truth in a book that, like any set of memoirs, stands or fall with truth itself? Vigoleis' pockets never received a single centimo. To be sure, the two crafty entrepreneurs didn't cash in millions, either. But many, many thousands of pesetas flowed into their Emmanuel-style strongbox.

The company and its owners flourished, especially once they intuited that all they had to do was pour wine—and let it be said to his shame, not always the best vintage—down Vigoleis' inventive gullet. Each time, the result was a copious flow of ideas, in confused abundance. I shall spare my reader further details, considering that it would require another bottle of wine to continue the list, and considering that my inventive ideas have never even yielded enough cash to buy ink for setting them down on paper. How much might Hitler have paid me directly in 1939 for my U-boat respirator? And would Don Darío, with his benighted entrepreneurship, have crossed out my adhesive pen if I had described its practical applications more accurately within the framework of the real world?

The company flourished, and its owners flourished, while Beatrice and Vigoleis kept on starving. Beatrice with her Lladó, Vigoleis with his mystics.

Like every self-respecting Spanish male, Don Darío hated the clergy, the priests, as the source of all that was evil in Iberia. He asked me to invent a gallows that would dispatch a cassocked felon in a single stroke. I referred him to my fellow countrymen in the Third Reich, who were now the experts in mass executions. A postcard to the *Führer* would suffice. I told Don Darío that the clergy were not my favorite people, either, those sinister mercenaries of the Lord, trained in fanaticism from childhood on, and woe to anybody who refuses to accept the faith! And yet, basically these fellows were just poor dolts with very little income, unless you totted up the not inconsiderable wherewithal they raked in on the side with their brothels, their bullfight arenas, and their schools—which in many cases were schools for scandal. But why string them up? They contributed a great deal to the country's picturesque image, and were thus invaluable for the tourist trade. Don Darío viewed them, of course, as more than just minions of the Almighty who went around handing out blessings, or just as shrewd businessmen who waylaid his own commercial schemes. Oh, if only all the clergymen in Spain would stick to cultivating the above-named activities—how harmless they would be! Then there would never have been an Inquisition, today there would be no General Franco, and God's Creation would belie its most painful contingency that allows life to go on only at the cost of other lives. God, conceived of as a monster—it's an idea that outside of the Book of Job I have found confronted frankly only in the writings of Pascoaes. In any case, I prefer mercantile priests, thieving priests, and whoring priests, men who can do fuller and more appealing justice to the idea of God's inscrutability, to the sanctimonious vultures and craven cowards who see in each and every human being nothing more than a child of the Devil.

Still, neither in Spain nor later in Portugal did I ever succeed in persuading the witch-hunters that a curate or an abbot commits less mischief if he goes about his work in the interest of financial creditors rather than the souls of the faithful. Would the pastor in my home town ever have driven my politically naive mother, a member of the Catholic Mothers' Society, into the arms of the *Führer* if he had gathered herbs on Süchteln Heights, if he had been a partner in the local railway enterprise or, more attractive still, owned the little corner cathouse? He was fanatically devoted to God and the Fatherland, and that's how he brought about the downfall—not of the Creator, but of his local congregation.

Don Darío regarded my theory as, quite simply, bonkers. Soon enough the Spanish Civil War taught him a lesson. Or rather, it was then too late, even for Don Darío. On his suit he sported not the blood of his ecclesiastical and secular enemies, but his own. He was brutally murdered.

I wrote and wrote, invented and invented. I constructed models, played at being a Wustmann describing Peoples and Fatherlands, and during sleepless nights longed inconsolably for my hour of death. Beatrice practiced and practiced at her Lladó, so persistently that I began thanking my lucky stars that she wasn't a soprano. And she read and read, and gave lessons, and mended and cleaned. What she was wishing for was not her death or money, not a hat from the Casa de Modas run by the German with hay fever, not some delectable porcupine dish. No, what she longed for was to hear Vigoleis finally giving his imprimatur to some product of his pen, instead of tossing it into the stove or on the manure pile. During all this time Zwingli did nothing at all, and yet of the three of us, he was the one who kept raking in the money. Certain of my inventions achieved success, but that didn't put any dough in my pocket. For that to happen, I would have to have come up with some specialized manufacturing techniques, and my inventive genius didn't carry that far. Every creative person is familiar with this defect; it's the one that all the parasites cash in on, and it's an age-old conundrum among the academic theologians.

Still and all, every day we had tropical fruit to eat. Zwingli saw to it that our bowls didn't remain empty. Before this period when he acted as our "house illuminator," I had often felt nostalgia for my days in Cologne, when with my monthly allowance I was able to buy a single orange each day, and sometimes even a banana, at a particularly friendly greengrocer's stand. In Spain we usually couldn't afford such things. Lemons were very expensive. Tropical fruit is a bargain when you can steal it directly from the tree. Once packed in crates, it gets affordable only after it crosses the borders. I had similar experiences in Portugal. Pineapple from Madeira for a song, whereas figs from the Algarve or grapes from the Douro were a luxury. Nevertheless, Zwingli was earning enough from my *pobreterías* to overcome the prevailing economic tensions. He himself liked Swiss cheese, the real kind that you can obtain in Switzerland only if you have the right connections at Parliament.

Our communal accommodations with my genius brother-in-law went along swimmingly. He did honor to his nickname "Oekolampadius". Wherever he went, he beamed forth like a lamp into the darkness. There were no womenfolk to steal his light from us, and the dirt carried into our house by Don Darío stayed in the streetside rooms.

Zwingli kept busy planning the foundation of his Academy. His card files were filling up, and *"Buschibuëb"* kept bringing home various island fruits such as apricots, which were normally reserved for the finest kind of pig swill. Our stock of Künzli tea never ran out. Wherever one looked, it was a scene of peace and concord. It was as if the word *puta* had been struck from our dictionary. Don Darío had his own *putas*, but we never got to see them. In this he was being discreet, like any Spaniard.

But one day this limping exploiter of my inventions arrived in an advanced state of anger. What was wrong? Had some priest stolen my idea for a rolling bordello, and then gone ahead and constructed one? Were my wagons already coursing through the Mallorcan countryside? Had some cardinal snuck away without paying his hotel bill? Had Count Keyserling, the hotel's most lavish resident, driven away guests he himself had attracted to the establishment by putting his "joviality" on excessive display? But no, it was only an American millionaire who had enraged my putative business partner. Upstairs at the hotel in his luxury-class rooms, this American millionaire was himself choking with rage at a damned stupid little Spaniard with a pince-nez and a mild limp.

Don Darío was sitting at his reception desk, calculating how much he had earned at his most recent bullfight, how much he would earn later by mobilizing his German inventor, how much he had lost through his most recent lover, and how much he would have to invest in his future lovers. Then he looked up from his ledger, and somebody approached the desk. "*Porra!* That's going too far!" And it was happening, so to speak, in his own house. He stands up and limps into the foyer, dragging his left leg behind him. There follows a moment of stasis, as the weight of his body rests solely on its right-leg support acting as a axle for the left; his left leg swings forward with an almost merry abandon, causing his body to jerk forward with what one might refer to as a step.

The American guest with the million-dollar bank account proceeds across the foyer with a mild limp. He explains that he has come to Palma for the express purpose of hearing a lecture by Keyserling and to watch Keyserling eat a meal—two talents that this epicurean philosopher loved to display in public. Now the Yankee culture-vulture is limping through the foyer; he is dragging his right leg. There follows a moment of stasis, during which the weight of his body rests solely on its left-leg support acting as an axle for the right; his right leg swings forward with an almost merry abandon, causing his body to jerk forward with what one might refer to as a step.

Don't make fun of foreigners' infirmities. This maxim holds equally for Spaniards and Americans. Don Darío was incensed when he saw the American imitating his *leve cojera* as if he had rehearsed it down to the finest detail— *caramba!* The American was incensed when he saw the Spaniard imitating his "slight limp" as if he had rehearsed it down to the finest detail. "Damnation!" The two impersonators met in the middle of the foyer, facing each other at the static points they had in common. All the rest was a flurry of curses, each making use of a language that was incomprehensible to the other, just as each had made use of his respective language to mock the other's physical impairment.

The hotel's reputation was now at stake, as well as the lives of the two game cocks. But salvation arrived at just the right moment, in the form of a gigantic man with crimson complexion, the eyes of a Kalmuk, a scraggly beard, and the paws of a longshoreman. This man stepped between the two combatants. With his right hand he grabbed the Spaniard, with his left the American. But instead of banging their heads together, which they actually deserved, he held them far apart and let them dangle in the air until he finished his discurso in Spanish and his speech in English. As cultured gentlemen, the both of them should be ashamed of themselves, he told them. Weren't they both lame enough as a result of their common affliction? This was spoken wisely; a philosopher wouldn't have handled the situation any more effectively—except perhaps Count Keyserling, whose savvy about human nature exceeded even that of Kessler with his *Peoples and Fatherlands*. Kessler would have let the two disputants mow each other down with their good legs. Indeed, he wouldn't even have looked up from his manuscript if he had been working on his memoirs in the foyer of the Príncipe. Keyserling was different. He felt it was his obligation to reconcile these representatives of the Old and the New World, a deed that he in fact accomplished, as we have just seen. The scales immediately fell from the eyes of the Spaniard and the American. Getting sight of each other's bum legs, they suddenly realized that they were both cripples. Keyserling, the founder of the School of Wisdom, had of course noticed this right away, and immediately caught scent of the bottle of wine that would be his reward for concluding the peace treaty.

The philosopher returned to his own hotel in a light-hearted mood, still grinning at the victory he had won on General Barceló Street, in the apartment of a nameless emigré, over his old schoolmate Harry Kessler. The man from Darmstadt had put the Weimaraner against the wall, and Harry had yielded to Hermann. "A gentleman's agreement" is how the philosopher characterized the détente they had reached. The diplomat saw it differently: it was pure swindle, he said. A thousand pardons, but it was nothing but fraud.

Count Hermann Keyserling may have been mistaken about Count Kessler, but not about the limping Don Darío. The latter ordered for a him a bottle of wine and a plate of roast turkey.

Zwingli loved his godmother very much, and that is why he begged money from her even at times when he didn't really need any. Psychologically speaking, this was a perfectly correct behavior. When someone's godmother is a millionaire and he doesn't keep asking her for more, that someone will soon come under suspicion of being either hypocritical or a legacy-hunter. Most cases of disinheritance can be traced to clumsy manners on the part of the potential heir. Excessive modesty awakens suspicion. Regular minor blood-lettings, coupled with the wholesale transfusions that become necessary from time to time, are the only way to win the heart of the potential deceased, especially when the potential beneficiary is aware that he can't be counted among the heirs who simply drop out of the sky post mortem. This was the sunny side of Zwingli's case. The side turned away from the sun had to do with certain events that still today can make half a dozen faces in Switzerland turn to stone as soon as anyone starts talking about them, even merely as elements in a historical narrative. Every family has its shady spots, and it was by reaching into this foggy, tenebrous realm that Zwingli made the sparks fly. And then one thing led to another.

On a particular fateful day he again put the bite on his godmother in a letter to Switzerland. I'm calling this day a fateful one because the tiny cross that you find on some old calendars indicating "good for bloodletting" had apparently been misplaced, astrologically speaking. The result: Zwingli received a registered letter written by someone else on his godmother's behalf, in German but with numerous offenses against the grammatical and orthographical rules—a type of *gaucherie* that I suppose a millionaire can easily afford, though I myself am wont to let Wustmann off his leash for much pettier misdemeanors. *Mais enfin*, the letter's message was clear. Zwingli cussed loudly in all of the languages at his disposal. His Lexicon of Invective came through brilliantly on this occasion, but the Swiss *Idiotikon*, which in this case was being virtually thrown at him, was not a book that he could simply ignore. I read the letter. With my mystical intuitions, which can also be brought to bear on financial matters, I immediately realized the ramifications of this handwritten ukase, a document that seemed to be a harbinger of the Last Will and Testament that would someday arrive.

Zwingli had lost a battle. The power residing in his pinky nail was thwarted. What was to be done?

I elucidated for him my theory of how to keep other people's property in your own pocket, that is, the concept of capitalism as midwife-toad. It was easy for me to develop such ideas, considering that I was too smart to fall for Communism and too stupid to follow Marx. I simply relied on the teachings of von Wiese und Kaiserswaldau on the one hand, and Heinrich Többen, the Münster prison warden, on the other.

On one occasion, in the amphitheater of his institution, Professor Többen brought forth for ostensibly educational purposes a certain thug who had several murders, manslaughters, confidence swindles, and what all on his conscience. The corpulent professor, who could turn loquacious in the presence of criminals and who had a talent for displaying his monsters with the determined shrewdness of an elephant driver, brought his patient to tears by recounting the fellow's childhood. The murderer wept the biggest teardrops I have ever seen. Then he pointed to an object now circulating around the auditorium: a metal spoon that he had deliberately swallowed in order to be admitted to the institution. "I'll never do that again!" he sobbed, and it was only the older students in the audience who realized that he was talking about the spoon, not about his murders and manslaughters. In front of me a female student started sobbing—the young man's father and mother long since lay in their cold, cold grave. Többen's romantic narrative had done the trick.

An older student gave her a poke in the ribs: "Get a hold of yourself! If Többen sees you, you'll be out of here in no time!" The professor didn't see her, but the girl was immediately served notice by a higher authority. The criminal himself interrupted his Papa's lecture, announcing that the professor did not permit emotional outbursts in the audience. The only person here who was allowed to weep was he himself, the serial murderer. Whereupon the professor called out to the prison guard that the prisoner claimed to know more than he himself; this was the last time he would bring this guy in for an educational demonstration. But the female student still received a serious reprimand when the swallowed spoon reached her; she lifted it with her fingertips and quickly passed it on. Többen interpreted this finger gesture as a criticism of the sanitary precautions taken in his "laboratory," an establishment recognized throughout Germany as exemplary in every way. So at least one suspect who didn't pass through Többen's hands could be classified as small fry.

Don Darío listened intently to my jailhouse recollections, but, *me cago en Dios*! What did that have to do with that money lady up in Basel? Zwingli, too, knit his brow as if to say, "What's all this supposed to mean?" My symbolic discourse was apparently not having the desired effect, so I would have to make things clearer. "Are you suggesting," Zwingli said, "that the way to turn on the money spigot is to start by telling sad childhood stories and get the tears flowing?"

"Precisely! A criminal and a millionaire, they both have consciences chock full of guilt, and they can only be assuaged by tearful stories. Do you want proof? Lift up thy pen, Zwingli Oekolampadius, and take dictation!"

I dictated a letter to his godmother. Christmas was just around the corner, so I had it easy. Our little tree served as Christian inspiration for this un-Christian scheme of mine. It took me but one line to neutralize the good lady's common sense. In the remainder of the letter, several pages long, I appealed directly to her heart, and from that organ to the complex of glands located in the corners of her eyes. I tore poor little infants from their mother's breasts, banished young children from their homes, and laid father and mother in their cold, cold grave. My letter was a hit, and that very evening it got sent off to Basel's highest taxpayer.

Don Darío, for whom we translated every word, dangled his pince-nez. He didn't know any Swiss millionaires, he said, but to wangle money from a Spanish one you'd have to go at him with *putas* and *curas* or—and he was thinking mainly of his arch-enemy Juan March—with a Toledo blade. I told him that Basel was a different kind of place, and I offered him a bet: ten *Fränkli* per tear, plus a sixfold security surcharge for a guilty conscience—just not for my own, of course.

I calculated just when the money transfer would arrive in Palma. On the appointed day, after summoning Don Darío, all four of us went to the post office, and—nothing! I had lost the bet, and I could have strangled old man Többen, thereby ensuring myself free bed and board for the rest of my life. This miserable day was a Saturday.

On the following Monday a transfer of 2000 francs arrived at the Banca March. I'll let my reader figure out how many tears were shed in Basel. I myself felt two tears moisten my eyes, tears of pride and gratitude for my genius. I experience such elation only upon success with an invention or a poem, or upon reaching a satisfying interpretation of an obscure passage of prose—as with Pascoaes, for example.

Zwingli offered me half of the transferred sum. But in his eyes I could see that he, too, was now developing an economic theory by imagining that I wouldn't accept any of this shameful booty. And he was right. "Thanks anyway!" I mentioned that I, too, was banking on the largesse of a millionaire: Mamú of the Royal Baking Powder Trust.

One week after this remarkable conquest of big capital, Zwingli fell ill with mysterious symptoms. Was it remote-control poisoning from his godmother's chemical laboratories? From Pilar's witch's kitchen? Dr. Solivellas calmly announced: typhus.

XXI

There you go again! You're not listening!" cried my mooching client, my cheapskate gadfly. "If you were my employee I would have fired you long ago! Repeat what I just told you!"

Unfortunately I wasn't Mr. Silberstern's employee, for if I was, he would have sent me packing, and I would have been forever rid of the miserly sadist. But I remained in his service nevertheless, as the unpaid dupe of a master who, as it says in Mamú's Bible, doth conceal the ways of the Almighty. And why didn't Mr. Silberstern just sack me? Hadn't he noticed that I wrote things for other people for nothing, created inventions for nothing, and plied my very existence for nothing? Vigoleis was the greatest chump who ever lived on the island of Mallorca. And that's how he has found his way into these pages.

I had in fact turned a deaf ear to what Mr. Silberstern, the man I sometimes absent-mindedly called Mr. Stern, was yelling at me during our businesslike promenade. My thoughts were taking me much deeper, down into the Tombs of the Huns in my home town.

Silberstern had sued the Third Reich for hundreds of thousands, his entire refugee fortune, amounting to half a million rust-proof Hitlerian marks. Converted into pesetas, my Adelfried was a solid millionaire, albeit a have-not compared to Zwingli's godmother, though such comparisons can be misleading. The only difficulty was that he had lost his legal suit. His lawyers were advising him to appeal, and Mr. Silberstern, putting his thumbs under his armpits, said to me, "Take dictation!"

I wrote, filling page after page with Silberstern's version of legalese. "You want three copies of everything?" I asked. I was given to understand that the

appropriate technical expression was "in triplicate"; that, secondly, since I had no comprehension of business protocol, I should refrain from asking such stupid questions; and that, thirdly, he had three legal advisors who were representing him in his suit against the Reich: his Jewish brother, the one with the two doctorates; an Aryan defense lawyer (a non-doctor); and a proxy counsel-attorney in Zurich (Dr. jur.) who was simply a Swiss and, to judge by his letters, had no particular interest in Silberstern's case. "Hopeless," I thought, but I took dictation anyway.

The correspondence ballooned. The Swiss attorney was given less and less to chew on, because certain facts were being withheld from him. In a surprisingly polite note he withdrew from the case. Besides, he was getting hot under the collar, as I found out later: he also had Aryan clients inside the Reich. His quitting meant less work for me.

What got written back and forth was utter nonsense, exceeded in its absurdity only by the Reich in whose baleful name all of this had to be put on paper. I told this to my boss, who then got upset and told me to keep my mouth shut. "The cobbler must stick to his last!" he said, and my "last" was making poems. "And yours is screwing whores," I thought, but kept this to myself and went on writing.

The result of my legal assistance was a letter from his Aryan attorney telling Silberstern that his case had received expedited attention—that is to say, it was denied. All was lost, with further appeal not only unnecessary but dangerous. Silberstern, a traveling wine merchant who had often been thrown out of the country and often snuck back in, was bursting with rage. But he said, "Take dictation! Justice is justice! I intend to appeal to the court of last resort!"

The last resort was, of course, the *Führer*. And so I wrote, "My dear *Führer*!" Silberstern scolded me, but then went on dictating. Letters, telegrams—there must have been much gleeful rubbing of hands in the Palma post office and no doubt also at the *Reichspost*. The litigant went on twiddling his thumbs, Vigoleis went on typing, and Beatrice went on threatening divorce if this farce with the lecher didn't come to a halt soon. But this was only the beginning. I learned the vocabulary of jurisprudence and, by training a philologist, I soon realized that the appearance and sound of a specific word may not have a specific thought behind it, and that a specific thought may be lacking a corresponding referent in the real world, but also that you can juggle all three of these variables and still be left with something in your hand. This "something" was sometimes Silberstern's non-Aryan *condition humaine*, at other times his money, and finally the blind spot in his eyes, so often bloodshot with fury. As a Jew, I told him, he was long since scheduled to perish, but now he was asking me to write letters again and again to his executioners. "Justice is justice" was all that this modern *Michael Kohlhaas* could say in reply.

"*Summum jus*, Herr Silberstern, *summa iniuria*. The adage wasn't written by St. Augustine, but one could easily ascribe it to him, unless he is in fact the originator. It contains all that I know about legal matters. In your case, what the judge is interested in is your head and your money, which will fall into his

lap when your head rolls. And since here on the island your head can at best fall into some *puta*'s lap, the judge will grab your money with the alacrity that is common to the mindless profession of the law. As for your Aryan attorney, he will not run the gauntlet for you unless you grant him as a fee your entire fortune, now frozen in banks in the Reich. You can cross out your brother with his two doctorates—he's due for hanging; his Aryan first name will give him away. The Privy Councilor, too, will end up on the gallows. All of you Silbersterns will have had it, together with your fortunes, which you yourself have admitted amount to several million marks. You keep trusting in legal codes and codicils, when you really ought to be trusting in your money. The court of last resort may still let you have everything back, but only if you're willing to do it the Jesuit way. For once, you should take a lesson from the Catholic Church. You'll get your money only by spending money."

Silberstern was sitting on a crate in our apartment, breathing heavily. Instead of twirling his thumbs, he now began twirling his greedy eyes. Words such as "money" and "*puta*" formed the core of his lilliputian vocabulary. Now he would have to pay attention. What's this would-be poet saying, anyway? A guy who can't even negotiate his own fee for legal counsel? Writers are stupid when they write what they write. "Take dictation!"

The documents kept piling up. Silberstern was in his element; he dictated for hours at a time. In order not to let Kessler's memoirs suffer, I had to stay up late at night, and did it willingly. I recuperated from the day's labor by typing out the Count's life history. After that, a few more pages of my Tombs of the Huns, although more than once, at the crack of dawn, Beatrice found me lying in a decidedly unheroic tomb of my own—fallen asleep over my manuscript.

Weeks went past on the island—maybe it was months. Then came the great moment when Silberstern was asked to formulate and notarize a declaration to be forwarded to the highest authorities in the Reich. His Aryan attorney informed him that the matter would proceed swiftly. Now it was *va banque* with Silberstern's pieces of silver.

I wouldn't have minded at all if this blockhead, this pretentious miser with a soul of corruption, were to lose all his usurious gains. But I didn't want the Nazis to get hold of them. So I started fighting with all the zeal I could muster for good or ill in another man's name. I presented him with an equation similar to the one I used in the case of Zwingli's godmother. The Többen coefficient remained the same, but this time I altered the larger unknown. Outlining my theory, I hammered away at the man with a "star" in his name, but he remained adamant. "The Reich is the Reich, and justice is justice!" "*Porra!*" "Don't you meddle in my personal affairs! Take dictation!" "All right— bye-bye, ye starry millions!"

I handed over the neatly typed documents to my boss. With beads of sweat on his brow he studied them carefully, signed them, and sauntered off to the post office. There's no helping a guy whose head is as fat as his ass.

It was already past midnight. The moon wandered slowly through the park of the beautiful daughters. The wind was rustling in the coconut palms, the field mice were out hunting, their piercing squeal sounding much like the bats that were coursing through the sultry air. In addition, the girls' monthly flags were swinging like little ghosts on the clothes line—a captivating *memento quia pulvis es* on this night of a million stars.

Beatrice lay sleeping next to me on the *Deutsche Allgemeine Zeitung*. She is an early bird, whereas I am a night owl. With the aid of two of my inventions I had made my typewriter almost soundless. Wet cloths damped what little of the tapping noise was still to be heard, while serving also as a coolant. Nothing disturbed my lover's sleep as I wrote down Kessler's past life and Vigoleis' future, which was still dormant in the Hunnish tombs near the banks of the Niers.

The mayor had just unveiled the "Tomb of the Unknown Brain" in the name of the *Führer*. Councilmen laid wreaths, the crowds shouted, the air was alive with the patriotic bloodthirst of the repressed Huns, and now the mayor yelled to his flock, "Germans! You now no longer have to think and write poetry! For this you must thank your *Führer*, who now will think and write for you in a way that no human brain has ever thought possible to think and write, not even our former nation of poets and..."—"thinkers" was the word he was looking for, but instead I heard a dull thump at our apartment door. I was startled, but unsure whether that was because of what I had just written, or the noisy interruption from outside.

Was it some drunks? Spaniards don't get drunk—with the exception of our *sereno*, who instead of guarding our house was at this moment squatting in some tavern on Atarazanas Square. Was it Nazi murderers? Those guys sneak around in their stocking feet, and in Spain they've been working most recently with chloroform and abductions. Was it the old lady upstairs? She has varicose veins, and sometimes she slips on the stairs and falls against our door. If it's her, I'll take her back up under the roof. But she's not in the habit of nosing around in the nighttime. I figured it was the Huns who did the thumping, and so I just went on typing. Whoever conjures up ghosts must not recoil in their presence, even if they are poor old ghosts that have trouble moving.

The second thump was very much of this world, and had nothing whatever to do with my manuscript. I went to the door and undid the lock.

There came rolling into the apartment a man's hat, whose price, quality, and circumstances of purchase were well known to me. Then came a flurry of letters, forms, and neatly typed documents—these items, too, familiar to me in every detail. Then Herr Silberstern lifted himself up from his second fall and staggered into the hall. I took a quick look down the stairwell, but heard and saw nothing. My first thought was: members of the German National Work Brigade were after the Jew. They intend to make him perish. He doesn't want to perish, and so he's come running to his legal advisor to dictate a letter of protest. I locked the door behind him.

Silberstern began a big harangue, his own kind of harangue, which was gibberish. It cost me a whole chapter of my novel, but it cost the Nazis the Jew's entire fortune.

Adelfried had not sent the documents to his attorney. My suspicions and my allusions to the Jesuits had addled his toad-like brain: "Suppose he's right, this pathetic poetizer who can't even afford to buy a bed? What if what he's telling me is true, that Germany has ceased to be a country governed by laws? It's a little strange that my Aryan lawyer signs all his letters to me, a Jew, with '*Heil Hitler!*' And are they really going to hang my Aryan lawyer for sending a Jew's money abroad?"

At the very same hour when the *Ciudad de Palma* was plowing its way through the leaden swells of the *Mare nostrum*, carrying in its postal sack the useless load of his undispatched legal documents, our litigant was swimming in the arms of a personage charging 2.50 pesetas, from which he was able to knock off half a peseta using sweaty sign language. Having completed this double transaction, the brother of Privy Councilor Silberstern betook himself to the door of his legal advisor, who he knew would still be pounding away at his typewriter. He slipped and fell on the stairway but then, raising a finger and still trembling at the thought, he let me know that she would have done it for 1.50 if only he had been able to say a few words of broken Spanish. "How would you have handled the situation?"

"Which situation? The babe or the Third Reich?"

"Don't make jokes! My fortune is at stake!"

Once again I expounded my economic theory, this time making it culminate in my general theory of private ownership. My recent coup in the Basel money market lifted my prestige, all the more since my new client knew the lady personally. But he added that I had badly underestimated the size of her bank account. Moving on, I mentioned that Count Kessler was likewise suing the Third Reich, that I was typing up his private documents, too, and that if Mr. Silberstern was willing to stick with me, he'd be on the right side of the law. This news had the effect of increasing my prestige still further, for although Silberstern didn't know the Count personally, he was on intimate terms with the Count's wine provisioner. He could name all the vintages that got poured at the Cranach Street residence in Weimar, whenever the intellectual elite of the world gathered there.

I asked my client to return the next day at 12 o'clock sharp, knowing that he would be here at half-past ten with the punctuality of all gossips. He arrived at half-past ten, and we discussed his urgent quarrel with the Reich. At the stroke of twelve a letter to his attorney was finished, telling him that as per a letter to be dispatched with the same post, the entire affair would be turned over to the Spanish National Bank in Madrid, allowing everything to be handled automatically, within the framework of German foreign-trade arrangements. We would await directives from Madrid, and had every intention of following them to the letter. Meanwhile we would also personally notify Dr. Köcher, the German Consul General in Barcelona.

It was a gigantic bluff. I figured that Silberstern's attorney, whose head was on the line, would fall for it—and he did. This gave me time actually to alert the National Bank in Madrid, and there, too my hunches proved correct. While hundreds of people were being murdered every day in his concentration camps, when dealing with foreign countries the *Führer* had to be careful to don the accepted white shirt of the diplomat instead of his normal brown attire. Cardinals, hundred-meter sprinters, shipowners, opera singers, six-day cycle racers, magnates: all such leading personalities would get to see only the gleam of white. This charade placated people's consciences. Foreign trade flourished as never before, and the world bowed down before the image of the Lord of the German Nation. And Silberstern, such was my thinking, ought to have his little profit from it.

His attorney in Frankfurt was now sitting between two stools. He sent expensive telegrams, which his client in Spain of course had to pay for. His Dr.- Dr. brother had long since been silenced, his Privy Councilor title long since vaporized. Adelfried again got the jitters, and I heard myself saying, "Don't give up! A Vigoleis can always find a way! Take dictation!"

For the first time in his life Herr Silberstern wrote down a text that was dictated to him. That is to say, it was still Vigoleis, but in this case he dictated a text to himself. Stern—beg your pardon, Silberstern—signed with a clammy hand. *Va banque.*

Some months later the Banco Nacional de Madrid informed Señor Don Alfredo Silberstern, Palma de Mallorca, Calle Cecilio Metello, that the Accounting Office of the Head Supervisor of the German Overseas Currency Management in Berlin had remitted the sum of..., in writing..., and that they awaited his further instructions.

Silberstern was now a millionaire—or more exactly, he had once again become a millionaire and, as such, a worthy member of the Silberstern clan with the Aryan first names. And I, Vigoleis, had once again demonstrated my prowess in dealing with millionaires. Who knew? Perhaps I was set to become the world's most-wanted adversary of big capital, without ever having read a word of Marx! I shook my own hand, since Silberstern declined to do so. He took all the credit for himself—that, too, was a stellar trait of his. Vigoleis' mission from now on was to remain in the service of this gentleman, who had just learned that justice could be justice after all. But I would no longer be his legal counsel. I would be his advisor in sexual affairs.

Silberstern detested me with a passion seldom encountered between human beings. It was my fault. If I had had the good sense, using the execrable mercantile German that twirled out of his thumbs, to present him with a bill—pardon, I mean a "debit notification"—for services rendered in the capacity of legal counsel in the case of Silberstern vs. Third Reich for fees outstanding amounting to the sum of 100,000 pesetas, he would have just rubbed his greedy hands, taken the envelope, and rapidly noted down how much below a 10% profit-share I should receive. He promised me 10% of the dowry if I would arrange a marriage for him with a rich *marrana*, one of the baptized Jewesses from Silversmith Street in Palma: not more than 30 and not less than 3 × 100,000 duros. Pedro and I actually took some steps in this cattle-trading maneuver. But General Franco was against it.

Here's what my gut was telling me: surely Silberstern would be accommodating to the tune of 10000 pesetas, or maybe with just a single peseta that he has wangled, centimo by centimo, out of some Pilar. "Vigoleis is such a dolt and a nincompoop," he'll be thinking, "that he'll consider it an honor to be working for me. And anyway, he can still learn. For example, our assault against the Third Reich! I'd like to meet anybody else who could pull that off like Adelfried, brother of Brunfried, both of us from the city of Würzburg! The German colony was astounded when the news of our legal coup made the rounds."

For two whole years Vigoleis served this master, the guy who was Aryan in front, non-Aryan behind, and in the middle the island's biggest *putafex*. He served him at dawn and at dusk, when the constellation was at zenith and again when it was below the horizon; during hours when even the most miserable slut has her bed all to herself, and always at the expense of his own work. Worse yet, and incomprehensible, was the fact that all of this affected an aspect of his existence that could have aroused the interest of Professor Többen in Münster: Beatrice's nerves. My reader, for whom cloven personalities may well be the most inscrutable subject in the world, may well be asking himself here the same question I have pondered over time and again: why has Vigoleis always let himself be flattened like a noodle? Effi Briest's father, in Fontane's novel of the same name, would say, "Hmm... that would take us far afield." God has his emissaries everywhere, and He prefers to utilize simple creatures in order to point out certain forces within His Creation, although in the world's labyrinth of obfuscations and exaggerations, this can lead to all kinds of false deductions. Would it be so very odd if He used Vigoleis to prove that an Aryan with a 2000-year-old Hunnish pedigree could, despite the long series of temptations, humiliations, extortions, and insults visited upon him by a constellation named Silberstern, avoid making him into an anti-Semite, no matter how often his friends and acquaintances made bets among themselves that he would turn out to be one? One of the *bons mots* to be heard on the island was that this Jew would turn Vigoleis into a Jew-baiter. But he never turned into one, and the person who was most amazed at this was the despicable Jew himself.

But was it truly gratitude, even if in microscopic form as Vigoleis liked to call it, that impelled Silberstern to do what he did when I told him that we were expecting company? A famous married couple would be arriving on the island: the Mengelbergs from Amsterdam, Carel and Rahel. We wanted to put them up at our place for a few days, after which they intended to move on with their rucksacks and their no less famous brother-in-law, the writer Helman. "They don't have a bed?" asked Silberstern. No, I told him, they don't have any money. They fled from Germany, where Carel had an important job at the Berlin Radio. But he also had Rahel, and the Nazis didn't like that. A woman could, of course, have the name Rahel and still be an Aryan, I went on, just as he was a Jew despite his Adelfried. But as he well knew, the Nazis were such nitpickers about such things. In any case, the three...

"Just a minute," said Adelfried. "Before you go on: are we talking about Willem Mengelberg, the conductor, the Concertgebouw?"—"Not exactly. The first names are different, the batons, the achievements, the fees, the attitudes— they're all different. It's the last name that's identical: Mengelberg."—"A son?"—"A nephew. His mother's maiden name is Huflattich, and his wife, Rahel, is first harpist at the Berlin Opera."—"You mean: used to be." —"You're right, used to be. Just as all of are used-to-be's."—"So you will swear to me that these people are genuine Mengelbergs?"—"I swear by all the Mengelbergs that they are the real McCoy."

Upon hearing this, Silberstern immediately declared his willingness to lend Mr. Mengelberg and his wife the mattress given to him by the Nina who jilted him back in Cologne. I could come pick it up, load it on my back, and lay it down for the Mengelbergs in one of our unused rooms. If this was in fact the nephew of the truly famous Willem M. of Amsterdam—did I know whom that man slept with? First with... and then with... and especially with...? And as for Rahel, she was the daughter of Hindemith—if it's the same one who was in the Leipzig Gewandhaus Orchestra... Yes, he knew them all, all of them! Fine people, the whole lot! All of them distinguished musicians! And that's why they could get to sleep on Nina's mattress. Would the writer Helman be joining them? Is he distinguished, too? "Much more so, Herr Stern— pardon, Silberstern. He's West Indian Rimbu aristocracy, hand-pulled with watermark."

"I'm telling you, not only will I let these eminent people sleep on Nina's mattress, they must sleep on it. They *must*, do you understand?"

I understood, and it seemed like gratitude. The human being in Silberstern was finally stirring, just as he himself had so often stirred on that mattress. I concluded that there must be something called compensatory bedroom justice.

It was already past midnight. As on p.612 above, the moon was wandering through the park of the beautiful daughters, where there was likewise a rustling, chirping, and fluttering of the coconut trees, the field mice, and the bats. The girls' monthly laundry was a reminder of the transitoriness of the years, once again in this night of a million stars and a single Mr. Silver Star, gentleman and millionaire.

There was a dull thump at our door. But this time I wasn't startled, because it was my own self, breaking down under the weight of the mattress. Bathed in sweat as if emerging from the sea, there I lay on the patamar. On top of me, at least fifty pounds of wool from contented Mallorquin sheep were redolent with lanolin, Nina, the brother of a Privy Councilor, plus the *sine qua non* of all mattresses.

"How come you smell so strange," asked Beatrice as I lay down next to her on the *Deutsche Allgemeine Zeitung*. "Where are you coming from?"

Unfortunately, Beatrice is one of those talented people who can tell whether a hard-boiled egg was laid in hay, straw, or into the farmer's open hand.

"What you're smelling is lanolin, Nina, the brother of a Privy Councilor, and what happens when people lie down on a mattress. When I take it back, it will have added further aromas: Carel, Rahel, Lou... Or should we let them have our heap of newspapers so we can sleep on a real bed for a change?"

Beatrice was already back asleep as I continued to ponder my special blend of aromas.

Next day, the famous people arrived. That night they slept on Nina's wool, while the philanthropic mattress-provider was accommodated in some establishment costing two pesetas, and Nina was offering her delights to some sheikh on his camel-hair blanket, beneath the stars of Marrakesh.

Once Silberstern had converted his Hitler Marks into pesetas, I told him that he could now afford a visit to the Casa Marguerita for one duro, tip included. The penny-pincher just laughed. I told him that now that he was again a millionaire he could afford a cardinal's mistress in her boudoir all decorated in scarlet silk. I knew of one, I said, a randy cookie, at the moment on leave of absence. My miserly client smiled.

He smiled and twiddled his thumbs. He was not one of those moneybags who try to pretend that they are poorer than a churchmouse—an animal that, according to Iberian legend, feeds on the rancid oil in liturgical lamps. No, this nickel-nurser was proud of his millions, and prouder still of the clever ruse that had filched his fortune, a non-Aryan's fortune, from the Nazis. I hastened to agree with him. Only someone of his stature could have pulled off a stunt like that one. It was further proof, I said, that there will always be a blind chicken around that can find some corn to peck. "But let's get down to business," I said. "What would you like me to do now?"

Well now, he said, he was approaching me on a rather delicate matter. Things were getting too expensive for him. If I was able, he said, I should figure out how much life was costing him, despite his modest needs and despite careful scrimping. So he had started thinking that he ought to look around for something reliable—a woman. It must be somebody he could talk to about these matters, and so the only kind of woman he was thinking about was a German citizen—because of the language and because of his feelings about the homeland. He was, he said, still attached to his German fatherland—unlike me, the by now thoroughly cosmopolized Vigoleis—"Or let's say I've been 'cosmocratized.'" Whenever our conversations hit the subject of Germany, this scum-bag's eyes went moist. His yearning for Würzburg was getting more and more intense. Whenever such strong emotions came to the fore, I told him that nostalgia was basically a question of money. I offered to buy him a rail ticket at "Viajes Marsans."

He knew a woman in Cologne or near Cologne, up there in my own German bailiwick. She was Aryan, he said, very Aryan—that he could swear to. But unfortunately, she looked Jewish. Her father was hit by a train, and her mother was still alive. She was getting by with a modest pension supervised by General Director Dr. Dorpmüller—he meant the mother, not Nina. Somebody had set the rail switch the wrong way. Nina was a *manniqueen*—surely I knew what that was—in one of the finest department stores on Hohestrasse in Cologne, where Mayor Adenauer's daughter was a regular customer. Everything was sewn by hand, and because of her non-Aryan looks Nina couldn't work there any more, and he wanted to send for her, and what did I think of that? A dependable girl! And what a set of boobs! And legs! And she's tall! And just think, she's educated, too!

I told him that with such qualities, plus a father who was hit by a train, I couldn't imagine any girl who would be better fit for calibrating my client's Mallorcan bedroom budget with his bank account. And so I advised him to send Fräulein Nina a postcard.

"A postcard? Don't you know that you don't send postcards to ladies? Nina is a perfect lady, I tell you!"

Adelfried Silberstern loved to write letters. His talent lay in his dictating skills, which allowed him to conceal his weakness: orthography. Orthography was not his concern, but his secretary's—that is to say, in this case, it was my concern. My client would have preferred a female employee, one with boobs. And with legs! No inhibitions, no panties, the kind of female employee who in novels and movies likes to jump on her boss' lap and eventually has the whole company tied to her little finger. Be that as it may, Silberstern's sense of importance was satisfied with Vigoleis. All he had to do was say, "Take dictation!" and then start twirling his thumbs and pacing back and forth.

It turned out to be long, this letter of mine to Nina, who lived between Cologne and Neuss, at the place where the now fatherless railroad-crossing cubicle stood. It was an epistle filled with nostalgic reminiscences and anticipatory aspirations, replete with "Do you remember" and "You see" and "Let me." The "Let me's" were in the majority. As he dictated, the roly-poly bridegroom's eyes bulged from their sockets. Pearls of lecherous sweat dripped from his nose, apparently the most active organ in a phenomenon of his type. His entreaties and erotic ambulations made him seem like a living page from the immolated treasures of his private collection of pornography. When the invitation to his bride was finished, the author stood in front of his scribe wringing his hands, and asked, "Well, what do you think?"

"Very few writers are able to dictate print-ready copy," I said. "Gerhart Hauptmann is said to have achieved a certain degree of perfection in this art, but he does that lying down. It's really quite remarkable, your combination of Bluebeard and traveling salesman. Your sentences will pierce the lady's heart. It's likely that you will become her destiny."

My words flattered the cheapskate. He punched his belly with delight, seeing himself in his mind's eye already sharing his shiny brass bedstead with Nina, sharing their daily bread and their nightly cavorting, sharing an *ensaimada* on Sundays and reminiscing about sharing finger-licking potato pancakes back in Cologne. Silberstern signed the letter, put his initials on the first carbon and a private symbol on the second. That was his businesslike custom. After all, Nina was a business transaction.

"There!" Silberstern licked the envelope, closed it, put his expensive hat on his brush-cut head, and was ready to march off to the post office.

"Wait, Herr Direktor!" I said. "Shouldn't we figure out first when the letter will arrive between Cologne and Neuss, just so we can at least imagine at which point the Nazi censor will break it open, make a few phone calls, see to it that Nina gets grabbed, and then make sure that she gets her hair shorn off for committing racial defilement with the "Jewish pig" Silberstern from Würzburg, currently residing in Palma de Mallorca? She'll be hanged in Klingelpütz Prison, and Adelfried will be murdered by Nazi thugs in the Balearic *Gau*."

Vigoleis is not a saint, although at certain times he has come close to a faint trace of saintliness as a result of selfless actions. Nor is he a Christian. Despite his poverty he still has enough clothes to put on. He's not a bad person, not a cynic, and he doesn't bear grudges. If Silberstern had paid him a fee for his legal counsel, just a few thousand pesetas as a gesture, so to speak, I am convinced that he never would have thought of badgering the man. This was simply his way of taking revenge. Or was it just a game, the way a cat plays with the mouse?

Silberstern had nothing to say. He broke out in a sweat and took his precious hat back off, no doubt thinking that he couldn't trust the moisture-proof quality of the leather lining. He wrung his pudgy hands, and drops of saliva appeared at the corners of his mouth. Just a moment ago he was riding toward triumph, but now he was a target of Hitler's minions! All that money! That brass bedstead!

I offered him consolation. If he would let me have my way once more, we could get Nina out of the Third Reich hale and hearty, just as we had done with his money. We would have to act smartly. The enemy was listening, and above all, we mustn't underestimate the enemy. We mustn't think of the enemy simply as a knave, but rather as a hyper-knave. I told him to go back home, light up his seven-branched candelabra, and thank Moses and the Prophets that his father hadn't given him a first name like Itzig or Isidor, but instead Adelfried. As "Adelfredo" he should send a postcard to Nina, despite the fact that she was a perfect lady, telling her that an old friend in Spain would be delighted if she were to pay him a visit sometime on Mallorca. "*Clima ideal*," no endemic diseases, no unsanitary kitchens, mortality rate 10.44 per 1000 inhabitants, average humidity...

"There you go again, Herr Doktor, making fun of me! What is all that supposed to mean, mortality, endymic, kitchens...?

"Those are points of comparison, Herr Stern, and they could serve as come-ons for your Nina. In Germany today, the mortality rate is 27.8 per 1000 citizens. I happen to know this figure precisely, because when I wake up every morning I see a column in the *Deutsche Allgemeine Zeitung* that contains statistical reports about such things. As for the word "endemic"—by the way, not "endymic," unfortunately not that—that is the way to describe National Socialism. It has turned out to be Germany's endemic illness. Nina is educated. She'll know right away what we're referring to."

"There you go again, making disparaging remarks about my homeland! And what's this about humidity?"

"Likewise for reasons of comparison. Average humidity 68%, highest elevation 1472 meters, free transportation and lodging, Sunday excursions alone or in group."

"Free transportation? I beg your pardon, you don't think I'm going to pay for her trip, do you? She should be happy that I'm letting her come!"

"Who else will pay for it, if not Silberstern? The *Führer*, perhaps? He's got other things to worry about. Or maybe the widow Jensen, out of her measly Dorpmüller pension? She's lucky if she gets 50 marks a month..."

"63.20. And she wouldn't have got anything if my brother the attorney hadn't written a letter to the railway authorities. Just think, her husband was standing on an unused spur when the train hit him!"

"One more reason why you'll have to pay for her trip. But first we'll have to find out whether Nina is still alive. If her looks are as non-Aryan as you say they are, she's in big trouble."

"Oh, but you don't know Nina! She's a superb woman, I'm telling you, and she can outfox the SS. I'm going to write her a card right away, and then you'll see that all I've been telling you is the God's honest truth. I have some pictures that I'll show you and your spouse. All of them decent, don't worry. Made by a photographer in Cologne. And besides, she's Catholic."

"What a shame. Unclothed women always reveal a clearer picture."

"I've got some of those, too, Herr Doktor. I'll bring them all."

"Do that. I'll give them to Count Kessler, who will pass them on with a few words of recommendation to the son of the current American ambassador in Madrid. You know, that fellow is in charge of the most luxurious nudist club in the Old World, here on Mallorca. That's where Nina can develop her talents. But first let's get to that postcard, so we can sneak her out of the Reich as quickly as possible."

Nina's reply, written on a postcard, was businesslike, although Mr. Silberstern thought he could read great happiness between the lines. But it caused him to wring his hands just the same. This would, he said, be his ruin. He was being asked to forward 400 marks for the travel expenses! For 300, he said, he himself could travel anywhere in the world. He made some calculations, pulled some grimy papers from his bulging briefcase, and showed me down to the penny how much he had paid for the trip from Aachen to Palma, third-class of course, but including baggage insurance and two salmon sandwiches.

Now a battle raged, and it was fought in sight of photos of the Cologne model that were spread out on the table. She was indeed one impressive broad, in certain respects similar to Kathrinchen of the Clock Tower, although Nina showed a sturdier maintenance of the parts of her physique devoted to love-making—presumably Mensendieck gymnastics. And yet there seemed to hover over her most intimate parts a trace of melancholy, which is after all an ingredient in the art of truly grand cocottes. Nina must have been insatiable, but at the same time unfathomable.

Over half an hour I persuaded the horny miser to transfer 500 marks to Cologne: 400 for transportation, 80 for new luggage, and 20 for a new goat for Mother Jensen. The latter item was mentioned by the solicitous Nina in a scribbled P.S. on her card: her Mom was doing OK, but in the meantime her goat had also been hit by a train. I told the skinflint that Dr. Dorpmüller could not be held responsible for this accident—that was the inevitable fate of any creature that did its munching at the edge of a railroad track. They would all end up under the wheels: goat, goose, or crossing-keeper. And besides, Mother Jensen was in large part responsible for the birth of this particular Venus; a nanny goat would hardly be an adequate form of recompense.

In addition to money, Silberstern also sent Nina some kisses, which were meant to hasten her departure. But the girl didn't arrive. The brass bedstead was polished up, the mattresses spread out—all Nina had to do, he told me, was to come and cuddle down next to her unappetizing master. Oh, but that wouldn't do, I told him. He would have to outfit a separate room for the lady, and surely his apartment was big enough for that. But why, he asked. She would be sleeping with him! Don't bet on it, I said. The local Aryan German colony would insist on separate sleeping quarters for an Aryan woman. Otherwise she would end up behind bars, and all his money would be out the window!

With sorrow in his heart, and because of what people might say, Silberstern purchased the new furniture. But Nina didn't arrive. While still engaging in his two peseta entertainments, Silberstern took out his misery on me. And patiently, I placed my neck under his foot. One day he asked me what I would do in similar circumstances. I told him I had no idea: I was good at giving advice to other people, just not to myself. But in a case like this one? Simple, I said. We would have to find out whether the bank had actually paid out the amount he had sent. No way, he said. Confidential transaction. All right, let's write to Mother Jensen, return reply requested, and ask her whether she has a new goat. Why not send a telegram directly to Nina? That would be an affront to the lady—unless, of course, she wasn't a lady after all.

Mother Jensen had received her goat. And a few painful, impatient weeks later Silberstern received a postcard from Nina, sent from Berlin: "So sorry. Letter will follow."

The letter said that she had gone for a spin with a boyfriend and 480 marks. In Berlin the guy went through all the cash with her, and then disappeared. She begged forgiveness and another 500 marks.

"Not one more penny! I wouldn't dream of it, that filthy sow! I've had it with all this deceit and insults!" But he knew how to force her. "Take dictation!"

I composed a long letter containing obscure threats, anticipated triumphs, rank violations of *consecutio temporum*, and ending with "Very sincerely yours, Silberstern." Now, he asked, wasn't that once again a top-notch letter after all this time?

No doubt about it, I said. Especially for a traveling wine merchant who was familiar with the law. "Abduction of a minor" was what it was called in jurisprudence. In former times it could bring you a jail sentence, and today it was a capital offense. His well-educated Nina, that canny, brainy girl, would take his letter to the police, which is to say to some Nazi with a medal for street-fighting, and the next time we visited Herr Hasenbank at the German Shop we would see the Silberstern Affair spread all over Julius Streicher's Nazi weekly *Der Stürmer*: "Jewish Swine Seduces Aryan Girl to Mallorca, Isle of Vice!" Watch out, I said. Nina could get dangerous. He was going too far, no chance of a retreat. He must transfer 500 marks minus one nanny goat. By telegraph!

Silberstern sent the money to the widow who held the little red flag at the railway crossing. He received a brief reply saying that the lady had always known that there were decent Jews, and that she was content that her daughter would be in excellent hands with this noble gentleman, especially in this day and age when one's life was in danger if one had a crooked nose. It was touchingly naive of the widow to write this way; it could have cost Nina her life right away on the railway platform. But Nina was carrying a guardian angel in her hand luggage. She later showed it to me.

Nina fulfilled all the promises displayed in her photos. At eight in the morning, just minutes after disembarking—Silberstern had taken a taxi to avoid creating a scene at the pier. At 8 am the super-broad was standing in our bible-paper room. Great Scott! If I were him, I too would have yanked her away from that railroad crossing and paid her trip in full. Face to face, her brow seemed somewhat less striking than in the photos, but that only increased one's expectations. The remainder met all the requirements one could place on a Nina, either in real life or in a book about a life. As she stood in our presence in her imposing corporeality, she had already cost Silberstern 1000 marks, and it would now be up to me to see to it that she cost him even more. But Beatrice, who was asked to join in the inspection, later told me that I wouldn't have to exert myself—everything would take its natural course. And that's exactly how it went.

The next day at the crack of dawn the magnanimous Mr. Silberstern again stood at our door, this time in a mood of sackcloth and ashes. Had she flown the coop so soon? No, on the contrary, she was still there, but she had locked herself in! How he wished now that he hadn't followed my advice and had a lock attached to her door! What did he care what people might say? She wasn't letting him in, and *par conséquence...* 1000 marks, and now this *affû-tage*! Despite the man's obvious distress, this business about *affûtage* sounded rather erudite, but as a lay philologist I didn't know what the word *affûtage* meant, and as a counsel specializing in legal and sexual matters I didn't dare look it up in my Dupiney. Surely it must mean something very lowdown, something in close connection with the brass bedstead. Beatrice, who at this early hour was unable to avoid the encounter, said that *affûtage* was strong language. The Nazis and their murderous scourges—those were examples of *affûtage*. Herr Silberstern crumbled. "That's just it," he cried. "That's just it! Nina has turned out to be a Nazi! Nina, my girlfriend from the most Catholic stretch of railroad in Germany! And an anti-Semite! And she always went to confession!"

I tried to console this victim of *affûtage* by telling him that a new Reformation had broken out. There were no more Catholics, only Nazis. This was the new German dispensation, bestowed by virtue of the Vatican Concordat. My own mother, who of course didn't raise goats at the edge of a railroad, was walking the selfsame path of sinister upheaval. But Nina? Surely she was out to gain something by her actions. A person wouldn't lock out such a generous Adelfried just because she was an anti-Semite. So I asked him, "What's up?"

"She wants to get to Lisbon. She told me so right away, at the harbor."

"Aha, so it's a small matter of extortion. What does she want to do in Lisbon? Has she got some other guy over there?"

"Some count, some highly placed gentleman. And she wants me to pay her way again, or she'll start making a huge fuss."

"A real count? Like Kessler? Or is it a con man like Count...?"

This new topic put the traveling wine merchant in his best businesslike form. It was Old Portuguese nobility! He mentioned the name, which was a truly grand one—of world-historical significance, at least in the 8th century. After that, the family enjoyed a great reputation solely inside the family itself. I mustn't reveal the name, because the Count is still living and is among the friends of my Portuguese friends, who were particularly attentive one day at the Pascoaes Estate when, telling tales as I always like to do, I recounted how Nina withheld her charms from Silberstern's brass bed, and had him pay her way to Lisbon for a visit with Count... all of my listeners knew this Count in person, and they all knew about his German affair. Nina? Yes indeed, that was her—a dancer, ballet. The Count was head over heels for her. Big family arguments. He threatened to make her his bride. *La ci darem la mano, la mi dirai di sí.* It's a shame, I said, that he didn't follow through. A certain amount of roadbed ballast from the rail line between Cologne and Neuss could have been of use to this noble dynasty. I was given stern looks, even though as a Habsburg bastard I felt I could very well have a say in the matter. The noble poet Pascoaes, who as a poet stood above all questions of bloodlines, later agreed with my assessment.

Nina had started early on to put her perfect physique in the service of her selfish desires. She traded successfully on this capital, and soon enough, as was only natural with a build like hers, she had no need to lead a goat to munch on desiccated weeds along the tracks, as piously Catholic as that particular line was between Neuss and Cologne. At our very first meeting, I felt the need to tell Nina that I had traveled that stretch of track dozens of times, and perhaps I had even sat in the train that was her father's tragic undoing. This information brought us closer together. Herr Silberstern wasn't pleased, and started calculating that my chronology must be wrong. So we dropped the subject.

When Nina was sixteen, she consulted her drab mirror for advice, took off her maidenly little dress, and became a full-fledged girl. At eighteen she was discovered at "Crazy Kunibert's" in downtown Cologne by a university student who once heard her belting out some song and, on the basis of these noises, drew certain conclusions about the usefulness of her voice for her future. Some months later, she was dancing and singing in Berlin, Paris, and Lisbon—one naked Nina together with 30 other naked Ninas. The troupe went on tour, embarking in Leixões for Rio de Janeiro. With no further ado, the Portuguese count, always quick on the draw, selected her from among the 30: "That one and none other!" For a shepherd, each sheep has its own personality. He got her all right, but their pastoral bliss lasted only a short while. They promised to meet again in Cologne. "*Minha alma!*" said the Count. "*Tschüss!*" said Nina.

This Count, who was also a baron and a marquis, horny as only a Portuguese can be, and Catholic, reacted to Nina's "I'm back!" telegram by traveling to Cologne. Together they prayed in the Cathedral and in St. Mary on the Capitol, and they also sought out the secular venues that had made Nina into Nina—above all, "Crazy Kunibert's." But they stayed away from the railroad crossing where Mother Jensen was now tending a goat and a goose. When the Count ran out of money and objects to hock—his last landholdings in Portugal had already gone under the hammer— he returned to the land of his forefathers, did some calculating, and married a *menina* who had no body to speak of, but owned some vineyards in the Douro Valley. Their union was consecrated; old nobility gave rise to new nobility, and two kids were already in the cradle when Nina showed up on Mallorca. Now she wanted nothing more than to dash off to her Conde in Lisbon.

What was Silberstern to do, buffeted as he was between vanity and avarice? "It's not the end of the world," I whispered to him., "so, better now than never." Once he'd got hooked on the charms of this super-chick, separation would be all the harder, even for just a few days. During this period, as Silberstern wrestled with the angel of his own stinginess, Nina kept everything under lock and key: her room, her chastity belt, and even her pretty lips. They communicated in writing, passing slips of paper under her door. She took meals only when the besieging general was out of the house. Behind her narrow brow there resided the instinct of all females who know how to hold off until their hour has come. Nina's hour now involved the Count. And now Silberstern's angel tapped on his wallet. Wringing his hands once again, he bought her a ticket to Lisbon. Nina saw fit to thank me for my service as an intermediary. Whereupon she shoved off, in regal fashion. The shabby Silberstern was left holding the bag, but he also had the satisfaction of entrusting his Nina to the care of a *conde, marquês,* and *barão* for one week.

Now Silberstern began to fret like an Albigensian undergoing the *endura*—or rather, since that simile does seem a little grandiose for this goofy erotomane, like a goat that for unexplained reasons suddenly refuses to eat anything. The bordellos of Palma were unable to cheer him up. Nina wasn't writing to him, not even a postcard view of her Count's castle. His money was gone, and the traveling coat he had bought her on Vigoleis' advice—gone too! It was enough, he lamented, to make him tear his hair out! That's fine with me, I thought, but please do that in your own apartment.

Was this one more night with millions of stars? Were dreams again floating around in the palm trees? Was the beautiful girls' pet armadillo once again poking along under the bushes? I just can't recall. And it doesn't really matter in which astrological sign Mother Nature was located as, hour after hour, I tapped my noiseless way through the Hunnish tombs of my pagan tribes. Like all history, this account pretty much wrote itself. In order to graft onto the Thousand-Year Reich a few memorable shoots, all I usually had to do was look in my hometown newspaper to watch the nationwide German depravity send forth its most grotesque sprouts. But then our doorbell rang, and after a moment or two of fear—I am a night owl—I opened for Mr. Silberstern and, pleading that the late hour belonged to me and my brainless characters, I asked him what was wrong this time. He looked terrible. I went to get him some water.

He said I had to come with him immediately—no time for Huns, no time for Kessler, no time for my own wife. No man who considered himself a man, he averred, would stand for anything like this! And on top of it all she had insulted *him*, the brother of Privy-Councilor Silberstern of Würzburg!

So it was Nina. Was she back? And was she back with him...?

In brief, with no ifs, ands, or buts, I was being asked to accompany him to the *Casa del Fortunón*—as Palma's outstanding tourist guide I was aware what kind of place that was— to let this "fortune" lady know in no uncertain terms exactly what was on his mind. He would be demanding the return of his money, or another lady entirely. The one he had got was simply not of his caliber. "One whole shiny duro! Just think of it, Herr Doktor!"

"I see. It's another case of *affûtage*, but this time in the literal sense of the word. That's not my specialty. And besides, I don't have the necessary probing instruments."

Resistance was useless. This disturber of my nocturnal peace was not to be shooed away. I just had to come with him, he said. One whole duro was at stake, as was his reputation as a German. I was to step in once again as interpreter and legal advisor... "Oh, but wait," I said. "If I'm supposed to be your advisor, then only in sexual matters. And as for having your honor besmirched as a German man, that's what the German consulate is for. As long as you haven't been officially deprived of your citizenship, you have a right to seek assistance. You know where the Consul lives. Take a taxi from the Alhambra."

At this, Silberstern went raging mad. He lowered his head like a bull and started threatening me. Fine, I was leaving him in the lurch. Fine, I didn't want to help him. Fine, but this wasn't the end of the matter. Not that he needed me at all—he would now go straight to my wife and ask for her opinion, her advice, her assistance, and...

The man was almost weeping with despair. Knowing the lay of our apartment, he placed his pigeon-toed feet on the first newspaper page in our hallway, with the intention of rushing from paper to paper on his way to our *sala immaculata*, where the pages were piled on top of each other, and where Beatrice lay fast asleep. Suddenly sensing the courage of my Huns, I grabbed my crazed client by the collar and thundered at him, "Don't you dare harass my wife with your thermopylic tribulations! If you do, you could suffer the same fate as Origenes—and by my own hand!"

This brought the lecher to his knees. Now all he did was whine. Was he speaking words in Hebrew? In any case, he presented the image of misery, and this made me feel sorry once again for the rogue. What else could I do for him, I asked. Silberstern squirmed out of his agony. New possibilities seemed to be glistening in his greedy, sex-mad eyes. "Something in writing," he said. "Write down a few lines to the *patrona*, asking her to give me credit, a chit good for making a switch—for the next time."

I prepared a document on azure-tinted notepaper. It was lightly perfumed, from which you may deduce that I raided Kessler's stock. It was the lateness of the hour and the bizarre nature of the situation that emboldened me to commit this larceny, for otherwise I have the deepest respect for other people's property. Silberstern, duly informed of the fact that his whoremongering ukase was written on paper hand-drawn by Gaspard Maillol, set off proudly for the city. There is nothing like a sense of justice accomplished to lift the spirits of a person who feels that the world is out of joint. And if that person has it in writing, on world-class hand-drawn paper... Months later Silberstern showed the document to our friend Bobby from the Folkwang School. He kept it in a special folder marked "Complicated." He had displayed it to the madam, and wiped clean the *affûtage* on that very same evening with a two peseta payoff. He was holding on to the document because it was written on a real count's personal stationery. And now he insisted on meeting the count in person. "Watch out," Bobby said. "This guy is worse than a ferret."

A few weeks went by, and finally the first sign of life arrived from Nina. And with it, I'm pained to say, came a bad omen. It was a telegram from Casablanca, where the blonde Rhenish maiden, now with her hair dyed just a little too black, was waiting in a ritzy-sounding hotel for the transfer of a considerable sum that would pay her hotel bill and her passage back to Mallorca. It was unthinkable, Silberstern said, that he would send her the money. He had other means of forcing his doll to return to him. Well and good, I replied, but why should he be wringing his hands? He should go ahead with his "other means." But he oughtn't to be surprised if Nina starts playing her trumps. "That tizzy? What do you mean, trumps? She can't even get her humps unless I pay for them!"

A single hint at possible intervention by the German Consulate General was sufficient to clear up this minor matter. For a few thousand pesetas, a miserly millionaire of the Silberstern ilk could be spared the guillotine. He received a grateful reply from the luxury Estoril spa in Portugal, saying she would be arriving soon via Marrakesh. "1000 kisses, Nina."

I explained to my client, who was now in the throes of yet another inner crisis, that the love bestowed by all first-rate females had its own special geography. He was making the mistake, I said, of drawing lines on the map simply as the crow flies. Nina was obviously a migratory bird with many separate breeding grounds and a deficient homing instinct. Patience!

On Mallorca anybody could be a count, a doctor, a professor, a best-selling writer or a neglected painter. A tall guy with the hairy legs of a jockey could present himself as the son-in-law of Franz von Papen's equestrian groom. A *grande dame* could live there on a minuscule pension, the same lady I was in the habit of entertaining with my pidgin-English tirades against the *Führer*-Pope Axis, quoting from books I had been sent from Amsterdam by *Het Vaderland* for review—some of them quite intelligent books, by the way. The lady smiled often, feeling flattered in her maternal solicitude. She soon knew by heart lines from the writings of Prince Hubertus zu Löwenstein, Wertheim, and Freudenberg. And we should just imagine, she added, all the great things her intelligent son was going to write...

Just as people on our island were able to maintain their various personalities, in similar fashion the men of Marrakesh inside their tents, where Nina was submitting to them on beautifully woven carpets, were no doubt all quite authentic. Surely they were all genuine sheikhs, and instead of offering her stockings from some Cologne bargain basement, they were favoring her with spikenard and saffran, precious incense, gold and silver trinkets, and for Widow Jensen, a stud camel in place of a puny goat. In return, Nina was presenting them what she received from her Creator: a pair of thighs like marble columns set upon golden pedestals; her sweet palate; and her breasts, which were like watering-troughs for the divinities. These sheikhs, descendants of Old-Testament power and glory, were naturally more skilled than Katrinchen's Spaniards at the Clock Tower. But a woman who has once shared the sack with a genuine sheikh could never be persuaded, for all the wealth of the world, to return to Silberstern's brass bedstead. Certainly not for a pair of cheap hosiery.

Back in Palma, once again ensconced in her detested master's living quarters, this Shulamite from the left bank of the Rhine had nothing on her mind except dancing. And soon enough she was doing just that at the "Trocadero," the just-completed, most lavish dance hall in the city, where a short time later an authentic Mengelberg would wield his baton in front of a combo made up of genuine gypsies, plus the arpeggios of a genuine Rahel. Dancing, dancing! This was all that Nina wanted to do—but never with the repulsive Silberstern, who in any case wouldn't be up to it.

A number of Spanish suitors lay at her feet. They gave her their excited *piropos* and made tempting offers. She allowed one of them to come close to her enchanting presence: this was a wealthy, handsome young fellow, and she gave him the key to her belt. He owned an elegant *piso*, a yacht, and a greyhound upon which Silberstern, a great fan of the dog races, once placed a winning bet. Instead of setting up shop with Adelfredo on Palma's market square, where neither of them could manage a word of Spanish, she preferred to amble about in the company of her *señorito*, thereby attracting the glances of so many other *señoritos* that the young man decided to abduct her. This *rapto* occurred in broad daylight, within sight of the brother of a twice-doctored German attorney—an indication that it is not always sufficient to have a powerful brother. Once again Silberstern came running to Barceló Street. This Nina was his Nina, he insisted. It was he who had brought her back. It was he who had busied himself with her clothing—not in the sense of un-clothing, to be sure, since things had not yet returned to the point of "racial defilement." It was he who was feeding her, and still he had to employ a maid. And what thanks was he getting? She was shacking up with a Spaniard.

Calm yourself, I said. I'll get her back for you. It would cost him a few of his crummy pesetas—not for snatching her away from her beau, which I could bring about at my own expense by means of a simple telephone call to the Spaniard. No, the real expense would be for her de-pilarization, for now his Nina was surely *beschmettet* from head to toe.

"Be-what?

"*Beschmettet*. It's a Dutchism I've learned, and it has something do with syphilis. We must face the facts directly."

Nina was gone for a whole month. Then a letter of hers arrived whose dreadful contents were mitigated only by the touchingly juvenile railroad-track German in which it was written. The *señorito* was holding her captive at his *finca*. He was a sadist, and he, too, was syphilitic. Adelfried could have her back, unconditionally, if only he would rescue her from the claws of this Spanish monster.

"What? Now I can have her back, now that she has the *schmette*?" It was enough to make him start tearing his hair out. "And to think that I had her come all the way from Cologne!"

I recommended Professor Scheidegger in Basel. For 3000 francs he would admit her to his purification plant, though it might cost as much as 5000—it all depended on the number of bacilli that the Spaniard had infested her with. After six months she could be back on the job.

Silberstern's reply to my matter-of-fact explanation consisted in two large tears. But he wasn't shedding them for Nina. They would have been more effective with her mother.

"It's the familiar emigration story," I said. "Some get it in the neck, others in the behind. And it's always aimed at your bank account."

I wrote the Spanish *señorito* that he was harboring a dangerous Third Reich spy, an activity that could come to the attention of counter-spies. She would be killed in any case, and if her corpse were found in his bed. Three days later a limousine stopped in front of our house: in it was Nina.

Nina was given a 3rd-class rail ticket back to the railroad crossing between Cologne and Neuss, plus a letter of recommendation for potential respectable employers—a document that, oddly enough, she insisted upon. Then she was off, back home to the Reich. But in the meantime her own Reich had expanded, and it began in Barcelona. Herr Silberstern escorted his squeeze, who for him was now hardly worth a sneeze, to the harbor. Always the cavalier. And who knew—she just *might*...

And now the mosaic of love again ran into the money, no matter how cheap each of the little stones was that Silberstern added to it. During this exciting epoch with Nina he had rid himself of *affûtage* by engaging in cash-free commerce.

A Mallorquin maiden with pigtail and *rebocillo*, and with bosom and legs swathed beneath seven protective layers of skirts and petticoats, moved into Silberstern's apartment. Beatrice sounded a warning: that man had better not any get funny ideas, for otherwise some island gang would lynch him.

After three days the young lady took flight. But she refrained from denouncing her employer, since at my insistence she got her month's wage in advance. So once again, disaster was avoided. But for how much longer?

Not much longer, as it turned out. For this was not life as Silberstern wanted to live it. "In Germany..." Over and over again I had to hammer it into this emigrant's skull that he wasn't living in Germany, and that even if he was experiencing a certain degree of erotic deprivation, he should consider that co-religionists of his were being crowded into concentrations camps, *sans* women and soon enough *sans* life itself.

The Bible came up with the idea that it isn't good for a man to stay alone; he should have a fitting helpmate. But the Bible doesn't offer an answer to the question of which helpmate would be fitting for an Adelfried Silberstern. And that's why Vigoleis had to do all that was humanly possible to close this gap. Indeed, whose rib would bring forth the right woman to grace this Adam's brass bedstead, above which hung the photos of all the females who had played a direct role in this piece of erotic furniture? There were about fifty of them—fifty stellar hours in the life of Herr Silberstern.

I vowed to myself that I would let my sun's rays shine upon this wretched client until vengeance was mine. One day I asked him to figure out whether it wouldn't be cheaper to get married than to hire both a housemaid and cathouse whores, quite apart from the moral advantages of having a stable household—a household, a German home in the barren diaspora! German domestic warmth! German *Gemütlichkeit*! And who but himself, I added, would have the wherewithal, intellectual and material, to create a model household in this foreign country, while back in Germany the households were fast becoming incubators of racist madness? Let the choice of a partner for you be my concern, I said, for my conscience tells me that I should make up for giving you such bad advice in connection with Nina. In any case, Nina was probably too close a neighbor of my own from the Lower Rhenish hinterlands.

I composed a personal ad, which produced an outcome different from what the suitor was imagining. He was looking for a housemaid, "later marriage not excluded"—which is to say, the kind of arrangement that the Dutch newspaper ads qualify with the phrase *met gebruik van* mijnheer, though of course it's vice-versa—"dowry desirable but not obligatory." The ad appeared in the largest newspapers of the Third Reich. The reactions were astounding. Even Silberstern was struck dumb by the realization that so many women wished to escape certain death. Jewish descent was one of the stipulations I mentioned in the ad. Yet Silberstern's reaction focused on his own vanity: so many women wanted to share his bed!

While sorting out the replies, it occurred to me that there were countless beautiful Jewesses in Germany—perhaps not beautiful to look at, but beautiful in the way they described their lot in the letters they wrote. Herr Silberstern wanted, he *had to have*, the most beautiful of them all, for after all, who would be paying the freight? Because he would be paying the freight, he would reject any beautiful woman who would soon enough leave him for another man. This had the effect of excluding any and all Ninas, plus any non-Ninas whose lives were not directly threatened, and it eventually came down to just one. And this one was a lady—but not in the sense of Adelfried's way of dealing with "ladies."

This case, one in a thousand, affected me most deeply. The woman in question, who in all innocence was applying to sweep floors for the anonymous suitor, was the widow of a well-known Berlin banker. Shortly after the Nazi takeover, he strung himself up on his bedroom window frame. His estate was confiscated. Their son—an only child, as I recall—was in a sanatorium. Her letter was brief: she would take on any job, and she had no money for transportation.

Herr Silberstern said that while she was not exactly a *beauté*, and while her age somewhat exceeded his needs, she apparently came from the loftiest social circles in Berlin, which included Rathenau and, no doubt, Kessler too. He asked me to get information from the Count immediately. He also inquired whether I thought she would sleep with him, although he did think it best if he asked the lady directly since she kept such exclusive company. My response was based on my readings concerning such social circles: without question, gentlemen were in the habit of sleeping with ladies if the gentlemen were perfect gentlemen and the ladies perfect ladies—unless, of course, they just couldn't stand each other. In the present case, I said, there should be no cause for concern—on the contrary. But first of all, this perfect lady had to be liberated from those finest Berlin social circles.

She came. She was short, thin, haggard, and dressed in clothes that seemed to indicate her decline from the mistress of a Berlin-Grunewald palace to the lowly domestic who would polish shoes for a miser—but woe to her if she put the shoe cream on too thick! Like Nina before her, we got to meet this first lady of Berlin high finance right after she stepped off the ship. Silberstern was in the best of moods. He folded his hands on his belly and twiddled his thumbs, proud as a peacock. Having come up short as a wine merchant, he had finally found the woman who would be subject to him and who, within 12 or 13 short hours, would literally lie beneath him in his bed of brass. Berlin high finance! Where Kaisers came and went!

Beatrice offered to assist the lady during her first days on the island, perhaps by looking in on her at noontime. Her French wouldn't be of help at the local markets. Herr Silberstern was touched. He said, "Do you see? Was I wrong? My connections are all educated people!"

Beatrice gave careful instructions to the new housemaid. She must be prepared for all eventualities. She must always lock her door and exercise patience. This was to be only a transitional position—we had already made contact with a wealthy Catalan industrialist who was looking for a German domestic.

Just 24 hours later, things went worse than we had bargained for. The perfect lady from Berlin simply refused. Her relationship with the brass bed was limited to polishing the metal and shaking out and spreading the linens. She did not lie down on it. This led to more hand-wringing and bitter accusations, which degenerated into true vulgarity when Silberstern learned that instead of shopping at the open market, this cultivated lady made purchases at the *Colmado Parisien* because she could converse in the language. We didn't own a bed, and so we weren't able to take this Cinderella in as our guest. And there was still no reply from Barcelona. But the lady told us that she had experienced even worse humiliation in Germany. She wanted nothing more than to retake her son into her custody, but the Nazis wouldn't let her. He was, she explained, somewhat feebleminded, and he would probably be killed.

The Catalan industrialist came in person on his own yacht to Mallorca to fetch his German domestic. We were delighted. Silberstern, close to despair, complained that once again everything had gone wrong. Everything!

Later we received a few letters from the lady. The Costa Brava was heaven on earth for her, she wrote, but she could never be happy while her son remained in Germany. Her Catalan employer offered to use his personal influence, but she rejected that idea. Her plan was to go back to Berlin herself.

One year later she wrote us a grateful note from Paris, where she was on her way to Germany. Her child had disappeared, and she was going to look for him. Then she, too, disappeared. No doubt she was setting out on the same journey as her child, like the millions of children of Israel.

If stones might ever be brought to tears, Silbersterns' daily lamentations could have done the job. His situation worsened. After his experience with the perfect lady, I suggested that he take in a young man as his valet. But just a few weeks later this fellow, too, was gone. The boy understood a few words of German, having worked for a time in Germany in the tropical fruit business like so many other Mallorquins. Silberstern tried training his "servant," as he called Jaime, in the business of snagging women. For this purpose Jaime had the use of a special bank account. But the birds he caught never ended up on his master's perch; the birdman himself listened to their chirpings in his own little spare room. It came to blows. Once again I insisted: find someone to marry! Find a German woman, if you will, but this time one who hails from circles that understand the true ways of the world.

"An artist?"

"An artist!"

"Like Rahel Mengelberg?"

"At least somebody extra-special like her."

"Well then, take dictation..."

The slaughter of Jews in Germany was proceeding apace, and so, in response to our new advertisement, this one aimed squarely at artist types. We received hundreds of applications. My table groaned under the weight of impoverished non-Aryan art. Prominent names came into view. Amid the unrelenting deluge, drowning souls were reaching out for Silberstern as a life-preserver. My intention was once again to extract a human being from hell at my client's expense and, once she was in Spain, to see to it that she got a decent roof over her head. But at the same time, this artist would have to be able to put the lecherous millionaire in his place. It took all my oratorical skills to dissuade horny Adelfried from going after a few dozen juicy prospects. I gave prime attention to a middle-aged woman who worked in films. I had a certain weakness for this type ever since I had contact with Victor E. van Vriesland's attractive film agent, though otherwise I knew nothing at all about movies and movie-making. I will never understand movies, but then again, over my lifetime I have seen perhaps 25 films in all.

This was to be the one. She was so famous that she didn't have to submit a photo—her face was familiar from the postcards you could buy at all the cinemas. As the divorced wife of an even more famous film director, she was in all respects savvy, and hence just the person I needed for this merry prank of mine, which was also an attempt to save a doomed soul. At first, Silberstern wouldn't have any of it, but then I flattered his vanity by telling him that he would soon be in all the newspapers of Spain, later of the whole world, for letting this particular star hover above his brass bedstead. Surely he was aware from his experience in selling wines, I said, that women with a bouquet like hers were immune to the aging process. As a film star, she had mastered the art of camouflage. Even her hands, those tell-tale fossils of maturing feminity, could surely be deceptive. "Shall we write?"

"Take dictation...!" Herr Silberstern was already imagining himself in the role of a celebrated Silver Star. His imbecilic egotism, constantly in conflict with his doltishness, made him salivate at the thought of winning this precious booty. He asked whether I thought she would also keep his apartment clean. What she would keep scrupulously clean, I thought to myself, was his bed, and she would know how to clean him out in other ways, too.

It wasn't easy to compose a letter to a movie star, but I finally wrote one in such a way that neither the undersigned nor the recipient would notice how they were both being misused. In retrospect I am just as proud of this epistolary accomplishment as I am of my Christian missive to Zwingli's millionaire aunt in Basel.

Her reply was encouraging. She even exceeded expectations by offering to travel to Palma and, following a decent probationary interval, giving her hand in marriage to Mr. Silberstern. Among their mutual acquaintances, it turned out, was Silberstern's brother, the Privy Councilor. She didn't send her photo, but requested one of her future breadwinner—causing me to take fright, though not because this might impair discretion, which she guaranteed. Silberstern gathered up all the pictures that had ever been taken of his not very attractive person during a life of wining and womanizing. Like the man himself, the pictures spoke volumes, and so we would have to be on our guard. If he sent her one, we would never again hear from this artist, whose own ulterior motives were in any case unclear to me. In order to escape the underworld, surely she had no need of a "star" such as this one. Heaven itself, whose existence I constantly doubt and decry, suddenly provided me with the means to get back at Vigoleis' exploiter and cost him a wad of money. "A cavalier," I told him as I handed him back his photos, "would never send his picture to a lady of her standing. He would send himself."

Was I crazy, he asked? Was I joking? If he went back to the Reich they would kill him on the spot. No, he would send the photos—all of them. "Take dictation!"

A gentleman like him, a lady like her, and an engagement that would attract the attention of the whole world—"Mr. Stern, that's why the Dear Lord created free Switzerland, the city of Zurich, and the Stork Hotel. But let's ask Beatrice how you call the hotel in French. That'll make it sound more cosmopolitan. The stork is, to be sure, a cosmopolitan bird, but there's something maternal about it that we want to avoid. The 'Baur au Lac' is out of the question—as an old capitalist you wouldn't need a place like that. Let me write her a few lines with my suggestion."

Struggle. Extremely rapid calculation of the expense. Vainglory, despair, thumb-twiddling, thumbs stuck in armpits, a recital of all of his future bride's scandalous liaisons, an engagement trip to the "Stork"... and then he asked me to start writing.

Reply from Berlin, by telegram. Agreed. *Cigogne*. The one who had to travel the longest distance should set the date.

Vigoleis rubbed his hands. If book publishers could only be as far-sighted as this movie actress, his literary production would long since be a financial success.

Having consented to this huge expense—there was no backing down—my pinchgut client wanted to board ship that very evening, and asked me to send a telegram. "Wait, my good man, " I cried. He mustn't go traveling just as he was, thinking that he could head straight for the Stork Hotel and, once at the Stork, directly into the lady's nest. Fine, but not in the kind of underpants I presumed he was wearing. Didn't he know that Catherine the Great once had a prince of the realm lashed to death for approaching her in that fashion—Catherine, who never behaved like that otherwise? Silberstern objected to my meddling in his laundry matters, but he went out anyway and bought a few pair of fancy underduds. As a millionaire, I told him, he mustn't appear at the hotel in such a shabby suit; he wasn't rich enough for that kind of reverse snobbery, so he would have to find a tailor. He agreed and said that he already knew a tailor, quite inexpensive, 60 pesetas with extras. Perfect, I said. But Palma had a *sastre* for just such cases as his: Bauzá, on the Plaza Cort, where Spanish generals had their work done—and also Count Kessler.

"The Count? You're making this up! Prove it!"

This I could readily do. I had paid the tailor's bill myself to save Kessler a trip downtown. 500 pesetas, the receipt signed by Paquita, beautiful Angelita's even more beautiful sister, who manned the cash register at Bauzá.

Dressed in new threads from head to toe, Adelfried set off for Zurich. But he was unable to put off his old Adam, whereas for me this was the crux of the matter all along. As a result, the meeting at the Stork was the expected fiasco. Silberstern had no more hair to tear out; he would have wrung his hands if he hadn't returned as a dead man.

Vengeance was mine, as with Pilar and Hedwig Courths-Mahler.

I gradually learned some, but not all, of the details of the encounter in Zurich, where the upper crust likes to gather. Silberstern stopped at the modest Hotel zur Krone, on the shores of the Limmat; the actress stayed at the Baur au Lac with some friends from the cinema. There was no opportunity for showing off new underwear. The meeting took place in the lobby of the Stork, and this bird showed no particular interest in bringing the two together. "Did you at least pay the lady's travel expenses?"—"Unfortunately yes, Herr Doktor, and promptly, too." What else could I expect of my client? "And did you get your money's worth otherwise, too? Little girls?" Zurich, he explained, had its own hidden sources of pleasure—rather expensive, though, since the Swiss government refuses to subsidize regular joy houses. That pushes up the prices! So nothing of that sort—too expensive.

One day after this leave-taking, he left for Barcelona. The trip was uneventful as far as Paris, but then some "elements" took their seats in his compartment, and to him they looked more than suspicious. They started whispering in German, and they began looking at him with glances aimed more at the Jew than at his snazzy Bauzá suit. He was overcome with Dachau panic. Spies! They'll grab you and string you up—racial defilement!—or they'll just toss you off the train! This was the time when Jews were getting found who had fallen out of trains all over the world. Silberstern knew this. Clumsy non-gymnast that he was, Silberstern snuck out of the compartment, and as the train slowed down a bit, at the risk of his life, he stepped outside and spent the night on the step. His expensive Bauzá hat went flying off. Some French Widow Jensen probably found it later next to the tracks somewhere between Clermont-Ferrand and Port-Bou. Adelfried was wearing his old hat when he returned from his trip and said, "Take dictation!"

So I started writing again. This time it was a letter to Nina's titled beau in Lisbon, the gentleman whose ancestral line would stand or fall with him—a detail I was of course unaware of at the time. He replied with the *courtoisie* of all Portuguese gentlemen: he would be happy to be of service. No, Portugal was not yet producing educational films, but Nina's friend should come over anyway and bring his colleague. He, the *conde*, *marquêz*, and *barão*, could be of assistance at all the preliminary discussions, capital transactions, etc. German experts, he wrote, were much in demand.

Silberstern had located a buddy with whom he now started planning a business venture. It was going to bring in millions, and—pure coincidence—it had to do with the cinema. This colleague, an educational-film expert from Berlin, was living in exile on Mallorca. He had made a name for himself, and it meant nothing that I had never heard of him. Bobby knew him, Beatrice knew him, everybody knew him. Silberstern's star was rising again.

Millions got transferred from Madrid to Lisbon. The correspondence grew to huge proportions, and it was complicated. I could have learned a lot from it, but didn't. Items of furniture were also sent to Portugal, since only death could separate Silberstern from his brass bedstead. Too much had happened, and not happened, to keep him off of his special *pilarière*. Like Mamú, he traveled with his own bed.

Whenever we ran out of centimos and I put the touch on Silberstern, he generously lent me money—up to 50 pesetas without an I.O.U., but only as a favor to me, and never even to his best friend. He always got it back to the last centimo. Honesty, this miser had discovered, was another one of Vigoleis' pathetic qualities. But now I owed him the postage for a letter I sent abroad, and for weeks I had forgotten to pay up the pittance.

When Mr. Silberstern took leave of us—"This time for good," he said—he mentioned that there was a small sum that needed taking care of. An ineffable shudder went through me. I thought—truly, dear reader, I actually thought—

that the skinflint would now pull out his bulging wallet, remove an envelope, and hand it to me, and that Vigoleis, who doesn't understand money and thus needs it all the more, would accept it with an obviously embarrassed smile. And I imagined that when Silberstern was finally gone, when the man I had derided, mocked, and ridiculed daily, the man who was driven into profligate expense, the one I had almost killed on the rail line between Clermont-Ferrand and Port-Bou! When this guy was gone—that is, as soon as he departed from our door—Vigoleis would open the envelope and collapse in shame: a check for 100,000 pesetas for services rendered in the court cases of Silberstern vs. Third Reich, Silberstern vs. Nina, Silberstern vs. diverse bordello madams, vs., vs., and vs. Vigoleis.

Silberstern was now reaching into his pocket. Vigoleis, having suddenly recovered, stammered, "Oh, but Mr. Silberstern, that's too, too kind of you! What I did was such a small matter..." This accursed brother of his brothers said, "Ah, but you mustn't say that, Herr Doktor. In business affairs, there is no such thing as a small matter. And as you know from our long-term collaboration, I can be quite meticulous. It has to do..." Meanwhile he had yanked out one of his greasy penciled notes. "Ah yes, it has to do with the postage for a letter sent abroad."

Vigoleis never became an anti-Semite, not even during this gut-wrenching moment. After all, there are some decent Christians, too.

When the ladies of Christian Science closed their New Testaments, my hour had arrived, the time for me to move my chair next to Mamú's and tell her stories from the Old Testament. The Scientists knew that I had an obscure relationship with a quirky fellow named Silberstern, who on the night of the Nazi takeover had almost lost his head—or at least his silverware. They also knew that Mamú preferred the Old Testament to the New, which was why she liked to listen to the tales spun by this particular Jacob. And finally, they knew that Mamú herself would never be able to pass the Aryan blood test, and that hence the contested baking-powder millions, despite their Royal camouflage, were dirty Jewish millions, whereas they themselves were devoted entirely to the New Testament, praying for the *Führer* like my mother, but in their own fashion and in their own languages, none of which, oddly enough, was German. Mamú was Jewish—and that explains her increasing fear of this bible-thumping gang. Bobby had presumed as much all along, while I was taken in by the "Royal" in the baking-powder logo. For the many-blooded Swiss citizen Beatrice, this aspect of things was no problem at all.

Shortly after the outbreak of the Civil War, Mamú fled the island under the efficiently organized protection of the American Consulate. But she still was in panic at the lethal threat posed to any Jew by the zealots of the Rome-Berlin-Burgos axis. Her fears were well founded. Several of the Christian Science dames had pinned to their blouses the emblem of the Holy War, the Most

Sacred Heart of Jesus, next to the swastika. This made them into the hyenas of a movement that would seek to annihilate their own organization. We said, "Mamú, find yourself a ship, the very next ship. Tomorrow might be too late. Jewish, and a millionaire..." She was even afraid of her German nanny, who had turned into a Nazi.

But she had to listen to my Old-Testament stories with all of their chapters and verses, insofar as Silberstern made manifest their eternally human significance. I held back nothing. Because Mamú's monthly checks were still arriving, she rewarded my palate for the things she was hearing from my loose tongue. We had the time of our lives together. She had praise for my triumph over the Third Reich, yet not enough praise to nab me a position as legal counsel in her very private suit against the Royal Powder Bakers. Her attorney in New York, she said, was doing excellent work. He had already made great strides and had the whole case under his expert care. She read me long letters from this lawyer who talked of "extreme importance"—so extreme that I prophesied that she would soon be a thousand times richer than all Silver Stars put together.

I earned a dish of kangaroo meat by recounting for her a *chronique scandaleuse* from the international world of music, one that our walking *Who's Sleeping With Whom?* expert revealed to Carel and Rahel Mengelberg as soon as they first entered our bible-paper room where, as fate would have it, I was taking dictation.

Carel Mengelberg, no prudish milquetoast but a world-class musician who knows that where you sing best is where you will settle down, since that's where your voice will be all the fuller and purer—Carel was astounded at all the goings-on inside his own artistic guild. "What? She with him, and he with her...?!" "You can take my word for it," said Silberstern, taking conceited pleasure in divulging some improbable or even impossible mingling of personalities, replete with when and where and with what consequences. "But now listen to this, ladies and gentlemen. What might have happened—I say *might* have happened—if this or that personality, or that time instead of some other time, or at that place rather than some other place..." He presented us with a string of Waterloo hypotheticals, the kind of "what if" questions that are considered moot only by people who don't realize that history actually consists of what doesn't really happen. In brief, without sins committed against the Sixth Commandment there would be no philharmonic enchantment for the masses. And when Carel swore to my pot-bellied client with a handshake that he was an authentic Mengelberg, no doubt about it, a Mengelberg from the Mengelberg family, nephew of *de groote Willem*, Silberstern said, "Excellent! I can get you an *angashement* at the Trocadero. First harp: Madame Rahel. The best of the best!"

Poor Mengelberg, genuine or not. He had arrived with only a dilapidated rucksack, intending to take a few hikes with his Rahel on the Golden Island, but now—conductor at the Trocadero! A lifetime position! Success and glory! Envious colleagues, an envious Uncle Willem! And he came without a suit of tails, with no money except one silver duro. Herr Silberstern promised to betake himself immediately to the nightclub to make the contractual arrangements.

When he actually left after three hours, the Mengelbergs straightaway sank down on Nina's bed, exhausted. Was it conceivable that ordinary people imagined such hanky-panky going on behind the musical scenes, inside the prompters' boxes and in the orchestra pits? They had remotely heard of such things—but were they really true? Was Willem Mengelberg in actuality a musically camouflaged "Wilhelm"? Was Abendroth a Schnabel, and was Schnabel an Edwin Fischer? I felt it necessary to interrupt such musings by announcing that they must send a registered letter to Carel's sister in San Cugat del Vallés, asking her to send him his tails by express, for our unlucky Star was at this very hour wending his way up the incline towards El Terreno, where the all-powerful owner of the Trocadero lived.

Carel's tails arrived in a mangled package. His sister Leentje—she, too, a genuine Mengelberg, unless we can get confused by Mr. Silberstern's behind-the-scenes magic—hadn't been living long enough in Spain to know how to send a suit of tails from Barcelona to Palma in such a way as to prevent it from running away by itself, resulting in a fall, or at least in a late delivery. And to prevent the little black armband from getting lost in transit. Happily, Don Matías, still observing his year of mourning, felt honored to lend the famous Dutch maestro his own black band for the occasion. As always several steps ahead of current events, I interpreted this gesture as a preliminary form of political collaboration: Why shouldn't Carel Mengelberg create a musical setting of "Thank God's Hymn to Freedom?" And Rahel, as swarthy as Rabindranath—why shouldn't she pluck her lyre in the wake of the Freedom March? And then: Carel as Director of the Tegucigalpa State Opera!

"Easy, there!" said Mengelberg's new impresario Silberstern. First we would have to make sure that the *angkashemang* at the bar was in perfect order, with 500 pesetas as a beginning wage for the conductor—harp included. With that they could get by quite well on Mallorca, he said, even as an "authenticious" Mengelberg. Beatrice, quizzed by four eyes at once, confirmed this.

So now Silberstern was the impresario for the composer and conductor Mengelberg, who just recently had made his mark leading the 110-man-strong Banda Municipal de Barcelona with the world premiere of his musical sketch "Catalunya Renaixent" in the *Palacio de Bellas Artes*. The Mallorcan debut was an event that I described in detail to Mamú, with the appropriate enumeration of orchestra personnel, instrumental desk arrangement, and who slept with whom. I portrayed for her the puffed-up impresario's darting about with flying coattails (I'm exaggerating, of course—coattails don't exist any more. Besides, to scrimp on the cost of fabric Silberstein kept his jackets tailless), and his dialogues with the boss of the Trocadero, who naturally had never heard the name of Mengelberg. According to the nightclub manager, if this Don Carlos was such a celebrity in the world of nightclub combos, and if Doña Raquel could slam the kettledrums, then let them come, by all means, and try things out with his ensemble.

We soon found out that Leentje needn't have sent her brother's formal suit. In the boss's honky-tonk, Carel could have mounted the stage in shorts, and Rahel could have plucked a few strings sporting only a bra and the Cassandra glances that were normal for her. "And do you know, Mamú, the end result of Silberstern's stupid puffery is simply that the event didn't meet the Mengelbergs' fond expectations, which were of a kind that not even a Mevrouw Beverwijn could fulfill. They'll get over it as soon as they start hiking. Valldemosa, Deyá—they're going to all those places on foot. No, Mamú, the real tragedy of the situation is something completely different, something awful. With all of their traveling back and forth between Palma and the Terreno, Carel discovered that the one duro they had in their possession, besides some small change, was phony. If you dropped it on a marble tabletop it wouldn't bounce back, but just lie there. It was a lead slug. The sound it would make is *plump*, a word that derives from the Latin *plumbum*, and not one Spaniard in the whole country would ever accept it. No, slugs like that one find their way into the pockets of foreigners. So now Carel was carrying this millstone around with him. Rahel didn't say anything, because unlike Carel she lives her life in regions other than the Aeolian clouds. To demonstrate the counterfeit, she pitched the duro onto the floor. All of us heard the etymological sound, and were filled with the "inner glow of poverty" that Rilke has made famous. The only one who could, would, and did master the situation was Silberstern. He asked for the duro so he could place a bet on a greyhound at the automatic machine. That, he explained, and the alms boxes in churches is where you can get rid of even the clumsiest counterfeit money. But his betting star was unlucky; he got caught trying to use the slug. The next day he came back and returned it, bowing and scraping to the original owners.

"But he's a millionaire, Vigo! He should be ashamed! He could simply have said, 'It made that sound. Here, Maestro, is a genuine duro in recompense.'"

Carel is myopic, and that has made his sense of hearing all the sharper. He can't tell by looking whether something is genuine or not. Aesthete that he is, and connoisseur of women that he is, he often took some female passer-by for Spain's most beautiful specimen of femininity. He would follow her, hoping to keep her before his eyes as if he were holding a tuning fork to his ear. He would simply run after her. Rahel, concerned for his welfare and bent on helping her creative partner avoid disappointment—although disappointment can also be inspiring—sounded a warning: that lady wasn't worth his trouble; Spain's beautiful women existed only on posters. But Carel, with his special intuition, disappeared from view. And when he returned to us breathless, he would always offer the same laconic report: "*Niet de moeite waard.*" As a bona fide Mengelberg of the musical guild his sense of hearing hadn't deceived him. But he didn't yet dare just to grab his "beautiful" prey and toss her to the ground like a duro to test her authenticity.

As far as duros were concerned, I myself had already made great strides. Sometimes I heard it make atonal sounds—an inexhaustible topic for a

Mengelberg. To make a coin sound just right, it was often only a matter of how you tossed it to the ground. I took our own real, genuine duro—it was also our very last—and made a few prestidigitory gestures unnoticed by the others (the Mengelbergs were too preoccupied with their own misery). I threw it down, and—it rang! Silver! You couldn't even hear the metallurgic deception perpetrated by the recently abdicated Spanish National Mint with the national currency. And anyway, why should we, the common people, worry about such things? Carel and Rahel, suddenly revived by the music of authenticity, now gave the subject their full attention. Rahel began an incredibly quick-paced lecture. Each of us felt that she was addressing us directly, whereas in reality she was talking to all of us together or to nobody in particular. Her subject was the duro. Never before, she said, had a revaluation of the *sevillano* achieved so much in such a short time. Rahel sketched out a plan. She conjured up worlds of possibilities for which our arch-miser Silberstern, so thoroughly versed in scrounging pennies, would readily have parted with at least three duros.

During my student days at Cologne, the economic philosophers claimed that money was a fiction. I had my reservations, which were supported by other academic departments, especially the Department of Theology. And now a genuine duro had certified for us the falsity of the economists' claim. Whereupon we all embraced, and left for Coll den Rebassa to go swimming. Carel paid the trolley fare—a Mengelberg, after all, doesn't act shabbily. It was warm in the sun, and plenty of beautiful women crossed Carel's path. Rahel was constantly amazed—how scarce beautiful women were in Spain!

Interested in matters of currency as in so many other subjects, Mamú wanted to know what happened with the bogus duro. She motioned to her servant to refill my glass.

"The next morning I pressed it into our milkman's hand. He was short-sighted, too, and since we had never cheated him, he didn't toss the *sevillano* on the floor, but innocently handed over our change. I breathlessly went back to our shredded-newspaper bed and reported to Beatrice that we were finally rid of the fake *sevillano*. It was the first time in my life that I had cheated someone, but I explained that the authentic Mengelbergs were worth such a prank. Suddenly our doorbell rang. It was the milkman. He said that lead-slug duros were making the rounds on the island, and often it was foreigners who were the first to get pulled in. All I could say was: right you are, and if it was OK with him we'd pay up at the end of the week".

"And then...?" Mamú never stopped halfway, which is why she kept going with her gigantic lawsuit.

"I put the *sevillano* in a metal box where Beatrice keeps souvenirs that we're both attached to. It's still in there, a reminder of the Mengelbergs, to whom we never confessed and never will confess that it was for their sake that I became a common extortionist. The left hand must never know what the right hand is doing—isn't that what your Science ladies are always saying?"

"So it's a talisman of friendship? How touching. That reminds me of my late Prince, who would have acted just as you did. I like your idea of friendship. And it is friendship, isn't it, that you have felt for the Mengelbergs?" She motioned, and her servant refilled again. It was an unadulterated Valdepeñas.

"It was friendship at first glance, Mamú. And nothing would have changed, even if Stern had used his *Who's Sleeping With Whom?* to show that the Mengelbergs were fake Mengelbergs. We liked them in spite of Carel's rucksack, which in my opinion just doesn't become him."

What did Beatrice think about friendship, Mamú inquired. The same as Vigo. In many respects Beatrice and I were contrary natures, but when it came to basic matters of life our ideas and feelings were at the same level. Friendship was one example. Stefan George was not.

Mamú's servant—for some time now it was none other than Jaime, the skirt-chasing fellow Silberstern had tossed out of his house—whom she was training to become her butler, once again responded to a gesture and rushed to fill our glasses. For Beatrice it was a Manzanilla.

At Mamú's everyone was treated fairly, as long as we did the same for her. She would of course have preferred that we squirted the wine in a beautiful arc down our throats, directly from a porrón. But her vintages were much too precious to be imbibed only for their value as nourishment, as the Southern Europeans are wont to do. You just can't squirt and taste at the same time. Admittedly it is impressive to watch a leather bag getting passed around a formal dinner table, especially if it involves expert *porronistas*. Not one drop on anybody's white shirt!

"And is your friend Silberstern now compiling his Roster of Musicians? If so, I'll send in my subscription right away!"

"If Hitler hadn't seized power over the German sleepyheads, the first volume, A - Adelfried, would already have been published. But now the editor is no longer *au courant*, Mamú. As it is, the emigrés are sleeping wherever and with whomever they can. And back in the Reich, this sort of thing is now regulated by the Reich Chamber of Intercourse, which issues its own pedigree lists."

At this moment Calpurnia rushed hurriedly into the room with a telegram. The maid hadn't become accustomed to the fact that messages are always urgent, even in the home of a millionaire, but that as soon as the messenger hands them over, these bits of news metamorphose into solemn communiqués concerning either access to new millions or harbingers of utter financial collapse. "Don't hurry," Mamú scolded her, but then she herself opened the telegram with alacrity—and Calpurnia lifted her swooning employer from the floor.

Vigoleis remained the single calm element in the tumult that arose over the unconscious woman. He preserved the dignity of big capital. At a wave of his hand, Jaime refilled his glass. It was a 1923 vintage.

As he was leaving the dining room he spied the telegram on the floor, picked it up and, contrary to his habits but in keeping with the spirit of the house, read the return address. "The Prince," he murmured. "This is going to get very interesting."

Some weeks later, or perhaps it was only days later, Mamú rode to the General's Street and wheezed her way up the stairs to our apartment. It goes without saying that she was beside herself, that her cheeks were quivering, and that first of all she had to sit down. She had received a letter from Budapest, her old bad-weather headquarters. But before she set out to explain matters, she inquired whether our notions about friendship, which we had explained to her earlier in connection with the Mengelbergs' duro, were just meaningless dinnertime chatter, or our true opinion.

I said to her: Mamú, true friendship can be tested only by money. If a friendship comes to an end because of money, then it never was a true friendship, never a so-called friendship based on virtue, never a Pythagorean friendship in the full sense of the term. Even a friendship between God and human beings can be destroyed by money... but at the moment, Mamú didn't want to hear this. She had come, she said, not as the head of her Mother Church but as a soul in distress, on a matter that the old hags must never learn about. This information calmed me somewhat. It couldn't be an insurmountable problem.

She wanted to know whether Beatrice still kept an account at her bank in Basel. Yes, a small amount for emergencies. Then came the fateful question: would Beatrice be willing to lend her this small amount, which could mean salvation for her at a time of her direst need?

With no further ado, Beatrice agreed. If Mamú was approaching us poor folk with such a request, her reasons must be so serious that she was side-stepping an appeal to the Scientist ladies, most of whom were as rich as Croesus.

Mamú, with tears in her eyes that gave heartwarming testimony to the caliber of our friendship, showed us the letter she had received from the Hungarian Pusta. "The Prince," I thought. Surely it was her Prince who was the cause of her reaching out to us.

This time, her 80-year-old skirt-chasing brother-in-law hadn't chased after one of his female serfs. Instead, he had gone for somebody else's bank account by way of check forgery—a considerable sum. If they caught him, this ennobled geezer with muttonchops would wander off to the penitentiary, where he would finish his days on bread and water and bereft of little girls. Because the Danube Monarchy was now extinct, the prestige of his exalted name was at stake. Mamú needed money right away to hire a lawyer in Budapest. Her check was already on its way. Just think: off to jail at age eighty!

"Finally at eighty, Mamú! But be that as it might, Beatrice will be deciding the man's fate. She loves Hungary. Her grandest memories of life at a castle are connected with the Colloredo-Mansfeld family."

Those were Bohemians, Beatrice interjected calmly. She added that her account held only 1000 francs, as Mamú already knew. Mamú should decide.

This tiny sum—I'm using the diminutive now in its most disparaging sense—was at a savings bank in Basel, a minuscule inheritance that Beatrice put away for emergency purposes. As she so often told me, we could touch it only when the floodwaters were already up to our necks. Now Beatrice and I have different opinions about floods and other life-threatening emergencies. At times I have had the impression that the waters were not just up to our necks, but in our throats, whereas she, with her Indian tenacity, has acted like a beaver. So she never sent the crucial telegram to her academic brother in Basel, not even during our *endura* at the Clock Tower, not even in sight of the Deucalian Cliff. As a person who lives his life in extremis, I admired her concept of utmost emergency. And so I repressed the whole idea of the Basel bank account.

Our friendship with Mamú held fast. It was not empty tabletalk, nor was it mere academic philosophy. The telegram got sent. Mamú received the *tusig Fränkli*, the Budapest attorney was given his orders, and 24 hours later her Prince emerged from his hiding place—where in the meantime he had done some further damage, but this time only to a skirt. Mamú was hoping that before nine months were up she would have won her own lawsuit, and soon our rescue action would be repaid threefold. "Interest at usurious rates?" "No," Mamú replied. "A small bonus for friendship's sake." She tapped her glass, and Jaime once again did as he was bidden.

Bobby, our seer from the Folkwang School, disapproved of this transaction. Our money was gone, he said. What a shame, considering what we might have used it for—maybe a little house in Valldemosa, where we could have lived together with Mamú.

Bobby was right. His microscopic eyes had penetrated through Mamú's millions to discover the tiny point in her life that had remained totally dark and obscure. Still, I told him that as a double-dealer she was forever charming—that he mustn't deny. And the Christian Science ladies were no doubt acting as her procurers.

"No doubt at all."

"What a shame! That pious little circle always struck me as so real in its Christian social fakery as to be just as believable as the Nail from Christ's Cross in the sacristy at the Valldemosa Charterhouse. But what it comes down to is the miracles it can perform."

Vigoleis never became an anti-Christian, not even following this crushing experience with Mamú. After all, there are some decent Jews, too.

XXII

You can catch a mouse with a slice of bacon. And you can also catch a Captain and Baron von Martersteig from Baron von Richthofen's squadron if the bacon, lean and mellow, is carved from noble German hogs and slathered on German sandwiches with a dollop of Düsseldorf mustard and some good German beer.

In the Bay of Palma a German steamer lay at anchor, a ship of the Woermann Line. But instead of letting loose a horde of tourists on the island, this ship had arrived at Mallorca with the special mission of luring people on board—German people. To be exact, all the Germans living here who were of an age to vote. The German colony was expected to say "Yes!" to the *Führer* in a secret ballot. As on a trip down the Rhine, a brass band on board presented the opportunity to link elbows, sing patriotic songs, and shed a nostalgic tear. Plus, as a personal reward from the *Führer* for voting "Yes," you'd receive two sandwiches smeared with lard, beer on tap, and all the mustard you wanted. In order to place the voting process under the sovereignty of the Third Reich, the voters had to be taken out beyond the legal limit of Spanish waters. This meant a delightful Mediterranean excursion with kit and caboodle. A fanfare, the anchor chains rattled—*Deutschland, Deutschland über alles...*

Starting weeks in advance, the German Consul had sent his agents from house to house passing out leaflets: German Man! German Woman!

I was approached by a cabinet maker from the German Labor Force, an expert carpenter who oughtn't to have degraded himself by espousing a movement he deemed ennobling. He reminded me of my patriotic duty. On Sunday at eight the steamer would sail out to sea. It was the Consul's wish to have the entire colony participate at the ballot box. We had an altercation concerning God, King, *Führer*, and Fatherland. It was all balderdash, I said, adding that I was just a human being like anybody else, but also that I had made construction plans for a desk, which I would like to show him so he could custom-build it for me. The craftsman explained that he was visiting me as an emissary of German culture, and if I didn't have it in my heart to comply, then perhaps my stomach might think otherwise—two sandwiches, sliced ham, beer, and mustard from the center of my own homeland, Düsseldorf! Now wasn't that something? "It says everything" I replied. Take the mustard, for example: I don't like it—too hot for me. The carpenter departed murmuring something about trying things a different way. I yelled after him, "Slabs of bacon for the onboard *Frühschoppen*!" I never was a fan of the German custom of *Frühschoppen*. At noon I met up with Martersteig.

"Hey there, it's you again! Vigoleis with a soft V as in Hannover!"

"And my captain isn't confronting the enemy? How are your monkeys? All ready for combat?"

He wasn't fleeing from Graves, and his book was almost finished. But, he said, that should not be an issue between us. I bowed, and he went on, saying that he had errands to do in the city, but then tomorrow—surely I knew?—the big sailing trip!

Sailing trip? Surely he didn't mean to say that he was falling for that voting fraud? His reply: he had always known that I wasn't a great strategist. He was of course going to cast his vote, a vote in solidarity with the entire German colony, which was going to vote unanimously with "No"—including the Consul, and including Vigoleis.

"Great heavens, man! Have you lost your senses? Are you fixed on setting a new record for crash landings? Here I was thinking that one such escapade would be enough in the life of a German hero. The Order *Pour le Mérite* never gets pinned twice on the same breast."

"Sandwiches with bacon, German beer on tap! Doesn't that say something?"

"You bet, it tells me everything. And more than everything, if such a thing is possible. Tomorrow your entire army of apes, living now for years as starving conscripts, will get betrayed for a mess of wurst, and Captain von Martersteig will be signing his own discharge papers. A dollop of mustard will put a seal on the transaction. Monkeys—dis-*missed!*"

At the Alhambra we drank an anise from Buñola, and parted as friends. It was all a joke, he said. He just wanted to see me hit the ceiling when talking about the Nazi gang that was out to take over our island. Why, among the Germans on Mallorca the two of us were already something like old gentry.

Early on *Führer* Sunday the vote-scrounging carpenter rang our bell, making me leap up from our newspaper pallet. It was half-past seven, which is early for a night-owl. He said he had brought a taxi to pick up any stragglers, in the name of the Consul. Quick—everybody else was ready to go! Herr von Martersteig, too? Yes, of course. It was going to be fine weather. The kids had little flags and balloons. I mustn't miss out on the fun.

"Kindly give the Consul greetings from his best *Führer*, and tell him that I don't want to get in the way of his other *Führer*. And when you have some time, come on back and we'll talk about making my desk. So long!"

The steamer left port without the island's best *Führer*. On board there was singing and dancing, balloting, elbow-linking, flirting, drinking, and a spreading of mustard on sandwiches. Porpoises followed in the ship's wake, and seagulls accompanied the floating ballot booth, where the Consul was in charge. And true enough, he hadn't gone wrong with his colony. The *Führer* emerged from the ballot-box unanimously victorious. After all, it was the *Führer* himself the voters had to thank for being allowed to vote on German soil in the middle of the Mediterranean while singing and dancing, gobbling sandwiches, guzzling beer, and passing gossip. The sea resounded with shouts of "Heil!" as the sun sent down its stinging rays. God lets the sun shine, they say, on the just and the unjust. But also on crazy people. Captain von Martersteig was pleased to let it shine on his gouty leg.

Toward the end of the trip—they were approaching the pier, the mustard was all gone, the balloons were wrinkled or busted, the beer dregs were but shallow pools in the steins—the Consul rose to make another speech. He thanked all of them for their loyalty to the *Führer*, to the Reich, to the Homeland. And he requested permission to request a small fee for the voyage, 13 pesetas per person; those on board were asked to consider that a steamboat like this one was, after all, expensive. The wealthier voters, those who were willing to give the *Führer* not only their love but their money, paid up, if a little reluctantly. The others were thinking, "Damn it all, we've just got stuck again!" But no one dared to utter a word of protest. A human life can be quickly tossed overboard and eaten up by the sharks.

For all with ears to hear, Captain von Martersteig told the story of the nautical flimflam: 13 pesetas, just think of it, for that money he could have ordered a few complete meals in a decent *fonda*. Polishing his monocle with a piece of onion skin, he added angrily that as far as the ballot-box was concerned, he had no idea how the others voted, but he had voted "No" and it still came out as "Yes." Was such a thing possible? A ballot mutating inside the box?

I told him I thought this was quite possible, considering that the *Führer* was the very image of his Creator.

You can catch a mouse with lard, and then drown it in a bucket. This particular cup passed from me. I had remained steadfast. Years later I was again put to the test. Instead of offering me a lard-slathered sandwich, this time the tempter approached me in his underpants. Having escaped the hell of the Spanish Civil War by the skin of our teeth, we found shelter with Beatrice's strictly academic brother in Basel. Contrary to the hopes of my touchingly *Führer*-blinded folks on the Lower Rhine, we refrained from making the three-minute trip across the border "to the bosom of the Reich" and into their collective Hunnish embrace. Were the familial bonds no longer effective? Was I immune to the blood of the ancient ancestral Thiudâ, to the magic of herbs and homeopathic nostrums? Well then, they would try to lure me back with textiles. One of my "Get a move on!" brothers sat down to write, asking whether I, Dear Brother, was aware that the glorious *Führer*, at his own expense, was offering each and every German refugee from Spain a 100% Egyptian cotton undershirt and a pair of longjohns, provided that the refugee would agree to return to the Reich. I wrote back that the Consul in Palma had duly informed me of the *Führer*'s offer, but what use could such discreet items of clothing be to a man who stood to lose his head, a part of the body he would need in order to feel ashamed of wearing underthings that were baiting him into the Underworld? So Vigoleis resisted this temptation, too.

In the Bay of Palma a German ship lay at anchor, a vessel of the Woermann Line that called at the port regularly. But this time it wasn't a balloting ark, but the *Monte Rosa* with many thousand tons displacement and many thousands of tourists on board.

Sure enough, the Consul had announced—not in his capacity as Consul, but as head of the Tourist Agency—that the day after tomorrow the *Monte Rosa* would be arriving from the Reich with 2000 tourists. I was his best *Führer*, and he needed me. Today was now the day after tomorrow, and the *Monte Rosa* had arrived in all the majesty implied by her name. She towered like a mountain above the blue harbor waters. Whenever the Consul needed me in the name of his *Führer*, he met with resistance, ridicule, and open hostility. But if I myself was to be his *Führer*, and his best one at that—well, *allons*! Besides, I was the only *Führer* he could depend on blindly, since I was also a seer. As a result, on tourist days such as this one I didn't get yelled at, shooed away, or issued a warning in the name of the Consul's other *Führer*. Our relationship stayed on the best of terms, although it didn't keep me from retching.

Beatrice came along. She was good with mixed groups because she could speak all the languages, the tourists could understand her, and she gave them reliable information. Forty more guides, locals and foreigners, were hired for this project, including members of the German Labor Force who, on this occasion at least, remained politically neutral. The only character who never applied for a job as tourist guide for 25 pesetas a day was Mr. Silberstern. Considering his obsession with money, his omniscience, and his talent for empty blather, why didn't he? That must remain an unwritten chapter.

Why did the Consul and the gentlemen of the German Labor Force seem so much friendlier on this day than on other days? Beatrice and I noticed this, and we both reached the same fairly obvious conclusion. It was June of 1934, and they didn't know how things would play out after the Röhm Purge. Now it wasn't only Jews who were getting murdered; the Nazis were finally getting at each other's throats. What would happen if the Nazi gang succeeded in liquidating itself entirely, down to the last man who got on the wrong side of his *Führer*? The local Party plenipotentiary, an odious, heavy-set school teacher from Westphalia with a doctorate and the medal of the Blood Order, acted as if he had never hurled anti-Semitic slurs at Beatrice. He was barely out of his racist diapers, so he was suspicious of any woman who failed to show blonde, full-bosomed devotion to the *Führer*. From suspicion to non-Aryan incrimination was for him a simple step. But today he was keeping his crazed epithets to himself. Röhm murdered by Nazis? Maybe he was thinking that there was some truth to our tale of Inca blood—the Incas aren't Jews, although who knows what they really are? He greeted Beatrice with a bow-legged bow. After all, there are so many different blood lines in this world of ours. The Old Testament alone lists more than a million of them, so isn't it possible that everybody is all mixed up with everybody else?

When the first motor launches landed at the pier, the Strength Through Joy tourists didn't head directly for the cars as they usually did. Instead, they headed for the newspapers. But damn it all, where were the kiosks? They weren't interested in the island, or in the best seat in the best car which, if you were lucky and if you had long legs, was the *Führer*'s car. No, the hordes wanted to know what was going on in the Third Reich. On board ship they had been kept in the dark about the outcome of the Röhm Revolt. Now it was Monday, and still nobody knew whether the *Führer*, too, had been wiped out. And who else? Will all of us who wear the swastika in our buttonholes be executed? Maybe it's best if we hide it under our lapels. "Excuse me, Herr *Führer*," said one of them as we were starting out, "Can you tell me if the *Führer* is still alive?" "As far as we *Führer*s know, unfortunately he is." My interrogator's expression remained unchanged, making it impossible to tell whether he was for or against the *Führer*'s demise. The Spanish newspapers on the island published extras, listing names and numbers. At the time, what they reported seemed exaggerated, but in retrospect, as is always the case with historical St. Bartholomew's Nights, the accounts were far short of what actually happened. Excitement grew, as more and more German citizens came on land. The names of the quick and the dead fluttered through the air, and we *Führer*s were bombarded with questions. They were demanding foreign newspapers—what a stupid country, where they don't even provide a newspaper in a decent language! We tried calming them down by telling them that we were on an island, and that the mail ship didn't arrive on Mondays. But was General Schleicher dead? Yes. And his wife, too? Yes. (Schleicher was a crook, Kessler told me, but he didn't deserve such an end to his career of machinations.)

After an hour's delay, the travel agency with its cadre of *Führer*s finally sent the first thousand tourists on their way. Beatrice and I were part of these groups. As usual with mass disembarkments, we traveled the route backwards—first on the little train from the harbor through the city to the main railroad station and then, after some complicated switching, on to Sóller. On the way, instead of my normal lecture about the island, its kings, churches, beggars, its art works and the Sureda dynasty, all the way to Sóller I sermonized on the dubious greatness, the rapid rise and certain demise of the Third *Reich*. At first I had as many listeners as my *Führer* compartment on the train could hold. But as my admonitions and prophecies became more and more bleak and impudent, as my accusations against derelict Christianity turned more and more sinful, more and more of my German fellow citizens simply tuned out and, since they couldn't make a hasty departure like Silberstern on the line between Clermont-Ferrand and Port-Bou, they gave their full attention to the Mallorcan landscape—which was, of course, what they had come to see.

The landscape was decidedly more beautiful than the image of Germany I was depicting, which I will suppress here because now it could be, or rather would almost have to be, interpreted retroactively as a simulacrum of the truth. For my views on Germany were just as dismal as Germany turned out to be in reality. The existence of concentration camps was summarily denied. No one was ready to admit that Jews were being killed by the thousands, only that one or the other Jew had been liquidated by mistake. But now what about these bullfights, these bloody entertainments staged by the Spaniards? Weren't they more barbaric than the racial purification commanded by the *Führer*?

The lady who asked this question was your typical German mother—my sole verbal opponent in this colloquy, by the way, who would probably strangle her entire brood if that would serve nationalist aims. She had a lofty position in the German National Women's Movement. I liked her. I like patriotic people who wouldn't flinch if they were told to shoot their own children for the sake of the Fatherland. Her eyes were steely, as were her mind and her heart— but why go into further anatomical details as if this were a Most Wanted poster? Everybody is familiar with this type of goose-stepping Valkyrie, without which no Fatherland can remain calm. She told me she was going to send in a formal protest and would get my name and address from the Consul— but I spared her the trouble. I gave her my business card, mentioned my catalogue of sins already known to the Consul and the authorities in my home town, and hinted that I was on the list of people to be done away with when the time came. "And when will the time come, Herr *Führer*?" "Well, Madam, for an answer to that question you must turn to the other *Führer*—unless he's already been stabbed, which I sincerely hope is the case!"

That was the big problem. Nobody knew whether the Great Leader was still alive. Otherwise this Nazi lady would have given me a haymaker and, with the help of a few fellow German citizens who were smirking with *Schadenfreude*, heaved me out the train window. You could have found my grave in Buñola, which is the town we were passing through at the moment.

On that particular day, contrary to my usual spiel for the tourists, I refrained from defending the bullfight as an institution when my fellow countrymen, who at the time were sending millions into the gas ovens, accused it of being a savage manifestation of the "Spanish folk soul." The multiple slaughter of the Röhm Purge, occurring within Hitler's sphere of influence, placed new and different demands on my tactics as a tourist guide. I was unable to focus my audience's attention on the small-scale but significant and bloody Spanish form of popular entertainment, in a manner that would do justice to a national pastime that I had come to admire. I would otherwise have explained to this gathering that Spaniards were no more brutal, no more archaically bewitched or inhumane than any other good Europeans including the Germans, who at that very moment were providing the world with laboratory evidence for psychotic epidemics. I would have presented my listeners with my usual comparisons: why was a bullfight to be considered sadistic, but not horse races, the force-feeding of geese, or quail hunting? Or swatting flies? Or training cavalry horses for combat in war? How about the nags forced to slave away in the mines? Or those anthelmintic tapeworms which, God knows, have just as much right to their parasitic existence as any human being? Not even to mention the shooting of pigeons, vivisection, and the plight of John Q. Public sitting at his melancholy office desk? Directly or indirectly, all of these things served to satisfy certain basic human needs.

But as soon as one segment of my audience took the side of quail hunting as a perfectly acceptable form of human endeavor, and another segment voiced a contrary opinion, somebody always would say, "But Herr *Führer*, what about the bloodshed?" That was indeed the big question, the one that hu-mankind has always evaded, ever since we started murdering our way up-wards as sentient beings, constantly learning how to live and how to kill. It was fortunate that we never really noticed it—I meant the blood that poured from the bull's wounds when the banderillas hit home, or the blood that flowed when a German soldier was given the Iron Cross First Class. Other-wise, why would anybody display that military decoration on the occasion of, for example, a baby's baptism? Is that a time when we want to be reminded of our mortality? That mass murderer in the Münster penitentiary, the guy who was hoping, praying, scheming that Professor Többen would bestow on him just such a commendation as a first-class homicide, may not have had it so wrong after all. Presumably he was now a member of the SS. Death in the afternoon, I explained, was Spain's traditional bloodless form of recreation.

"But certainly you don't mean to imply that the bull doesn't suffer terrible agony when his blood starts flowing—that 'bloodless' blood of yours, Herr *Führer*!"

"A bull reacts to pain no differently than a crazed human being, for example a soldier in the midst of the most sacred battle for liberation—Hölderlin's youthful hordes, if you will. The thrill of combat can constrict a person's con-sciousness to the point where he feels no more pain. A bull in the arena feels only heroic rage, and that can be a glorious spectacle. After spending so much time ruminating in some gloomy pen, now he lowers his horns and charges after the gaudy dude who is challenging him for a place in the sun. When the juice of life starts bursting forth, not even the old British spinsters in attendance pay any heed—the ladies who along with their parasols have brought with them their readiness for hysterical protest. Spaniards get plenty angry at these ladies who sit there as if it were five o'clock teatime at a café terrace on the Borne. At the bullfights you get to see such an interesting crowd, such an array of colorful, noisy people, half of them on the sunny side of the arena, the other half in the shade, the whole assembly rising up toward the sky. You see, that's Spain! You accept it all, and it's marvelous. The way the troop marches into combat, the torero, trumpets and drumbeats, the formal greeting in front of the president's tribune, the countless beautiful women who, when seen from the cheap seats occupied by the English spinsters, look like the most beautiful women in all of Spain. In the bullfight arena, Carel Mengelberg would have his choice among them. And the mothers with babies at their breasts.

"Now just look at that! The president has thrown the key to the *toril* down onto the sand, a colorfully garbed fellow picks it up and hands it to another colorfully garbed fellow, who then opens up the bull pen. Around the entire stadium there is a deathly silence, rising up from thousands of human hearts. Only the sun moves one heartbeat onward. And then comes the yelling. Sud-denly the bull is standing there with lowered horns, a colossus in the ring, tak-ing on the challenge. And one by one the English ladies collapse stiffly onto their seats, paralyzed with fear. One of them even goes so far as to perform an act that is permissible here only down on the arena floor: she contends with death itself and loses—a *suerte de capa* that lasts but a few seconds. The Spanish caballeros pick her up and, accustomed as they are to fainting attacks among the female British audience, lean her up against another lady who, while still conscious, is standing there as stiff as a board. Then they turn back with renewed interest to the game of catch being played down below."

"But Herr *Führer*, why do those ladies go to watch such things? If they are so afraid, why don't they just stay away?"

"When Cook's pilgrims go to Rome they want to see the Holy Father. In Paris it's naked women, in Lourdes it's a miracle, and in Spain it's a *corrida de toros*. You can watch a game of football anywhere in the world. If the Spaniards were the brutal monsters the animal lovers talk about, they would take all the spoilsports who for no reason fall over in a faint at a bullfight or, as on the rarest of occasions, fall over dead as though they were back home somewhere—they would take these people and kick them under their seats or hurl them down onto the arena floor. But that never happens. One time and one time only, I was a witness as an enraged *aficionado*, which is what they call someone who is a fan of the bullfights, took the parasol away from a female spoilsport who had simply fainted away, broke it in two, and when she came to, gave it back to her with the words, 'Don't let me ever see you here again, do you hear me!' Whereupon the lady mumbled something about not having understood what the man had said. I stepped in as interpreter and told her that this fellow, superstitious like all Spaniards, broke her parasol in order to ward off evil magic. Fainting at a bullfight signifies death for the torero— 'or for you, milady! It always means death!' The lady, already a full shade paler, offered her hand to the Spaniard. That is to say, she started to offer it, but that didn't work. Down in the arena a death was taking place that she had been spared: *a suerte suprema*. The spell was broken, and while the British lady pulled up her woolen stockings the crowd went berserk, clapping and stamping their feet. Beatrice was beside herself...."

"Beatrice? Who is that? Excuse me for interrupting."

"My wife..."

"Oh, of course. She's Spanish? From Valencia or somewhere...?"

"From Kleinbasel, the other side of the bridge. Beatrice is beside herself, clapping and shouting *Olé!* Hats, skirts, *mantillas* get thrown down onto the arena floor, where the bullfighter, having come within a hair's breadth of getting killed himself, accepts thanks from the most beautiful specimen of Spanish womanhood. It is only now that one notices that blood has been shed—just as it is when you visit the dentist and he says, "Now rinse." Chulos arrive on the scene with a mule team and drag away the bull's enormous carcass. Other workers rake sand over the black pools of blood, and then the *aficionados* start arguing among themselves so vehemently that it looks as if they, too, want to shed some blood."

"But excuse me, Herr *Führer*. What about those horses that they say always get slit open? You don't have to give us the details, but you must have seen that kind of thing?"

This is an embarrassing question, often asked and difficult to reply to. But
I'm able to parry it just as a powerful bull shakes off a badly applied bander-
illa. I refer my interrogator to Montaigne, who, I say, in the second volume of
his essays provides an incontrovertible answer. I say this while trusting that
no one would ever admit ignorance of a literary passage that was never written, and one that I myself have never read.

In Sóller matters were getting so tense that the nautical-travel boss asked the
land-travel boss to pick out his best guide. The German citizens would have
to be distracted by holding a general roll-call. Vigoleis would take care of this.
"Get them to think about other things. But do it so that it's all Greek to them.
We've got three hours to kill."

Vigoleis gave a lecture—a very good one, I was told—on the choice of Spain
as a new homeland. Nothing political, and therefore edifying and even constructive. But Vigoleis can never stick to his subject. He's not a nuclear scientist, and always finds more interesting things going on at the margins of
any problem. Soon enough he was talking about the rise and decline of the
House of Sureda, although it wasn't very clear just who did the rising and
who did the declining. Afterwards we would be visiting the *Cartuja*, so I explained that each and every stone at that place breathed the breath of a
Sureda. And then there was the cute story of the Cell Rebellion: for years,
two particular cells at the monastery were shown to visitors as the places
where Chopin and George Sand had kept house. But all of a sudden someone
claimed that the famous couple had made love a few cells farther on, or
downstairs off the corridor. This led to trench warfare, since the precise
location for the lovemaking would bring in hard cash for whoever owned it.
Foreign tourists, it was said, must be shown only the genuine article, as in a
museum. The two cell owners battled it out. There were experiments with a
dowsing rod and with telepathy. Finally Count Hermann Keyserling stepped
in and uttered the philosophical words that saved the day: "The two cell
suites are in different corridors, so why don't you show both of them?" The
second cloister apartment was quickly furnished in identical fashion with the
one sanctioned by tradition. Then began a scramble to find the proper tour
guides, who were bribed with cigarettes, wine, and anise. On days when the
tourists arrived in crowds, the groups were kept apart and nobody noticed.
It was only when just a few people had to be dragged through the *Cartuja*
that things got dicey, since the sacred hallways then took on the aspect of a
bordello, in which the madam makes the assignments, and each girl has a
separate room.

I lack historical intuition, I don't smoke, and I spat out the terrible wine offered me by the hostile cell-owners. From the start, I left it up to my tourists
themselves to smell out the authentic cell apartment. Chopin's piano, I explained, the one he played on when he was here, had in any case long since

been removed to Paris. Later, in Valldemosa, I would show my group the very house lived in by the man who sold it in person to a French antiques dealer. The man I had in mind was my friend Don José, personal physician to His Royal Highness Archduke Ludwig Salvator of Austria. Soon enough, I heard myself talking about the disobedient dog responding to the name Pistola, the clinic pet that ran away as if shot from a cannon whenever its instinctive Izibencan cowardice came to the fore. If we were lucky, I told my group, Don José himself would be standing in his doorway. I would point him out to them, considering that personal physicians have gone out of fashion. If he wasn't standing there—which was most often the case, but I didn't say so—I would point to some other man and some other dog. This always worked. Great is the power of suggestion. Any *Führer* can testify to this, whether he is guiding tourists or entire nations. It's only people leading bears around who have to be on their guard. They solve this problem by carrying a long cudgel to keep the chained animal from molesting the guide himself.

On this historical Day of the *Führer* I closed my oration, as always, with a discreet bow to my audience and a studiously humble word of thanks for their kind attention. Stormy applause! Bravos! Hurrahs! Waves of gratitude as never before: "Long live our *Führer*!" No people on earth, I was thinking, has been so unlucky as the Germans in their choice of a *Führer*. And yet I had to admit that they were better off raising Vigoleis on their shields as *Führer* here on the Plaza Grande in Sóller, than that other bigwig back in the Thousand-Year *Reich*. Assuming that the latter hadn't already been massacred.

The bloodthirsty German Mother in the crowd was steaming with indignation. Others, too, and not only women, regarded such a spontaneous demonstration of reverence for their *Führer* as out of place, in particular those who had heard my earlier Speech to the German Nation in the train compartment. But no one dared to murder me. The big unanswered questions were of course: who can ever be the genuine leader of a genuine nation? How do you bring down a bogus leader? How and when will he kick the bucket? These problems could obviously not be solved on the island of Mallorca; on this day they couldn't even be put up for discussion. They were being answered back in the *Reich* with revolvers, and without a trace of doggish Ibizencian timidity.

Beatrice, too, wouldn't soon forget this day. Her great moment occurred with an ocean view, at the seaside cliff with its wave-spilled gorge, the Ponta de la Foradada. This was a favorite spot, one that delighted the tourists even when it was raining. Beatrice loved places where nature revealed itself with a purity otherwise seen only on picture postcards. The whole group focused its eyes on the big hole in the cliff, admired the rocky arch formation, speculated on its diameter, compared the sight with other famous holes at other locations in the world, and gazed into its depths. "Yes indeed, 400 meters! And just look over there to the right, do you see something moving? No, a little farther, under the rock with the tin can on top of it. That's an octopus! Look how its arms throw ghostly shadows! With just a single reach of its tentacle it could grab a person and pull him down..." But I don't want to interrupt Beatrice's harangue. In brief, while nature was unfolding its marvels to a grateful assembly, one gentleman kept staring at the group's guide, with the result that his bile got the better of him. Mixed in with the bile was this fellow's honorable Teutonic blood, and there began a swelling and heaving to match the foaming ocean surf far down below. He looked around in a fury, and shortly found the person he could address with his grievance, who was none other than Vigoleis. He cried out, "Herr *Führer*, this is going too far! I protest! Where can I register a complaint?"

I pointed to my badge and told him he could start with me, and that I would pass his words on to higher authorities. Had he not had enough to eat in Sóller? Was he taking into consideration that today's tour had unusually numerous participation? Could I offer him another sandwich...?

The gentleman, a German compatriot of the nationalist persuasion, pointed to Beatrice and said that he had been bothered by that suspect person all along, especially when every time he heard her speak she was using a different language. It was an insult, he said, on a tour with Strength Through Joy, on a German ship, to be served up a Jew as a guide at a time when the *Reich* was trying to get rid of those people. And this woman is supposed to be some kind of *Führer*? Incredible! This was followed by the usual obscenities. This was a German group, so there was no need to tolerate the use of foreign languages. The world would just have to learn to employ the German tongue. Anybody who claimed to be a guest on German ships of the line must speak German, and not the gibberish this lady was talking.

This man, feeling so humiliated in his racist proclivities, was unfortunately making a valid point. Aboard the *Monte Rosa* were many non-Germans, bunched together in Babel-like fashion. Beatrice greatly enjoyed leading such a group, passing from one language into another, since it allowed her to forget for the length of one difficult day her inborn mistrust of the human race.

The gentleman worked himself into such a lather that he could hardly restrain himself from rushing at Beatrice. As long as he exhibited such self-control, I felt I could let him bluster away. The scene had already upset a number of other tourists. The only person noticing nothing was the foreign tarantula, the 'lady' who had stung my compatriot so fiercely. This guy was probably some fancy Party official, since nobody tried to stop his harangue. On the contrary, the group moved sullenly away—the hole in the cliff no longer had their attention. My German compatriot kept up his barrage of expletives. I nodded in his direction, a gesture that he took to mean encouragement—and this prevented me from doing what I wanted most to do. Once he was finished tossing up his bile, I wanted to grab him by the sleeve and whisper to him, "Watch out! One never knows the company one is in. This 'lady'—you could get yourself into trouble with her, diplomatic trouble.

The woman you regard as a Jewish sow is no more and no less than Madame
Enderun, wife of the Persian Consul to the Balearics. As such she is hyper-
Aryan, maybe even Ur-Aryan. Have things come the point where the *Führer*
is willing to unleash international incidents?"

Madame Enderun, now surrounded by a little band of steadfast admirers,
finally noticed that something unpleasant was going on. The Ponta de la
Foradada was no longer an attraction. At this moment the Center of Creation
was the irate Teuton, all in a froth. Another gentleman in the group had listened to his tirade, and felt that this was the moment to do something about
it. This was a quite ordinary guy in his sixties, with a battered Panama hat, a
starched collar, and a flat-black necktie. From his vest, on a heavy silver chain,
hung a medallion that no doubt bore his family crest. His shoes were of crude
leather, his hiking stick had wrought-iron inserts, and his speech was replete
with gutterals. Woe to whoever maligns a citizen of Switzerland!

The German guy, the *chaibe Schwob*, was now summarily upbraided in the
mode of *Schwyzerdütsch* that gets spoken in Basel and environs. He was given
a thorough dressing-down. But did he understand a word of it? If so, he
learned that a specific aristocratic family had been living in Basel since the
11th century, and that this lady, *hei jo*—the hiking stick was pointed toward
Beatrice—was part of the very same family with all its ck's and ck-dt's in spite
of her Spanish skin color. And he was told, in addition, just what a *Löli* was,
how he should be ashamed of himself and that—here the hiking stick was
again pointed, but now directly at the Schwob, who stepped back a pace—
goddamned Prussian that he was, he should immediately get out of sight,
or else...

William Tell had shot his arrow!

Several other Swiss tourists stepped forward from guarding Beatrice and assumed a threatening stance, which announced that they wouldn't abide a fellow citizen being defamed, thus forcing the defamer to face a small crowd.
The Swiss hiker warned the German that he was obviously outnumbered. I
told my fuming compatriot that it would be best if he just gave up, and added
that the man from Basel bore the renowned name of Strub.

Condemnation of the German's behavior resounded from a dozen throats.
But he kept standing there, like an owl at midday being attacked by flocks of
angry birds. He was speechless, since he was unaware whether his true *Führer*
was alive or dead. Just one push of a Basel hiking stick, and this racist crack-
pot would have plunged into the arms of the octopus down below, his ghostly
shade wafting down over a Mallorcan cliff.

Back at my official *Führer* car, the tourists were waiting impatiently. What
was that scene all about at the Foradada, they asked. Did it have to do with
the lady guide? Was somebody mad at her? She was probably a Jewess, as you
might expect in this day and age. But then again, in a foreign country one
shouldn't be quite so picky, should one? It's too bad about the beautiful landscape, though, and with the ocean so very, very blue, and that green octopus
down there! Politics should be left back home, or maybe some people

shouldn't even leave home if they're political. But then again, that fellow probably was right to protest. The trip was happening with German money, and people had a right to demand German treatment.

I gave my charges the long and involved personal history of Madame Enderun, the daughter of the Persian Consul General in Madrid, who owned a *finca* on the island of Mallorca. I told them I would show them his estate, with its subtropical garden and all. The German protester, I said, had been thinking that she was just another Jewish sow, which caused the Swiss delegation to man the ramparts, since Madame Enderun had attended Basel University, and besides many other languages spoke Swiss German. As that German fellow must have known, dialects are a binding force.

If she was Persian—and that man actually took her for a Jewess—then she was not only Aryan but hyper-Aryan. And her father, the Consul General— "What a delightful posting," interjected a German lady. "My husband hasn't got quite that far yet!" "You're absolutely right about postings like that one, " I replied. "It's my lifelong dream to become a Chief Executive Officer or a Consul General, but..."

My interlocutor suggested that I ought to try out some courtship with the woman in question—try making the right kind of connection. Hadn't he already seen me in Valldemosa and Sóller in her company, more than once? If I did things right, maybe I wouldn't end up as a Consul General, but maybe as a special son-in-law with—how had I put it?—a *finca*. That was it, a *finca*!

"Over there!" I cried out. "That's the Enderun estate!" I was pointing toward a *finca* that we were passing by on the dusty road at the moment.

That day, the *Monte Rosa* left the Palma harbor rather late. People said that the delayed departure had to do with events taking place in Germany. This left the tourists with a few hours to kill in Palma.

Beatrice and I, as completely dead as we wished the German *Führer* to be, sat on the Plaza Atarazanas drinking the dust out of our throats. Suddenly we were joined by the ladies and gentlemen from my tour group, who sat down a few tables away from us. The man who had quizzed me raised a teasing finger, as did the lady with him. "Aha!" they called across the café aisle. "Everything going on schedule?"

"Perfectly, " I called back. "We've just got engaged!"

A roll-call aboard the *Monte Rosa* showed that about a hundred of the German citizens were missing. News reports from the native soil were such that they preferred not to return home. One can get hanged anywhere in the world, so who needs a fatherland?

The next day I went to the travel agency and received the 50 pesetas wage for myself and my Persian bride. The agency manager, none other than the German Consul himself, was once again in full control, just like his main *Führer*, if not like his best one. The Röhm Revolt had been suppressed. Some heads were still rolling, and Herr von Papen's son-in-law, whom I met on the streets of the city, had left his legs unpowdered. That was his ceremonial form of mourning.

XXIII

We buried a great painter, Jacobo Sureda.

Elly Sackett, an American banker's daughter, had given support to Jacobo the man, while Mother Ey in Düsseldorf championed the artist. He was the best painter on Mallorca, which is saying a great deal, since the island was teeming with painters. Pedro had but one desire, and that was to achieve as much with brush and palette as his brother. So he painted more and more intensely, while Jacobo painted less and less. Jacobo's lung ailment got worse from year to year. When we got to know him during our first island winter, the season that stood completely under the sign of the hellcat Pilar, his health was comparatively good. He was able to afford an annual visit to the St. Blasien spa in the Black Forest. He loved Germany, a country where he was no longer a stranger. Mother Ey had discovered him. She was in rapture over the young consumptive nobleman, who began as a poet and who personally set the type and printed his own first small volume of verse using the press owned by his friend Josef Weisemberger. The title was *El prestidigitador de los cinco sentidos*, and the poems did justice to the title: magically expressionistic, and deploying all of the five senses. When Jacobo died, his best paintings were hanging in Mother Ey's gallery—or rather, they were in Mother Ey's hands, since the Nazis had liquidated her gallery, accusing her of sponsoring "degenerate art." It is probable that Don Jacobo's pictures were likewise annihilated as "degenerate art." They have never been found.

I never knew Mother Ey in person. Our only halfway intimate contact occurred when I slept on a historic mattress she had once reclined upon. Judging from the stories I heard from Pedro and Don Juan Sureda, from Jacobo himself and from our Folkwang School teacher, I understood perfectly why it was that Don Juan paid equally intense reverence to the mattress and bed linens used by *Señora Huevo*, as the Sureda children called her, just as to the beds once occupied through sleepless nights by His Catholic Majesty and his rival Don Miguel de Unamuno. The castellan protected Josef Weisemberger's mattress, too, from profanation, and he no doubt had his special reasons. Was it because this German was a friend of his most talented child? Perhaps. I am unfamiliar with this man's contributions to the world of art; I only know that in the House of Sureda his name will outlast the mattress he slept on. Josef Weisemberger was the first person to walk the streets of Mallorca in wintertime without a hat. Baedeker fans, those who are sworn to historical accuracy, should make note of the fact that this particular honor does not belong to Chopin.

Jacobo died of a pulmonary hemorrhage in his attractive artist's home Ca's Potecari in Génova, cradled in Pedro's arms. In Barcelona he had undergone a difficult operation performed by a Catalan surgeon, a pupil of Sauerbruch's, who did his work so badly that the operation was a success, but the patient succumbed. We had argued that he should go to Germany to be operated on by Sauerbruch himself. Elly Sackett would have financed this. But Don Jacobo didn't want to go to Germany, because it was no longer his Germany. Should we summon Sauerbruch to Spain? Count Kessler, who took an interest in the Sureda case, told me that Sauerbruch would come immediately by plane with an assistant surgeon and a nurse, and the result would be one cured patient and one devastated bank account. Kessler himself had once been duped by the same "pork butcher" (the term was not Kessler's) many years before, when he lay sick in London. A rather hesitant diagnosis by his English physician upset Kessler's sister. She kept telling him he should ask Sauerbruch to come to England; after all, the two men knew each other. Sauerbruch flew over, tapped the Count's chest, auscultated, reassured the patient, wrote out prescriptions, and casually inquired whether the Count would mind if he, Sauerbruch, stayed on a day longer to dine with the King's personal physician. Kessler had no objections, and in fact he arranged the dinner. The surgeon's bill for medical treatment and time spent in London was in the thousands, an amount that caused even a Count Kessler to blanch. He was about to sue the "blackguard" (Kessler's term), but his sister took over the entire expense to spare her beloved brother all the anguish of a lawsuit. I had already heard a similar account of Sauerbruch's padded bills from my uncle, Bishop Jean in Münster. A scion of the Westphalian Droste clan had an only son who was deathly ill. The professors at the university clinic all said: call in Sauerbruch. He came, he carved, he sewed, and left the patient out of danger. His rich, generous, happy Papa wrote out a check for the doctor on the very same day, for the fat sum of, let's say, 50,000 marks. The surgeon telegraphed back: "50,000 is what one offers a clinical assistant, not a Sauerbruch. Signed: Sauerbruch".

What an amazing message! It is a mark of true greatness if at the proper moment you can formulate words that can become proverbial. That is how I ought to have come back at Adelfried Silberstern on the subject of my consultation fee. "Zero point zero pesetas is what one offers one's lawyer brother, not a legal and sexual consultant named Vigoleis. Signed: Vigoleis."

I would give anything for a painting by Jacobo Sureda, especially for one created during the period of his physical decline—his *Almocrebe*, for instance, which presents Spain's pride, misery, poverty, and steadfastness, depicted in the figures of a jackass, its master, and the shadows they cast across the baking soil. The picture wasn't large; it would fit nicely in the place where I have hung a map of Mallorca, a sight that fills me with longing for my Island of Second Sight, now extinct. That is to say, I am overcome by *saudade*, as the Portuguese call it, and as Pascoaes—my Pascoaes!—uniquely delineates it in book after book. Or rather, as he once delineated it, for now he is dead. Just now, before I start explaining how I first encountered his work, I have received the news of his heroic, tragic demise, the death of the last Portuguese mystic, the man who intoned the swan song of Iberian mysticism.

In the senior apartments at the Suredas' house things were constantly topsy-turvy. But one day Pedro told me that the place was now a madhouse. Papá, Mámá, and everybody else had gone completely off their rockers, and now they were obliged to use the WC at their next-door neighbor's. Papá was locking himself in the toilet for hours at a time and reciting out loud. Pixedes, a housemaid who had stayed on longer than most because Papá went through a quiet phase, had now run away also. Pedro brought with him blankets and sleepwear, since nights at home were unbearable. Had more "golden veins" made their appearance? And which language had Don Juan opted for now?

"He's not cramming any new ones. At first we thought it was Arabic, which he's always been interested in. And it was our idea that while learning it, he forgot the trick with the door latch and couldn't let himself out, just like that nun. What surprised us was when we first heard him yelling, 'Paul, Paul, open up Spain!' Pixedes packed her bundle and fled the house. Pazzis is desperate, because it's not golden knots any more, it's religious fanaticism that's broken out in our house."

"Religious fanaticism? Not bad for Spain. Great tradition! How can you tell?"

"He starts shouting, 'Woe is me, woe is me if I do not preach the Gospel!' Or 'When will I be free of this mortal body?'"

There was no contradicting Pedro; this was clearly a case of religious hallucinations. If I had been the maid Pixedes, I too would have flown the coop. As Vigoleis, however, I kept listening. It's one thing to use a bathroom for meditation, learning grammar, or doing a crossword puzzle. But for preaching? I pictured the Sureda family gathered together and flinching at each new outburst of their patriarch's heretical phantasms, a form of blasphemy that no amount of patient reasoning could ever suppress. I saw them sticking the man's trumpet in his ear and shouting, "Cease and desist! For thou knowest that thou art cursing the Lord!"

But from inside the room in question the tirade continued: "Christianity is the religion of the evening, which veils all things in its twilight. But then the heavens, which during the day are kept from sight by the azure air, open up a thousand tiny, gleaming windows. Christianity is the religion of the final hour, the time when our only salvation is to be found in hope, the somewhat desperate hope of St. Paul. Let us seek our salvation in hope!"

"Papá, come out of there! Papáááá, come out!"

"God perceived the imperfect nature of his Creation, and He was unable to undo it. But then Noah entered the Ark. Now Creation could only be modified, and the crime only eventually atoned for. That is the profound meaning of Golgotha. Jesus, the Son, is God's bad conscience."

The family left their pontificating father to his own fate. Pedro fled to General Barceló Street. Juanito took succor in devotional exercises; together with his pious sisters he prayed for Papá, though he didn't overdo it. He was the only one in the family who eschewed exaggeration, for he was lazy and always tired, though not as a result of general dynastic torpor. Only Doña Pilar, the princess, stood firmly rooted in reality. Her Juan had not gone crazy, and he hadn't turned more Quixotesque than otherwise. He had simply found a certain book—where? At a literary *tertulia*, of course. It was a book that had inwardly captivated him and was now keeping him outwardly captive at the odd location that could no longer be kept secret. She didn't scold him, since from long years of marriage she knew that he would eventually come forth. The Suredas always came forth. The family coat of arms features a ferret. When he finally came forth, she would simply take the book out of his hands, and peace and tranquility would return to their home.

"Does anybody know which book it is that's causing Don Juan such ecstasies? What kind of new gospel is he reading?"

"It's a book about St. Paul, written by some Portuguese writer. That's all we know."

Doña Pilar actually succeeded in wrenching the book from her mystically transported husband, the book from which he continued to recite passages out loud at night, in bed, albeit only certain passages that received his imprimatur. During the daylight hours, pursuing his career as a Spanish grandee on the Promenade, at the cafés, in the clubs, or in the *palacios* of other grandees who were not yet financially ruined, he hid the book from sight. It was, after all, heretical in the highest degree, a threat to the salvation of his family's souls, especially his daughters', and it belonged on the Index. Doña Pilar, less concerned about saving souls than about the stability of her household, sneaked a peek at her husband and, when he left the house, took the book out of its hiding place. Don Juan, finding the place empty, went into a fit of rant: "Stolen!" He suspected one of his friends, a doctor whom he considered not only capable of robbing a tabernacle but also worthy of such an act. In the middle of the night he drummed the man out of bed. "You have stolen my Paul! Woe is me if I don't preach the Gospel!"

Unlike many doctors who are enraged when somebody gets them out of bed for some petty ailment, this one kept calm. Since he hadn't stolen the book, he wrote Don Juan a prescription for a purge, the Spanish panacea, and dismissed the despondent *hidalgo*.

But I still didn't know which book Don Juan had found, and my curiosity increased. A book that could aggravate that man's inborn nuttiness must indeed be one of the world's greatest works of literature. I pocketed a duro, apparently our very last.

"That's our last duro!" Beatrice cried out after me.

"I know! But we're always living down to our last everything. *Ciao*!"

At the time, there was one bordello for every 1000 inhabitants of Palma. Which is to say, the statistics were even more favorable if one added the *casas* that were not officially sanctioned. More significant still were the figures for intellectual activity: one bookstore per 40,000 citizens. Not counting Mulet's lending library, where it was sometimes possible to obtain certain volumes under the counter, Palma had two such stores. My search for St. Paul, the disturber of Don Juan's peace and his family's sanity, led me to Palma's premier bookstore, the one on the Plaza Cort.

A book about St. Paul. What did I know about St. Paul? Precious little. I knew that Nietzsche called him the "dysangelist" and saw in him a hate-filled rabble-rouser, the incarnate loathing of the Roman Empire as of the world itself, the Eternal Jew, and what not else? Unamuno dealt with him in his *Agony of Christianity*, which he regarded as deriving from Paul's personal agony. Cervantes calls him the Knight Errant of Life, the patron saint of death who arrived at ultimate serenity. The Nazis, too, were busying themselves with this personage; for them he was the Jewish sub-human, and they placed him on their index together with his Master and all the disciples. I also knew Karl Barth's *Epistle to the Romans*, a cold, arrogant piece of writing. I hadn't read Schweitzer's *The Mysticism of the Apostle Paul*.

I made the acquaintance of Barth's book when I was studying in Münster. The work caused quite a stir. Divinity students were discussing it heatedly, either in the university corridors or over plates of fried potatoes and pancakes in the dining hall. This was the period when Professor Magon was giving his famous lectures on Kierkegaard, who was not yet fashionable but who drew crowds into a large lecture hall. Kierkegaard was "in the air" at the time, along with Johann Georg Hamann, the "Wizard of the Northland," with his *Diary of a Christian*. Hitler, too, was "in the air" with his *Mein Kampf*, considered by some as a work of divine revelation, by others as a brick to toss at Jewish store windows. Dr. Robert Ley's mouse-catchers were already at work. They entered Jewish restaurants, ordered potato salad, took a dissected mouse out of a matchbox and stuck it in the salad, started complaining loudly, and then smashed the windows. That was the year 1927. Professor Wätjen was still teaching during this incipient German riffraff rebellion, delivering his fawning lectures on the history of the Hanseatic League before select audiences. His talks were social occasions. Amidst a clanking of spurs, generals with glistening monocles kissed the hands of beautiful ladies. The ladies played the coquettes with their fur boas and wrote down a few of Wätjen's elegant formulations with gold-plated pens in gold-embossed notebooks. When some insignificant general of the accursed *Reichswehr* kicked the bucket, the entire lecture-hall audience emptied out to follow the cortege to his grave.

René van Sint-Jan rubbed his carefully groomed Flemish beard, submitting Vigoleis, student of Netherlandic philology, to a test to see whether he qualified for admission to his advanced seminar. If so, he would have two pupils instead of just one. For *almae matres* as for flesh-and-blood mothers, the only-child system is not to be recommended. He handed his seminar candidate a poem by Pieter Corneliszoon Hooft and said, "Here, interpret this." Vigoleis read through the work slowly. It was one of those charming, playful verses dedicated to a *schoon nymfelyn* named Meisken Ina Quekel, who is courted successively under the names Diana, Iphigenia, Dia, or Amaryllis. *Amaryl de deken zacht / Van de nacht...*

I stumbled over the very first word, as if I had never been confronted with pastoral poetry before. There was no need in the world for me to know that certain tuberous plants go by the name Amaryllidae, but I happened to know it. The blood that had leaped to my head flowed calmly back down into my circulatory system. Taking botany as my point of departure, I focused on what I took to be the verb *amarylleren*. I cleared my throat and began to translate: "Let us, gently like the flowers, smooth out our nocturnal berth..." Today I would call that thing a *pilarière*. The professor smoothed out his beard, and kept smoothing it ever so pensively as I waxed more and more audacious in my exegesis of the poem, fully conscious of the academic failure facing a low-semester student who at the same was supposed to offer proof of his talent and overall intelligence. But this student didn't fail either test. Mijnheer van Sint-Jan told me that he actually ought to flunk me, but that he would desist for two reasons: first, his other candidate would be staying on only for a half-semester longer, after which he would be getting his doctorate, leaving the professor with no more students at all and forcing him to shut down his seminar. Second, he was interested in my "case": a gift for thought-associations that was as amazing as it was academically dangerous, but all in all a knack that, if nurtured in the proper pedagogical manner, could bear interesting fruit. Besides, the two of us would soon be *entre nous*. He welcomed me, and said that he would support me in his department. And he had a dissertation topic that would suit me perfectly.

My uncle Jean on Münster's Cathedral Square had also welcomed me. He also considered me dangerous because of my hopping from subject to subject, and for that very reason preferred that he and I meet alone—which was just fine with me. Over dinner he sent away his servant, and we got along famously.

Professor Günther Wohlers taught an academic course in journalism before a no less select audience: Vigoleis and the overbred son of an aristocratic line. This fellow made his doctorate under Wätjen with a thesis on Lord Grey, but his dissipating womanizing kept him short of the coveted *summa cum laude*. His breakfasts consisted of a banana and strawberry-flavored sparkling wine, whereas Professor Wohlers, with our permission, always brought along to the seminar a stein of beer. As for myself, I practiced abstinence, out of continued abhorrence of the ur-German custom of alcohol-laced *Frühschoppen*, particularly when pursued in a university classroom.

On Sundays after the last Mass in the cathedral, where Donders' sermons attracted even godless listeners, the fraternity students, those with and those without their special "colors," marched around Cathedral Square—an *al fresco* ballet that never ceased to strike me as a gigantic prison courtyard where the inmates are allowed a few minutes of exercise.

Old Professor Mausbach, a sly little peasant type, taught us his notions of morality and cultural politics.

That was my little world at the time, the world that coursed around me and gave me direction. It was largely by accident that my closest friends were students of Protestant theology. It was stimulating for me to get to know the hearts and souls of these young people who, a few years later, would don their robes and bands, ascend the pulpit, and declaim the Word of God with the same lips as would sing the German National Anthem as the times required. They were firmly set on rendering to God that which was God's, and to the devil (Caesar) that which was the devil's (Caesar's), even if the latter, such as for example Adolf Hitler, lacked the proper imperial format. "Our Father" and "God Save the King"—for me, that just didn't rhyme. I was of course familiar with Catholic attitudes. Oddly enough, the Protestant fellows were intensely interested in my opinions. They knew that I was a sometime "writer," and the fact that I did my writing for a posthumous readership was in their eyes just as impressive as the fact that I was a *propinquus* of Auxiliary Bishop Dr. Johannes Seifes, highly regarded in Protestant circles for his tolerant ideas.

Incidentally, it was these same students of divinity who hung on me the nickname Vigoleis. In a seminar on the origins of the novel, taught by the highly dramatic Papa Schwering, I discovered in the chapbook narrative *Wigalois* by Wirnt von Gravenberg a few picaresque motifs that a hundred years or more of literary scholarship hadn't brought to light. I was pioneering in philological *terra incognita*, and even Schwering could easily have rewarded me for this with a formal doctorate. If I'm not mistaken—and here I'm truly not—the divinity students, by nature lacking in imagination, thought that my discoveries were ingenious, and they baptized me "*Wigalois*," the Knight of the Wheel, by which they meant the emblem on the writer's illustrated armor helmet. By my own interpretation, the emblem stood for the little wheel spinning inside Wirnt's head, and I was proud of this. But I revised the name *Wig-alois*, "because of Alois," to Vigoleis, a variant form also to be found in the documents, thereby alluding instinctively to the Iberian regions where Wirnt's story takes place. By doing so, I turned the tables on my fellow students: what they had meant as a tease now became for me a knightly honorific. What I didn't realize at the time was that by bestowing upon myself such an exalted sobriquet I was entering the company of Jacopone da Todi, the Umbrian poet of the Laude, who likewise endorsed his own nickname. I was even less aware that ten years later, on the island of Mallorca, this echt-Münster type of anabaptism would save my life.

The divinity students gave me a copy of The Epistle to the Romans, asking me to read it and then make an oracular pronouncement on whether the author believed in God or not. My soothsaying decision: if God was a writer, as we often were told He was, then Barth believed in Him in the same way that Bohr believed in his model of the atom, Planck in his quanta, and Professor Többen in his convicts. Life would be so nice if the academic departments of theology and law no longer had to be subsidized. It would be Paradise. No bird would gobble up a mosquito, and yet would go on living. No wolf would kill a sheep, and yet would go on living. No Adam...

... and there I was, standing in front of the bookstore on the Plaza Cort and feeling the necessity to suppress my recollections of student days. Or was it that I just didn't want to sacrifice our last duro for a St. Paul?

The lady at the store said she had never heard of a book on *San Pablo*, and certainly not one by a Portuguese writer. By a Portuguese! She laughed, just as everyone in Spain laughs at Portugal. And she asked me whether I knew the couplet, *Los portugueses pocos y estos pocos locos*. From my geography lessons I knew that Portugal had a small population, and that it was a little Iberian offshoot next to the Atlantic. But that the few Portuguese citizens were also crazy—could such a thing be possible? Once you've been to Spain and met Don Juan, Don José, Don Matías, and Don Pedro, is there a surpassing degree of *locura*? A Seventh Heaven of screwiness, so to speak?

I was on the right track. Beatrice would never see this duro again. I remained undeterred. I asked if I might be permitted to look on the shelves by myself. Yes, was the reply. In fact I would have to go take a look for myself, since she didn't want to be bothered, and certainly not with questions about books. Imagine what things would be like if just anyone could come in off the street and ask for a *San Pablo*—written by a Portuguese! Because in my own personal library the books are arranged neither by language, author, nor subject, it took me only minutes to find what I was looking for: a volume printed in Barcelona by Editorial Apolo—Verdaguer's publisher, and as such a recommendation in and of itself. The cover showed an Iberian portrait of Saint Paul. Title: *San Pablo*; author: Teixeira de Pascoaes; foreword: Miguel de Unamuno. This four-leaf clover could not have been more impressive. Three copies still stood on the shelf. I stuck one under my arm and asked the price. The lady didn't move, but instead sent a hostile glance at my book. I felt embarrassed, as always in the presence of an illiterate. All of a sudden I was ashamed of knowing the alphabet by heart. It was not until we reached Portugal and the mountainous region of Travanca, where the wolves circled our house at night and only one person was barely able to read and write, that I learned to my amazement that one must approach this problem from a completely different angle.

In any case, I was making no headway with the bookstore clerk. But fortunately, at this moment a gentleman entered the store from a back room, and I immediately turned to him, suspecting that he was the bookseller himself, which he was. "How much?" I showed him the book, a gesture that caused the man to go into a mild fit. Speaking Mallorquin, a dialect I had little comprehension of, he hissed at his wife and then, politely switching to Castilian, he explained that this spouse of his was constantly committing stupidities such as, for example, thinking that a bookstore was like a bakery, where you kept giving away the merchandise until nothing was left on the shelves. So it was hardly to be expected that the poor woman knew anything at all about literature. Was it my wish to abscond with *San Pablo*? He was glad to have arrived on the scene when he did, for otherwise this copy of the book would also have disappeared, never to be seen again! Such things just didn't happen in his store. He urged me to consider that there were only three copies left—three! A week ago there had been two dozen, and before that about fifty. The book was selling like hotcakes, and it was Miguel's fault. Although I appeared to be a foreigner, surely I was aware that the man he meant was Unamuno. "So please, Sir, hand me the book. It belongs up there on the shelf. This is a bookstore, not a bakery."

The bookseller replaced my copy next to the other dead stock on the shelf. Stunned, I remained silent. Don Joaquín Verdaguer had once recounted for me a similar story, and I thought it was just an example of his clever broma, one of his Lichtenbergian vignettes.

"How much does a book like that cost," I finally dared to inquire. "Maybe I can't even afford it."

"Perhaps. It's difficult to judge the purchasing power of book buyers. But a book from Editorial Apolo—8 pesetas."

"I'm happy to hear that. All I have is one duro."

"Fine. You're a customer after my own heart. You keep your duro, and I'll keep my book."

"Could I just write down the author's name?"

"That won't be necessary. I'll give you the publisher's brochure, and you can try at the new store on San Miguel, just opened up. New-fangled place, you know. They'll sell anything—anything, I tell you." As I left his establishment he shouted after me that nowadays literature was going to the dogs—illiterates were buying up every last thing. Did he mean me, or his wife? Probably both of us.

Mulet didn't have the book, but he knew of this Portuguese writer, and offered to have a copy of *San Pablo* sent over from Barcelona. It would be there in a few days, maybe the day after tomorrow—no, not "maybe" but definitely. This meant that I had a few weeks time, and that I would have to do some fancy work with the duro we obtained through our friendship with the Mengelbergs. I was obliged to enter into negotiations with the beggar on the cathedral steps. After submitting to his usual reprimands, I pretended that I was simply a passer-by who would gladly give him something, but that I had just discovered that my last duro was a genuine *sevillano*, and thus I would have to walk all the way home to Génova. The beggar suggested fifty-fifty. I gave him the 5 pesetas, and in return I received 2.50 and blessings from all the saints, plus 100 days indulgence. I was still lacking two reales, but surely Mulet would offer me that much credit. After all, I wasn't his only *intelectual con su carcoma*, to quote the title of a novel by Mario Verdaguer.

São Paulo by Teixeira de Pascoaes turned out to be the great adventure of my life. Don Juan Sureda Bimet: your Catholic German thanks you and your golden veins, along with Pascoaes and his Iberian St. Paul, for having transported him to the Heaven of the godless.

I had come upon a religious genius.

Almost twenty years have passed since I first read a line of Pascoaes. From the first page onward I knew that I was being touched by a genius who would command my total loyalty. On the final pages I pondered with the Lusitanian seer where on this earth the apostle's poor, emaciated body might have been returned to the soil, this body so worn down by inexpressible anguish. "Was it in Spain? In Rome? In Asia? In Macedonia? Did Lydia and Timothy close his eyelids and bury him amid showers of tears?" At that time, archeological excavations in Catalonia made it seem certain that the apostle had indeed made his questionable Iberian journey. In Unamuno's eyes, this caused the Pascoalinian St. Paul to become doubly Iberian. Upon reading Pascoaes' book Unamuno issued the summons, "*San Pablo*, open up Spain!" I knew right away that I would be this writer's translator. And that is just what I am. But what is more, I became his private humanist, as Menno ter Braak has called me. God willing—that is, the "godless God" of Pascoaes—I will also be his biographer.

I read the work in a single sitting, a feat that I rarely accomplish with a book, especially when the topic is religion. It discussed problems that had plagued me for years. The author dealt with questions that lay beyond the ultimate questions in a fascinating, often obscure, often spare style of writing: the sins of God, the restoration of the world, the unity of crime and redemption, mankind not as sinner but as sin itself and, as a logical extension of this idea that was so familiar to me, theologians as God's gravediggers, reality as the forecourt of the magical temple of illusion, and the *mysterium tremendum* in the company of the *tremenda*... Dear reader, do go out and purchase and read St. Paul for yourself and you will learn all that I owed to Don Juan's golden veins, and just what a treasure I had obtained for one genuine duro, a second phony one, and a little bit of credit from my friend Mulet. Take this book and read, at the risk of seeing your own personal Pixedes head for the hills. It is your problem whether you have to pay for the volume with your last penny. Your bookseller will at all events greet you with open arms, for in the meantime Pascoaes has become a writer for the "happy few"—which is to say, he is now a white elephant.

As I read on, I caught myself mentally translating whole passages, assuring myself that I was going to transfer *São Paolo* into my own language. It occurred to me that the Spanish version could not be "correct" in all respects, that the translator hadn't achieved his aims, unless my own premonitions about the work were themselves incorrect or overshot the mark. Later, when I compared the Spanish with the original, I found that I had been right all along. My instincts had not atrophied, Spain had not yet worn me down to the point where I would put off until tomorrow what I ought to start doing today: learn Portuguese in order to comprehend more of this extraordinary writer. Portuguese had the reputation of being a more difficult language than

Spanish. To be equal to the task I would have to feed my brain with more phosphorus. I wrote to the author and asked him for the rights to a German edition of his *São Paulo*. Pascoaes, the Squire of Pascoaes, replied by return mail—a gesture of special distinction, as I later learned. It meant a great deal to him to be translated into German, a language with which he was not familiar. Germany was for him more the land of the nebulous philosopher of Königsberg than that of the Olympian Poet of Weimar. We began a correspondence that, with the exception of the seven years when we lived at his estate Pascoaes, lasted until just a few weeks before his death.

My Hunnish graves, my consultancy in legal and sexual affairs, Count Kessler, Leopold Fabrizius—all of these things now took a back seat to my departure into the realm of *saudade*. The worst to suffer was our cache of savings for postage, for precisely 37 publishers rejected my Pascoaes manuscript until Rascher in Zurich finally dared to undertake this adventure of the spirit. This meant that I had broken the boomerang record for literature, which up to that time was held by Remarque with 33 rejections of his *All Quiet on the Western Front*. I wrote Pascoaes about this. He replied, saying that in an epoch when for every thousand persons who could write a book there might be a single one who could read one, it was indeed a triumphant accomplishment to have located 37 German readers for his book.

XXIV

Gypsies: those were the filthy women with skirts that stirred up dust, wearing heavy gold earrings, striding along barefoot and carrying a suckling infant tied inside a colorful shawl around their waist, leaving their hands free for thievery. That's how I got to know them in my childhood, the dark-skinned bands of people who went about from place to place in stolen wagons drawn by stolen horses, getting their food by stealing. Their children didn't have to go to school, nor did they have to go to church—the latter being the privilege for which I envied them most. They trained their kids in larceny, and celebrated bloodthirsty weddings in their camps at the outskirts of town with dancing bears, knifings, campfires, tambourines, and loud chatter. Whenever the gypsies passed from door to door through our town begging and soothsaying, the pugnacious protectors of public order on the steps of the town hall whetted their sabers, used their practiced thumbs to wipe the stains from the blood grooves, and waited just as long as it took for headquarters to draft, compose, sign, and seal the expulsion command. Then it was simply a matter of "That's it, you bandits! Off with you to the next town!" My mother counted the heads of her loved ones, and then all of us counted our chickens while our neighbor, whose loved ones were horses, counted his horses.

The personage who was now running around in Don José's house in Valldemosa—or rather who now, at the moment when I wish to introduce her, was sitting around his house with crossed legs and smoking with a long ivory cigarette holder, wearing high-heel shoes instead of going barefoot—this woman was as swarthy as the night and wore her gleaming hair sharply parted in the middle. Her earrings were so heavy that they made her earlobes hang down like pendulums, and every one of her fingers sported a ring. She was indeed a gypsy, and thus she must be none other than Doña Soledad, the authentic Andalusian *gitana* Bobby had already written us about. By examining palms, cards, and coffee grounds she could read the future and the past, and with her talent for synthesizing could draw conclusions about the present. What was more, it wasn't necessary to keep doors or drawers locked when she was around. Doña Soledad wasn't a thief. We were invited to come out for the weekend; Clarita was expecting us. We were to bring Pedro along, Bobby wrote in a P.S., and added in the margin, "There'll be armadillo with champignon sauce." So off we went to Valldemosa. We had never met a gypsy who didn't steal but was otherwise authentic. Not even in the Balkans had Beatrice seen anything like it.

Doña Soledad, wearing a red carnation in her hair and with a question-mark curl at her brow, hailed from the *cuevas* near Granada. She was rich, and no longer needed to filch anything. In the evening she performed gypsy dances. Pedro beat the tambourine and clacked the castanets. Soledad spoke fluent French, but what made her most appealing, especially to Beatrice, was the fact that she didn't eat with her knife. Things got a little dicey when she started eating with her fingers, but Pedro explained that this wasn't a gypsy custom, but the proper and polite way to consume armadillo.

Beatrice's fortune came first. A man had entered her life—not a major event, to be sure. In fact, more like the opposite. There were no signs that this man would be leaving her just as quickly. She should have patience, and not despair. As for the gentleman in question, certain foreign bodies had entered his life, too, although it wasn't quite clear whether these were women or perhaps books—in any case they were hard, there was a collision, and that brought an end to it. In addition she saw a voyage, a ship, cannons, once again something hard, a coil of rope. "Do you see a bed?" I inquired. No, not a bed. So we would have to keep sleeping on newspapers. Doña Soledad, as clairvoyant as she was, failed to understand my question. Then she asked, "You've told me everything? Added nothing? Then show me your hand."

The gypsy woman unveiled my past life by taking one look at my left palm. It wasn't pretty. Then she gazed at my other palm: a woman would enter my life. "A gypsy?" I asked.

"No, why?"

The reason was plain enough: I would love to be abducted by a real gypsy woman. Pilar had certain gypsy-like traits, but she saw everything wrong. And anyway, she wasn't born in a cave in Sacro Monte. The fiery stream coursing between her hand and mine didn't stop. She saw a person who was both close to me and far away. That person was in danger. Something was going to happen to him. He was going to die. I was hoping that it was Mr. Silberstern.

That person was a good person... Oh well, too bad, it wasn't my exploiter after all. And then Doña Soledad suddenly espied policemen. I was going to have difficulties with the police, though everything depended on my behavior—I held my fate in my own hand. With these words she let go of my hand, which prevented me from imagining that my fate bore the name Soledad Torres Medina. Was that all she saw? No, I would be traveling at sea—cannons, coils of rope, as with Doña Beatriz. Were we going to drown? No, this island was going to drown.

It was all very exciting. Don José put on a wax nose, the better to fill his role as a seer. Nephew Manola, the Sureda dynasty's fair-haired boy, principal heir and favorite painter, threatened to have a nervous breakdown in front of the church the next day, Sunday, unless Tio José gave him 100 pesetas. Everyone's eyes turned to Ludwig Salvator's personal physician, who had of course mastered worse situations during his lifetime. Peering over his extended nose, he looked over at Bobby who, simply using his optical eyes, had evolved into something like the domestic oracle of this *hospedage*. Bobby, in turn, looked at the gypsy, who had just taken hold of his hand. One brief touch, one glance at his palm, and she turned pale and immediately let go. A curt shriek told us that she had seen Bobby's future. But what was it that the Andalusian professional clairvoyant actually saw in the lines of this Folkwang student's hand? Beatrice, who also can read palms and tell a person's fortune, would have handled a delicate situation like this one quite differently. She would have pulled herself together, declared that she was so tired she was seeing double, and said, "Some other time."

The fright that we all experienced caused Don José to forget to award his nephew the obolus he was demanding in order to prevent his nervous collapse on the morrow. Bobby and Pedro were pleased at this turn of events, for the next day, at the portal of the *Cartuja*, we would witness how the talented painter would go about extorting his uncle, throwing himself on the ground and, like the mimic of a gigantic spitting cicada, gathering enough froth at his mouth to make a pushover of his Tio José. And that is actually how it happened. But we also got a small bonus, for when Don José saw his nephew go into an epileptic fit, he too collapsed to the ground and was in need of Samaritan aid. Bobby took care of this.

Back home, the two epileptics negotiated the appropriate economic arrangements, but not before Don José, once again in command of his physical and physicianly shrewdness, turned violently angry and hurled a chair at Manolo. The latter, likewise in full command of his faculties, quickly ducked and fell to the floor, and the chair went flying through the large window pane into the street below. Pistola fetched the debris without chewing a single piece. There followed a grand feast of reconciliation, with gypsy folk songs, superb wines, new glances into the future, and a unanimous protest from our hosts when we announced that we had to return to Palma. The weekend was at an end, but being outvoted we decided to stay on for a whole week more. One more week would eventually turn into two or three—a round month, let us say. We both needed a vacation, they told us. Vigo could continue writing his Hunnian epic or study his Lusitanian mystic, and Beatrice would have a grand piano at her disposal. We accepted, but Beatrice would have to go back to the city the next day to retrieve a few things: some clothes, books, sheet music. She would also have to start up my self-watering flower pots. And so Doña Beatriz departed alone.

Upon her return I saw in her face that something had gone wrong. "Burglary," she said. "The place was ransacked, but thank heavens they didn't find your Hunnish Tombs." She pulled my almost finished manuscript from her *cenaia*. I had put it in a waterproof envelope and sunk it down in a well, thinking that this might save it in case of a house fire. But meanwhile the Nazis had struck! I rode into the city to examine the damage. Our lock had been opened with a crowbar. I bought a new one, this time with the Yale trademark, with bolts to fit, and I filed down the key so it would fit snugly.

Mamú thought that our burglary was "thrilling." She asked me if I suspected anybody in particular. Well yes: the Nazis, or the heinous pillars of Christian Science, or perhaps both of these in subversive concert. "Then it's a matter for the police," said Mamú, and she summoned her chauffeur. Auma's personal attorney in matters of state and matters of love, the man who sat at her feet, reverted for a brief moment to his professional world of jurisprudence and warned us not to inform the local authorities. He was sure that I already knew that the island police who monitored foreigners were especially suspicious of outlanders who made trouble of any kind. Therefore, he said, I should take matters into my own hands.

"But how?"

"I thought you were an inventor."

I asked Mamú's chauffeur to take me in her car to Bonanova for a visit with Count Kessler. I possessed manuscripts of his as well as letters and other documents, and thus he was also involved in the burglary case. When I entered his house he was seated at his desk, a piece of furniture obviously designed by anybody else in this world but his private interior architect Henry van de Velde. This desk was a semi-circular affair, a work space for a housemaid, covered with a simple cotton fabric with printed pattern and fringe. That is where I encountered the Count, at the time the most famous man on the island, committing his thoughts and memories to paper for posterity.

"A burglary, you say? And they didn't touch my manuscripts? Well, that's understandable, considering that everything is slated to be published by S. Fischer, back in the *Reich*. The spies knew all about this, and they had their specific orders." But they didn't know the whole story, the Count continued. That miserable Consul wasn't even aware that he, Kessler, despite being exiled from Germany, had the status of an "exterritorial." The local police authorities, too, were oblivious—but their ignorance could be called charming in comparison. But no matter. Although the thugs seemed to be aiming at me, Thälmann, Enemy Number One, at the moment the Count was most interested in obtaining a dog. He had the address of some German living somewhere in a hidden corner of the island, a man with a litter to select from.

A few weeks later Kessler arrived at our door in a state of excitement. Something awful had happened to him. Had he been personally burglarized? Had his new dog, the pup from the secret German litter, raised its right paw to the Nazis and licked clean all the fingerprints from all his doorknobs and file cabinets?

Count Kessler had paid a visit to the clandestine dog breeder and told him who he was and what he was looking for. He needed a watchdog, trained to spot his true enemy, Hitler. "Hitler? Who's that?" the man asked.

"Just imagine. Here's a man who has lived on this island for decades, breeding dogs. He hasn't the faintest idea of what's going on in the world outside. He's hearing the name 'Hitler' for the first time from my lips. And now I have disturbed his domestic comfort in an effort to secure my own domestic security. Now I think I have made a big mistake. I should have bought some local breed."

I consoled the Count by pointing out the well-known cowardice of the Balearic species, insisting that there wasn't much to gain with such a purchase. I was aware, I told him, of how profoundly disturbed he must have been, as former President of the German Society for Peace, and as a diplomat familiar with the wish-dreams of all humanity, during his visit to the Mallorcan dog pound. But it was no different with the natives in the African jungle, I went on. They know nothing at all about Jesus Christ, and they eat each other up if that suits their appetite. Then along comes a troop of missionaries who capsize their domestic harmony, leaving them to do the best they can with a switch to vegetarianism.

What was it that Doña Soledad predicted for us? I was destined to have difficulties with the police—but that would depend on my own behavior. I avoided contact with the authorities, steered clear of difficulties, and thereby fulfilled the *gitana's* prophecy. Her reputation grew. But then she gazed at the moist hands of an elderly gentleman from Palma and foresaw a true bloodbath on our island. With that her clairvoyance became all too prophetic. Henceforth she was shunned.

A few weeks later I received a telegram informing me that my father had died. My first thought was: the Nazis! I didn't dare go back home for the funeral. One grave was enough, I figured. Surely one should love one's enemies, but the Bible says nothing about helping one's enemies to love one back. Our gypsy had once again prophesied correctly.

Some years later we sat on coils of rope on board a British destroyer. All around us we had refugees, cannons, misery, and whining. Behind us was our island, sinking in the flames of civil war in night and fog—just as the gypsy had foretold. This was our voyage across the waters.

Her predictions for Bobby likewise came true. Taken all together, it was what Henri Bergson called the phenomenon of *déjà vu*.

XXV

Count Harry Kessler dug deeper and deeper into his glorious past. He was up to his ears in his notes, diaries, letters by the thousands, memoranda, finished manuscripts, and other documents in a perpetual state of Wustmann-ian half-completion. There was hardly a single current event that could ferret him out of his burrow. He claimed that since he was in the process of retrieving the past, he surely ought to know whether he went to school with Hermann Keyserling—although he realized that Hermann wasn't talking about his school in Darmstadt. He simply couldn't recall the two of them having school years in common, although Keyserling insisted that they had. This must imply, he said, that he was writing his memoirs without being able to remember his own self. I begged leave to point out that similar cases occur in world litera-ture: *Don Quixote*, for example. He replied that rather than making fun of him I should just tell him how he could steer clear of that obnoxious fellow. Why, Keyserling was probably going to follow his steps to General Barceló Street! And what was that man after? He needed accomplices for his private harlequinade. For weeks there had been announcements of a session of Count Hermann Keyserling's School of Wisdom to be held at the Hotel Príncipe Alfonso. And since they went to school together, Keyserling was thinking that he, Kessler, was bound by conscience to assist him at this overseas outpost of German philosophy. But Kessler could remember nothing about schooldays in common...

There are lots of things I can't remember, but schooldays are not among them; they are forever hammered into my memory. In this respect I differ from Kessler, who from the day he was born was destined for a career at the end of which he would put down his recollections on paper. I was destined for a career at the end of which only I myself would get put down. And that's why I have never made notes, never kept a diary, never scribbled things on slips of paper and placed them, like Don Juan Sureda, in boxes and suitcases—build-ing-blocks for my applied recollections. If I ever had, then no sooner would neatnik Beatrice have wiped up Kessler's boot marks from our floor than I would have committed my "Conversations with Kessler" to paper with the verbatim quality of fresh memory, which permits only subtle differentiations such as that between "crook" and "blackguard."

Still, nuances of this kind could have no effect on the moral depravity of the person so labeled, especially since that person was a book publisher whom Kessler was intending to pillory in his fourth volume. Speaking of his own publisher, he said that this man would turn out to be his coffin nail. But that, too, strikes me as a matter of subtle nuance. Publishers, he explained, were a writer's eternal gadflies. Having bad luck with a publisher meant that the writer could simply fail—and he was beginning to have bad luck. Or did he say "misfortune"? When I once asked him about such details, Kessler told me that when recording actual conversations it was not verbal but psychological accuracy that was important. This is what Bismarck must have said, given all that one knows about the man, or noted down after speaking with him, or has read in Bismarck's own writings, or the like. An insight like this one from Kessler has reassured me while I write down these recollections of mine, in which a single publisher can at once embody verbal reality as a crook, psychological reality as a scamp, and historical reality as my coffin nail. It goes without saying that, besides, the publisher is a scoundrel.

Count Kessler recounted for us many episodes in his life that were meant for the later volumes of his memoirs. He explained the context of each event, and told us where it would fit in his personal narrative. If I had kept careful notes for my own "memoirs," I could offer a little assistance to the world's historical memory, now that everything is in the past and will no doubt soon be forgotten.

"What does Keyserling want from you? He is his own man as a philosopher and as a person, and in my opinion he doesn't need anybody else to help him out. And besides, he lives in the Príncipe, where they idolize him as the establishment's most effective advertisement. That's what my brother-in-law Don Helvecio has told me."

"It's so distressing, my friend. He wants to rig one of his sessions and have me play the part of an anonymous member of the audience. It's a hoax, and I just won't have any part in it."

The Wise Man of Darmstadt was once again staying at the Príncipe, where he was eating his way through the menu and drinking the vin *à discrétion* in such quantities that the management might have considered taking countermeasures if he weren't the hotel's greatest attraction. As often as he checked in, the No Vacancy sign went up. And ever since his *South American Meditations* was published, at Zwingli's instigation the hotel offered him unlimited credit.

Don Joaquín Verdaguer once described for me the way Count Keyserling conducted his School of Wisdom in the pine grove of the Hotel Formentor, on the Formentor peninsula. He sat on the ground with his legs crossed. Seated around him, likewise with legs crossed, were his pupils and auditors from all over the world. On a certain fateful day, the famous-notorious Spanish writer and aphorist Don Ramón Gómez de la Serna, an intellectual acrobat and prestidigitator, joined the throng, hunkered down, crossed his own legs, and pretended to be a run-of-the-mill participant and not the "Ramón" he was known as by every Spaniard. His forte was his so-called *greguerías*, which means "bird chatter": dazzling conceits that arise from his peculiar Donramonistic world-view. A regular visitor to Madrid's *rastro*, the city's central flea- and knickknack-market, Ramón studied the stuff offered for sale and, following intensive examination, deduced new aspects concerning those particular objects' mode of existence. Then he began unfolding his existential philosophy. Ramón was practicing existentialism well before this sort of thing became a fad. It is likely that he busied himself with the God's Eye in chamber pots, although I have yet to come across any aphorism of his concerning this branch of the ceramic arts. In addition, Ramón collected epitaphs, and when he made appearances as a lecturer he liked to balance on a rope stretched above the stage. But at Keyserling's school on the Formentor peninsula he refrained from stretching a rope between the pine trees. Like every other mortal disciple, he took his seat amid the ants, eye-to-eye with the Darmstadt conveyor of wisdom.

The Sage asked his pupils to name a subject on which he could improvise. He would then (now there were smiles around the whole circle) end up by pronouncing a compelling judgment. Now any teacher knows how hard it is to think up a clever topic. And once you have found a topic, at least half of the solution to its problems will be obvious. Ramón knew this, too, and so he motioned to an expectant waiter standing at the edge of the Wisdom School—one must recall that the Hotel Formentor had the reputation as the best hotel in Spain—and asked him to fetch a coffee pot. The *camerero* rushed away and returned carrying a luxury article. Ramón handed it to the German philosopher saying, "Here's your topic: The Coffee Pot."

Keyserling—I am following Verdaguer's account of the incident—had already imbibed a quantity of wine, and was now even more flushed than in his normal standing state. Thus no one noticed his embarrassment, which would have been all the greater had he realized that the man presenting him with his topic was none other than Gómez de la Serna. Well now, what might a profound German philosopher have to say about The Coffee Pot? Keyserling turned the pot around and around, meditating all the while. Finally, with a rapid gesture like a circus seal he placed it in front of his snout and started explaining what he, as a German philosopher in general, and as a Darmstadt Keyserling in particular, had to say about this utensil. He accomplished this brilliantly, deploying wit, paradoxes, scorn, and profundity, getting quickly to the heart of the matter so adroitly that everyone in the squatting circle was simply amazed. Who would have thought that so much wisdom could be derived from a simple coffee pot, from a Coffee Pot *an sich?*

Keyserling, who was himself surprised at how well he had done this trick, took a deep bow and placed the vessel on the ground on top of an ant hill. Then he, too, motioned to the waiter, asked him to bring over a *porrón*, and proceeded to pour the red liquid in an archaically measured arc into his eloquent gullet. This feat, too, he accomplished without staining his shirt. There was more applause. He was the hero of the pine grove, just as he loved to be the hero anywhere and everywhere. Then he casually inquired whether anyone else might have something to say on the subject of The Coffee Pot, while remaining convinced that no one could ever top him on a subject he had treated so exhaustively.

All those present who recognized Ramón—and who among the Spaniards here did not know him?—looked over at Ramón. He asked for the pot, blew away the ants, and started in. Our brilliant guest, he said, has discussed the brilliant surface of this brilliant object quite brilliantly, but nonetheless superficially. He, Ramón—and with the mention of the name, the Wise Man from

Darmstadt underwent his initial shock—asked if he might be permitted to say a few words concerning the darker recesses of the topic at hand. Whereupon Ramón Gómez de la Serna began regaling the circle with his *greguerías*, proving two things at once: that German philosophy was lacking in depth, and that a coffee pot was an ultimately inexhaustible subject.

When the pupils arose from their squatting position and brushed the ants from their lower extremities, they noticed that the Sage was reeling slightly. Had his legs, too, gone to sleep? Or had he sat down in the middle of an anthill? He retired to his deluxe hotel suite as a vanquished philosopher, and as such he quickly departed from the hotel and the island.

Kessler was unfamiliar with this saga of the coffee pot, which had taken place some few years back. When I recounted it for him, he said, "Aha! So that's what's behind this piece of trickery! Keyserling had better watch out!"

Keyserling's plan was to assemble a select audience in the small auditorium at the Príncipe, treat them with some nuggets of wisdom, then ask for a random topic from his listeners and, after a minute for meditation, deliver an exhaustive discourse on the subject. Quite a number of philosophy *aficionados* had arrived from the Spanish mainland, people who out of sheer ennui were preoccupied with problems of life-enhancing wisdom—a dangerous kind of audience in a country that has never produced a real philosopher, since every citizen already possesses his own philosophy of idleness. Ramón was not invited; Hermann wasn't about to take any risks. So it was a stroke of luck that this other *conde*, his old schoolmate Harry, was staying on the island. It was Hermann himself who recommended Mallorca as a suitable place of exile and a site conducive to the writing of memoirs. Counts of a feather will flock together, so they soon found each other.

Hermann began their conversation by railing against the Nazis, especially Goebbels, who had detained his wife as a hostage at the Darmstadt School. He, Hermann, was forced to take an oath stipulating that during his lecture tour in Spain he would keep philosophy and politics strictly separate, a feat that has been one of philosophy's great accomplishments since the days of Plato. Then Hermann cooked up his fairy tale about his and Harry's common schooldays. God only knows where that common school was located, for Keyserling was born in Livonia and Kessler in Paris, 12 years apart—although such a time differential is perhaps irrelevant when dealing with minds that functioned at such a sublime remove from space and time. According to Hermann's fable, Harry, the older of the two, had more than once had to repeat a whole school year—a most unlikely sequence of events given Harry's superior intelligence, even for a youngster brought up on a remote country estate.

In short, Keyserling badgered poor Harry so relentlessly that he finally surrendered, in order to maintain his composure and his ability to go on with his own work. He agreed to attend the lecture at the Príncipe, make believe he was just some guy in the audience, and suggest a topic for Hermann to discourse upon. Conde de Keyserling would make a few introductory remarks, greeting his guests in six or seven different languages—but of course only after consuming a liter of red wine and a few armadillos. Then he would ask for the evening's topic from his esteemed audience: "Just step right up, ladies and gentlemen, and don't be shy, because this mental acrobat can handle anything." His circus-barker railery would give rise to genteel merriment, perhaps even some genuine surprise at so much un-academic clowning. But no one would come forth with a topic. Each member of the audience would be thinking, "Let somebody else make a fool of himself." Keyserling knew from experience that the first few minutes were non-threatening. The moment would arrive when the piston reached the dead point. The danger would be past, the lecturer himself could breathe easily and suggest a few subjects to choose from—unless, of course, some Ramón stood up... That would have to be avoided, and so, Harry my old friend, why don't you and I think up a topic, and you pretend to be an *aficionado* in the audience? The big advantage was that nobody at all would recognize him.

Kessler told me that this kind of chicanery disgusted him. But now he couldn't get rid of the man. What should he do?

"Play along with him, Count Kessler! Suggest some topic to Keyserling, give him three days to prepare his spiel, and when he gets up there on the stage and motions to his accomplice, you trip him up by announcing a completely different subject. One swindle is worth another. But both topics must be of a kind to give him real trouble. It's time that the charlatan got his comeuppance!"

Count Kessler was unwilling to enter into this double-dealing fakery, out of a real fear that the Baltic philosopher would strangle him alive *coram publico*. He agreed only to concoct for his schoolmate a particularly thorny subject: "The Machine as the Upstart of Our Century."

In the meantime Count Keyserling gave a two-hour public lecture in a large theater in Palma on a subject dear to his heart: "Spanish-Mediterranean Culture as the New Hellas." He spoke without notes, partly in Spanish, partly in Catalan, and was a huge success. All the Hondurans were on hand, as were all the island's anarchists, a few clergymen, several aristocrats, and even a nursing mother whose presence the Kalmuck count found particularly touching and inspirational—again and again his glances wandered in the direction of the place where Young Hellas was getting suckled. My friend Enorme was sitting next to me. As a Krausite he was interested in Keyserling, and as a conspirator he had already been clued in by me concerning the conspiracy being hatched by the two counts. Enorme and I decided that the best way to outwit the philosopher was for us to shout some questions from the audience that would take him out on political thin ice.

With Zwingli's help, Keyserling arranged everything perfectly. Rows of seats were set up in the auditorium of the Príncipe with a respectful space in front of the stage; a long green table, and to the right and to the left of the table some artificial palms, just as at Pilar's, but bigger. The select audience was truly *crème de la crème*, and Zwingli knew most of them. They represented literature, music, the visual arts, journalism, banking and industry, as well as the feared *aficionados* of all the above fields of activity. They spoke a good dozen different languages, and Conde de Keyserling, flushed with a red vintage, chatted with each of them in the appropriate tongue. He was in his element, the *grand monde*, the sounding-board for his boundless wisdom. Many beautiful women had also arrived; all around the hall there was a swishing of fans, a sparkling of jewelry, an aroma of intellectual excitement. A thin and wordless Count Kessler pressed his way through the noisy crowd, visibly annoyed, and intent upon avoiding his old schoolmate. As soon as he spied us, he rushed over, and I introduced him to the Krausite Don Sacramento, whom Kessler took for a Mexican. Then Zwingli arrived in his capacity as Don Helvecio. He asked us to take first-row seats that he had reserved for us. Kessler declined such a prominent focal point. Like his ancestor Johannes in St. Gall, he took a seat on the hindmost bench.

The event proceeded on schedule. Kessler, the programmed "anonymous man in the audience," sat anonymously in the audience. Then he was approached by the Reverend Don Francisco Sureda Blanes, a Mallorquin writer, amateur philosopher, and Ramón Lull researcher. He was the organizer of this *charla*, he knew Count Kessler, and right away fished him out of his anonymity. He pulled the reluctant count forward to the green table, where some members of the lecture committee had already gathered. For the most part these were local dignitaries, but they also included a foreigner who was being celebrated throughout Spain: Francis de Miomandre, a hispanist who had produced a monumental new translation of *Don Quijote* into French.

Don Darío whispered to me that even though Conde de Keyserling had quaffed a lot of wine, he wasn't even tipsy.

Taller than everyone else in the hall by a head, a head that was now redder than ever and that (it must be told) emerged from a pink shirt with green necktie, his beard fluttering smartly, his eyes twinkling with excitement—there he stood before us, and listened as Reverend Don Francisco introduced him: "You have come to witness something that has never been seen before..." I realized right away that when God created a Keyserling, He could not have had this particular Keyserling in mind, for the little ditty we learned as Lower-Rhineland kids went this way: "When God's breath became a paltry thing, He created the famous Count Keyserling." To create this Hermann, God would have required His full diapason. The ditty is more fitting for his cousin Eduard Keyserling, the melancholy narrator of Baltic aristocratic family chronicles, a personage whom a mild zephyr could have blown off the face of the earth.

Count Keyserling spoke Spanish fluently, but a certain agitation in his audience told him that people were not following his words. How about English? No? Then let's try French. He was willing to obey the wishes of his esteemed listeners. Applause from all present except Vigoleis and Don Sacramento. Although both of us were in full command of the French language, we lacked the conversational practice that would allow us to play our trick on the celebrated philosopher. With Spanish we could have pulled it off. Keyserling could tote up his first two victims.

His circus act went along as planned. The mental acrobat in his pink shirt and dashing white beard invited the audience to present him with the evening's subject for discussion. "And please, don't hold back. This is a master class, so is anyone brave enough? No one? Nobody at all? Is this so difficult? No one from the green table, either? What's the matter?" The Conde wrung his hands as if conjuring a genie. I noticed how he now winked toward Harry Kessler, and how the latter, the anti-clown, glanced off into the corner where we were sitting. If he didn't stand up right away, Hermann would lose, for someone in the first row was clearing his throat—presumably it was somebody's Adam's apple being rolled up and then back down. There was deathly silence, and everyone gazed forward toward the man with the breathing problem. At this moment, Count Kessler arose from his seat at the green table.

I cannot offer a historically accurate portrait of Harry Kessler, for I neither believe in historical exactitude, nor have I ever kept written notes. But this much I recall of that evening's gala philosophical spectacular: Count Kessler had on his natty Bauzá suit, which I could describe down to the last button— not because my client Silberstern was so interested in the Count's wardrobe, but because I myself had, by coincidence, asked the haberdasher at Bauzá to make me a suit from the very same fabric and with the very same cut. It was on this very same gala evening that the Count and I discovered that we shared the same tailor, the same taste in clothing, and the same trust in the potential sales value of his book *Peoples and Fatherlands*.

Kessler, who had given a thousand speeches in front of more hostile audiences than this one, spoke slowly, with almost touching modesty and with a firm voice. No one besides us two and Keyserling could have interpreted the faint rosy flecks on his cheeks as a sign of trepidation. As a phony he was playing his role quite convincingly. He began by saying that it was not easy to offer a topic to a philosopher of Keyserling's standing. It would be necessary to reach, or at least to approach, the Count's level of competency. "Well now, *mon cher* Keyserling, how about this: '*La machine comme parvenue de notre siècle*'?"

There it was! Drumroll and crack of the whip! The clown leaps into the ring and pulls a bunny from his nose. Count Kessler sat down. If now he just wouldn't look over to the place where Thälmann is sitting—if he could just go on with his thoughts about "*Times and Faces*"—his private faces, his private times—while the other Count clears his throat.

An electric fan sent a breeze across the green table. The artificial palms started rustling, and the philosopher's beard, caught by the puffs of air, blew out horizontally. Don Quixote in person!

Hermann played his role better than Harry, for he was everything at once: philosopher, tippler, diplomat, Don Quixote, Sancho Panza, magician. And because his published works legitimized him for decades into the future, unlike Harry he didn't need to keep his mind focused on the past. Well now: "The Machine As Upstart"? Hermann squinted and surveyed his mixed audience. Then he tested the ropes that would lift him up to his trapeze. Were all the rings and hooks secure? Taking the measure of this Upstart would be child's play for Hermann. Drumbeat! Crack of whip! The pink shirt takes a bow, the green necktie shimmers menacingly. *"Mesdames et messieurs, la machine comme parvenue...nous verrons."*

Hermann had obviously not wasted his time with the bottle. He had prepared everything exactly to his taste, and his performance earned him a *summa cum laude.* The way he attacked the topic was simply ingenious. He immediately went for the depths—Harry hadn't tossed him a coffee pot. Hermann didn't just go foraging on the surface, he plunged to the very bottom and revealed the ocean's darkest secrets: fish with rear-end lights, lanceolate eyes, phosphorescent jellyfish, high-voltage sea monsters—these were the precursors, an entire aquarium full, of all of Nature's "upstarts" that were eventually to reach *terra firma.* Hermann then ascended slowly to the surface, and slithered ahead as Wisdom's amphibian. He ended his oration with an even more ingenious conclusion—the nature of which I can't remember. After an hour, both the subject and the lecturer were obviously exhausted.

There was loud applause, honestly proffered and well deserved. Dr. Sureda Blanes thanked the speaker in the name of Lullian Science and all of its devotees in attendance, for the great German philosopher's brilliant impromptu discourse on such an extraordinary subject. An exhaustive discourse, he went on, again speaking for all those present. Surely there was nothing to add to the Count's explanations—or perhaps there was? If not, then if the audience so desired, we could proceed to the general discussion, for Conde de Keyserling would surely give us the pleasure of taking up some of the more obscure points... Hermann nodded, *mais naturellement*—just ask away! Darmstadt was ready to provide all the answers.

No one budged. Someone had turned the electric fan back on, and it blew the pearl fisher's beard out toward the audience. His green tie glistened, the palms swayed. The gentlemen at the green table were also swaying, and Harry too, who looked as if he wanted to say something. A few words of thanks? He stood up, and the custom tailoring of his Bauzá suit presented a *distingué* contrast to his would-be schoolmate's pink shirt. The latter gestured to him as if to say, "Well, I'll let you speak a few nice words, Harry, but keep it brief. If the audience likes what you say, we'll take that as a recommendation for a repeat performance sometime, and then we can take off and enjoy a bottle together. I've got it all prepared."

Harry did express his thanks—oh yes, indeed. His old friend, he said, had made some interesting points concerning the proposed topic. But—a thousand pardons—although Count Keyserling certainly had profound things to say about the subject at hand, he hadn't truly plumbed the depths—a thousand pardons. Would he be permitted to add a few comments of his own? He had made some notes. Ten minutes, and no more?

There was commotion in the hall, commotion at the green table, commotion beneath the pink shirt. Don Francisco spoke up: "Go ahead, *Señor Conde!*" There were echoes of "Go ahead!" from the audience in many languages.

Then Hermann, circus M.C. and clown in one and the same person, said, "Fine!" and clapped his hands smartly. No one followed his example, so now Harry, his head bent ever so slightly forward, commenced his act of revenge on the louche impostor and his phony story about their schooldays together. One by one, Harry hauled up to the surface all of Hermann's deep-sea monsters, luminescent animals, medusas, and jellyfish, and burst them apart. When the aquarium was totally empty, Hermann was done for, stripped down to his dawn-colored shirt. The one Count had no need to administer the coup de grâce to the other Count. The entire audience took over this task. They gave Conde Harry de Kessler a thunderous ovation, a tribute that Conde de Keyserling couldn't out-clap with his gigantic paws. As a self-defined Sage, he clearly knew when the jig was up.

Count Kessler looked over to our corner of the hall. We waved to him. He gestured his thanks. Afterwards he told us that he felt so ashamed on our account that he was worrying how he could possibly set things aright. He succeeded admirably.

Hermann retreated to his hotel suite and, all alone, drank up the chilled bottles, all six of them. Then he summoned Don Helvecio to his room and discussed with him his departure. He wasn't interested in a return engagement at Formentor. He had urgent commitments in Barcelona, Madrid, Salamanca...

The local newspapers took notice of the Príncipe event. Who was this Count Kessler, the man whose age, compendious knowledge, and cleverness had so astonishingly outpointed the famous, popular, hispanophile Count Keyserling? He was reported to be a foreign guest on the island, and a renowned personage on all the continents. But why had Mallorca not heard of him before? It was said that he was composing his memoirs, and the hope was that they would be published in Spanish, too.

During the following days Count Kessler was inundated with letters of invitation: *conferencias* here, *conferencias* there, requests for pre-publication copies of his memoirs and for copies of his *Notes on Mexico*. Kessler rejected all of them. It was not his intention, he said, to claim the spotlight. He had simply wished to give the insistent Hermann a lesson. Hermann, for his part, cursed the day when he shared his platonic schooldays with Harry.

Harry once again submerged into his days of imperial glory. Hermann, after a return to the Spanish mainland, enjoyed continued acrobatic success as the prophet of an Iberian Hellas.

I was not aware that the German publisher Samuel Fischer was known to his friends as "Sami." And thus at first I couldn't understand why Count Kessler was so upset at reading this man's obituary, or that he, who even in exile observed all the forms of etiquette, came knocking at our door late in the evening—a type of behavior that we could have expected only from Herr Silberstern.

"Sami is dead. May I come in?" To judge by the newspapers that we found in our corridor, it must have been a night between Saturday and Sunday. Kessler made no attempt to take his shoes off. He was in distress, and kept saying how horrible it was that Sami was dead. Not until he added, leaning against the bookcase in our bible-paper room, that Sami's successor would no doubt turn out to be his coffin nail, did I realize that the person he was mourning was none other than the famous S. Fischer. There would be trouble, he told us. All their wonderful collaboration on the literary journal Pan was now over with, all the leisure he, Kessler, needed for the later volumes of his memoirs. Then he wandered off in recollections of the post-Bismarck years: the heyday of Naturalist drama: Gerhart Hauptmann, Hofmannsthal, Eberhard von Bodenhausen, all the great European writers that Sami had assembled from near and far: Ibsen, Dostoevsky, Georg Brandes.

Conversing further on, he eventually focused on an episode to be recounted in the final volume of his memoirs, which he intended to finish with his flight from Germany. It was a scene that took place in the Hotel Adlon in Berlin. He was involved in negotiations in a private room with personages whose names I have of course forgotten. A waiter arrives and says, "Gentlemen, the *Reichstag* is on fire!" Someone grabs Kessler's arm and whispers to him that it is high time that he pack his bags and escape to England or France. Kessler doesn't even take the time to return to his apartment on Köthener Strasse, the rooms designed and decorated by Henry van de Velde. Instead, he takes the very next train to Paris. His head was on the list of those to be liquidated when the Nazis faked a Communist assassination attempt against the *Führer*. Kessler had a copy of that list, given to him by friends of his at the German embassy in London.

That business about Sami Fischer's successor as Harry's "coffin nail" made a big impression on me, since I was thinking that a writer of such universal renown as Count Kessler must be immune to the vagaries and chicaneries of any publisher, especially his own publisher. Today I know that an author must consider himself fortunate if his publisher doesn't send him, along with a publishing contract, a finished coffin—one that would probably be a few sizes too small. It's a lucky thing for the future of literature that most writers feel so sheltered from death that even in sight of the proverbial four boards, they continue to compose their own epitaphs.

Count Kessler left the island in the spring of 1936. His health was ruined; he was spitting blood, and he looked terrible. Before he departed, in Barcelona and in the Galerías Costa in Palma he arranged exhibitions of highly acclaimed works from his Cranach Press.

We agreed that I should continue *par distance* as his scribe. He would send me his manuscripts, and I would edit them with my Wustmannian marginal notes. A few letters and manuscript packages went between General Barceló Street and his new refuge, the Hostellerie des Compagnons de Jéhu in Pontanevaux. The outbreak of the Civil War brought all this to an end.

Count Kessler was lucky to have reached French soil when the disaster started. He would not have survived the Franco night of July 18th-19th, 1936. The gun-toting Nazi from Königsberg, the one who took upon himself the purging of the German colony, would have made short work of him. For quite a while a rumor spread that Kessler had been shot on Mallorca. Under normal circumstances the Nazis could have left him alone for a few more years, since he was relatively harmless. He never gave reckless speeches against the Third *Reich*, and was not involved in any conspiracies. It is only because the collaboration between him and his Wustmannian, Thälmannian, Thelemannian amanuensis worked so well that he hadn't sought out some politically innocuous secretary. There were times when he was anxious about my unpredictability. Only the completion of his fourth and final volume of memoirs could have given Hitler reason to eliminate him. "That must never be written," I was told later, by a man sitting next to me on a coil of rope on a British destroyer, a man who had reason to fear the same fate. It was the writer Franz Blei, Kessler's friend from the time of their collaboration on the literary journal *Pan*.

XXVI

It's always the same when a person is going down the drain: those nearest to him never notice the problem until it is too late. That's how it was with Zwingli. One day we observed that he had stopped taking baths, that he no longer did us his customary little favors, that again and again we had to tell his limping business partner that Don Helvecio hadn't come back to us, and that his clothes got dirtier and shabbier. In short, a woman!

She was a dancer of the unclothed variety, her name was Konákis, which suggested Greek origins—or rather the Greek origins of her art. For although she pretended to be a child of Hellas, she was Italian, came from Chicago, and had Irish blood. She could be sporadically observed in the altogether at the dingiest of nightclubs, where she was lauded and serenaded for her beauty.

Like many high-bred women, Konákis preferred men who exuded the aroma of the cave. She, too, yearned to be abducted and thrown into the bushes by hairy chimpanzee fists, and to view above her a powerful male chest with hair containing clumps of earth that she could pluck out one by one, chanting "He loves me, he loves me not," only to have the depilated savage take out his bloody lust on her. Zwingli had fished up Konákis at the Torre del Reloj. Now he was in her thrall, and quickly went primitive in order to grab hold of her all the more securely. Without such a mutation he wouldn't have been nearly earthy enough for her. What the two of us were mourning as yet another form of deterioration was for Zwingli, on the contrary, a new awakening. The horn on his pinky once again showed the old signs of accumulated grime. His brain was hatching audacious plans, and producing so much dandruff that a light snowfall occurred whenever he shook his head, which he now often did.

In the center of the city he rented a half-derelict villa for his Academy. His millionaire sponsor was still hiding behind his bank account, but was expected to arrive on Mallorca, where rooms in the Príncipe were long since awaiting him. Yet because this man was still invisible, Zwingli was hard at work with his local genius for the founding of institutions, Don Darío. My inventions had already earned them "quite a wad." They were now investing the wad in higher art education. This started with a series of sketching classes with nude models for beginners and advanced students, plus a master class. There were peepholes for the "*aficionados* of nudity," and the entire enterprise went forward under the aegis of Spain's famous painter Doña Pilar, whose full surname was several lines long although her single noble title would suffice to fill the classroom with standing-room-only. It goes without saying that Pedro's mother had no idea what mischief was being perpetrated in the name of her *alba*. She learned about it from her indignant relatives, who had seen their name emblazoned on banners, posters, and leaflets. One more crazy Sureda escapade? That's what people were asking. The sketching classes were a front, they said. This was surely a bordello with a fancy new cachet.

It was a fact that Zwingli could hardly keep control of the applications for his academy. He had only a single model: Konákis. Old geezers, bored with their sterile club activities, applied for admission as beginners. They were loath to pass from this life without sketching a live nude. They had never done anything like it, and didn't even know that it could be done. For them, women's bodies existed to be fallen in love with, stared at, slept with, married, locked in, beaten, sent to church, and allowed annually to enjoy the heaven-sent gift of pregnancy. But now a domestic animal of this kind could be possessed with the aid of an artist's pencil at Don Helvecio's International Academy of Art. Who could resist?

The posters and brochures announced that, in addition to the modeling studio, there were two further new affiliated educational institutions: one for foreign languages and one for herbal tea.

Zwingli distributed thousands of advertisements across the entire island. He hired minions to cruise the Borne, shout the name of the new academy, and pass out fliers to pedestrians. One time I heard my own name being called out. Curious as to what Vigoleis had now got himself into, I took one of the brochures and learned that the new Academy had obtained for its faculty a certain Professor Vigoleis, trained at German and Dutch universities, widely traveled, and famous as the inventor of the One-Chair System of Pedagogy. Attendance at his ¾ hour One-Chair seminar was listed as costing 25 pesetas, instruction in any of the major languages, and "Please turn." When I turned, I found this: *Mens sana non potest vivere in corpore sicco*—Rabelais' parody of Juvenal's famous motto: "A healthy mind cannot live inside a dried-up body." *Ergo*: "Drink Pastor Künzli's Herbal Tea! Samples served at the Academy!" The trinity of wine, women, and song was hailed in this broadsheet, along with the little deviancies that can make such a combination so fruitful. The wine was Künzli Tea, the woman's name was Konákis, and the song would have to come forth from Vigoleis' throat.

Elated by my appointment to the faculty of the new Academy, I rushed home. This was, finally, going to be my great stroke of luck. Beatrice must be the first to hear about it.

In front of our house, furniture was being loaded into vans. Zwingli was in charge of the procedure with his pinky nail. Next to him on our balcony stood Konákis, a desirable specimen of Mother Nature even when fully clothed. Neither of them noticed my arrival. I ducked beneath a desk some guy was lifting, and entered the stairway.

I found Beatrice in our spare room. Had she been crying? After so many years and so much trouble in a constantly vulnerable marriage, it is difficult to be sure in retrospect. There is no question that she had reason to shed tears, not to mention tearing her hair out. I could claim the privilege of all writers of memoirs and have her behave here in just this way, but only if she had a natural inclination toward theatrical masochism. Just this much: brother and sister had just emerged from a terrible fight. She had tossed water at him, and he had tossed bottles of medicine at her, with his Greek squeeze goading her earthy troglodyte companion to clobber his prude of a sister. Beatrice accused Zwingli of exploiting the honorable name of Pedro's mother, telling him that she knew full well that his new establishment was nothing but a brothel camouflaged as an academy of art. With that, Beatrice had uttered the fateful word, and the above-named objects started flying about our apartment. Zwingli's choice of bottles of medicine to toss must be understood in the context of the bout of typhus from which he had just recovered, a disease we had nursed him through for several months. We had to summon Dr. Solivellas, because neither brother nor sister had any further confidence in their grandfather's homeopathic drops. Zwingli didn't trust Spanish hospitals. Vigoleis didn't trust Zwingli. And so forth...

It's such a shame. If Konákis hadn't been on the scene in her fully clothed state, instead of squabbling, brother and sister would have embraced each other, and Zwingli would have moved off to his Institute of Female Art. But as it was, he now burned all his bridges behind him. The only thing he took with him, at Konákis' insistence, was the list of my inventions. I was flattered.

I soon convinced Beatrice that we should be happy that Zwingli's cathouse academy was not to be located inside our own apartment. I meant this as a form of consolation, but quickly enough it became a fly in the ointment. Beatrice was unable to rid herself of the idea that the very possibility of such a development had desecrated our living quarters. She was unwilling to stay where we were, yet she wasn't suggesting that we once again try jumping into the ocean. A move to the Archduke's palace at Miramar would be possible only when Mamú's millions were finally available. But in the meantime, Mamú wasn't even in a position to pay back the *tusig Fränkli* we had lent her.

"OK, let's move out," I said. "You're sick of this apartment. For you it stinks of this Konákis woman. I'll go look for another place."

I found a new apartment on the 7th floor of a new building on a street we knew, one named after a more than familiar personage: the Avenida del Archiduque Luis Salvador. "Salvador" means "redeemer." The Suredas had recently moved with kit and caboodle into a flat just a few doors away from us. Could we have hoped for a nicer neighborhood? When we negotiated the rent, the paint was still wet, but that didn't mean that we were "dry renters". This *piso* had a bathroom, a custom-made kitchen, and a roof garden with ocean view. Our finances were in satisfactory condition, but our health had gone to the dogs. It was over-exertion, Dr. Solivellas told us. We should go out into the countryside, into the mountains, for three or four months. For that length of time the two of us should do no work at all, for up to now we had knocked ourselves out like slaves. He offered us his cottage at the seaside near Pollensa. But mountain air would be better, he said. Valldemosa, Génova, Monasterio de Lluch...

Mamú had a woman friend who didn't belong to the Christian round table, a Swedish painter of indeterminable age but of quite determinable lineage. She called her Swedish king "Uncle," an appellation she employed every year during the vacations she spent at court with her relatives. One of her passions was tennis. Her name was Agnes, so on our island she was known as Doña Inés. She let us use her house in Génova for four summer months. So our switch to the new address on Archduke Luis Street was in effect a twofold removal.

Don Matías was overcome with sadness when I told him that this was the very last loaf of bread from Jaume's oven we would be consuming here, on our last day on the street named after the General we had come to love and admire. Oh my good friend, he said, let's not lose sight of each other! Why were we moving to a new apartment when important things were about to happen in Honduras? The new flag was ready. The Honduran nation was ready. Don Patuco had packed his military knapsack, and the only thing left was the official *pronunciamiento*. "When are you moving out?" I told him that we expected the moving van to arrive at dawn. Our furniture would be placed in storage for a while, and we would then be on our way to Génova and the house owned by Princess Inés, whose behavior on the island was so democratic in nature that she was known as Citizen Agnes.

Mamú, too, chided us. Our decision to move was too hasty. Why change our address, when her millions would become liquid in just a few weeks, and all of us could establish princely new lodgings in Miramar? I told her that it was just one step from the Archduke's Street to his regal palace. As soon as the first promising droplets of financial rain started falling upon us, we would gladly make the additional move. "Don't you trust me?" That's not what it's about, I said. It was just that with Mamú, things seemed to be proceeding at an un-American pace, although this was not her own fault. It was the fault of the lawyers on both sides of her case, whose work she, as a devout Christian Scientist, was apparently unwilling to disturb. "Live and let live"—wasn't that the motto of her late husband?

No matter where Vigo and Beatrice met friends during this period, they both had to explain the reasons behind their good fortune. An apartment with bath and roof garden, one whole duro cheaper than their previous one. A vacation at the Casa Inés, a rosy future in the palace of the Archiduque. All that remained for us to wish for was the success of the published German version of the Lusitanian mystic Pascoaes, my *"Hun-less Tombs of the Huns,"* and one or another of my inventions. This would take us both out of all our trouble. We had withstood a great deal of starving and unhappiness. Our final gesture in the direction of triumph for us little people was the acquisition of a bullet-proof vest, which we wore by turns. Not long ago in our vicinity, the Nazis had dispatched an enemy of the German nation with a shot from a revolver.

Our move took place without incident. The men arrived shortly after noon, early enough to establish ourselves in our new digs in Génova on the same day. We left all our other things in disarray in our old apartment.

Our main concern now was to take a rest—one week, perhaps two weeks. Let's do nothing at all. Give me a few days to finish the final chapter of my "Huns," and then I would send the completed manuscript to the publisher Querido in Amsterdam.

I had installed a second security lock in the door of our old apartment. If someone wanted to break into our *pisa*, he would have to break down the wall. We closed off everything with four twists of the locks, and an hour later we opened the door to the Casa Inés by means of a prehistoric bone. This door, painted green, featured the coat of arms of the Swedish royal dynasty—a token emblem placed there in understandable family pride by the painter who later saved our lives and the lives of dozens of other people.

We had four months ahead of us, and to us they seemed more endless than the shimmering blue ocean we now had at our feet, quivering beneath the cloudless skies we had enjoyed for all the past months. But how much water was left in the local wells? A neighbor of ours guessed that we had two or three more weeks' worth if we were willing to conserve—which most foreigners weren't willing to do. Rain? Hardly a chance. I resolved to forego bathing until the next rainfall.

The painter who owned the place had laid out a rock garden, whose un-Spanish cuteness was in stark contrast to the luxuriant abundance of indigenous plants, agaves and yard-tall stands of cactus that formed a border between the terraced house plot and a steep hill in the back.

Our aristocratic gardener had not been able to improve on the background of this vista: the Cala Mayor inlet, opening into the Bay of Palma. As we looked out, tiny lights began to sparkle on the water, fishermen with their fire baskets, setting out for the catch. Standing watch over all this was the constellation of Orion.

Our day was at an end.

* * *

Our day was at an end, and it also was supposed to mark the end of the first volume of these applied recollections of mine. That would have been a happy ending for a book that begins unhappily. We would find Vigoleis and Beatrice sleeping in the heavenly bed of a real princess, their shimmering linen sheet strewn with Keating's Gold Insecticide Powder, hummed into slumber beneath a gossamer net by mosquitoes, and left unplagued by bad dreams during this night under Orion, who outshone the threefold constellation of my would-be assassins. Outside, the fireflies sparkled and the crickets fiddled furiously in anticipation of the big rains to come—to our dreamy ears it sounded like Bach fugues played on the organ that Mamú was going to have installed in Miramar—she had already received a cost estimate from an organ builder in San Sebastián. Somewhere on the island, my personal *burro* was rearing up on his bed of fermenting straw, waiting to be pushed into his stall at the Archduke's fly-free stables.

This is where my book should stop, with Orion holding his glistening pilgrim staff over our heroes' slumber. Peace all across the island, peace in our hearts, peace in each and every cricket's burrow. You, dear reader, already know from my countless hints that much blood has yet to be shed, especially the blood of Vigoleis, who after precisely five nights was slated to be one of the bullet-riddled corpses. By replying to the German Consul's hesitant query, "What? You haven't been shot?" with the touchingly foolish counter-query, "Am I supposed to be?" he has earned the right to postpone his *Finis operis* by the length of one more Book, although it's going to be a Book with only one chapter—meaning, of course, with no chapter at all. A book of extended leave-taking. I myself am no longer frightened. I was supposed to be bumped off, and yet I was still standing. Any reader can shoot me now by slamming the book shut. If he does so, he will be spared the sight of other people's fright—Angelita's, for example, who didn't believe her eyes when she saw us still alive. Every one of our not yet gunned down, drowned, hanged, or crucified friends got the cold shivers when we knocked at their sealed front doors to say goodbye. Some of them slammed their doors shut in a faint. In most cases, I was able to shove one foot inside and, using the password, let them see my true face. These people let us in and bolted the lock behind us, whereupon we, the Resurrected Ones, started giving report after report.

For a certain length of time back then on the island, anyone who hadn't been killed was considered to have risen from the dead. I'll be brief about this, although I could fill chapter after chapter with descriptions of encounters during the first, second, and third months of the insurrection: my encounter with the limping Don Matías, with Don Gracias a Dios, who was now redeeming himself by composing patriotic verse hailing the Spanish *pronunciamiento*—like so many other foreign conspirators.

In Jaume's bakery, the Hondurans had already held a little memorial ceremony for the murdered Don Vigoleis. But now here he was, out on the street, stretching out a hand that at first no one dared to touch. The amazing thing in those days was that nobody had the courage to say to us, "How did you escape getting killed? You're both supposed to have been shot!" In Don Matías I still saw the old Krausite and Decipherer of the World, my flour-sack buddy. But now this pseudo-Honduran was holding back his feelings. He had become as stiff as the little vest he was again wearing. I inquired as to the welfare of the one-armed general Don Patuco, explaining that I was being guided by this man's inspired warnings against priests with forked tongues and generals with two arms. I was on my guard, since General Franco still had both of his arms. Don Matías suddenly went pale. "Be quiet," he whispered. "If anybody hears you, you'll be shot. They'll think we're in a conspiracy." As for himself, he was now for Franco, and his daughter Encarnación was for Franco. After all, a man could have two arms and still be a swell guy and a successful revolutionary... "What about Ulua the cobbler?" He got thrown down a well. They put a stone on top. His wife was thrown down another well. Stone on top. Their son got away with false papers to Uruguay.

In this way, I could fill many pages of this final, chapter-less Book. By doing so, I could easily lose sight of the two of us—not a bad ending, perhaps, for a pair of heroes who entered my story namelessly, plagued by fleas and bad dreams on board a ship taking them to the island—just two out of hundreds of people. That was years ago.

They left the island as two out of thousands, unmolested by dreams, since they were kept wide awake by the reality around them. But they weren't able to sleep, either—certainly not the kind of peaceful slumber enjoyed by Vigoleis and Beatrice in the celestial bed owned by Doña Inés, who like a girl in a fairy tale could call a king "Uncle," and who greeted her polyglot house tenants with a strip of embroidery on our pillow saying *Godnatt!*

Vigoleis turned the pillow over; he didn't want any pearly greeting pressing into his cheek. Besides, the same idea sounds better in Mallorquin: *Bona-nit*! *Bona-nit* contains everything: the mouse rustling around in the palms, the bat's shadow on the window pane, the octopus' play of shadow beneath the seaside cliffs, the sea itself, the moon in the sea, the millions of stars, the Queen of the Night opening her chalice, and the red star at Orion's shoulder, Bed-el-shauza, who with his very name proclaims the glory of the night.

Bona-nit!

EPILOGUE

The world is simply the sedan chair
that carries us from heaven to hell.
The carriers are God and the Devil;
the Devil is out in front.
Johann Wilhelm Ritter

Over and over again while setting down these island recollections of mine, whose origins were anything but arbitrary but whose future is anything but secure, I have noticed that the overture to any given chapter has determined that chapter's structure and length. Since it has taken me so long to realize that mysterious tectonic forces are at work here—as in writing poetry—I might do well to exploit this insight into my work habits when shaping my Epilogue, the only section of my memoir that I am writing with an eye toward its length and toward the way it will come to an end—as both I and my reader so eagerly anticipate.

If, for example, I were to begin with a factual account of how Beatrice, performing her first domestic chores in the Casa Inés, prepared the small guest room for Frederico García Lorca, then I would have to get lost in all the details of Lorca's planned trip to Mallorca, and how his failure to make it became so fateful for him—and right there I would have transgressed the limits of space. It would be even more dangerous, albeit more tempting, to begin in this fashion: "Beatrice, look over there, to the right. Yes, directly above the seventh cactus from the left, that's it, down below Son Maroix, that white speck. That's the terrace at the house I was going to rent, the one I should have rented, for Henny Marsman." The result would be more than a single chapter, it would be an entire book about my friendship with Marsman, Holland's great poet and the editor for my Dutch editions of Pascoaes. I would relate our picaresque encounter on Mallorca and our re-encounter in Basel; the way-stations Dornach, Arlesheim, Locarno, and Auressio; the haunted Casa Peverada; Schulenburg's "Monda"; our weeks together in the ski lodge in Bogève in the Haute Savoie; our flight to Portugal, where Marsman intended to rejoin us and where, at Pascoaes' country estate, the mystic's aged little mother prepared the royal guest room for Holland's King of Poetry with the same loving care as Beatrice gave to the room for Lorca at the Casa Inés. Neither poet ever reached his destination. Lorca was executed on the Spanish mainland. Marsman drowned in the Channel as he fled to Portugal, his ship torpedoed.

On the other hand, what if I were to start out by telling about the last snail we wanted to cook for ourselves, but which escaped us—or rather, which escaped none other than our clever friend Bobby, the young fellow who could surmount any problem the island posed to its foreign guests, excepting of course his own personal problems and those of the private physician's gynecology? Just imagine—a single vineyard snail got away from him! But I'd better begin at the beginning. Period.

I shall never comprehend why people like us Vigotrices, for whom destiny has reserved no firm place of residence on the globe, have not sung the praises of the sardine, the kind you can get in cans either in olive oil or *en escabeche* for two reales a can. Consume them with a piece of bread, and you have stilled your hunger for the next ten minutes, or however long it takes until you can get the next can. Doña Inés had piled up many such *latas*, and she invited us to eat our way through the entire pile, at cost. This was how she re-provisioned her household on an annual basis. Crisp, succulent lettuce grew in her herbal garden, there were jugs of wine and oil, and an old sailor next door brought us our bread. I'm mentioning all this in order to explain that during our first days, without ever leaving the house, we did not suffer hunger. Intellectual nourishment was also to be found on Doña Inés' shelves, preserved like the sardines: St. Augustine, Cervantes, Pascoaes, Novalis. That's all that I took with us into our place of solitude, but naming those names here might seem erudite indeed. Reading the urbane, devout Thagastian bishop's works under the sign of Orion was an experience I shall never forget.

Suddenly there is a gunshot; I look up from my book and gaze in the direction where the explosion is still echoing. A large, many-colored bird drops from the blazing sky to the dark-green foliage of the orange orchard. I catch myself recalling certain verses by Goethe and, turning back to Augustine, I say, "Damn it all, Beatrice, those bratty kids have just shot down another hoopoe! By the time Bobby arrives they'll be extinct!"

Otherwise, nothing at all disturbed the peace on our island. Just once I saw an eagle. It was flying so low that I could follow precisely its broad sweeping shadow across the red earth.

Sunday began as bright as never before. During the night we had heard more gunfire. "What are they hunting for in the nighttime?" Beatrice asked. "Bats," I said. "Great substitute for clay pigeons, and cheaper." The ocean lay calm and contented in the Bay. Not a single sail, not a single wake from a ship already beyond the horizon. Not a single breeze to create on the sea's surface the familiar shimmering moiré effect. The sky, too, was leaden.

At around noontime some airplanes arrived. They circled Palma and the harbor of Porto-Pí. Oh look! Now they're diving. And way up, that little dot must be a skywriter. Pretty soon we'll see his ad, *Mallorca clima ideal*, and right behind it the word Persil, which will of course earn him more money.

Now and then we heard more shots. Hoopoes, I thought. Maybe ravens, or quail. Sunday hunters? Do they exist in Spain, too?

Several days passed. Beatrice took a short walk into the village, if that is what you could call the dozen houses in Génova, and reported casually that Doña Inés apparently owed some money at the store. The people there ogled her strangely, and hardly even greeted her. Crabby people, Beatrice said; she wasn't going back. They were probably afraid that we, too, would ask for credit and then disappear from sight. Such behavior was now rather common in the island. That's how many emigrés kept themselves above water.

A few days later Pedro Sureda arrived—in uniform! And unshaven, and minus his usual loquacity. No jokes, no dance steps, no clapping on shoulders. Pedro, too, just stared at us, as if we were deep in debt, and apparently we actually were in some kind of trouble without realizing it. We owed our lives to a few people who were now beginning to demand the settling of old scores. Someone had told Pedro that we had been shot on orders from on high, and he had come by to see for himself. The fact was that our good friend Pedro simply couldn't imagine Vigoleis, the fellow with the pronounced death wish, as a corpse. Seeing that we were still alive, he was relieved for the moment. But this is not something that he told us on that day of our resurrection. He, too, remained silent. Why? It wasn't until the eve of our escape, in a café at a corner of the Apuntadores that was swarming with uniforms of all conceivable political persuasions—some real generals were among them—that Pedro broke his silence. Back then, he said, he had wanted to make sure that I was dead.

He gave us the following report: *Pronunciamiento*! Our buddy General Franco had mounted a sudden attack in Morocco, and the conflagration spread to the mainland. During the very first night our island had fallen to the insurrection. So it wasn't clay pigeons after all? People make for better target practice. It was war, but it was a Holy War, one being fought for the greater glory of God and His generals.

The background of the insurrection is obscure, and to this very hour no historian has been able to explain it thoroughly. In all our years on the island I was never able to get a clear picture of Spanish politics. For one thing, I have no sense at all of such developments. Worse still, I just don't care who wants to exert control over me. As an honorary guest of the island, as an exterritorial and thus exempt from paying taxes, my interest in Spanish politics was all the more feeble. Yet of one thing I was sure: what was happening in Germany, the herding of an entire nation under the leadership of a single bleating sheep, could never happen in Spain. As I had got to know them, the Spaniards seemed much too self-centered for such foolishness, too convinced of their own importance. They were very much their own persons, and would never fall victim to massification. All the rest of Spanish politics, insofar as a foreigner could take notice of it, seemed simply ludicrous.

As an example, let me cite the reaction of cloisters involving both sexes to a stern decree from the Republican government, stripping monks and nuns of the privilege of teaching school. Two religious orders housed on our street maintained separate educational institutions, for boys and for girls. We ran across nuns and monks every day, and exchanged greetings with them. I had many a stimulating chat with one or the other schoolmaster in front of our house. Those people were highly educated. I never spoke with any of the nuns, for that would have been sinful. Some of them were quite beautiful. They gazed out wanly from between the black blinders of their habits, revealing to an onlooker the passionate fires that were consuming them inwardly.

The School Secularization Law was meant as a coup against the clerical orders. But all it did was create for them the simple problem of choosing the proper attire: off with the robes and habits, on with the middle-class duds. The Pope issued the proper licenses, while the Brothers and Sisters closed their schools for three days. They sailed to Barcelona and returned as bourgeois personalities: Señor González and Señorita Sánchez, Don José and Doña Carmen, the men wearing collars, neckties, and straw hats, the ladies in jacket and skirt or, for those with shaved heads, combination wig-hats. The political Left was furious; the Right was delighted. The satirical papers had a field day in all the parties. Then, as new elections approached and attempts were made to force a victory for the Right, everyone including the nuns had to step up to the ballot box. Even nuns living in lifelong seclusion were given a free day, and re-emerged into God's sunlight. They instantly became the butt of jokes, but they took all this with dignity and recitations of the Rosary.

Clothes make the man—and they make for hostility, too. In Mulet's *tertulia* the politicking now became hot and heavy, opinion clashing against opinion. As far as internal Spanish problems were concerned, I stayed out of these quarrels, explaining that I had even less comprehension of such matters than the members of the Cortes themselves. But when the subject of the Third *Reich* came up, I leaped willingly into the fray.

After Pedro disappeared like a thief in the night, we sat for a long time at the edge of the well and listened. The constellation of Orion was still up there in all its eternal glory, but the night sounds were different. That is, they now had a different meaning. There were gunshots. We heard shouts, children whimpered, dogs started barking. The night around us and below us was speaking to us, but no longer in the familiar language of island nights. Not long before this, I had translated a passage in Pascoaes' *Saint Paul* about the rampaging Saul of Tarsus, a passage that the publisher Rascher's bumbling Leipzig affiliate had taken for a caricature of the Propaganda Apostle Goebbels: "He broke into houses, took the occupants captive, convicted them, and threw them into prison. He was acting as a criminal in the name of the law." The Disciple Goebbels was likewise breaking into houses, taking captives, and killing them in the name of Audhumla, the Primeval Cow. On the island of Mallorca, mass murder was occurring in the name of the Immaculate Conception of the Virgin and the Sacred Heart of Jesus. That is just how the flag-wavers behaved: they took prisoners and killed them by the thousands— no one has ever calculated how many thousands. The other side, the Red side, killed in the name of Liberty, Equality, and Fraternity. All of them were on a rampage in the name of the Fatherland. Isn't that what it's all about, justifying what we are doing by doing it in the name of what is nameless?

Our island was the scene of the Spanish War's most dreadful carnage. The butchery committed by Right and Left on the mainland was nothing when compared to the Divine Scourge that descended upon the Balearics. There was no escape. Everybody on the lists was cut down. You couldn't get through to your political allies on the other side; you were sitting in a trap. The initial salvo of the *pronunciamiento* caused the island to collapse into the hands of the Catholic General Staff, which proclaimed a Holy War. It was a sudden regression to the Middle Ages. The coup on Mallorca was ignited by a no doubt authentic grandee, Marqués de Zayas, who together with some accomplices was imprisoned in San Carlos Fortress for having planted a bomb at the Trade Union headquarters. He was liberated, and from that moment on he was a rampaging Saul. I have no idea whether he ever turned into a Saint Paul.

War, the Holy War Against the Saracens, as it was called on the island, had erupted. But no matter how holy a war is, no matter which side claims that God is on its side, no war can go on without gold. The contributions poured in, and whoever refused to contribute voluntarily was shot. Liturgical vessels, some of them of the high-karat variety, were melted down together with secular utensils and sent to the German *Führer*, who promised to deliver warplanes, weapons, and all kinds of technical assistance. The Third *Reich*, constantly in search of foreign trade, delivered promptly, but of course only such goods as it had no need for at home. I saw Heroes of the Iron Cross, sporting their uniform buckles with the blasphemous motto *Gott mit uns*, which neatly matched the maxim proclaimed by Franco: "To die in battle is the highest honor. One dies only once. Death comes painlessly, and dying is not as terrible as it looks. It is more terrible to go on living as a coward. Long live Spain! Long live Christ the King! Long live Franco!"

An old priest, well known as a preacher at the Cathedral, thought rather differently. That is to say, he had grown so senile in his service to the Creator that he couldn't think at all any more, and that was his undoing. He mounted the Cathedral pulpit and preached. All his life long he had done nothing besides preach. He had a reputation for being a gripping speaker—a Spanish Monsignor Donders. Many thousands had already been murdered, and the killing went on like the war itself, week after week, as wars tend to do. The combatants were unable to stop. Besides, the problem of available gold hadn't been solved; there were negotiations with representatives of worldly and celestial powers. In the midst of all this, appealing to the fateful message of Christ, Monseñor uttered the even more fateful admonition: "Thou shalt not kill!"

Two young brats, members of the Boys' Militia in paramilitary uniforms showing genuine Mallorquin-embroidered Sacred Heart insignias with their divine shooting arrows—these two kids nudged each other and said to each other, "This is sabotage! If these people listen to him, it's all over with God's cause!" They screamed up to the pulpit, "Shut your trap, you old fart! It's our turn now!"

The priest, confused as he was, made further appeals to the Lord, just as he had been taught at the seminary 60 years earlier. And lo, he had learned nothing more since then. What is more, God was apparently no longer with him. These two jerks, 13 or 14 years old, like all such little pissers the Great Hope of their Fatherland, tore him down from his pulpit, put their fists to his nose, and dragged him past the silent congregation to the Cathedral portal. The gunshots echoed down the ranks of pews. Holy Mass continued, and when it was over the Bishop blessed the Lord's appointed executioners. In all nations and at all times, sabotage is in wartime a capital offense. During the period in question, the harried Bishop of Mallorca could scarcely keep up with all the blessings he had to perform. He blessed everything: Italian and German airplanes; Italian and German sailors; the nightly death squads; the Italian warrior Conte di Rossi; the hydrocephalic German steel helmets that not even Nazi heads could fit into; and the streets that, as in all revolutions, were renamed in the interest of posterity, whereas it seems to me that it would be smarter to memorialize heroic deeds in brain cells *à la* Professor Wernicke. But then again, revolutions are never smart.

The Bishop kept on blessing all kinds of things. Christians who neglected their Easter Duty were shot, including those who lost the written confirmation that was sent through the mail. Holy Mother Church prevailed. She was never as powerful as now, yet at the same time She never trembled before Her own power so much as during the Holy War on Mallorca. The killing went on out of fear. The archepiscopal prelate kept on blessing out of fear, the same Prince of the Church whom Bernanos pillories in his book on Mallorca, *Les grands cimitières sous la lune*. But instead of calling this man of the Church an outright criminal or a Grand Inquisitor, as I would have done, the French writer identifies him with this even more baneful appellation: *Le personnage que les convenances m'obligent toujours à nommer son Excellence l'évèque-archivèque de Palma*. This man was the very same fellow, His Eminence Don José, to whom my uncle in Münster had written a letter of recommendation on my behalf. When I began to notice in which direction the Mallorcan winds of danger were blowing, I fished out this handwritten missive and henceforth carried it with me at all times. It was the most helpful report card I have ever received in my whole life: *Propinquus meus, oriundus ex familia vere catholica* (post-1933: a-catholica) *officiis catholicis semper optime satesfecit* (My uncle had a marvelous way of interpreting a Catholic's "duties") *et dignus est ut in omnibus suis studiis adiuvetur*. This letter, countersigned by the exalted personage mentioned in Bernanos' book, and with an ecclesiastical seal affixed, proved to be more effective than any bullet-proof vest. But it wasn't the Spaniards who wanted to kill me. It was the Nazis. The two of us, Beatrice and I, were on the list of those to be executed, hand in hand as in a wedding photo.

There are times when people who don't believe in God, and thus cannot be expected to knife their fellow men in the name of the Lord, can incur the hatred of believers and fall prey to their lust for murder. This was the situation on our island as the woeful fanatics of the faith mounted their trials of heretics. These were the same men and boys who during Holy Week, garbed in penitent robes and with their hoods pointed devoutly toward Heaven, accompanied the Blessed Sacrament through the town, gazing furtively at the pretty girls on the sidewalks while the ladies standing on the piously decorated balconies competed with one another in coquettish devotion to the Lamb of God. Do those guys with the hoods on really believe in God? Are those boys with the Sacred Heart on their shirts the same ones who have been tossing their Dads and Moms into wells and heaving stones on top? A moot question. Whoever loves God and the Fatherland but is unwilling to strangle Dad and Mom if they are against God and Fatherland—that person is unworthy to go on living beneath God's benevolent sun. That's why I am reluctant to judge the murderers of Mallorca. They simply made me uncomfortable.

When we went to Mamú's house, she was in the company of several Christian Science ladies, and it was the day after Pedro's visit with us in Génova. She would love to have embraced us both, but her age and her corpulence— the abundance of good food had caused her to gain weight, although her kidneys were in working order—prevented her from doing this. She told us that she had written us notes, sent out emissaries, and mobilized her chauffeur, all to no avail—we were unaccounted for. People on the street where we used to live said, "Those two? They were liquidated on the very first night!"

Mamú went into a panic. She was Jewish! It wasn't the Spaniards she was afraid of, but the German agents, and... and... She didn't dare to take a closer look at some of her ladies who, in addition to the swastika, had embroidered the Sacred Heart and the Fasces on their blouses. At the time in question, everyone carried with him his own talisman. Was my episcopal letter from Münster any better? I have long since forgiven these ladies. They loved Jesus, but also Hitler. They were just too feminine to feel otherwise.

In such surroundings, Mamú could not remain safe. I considered her household nanny, who was never devoted to Jesus but all the more fervently devoted to Hitler, as a particularly dangerous kind of domestic company. We urged her: "Mamú, get out of here!"

All the various countries had alerted their consulates. The foreigners were leaving the island in droves. The hotels were either empty or were requisitioned as prisons. Mallorca's ideal climate was now in the service of the Holy War. There was not a drop of rain, and at all the places where earlier you could see bare-ass foreigners reclining on the beach or swimming, you now saw reclining or floating corpses, equally bare-ass. The banks closed their counters; foreign accounts were frozen. When a man named Vigoleis went to the savings bank to get some emergency cash—it wasn't much, but it would have sufficed for six months at the Casa Inés—he was told that his money had already been withdrawn for the Holy War, and he was asked if he was perhaps not in favor of the Holy War. Vigoleis replied that he was a German, and a Catholic. The bank manager, whose office he reached by telling this series of lies, shook his hand warmly. Now we were penniless. I didn't even have the fare for the tram to get me back to Génova, so I went there on foot. I had ceased to exist as a capitalist. Strangely enough, I still didn't realize that I had no right to go on existing at all.

One look at me, and Beatrice understood right away that we were poor once again. Despite all the various faces that Heaven has granted me, I am unable to pretend. You only have to look at me when I am telling the truth to tell that I really ought to be lying. That's when I blush. To quote St. Augustine, I am one of those stupid men who never have to take back anything they have spoken.

Bankruptcy! It was our old, familiar domestic affliction, one that we had almost got ourselves accustomed to. We didn't go to pieces as a result. Worse yet was what I observed in Palma before making the trek back to Génova. I had gone to our old apartment to retrieve a few things. Our avenida was swarming with firearms, and those brandishing them were mostly young kids. The Holy War had evolved into a fracas involving adolescents. Cannons were set in place, and machine guns were aimed at exits and entryways along the entire street. I was halted repeatedly and asked to show my papers. I pulled out my episcopal letter of recommendation, and offered explanations. "Foreigner?" these squirts started asking. Yes, a Catholic from Germany. "*Heil Hitler*," they then shouted, and let me pass. Hitler and the Pope were the two-armed General Franco's great models. No wonder, then, that his pimply-faced minions revered them too. Moreover, the Germans had sent their special General Faupel to Madrid, where he was instructed to hold up Franco by both of his arms—which was apparently necessary. But why was there such a rattling of sabers on this particular street?

Opposite our house stood the Main Headquarters of the Blue Shirts, the Falange. For a brief moment I felt a chill in the seat of my lily-white linen pants, although it was 102 degrees in the shade of this Holy War. But I collected myself and strode quickly and proudly into our house. At the top of the stairs I ran into the woman who lived in the apartment to the right of us next door, to whom we had failed to make the customary initial visit when occupying the place. She ran down toward me several steps, grabbed my arm, and told me to open our blinds on the street side immediately: there were snipers, and closed blinds were a target. She was the wife of a Falange officer. She had informed the Falange boss that the next-door apartment was occupied by a German who had gone off on vacation to the mountains, and that she would guarantee the security of the building. But now, near twelve noon, the deadline was almost up. If by then all the blinds were not open, they would start shooting. There were just a few minutes left. I ran into our apartment, raced to our windows, and threw open the blinds. In the Blue House on the other side of the street they had already set up a machine gun on the top floor. I didn't like this kind of punctuality. A Spaniard who is ready to shoot today instead of tomorrow—how very odd! I saluted across the street, and the kids saluted back. It was like ships passing in the night.

I packed a few books, took with me the beginning of my translation of Jerome with the intention of continuing this Pascoaes work in Génova, pinned one of my pretentious business cards to the door, turned the lock four times, stuck some clumps of wax here and there as a security measure, and left the menacing neighborhood.

Once a day, in keeping with my sound digestive regularity, I stepped out with newspaper in hand into the Princess' cactus grove. At the same time, another man, our neighbor the sailor, whose digestion was apparently coordinated with mine, also approached the rows of cactus. This spiky venue, conducive to discreet soul-searching, was large enough to permit visitors to avoid speaking with one another if that was what they wished. But rather than wishing to avoid each other, the two of us sought each other out. The old seadog kept me informed about developments of the insurrection. I combined what he told me with events I witnessed myself, wrote some war reportage and sent my articles to foreign newspapers. To get this done we had to go to the harbor in Palma, where Beatrice made friends with sailors on foreign warships who, for a few cigarettes, agreed to deliver my letters. Evading the censors in this way was a capital offense, but that didn't prevent us from sending off reports once a week. Apart from my sailor friend, I learned all I needed to know about the crusade against the infidels from a well-placed personage in Palma. To raise the Cross of Christ it takes people who aren't deterred by thousands of other crosses. On Mallorca, there were plenty of people like that. And I figured that this, too, had to be reported openly.

Bobby occasionally came to visit, just as in peacetime. Life went on in the daytime, whereas the nights were devoted to bloodshed. Bobby had witnessed a thing or two in Valldemosa, up in the mountains of his new homeland. Doña Clara sent a message, saying that if we had nothing more to eat we should go to her place and await the end of the war in her *hospedage*. Where there was food for a group of twelve, two more hungry mouths wouldn't bring about starvation. But we still had a little money, and Doña Inés' sardine cans hadn't been used up yet.

After several weeks, when Bobby returned telling tales of more horror, he found us emaciated. Our money was gone, our bank account was frozen, the sardine cans were empty, and the jug of oil was down to the last half-inch. For three weeks we had been living on tea, vineyard snails, and prickly pears. It was a stroke of luck that Doña Inés' rock garden was crawling with snails, if one is willing to accept the word 'crawling' as referring statically to the great multiplicity, and not dynamically to the back-and-forth weaving and slithering of these tasty creatures. By day they were invisible; like the crusading gangsters, they emerged from their hiding places only at night. While all around us we could hear the death squads in action, while motorcycles roared, and while the populace of the island was getting thinned out according to the perceived degree of Christian faith, or lack of the same, the two of us searched the ground for snails using dimmed candles. One night Bobby took a snail census: he knew exactly how many there were, and figured out their marching routes and crossways. The mollusks had long since ceased being a delicacy, but now, just as in an emergency the Devil will eat flies, we hunted down our creepy-crawlies. Our Folkwang huntsman Bobby, absolutely convinced of his prowess, led me to the places where his calculations told him we could still locate the animals: four underneath that potsherd, two under that moldy cactus leaf, seven under the jagged agave, and two more down near their copulation stone. He would snatch them blindly, if our sailor neighbor hadn't already squished them with his feet. Our neighbor, however, had done just that, and so all of a sudden we came up with no snails at all. But wait, Bobby said. Let's not be so pessimistic. There was one more snail out there, he said, and since on occasion he was able to hear his own beard growing, we were confident that he would get on the trail of our very last snail. We had just one match left to cook our last meal. This was one of those Southern nights that are luminescent, and snail trails also glow in the dark. But after a full hour Bobby returned minus a catch, his face flushed with frustration. I went out in the garden myself to try my luck. Nothing doing. Our last snail had got the jump on us, and we couldn't catch up.

"Well, we'll just have to leave," said Beatrice. Prolonged hunger can make a person irritable, and snails with prickly pear à la vinaigrette make for very sour fodder. One more week of this stimulating diet and we bleeding-heart pacifists, too, would have reached for a revolver and taken up combat against those outside who were fighting for the glory of God and filling His consecrated cemeteries. We were already benumbed. As for myself, I am willing to confess that the execution of 14 people, for whose death I was unknowingly responsible, did not deprive me of my senses. It would take too long to set forth the tragic details of a mistake that caused the Christian crusaders to commit new acts of terror. When we heard shooting in the vicinity of the Casa Inés, when we heard the screaming of women and children, my heart did not burst. It was the most awful night of my life—the night when my heart did not cease its beating.

It's an amazing thing about any war, that after committing a few atrocities, a human being can regress to the womb of primeval atrocity.

We had eaten our next-to-last snail, and the last one had escaped, so there was no sense in our staying in Génova. The next day we went to the English Consulate and asked to be evacuated on a warship. No problem, we were told. His Majesty's Navy stood ready to rescue anybody from this hell, no matter the nationality. "Your nationality?"

"We're Germans." That would be all right, we learned, but the protocol of international cooperation would require that the German Consulate stamp my passport as valid for evacuation. Beatrice, who in the meantime had become my passport-validated spouse—a stupid move that deprived her of her bullet-proof Swiss passport—and I just stared at the British official. Was he crazy? A passport stamp that would allow us to flee? From the Nazi Consul, who had already threatened us with documents from back home? I started explaining my unusual situation: I was an early emigré from Germany, but anti-Nazi. Couldn't this man understand that it would be impossible for me to approach the German Consulate? Beatrice interrupted, asking if we might speak with the British Consul in person. We knew the gentleman; Count Kessler had maintained good relations with him. He wasn't there; he had been called off to the interior of the island with the urgent task of rescuing British subjects from the threat of execution by reason of mistaken identity.

Doubtless this was the same kind of mistake that almost led to the execution of the Admiral of the British Mediterranean Fleet when he was seen stepping out of a jolly boat on the sandy beach at Coll de Rebassa, all alone and dressed in a white civilian tropical suit. He wanted to take a swim, and that was prohibited under pain of death; every island beach was now a death zone. A swarm of kids, armed to the teeth, let out Indian war whoops and surrounded the man. The Admiral, of middling height and slim, his features the typical English hybrid of old salt and university scholar—we later made his acquaintance on board his ship—remained as composed as Karl May's Old Shatterhand at the martyr's stake. "What's wrong, fellows?" he asked. But the fellows didn't understand English, and weren't in a joking mood. All of them had cocked their pistols, and now they were waiting to see who would take the first shot. It was a sure thing that this spy would have to be knocked off.

They couldn't agree among them, and that is the only reason why the Admiral wasn't summarily blasted into the sand. They got hold of a truck, and delivered their precious booty to Manacor. His Lordship offered no resistance. He couldn't speak Spanish, and at Manacor they took him for a kook who was pretending to be the Admiral of the Mediterranean Fleet. They were used to cases like this one: even in peacetime, people on the island pretended to be all kinds of things they weren't, and now in the midst of a war! This was a time when army generals were being canonized and worshiped. Even so, a few of the Manacor officers were taken aback. This kook's behavior seemed to manifest a degree of hallucination unknown in Spain. They sent for an interpreter, who after a brief conversation advised them to send this Sir, unexecuted, to Palma. If it was found out that the guy was truly a nut case and hence a spy, he could still be shot in the head.

Meanwhile, in Palma a minor palace revolt had occurred involving rival factions of generals and commanders-in-chief of all nationalistic colorations, some of them the sworn enemies of some others. Carlists, Falangists, legionnaires, militiamen, paramilitaries, Guardia Civil: all of them were busy combing their brilliantine-soaked hair when news arrived that the Admiral of the British Mediterranean Fleet had been shot while swimming at Coll de Rebassa. The officers of the flagship London came to retrieve their boss, who was handed over to them unharmed. The Spaniards were happy to have avoided an international incident. That evening, I was later told by a reliable source who was also a direct participant, all the generals threw a huge party for their whores. The kids had their pistols taken away from them for 24 hours.

After leaving the British Consulate we went over to the French. Evacuation? Yes. Are you Swiss citizens? No. German? Yes. Two seconds later we were back out on the street. It couldn't go any faster, since there were several doors between the street and the old Verdun warrior we had spoken with. Try explaining to a French consul that you are among the little band of degenerate Germans who aren't out to lead their Fatherland to victory! But now, what reason would the German Consul have to refuse us, seeing that he considered me his best *Führer*. "Beatrice, will you come with me, or should I go alone?"

We went together. Beatrice had loaded her face-powder box with pepper, for all eventualities.

The German Consulate was now located in El Terreno, the fashionable residential section of the city, on the second floor of the Consul's villa. There were no identifying signs outside. For fear of flying bricks, the *Führer's* representative had unscrewed the plaque with the national insignia. All the other consulates had put up gigantic flags and painted their national colors on the roofs, a precaution during the continual aerial bombardments originating in Barcelona. Their automobiles, too, carried big fluttering flags, a spectacle outdone only by the adventurer from the Holy See Conte di Rossi, lord of the island, who mounted on his Bugatti a black flag with larger-than-life skull and crossbones.

So the Consul is getting the willies, I thought. He's unsure of his position. My own courage, a bookworm's courage, took heart at this idea. The stubborn fellow let us wait for about an hour.

In the course of my story I have been unable to resist the urge to throw out hints concerning the Consul's crucial query about my having been shot. So now that the moment for that query has arrived, I fear I have squandered the narrative effect it might otherwise have. Instead of letting my recollections resemble a perpetuum mobile, I ought to have proceeded in strict chronological fashion with the aid of file cards to mark the temporal divisions. Every section should have been clearly delineated, all my sources neatly identified, the veracity of every assertion beyond question. Even memory lapses would be accounted for; that is how Count Kessler went about it, to cite just one example. I can depend on my Vigoleis only to the extent that he, the hindmost part of history, has no idea what his head has in mind—to quote Lichtenberg. But there are organisms that move more efficiently with their tails than with their heads. Like the whales, they can whip themselves right out of their milieu with a single whack of their flukes. When they plunge back into their element, it causes an earthquake. In this sense, we could say that the recollections of Vigoleis are being written with his tail. Count Kessler was one of the last remnants of a cerebral culture that is no longer with us. I regard it as one of the most vexing puzzles of my lifetime that he, such an intellectually superior individual, could ever don a uniform—and the Kaiser's uniform at that. This very topic would have found its place in the third volume of his memoirs. It's a shame that Kessler didn't write his book backwards. When I once broached the subject with him, he reacted only with a pitying smile, as so often when I brought up matters or made suggestions that were foreign to his way of thinking. Did he think of me only as the idiot he first encountered when he found me stark naked under our Unlulunkulu? If so, then his polite silence was just the proper kind of behavior.

Yet if he had begun at the hind end of his story, he would have exposed himself to the danger of being shot by the Nazis immediately following the publication of Volume One, just as the Mexicans wanted his head because he, as the first European, reported in his 1898 *Notes on Mexico* on the satanic *Ley fuga* ("shot while trying to escape") enforced by the dictator Porfirio Diaz. In Mexico he was placed on the Most Wanted list. It was terrible, the writer thought, to be shot while trying to escape. But in 1921 he saw fit to add a footnote to the new edition of his book, saying, "In Germany since the revolution we have unfortunately also had experience with the *Ley fuga*." And something similar: the suppression of a conspiracy against Don Porfirio, discovered by the governor of Veracruz, who asked the dictator for instructions. Porfirio Diaz telegraphed back, *"Matan los todos!"*—Kill them all! That same night, Kessler writes, the governor arrested nine young men aged nineteen and twenty in their homes and ordered them shot under their own roofs. The bodies, with bullet holes in the back, were handed over to their parents. So what was happening on Mallorca, or for that matter in the Third *Reich*, was not so original after all. But perhaps it was more historical.

A stronger claim to imaginative planning, albeit one involving a leap backwards by two thousand years, could be made for the crucifixions that took place on Mallorca. There were rumors that people who didn't believe in God, or who were branded as deniers of the Divinity (the Inquisition itself never created a reliable test; even Szondi is evasive on this point) were crucified by bands of extremely devout Falange fanatics, nailed to the famous 1000-year-old olive trees that were not only the pride of the island, but also a huge advertising success for the travel agencies. Gustave Doré himself was fascinated by the bizarre shapes of these olive trees. He used them as a model for the images of Hell in Dante's Divine Comedy. In other words, these were very special trees, perfect for committing carnage in the name of religion. In earlier times trees were likewise used for massacres when not enough crosses could be built in time. So again: it's all been done before. But is it really true? Were people actually nailed to the olive trees on Mallorca? I could find no eyewitnesses who could have confirmed this. I heard only whispered rumors.

Bernanos, who tracked down all kinds of inhumane acts, nowhere mentions a single instance of crucifixion, and we must bear in mind that this writer, with a conscientious zeal motivated by a bad conscience, would have recorded anything that could serve—for his own private purposes—to exculpate his soul. To use the term "bad conscience" is, from the point of view of psychology, to speak quite superficially when applied to a thinker for whom the problem of Original Sin was a simple matter, but who fell for the abysmally stupid slogans of the Spanish monarchists in a manner matched only by a certain provincial German Nobel-Prize-winning philosopher who swallowed Hitler's double-talk. When Bernanos once invited me to come and discuss a German translation of his *Journal d'un curé de campagne*, I refused. Tell me what company you keep, and I'll tell you what you're in for. Bernanos frequented the same exalted Catholic and aristocratic company on the island to which we had also found access, and which was the source of the Revolution. Does this mean that I should have gone against myself? A court jester can take liberties that a king must forego. If at the time I had read more of Bernanos' work, I would have told myself, "Sooner or later this guy is going to have to wake up." Miguel de Unamuno underwent an even more serious kind of blinding. He actually saw in the two-armed General Franco the Redeemer of Spain, and he suffered greatly as a result. With him, I was sure that the scales would fall from his eyes. It didn't take long for him to recover, but he was soon put under arrest and didn't survive the incarceration.

A big one-armed general contributed to the performance of this miracle. No, not our Patuco—unfortunately not him. Millán Astray provided the immediate cause for Unamuno's uttering his famous pun, a *faux pas* that cost him his life. In front of his students in Salamanca, Unamuno waxed prophetic: Franco and his minions would, to be sure, be victorious (*vencerán*), but they would fail to convince (*convencerán*), and his beloved Spain would emerge from the Revolution—"Like you, General"—and he pointed to the one-armed Astray.

It was high time that this university professor got tossed in jail. Unamuno was famous for his words, which took wing as soon as he spoke them. Just hours later these words of his were circulating in *tertulias* in the remotest provinces of Spain, along with dozens of other *bons mots* about the King, dozens about Primo de Rivera, one *bon mot* more clever than the other. Such utterances have been known to dethrone kings. Franco was aware of this, and he also realized that an apostate Unamuno was more dangerous than a Don Miguel who was against the New Redeemer from the beginning. Don Miguel had to be muzzled. *Ley fuga*? The circumstances didn't permit this to happen, and so they employed "protective custody." Necessity breeds invention, and it also strengthens group solidarity. To grab the Rector of Salamanca University, a religious thinker of world renown, and in front of all his students simply to...

"You? Haven't you been shot?"

There you have it, dear reader, the question concerning our hero's destiny from the mouth of the German Consul himself. It shook me awake from my reveries, and before I uttered my already familiar counter-query, as the victim of my complicated instincts I probably gave way to a very Prussian urge to leap up, stand at attention, and shout, "Am I supposed to be?" When, says St. Paul, will I be delivered from this mortal body? When will the rebellious citizen Vigoleis be delivered from the poisonous garb of his nationality? Anyone who was raised among wild animals will, even years later, start grunting as soon as the barking of a jackal reaches his ears. Madame de Manziarly records just such a regression to Paradise in her *Pérégrinations asiatiques*.

The Consul let us have it. He sat down behind his desk. I was seated next to Beatrice, whose expression was stony. She had taken her powder box out of her purse. Ever since Consul General Dr. Köcher in Barcelona had blessed our union and—lucky for us—reduced the fee according to the poverty laws, she had been a citizen of the German *Reich*. Now she was looking straight through the official representative of her obligatory fatherland—which is not to say that she saw through him.

In the course of a lengthy scolding we learned the following: on the night when the rebellious generals first struck on the mainland, on Mallorca, a number of German emigrés were arrested and put in jails where they were to be tried. Among them was the famous Captain Kraschutzki, who had taken part in a mutiny in Kiel in 1918. For many years he lived as a stateless person on Mallorca, where he bred chickens. He, the Consul, had arranged the release of all of these people with the exception of Kraschutzki, since he lacked jurisdiction over individuals who had lost their citizenship. Franz Blei told us later that all the rest of those people had also been shot to death. Our own names were likewise on the liquidation list. And quite naturally so; we didn't deserve any other fate, since we were against the *Führer*. A squad had entered our house on Barceló and asked questions. The hens had flown the coop. Where to? Pepe, my loitering friend from Palma Harbor, knew our new address but refused to reveal it. They shot him, and left his body behind. For three weeks afterward, a truckload of a dozen Falange goons, accompanied by a German interpreter, drove across the whole island looking for us. They eventually gave up the search. The Consulate was informed that we had been shot. But now, months later, these two sub-humans suddenly reappear and betake themselves straightaway to the monster's lair!

Were we aware, the Consul inquired, that our presence in his office could compromise him? How so? Well, it was his duty to inform the leadership of the Falange that two presumably executed individuals were giving themselves up at his consulate. "Giving themselves up?" Well, at least that they were making an appearance there. Beatrice toyed with her pepper powder. Was she getting ready to blow out the man's eyesight? I gestured to her and then said that all of this was news to us; we had known for quite a while that my fellow German citizens were intent on doing us in; he himself had repeatedly referred to certain ominous documents from my home town. Now he and the others, I went on, the whole brownshirt gang, were the victors, and we had lost the game. So—"Please?" "Please what?" Well, I said, now he must not shirk his duty as an employee of his other *Führer*. He must call up the Falange and pass the case on. Just two shots, and everybody would be happy. "What are you saying?" He must do his duty, I replied, and call up the Blue House! The Consul went pale: had I gone crazy? Not at all, I said; if I were crazy, I would be a Nazi. So now get to work! Orders are orders!

The Consul still couldn't comprehend the situation. So I stood up, turned to Beatrice and asked her if she would allow me (ladies first!), lifted the receiver and was about to push it into the Consul's hand. "Tell the Falange what's going on here. We are under martial law. Do your duty!"

The Consul slammed the receiver down. I sat down again next to my German wife from the house of ck-dt and with Indian blood in her veins. She had replaced the powder box in her purse. There would be no need for pepper. The Consul was giving up the fight.

Today neither Beatrice nor I can recall how long it took for the Consul to go back into an official rage at us. He gave us a thorough dressing down. His recital of our political transgressions was lengthy, and is already familiar to my reader. But my reader is not yet familiar with the way the Consul sought to conceal his cowardice. He was, he told us, a student of human nature; he knew very well what kind of characters we were, and he could easily explain to the *Führer* why he wasn't handing us over to the Blue House for execution. I was a confused individual, caught up in philosophical fantasies—a rough exterior, but a solid core. My heart was in the right place, and one fine day it would beat mightily for Nation and *Führer*. It was his conviction that I could yet turn into a valuable member of the new folk community that was persuading him to save my life. And now, what had I actually come for?

I told him, and he burst out laughing. Escape on an English ship? Completely out of the question! We were still Germans, and so: back to the homeland on S.M.S. Deutschland, the pocket battleship currently cruising Spanish waters. We would be allowed to take with us all our belongings; suitcases, boxes, items of furniture, books (we had starved our way to amassing a sizeable library)—none of this would have to remain behind. And upon arrival back home, we would be placed in a re-education camp. My wife, in particular, would have to learn how to be a real German woman.

I suddenly took fright; Beatrice was opening her pocketbook and taking out her cosmetics. It seemed the worst psychological moment to blow pepper into the Consul's eyes. But before I could give Beatrice a warning with my foot, she had already begun to put on her makeup, all the while smiling at the *Führer*'s representative. Why, of course! She was now sitting there as a German woman, and German women no longer wore makeup. That's exactly why she was applying makeup.

I told the man that we weren't interested in returning to the homeland. I would go back to the River Niers only after the whole mob of Nazis and their *Führer* had gone to the devil. We wanted to go to Switzerland. "That's absurd! How in heaven's name...?" He refused to stamp our passports. "What? Insult the *Führer* and then demand a passport stamp? Not on your life!" He asked us if we didn't feel ashamed, if we didn't know how to behave in his presence and under his protection. If we had disagreements with the New Order, he said, we should keep those to ourselves, seeing as we were German citizens and thus wards of the glorious *Führer*. This was strong language. The two of us, wards of a criminal, a Professor Többen-type murderer? I stood up, grabbed our passports, pointed to the larger-than-life photo of the *Führer* and asked Beatrice if she wished to continue living under the protection of that man. Neither of us wanted that, and so I slapped both of the brown documents on the Consul's desk, and we abruptly left. I had just canceled our citizenship. We were free again.

We were still rushing through the front yard of the villa when we heard footsteps behind us. The Consul grabbed my shoulder and stuttered, "This is madness! Don't you realize that if you are caught without papers you will be immediately shot?" He stuffed our passports into my inside coat pocket. I calmly replied that since we already knew that we were to be liquidated, it didn't matter much where and how that was going to happen.—

"Well then just go away! *Heil Hitler!*"

It was of course our fervent desire to leave this inhospitable place, but—had our kind friend put his stamp in our passports? I thumbed through them—nothing! The Consul went back into his house, and we followed him. Without the stamps, our journey to Canossa would have been senseless. Upstairs again: he's back behind his desk, we're sitting on the chairs. Another tirade. Pepper at the ready, a life-and-death tug-of-war. New accusations. An amplified list of our transgressions, followed by further threats. I: "And the stamps?" He: was it true that I had a caricature of the *Führer* hanging on the wall of my study, a horrible misrepresentation of the features of the heaven-sent Redeemer of the Nation, a thing that I put up there to show my Spanish friends and make insulting comments on? I denied this. I said it was a lie that there was any such caricature hanging on the wall of my study. The Consul: such insolence! I was a liar on top of everything else. He had evidence and witnesses. He named some names.

The Consul was purple with rage. I quieted him down by saying that what he was taking as a political matter was for me purely a question of philology, since by training I was in fact a philologist, albeit a failed one. The incident under discussion revolved around the difference between "have" and "had"— that is, around the verb "to have" and its conjugation. I unfortunately no longer owned the caricature, I told him. It was stuck to the wall, and when we moved it got torn. Egg-white is a strong kind of glue. Thus I once "had" the drawing, but I no longer "have" it. I begged his pardon for my linguistic fastidiousness. With a smile, I handed him our passports. Still in a rage, he banged down his stamp in both of them and told us to beware: the Deutschland would let us take all our possessions with us, whereas the British would allow us only to take hand-baggage on board—small suitcases, a box... He added that if the police stopped us and identified us as the two Barceló Street residents on the liquidation list, we were to appeal to the German Consulate. For a period of 24 hours he would guarantee our lives in the name of the magnanimous *Führer*, whose loyal servant I would no doubt become in due time. Not a hair on our heads would be harmed; the *Führer* was in need of heads. Considering the circumstances, this was a fine compliment—the finest that a clairvoyant Consul could offer to two documented heads that had not yet rolled in the name of the *Führer*, and that would not roll in the *Führer*'s name for the next twenty-four hours. We could only hope that no one noticed that our heads were steaming with anger. Our knees felt like jelly as we walked through the consulate yard for the fourth time.

We were now officially stamped for our escape. This was bureaucratic lunacy. The English, such a great power on the high seas, were miserable pencil-pushers on dry land.

We could stay alive for 24 hours, but by the end of that grace period we

would be safely aboard ship. What lay behind us were three months of shut-
tling between Génova and Palma visiting friends and then going to the harbor.
We had smuggled eyewitness reports and letters without realizing that we were
ourselves scheduled to be shot.

Pause for a council of war. I recovered my composure and tossed Beatrice's
peppered powder box into a ditch. Beatrice was shivering so violently that I
feared she might misuse the box and blind herself. But what now? We should
go separately, one of us to Génova to pack our little bundles, the other to our
apartment in the city to do what was necessary, especially to pick up my
Tombs of the Huns manuscript. Beatrice volunteered for the latter chore. If
she was stopped by the gendarmes, as a woman she would be a more effective
protection against our premature death than I would be with my episcopal
letter of recommendation. But first we had to go to the English Consulate.

There they put our names on the international list of refugees. Then we
learned that the destroyer due to arrive at Mallorca that very evening had
changed its course. There would be another ship. "When?" They couldn't tell
us exactly—maybe tomorrow, but it could be several days. We were asked to
stay in contact with the consulate—call them three times a day or come in
person. We turned numb. We were living outside the city in Génova without
a telephone, we had no more money, and they were after us. Had the German
Consul paid us the prescribed 200 marks refugee allowance? "No." "Sorry."
This meant that for the British our case was closed.

But it was only logical: whoever rejects the *Führer*'s bribe for returning to
the homeland mustn't expect him to offer some grudge money.

We had to change our plans. We must stay together. Taking all possible
measures for our security, we went to our city apartment. The concierges told
us that someone had repeatedly come asking for me. Apparently I was on
some search list. Well, I said, I was busy both day and night—interpreting for
the Falange.

The clumps of wax at our apartment door were undisturbed. We locked
ourselves in and, in a fit of panic that I have never been able to understand, I
took the manuscript of my brainless Huns and began thinking how to give it
an anti-heroic burial. This book, which depicted the outbreak of mass insanity
in my home town, was about to fall victim to another form of insanity. Certain
that we would be staying on the island for some time yet, we figured that if I
were caught with the manuscript I would surely be shot.

Our apartment had no stove. Should we start a fire on the terrace? The
smoke would alarm the Blue House. That left only the toilet. I tore the pages
to shreds, tore the shreds to smaller shreds, and sent my creation chapter by
chapter to the same destination that no doubt some of my readers would
have chosen for it. I tore up the pages and pulled the chain, tore again and
pulled again, with ever greater intervals in between tearing and pulling, since
the cistern on our roof was almost empty, and the bowl was filling up more
and more slowly. Desperate as I was, this afforded me a certain pleasure at
my own downfall. In between page-tearings and chain-pullings I read

through a few passages, made some editing and deleting, and then once more pulled the chain. This game of cowardly egotism lasted a full three hours. If my opus was to go the way of all sewage, it at least ought to go in print-ready condition.

What a memorable auto-da-fé! I, who already had annihilated so many of my artistic creations, discovered at this moment that I was a born writer. Not one word of mine was to leave the house without my own imprimatur. After drowning all my Huns, whom I had got to like while writing about them, in place of the still unwritten final chapter I flushed down a bunch of suspect letters into the *cloaca maxima Maioricensis*. Then I asked Beatrice, who was standing guard like a *dame de pissoir*, for some paper for myself.

We spent the night at the Casa Inés. There, too, we arranged our belongings provisionally and left instructions as to what to do with them. Early the next day we walked to Palma, each of us carrying a small bundle in each hand, just as the Consul had told us. At the English Consulate we learned to our horror that no ship had arrived and that none was expected soon.

What now? No money, and no house. That meant hiking back and forth to Génova in the blazing sun. And we hadn't eaten a thing in two days.

Our grace period was over. We were doomed.

"It is folly to try curing the incurable" Thus spake Zarathustra. So let them perish!

"But it takes more courage to make an end of things than to create a new verse—all physicians and poets know this." Thus, too, spake Zarathustra, or thus speaks life itself—which amounts to the same thing.

Where could we go? On the steps of the English Consulate, our bundles at our feet, we told each other that if the anarchist Count's and the anarchist Countess' offer—"Our home is your home"—was not just a local figure of speech but a sign of genuinely anarchistic generosity, then we could make our way to the Pensión del Conde—if in fact the Conde was still alive.

Old, familiar paths, familiar faces, but no *olás* and *olés*. Hadn't Josefa, the maid with the smoking bosom, made the sign of the cross? Doña Inés opened the gate a crack, made the little shriek appropriate to the occasion, and let us inside. "You? You're alive?" It was still the same vestibule, the same paintings, the same rocking chairs. But the Countess looked different: tinier, paler, thinner. We knew several languages? That was important now, she said. She went to fetch Alonso.

Don Alonso welcomed us in a whisper. A place to sleep? Fine, as long as the rebels didn't blow up his house, which could happen any day now, at any hour. It was, he said, a miracle of his anarchist Madonna that the house was still standing. House searches once every week—fine, although he had declared himself *pro forma* in favor of the Holy War in order to keep his conspirators in hiding. He could have used us during the first days, he said, but on Barceló Street he was told we had been eliminated—*despachados* was the term used. The Count gave a soft whistle. Doors opened, and conspirators appeared from all corners of the house, men and women by the dozens, most of them intellectuals, to judge by the way they looked. I got the cold shivers. We had escaped the neighborhood of the Blue House only to find ourselves now in the Citadel of Anarchism. It was only the drawing-room anarchists who had left the scene; these were people who were ready for anything.

We, too, were ready for anything. After a snack—something I had been dying for—we were mobilized for the cause. Upstairs under the red-hot roof was an attic alcove, formerly a dovecote. There they had put together the parts of a radio transmitter in such a way that it could be disassembled on a moment's notice. Everyone in the house knew exactly where to betake himself in case of a house search. Don Alonso, the ingenious tinkerer, had planned everything. A number of anarchist priests, amazing people, were serving as fronts to the world outside. But house-raiding squads sometimes came down from the roof. To warn against them, guards were posted, including dogs. The radio was turned on, and we took up our listening post. The skylights and walls were made soundproof with blankets, and as a further precaution they threw a flea-ridden manta over our heads. We heard radio static. It was our job to monitor foreign broadcasts and to translate. They wanted to know what the outside world was thinking and saying about the Holy War. Beatrice listened to a few sentences, and then she translated while I listened on and translated in turn. It worked like a charm. In this fashion, we two candidates for execution didn't lose any time at all. We earned our keep by sweating and getting bitten by fleas. I would like to have put on a bathing suit for these listening sessions, but Spaniards observe etiquette in all situations.

We waited ten days for the English ship, days during which more than one tragedy occurred inside our fortress. One of the priests fell in love with a school teacher. But he wanted to keep on saying Mass until the war was over, when he would finally hang up his cassock and begin a new life with his *novia* somewhere on the mainland. A Communist sailor, a fellow who wanted nothing to do with anarchism, became rebellious and had to be bound and gagged. A citizen of Manacor hanged himself from a rafter when he learned that his entire family had been killed in a raid in his home town. Don Alonso cut the rope; groaning, the man came to. It's not easy to break your own neck. In this house there was always something going on, and always in whispers. Vigoleis held forth on the subjects of human dignity, free will, peoples and fatherlands—sublime topics all, while the murderous rampages continued on the island outside our doors.

We maintained contact with the English Consulate. One of us went there every morning, every noontime, and every evening.

Bobby offered to take all of our belongings from our risky apartment to Valldemosa, where they would be in safe keeping. Doña Clara insisted that we stay during the winter in her *hospedage*, but we declined. We didn't want to put anyone's life in danger. We were marked people.

Don Joaquín Verdaguer, the author of a serio-comic catechism for pipe smokers, had run out of shag. Deprived of his customary puffing, his pipe couldn't fall out of his mouth when he opened his door in response to our knocking. He turned white as a sheet when we announced that we had come to say goodbye.

Don Joaquín is the one who told us all about the plans for our execution.

Our names were on a list drawn up by the Germans. The Spaniards weren't particularly interested in liquidating us, but considering that an overall cleansing operation was to take place, they didn't shirk from eliminating us along with all the others. One favor deserves another. Verdaguer's account tallied on many points with the one given us by the German Consul. After three weeks of fruitless searching, the leader of the Spanish death squad had had enough; he wanted to let us get away. But then someone told him that these two Germans were good friends of his, Don Joaquín Verdaguer's, so maybe he could provide further information. Verdaguer was grilled. He told them everything he knew about me: I was a member of the literary *tertulia* run by the man Mulet, but besides that, nothing suspicious. "Involvement in Spanish politics?" No such thing that he knew of, and highly improbable besides. But the best source of information was the owner of the lending library, Señor Don Jaime Escát, who would doubtless also give them a positive report.

The executioner's deputy looked up Don Jaime. He found him in the back room of his library, where he and I had so often talked politics and philosophy, and where Don Jaime had been almost drunk with joy at the news of a Red Azaña victory in the elections. It was there that he had asked Vigoleis to drink a toast to the Red Flag. "Oh you Spaniards and your politics!" Vigoleis had said. He, Vigoleis, would turn old and grey before he could comprehend one iota of Spanish politics, and besides, it didn't interest him in the least. And besides that, he as a foreign guest in the country had no business getting mixed up in internal Spanish affairs. As for Hitler, however, he was a prime authority.

Don Jaime, Verdaguer continued, asked the executioner just why he was looking for this damnable German Catholic. Of course he knew me, he told the man; he knew me all too well. The squad leader pulled out his execution orders: husband and wife, up against the wall, both of them! Whereupon Don Jaime leaped up and cried, "Ha! Give me that! That's my affair! I'll get them both, and I'll take care of them myself, those traitors! I'll shoot 'em myself!" Whereupon Don Jaime lifted his lapel and identified himself as the boss of the island's Secret Police. The squad leader handed over his written orders, was given a receipt for the prospective liquidation of Vigoleis and Beatrice, and with that he was rid of his burdensome chore. No doubt he thought to himself that if the boss himself wanted to take on the job, those two must be truly dangerous criminals. Great! Let him do what he wants! But no sooner had the guy left the library when Don Jaime burned the execution orders and told a petrified Mulet how fortunate it was that this Catholic German never bothered himself with Spanish politics, for otherwise he would have searched him out and had him shot. But the Nazis, he said, ought to get rid of their opponents on their own time. For him, Don Jaime, the case was closed.

Now it was only the Christian Scientist ladies who could deliver me up to my enemies. I was terribly afraid of them.

By the way, none of the frequenters of Mulet's *tertulia* had ever been aware that the organizer of that institution was for years a secret member of the Franco movement. His reputation was that of a radical leftist.

I still had debts with Bauzá, the premier Mallorcan tailor. I couldn't pay them, but I didn't want to escape from the island without giving the store my Swiss address. "Debts?" the proprietor asked. "Have you gone crazy? And what am I supposed to do with your address in Switzerland?" Now you are really going to get shot, I told myself. They were shooting people who, although they believed in God, were causing economic difficulties for other believers. This war, the Bauzá man went on, would be over soon. Franco would be the winner, and then we would return to the island. Paquita had told him how much we loved Mallorca. So now, in order that we wouldn't crash in on our Swiss relatives in shabby clothes, which would cast wrong signals about Franco and the Holy War, he was prepared to have two more suits made for me. He clapped his hands, and his staff rushed to his side. They showed me some select English yarns. I know a thing or two about fine fabrics, and this display caused me to take fright once again. This was highest-quality stuff. I lied, telling them that my departure was set for the next day. "Not a problem," was the answer. The custom work would be ready in 24 hours. I could pay when we returned; they had no use for more money; making uniforms was now more profitable than in peacetime. I was sweating tacks. The world around me had gone insane. First I was scheduled for the firing squad, then I was listed to receive a bribe from the *Führer*'s own cash box, and now, for reasons of international prestige, General Franco was about to have two suits custom-made to fit my body. I shook a few hands and left the store in haste.

But the English rescue ship didn't arrive.

Suddenly Beatrice remembered that we had left two books from the lending library in our apartment. We mustn't leave without returning them—they were, after all, books! Once again she ventured into the most dangerous area of the city, retrieved our books, and took them to Mulet. When Mulet saw her entering his shop he was at first speechless. Then he said, "Are the two of you bound and determined to be executed?" No, said Beatrice, but books were books, and borrowed books were meant to be returned, even in wartime. We even returned Mamú's precious binoculars, a piece of her late Prince's military gear that she had lent us. Mamú had already fled from the island, so we gave this item to her cook. Stupidity never ceases, even in wartime. What am I saying? There is nothing like war to bring forth the most sublime forms of human brainlessness.

Once when I was strolling along the Borne, I spied the sign for the *Fomento del turismo*, and I thought to myself, "Go on in, the boss was always nice to you. He's an old German ex-pat, totally Iberianized by now, 30 years of experience with foreigners." His name was Müller, or maybe Schulze, and that was all he had left of his German origins, but this was a common affliction among former Germans. We had a chat, but the fellow avoided any mention of murder and manslaughter—an understandable omission with a state employee, and anyway, conversations can soon come to an end in times of widespread carnage. He told me that sometimes he was consulted as an interpreter, and one time—sure enough, they were looking for some notorious German, some writer or other, some dangerous character who lived on the Calle del General Barceló. They couldn't locate the guy, but for three weeks they took Müller/Schulze out on a truck as an interpreter. Both of the suspects were supposed to be killed—the guy's wife was supposedly from Switzerland.

But those two weren't killed, I said, adding that the lackadaisical Spanish methods had allowed them to escape. Did he know the couple, I asked? Nope—never saw them. The guy was some kind of struggling writer, his wife gave lessons. Failures, both of them. Did he consider myself as a failure? Of course not; I was the best tourist guide on the island. He laughed. Then I told him who I was. Once again, laughter from Herr Meier or Herr Schulze. We both placed our elbows on his office counter. I showed him my passport. When it finally dawned on him that I was identical with my doomed *Doppelgänger*, he quickly stepped out in front of the counter, grabbed my arm, and shoved me out the door. "Get out of here, for God's sake! You're going to be shot, and I don't want to be any part of it!" I was on the point of telling him that my execution had been delayed, but I was already standing outside on the Borne. Herr Müller bolted the door of his tourist office behind me.

Wherever I went, I was redundant. In similar circumstances, Hamlet would have said, "Oh that this too too solid flesh would melt, thaw, and resolve itself into a dew!" Vigoleis wended his way, somewhat less classically, once again to the British Consulate. "Good news, just arrived! Be at the port tomorrow at 4 a.m. H.M.S. *Grenville*, a destroyer." A dyed-in-the-wool Englishman would have said, "God bless you!" I shouted, "*Porra!*" and sped away.

"Grenville? Grenville?" Beatrice didn't seem to like the name. She searched her memory and said that it was not at all a good omen if the destroyer in question was named after the famous ocean-going hero during the reign of Queen Elizabeth. The Spaniards had capsized him in a battle off the Azores.

"The evil eye, across the centuries?"

That evening we went to the Suredas to say goodbye.

The Suredas are, on a national level, a decidedly fertile dynasty, one that has bequeathed divine right from father to son. Seldom do their parcels of land lie fallow or wither back to wilderness, as sometimes happens when one scion or another devotes himself to art or the sciences, becomes a purely intellectual being, gets beyond all the political nonsense in his country, and thus becomes irrelevant to the cause of patriotism. Pedro Sureda is one such example. Families like this one are the joy and the natural habitat of all monarchies. If the monarch should fall from his throne because he is unwilling to relinquish the Imperial Apple in favor of the Adam's apple beneath a stiff bourgeois collar, or to give up the crown in favor of a soft fedora, then dynasties whose regal legitimacy exists solely on insignias, or in ancestral portraits hanging on their walls, will go on dreaming of royal power and majesty, ermine robes and dalmatic capes. At times when they get impatient in sight of the empty throne, they will band together to heave the King back up where he historically belongs.

All of the Suredas remained loyal to the Spanish King, with the exception of Pedro, who was too much of an artist to wish to serve any other master. Besides, he was unwilling to crawl in the dust. That is why all of the Suredas looked upon the two-armed General as the man to reinstate the Old King or to bestow a New King on the country. That is exactly what Franco promised the Mallorcan monarchists during a visit to the island several years previous. History knows of no instance of a general going back on his word. It knows only of instances when he didn't keep his word—but that is just a matter of time.

The reception took place at the home of Pedro's sister Celerina, in a large salon with stable chairs. Not a single chair leg was missing or rotting with age. The door to the secret chamber was not a secret. There were plates and cups for each guest, and whoever wished to stay overnight, or was forced to by the curfew, could choose a bed without sinning against some famous personage. In a word, Celerina had a rich husband.

The large cemeteries under the island moon were getting larger. The Holy War continued planting its crosses. So the mood was morose as we, who clung illegally to what was left of our little lives, joined the circle of visitors invited and arranged in accordance with Mallorquin custom. There were several relatives in the group, but also friends of the family who had come to wish us well on our departure. All these people liked us; many of them had taken us to their hearts. Moreover, the ones who knew about our adventures, the members of the nobility in particular, were impressed that we hadn't done any stealing in the process of scrambling out of our misery.

Each and every face reflected the mixture of terror, pity, eschatological expectation, and the peculiar glow that we later discerned in Portugal in similarly decadent noble families. It expressed a certain anticipation: just a few more shots, just a few more heads, and all will be accomplished. Behold, the King has arrived!

"Why flee at this late phase of the war?" they asked. "Ridiculous! What for?" The grand deluxe train was already under steam, they said. "But what's with you? Why are you leaving?"

Thus I had to relate the same story all over again, now for the twelfth time, as in a mortuary when you spell it all out in detail for the benefit of the aunts, the neighbors, and the milkman.

The ballad of our fishy heroism evoked a great deal of interest among the aunts with lorgnette and reticule, and among their fawning young heirs; among elderly gentlemen with sideburns and medals; among officers with pomade in their hair, pomade on their fingernails, and swagger sticks in their tunic pockets; and with the unassuming Princess, who was seated on a stool as if she were working at her easel. It is no wonder, then, that I soon started stretching the boundaries of my historical account, striding through our 24-hour life-and-death grace period not with wobbly knees, but with a firm gait. Don Juan's ear trumpet was constantly at my mouth, even when I had to change places and explain to a hard-of-hearing lady some detail of our uniquely perpetual execution. The grandee followed me around all bent over, a vassal of his own deafness, which over the years worsened at the same rate as the tufts of hair grew out of his ears. As a courtesy to him, I shouted a few words into his trumpet, then quickly resumed speaking to normal ears. Deaf people are grateful for any little particle of language that gets tossed to them. They chew on it until it turns to poison inside. That's why deaf people are malicious; they're always thinking that people are putting the wrong morsels of speech into their trumpets.

Everybody felt that Papá's constant trumpet-waggling was disturbing the leave-taking festivities. But didn't he, too, have a right to hear our story? Alas, later on we found out that he wasn't at all interested. Nor was Don Juan Sureda eager to learn what his friend, the Catholic German, or the other crusaders, thought about the Holy War. Pedro told me that Papá had breathed a sigh of relief when he heard that Vigoleis hadn't been shot, that he was still alive, but that no one knew where he was—presumably at some hideaway in the mountains. Search for him, Don Juan immediately said. He mustn't leave the island or be sentenced before he could speak with him. If Vigoleis was put in the slammer prior to getting drilled, he, Juan Sureda Bimet, would arrange for his release on the basis of his personal connections, which included the King and his *Generalissimus*. He needed Vigoleis, he said. But what for? For some Catholic mission or other? No one in the family knew. Papá had kept silent.

As soon as I entered the salon, Don Juan came right up to me, stuck his horn under my nose, and started nudging me with it, much as lambs nudge the udder to make the milk start flowing. He sputtered a few words; I thought I heard the word *diferencia*, and then the name "Goethe." But by then I was already in conversation with some of the others present, with Don Juan in my wake. I related the German Consul's winged words to us, which earned me generous applause. Don Juan nudged me with his horn. "Well, old fellow," I said to a friend of the family who had always boasted of his anarchistic ideas, "not yet in your coffin? You have only Don Juan to thank for that, the man who has permeated your whole clan with his monarchistic notions"—again a nudge of the ear trumpet under my nose, and again the words "difference" and "Goethe." I bent down to kiss the feeble hand belonging to an elderly lady, and the elderly lady blessed my scalp, telling me that I was not meant to be a martyr of the revolution. Someone interjected, "Well now, he really ought to have been shot! No tourist guide has ever told as many lies as he has. He gave the foreigners a completely false image of our island. The officials have received dozens of complaints. Not one date was correct, not one name, not one anecdote. So—shoot him!"

Finally Don Juan grabbed a chair next to mine, tore me away from a chat with the Princess, and held his trumpet in front of my mouth so threateningly that, for the first time since the outbreak of the insurrection, I thought my final hour had arrived.

Don Juan urgently wanted his Catholic German to tell him the semantic difference between the word *übersetzen* with the accent on *setzen*, and the word *übersetzen* with the accent on *über*. And what about the word *überwinden*, or the word...? There were loud protests. Don Juan heard them, or rather he overheard them. Speaking half in Spanish and half in German, he expressed the opinion that the classic German writers—among them, unfortunately, Goethe—constantly misused these compound verbs. Would I be willing, he asked, to clear this matter up, here and now and once and for all? If so, then whoever felt he had a right to end my life was welcome to shoot me forthwith. Revolutions, he explained, have a way of taking their own course, but literary study takes hard work, even while the bombs are going off.

I was about to give vent to my philological prowess when Pedro dragged me away from the ear trumpet. This was our last evening together, the Princess explained as if in apology; perhaps they would never see us again. "Never again," the entire Sureda clan trumpeted into the deaf man's ear as he tapped the air with his bugle, waiting for his oracle to make a pronouncement. I, the *Übersetzer* who was planning my *Übersetzung* to France, began a discourse on the linguistic "*über*" muddle, taking examples from my own life experience, but I was soon shouted down, so Don Juan didn't hear what I had to say. An object came flying across the salon and landed right in the bell of the trumpet. The discussion came to a muffled end. The object smelled of sweaty feet. A young male Sureda from the house of Verdugo, a decadent scion in a decadent era, had thrown one of his socks at his father. Five centuries previous, a similar Sureda would have had his father's head cut off. Outside on the island, other sons were throwing their fathers into wells, hanging them, or crucifying them. The Lord's Ten Commandments have no meaning during the Lord's own wars.

That wasn't a very pleasant farewell gathering, Beatrice said. It was all just because of the old *hidalgo*. I myself thought it was the nicest farewell I had ever survived. Beatrice would have preferred to go home right away.

At the very moment when the sock got tossed into the trumpet, agents came searching for us at the Pensión del Conde. If we had been there, they could have just lifted us out of our rocking chairs. Vigoleis, the Übersetzer, would soon have experienced his *Übersetzung* into the Great Beyond, his wife Beatrice along with him.

It began with somebody's letter to his fiancée on the mainland. Would we be willing to post it in Marseille? Just a brief cordial message, nothing more. This was prohibited under pain of death, as everyone knew, and at the English Consulate they reminded us of this in no uncertain terms. Even the consular mail was being censored, now that the police had established that consulates were spreading "false tales of atrocities" to foreign countries. The German Consul actually pretended to be shocked by such horror stories. He claimed to know nothing about murder and manslaughter on the island.

And it ended with Beatrice once again emptying her little cosmetics kit and placing more and more letters inside. Everyone had relatives on the mainland, but—heaven forbid, nothing of a political nature! One of the anarchist priests handed me a thick letter with the query, "Are you willing to risk this for the Lord's sake? It contains the truth about what's happening on our island." It was addressed to the Archbishop of Paris. I thanked the clergyman for his confidence and stuck the letter in my breast pocket, where I also carried with me my uncle's letter of recommendation. But first I placed some important-looking seals on the letter to the Archbishop.

It was madness to agree to this courier service: 200 letters, more or less! Could there possibly be so many loved ones back home?

Angelita, too, the beautiful Angelita, asked us to take something along. She was the only one who had no loved ones across the ocean, but she packed a basket of provisions for us, delicacies from a secret hoard in her shop. Did such things still exist? *Sobrasadas*? *Turrón*? Her aunts wept, and the volatile Paquita was also rather moved. But she tapped her temple with her finger. As the cashier at Bauzá, the premier clothing store on the island, she knew that I was leaving Mallorca without my custom-cut Bauzá suit.

To make a decent escape is also to be like Don Quixote.

This time, our exit from the Pensión del Conde took place without fanfare, without the other tenants lining up to say farewell, and without *porra*! and *puta*! There was no Beppo there to toss a handful of dirt at us.

Don Alonso had scrounged up a taxi to fetch us at the most god-awful early hour I have ever crept out of bed. The driver was reliable, he told us, and had exact instructions. Josefa, the cook, gave me her blessing. If here and now I let the Vesuvius of her mighty bosom send forth smoke one last time, it is only because my memory retains the touching image of that sacrificial altar of hers. For like Don Joaquín's pipe, hers too had long since gone cold.

They didn't like to see us go. As amateur conspirators we had earned everyone's respect. The Spaniards have a special liking for *aficionados*. In these circles, no one expected the war to end soon. But all of them, except for the priests, thought it would end well.

Our taxi driver was one of those Spanish proletarians with the air of a *grandseigneur*. His co-pilot was no less splendid in his nameless valor. He played the role of herald: "Make way for Catholic Germans on a special mission!" he shouted as we turned onto the Paseo Sagrera and a few dozen rifles blocked our progress. The car stopped. Pistols banged against all the windows. The copilot yelled at the gang and waved a bill of lading. "Friends of the *Movimento Salvador*! Deputies of the Caudillo! Mission to the *Führer*! To the harbor! The cruiser won't wait!" We were allowed to pass through unharmed. There was a clicking of boot heels. German steel helmets, paid for with Mallorcan money, wiggled on heads that were racially too small for them. We sat in the back, fully composed and conscious of our mission. On my lap sat my one and only piece of property, my typewriter. On Beatrice's lap was our suitcase containing, instead of my "Tombs of the Huns," some much more dangerous written material. A second armed patrol let us pass, but a third didn't fall for our ruse. Halt! Passports! Out of the car for inspection! An officer waved to some of his men to approach the car.

We stayed seated. We were exterritorials! Earlier on I had once accompanied Kessler on a visit to the Immigration Police in Palma, so I knew how ambassadors and envoys were supposed to behave. I had clipped my uncle's letter to my passport in such a way as to make the Archbishop of Mallorca's signature and seal immediately visible. The officer studied the Latin text and peered in at me. "Special mission?" Yes, I said, and showed him the letter from the priest to the Archbishop of Paris—we were in the special service of the Church. He made a gesture, his men snapped to attention, and the officer saluted with his sword. It was all very ceremonial, somewhat like a Solemn High Mass. It could have been our funeral. One minute later we were at the pier.

The scene that now presented itself to our eyes reminds me today of certain illustrations in the old Swiss Chronicle by Reverend Diebold Schilling. I say "today," for although what we saw on that October morning was no less colorful and quaint, it was by no means a romantic image. But that, too, is only half of the truth. The scene was romantic enough, but we just couldn't appreciate it.

As I squeezed forward to get out of the car, I noticed that my seat was sopping wet. It was dry when we had entered the taxi. We were surrounded by a thicket of pointed rifles, each rifle containing at least one bullet and ready to fire. The miracle was that there were still any living people on the island. Even the Spaniards aren't capable of such rapid procreation. But come to think of it, no matter where you can hear gunshots, at your county fair or on New Year's Eve or in a war, humans can still activate their libidinous genes. Thus it is likely that the human race will survive the atomic fireworks that will happen in the future.

Flags were fluttering on tall staffs—the standards of the various consulates. Gathered around them were larger and smaller groups of refugees.

Men with arm bands and clipboards, in some cases the consuls themselves or their deputies for refugee affairs, were scampering about. If we had been Dutch citizens, for example, we would have joined half a dozen others with *Oranje boven* snapping above them in the breeze, signifying that they were now in safety. These Hollanders had regained all of the jovial, weather-proof, and infectious *joie de vivre* that makes them so unpopular with one another in railroad stations and landing piers anywhere in the world. It was certain that none of them had any early-morning garden snails run away from them on the island. We weren't Dutch, but neither were we the citizens of any other country that was showing its colors here at the harbor.

One particular group here wasn't showing any colors at all, for the simple reason that it wasn't allowed to, but not because it was politically neutral. I recognized a few faces of German emigrés who had lost their citizenship, a cluster of nobodies, the German nation's rubbish. Even here on the island, where lead bullets were a dime a dozen, they weren't considered worth the price of a spoonful of gunpowder. There were Jews among them, politically innocuous people who had kept their mouths shut. We had nothing in common with them, for we had indeed displayed our colors.

Off to one side, set apart from the picturesque crowd, we saw another flag hanging on a stick, a miserable little rag so tiny that it couldn't catch any of the morning wind and flutter proudly as the patriotic songs would have it do. It was the *Führer*'s swastika. Beneath this sign and its promise of a thousand years of glory, there stood the local power center of the Third *Reich*: our Herr Konsul and a short, shabbily dressed compatriot of his with the party insignia at his lapel and a little mongrel on his arm. He was unshaven, but refugees don't have to shave. And as we found out later, he wasn't a refugee at all. He was some higher *Reich* functionary, sent here on a mission that stipulated outward grubbiness, maybe Strength Through Joy and a little murder plot. But that was his own affair.

Then came no-man's-land, and beyond that an enormous pile that I recall as being as high as a house. Trunks, suitcases, crates, bales—the sight of it gave us a shock. Could this be the baggage belonging to the evacuees? Hardly possible.

The Consul of the Third *Reich* caught sight of us. He watched our every move. Beatrice wanted to find out more about all the baggage. But of course, the English consular official told her. We could take with us as much as we wanted to—there were no limits.

Following this new thunderclap, the two of us gathered around the invisible flag of Vigoleis: a white cross on a white background, or a black cross on black—whichever way one wants to symbolize The Void. A sailor approached us and inquired whether we were refugees or service personnel. We gave him our explosive bundle, which he quickly stowed in the jolly boat. So that danger was past.

Then came the German Consul.

This bastard, I thought, has robbed us of all our belongings with his lying hogwash, trying to lure us on board the Deutschland. He began with some vacuous chatter. I remained cold as a stone, and Beatrice was non-existent. A mob of Spanish gendarmes was all around us, and it seemed advisable to be on our best behavior. So I took up a conversation with the Consul, saying that it was still not our intention to return to Germany. As he knew, we had relatives in Basel. But proximity to the Fatherland, he countered, would surely make us change our minds once we heard the voice of the homeland beckoning across the border... And then, his voice turning softer, he asked if I would be willing to do him a favor. Just a small matter, he said, but personally important for him. He waxed sentimental. His aged father was living in—was it Hamburg?—and hadn't heard from his son in a long time. He was worried, since even as a Consul he wasn't permitted to send private correspondence— only official, censored dispatches. He had a letter, a few lines from a son to his Dad, and would I be so kind as to put it in a mailbox in Marseille? He would give me a few international reply forms...

Vengeance is mine, saith the Lord, saith the whore Pilar, saith practially any decent human being. Here and now, at this early morning hour at the pier in Palma, vengeance was finally being handed to Vigoleis. One simple wave on my part, the enunciation of the one word *Oiga*! and a Spanish officer would come to where we were standing. The sequel would take place in keeping with the protocol of martial law. Probably behind the customs office, to avoid frightening the refugees.

I think of myself as an act of vengeance perpetrated by obscure, possibly cosmic forces, cursed with a life that constantly confronts me with stupid questions. So I figured that I had nothing to gain by letting the Consul get shot. I remained silent. I pointed to the man with the dog and the party button on his lapel, those two shoddy emblems of authority, who was now standing guard alone next to the *Führer*'s flag.

I said, "Herr Dede, there is no reason in the world why I should do you a favor. You are a bad person. Because of you, we are leaving this island as beggars. But give me your letter. I'll take care of it."

The Consul gave me the letter with a trembling hand. I calmly placed it in the same pocket as the episcopal documents I was carrying. Then I continued:

"By giving me this letter you have placed the life of a German Consul in my hands. One little gesture on my part, and in accordance with martial law you will be shot. You know better than I do that these people aren't fooling around, even though you deny any knowledge of the atrocities that are happening. But have no fear, I will not betray you. The satisfaction I now feel, seeing that you, a party member and the Consul of your *Führer*, don't trust that filthy guy over there standing next to your criminal flag, is worth more to me than all the private belongings we are leaving behind us. You're showing that you have more confidence in an enemy of your Movement, someone you have got to know personally. That is a hopeful sign for us refugees. I thank you."

At this moment a siren went off. We climbed aboard the jolly boat. H.M.S. *Grenville* lay at anchor far out in the bay. A few minutes later, we were standing on English territory and in English custody.

The boss of the Spanish Harbor Censorship Office, who ought to have inspected hand baggage, had overslept. His loudly honking limousine raced along the pier—too late. To keep up appearances he boarded a *lancha*, followed us out in a wide swing of the boat and, making an even wider swing, straightaway returned to his Pilar.

We owe it to my uncle's episcopal letter, but also to some insatiable Spanish whore, that we escaped the harbor at Palma without getting shot.

Round about us the grey veils of night had completely lifted. We stepped upon the afterdeck sleepless, spiritually drained, and lightly shivering in the breeze that was now sweeping in from the horizon to reveal the gorgeous spectacle of the slowly receding island palisades. Crimson and gold flames appeared on the cliffside crags and were reflected on the rocky shoreline. Here and there the sea had its black sheen, as yet untouched by the breath of the dawning day. Seagulls were our airborne harbor pilots.

On board the Grenville the nationalities remained apart in groups. We found places to sit on coils of rope. A gentleman was seated there already, a goateed fellow with a blue beret—I immediately recognized Franz Blei, the Austrian writer whose works I always enjoyed reading. I sat down next to him. At my other side sat a man dressed like a Mallorquin peasant, bent forward and brooding. All of a sudden he let out frightful yells, truly bellowing. They had crucified his son, he shouted. And still he couldn't believe in God—not he, no, never! They could nail him to a cross, and he still wouldn't believe, not on his life! Then he again collapsed. I heard him weeping. He wasn't a Mallorquin; he spoke the Spanish of South America.

The English officers and sailors were splendid hosts on board His Majesty's ship. We had everything we needed. If exhausted mothers needed a rest in their cabins, officers played nanny. The meals were first-rate—just as in peacetime, to use an age-old comparison beloved by our civilization.

I continued my chat with Franz Blei: about the world situation, about Kessler, about the difficulty of traveling as an anti-Nazi with a German passport. Then the peasant started bellowing again.

He was from Argentina, and he had settled on Mallorca several years ago. He had a small farm, a wife, and many children. His oldest son was arrested by the religious fanatics and hanged from an olive tree for the atheism he refused to recant. "Crucify him!" the gang had shouted. He gave up the spirit within sight of his father. The father, his child's screams still echoing within him, took heart and fled. But how? He no longer knew. He left everything and everybody behind: his wife, his other children, his farm, everything. Now here he was, half crazed, bellowing his pain and his atheism out across the ocean. If he had been caught, he would have suffered the same fate: *Ibis ad crucem!*

There were other Argentinian farmers on board, quite a lot of them, with their whole families. Obstinate characters, they refused to eat the snow-white bread offered them by the Englishmen. They demanded their familiar country bread with the dark crust. I spoke with one of them, a friend of the fellow who had lost his son. God? he said. What was a farmer supposed to know about God? God is the one who sends rain when rain wasn't wanted. Who sends drought when the earth longs for a drop of rain. Farmers didn't know anything about God. God was something for priests and nuns. As for the death on a cross that was costing his friend his sanity, what was there to say? Maybe somebody else could understand it, but he certainly didn't. Pepe's son was nailed to a cross because the boy didn't believe in God, and people had told him—he himself couldn't read—that Jesus Christ, the guy in the Bible, was crucified too. This guy Christ, the one in the holy book, actually believed in God, or at least that's what he kept on saying. But maybe all this stuff the priests were spreading around was a bunch of lies to keep people stupid. As far as he was concerned,—"*Me cago en Dios!*"

I was thunderstruck.

Off on the horizon we spied a little cloud. Or was it a sail? Fog? The farmers pointed it out to each other. Full speed ahead, we sailed toward the spot, right through a sky that soon changed from azure to black. Suddenly we couldn't see our hands in front of our eyes. The foghorns started barking, the engines were stifled, and the rolling and heaving ceased. The Grenville seemed to be running on without steam. It was uncanny here amidst the cold bank of fog, for what seemed like hours. Suddenly the cloud lifted, the foghorns went silent, and the destroyer leaped full speed ahead into a resurrected world. Blue, blue, as far as the eye could see.

An officer came on deck and raised his hand as if to command attention. Aha, I thought, a speech! That's part of his duties, and at the end we'll all stand up and sing "God save the King!"

The officer made it short and sweet: change of course. Instead of heading for Marseille, we would land at Genoa, where other ships would take passengers to their various destinations.

Italy! From the frying pan into the fire! Were the two of us destined, after all was said and done, to be buried in my home town's Hunnish tombs? Nailed to the *Führer's* hooked cross? Somebody shouted, "Mussolini!"

Franz Blei rose from his sitting position. In the interest of historical accuracy I should stress that he stood up on one of the coils of rope. He turned to the officer. He was not speaking for himself, he said, for as an Austrian he was still a free individual. But persecuted Germans were on board this ship, as well as stateless persons, and it was unconscionable to land these people on Italian soil. For all of them, that would mean Third *Reich*, concentration camps, death! Whereupon Franz Blei stepped down from his podium and again took his seat on the rope coil. The officer said nothing and disappeared down a hatch.

Nothing but water and a black-azure sky, a leaping dolphin, and the music of our stuttering sea journey. Not a cloud in the sky, not a cloud on the horizon. The ship's wake told us that we were making the wide course change in the direction of Mussolini.

The father of the crucified boy regained his senses. The Englishmen's white bread, their pap for sucklings, had performed a miracle. Fortunately the man had one last dark crust in his breast pocket.

"God," said Franz Blei, who also noticed this, "God will bless anybody's true bread."

The officer came back on deck with a new announcement. The ship had made contact with the admiral on board their flagship *H.M.S. London* in the harbor at Barcelona. His British Majesty's Mediterranean Fleet, the radio communication had said, would not discharge any passenger against his will in a hostile country. Grenville, however, would not be heading for Marseille; she had orders to go to Genoa. We would be landing at Barcelona, where the refugees would spend the night on the flagship and would depart the next day on another destroyer for Marseille. "All right?"

"All right," said Franz Blei, to whom the officer had directed his last question. "God bless the King!"

"God bless him!" added Beatrice with a sigh of relief. She has a weakness for anything British, and she is familiar with such slogans. This ocean-going coup of Olde England left me speechless. Such grandeur on the high seas, while their landlubber Consul kept strictly to his orders! One wave to the steersman sufficed to make our ship curve toward liberty. We noticed the change of course by watching the ship's wake. The circle was closing; with redoubled speed our destroyer first headed back to where we came from, but then wheeled sharply to port.

Nature herself provided the final thrill, but I don't want to make it sound melodramatic. Once again the sirens wailed, and once again we were inside a cloud. Was anybody else noticing this? A ghoulish whiteness surrounded us. The ship's deck was rigid. The world was soundless. The azure maritime day was invisible above us, and down below was night, veiling our destination.

Our destination: freedom.

Ever since man was forced to depart from Paradise and enter the nature reserve of his own culture, a place where he can survive only so long as he retains his instinct for creating borders beyond which he is in danger of being executed, the history of his freedom has been a history devoid of meaning. One cannot retell this history without causing acute embarrassment. That is why I have allowed Nature to enter here, allowing Her to arrange a large bank of fog that will now descend upon this final scene in the recollections of Vigoleis, instead of some dazzling, fanciful

finis operis.

Correction:

In my "Notice to the Reader" you will have read that "all the people in this book are alive or were at one time." What I meant by that pronouncement was that my book is not of the kind inspired by poetic fantasy, but one that takes actual fact as its point of departure—or if you prefer another formulation, it is a book of recollections shaped by poetic means. This makes it different from works whose exclusively poetic authors say, in order to avoid legal complications or other intrusions into their *métier*, that all their characters are fictional, and that any similarity to persons living or dead is purely coincidental.

For this reason, there can be no talk of "pure coincidence" concerning the living or dead persons in my book. Each and every character in it makes an appearance in the flesh, in his or her own shadowless image, although in certain cases where political entities or individual grudges might present a danger, my reader must be detoured away from precise identification. This was decidedly not the case with my Kathrinchen from the Rhineland, who appears in my memoirs as the complete nymphomaniac that she was in reality. The same is true for her male counterpart, the piggish lecher Silberstern, although I must admit that with this particular fellow, a man who was worth his weight in gold, I have altered his surname from "gold" to "silver." This admission will no doubt be of help to his family. Here and there in my book I have changed certain phonemes within proper names, but the bearers of these names appear as they actually lived. I changed nothing at all that concerns my own person. As the author, and as a human being, I felt that I had no choice but to expose myself to any and all personal attacks.

Many of my acquaintances had already passed on from this world before I decided in the year 1952 to set down my recollections, aided by nothing more than my magically comprehensive, logarithmic memory and that of my constantly courageous and loyal partner Beatrice. Other people gave me their blessing as I naively wrote out my memories, and even later when they appeared in print. Today, as I write this Afterword with the intention of canceling an erroneous inhumation, the number of departed souls from our Mallorcan world has already risen sharply, and I don't even get to read all the obituaries. Zwingli, the real-life originator of my second-sighted island adventures, the man who, like his sister and me, was listed to be liquidated during the Spanish insurrection, was lowered into an early grave in Santa Fe de Bogotá. Mamú, our lady in charitable Christian memory; Don Juan Sureda; both of the Counts, Kessler and Keyserling; Villalonga; Mulet the Great—All of them are now no longer with us.

Risen from the dead is solely Captain Heinz Kraschutzki, about whom I reported previously that he was executed, and about whom I report that he was involved in the 1918 naval mutiny at Kiel, and that he raised chickens on Mallorca. I wrote this in response to what I heard about him on our island at the time, an account of his life that none of my painstaking research in libraries in Amsterdam and The Hague has put into question. I am not one of those writers who invent things from whole cloth, nor could anything be further from my intentions than to besmirch any person's reputation, either by detracting from his real life or by concocting a phony life for him.

This particular hero of my applied recollections wrote to me in the spring of 1957, saying that everything I said about him in my book was wrong. But unlike what I might have expected of him in accordance with my further advisory to accept the characters "in dual cognizance of their identity," he submitted his complaint in full cognizance of his own person, which he claimed was the victim of mistaken, though happily not willfully falsifying, assertions. First of all, he explained, he never took part in a mutiny in Kiel. At the time in question—I am keeping strictly to what he told me in his letter, which is no doubt of importance for the history of World War I—he was captain of the minesweeper *M 100*, whose home port was Bremerhaven, and he was on the high seas when the naval mutiny occurred. Upon returning to port, where the city had already fallen into the hands of a military soviet, his crew unanimously elected him as a delegate to the existing revolutionary council. Thus it was only after the uprising that he entered the Bremerhaven military regime. Hence, I read further in this admonitory letter from a sailor I thought was dead and who was claiming to have been mistreated by others as well, there was no mutiny on his ship. If the relationship between captain and crew had in all cases been like that on *M 100*, he went on, there would never have been any mutinies at all.

Secondly, he wrote, he never engaged in chicken farming on Mallorca. In fact he had never in his life owned a single chicken. Thirdly, he was never executed there, although the radio and three newspapers of national renown had published obituaries (incidentally, they also published my own obituary). He cited the newspapers by name, and one of the obituaries was printed under my byline. When I wrote it, I had no idea at all that sometime later my pen would bring forth my insular recollections, including an account of the execution of Herr Heinz Kraschutzki. He was still very much alive, he wrote, despite the fact that in Spain he had been sentenced to "only" thirty years in prison, of which he served nine years, two months, and four days.

In addition, this resurrected man complains in his letter that I had no right "*an sich*" to publish details of the life of living person that could potentially harm that person. But he was reluctant to make a direct accusation against me, since I had presumably been misled by the press accounts of his passing.

I was not particularly moved by this message from what I had been thinking was a voice from the next world. My joy at a man's resurrection, coupled with my shame at having offended the same man's reputation—these things lay far behind me. For in the meantime I had learned from my friend, the writer Karl Otten, who like Kraschutzki and all the rest of us was a victim of Nazi persecution on the explosive island of Mallorca, that the information given to me by the German Consul, which was the basis for the account in my book, was erroneous. In a later letter, Herr Kraschutzki asked me what possible motivation the Hitlerian Consul might have had to list a person among the deceased, when he knew full well that this person was still living.

In times when murder is rampant, puzzles will multiply. Even so, I hastened to reply to the ex-captain of the German Navy that in a subsequent edition of my book, in accordance with his wishes, I would duly absolve him of (1) mutiny and (2) chicken-farming, and I promised (3) that I would restore him to life in all its blissful abundance. I should add that I could not resist expressing my disappointment that he had never made personal acquaintance with a chicken, in the legal sense of "chicken ownership" *(detentio gallinae)*. I informed him that I myself had never owned a single chicken, although for several years I had intercourse with chickens, with thousands of chickens to be exact, on my brother's farm, where I also had found opportunity to observe their egg-laying secrets and repeatedly to be amazed by their proverbial stupidity. Yet I was also aware, I told Mr. Kraschutzki, of their obsession with any and all forms of chicken feed, as with their active herding instinct, which one might refer to as a biological extension of their hunger for corn kernels. Beyond this, I knew of the frustration experienced by chicken breeders in seasons when the eggs yield more roosters than hens—a state of affairs in the barnyard that could be called, if I remember correctly, a form of sexual mutiny.

I am mentioning all this simply as a marginal comment on the recantation I sent to Herr Kraschutzki, although my reader will have noticed that here, too, one thing quickly leads to another. I wrote to the sailor further that I was sorry he hadn't been a mutineer. I would have liked him better as a mutineer. In fact—and this has nothing more to do with the special case of a man who avoided getting murdered against all sense of law and liberty—in fact, I consider military revolts on land, on the sea, and in the air as a distinctly honorable method of atoning for the type of sins one has committed by putting on a killer's uniform in the first place. As I see it, a rebellious soldier is more courageous than one who sticks to his post wearing a murderer's decoration on his cowardly breast until he hears the trumpet calling him to his own demise.

This completes my act of contrition with respect to Captain Heinz Kraschutzki. Let him now rejoin the living characters in my book—*sans* chickens, to be sure, and absolved of being a mutineer against God, King, and Fatherland, those three entities that have caused so much trouble for humankind in the upwards as well as the downwards direction, but especially downwards, where the soldier makes his appearance, standing rigidly at attention with his brain in his boots. Since the Stone Age we have never come to grips with spiritual ossification. Perhaps there are some who wish to believe that man is a rational being who can get beyond acting with tooth and claw. But here, too, let truth be told.

Ascona. Casa Rocca Vispa . July 8, 1960

Additional Correction:

I cite a character in my island memoirs, Bobby, as presenting his business card with the same typographic design as the printing of this book. This refers solely to the first edition, whose colophon reads as follows:

"*The Island of Second Sight* by Albert Vigoleis Thelen was set in Poliphilus and printed in the autumn of 1953 by Drukkerij G. J. Thieme in Nijmegen, under commission from G. A. van Oorschot, publisher on the Herengracht, Amsterdam, and bound by Elias P. van Bommel in Amsterdam. The typographic design is by Helmut Salden, Wassenaar. The licensed German-language edition is published by the Eugen Diederichs Verlag, Düsseldorf."

Blonay. La Colline en Malaterraz, September 7, 1970

Further Correction:

For years there have been reports that I was dead. Yet it is not the purpose of this supplement to my island recollections to contradict advisories concerning my interment. Recently the announcements about my biting the dust have become more numerous. There have even been some messages of condolence, which I have found just as touching as they are amusing, because when the fateful hour finally arrives I'll be in no position to savor them, either in heaven or in hell. I will have disappeared into the void, *dans le néant*. And that's just as it should be.

But people whom I have myself caused to die with strokes of my pen, people who since then have proven to be very much alive—in my applied recollections I have restored such individuals to life, as in the case of Navy Captain Kraschutzki.

In the book, I reproduced the death notice of an uncle of my mother's, from the Scheifes farm in St. Hubert. I added an assertion that God had forgiven this murderer, but that he had not escaped the secular arm of the law. He was hanged, I wrote, basing my conclusion on oral reports from my grandmother and my mother. This family oral tradition is erroneous. I am seizing the opportunity presented by this new edition of my book to set things straight.

Not long ago I received a copy of the local newsletter from the village of St. Hubert, the *Hubertus Messenger*, No. 98, dated October, 1974. Under the headline 'St. Hubert Enters World Literature?' the death certificate is quoted together with my explanation of the murderous deed. The author of this notice added the following commentary:

"The death notice for Heinrich Hermann Scheifes, which A. V. Thelen incorporated into his novel, was quoted together with other information in Footnote 29 of the article 'Diary of the Remarkable Events, Recorded by C. Pielen in St. Hubert' in the *Hubertus Messenger*, No. 42. It should be noted that not only has God forgiven this unhappily culpable man, but the civil authorities were also merciful toward him. Following early release from prison, he lived for a long time in the vicinity of Stenden-Rahm, where he passed away. Given all that we know about the man, it is clear that he was not a murderer. Signed: Ma."

It was not wanton macabre fantasy that caused me to let this putative murderer hang from a tree. Rather, I was following carefully the legend about him that was current within my own family. This now takes me straightaway to the topic of the credibility of my Applied Recollections. What is a "legend"? Here in my *Island*, you can read Pascoaes' opinion that legend corrects history, and in another passage, that truth is no different from legend. On the other hand, in Conde-Duque de Olivares by the eminent man of science Gregorio Marañón, we find the statement that "legend is a caricature of truth." One step further on this controversial subject, and I have arrived at Ernst Bertram and his book on Nietzsche, his *"Attempt at a Mythology."* Bertram's Introduction is concerned specifically with the nature of legend, and it has often been contested: what remains of history, he says, is quite simply legend.

I am therefore grateful to the *Hubertus Messenger*, which has herewith permitted me to return an executed but now half-cleansed man to his world and to my reader, by removing the noose from his neck.

Further, there is need for supplementary information in reference to p. 518, where, in keeping with what Pedro reported to us at the time, I remark in passing that several children had died. This, too, is erroneous, for now it is necessary to add two more children. Permit me to explain this unfortunate omission:

In the autumn of 1976, Vigoleis and Beatrice finally decided to make a return trip to Mallorca to enjoy a reunion with Pedro, and to make the acquaintance of his wife and their three children. Besides, Pedro had expressed his desire to create on canvas a portrait of myself in old age.

After 40 years, during the exact week of our former departure and overcome with emotion, we fell into each others' arms. And like 40 years previous, Beatrice received a kiss on her hand from this Spanish grandee—nothing had changed, except that we had grown old. During this visit we often retraced our own steps. But the island was no longer our island. It had turned into an encampment for international tourism. Where ships of the Woermann Line once discharged hordes of Strength Through Joy passengers, now each and every hour thundering jets spewed forth travelers onto the island.

Our first destination was the Street of General Barceló, the Calle del General Barceló, House No. 23. The street itself had not much changed, although the house numbers had. But inside the front door we found our old address number. A little farther on, at the corner, we sought out Jaume's and Don Matías' bakery, but it was no longer there. Then we turned into the Calle de las Apuntadores, heading for the Count's *pensión* and the little store run by pretty Angelita. But great heavens! Our little street was unrecognizable! It now was one single bazaar, with tavern after tavern, each one offering, on posted menus and in pub windows, selections to suit the taste of Teutonic customers: sauerkraut, fresh-ground coffee, and similar items of German gourmandise. What had once been the aunts' shop was now a *restaurante*. And yet—may I continue serving as a Baedeker?—the little palace that had harbored the Pensión del Conde was still there, but in more decayed condition. The tree-shaking monkey Beppo's coconut palm in the inner courtyard was withered. And upstairs, everything was transformed. The place was teeming with hippies, who had established here an international convention center. I felt very uncomfortable moving about in such company and stumbling over them. They were living in their own world, and the new proprietor of this rooming house, a bearded fellow, asked us with a scowl why we had entered the place. I explained the reason for our visit to the Conde's *Pensión*, but he was unable to provide us with any information. He knew nothing about this Count. Besides, amid all the noise produced by the unruly crowd of kids, we were hardly able to make ourselves understood. Where at one time noble personages had found shelter, a brand new style of living held sway. So we left the premises, I with my head bowed.

The Borne? Well, this once exclusive boulevard was now a platform for strip-teasing blonde Valkyries. Other ladies sat beneath café parasols quaffing their beer, their loins yearning for musclebound Spanish machismo. Their male partners, meanwhile, spent their time ogling the Spanish beauties passing by in blue jeans.

In Valldemosa we visited Pedro's little cottage studio. The new owner allowed us to examine, room by room, the palatial quarters that Don Juan Sureda had completely squandered.

There was much that we had no desire to see again. Besides Pedro, the only other old friend we met with was his brother-in-law Don Eduardo, well above 80 years of age—an impressive character.

Pedro's true home is now his studio in an old mill, Es Molí in Sa Cabaneta, situated on untouched land a few kilometers north of Palma. It is a magical place. What you'll find there is a well, some donkeys, a grove of cactus, a flock of pigeons. Just a year prior to our visit, our painter friend was able to afford the installation of electric lighting.

To mention only one of our excursions, we drove out to Felanitx, where everything was just as we remembered it, and we had dinner in an old *taberna*. We chatted with the owner, who just then was celebrating the name-day of one of his children with a grand meal, to which he immediately invited us. We had roast dove—not the kind from Brindisi but from Binisalem, and a Felanitx white. As a gesture of thanks to our host, I spoke a few words in honor of his son's eponymous saint, invoking blessings upon all who were gathered here at the festive table. In return, we two old, odd strangers received copious heartfelt thanks in the Spanish tradition.

Pedro's inquisitive ways had also affected his wife Catalina and his disconcertingly beautiful grown-up daughters. These two were dying to meet Vigo and Beatrice. I had a great deal to tell them, since they wanted to hear all the stories of the House of Sureda that are recorded in this book, and with which they were of course already familiar directly from us, and in particular from me, the one who has made literature out of the chronicles of their distinguished heritage. I didn't hesitate for very long. Once having started, I wove into my narration several other grotesque episodes from our personal experience. My Spanish tongue became quite fluent once again. But I asked Pedro and his family to speak in their local dialect, the language so dear to me even though I couldn't grasp every word. When I was posing for Pedro, he always asked me to go on palavering. I soon discovered that my constant chatter was enlivening the painter's creative spirit. In this way, the 40 years that separated us soon vanished, and the portrait turned out to be a masterpiece.

We soon learned something about Pedro's family history that he had never mentioned: during his parents' artistic sojourn in England, in addition to his mother's paintings and his father's higgledy-piggledy collection of ticket stubs, brochures, museum catalogues, etc., two children made their appearance. So here and now, I am allowing these unborn creatures (which they had been for us all along) to join the ranks of humanity. I know nothing more about them. I forgot to ask Pedro about their fate, or even just about their lives. Perhaps they never crossed the Channel. When I experience something unusual in my life in this world, I never say to myself, "Aha! You can use that in your manuscript!"

At any rate, before we left the island I promised Pedro that I would fill in this gap in my memoirs, trusting at the same time that this would firm up the credibility of my jottings. For it is difficult enough to separate the rock-hard reality of certain of my characters from the ostensibly shameless dissimulation that can likewise be found in my account. All of it had to be written down just as someone experienced it, especially if this someone was prone to fall for other people's prevarications. Many of the personages in my book took me and my Vigoleis for suckers. We were fooled—thereby enriching my life, by the way, and eventually that of my recollections. *Poetry and Truth*, 'bizarre mystification' and reality—I play my games with what I have actually experienced, to the despair of scholarly exegetes of the picaresque novel, those who insist upon the fictionality of my 'Applied Recollections,' although in the process they themselves are striding out on the path of untruth.

All this loquacity, some readers might be thinking, just for the sake of two nameless human offspring? Yes, indeed. By reason of their right to life they belong in my book, where, Lord knows, so much weirdness has been left out. Consider, if you will, that I excised a good 500 pages from a manuscript that took me exactly nine months to produce. In keeping with my penchant toward nihilism, I burned them in the coal stove in our apartment on Helmersstraat in Amsterdam: an anti-herostratic, barbaric act that caused unspoken distress for Beatrice, but one that to this day she has never held against me.

Barbaric? Perhaps. But is this the dangerous "Perhaps" to be found in Nietzsche's *Beyond Good and Evil*? In case of doubt, let truth once more be told.

Lausanne-Vennes, on the street of the poet Ysabelle de Montolieu,
Spring 1981